'The owner of the most powerful imagination in science fiction'
Ken Follett

'The most sprawling, demanding, and impossible-to-ignore saga
that space opera has ever seen' *sfreviews.net*

'The sheer scale of blazing action and galactic pursuit is genuinely impressive. Nanonics-enhanced warriors, intelligent space
habitats, X-ray lasers, gamma pulsers, illicit antimatter bombs,
whole arsenals of tasty assault weapons and improvised means of
destruction . . . *The Neutronium Alchemist* is high space opera, a
real page-turner' *SFX*

'Thoroughly engrossing . . . immensely satisfying. An excellent
book. One that engages the intellect as well as the emotions.
A tale that drags the reader on a corkscrew rollercoaster ride of
dazzling imagination and electrifying excitement' *Starburst*

'This is thrilling stuff . . . compulsively readable and abundantly
full of ideas' *The Times*

'Reaches another level of excellence . . . Brilliant' *Locus*

'One of the most popular authors of "space operas" in Britain
today, writing vast doorsteps of novels that combine fantastic
speculation with incredibly detailed imagining of the lives we will
lead after the 30th century . . . Hamilton's storytelling is crystal
clear' *Guardian*

'A huge achievement in science fiction' *SciFiNow*

# THE NEUTRONIUM ALCHEMIST

**Peter F. Hamilton** was born in Rutland in 1960 and still lives in that county. He began writing in 1987, and sold his first short story to *Fear* magazine in 1988. He has written many bestselling novels, including the Greg Mandel series, the Night's Dawn trilogy, the Commonwealth Saga, the Void trilogy, two short story collections and several standalone novels.

*Find out more about Peter F. Hamilton at*
www.peterfhamilton.co.uk
*or discover more Pan Macmillan and Tor UK books at*
www.torbooks.co.uk

## By Peter F. Hamilton

### The Greg Mandel series
Mindstar Rising
A Quantum Murder
The Nano Flower

### The Night's Dawn trilogy
The Reality Dysfunction
The Neutronium Alchemist
The Naked God

### The Commonwealth Saga
Pandora's Star
Judas Unchained

### Chronicle of the Fallers
The Abyss Beyond Dreams

### The Void trilogy
The Dreaming Void
The Temporal Void
The Evolutionary Void

### Short story collections
A Second Chance at Eden
Manhattan in Reverse

Fallen Dragon
Misspent Youth
The Confederation Handbook
(a vital guide to the Night's Dawn trilogy)
Great North Road

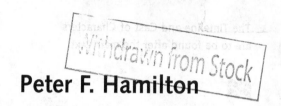

# Peter F. Hamilton

# THE NEUTRONIUM ALCHEMIST

### Book Two of the Night's Dawn trilogy

**PAN BOOKS**

**The Timeline and Cast of Characters**
**are to be found after the main text.**

First published 1997 by Macmillan

This edition published 2012 by Pan Books
an imprint of Pan Macmillan
20 New Wharf Road, London N1 9RR
Associated companies throughout the world
www.panmacmillan.com

ISBN 978-1-4472-0858-7

9 8

A CIP catalogue record for this book is available from
the British Library.

Typeset by SetSystems Ltd, Saffron Walden, Essex
Printed and bound by CPI Group (UK) Ltd, Croydon, CR0 4YY

# 1

It seemed to Louise Kavanagh as though the fearsome midsummer heat had persisted for endless, dreary weeks rather than just the four Duke-days since the last meagre shower of rain. Air from the Devil's cookhouse, the old women of the county called this awful unbreathable stillness which blanketed the wolds. It complemented Louise's mood perfectly. She didn't feel much of anything these days. Destiny had apparently chosen her to spend her waking hours doing nothing but wait.

Officially, she was waiting for her father, who was away leading the Stoke County militia help quell the insurrection which the Democratic Land Union had mounted in Boston. The last time he'd phoned was three days ago, a quick, grim call saying the situation was worse than the Lord Lieutenant had led them to believe. That had made Louise's mother worry frantically. Which meant Louise and Genevieve had to creep round Cricklade Manor like mice so as not to worsen her temper.

And there had been no word since, not of Father nor any of the militia troops. The whole county was crackling with rumours, of course. Of terrible battles, and beastly acts of savagery by the Union irregulars. Louise tried hard to close her ears to them, convinced it was just wicked propaganda put about by Union sympathizers. Nobody really knew anything. Boston could have been on another planet as far as Stoke

County was concerned. Even bland accounts of 'disturbances', reported on the nightly news programmes, had ceased after the county militias encircled the city. Censored by the government.

All they could do was wait helplessly for the militias to triumph, as they surely would.

Louise and Genevieve had spent yet another morning milling aimlessly around the manor. It was a tricky task; sitting about doing nothing was so incredibly boring, yet if they drew attention to themselves they would be given some menial domestic job to do. With the young men away, the maids and older menservants were struggling with the normal day-to-day running of the rambling building. And the estate farms outside, with their skeleton workforce, were falling dismayingly far behind in their preparations for the summer's second cereal crop.

By lunchtime, the ennui had even started to get to Louise, so she had suggested she and her sister went riding. They had to saddle the horses themselves, but it was worth it just to be away from the manor for a few hours.

Louise's horse picked its way gingerly over the ground. Duke's hot rays had flayed open the soil, producing a wrinkled network of cracks. The aboriginal plants which had all flowered in unison at midsummer were long dead now. Where ten days ago the grassland had been dusted with graceful white and pink stars, small shrivelled petals now skipped about like minute autumn leaves. In some hollows they had drifted in loose dunes up to a foot deep.

'Why do you suppose the Union hates us so?' Genevieve asked querulously. 'Just because Daddy's got a temper doesn't mean he's a bad man.'

Louise procured a sympathetic smile for her younger sister. Everyone said how alike they were, twins born four years apart. And indeed it was a bit like looking into a mirror at times; the same features, rich dark hair, delicate nose, and almost oriental eyes. But smaller, and slightly chubbier. And right now, brokenly glum.

Genevieve had been sensitive to her moodiness for the last week, not wanting to say anything significant in case it made big sister even more unaccountably irritable.

She does idolize me so, Louise thought. Pity she couldn't have chosen a better role model.

'It's not just Daddy, nor even the Kavanaghs,' Louise said. 'They simply don't like the way Norfolk works.'

'But why? Everybody in Stoke County is happy.'

'Everybody in the county is provided for. There's a difference. How would you feel if you had to work in the fields all day long for every day of your life, and saw the two of us riding by without a care in the world?'

Genevieve looked puzzled. 'Not sure.'

'You'd resent it, and you'd want to change places.'

'I suppose so.' She gave a sly grin. 'Then I'd be the one who resented them.'

'Exactly. That's the problem.'

'But the things people are saying the Union is doing...' Genevieve said uncertainly. 'I heard two of the maids talking about it this morning. They were saying horrible things. I ran away after a minute.'

'They're lying. If anybody in Stoke County knew what was going on in Boston, it would be us, the Kavanaghs. The maids are going to be the last to find out.'

Genevieve shone a reverent smile at her sister. 'You're so clever, Louise.'

'You're clever too, Gen. Same genes, remember.'

Genevieve smiled again, then spurred her horse on ahead, laughing gladly. Merlin, their sheepdog, chased off after her, kicking up whirling flurries of brown petals.

Louise instinctively urged her own horse into a canter, heading towards Wardley Wood, a mile ahead of her. In summers past the sisters had claimed it as their own adventure playground. This summer, though, it held an added poignancy. This summer it contained the memory of Joshua Calvert. Joshua and the things they'd done as they lazed by the side of the rock pools. Every outrageous sexual act, acts which no true well-born Norfolk lady would ever commit. Acts which she couldn't wait for them to do again.

Also the acts which had made her throw up for the last three mornings in a row. Nanny had been her usual fuss the first two times. Thankfully, Louise had managed to conceal this morning's bout of nausea, otherwise her mother would have been told. And Mother was pretty shrewd.

Louise grimaced forlornly. *Everything will be fine once Joshua comes back.* It had become almost a mantra recently.

Dear Jesus, but I hate this waiting.

Genevieve was a quarter of a mile from the wood, with Louise a hundred yards behind her, when they heard the train. The insistent tooting carried a long way in the calm air. Three short blasts, followed by a long one. The warning signal that it was approaching the open road crossing at Collyweston.

Genevieve reined her horse in, waiting for Louise to catch up with her. 'It's coming into town!' the younger girl exclaimed.

Both of them knew the local train times by heart. Colsterworth had twelve passenger services a day. This one wasn't one of them.

'They're coming back!' Genevieve squealed. 'Daddy's back!'

Merlin picked up on her excitement, running round the horse, barking enthusiastically.

Louise bit her lip. She couldn't think what else it could be. 'I suppose so.'

'It is. It is!'

'All right, come on, then.'

\*

Cricklade Manor lurked inside its picket of huge geneered cedars, an imposing stone mansion built in homage to the stately homes of an England as distant in time as in space. The glass walls of the ornate orangery abutting the east wing reflected Duke's brilliant yellow sunlight in geometric ripples as the sisters rode along the greensward below the building.

When she was inside the ring of trees, Louise noticed the chunky blue-green farm ranger racing up the long gravel drive. She whooped loudly, goading her horse to an even faster gallop. Few people were allowed to drive the estate's powered vehicles. And nobody drove them as fast as Daddy.

Louise soon left Genevieve well behind, with an exhausted Merlin trailing by almost quarter of a mile. She could see six figures crammed into the vehicle's seats. And that was definitely Daddy driving. She didn't recognize any of the others.

Another two farm rangers turned into the drive just as the first pulled up in front of the manor. Various household staff and Marjorie Kavanagh hurried down the broad steps to greet it.

Louise tumbled down off her horse and rushed up to her father. She flung her arms around him before he knew what was happening. He was dressed in the same military uniform as the day he left.

'Daddy! You're all right.' She rubbed her cheek against the coarse khaki-green fabric of his jacket, feeling five years old again. Tears were threatening to brim up.

He stiffened inside her manic embrace, head slowly tipping down to look at her. When she glanced up adoringly she saw a look of mild incomprehension on his strong ruddy face.

For a horrible moment she thought he must have found out about the baby. Then a vile mockery of a smile came to his lips.

'Hello, Louise. Nice to see you again.'

'Daddy?' She took a step backwards. What was wrong with him? She glanced uncertainly at her mother, who had just reached them.

Marjorie Kavanagh took in the scene with a fast glance. Grant looked just awful; tired, pale, and strangely nervous. Gods, what had happened in Boston?

She ignored Louise's obvious hurt, and stepped up to him. 'Welcome home,' she murmured demurely. Her lips brushed his cheek.

'Hello, dear,' Grant Kavanagh said. It could have been a complete stranger for all the emotion in the voice.

He turned, almost in deference, Marjorie thought with growing bewilderment, and half-bowed to one of the men accompanying him. They were all strangers, none of them even wore Stoke County militia uniforms. The other two farm rangers were braking behind the first, also full of strangers.

'Marjorie, I'd like you to meet Quinn Dexter. Quinn is a ... priest. He's going to be staying here with some of his followers.'

The young man who walked forward had the kind of gait Marjorie associated with the teenage louts she glimpsed occasionally in Colsterworth. Priest, my arse, she thought.

Quinn was dressed in a flowing robe of some incredibly black material; it looked like the kind of habit a millionaire monk would wear. There was no crucifix in sight. The face which smiled out at her from the voluminous hood was coldly vulpine. She noticed how everyone in his entourage was very careful not to get too close to him.

'Intrigued, Father Dexter,' she said, letting her irony show.

He blinked; and nodded thoughtfully, as if in recognition that they weren't fooling each other.

'Why are you here?' Louise asked breathlessly.

'Cricklade is going to be a refuge for Quinn's sect,' Grant Kavanagh said. 'There was a lot of damage in Boston. So I offered him full use of the estate.'

'What happened?' Marjorie asked. Years of discipline necessary to enforce her position allowed her to keep her voice level, but what she really wanted to do was grab hold of Grant's jacket collar and scream it in his face. Out of the corner of her eye she saw Genevieve scramble down off her horse, and run over to greet her father, her delicate face suffused with simple happiness. Before Marjorie could say anything, Louise thrust out an arm, and stopped her dead in her tracks. Thank God for that, Marjorie thought; there was no telling how these aloof strangers would react to excitable little girls.

Genevieve's face instantly turned woeful, staring up at her untouchable father with widened, mutinous eyes. But Louise kept a firmly protective arm round her shoulder.

'The rebellion is over,' Grant said. He hadn't even noticed Genevieve's approach.

'You mean you rounded up the Union people?'

'The rebellion is over,' Grant repeated flatly.

Marjorie was at a loss what to do next. Away in the distance she could hear Merlin barking with unusual aggression. The fat old sheepdog was lumbering along towards the group outside the manor.

'We shall begin straight away,' Quinn announced abruptly. He started up the steps towards the wide double doors, long pleats of his robe swaying leadenly around his ankles.

The manor staff clustering with considerable curiosity on top of the steps parted nervously. Quinn's companions surged after him.

Grant's face twitched in what was nearly an apology to Marjorie as the new arrivals clambered out of the farm rangers to hurry up the steps after their singular priest. Most of them were men, all with exactly the same kind of agitated expression.

They look as if they're going to their own execution, Marjorie thought. And the clothes a couple of them wore were bizarre. Like historical military costumes; grey greatcoats with broad scarlet lapels and yards of looping gold braid. She strove to remember history lessons from too many years ago, images of Teutonic officers hazy in her mind.

**7**

'We'd better go in,' Grant said encouragingly. Which was absurd. Grant Kavanagh neither asked nor suggested anything on his own doorstep, he gave orders.

Marjorie gave a reluctant nod, and joined him. 'You two stay out here,' she told her daughters. 'I want you to see to Merlin, then stable your horses.' While I find out just what the hell is going on around here, she completed silently.

The two sisters were virtually clinging together at the bottom of the steps, faces heavy with doubt and dismay. 'Yes, Mother,' Louise said meekly. She started to tug on Genevieve's black riding jacket.

Quinn paused on the threshold of the manor, giving the grounds a final survey. Misgivings were beginning to stir his mind. When he was back in Boston it seemed only right that he should be part of the vanguard bringing the gospel of God's Brother to the whole island of Kesteven. None could stand before him when his serpent beast was unleashed. But there were so many lost souls returning from the beyond; inevitably some dared to disobey, while others wavered after he had passed among them to issue the word. In truth he could only depend upon the closest disciples he had gathered.

The sect acolytes he had left in Boston to tame the returned souls, to teach them the real reason why they had been brought back, agreed to do his bidding simply from fear. That was why he had come to the countryside, to levy the creed upon all the souls, both the living and the dead, of this wretched planet. With a bigger number of followers inducted, genuinely *believing* the task God's Brother had given them, then ultimately their doctrine would triumph.

But this land which Luca Comar had described in glowing terms was so empty, kilometre after kilometre of grassland and fields, populated by dozing hamlets of cowed peasants; a temperate climate version of Lalonde.

There had to be more to his purpose than this. God's Brother would never have chosen him for such a simple labour.

There were hundreds of planets in the Confederation crying out to hear His word, to follow Him into the final battle against the false gods of Earth's religions, where Night would dawn for evermore.

After this evening I shall have to search myself to see where He guides me; I must find my proper role in His plan.

His gaze finished up on the Kavanagh sisters, who were staring up at him, both trying to be courageous in the face of the strangeness falling on their home as softly and inexorably as midwinter snow. The elder one would make a good reward for disciples who demonstrated loyalty, and the child might be of some use to a returned soul. God's Brother found a use for everything.

Content, for the moment, Quinn swept into the hall, relishing the opulence which greeted him. Tonight at least he could indulge himself in decadent splendour, quickening his serpent beast. For who did not appreciate absolute luxury?

The disciples knew their duties well enough, needing no supervision. They would flush out the manor's staff and open their bodies for possession. A chore repeated endlessly over the last week. His work would come later, selecting those who were worthy of a second chance at life, who would embrace the Night.

\*

'What—!' Genevieve began hotly as the last of the odd adults disappeared inside the manor's entrance.

Louise's hand clamped over her mouth. 'Come on!' She pulled hard on Genevieve's arm, nearly unbalancing the younger girl. Genevieve reluctantly allowed herself to be steered away.

'You heard Mother,' Louise said. 'We're to look after the horses.'

'Yes, but . . .'

'I don't know! All right? Mother will sort everything out.'

The words brought scant reassurance. What had happened to Daddy?

Boston must have been truly terrible to have affected him so.

Louise undid the strap on her riding hat, and tucked it under an arm. The manor and its grounds had become very quiet all of a sudden. The big entrance hall doors swinging shut had acted like a signal for the birds to fall still. Even the horses were docile.

The funereal sensation was broken by Merlin who had finally reached the gravel driveway. He barked quite piteously as he nosed round Louise's feet, his tongue lolling out as he wheezed heavily.

Louise gathered up the reins of both horses and started to lead them towards the stables. Genevieve grabbed Merlin's collar and hauled him along.

When they reached the stable block at the rear of the west wing there was nobody there, not even the two young stable lads Mr Butterworth had left in charge. The horses' hoofs made an almighty clattering on the cobbles of the yard outside, the noise reverberating off the walls.

'Louise,' Genevieve said forlornly. 'I don't like this. Those people with Daddy were really peculiar.'

'I know. But Mother will tell us what to do.'

'She went inside with them.'

'Yes.' Louise realized just how anxious mother had been for her and Genevieve to get away from Daddy's friends. She looked round the yard, uncertain what to do next. Would Mother send for them, or should they go in? Daddy would expect to talk with them. The old Daddy, she reminded herself sadly.

Louise settled for stalling. There was plenty to do in the stables; take the saddles off, brush the horses down, water them. She and Genevieve both took off their riding jackets and set to.

It was twenty minutes later, while they were putting the saddles back in the tack room, when they heard the first scream. The shock was all the more intense because it was male. A raw-throated yell of pain which dwindled away into a sobbing whimper.

Genevieve quietly put her arm around Louise's waist. Louise could feel her trembling, and patted her softly. 'It's all right,' she whispered.

The two of them edged over to the window and peered out. There was nothing to see in the courtyard. The manor's windows were black and blank, sucking in Duke's light.

'I'll go and find out what's happening,' Louise said.

'No!' Genevieve pulled at her urgently. 'Don't leave me alone. Please, Louise.' She was on the verge of tears.

Louise's hold tightened in reflex. 'OK, Gen, I won't leave you.'

'Promise? Really truly promise?'

'Promise!' She realized she was just as frightened as Genevieve. 'But we must find out what Mother wants us to do.'

Genevieve nodded brokenly. 'If you say so.'

Louise looked at the high stone wall of the west wing, sizing it up. What would Joshua do in a situation like this? She thought about the layout of the wing, the family apartments, the servants' utility passages. Rooms and corridors she knew better than anyone except for the chief housekeeper, and possibly Daddy.

She took Genevieve by the hand. 'Come on. We'll try and get up to Mother's boudoir without anyone seeing us. She's bound to go there eventually.'

They crept out into the courtyard and scuttled quickly along the foot of the wall to a small green door which led into a storeroom at the back of the kitchens. Louise expected a shouted challenge at any moment. She was panting by the time she heaved on the big iron handle and nipped inside.

The storeroom was filled with sacks of flour, and vegetables piled high in various wooden bays. Two narrow window slits, set high in the wall, cast a paltry grey light through their cobweb-caked panes.

Louise flicked the switch as Genevieve closed the door. A couple of naked light spheres on the roof sputtered weakly, then went out.

'Damnation!' Louise took Genevieve's hand, and threaded her way carefully round the boxes and sacks.

The utility corridor beyond had plain white plaster walls, and pale-yellow flagstones. Light spheres every twenty feet along its ceiling were flickering on and off completely at random. The effect made Louise feel mildly giddy, as if the corridor was swaying about.

'What's doing that?' Genevieve whispered fiercely.

'I've no idea,' she replied carefully. A dreadful ache of loneliness had stolen up on her without any warning. Cricklade didn't belong to them any more, she knew that now.

They made their way along the disconcerting corridor to the antechamber at the end. A cast-iron spiral staircase wound up through the ceiling.

Louise paused to hear if anyone was coming down. Then, satisfied they were still alone, started up.

The manor's main corridors were a vast contrast to the plain servant utilities. Wide strips of thick green and gold carpet ran along polished golden wood planks, the walls were hung with huge traditional oil paintings in ostentatious gilt frames. Small antique chests stood at regular intervals, holding either delicate objets d'art or cut-crystal vases with fragrant blooms of terrestrial and xenoc flowers grown in the manor's own conservatory.

The outside of the door at the top of the spiral stair was disguised as a wall panel. Louise teased it open, and peeped out. A grand stained-glass window at the far end of the corridor was sending out broad fans of coloured light to dye the walls and ceiling with tartan splashes. Engraved light spheres on the ceiling were glowing a lame amber. All of them emitted an unhealthy buzzing sound.

'Nobody about,' Louise said.

The two of them darted out and shut the panel behind them. They started edging towards their mother's boudoir.

A distant cry sounded. Louise couldn't work out where it came from. It wasn't close, though; thank sweet Jesus.

'Let's go back,' Genevieve said. 'Please, Louise. Mummy knows we went to the stables. She'll find us there.'

'We'll just see if she's here first. If she's not, then we'll go straight back.'

They heard the anguished cry again, even softer this time.

The boudoir door was twenty feet away. Louise steeled herself, and took a step towards it.

'Oh God, *no*! No, no, no. Stop it. Grant! Dear God, help me!'

Louise's muscles locked in terror. It was her mother's voice – Mother's scream – coming from behind the boudoir door.

'Grant, no! Oh, please. *Please*, no more.' A long, shrill howl of pain followed.

Genevieve was clutching at her in horror, soft whimpers bubbling from her open mouth. The light spheres right outside the boudoir door grew brighter. Within seconds they glared hotter than Duke at noon. Both of them burst apart with a thin pop, sending slivers of milky glass tinkling down on the carpet and floorboards.

Marjorie Kavanagh screeched again.

'Mummy!' Genevieve wailed.

Marjorie Kavanagh's scream broke off. There was a muffled, inexplicable thud from behind the door. Then: 'RUN! RUN, DARLING. JUST RUN, NOW!'

Louise was already stumbling back towards the concealed stairway door, holding on to a distraught, sobbing Genevieve. The boudoir door flew open, wood splintering from the force

**13**

of the blow which struck it. A solid shaft of sickly emerald light punched out into the corridor. Spidery shadows moved within it, growing denser.

Two figures emerged.

Louise gagged. It was Rachel Handley, one of the maids. She looked the same as normal. Except her hair. It had turned brick-red, the strands curling and coiling around each other in slow, oily movements.

Then Daddy was standing beside the chunky girl, still in his militia uniform. His face wore a foreign, sneering smile.

'Come to Papa, baby,' he growled happily, and took a step towards Louise.

All Louise could do was shake her head hopelessly. Genevieve had slumped to her knees, bawling and shaking violently.

'Come on, baby.' His voice had fallen to a silky coo.

Louise couldn't stop the sob that burped from her lips. Soon it would become a mad scream which would never end.

Her father laughed delightedly. A shape moved through the liquid green light behind him and Rachel.

Louise was so numbed she could no longer even manage a solitary gasp of surprise. It was Mrs Charlsworth, their nanny. Variously tyrant and surrogate mother, confidante and traitor. A rotund, middle-aged woman, with prematurely greying hair, and an otherwise sour face softened by hundreds of granny wrinkles.

She stabbed a knitting needle straight at Grant Kavanagh's face, aiming for his left eye. 'Leave my girls alone, you bloody fiend,' she yelled defiantly.

Louise could never quite remember exactly what happened next. Blood and miniature lightning forks. Rachel Handley letting out a clarion shriek. Shattered glass erupting from the frames of the oil paintings down half the length of the corridor as the blazing white lightning strobed violently.

Louise crammed her hands over her ears as the shriek

threatened to crack open her skull. The lightning died away. When she looked up, instead of her father there was a hulking humanoid shape standing beside Rachel. It wore strange armour, made entirely of little squares of dark metal, embossed with scarlet runes, and tied together with brass wire. 'Bitch!' it stormed at a quailing Mrs Charlsworth. Thick streamers of bright orange smoke were belching out of its eye slits.

Rachel Handley's arms turned incandescent. She clamped her splayed fingers over Mrs Charlsworth's cheeks, teeth bared in exertion as she pushed in. Skin sizzled and charred below her fingertips. Mrs Charlsworth mewed in agony. The maid released her. She slumped backwards, her head lolling to one side; and she looked at Louise, smiling as tears seeped down her ruined cheeks. 'Go,' she mouthed.

The grievous plea seemed to kick directly into Louise's nervous system. She pushed her shoulders into the wall, levering herself upright.

Mrs Charlsworth grinned mirthlessly as the maid and the burly warrior closed on her to consummate their vengeance. She raised the pathetic knitting needle again.

Ribbons of white fire snaked round Rachel's arms as she grinned at her prey. Small balls of it dripped off her fingertips, flying horizontally towards the stricken woman, eating eagerly through the starched grey uniform. A booming laugh emerged from the clinking armour, mingling with Mrs Charlsworth's gurgles of pain.

Louise put her arm under Genevieve's shoulder and lifted her bodily. Flashes of light and the sounds of Mrs Charlsworth's torture flooded the corridor behind her.

I mustn't turn back. I mustn't.

Her fingers found the catch for the concealed door and it swung open silently. She almost hurled Genevieve through the gap into the gloom beyond, heedless of whether anyone else was on the stairs.

The door slid shut.

'Gen? Gen!' Louise shook the petrified girl. 'Gen, we have to get out of here.' There was no response. 'Oh dear Jesus.' The urge to curl into a ball and weep her troubles away was strengthening.

If I do that, I'll die. And the baby with me.

She tightened her grip on Genevieve's hand, and hurried down the spiral stairs. At least Genevieve's limbs were working. Though what would happen if they met another of those ... people-creatures was another question altogether.

They'd just reached the small anteroom at the bottom of the spiral when a loud hammering began above. Louise started to run down the corridor to the storeroom. Genevieve stumbled along beside her; a low determined humming came from her lips.

The hammering stopped, and there was the brassy thump of an explosion. Tendrils of bluish static shivered down the spiral stair, grounding out through the floor. Red stone tiles quaked and cracked. The dimming light spheres along the ceiling sprang back to full intensity again.

'Faster, Gen!' she shouted.

They charged into the storeroom and through the green door leading to the courtyard. Merlin was standing in the wide open gateway of the stable block, barking incessantly. Louise headed straight for him. If they could take a horse they'd be free. She could ride better than anyone else at the manor.

They were still five yards short of the stables when two people ran out of the storeroom. It was Rachel and her father. *Except it's not really him*, she thought desperately.

'Come back, Louise,' the dark knight called. 'Come along, sweetie. Daddy wants a cuddle.'

Louise and Genevieve dashed round the gates. Merlin stared out at the yard for a second, then turned quickly and followed them inside.

Globules of white fire smashed into the stable doors, breaking apart into complex webs which probed the woodwork with the tenacity of a ghoul's fingers. Glossy black paint blistered and vaporized, the planks began to blaze furiously.

'Undo the stall doors,' Louise called above the incendiary roar of the fire, and the braying, agitated horses. She had to say it again before Genevieve fumbled with the first bolt. The horse inside the stall shot out into the aisle which ran the length of the stable.

Louise rushed for the far end of the stables. Merlin was yapping hysterically behind her. Fire had spread from the doors to straw bundled loosely in the manger. Orange sparks were flying like rain in a hurricane. Thick arms of black smoke coiled insidiously along the ceiling.

The voices from outside called again, issuing orders and promises in equal amounts. None of which were real. Treachery on the grandest scale.

Screams were being added to the clamour in the courtyard now. Quinn's disciples had inevitably gained the upper hand; Cricklade's few remaining free servants were being hunted and possessed without any attempt at stealth.

Louise reached the stall at the end of the stables, the one with Daddy's magnificent black stallion, a bloodline geneered to a perfection which nineteenth-century sporting kings could only dream of. The bolt slid back easily, and she grabbed the bridle before he had a chance to arrow into the aisle. He snorted furiously at her, but allowed her to steady him. She had to stand on a bale of hay in order to mount him.

The fire had spread with horrendous speed. Several of the stalls were burning now, their stout old timber walls shooting out wild sulphurous flames. Merlin was backing away from them, his barking fearful. Over half a dozen horses were milling in the aisle, whinnying direly. Flames had cut them off from the stable doors, the noisy inferno pressing them back from their one exit. She couldn't see Gen.

'Where are you?' she shouted. 'Gen!'

'Here. I'm here.' The voice was coming from an empty stall.

Louise urged the stallion forwards down the aisle, yelling wildly at the panicking horses in front of her. Two of them reared up, alarmed by this new, unexpected threat. They began to move en masse towards the flames.

'Quick!' Louise yelled.

Genevieve saw her chance, and sprinted out into the aisle. Louise leant over and grabbed her. At first she thought she'd miscalculated the girl's weight, feeling herself starting to slide downwards. But then Genevieve snatched at the stallion's mane, causing it to bay sharply. Just as Louise was sure her spine would snap, or she'd crash headfirst onto the aisle's stone flagging, Genevieve levered herself up to straddle the base of the stallion's neck.

The stable doors had been all but consumed by the eerily hot fire. Their remaining planks sagged and twisted on the glowing hinges, then lurched onto the cobbles with a loud bang.

With the intensity of the flames temporarily reduced, the horses raced for the door and their chance of freedom. Louise dug her heels into the stallion's flanks, spurring it on. There was an exhilarating burst of speed. Yellow spires of flame splashed across her left arm and leg, making her cry out. Genevieve squealed in front of her, batting frantically at her blouse. The stench of singed hair solidified in her nostrils. Thin layers of smoke stretching across the aisle whipped across her face, stinging her eyes.

Then they were through, out of the gaping door with its wreath of tiny flames scrabbling at the ruined frame, chasing after the other horses. Fresh air and low sunlight washed over them. The hefty knight in the dark mosaic armour was standing ahead of them. Streamers of bright orange smoke were still pouring from his helmet's eye slits. Sparks of white fire danced across his raised gauntlets. He started to point a rigid forefinger at them, the white fire building.

But the posse of crazed horses couldn't be deflected. The

first one flashed past stark inches from him. Alert to the danger they presented, even to someone with energistic power, he began to jump aside. That was his mistake. The second horse might have missed him if he'd stayed still. Instead, it struck him almost head on. The screaming horse buckled on top of him, forelegs snapping with an atrocious crack as inertia sent it hurtling forwards regardless. The knight was flung out sideways, spinning in the air. He landed bonelessly, bouncing a full foot above the cobbles before coming to a final rest. His armour vanished immediately, revealing Grant Kavanagh's body, still clad in his militia uniform. The fabric was torn in a dozen places, stained scarlet by the blood pumping from open wounds.

Louise gasped, instinctively pulling the reins to halt the stallion. Daddy was hurt!

But the flowing blood swiftly staunched itself. Ragged tears of flesh started to close up. The uniform was stitching itself together. Dusty, grazed leather shoes became metallic boots. He shook his head, grunting in what was little more than dazed annoyance.

Louise stared for a second as he started to raise himself onto his elbows, then spurred the horse away.

'Daddy!' Genevieve shouted in anguish.

'It's not him,' Louise told her through clenched teeth. 'Not now. That's something else. The Devil's own monster.'

Rachel Handley stood in front of the arched entrance to the courtyard. Hands on hips, aroused wormlet hair threshing eagerly. 'Nice try,' she laughed derisively. A hand was raised, palm towards the sisters. The awful white fire ignited around her wrist, wispy talons flaring from her fingers. Her laugh deepened at the sight of Louise's anguish, cutting across Merlin's miserable barking.

The bullet-bolt of white fire which caught Rachel Handley an inch above her left eye came from somewhere behind Louise. It bored straight through the maid's skull, detonating in the centre of the brain. The back of her head blew off in a gout of charred gore and rapidly dissipating violet flame. Her body remained upright for a second, then the muscles spasmed once before losing all tension. She pitched forwards. Bright arterial blood spilled out of her ruined, smoking brainpan.

Louise twisted round. The courtyard was empty apart from the woozy figure of her father still clambering to his feet. A hundred empty windows stared down at her. Faint screams echoed over the rooftops. Long swirls of flame churned noisily out of the stable block's wide doors.

Genevieve was shaking violently again, crying in convulsive gulps. Concern for the little girl overcame Louise's utter confusion, and she spurred the stallion once more, guiding it round the vile corpse and out through the courtyard's entrance.

*

From where he was standing beside the window of the third-floor guest suite, Quinn Dexter watched the girl riding the superb black horse hell-for-leather over the manor's greens-ward and towards the wolds. Not even his awesome energistic strength could reach the fleeing sisters from this distance.

He pursed his lips in distaste. Someone had aided them. Why, he couldn't think. The traitor must surely know they would never go unpunished. God's Brother saw all. Every soul was accountable in the end.

'They'll head for Colsterworth, of course,' he said. 'All they're doing is postponing the inevitable for a couple of hours. Most of that poxy little town already belongs to us.'

'Yes, Quinn,' said the boy standing behind him.

'And soon the whole world,' Quinn muttered. And then what?

He turned, and smiled proudly. 'It is so nice to see you again. I never thought I would. But He must have decided to reward me.'

'I love you, Quinn,' Lawrence Dillon said simply. The body

**20**

of the stable lad he had possessed was completely naked, the scars from the act of possession already nothing more than faint, fading pink lines on the tanned skin.

'I had to do what I did on Lalonde. You know that. We couldn't take you with us.'

'I know, Quinn,' Lawrence said devoutly. 'I was a liability. I was weak back then.' He knelt at Quinn's feet, and beamed up at the stern features of the black-robed figure. 'But I'm not any more. Now I can help you again. It will be like before, only better. The whole universe will bow before you, Quinn.'

'Yeah,' Quinn Dexter said slowly, savouring the thought. 'The fuckers just might.'

\*

The datavised alert woke Ralph Hiltch from a desultory sleep. As an ESA head of station, he'd been assigned some temporary quarters in the Royal Navy wardroom. Strange impersonal surroundings, and the emotional cold turkey from bringing Gerald Skibbow to Guyana had left his thoughts racing as he lay on the bunk after a three-hour debrief session last night. In the end he'd wound up accessing a mild trank program to relax his body.

At least he hadn't suffered any nightmares; though Jenny was never very far from the surface of his mind. A final frozen image of the mission: Jenny lying under a scrum of man-apes, datavising a kamikaze code into the power cell at her side. An image which didn't need storing in a neural nanonics memory cell in order to retain its clarity. She'd thought it was preferable to the alternative. But was she right? It was a question he'd asked himself a lot during the voyage to Ombey.

He swung his legs over the side of his bunk, and ran fingers through hair that badly needed a wash. The room's net processor informed him that Guyana asteroid had just gone to a code three alert status.

'Shit, now what?' As if he couldn't guess.

His neural nanonics reported an incoming call from Ombey's ESA office, tagged as the director, Roche Skark, himself. Ralph opened a secure channel to the net processor with a sense of grim inevitability. You didn't have to be psychic to know it wasn't going to be good.

'Sorry to haul you back to active status so soon after you arrived,' Roche Skark datavised. 'But the shit's just hit the fan. We need your expertise.'

'Sir?'

'It looks like three of the embassy personnel who came here on the *Ekwan* were sequestrated by the virus. They've gone down to the surface.'

'*What?*' Panic surged into Ralph's mind. Not that abomination, not loose here in the Kingdom. Please God. 'Are you certain?'

'Yes. I've just come out of a Privy Council security conference with the Princess. She authorized the code three alert because of it.'

Ralph's shoulders slumped. 'Oh God, and I brought them here.'

'You couldn't have known.'

'It's my job to know. God damn, I grew slack on Lalonde.'

'I doubt any of us would have done anything different.'

'Yes, sir.' Pity you couldn't sneer with a datavise.

'In any case, we're right behind them. Admiral Farquar and my good colleague Jannike Dermot over at the ISA have been commendably swift in implementing damage limitation procedures. We estimate the embassy trio are barely seven hours ahead of you.'

Ralph thought about the damage one of those things could inflict in seven hours, and put his head in his hands. 'That still gives them a lot of time to infect other people.' Implications began to sink through his crust of dismay. 'It'll be an exponential effect.'

'Possibly,' Roche Skark admitted. 'If it isn't contained very quickly we may have to abandon the entire Xingu continent. Quarantine procedures are already in place, and the police are being told how to handle the situation. But I want you there to instil a bit of urgency, kick a bit of arse.'

'Yes, sir. This active status call, does that mean I get to go after them in person?'

'It does. Technically, you're going down to advise the Xingu continent's civil authorities. As far as I'm concerned you can engage in as much fieldwork as you want, with the proviso that you don't expose yourself to the possibility of infection.'

'Thank you, sir.'

'Ralph, I don't mind telling you, what this energy virus can do scares the crap out of me. It has to be a precursor to something, some form of invasion. And safeguarding the Kingdom from such threats is my job. Yours too, come to that. So stop them, Ralph. Shoot first, and I'll whitewash later if needs be.'

'You've got it, sir.'

'Good man. The Admiral has assigned a flyer to take you down to Pasto city spaceport, it's leaving in twelve minutes. I'll have a full situation briefing data package assembled ready for you to access on the way down. Anything you want, let me know.'

'I'd like to take Will Danza and Dean Folan with me, and authorized to fire weapons on the surface. They know how to deal with people who have been sequestrated. Cathal Fitzgerald, too; he's seen the virus at work.'

'They'll have the authorization before you land.'

*

Duchess had risen above the horizon by the time Colsterworth came into view. The red-dwarf sun occupied a portion of the horizon diametrically opposite Duke, the two of them struggling to contaminate the landscape below with their own unique spectrum.

Duchess was winning the battle, rising in time to Duke's fall from the sky. The eastward slopes of the wolds were slowly slipping from verdant green to subdued burgundy. Aboriginal pine-analogue trees planted among the hedgerows of geneered hawthorn became grizzled pewter pillars. Even the stallion's ebony hide was darkening.

Duke's golden glow withdrew before the strengthening red tide.

For the first time in her life, Louise resented the primary's retreat. Duchess-night was usually a magical time, twisting the familiar world into a land of mysterious shadows and balmy air. This time the red stain had a distinctly ominous quality.

'Do you suppose Auntie Daphnie will be home?' Genevieve asked for what must have been the fifth time.

'I'm sure she will,' Louise replied. It had taken Genevieve a good half-hour to stop crying after they'd escaped from Cricklade. Louise had concentrated so hard on comforting her sister, she'd almost stopped being afraid herself. Certainly it was easy to blank what had happened from her mind. And she wasn't quite sure exactly what she was going to say to Aunt Daphnie. The actual truth would make her sound utterly mad. Yet anything less than the truth might not suffice. Whatever forces of justice and law were dispatched up to Cricklade would have to be well armed, and alert. The chief constable and the mayor had to believe what they faced was deadly real, not the imaginings of a half-hysterical teenage girl.

Fortunately she was a Kavanagh. People would have to listen. And please, dear Jesus, make them believe.

'Is that a fire?' Genevieve asked.

Louise jerked her head up. Colsterworth was spread out along a couple of miles of a shallow valley, growing up from the intersection of a river and the railway line. A somnolent little market town with ranks of neat terrace houses set amid small, pretty gardens. The larger homes of the important families occupied the gentle eastern slope, capturing the best view over the countryside. An industrial district of warehouses and small factories cluttered the ground around the wharf.

Three tall spires of filthy smoke were twisting up from the centre of the town. Flames burned at the base of one. Very bright flames. Whatever the building was, it glowed like molten iron.

'Oh no,' Louise gasped. 'Not here, too.' As she watched, one of the long river barges drifted past the last warehouse. Its decks were alight, the tarpaulin-covered cargo hold puffing out mushrooms of brown smoke. Louise guessed the barrels it carried were exploding. People were jumping off the bows, striking out for the bank.

'Now what?' Genevieve asked in a woeful voice.

'Let me think.' She had never considered that anywhere other than Cricklade was affected. But of course her father and that chilling young priest had stopped at Colsterworth first. And before that . . . A midwinter frost prickled her spine. Could it all have started at Boston? Everyone said an insurrection was beyond the Union's ability to mount. Was the whole island to be conquered by these demons in human guise?

And if so, where do we go?

'Look!' Genevieve was pointing ahead.

Louise saw a Romany caravan being driven at considerable speed along one of the roads on the edge of town below them. The driver was standing on the seat, striking at the cob horse's rump with a whip. It was a woman, her white dress flapping excitably in the wind.

'She's running away,' Genevieve cried. 'They can't have got to her yet.'

The notion that they could join up with an adult who would be on their side was a glorious tonic for Louise. Even if it was just a simple Romany woman, she thought uncharitably. But then didn't Romanies know about magic? The manor staff said they practised all sorts of dark arts. She might even know how to ward off the devils.

Louise took in the road ahead of the racing caravan with a keen sweep, trying to work out where they could meet it. There was nothing directly in front of the caravan, but three-quarters of a mile from the town was a large farmhouse.

Frantic animals were charging out of the open farmyard gate into the meadows; pigs, heifers, a trio of shire-horses, even a Labrador. The house's windows flashed brightly, emitting solid beams of blue-white light which appeared quite dazzling under the scarlet sky.

'She's heading straight for them,' Louise groaned. When she checked the careering caravan again it had just passed the last of Colsterworth's terraced houses. There were too many trees and bends ahead for the driver to see the farmhouse.

Louise sized up the distance to the road, and snapped the bridle. 'Hang on,' she told Genevieve. The stallion charged forwards, dusky red grass blurring beneath its hoofs. It jumped the first fence with hardly a break in its rhythm. Louise and Genevieve bounced down hard on its back, the younger girl letting out a yap of pain.

A jeering crowd had emerged on the road behind the caravan, milling beneath the twin clumps of geneered silver birch trees which marked the town's official boundary. It was almost as if they were unwilling, or unable, to venture out into the open fields. Several bolts of white fire were flung after the fleeing caravan, glinting stars which dwindled away after a few hundred yards.

Louise wanted to weep in frustration when she saw people walking out of the farmhouse and start down the road towards Colsterworth. The Romany woman still hadn't noticed the danger ahead.

'Shout at her! Stop her!' she cried to Genevieve.

They covered the last three hundred yards bellowing wildly.

It was to no avail. They were close enough to the caravan to see the foam coating the nose of the piebald cob before the Romany woman caught sight of them. Even then she didn't stop, although the reins were pulled back. The huge beast started to slow its frantic sprint to a more reasonable trot.

The stallion cleared the hedge and the ditch running alongside the road in an easy bound. Louise whipped it round to match the caravan's pace. There was a tremendous clattering coming from inside the wooden frame with its gaudy paint-work, as if an entire kitchen's worth of pots and pans were being juggled by malevolent clowns.

The Romany woman had long raven hair streaming out behind her, a brown face with round cheeks. Her white linen dress was stained with sweat. Defiant, wild eyes stared at the sisters. She made some kind of sign in the air.

A spell? Louise wondered. 'Stop!' she begged. 'Please stop. They're already ahead of you. They're at that farmhouse, *look*.'

The Romany woman stood up, searching the land beyond the cob's bobbing head. They had another quarter of a mile to go until they reached the farmhouse. But Louise had lost sight of the people who had come out of it.

'How do you know?' the woman called out.

'Just *stop*!' Genevieve squealed. Her small fists were bunched tight.

Carmitha looked the little girl over, then came to a decision. She nodded, and began to rein back.

The caravan's front axle snapped with a prodigious crunch-ing sound.

Carmitha just managed to grab hold of the frame as the whole caravan pitched forward. Sparks flew out from under-neath her as the world tilted sharply. A last wrenching snap and the caravan ground to a halt. One of the front wheels trundled past Olivier, her cob horse, then rolled down into the dry ditch at the side of the road.

'Shit!' She glared at the girls on the big black stallion, their soot-stained white blouses and grubby desolate faces. It must have been them. She'd thought they were pure, but you just couldn't tell. Not now. Her grandmother's ramblings on the

**27**

spirit world had been nothing more than campsite tales to delight and scare young children. But she did remember some of the old woman's words. She raised her hands so and summoned up the incantation.

'What are you doing?' the elder of the two girls yelled down at her. 'We have to get out of here. Now!'

Carmitha frowned in confusion. The girls both looked terrified, as well they might if they'd seen a tenth of what she had. Maybe they were untainted. But it if wasn't them who wrecked the caravan . . .

She heard a chuckle, and whirled round. The man just appeared out of the tree standing on the other side of the road from the ditch. Literally out of it. Bark lines faded from his body to reveal the most curious green tunic. Arms of jade silk, a jacket of lime wool, big brass buttons down the front, and a ridiculous pointed felt hat sprouting a couple of white feathers.

'Going somewhere, pretty ladies?' He bowed deeply, and doffed his hat.

Carmitha blinked. His tunic really was green. But it shouldn't have been, not in this light. 'Ride!' she called to the girls.

'Oh, no,' his voice sounded indignant, a host whose hospitality has proved inadequate. 'Do stay.'

One of the small kittledove birds in the tree behind him took flight with an indignant squawk. Its leathery wings folded back, and it dived towards the stallion. Intense blue and purple sparks fizzed out of its tail, leaving a contrail of saffron smoke behind it. The tiny organic missile streaked past the stallion's nose, and skewered into the ground with a wet thud.

Louise and Genevieve both reached out instinctively to pat and gentle the suddenly skittish stallion. Five more kittledoves were lined up on the pine's branches, their twittering stilled.

'In fact, I insist you stay,' the green man said, and smiled charmingly.

'Let the girls go,' Carmitha told him calmly. 'They're only children.'

His eyes lingered on Louise. 'But growing up so splendidly. Don't you agree?'

Louise stiffened.

Carmitha was about to argue, maybe even plead. But then she saw four more people marching down the road from the farmhouse and the fight went out of her. Taking to her heels would do no good. She'd seen what the white fireballs could do to flesh and bone. It was going to be bad enough without adding to the pain.

'Sorry, girls,' she said lamely.

Louise gave her a flicker of a smile. She looked at the green man. 'Touch me, peasant, and my fiancé will make you eat your own balls.'

Genevieve twisted round in astonishment to study her sister. Then she grinned weakly. Louise winked at her. Paper defiance, but it felt wonderful.

The green man chortled. 'Dearie me, and I thought you were a fine young lady.'

'Appearances can be deceptive,' she told him icily.

'I will enjoy teaching you some respect. I will personally see to it that your possession takes a good many days.'

Louise glanced briefly in the direction of the four men from the farmhouse who were now standing beside the placid cob. 'Are you quite sure you have mustered sufficient forces? I don't want you to be too frightened of me.'

The green man's laboured smile vanished altogether, as did his debonair manner. 'Know what, bitch? I'm going to make you watch while I fuck your little sister in half.'

Louise flinched, whitening.

'I believe this has gone far enough.' It was one of the men who'd arrived from the farm. He walked towards the green man.

Louise noticed how his legs bowed outward, making his shoulders rock slightly from side to side as he walked. But he was handsome, she acknowledged, with his dark skin and wavy jet-black hair tied back in a tiny ponytail. Rugged; backed up by a muscular build. He couldn't have been more than about twenty, or twenty-one – the same age as Joshua. His dark-blue jacket was dreadfully old-fashioned, it had long tails which came to a point just behind his knees. He wore it over a yellow waistcoat, and a white silk shirt that had a tiny turn-down collar complemented with a black ruffled tie. Strange apparel, but elegant, too.

'What's your problem, boy?' the green man asked, scornfully.

'Is that not apparent, sir? I find it difficult to see how even a gentleman of your tenor can bring it upon himself to threaten three frightened ladies.'

The green man's mouth split into a wide smile. 'Oh you do, do you?' White fire speared out of his fingers. It struck the newcomer's blue jacket, and flared wide into clawing braids. He stood calmly as the coils of incandescence scrabbled ineffectively across him, as if he wore an overcoat of impervious glass.

Unperturbed by his failure, the green man swung a fist. It didn't connect. His opponent ducked back with surprising speed. A fist slammed into the side of the green man's torso. Three ribs shattered from the enhanced blow. He had to exert some of his own energistic strength to stave off the pain, and repair the physical damage. 'Fuck,' he spat, shocked by this inexplicable recalcitrance on the part of someone who was supposed to be a comrade. 'What the hell are you doing?'

'I would have thought that obvious, sir,' the other said behind raised fists. 'I am defending the honour of these ladies.'

'I don't believe this,' the green man exclaimed. 'Look, let's just get them possessed, and forget it. OK? Sorry I mouthed off. But that girl has the Devil's own tongue.'

'No, sir, I will not forget your threat to the child. Our Lord may have deemed me unworthy to join Him in Heaven. But still I count myself as more than a beast who would commit rapine upon such a delicate flower.'

'Delicate . . . You have got to be fucking joking.'

'Never, sir.'

The green man threw his hands in the air. He turned to the other three who had accompanied his opponent from the farm. 'Come on, together we can boil his crazy brain and send him back to the beyond. Or maybe you can ignore them pleading to be let back into the world,' he added significantly.

The three men exchanged an uneasy glance.

'You may indeed best me,' the man in the blue jacket said. 'But if I have to return to that accursed nowhere, I will take at least one of you with me, possibly more. So come then, who will it be?'

'I don't need any of this,' one of the three muttered. He pushed his way past the other two, and started to walk down the road toward the town.

The man in the blue jacket gave the remaining two an enquiring look. Both of them shook their heads, and set off down the road.

'What is it with you?' the green man shouted furiously.

'I believe that is a rhetorical question.'

'OK, so who the hell are you?'

For a moment his handsome face faltered in its resolution. Pain burned in his eyes. 'They called me Titreano, once,' he whispered.

'OK, Titreano. It's your party. For now. But when Quinn Dexter catches up with you, it's going to be the morning after like you've never fucking believed.'

He turned on a heel, and stalked off along the road.

Carmitha finally remembered to breathe again. 'Oh my God!' Her knees gave out, and she sat down fast. 'I thought I was dead.'

Titreano smiled graciously. 'You would not have been killed. What they bring is something far worse.'

'Like *what*?'

'Possession.'

She gave him a long mistrustful stare. 'And you're one of them.'

'To my shame, my lady, I am.'

Carmitha didn't know what the hell to believe.

'Please, sir?' Genevieve asked. 'What should we do now? Where can Louise and I go?'

Louise patted Gen's hands in caution. This Titreano was one of the devils after all, no matter how friendly he appeared to be.

'I do not know this place,' Titreano said. 'But I would advise against yonder town.'

'We know that,' Genevieve said spryly.

Titreano smiled up at her. 'Indeed you do. And what is your name, little one?'

'Genevieve. And this is my sister, Louise. We're Kavanaghs, you know.'

Carmitha groaned, and rolled her eyes. 'Christ, that's all I need right now,' she mumbled.

Louise gave her a puzzled frown.

'I regret I have not heard of your family,' Titreano said in what sounded like sincere regret. 'But from your pride, I venture it is a great one.'

'We own a lot of Kesteven between us,' Genevieve said. She was beginning to like this man. He'd stood up to the horrors, and he was polite. Not many grown-ups were polite to her, they never seemed to have the time to talk at all. He was very well-spoken, too.

'Kesteven?' Titreano said. 'Now that is a name I do know. I believe that it is an area of Lincolnshire. Am I correct?'

'Back on Earth, yes,' Louise said.

'Back on Earth,' Titreano repeated incredulously. He glanced over at Duke, then switched to Duchess. 'Exactly what is this world?'

'Norfolk. It's an English-ethnic planet.'

'The majority,' Carmitha said.

Louise frowned again. Whatever was wrong with the Romany woman?

Titreano closed his eyes, as if he felt some deep pain. 'I sailed upon oceans, and I thought no challenge could be greater,' he said faintly. 'And now men sail the void between stars. Oh, how I remember them. The constellations burning so bright at night. How could I ever have known? God's creation has a majesty which lays men bare at his feet.'

'You were a sailor?' Louise asked uncertainly.

'Yes, my lady Louise. I had the honour to serve my king thus.'

'King? There's no royal family in the Earth's English state any more.'

Titreano slowly opened his eyes, revealing only sadness. 'No king?'

'No. But our Mountbatten family are descended from British royalty. The Prince guards our constitution.'

'So nobility has not yet been overthrown by darkness. Ah well, I should be content.'

'How come you didn't know about old England?' Genevieve asked. 'I mean, you knew about Kesteven being a part of it.'

'What year is this, little one?'

Genevieve considered protesting about being called 'little one', but he didn't seem to mean it in a nasty way. 'Year 102 since settlement. But those are Norfolk years; they're four Earth years long. So back on Earth it's 2611.'

'2611 years since Our Lord was born,' Titreano said in awe. 'Dear Heaven. So long? Though the torment I endured felt as if it were eternal.'

'What torment?' Genevieve asked with innocent curiosity.

'The torment all us damned souls face after they die, little one.'

Genevieve's jaw dropped, her mouth forming a wide O.

'You've been dead?' Louise asked, not believing a word of it.

'Yes, lady Louise. I was dead, for over eight hundred years.'

'That's what you meant by possession?' Carmitha said.

'Yes, my lady,' he said gravely.

Carmitha pinched the top of her nose, wrinkling her brow. 'And how, exactly, did you come back?'

'I do not know, except a way was opened into this body's heart.'

'You mean that's not your body?'

'No. This is a mortal man by the name of Eamon Goodwin, though I now wear my own form above his. I hear him crying inside me.' He fixed Carmitha with a steady eye. 'That is why the others pursue you. There are millions of souls lost in the torment of beyond. All seek living bodies so they may breathe again.'

'Us?' Genevieve squeaked.

'Yes, little one. You. I'm sorry.'

'Look, this is all very interesting,' Carmitha said. 'Complete drivel, but interesting. However, just in case you haven't caught hold, right now we are drowning in deep shit. I don't know what you freaks really are, possessed zombies or something nice and simple like xenocs with psychic powers. But when that green bastard reaches Colsterworth he's going to be coming back with a lot of friends. I've got to unhitch my horse, and we three' – her gesture took in the sisters – 'have got to be long gone.' She arched an eyebrow. 'Right, Miss Kavanagh?'

'Yes,' Louise nodded.

Titreano glanced at the passive cob, then the stallion. 'If you are serious in your intent, you should travel together in your caravan. None of you has a saddle, and this mighty beast has the look of Hercules about him. I'll wager he can maintain a steady pace for many hours.'

'Brilliant,' Carmitha snorted. She hopped down onto the hard-packed dirt of the road, and slapped the side of her ruined caravan. 'We'll just wait here for a wheelwright to come along, shall we?'

Titreano smiled. He walked over to the ditch where the wheel had fallen in.

Carmitha's next acidic phrase died unspoken as he righted the wheel and pushed it (one handed!) up out of the ditch, treating it as though it was a child's hoop. The wheel was five feet in diameter, and made of good, heavy tythorn wood. Three strong men would struggle to lift it between them.

'My God.' She wasn't sure if she should be thankful or horrified at such a demonstration. If all of them were like him, then hope had deserted Norfolk long ago.

Titreano reached the caravan, and bent down.

'You're not going to . . .'

He lifted it by the front corner; two, three feet off the road. Carmitha watched as the broken axle slowly straightened itself. The splintered fracture in the middle blurred, then for a brief moment the wood appeared to run like a liquid. It solidified. And the axle was whole again.

Titreano jemmied the wheel back on to the bearing.

'What are you?' Carmitha whispered weakly.

'I have already explained, my lady,' Titreano said. 'What I can never do is bring you to believe what I am. That must come of its own accord, as God wills.'

He went over to the stallion, and held his arms up. 'Come on, little one, down you come.'

Genevieve hesitated.

'Go on,' Louise said quietly. Plainly, if Titreano had wanted to harm them, he would have done it by now. The more she saw of these strange people, the more her heart blackened. What could possibly fight such power?

Genevieve smiled scampishly, and swung a leg over the stallion. She slithered down his flank into Titreano's grip.

'Thank you,' she said as he put her down. 'And thank you for helping us, too.'

'How could I not? I may be damned, but I am not devoid of honour.'

Louise got most of the way down the stallion before she accepted his steadying hand. She managed a fast, embarrassed grin of thanks.

'I'm sore all over,' Genevieve complained, hands rubbing her bottom.

'Where to?' Louise asked Carmitha.

'I'm not sure,' the Romany replied. 'There should be a lot of my folk in the caves above Holbeach. We always gather there if there's any kind of trouble abroad. You can hold those caves for a long time; they're high in the cliffs, not easy to reach.'

'It would be a short siege this time, I fear,' Titreano said.

'You got a better idea?' she snapped back.

'You cannot stay on this island, not if you wish to escape possession. Does this world have ships?'

'Some,' Louise said.

'Then you should try to buy passage.'

'To go where?' Carmitha asked. 'If your kind really are after bodies, exactly where would be safe?'

'That would depend on how swiftly your leaders rally. There will be war, many dreadful battles. There can be nothing less. Both our kinds are fighting for their very existence.'

'Then we must go to Norwich, the capital,' Louise said decisively. 'We must warn the government.'

'Norwich is five thousand miles away,' Carmitha said. 'A ship would take weeks.'

'We can't hide here and do nothing.'

'I'm not risking myself on some foolhardy errand, girl. Fat lot of good you precious landowners will be, anyway. What has

Norfolk got which can fight off the likes of him.' She waved a hand towards Titreano.

'The Confederation Navy squadron is still here,' Louise said, her voice raised now. 'They have fabulous weapons.'

'Of mass destruction. How's that going to help people who have been possessed? We need to break the possession, not slaughter the afflicted.'

They glared at each other.

'There's an aeroambulance based at Bytham,' Genevieve said brightly. 'That could reach Norwich in five hours.'

Louise and Carmitha stared at her. Then Louise broke into a grin, and kissed her sister. 'Now who's the clever one?'

Genevieve smiled round pertly. Titreano made a face at her, and she giggled.

Carmitha glanced down the road. 'Bytham's about a seven-hour journey from here. Assuming we don't run into any more problems.'

'We won't,' Genevieve said. She took hold of Titreano's hand. 'Not with you with us.'

He grinned half-heartedly. 'I . . .'

'You're not going to leave us alone?' a suddenly stricken Genevieve asked.

'Of course not, little one.'

'That's that, then.'

Carmitha shook her head. 'I must be bloody mad even thinking of doing this. Louise, tether your horse to the caravan.'

Louise did as she was told. Carmitha climbed back up on the caravan, regarding it suspiciously as she put her weight on the driver's seat. 'How long is that repair going to last for?'

'I'm not quite sure,' Titreano said apologetically. He helped Genevieve up beside Carmitha, then hoisted himself up.

When Louise clambered up, the narrow seat was cramped. She was pressed against Titreano, and not quite sure how she should react to such proximity. If only it were Joshua, she thought wistfully.

Carmitha flicked the reins, and Olivier started forward at an easy trot.

Genevieve folded her arms in satisfaction, and cocked her head to look up at Titreano. 'Did you help us at Cricklade as well?'

'How's that, little one?'

'One of the possessed was trying to stop us from riding away,' Louise said. 'She was hit by white fire. We wouldn't be here otherwise.'

'No, lady Louise. It was not I.'

Louise settled back into the hard seat, unhappy the mystery hadn't been solved. But then by today's standards it was one of the lesser problems confronting her.

Olivier trotted on down the road as Duke finally disappeared below the wolds. Behind the caravan, more of Colsterworth's buildings had started to burn.

*

Guyana's naval spaceport was a standard hollow sphere of girders, almost two kilometres in diameter. Like a globular silver-white mushroom on a very thin stalk, it stuck out of the asteroid's rotation axis; the massive magnetic bearings on the end of the connecting spindle allowed it to remain stationary while the colossal rock rolled along its orbital track. The surface was built up from circular docking-bays linked together by a filigree of struts and transit tubes. Tanks, generators, crew stations, environmental maintenance machinery, and shark-fin thermo-dump panels were jumbled together in the gaps between bays, apparently without reference to any overall design logic.

Narrow rivers of twinkling star-specks looped around it all, twining in elaborate, interlocked figure-eights. The rivers had a current, their points of light drifting in the same direction at the same speed; cargo tugs, personnel commuters, and MSVs, firing their reaction drives to maintain the precise vectors fed to them by traffic control. Ombey's code three defence alert had stirred the spaceport into frantic activity for the second time in twenty-four hours. But this time instead of preparing to receive a single craft, frigates and battlecruisers were departing. Every few minutes one of the big spherical Royal Kulu Navy ships would launch from its docking-bay, rising through the traffic lanes of smaller support craft with an arc-bright glare of secondary fusion drives. They were racing for higher orbits, each with a different inclination, Strategic Defence Command positioning them so they englobed the entire planet, giving full interception coverage out to a million kilometres. If any unidentified ship emerged from a ZTT jump within that region, it would be engaged within a maximum of fifteen seconds.

Amid the departing warships a lone navy flyer rose from the spaceport. A flattened egg-shape fuselage of dark blue-grey silicolithium-composite, fifty metres long, fifteen wide. Coherent magnetic fields wrapped it in a warm golden glow of captured solar wind particles. Ion thrusters fired, manoeuvring it away from the big frigates. Then the fusion tube in the tail ignited, pushing it down towards the planet seventy-five thousand kilometres below.

The one-gee acceleration sucked Ralph Hiltch gently back into his seat, making the floor stand to the vertical. On the seat next to him, his flight bag rolled over once to lie in the crook of the cushioning.

'This vector will get us to Pasto spaceport in sixty-three minutes,' Cathal Fitzgerald datavised from the pilot's seat.

'Thanks,' Ralph replied. He widened the channel to include the two G66 troopers. 'I'd like you all to access the briefing that Skark gave me. This kind of information could be critical, and we need all the breaks we can get around here.'

That earned him a grin and a wave from Dean Folan, a

noncommittal grimace from Will Danza. They were both sitting on the other side of the aisle. The sixty-seater cabin seemed deserted with just the four of them using it.

None of his little team had complained or refused to go. Privately he'd made it quite clear they could pull out without any indiscipline action being entered on their file. But they'd all agreed, with varying degrees of enthusiasm – even Dean, who had the best excuse of all. He'd been in surgery for seven hours last night, the asteroid's Navy clinic had to rebuild sixty per cent of his arm. The boosted musculature, ruined by the hits he'd taken in Lalonde's jungle, had to be completely replaced with fresh artificial tissue, along with various blood vessels, skin, and nerves. The repair was still wrapped in a green sheath of medical nanonic packaging. But he was looking forward to levelling the score, he'd said cheerfully.

Ralph closed his eyes and let the briefing invade his mind, neural nanonics tabulating it into a sharply defined icono-graphic matrix. Details of the Xingu continent: a four and a half million square kilometre sprawl in the northern hemi-sphere, roughly diamond-shaped, with a long mountainous ridge of land extending out from its southern corner. The ridge crossed the equator; and Ombey's broad tropical zones meant the entire continent was an ideal farming region, with the one exception of the semi-desert occupying the centre. So far only two-fifths of it was inhabited, but with a population of seventy million it was the second most prosperous continent after Esparta, where the capital, Atherstone, was situated.

After Xingu came the embassy trio, Jacob Tremarco, Savion Kerwin, and Angeline Gallagher. Their career files contained nothing exceptional, they were all regular Kulu Foreign Office staffers, loyal, boring, bureaucrats. Visuals, family histories, medical reports. It was all there, and none of it particularly useful apart from the images. Ralph stored them in a neural nanonics memory cell, and spliced them with a general charac-teristics recognition program. He hadn't forgotten that strange image-shifting ability the sequestrated had demonstrated back on Lalonde. The recognition program might give him a slight edge if one of them attempted a disguise, though he didn't hold out much hope.

The most promising part of the data package was the series of measures Admiral Farquar and Leonard DeVille, Xingu's Home Office Minister, had implemented to quarantine the continent and trace the embassy trio. All civil traffic was being systematically shut down. Search programs were being loaded into the continent's data cores, watching for a trail of unexplained temporary glitches in processors and power circuits. Public area security monitor cameras had been given the visual pattern of the trio, and police patrols were also being briefed.

Maybe they'd get lucky, Ralph thought. Lalonde was a backward colony on the arse edge of nowhere, without any modern communications or much in the way of civil authority. But Ombey was part of the Kingdom, the society he'd sworn to defend with his life if need be. Because, years ago at university, when he'd discreetly been offered a commission in the agency, he'd considered Kulu a worthwhile society. The richest in the Confederation outside Edenism. Strong economically, and militarily; a technology leader. It had a judicial system which kept the average citizen safe on the streets, and was even reasonably fair by modern standards. Medical care was socialized. Most people had jobs. Admittedly, ruled by the Saldanas, it was hardly the most democratic of systems, but then short of the Edenist Consensus few democratic societies were truly representative. And there were a lot of planets which didn't even pretend to be egalitarian. So he'd swallowed any niggling self-suspicion of radicalism, and agreed to serve his King until his death.

What he'd seen of the galaxy had only served to strengthen his conviction that he'd done the right thing in taking the oath. The Kingdom was a civilized place compared to most, its citizens were entitled to lead their lives without interference.

And if that meant the ESA occasionally having to get its hands dirty, then so be it, as far as Ralph was concerned. A society worth having is worth protecting.

And thanks to its own nature, Ombey should definitely be able to cope better than Lalonde, although the very systems which made it more able also gave the enemy a greater opportunity to spread its subversion. The virus carriers had been slow to travel on Lalonde. Here they would suffer no such restrictions.

Cathal Fitzgerald cut the flyer's fusion drive when they were two hundred kilometres above Xingu. Gravity took over, pulling the flyer down. Its magnetic field expanded, applying subtle pressures to the tenuous gases pushing against the fuselage. Buoyant at the centre of a sparkling cushion of ions, the flyer banked to starboard, and began a gentle glide-spiral down towards the spaceport below.

They were a hundred and fifty kilometres high when the flight computer datavised a priority secure signal from Roche Skark into Ralph's neural nanonics.

'We might have a problem developing,' the ESA director told him. 'A civil passenger flight from Pasto to Atherstone is having trouble with its electronic systems, nothing critical but the glitches are constant. I'd like to bring you in on the Privy Council Security Committee to advise.'

'Yes, sir,' Ralph acknowledged. The datavise broadened to a security level one sensenviron conference. Ralph appeared to be sitting at an oval table in a plain white bubble room with walls at an indeterminate distance.

Admiral Farquar was sitting at the head of the table, with Roche Skark and Jannike Dermot flanking him. Ralph's neural nanonics identified the other three people present. Next to the ISA Director was Commander Deborah Unwin, head of Ombey's strategic-defence network; Ryle Thorne, Ombey's national Home Office Minister, was placed next to her. Ralph found himself with Roche Skark on one side and Leonard DeVille on the other.

'The plane is seven minutes from Atherstone,' Deborah Unwin said. 'We have to make a decision.'

'What is the plane's current status?' Ralph asked.

'The pilot was instructed to turn back to Pasto by my flight controllers as part of the quarantine procedures. And that's when he reported his difficulties. He says he'll be endangering the passengers if he has to fly all the way back to Pasto. And if it's a genuine malfunction he will be.'

'We can hardly go around using our SD platforms on civil aircraft just because they have a dodgy processor,' Ryle Thorne said.

'On the contrary, sir,' Ralph said. 'In this situation we have to maintain a policy of guilty until proven innocent. You cannot allow that plane to land in the capital, not under any circumstances. Not now.'

'If he has to fly back to Xingu he may well kill everyone on board,' the minister protested. 'The plane could be downed in the ocean.'

'Atherstone has a high proportion of military bases in the surrounding district,' Admiral Farquar said. 'If necessary the plane can simply sit on a landing pad surrounded by marines until we work out a satisfactory method of detecting if the virus is present.'

'Is the pilot using his neural nanonics to communicate with flight control?' Ralph asked.

'Yes,' Deborah said.

'OK, then it's a reasonable assumption that he's not been sequestrated. If you can guarantee a landing pad can be guarded securely, I say use it. But the plane must remain sealed until we find out what's happened to the embassy trio.'

'Good enough,' Admiral Farquar said.

'I'll put the marines at Sapcoat base on active status as of now,' Deborah said. 'That's over a hundred kilometres from Atherstone. The plane can reach it easily enough.'

'A hundred kilometres is a safe enough distance,' Ryle Thorne said smoothly.

Ralph didn't like the minister's attitude; he seemed to be treating this as if it was a minor natural incident, like a hurricane or earthquake. But then the minister had to go back to his constituents every five years and convince them he was acting in their best interests. Ordering SD platforms to fire on their fellow citizens might be hard to explain away in public relations terms. That was one of the reasons the royal Saldanas had a parliament to advise them. An insulating layer around the blame. Elected politicians were always culpable and replaceable.

'I'd also suggest that once the plane's landed you use an orbital sensor satellite to mount a permanent observation on it,' Ralph said. 'Just in case there's any attempt to break out. That way we can use the SD platforms as a last resort; sterilize the entire area.'

'That strikes me as somewhat excessive,' Ryle Thorne said, with elaborate politeness.

'Again, no, sir. On Lalonde the enemy were able to use their electronic-warfare capability to interfere with the LDC's observation satellite from the ground, they fuzzed the images to quite a degree. I'd say this fall-back option is the least we should be doing.'

'Ralph was brought in because of his experience in combating the virus,' Roche Skark said, smiling at the minister. 'He got off Lalonde precisely because he instigated these kind of protective measures.'

Ryle Thorne gave a short nod.

'Pity he didn't protect us from the virus,' Jannike muttered. Except in a sensenviron context nothing was really *sotto voce*; all utterances were deliberate.

Ralph glanced over at her, but the computer-synthesized image of her face gave nothing away.

*

Chapman Adkinson was getting mighty tired of the continual stream of datavises he was receiving from flight control. Worried, too. He wasn't dealing with civil flight control at Atherstone any more, they'd gone off-line eight minutes ago. Military protocols were being enforced now, the whole planet's traffic control was being routed through the Royal Navy operations centre on Guyana. And they were none too sympathetic to his condition.

Esparta was rolling by below the plane; one of the lush national parks which surrounded the capital. A jungle scarred only by the occasional Roman-straight motorway and dachas belonging to the aristocracy. The ocean was five minutes behind them.

His neural nanonics were accessing the external sensors, but the visual image was only being analysed in secondary mode, mainly to back up the inertial-guidance system which he no longer wholly trusted. He was concentrating on schematics of the plane's systems, twenty per cent of the on-board processors were suffering from random drop-outs. Some had come back on-line after a few seconds, others remained dead. The diagnostic programs he ran simply couldn't pinpoint the problem. And, even more disturbing, in the last fifteen minutes he'd been experiencing spikes and reductions in the power circuits.

That was what had made him argue with the military controllers. Processor glitches were an acceptable menace, there was so much redundancy built into the plane's electronic architecture it could survive an almost total shutdown; but power loss was in a different hazard category altogether. Chapman Adkinson had already decided that if they did try and force him to fly back over the ocean he was going to ditch there and then, and to hell with the penalties they'd load into his licence. The biohazard in Xingu couldn't be that lethal, surely?

'Chapman, stand by for some updated landing coordinates,' Guyana's flight controller datavised. 'We're diverting you.'

'Where to?' Chapman asked sceptically.

'Sapcoat base. They're prepping a clean reception area for you. Looks like the passengers are going to have to stay on board for a while once you're down.'

'As long as we get down.'

The coordinates came through, and Chapman fed them directly into the flight computer. Twelve minutes to Sapcoat. He could accept that. The plane banked gently to port, and began to curve away from the city which lay somewhere beyond the horizon's black and silver heat shimmer.

It was a signal for the glitches to quadruple. Circuits began to drop out at a frightening rate. A quarter of the systems schematic flicked to a daunting black, leaving only ghostly colourless outlines where functional hardware had been a moment before. Power to the two rear starboard compressors failed completely. He could hear the high-pitched background whine deepening as the blades slowed. The flight computer's compensation program went primary, but too many control surfaces had shut down for it to be truly effective.

'Mayday, mayday,' Chapman datavised. Even his primary transmitter had failed. Back-up processors were activated. The fuselage began to vibrate and judder, as the plane was ploughing through a patch of choppy air.

'What is it?' flight control asked.

'Losing power and height. Systems failure rate increasing. Shit! I just lost the tail rudder databus.' He datavised an emergency code into the flight computer. A silvery piston slid out of the horseshoe console in front of him, a dull chrome-red pistol grip on the end. It reached his lap, and rotated silently through ninety degrees. Chapman grabbed it. Manual control. Christ, I've never used one outside of Aviation Authority simulations!

The datavise bandwidth to the flight computer started to shrink. He prioritized the schematic to display absolute essentials. Holographic displays on the console came alive, duplicating the information.

'Find me a flat patch of land – now, damn it!' How he was going to bring the plane down in VTOL configuration with both the starboard compressors out wasn't something he wanted to think about. Maybe a motorway, and use it like a runway?

'Request denied.'

'*What?*'

'You may not land anywhere but the authorized coordinate.'

'Fuck you! We're going to crash.'

'Sorry, Chapman, you cannot land anywhere outside Sapcoat.'

'I can't *reach* Sapcoat.' His datavised control linkage to the flight computer began to fail. The pistol grip shifted slightly in his hand, and he felt the plane tilt in tandem.

Careful! he told himself. A firm pressure on the grip, and the nose began to edge back. The holographic horizon graphic showed he was still in a shallow dive. More pressure, and the descent rate slowed.

The door into the cockpit slid open. Chapman Adkinson was wired too tight to care. It was supposed to be codelocked, but the way hardware was crashing . . .

'Why have you altered course?'

Chapman shot a quick glance over his shoulder. The guy was dressed in a cheap suit, five years out of date. He wasn't just calm, he was serene. Incredible! He must feel the plane's buffeting.

'Technical problem,' Chapman managed to gasp. 'We're putting down at the nearest landing pad that can handle an emergency.' The pistol grip was fighting his every movement.

And now the holographic displays were wobbling. He wasn't sure if he could trust them any more. 'Get back into your seat now, feller.'

The man simply walked up behind the pilot's chair, and slid his head over Chapman's shoulder, peering out of the narrow curving windscreen. 'Where is Atherstone?'

'Look, pal—' Pain lanced deep into his thigh. Chapman grunted roughly at the shock of it. The man's left index finger was resting lightly on his leg, a small circle of his uniform's trouser fabric was burning around it.

Chapman swatted at the small blue flames, eyes blinking away sudden tears. His thigh muscle was smarting abominably.

'Where is Atherstone?' the man repeated. 'I have to go there.'

Chapman found his calmness more unnerving than the plane's failure. 'Listen, I wasn't joking when I said we had technical problems. We're going to be lucky if we make it over this sodding jungle. Forget about Atherstone.'

'I will hurt you again, harder this time. And I will keep on hurting you until you take me to Atherstone.'

I'm being hijacked! The realization was as staggering as it was improbable. Chapman gagged at the man. 'You have got to be kidding!'

'No joke, Captain. If you do not land in the capital, I will see to it you don't land anywhere.'

'Holy Christ.'

'Atherstone. Now where is it?'

'To the west somewhere. Christ, I'm not sure where. Inertial guidance has packed up.'

A mirthless smile appeared on the man's face. 'Then head west. It is a big city. I'm confident we'll see it from this height.'

Chapman did nothing. Then winced as the man reached past him. He put his hand on the windscreen, palm flat. Horrifyingly deep white cracks splintered outward.

'Atherstone.' It was an order.

'OK. Just take your goddam hand off that.' The windscreen was artificial sapphire, for God's sake. You couldn't crack it by leaning on it. A neural nanonics status check showed him half his synaptic augmentation had crashed, and virtually all the memory cells had shut down. But there was enough capacity for a datavise. 'Code F emergency,' he shot at the flight computer. Followed by a small prayer that it hadn't glitched completely yet.

'ISA Duty Officer,' came the response. 'What's happening?'

Chapman used the last of his neural nanonics' capacity to issue a metabolic override, keeping his face perfectly composed. He must not betray the silent conversation by a twitch of emotion. 'Attempted hijacking. And the plane's falling apart around me.'

'How many hijackers?'

'Just one, I think. Can't access the cabin cameras.'

'What does he want?'

'He says he wants to go to Atherstone.'

'What sort of weapon is he using?'

'Not sure. Nothing visible. Some kind of implant. Maybe a thermal induction field generator. He burnt my leg, and damaged the windscreen.'

'Thank you. Hold, please.'

Like I can do something else, Chapman thought acidly. He flicked a curious glance at the man, who was still standing to one side of the chair. His face was as emotionless as Chapman's.

The plane rocked alarmingly. Chapman tried to damp it down by swaying the pistol grip to compensate for the erratic motion. On a plane with fully responsive control surfaces it might have worked, here it just slewed the tail round. He noticed the nose had dropped a couple of degrees again.

'If you don't mind me asking, what's so bloody important in Atherstone that you've got to pull this crazy stunt?'

'People,' the man said blandly.

Some of the man's calmness was infiltrating Chapman's own

mind. He pulled back on the pistol grip, easing the nose up until they were level again. Nothing to it. At least there were no more systems dropping out, the malfunctions appeared to have plateaued. But landing would be a bitch.

'Chapman,' the ISA duty officer datavised. 'Please try and give us a visual of the hijacker. It's very important.'

'I'm down to about two kilometres altitude here, seventy per cent of my systems have failed, and all you want is to see what he looks like?'

'It will help us evaluate the situation.'

Chapman gave the man a sideways glance, loading the image into one of his remaining three functional memory cells. His datavise bit rate was now so low it took an entire second to relay the file.

Ralph Hiltch watched the pixels slowly clot together above the bubble room's table. 'Savion Kerwin,' he said, unsurprised.

'Without a doubt,' Admiral Farquar acknowledged.

'That plane left Pasto ninety minutes after their spaceplane landed,' Jannike Dermot said. 'They obviously intend to spread the virus as wide as possible.'

'As I've been telling you,' Roche Skark said. 'Ralph, do you think he's infected anyone else on the plane?'

'Quite possibly, sir. The flight computer and Chapman's neural nanonics are obviously being assaulted by a very powerful electronic-warfare field. It might be several of them acting in unison, or it could just be Savion Kerwin's proximity to the electronic systems, after all the flight computer is housed below the cockpit decking. But we really can't take the chance.'

'Agreed,' Admiral Farquar said.

Chapman Adkinson waited for fifteen seconds after he'd datavised the visual file. The crippled flight computer reported the communication channel was being maintained. Nothing happened, there was no update from the ISA officer.

A Royal Kulu Navy Reserve officer himself, Chapman knew of the response procedures for civil emergencies. Rule of thumb: the longer it took to come to a decision, the higher up the command structure the problem was being bumped. This one must be going right to the top. To the people authorized to make life-or-death decisions.

Intuition or just a crushing sense of doom, Chapman Adkinson started laughing gleefully.

The man turned to give him a strange look. 'What?'

'You'll see, feller, soon enough. Tell me, are you the biohazard?'

'Am I a—'

The X-ray laser struck the plane while it was still eighty kilometres away from Atherstone. Ombey's low-orbit SD platform weapons could hit combat wasps while they were still two and a half thousand kilometres distant. The plane was a mere three hundred kilometres beneath the platform which Deborah Unwin activated. Oxygen and nitrogen atoms in the lower atmosphere simply cracked into their subatomic constituents as the X-ray punched through the air, a searing purple lightning bolt eighty kilometres long. At its tip, the plane detonated into an ionized fog which billowed out like a miniature neon cyclone. Scraps of flaming, highly radioactive wreckage rained down on the pristine jungle below.

# 2

He was actually born in the United States of America, though few people ever liked to admit that particular fact, then or afterwards. His parents were from Naples; and southern Italians were universally looked down on and despised even by other poor immigrant groups, let alone the superior intellectuals of the time who openly stated their hatred of such an inferior breed of humans. As a consequence, few biographers and historians ever admitted the simple truth. He was, above all, a bona fide made in America monster.

His birthplace was Brooklyn, on the chilly winter's day of 17 January 1899, the fourth son of Gabriele and Teresina. At that time the district was home to a seething mass of such burgeoning immigrant families trying to build fresh lives for themselves in this new land of promise. Work was hard, labour cheap, the infamous city political machine strong, and the street gangs and racketeers prominent. But amongst all these difficulties his father managed to earn enough to support his family. And as a barber he did so independently and honestly, rare enough in that time and place.

Gabriele's son never followed that route; there were just too many odds stacked against him. The whole Brooklyn environment seemed designed to turn its young male population from the good.

After being expelled from school at fourteen for fighting

with his (female) teacher he began running errands for the local Association chief. One of the lowest of the low. But he learned; of men's vices and what they would do to obtain them, of the money to be made, of loyalty to his own, and most of all what people gave the Association's leader: respect. A commodity no one ever showed him or his father. Respect was the key to the world. A man who was respected had everything, a prince among men.

It was during this criminal apprenticeship that the ultimate seeds of his destruction were sown, ironically by himself. He contracted syphilis in one of the many seedy brothels which local boys of his age and background visited on a regular basis. Like most people he survived the first stage, the boils on his tender genitalia healing within a couple of weeks. Nor did the second stage disturb him to any great extent; an equally short time spent suffering what he convinced himself was a bad case of flu.

Had he visited a doctor he would have been told that it is the tertiary stage which proves lethal in a fifth of those infected, eating away at the frontal lobes of the brain. But once the second stage has passed, the malicious disease becomes dormant for a long time, sometimes measurable in decades, lulling its victim into a false sense of security. He saw no reason to share the humiliating knowledge.

Paradoxically, it was this very disease which contributed to his inexorable rise over the next fifteen years. Because of the nature of its attack on the brain it amplified its victim's personality traits. Traits which in his case had been forged in turn-of-the-century Brooklyn. They comprised contempt, hostility, anger in tandem with violence, greed, treachery, and guile. Excellent survival qualities for that particular dead-end district, but in a more civilized environment they set him apart. A barbarian in the city.

In 1920 he moved to Chicago. Within months he was heavily involved with one of the major syndicates. Until that era the syndicates ran the rackets and the brothels and the gambling joints, and raked in a good deal of hard currency. And at that relatively insignificant level they might well have remained. But that was the year when Prohibition came into effect throughout the nation.

The speakeasies opened, the back-alley breweries flourished. Money flooded into the coffers of the syndicates, millions upon millions of easy, dirty dollars. It gave them a power base they had never dreamed of before. They bought the police, they owned the mayor and most of City Hall, they intimidated the crusading newspapers and laughed at the law. But money brought its own special problem. Everybody could see how vast the market was, how profitable. They all wanted a cut.

And that was where he finally came into his own. Whole districts of Chicago degenerated into war zones as gangs and syndicates and bosses fought like lions for territory. With the neurosyphilis gradually eroding his rationality he emerged from the ranks of his contemporaries as the most ruthless, the most successful, and the most feared gang boss of them all. Quirks became vainglorious eccentricities; he opened soup kitchens for the poor; for slain colleagues he threw funeral parades which brought the entire city to a halt; he craved publicity and held press conferences to promote his magnanimity in giving people what they really wanted; he sponsored broke jazz musicians. His flamboyance became as legendary as his brutality.

At its height his tyranny was sufficient to be raised by the White House. Nothing the authorities did ever seemed to make the slightest difference. Arrests, inquiries, indictments; he bought his way out with his money, while his reputation (and associates) kept witnesses silent.

So government did what government always does when confronted with an opposition which can't be brought down by fair and legal means. It cheated.

His trial for tax evasion was later described as a legal lynching. The Treasury made up new rules, and proved he was guilty of breaking them. A man who was both directly and indirectly responsible for the deaths of hundreds of people was sentenced to eleven years in jail over delinquent taxes to the total of $215,080.

His atrocious reign was ended, but his life took another sixteen years to wither. In his latter years, with the neurosyphilis raging in his head, he lost all grip on reality, seeing visions and hearing voices. His mind now roamed through a purely imaginary state.

His body ceased to function in a peaceful enough manner on 25 January 1947, in a big house in Florida, surrounded by his grieving family. But when you are already utterly insane, there is little noticeable difference from your very own delusory universe and the distorted torment of the beyond into which your soul slips.

Over six hundred years passed.

The entity which emerged from the beyond into the fractured, bleeding body of Brad Lovegrove, fourth assistant manager (urban sanitation maintenance division) of the Tarosa metamech corp of New California, didn't even realize he was back in living reality. Not to start with, anyway.

The first possessed being to reach New California did so on a cargo starship from Norfolk, one of the twenty-two insurgents Edmund Rigby had created in Boston. His name was Emmet Mordden, and as soon as he reached the planet's surface he began the process of conquest; snatching people off the streets and the autoways, inflicting agonizing injuries to weaken their spirits and open their minds to receive the souls in the beyond.

It was a small band of possessed filtering unobtrusively through the boulevards of San Angeles in the days which followed, slowly building up their own ranks. Like all of the possessed emerging across the Confederation they had no distinct strategy, simply a single driving impulse to bring more souls back from the beyond.

But this one among them was of no use to the cause. His

mind shattered, he could relate to no external stimuli. He shouted hysterical warnings to his brother Frank, he wept, he delivered huge monologues about his shoe factory where he promised he'd give them all work, tiny spits of energy would fly from him without warning, he giggled constantly, he shat his pants and started slinging it about. Whenever they brought him food his energistic ability would turn it to the image of hot spicy pasta which gave off an appalling stink.

After two days, the growing cabal simply left him behind in the disused shop they'd been using as a base. Had they bothered to check him before they left they would have noticed that the behaviour was slightly more moderate, the talk more coherent.

Psychotic thought patterns which had formed in the early 1940s and run on unchecked for six centuries had finally begun to operate within a healthy neuron structure once more. There were no chemical imbalances, no spirochaete bacteria, not even traces of mild alcohol toxicology, for Lovegrove didn't drink. His sanity gradually returned as thought processes began to move in more natural cycles.

He felt his mind and memories coming together as though he was emerging from the worst cocaine trip ever (his long-time vice back in the 1920s). For hours he simply lay on the floor trembling as events tumbled through his expanding consciousness. Events which sickened the heart, but which belonged to him nonetheless.

He never heard the shop's service door open, the surprised grunt of the realtor agent, the heavy footsteps marching towards him. A hand closed round his shoulder, and shook him strongly.

'Hey, dude, how did you get in here?'

He flinched violently, and looked up to see a man in a very strange helmet, as if glossy green beetle wings had folded over his skull. Blank, golden bubble eyes stared down at him. He screamed, and spun over. The equally startled realtor took a pace backwards, reaching for the illegal nervejam stick in his jacket pocket.

Despite six hundred years of technological development he could still recognize a hand weapon when he saw one. Of course, the real give-away was the expression of superiority and nervous relief on the realtor's face; the one every frightened man wears when a piece has suddenly swung the odds back in his favour.

He drew his own gun. Except it wasn't exactly a draw – no holster. One second he wanted a gun, the next his fingers were gripping a Thompson sub-machine-gun. He fired. And the once-familiar roar of the weapon nicknamed a trench broom hammered his ears again. A curiously white flame emerged from the barrel as he trained it on the cowering figure of the realtor, fighting the upwards kick.

Next, all that was left was a mangled jerking body pumping gallons of blood onto the bare carbon-concrete floor. The craterous wounds were smoking, as if the bullets had been incendiaries.

Bulge-eyed and horrified, he stared at the corpse for a moment, then barfed helplessly. His head was whirling as though the eternal nightmare was returning to clasp him once more.

'Christ no,' he groaned. 'No more of that crap. Please.' The Thompson sub-machine-gun had vanished as mysteriously as it had appeared. Ignoring the nausea which sent shivers down every limb he staggered out through the door and into the street. Crazy images mugged him. His head slowly tipped back to view the pulp-magazine fantasy into which he had emerged. Low wispy clouds scudding in from the ocean were sliced apart by the chromeglass sword-blade skyscrapers which made up downtown San Angeles. Prismatic light gleamed and sparkled off every surface. A city of a hundred towering multicoloured mirrors. Then he saw the naked crescent of a small reddish moon directly overhead. Starship exhausts swarmed casually across the cobalt sky like incandescent fireflies. His jaw dropped in absolute bewilderment. 'Goddam, what the hell *is* this place?' demanded Alphonse Capone.

\*

Ombey's rotation had carried the Xingu continent fully into the centre of the darkside as the Royal Navy flyer Ralph Hiltch was using passed over the outskirts of Pasto. The city was situated on the western coast, growing out from the Falling Jumbo seaport in a sustained hundred-year development spree. It was flat country, ideal for urbanization, placing minimal problems in the path of the ambitious civil engineers. Most of the level districts were laid out in geometric patterns, housing estates alternating with broad parks and elaborate commercial districts. Hills, such as they were, had been claimed by the richer residents for their chateaux and mansions.

Accessing the flyer's sensor suite, Ralph could see them standing proud in their own lakes of illumination at the centre of large sable-black grounds. The narrow, brightly lit roads which wound round the hills were the only curves amid the vast grid of brilliant orange lines spread out below him. Pasto looked so beautifully crisp and functional, a grand symbol of the Kingdom's economic prowess, like a merit badge pinned on the planet.

And somewhere down there, amid all that glittering regimented architecture and human dynamism, were people who could bring the whole edifice crashing down. Probably within a couple of days, certainly no more than a week.

Cathal Fitzgerald angled the flyer towards the big cube-shaped building which was the Xingu Police Force headquarters. They landed on a roof pad, at the end of a row of small arrowhead-planform hypersonic planes.

Two people were waiting for Ralph at the bottom of the airstairs. Landon McCullock, the police commissioner; a hale seventy-year-old, almost two metres tall, with thick crew-cut ginger hair, dressed in a midnight-blue uniform with several silver stripes on his right arm. Beside him was Diana Tiernan, the Police Department's Technology Division chief, a fragile, elderly woman who was dwarfed by her superior officer, a contrast which tended to emphasize her scholarly appearance.

'I appreciate you coming down,' Landon said, as he shook hands with Ralph. 'It can't have been an easy choice for you to face this thing again. The data package briefing I've had from Admiral Farquar gave me a nasty jolt. My people aren't exactly geared up to cope with this kind of incident.'

'Who is?' Ralph said, a shade too mordantly. 'But we coped on Lalonde; and we aim to do a little better here.'

'Glad to hear it,' Landon said gruffly. He nodded crisply to the other three ESA agents coming down the airstairs and Will and Dean carrying their combat gear in a couple of bulky bags. His lips twitched in a memory-induced smile of admiration as he eyed the two G66 division troops. 'Been a while since I was at that end of an operation,' he murmured.

'Any update on the plane which was shot down?' Ralph asked as they all walked towards the waiting lift.

'Nobody survived, if that's what you mean,' Diana Tiernan said. She gave Ralph a curious look. 'Was that what you meant?'

'They're tough bastards,' Will said curtly.

She shrugged. 'I accessed a recording of Adkinson's datavise. This energy-manipulation ability Savion Kerwin demonstrated seemed quite extraordinary.'

'He didn't show you a tenth of what he could do,' Ralph said.

The lift doors closed, and they descended to the command centre. A windowless room which took up half of the floor, it had been designed to handle every conceivable civil emergency, from a plane crash in the heart of a city to outright civil war. Twenty-four separate coordination hubs were arranged in three rows, circles of consoles with fifteen operators apiece. Their access authority to the continent's net was absolute, providing them with unparalleled sensor coverage and communication linkages.

When Ralph walked in every seat was taken, the air seemed almost solid with the laserlight speckles thrown off by hundreds of individual AV projection pillars. He saw Leonard DeVille sitting at Hub One, a raised ring of consoles in the middle of the room. The Home Office Minister's welcoming handshake lacked the sincerity of McCullock's.

Ralph was quickly introduced to the others at Hub One: Warren Aspinal, the Prime Minister of the Xingu continental parliament; Vicky Keogh, who was McCullock's deputy; and Bernard Gibson, the police Armed Tactical Squad commander. One of the AV pillars was projecting an image of Admiral Farquar.

'All air traffic was shut down twenty minutes ago,' said Landon McCullock. 'Even the police patrol plane flights are down to a complete minimum.'

'And the crews of those that are still in the air have been required to datavise files from their neural nanonics to us here,' Diana said. 'That way we can be reasonably certain that none of them have been infected by Tremarco or Gallagher.'

'There was an awful lot of traffic using the city roads when I flew over,' Ralph said. 'I'd like to see that shut down now. I can't emphasize enough that we must restrict the population's movement.'

'It's only ten o'clock in Pasto,' Leonard DeVille said. 'People are still on their way home, others are out for the evening and will want to return later. If you shut down the city's ground traffic now you will cause an astounding level of confusion. One which would be beyond the police force's ability to resolve for hours. And we must have the police in reserve to deal with the embassy people when we detect them. We thought it made more sense to allow everyone to go home as normal, then introduce the curfew. That way, the vast majority will be confined to their houses come tomorrow morning. And if Tremarco and Gallagher have started infecting them, any outbreak will be localized, which means we should be able to isolate it relatively easily.'

Sit down and make an impact, why not? Ralph thought sourly. I'm supposed to listen and advise, not barge in and act like a loudmouth arsehole. Damn, but Kerwin and the plane have me hyped too hot.

Trying to hide how foolish he felt, he asked: 'What time will you introduce the curfew?'

'One o'clock,' the Prime Minister said. 'Only diehard night-birds will still be out and about then. Thank heavens it's not Saturday night. We really would have been in trouble then.'

'OK, I can live with that,' Ralph said. There was a quick victory smile on DeVille's face, which Ralph chose to ignore. 'What about the other cities and towns; and more importantly the motorways?'

'All Xingu's urban areas are having their curfew enacted at one o'clock,' McCullock said. 'The continent's got three time zones, so it'll be phased in from the east. As for the motorways, we're already shutting down their traffic, so cities and major towns are going to be segregated. That wasn't a problem, all motorway vehicles are supervised by the Transport Department route- and flow-management computers. It's the vehicles on the minor roads which are giving us a headache; they're all switched to autonomous control processors. And even worse are the farm vehicles out there in the countryside, half of those bloody things have manual steering.'

'We estimate it will take another three hours to completely shut down all ground traffic movement,' Diana said. 'At the moment we're setting up an interface between Strategic Defence Command and our police Traffic Division. That way when the low-orbit SD sensor satellites locate a vehicle moving on a minor road they'll perform an identification sweep and cata-logue it. Traffic Division will then datavise the control processor

**61**

to halt. For manually operated vehicles we'll have to dispatch a patrol car.' A hand waved lamely in the air. 'That's the theory, anyway. A continent-wide detection and identification operation is going to tie up an awful lot of processing power, which we really can't spare right now. If we're not very careful we'll wind up with a capacity shortfall.'

'I thought that was impossible in this day and age,' Warren Aspinal interjected mildly.

Diana's humour became stern. 'Under normal circumstances, yes. But what we're attempting to do has no precedent.' She offered the others sitting at Hub One a reluctant shrug. 'My team have got three AIs in the basement and two at the university which are attempting to access and analyse every single processor in the city simultaneously. It's a refinement of Admiral Farquar's idea of tracking the energy virus through the electronic distortion it generates. We've seen it demonstrated on Adkinson's plane, so we know the approximate nature of the beast. All we have to do is perform the most massive correlation exercise ever mounted; find out which processors have suffered glitches during the last eight hours, and cross-reference the time and geographical location. If it happened to several unrelated processors in the same area at the same time, then it's a good chance the glitch was caused by someone who has the virus.'

'Every processor?' Vicky Keogh queried.

'Every single one.' Just for a moment, Diana's dried up face wore an adolescent's smile. 'From public net processors to street light timers, AV adverts, automatic doors, vending machines, mechanoids, personal communication blocks, household supervisor arrays. The lot.'

'Will it work?' Ralph asked.

'No reason why not. As I said, there's a possible capacity problem, and the AIs might not manage to format the correlation program within the time-frame we need. But when the program comes on-line it should provide us with the electronic equivalent of footprints in snow.'

'And then what?' Warren Aspinal asked quietly. 'That's what you were really brought down here for, Ralph. What do we do with these people if we find them? There is something of a political dimension involved in using the SD systems every time we locate one of the afflicted. I don't dispute the necessity of eliminating Adkinson's plane. And people will certainly agree to us using force to obliterate the threat to start with. But ultimately we have to find a method of eradicating the energy virus itself, and without damaging the victim. Not even the Princess can go on authorizing such destruction for ever, not when it's aimed against the Kingdom's own subjects.'

'We're working on it,' said Admiral Farquar. 'Gerald Skibbow is going into personality debrief right now. If we can find out how he was infected, and how he was purged, then we ought to be able to come up with a solution, some kind of countermeasure.'

'How long will that take?' Leonard DeVille asked.

'Insufficient information,' the Admiral answered. 'Skibbow isn't very strong. They're going to have to go easy on him.'

'Yet if our preparations are to mean anything,' Landon McCullock said, 'we have to catch the embassy duo tonight, or tomorrow morning at the latest. And not just them, but anyone they've come into contact with. This situation could escalate beyond our ability to contain. We must have a policy ready for dealing with them. So far the only thing we know that works is overwhelming firepower.'

'I've got two things to offer,' Ralph said. He looked at Bernard Gibson, and gave him a penitent smile. 'Your squads are going to have to take the brunt of this, especially to start with.'

The police AT squad commander grinned. 'What we get paid for.'

'OK, here it is, then. First off, contact with someone who is carrying the energy virus doesn't necessarily mean you contract it yourself. Will and Dean are excellent proof of that. They captured Skibbow, they manhandled him, they were in very close proximity to him for hours, and they're both fine. Also, I was on the *Ekwan* with the embassy trio for a week, and I wasn't infected.

'Secondly, despite their power they can be intimidated into submission. But you have to be prepared to use ultraviolence against them, and they have to know that. One hint of weakness, one hesitation, and they'll hit you with everything they've got. So when we do find the first one, it'll be me and my team which heads the actual assault. OK?'

'I'm not arguing so far,' Bernard Gibson said.

'Good. What I envisage is spreading the experience of an assault in the same fashion the virus is spread. Everyone who is with me on the first assault will be able to familiarize themselves with what has to be done. After that you assign them to head their own squads for the next round of captures, and so on. That way we have your whole division brought up to speed as swiftly as possible.'

'Fine. And what do we do with them once we've subdued them?'

'Shove them into zero-tau.'

'You think that's what got rid of Skibbow's virus?' Admiral Farquar asked sharply.

'I believe it's a good possibility, sir. He was extremely reluctant to enter the pod in *Ekwan*. Right up until then he was quite docile. When he found out we were going to put him in the pod, he became almost hysterical. I think he was frightened. And certainly when he came out at this end the virus was gone.'

'Excellent,' Warren Aspinal smiled at Ralph. 'That course of action is certainly more palatable than lining them all up against a wall and shooting them.'

'Even if zero-tau isn't responsible for erasing the virus, we know it can contain them the same way it holds ordinary people,' Ralph said. 'We can keep them in stasis until we do find a permanent solution.'

'How many zero-tau pods have we got available?' Landon asked Diana.

The Technology Division chief had a long blink while her neural nanonics chased down the relevant files. 'Here in the building there are three. Probably another ten or fifteen in the city in total. They tend to be used almost exclusively by the space industry.'

'There's five thousand unused pods in the *Ekwan* right now,' Ralph pointed out. 'That ought to be enough if this AI correlation program works. Frankly, if we need more than that, we've lost.'

'I'll get some maintenance crews to start disconnecting them straight away,' Admiral Farquar said. 'We can send them down to you in cargo flyers on automatic pilot.'

'That just leaves us with forcing infected people into them,' Ralph said. He caught Bernard's gaze. 'Which is going to be even worse than capturing them.'

'Possible trace,' Diana announced without warning as she received a datavise from one of the AIs. Everyone sitting at Hub One turned their attention on her. 'It's a taxi which left the spaceport twenty minutes after the embassy trio's space-plane arrived. The vehicle's processor array started suffering some strange glitches five minutes later. Contact was lost after a further two minutes. But it can't have been a total shutdown, because traffic control has no record of a breakdown in that sector this afternoon. It simply dropped out of the route-and-flow control loop.'

*

The warehouse which housed Mahalia Engineering Supplies was sealed up tight, one of twenty identical buildings lined up along the southern perimeter of the industrial park, separated from its neighbour by strips of ancient concrete and ranks of spindly trees planted to break the area's harshness. It was seventy metres long by twenty-five wide and fifteen high; dark-grey composite panels without a single window. From outside it looked inert, innocuous, if somewhat spurned of late. Furry tufts of Ombey's aboriginal vegetation were rooting in the gutters. Denuded chassis of ancient farm vehicles were stacked three or four deep along one wall, sleeting rust onto the concrete.

Ralph focused his shell-helmet's sensors on the broad roll-up door in the centre of the end wall fifty metres in front of him. It had taken him and his team four minutes to get here from police headquarters in one of the force's hypersonics, following the city-wide trail of route-and-flow processor drop-outs located by Diana and the AIs. Three police Armed Tactical squads had also been dispatched to the industrial park, under orders from Bernard Gibson. In total, eight of the little planes had landed, encircling the warehouse at a five hundred metre distance.

There wasn't a single crack of light leaking round the door. No sign of life. Infra-red didn't reveal much, either. He scanned along the side of the building again.

'The conditioning unit is on,' Ralph observed. 'I can see the motor's heat, and the grille's venting. Someone's in there.'

'Do you want us to infiltrate a nanonic sensor?' Nelson Akroid asked. He was the AT squad's captain, a stocky man in his late thirties, barely coming up to Ralph's shoulder. Not quite the image one expected from someone in his profession, although Ralph was used to the more bulky G66 troops. But then he suspected Nelson Akroid would be a healthy opponent in any hand-to-hand fighting, he had the right kind of subdued competence.

'It's a big building, plenty of opportunities for ambush,' Nelson Akroid said. 'We'd benefit from positioning them exactly. And my technical operators are good. The hostiles would never know they'd been infiltrated.' He sounded eager, which could be a flaw given this situation. Ralph couldn't imagine him and his squad seeing much active duty on Ombey. Their lot was more likely endless drills and exercises, the curse of any specialist field.

'No nanonics,' Ralph said. 'We could never depend on them anyway. I want the penetration team to deploy using standard search and seizure procedures. We can't believe any information from a sensor, so I want them going in fully alert.'

'Yes, sir.'

'Diana?' he datavised. 'What can the AIs tell me?'

'No change. There are no detectable glitches in the warehouse processors it can access. But there's very little electronic activity in there anyway, the office and administration systems are all switched off, so that doesn't mean much.'

'What's the taxi's maximum capacity?'

'Six. And the Industry Department says Mahalia employs fifteen staff. They service and distribute parts for agricultural machinery right across the continent.'

'OK, we'll assume the worst case. A minimum of twenty-one possible hostiles. Thanks, Diana.'

'Ralph, the AIs have discovered another two possible glitch traces in the city's route-and-flow network. I instructed them to concentrate on vehicle traffic around the spaceport in the period after the embassy trio arrived. Another taxi suffered a lot of problems, and the other's a freight vehicle.'

'Shit! Where are they now?'

'The AIs are running search routines; but these two are proving harder to find than the first taxi. I'll keep you updated.'

The channel closed. Ralph reviewed the AT squad as they closed in on the warehouse, black figures who seemed more mobile shadows than solid people. They know their job, he admitted grudgingly.

'Everyone's in place, sir,' Nelson Akroid datavised. 'And the AIs have taken command of the security cameras. The hostiles don't know we're here.'

'Fine.' Ralph didn't tell him that if Tremarco or Gallagher were in there they'd know for sure that the AT squad was outside. He wanted the squad charged up and professional, not shooting at phantoms.

'Stand by,' Ralph datavised to the squad. 'Status of the assault mechanoids, please?'

'On-line, sir,' the AT squad's technical officer reported.

Ralph gave the roll-up door another scan. Like Pandora's box, once it was open there would be no going back. And only he, Roche Skark, and Admiral Farquar knew that if the virus carriers got past the AT squad the industrial park would be targeted by SD platforms.

He could feel the low-orbit observation satellite sensors focusing on him.

'OK,' he told the squad. 'Go.'

*

The assault mechanoid which Ombey's AT squads employed looked as if the design team had been accessing too many horror sensevises for inspiration. Three metres high at full stretch, it had seven plasmatic legs, resembling tentacles with hoofs, which could move it over the most jumbled terrain at a sprint that even boosted humans couldn't match. Its body was a segmented barrel, giving it a serpentine flexibility. There were sockets for up to eight specialist limb attachments, varying from taloned climbing claws to mid-calibre gaussrifles. Control could be either autonomous, operating under a pre-loaded program, or a direct waldo datavise.

Five of them charged across the parking yard outside the warehouse, covering the last thirty metres in two seconds. Long whiplike cords lashed out from the top of their bodies, slashing against the door's centimetre-thick composite. Where they hit, they stuck, forming a horizontal crisscross grid four metres above the ground. A millisecond later the cords detonated; the shaped electron explosive charge was powerful enough to cut clean through a metre of concrete. The ruined door didn't even have time to fall. All five assault mechanoids slammed against it in a beautiful demonstration of synchronized mayhem. What was left of the door buckled and burst apart, sending jagged sections tumbling and bouncing down the warehouse's central aisle.

With a clear field of fire established, the mechanoids sent a fast, brutal barrage of short-range sense-overload ordnance blazing down the length of the building. Sensors instantly pinpointed the designated-hostile humans flailing around in panic, and concentrated their fire.

Behind the assault mechanoids the AT squad flashed through the smoking doorway. They scuttled for cover between the stacks of crates, scanning the deeper recesses of the warehouse for hidden hostiles. Then, with the mechanoids taking point duty down the central aisle, they began to fan out in their search and seizure formation.

Mixi Penrice, proprietor of Mahalia Engineering Supplies, had been struggling to remove the linear motor from the stolen taxi's rear axle when the assault mechanoids crashed into the warehouse door. The noise of the shaped electron explosive charges going off was like standing next to a lightning strike.

Shock made him jump half a metre in the air, not an easy feat given he was about twenty kilos overweight. Terrible lines of white light flared at the far end of the warehouse, and the door bulged inwards briefly before it disintegrated. But he wasn't so numbed that he didn't recognize the distinctive silhouette of the assault mechanoids sprinting through the swirl of smoke and composite splinters. Mixi shrieked, and dived for the floor, arms wrapping round his head. The full output of the sense-overload ordnance struck him. Strobing light which seemed to shine through his skull. Sound that was trying hard to shake every joint apart. The air turned to rocket exhaust, burning his tongue, his throat, his eyes. He vomited. He voided both his bladder and his bowels; a combination of sheer fright and nerve short-out pulses.

Three minutes later, when pain-filled consciousness returned, he found himself lying flat on his back, shaking spastically, with disgustingly thick liquids cooling and crusting across his clothes. Five large figures wearing dark armour suits were standing over him, horribly big guns trained on his abdomen.

Mixi tried to clasp his hands together in prayer. It was the day which in his heart he'd always known would come, the day when King Alastair II dispatched all the forces of law and order in his Kingdom to deal with Mixi Penrice, car thief and trader in stolen parts. 'Please,' he blabbed weakly. He couldn't hear his own voice; too much blood was running out of his ears. 'Please, I'll pay it all back. I promise. All the systems we flogged off, every penny we got. I'll tell you who my fences are. I'll give you the name of the bloke who wrote the program which screws up the road network processors. You can have it all. Just, please, don't kill me.' He started sobbing wretchedly.

Ralph Hiltch slowly pulled back his shell-helmet's moulded visor. 'Oh *fuck!*' he yelled.

*

The white-plaster and stone interior of Cricklade's family chapel was comfy and sober without the exorbitant lavishness prevalent throughout the rest of the manor. Its history was cheerful, anyone walking into it for the first time was immediately aware of that; you only had to close your eyes to see the innumerable christenings, the grand marriage ceremonies of the heirs, Christmas masses, choral evenings. It was as much a part of the Kavanaghs as the rich land outside.

Now though, its gentle sanctity had been methodically

violated. Icon panels defaced, the dainty stained-glass windows broken, the statues of Christ and the Virgin Mary smashed. Every crucifix had been inverted; red and black pentagons daubed on the walls.

The despoiling soothed Quinn as he knelt at the altar. Before him an iron brazier had been set up on top of the thick stone slab. Avaricious flames were busy consuming the Bibles and hymn books it contained.

His body's lusts satiated by Lawrence, fed on gourmet food, and over-indulged on the bottles of vintage Norfolk Tears from the cellar, he felt miraculously calm. Behind him, the ranks of novices stood to attention as they waited to be inducted into the sect. They would stand there, motionless, for all of eternity if necessary. They were that scared of him.

Luca Comar stood in front of them like some masterful drill sergeant. His dragon armour glinted dully in the firelight, small plumes of orange smoke snorting from his helmet's eye slits. He had worn the guise almost continually since possessing Grant Kavanagh's body. Compensating for some deep psychological fracture, Quinn thought. But then everyone returning from beyond was flaky to some degree.

Quinn allowed his contempt to rise, the raw emotion bubbling into his brain. The hem of his robe gave a small flutter. Here on Norfolk such pitiful masquerades would triumph, but on few other worlds. Most Confederation planets would fight back against the incursions of the possessed, and those were the planets which counted. The planets where the real war would be fought, the universal war for belief and devotion between the two celestial brothers. Norfolk was irrelevant to that struggle, it could contribute nothing, no weapons, no starships.

He lifted his gaze above the flames darting out of the brazier. A vermilion sky was visible through the gaping rents in the broken window. Less than a dozen first magnitude stars twinkled above the wolds, the rest of the universe had been washed out in the red dwarf's sullied glow. The tiny blue-white lights seemed so delicate and pure.

Quinn smiled at them. His calling finally revealed. He would bring his divine gift of guidance to the lost armies which God's Brother had seeded throughout the Confederation. It would be a crusade, a glorious march of the dead, folding the wings of Night around every spark of life and hope, and extinguishing it for ever.

First he would have to raise an army, and a fleet to carry them. A frisson of his own, very personal desire kindled in his mind. The serpent beast speaking right into his heart. Banneth! Banneth was at the very core of the Confederation, where the greatest concentration of resources and weapons lay.

The obedient novices never moved when Quinn rose to his feet and turned to face them. There was an amused sneer on his snow-white face. He jabbed a finger at Luca Comar. 'Wait here, all of you,' he said, and stalked down the aisle. Dark magenta and woad moiré patterns skipped across the black fabric of his robe, reflections of his new-found determination. A click of his fingers, and Lawrence Dillon scurried after him.

They passed quickly through the ransacked manor and down the portico's stone steps to the farm rangers parked on the gravel. A smudge of smoke on the horizon betrayed Colsterworth's position.

'Get in,' Quinn said. He was on the verge of laughter.

Lawrence clambered into the front passenger seat as Quinn switched the motor on. The vehicle sped down the drive, sending pebbles skidding onto the grass verge.

'I wonder how long they'll stay in there like that?' Quinn mused.

'Aren't we coming back?'

'No. This crappy little world is a dead end, Lawrence. There's nothing left for us here, no purpose. We have to get off; and there aren't many navy starships in orbit. We've got to reach one before they all leave. The Confederation will be waking to the threat soon. They'll recall their fleets to protect the important worlds.'

'So where are we going if we do get a frigate?'

'Back to Earth. We have allies there. There are sects in every major arcology. We can gnaw at the Confederation from within, corrupt it completely.'

'Do you think the sects will help us?' Lawrence asked, curious.

'Eventually. They might need a little persuading first. I'll enjoy that.'

*

The AT squad had the exclusive shop completely surrounded. Moyce's Of Pasto occupied a more hospitable section of the city than the Mahalia warehouse. The building's design an indulgent neo-Napoleonic, overlooking one of the main parks. It catered to the aristocracy and the wealthy, trading mainly on snob value. The shop itself was only a fifth of the business, Moyce's main income came from supplying goods and delicacies to estates and the upwardly mobile clear across the continent. There were eight separate loading-bay doors at the back of the building to accommodate the fleet of lorries which were dispatched every night. Their feed roads merged into a single trunk road which led down into a tunnel where it joined one of the city's three major underground ring motorways.

At ten past midnight its distribution centre was normally busy loading lorries with the day's orders. Nothing had emerged in the four minutes it had taken the AT squad to deploy. However, there was one vehicle parked outside the end loading-bay, obstructing the road: the taxi which the AI cores had traced from the spaceport. All its electrical circuits had been switched off.

Fifteen assault mechanoids dashed up the slope to the loading-bay doors, their movements coordinated by the Squad's seven technical officers. Three of the doors were to be broken down, while the others were to be blocked and guarded. One had been assigned to the taxi.

Six of the assault mechanoids lashed out with their electron-explosive whips. Squad members were already running up the feed roads behind them.

Not all of the whips landed on target. Several detonations chopped into support pillars and door joists. Brick-sized lumps of stone came flying back down the feed roads. Two of the assault mechanoids were hit by the chunks, sending them cartwheeling backwards. The entire central loading-bay collapsed, bringing with it a large section of the first-storey floor. An avalanche of crates and cylindrical storage pods tumbled down onto the road, burying a further three assault mechanoids. They started to fire their sense-overload ordnance at random, flares and sonic shells punching out from the wreckage amid huge fountains of white packaging chips. Crumpled kitchen units and patio furniture skittered down the mound.

The AT squad members dived for cover as another two mechanoids started to gyrate in a wild dance. Their ordnance sprayed out, slamming into walls and arching away over the park. Only three of the remaining assault mechanoids were actually firing ordnance into the two loading-bays which had been broken open.

'Pull them back!' Ralph datavised to the technical officers. 'Get those bloody mechanoids out of there.'

Nothing happened. Sense-overload ordnance was squirting out everywhere. The assault mechanoids continued their lunatic dance. One pirouetted, twining its seven legs together, and promptly fell over. Ralph watched a dozen flares shoot straight upwards, illuminating the whole area. Black figures were lying prone on the feed roads, horribly exposed. A sense-overload flare speared straight into one of them; then it expanded strangely, creating a web of rippling white light. The suited figure thrashed about.

'Shit,' Ralph grunted. It wasn't a flare, it was the white fire. They were in the distribution centre! 'Shut down those mechanoids now,' he datavised. His neural nanonics reported that several of his suit systems were degrading.

'No response, sir,' a technical officer replied. 'We've lost them completely, even their fall-back routine has failed. How did they do that? The mechanoids are equipped with military-grade electronics, a megaton EMP couldn't glitch their processors.'

Ralph could imagine the officer's surprise, he'd undergone it himself back on Lalonde as the awful realization struck. He stood up from behind the parapet on top of the tunnel entrance, and lifted the heavy-calibre recoilless rifle. Targeting graphics flipped up over his helmet's sensor image. He fired at an assault mechanoid.

It exploded energetically, its power cells and ordnance detonating as soon as the armour-piercing round penetrated its flexing body. The blastwave shifted half of the precariously tangled wreckage in front of the collapsed loading-bay. More crates thumped down from the sagging first storey. Three assault mechanoids were sent lurching back down the feed roads, plasmatic legs juddering in fast undulations. Ralph shifted his aim, and took out another one just as it started to lumber upright.

'Squad, shoot out the mechanoids,' he ordered. His communication block informed him that half of the command channels had shut down. He switched on the block's external speaker, and repeated the order, bellowing it out across the feed roads at a volume which could be heard above the detonating mechanoids.

A streak of white fire lanced down from one of Moyce's upper windows. The threat-response program in Ralph's neural nanonics bullied his leg muscles with nerve-impulse overrides. He was flinging himself aside before his conscious mind had registered the attack.

Two more mechanoids exploded as he hit the concrete behind the parapet. He thought he recognized the heavy-calibre gaussrifle which the G66 troops used. Then an insidious serpent of white fire was coiling round his knee. His neural nanonics instantly erected analgesic blocks across his nerves, blanking out the pain. A medical display showed him skin and bone being eaten away by the white fire. The whole knee joint would be ruined in a matter of seconds if he couldn't extinguish it. Yet both Dean and Will said smothering it like natural flames made hardly any difference.

Ralph assigned his neural nanonics full control of his musculature, and simply designated the window which the white fire had emerged from. With detached interest he observed his body swivelling, the rifle barrel swinging round. His retinal target graphics locked over a window. Thirty-five rounds pummelled the black rectangle, a mixed barrage of high explosive (chemical), shrapnel, and incendiary.

Within two seconds the room had ceased to exist. Its carved stone frontage disintegrated behind a vast gout of flame, and showered down on the mêlée below.

The white fire round Ralph's knee vanished. He pulled a medical nanonic package from his belt, and slapped it on the charred wound.

Down on the feed roads most of the AT squad had switched to their communication-block speakers. Orders, warnings, and cries for help reverberated over the sound of multiple explosions. A vast fusillade of heavy-calibre rifle fire was pounding into the loading-bays. Comets of white fire poured out in retaliation.

'Nelson,' Ralph datavised. 'For Christ's sake, make sure the troops out front don't let anyone escape. They're to hold position and shoot to kill now. Forget the capture mission; we'll try it back here, but nobody else is to attempt anything fancy.'

'Yes, sir,' Nelson Akroid answered.

Ralph went back to the speaker. 'Cathal, let's try and get in there. Isolation procedure. Separate them, and nuke them.'

'Sir.' The cry came back over the parapet.

At least he's still alive, Ralph thought.

'Do you want stage two yet?' Admiral Farquar datavised.

'No, sir. They're still contained. Our perimeter is holding.'

'OK, Ralph. But the second there's a status change, I need to know.'

'Sir.'

His neural nanonics reported the medical package had finished knitting to his knee. The weight load it could take was down forty per cent. It would have to do. Ralph tucked the heavy-calibre rifle under his arm, then bending low he ran for the end of the parapet and the steps down to the trunk road.

Dean Folan signalled his team members forward, scurrying round the side of the big mound of crates and into the loading-bay area. Flames had taken hold amid the fragments piled outside.

It was dark inside. Projectile impacts had etched deep pocks into the bare carbon-concrete walls. Rat-tail tangles of wire and fibre-optic cable hung down from the fissured ceiling, swaying gently. Through the helmet's goggle lenses he could see very little, even with enhanced retinas on full sensitivity. He switched his shell-helmet sensors to low light and infra-red. Green and red images merged to form a pallid picture of the rear of the bay. Annoying glare spots flickered as small flames licked at the storage frames which lined the walls. Discrimination programs worked at eliminating them.

There were three corridors leading off straight back from the rear of the bay, formed by the storage frames. Metal grids containing crates and pods ready for the lorries, they looked like solid walls of huge bricks. Cargo-handling mechanoids had stalled on their rails which ran along the side of the frames, plasmatic arms dangling inertly. Water was pouring out of five or six broken ceiling pipes, spilling down the crates to pool on the floor.

Nothing moved in the corridors.

Dean left his gaussrifle at the head of the middle corridor, knowing it would be useless at close range, the electronic-warfare field would simply switch it off. Instead, he drew a semi-automatic rifle; it had a feed loop connected to his backpack, but the rounds were all chemical. The AT squad had grumbled about that at the start, questioning the wisdom of abandoning their power weapons. Nobody had complained much after the mechanoids went berserk, and their suit systems suffered innumerable drop-outs.

Three of the team followed him as he advanced down the corridor, also carrying the same semi-automatics. The rest of them spread out round the bay, and edged down the other two corridors.

A figure zipped across the end of the corridor. Dean fired, the roar of the semi-automatic impressively loud in the confined space. Plastic splinters from the crates ricocheted through the air as the bullets chiselled into them.

Dean started running forward. There was no corpse on the floor.

'Radford, did you see him?' Dean demanded. 'He was heading towards your corridor.'

'No, chief.'

'Anybody?'

All he got was a series of negatives, some shouted some datavised. No doubt the hostiles were about, his suit blocks were still badly affected by the electronic-warfare field. His injured arm was itchy, too.

He reached the end of the corridor. It was a junction to another three. 'Hell, it's a sodding maze back here.'

Radford arrived at the end of his corridor, semi-automatic sweeping the storage frames.

'OK, we fan out here,' Dean announced. 'All of you: keep two other squad members in visual range at all times. If you lose sight of your partners, then stop immediately and re-establish contact.'

He picked one of the corridors leading deeper into the shop, and beckoned a couple of the squad to follow him.

A creature landed on top of Radford; half man, half black lion, features merged grotesquely. Its weight carried him effortlessly to the floor. Dagger claws scraped at Radford's armour suit. But the integral valency generators had stiffened the fabric right from the moment of impact, protecting the vulnerable human skin inside. The creature howled in fury, thwarted at the very moment of triumph.

Radford's suit systems as well as his neural nanonics began to fail. Even his shocked yell was cut off as the communication-block speaker died. The suit's fabric started to give way, slowly softening. One of the claw tips screwed inwards, hungry for flesh.

Even amid his frantic twisting and bucking to throw off the creature Radford was aware of a whisper which bordered on the subliminal. One that had surely been there all his life, but only now with the prospect of death sharpening his perception was he fully conscious of it. It began to expand, not in volume, but in harmony. A whole chorus of whispers. Promising love. Promising sympathy. Promising to help, if he would just—

Bullets smashed into the flanks of the creature, mauling the fur and long muscle bands. Dean kept his semi-automatic steady as the thing clung to Radford's body. He could see the armour suit fabric hardening again. The claws slipping and skidding.

'Stop!' one of the team was shouting. 'You'll kill Radford.'

'He'll be worse than dead if we don't,' Dean snarled back. Spent casings were hurtling out of the rifle at an astounding rate. Still the beast wouldn't let go, its great head shaking from side to side, emitting a continual wail of pain.

The team was rushing en masse towards Dean down the narrow corridors between the storage frames. Two more were shouting at him to stop.

'Get back!' he ordered. 'Keep watching for the rest of the bastards.' His magazine was down to eighty per cent. The rifle didn't have the power to beat the creature, all it had to do was hang on. Blood was running down its hind legs, the fur where the bullets struck a pulped mass of raw flesh. Not enough damage, not nearly enough.

'Someone else fire at it, for Christ's sake!' Dean yelled frantically.

Another rifle opened up, and the second stream of bullets caught the creature on the side of its lycanthropic head. It let go of Radford, to be flung against the storage frame. The rampant wail from its gaping fangs redoubled.

Dean boosted the communication block's volume to its highest level. 'Surrender or die,' he told it.

It might have had a beast's form, but the look of absolute hatred came from an all-too-human eye.

'Grenade,' Dean ordered.

A small grey cylinder thumped into the bloody body.

Dean's armour suit froze for a second. His collar sensors picked up the detonation. Explosion followed by implosion. The outline of the beast collapsed into a middle-aged man, colour draining away. For a millisecond the man's silhouette was captured perfectly, sprawled against the storage frame. Then the bullets resumed their attack. This time, he had no defence.

Dean had seen worse carnage, though the limited space between the storage frames made it appear terrible. Several of the AT squad obviously didn't have his experience, or phlegmatism.

Radford was helped to his feet, and mumbled a subdued thanks. The sound of other teams from the AT squad shooting somewhere in the building echoed tinnily down the corridors.

Dean gave them another minute to gather their composure, then resumed the sweep. Ninety seconds after they started, Alexandria Noakes was calling for him.

She'd discovered a man hunched up in a gap between two crates. Dean rushed up to find her prodding the captive out of his hiding place with nervous thrusts of her rifle. He levelled his own rifle squarely on the man's head. 'Surrender or die,' he said.

The man gave a frail little laugh. 'But I am dead, señor.'

\*

Eight police department hypersonics had landed in the park outside Moyce's Of Pasto. Ralph limped wearily towards the one which doubled as a mobile command centre for the AT squad. There wasn't that much difference from the rest, except it had more sensors and communication gear.

It could have been worse, he told himself. At least Admiral Farquar and Deborah Unwin had stood down the SD platforms, for now.

Stretchers with injured AT squad members were arranged in a row below a couple of the hypersonics. Medics were moving among them, applying nanonic packages. One woman had been shoved into a zero-tau capsule, her wounds requiring immediate hospital treatment.

A big crowd of curious citizens had materialized, milling about in the park and spilling out across the roads. Police officers had thrown up barricades, keeping them well away.

Nine bulky fire department vehicles were parked outside Moyce's Of Pasto. Mechanoids trailing hoses had clambered up the walls with spiderlike tenacity, pumping foam and chemical inhibitors into smashed windows. A quarter of the roof was missing. Long flames were soaring up into the night sky out of the gap. Heat from the inferno was shattering the few remaining panes, creating more oxygen inflows.

It was going to be a long time before Moyce's would be open for business again.

Nelson Akroid was waiting for him at the foot of the command hypersonic's airstair. His shell-helmet was off, revealing a haggard face; a man who has seen the ungodly at play. 'Seventeen wounded, three fatalities, sir,' he said in a voice close to breaking. His right hand was covered by a medical nanonic package. Scorch marks were visible on his armour suit.

'And the hostiles?'

'Twenty-three killed, six captured.' He twisted his head round to stare at the blazing building. 'My teams, they did all right. We train to cope with nutters. But they beat those things. Christ—'

'They did good,' Ralph said quickly. 'But, Nelson, this was only round one.'

'Yes, sir.' He straightened up. 'The final sweep through the building was negative. What we could get to. I had to pull them out when the fire took hold. I've still got three teams covering it in case there are any hostiles still in there. They'll do another sweep when the fire's out.'

'Good man. Let's go see the prisoners.'

The AT squad was taking no chances; they were holding the six captives out on the park, keeping them a hundred metres apart. Each one stood in the centre of five squad members, five rifles trained on them.

Ralph walked over to the one Dean Folan and Cathal Fitzgerald were guarding. He datavised his communication block to open a channel to Roche Skark. 'You might like to see this, sir.'

'I accessed the sensors around Moyce's when the AT squad went in,' the ESA director datavised. 'They put up a lot of resistance.'

'Yes, sir.'

'If that happens each time we locate a nest of them, you'll wind up razing half the city.'

'The prospects for decontaminating them aren't too good,

either. They fight like mechanoids. Subduing them is tricky. These six are the exception.'

'I'll bring the rest of the committee in on the questioning. Can we have a visual, please?'

Ralph's neural nanonics informed him that other people were coming on-line to observe the interview; the Privy Council Security Committee over in Atherstone, and the civil authorities in Pasto's police headquarters. He instructed his communication block to widen the channel's bandwidth to a full sensevise, allowing them to access what he could see and hear.

Cathal Fitzgerald acknowledged him with the briefest nod as he approached. The man he was guarding was sitting on the grass, pointedly ignoring the semi-automatics directed at him. There was a slim white tube in his mouth. Its end was alight, glowing dully. As Ralph watched, the man sucked his cheeks in, and the coal glow brightened. He removed the tube from his mouth and exhaled a thin jet of smoke.

Ralph exchanged a puzzled frown with Cathal, who merely shrugged.

'Don't ask me, boss,' Cathal said.

Ralph ran a search program through his neural nanonics memory cells. The general encyclopedia section produced a file headed: Nicotine Inhalation.

'Hey, you,' he said.

The man looked up, and took another drag. '*Si*, señor.'

'That's a bad habit; which is why no one has done it for five centuries. Govcentral even refused an export licence for nicotine DNA.'

A sly, sulky smile. 'After my time, señor.'

'What's your name?'

'Santiago Vargas.'

'Lying little bastard,' Cathal Fitzgerald said. 'We ran an ident check. He's Hank Doyle, distribution supervisor for Moyce's.'

'Interesting,' Ralph said. 'Skibbow claimed to be someone else when he was caught: Kingsford Garrigan. Is that what the virus is programmed to do?'

'Don't know, señor. Don't know any virus.'

'Where does it come from? Where do you come from?'

'Me, señor? I come from Barcelona. A beautiful city. I show you round some time. I lived there many years. Some happy years, and some with my wife. I died there.'

The cigarette glow lit up watery eyes which watched Ralph shrewdly.

'You died there?'

'*Si*, señor.'

'This is bullshit. We need information, and fast. What's the maximum range of that white fire weapon?'

'Don't know, señor.'

'Then I suggest you run a quick memory check,' Ralph said coldly. 'Because you're no use to me otherwise. It'll be straight into zero-tau with you.'

Santiago Vargas stubbed his cigarette out on the grass. 'You want me to see how far I can throw it for you?'

'Sure.'

'OK.' He climbed to his feet with indolent slowness.

Ralph gestured out over the deserted reaches of the park. Santiago Vargas closed his eyes, and extended his arm. His hand blazed with light, and a bolt of white fire sizzled away. It streaked over the grass flinging out a multitude of tiny sparks as it went. At a hundred metres it started to expand and dim, slowing down. At a hundred and twenty metres it was a tenuous luminescent haze. It never reached a hundred and thirty metres, evaporating in mid-air.

Santiago Vargas wore a happy smile. 'All right! Pretty good, eh, señor? I practice, I maybe get better.'

'Believe me, you won't have the opportunity,' Ralph told him.

'OK.' He seemed unconcerned.

'How do you generate it?'

'Don't know, señor. I just think about it, and it happens.'

'Then let's try another tack. Why do you fire it?'

'I don't. That was the first time.'

'Your friends didn't have any of your inhibitions.'

'No.'

'So why didn't you join them? Why didn't you fight us?'

'I have no quarrel with you, señor. It is the ones with passion, they fight your soldiers. They bring back many more souls so they can be strong together.'

'They've infected others?'

'*Si.*'

'How many?'

Santiago Vargas offered up his hands, palms upward. 'I don't think anyone in the shop escaped possession. Sorry, señor.'

'Shit.' Ralph glanced back at the burning building, just in time to see another section of roof collapse. 'Landon?' he datavised. 'We'll need a full list of staff on the night-time shift. How many there were. Where they live.'

'Coming up,' the commissioner replied.

'How many of the infected left before we arrived?' he asked Santiago Vargas.

'Not sure, señor. There were many trucks.'

'They left on the delivery lorries?'

'*Si.* They sit in the back. You don't have no driver's seat these days. All mechanical. Very clever.'

Ralph stared in dismay at the sullen man.

'We've been concentrating on stopping passenger vehicles,' Diana Tiernan datavised. 'Cargo traffic was only a secondary concern.'

'Oh, Christ, if they got on to the motorways they could be halfway across the continent by now,' Ralph said.

'I'll reassign the AI vehicle search priority now.'

'If you find any of Moyce's lorries that are still moving,

target them with the SD platforms. We don't have any other choice.'

'I agree,' Admiral Farquar datavised.

'Ralph, ask him which of the embassy pair was in Moyce's, please,' Roche Skark datavised.

Ralph pulled a processor block from his belt, and ordered it to display pictures of Jacob Tremarco and Angeline Gallagher. He thrust it towards Vargas. 'Did you see either of these people in the shop?'

The man took his time. 'Him. I think.'

'So we've still got to find Angeline Gallagher,' Ralph said. 'Any more city traffic with glitched processors?'

'Three possibles,' Diana datavised. 'We've already got two of them located. Both taxis from the spaceport.'

'OK, assign an AT squad to each taxi. And make sure there are experienced personnel in both of them. What was the third trace?'

'A Longhound bus which left the airport ten minutes after the embassy trio landed; it was a scheduled southern route, right down to the tip of Mortonridge. We're working on its current location.'

'Right, I'm coming back to the police headquarters. We're finished here.'

'What about him?' Nelson Akroid asked, jerking a thumb at the captive.

Ralph glanced back. Santiago Vargas had found another cigarette from somewhere, and was smoking it quietly. He smiled. 'Can I go now, señor?' he asked hopefully.

Ralph returned the smile with equal honesty. 'Have the zero-tau pods from *Ekwan* arrived yet?' he datavised.

'The first batch are due to arrive at Pasto spaceport in twelve minutes,' Vicky Keogh replied.

'Cathal,' Ralph said out loud. 'See if Mr Vargas here will cooperate with us for just a little longer. I'd like to know the limits of the electronic-warfare field, and that illusion effect of theirs.'

'Yes, boss.'

'After that, take him and the others on a sightseeing trip to the spaceport. No exceptions.'

'My pleasure.'

*

The Loyola Hall was one of San Angeles's more prestigious live-event venues. It seated twenty-five thousand under a domed roof which could be retracted when the weather was balmy, as it so frequently was in that city. There were excellent access routes to the nearby elevated autoway, the subway station was a nexus for six of the lines which ran beneath the city; it even had seven landing pads for VIP aircraft. There were five-star restaurants and snack bars, hundreds of restrooms. Stewards were experienced and friendly. Police and promoters handled over two hundred events a year.

The whole site was an operation which functioned with silicon efficiency. Until today.

Eager kids had been arriving since six o'clock in the morning. It was now half-past seven in the evening. Around the walls they were thronging twenty deep; scrums outside the various public doors needed police mechanoids to maintain a loose kind of order, and even they were in danger of being overwhelmed. The kids had a lot of fun spraying them with soft drinks and smearing ice creams over the sensors.

Inside the hall every seat was taken, the tickets bought months ago. The aisles were filled with people, too, though how they had got in past the processor-regulated turnstiles was anyone's guess. Touts were becoming overnight millionaires, those that weren't being arrested or mugged by gangs of motivated fourteen-year-olds.

It was the last night of Jezzibella's 'Moral Bankruptcy' tour.

The New California system had endured five weeks of relentless media saturation as she swept across the asteroid settlements and down to the planetary surface. Rumour, of AV projectors broadcasting illegal activent patterns during her concerts to stimulate orgasms in the audience (not true, said the official press release, Jezzibella has abundant sexuality of her own, she doesn't need artificial aids to boost the Mood Fantasy she emotes). Hyperbole, about the President's youngest daughter being completely infatuated after meeting her, then sneaking out of the Blue Palace to go backstage at her concert (Jezzibella was delighted and deeply honoured to meet all members of the First Family, and we are not aware of any unauthorized entry to a concert). Scandal, when two of the band, Bruno and Busch, were arrested for violating public decency laws in front of a senior citizens holiday group, their bail posted at NC$1,000,000 (Bruno and Busch were engaged in a very wonderful, sensitive, and private act of love; and that bunch of filthy old perverts used enhanced retinas to spy on them). Straight hype, when Jezzibella visited (as a private citizen – so no sensevises, please) a children's ward in a poor district of town, and donated half a million fuseodollars to the hospital's germ-line treatment fund. Editorial shock at the way she flaunted her thirteen-year-old male companion, Emmerson (Mr Emmerson is Jezzibella's second cousin, and his passport clearly states he is sixteen). A lot of spectator fun, and official police cautions, derived from the extraordinarily violent fights between her entourage's security team and rover reporters. The storm of libel writs issued by Leroy Octavius, her manager, every time anyone suggested she was older than twenty-eight.

And in all those five weeks she never gave an interview, never made a single public utterance outside of her stage routine. She didn't have to. In that time, the regional office of Warner Castle Entertainment datavised out thirty-seven million copies of her new MF album *Life Kinetic* across the planet's communication net to worshipful fans; her back catalogue sold equally well.

The starship crews who normally made a tidy profit from selling a copy of an MF album to a distributor in star systems where they hadn't been officially released yet cursed their luck when they arrived on planets where Jezzibella had passed through in the last eighteen months. But then that was the point of being a touring artist. A new album every nine months, and visit ten star systems each year; it was the only way you could beat the bootleggers. If you weren't prepared to do that, the only money you ever got was from your home star system. Few made the transition from local wonder to galactic mega-star. It took a lot of money to travel, and entertainment companies were reluctant to invest. The artist had to demonstrate a colossal degree of professionalism and determination before they were worth the multimillion-fuseodollar risk. Once they'd breached the threshold, of course, the old adage of money making more money had never been truer.

High above the costly props and powerful AV stacks on stage, an optical-band sensor was scanning the crowd. Faces merged into a monotonous procession as it swept along the tiers and balconies. Fans came in distinct categories; the eager exhilarated ones, mostly young; boisterous and expectant, late teens; impatient, already stimmed out, nervous, fearfully worshipful, even a few who obviously wanted to be somewhere else but had come along to please their partner. Every costume Jezzibella had ever worn in an MF track was out there somewhere, from the simple to the peacock bizarre.

The sensor focused on a couple in matching leathers. The boy was nineteen or twenty, the girl at his side a bit younger. They had their arms around each other, very much in love. Both tall, healthy, vital.

Jezzibella cancelled the datavise from the sensor. 'Those two,' she told Leroy Octavius. 'I like them.'

The unpleasantly overweight manager glanced at the short AV pillar sticking out of his processor block, checking the two blithesome faces. 'Roger dodger. I'll get on it.'

There was no quibbling, not the faintest hint of disapproval. Jezzibella liked that; it was what made him such a good manager. He understood how it was for her, the things she required in order to function. She needed kids like those two. Needed what they'd got, the naïvety, the uncertainty, the delight at life. She had none of that left, now, not the sweet side of human nature. The eternal tour had drained it all away, somewhere out amongst the stars; the one energy which could leak out of a zero-tau field. Everything became secondary to the tour, feelings weren't allowed to interfere. And feelings suppressed long enough simply vanished. But she couldn't have that, because she needed an understanding of feelings in order to work. Circles. Her life was all circles.

So instead of her own emotions, she familiarized herself with this alien quality which others owned, examining it as if she was performing a doctoral thesis. Absorbed what she could, the brief taste allowing her to perform again, to fake it through yet one more show.

'I don't like them,' Emmerson said petulantly.

Jezzibella tried to smile at him, but the whole charade of pandering to him bored her now. She was standing, stark naked, in the middle of the green room while Libby Robosky, her personal image consultant, worked on her dermal scales. The bitek covering was a lot more subtle than a chameleon layer, allowing her to modify her body's whole external texture rather than simply changing colour. For some numbers she needed to have soft, sensitive skin, a young girl who quivered at her first lover's touch; then there was the untainted look, a body which was naturally graceful without workouts and fad diets (like the girl she'd seen through the hall's sensor); and of course the athlete/ballerina body, supple, hard, and muscular – a big favourite with the boys. It was the feel of her which everyone out there in the hall wanted to experience; Jezzibella in the flesh.

But the tiny scales had a short lifetime, and each one had to be annealed to her skin separately. Libby Robosky was an undoubted wizard when it came to applying them, using a modified medical nanonic package.

'You don't have to meet them,' Jezzibella told the boy patiently. 'I can take care of them by myself.'

'I don't want to be left alone all night. How come I can't pick someone out of the audience for myself?'

As the reporters had been allowed to discover, he really was only thirteen. She'd brought him into the entourage back on Borroloola, an interesting plaything. Now after two months of daily tantrums and broodiness the novelty value had been exhausted. 'Because this is the way it has to be. I need them for a reason. I've told you a hundred times.'

'OK. So why don't we do it now, then?'

'I have a show in quarter of an hour. Remember?'

'So what?' Emmerson challenged. 'Skip it. That'll cause a real publicity storm. And there won't be any backlash 'cos we're leaving.'

'Leroy,' she datavised. 'Take this fucking brat away before I split his skull open to find out where his brain went.'

Leroy Octavius waddled back over to where she stood. His bulky frame was clad in a light snakeskin jacket that was an optimistic size and a half too small. The tough, thin leather squeaked at every motion. 'Come on, son,' he said in a gruff voice. 'We're supposed to leave the artists to it this close to a show. You know how spaced out they get about performing. How about you and I have a look at the food they're laying on next door?'

The boy allowed himself to be led away, Leroy's huge hand draped over his shoulder, casually forceful.

Jezzibella groaned. 'Shit. Why did I ever think his age made him exciting?'

Libby's indigo eyes fluttered open, giving her a quizzical look. Out of all the sycophants, hangers-on, outright parasites, and essential crew, Jezzibella enjoyed Libby the most. A grandmotherly type who always dressed to emphasize her age. She had the stoicism and patience to absorb any tantrum or crisis with only the vaguest uninterested shrug.

'It was your hormones which went a-frolicking at the sight of his baby dick, poppet,' Libby said.

Jezzibella grunted, she knew the rest of the entourage hated Emmerson. 'Leroy,' she datavised. 'I paid that hospital we visited enough fucking money; have they got a secure wing we could leave the juvenile shit in?'

Leroy gave a backwards wave as he left the green room. 'We'll talk about what we're going to do with him later,' he replied.

'You fucking finished yet?' Jezzibella asked Libby.

'Absolutely, poppet.'

Jezzibella composed herself, and ordered her neural nanonics to send a sequence of encoded impulses down her nerves. There was an eerie sensation of wet leather slithering on the top of her ribcage, all four limbs shivered. Her shoulders straightened of their own accord, belly muscles tightened, sinuous lines hardened under skin that was turning a deeper shade of bronze.

She dug deep into her memory, finding the right sensation of pride and confidence. Combined with the physique it was synergistic. She was adorable, and knew it.

'Merrill!' she yelled. 'Merrill, where the fuck's my first-act costume?'

The flunky hurried over to the big travelling trunks lined up along a wall, and began extracting the requisite items.

'And why haven't you shitheads started warming up yet?' she shouted at the musicians.

The green room abruptly became a whirlwind of activity as everyone found legitimate employment. Private, silent datavises flashed through the air as they all discussed the impending frailty of Emmerson's future. It diverted them from how precarious their own tenures were.

*

Ralph Hiltch accessed various reports as he flew back over the city. The priority search which Diana Tiernan's department had initiated was producing good results. According to the city's route-and-flow road-processor network, fifty-three lorries had left Moyce's that evening. The AIs were now chasing after them.

Within seven minutes of Diana assigning the lorries full priority, twelve had been located. All outside the city. The coordinates were datavised into the Strategic Defence Command up in Guyana, and sensor satellites triangulated the targets for low-orbit weapons platforms. A dozen short-lived violet starbursts blossomed across Xingu's southern quarter.

By the time Ralph's hypersonic landed another eight had been added to the total. He'd stripped off his damaged lightweight armour suit in the plane, borrowing a dark-blue police one-piece fatigue. It was baggy enough to fit over his medical nanonic package without restriction. But for all the package's support he was still limping as he made his way over to Hub One.

'Welcome back,' Landon McCullock said. 'You did a good job, Ralph. I'm grateful.'

'We all are,' Warren Aspinal said. 'And that's not just a politician speaking. I have a family in the city, three kids.'

'Thank you, sir.' Ralph sat down next to Diana Tiernan. She managed a quick grin for him. 'We've been checking up on the night shift at Moyce's,' she said. 'There were forty-five on duty this evening. As of now, the AT squads have accounted for twenty-nine during the assault, killed and captured.'

'Shit. Sixteen of the bastards loose,' Bernard Gibson said.

'No,' Diana said firmly. 'We think we may have got lucky.

I've hooked the AIs into the fire department's mechanoids, their sensors are profiled for exploring high-temperature environments. So far they've located a further five bodies in the building; and there's still thirty per cent which hasn't been covered. Even so, that accounts for all but eleven of the night shift.'

'Still too many,' Landon said.

'I know. But we're certain that six of the lorries zapped so far contained a shift member. Their processors and ancillary circuits were suffering random failures. It matched the kind of interference which Adkinson's plane suffered.'

'And then there were five,' Warren Aspinal said quietly.

'Yes, sir,' Diana said. 'I'm pretty sure they're in the remaining lorries.'

'Well, I'm afraid "pretty sure" isn't good enough when we're facing a threat which could wipe us out in less than a week, Chief Tiernan,' said Leonard DeVille.

'Sir.' Diana didn't bother to look at him. 'I wasn't making wild assumptions. Firstly, the AIs have confirmed that there was no other traffic logged as using Moyce's since Jacob Tremarco's taxi arrived.'

'So they left on foot.'

'Again, I really don't think that is the case, sir. That whole area around Moyce's is fully covered by security sensors, both ours and the private systems owned by the companies in neighbouring buildings. We accessed all the relevant memories. Nobody came out of Moyce's. Just the lorries.'

'What we've seen tonight is a continuing pattern of attempted widespread dispersal,' Landon McCullock said. 'The embassy trio have been constant in their attempt to distribute the energy virus as broadly as possible. It's a very logical move. The wider it is spread, the longer it takes for us to contain it, and the more people can be infected, in turn making it more difficult for us to contain. A nasty spiral.'

'They only have a limited amount of time in the city,' Ralph chipped in. 'And the city is where we have the greatest advantage when it comes to finding and eliminating them. So they'll know it's a waste of effort trying to spread the contamination here, at least initially. Whereas the countryside tilts the balance in their favour. If they win out there, then Xingu's main urban areas will eventually become cities under siege. Again a situation which we would probably lose in the long run. That's what happened on Lalonde. I imagine that Durringham has fallen by now.'

Leonard DeVille nodded curtly.

'The second point,' said Diana, 'is that those infected don't seem able to halt the lorries. Short of them using their white-fire weapon to physically destroy the motors or power systems the lorries aren't stopping before their first scheduled delivery point. And if they do use violence against a lorry the motorway processors will spot it straight away. From the evidence we've accumulated so far it seems as though they can't use their electronic-warfare field to alter a lorry's destination either. It's powerful, but not sophisticated, not enough to get down into the actual drive control processors and tamper with on-line programs.'

'You mean they're trapped inside the lorries?' Warren Aspinal asked.

'Yes, sir.'

'And none of the lorries have reached their destination yet,' Vicky Keogh said, with a smile for the Home Office Minister. 'As Diana said, it looks like we got lucky.'

'Well thank God they're not omnipotent,' the Prime Minister said.

'They're not far short,' Ralph observed. Even listening to Diana outline the current situation hadn't lifted his spirits. The crisis was too hot, too now. Emotions hadn't had time to catch up with events: pursuing the embassy trio was like space warfare, everything happening too quick for anything other than simplistic responses, there was no opportunity to take stock and think. 'What about Angeline Gallagher?' he inquired. 'Have the AIs got any further leads?'

'No. Just the two taxis and the Longhound bus,' Diana said. 'The AT squads are on their way.'

*

It took another twelve minutes to clear the taxis. Ralph stayed at Hub One while the interception operations were running, receiving datavises from the two squad commanders.

The first taxi was laid up beside one of the rivers which meandered through Pasto. It had stopped interfacing with the route-and-flow processors as it drew up next to a boathouse. Road monitor cameras had been trained on the grey vehicle for eleven minutes, seeing no movement from it or the boathouse.

The AT squad members closed in on it, using standard leapfrog advancement tactics. Its lights were off, doors frozen half-open, no one inside. A technical officer opened a systems-access panel and plugged his processor block into it. The police AI probed the vehicle's circuitry and memory cells.

'All clear,' Diana reported. 'A short circuit turned the chassis live, blew most of the processors, and screwed the rest. No wonder it showed up like one of our hostiles.'

The second taxi had been abandoned in an underground garage below a residential mews. The AT squad arrived just as the taxi company's service crew turned up to take it away on their breakdown hauler. Everyone at Hub One witnessed the scenes of hysterics and anger as the AT squad took no chances with the three service crew.

After running an on-the-spot diagnostic, the crew discovered the taxi's electron matrix was faulty, sending huge power spikes through the on-board circuitry.

'Gallagher has to be on the bus,' Landon McCullock said as he cancelled his datavise to the AT squad, the service crew's inventive obscenities fading from his borrowed perception.

'I can confirm that,' Diana said. 'The damn thing won't

respond to the halt orders we're issuing via the motorway route-and-flow processors.'

'I thought you said they couldn't alter programs with their electronic-warfare technique,' Leonard DeVille said.

'It hasn't altered its route, it just won't respond,' she shot back. An almost uninterrupted three-hour stint spent interfacing with, and directing, the AIs was beginning to fatigue her nerves.

Warren Aspinal gave his political colleague a warning frown.

'The AT squad teams will be over the bus in ninety seconds,' Bernard Gibson said. 'We'll see exactly what's going on then.'

Ralph datavised a tactical situation request into the hub's processor array. His neural nanonics visualized a map of Xingu, a rough diamond with a downward curling cat's tail. Forty-one of Moyce's delivery lorries had been located and annihilated now, green and purple symbols displaying their movements, the locations when they were targeted. The bus was a virulent amber, proceeding down the M6 motorway which ran the length of Mortonridge, the long spit of mountainous land which poked southwards across the equator.

He switched to accessing the sensor suite on the lead hypersonic. The plane was just decelerating into subsonic flight. There was nothing any discrimination filter program could do about the vibration as it aerobraked. Ralph had to wait it out, impatience heating his blood feverishly. If Angeline Gallagher wasn't on the bus, then they'd probably lost the continent.

The M6 was laid out below him in the clear tropical air. The hypersonic's shaking damped out, and he could see hundreds of stationary cars, vans, buses, and lorries parked on the motorway's service lanes. Headlights illuminated the lush verges, hundreds of people were milling round, some even settling down for midnight picnics by their vehicles.

The static pageant made the bus easy to spot, the one moving light source on the motorway, heading south at about two hundred kilometres an hour. It roared on past the riveted spectators lining the lane barrier, immune to the priority codes being fired into its circuitry from the motorway's route-and-flow processors.

'What the hell is that thing?' Vicky Keogh voiced the unspoken question of everyone accessing the hypersonic's sensor suite.

The Longhound bus company had a standardized fleet of sixty-seaters made on the Esparta continent, with a distinct green and purple livery. They were used all over Ombey, stitching together every continent's cities and towns with an extensive, fast, and frequent service. The principality didn't yet have the economy or population to justify vac-train tubes linking its urban areas like Earth and Kulu, so the Longhound buses were a familiar sight on the motorways, more or less everyone on the planet had ridden on one at some time in their lives.

But the runaway vehicle speeding down the M6 looked nothing like a normal Longhound. Where the Longhound's body was reasonably smooth and trim, this had the kind of sleek profile associated with the aerospace industry. A curved, wedge-shaped nose blending back into an oval cross-section body, with sharp triangular fin spoilers sprouting out of the rear quarter. It had a dull silver finish, with gloss-black windows. Greasy grey smoke belched out of a circular vent just behind the rear wheel set.

'Is it on fire?' a disconcerted Warren Aspinal asked.

'No, sir,' Diana sounded ridiculously happy. 'What you're seeing there is its diesel exhaust.'

'A what exhaust?'

'Diesel. This is a Ford Nissan omnirover; it burns diesel in a combustion engine.'

The Prime Minister had been running his own neural nanonics encyclopedia search. 'An engine which burns hydro-carbon fuel?'

'Yes, sir.'

'That's ridiculous, not to mention illegal.'

'Not when this was built, sir. According to my files, the last one rolled off the Turin production line in AD 2043. That's the city of Turin on Earth.'

'Have you a record of any being imported by a museum, or a private vehicle collector?' Landon McCullock asked patiently.

'The AIs can't find one.'

'Jenny Harris reported a phenomenon similar to this back on Lalonde,' Ralph said. 'She saw a fanciful riverboat when I sent her on that last mission. They'd altered its appearance so it seemed old-fashioned, something from Earth's pre-technology times.'

'Christ,' Landon McCullock muttered.

'Makes sense,' Diana said. 'We're still getting a correct identification code from its processors. They must have thrown this illusion round the Longhound.'

The hypersonic closed on the bus, sliding in over the motorway, barely a hundred metres up. Below it, the omnirover was weaving from side to side with complete disregard for the lane markings. The ceaseless and random movement made it difficult for the pilot to stay matched directly overhead.

Ralph realized what had been bothering his subconscious, and requested a visual sensor to zoom in. 'That's more than just a holographic illusion,' he said after studying the image. 'Look at the bus's shadow under those lights, it matches the outline.'

'How do they do that?' Diana asked. Her voice was full of curiosity, with a hint of excitement bleeding in.

'Try asking Santiago Vargas,' Vicky Keogh told her sharply.

'I can't even think of a theory that would allow us to manipulate solid surfaces like that,' Diana said defensively.

Ralph grunted churlishly, he'd had a similar conversation back on Lalonde when they were trying to figure out how the

LDC's observation satellite was being jammed. No known principle. The whole concept of an energy virus was a radical one.

Possession, Santiago Vargas called it.

Ralph shivered. His Christian belief had never been that strongly rooted, but in a good Kingdom subject it was always there. 'Our immediate concern is what we do about the bus. You might manage to land AT squad teams on the thing if they were equipped with airpack flight suits, but they can hardly jump down from the hypersonic.'

'Use the SD platforms to chop up the motorway ahead of it,' Admiral Farquar suggested. 'Force it to stop that way.'

'Do we know how many people were onboard?' Landon McCullock asked.

'Full complement when it left Pasto spaceport, I'm afraid,' Diana reported.

'Damn. Sixty people. We have to make at least an effort to halt it.'

'We'd have to reinforce the AT squads first,' Ralph said. 'Three hypersonics isn't enough. And you'd have to stop the bus precisely in the centre of a cordon. With sixty possible hostiles riding on it, we'd have to be very certain no one broke through. That's wild-looking countryside out there.'

'We can have reinforcements there in another seven minutes,' Bernard Gibson said.

'Shit—' It was a datavise from the pilot. A big javelin of white fire streaked up from the bus, punching the hypersonic's belly. The plane quaked, then peeled away rapidly, almost rolling through ninety degrees. Bright sparkling droplets of molten ceramic sprayed out from the gaping hole in its fuselage to splash and burn on the motorway's surface. Its aerodynamics wounded, it started juddering continuously, losing height. The pilot tried desperately to right it, but he was already too low. He came to the same conclusion as the flight computer, and activated the crash-protection system.

Foam under enormous pressure fired into the cabin, swamping the AT squad members. Valency generators turned it solid within a second.

The plane hit the ground, ploughing a huge gash through the vegetation and soft black loam. Nose, wings, and tailplane crumpled and tore, barbed fragments spinning off into the night. The bulky cylinder which was the cabin carried on for another seventy metres, flinging off structural spars and smashed ancillary modules. It came to a jarring halt, thudding into a steep earthen bluff.

The valency generators cut off, and foam sluiced out of the wreckage, mingling with the mud. Figures stirred weakly inside.

Bernard Gibson let out a painful breath. 'I think they're all OK.'

One of the other two hypersonics was circling back towards the crash. The second took up position a respectful kilometre behind the bus.

'Oh, Christ,' Vicky Keogh groaned. 'The bus is slowing. They're going to get off.'

'Now what?' the Prime Minister demanded. He sounded frightened and angry.

'One AT squad can't possibly contain them,' Ralph said. It was like speaking treason. I betrayed those people. My failure.

'There are sixty people on that bus,' an aghast Warren Aspinal exclaimed. 'We might be able to cure them.'

'Yes, sir, I know that.' Ralph hardened his expression, disguising how worthless he felt, and looked at Landon McCullock. The police chief obviously wanted to argue; he glanced at his deputy, who shrugged helplessly.

'Admiral Farquar?' Landon McCullock datavised.

'Yes.'

'Eliminate the bus.'

Ralph watched through the hypersonic's sensor suite as the laser blast from low orbit struck the phantasmic vehicle. Just for an instant he saw the silhouette of the real Longhound inside the illusory cloak, as if the purpose of the weapon was really to expose truths. Then the energy barrage incinerated the bus along with a thirty-metre diameter circle of road.

When he looked round the faces of everyone sitting at Hub One, he saw his own dismay and horror bounced right back at him.

It was Diana Tiernan who held his gaze, her kindly old face crumpled up with tragic sympathy. 'I'm sorry, Ralph,' she said. 'We weren't quick enough. The AIs have just told me the bus stopped at the first four towns on its scheduled route.'

# 3

Al Capone dressed as Al Capone had always dressed: with style. A double-breasted blue serge suit, a Paisley pattern silk tie, black patent-leather shoes, and a pearl grey fedora, rakishly aslant. Gold rings set with a rainbow array of deep precious stones glinted on every finger, a duck-egg diamond on his pinkie.

It hadn't taken him long to decide that the people in this future world didn't have much in the way of fashion sense. The suits he could see all followed the same loose silk design, although their colourful slimline patterns made them appear more like flappy Japanese pyjamas. Those not in suits wore variants on vests and sports shirts. Tight fitting, too, at least for people under thirty-five. Al had stared at the dolls to start with, convinced they were all hookers. What kind of decent gal would dress like that, with so much showing? Skirts which almost didn't cover their ass, shorts that weren't much better. But no. They were just ordinary, smiling, happy, everyday girls. The people living in this city weren't so strung up on morality and decency. What would have given a Catholic priest apoplexy back home didn't raise an eyebrow here.

'I think I'm gonna like this life,' Al declared.

Strange life that it was. Reincarnated as a magician; a real magician, not like the fancy tricksters he'd booked for his clubs back in Chicago. Here, whatever he wanted appeared out of nowhere.

That had taken a long while to get used to. Think and ... pow. There it was, everything from a working Thompson to a silver dollar glinting in the hot sun. Goddam useful for clothes, though. Brad Lovegrove had worn overalls of shiny dark red fabric like some kind of pissant garbage collector.

Al could hear Brad Lovegrove whimpering away inside him; like having a leprechaun nesting at the centre of his brain. He was bawling like a complete bozo, and making about as much sense. But there was some gold among the dross, twenty-four-carat nuggets. Like – when he had first got his marbles together Al had thought this world was maybe Mars or Venus. Not so. New California didn't even orbit the same sun as Earth. And it wasn't the twentieth century no more.

Jee-zus, but a guy needed a drink to help keep that from blowing his head apart.

And where to get a drink? Al imagined the little leprechaun being squeezed, as if his brain was one giant muscle. Slowly contracting.

A macromall on the intersection between Longwalk and Sunrise, Lovegrove squealed silently. There's a specialist store there with liquor from every Confederation planet, probably even got Earth bourbon.

Drinks from clear across the galaxy! How about that?

So Al started walking. It was a lovely day.

The sidewalk was so wide it was more like a boulevard in itself; there were no paving slabs, instead the whole strip had been made from a seamless sheet, a material which was a cross between marble and concrete. Luxuriant trees sprouted up through craters in the surface every forty yards or so, their two-foot sprays of floppy oval flowers an impossible shade of metallic purple.

He spotted a few trashcan-sized trucks trundling sedately among the walkers enjoying the late-morning sunshine, machinery smoother than Henry Ford had ever dreamed of.

Utility mechanoids, Lovegrove told him, cleaning the sidewalk, picking up litter and fallen leaves.

The base of each skyscraper was given over to classy delis and bars and restaurants and coffee shops; tables spilled out onto the sidewalk, just like a European city. Arcades pierced deep into the buildings.

From what Al could see, it was the same kind of rich man's playground set-up on the other side of the street, maybe a hundred and fifty yards away. Not that you could walk over to be sure, there was no way past the eight-foot-high glass and metal barrier which lined the road.

Al stood with his face pressed to the glass for some time, watching the silent cars zoom past. Big bullets on wheels. All of them shiny, like coloured chrome. You didn't even have to steer them no more, Lovegrove told him, they did it themselves. Some kind of fancy electrical engine, no gas. And the speed, over two hundred kilometres an hour.

Al knew all about kilometres; they were what the French called miles.

But he wasn't too sure about using a car that he couldn't drive himself, not when it travelled that fast. And anyway, his presence seemed to mommick up electricity. So he stuck to walking.

The skyscrapers gave him vertigo they were so tall, and all you could see when you looked up at them was reflections of more skyscrapers. They seemed to bend over the street, imprisoning the world below. Lovegrove told him they were so high that their tops were designed to sway in the wind, rocking twenty or thirty metres backwards and forwards in slow motion.

'Shut up,' Al growled.

The leprechaun curled up tighter, like a knotted snake.

People looked at Al – his clothes. Al looked at people, fascinated and jubilant. It was a jolt seeing blacks and whites mixing free, other types too, light-skinned Mediterranean like his own, Chinese, Indian. Some seemed to have dyed their hair completely the wrong colour. Amazing.

And they all appeared so much at ease with themselves, owning a uniform inner smile. They had a nonchalance and surety which he'd never seen before. The Devil which drove so many people back in the twenties was missing, as if the city elders had abolished worry altogether.

They also had astonishingly good health. After a block and a half Al still hadn't seen anyone remotely overweight. No wonder they wore short clothes. A world where everyone was in permanent training for the big game, even the seventy-year-olds.

'You still got baseball, ain't you?' Al muttered under his breath.

Yes, Lovegrove confirmed.

Yep, Paradise all right.

After a while he took off his jacket and slung it over his shoulder. He'd been walking for quarter of an hour, and it didn't look as if he'd got anywhere. The massive avenue of skyscrapers hadn't changed at all.

'Hey, buddy,' he called.

The black guy – who looked like a prize fighter – turned, and gave an amused grin as he took in Al's clothes. His arm was round a girl: Indian skin, baby blonde hair. Her long legs were shown off by a pair of baggy culottes.

Cutie pie, Al thought, and grinned at her. A real sweater girl. It suddenly struck him that he hadn't hit the sack with a woman for six centuries.

She smiled back.

'How do I call a cab around here?'

'Datavise the freeway processors, my man,' the black guy said expansively. 'City runs a million cabs. Don't make a profit. But then that's what us dumb taxpayers are for, to make up the shortfall, right?'

'I can't do the data thing, I ain't from around here.'

The girl giggled. 'You just get off a starship?'

Al tipped the rim of his fedora with two fingers. 'Kind of, lady. Kind of.'

'Neat. Where you from?'

'Chicago. On Earth.'

'Hey, wow. I never met anyone from Earth before. What's it like?'

Al's grin lost its lustre. Jee-zus, but the women here were forward. And the black guy's thick arm was still draped over her shoulder. He didn't seem to mind his girl making conversation with a total stranger. 'One city's just like another,' Al said; he gestured lamely at the silver skyscrapers, as if that was explanation enough.

'City? I thought you only had arcologies on Earth?'

'Look, you going to tell me how to get a fucking cab, or what?'

He'd blown it. The moment he saw the man's expression harden, he knew.

'You want us to call one for you, buddy?' The man was taking a longer, slower look at Al's clothes.

'Sure,' Al bluffed.

'OK. No problem. It's done.' A phoney smile.

Al wondered exactly what it was the man had actually done. He didn't have no Dick Tracy wrist radio to call for a cab, or anything. Just stood there, smiling, playing Al for a sucker.

Lovegrove was filling Al's head with crap about miniature telephones in the brain. He had one fitted himself, he said, but it had packed up when Al possessed him.

'Going to tell me about Chicago now?' the girl asked.

Al could see how worried she was. Her voice, mannerisms, the way she had merged into her man's encircling arm. They all telegraphed it, and he knew how to read the signs. Fear in other people was wholly familiar.

He thrust his face forward towards the black guy, snarling

at the wiseass bastard. Just for an instant three long scars pulsed hotly on his left cheek. 'Gonna remember you, cocksucker. Gonna find you again. Gonna teach you respect, and buddy it's gonna be the real hard way to learn.' The old rage was burning in his body now, limbs trembling, voice rising to a thunderous roar. 'Nobody shits on Al Capone! You got that? Nobody treats me like some dog turd you trod in. I fucking ruled Chicago. I owned that city. I am not some asswipe street punk you can take for a ride. I. Deserve. RESPECT.'

'Bastard Retro!' The man swung a punch.

Even if Lovegrove's body hadn't been enhanced with the energistic power which possessing souls exuded in the natural universe Al would probably have beaten him. His years in Brooklyn had pitched him into countless brawls, and people had quickly learned to steer clear of his awesome temper.

Al ducked instinctively, his right fist already coming up. The blow was focused, mentally and physically. He struck the man perfectly, catching him on the side of his jaw.

There was an ugly sound of bone shattering. Dead silence. The man flew backwards five yards through the air, hitting the sidewalk in a crumpled sprawl. He slid along the carbon concrete composite for another couple of yards before coming to rest, completely inert. Blood began to splatter from his mouth where serrated bone had punctured his cheek and lip.

Al stared, surprised. 'Goddam!' He started to laugh delightedly.

The girl screamed. She screamed and screamed.

Al glanced round, suddenly apprehensive. Everyone on the broad sidewalk was looking at him, at the injured black guy. 'Shut up,' he hissed at the loopy broad. 'Shut up!' But she wouldn't. Just: scream, and scream, and scream. Like it was her profession.

Then there was another sound, cutting through her bawling, rising every time she took a breath. And Al Capone realized it wasn't just handguns he could recognize after six hundred years. Police sirens hadn't changed much either.

He started to run. People scattered ahead of him the way kittens ran from a pit-bull. Cries and yells broke out all around.

'Stop him!'

'Move.'

'Stinking Retro.'

'He killed that dude. One punch.'

'No! Don't try to—'

A man was going for him. Beefy and hard-set, crouched low for a pro football tackle. Al waved a hand, almost casually, and white fire squirted into the hero's face. Black petals of flesh peeled back from the bone, sizzling. Thick chestnut hair flamed to ash. A dull agonized grunt, cutting off as pain overloaded his consciousness, and the man collapsed.

Then all hell really did hit the fan. Anxious people became a terrified mob. Stampeding away from him. Fringe onlookers got caught, and bowled over by thudding feet.

Al glanced back over his shoulder to see a section of the road barrier fold down. The squad car glided over it towards him. An evil-looking black and blue javelin-head, airplane-smooth fuselage. Dazzlingly bright lights flashed on top of it.

'Hold it, Retro,' a voice boomed from the car.

Al's pace slackened. There was an arcade ahead of him, but its arching entrance was wide enough to take the squad car. Goddam! Alive again for forty minutes, and already running from the cops.

What else is new?

He stopped, and turned full square to face them, silver-plated Thompson gripped in his hands. And – oh shit – another two squad cars were coming off the road, lining up directly towards him. Big slablike flaps were opening like wings at their rear, and *things* came running out. They weren't human, they weren't animal. Machine animals? Whatever, they sure didn't look healthy. Fat dull-metal bodies with stumpy gun barrels protruding. Far too many legs, and all of those rubber, no knees or ankles.

Assault mechanoids, Lovegrove said. And there was a tinge of excitement in the mental voice. Lovegrove expected the things to beat him.

'They electric?' Al demanded.

Yes.

'Good.' He glared at the one taking point, and cast his first sorcerer's spell.

Police Patrol Sergeant Alson Loemer was already anticipating his promotion when he arrived at the scene. Loemer had been delighted as his neural nanonics received the updates from the precinct house. With his outlandish clothes, the man certainly looked like a Retro. The gang of history-costumed terrorists had been running the police department ragged for three days, sabbing city systems with some new style of plasma weapon and electronic-warfare field. Other acts too. Most officers had picked up strong rumours of snatches going down, people being lifted at random from the streets at night. And not one Retro had been brought to book. The news companies were datavising hiveloads of untamed speculation across the communication net: a religious group, a band of offplanet mercenaries, even wackier notions. The mayor was going apeshit, and leaning on the police commissioner. Smooth people from an unnamed government Intelligence agency had been walking round the corridors at the precinct house. But they didn't know anything more than patrol officers.

Now he, Sergeant Loemer, was going to nail one of those suckers.

He guided the patrol car over the folded barrier and onto the sidewalk. The crim was dead ahead, running for the base of the Uorestone Tower. Two more precinct cars were riding with Loemer, closing on the crim, hemming him in. Loemer deployed both of his patrol car's assault mechanoids, and datavised in their isolate and securement instructions.

That was when the patrol car started to glitch, picking up speed. The sensors showed him frightened citizens in front, racing to escape; one of the assault mechanoids wobbled past, shooting wildly. He fired shutdown orders into the drive processor. Not that it made much difference.

Then the Retro started shooting at the patrol cars. Whatever the gun was, it ripped straight through the armour shielding, smashing the axles and wheel hubs. Metal bearings screeched in that unique, and instantly recognizable, tone which heralded imminent destruction. Loemer thumped the manual safety cut out, killing power instantly.

The patrol car slewed round, and bounced off the road barrier to smack straight into one of the regree trees planted along the sidewalk. The internal crash alarm went off, half-deafening an already dazed Loemer, and the emergency side hatch jettisoned. Loemer's bubble seat slid out along its telescoping rails. The translucent bubble's thick safety-restraint segments peeled back, allowing him to drop, wailing, to his knees as the air around him spewed out a terrible volley of sense-overload impulses. His neural nanonics were unable to datavise a shutdown code into the crazed assault mechanoids. The last thing he saw as he fell onto the ground was the ruined regree tree starting to keel over directly above him.

Even Al was bruised by the wild strafing of the sense-overload ordnance. The manic glee as he watched the patrol cars skid and smash was swiftly curtailed by the onslaught of light, sound, and smell. His energistic ability could ward off the worst of it, but he turned and began a stumbling run towards the arcade entrance. Behind him the assault mechanoids continued to deluge the street with their errant firepower, lumbering about like drunks. Two ran into each other, and rebounded, falling over. Legs thrashed about in chaos, beetles flipped on their backs.

The sidewalk was littered with prone bodies. Not dead, Al thought, just terribly battered. Jee-zus, but those mechanical soldier contraptions were nasty pieces of work. And unlike real police, you wouldn't be able to buy them.

Maybe New California wasn't quite paradise after all.

Al staggered his way along the arcade, caught up in the flow of people desperate to escape the havoc. His suit faded away, the sharp colour and cut reverting to Lovegrove's original drab overall.

He picked up a little girl whose eyes were streaming tears, and carried her. It felt good to help. Those goddam brainless pigs should have made sure she was out of the way before they came at him with guns blazing. It would never have happened back in Chicago.

Two hundred yards from the arcade entrance he stopped among a group of anxious, exhausted people. They'd come far enough from the sense-overload ordnance to be free of its effects. Families clung together, others were calling out for friends and loved ones.

Al put the little girl down. Still crying, which he thought was due to the Kaiser gas rather than any kind of injury. Then her mother came rushing up and hugged her frantically. Al was given profuse thanks. A nice dame. Cared about her children and family. That was good, proper. He was sorry he wasn't wearing his fedora so he could tip it to her.

Just how do people express that kind of formal courtesy on this world, anyhow?

Lovegrove was puzzled by the question.

He carried on down the arcade. Cops would be swarming all over the joint in a few minutes. Another hundred and fifty yards, and he was out on the street again. He started walking. Direction didn't matter, just away. This time he kept Lovegrove's overalls on. No one paid him any attention.

Al wasn't entirely sure what to do next. Everything was so

strange. This world, his situation. Mind, strange wasn't the word for it, more like overwhelming. Or just plain creepy. Bad to think that the priests had been right about the afterworld, heaven and hell. He never went to church much, much to his momma's distress.

I wonder if I've been redeemed, paid my celestial dues. Is that why I'm back? But if you got reincarnated didn't you start off as a baby?

They weren't the kind of thoughts he was used to.

A hotel, he told Lovegrove, I need to rest up and have a long think about what to do.

Most of the skyscrapers had some sort of rentable accommodation, apparently. But it would have to be paid for.

Al's hand automatically went to a leg pocket. He drew out a Jovian Bank credit disk, a thick, oversize coin, sparkly silver on one side, magenta on the other. Lovegrove obediently explained how it worked, and Al put his thumb on the centre. A hash of green lines wobbled over the silver side.

'Goddam!' He tried again, concentrating, wishing. Doing the magic.

The green lines began to form figures, crude at first, then sharp and regular. You could store an entire planet's Treasury in one of these disks, Lovegrove told him. Al's ears pricked up at that. Then he was aware of something being not quite right. A presence, close by.

He hadn't really thought about the others. Those who had been there when he came into Lovegrove's body. The same ones who had deserted him in the disused shop. But if he closed his eyes, and shut out the sounds of the city, he could hear the distant Babelesque clamour. It came from the night-mare domain, the pleas and promises to be brought forth, to live and breathe again.

That same perception gave him a most peculiar vision of the city. Walls of thick black shadow amid a universal greyness.

People moved through it all, distorted whispers echoing all around, audible ghosts. Some different from others. Louder, clearer. Not many of them among the multitude.

Al opened his eyes and looked down the road. A section of the barrier was folding down neatly. One of the bullet cars drew to a halt beside it. The gull-wing door slid up, and inside was a proper car, a genuine American convertible wearing the streamlined image of the New California vehicle like a piece of clothing. It was low-slung, with a broad hood and lots of chrome trim. Al didn't recognize the model, it was more modern than anything in the twenties, and his memory of the thirties and forties wasn't so hot.

The man in the red leather driving seat nodded amicably. 'You'd better get in,' he said. 'The cops are going to catch you if you stay out on the street. They're a mite worked up about us.'

Al glanced up and down the sidewalk, then shrugged and climbed in.

Inside, the image of the bullet car tinted the air like a stained soap bubble.

'The name's Bernhard Allsop,' the man behind the steering column said. He swung the car out into the road. Behind them the barrier rose up smoothly. 'I always wanted me an Oldsmobile like this beauty, never could afford it back when I was living in Tennessee.'

'And this is real now?'

'Who knows, boy? But it sure feels real. And I'm mighty grateful for the opportunity to ride one. You might say I thought it had passed me by.'

'Yeah. I know what you mean.'

'Caused a bit of commotion back there, boy. Them pigs is riled good and proper. We were monitoring what passes for their radio band these days.'

'I just wanted a cab, that's all. Someone tried to get smart.'

'There's a trick to riding round this town without the police knowing. Be happy to show you how some time.'

'Appreciate it. Where are we going?'

Bernhard Allsop grinned and winked. 'Gonna take you to meet the rest of the group. Always need volunteers, they're kinda hard to come by.' He laughed, a high-pitched stuttering yodel reminding Al of a piglet.

'They left me behind, Bernhard. I don't have anything to say to them.'

'Yeah, well. You know how it was. You weren't altogether there, boy. I said we should have taken you along with us. Kin is kin, even though it ain't exactly family here, know what I mean? Glad to see you came through in the end, though.'

'Thank you.'

'So what's your name, boy?'

'Al Capone.'

The Oldsmobile swerved as Bernhard flinched. His knuckles whitened as he tightened his grip on the wheel; then he risked an anxious sideways glance at his passenger. Where before there had been a twenty-year-old man dressed in a set of dark red overalls, there was now a debonair Latin-ethnic character in a double-breasted blue suit and pigeon-grey fedora.

'You shitting me?'

Al Capone reached into his suit, and produced a miniature baseball bat. A now highly apprehensive Bernhard Allsop watched it grow to full size. It didn't take much imagination to figure out what the black stains around the end were.

'No,' Al said politely. 'I'm not shitting you.'

'Holy Christ.' He tried to laugh. 'Al Capone.'

'Yeah.'

'Holy Christ. Al Capone in my car! Ain't that something?'

'That's certainly something, yeah.'

'It's a pleasure, Al. Christ, I mean that. A real pleasure. Hell, you were the best Al, the top man. Everybody knew that. Ran a bit of moonshine in my day. Nothing much, a few slugs, is all. But you, you ran it for a whole city. Christ! Al Capone.' He slapped the steering wheel with both hands, chortling. 'Damn, but I can't wait to see their faces when I bring you in.'

'Bring me in to what, Bernhard?'

'The group, Al, the group. Hey, you don't mind if I call you Al, do you? I don't want to give no offence, or nothing. Not to you.'

'That's OK, Bernhard, all my friends call me Al.'

'Your friends. Yes, sirree!'

'What does this group of yours do, exactly, Bernhard?'

'Why, get larger, of course. That's all we can do for now. Unity is strength.'

'You a Communist, Bernhard?'

'Hey! No way, Al. I'm an American. I hate the filthy Reds.'

'Sounds like you are to me.'

'No, you got it all wrong. The more of us there are, the better chance we stand, the stronger we are. Like an army; a whole load of people together, they got the strength to make themselves felt. That's what I meant, Al. Honest.'

'So what does the group have in mind for when they get big and powerful?'

Bernhard gave Al another sideways glance, puzzled this time. 'To get out of here, Al. What else?'

'To get out of the city?'

'No. To take the planet away.' He jabbed a thumb straight up. 'From that. From the sky.'

Al cast a sceptical eye upwards. The skyscrapers were flashing past on either side. Their size didn't bother him so much now. Starship drives still speckled the azure sky, streaked flashbulbs taking a long time to pop. He couldn't see the odd little moon any more. 'Why?' he asked reasonably.

'Damn it, Al. Can't you feel it? The emptiness. Man, it's horrible. All that huge nothing trying to suck you up and swallow you whole.' He gulped, his voice lowering. 'The sky is like there. It's the beyond all over again. We gotta hide. Someplace where we ain't never going to die again, somewhere that don't go on for ever. Where there's no empty night.'

'Now you're sounding like a preacher man, Bernhard.'

'Well, maybe I am a little bit. It's a smart man who knows when he's beat. I don't mind saying it to you, Al. I'm frightened of the beyond. I ain't never going back there. No, sirree.'

'So you're going to move the world away?'

'Damn right.'

'That's one fucking big ambition you've got there, Bernhard. I wish you a lot of luck. Now just drop me off at this intersection coming up here. I'll find my own way about town now.'

'You mean you ain't going to pitch in and help us?' an incredulous Bernhard asked.

'Nope.'

'But you gotta feel it, too, Al. Even you. We all can. They never stop begging you, all those other lost souls. Ain't you afraid of going back there?'

'Can't say as I am. It never really bothered me any while I was there first time around.'

'Never bothered ... ! Holy Christ, you are one tough sonofabitch, Al.' He put his head back and gave a rebel yell. 'Listen, you mothers, being dead don't bother Al Capone none! God damn!'

'Where is this safe place you're taking the planet to, anyhow?'

'Dunno, Al. Just follow Judy Garland over the rainbow, I guess. Anywhere where there ain't no sky.'

'You ain't got no plans, you ain't got no idea where you're going. And you wanted me to be a part of that?'

'But it'll happen, Al. I swear. When there's enough of us, we can do it. You know what you can do by yourself now, one man. Think what a million can do, two million. Ten million. Ain't nothing going to be able to stop us then.'

'You're going to possess a million people?'

'We surely are.'

The Oldsmobile dipped down a long ramp which took it into a tunnel. Bernhard let out a happy sigh as they passed into its harsh orange-tinged lighting.

'You won't possess a million people,' Al said. 'The cops will stop you. They'll find a way. We're strong, but we ain't no bullet-proof super heroes. That stuff the assault mechanoids shoot nearly got me back there. If I'd been any closer I'd be dead again.'

'Damn it, that's what I been trying to tell you, Al,' Bernhard complained. 'We gotta build up our numbers. Then they can't never hurt us.'

Al fell silent. Part of what Bernhard said made sense. The more possessed there were, the harder it would be for the cops to stop them spreading. But they'd fight, those cops. Like wild bears, once they realized how big the problem was, how dangerous the possessed were. Cops, whatever passed for the Federal agents on this world, the army; all clubbing together. Government rats always did gang up. They'd have the starship weapons, too; Lovegrove burbled about how powerful they were, capable of turning whole countries to deserts of hot glass within seconds.

And what would Al Capone do on a world where such a war was being fought? Come to that, what would Al Capone do on any modern world?

'How are you snatching people?' he asked abruptly.

Bernhard must have sensed the change in tone, in purpose. He suddenly got antsy, shifting his ass round on the seat's shiny red leather, but keeping his eyes firmly on the road ahead. 'Well gee, Al, we just take them off the street. At night, when it's nice and quiet. Nothing heavy.'

'But you've been seen, haven't you? That cop called me a Retro. They even got a name for you. They know you're doing it.'

'Well, yeah, sure. It's kinda difficult with the numbers we're working, you know. Like I say, we need a *lot* of people. Sometimes we get seen. Bound to happen. But they haven't caught us.'

'Not yet.' Al grinned expansively. He put his arm round Bernhard's shoulder. 'You know, Bernhard, I think I will come and meet this group of yours after all. It sounds to me that you ain't organized yourselves too good. No offence, I doubt you people have much experience in this field. But me now . . .' A fat Havana appeared in his hand. He took a long blissful drag, the first for six hundred years. 'Me, I had a lifetime's experience of going to the bad. And I'm gonna give you all the benefit of that.'

\*

Gerald Skibbow shuffled into the warm, white-walled room, one arm holding on tightly to the male orderly. His loose powder-blue institute gown revealed several small medical nanonic packages as it shifted about. He moved as would a very old man in a high-gravity environment, with careful dignity. Needing help, needing guidance.

Unlike any normal person, he didn't even flick his eyes from side to side to take in his newest surroundings. The thickly cushioned bed in the centre of the room, with its surrounding formation of bulky, vaguely medical apparatus, didn't seem to register on his consciousness.

'OK, now then, Gerald,' the orderly said cordially. 'Let's get you comfortable on here, shall we?'

He gingerly positioned Gerald's buttocks on the side of the bed, then lifted his legs up and round until his charge was lying prone on the cushioning. Always cautious. He'd prepared a dozen candidates for personality debrief here in Guyana's grade-one restricted navy facility. None of them had exactly been volunteers. Skibbow might just realize what he was being prepped for. It could be the spark to bring him out of his trauma-trance.

But no. Gerald allowed the orderly to secure him with the webbing which moulded itself to his body contours. There was no sound from his throat, no blink as it tightened its grip.

The relieved orderly gave a thumbs up to the two men sitting behind the long glass panel in the wall. Totally immobilized, Gerald stared beyond the outsized plastic helmet that lowered itself over his head. The inside was fuzzy, a lining of silk fur which had been stiffened somehow. Then his face was covered completely, and the light vanished.

Chemical infusions ensured there was no pain, no discomfort as the nanonic filaments wormed their way around his dermal cells and penetrated the bone of the skull. Positioning their tips into the requisite synapses took nearly two hours, a delicate operation similar to the implanting of neural nanonics. However, these infiltrations went deeper than ordinary augmentation circuitry, seeking out the memory centres to mate with neurofibrillae inside their clustered cells. And the incursion was massive, millions of filaments burrowing along capillaries, active superstring molecules with preprogrammed functions, knowing where to go, what to do. In many respects they resembled the dendritic formation of living tissue in which they were building a parallel information network. The cells obeyed their DNA pattern, the filaments' structure was formatted by AIs. One process designed by studying the other, but never complementary.

Impulses began to flow back down the filaments as the hypersensitive tips registered synaptic discharges. A horribly jumbled montage of random thoughtsnaps, memories without order. The facility's AI came on-line, running comparisons, defining characteristics, recognizing themes and weaving them into coherent sensorium environs.

Gerald Skibbow's thoughts were focused on his apartment in the Greater Brussels arcology. Three respectably sized rooms on the sixty-fifth floor of the Delores pyramid. From the triple-glazed windows you could see a landscape of austere geometries. Domes, pyramids, and towers, all squashed together and wrapped up within the intestinal tangle of the elevated bahn tubes. Every surface he could see was grey, even the dome glass, coated with decades of grime.

It was a couple of years after they had moved in. Paula was about three, totter-running everywhere, and always falling over. Marie was a tiny energetic bundle of smiles who could emit a vast range of incredulous sounds as the world produced its daily marvels for her.

He was cradling his infant daughter (already beautiful) in his lap that evening, while Loren was slumped in an armchair, accessing the local news show. Paula was playing with the second-hand Disney mechanoid minder he'd bought her a fortnight ago, a fluffy anthropomorphized hedgehog that had an immensely irritating laugh.

It was a cosy family, in a lovely home. And they were together, and happy because of that. And the strong arcology walls protected them from the dangers of the outside world. He provided for them, and loved them, and protected them. They loved him back, too; he could see it in their smiles and adoring eyes. Daddy was king.

Daddy sang lullabies to his children. It was important to sing, if he stopped then the hobgoblins and ghouls would come out from the darkness and snatch children away—

Two men walked into the room, and quietly sat down on the settee opposite Gerald. He frowned at them, unable to place their names, wondering what they were doing invading his home.

Invading . . .

The pyramid trembled as if caught by a minor earthquake, making the colours blur slightly. Then the room froze, his wife and children becoming motionless, their warmth draining away.

'It's OK, Gerald,' one of the men said. 'Nobody is invading. Nobody is going to hurt you.'

Gerald clutched at baby Marie. 'Who are you?'

'I'm Dr Riley Dobbs, a neural expert; and this is my colleague, Harry Earnshaw, who is a neural systems technician. We're here to help you.'

'Let me sing,' a frantic Gerald yelled. 'Let me sing. They'll get us if I stop. They'll get us all. We'll be dragged down into the bowels of the earth. None of us will ever see daylight again.'

'There's always going to be daylight, Gerald,' Dobbs said. 'I promise you that.' He paused, datavising an order into the AI.

Dawn rose outside the arcology. A clean dawn, the kind which Earth hadn't seen for centuries; the sun huge and red-gold, casting brilliant rays across the dingy landscape. It shone directly into the apartment, warm and vigorous.

Gerald sighed like a small child, and held his hands out to it. 'It's so beautiful.'

'You're relaxing. That's good, Gerald. We need you relaxed; and I'd prefer you to reach that state by yourself. Tranquillizers inhibit your responses, and we want you to be clear headed.'

'What do you mean?' Gerald asked suspiciously.

'Where are you, Gerald?'

'At home.'

'No, Gerald, this is long ago. This is a refuge for you, a psychological retreat into the past. You're creating it because something rather nasty happened to you.'

'No. Nothing! Nothing nasty. Go away.'

'I can't go away, Gerald. It's important for a lot of people that I stay. You might be able to save a whole planet, Gerald.'

Gerald shook his head. 'Can't help. Go away.'

'We're not going, Gerald. And you can't run from us. This isn't a place, Gerald, this is inside your mind.'

'No no no!'

'I'm sorry, Gerald, truly, I am. But I cannot leave until you have shown me what I want to see.'

'Go away. Sing!' Gerald started to hum his lullabies again.

Then his throat turned to stone, blocking the music inside. Hot tears trickled down his cheeks.

'No more singing, Gerald,' Harry Earnshaw said. 'We're going to play a different game. Dr Dobbs and I are going to ask you some questions. We want to know what happened to you on Lalonde—'

The apartment exploded into a blinding iridescent swirl. Every sensory channel splice into Gerald Skibbow's brain thrummed from overload.

Riley Dobbs shook himself as the processor array broke the direct linkage. In the seat next to him Harry Earnshaw was also stirring.

'Sod it,' Dobbs grumbled. In the room through the glass, he could see Skibbow's body straining against the webbing. He hurriedly datavised an order into the physiological control processor for a tranquillizer.

Earnshaw studied the neural scan of Skibbow's brain, the huge electrical surge at the mention of Lalonde. 'That is one very deep-seated trauma. The associations are hot-wired into almost every neural pathway.'

'Did the AI pull anything out of the cerebral convulsion?'

'No. It was pure randomization.'

Dobbs watched Skibbow's physiological display creep down towards median. 'OK, let's go in again. That trank should take the edge off his neurosis.'

This time the three of them stood on a savanna of lush emerald-green knee-high grass. Tall snow-capped mountains guarded the horizon. A bright sun thickened the air, deadening sounds. Before them was a burning building; a sturdy log cabin with a lean-to barn and a stone chimney.

'Loren!' Gerald shouted hoarsely. 'Paula! Frank!' He ran towards the building as the flames licked up the walls. The roof of solar-cell panels began to curl up, blistering from the heat.

Gerald ran and ran, but never got any nearer. There were

faces behind the windows; two women and a man. They did nothing as the flames closed around them, simply looked out with immense sadness. Gerald sank to his knees, sobbing.

'Wife Loren, and daughter Paula with her husband Frank,' Dobbs said, receiving their identities direct from the AI. 'No sign of Marie.'

'Small wonder the poor bastard's in shock if he saw this happen to his family,' Earnshaw remarked.

'Yeah. And we're too early. He hasn't been taken over by the energy virus yet.' Dobbs datavised an order into the AI, activating a targeted suppression program, and the fire vanished along with the people. 'It's all right, Gerald. It's over. All finished with. They're at peace now.'

Gerald twisted round to glare at him, his face deformed by rage. 'At peace? At peace! You stupid ignorant bastard. They'll never be at peace. None of us ever will. Ask me! Ask me, you fucker. Go on. You want to know what happened? This, this happened.'

Daylight vanished from the sky, replaced by a meagre radiance from Rennison, Lalonde's innermost moon. It illuminated another log cabin; this one belonged to the Nicholls family, Gerald's neighbour. The mother, father, and son had been tied up and put in the animal stockade along with Gerald.

A ring of dark figures encircled the lonely homestead, distorted human shapes, some atrociously bestial.

'My God,' Dobbs murmured. Two of the figures were dragging a struggling, screaming girl into the cabin.

Gerald gave a giddy laugh. 'God? There is no God.'

\*

After nearly five hours of unbroken and mercifully uneventful travel, Carmitha still hadn't convinced herself they were doing the right thing in going to Bytham. Every instinct yelled at her to get to Holbeach and surround herself with her own kind, use them like a fence to keep out the nemesis which prowled the land, to be safe. That same instinct which made her queasy at Titreano's presence. Yet as the younger Kavanagh girl predicted, with him accompanying them nothing had happened to the caravan. Several times he had indicated a farmhouse or hamlet where he said his kind were skulking.

Indecision was a wretched curse.

But she now had few doubts that he was almost what he claimed to be. An old Earth nobleman possessing the body of a Norfolk farmhand.

There had been a lot of talk in the last five hours. The more she heard the more convinced she became. He knew so many details. However, there was one small untruth remaining which bothered her.

After Titreano had spoken about his former life to the fascination of the sisters, he in turn became eager to hear of Norfolk. And that was when Carmitha finally began to lose patience with her companions. Genevieve she could tolerate; the world as seen through the eyes of a twelve-(Earth)-year-old was fairly bizarre anyway, all enthusiasms and misunderstandings. But Louise, now; that brat was a different matter. Louise explained about the planet's economy being built around the export of Norfolk Tears, about how the founders had wisely chosen a pastoral life for their descendants, about how pretty the cities and towns were, how clean the countryside and the air were compared to industrialized worlds, how nice the people, how well organized the estates, how few criminals there were.

'It sounds as though you have achieved much that is worthy,' Titreano said. 'Norfolk is an enviable world in which to be born.'

'There are some people who don't like it,' Louise said. 'But not very many.' She looked down at Genevieve's head, cradled in her lap, and smiled gently. Her little sister had finally fallen asleep, rocked by the gentle rhythm of the caravan.

She smoothed locks of hair back from Genevieve's brow. It

was dirty and unkempt, with strands shrivelled and singed from the fire in the stable. Mrs Charlsworth would have a fit of the vapours if she saw it. Landowner girls were supposed to be paragons of deportment at all times, Kavanagh girls especially.

Just thinking of the old woman, her sacrifice, threatened to bring the tears which had been so long delayed.

'Why don't you tell him the reason those dissidents don't like it here?' Carmitha said.

'Who?' Louise asked.

'The Land Union people, the traders flung in jail for trying to sell medicine the rest of the Confederation takes for granted, the people who work the land, and all the other victims of the landowner class, me included.'

Anger, tiredness, and despair spurted up together in Louise's skull, threatening to quench what was left of her fragile spirit. She was so very tired; but she had to keep going, had to look after Gen. Gen and the precious baby. Would she ever see Joshua again now? 'Why are you saying this?' she asked jadedly.

'Because it's the truth. Not something a Kavanagh is used to, I'll warrant. Not from the likes of me.'

'I know this world isn't perfect. I'm not blind, I'm not stupid.'

'No, you know what to do to hang on to your privileges and your power. And look where it's got you. The whole planet being taken over, being taken away from you. Not so smart now, are you? Not so high and mighty.'

'That's a wicked lie.'

'Is it? A fortnight ago you rode your horse past me when I was working in one of your estate Roseyards. Did you stop for a chat then? Did you even notice I existed?'

'Come now, ladies,' Titreano said, uneasily.

But Louise couldn't ignore the challenge, the insult and the vile implication behind it. 'Did you ask me to stop?' she demanded. 'Did you want to hear me chat about the things I love and care about the most? Or were you too busy sneering at me? You with your righteous poverty. Because I'm rich I'm evil, that's what you think, isn't it?'

'Your family is, yes. Your ancestors made quite sure of that with their oppressive constitution. I was born on the road, and I'll die on it. I have no quarrel with that. But you condemned us to a circular road. It leads us nowhere, in an era when there is a chance to travel right into the heart of the galaxy. You shackled us as surely as any house would. I'll never see the wonder of sunrise and sunset on another planet.'

'Your ancestors knew the constitution when they came here, and they still came. They saw the freedom it would give you to roam like you always have done, like you cannot do on Earth any more.'

'If that's freedom, then tell me why can't we leave?'

'You can. Anyone can. Just buy a ticket on a starship.'

'Fat bloody chance. My entire family working a summer cupping season couldn't raise the price of one ticket. You control the economy, too. You designed it so we never earn more than a pittance.'

'It's not my fault you can't think of anything other than grove work to do. You have a caravan, why don't you trade goods like a merchant? Or plant some rosegroves of your own? There's still unsettled land on hundreds of islands.'

'We're not a landowning people, we don't want to be tied down.'

'Exactly!' Louise shouted. 'It's only your own stupid prejudices that trap you here. Not us, not the landowners. Yet we're the ones who you blame for your own inadequacies, just because you can't face up to the real truth. And don't think you're so unique. I want to see the whole Confederation, too. I dream about it every night. But I'll never be able to fly in a starship. I'll never be allowed, which is much worse than you. You made your own prison. I was born into mine. My obligations bind me to this world, I have to sacrifice my entire life for the good of this island.'

'Oh, yes. How you noble Kavanaghs suffer so. How grateful I am.' She glared at Louise, barely noticing Titreano, and not paying any attention to where the cob was trotting. 'Tell me, little Miss Kavanagh, how many brothers and sisters do you think you have in your high-born family?'

'I have no brothers, there's only Genevieve.'

'But what of the half-bloods?' Carmitha purred. 'What of them?'

'Half-bloods? Don't be foolish. I have none.'

She laughed bitterly. 'So sure of yourself. Riding high above us all. Well I know of three, and those are just the ones born to my family. My cousin carried one to term after last midsummer. A bonny little boy, the spitting image of his father. Your father. You see, it isn't all work for him. There's pleasure, too. More than to be found in your mother's bed.'

'Lies!' Louise cried. She felt faint, and sick.

'Really? He lay with me the day before the soldiers went to Boston. He got his money's worth of me. I made sure of that; I don't cheat people. So don't you talk to me about nobility and sacrifice. Your family are nothing more than titled robber barons.'

Louise glanced down. Genevieve's eyes were open, blinking against the red light. Please don't let her have heard, Louise prayed. She turned to look at the Romany woman, no longer able to stop her jaw from quivering. There was no will to argue any more. The day had won, beaten her, captured her parents, invaded her home, burned her county, terrorized her sister, and destroyed the only remaining fragment of happiness, that of the past with its golden memories. 'If you wish to hurt a Kavanagh,' she said in a tiny voice, 'if you wish to see me in tears for what you claim has happened, then you may have that wish. I don't care about myself any more. But spare my sister, she has been through so much today. No child should have to endure more. Let her go into the caravan where she can't hear your accusations. Please?' There was more to say, so much more, but the heat in her throat wouldn't let it come out. Louise started sobbing, hating herself for letting Gen see her weakness. But allowing the tears to flow was such an easy act.

Genevieve put her arms round her sister, and hugged her fiercely. 'Don't cry, Louise. Please don't cry.' Her face puckered up. 'I hate you,' she spat at Carmitha.

'I hope you are satisfied now, lady,' Titreano said curtly.

Carmitha stared at the two distraught sisters, Titreano's hard, disgusted face, then dropped the reins, and plunged her head into her hands. The shame was beyond belief.

Shit, taking out your own pathetic fear on a petrified sixteen-year-old girl who'd never hurt a living soul in her life. Who'd actually risked her own neck to warn you about the possessed in the farmhouse.

'Louise.' She extended an arm towards the still sobbing girl. 'Oh, Louise, I'm so sorry. I never meant to say what I did. I'm so stupid, I never think.' At least she managed to stop herself from asking 'forgive me'. Carry your own guilt, you selfish bitch, she told herself.

Titreano had put his own arm around Louise. It didn't make any difference to the broken girl. 'My baby,' Louise moaned between sobs. 'They'll kill my baby if they catch us.'

Titreano gently caught her hands. 'You are . . . with child?'

'Yes!' Her sobbing became louder.

Genevieve gaped at her. 'You're pregnant?'

Louise nodded roughly, long hair flopping about.

'Oh.' A small smile twitched across Genevieve's mouth. 'I won't tell anyone, I promise, Louise,' she said seriously.

Louise gulped loudly, and looked at her sister. Then she was laughing through her tears, clutching Genevieve to her. Genevieve hugged her back.

Carmitha tried not to show her own surprise. A landowner girl like Louise, the highest of the high, pregnant and unmarried! I wonder who . . .

'OK,' she said with slow determination. 'That's another

reason to get you two girls off this island. The best yet.' The sisters were regarding her with immense distrust. Can't blame them for that. She ploughed on: 'I swear to you here and now, Titreano and I will make sure you get on the plane. Right, Titreano?'

'Indeed, yes,' he said gravely.

'Good.' Carmitha picked up the cob's reins again, and gave them a brisk flip. The horse resumed its interminable plodding pace.

One good act, she thought, a single piece of decency amid the holocaust of the last six hours. That baby was going to survive. Grandma, if you're watching me, and if you can help the living in any way possible, now would be a good time.

And – the thought wouldn't leave her alone – a boy who wasn't intimidated by Grant Kavanagh, who'd dared to touch his precious daughter. A lot more than just touch, in fact. Foolhardy romantic, or a real hero prince?

Carmitha risked a quick glance at Louise. Either way, lucky girl.

\*

The long-base van which nosed down into the third sub-level car park below City Hall had the stylized palm tree and electron orbit logo of the Tarosa metamech corp emblazoned on its sides. It drew up in a bay next to a service elevator and six men and two women climbed out, all wearing the company's dull-red overalls. Three flatbed trolleys, piled high with crates and maintenance equipment, trundled down obediently out of the rear of the van.

One of the men walked over to the elevator, and pulled a processor block out of his pocket. He typed something on the block's surface, paused, then typed again. A nervous glance at his impassive workmates as they watched him.

The building management processor array accepted the

coded instruction which the block had datavised, and the elevator doors hissed open.

Emmet Mordden couldn't help the way his shoulders sagged in sheer relief as soon as the doors started to move. In his past life he'd suffered from a weak bladder, and it seemed as though he'd brought the condition with him to the body he now possessed. Certainly his guts were dangerously wobbly. Being in on the hard edge of operations always did that to him. He was strictly a background tech; until, of course, the day in 2535 when his syndicate boss got greedy, and sloppy with it. The police claimed afterwards that they'd given the gang an opportunity to surrender, but by then Emmet Mordden was past caring.

He shoved the processor block back into his overalls pocket while he brought out his palm-sized tool kit. Interesting to see how technology had advanced in the intervening seventy-five years; the principles were the same, but circuitry and programs were considerably more sophisticated.

A key from the tool kit opened the cover over the elevator's small emergency manual control panel. He plugged an optical cable into the interface socket, and the processor block lit up with a simple display. The unit took eight seconds to decode the elevator monitor program commands, and disable the alarm.

'We're in,' he told the others, and unplugged the optical cable. The more basic the electronic equipment, the more chance it had of operating in proximity to possessed bodies. By reducing the processor block functions to an absolute minimum he'd found he could make it work, although he still fretted about the efficiency.

Al Capone slapped him on the shoulder as the rest of the work crew and the flatbeds squeezed in to the elevator. 'Good work there, Emmet. I'm proud of you, boy.'

Emmet gave a fragile grin of gratitude, and pressed the door close button. He respected the resolve which Al had bestowed to the group of possessed. There had been so much bickering before about how to go about turning more bodies over for possession. It was as though they'd spent ninety per cent of their time arguing amongst themselves and jockeying for position. The only agreements they ever came to were grudgingly achieved.

Then Al had come along, and explained as coolly as you like that he was taking charge now thank you very much. Somehow it didn't surprise Emmet that a man who displayed such clarity of purpose and thought would have the greatest energistic strength. Two people had objected. And the little stick held so nonchalantly in Al Capone's hand had grown to a full-sized baseball bat.

Nobody else had voiced any dissension after that. And the beauty of it was, the dissenters could hardly go running to the cops.

Emmet wasn't sure which he feared the most, Al's strength or his temper. But he was just a soldier who obeyed orders, and happy with it. If only Al hadn't insisted he come with them this morning.

'Top floor,' Al said.

Emmet pressed the appropriate button. The elevator rose smoothly.

'OK, guys, now remember with our strength we can always blast our way out if anything goes wrong,' Al said. 'But this is our big chance to consolidate our hold over this town in one easy move. If we get rumbled, it's gonna be tough from here on. So let's try and stick to what we planned, right?'

'Absolutely, Al,' Bernhard Allsop said eagerly. 'I'm with you all the way.'

Several of the others gave him barely disguised glances of contempt.

Al ignored them all, and smiled heartily. Jee-zus, but this felt good; starting out with nothing again apart from his ambition.

But this time he knew the moves to make in advance. The others in the group had filled him in on chunks of history from the last few centuries. The New California administration was a direct descendant of the old US of A government. The Feds. And Al had one or two old scores to settle with those bastards.

The elevator doors chimed gently as they opened on the one hundred and fiftieth floor. Dwight Salerno and Patricia Mangano were out first. They smiled at the three staff members who were in the corridor, and killed them with a single coordinated blast of white fire. Smoking bodies hit the floor.

'We're OK, they didn't get out an alarm,' Emmet said, consulting his processor block.

'Get to it, people,' Al told his team proudly. This wasn't the same as the times with his soldiers like Anselmi and Scalise back on Cicero's streets. But these new guys had balls, and a cause. And it felt righteous to be a mover again.

The possessed spread out through the top floor. Tarosa metamech uniforms gave way to clothes of their own periods. A startlingly unpleasant variety of weapons appeared in their hands. Doors were forced open with precisely applied bolts of white fire. Rooms searched according to the list. Everyone following their assignment to the letter. Capone's letter.

It was six o'clock in the morning in San Angeles, and few of the mayor's staff were at work. Those that had turned up early found Retros bursting in to their offices and hauling them out at gunpoint. Their neural nanonics failed, desktop blocks crashed, net processors wouldn't respond. There was no way to get a warning out, no way to cry for help. They found themselves corralled in the Deputy Health Director's office, seventeen of them, clinging together in panic and mutual misery.

They thought that would surely be the worst of it, crammed into the one room for hours or maybe a couple of days while negotiations for their release were conducted with the terrorists. But then the Retros started taking them out one at a time, summoning the toughest first. The sound of screams cut back clean through the thick door.

Al Capone stood by the long window wall of the mayor's office, and looked out at the city. It was a magnificent view. He couldn't remember being so high off the ground in his life before. This skyscraper made the Empire State Building look puny, for God's sake. And it wasn't even the tallest in the city.

The skyscrapers only occupied the central portion of San Angeles, fifty or sixty of them bunched together to form the business, finance, and administration district. Beyond that the vast urban sprawl clung to the shallow folds of the land, long grey lines of buildings and autoways, interspaced with the equally regular squares of green parks. And to the east was the brilliant glimmer of the ocean.

Al, who had always enjoyed Lake Michigan in the summer, was fascinated by the glistening turquoise expanse as it reflected the first light of a new day. And the city was so clean, vibrant. So different to Chicago. This was an empire which Stalin and Genghis Khan would both envy.

Emmet knocked on the door, and popped his head round when he didn't receive an answer. 'Sorry to bother you, Al,' he ventured cautiously.

'That's OK, boy,' Al said. 'What've you got for me?'

'We've rounded up everyone on this floor. The electronics are all fucked, so they can't get word out. Bernhard and Luigi have started to bring them to possession.'

'Great, you've all done pretty goddam good.'

'Thanks, Al.'

'What about the rest of the electrics, the telephones and math-machine things?'

'I'm getting my systems plugged into the building network now, Al. Give me half an hour and I should have it locked down safe.'

'Good. Can we go to stage two?'

'Sure, Al.'

'OK, boy, you get back to your wiring.'

Emmet backed out of the office. Al wished he knew more about electrics himself. This future world depended so much on their clever mini-machines. That had to be a flaw. And Al Capone knew all about exploiting such weaknesses.

He let his mind slip into that peculiar state of otherness, and felt round for the rest of the possessed under his command. They were positioned all around the base of City Hall, strolling casually down the sidewalk, in cars parked nearby, tucking into breakfast in arcade diners.

Come, he commanded.

And the big ground-floor doors of City Hall opened wide.

\*

It was quarter to nine when Mayor Avram Harwood III arrived in his office. He was in a good mood. Today was the first day in a week when he hadn't been bombarded with early morning datavises from his staff concerning the Retro crisis. In fact there hadn't been any communication from City Hall at all. Some kind of record.

He took the express elevator from his private car bay up to the top floor, and stepped out into a world which wasn't quite normal. Nothing he could clarify, but definitely wrong. People scurried past as usual, barely pausing to acknowledge him. The elevator doors remained open behind him, the lights inside dying. When he tried to datavise its control processor there was no response. Attempting to log a routine call to maintenance he found none of the net processors were working.

Damn it, that was all he needed, a total electronics failure. At least it explained why he hadn't received any messages.

He walked into his office to find a young, olive-skinned man lounging in his chair, a fat soft stick in his mouth with one end on fire. And his clothes . . . Retro!

Mayor Harwood spun round, ready to make a dash for the

door. It was no good. Three of them had moved in to block the opening. They were all dressed in the same kind of antique double-breasted suits, brown hats with broad rims, and carrying primitive automatic rifles with circular magazines.

He tried to datavise a citizen's distress call. But his neural nanonics crashed, neatly tabulated icons retreated from his mind's eye like cowardly ghosts.

'Sit down, Mr Mayor,' Al Capone said munificently. 'You and I have some business to discuss.'

'I think not.'

A Thompson's butt slammed into the small of Avram Harwood's back. He let out a cry at the pain, and the world went dizzyingly black for a second. One of his big armchairs hit the back of his legs, and he fell down into the cushions, clutching at his spine.

'You see?' Al asked. 'You ain't calling the shots no more. Best you cooperate.'

'The police will be here soon. And mister, when they arrive they are going to fillet you and your gang. Don't think I'll help you negotiate, the Commissioner knows my policy on hostage situations. No surrender.'

Al winked broadly. 'I like you, Avvy. I do. I admire a man who stands up for himself. I knew you wouldn't be no patsy. It takes smarts to get to the top in a city like this, and plenty of them. So why don't you have a word with that Commissioner of yours. Clear the air some.' He beckoned.

Avram Harwood twisted round as Police Commissioner Vosburgh walked into the office.

'Hi there, Mr Mayor,' Vosburgh said blithely.

'Rod! Oh Christ, they got you too . . .' The words shrank as Vosburgh's familiar face *twisted*. A feral-faced stranger sneered down at him, hair was visibly sprouting out of his cheeks. Not a beard, more like thick prickly fur.

'Yeah, they got me too.' The voice was distorted by teeth

which were too long for a human mouth. He burst into a wild laugh.

'Who the hell are you Retro people?' an aghast Avram Harwood asked.

'The dead,' Al said. 'We've come back.'

'Bullshit.'

'I ain't arguing with you. Like I told you, I'm here to make a proposition. One of my guys – comes from just after my time – he said people took to calling it an offer you can't refuse. I like that, it's great. And that's what I'm making here to you, Avvy, my boy. An offer you can't refuse.'

'What offer?'

'It's like this: souls ain't the only thing I'm resurrecting today. I'm gonna build up an Organization. Like I had me before, only with a shitload more clout. I want you to join it, join me. Just as you are. No catch; you have my word. You, your family, maybe a few close friends, they don't get possessed. I know how to reward loyalty.'

'You're crazy. You're absolutely berserkoid. Join you? I'm going to see you destroyed, all of you deviant bastards, and then I'm going to stamp on the pieces.'

Al leant forwards and rested his elbows on the desk, staring earnestly at the Mayor. 'Sorry, Avvy. That's one thing you ain't gonna do. No fucking way. See, people hear my name, and they think I'm just a bigshot hoodlum, a racketeer who made good. Wrong. I used to be a fucking king. King Capone the first. I got the politics tied up. So I know which strings to pull in City Hall and the precinct houses. I know how a city works. That's why I'm here. I'm launching the biggest heist there's ever been in all of history.'

'What?'

'I'm gonna steal your world, Avvy. Take the whole caboodle from under your nose. These guys you see here, the ones you called Retros, they didn't know what the Christ they were doing before. Because just between you and me shutting off the sky like it's some kind of window with thick drapes is a bit of a wacko idea, you know? So I've straightened them out. No more of that bullshit. Now we're playing straight hardball.'

Avram Harwood lowered his head. 'Oh Christ.' They were insane. Utterly demented. He began to wonder if he would see his family again.

'Let me lay it out for you here, Avvy. You don't take over a society from the bottom like the Retros were trying to do. You know, little bit at a time until you're in the majority. Know why that's a crappy way to get on top? Because the goddam self-righteous majority is gonna find out and fight like fuck to stop you. And they get led by people like you, Avvy. You're the generals, the dangerous ones, you organize the lawyers and the cops and the special Federal agents to stop it happening. To protect the majority that elects you from anything which threatens you or them. So instead of an assways-first revolution, you do what I'm doing. You start at the top and work down.' Al got up and walked over to the window wall. He gestured at the street far below with his cigar. 'People are coming in to City Hall, Avvy. The workers, the police captains, the attorneys, your staff, tax clerks. All of them; the ones who'd lead the fight against me if they knew what I was. Yeah. They're coming in, but they ain't going out again. Not until we've made our pitch to each and every one of them.' Al turned to see Avram Harwood staring at him in horror. 'That's the way it is, Avvy,' he said softly. 'My people, they're working their way up from the ground floor. They're coming all the way up here. And all the people sitting in their offices who would normally fight against me. Why, they're going to be the ones who lead our crusade out into the world. Ain't that right, guys?'

'You got it, Al,' Emmet Mordden said. He was hunched over a couple of processor blocks at one end of the desk, monitoring the operation. 'The first twelve floors are all ours now. And we're busy converting everyone on thirteen to eighteen. I make that approximately six and a half thousand people possessed so far this morning.'

'See?' Al waved his cigar expansively. 'It's already begun, Avvy. Ain't nothing you can do about it. By lunch I'm gonna own the entire city administration. Just like the old days when Big Bill Thompson was in my pocket. And I got even bigger plans for tomorrow.'

'It won't work,' Avram Harwood whispered. 'It can't work.'

'Course it will, Avvy. The thing is ... returned souls. They ain't altogether marbles intacto. Capeesh? It's not just an Organization I'm building. Shit. We can be honest in here, you and me. It's a whole new government for New California. I need people who can help me run it. I need people who can run the factory machines. I need people who can keep the lights on and the water flowing, who're gonna take the garbage away. Fuck, if all that goes down the pan, my citizens, they're gonna come gunning for me, right? I mean, that's what the Retros didn't think about. What happens after? You still gotta keep things running smoothly.' Al sat on the arm of Avram Harwood's comfy chair, and put a friendly arm round his shoulder. 'Which is where you come in, Mr Mayor. Plenty of people want to run it. Everyone in this room, they all want to be my lieutenants. But it's the old problem. Horses for courses. Sure they're keen, but they ain't got the talent. But you, you my boy, you have got the talent. So how about it? Same job as before. Better salary. Perks. Fancy girl or two on the side if you like. So what do you say? Huh, Avvy? Say yeah. Make me happy.'

'Never.'

'What? What was that, Avvy? I didn't hear too good.'

'I said NEVER, you psychopathic freak.'

Very calmly, Al rose to his feet. 'I ask. I go down on my fucking knees, and ask you to help me. I ask you to be my friend. You, a wiseass I ain't never even seen before. I open my goddam heart to you. I'm bleeding across the floor for you

**139**

here. And you say no? No. To me!' Three scars burned hot and bright on his cheek. Everyone else in the office had retreated into a daunted silence.

'Is that what you're saying, Avvy? No?'

'You got it, shithead,' Avram Harwood shouted recklessly. Something wild was running free in his brain, a mad glee at confounding his adversary. 'The answer is never. Never. Never.'

'Wrong.' Al flicked his cigar onto the thick carpet. 'You got it way wrong, buddy. The answer is yes. It is always yes when you talk to me. It is yes fucking please Mr Capone *sir*. And I'm going to fucking well hear you say it.' A fist thumped on his chest for emphasis. 'Today is the day you say yes to me.'

Mayor Avram Harwood took one look at the stained baseball bat which had materialized in Al Capone's hands, and knew it was going to be bad.

*

Duke-dawn failed. There was no sign of the primary sun's comforting white light brushing the short night before it as the bright disc rose above the wolds. Instead a miscreant coral phosphorescence glided out over the horizon, staining the vegetation a lustreless claret.

For a harrowingly confused moment Louise thought that Duchess was returning, racing round the underside of the planet after it had set scant minutes ago to spring up ahead of the lumbering Romany caravan. But after a minute's scrutiny she realized the effect was due to a high haze of reddish mist. It really was Duke which had risen.

'What is it?' Genevieve enquired querulously. 'What's wrong?'

'I'm not sure.' Louise scanned the horizon, leaning round the corner of the caravan to check behind them. 'It looks like a layer of fog really high up, but why is it that colour? I've never seen anything like it before.'

'Well, I don't like it,' Genevieve announced, and folded her arms across her chest. She glared ahead.

'Do you know what's doing that?' Carmitha asked Titreano.

'Not entirely, my lady,' he said, appearing troubled. 'And yet, I sense there is a rightness to it. Do you not feel comforted by its presence?'

'No, I bloody don't,' Carmitha snapped. 'It's not natural, and you know it.'

'Yes, lady.'

His subdued acknowledgement did nothing to alleviate her nerves. Terror, uncertainty, lack of sleep, not having eaten since yesterday, remorse, it was all starting to add up.

The caravan trundled on for another half a mile under the brightening red light. Carmitha steered them along a well-worn track below a forest. Here, the land's gentle undulations were gradually increasing to form deeper vales and rolling hills. Dried up stream beds crisscrossed the slopes, emptying into the deeper gullies which ran along the floor of each valley. There was more woodland than out on the open wolds, more cover from, and for, prying eyes. All they had to go on was Titreano's strange sixth sense.

Nobody spoke, too tired or too fearful. Louise realized the birds were missing from the air. The characterless forest loomed up like a shaggy cliff face mere yards away, bleak and repellent.

'Here we are,' Carmitha said as they rounded a curve in the track. It had taken longer than she thought. Eight hours at least. Not good for poor old Olivier.

Ahead of them the slope dipped down to expose a broad valley with heavily forested sides. The alluvial floor was a chess-board of neat fields, all marked out by long drystone walls and geneered hawthorn hedges. A dozen streams bubbling out from the head of the valley funnelled into a small river which meandered off into the distance. Red sunlight glinted off a narrow sliver of water running along the centre of its baked clay banks.

Bytham was situated about three miles down the valley, a cluster of stone cottages split in half by the river. Over the centuries the community had grown outwards from a single humpbacked stone bridge. At the far end, a narrow church spire rose above the thatched roofs.

'It looks all right,' Louise said cautiously. 'I can't see any fires.'

'Quiet enough,' Carmitha agreed. She hardly dared consult Titreano. 'Are your kind out there?' she asked.

His eyes were closed, yet his head was thrust forwards, as though he were sniffing the air ahead. 'Some of them,' he said, regretfully. 'But not all of the village has been turned. Not yet. People are wakening to the fact that great evil stalks this land.' He glanced at Louise. 'Where is your aerial machine berthed?'

She blushed. 'I don't know. I've never been here before.' She didn't like to admit that apart from accompanying Mother on a twice-yearly train trip to Boston for a clothes buying spree she'd hardly ever ventured outside Cricklade's sprawling boundaries.

Carmitha pointed to a circular meadow half a mile outside the town, with two modest hangars on the perimeter. 'That's the aerodrome. And thank God it's on this side of the village.'

'I suggest we make haste, lady,' Titreano said.

Still not quite trusting him, Carmitha nodded reluctantly. 'One minute.' She stood up, and hurried back into the caravan. Inside, it was a complete mess. All her possessions had been slung about by her madcap dash from Colsterworth, clothes, pots and pans, food, books. She sighed at the shards of broken blue and white china lying underfoot. Her mother always claimed the crockery had come with the family from Earth.

The chest under her bed was one article which hadn't moved. Too heavy. Carmitha knelt down and spun the combination lock.

Louise gave the Romany woman an alarmed look when she

emerged from the caravan. She was carrying a single-barrelled shotgun and a belt of cartridges.

'Pump action,' Carmitha said. 'It holds ten rounds. I've already loaded it for you. Safety's on. You hold it, get used to the weight.'

'Me?' Louise gulped in surprise.

'Yes, you. Who knows what's waiting for us down there. You must have used a shotgun before?'

'Well, yes. Of course. But only on birds, and tree rats, and things. I'm not a very good shot, I'm afraid.'

'Don't worry. Just point it in the general direction of any trouble, and shoot.' She gave Titreano a dry grin. 'I'd give it to you, but it's rather advanced compared to the kind of guns you had in your day. Better Louise carries it.'

'As you wish, my lady.'

Now Duke was higher in the sky it was doing its best to burn away the red mist which hung over the land. Occasionally a beam of pure white sunlight would wash over the caravan, making all four of them blink from its glare. But for the most part, the veil remained unbroken.

The caravan reached the valley floor, and Carmitha urged the cob into a faster trot. Olivier did his best to oblige, but his reserves of strength were clearly ebbing.

As they drew nearer to the village they heard the church bell tolling. It was no glad peal calling the faithful to morning service, just a monotonous strike. A warning.

'The villagers know,' Titreano announced. 'My kind are grouping together. They are stronger that way.'

'If you know what they're doing, do they know about you?' Carmitha asked.

'Yes, lady, I would fear so.'

'Oh, just wonderful.' The road ahead was now angling away from the direction in which the aerodrome lay. Carmitha stood on the seat, and tried to work out where to turn off. The hedges and walls of the fields were spread out before her like a maze. 'Bugger,' she muttered under her breath. Both of the aerodrome's hangars were clearly visible about half a mile away, but you'd have to be a local to know how to get to them.

'Do they know we're with you?' Carmitha asked.

'Probably not. Not over such a distance. But when we are closer to the village, they will know.'

Genevieve tugged anxiously at Titreano's sleeve. 'They won't find us, will they? You won't let them?'

'Of course not, little one. I gave my word I will not abandon you.'

'I don't like this at all,' Carmitha said. 'We're too visible. And when they realize there's four of us riding on it, your side is going to know you're travelling with non-possessed,' she said accusingly to Titreano.

'We can't turn round now,' Louise insisted, her voice high and strained. 'We're so close. We'll never have another chance.'

Carmitha wanted to add that there might not even be a pilot at the aerodrome; come to that she hadn't actually seen the distinctive shape of the aeroambulance itself yet. Could be in a hangar. But with the way their luck was turning out right now . . .

Both the sisters were obviously near the end of their tether. They looked dreadful, filthy and tired, close to breaking down in tears – for all Louise's outward determination.

Carmitha was surprised to realize just how much she had begun to respect the elder girl.

'You can't go back, no,' Carmitha said. 'But I can. If I take the caravan back to the woods the possessed will think we're all running away from Titreano here.'

'No!' Louise said in shock. 'We're together now. We've only got each other. There's only us left in the whole world.'

'We are not all that's left. Don't ever think that. Outside Kesteven, people are going about their lives just like before. And once you get to Norwich, they'll be warned.'

'No,' Louise mumbled. But there was less conviction now.

'You know you have to go,' Carmitha continued. 'But me. Hell, I'll be a lot better off by myself. With my lore I can lose myself in the forests; the possessed will never find me. I can't do that with you three tagging along. You know us Romanies belong with the land, girl.'

The corners of Louise's mouth turned down.

'Don't you?' Carmitha said sternly. She knew she was still being selfish; just plain didn't want to admit she couldn't stand seeing their delicate hopes burnt to cinders when they reached the aerodrome.

'Yes,' Louise said docilely.

'Good girl. OK, this section of road is wide enough to turn the caravan round. You three had better get down.'

'Are you sure of this, lady?' Titreano asked.

'Absolutely. But I'm holding you to your promise of guarding these two.'

He nodded sincerely, and dropped down over the side.

'Genevieve?'

The little girl glanced up shyly, her lower lip pressed against her teeth.

'I know we didn't get on too well, and I'm sorry we didn't. But I want you to have this.' Carmitha reached behind her neck, and unfastened the pendant's chain. The silver bulb which glinted in the pink light was made from a fine mesh, much dinted now; but through the grid a filigree of thin brown twigs was just visible. 'It used to be my grandma's; she gave it to me when I was about your age. It's a charm to ward off evil spirits. That's lucky heather inside, see? Genuine heather; it grew on Earth in the time before the armada storms. There's real earth magic stored in there.'

Genevieve held the bauble up in front of her face, studying it intently. A fast smile lit up her delicate features, and she lunged forward to hug Carmitha. 'Thank you,' she whispered. 'Thank you for everything.' She climbed down into Titreano's arms.

Carmitha gave an edgy smile to Louise. 'Sorry it turned out the way it did, girl.'

'That's all right.'

'Hardly. Don't lose faith in your father because of what I said.'

'I won't. I love Daddy.'

'Yes, I expect you do. That's good, something to hold on to. You are going to be facing a few more dark days yet, you know.'

Louise started tugging at a ring on her left hand. 'Here. It's not much. Not lucky, or anything special. But it is gold, and that's a real diamond. If you need to buy anything, it'll help.'

Carmitha eyed the ring in surprise. 'Right. Next time I need a mansion I'll remember.'

They both grinned sheepishly.

'Take care, Carmitha. I want to see you when I come back, when all this is over.' Louise twisted round, preparing to climb down.

'Louise.'

There was such disquiet in the voice that Louise froze.

'There's something wrong about Titreano,' Carmitha said quietly. 'I don't know if I'm just being paranoid, but you ought to know before you go any further with him.'

A minute later Louise clambered gingerly down the side of the caravan, keeping hold of the pump-action shotgun, the cartridge belt an uncomfortable weight around her hips. When she was on the dirt track she waved up at Carmitha. The Romany waved back, and flicked the Cob's reins.

Louise, Genevieve, and Titreano watched the caravan turn round and head back up the rucked road.

'Are you all right, lady Louise?' Titreano asked courteously.

Her fingers tightened round the shotgun. Then she took a breath, and smiled at him. 'I think so.'

They struck out for the aerodrome, scrambling through

ditches and over hedges. The fields were mostly ploughed, ready for the second cereal crop, difficult to walk on. Dust puffed up from each footfall.

Louise glanced over at Genevieve who was wearing Carmitha's pendant outside her torn and dusty blouse, one hand grasping the silver bulb tightly. 'Not long now,' she said.

'I know,' Genevieve replied pertly. 'Louise, will they have something to eat on the aeroambulance?'

'I expect so.'

'Good! I'm starving.' She trudged on for another few paces, then cocked her head to one side. 'Titreano, you're not dirty at all,' she exclaimed in a vexed tone.

Louise looked over. It was true; not a scrap of dirt or dust had adhered to his blue jacket.

He glanced down at himself, rubbing his hands along the seams of his trousers in a nervous gesture. 'I'm sorry, little one, it must be the fabric. Although I do confess, I don't remember being immune to such depredations before. Perhaps I should bow to the inevitable.'

Louise watched in some consternation as mud stains crept up from his ankles, discolouring his trousers below the knee. 'You mean you can change your appearance whenever you want?' she asked.

'It would seem so, lady Louise.'

'Oh.'

Genevieve giggled. 'You mean you want to look all silly like that?'

'I find it . . . comfortable, little one. Yes.'

'If you can change that easily, I think you ought to adopt something which will blend in a bit better,' Louise said. 'I mean, Gen and I look like a pair of tramps. And then there's you in all your strange finery. What would you think of us if you were one of the aeroambulance crew?'

'Finely argued, lady.'

For the next five minutes as they crossed the fields Titreano went through a series of alterations. Genevieve and Louise kept up a stream of suggestions, arguing hotly, and explaining textures and styles to their mildly befuddled companion. When they finished he was dressed in the fashion of a young estate manager, with fawn cord trousers, calf-length boots, a tweed jacket, check shirt, and grey cap.

'Just right,' Louise declared.

'I thank you, lady.' He doffed his cap, and bowed low.

Genevieve clapped delightedly.

Louise stopped at another of the interminable walls, and found a gap in the stone to shove her boot toe in. An unladylike action she was becoming highly adept at. Straddling the top of the wall she could see the aerodrome's perimeter fence two hundred yards away. 'Almost there,' she told the others cheerfully.

\*

The Bytham aerodrome appeared to be deserted. Both hangars were closed up; nobody was in the control tower. Away on the other side of the mown field the row of seven cottages used by station personnel was silent and dark.

The only sound was the persistent clang of the church bell in the village. It hadn't stopped ringing the whole time they had walked across the fields.

Louise peered round the side of the first hangar, clutching the shotgun. Nothing moved. A couple of tractors and a farm ranger were parked outside a small access door. 'Are there any possessed here?' she whispered to Titreano.

'No,' he whispered back.

'What about normal people?'

His brown face creased in concentration. 'Several. I hear them over in yon houses. Five or six are malingering inside this second barn.'

'Hangar,' Louise corrected. 'We call them hangars nowadays.'

'Yes, lady.'

'Sorry.'

They swapped a nervous grin.

'I suppose we'd better go and see them, then,' she said. 'Come here, Gen.' She pointed the shotgun at the ground and took her sister's hand as they walked towards the second hangar.

She really wished Carmitha hadn't given her the weapon. Yet at the same time it imbued her with an uncommon sense of confidence. Even though she doubted she could ever actually fire it at anyone.

'They have seen us,' Titreano said quietly.

Louise scanned the corrugated panel wall of the hangar. A narrow line of windows ran the entire length. She thought she saw a shiver of motion behind one. 'Hello?' she called loudly.

There was no reply.

She walked right up to the door, and knocked firmly. 'Hello, can you hear me?' She tried the handle, only to discover it was locked.

'Now what?' she asked Titreano.

'Hey!' Genevieve shouted at the door. 'I'm hungry.'

The handle turned, and the door opened a crack. 'Who the hell are you people?' a man asked.

Louise drew herself up as best she could manage, knowing full well what she must look like to anyone inside. 'I am Louise Kavanagh, the heir of Cricklade, this is my sister Genevieve, and William Elphinstone, one of our estate managers.'

Genevieve opened her mouth to protest, but Louise nudged her with a toe.

'Oh really?' came the answer from behind the door.

'Yes!'

'It is her,' said another, deeper voice. The door opened wide to show two men gazing out at them. 'I recognize her. I used to work at Cricklade.'

'Thank you,' Louise said.

'Until your father fired me.'

Louise didn't know whether to burst into tears or just shoot him on the spot.

'Let them in, Duggen,' a woman called. 'The little girl looks exhausted. And this is no day to settle old grudges.'

Duggen shrugged, and moved aside.

A line of dusty windows was the sole source of illumination inside. The aeroambulance was a hulking dark presence in the middle of the concrete floor. Three people were standing below the plane's narrow, pointed nose; the woman who had spoken, and a pair of five-year-old twin girls. She introduced herself as Felicia Cantrell, her daughters were Ellen and Tammy; her husband Ivan was an aeroambulance pilot, the man who had opened the door. 'And Duggen you already know, or at least he knows you.'

Ivan Cantrell took a vigilant look out of the hangar door before closing it. 'So would you like to tell us what you're doing here, Louise. And what happened to you?'

It took her over fifteen minutes to produce a patched-up explanation which satisfied them. All the time guarding her tongue from uttering the word possession, and mentioning who Titreano really was. As she realized, those two items would have got her ejected from the hangar in no time at all. Yet at the same time she was pleased with her white lies; the Louise who had woken to a normal world yesterday would have just blurted the truth and imperiously demanded they do something about it. This must be growing up, after a fashion.

'The Land Union with modern energy weapons?' Duggen mused sceptically when she was finished.

'I think so,' Louise said. 'That's what everyone said.'

He looked as if he was about to object when Genevieve said: 'Listen.'

Louise couldn't hear a thing. 'What?' she asked.

'The church bells, they've stopped.'

Duggen and Ivan went over to the windows and looked out.

'Are they coming?' Louise mouthed to Titreano.

He nodded his head surreptitiously.

'Please,' she appealed to Ivan. 'You have to fly us out of here.'

'I don't know about that, Miss Kavanagh. I don't have the authority. And we don't really know what's happening in the village. Perhaps I ought to check with the constable first.'

'Please! If you're worried about your job, don't be. My family will protect you.'

He sucked in his breath, blatantly unhappy.

'Ivan,' Felicia said. She stared straight at him, pointing significantly to the twins. 'Whatever is going on, this is no place for children to be. The capital will be safe if anywhere is.'

'Oh, hell. All right, Miss Kavanagh. You win. Get in. We'll all go.'

Duggen started to open the big sliding doors at the end of the hangar, allowing a thick beam of pink-tinted sunlight to strike the aeroambulance. The plane was an imported Kulu Corporation SCV-659 civil utility, a ten-seater VTOL supersonic with a near-global range.

'It has the essence of a bird,' Titreano murmured, his face gently intoxicated. 'But with the strength of a bull. What magic.'

'Are you going to be all right inside?' Louise asked anxiously.

'Oh yes, lady Louise. This is a voyage to be prized beyond mountains of gold. To be granted this opportunity I shall give full praise to the Lord tonight.'

She coughed uncomfortably. 'Right. OK, we'd better get in; up that stair on the other side, see?'

They followed Felicia and the twins up the airstairs. The plane's narrow cabin had been customized for its ambulance role, with a pair of stretchers and several cabinets of medical equipment. There were only two seats, which the twins used. Genevieve, Titreano, and Louise wound up sitting together on one of the stretcher couches. Louise checked the safety on the shotgun once again, and wedged it below her feet. Surprisingly, no one had objected to her carrying it on board.

'This is all we need,' Ivan called back from the pilot's seat as he started to run through the preflight check list. 'I've got half a dozen systems failures showing.'

'Any critical?' Duggen asked as he closed the hatch.

'We'll survive.'

Felicia opened one of the cabinets, and handed Genevieve a bar of chocolate. The girl tore the wrapper off, and sat munching it with a huge contented smile.

If she craned forwards, Louise could just see the windscreen beyond Ivan. The plane was rolling forwards out of the hangar.

'There are some houses on fire in the village,' the pilot exclaimed. 'And some people running down the road towards us. Hang on.'

There was a sudden surge in the bee-hum from the fans, and the cabin rocked. They were airborne within seconds, climbing at a shallow angle. The only things visible through the windscreen were daubs of insubstantial pink cloud.

'I hope Carmitha is all right down there,' Louise said guiltily.

'I feel certain she will remain free from harm, lady. And it gladdens me that you resolved your quarrel with her. I admire you for that, my lady Louise.'

She knew her cheeks would be blushing, she could feel the heat. Hopefully the smears of mud and dust would be veiling the fact. 'Carmitha said something to me before she left. Something about you. It was a question. A good one.'

'Ah. I did wonder what passed between you. If you care to ask, I will answer with such honesty as I own.'

'She wanted me to ask where you really came from.'

'But lady Louise, I have spoken nothing but the truth to you in this matter.'

'Not quite. Norfolk is an English-ethnic planet; so we do learn something of our heritage in school. I know that the England of what you say is your time was a pure *Anglo*-Saxon culture.'

'Yes?'

'Yes. And Titreano is not an English name. Not at that time. After that possibly, when immigration began in later centuries. But if you had been born in Cumbria in 1764 as you claim, that could not be your name.'

'Oh, lady, forgive me any mistrust I have inadvertently caused you. Titreano is not the name I was born with. However, it is the one I lived with in my latter years. It is the closest rendering the island people I adopted could come to my family name.'

'And that is?'

The dignity vanished from his handsome features, leaving only sorrow. 'Christian, my lady Louise. I was baptized Fletcher Christian, and was proud to be named so. In that I must now be alone, for I have brought naught but shame to my family ever since. I am a mutineer, you see.'

# 4

Ralph Hiltch was gratified and relieved by the speed with which Ombey's senior administration reacted to what they'd taken to calling the Mortonridge crisis. The people at Hub One were joined by the full complement of the Privy Council Security Committee. This time Princess Kirsten herself was sitting at the head of the table in the white bubble room, relegating Admiral Farquar to a position adjacent to her. The table top mutated into a detailed map showing the top half of Mortonridge; the four towns which the rogue Longhound bus had visited, Marble Bar, Rainton, Gaslee, and Exnall, glinted a macabre blood-red above the rumpled foothills. Flurries of symbols flickered and winked around each of them, electronic armies harassing their foes.

Once the last of Moyce's delivery lorries had been tracked down and eliminated, Diana Tiernan switched the entire capacity of the AIs to analysing vehicles that had left the four towns, and stopping them. In one respect they were fortunate: it was midnight along Mortonridge, and the volume of traffic was much reduced from its daytime peak. Identification was reasonably easy. Deciding what to do about both cars and towns was less so.

It took twenty minutes of debate, arbitrated by the Princess, before they thrashed out an agreed policy. In the end, the deciding factor was Gerald Skibbow's completed personality debrief, which was datavised down from Guyana. Dr Riley Dobbs appeared before the committee to testify its provenance; an apprehensive man, telling the planetary rulers that they were being assaulted by the dead reborn. But it did provide the justification, or spur, necessary for the kind of action which Ralph was pressing for. And even he sat through Dobbs's report in a state of cold incredulity. If I'd made a mistake, shown a single gram of weakness . . .

The expanded Security Committee decided that all ground vehicles which had left the Mortonridge towns were to be directed to three separate holding areas established along the M6 by the police AT squads. Refusal to comply would result in instantaneous SD fire. Once at the holding area, they would be required to wait in their vehicles until the authorities were ready to test them for possession. Failure to remain in the vehicle would result in the police AT squads opening fire.

For the towns, a complete martial law curfew was to be effected immediately, no vehicular traffic or pedestrians allowed. Low-orbit SD sensor satellites would scan the streets constantly in conjunction with the local police patrols. Anyone found disobeying the prohibition would be given exactly one opportunity to surrender. Weapons engagement authorization was granted to all the police personnel responsible for enforcing the curfew order.

At first light tomorrow the operation to evacuate the four towns would begin. Now that Diana Tiernan and the AIs were reasonably satisfied that no possessed were left anywhere else on the continent, Princess Kirsten agreed to dispatch marine troops from Guyana to assist with the evacuation. All Xingu police reserves would be called in, and together with the marines they would encircle the towns. Squads would then move in to conduct a house-to-house examination. Non-possessed members of the population were to be escorted out and flown on military transports to a Royal Navy ground base north of Pasto where they would be housed for the immediate future.

As for the possessed, they would be given a stark choice: release the body or face imprisonment in zero-tau. No exceptions.

'I think that covers everything,' Admiral Farquar said.

'You'd better make it clear to the marine commanders that they're not to use assault mechanoids under any circumstances,' Ralph said. 'In fact, the more primitive the systems they deploy, the better.'

'I don't know if we've got enough chemical-projectile weapons in store for everyone,' the admiral said. 'But I'll see that all our current stock is issued.'

'It wouldn't be too difficult for Ombey's engineering factories to start production of new projectile rifles and ammunition,' Ralph said. 'I'd like to see what can be done in that direction.'

'It would take at least a couple of days to set up,' Ryle Thorne said. 'Our current situation should have been settled by then.'

'Yes, sir,' Ralph said. 'If we truly have got all the possessed trapped on Mortonridge this time. And if no more sneak on to the planet.'

'Starship interception has been one hundred per cent throughout the Ombey system for the last five hours,' Deborah Unwin said. 'And you were the first ship to arrive from Lalonde, Ralph. I guarantee no more possessed will escape from orbit down to the planet.'

'Thank you, Deborah,' Princess Kirsten said. 'I'm not doubting the competence of your officers, nor the efficiency of the SD network, but I have to say I think Mr Hiltch is correct in requesting contingency arrangements. What we've seen so far is simply the very first encounter with the possessed; and combating them is absorbing nearly all of our resources. We have to assume that other planets will not be as successful as us in containing the outbreaks. No, this problem is not one which is going to go away in the near or even mid-future. And, as is likely, it is proved beyond reasonable doubt that there is both an afterlife and an afterworld, the philosophical implications are quite extraordinary, and profoundly disturbing.'

'Which brings us to our second problem,' Ryle Thorne said. 'What are we going to tell people?'

'Same as always,' Jannike Dermot said. 'As little as possible, certainly to start with. We really can't risk the prospect of a general panic right now. I would suggest we use the energy virus as a cover story.'

'Plausible,' Ryle Thorne agreed.

The Home Secretary, the Princess, and her equerry put together a statement for general release the next morning. It was instructive for Ralph to see the Saldana body politic at work in the flesh, as it were. There was no question of the Princess herself delivering the statement to the news companies. That was the job of the Prime Minister and the Home Secretary. A Saldana simply could not announce such appalling news. It was the function of royalty to offer comments of support and sympathy to the victims at a later date, and people were going to need all the comfort they could get when that byte of official news hit the communication net.

*

The town of Exnall sat two hundred and fifty kilometres below the neck of Mortonridge, where the peninsula joined the main body of the continent. It had been founded thirty years ago, and had grown with confidence ever since. The soil around it was rich, the haunt of any number of aboriginal plant species, many of which were eatable. Farmers came in their hundreds to cultivate the new species alongside terrestrial crops which thrived in the moist tropical climate. Exnall was a town dominated by agriculture; even the light industries attracted by the council produced and serviced farm machinery.

But by no means a hick town, Chief Inspector Neville

Latham thought as his car drove along Maingreen, which ran straight through the centre. Exnall had amalgamated with the local harandrid forest instead of chopping it down to make way for buildings as other Mortonridge towns had done. Even twenty minutes after midnight Maingreen looked superb, the mature trees importing an air of rustic antiquity for the buildings, as if the two had been coexisting for centuries. Street lights hanging from overhead cables cast a glareless haze of orange-white light, turning the harandrids' dripping leaves a spooky grey. Only a couple of bars and the all-nighter coffee shop were open, their liquid glass windows swirling in abstract patterns, making it impossible to see exactly what was happening inside. Not that anything wild ever did take place; Neville Latham knew that from his days as a patrol officer twenty years ago. Terminal drunks and stim victims slummed the bars, while night shift workers took refuge in the coffee shop, along with the duty police officers.

The car's drive processor datavised an update request, and Neville directed it off Maingreen and into the police station's car park. Almost all of Exnall's twenty-five-strong police complement were waiting for him in the station's situation management room. Sergeant Walsh stood up as he entered, and the rest stopped talking. Neville took his place at the head of the room.

'Thank you all for coming in,' he said briskly. 'As you know from the level two security datavise you've received, the Prime Minister has decreed a continent-wide curfew to come into effect from one o'clock this morning. Now, I'm sure we've all accessed the rumours streaming the net today, so I'd like to clarify the situation for you. First the good news; I've been in communication with Landon McCullock who assures me that Ombey has not been contaminated by a xenoc biohazard as the media has been hinting. Nor are we under any sort of naval assault. However, it seems someone has released an extremely sophisticated sequestration technology down here on Xingu.'

Neville watched the familiar faces in front of him register various levels of apprehension. The ever-dependable Sergeant Walsh remained virtually emotionless, the two detectives, Feroze and Manby, wary and working out angles, genuine disquiet among the junior patrol officers – who knew full well they'd have the dirty job of actually going out in their cars and enforcing the curfew order.

He waited a few moments for the grumbles to subside. 'Unfortunately, the bad news is that the Privy Council Security Committee believes several examples of this technology may already be loose here in Exnall. Which means we are now under a full state of martial law. Our curfew has to be enforced one hundred per cent, no exceptions. I know this is going to be difficult for you, we've all got family and friends out there, but believe me the best way to help them now is to make sure the order holds. People must not come into contact with each other; which is how the experts think this technology spreads. Apparently it's very hard to spot anyone who has been sequestrated until it's too late.'

'So we just sit in our homes and wait?' Thorpe Hartshorn asked. 'For how long? For what?'

Neville held up a placatory hand. 'I'm coming to that, Officer Hartshorn. Our efforts will be supported by a combined team of police and marines who are going to seal off the entire area. They should be here in another ninety minutes. Once they arrive all the houses in the town will be searched for any victims of the sequestration, and everyone else is going to be evacuated.'

'The whole town?' Thorpe Hartshorn asked suspiciously.

'Everybody,' Neville confirmed. 'They're sending over a squadron of military transports to take us away. But it's going to take a few hours to organize, so it falls upon us to ensure that the curfew is maintained until then.'

*

DataAxis, Exnall's sole news agency, was at the other end of Maingreen from the police station; a shabby, three-storey flat-roof office module which made few creditworthy concessions to the sylvan character of the town. The agency itself was a typical small provincial outfit, employing five reporters and three communication technicians who between them combed the whole county for nuggets of information. Given the nature of the area, their brief was wide-ranging, dealing in local human interest stories, official events, crime (such as it was), and the horrendously mundane crop price sheets which the office processors handled with little or no human supervision. Out of this fascinating assortment of articles they had managed to sell precisely four items to Ombey's major media companies in the last six weeks.

But that had certainly changed today, Finnuala O'Meara thought jubilantly as the desktop processor finished decrypting the level two security datavise from Landon McCullock to Neville Latham. She'd spent a solid ten hours fishing the net streams today, digesting every rumour since yesterday's Guyana alert. Thanks to the trivia and paranoid nightmares which every bulletin site geek on the planet had contributed she'd felt completely stimmed out and ready to pack it in. Then an hour ago things got interesting.

AT squads had seen action in Pasto. Violent action by all accounts – and still no official media release on that from the police. The motorways were being shut down clean across the continent. Reports of SD fire on vehicles abounded; including a clear account of a runaway bus being vaporized not a hundred and fifty kilometres south of Exnall. And now Xingu's Police Commissioner, in person, informing Neville Latham that an unknown, but probably xenoc, sequestration virus was loose in Exnall.

Finnuala O'Meara datavised a shutdown order into the desktop processor block, and opened her eyes. 'Bloody hell,' she grunted.

Finnuala was in her early twenties, eleven months out of university in Atherstone. Her initial delight at landing a job within two days of qualifying had, during the first quarter of an hour at the agency, turned into dismay. The Exnall agency didn't deal in news, it churned out anti-insomnia treatments. Dismay had slumped to surly anger. Exnall was everything which was rotten with small towns. It was run by a clique, a small elite group of councillors and businessmen and the richer local farmers, who made the decisions which counted at their dinner parties and out on their golf course.

It was no different from her own home town. The one over on the Esparta continent where her parents never quite made the leap to real money contracts. Because they lacked the connections. Excluded, by class, by money.

She did nothing for half a minute after the decrypted datavise slipped from her mind, sitting staring at the desktop processor. Accessing the net's police architecture was illegal enough, owning a level two decryption program was grounds for deportation. But she couldn't ignore this. Couldn't. It was everything she'd become a reporter for.

'Hugh?' she called.

The communication technician sharing the graveyard shift with her cancelled the Jezzibella album he was running, and gave her a disapproving look. 'What?'

'How would the authorities announce a curfew to the general public, one where everyone is confined to their house? Specifically, a curfew here in Exnall.'

'Are you having me on?'

'No.'

He blinked away the figments of the flek, and accessed a civil procedures file in his neural nanonics. 'OK I've found it; it's a pretty simple procedure. The Chief Inspector will use his code rating to load a universal order into the town's net for every general household processor. The message will play as soon as the processor is accessed, no matter what function you asked for – you tell it to cook your breakfast or vacuum the floor, the first thing it will do is tell you about the curfew.'

Finnuala patted her hands together, charting out options. 'So people won't know about the curfew until tomorrow morning after they wake up.'

'That's right.'

'Unless we tell them first.'

'Now you really are winding me up.'

'No way.' The smile on her face was carnivorous. 'I know what that prat Latham is going to do next. He'll warn his friends before anyone else, he'll make sure they're ready to be evacuated first. It's his style, this whole bloody town's style.'

'Don't be so paranoid.' Hugh Rosler said edgily. 'If the evacuation is under McCullock's command, nobody will be able to pull a fast one from this end.'

Finnuala smiled sweetly, and datavised an order into the desktop processor block. It accessed the net's police architecture again, and the monitor programs she designated went into primary mode.

The results simmered into Hugh's mind as a cluster of grey, dimensionless icons. Someone at the police station was datavising a number of houses in the town and outlying areas. They were personal calls, and the households they were being directed at were all depressingly familiar.

'He already is,' Finnuala said. 'I know these people as well as you do, Hugh. Nothing changes, not even when our planet is under threat.'

'So what do you want to do?'

'What this agency is supposed to do: inform people. I'll assemble a package warning everyone about the sequestration; but instead of just releasing it on the media circuit I want you to program the agency processor to datavise it to everyone in Exnall right away, coded as a personal priority message. That way we'll all have an equal chance to get clear when the military transports arrive.'

162

'I don't know about this, Finnuala. Maybe we ought to check with the editor first . . .'

'Bugger the editor,' she snapped. 'He already knows. Look who was seventh on Latham's list. Do you think his priority is to call us? Do you? Right now he's getting his fat wife and their backward brat dressed ready to take off for the landing site. Are your wife and kids being told, Hugh? Are they being made safe?'

Hugh Rosler did what he always did, and offered no resistance. 'All right, Finnuala, I'll modify the processor's program. But by Christ, you'd better be right about this.'

'I am.' She stood up and pulled her jacket off the back of the chair. 'I'm going down to the police station, see if I can get a personal comment from that good man Chief Inspector Latham on the crisis facing his little fiefdom.'

'You're pushing it,' Hugh warned.

'I know.' She grinned sadistically. 'Great, isn't it.'

*

Ralph knew he didn't have anything to prove any more. The AT squads were alert to the terrible danger, they'd been fully blooded. So there was no practical reason for him to take a police hypersonic out to Mortonridge. Yet here he was with Cathal, Will, and Dean heading south at Mach 5. His justification . . . well, the marine brigade coming down from the orbital bases would need to be brought up to speed. And he might have some advice invaluable to those on the ground.

In reality, he needed to see those towns cordoned off for himself. The threat contained, pinned down ready for extermination.

'It looks like your idea about zero-tau was on the ball,' Roche Skark datavised. 'All six prisoners we captured at Moyce's have now been placed in the pods shipped down from Guyana. Four of them fought like lunatics before the AT squads could force them in. The other two were apparently cured before they went in. In both cases the possessors just gave up and left the bodies rather than undergo exposure to temporal stasis.'

'That's about the best news I've had for ten hours,' Ralph replied. 'They can be beaten, squeezed out without killing the body they're possessing. It means we're not just fighting a holding action.'

'Yes. Well, full credit to you for that one, Ralph. We still don't know why the possessed can't tolerate zero-tau, but no doubt the reason will turn up in debrief at some time.'

'Are you shoving the cured prisoners into personality debrief?'

'We haven't decided. Although I think it's inevitable eventually. We must not get sidetracked from neutralizing the Mortonridge towns. Frankly, the science of it all can wait.'

'What sort of state are the prisoners in?'

'Generally similar to Gerald Skibbow, disorientated and withdrawn, but their symptoms are nothing like as severe as his. After all they were only possessed for a few hours. Skibbow had been under Kingston Garrigan's control for several weeks. Certainly they're not classed as dangerous. But we're placing them in secure isolation wards for the moment, just in case. It's the first time I've agreed with Leonard DeVille all day.'

Ralph snorted at the name. 'I meant to ask you, sir. What is it with DeVille?'

'Ah, yes; sorry about him, Ralph. That's pure politics between us and our dear sister agency. DeVille is one of Jannike's puppets. The ISA keeps tabs on all major Kingdom politicians, and those who are squeaky clean are nudged forward. DeVille is obnoxiously pure in heart, if devious in mind. Jannike is grooming him as a possible replacement for Warren Aspinal as Xingu's Prime Minister. Ideally, she'd like him in charge of the hunt operation.'

'Whereas you had the Princess appoint me as chief advisor . . .'

'Exactly. I'll have a word with Jannike about him. It's probably heretical of me, but I think the problem the possessed present us might be slightly more important than our little internal rivalries.'

'Thank you sir. It'd be nice to have him off my back.'

'I doubt he'd be much more of a problem anyway. You've done some sterling work tonight, Ralph. Don't think it's gone unnoticed. You've condemned yourself to a divisional chief's desk for the rest of eternity now. I can assure you the boredom is quite otherworldly.'

Ralph managed a contemplative smile in the half-light of the hypersonic's cabin. 'Sounds attractive right now.'

Roche Skark cancelled the channel.

With his mind free, Ralph datavised a situation update request to Hub One. The squadron of Royal Marine troop flyers was already halfway down from Guyana. Twenty-five police hypersonics carrying AT squads were arrowing across the continent, converging on Mortonridge. All motorway traffic had now been shut down. An estimated eighty-five per cent of non-motorway vehicles had been located and halted. Curfew orders were going out to every general household processor in Xingu. Police in the four Mortonridge towns were preparing to enforce the martial law declaration.

It looked good. In the computer, it looked good. Secure. But there must be something we missed. Some rogue element. There always is. Someone like Mixi Penrice.

Someone . . . who abandoned the Confederation marines in Lalonde's jungle. Who left Kelven Solanki and his tiny, doomed command to struggle against the wave of possessed all alone.

All actions which were fully justifiable in the defence of the realm. Maybe I'm not so dissimilar to DeVille after all.

\*

Twenty minutes after Neville Latham had issued his assignment orders, the station situation management room had settled down into a comfortable pattern. Sergeant Walsh and Detective Feroze were monitoring the movement of the patrol cars, while Manby was maintaining a direct link to the SD centre. Any sign of human movement along the streets should bring a patrol car response within ninety seconds.

Neville himself had taken part in issuing dispatch orders to the patrol officers. It felt good to be involved, to show his people the boss wasn't afraid of rolling up his sleeves and getting stuck in there. He'd quietly accepted the fact that for someone his age and rank Exnall was a dead-end posting. Not that he was particularly bitter; he'd realized twenty-five years ago he wasn't cut out for higher office. And he fitted in well here with these people, the town was his kind of community. He understood it. When he retired he knew he would be staying on.

Or so he'd thought until today. Judging from some of the latest briefing updates he'd received from Pasto, after tomorrow there might not be much of Exnall left standing for him to retire to.

However, Neville was determined about one thing. Non-entity he might be, but Exnall was going to be protected to the best of his ability. The curfew would be carried out to the letter with a competence which any big city police commander would envy.

'Sir,' Sergeant Walsh was looking up from the fence of stumpy AV pillars lining his console.

'Yes, Sergeant.'

'Sir, I've just had three people datavise the station, wanting to know what's going on, and is the curfew some kind of joke.'

Feroze turned round, frowning. 'I've had five asking me the same thing. They all said they'd received a personal datavise telling them a curfew was being effected. I told them they should check their household processor for information.'

'Eight people?' Neville queried. 'All receiving personal messages at this time of night?'

Feroze glanced back at one of his displays. 'Make that fifteen, I've got another seven incoming datavises stacked up.'

'This is absurd,' Neville said. 'The whole point of my universal order was to explain what's happening.'

'They're not bothering to access it,' Feroze said. 'They're calling us direct instead.'

'Eighteen new datavises coming in,' Walsh said. 'It's going to hit fifty any minute.'

'They can't be datavising warnings to each other this fast,' Neville murmured, half to himself.

'Chief,' Manby was waving urgently. 'SD control reports that house lights are coming on all over town.'

'What?'

'Hundred and twelve datavises, sir,' Walsh said.

'Did we mess up the universal order?' Neville asked. At the back of his mind was the awful notion that the electronic-warfare capability Landon McCullock warned him about had glitched the order.

'It was straight out of the file,' Feroze protested.

'Sir, we're going to run out of net access channels at this rate,' Walsh said. 'Over three hundred datavises coming in now. Do you want to reprioritize the net management routines? You have the authority. We'd be able to re-establish our principal command channels if we shut down civilian data traffic.'

'I can't—'

The door of the situation management room slid open.

Neville twisted round at the unexpected motion (the damn door was supposed to be codelocked!), only to gasp in surprise at the sight of a young woman pushing her way past a red-faced Thorpe Hartshorn. A characteristics recognition program in his neural nanonics supplied her name: Finnuala O'Meara, one of the news agency reporters.

Neville caught sight of a slender, suspicious-looking processor block which she was shoving back into her bag. A codebuster? he wondered. And if she has the nerve to use one inside a police station, what else has she got?

'Ms O'Meara, you are intruding on a very important official operation. If you leave now, I won't file charges.'

'Recording and relaying, chief,' Finnuala said with a hint of triumph. Her eyes with their retinal implants were unblinking as they tracked him. 'And I don't need to tell you this is a public building. Knowing what happens here is a public right under the fourth coronation proclamation.'

'Actually, Miss O'Meara, if you bothered to fully access your legal file, you'd know that under martial law all proclamations are suspended. Leave now, please, and stop relaying at once.'

'Does that same suspension give you the right to warn your friends about the danger of xenoc sequestration technology before the general public, Chief Inspector?'

Latham blushed. How the hell did the little bitch know that? Then he realized what someone with that kind of command access to the net could do. His finger lined up accusingly on her. 'Have you datavised personal warnings to people in this town?'

'Are you denying you warned your friends first, Chief Inspector?'

'Shut up, you stupid cow, and answer me. Did you send out those personal alarm calls?'

Finnuala smirked indolently. 'I might have done. Want to answer my question now?'

'God in Heaven! Sergeant Walsh, how many calls now?'

'One thousand recorded sir, but that's all our channels blocked. It may be a lot more. I can't tell.'

'How many did you send, O'Meara?' Neville demanded furiously.

She paled slightly, but stood her ground. 'I'm just doing my job, Chief Inspector. What about you?'

'How many?'

She arched an eyebrow, aspiring to hauteur. 'Everybody.'

'You stupid— The curfew is supposed to be averting a panic; and it would have done just that if you hadn't interfered. The only way we're going to get out of this with our minds still our own is if people stay calm and follow orders.'

'Which people?' she spat back. 'Yours? The mayor's family?'

'Officer Hartshorn, get her out of here. Use whatever force is necessary, and some which isn't if you want. Then book her.'

'Sir.' A grinning Hartshorn caught Finnuala's arm. 'Come along, miss.' He held up a small nervejam stick in his free hand. 'You wouldn't want me to use this.'

Finnuala let Hartshorn tug her out of the situation management room. The door slid shut behind them.

'Walsh,' Neville said. 'Shut down the town's communication net. Do it now. Leave the police architecture functional, but all civil data traffic is to cease immediately. They mustn't be allowed to spread this damn panic any further.'

'Yes, sir!'

\*

The police hypersonic carrying Ralph had already started to descend over the town of Rainton when Landon McCullock datavised him.

'Some bloody journalist woman started a panic in Exnall, Ralph. The Chief Inspector is doing his best to damp it down, but I'm not expecting miracles at this point.'

Ralph abandoned the hypersonic's sensor suite. The image he'd received of Rainton was all in the infra-red spectrum, rectangles of luminous pink glass laid out over the black land. Glowing dots converged in the air above it, marine troop flyers and police hypersonics ready to implement the isolation. Given they were the forces of salvation, their approach formation looked strangely like the circling of giant carrion birds.

'I suggest you or the Prime Minister broadcasts to them directly, sir. Appeal to them to follow the curfew order. Your word should carry more weight than some local dignitary. Tell them about the marines arriving; that way they'll also see that you're acting positively to help them.'

'Good theory, Ralph. Unfortunately Exnall's Chief Inspector has shut down the town's net. Only the police architecture is functional right now. The only people we can broadcast to are the ones sitting in the patrol cars.'

'You have to get the net back on-line.'

'I know. But now it seems there's a problem with some of the local management processors.'

Ralph squeezed his fists, not wanting to hear. 'Glitches?'

'Looks like it. Diana is redirecting the AIs to interrogate Exnall's electronics. But there aren't nearly enough channels open for them to be as effective as they were in Pasto.'

'Hellfire! OK, sir, we're on our way.' He datavised a quick instruction to the pilot, and the hypersonic rose above its spiralling siblings before streaking away to the south.

*

Two hundred and fifty kilometres above Mortonridge, the SD sensor satellite made its fourth pass over Exnall since the network had been raised to a code three alert status. Deborah Unwin directed its high-resolution sensors to scan the town. Several specialist teams of security council analysts and tactical advisors were desperate for information about the town's on-the-ground situation.

But they weren't getting the full picture. In several places the satellite images were fuzzy, edges poorly defined. Switching to infra-red didn't help; red ripples swayed to and fro, never still.

'Just like the Quallheim Counties,' Ralph concluded morosely when he accessed the data. 'They're down there, all right. And in force.'

'It gets worse,' Deborah datavised. 'Even in the areas relatively unaffected we still can't get a clear picture of what's going on below those damn harandrid trees. Not at night.

All I can tell you is that there are a lot of people out on the streets.'

'On foot?' Ralph queried.

'Yes. The AI's loaded travel-proscription orders into all the processor-controlled vehicles in the town. Some people will be able to break the order's code, of course, but basically the only mechanical transport left in Exnall right now is the bicycles.'

'So where are all the pedestrians going?'

'Some are taking the main link road to the M6, but it looks like the majority are heading for the town centre. I'd say they're probably converging on the police station.'

'Damn it, that's all we need. If they congregate in a crowd there's no way we'll be able to stop the possession from spreading. It'll be like a plague.'

*

Frank Kitson was angry in a way he hadn't been for years. Angry, and just a bit alarmed, too. First, woken up in the dead of night by a priority message from some O'Meara woman he'd never heard of. Which turned out to be a paranoid fantasy about xenoc takeovers and martial law. Then when he tried to datavise the police station about it he couldn't get through to the duty officer. So he'd seen the lights on next door, and datavised old man Yardly to see if he knew what was going on. Yardly had received the same priority datavise, as had some of his family, and he couldn't get through to the police either.

Frank didn't want to make a fool of himself by appearing panicky, but something odd was definitely going down. Then the communication net crashed. When he accessed the general household processor for an emergency channel to the police station there was an official message in the processor's memory from Chief Inspector Latham announcing the curfew, setting out its rules, and assuring all the citizens they would be evacuated in the morning. Genuinely worried now, Frank told his little family to get ready, they were leaving right away.

The car processor refused to acknowledge his datavise. When he switched the car to manual override, it still wouldn't function. That was when he set off to find a police officer and demand to be told just what the hell was going on. It was a few minutes short of one o'clock when the curfew was officially due to start. And in any case, he was an upstanding subject of the King, he had every right to be on the street. The curfew couldn't possibly apply to him.

A lot of other people seemed to have the same idea. Quite a group of them marched down the wide road out of their tranquil residential suburb heading for the town centre, shoulders set squarely against the night air. Some people had brought their kids, the children sleepy, their voices piping and full of queries. Comments were shouted back and forth, but no one had any answers to what was actually going on.

Frank heard someone call his name, and saw Hanly Nowell making his way towards him.

'Hell of a thing,' he told Hanly. They worked for the same agrichemical company; different divisions, but they drank together some nights, and their two families went on joint outings occasionally.

'Sure,' Hanly looked distracted. 'Did your car pack up?'

Frank nodded, puzzled by how low Hanly was keeping his voice, almost as if he didn't want to be overheard. 'Yes, some kind of official Traffic Division override in the processor. I didn't even know they could do that.'

'Me neither. But I've got my four-wheeler. I can bypass the processor in that, go straight to manual drive.'

They both stopped walking. Frank threw cautious glances at the rest of the loose group as they passed by.

'Room in it for you and the family,' Hanly said when the stragglers had moved away.

'You serious?' Maybe it was the thick grey tree shadows which flapped across the street creating confusing movements of half-light, but Frank was sure Hanly's face was different somehow. Hanly always smiled, or grinned, forever happy with life. Not tonight, though.

Guess it's getting to him, too.

'Wouldn't have offered otherwise,' Hanly said generously.

'God, thanks, man. It's not for me. I'm scared for the wife and Tom, you know?'

'I know.'

'I'll go back and get them. We'll come round to your place.'

'No need.' And now Hanly was smiling. He put an arm round Frank's shoulders. 'I'm parked just round the corner. Come on, we'll drive back to your house. Much quicker.'

Hanly's big off-road camper was sitting behind a thick clump of ancient harandrids in a small park. Invisible from the street.

'You thought about where we can go to get clear?' Frank asked. He was keeping his own voice low now. There were still little groups of people walking about through the suburb, all making their way to the town centre. Most of them would probably appreciate a ride out, and wouldn't be too fussy how they got it. He was bothered by how furtive and uncharitable he'd become. Focusing on survival must do that to a man.

'Not really.' Hanly opened the rear door, and gestured Frank forwards. 'But I expect we'll get there anyway.'

Frank gave him a slightly stiff smile, and climbed in. Then the door banged shut behind him, making him jump. It was pitch-black inside. 'Hey, Hanly.' No answer. He pushed at the door, pumping the handle, but it wouldn't open. 'Hanly, what the hell you doing, man?'

Frank had the sudden, awful realization that he wasn't alone inside the camper. He froze, spread-eagle against the door. 'Who's there?' he whispered.

'Just us chickens, boss.'

Frank whirled round as a fearsome green-white light bloomed inside the camper. Its intensity made him squeeze his eyes tight shut, fearing for his retinas. But not before he'd seen the sleek wolverine creatures launching themselves at him, their huge fangs dripping blood.

*

From his seat in the situation management room, Neville Latham could hear the crowd outside the police station. They produced an unpleasant ebb and flow of sound which lapped at the building, its angry tone plain for all to hear.

The final impossibility: a mob in Exnall! And while he was supposed to be enforcing a curfew. Dear Lord.

'You must disperse them,' Landon McCullock datavised. 'They cannot be allowed to group together for any length of time, it would be a disaster.'

'Yes, sir.' *How?* he wanted to shout at his superior. I've only got five officers left in the station. 'How long before the marines land?'

'Approximately four minutes. But, Neville, I'm not allowing them in to the town itself. Their priority is to establish a secure perimeter. I have to think of the whole continent. What's loose in Exnall cannot be allowed out.'

'I understand.' He glanced at the desktop processor's AV projector, which was broadcasting Exnall's status display. The SD sensor satellite wasn't producing as many details as he would have liked, but the overall summary was accurate enough. Approximately six hundred people were milling along Maingreen outside the station, with dribs and drabs still arriving. Neville made his decision, and datavised the communication block for a channel to each patrol car.

It was all over now, anyway: career, retirement prospects, probably his friends, too. Ordering the police to open fire with sonics on his own townsfolk wouldn't make the recriminations appreciably worse. And it would be helping them, even though they'd never appreciate the fact.

*

Eben Pavitt had arrived at the police station ten minutes ago, and still hadn't managed to get anywhere near the doors to make his complaint. Not that it would do him much good if he had got up there. He could see those at the front of the building hammering away at the thick glass doors to no avail. If that pompous dickbrain Latham was in there, he wasn't doing his duty and talking to the crowd.

It was beginning to look like his walk (two bloody kilometres, dressed in a thin T-shirt and shorts) had all been for nothing. How utterly bloody typical that Latham should bungle tonight. Ineffective warnings. Sloppy organization. Cutting people off from the net. The Chief Inspector was supposed to be helping the town, for crying out loud.

By God, my MP is going to hear about this.

If I get out in one piece.

Eben Pavitt glanced uneasily at his fellow townsfolk. There was a constant derisory shouting now. Several stones had been thrown at the police station. Eben disapproved of that, but he could certainly understand the underlying frustration.

Even Maingreen's overhead street lights seemed to be sharing the town's malaise, they weren't as bright as usual. Away in the distance, above the fringes of the crowd, he could see several of them flickering.

He wasn't going to achieve anything here. Perhaps he should have hiked straight out of town? And it still wasn't too late, if he started now.

As he turned round, and started to push his way through the press of aggrieved people, he thought he saw a large flyer curving through the sky above the western edge of town. Trees and the wayward street lights swiftly cut it from his view, but there wasn't much else that gold-haze blob could be. And the size could only mean a military transport of some kind.

He grinned secretively. The government was doing something positive. Perhaps all was not lost after all.

Then he heard the sirens. Patrol cars were racing along

Maingreen, approaching the crowd from both ends. Those people around him were straining to catch a glimpse of the latest distraction.

'LEAVE THE AREA,' an amplified voice bellowed from the police station. 'THE TOWN IS NOW UNDER MARTIAL LAW. RETURN HOME AND REMAIN THERE UNTIL YOU RECEIVE FURTHER INSTRUCTIONS.'

Eben was sure the distorted voice belonged to Neville Latham.

The first patrol cars braked dangerously close to people on the edge of the main crowd, as if their safety systems had somehow become uncoupled. Several jumped clear hurriedly, two or three lost their footing and fell over. One man was struck by a patrol car, sending him cannoning into a woman. They both went sprawling.

A deluge of boos was directed at the patrol cars. Eben didn't like the mood emerging among his fellow citizens. These weren't the usual peaceable Exnall residents. And the police reaction was unbelievably provocative. A lifelong law abider, Eben was shocked by their actions.

'LEAVE THE AREA NOW. THIS IS AN ILLEGAL ASSEMBLY.'

A single lump of stone tumbled through the air above the bobbing heads of the crowd. Eben never did see the arm which flung it. One thing remained certain, though, it was thrown with incredible force. When it hit the patrol car it actually managed to fracture the bonded-silicon windscreen.

Several taunting cheers went up. Suddenly the air was thick with improvised missiles raining down on the patrol cars.

The response was predictable, and immediate. A couple of assault mechanoids emerged from the rear of each patrol car. Sense-overload ordnance shot out, red flares slicing brilliant ephemeral archways across the stars.

They should have been warning shots. The mechanoids had

a direct-attack prohibition loaded into their processors which only Neville Latham could cancel.

The ordnance activated two metres above the compressed bustle of bodies at the heart of the crowd. The effect was almost as bad as if live ammunition had been fired straight at them.

Eben saw men and women keel over as though they'd been electrocuted. Then his eyes were streaming from intolerable light and wickedly acidic gas. Human screams vanished beneath a hyper-decibel whistle. His neural nanonics sensorium-filter programs were unable to cope (as the ordnance designers intended), leaving him blind, deaf, and virtually insensate. Heavy bodies thudded into him, sending him spinning, stumbling for balance. Pinpricks of heat bloomed across his bare skin, turning to vicious stings. He felt his flesh ballooning, body swelling to twice, three times its normal size. Joints were seizing up.

Eben thought he was screaming. But there was no way to tell. The solid sensations, when they started to return, were crude ones. His bare legs scraping over damp grass. Limp arms banging against his side. He was being dragged along the ground by his collar.

When he'd regained enough rationality to look around, the scenes of suffering on Maingreen outside the police station made him want to weep with rage and helplessness. The crazed assault mechanoids were still pummelling people with their ordnance from point-blank range. A direct hit brought instant death, for those nearby the activation was outright torture.

'Bastards,' Eben rasped. 'You bastards.'

'Pigs are always the same.'

He looked up at the man who was pulling him away from the mêlée. 'Christ, thanks, Frank. I could have died if I'd stayed in there.'

'Yeah, I suppose you could have,' Frank Kitson said. 'Lucky I came along, really.'

\*

The police hypersonic landed next to the five big marine troop flyers. They were strung out along the link road which connected Exnall to the M6; a quintet of dark, menacingly obese arachnids whose landing struts had dinted the carbon concrete. The start of the town's harandrid forest was two hundred metres away, a meticulous border where the aboriginal trees finished and the cultivated citrus groves began.

As he came down the hypersonic's airstair, Ralph's suit sensors showed him the marine squads fanning out along the edge of the trees. Some kind of barrier had already been thrown across the road itself. So far a perfect deployment.

The marine colonel, Janne Palmer, was waiting for Ralph in the command cabin of her flyer. It was a compartment just aft of the cockpit with ten communications operatives and three tactical interpretation officers. Even though it was inside and well-protected, the colonel was wearing a lightweight armour suit like the rest of her brigade. Her shell-helmet was off, showing Ralph a surprisingly feminine face. The only concession to military life appeared to be her hair, which was shaved down to a two-millimetre stubble of indeterminable colour. She gave him a fast nod of acknowledgement as he was escorted in by a young marine.

'I accessed a recording of the operation at Moyce's,' she said. 'These are one tough set of people we've got here.'

'I'm afraid so. And it looks like Exnall is the worst infestation out of all the four Mortonridge towns.'

She glanced into an AV pillar's projection. 'Nice assignment. Let's hope my brigade can handle it. At the moment I'm trying to establish a circular perimeter roughly fifteen hundred metres outside the town. We should have it solid in another twenty minutes.'

'Excellent.'

'That forest's going to be a bitch to patrol. The SD sensor sats can't see shit below the trees, and you're telling me I can't rely on our usual observation systems.'

''Fraid not.'

'Pity. Aerovettes would be exceptionally handy in this case.'

'I must advise against using them. The possessed can really screw our electronics. You're far better off without them. At least that way you know the information you're receiving is accurate, even though there isn't much of it.'

'Interesting situation. Haven't handled anything like this since tac school, if then.'

'Diana Tiernan told me the AIs have got very few datalinks left into Exnall. We've definitely lost most of the communication net. Even the police architecture has failed now. So the exact situation inside is unknown.'

'There was some kind of fight outside the police station which finished a couple of minutes ago. But even if that crowd which gathered along Maingreen have all been possessed, that still leaves us with a lot of the population which have escaped so far. What do you want to do about them?'

'Same as we originally planned. Wait until dawn, and send in teams to evacuate everyone. But I wish to Christ that curfew had held. It did in all the other towns.'

'Wishes always wind up as regrets in this game, I find.'

Ralph gave her a speculative look, but she was concentrating on another AV projection. 'I think our main concern right now is to contain the possessed in Exnall,' he said. 'When it's light we can start worrying about getting the rest out.'

'Absolutely.' Janne Palmer stared straight at the ESA operative, and gave him a regretful grin. 'And come dawn I'm going to need the best information I can acquire. A lot of lives are going to depend on me getting it right. I don't have any special-forces types in my brigade. This was a rush operation. But what I do have now is you and your G66 troops. I'd like you to go in and make that assessment for me. I believe you're the best qualified, in all respects.'

'You don't happen to know Jannike Dermot, do you?'

'Not personally, no. Will you go in for me? I can't order you to; Admiral Farquar made it quite plain you're here to advise, and I have to take that advice.'

'Considerate of him.' Ralph didn't even need any time to decide. *I made that choice when I put the armour suit on again.* 'OK, I'll go and tell my people we're on-line again. But I'd like to take a squad of your marines in with us. We might need some heavy-calibre firepower support.'

'There's a platoon assembled and waiting for you in flyer four.'

*

Finnuala O'Meara had passed simple frustration a long time ago. Over an hour, in fact. She had been sitting on a bunk in the police station's holding cell for an age. Nothing she did brought the slightest response from anyone, not datavises into the station processor, nor shouting, or thumping on the door. Nobody came. It must have been that prick Latham's orders. Let her cool off for a few hours. Jumped-up cretin.

But she could nail him. Any time she wanted, now. He must know that. Which was probably why he'd kept her in here while the rest of her story played out, denying her a complete victory. If only her coverage had been complete she would have been able to dictate her own terms to a major.

She'd heard the noises from outside, the sound of a crowd gathering and protesting. A large crowd, if she was any judge. Then the sirens of the patrol cars rushing along Maingreen. Speakers blaring a warning, pleas and threats. Strange monotonous thumps. Screams, glass smashing.

It was awful. She belonged outside, drinking down the sight.

After the riot, or whatever, it had become strangely quiet.

Finnuala had almost drifted off to sleep when the cell door did finally open.

'About bloody time,' she said. The rest of the invective died in her throat.

A huge mummy shuffled laboriously into the cell, its bandages a dusty brown, with lime-green pustulant fluids weeping from its hands. It was wearing Neville Latham's immaculate peaked cap. 'So sorry to keep you waiting,' it apologized gruffly.

*

Colonel Palmer's field command officers informed Ralph's reconnaissance team about the woman as they were about to enter Exnall. Datavise bandwidth was being suppressed by the now-familiar electronic-warfare field, preventing anything other than basic conversation. They certainly couldn't receive a full sensevise, or even a visual image, so they had to rely on a simple description instead.

As far as the SD sensor satellites could tell, the town's entire population had retreated back into the buildings. Earlier on there had been a considerable amount of movement under the umbrella of harandrids, blurred infra-red smears skipping about erratically. Then as dawn rose even those beguiling traces vanished. The only things left moving in Exnall were the treetops swaying back and forth in the first morning zephyr. Roofs, and even entire streets, appeared blurred, as if a gentle rain was pattering on the satellite's lenses. Visually, the town was a complete hash, except for a solitary circle, fifteen metres across, in front of a diner which served the link road to the M6. And in the middle of that was the woman.

'She's just standing there,' Janne Palmer datavised. 'She'll be able to see anything approaching up the link road into town.'

'Any weapons apparent?' Ralph asked. Along with the twelve-strong platoon the colonel had assigned him, he was crouched down at the side of the road, a hundred metres short of the first houses. They were using a small embankment for cover as they crept in towards the town.

His head was ringing with a mental version of tinnitus, which he suspected was due to the stimulants. After only two hours' sleep in the last thirty-six he was having to use both chemical and software excitants to keep his edge. But he couldn't afford to relax his guard, not now.

'Definitely not,' Janne Palmer told him. 'At least not any heavy-calibre hardware, anyway. She's wearing a jacket, so she could be concealing a small pistol inside it.'

'Not that it makes any difference if she's possessed. We've not seen them use a weapon yet.'

'Quite.'

'Dumb question, but is she alive?'

'Yes. We can see her chest moving when she breathes, and her infra-red signature is optimum.'

'She's some kind of bait, do you think?'

'No, too obvious. I'd guess some kind of sentry, except they must know we're here. Several squads have skirmished while we were setting up the perimeter.'

'Hell, you mean they're loose in the woods?'

''Fraid so. Which means I can't confirm that all the possessed are inside the cordon. I've requested some more troops from Admiral Farquar to start searching the locality. The request is up before the Security Committee as we speak.'

Ralph cursed silently. Possessed roaming round in this area would be nigh on impossible to track down. The Mortonridge countryside was a rugged nightmare. Pity we haven't got any affinity-bonded hounds, he thought. The ones I saw the settlement supervisors use back on Lalonde would have been perfect for the job. And I can just see Jannike Dermot's face if I make that suggestion to the Security Committee. But ... hell, they're what we need.

'Ralph, one moment please,' Colonel Palmer datavised.

'We've run an ident check on our lady sentry. It's confirmed, she's Angeline Gallagher.'

'Hell. That changes everything.'

'Yes. Opinion here is that she's wanting to talk. She's not stupid. Allowing herself to be seen like this must be their equivalent of a white flag.'

'I expect you're right.' Ralph gave the platoon's lieutenant an order to halt their advance while the Security Committee came on-line. The marines formed themselves into a defensive circle, scanning the trees and the nearby houses with their most basic sensors. Ralph let his automatic rifle hang at his side as he squatted in the middle of some thick marloop bushes. He had a terrible intimation that Gallagher (or rather her possessor) wasn't about to lay out some convenient terms of surrender. There never can be surrender between us, he acknowledged gloomily.

So what could she want to say?

'Mr Hiltch, we concur with Colonel Palmer that the woman wants to negotiate,' Princess Kirsten datavised. 'I know it's a lot to ask after all you've been through, but I'd like you to go in there and talk to her.'

'We can set up SD groundstrike coverage to support you,' Deborah Unwin datavised. 'Put you in the eye of a hurricane, so to speak. Any tricks or attempts to overwhelm you, and we'll laser out a two hundred metre circle with you at the centre. We know they can't withstand the SD platform's power levels.'

'It's all right,' Ralph told his invisible audience. 'I'll go in. After all, I was the one who brought her here.'

*

Strangely enough, Ralph didn't think of very much at all when he was walking the last five hundred metres along the road. All he wanted to do now was get the job over. The road which had started at the mouth of a titanic river on a different, distant planet finished inside a pretty rural town on the rump of nowhere. If there was an irony to be had in those circumstances, Ralph couldn't taste it.

Angeline Gallagher's possessor waited calmly outside the cheap single-storey diner as he walked towards her. Dean, Will, and Cathal accompanied him for most of the way; then when they were still a hundred metres away from her he told them to wait and carried on alone. Nothing moved in any of the simple, elegant buildings which lined the link road. But he knew they were waiting behind the walls and blanked windows. The conviction grew inside him that they weren't showing themselves because it wasn't yet their time to do so. Their part in the drama would come later.

This was a certainty he'd never known before, a kind of psychic upswelling. And with it his intimation of disaster grew ever stronger.

The closer he got to the woman, the less the electronic-warfare field affected his implants and suit blocks. By the time he was five metres away, the Security Committee was receiving a full sensevise again.

He stopped. Squared his shoulders. Took off his shell-helmet.

Her smile was almost pitying in its sparsity. 'Looks like we've arrived at the crunch time,' she said.

'Who are you?'

'Annette Ekelund. And you are Ralph Hiltch, the ESA's Head of Station on Lalonde. I might have known you would be the one they set on us. You've done quite a good job so far.'

'Could we cut the bullshit. What do you want?'

'Philosophically, to live for ever. Practically, I want you to call off the police and marines you've got circling this town along with the other three we've managed to occupy. Right now.'

'No.'

'I see you've already learned not to make threats. No: or

else. No: if you don't you'll regret it. That's good. After all, what can you threaten me with?'

'Zero-tau.'

Annette Ekelund frowned as she considered the response. 'Yes. Possibly. It is, I admit, certainly frightening enough for us. But there's no finality to that, not any more. If we flee our possessed bodies to escape zero-tau, we can still return. There are already several million possessed walking upon the Confederation worlds. Within weeks, that number will be hundreds of millions, a few days later billions. I will always have a way back now. As long as a single human body is left alive my kind can resurrect me. Do you understand now?'

'I understand the zero-tau option works. We will put you in the pods; and we will keep putting you in the pods until there are no more of you left. Do you understand that?'

'I'm sorry Ralph, but as I said, you simply cannot threaten me. Have you worked out why yet? Have you worked out the real reason I will win? It is because you will ultimately join me. You are going to die, Ralph. Today. Tomorrow. A year from now. If you're lucky, in fifty years' time. It doesn't matter when. It is entropy, it is fate, it is the way the universe works. Death, not love, conquers all in the end. And when you die, you will find yourself in the beyond. That is when you and I will become brother and sister in the same fellowship. United against the living. Coveting the living.'

'No.'

'Do not speak about something you know nothing about.'

'I still do not believe you. God is not that cruel. There will be more to death than this emptiness you found.'

She laughed bitterly. 'Fool. Know-nothing fool.'

'But a living fool. A fool you have to contend with here and now.'

'There is no such thing as God, Ralph. Only humans are stupid enough to create religions. Have you noticed that? None of the xenocs we've encountered need to bandage their insecurities and fears with promises of incorporeal glory that are every soul's due. Oh, no, Ralph; God is merely the term an ignorant primitive uses when he wants to say quantum cosmology. The universe is an entirely natural structure, one which is exceptionally vicious in its attitude to life. And now we have an opportunity to leave it for good, a chance of salvation. We're not going to let you stop us, Ralph.'

'I can, and I will.'

'Sorry, Ralph, but your intransigent belief in humanity is your principal weakness, one which you share with the rest of this Kingdom's devout population. We intend to exploit that to the full. What I'm about to say might seem inhuman, but then, that's what you think I am anyway. As I told you, the dead cannot lose this fight, for you have no lever on us. We cannot be threatened, coerced, or pleaded with. Like death itself, we are an absolute.'

'What is it you have to say?'

'Am I talking to this planet's authorities, the Saldana Princess?'

'Yes. She's on-line.'

'Good. Then I say this. You almost managed to exterminate us last night, and if our fight continues along those same lines today then a great many people will be killed. A situation neither of us would welcome. Therefore I propose a stand-off solution. We will keep Mortonridge for ourselves, and I pledge none of us will leave it. If you do not believe me, and I expect trust to be lacking on your part, you have the physical power to set up a blockade across the neck of this land where it joins the continent.'

'No deal,' Princess Kirsten datavised.

'The Kingdom will not abandon its subjects,' Ralph said out loud. 'You ought to know that by now.'

'We acknowledge the Kingdom's strength,' Annette Ekelund said. 'And that is why we propose this ceasefire. The outcome of the struggle between the living and our kind will not be decided by what transpires here. We are too evenly matched. However, not every Confederation planet is as advanced or as competent as Ombey.' She raised her head, closing her eyes as she did so; looking blindly up at the sky. 'Out there is where both our fates are being decided right now. You, like I, will have to wait for the outcome to be determined by others. We know that we will triumph. Just as your misplaced faith tells you that the living will be victorious.'

'So you're saying we should just sit it out on the sidelines?'

'Yes.'

'I don't even have to ask the Security Committee for their opinion on that one. We're not the sideline, we're the front line, we are a major part of the struggle against you. If we can show other planets that it is possible to stop you from spreading, banish you from the bodies you've captured, then they will have faith in their own ability.'

Annette Ekelund nodded sadly. 'I understand. Princess Saldana, I have tried reason; now I must use something stronger to convince you.'

'Ralph, our satellite sensors just came back on-line,' Deborah Unwin reported. 'We can see a lot of movement down there. Oh Christ, they're swarming out of the houses. Ralph, get out of there. Now. Do it now! Run.'

But he stood his ground. He knew the Ekelund woman wasn't threatening him personally. This was to be a demonstration. The one he'd anticipated, and dreaded all along.

'Do you want groundstrike support?' Admiral Farquar datavised.

'Not yet, sir.' His enhanced retinas showed him doors opening all the way along the street, people emerging onto the pavements.

At Ekelund's invisible signal, the possessed were bringing out their hostages. The illusory bodies on display were deliberately gaudy, ranging from historical warlords to fictitious creatures, blighted monsters, and necromantic demigods. Fantasies chosen to emphasize the impossible gulf between them and their frightened prisoners.

Each of the sorcerous apparitions was paired off with one of Exnall's surviving non-possessed residents. Like their captors, they were a cross-section of the community, young and old, male and female; dressed in nightgowns, pyjamas, hurriedly thrown on shirts, even naked. Some struggled, the die-hards and the fatalists; but most had been tyrannized into obedience.

The possessed restrained them with the greatest of ease as they hustled them forwards, their energistic ability giving them a mechanoid's strength. Children wailed fearfully as they were gripped by hands and claws as hard as stone. Men grimaced in subdued fury.

A symphony of cries and hopeless shouts laid siege to Ralph's ears.

'What the hell are you doing?' he yelled at Ekelund. His arm swept round. 'For Christ's sake, you're hurting them.'

'This is not all,' Annette Ekelund said impassively. 'Tell your people to look four kilometres southwest of the town at a lake called Otsuo. There is an abandoned off-road camper there belonging to one of Exnall's residents.'

'Hang on, Ralph,' Deborah Unwin datavised. 'We're scanning now. Yep, there's a vehicle parked there all right. Registered to a Hanly Nowell, he works at an agrichemical plant in the town's industrial precinct.'

'OK,' Ralph said. 'It's there. Now tell your people to ease off those hostages.'

'No, Ralph,' Annette Ekelund said. 'They will not ease off. What I am trying to make clear to you is the fact that we have spread beyond this town. I could only know where the vehicle was if I ordered the driver to leave it there. And it is not the only one, not from this town nor the others. We have escaped the clutches of your marines, Ralph. I organized the four towns which the Longhound bus visited very carefully; we were busy last night while you were chasing after the possessed in Pasto. My followers spread out along the whole peninsula, on foot, on horseback, on bikes, in manual-control vehicles. Even I don't know where they all are any more. The marines barricading the towns are worthless. Now you will have to block off Morton-ridge in its entirety to prevent us from contaminating the rest of the continent.'

'No problem.'

'I'm sure. But you'll never retake this land from us, not now. You can't even claim back this single town, not without committing genocide. You've already seen what a single one of us can achieve when we have to defend ourselves. Imagine that destructive power focused with evil intent. Suburban fusion plants ruptured, hospitals incinerated, day clubs crashing down on their young occupants. So far we have never killed anyone, but if we choose to do so, if you leave us with no alternative, this planet will suffer enormously.'

'Monster!'

'And I'll do it, Ralph. I'll give the order for my followers to start the campaign. It will come right after my order for every non-possessed in Exnall to be murdered. They're going to be killed right here on the streets in front of you, Ralph. We will crush their skulls, snap their necks, strangle them, cut their bellies open and leave them to bleed to death.'

'I don't believe you.'

'No, you don't want to believe me, Ralph. There is a difference.' Her voice became smooth, taunting him. 'What have we got to lose? These people you see around you will join us one way or the other. That is what I'm trying to tell you. Either their bodies will be possessed, or they will die and possess in turn. Please, Ralph, don't allow yourself and others to suffer because of your stupid beliefs. We will win.'

Ralph wanted to kill her, hating and fearing the serene way she talked about slaughter, knowing she wasn't bluffing. The most basic human urge, to wipe out your enemy hard and fast, came firing up from his subconscious. His neural nanonics had to reduce his heart rate. One hand moved fractionally towards the pistol holster on his belt.

And I can't do it. Can't kill her. Can't end it all with the one act of barbarism which we've always resorted to. Dear God, she's already dead.

Annette Ekelund's eyes followed the tiny motion of his hand. She smiled and turned to beckon one of the figures that had emerged from the diner.

Ralph watched numbly as a mummy wearing a peaked police cap shuffled forwards. The girl held in its solid embrace couldn't have been more than fifteen. All she wore was a long mauve T-shirt. Her bare legs were grazed and streaked with dirt. She'd been crying profusely. Now she could only whimper as she was dragged towards him.

'Nice looking girl,' Annette Ekelund said. 'A fine body, if a little young. But I can alter that. You see, if you blow big chunks out of this body of Angeline Gallagher's, Ralph, the girl will become the one I possess next. My colleague here will break her bones, rape her, rip the skin from her face, hurt her so terribly she'll make a pact with Lucifer himself to make it stop. But it won't be Lucifer who answers her from the afterlife, only me. I shall come forth again; and you and I will be right back where we started, except that Gallagher's body will be dead. Will she thank you for that, do you think, Ralph?'

Nerve impulse overrides prevented Ralph's hands from tearing Ekelund's head from her shoulders. 'What do you want me to say?' he datavised to the Security Committee.

'I don't think we have any choice,' Princess Kirsten replied. 'I cannot allow thousands of my people to be killed out of hand.'

'If we leave, they'll be possessed,' Ralph warned her. 'Ekelund will do exactly what she described to this girl, and all the others. Not just here, but right along the whole length of Mortonridge.'

'I know, but I have to consider the majority. If the possessed are outside the marine cordons, then we've already lost Mortonridge. I cannot lose Xingu, too.'

'There are two million people living on Mortonridge!'

'I am aware of that. But at least if they're possessed they will still be alive. I think that Ekelund woman is right; the overall problem of possession isn't going to be solved here.' There was a moment's pause. 'We're cutting our losses, Ralph. Tell her she can have Mortonridge. For now.'

'Yes, ma'am,' he whispered.

Annette Ekelund smiled. 'She agreed, didn't she?'

'You may have Mortonridge,' Ralph relayed imperturbably as the Princess started to outline the conditions. 'We will instigate an immediate evacuation procedure for people from areas you have not yet reached; any attempt to sabotage vehicles will result in SD strikes against areas where we know you are concentrated. If any of you try to pass the cordon we establish between Mortonridge and the main body of the continent you will be put into zero-tau. If any of you are found outside the cordon you will be put into zero-tau. If there is any terrorist assault against any Ombey citizen or building we will send in a punitive expedition and throw several hundred of you into zero-tau. If you attempt to communicate with other offplanet possessed forces, you will again be punished.'

'Of course,' Ekelund said mockingly. 'I agree to your terms.'

'And the girl comes with me,' Ralph declared.

'Come, come, Ralph, I don't believe the authorities actually said that.'

'Try me,' he challenged.

Ekelund glanced at the sobbing girl then back to Ralph. 'Would you have bothered if she was a wizened old grandmother?' she asked sarcastically.

'But you didn't choose a wizened old grandmother, did you? You chose her because you knew how protective we are towards the young. Your error.'

Ekelund said nothing, but made a sharp irritated gesture to the mummy. It let the girl go. She floundered, trembling so badly she could hardly stand. Ralph caught her before she fell. He winced at the weight that put on his injured leg.

'I'll look forward to the day you join us, Ralph,' Ekelund said. 'However long it takes. You'll be quite an asset. Come and see me when your soul finally obtains a new body to live in.'

'Fuck you.' Ralph scooped the girl up, and started to walk down the road. He ignored the hundreds of people standing in front of the prim buildings, the indifferent possessed and their wailing distraught victims, the ones he'd failed so completely. Staring resolutely ahead, concentrating on putting one foot in front of the other. He knew if he took it all in, acknowledged the magnitude of the disaster he'd wrought, he'd never be able to carry on.

'Enjoy your magnificent victory with the girl,' Annette Ekelund called after him.

'This one is only the beginning,' he promised grimly.

# 5

At a point in space four light-years distant from the star around which Mirchusko orbited, the gravity density suddenly leapt upwards. The area affected was smaller than a quark, at first. But once established, the warp rapidly grew both in size and in strength. Faint strands of starlight curved round the fringes, only to be sucked in towards the centre as the gravity intensified further.

Ten picoseconds after its creation, the shape of the warp twisted from a spherical zone to a two-dimensional disc. By this time it was over a hundred metres in diameter. At the centre of one side, gravity fluctuated again, placing an enormous strain on local space. A perfectly circular rupture appeared, rapidly irising open.

A long grey-white fountain of gas spewed out from the epicentre of the wormhole terminus. The water vapour it contained immediately turned to minute ice crystals, spinning away from the central plume, twinkling weakly in the sparse starlight. Lumps of solid matter began to shoot out along the gas jet, tumbling off into the void. It was a curious collection of objects: sculpted clouds of sand, tufts of reed-grass with their roots wriggling like spider legs, small fractured dendrites of white and blue coral, broken palm tree fronds, oscillating globules of saltwater, a shoal of frantic fish, their spectacularly coloured bodies bursting apart as they underwent explosive decompression, several seagulls squirting blood from beaks and rectums.

Then the crazy outpouring reduced drastically, blocked by a larger body which was surging along the wormhole. *Udat* slipped out into normal space, a flattened teardrop over a hundred and thirty metres long, its blue polyp hull enlivened with a tortuous purple web. Straight away the blackhawk changed the flow of energy through the vast honeycomb of patterning cells which made up the bulk of its body, modifying its gravitonic distortion field. The wormhole terminus began to close behind it.

Almost the last object to emerge from the transdimensional opening was a small human figure. A woman: difficult to see because of the black SII spacesuit she wore, her limbs scrabbling futilely, almost as though she was clawing at the structure of space-time in order to pursue the big blackhawk as it drew away from her. Her movements slowly calmed as the suit's sensor collar revealed stars and distant nebulas again, replacing the menacingly insubstantial pseudofabric of the wormhole.

Dr Alkad Mzu felt herself shudder uncontrollably, the relief was so intoxicating. Free from the grip of equations become energy.

I understand the configuration of reality too well to endure such direct exposure. The wormhole has too many flaws, too many hidden traps. A quasi-continuum where time's arrow has to be directed by an artificial energy flow; the possible fates lurking within such a non-place would make you welcome death as the most beautiful of consorts.

The collar sensors showed her she had picked up a considerable tumble since losing her grip on the rope ladder. Her neural nanonics had automatically blocked the impulses from her inner ears as a precaution against nausea. There were also a number of analgesic blocks erected across the nerve paths from her forearms. A physiological-status display showed her the damage inflicted on tendons and muscles as she'd forced herself to hang on as the *Udat* dived for safety. Nothing drastic, thankfully. Medical packages would be able to cope once she got the suit off.

'Can you retrieve me?' she datavised to the *Udat*'s flight computer. 'I can't stop spinning.' As if they couldn't see that. But the bitek starship was already seven hundred metres away, and still retreating from her. She wanted an answer, wanted someone to talk to her. Proof she wasn't alone. This predicament was triggering way too many thirty-year-old memories. Dear Mary, I'll be calling it déjà vu next. 'Calling *Udat*, can you retrieve me?' Come on, answer.

On the *Udat*'s bridge Haltam was busy programming the medical packages which were knitting to the base of Meyer's skull. Haltam was the *Udat*'s fusion specialist, but doubled as ship's medical officer.

The captain was lying prone on his acceleration couch, unconscious. His fingers were still digging into the cushioning, frozen in a claw-like posture, nails broken by the strength he'd used to maul the fabric. Blood dribbling out of his nose made sticky blotches on his cheeks. Haltam didn't like to think of the whimpers coming from Meyer's mouth just before the blackhawk had swallowed out of Tranquillity, snatching Alkad Mzu away from the Intelligence agents imprisoning her within the habitat. Nor did he like the physiological display he was accessing from Meyer's neural nanonics.

'How is he?' asked Aziz, the *Udat*'s spaceplane pilot.

'None too good, I think. He's suffered a lot of cerebral stress, which pushed him into shock. If I'm interpreting this display right, his neural symbionts were subjected to a massive trauma. Some of the bitek synapses are dead, and there's minor haemorrhaging where they interface with his medulla oblongata.'

'Christ.'

'Yeah. And we don't have a medical package on board which can reach that deep. Not that it would do us a lot of good if we had. You need to be a specialist to operate one.'

'I cannot feel his dreams,' *Udat* datavised. 'I always feel his dreams. Always.'

Haltam and Aziz exchanged a heavy glance. The bitek starship rarely used its link with the flight computer to communicate with any of the crew.

'I don't believe the damage is permanent,' Haltam told the blackhawk. 'Any decent hospital can repair these injuries.'

'He will waken?'

'Absolutely. His neural nanonics are keeping him under for the moment. I don't want him conscious again until the packages have knitted. They ought to be able to help stabilize him, and alleviate most of the shock.'

'Thank you, Haltam.'

'Least I can do. And what about you? Are you all right?'

'Tranquillity was very harsh. My mind hurts. I have never known that before.'

'What about your physical structure?'

'Intact. I remain functional.'

A whistle of breath emerged from Haltam's mouth. Then the flight computer informed him that Alkad Mzu was datavising for help. 'Oh hell,' he muttered. The coverage provided by the electronic sensor suite mounted around the outside of the starship's life-support horseshoe was limited. Normally, *Udat*'s own sensor blisters provided Meyer with all the information he needed. But when Haltam accessed the suite, the infra-red sweep found Mzu easily, spinning amid the thin cloud of dispersing debris which had been sucked into the wormhole with them.

'We've got you located,' he datavised. 'Stand by.'

'*Udat*?' Aziz asked. 'Can you take us over to her, please?'

'I will do so.'

Haltam managed a nervous, relieved smile. At least the

blackhawk was cooperating. The real big test would come when they wanted a swallow manoeuvre.

*Udat* manoeuvred itself to within fifty metres of Mzu, and matched her gentle trajectory. After that, Cherri Barnes strapped on a cold-gas manoeuvring pack and hauled her in.

'We have to leave,' Alkad datavised as soon as she was inside the airlock. 'Immediately.'

'You didn't warn us about your friends on the beach,' Cherri answered reproachfully.

'You were told about the observation agents. I apologize if you weren't aware of how anxious they were to prevent me from escaping, but I thought that was implicit in my message. Now, please, we must perform a swallow manoeuvre away from here.'

The airlock chamber pressurized as soon as the outer hatch closed, filling with slightly chilled air. Cherri watched Mzu touch the seal catches on her worn old backpack with awkward movements. The small incongruous pack fell to the floor. Mzu's SII suit began flowing off her skin, its oil-like substance accumulating in the form of a globe hanging from the base of her collar. Cherri eyed their passenger curiously as her own suit reverted to neutral storage mode. The short black woman was shivering slightly, sweat coating her skin. Both hands were bent inward as though crippled with arthritis; twisted, swollen fingers unmoving.

'Our captain is incapacitated,' Cherri said. 'And I'm none too certain about *Udat* either.'

Alkad grimaced, shaking her head. Oh, what an irony. Depending on the *Udat*'s goodwill, it of all starships. 'Ships will be sent after us,' she said. 'If we remain in this location I will be captured, and you will probably be exterminated.'

'Look, just what the hell did you do to get the Kingdom so pissed at you?'

'Better you don't know.'

'Better I do, then I'll know what we're likely to be facing.'

'Trouble enough.'

'Try to be a little more specific.'

'Very well: every ESA asset they can activate throughout the Confederation will be used to find me, if that makes you feel any happier. You really don't want to be around me for any length of time. If you are, you will die. Clear enough?'

Cherri didn't know how to answer. True, they'd known Mzu was some kind of dissident on the run, but not that she would attract this kind of attention. And why would Tranquillity, presumably in conjunction with the Lord of Ruin, help the Kulu Kingdom try and restrain her? Mzu was adding up to real bad news.

Alkad datavised the flight computer, requesting a direct link to the blackhawk itself. '*Udat*?'

'Yes, Dr Mzu.'

'You must leave here.'

'My captain is hurt. His mind has darkened and withered. I am in pain when I try to think.'

'I'm sorry about Meyer, but we cannot stay here. The blackhawks at Tranquillity know where you swallowed to. The Lord of Ruin will send them after me. They'll take us all back.'

'I do not wish to return. Tranquillity frightens me. I thought it was my friend.'

'One swallow manoeuvre, that's all. A small one. Just a light-year will suffice, the direction is not important. No blackhawk will be able to follow us then. After that we can see what's to be done next.'

'Very well. A light-year.'

Cherri had already unfastened her spacesuit collar when she felt the familiar minute perturbation in apparent gravity which meant *Udat*'s distortion field was altering to open a wormhole interstice. 'Very clever,' she said sardonically to Mzu. 'I hope to hell you know what you're doing. Bitek starships don't usually make swallows without their captain providing some supervision.'

'That's a conceit you really ought to abandon,' Alkad said tiredly. 'Voidhawks and blackhawks are considerably more intelligent than humans.'

'But their personalities are completely different.'

'It's done now. And it would appear we are still alive. Were there any more complaints?'

Cherri ignored her, and started to pull on a one-piece ship-suit.

'Could you sling my backpack over my shoulder, please?' Alkad asked. 'I don't have the use of my hands at this moment. Our exit from Tranquillity was more precipitous than I imagined. And I'll need some medical packages.'

'Fine. Haltam can apply the packages for you; he'll be in the bridge tending to Meyer. I'll take the backpack for you.'

'No. Put it over my shoulder. I will carry it.'

Cherri sighed through clenched teeth. She urgently wanted to see for herself how bad Meyer was. She was worried about the way *Udat* would react if the captain was unconscious for too long. She was coming down off the adrenalin high of the escape, which was like a hit of pure depression. And this small woman was about as safe as her own weight in naked plutonium.

'What have you got in it?'

'Do not concern yourself about that.'

Cherri grabbed the backpack by its straps, and held it up in front of Mzu's impassive face. There couldn't have been much in it, judging by the weight. 'Now look—!'

'A great deal of money. And an even larger amount of information; none of which you would have the faintest comprehension of. Now, you are already harbouring me on board which in itself is enough to get you killed if I'm discovered. And if the agency knew you had physically held up the backpack containing the items it does, they would throw you straight into personality debrief just to find out how much those items weigh. Do you really want to compound matters by taking a look inside?'

What Cherri wanted to do was swing the backpack at Mzu's head. Meyer had made the worst error of judgement in his life agreeing to this absurd rescue mission. All she could do now was pray it turned out not to be a terminal mistake.

'As you wish,' Cherri said with fragile calm.

\*

San Angeles spaceport was situated on the southern rim of the metropolis. A square ten kilometres to a side, a miniature city chiselled from machinery. Vast barren swaths of carbon concrete had been poured over the levelled earth and then divided up into roads, taxi aprons, and landing pads. Hundreds of line company hangars and cargo terminals hosted a business which accounted for a fifth of the entire planet's ground-to-orbit traffic movements.

Among the numbingly constant lines of standardized composite-walled hangars and office-block cubes only the main passenger terminal had been permitted a flight of fancy architect. It resembled the kind of starship which might have been built if the practicalities of the ZTT drive hadn't forced a uniform spherical hull on the astroengineering companies. A soft-contoured meld between an industrial microgee refinery station and a hypersonic biplane, dominating the skyline with its imperious technogothic silhouette. On the long autoway ride out from the city it gave approaching drivers the impression it was ready to pounce jealously on the tiny delta-planform spaceplanes which scuttled underneath its sweeping wings to embark passengers.

Jezzibella didn't bother looking at it. She sat in the car with her eyes closed for the whole of the early morning journey, not asleep, but brain definitely in neutral. Those kids from the concert – whatever their names were – had proved worthless last night, their awe of her interfering with their emotions. Now she just wanted out. Out of this world. Out of this galaxy. Out of this universe. Forever living on the hope that the waiting starship would take her to a place where something new was happening. That the next stop would be different.

Leroy and Libby shared the car with her, silent and motionless. They knew the mood. Always the same when she was leaving a planet. Always a fraction more intense every time.

Leroy was pretty sure the unspoken yearning was one reason she appealed to the kids, they identified with that integral sense of bewildered desperation and loss. Of course, it would have to be watched. Right now it was just an artist's essential suffering, a perverted muse. But eventually it could develop into full depression if he wasn't careful.

Another item to take care of. More stress. Not that he'd have it any other way.

The eleven cars which made up the Jezzibella tour convoy slid into the VIP parking slots below one of the terminal's flamboyant wings. Leroy had chosen such an early hour for the flight because it was the terminal's slackest time. They ought to be able to clear the official procedures without any problems.

Maybe that was the reason why none of the bodyguards sensed anything wrong. Always scanning for trouble with augmented senses, the absence of people was a relief rather than a concern.

It wasn't until Jezzibella asked: 'Where the fuck are the reporters?' that Leroy noticed anything amiss. The terminal wasn't merely quiet, it was dead. No passengers, no staff, not even a sub-manager to greet Jezzibella. And certainly no sign of any reporters. That wasn't odd, that was alarming. He'd leaked their departure schedule to three reliable sources last night.

'Just fucking great, Leroy,' Jezzibella growled as the entourage went through the entrance. 'This exit is really up there in fucking mythland, isn't it? Because I certainly don't fucking believe it. How the hell am I supposed to make a fucking impression when the only things watching me leave are the fucking valeting mechanoids?'

'I don't understand it,' Leroy said. The cavernous VIP vestibule carried on the never-was illusion of the terminal building: ancient Egypt discovers atomic power. A marble fantasyville of obelisks, fountains, and outsize gold ornaments, where ebony sphinxes prowled round the walls. When he datavised the local net processor all he got was the *capacity engaged* response.

'What's to understand, dickbrain? You screwed up again.' Jezzibella stomped off towards the wide wave-effect escalator which curved up towards one of the terminal's concourses. She could remember coming down it when she arrived, so it must be the way to the spaceplanes. The bastard local net processor wouldn't even permit her to access a floor plan. Cock-up planet!

She was five metres from the top (her retinue scurrying to catch up) when she saw the man standing waiting for her beside the arched entrance of the concourse. Some oaf in a terminal staff suit uniform, officious smile in place.

'I'm sorry, lady,' he said, when she drew level with him. 'You can't go any further.'

Jezzibella said: 'Oh, really?'

'Yes. We've got a priority flight operation in progress today, everything has been rescheduled.'

Jezzibella smiled, her skin softening. A delectably young wide-eyed ingénue looking for a *real man* to guide her. 'That's such a pity. I'm booked to leave this morning.'

'I'm afraid there will be a short delay.'

Still smiling, Jezzibella slammed her knee into his crotch.

Isaac Goddard had been pleased at his assignment. Putting the brakes on inconvenient civilians wandering through the terminal was an important task, Al Capone wouldn't give it to just anyone. And now it meant he got to meet this century's superstar, too. Lee Ruggiero, whose body he possessed, was full of admiration for Jezzibella. Looking at her up close, Isaac could see why. So sweet and vulnerable. Shame he had to use force to stop her. But the timing of the spaceplane flights was vital. Al had emphasized that often enough.

He was readying his energistic powers to deal with her bodyguards, who had now caught her up, when she did her level best to ram his testicles into his eye sockets via his intestinal tract.

The energistic power which was the inheritance of every possessed was capable of near-miraculous feats as it bent the fabric of reality to a mind's whim. As well as its destructive potential, items could be made solid at the flicker of a thought. It was also capable of reinforcing a body to resist almost any kind of assault as well as enhancing its physical strength. Wounds could be healed at almost the same rate they were inflicted.

But first the wish had to be formulated, the energistic flow regulated appropriately. Isaac Goddard never had a chance to wish for anything. A uniquely male agony blew apart every coherent thought current stealing through his captured brain. Pain was all that remained.

His face white, he slowly sank to the floor before Jezzibella. Tears trickled down his cheeks as his mouth laboured soundlessly.

'If it's all the same to you,' Jezzibella said brightly. 'I really would like to leave this shit tip of a planet right now.' She strode away.

'Oh, hey, come on, Jez,' Leroy called as he chased after her down the concourse, forcing himself into a fast waddle. 'Give me a break. You can't go around doing things like that.'

'Why not, for shit's sake? Worried this fucking great army of witnesses will all testify in court?'

'Look, you heard him. There's some kind of special flight schedule this morning. Why don't you wait here, and I'll find out what's going on. Huh? I won't be long.'

'I'm the fucking special flight, shithead! *Me, me.*'

'Christ! Grow up, will you! I don't manage bloody teen-scream acts. I only do adults.'

Jezzibella stopped in surprise. Leroy never shouted at her. She pouted prettily. 'I've been bad.'

'You got it.'

'Forgive me. I was all worked up over Emmerson.'

'I can understand that. But he's not coming on the starship with us. Panic over.'

The mock smile faltered. 'Leroy ... Please, I just want to leave. I hate this fucking place. I'll behave, really. But you have got to get me away from here.'

He rubbed his fat fingers over his face; sweat was making hair stick to his brow. 'OK. One miracle evacuation flight coming up.'

'Thanks, Leroy. I don't have your defences, you know? The world's different for you. Hard and easy all together.'

Leroy tried to datavise a net processor. But he couldn't get a single response, the units were all inert. 'What the hell is going on here?' he asked in annoyance. 'If these flights were that big a deal, why weren't we informed?'

'Guess that's my fault,' Al Capone told him.

Jezzibella and Leroy turned to see a group of ten men walking down the concourse towards them. They all wore double-breasted suits, and carried sub-machine-guns. Somehow the idea of running from them seemed ludicrous. More gangsters were emerging from side corridors.

'You see, I don't want people informed,' Al explained. 'At least not for a while. After that, I'm gonna speak to this whole goddam planet. Loud and clear.'

Two of Jezzibella's bodyguards caught sight of the approaching gangsters. They began to run forwards, drawing their thermal-induction pistols.

Al clicked his fingers. The bodyguards let out simultaneous yelps of pain as their pistols turned red hot. They dropped them fast. That was when a ripple of onyx flooring rose up and tripped them.

Jezzibella watched in astonishment as both bulky men went skidding into the wall. She looked from them back to Al, and grinned. 'Magnifico.'

She desperately wanted to record the scene, but her fucking neural nanonics were crashing. Fucking typical!

Al watched the beef boy back away fearfully. But the dame … she just stood there. This weird expression on her face, fascination and interest making her eyes narrow demurely. Interest in him, by damn! She wasn't afraid. She was pure class, this one. She was also one hell of a looker. Minx face, and a body the likes of which simply didn't exist in the twenties.

Lovegrove was itching for a peek at her, busy telling him who Jezzibella was. Some kind of hotshot nightclub singer. Except there was more to it than just singing and playing the ivories these days, a lot more.

'So what are you going to tell us?' Jezzibella asked, her voice husky.

'What?' Al asked.

'When you speak to the planet. What are you going to say?'

Al took his time lighting a cigar. Making her wait, showing exactly who was in control. 'I'm gonna tell them that I'm in charge now. Number one guy on the planet. And you've all gotta do what I say. *Anything* I say.' He winked broadly.

Jezzibella put on a disappointed expression. 'Waste of talent.'

'*What?*'

'You're the guys the police are calling Retros, right?'

'Yeah,' Al said cautiously.

She flicked a casual finger towards her dazed bodyguards. 'And you've got the balls and the power to take over a whole planet?'

'You catch on quick.'

'So why waste it on this dump?'

'This dump has eight hundred and ninety million people living on it, lady. And I'm gonna be the fucking emperor of them all before the evening.'

'My last album has sold over three billion so far, probably triple that number in bootlegs. Those people want me to be their empress. If you're going for broke, why not choose a decent planet? Kulu, or Oshanko, or even Earth.'

Not taking his eyes off her, Al called over his shoulder: 'Hey, Savvy Avvy, get your crummy ass up here. Now!'

Avram Harwood scuttled forwards, his head bowed, shoulders drooping. Each step was obviously painful for him, he was favouring his right leg. 'Yes, sir?'

'New California is the greatest goddam planet in the Confederation, ain't that right?' Al asked.

'Oh, yes, sir. It is.'

'Is your population bigger than Kulu?' Jezzibella asked in a bored tone.

Avram Harwood twitched miserably.

'Answer her,' Capone growled.

'No, ma'am,' Harwood said.

'Is your economy larger than Oshanko's?'

'No.'

'Do you export as much as Earth?'

'No.'

Jezzibella inclined her head contemptuously on one side, pushing her lips out towards Al. 'Anything else you want to know?'

Her voice had suddenly become very stern. Al started to laugh in sincere admiration. 'God damn! Modern women.'

'Can you all do that heat trick with the fingers?'

'Sure can, honey.'

'Interesting. So how is taking over this spaceport tied in with conquering the planet?'

Al's first instinct was to brag. About the synchronized flights up to the orbiting asteroids. About taking out the SD personnel. About using the SD network firepower to open up the whole planet to his Organization. But they were short on time. And this was no backwoods girl, she'd understand if he explained it. 'Sorry, babe, but we're kinda in a hurry. It's been a ball.'

'No it hasn't. If you'd had a ball with me, you'd know about it.'

'Hot shit—'

'If it's tied in with spaceplane flights, you're either going up to starships or the orbiting asteroids. But if you're taking over the planet, it can't be the starships. So it has to be the asteroids. Let me guess, the strategic-defence network.' She watched the alarmed expressions light up on the faces of the gangsters. All except Mayor Harwood; but then he was already hopelessly adrift in some deep private purgatory. 'How did I do?'

Al could only gawp. He'd heard of lady spiders like this; they knitted fancy webs or did hypnosis, or something. It ended up that the males just couldn't escape. Then they got screwed and eaten.

*Now I know what they go through.*

'You did pretty good.' He was envious of her cool. Envious of a lot of things, actually.

'Al?' Emmet Mordden urged. 'Al, we have to get going.'

'Yeah, yeah. I ain't forgotten.'

'We can send this group down to Luciano's people for possessing.'

'Hey, who the fuck's in charge here?'

Emmet took a frightened pace backwards.

'In charge, but not in control,' Jezzibella teased.

'Don't push it, lady,' Al warned her sharply.

'True leaders simply tell people to do what they want to do anyway.' She licked her lips. 'Guess what I want to do?'

'Fuck this. Modern women. You're all like goddam whores. I ain't never heard anything like it.'

'The talk isn't all you've never had before.'

'Holy Christ.'

'So what do you say, Al?' Jezzibella switched her voice back to a liquid rumble. She almost didn't have to fake it. She was so turned on, excited, stimulated. You name it. Caught up in a terrorist hijack. And such strange terrorists, too. Wimps with a personal nuclear capability. Except the leader, he was massively focused. Not bad looking, either. 'Want me to tag along on your little *coup d'état* mission? Or are you going to spend the rest of every waking day wondering what it would have been like? And you will wonder. You know you will.'

'We got a spare seat on the rocketship,' Al said. 'But you've got to do as you're told.'

She batted her eyelashes. 'That'll be a first.'

Amazed at what he'd just said, Al tried to play back their conversation in his mind to see how he'd gotten to this point. No good, he couldn't figure it. He was acting on pure impulse again. And that felt first-class. Like the good old days. People never did know what he was going to do next. It kept them on edge, and him on top.

Jezzibella walked over to him, and tucked her arm in his. 'Let's go.'

Al grinned round wolfishly. 'OK, wiseasses, you heard the lady. Mickey, take the rest of this bunch down to Luciano. Emmet, Silvano, take your boys to their spaceplanes.'

'Leave me my manager, and the old woman, oh and the band too,' Jezzibella said.

'What the hell is this?' Al demanded. 'I ain't got room in my Organization for freeloaders.'

'You want me to look good. I need them.'

'Jee-zus, you're pushy.'

'You want a girl who's a pushover, find yourself a teenage bimbo. Me, it's the whole package or nothing.'

'OK, Mickey, lay off the cornholers. But the rest of them get the full treatment.' He shoved his hands out towards her, palms held up imploringly. 'Good enough?' The sarcasm wasn't entirely feigned.

'Good enough,' Jezzibella agreed.

They grinned knowingly at each other for a moment, then led the procession of gangsters down the concourse to the waiting spaceplanes.

*

The wormhole terminus opened smoothly six hundred and eighty thousand kilometres above Jupiter's equator, the absolute minimum permitted distance from the prodigious band of orbiting habitats. *Oenone* flew out of the circular gap, and immediately identified itself to the Jovian strategic-defence network. As soon as their approach authorization had been granted, the voidhawk accelerated in towards the Kristata habitat at an urgent five gees. It was already asking the habitat to assemble a medical team to meet it as soon as it docked.

**Of what nature?** Kristata asked.

At which point Cacus, their medical officer, took over, using the voidhawk's affinity to relay a list of the grisly physical injuries inflicted on Syrinx by the possessed occupying Pernik Island. **But most importantly we're going to need a psychological trauma team,** he said. **We put her in zero-tau for the flight, naturally. However, she did not respond to any level of mentalic communication after she was brought on board, other than a purely autonomic acknowledgement of** *Oenone*'s **contact. I'm afraid the intensity of the withdrawal is one which approaches catatonia.**

**What happened to her?** queried the habitat. It was unusual for a voidhawk to fly without its captain's guidance.

**She was tortured.**

Ruben waited until the medical discussion was under way

before asking *Oenone* for an affinity link with Eden itself. Arriving at Jupiter he could actually feel his body relaxing in the bridge couch despite the acceleration pressure. The events which would play out over the next few hours were going to be strenuous, but nothing like as bad as Atlantis and the voyage to the Sol system.

*Oenone*'s instinct had been to rush directly to Saturn and the Romulus habitat as soon as Oxley had brought Syrinx on board. The yearning to go home after such a tremendous shock was as much a voidhawk trait as a human one.

It had been down to Ruben to convince the frantic, frightened voidhawk that Jupiter would be preferable. Jovian habitats had more advanced medical facilities than those orbiting Saturn. And of course, there was the Consensus to inform. This was a threat which simply had to rank higher than individual concerns.

Then there was the flight itself. *Oenone* had never flown anywhere without Syrinx's subliminal supervision, much less performed a swallow manoeuvre. Voidhawks could fly without the slightest human input, of course. But as ever there was a big difference between theory and practice. They identified so much with the needs and wishes of their captains.

The crew's general affinity band had rung with a powerful cadence of relief when the first swallow manoeuvre passed off flawlessly.

Ruben knew he shouldn't have doubted *Oenone*, but his own mind was eddying with worry. The sight of Syrinx's injuries ... And worse, her mind closed as if it were a flower at night. Any attempt to prise below her churning surface thoughts had resulted in a squirt of sickening images and sensations. Her sanity would surely suffer if she was left alone with such nightmares. Cacus had immediately placed her in zero-tau, temporarily circumventing the problem.

**Hello, Ruben,** Eden said. **It is pleasant to receive you again.**

*Though I am saddened by the condition of Syrinx, and I sense that Oenone is suffering considerable distress.*

Ruben hadn't conversed directly with the original habitat for over forty years, not since his last visit. It was a trip which most Edenists made at some time in their life. Not a pilgrimage (they would hotly deny that) but paying their respects, acknowledging the sentimental debt to the founding entity of their culture.

*That's why I need to speak with you,* Ruben said. *Eden, we have a problem. Would you call a general Consensus, please?*

There was no hierarchy in Edenism, it was a society proud of its egalitarianism; he could have made the same request of any habitat. If the personality considered the request valid, it would be forwarded to the habitat Consensus, then if it passed that vote a general Consensus would be called, comprising every single Edenist, habitat, and voidhawk in the Sol system. But for this issue, Ruben felt obliged to make his appeal direct to Eden, the first habitat.

He gave an account of what had happened on Atlantis, followed by the précis which was Laton's legacy. When he finished, the affinity band was silent for several moments.

*I will call for a general Consensus,* Eden said. The habitat's mental voice was uncharacteristically studious.

Relief mingled with a curious frisson of worry among Ruben's thoughts. At least the burden which *Oenone*'s crew had carried by themselves during the flight was to be shared and mitigated – the fundamental psychology of Edenism. But what amounted to the habitat's shock at the revelation of souls returning to possess the living was deeply unsettling. Eden had been germinated in 2075, making it the oldest living entity in the Confederation. If anything had the requisite endowment of wisdom to withstand such news then surely it must be the ancient habitat.

Disquieted by the habitat's response, and chiding himself for expecting miracles, Ruben settled back in the acceleration couch and used the voidhawk's sensor blisters to observe their approach flight. They were already twenty-five thousand kilometres from Europa, curving gently round its northern hemisphere. The moon's ice mantle glinted a grizzled oyster as distant sunlight skittered over its smooth surface, throwing off the occasional dazzling mirror-flash from an impact crater.

Behind the moon, Jupiter occluded half of the universe. They were close enough that the polar regions were invisible, distilling the planet to a simple flat barrier of enraged orange and white clouds. The gas giant was in one of its more active phases. Vast hurricane storm-spots geysered through the upper cloud bands, swirling mushroom formations bringing with them a multitude of darker contaminates from the lower levels. Colours fought like armies along frenzied boundaries of intricate curlicues. Never winning, never losing. There was too much chaos for any one pattern or shade to gain the ultimate triumph of stability. Even the great spots, of which there were now three, had lifetimes measurable in mere millennia. But for raw spectacle they were unmatched. After five centuries of interstellar exploration, Jupiter remained one of the largest gas giants ever catalogued, honouring its archaic title as the Father of Gods.

A hundred thousand kilometres in from Europa, the habitats formed their own unique constellation around their lord; drinking down its magnetosphere energy, bathing in the tempestuous particle winds, listening to the wild chants of its radio voice, and watching the ever-changing panorama of the clouds. They could never live anywhere else but above such worlds; only the magnetic flux spun out by gas giants could generate the power levels necessary to sustain life within their dusky-crimson polyp shells. There were four thousand two hundred and fifty mature habitats in Jupiter orbit, nurturing a total Edenist population of over nine billion individuals. The second largest civilization in the Confederation – in numerical terms.

Only Earth with its guesstimated population of thirty-five billion was bigger. But the standard of civilization, in both economic and cultural terms, was peerless. Jupiter's citizens had no underclass, no ignorance, no poverty, and no misfits, barring the one-in-a-million Serpent who rejected Edenism in its entirety.

The reason for such enviable social fortune was Jupiter itself. To build such a society, even with affinity enhancing psychological stability, and bitek alleviating a great many mundane physical problems, required vast wealth. It came from helium$_3$, the principal fusion fuel used throughout the Confederation.

In comparison with other fuels, a mix of He$_3$ and deuterium produced one of the cleanest fusion reactions possible, resulting mainly in charged helium with an almost zero neutron emission. Such an end product meant that the generator systems needed little shielding, making them cheaper to build. Superenergized helium was also an ideal space drive.

The Confederation societies were heavily dependent on this form of cheap, low-pollution fusion to maintain their socioeconomic index. Fortunately deuterium existed in massive quantities; a common isotope of hydrogen, it could be extracted from any sea or glacial asteroid. He$_3$, however, was extremely rare in nature. The operation to mine it from Jupiter began in 2062 when the then Jovian Sky Power Corporation dropped its first aerostat into the atmosphere to extract the elusive isotope in commercial quantities. There were only minute amounts present, but minute is a relative term in the context of a gas giant.

It was that one tentative high-risk operation which had transformed itself, via political revolution, religious intolerance, and bitek revelation, into Edenism. And Edenists continued to mine He$_3$ in every colonized star system which had a gas giant (with the notable exception of Kulu and its Principalities), although cloudscoops had replaced aerostats long ago as the actual method of collection. It was the greatest industrial enterprise in existence, and also the largest monopoly. And with the format for developing stage one colony worlds now institutionalized, it looked set to remain so.

Yet as any student of ekistics could have predicted, it was Jupiter which remained the economic heart of Edenism. For it was Jupiter which supplied the single largest consumer of He$_3$: Earth and its O'Neill Halo. Such a market required a huge mining operation, as well as its associated support infrastructure, and on top of that came their own massive energy requirements.

Hundreds of industrial stations flocked around every habitat, varying in size from ten kilometre diameter asteroidal mineral refineries to tiny microgee-research laboratories. Tens of thousands of spaceships congested local space, importing and exporting every commodity known to the human and xenoc races of the Confederation. Their assigned flight vectors wove a sluggish, ephemeral DNA coil around the five hundred and fifty thousand kilometre orbital band.

By the time *Oenone* was two thousand kilometres away from Kristata the habitat was becoming visible to its optical sensors. It shone weakly of its own accord, a miniature galaxy with long, thin spiral arms. The habitat itself formed the glowing core of the nebula, a cylinder forty-five kilometres long, rotating gently inside a corona of St Elmo's fire sparked by the agitated particle winds splashing across its shell. Industrial stations glimmered around it, static flashing in crazed patterns over external girders and panels, their metallic structures more susceptible to the ionic squalls than bitek polyp. Fusion drives formed the spiral arms, Adamist starships and inter-orbit craft arriving and departing from the habitat's globe-shaped counter-rotating spaceport.

A priority flight path had been cleared through the other ships, allowing *Oenone* to race past them towards the docking-ledges ringing Kristata's northern endcap, although the starship was actually decelerating now, pushing seven gees. Ruben observed the habitat expand rapidly, its central band of star-scrapers coming into focus. It was virtually the only aspect of the external vista which had changed after travelling a hundred thousand kilometres from their swallow emergence point. Jupiter remained exactly the same. He couldn't even tell if they were closer to the gas giant or not, there were no valid reference points. It seemed as though *Oenone* was flying between two flat plains, one comprised of ginger and white clouds, the other a midnight sky.

They swept round the counter-rotating spaceport and headed in for the northern endcap. The violet haze of glowing particles was murkier here, disrupted by slithering waves of darkness as the energized wind broke and churned against the four concentric docking-ledge rings. *Oenone* experienced a prickle of static across its blue polyp hull as it slipped over the innermost ledge at a shallow tangent, for a moment the tattered discharge mimicked the purple web pattern veining its hull surface. Then the bulky voidhawk was hovering directly above a docking pedestal, slowly twisting round until the feed tubes were aligned correctly. It settled on the pedestal with all the fuss of a falling autumn leaf.

A convoy of service vehicles rolled towards it. The ambulance was the first to reach the rim of the saucer-shaped hull, its long airlock tube snaking out to mate with the crew toroid. Cacus was still discussing Syrinx's status with the medical team as the zero-tau pod containing her body was rolled into the ambulance.

Ruben realized *Oenone* was hungrily ingesting nutrient fluid from the pedestal tubes. **How are you?** he asked the voidhawk belatedly.

**I am glad the flight is over. Syrinx can begin to heal now. Kristata says all the damage can be repaired. Many doctors are part of its multiplicity. I believe what it says.**

**Yes, she'll heal. And we can help. Knowing you are loved is a great part of any cure.**

**Thank you, Ruben. I am glad you are my friend, and hers.**

Rising from his acceleration couch, Ruben felt a flush of sentiment and admiration at the voidhawk's guileless faith. Sometimes its simple directness was like a child's honesty. Unarguable.

Edwin and Serina were busying themselves powering down the crew toroid's flight systems, and supervising the service vehicles as umbilicals were plugged into the ledge's support machinery. Tula was already conversing with a local cargo depot about storing the few containers remaining in the lower hull cradles. Everyone seemed to have acknowledged that they would be here for some time, even *Oenone*.

Ruben thought of her injuries again and shivered in the bridge's warm air. **I'd like to talk to Athene, please,** he asked the voidhawk. The final duty, which he'd put off as long as possible, terrified Athene would pick up his shame. He felt so responsible for Syrinx. If I hadn't let her rush down there. If I'd gone with her . . .

**Individuality is to be cherished,** the voidhawk told him stiffly. **She decides for herself.**

He barely had time to form a rueful grin when he was aware of the voidhawk's potent affinity reaching out across the solar system to Saturn and the Romulus habitat.

**It's all right, my dear,** Athene told him as soon as they swapped identity traits. **She's alive, and she has *Oenone*. That is enough no matter what the damage those fiends inflicted. She will come back to us.**

**You know?**

**Of course. I always know when one of Iasius's children returns home, and *Oenone* informed me straight away. Since Eden called for a Consensus I've been listening to the details.**

**There will be a general Consensus?**

**Certainly.**

Ruben felt the old voidhawk captain's lips assume an ironic smile.

**You know,** she said, **we haven't called one since Laton destroyed Jantrit. And now he's back. I suppose there is a certain inevitability about it.**

**He was back,** Ruben said. **We really have seen the last of him now. It's funny, in a way I almost regret his suicide, however noble. I think we're going to need that kind of ruthlessness in the weeks ahead.**

The general Consensus took several minutes to gather; people had to be woken, others had to stop work. All across the solar system Edenists merged their consciousness with that of their home habitats, which in turn linked together. It was the ultimate democratic government, in which everyone not only voted but also contributed to and influenced the formation of policy.

*Oenone* presented Laton's précis first, the message he had delivered to the Atlantean Consensus. He stood before them, a tall, handsome man with Asian-ethnic features and black hair tied back in a small ponytail, dressed in a unfussy green silk robe, belted at the waist. Alone in a darkened universe. His studied attitude showing he knew they were his judges, and yet not quite caring.

'No doubt you have assimilated the account of events on Pernik Island and what happened at Aberdale,' he said. 'As you can see this whole episode started with Quinn Dexter's sacrifice ritual. However, we can safely conclude that the breakthrough from beyond which occurred in the Lalonde jungle was unique. These idiot Satanists have been dancing through the woods at midnight for centuries, and they've never succeeded in summoning up the dead before. Had souls ever returned at any time in the past we would know about it; although I concede there have always been rumours of such incidents throughout human history.

'Unfortunately, I was never able to ascertain the exact cause of what I can only describe as a rupture between our dimension and this "beyond" where souls linger after death. Something must have happened to make this ritual different from all the others. This is the area where you should concentrate your research effort. The spread of possession is not a threat which can be countered on an individual basis, though I'm sure Adamist populations will demand military action whenever it breaks out. Resist such futile actions. You must discover the root cause, close the dimensional rupture. Such a method is the only long-term chance for success you have. I believe that only Edenism has the potential to challenge this problem with the necessary commitment and resources. Your unity may be the only advantage which the living have. Use it.

'I assure you that though the possessed remain unorganized, they do have a common and overriding goal. They seek strength through numbers, and they will not rest until every living body is possessed. Now you are warned, you should be able to protect yourself from anything like Pernik happening again. Simple filtering subroutines will safeguard the habitat multiplicities, and they in turn can detect possessed individuals claiming to be Edenists with a more detailed interrogation of personality traits.

'My last observation is more philosophical than practical, although equally important in the long run should you triumph. You are going to have to make considerable adjustments to your culture now you know humans have an immortal soul. In making this adaptation, I cannot overemphasize how important corporeal existence is. Do not think death is an easy escape option from suffering, or life as simply a phase of being, for when you die it is truly the end of a part of yourself. But nor would I want you to worry about being trapped in beyond for all of time, I doubt one in a billion Edenists ever would be. Think of what the returning souls are, who they are, and you will see what I mean. Ultimately you will know for yourself, as we all do. What I discovered on confronting the final reality is the belief that our culture is supreme among corporeal societies. I only wish I could have returned to it for just a little while longer knowing what I now know. Not that you would have me back, I suspect.'

A final knowing smile, and he was gone for the last time.

First, Consensus decided, we must safeguard our own culture. Although we are relatively immune from infiltration, we must consider the longer term prospect of physical assault should the possessed gain control of a planetary system with military starships. Our protection will be achieved most effectively by supporting the Confederation, and preventing the spread of possession. To this end, all voidhawks will be recalled from civil flight activities to form an expanded defence force, one-third of which will be assigned to the Confederation Navy. Our scientific resources must be targeted as Laton suggested to discover the origin of the initial breakthrough, and achieve understanding of the energistic nature of the possessing souls. We must discover a permanent solution.

We acknowledge the views of those among us that favour a policy of isolation, and will retain it as an option should it appear the possessed are gaining the upper hand. But to be left alone in the universe after the possessed remove the Adamist planets and asteroids they have conquered is not a future we consider to be optimum. This threat must be faced in conjunction with the entire human race. We are the problem, we must cure ourselves.

\*

Louise Kavanagh woke to the blessed smell of fresh clean linen, the pleasing sensation of crisp sheets pressing against her. When she opened her eyes the room she found herself in was even larger than her bedroom back at Cricklade. On the opposite wall, thick curtains were drawn across the windows, permitting very little light to enter. The gloomy chinks didn't even tell her what colour the light outside was. And that was tremendously important.

Louise pushed back the sheets and padded over the pile

carpet to draw one of the high curtains. Duke's golden haze surged in. She studied the sky anxiously, but it was a clear day outside. There weren't even any rain clouds, and certainly none of the spirals of gauzy red mist. She had seen her fill of that banshee's breath yesterday as the aeroambulance flew across Kesteven; broad translucent whorls of it swirling above every town and village they passed. Streets, houses, and fields below the downy substance were all tarnished a lurid carmine.

They're not here yet, Louise thought in relief. But they'll come, sure as winter.

Norwich had been a city in panic when they arrived yesterday. Though the authorities weren't entirely sure what they were panicking over. The only news which had reached the capital from islands afflicted by the relentless march of the possessed were muddled claims of uprisings and invasions by offworld forces carrying strange weapons. But the Confederation Navy squadron orbiting Norfolk assured the Prince and Prime Minister that no invasion had occurred.

Nonetheless a full mobilization of the Ramsey Island militias had been ordered. Troops were digging in around the capital. Plans were being drawn up to free those islands like Kesteven which had been lost to the enemy.

Ivan Cantrell had been ordered to land his plane on a remote part of the city's aerodrome. Soldiers had surrounded the vehicle as they touched down, nervous men in ill-fitting khaki uniforms, squeezing the stocks of rifles which had been antique back in their grandfathers' time. But dotted among them were several Confederation Navy marines, clad in sleek one-piece suits which seemed like an outgrowth of rubbery skin. And their dull-black weapons were definitely not obsolete. Louise suspected a single shot from one of those blank muzzles would be quite capable of destroying the aeroambulance.

The soldiers had calmed considerably when the Kavanagh sisters had climbed down the plane's airstairs followed by Felicia Cantrell and her girls. Their commanding officer, a captain called Lester-Swindell, accepted that they were refugees, but it took another two hours of questioning before they were 'cleared'. At the end Louise had to call Aunt Celina to come and vouch for her and Genevieve. She really hadn't wanted to, but by that time there was little choice. Aunt Celina was Mother's elder sister, and Louise never could quite believe the two could possibly be related, the woman was completely brainless, a simpering airhead concerned only with the Season and shopping. But Aunt Celina was married to Jules Hewson, the Earl of Luffenham, and he was a senior adviser to the Prince's Court. If the Kavanagh name didn't carry quite the weight here on Ramsey which it did on Kesteven, his certainly did.

Two minutes after Aunt Celina had blustered and whinnied her way into the office, Louise and Genevieve were outside being bundled into her carriage. Fletcher Christian, *a Cricklade farmhand who helped us escape, Auntie,* was told to ride on the bench with the driver. Louise wanted to protest, but Fletcher gave her a wink, and bowed deeply to Aunt Celina.

Louise dropped her gaze from the unblemished sky over Norwich. Balfern House was in the centre of Brompton, the most exclusive borough of the capital city, but even so it stood in its own extensive grounds. There had been two policemen on duty outside the iron gates as they drove in yesterday evening.

Safe for the moment, then, she told herself. Except she had brought one of the possessed right into the heart of the capital. Into the core of government, in fact.

But Fletcher Christian was her secret, hers and Genevieve's; and Gen wouldn't tell. It was funny, but she trusted Fletcher now; more so than the Earl and the Prime Minister. He had already proved he would, and could protect her from the other possessed. And she in turn was charged with protecting Genevieve. Because Heaven knows the militia soldiers and Confederation marines can't, not against *them.*

She slumped her shoulders and walked the length of the room, pulling back the remaining curtains. *What do I do next? Tell people the truth about what they're facing? I can just imagine Uncle Jules listening to that. He'll think I'm hysterical. Yet if they don't know, they'll never be able to protect themselves.*

It was a horrible dilemma. And to think she'd always expected her problems to end once they reached the safety of the capital. *That something would be done. That we could rescue Mummy and Daddy. A schoolgirl's dream.*

Carmitha's shotgun was resting against the side of the bed. Louise smiled fondly at the weapon. Aunt Celina had fussed and faffed so when she insisted on bringing it with them from the aerodrome, bleating that Young Ladies simply did not know about such things, let alone carry them on their person.

It was going to go hard on Aunt Celina when the possessed caught up with her. Louise's smile faded. *Fletcher*, she decided, *I must ask Fletcher what to do next.*

*

Louise found Genevieve sitting in the middle of her bed in the next room, knees tucked up under her chin, sulking silently. They both took one look at each other, and burst out laughing. The maids, on Aunt Celina's strict instruction, had provided them with the most fanciful dresses, brightly coloured silk and velvet fabrics with huge ruffed skirts and puffball sleeves.

'Come on.' Louise took her little sister's hand. 'Let's get out of this madhouse.'

Aunt Celina was taking breakfast in the long glass-walled morning room which looked out over the garden's lily ponds. She sat at the head of the teak table, an empress marshalling her troops of liveried manservants and starch-uniformed maids. A gaggle of overweight corgies snuffled hopefully round her chair to be rewarded with the odd titbit of toast or bacon.

'Oh, that's so much better,' she declared when the sisters

were ushered in. 'You did look simply awful yesterday. Why, I barely recognized you. Those dresses are so much prettier. And your hair is so shiny now, Louise. You look a picture.'

'Thank you, Aunt Celina,' Louise said.

'Sit down, my dear, and do tuck in. You must be famished after such a terrible ordeal. Such dreadful things you've seen and endured, more than any gal I know. I gave thanks to God last night that you both reached us in one piece.'

One of the maids put a plate of scrambled eggs in front of Louise. She felt her stomach curdle alarmingly. Oh, please Jesus, don't let me throw up now. 'Just some toast, please,' she managed to say.

'You remember Roberto, don't you, Louise?' Aunt Celina said. Her voice became slippery with pride. 'My dear son, and such a strapping lad, too.'

Louise glanced at the boy sitting at the other end of the table, munching his way through a pile of bacon, eggs, and kidneys. Roberto was a couple of years older than her. They hadn't got on the last time he visited Cricklade. He never seemed to want to do anything. And now he'd put on at least another stone and a half, most of it round his middle.

Their eyes met. He was giving her what she now called the William Elphinstone look. And the dratted dress with its tight bodice flattered her figure.

She was rather surprised when her steely stare made him blush and shift his gaze hurriedly back to his plate. I've got to get out of here, she thought, out of this house, this city, away from these stupid bovine people, and most of all out of this bloody dress. I don't need Fletcher to tell me that.

'I never did know why your mother went to live on Kesteven,' Aunt Celina said. 'It's such a wild island. She should have stayed here in the city. Could have had her pick of the court, you know, your dear mother. Divine creature she was, simply divine when she was younger. Just like you two. And now who knows what dreadful things have happened to her in this horrid rebellion. I told her to stay, but she simply wouldn't listen. Wild, it is. Wild. I hope the navy squadron shoots every one of those savages. They should cleanse Kesteven, laser it clean right down to the bedrock. Then you two darlings can come and live here safely with me. Won't that be wonderful?'

'They'll come here, too,' an indignant Genevieve said. 'You can't stop them, you know. Nobody can.'

Louise jabbed her with a toe, and glared. Genevieve simply shrugged, and tucked in to her eggs.

Aunt Celina blanched theatrically, her handkerchief flapping in front of her face. 'Why, my darling child, what a simply dreadful thing to say. Oh, your mother should never have left the capital. Gals are brought up properly here.'

'I'm sorry, Aunt Celina,' Louise said swiftly. 'Neither of us is thinking straight right now. Not after . . . you know.'

'Of course I understand. You must both visit a doctor. I should have summoned one last night. Goodness knows what you picked up tramping round the countryside for days on end.'

'No!' A doctor would discover her pregnancy in minutes. And Heaven knows how Aunt Celina would react to that. 'Thank you, Aunt Celina. But really, it's nothing a few days' rest won't cure. I was thinking, we could tour Norwich now we're here. It would be a real treat for us.' She smiled winningly. 'Please, Aunt Celina.'

'Yes. Please may we?' Genevieve chipped in.

'I don't know,' Aunt Celina said. 'This is hardly the time for sightseeing, what with the militias forming up. And I promised Hermione I would attend the Red Cross meeting today. One must do what one can to support our brave menfolk in such times. I really can't spare the time to show you round.'

'I could,' Roberto said. 'I'd enjoy it.' His eyes were lingering on Louise again.

'Don't be silly, darling,' Aunt Celina said. 'You have school today.'

'Fletcher Christian could chaperone us,' Louise said quickly. 'He's more than proved his worth. We'd be completely safe.' From the corner of her eye she could see Roberto frowning.

'Well—'

'Please!' Genevieve wheedled. 'I want to buy you some flowers, you've been so kind.'

Aunt Celina clasped her hands together. 'Oh, you are a little treasure, aren't you. I always wanted a little gal of my own, you know. Of course you can go.'

Louise blew her cheeks out in thanks. She could just imagine what would have happened if they'd tried pulling that routine on Mother. Genevieve had gone back to her eggs, her face a perfect composure of purity.

At the other end of the table, Roberto was chewing thoughtfully on his third slice of toast.

*

The sisters found Fletcher Christian in the servants' quarters. With so many of Balfern House's staff called away to their militia regiments he had been put to work by the cook bringing sacks up from the storerooms.

He gave both girls a measured look as he lowered a big string bag of carrots onto the kitchen floor, and bowed gracefully. 'How splendid you look, my young ladies, so refined. I always imagined you more suited to finery such as this.'

Louise gave him a very sharp stare. And then they were both grinning at each other.

'Aunt Celina has lent us the use of a carriage,' she said in her grandest tone. 'And she's also given you leave to accompany us, my man. Of course, should you prefer to remain here doing what you seem to do so well . . .'

'Ah, my lady Louise, I see you are a cruel one. But justly do I deserve such mockery. It would be my honour to accompany you.'

He picked up his jacket under the disapproving gaze of the

cook, and followed Louise out of the kitchen. Genevieve picked up her skirt hems, and ran on ahead of them through the house.

'The little one seems none the worse for all she has been through,' Fletcher observed.

'Yes, thank the Lord. Was it truly awful for you last night?' Louise asked once they were out of earshot of the other servants.

'The room was dry and warm. I've made my bunk in sorrier circumstances.'

'I apologize for bringing you here, I'd forgotten quite how bad Aunt Celina was. But I couldn't think of anyone else who could extract us from the aerodrome as quickly.'

'Pay it no further heed, my lady. Your aunt is a model of enlightenment compared to some of the matrons I knew in my own youth.'

'Fletcher.' She put her hand on his arm, and slowed their pace. 'Are they here?'

His sturdy features turned melancholy. 'Yes, my lady Louise. I can feel several dozen encamped throughout the city. And their numbers grow with every passing hour. It will take many days, perhaps a week. But Norwich will surely fall.'

'Oh, dear Jesus, when will this ever end?'

She was aware of his arm around her as she trembled. Hating herself for being weak. Oh, where are you, Joshua? I need you.

'Speak not of evil, and it will pay you no heed,' Fletcher said softly.

'Really?'

'So my mother assured me.'

'Was she right?'

His fingers touched her chin, tilting her face up. 'That was a long time ago, and far away. But today I think if we avoid their attentions, then you will remain out of harm's way for longer.'

'Very well. I've been giving this some serious thought, you

know; how to keep Genevieve and the baby truly safe. And there's only one way to do it.'

'Yes, my lady?'

'Leave Norfolk.'

'I see.'

'It's not going to be easy. Will you help me?'

'You do not have to ask that of me, lady, you know I will offer you and the little one what aid I can.'

'Thank you, Fletcher. The other thing was; do you want to come with us? I'm going to try and reach Tranquillity. I know someone there who can help us.' If anyone can, she added silently.

'Tranquillity?'

'Yes, it's a sort of palace in space, orbiting a star a long way away from here.'

'Ah, lady, what a temptress you are. To sail the stars I once sailed by. How could I resist such a request?'

'Good,' she whispered.

'I imply no criticism, lady Louise. But do you really know how to prepare for such an endeavour?'

'I think so. There was one thing I learned from both Daddy and Joshua, Carmitha, too, in a way; and that is: money makes everything possible.'

Fletcher smiled respectfully. 'A worthy saying. And do you have this money?'

'Not on me, no. But I'm a Kavanagh, I can get it.'

# 6

Ione Saldana's palatial cliff-base apartment was empty now, apart from herself; the guests from the Tranquillity Banking Regulatory Council had been ushered out politely but insistently, the convivial party most definitely over. And they had known better than to argue. Unfortunately, they were also astute enough to know they wouldn't be turned out unless it was a real crisis. Word would already be spreading down the length of the giant habitat.

She had reduced the output of the ceiling's electrophorescent cells to a sombre starlight glimmer. It allowed her to see out through the glass wall which held back the sea, revealing a silent world composed entirely from shades of aquamarine. And now even that was darkening as the habitat's light-tube allowed night to claim the interior. Fish were reduced to stealthy shadows slithering among the prickly coral branches.

When Ione was younger she had spent hours staring out at the antics of the fish and sand-crawling creatures. Now she sat cross-legged on the apricot moss carpet before her private theatre of life, Augustine nesting contentedly in her lap. She stroked the little xenoc's velvety fur absently, eyes closed to the world.

**We can still send a squadron of patrol blackhawks after Mzu,** Tranquillity suggested. **I am aware of the *Udat*'s wormhole terminus coordinate.**

So are the other blackhawks, she replied. But it's their crews I worry about. Once they're away from our SD platforms, there really is nothing we can do to enforce their loyalty. Mzu would try to make a deal with them. She'd probably succeed, too. She's proved astonishingly resourceful so far. Fancy even lulling us into complacency.

I was not complacent, the habitat personality said irksomely. I was caught off guard by the method. Which in itself I find disturbing. It implies a great deal of thought went into her escape. One wonders what her next move will be.

I've got a pretty good idea, unfortunately. She'll go for the Alchemist. There's no other reason for her to behave like this. And after she's got it: Omuta.

Indeed.

So no we don't send the blackhawks after her. She may lead them to the Alchemist. That would give us an even worse situation than the one we've got now.

In that case, what do you want to do about the Intelligence agency teams?

I'm not sure. How are they reacting?

*

Lady Tessa, the head of the ESA's Tranquillity station, had been badly frightened by the news of Alkad Mzu's escape, a fact which she managed to conceal behind a show of pure fury. Monica Foulkes stood in front of her in the starscraper apartment which doubled as the ESA team's headquarters. She had reported to Lady Tessa in person rather than use the habitat's communication net. Not that Tranquillity was unaware (hardly!), but there were a great number of organizations and governments who knew nothing of Mzu's existence, nor the implications arising from it.

It was twenty-three minutes since the physicist's escape, and a form of delayed shock had begun to infiltrate Monica's body as her subconscious acknowledged just how lucky she'd been to avoid vanishing down the *Udat*'s wormhole. Her neural nanonics were helpless to prevent the cold shivers which spiralled their way round her limbs and belly muscles.

'I won't even dignify your performance by calling it a disaster,' Lady Tessa stormed. 'Great God Almighty, the principal reason we're here is to make sure she remained confined to the habitat. Every agency endorses that policy, even the bloody Lord of Ruin supports it. And you let her stroll out right in front of you. I mean, Jesus Christ, what the hell were you all doing on that beach? She stops to put on a spacesuit, and you didn't even move in closer to investigate.'

'It was not exactly a *stroll*, Chief. And I'd like to point out for the record that we are just an observation team. Our operation in Tranquillity has always been too small to guarantee Mzu remains inside should she make a determined effort to leave, or if someone uses force to extract her. If the agency wanted to be certain, it should have allocated a bigger team to monitoring her.'

'Don't datavise the rule flek at me, Foulkes. You're boosted, you've got weapons implants' – she flinched, and glanced up at the ceiling as though expecting divine censure – 'and Mzu is in her sixties. There is no way she should have ever got near that bloody blackhawk, let alone have it snatch her away.'

'The blackhawk tipped the physical balance heavily in her favour. It simply wasn't a contingency we allowed for. Tranquillity had two serjeants eliminated during our attempt to stop her boarding. Personally, I'm surprised the starship was allowed to swallow inside at all.' Now Monica glanced guiltily round the naked polyp walls.

Lady Tessa's baleful expression didn't alter, but she did pause. 'I doubt there was much it could do. As you say, that swallow manoeuvre was completely unprecedented.'

'Samuel claimed that not many voidhawks could be that precise.'

'Thank you. I'll be sure to include that most helpful unit of data in my report.' She got up out of the chair, and walked over to the oval window. The apartment was two-thirds of the way down the StEtalia starscraper, where gravity was approaching Earth standard. It was a location which gave her a unimpeded view across the bottom of the vast curving burnt-biscuit-coloured habitat shell, with just a crescent of the counter-rotating spaceport showing beyond the rim as if it were a metallic moon rising. Today, as for the last four days, there were few starships arriving or departing from its docking-bays. Big SD platforms glinted reassuringly against the backdrop of Mirchusko's darkside as they caught the last of the sunlight before Tranquillity sailed into the penumbra.

And what use would they be against the Alchemist? Lady Tessa wondered sagely. A doomsday device that's supposed to be able to kill stars.

'What's our next move?' Monica asked. She was rubbing her arms for warmth in an attempt to stop the shaking. Grains of sand were still falling out of her sweater's sleeves.

'Informing the Kingdom is our primary responsibility now,' Lady Tessa said in a challenging tone. There was no reaction from the AV pillar sticking up out of her desktop processor block. 'But it's going to take time for them to respond and start searching. And Mzu will know that. Which means she's got two options, either she takes the *Udat* straight to the Alchemist, or she loses herself out there.' She tapped a gold-chromed fingernail on the window as the myriad stars drifted past in slow arcs.

'If she was smart enough to get away from all the agency teams tagging her, she'll know that she'll never stay lost, not for ever,' Monica said. 'Too many of us are going to be looking now.'

'And yet the *Udat* doesn't have any special equipment rigged. I checked the CAB registry, it hasn't had any refitting for eight months. Sure, it has got standard interfaces for combat-wasp cradles and heavy-duty close-defence weapons. Almost every blackhawk has. But there was nothing unusual.'

'So?'

'So if she does take *Udat* straight to the Alchemist, how will they fire it at Omuta's sun?'

'Do we know what equipment is necessary to fire it?'

'No,' Lady Tessa admitted. 'We don't even know if it does need anything special. But it was different, new, and unique; that means it's non-standard. Which may give us our one chance to neutralize this situation. If there is any hardware requirement involved, she's going to have to break cover and approach a defence contractor.'

'She might not have to,' Monica said. 'She'll have friends, sympathizers; certainly in the Dorados. She can go to them.'

'I hope she does. The agency has kept the Garissan survivors under surveillance for decades, just in case any of them try to pull any stupid revenge stunts.' She turned from the window. 'I'm sending you there to brief their head of station. It's a reasonable assumption she'll turn up there eventually, and it may help having someone familiar with her on the ground.'

Monica nodded in defeat. 'Yes, Chief.'

'Don't look so tragic. I'm the one who's going to have to report back to Kulu and tell the Director we lost her. You're getting off lightly.'

*

The meeting in the Confederation Navy bureau on the forty-fifth floor of the StMichelle starscraper was synchronous with that of the ESA in both time and content. In the bureau it was an aghast Commander Olsen Neale who accessed the sensevise memory of Mzu's abrupt exit from the habitat as recorded by a thoroughly despondent Pauline Webb.

When the file ended he asked a few supplementary questions, and came to the same conclusions as Lady Tessa. 'We can assume she has access to the kind of money necessary to buy whatever systems she needs to use the Alchemist, and install them in a combat-capable ship,' he said. 'But I don't think it'll be the *Udat*; that's too high profile now. Every Navy ship and government is going to be hunting it inside a week.'

'Do you think the Alchemist really does exist, then, sir?' Pauline asked.

'CNIS has always believed so, even though it could never track down any solid evidence. And after this, I don't think there can be any doubt. Even if it wasn't stored in zero-tau, don't forget she knows how to build another one. Another hundred, come to that.'

Monica hung her head. 'Shit, but we screwed up big-time.'

'Yes. I always thought we were a little over-dependent on the Lord of Ruin's benevolence in keeping her here.' He made a finger-fluttering gesture with one hand, and muttered: 'No offence.'

The AV pillar on his desktop processor block sparkled momentarily. 'None taken,' said Tranquillity.

'We also got complacent with how static the whole situation had become. You were quite right when you said she'd fooled us for quarter of a century. Bloody hell, but that is an awful long time to keep a charade going. Anyone who can hate for that long isn't going to be fooling around. She's gone because she thinks she has a good chance to use the Alchemist against Omuta.'

'Yes, sir.'

Olsen Neale made an effort to suppress his worry and formulate some kind of coherent response to the situation. One he didn't have a single contingency plan for. No one at CNIS ever believed she could actually escape. 'I'll leave for Trafalgar right away. Our first priority is to inform Admiral Lalwani that Mzu's gone, so she can start activating our assets to find her. Then the First Admiral will have to beef up Omuta's defences. Damn, that's another squadron which the navy can't spare, not now.'

'The Laton scare will make it difficult for her to travel,' Pauline said.

'Let's hope so. But just in case, I want you to go to the Dorados and alert our bureau that she may put in an appearance soon.'

\*

Samuel, of course, didn't have to physically meet with the other three Edenist intelligence operatives in the habitat. They simply conferred with each other via affinity, then Samuel and a colleague called Tringa headed for the spaceport. Samuel chartered a starship to take him to the Dorados, while Tringa found one which would convey him to Jupiter so he could warn the Consensus.

\*

The same scenario was played out by the other eight national Intelligence agency teams assigned to watch Mzu. In each case, it was decided that alerting their respective directors was the primary requirement; three of them also dispatched operatives to the Dorados to watch for Mzu.

The spaceport charter agents who had been suffering badly from the lack of flights brought on by the Laton scare suddenly found business picking up.

\*

So now you have to decide if you're going to allow them to inform their homeworlds, Tranquillity said. For once the word gets out, you will be unable to control further events.

I didn't really control events before. I was like an umpire ensuring fair play.

Well, now is your chance to get down off your stool and take part in the game.

Don't tempt me. I have enough problems right now with the Laymil's Reality Dysfunction. If dear grandfather Michael was right, that may yet turn out to be a lot more trouble than Mzu's Alchemist.

I concede the point. But I do need to know if I am to permit the agency operatives to depart.

Ione opened her eyes to look through the window, but the water outside was sable black now, there was nothing to see apart from a weak reflection of herself in the glass. For the first time in her life she began to understand what loneliness was.

You have me, Tranquillity assured her gently.

I know. But in a way you are a part of me. It would be nice to have someone else's shoulder to lean on occasionally.

A someone such as Joshua?

Don't be so bitchy.

I'm sorry. Why don't you ask Clement to come to the apartment? He makes you happy.

He makes me orgasm, you mean.

Is there a difference?

Yes, but don't ask me to explain it. It's just that I'm looking for more than physical contentment right now. These are big decisions I'm making here. They could affect millions of people, hundreds of millions.

You have known this time would come ever since you were conceived. It is what your life is for.

Most of the Saldanas, yes. They make a dozen decisions like this before lunch every day. Not me. I think the family's arrogance gene might be inactive in my case.

It is more likely to be a hormonal imbalance due to your pregnancy which is making you procrastinate.

She laughed out loud, the sound echoing round the vast room. You really don't understand the difference between your thought processes and mine, do you?

I believe I do.

Ione had the silliest vision of a two kilometre long nose sniffing disdainfully. Her laugh turned to a giggle. OK, no more procrastination. Let's be logical. We blew it with safeguarding Mzu, and now she's presumably on her way to exterminate Omuta's star.

And you and I certainly don't have the kind of resources available to the ESA and other agencies to track her down and stop her. Right?

An elegant summary.

Thank you. Therefore, the best chance to stop her will be to let the Intelligence community off the leash.

Granted.

Then we let them out. At least that way Omuta stands a chance of survival. I don't think I really want a genocide on my conscience. Nor, I suspect, do you.

Very well. I will not restrict their starships from departing.

Which just leaves us with what's going to happen afterwards. If they do catch her, someone is going to wind up with the technology to build Alchemist devices. As Monica said on the beach, every government will want it to safeguard their own particular version of democracy.

Yes. The old term for a nation acquiring such an overwhelming military advantage is a 'superpower'. At the very least, the emergence of such a nation will result in an arms race as other governments try to acquire the Alchemist technology, which will not benefit the general Confederation economy. And if they succeed, the Confederation will be plunged into a deterrence cycle; a balance of terror.

And it was all my fault.

Not quite. Dr Alkad Mzu invented the Alchemist. From that moment on all subsequent events were inevitable. There is a saying that once you have released the genie from the bottle, he cannot be put back.

Maybe not. But it wouldn't hurt to have a go.

\*

From the air Avon's capital, Regina, was almost indistinguishable from any big city on a fully developed and industrialized planet within the Confederation: dark gritty stain of buildings which crept a little further outward into the green countryside with every passing year. Only the steeper hill slopes and crinkled watercourses inconvenienced the encroachment to any degree, although in the central districts even they had been tamed with metal and carbon concrete. Again, as normal, a clump of skyscrapers occupied the very heart of the city, forming the commercial, financial, and government administration district. A lavish display of crystal spires, thick composite cylinders, and gloss-metal neo-modern towers, reflecting the planet's economic strength.

The one exception to the standard urban layout was a second, smaller, cluster of silver and white skyscrapers occupying the shore of a long lake on the city's easternmost district. Like the Forbidden City of the ancient Chinese Emperors, it existed aloof from the rest of Regina, yet it held sway over billions of lives. Home to one and a half million people, it was sixteen square kilometres of foreign diplomatic compounds, embassies, legal firms, multistellar corporation offices, navy barracks, executive agencies, media studios, and a thousand catering and leisure company franchises. This overcrowded, overpriced, bureaucratic mother-hive formed a protective ring around the Assembly building which straddled the lakeshore, itself looking more like a domed sports stadium than the very seat of the Confederation.

The stadium analogy was continued inside the main chamber, with tiered ranks of seats circling the central Polity Council table. First Admiral Samual Aleksandrovich always likened it to a gladiatorial arena, where the current Polity Council members had to present and defend their resolutions. It was ninety per cent theatre; but politicians, even in this day and age, clung to the public stage.

As one of the four permanent members of the Polity Council, the First Admiral had the right and authority to summon a full session of the Assembly. It was a right which earlier First Admirals had exercised only three times in the Confederation's history; twice to request additional vessels from member states to prevent inter-system wars, and once to ask for the resources to track down Laton.

Samual Aleksandrovich hadn't envisaged himself being number four. But there really hadn't been time to consult with the President after the voidhawk from Atlantis arrived at Trafalgar. And after reviewing the report it carried, Samual Aleksandrovich was convinced that time was a crucial issue. Mere hours could make a colossal difference if the possessed were to be prevented from infiltrating unsuspecting worlds.

So now here he was in his dress uniform walking towards the Polity Council table under the bright lights shining out of a black marble ceiling; Captain Khanna on one side, Admiral Lalwani on the other. The chamber's tiers were full of diplomats and aides shuffling to their designated seats, their combined grumbling sounding like a couple of bulldozers attacking the foundations. A glance upward showed him the media gallery was packed. Everybody wanted in on the phenomenon.

You wouldn't if you knew, he thought emphatically.

The President, Olton Haaker, wearing his traditional Arab robe, took his seat at the horseshoe oak table along with the other members of the Polity Council. Samual Aleksandrovich thought Haaker looked nervous. A telling sign, the old Brezni-kan was a superb, not to mention wily, diplomat. This was his second five-year term of office; and only four of the last fifteen presidents had managed to gain re-nomination.

Rittagu-FHU, the Tyrathca Ambassador, walked imperiously across the chamber floor, minute particles of bronze-coloured powder shaking out of her scales to dust the tiles below her. She reached one end of the table, and eased her large body onto a broad cradle arrangement. Her mate hooted softly at her from a similar cradle in the front tier.

Samual Aleksandrovich wished it was the Kiint who held the xenoc Polity Council seat this term. The two xenoc member races alternated every three years; although there were those in the Assembly who said that the xenocs should join the rota for the Polity Council seats like every human government had to.

The Assembly speaker called for silence, and announced that

the First Admiral had been granted the floor under article nine of the Confederation Charter. As he got to his feet, Samual Aleksandrovich studied the blocs in the tiers which he would have to carry. The Edenists, of course, he already had. Earth's Govcentral would probably follow the Edenists, given their strong alliance. Other key powers were Oshanko, New Washington, Nanjing, Holstein, Petersburg, and inevitably, the Kulu Kingdom, which probably had the most undue influence of all – and thank God the Saldanas were keen supporters of the Confederation.

In a way he was angry that an issue as vital as this (surely the most vital in human history?) would be dependent on who was speaking with who, whose ideologies clashed, whose religions denounced the other. The whole point of ethnic-streaming colonies, as Earth had painfully discovered centuries ago during the Great Dispersal, was that foreign cultures can live harmoniously with each other providing they don't have to live jammed together on the same planet. And the Assembly allowed that wider spirit of cooperation to continue and flourish. In theory.

'I have asked for this session because I wish to call for a full state of emergency to be declared,' Samual Aleksandrovich said. 'Unfortunately, what started off as the Laton situation has now become immeasurably graver. If you would care to access the sensevise account which has just arrived from Atlantis ...' He datavised the main processor to play the recording.

Diplomats they might have been, but even their training couldn't help them maintain poker faces as the events of Pernik Island unravelled inside their skulls. The First Admiral waited impassively as the gasps and grimaces appeared simultaneously throughout the chamber. It took quarter of an hour to run, and many broke off during the playback to check the reactions of their colleagues, or perhaps even to make sure they were receiving the right recording, and not some elaborate horrorsense.

Olton Haaker got to his feet when it finished, and stared at Samual Aleksandrovich for a long time before speaking. The First Admiral wondered exactly how he was taking it, the President's Muslim faith was a strong one. *Just what does he think about djinns coming forth?*

'Are you certain this information is genuine?' the President asked.

Samual Aleksandrovich signalled Admiral Lalwani, the CNIS chief, who was sitting in one of the chairs behind him. She got to her feet. 'We vouch for its authenticity,' she said, and sat down again.

A number of intense stares were directed at Cayeaux, the Edenist Ambassador, who bore them stoically.

*How typical to blame the messenger,* the First Admiral thought.

'Very well, what exactly are you proposing we should do?' the President asked.

'Firstly, the vote for a state of emergency will provide a considerable reserve of national naval ships for the Confederation Navy,' the First Admiral said. 'We shall require all those national squadrons pledged to us to be transferred over to their respective Confederation fleets as soon as possible. Preferably within a week.' That didn't go down well, but he was ready for it. 'Combating the threat we now face cannot be achieved by confronting it in a piecemeal fashion. Our response has to be swift and overwhelming. That can only be achieved with the full strength of the navy.'

'But to what end?' the Govcentral Ambassador asked. 'What possible solution can you provide for the dead coming back? You can't be considering killing those who are possessed.'

'No, we cannot do that,' the First Admiral acknowledged. 'And unfortunately they know it, which will provide them with a huge advantage. We are faced with what is essentially the greatest hostage scenario ever. So I propose we do what we always do in such situations, and that is play for time while a genuine solution is found. Whilst I have no idea what that will be, the overall policy we must adopt I consider to be very clearcut. We must prevent the problem from spreading beyond those star systems in which it has already taken hold. To that end, I would ask for a further resolution requiring the cessation of all civil and commercial starflights, effective immediately. The number of flights is already reducing sharply because of the Laton crisis, reducing it to zero should not prove difficult. Once a Confederationwide quarantine is imposed, it will become easier to target our forces where they will be most effective.'

'What do you mean, effective?' the President demanded. 'You just said we cannot consider an armed response.'

'No, sir, I said we cannot consider it as the ultimate solution. What it can, and must, be used for is to prevent the spread of possessed from star systems which they have infiltrated. If they ever manage to conquer an industrialized system, they will undoubtedly commit its full potential against us to further their aim; which, as Laton has told us, is total annexation. We have to be ready to match that, probably on several separate fronts. If we do not they will multiply at an exponential rate, and the entire Confederation will fall, every living human will become possessed.'

'Are you saying we just abandon star systems that have been taken over?'

'We must isolate them until we have a solution which works. I already have a science team examining the possessed woman we hold in Trafalgar, hopefully its research may produce some answers.'

A loud murmur of consternation spiralled round the tiers at that disclosure.

'You have one captured?' the President enquired in surprise.

'Yes, sir. We didn't know exactly what she was until the voidhawk from Atlantis came. But now we do, our investigation can proceed along more purposeful lines.'

'I see.' The President seemed at a loss. He glanced at the Speaker, who inclined his head.

'I second the motion of the First Admiral for a state of emergency,' the President said formally.

'One vote down, eight hundred to go,' Admiral Lalwani whispered.

The speaker rang the silver bell on the table in front of him. 'As, at this time, there would seem little to add to the information the First Admiral has presented to us, I will now call upon those here present to cast their votes on the resolution before you.'

Rittagu-FHU emitted a piping hoot, and rose to her feet. Her thick head swung round to look at the First Admiral, a motion which sent the chemical program teats along her neck bobbling, delivering a leathery slapping sound. She worked her double lips elaborately, producing a prolonged gabble. 'Speaker statement not true,' the translator block on the table said. 'I have much to add. Elemental humans, dead humans; these are not part of Tyrathca nature. We did not know such things were possible for you. We impugn these assaults upon what is real today. If you all have this ability to become elemental, then you all threaten the Tyrathca. This is frightening for us. We must withdraw from contact with humans.'

'I assure you, Ambassador, we did not know of this ourselves,' the President said. 'It frightens us as much as it does you. I would ask you to retain at least some lines of communication until this situation can be resolved.'

Rittagu-FHU's fluting reply was translated as: 'Who says this?'

Olton Haaker's weary face reflected his puzzlement. He flicked a glance at his equally uncertain aides. 'I do.'

'But who speaks?'

'I'm sorry, Ambassador, I don't understand.'

'You say you speak. Who are you? I see Olton Haaker standing here today, as he has stood many times. I do not know if it is Olton Haaker. I do not know if it is an *elemental* human.'

'I assure you I'm not!' the President spluttered.

'I do not know that. What is the difference?' She turned her gaze on the First Admiral, big glassy eyes displaying no emotions he could ever understand. 'Is there a way of knowing?'

'There seems to be a localized disturbance of electronic systems in the presence of anyone possessed,' he said. 'That's the only method of detection we have now. But we're working on other techniques.'

'You do not know.'

'The possessions started on Lalonde. The first starship to reach here from that planet was *Ilex*, and it came directly. We can be safe in assuming that no one in the Avon system has been possessed yet.'

'You do not know.'

Samual Aleksandrovich couldn't answer. *I'm sure, but the damn creature is right. Certainty is no longer possible. But then humans have never needed absolutes to convince themselves. The Tyrathca have, and it's a difference which divides us far greater than our biology.*

When he appealed silently to the President, he met a blank face. Very calmly, he said: 'I do not know.'

There was a subliminal suggestion of a mass sigh from the tiers, maybe even resentment.

*But I did what was right, I answered her on her own terms.*

'I express gratitude that you speak the truth,' Rittagu-FHU said. 'Now I do what is my task in this place, and speak for my race. The Tyrathca this day end our contact with all humans. We will leave your worlds. Do not come to ours.'

Rittagu-FHU stretched out a long arm, and a nine-fingered circular hand switched off her translator block. She hooted to her mate, and together they made their way to the exit.

The vast chamber was utterly silent as the door slid shut behind them.

Olton Haaker cleared his throat, squared his shoulders, and faced the Kiint ambassador who was standing passively in the bottom tier. 'If you wish to leave us, Ambassador Roulor, then of course we shall provide every assistance in returning you and the other Kiint ambassadors to your homeworld. This is a human problem after all, we do not wish to jeopardize our fruitful relationship by endangering you.'

One of the snow-white Kiint's tractamorphic arms uncurled to hold up a small processor block, its AV projection pillar produced a moiré sparkle. 'Being alive is a substantial risk, Mr President,' Roulor said. 'Danger always balances enjoyment. To find one, you must face and know the other. And you are wrong in saying that it is a human problem. All sentient races eventually discover the truth of death.'

'You mean you knew?' Olton Haaker asked, his diplomatic demeanour badly broken.

'We are aware of our nature, yes. We confronted it once, a great time ago, and we survived. Now you must do the same. We cannot help you in this struggle which you are facing, but we do sympathize.'

*

Starflight traffic to Valisk was dropping off; ten per cent in two days. Even though Rubra's subsidiary thought routines managed the habitat's traffic control, the statistic hadn't registered with his principal personality. It was the economics of the shortfall which finally alerted him. The flights were all scheduled charters, bringing components to the industrial stations of his precious Magellanic Itg company. None of them were blackhawk flights from his own fleet, it was only Adamist ships.

Curious, he reviewed all the news fleks delivered by those starships which had arrived recently, searching for a reason, some crisis or emergency in another section of the Confederation. He drew a blank.

It was only when his principal personality routine made its

weekly check on Fairuza that Rubra realized something was wrong inside the habitat as well. Fairuza was another of his protégés, a ninth-generation descendant who had showed promise from an early age.

Promise, as defined by Rubra, consisted principally of the urge to exert himself as leader of the other boys at the day club, snatching the biggest share, be it of sweets or game processor time; a certain cruel streak with regard to pets; contempt for his timid, loving parents. It marked him out as a greedy, short-tempered, bullying, disobedient, generally nasty little boy. Rubra was delighted.

When Fairuza reached ten years of age, the slow waves of encouragement began to twist their way into his psyche. Dark yearnings to go further, a feeling of righteousness, a sense of destiny, a quite insufferable ego. It was all due to Rubra's silent desires oozing continually into his skull.

The whole moulding process had gone wrong so often in the past. Valisk was littered with the neurotic detritus of Rubra's earlier attempts to create a dynamic ruthless personality in what he considered his own image. He wanted so much to forge such a creature, someone worthy to command Magellanic Itg. And for two hundred years he had endured the humiliation of his own flesh and blood failing him time and again.

But Fairuza had a resilient quality which was rare amongst his diverse family members. So far he had displayed few of the psychological weaknesses which ruined all the others. Rubra had hopes for him, almost as many hopes as he once had for Dariat.

However, when Rubra summoned the subroutine which monitored the fourteen-year-old youth, nothing happened. A giant ripple of surprise ran down the entire length of the habitat's neural strata. Servitor animals flinched and juddered as it passed below them. Thick muscle rings regulating the flow of fluids inside the huge network of nutrient capillaries and water channels buried deep in the polyp shell spasmed, creating surges and swirls which took the autonomic routines over half an hour to calm and return to normal. All eight thousand of Rubra's descendants shivered uncontrollably, and for no reason they could understand, even the children who had no knowledge of their true nature yet.

For a moment, Rubra didn't know what to do. His personality was distributed evenly through the habitat's neural strata, a condition the original designers of Eden had called a homogenized presence. Every routine and subroutine and autonomic routine was at once whole and separate. All perceptual information received by any sensitive cell was immediately disseminated for storage uniformly along the strata. Failure, any failure, was inconceivable.

Failure meant his own thoughts were malfunctioning. His mind, the one true aspect of self left to him, was flawed.

After surprise, inevitably, came fear. There could be few reasons for such a disaster. He might finally be succumbing to high-level psychological disorders. It was a condition the Edenists always predicted he would develop after enduring centuries of loneliness coupled with frustration at his inability to find a worthy heir.

He began to design a series of entirely new routines which would analyse his own mental architecture. Like undercover wraiths, these visitants flashed silently through the neural strata on their missions to spy on the performance of each subroutine without it being aware, reporting back on his own performance.

A list of flaws began to emerge. They made a strange compilation. Some subroutines, like Fairuza's monitor, were missing completely, others were inactive, then there were instances of memory dissemination being blocked. The lack of any logical pattern bothered him. Rubra didn't doubt that he was under attack, but it was a most peculiar method of assault. However, one aspect of the attack was perfectly clear: whoever was behind the disruptions had a perfect understanding of both affinity and a habitat's thought routines. He couldn't believe it was the Edenists, not them with their repugnant superiority. They considered time to be their premier weapon against him; the Kohistan Consensus was of the opinion that he could not sustain himself for more than a few centuries. And a covert undeclared war on someone who didn't threaten them was an inconceivable breach of their culture's ethics. No, it had to be someone else. Someone more intimate.

Rubra reviewed the monitor subroutines which had been rendered inactive. There were seven: six of them were assigned to ordinary descendants, all of them under twenty; as they weren't yet involved with Magellanic Itg they didn't require anything more than basic observation to keep an eye on them. But the seventh ... Rubra hadn't bothered to examine him at any time during the last fifteen years of their thirty-year estrangement, his greatest ever failure: Dariat.

The intimation was profoundly shocking. Somehow Dariat had achieved a degree of control over the habitat routines. But then Dariat had managed to block all Rubra's attempts to gain access to his mind through affinity ever since that fateful day thirty years ago. Dariat, for all his massive imperfections, was unique.

Rubra reacted to the revelation by erecting safeguards all around his primary personality pattern; input filters which would scrutinize all the information reaching him for Trojan viruses. He wasn't certain exactly what Dariat was trying to achieve by interfering with the subroutines, but he knew the man still blamed him for Anastasia Rigel's death. Ultimately Dariat would try to extract his vengeance.

What remarkable determination. It actually rivalled his own.

Rubra hadn't been so stimulated for decades. Maybe he could still negotiate with Dariat; after all, the man was not yet fifty, there was another half-century of useful life left in him. And if they couldn't come to an agreement, well ... he could always be cloned. All Rubra needed for that was a single living cell.

With his mentality as secure as he could make it, he formed a succession of new orders. Again, they were different to anything which existed in the neural strata before; fresh patterns, a modified routing hierarchy. Invisible to anyone accustomed to the standard thought routines. The clandestine command went out to every optically sensitive cell, every affinity capable descendant, every servitor animal: find a match for Dariat's visual image.

It took seven minutes. And it wasn't quite what Rubra was expecting.

A number of the observation routines on the eighty-fifth floor of the Kandi starscraper had been tampered with. The Kandi was used mainly by the less wholesome of Valisk's residents, which, given the overall content of the population, meant that the starscraper was just about the last resort for the real lowlife. It was in the apartment of Anders Bospoort, vice lord and semi-professional rapist, where the greatest anomaly was centred. One of the observation subroutines had been altered to include a memory segment. Instead of observing the apartment, and feeding the processed image directly into a general event analysis routine it was simply substituting an old visualization of the rooms for the real-time picture.

Rubra solved the problem by wiping the old routine entirely, and replacing it with a viable one. The apartment he was now looking round was a shambles, furniture out of place and smothered by every kind of male and female clothing, plates of half-eaten food discarded at random, empty bottles lying about. High-capacity Kulu Corporation processor blocks and dozens of technical encyclopedia fleks were piled up on the tables – not exactly Bospoort's usual bedtime material.

With the restoration of true sight and sound came an olfactory sense; a stiff price to pay, the feculent stink in the apartment was dreadful. The reason was simple: Dariat's obese corpse was lying slumped at the foot of the bed in the master bedroom. There was no sign of foul play, no bruising, no stab wounds, no energy beam charring. Whatever the cause, it had left an appallingly twisted grin scrawled across his chubby face. Rubra couldn't help but think that Dariat had actually enjoyed dying.

*

Dariat was inordinately happy with his new, captive, body. He had quite forgotten what it was like to be skinny; to move fast, to slither adroitly between the closing doors of a lift, to be able to wear proper clothes instead of a shabby toga. And youth, of course, that was another advantage. A more vital physique, lean and strong. That Horgan was only fifteen years old was of no consequence, the energistic power made up for everything. He chose the appearance of a twenty-one-year-old, a male in his physical prime, his dark skin smooth and glossy, hair worn thick, long, and jet black. His clothes were white, simple cotton pantaloons and shirt, thin enough to show off the panther flex of muscles. Nothing as gross-out as Bospoort's ridiculous macho frame which Ross Nash wore, but he'd certainly drawn the eye of several girls.

In fact, possession with all its glories was almost enough to make him renege on his task. Almost, but not quite. His agenda remained separate from the others, for unlike them he wasn't scared of death, of returning to the beyond. He believed in the spirituality Anastasia had preached, now as never before. The beyond was only part of the mystery of dying; God's creativity was boundless, of course more continua existed, an after-afterlife.

He pondered this as he walked with his fellow possessors towards the Tacoul Tavern. The others were all desperately intent on their mission, and so humourless.

The Tacoul Tavern was a perfect microcosm of life in Valisk. Its once stylish black and silver crystalline interior was a form now abandoned even by designers of retro chic, its food came out of packages where once its cuisine was prepared by chefs in a five-star kitchen, its waitresses were really too old for the short skirts they wore, and its clientele neither questioned nor cared about its inexorable decline. Like most bars it tended to attract one type of customer, in this case the starship crews.

There were a couple of dozen people seated at the various rock-mushroom tables when Dariat followed Kiera Salter inside. She sauntered over to the bar and ordered a drink for herself. Two men offered to buy it for her. While the charade played out, Dariat chose a table by the door, and studied the big room. They'd done well, five of the drinkers had the tell-tale indigo eyes of Rubra's descendants, and all of them wore ship-suits with a silver star on the epaulette: blackhawk captains.

Dariat concentrated on the observation routines operating in the neural strata behind the Tavern's walls, floor, and ceiling. Abraham, Matkin, and Graci, who also possessed affinity capable bodies, were doing the same thing, all four of them sending out a multitude of subversive commands to isolate the room and everything which happened in it from Rubra's principal personality.

He had taught them well. It took the foursome barely a minute to corrupt the simple routines, turning the Tacoul Tavern into a perceptual null zone. To complete the act, the muscle-membrane door contracted quietly, its grey pumicelike surface becoming an intractable barrier, sealing everyone inside.

Kiera Salter stood up, dismissing her would-be suitors with a contemptuous gesture. When one of them rose and started to say something, she struck him casually, an open-handed slap across his temple. The blow sent him flailing backwards. He struck the polyp floor hard, yelling with pain. She laughed and blew him a kiss as he dabbed at the blood seeping from his nose. 'No chance, lover boy.' The long leather purse in her hand morphed into a pump-action shotgun. She swung it round to point towards the startled patrons, and blew one of the ceiling's flickering light globes to pieces.

Everyone ducked as splinters of pearl-white composite rained down. Several people were attempting to datavise emergency calls into the room's net processor. Electronics were the first thing the possessed had disabled.

'OK, people,' Kiera announced, with a grossly stressed American twang. 'This is a stick-up. Don't nobody move, and shove your valuables in this here sack.'

Dariat sighed in contempt. It seemed altogether inappropriate that a complete bitch like Kiera should possess the body of such a physically sublime girl as Marie Skibbow. 'There's no need for all this,' he said. 'We only came for the blackhawk captains. Let's just keep focused on that, shall we?'

'Maybe there's no need,' she said, 'but there's certainly plenty of want.'

'You know what, Kiera, you really are a complete arsehole.'

'That so?' She flung a bolt of white fire at him.

Waitresses and customers alike shouted in alarm and dived for cover. Dariat just managed to deflect the bolt, thumping it aside with a fist he imagined as a fat table-tennis bat. The white fire bounced about enthusiastically, careering off tables and chairs. But not before the strike gave him a vicious electric shock, jangling all the nerves in his arm.

'Give the lectures a rest, Dariat,' Kiera said. 'We do what we're driven to do.'

'Nobody drove you to do that. It hurt.'

'Oh, get real, you warped slob. You'd enjoy yourself a lot more if you didn't have that morals bug stuffed so far up your arse.'

Klaus Schiller and Matkin sniggered at his discomfort.

'You're screwing up everything with this childishness,' Dariat said. 'If we are to acquire the blackhawks we cannot afford your indiscipline. The Lord Tarrug is making you dance to his tune. Contain yourself, listen to your inner music.'

She shouldered the shotgun and levelled an annoyed finger at him. 'One more word of that New Age bullshit, and I swear

I'll take your head clean off. We brought you along so that you could deal with the habitat personality, that's all. I'm the one who lays down our goals. I have concrete bloody policies; policies which are going to help us come up trumps. Policies with attitude. What the fuck have you got to offer us, slob? Chop away at the habitat's floor for a century until we find this Rubra's brain, then stamp on it. Is that it? Is that your big, useful plan?'

'No,' he said with wooden calm. 'I keep telling you, Rubra cannot be defeated by physical means. This policy you have for taking over the habitat population isn't going to work until we've dealt with him. I think we're making a mistake with the blackhawks, not even their physical power can help us beat him. And if we start taking them over, we risk drawing attention to ourselves.'

'As Allah wills,' Matkin muttered.

'But don't you see?' Dariat appealed to him. 'If we concentrate on annihilating Rubra and possessing the neural strata, then we can achieve anything. We'll be like gods.'

'That is close to blasphemy, son,' Abraham Canaan said. 'You should have a little more care in what you say.'

'Shit. Look, godlike, OK? The point is—'

'The point, Dariat,' Kiera said, aligning the shotgun on him for emphasis, 'is that you are steaming for vengeance. Don't try and plead otherwise, because you are even insane enough to kill yourself in order to achieve it. We know what we are doing, we are multiplying our numbers to protect ourselves. If you don't wish to do that, then perhaps you need a little more time in the beyond to set your mind straight.'

Even as he gathered himself to argue, he realized he'd lost. He could see the blank expressions hardening around the other possessed, while his mind simultaneously perceived their emotions chilling. Weak fools. They really didn't care about anything other than the now. They were animals. But animals whose help he would ultimately need.

Kiera had won again, just as she had when she insisted on him proving his loyalty through self-sacrifice. The possessed looked to her for leadership, not him.

'All right,' Dariat said. 'Have it your way.' For now.

'Thank you,' Kiera said with heavy irony. She grinned, and sauntered over to the first blackhawk captain.

During the altercation, the rest of the Tacoul Tavern had been as quiet as people invariably become when total strangers are discussing your fate two metres in front of you. Now the discussion was over. Fate decided.

The waitresses squealed, huddling together at the bar. Seven of the starship personnel made a break for the closed muscle-membrane door. Five actually launched themselves at the possessed, wielding whatever came to hand: fission blades (which malfunctioned), broken bottles, nervejam sticks (also useless), and bare fists.

White fire flared in retaliation: globes aimed at knees and ankles, disabling and maiming; whip tendrils which coiled around legs like scalding manacles.

With their victims thrashing about on the floor, and the stink of burnt flesh in the air, the possessed closed in.

Rocio Condra had been trapped in the beyond for five centuries when the time of miracles came. An existence of madness, which he could only liken to the last moment of smothering being drawn out and out and out ... And always in total darkness, silence, numbness. His life had replayed itself a million times, but that wasn't nearly enough.

Then came the miracles, sensations leaking in from the universe outside. Cracks in the nothingness of the beyond which would open and shut in fractions of a second, akin to storm clouds of soot parting to let through the delicious golden sunlight of dawn. And every time, a single lost soul would fly into the blinding, deafening deluge of reality, out into freedom and beauty. Along with all the others left behind, Rocio would howl his frustration into the void. Then they would redouble their pleas and prayers and pledges to the obdurate, indifferent living, offering them salvation and ennoblement if they would just help.

Perhaps such promises actually worked. More and more of the cracks were appearing, so many that they had become a torment in their own right. To know there was a route out, and yet always denied.

Except now. This time ... This time the glory arose all around Rocio Condra so loud and bright it nearly overwhelmed him. Furled with the torrent was someone crying for help, for the agony to stop.

'I'll help,' Rocio lied perilously. 'I'll stop it happening.'

Pain flooded into him as the frantic thoughts clung to his false words. It was far, far more than the usual meshing of souls in search of bitter sustenance. He could feel himself gaining weight and strength as their thoughts entwined. And the pain surged towards ecstasy. Rocio could actually feel legs and arms jerking as agonizing heat played over skin, a throat which had been stung raw from screaming. It was all quite delicious, the kind of high a masochist would relish.

The man's thoughts were becoming weaker, smaller, as Rocio pushed and wriggled himself deeper into the brain's neural pathways. As he did so, more of the old human experiences made their eminently welcome return, the air rushing into his lungs, thud of a heart. And all the while his new host was diminishing. The way Rocio pushed him down, confining his soul, was almost instinctive, and becoming easier by the second.

He could hear the other lost souls of the beyond shrieking their outrage that he was the one to gain salvation. The bitter threats, the accusations of unworthiness.

Then there was just his host's feeble protests, and a second oddly distant voice begging to know what was happening to its beloved. He squeezed the host's soul away, expanding his own mind to fill the entire brain.

'That's enough,' a woman's voice said. 'We need you for something more important.'

'Leave me!' he coughed. 'I'm almost in, almost—' His strength was growing, the captive body starting to respond. Tear-drowned eyes revealed the wavery outline of three figures bending over him. Figures which must surely be angels. A gloriously pretty girl clad only in a resplendent white corona.

'No,' she said. 'Get into the blackhawk. Now.'

There must have been some terrible mistake. Didn't they understand? This was the miracle. The redemption. 'I'm in,' Rocio told them. 'Look, see? I'm in now. I've done it.' He made one of his new hands rise, seeing blisters like big translucent fungi hanging from every finger.

'Then get out.'

The hand disintegrated. Blood splattered across his face, obliterating his sight. He wanted to scream, but his vocal cords were too coarsened to obey.

'Get into the blackhawk, you little pillock, or we'll send you right back into the beyond again. And this time we'll never let you return.'

Another burst of quite astonishing pain, followed by equally frightening numbness, told him his right foot had been destroyed. They were gnawing away at his beautiful new flesh, leaving him nothing. He raged barrenly at the unfairness of it all. Then strange echoey sensations blossomed into his mind.

**See?** Dariat asked. **It's simple, apply your thoughts like _this_.**

He did, and affinity opened, joining him with the *Mindori*.

**What is happening?** the frantic blackhawk asked.

Rocio's entire left leg was obliterated. White fire engulfed his groin and the stumpy remnant of his right leg.

**Peran!** the blackhawk called.

Rocio superimposed the captain's mind-tone over his own thoughts. **Help me, _Mindori_.**

**How? What is happening? I could not feel you. You closed yourself to me. Why? You have never done that before.**

**I'm sorry. It's the pain, a heart attack. I think I'm dying. Let me be with you, my friend.**

**Come. Hurry!**

He felt the affinity link broaden, and the blackhawk was there waiting for its captain, its mind full of love and sympathy; a gentle and trusting creature for all its size and indomitable power. Kiera Salter exerted still more of her own particular brand of pressure.

With a last curse at the devils who left him no choice, Rocio abandoned that cherished human body, sliding himself along the affinity link. This transfer was different to the one which had brought him back from beyond. That had been a forced entry, this was a welcome embrace from an unsophisticated lover, drawing him in to secure him from harm.

The energistic nexus which his soul engendered established itself within the waiting neural cells at the core of the blackhawk, and the linkage which connected him to the captain's body snapped as the skull was smashed apart by Kiera's triumphant fist.

The *Mindori* sat on its pedestal on the second of Valisk's three docking-ledges, patiently sucking nutrient fluid into its storage bladders. Beyond the eclipse of the habitat's non-rotating spaceport, the gas giant Opuntia was a pale cross-hatching of lime-green storm bands. The sight was a comforting one to the blackhawk. It had been birthed in Opuntia's rings, taking eighteen years to grow into the lengthy hundred and twenty-five metre cone of its mature form. Even among blackhawks, whose profiles varied considerably from the standard voidhawk disc shape, it was an oddity. Its polyp hull was a dusky green speckled with purple rings, while three fat finlike protuberances angled up out of its rear quarter. Given its squashed-missile appearance, the only option for the life-support module was a swept-back teardrop, which sat like a metallic saddle over the midsection of its upper hull.

Like all blackhawks and voidhawks its distortion field was

folded around the hull, barely operative while it was docked. A condition which ended as soon as Rocio Condra's soul invaded its neural cells. The number of neurons he now possessed was considerably larger than a human brain, increasing the amount of energistic power produced by the transdimensional twist. He extended himself out from the storage cluster *Mindori* had designated, breaking straight through the subroutines designed to support him.

The startled blackhawk managed to ask: **Who are you?** before he vanquished its mind. But he couldn't assume control of a blackhawk's enormously complex functions as easily as he could a human body. There was no instinct to guide him, no old familiar nerve impulse sequences to follow. This was an alien territory, there hadn't been any starships at all during his life, let alone living ones.

The autonomic routines, those regulating the *Mindori*'s organs, were fine, he just left them operating. However, the distortion field was controlled by direct conscious thought.

A couple of seconds after he gained possession it was billowing outwards uncontrollably. The blackhawk tipped back, pulling the pedestal feed tubes from their orifices. Nutrient fluid fountained out, flooding across the ledge until the habitat hurriedly closed the muscle valves.

*Mindori* rocked forwards then rose three metres above the mushroom-shaped pedestal as Rocio frantically tried to contain the oscillating fluxes running wild through his patterning cells. Unfortunately he couldn't quite coordinate the process. Mass-detection, the blackhawk's primary sense, came from a sophisticated secondary manipulation of the distortion field. Rocio couldn't work out where he was, let alone how to return to where he'd been.

**What the hell are you doing?** an irate Rubra asked.

*Mindori*'s stern swept round in a fast arc, lower fins almost scraping the ledge surface. The driver of a service vehicle slammed on the brakes, and reversed fast as the huge bitek starship swished past less than five metres in front of her cabin's bubble windscreen.

**Sorry,** Rocio said, frenziedly searching through the blackhawk's confined memories for some kind of command routine. **It's a power flux. I'll have it choked back in a second.**

Two more blackhawks had started similar gyrations as returned souls invaded their neurons. Rubra shot them vexed questions as well.

Rocio managed to regulate the field somewhat more effectively, and tie in the mass forms he was sensing to the images from the sensor blisters. His hull was slithering dangerously close to the rim of the docking-ledge.

He reconfigured the distortion field to impel him in the other direction. Which was fine, until he realized exactly how fast he was heading for the shell wall. And another (nonpossessed) blackhawk was sitting in the way.

**Can't stop,** he blurted at it.

It rose smooth and fast, shooting sixty metres straight up, protesting most indignantly. The *Mindori* skidded underneath, and just managed to halt before its rear fins struck Valisk's shell.

The remaining two blackhawk captains in the Tacoul Tavern were finally sacrificed to Kiera's strategy; and their ships shot off their respective pedestals like overpowered fireworks. Rubra and the other blackhawks fired alarmed queries after them. Three of the non-possessed blackhawks, thoroughly unnerved by their cousins' behaviour, also launched themselves from the ledge. A collision appeared imminent as the giant ships cavorted in the kilometre gap between the two ledges. Rubra began broadcasting flight vectors at them to try and steer them apart, demanding instant obedience.

By now, Rocio had mastered the basics of distortion-field dynamics. He manoeuvred his prodigious bulk back towards the original pedestal. After five attempts, edging round in jerky spirals, he managed to settle.

**If you've all *quite* finished**, Rubra said, as the agitated flock of blackhawks settled nervously.

Rocio sheepishly acquiesced to the admonishment. He and the other four possessed blackhawks exchanged private acknowledgements, swapping snippets of information on how to control their new bodies.

After experimenting for half an hour Rocio was pleasantly surprised with what he could see and feel. The gas giant environ was bloated with energy of many types, and a great deal of loose mass. There were overlapping tides of magnetic, electro-magnetic, and particle energy. Twenty moons, hundreds of small asteroids. They all traced delicate lines across his consciousness, registering in a multitude of fashions: harmonics, colours, scents. He had far more sensations available than those produced by a human sensorium. And any sense at all was better than the beyond.

The affinity band fell into a subdued silence as they waited to see what would happen next.

# 7

The overloaded spaceplane ascended cleanly enough through Lalonde's stratosphere, racing away from Amarisk's mountainous eastern coastline. It wasn't until the craft reached an altitude of a hundred kilometres, where the ions had thinned out to little more than a static-congested vacuum, that Ashly Hanson had to switch from the induction rams to the reaction drive. That was when their problems began. He had to redline the twin rocket engines in the tail, shunting up the voltage from the power cells, boosting the plasma temperature to dangerous heights. Coolant shunts emitted caution warnings, which he balanced against the craft's performance, heeding some, ignoring others. The job was his personal milieu: true piloting, knowing just how far he could push the systems, when to take calculated risks.

Power reserves, fuel levels, and safety margins formed fabulously elaborate interacting multi-textural graphics inside Ashly's mind as he continued the magic juggling act. The factors were slowly coming together, enabling him to decide on his best-case option: escape velocity at a hundred and twenty kilometres' altitude. In theory that would leave seven kilos of reaction mass in the tanks. 'But not a nice height,' he muttered to himself. Never mind, it gave them the ability to rendezvous with *Lady Mac*.

The reasons for the spaceplane's overstressed loading parameters, all twenty-nine of them, were chattering and whooping happily behind him, impervious to the efforts of Father Elwes and Kelly Tirrel to shush them. It wouldn't last, Ashly thought with an air of inevitable gloom, kids always threw up in zero-gee, especially ones as young as these.

He datavised the flight computer for a channel to *Lady Mac*. It took a while for the communication processor to lock on to Lalonde's satellite, and even then the bandwidth was reduced. Sore evidence of the malicious forces swirling invisibly round the doomed planet.

'Joshua?'

'Tracking you, Ashly.'

'You're going to have to manoeuvre to make rendezvous. I'm even having to expend my RC thruster reaction mass to achieve orbit. This is the vector.' Ashly datavised over the file from the spaceplane's flight computer.

'Jesus, that's cutting it fine.'

'I know. Sorry, but the kids weigh too much. And you're going to have to replace the reaction engines altogether when we reach port. I had to pump them over the safeties. A full structural-stress test probably wouldn't hurt, either.'

'Ah well, our no claims bonus got blown to shit in the battle anyway. Stand by for rendezvous in twelve minutes.'

'Thank you, Joshua.'

The contented babble coming from the spaceplane's cabin was quietening considerably. Acceleration had now declined to a twentieth of a gee as the orbital injection burn was finalized. Both rocket engines cut out. The flight computer reported four kilos of reaction mass were left in the tanks.

Then the first damp groan could be heard from the rear of the cabin. Ashly braced himself.

\*

Acceleration warnings sounded in the *Lady Macbeth*'s cabins. The Edenists working under the direction of Sarha Mitcham and Dahybi Yadev to prepare for the influx of some thirty children hurried to the couches and temporary mattresses. They all wore variants of the same haunted grey expression on their faces. Given what they'd been through in the last thirty hours, such consternation was understandable. The high-pitched hooting conjured up all the wrong associations.

'Don't worry,' Joshua announced. 'No killer gees this time, we're just manoeuvring.'

He was alone on the bridge, lights reduced to a pink glimmer, sharpening the resolution of the console hologram displays and AV projections. Strangely enough, the solitude felt good. He was now what he had always wanted to be – or thought he had – a starship captain, devoid of any other responsibility. Overseeing the flight computer and simultaneously piloting the big vessel along their new course vector towards the inert spaceplane didn't leave him with much time to brood on the consequences of their recent actions: Warlow dead, the mercenary team lost, the planet conquered, the rescue fleet broken. The whole shabby disaster really wasn't one he wanted to reflect on, nor the wider implications of having the possessed loose in the universe. Better to function usefully, to lose oneself in the mechanics of the problem at hand.

In a way his emotional climbdown was akin to a sense of release. The battles which they'd personally fought in, they'd won. Then they'd rescued the Edenists, the children, and now Kelly. And in a little while they were going home.

At the end, what more could you ask?

The unsuppressible guilt was his silent answer.

Joshua stabilized *Lady Mac* a kilometre above the spaceplane, allowing orbital mechanics to bring the two together. Both craft had fallen into the penumbra, reducing the planet below to a featureless black smear. Visually dead, only radar and infra-red could distinguish between oceans and continents.

He ordered the flight computer to establish communication

circuits with the small number of low-orbit observation satellites remaining. The image they provided built up quickly.

Amarisk had emerged completely into the daylight hemisphere now. He could see the continent was completely dominated by the huge red cloud. The vast patch must already cover nearly a quarter of the land, and it was expanding rapidly out from the Juliffe basin, its leading edges moving at hurricane velocities. Yet it still retained its silky consistency, a uniform sheet through which no glimpse of the ground below was possible. The grey blemish which had hung above the Quallheim Counties during the mercenaries' brief campaign had also vanished. Even the mountains where the Tyrathca lived proved no barrier; the cloud was bubbling round them, sealing over valleys. Only the very tallest peaks were left unclaimed, their jagged snowcaps sticking up from the red veil, icebergs bobbing through a sea of blood.

The sight had repelled Joshua before, now it frightened him. The sheer potency it intimated was appalling.

Joshua flicked back to the images coming in from the *Lady Mac*'s extended sensor clusters. The spaceplane was five hundred metres away, its wings already folded back. He played the starship's equatorial ion thrusters, and moved in, bringing the docking cradle round to engage the latches in the spaceplane's nose-cone.

Sitting in his pilot's seat, watching the performance through the narrow windscreen, Ashly was, as ever, amazed by Joshua's ability to control the huge spherical starship's motions. The docking cradle which had telescoped out of the hangar bay swung round gracefully until it was head-on, then slid over the squashed-bullet nose. Naturally the alignment matched first time.

Various clunking sounds were transmitted through the stress structure, and the spaceplane was slowly drawn inside the *Lady Mac*'s narrow cylindrical hangar. Ashly shuddered as another warm, sticky, smelly globe of fluid landed on his ship-suit. He didn't make the mistake of trying to swat it, that just broke the larger portions into smaller ones. And you could inhale those.

'Eight of you are going to have to stay inside the spaceplane cabin,' Sarha datavised as the hangar's airlock tube mated to the spaceplane.

'You're kidding me,' a dismayed Ashly replied.

'Bad luck, Ashly. But we're maxing out our life support with so many people on board. I really need the spaceplane carbon dioxide filters.'

'Oh, God,' he said miserably. 'OK. But send in some hand-held sanitizer units, and quickly.'

'They're already in the airlock waiting for you.'

'Thanks.'

'Send out the smallest children first, please. I'm going to cram them into the zero-tau pods.'

'Will do.' He datavised the flight computer to open the airlock hatch, then left his seat to talk with Father Elwes about which children should go where.

*Lady Macbeth*'s two undamaged fusion-drive tubes ignited as soon as the spaceplane was stowed inside the hull. She rose away from the planet at a steady one gee, heading up towards a jump coordinate which would align her on Tranquillity's star.

Far behind her, the middle section of the red cloud rippled and swirled in agitation. A tornado column swelled up from the centre, extending a good twenty kilometres above the twisting currents of cumulus. It flexed blindly for several minutes, like a beckoning – or clawing – finger. Then the *Lady Macbeth*'s sensor clusters and thermo-dump panels began to retract into their jump positions below the hull. Her brilliant blue-white fusion exhaust shrank away, and she coasted onwards and upwards for a brief minute until an event horizon claimed her.

The questing finger of cloud lost its vigour, and slowly bowed over in defeat, its glowing vapour reabsorbed into the now quiescent centre of the shroud. The leading edges continued their advance.

*

The view from the Monterey's Hilton was as spectacular as only a three hundred and fifty million dollar building could provide. Al Capone loved it. The Nixon suite was on the bottom floor of the tower, giving it a standard gravity. New California glided slowly past the curving radiation-shielded window which made up an entire wall of the master bedroom. The planet gleamed enticingly against the jet-black starfield. His one disappointment was that from here the stars didn't twinkle like they used to when he watched them at night above his summer retreat cottage at Round Lake. That aside, he felt like a king again.

The Hilton was a sixty-storey tower sticking out of the Monterey asteroid, orbiting a hundred and ten thousand kilometres above New California. Apart from Edenist habitat starscrapers (which it was modelled on) there were few structures like it in the Confederation. Tourists could rarely look down on terracompatible planets in such a fashion.

Which was stupid, Al thought, big business could make a packet out of hotels like the Hilton. But he couldn't spend all day looking at New California. He could sense his Organization's top lieutenants waiting patiently outside the suite. They'd learned quickly enough not to interrupt when he wanted his privacy, but they did need orders, to be kept on their toes. Al knew just how fast things would fall apart if he didn't ride them hard. The world might be different, but the nature of people didn't change.

As if on cue, Jezzibella purred, 'Come back here, lover.'

Well, maybe some people did, women never acted like her back in the 1920s and 30s. Then they were either whores or wives. But Al was beginning to suspect there weren't many girls quite like Jezzibella in this century, either: one minute all cute and kittenish, the next an animal as strong and demanding as

**265**

himself. Al had his energistic strength now, which meant he could do some pretty incredible things with his wang. Things which even Jezzibella hadn't known about. Performances which made him proud, for a while anyway, because they were the only times he could make her beg him for more, to keep going, tell him how stupendous he was. Most of the time it was the other way round. Shit, she even kissed like a boy. Trouble was, after he'd done all those fantastic things to her hot-rod body, she wanted them doing again, and again, and again . . .

'Please, baby. I really liked the Egyptian position. Only you are big enough to make that work.'

With a half-hearted sigh Al left the window and walked back to the sunken bed she was lying on. The oomph girl had no shame, she was absolutely naked.

He grinned and let the front of his white robe fall open. Jezzibella hooted, and applauded as his erection rose. Then she flopped back, character shifting in an instant. Al looked down on a scared-for-her-cherry-schoolgirl.

His entry was fierce, without any attempt at finesse. It made her cry out in disbelief, pleading for him to stop, to be kind. But she couldn't resist, no girl could, not a lover like him. In minutes his vigorous pumping had turned her cries to rolling moans of delight, her snarl to a smile. Her body was responding, the two of them moving in a slick acrobatic rhythm. He made no attempt to control himself, to wait for her, he climaxed when he was ready, oblivious to anything else.

When his drowsy eyes opened, he saw her staring drunkenly up at the ceiling, the tip of her tongue licking her lips. 'That was a good fantasy fuck,' she drawled. 'We'll have to do that one again.'

Al gave up. 'I gotta get going. I gotta sort the boys out, you know how it is.'

'Sure, baby. What are you going to get them to do?'

'Christ, you dumb broad. I'm running the whole fucking planet now. You think that just falls into place? I gotta million problems need looking at. Soldiers, they need orders else they go sour.'

Jezzibella pouted, then rolled over to grab the processor block which lay on the side of the bed. She typed on it, and frowned. 'Al, honey, you must pull in that field of yours.'

'Sorry,' he muttered, and made an effort to calm his thoughts. It was the best way to make the electric gadgets work.

Jezzibella whistled in appreciation as she read the data running down the block's screen (she'd long since given up trying to datavise when she was in Al's presence). According to the information assembled by Harwood's office, there were nearly forty million possessed on New California now. Hooking up with Al, that wild impulse back at the San Angeles spaceport, looked like being the smartest move she'd ever made. This was the anarchy ride she'd been hunting for most of her life. The buzz of power she got from being with Al – very literally one of life and death – stimmed her higher than any adulation the fans gave during a concert.

How could anyone know that a gangster from the past would have such a genius for assembling a power structure which could hold an entire planet in bondage? But that was what he'd done. 'You just gotta know what strings to jerk,' he'd told her on the flight up to the orbiting asteroids.

Of course all forty million possessed weren't perfectly loyal to him, they weren't even recruited into the Organization. But then neither had the vast majority of Chicago's citizens sworn fealty to him. Nonetheless, willing or not, they had been his vassals. 'All we gotta do is have an Organization in place and ready when the possessed start to emerge,' he explained. 'Back in Chicago, they called me a mobster because there was another administration trying to run things parallel to mine: the government. I lost out because the fuckers were bigger and stronger. This time, I ain't making that mistake. This time there's only gonna be me from the word go.'

And he'd been true to his word. She'd watched him at work

that first day, just after they'd captured the orbiting asteroids and the SD network. Sitting quietly in the background of the Monterey naval tactical operations room which the Organization soldiers had taken over as their headquarters. Watching and learning just what she'd gone and gotten herself involved in. And what she saw was the building of a pyramid, one constructed entirely from people. Without once losing his temper, Al issued orders to his lieutenants, who issued them to their seconds, and so on down the line. A pyramid which was constantly growing, absorbing new recruits at the bottom, adding to the height, to the power of the pinnacle. A pyramid whose hierarchy was established and maintained with the coldly ruthless application of force.

The first targets to be blasted into lava by the SD platforms had been government centres, everything from the Senate palace and the military bases right down to county police stations – Al really hated the police: 'Those cocksuckers murdered my brother,' he'd growl darkly when she questioned him on it – even little town halls in country smallvilles were reduced to cinders after they opened for business in the morning. For eight hours, the platforms had fired energy pulses down on the hapless, helpless planet they had been constructed to defend. Any group which could organize resistance was systematically wiped out. After that, the possessed were free to sweep across the land.

But Al's Organization people were among them, directing the onward march, finding out exactly who had returned from the beyond, when they came from, what they did in their first life. Their details would be sent up to the office which Avram Harwood had set up in Monterey, where they would be studied to gauge their potential usefulness. A select few would then be made an offer which— 'They just can't refuse,' Al chortled jubilantly.

They were a tiny minority, but that was all it ever took to govern. No rival could ever develop. Al had seen to that; he had the firepower to support his Organization if anyone stepped out of line. And when he captured the SD network, he acquired the ultra-hardened military communications net which went with it, the only one which had a chance of remaining functional in the territories of the possessed. So even if there were objectors among the newly emerged possessed (and there certainly were) they couldn't get in contact with others who thought along the same lines to create any decent kind of opposition.

In the end Jezzibella had felt privileged. It was a pivotal moment of history, like watching Eisenhower dispatching his D-day forces, or being with Richard Saldana as he organized the exodus from the New Kong asteroid to Kulu. Privileged and ecstatic.

More statistics ran down the processor block's screen. There were over sixteen million non-possessed left in the areas where the Organization ruled supreme. Harwood's office had declared they should be left alone to keep the utilities and services going, and by and large the Organization ensured they were left alone – for now. How long that would last, though, Jezzibella had her doubts.

Transport was also being orchestrated to invade the cities and counties which remained uncontaminated. According to the tactical estimates there would be a hundred million possessed living on New California by this time tomorrow. The Organization would achieve absolute control of the entire planet within a further three days.

And yesterday all she'd had to entertain her were a couple of fresh, gawky kids and the tiresome antics of the entourage.

'It's looking pretty fucking fantastic, Al,' she said. 'Guess you've got what it takes.'

He slapped her buns playfully. 'I always have. Things here ain't so different from Chicago. It's just a question of size; this is one fuck of a lot bigger, but I got Savvy Avvy's boys to help sort out that side of things, keeping track and all. Avvy didn't get to be mayor of San Angeles the way Big Jim Thompson made it into City Hall back in Chicago. No, sir, he's got a flair for paperwork.'

'And Leroy Octavius, too.'

'Yep. I see why you wanted to keep him now. I could do with a load more like him.'

'To do what?'

'To keep going, of course. At least for a few days more.' He slumped his shoulders, and rubbed his face in his hands. 'Then it's really gonna hit the fan. Most of the dumbasses down there want to do this magic disappearing act. Jee-zus, Jez, I ain't so sure I can stop them.' Eight times in the last day he'd ordered Emmet Mordden to use the SD platforms to sharpshoot buildings and city blocks over which the wisps of red cloud were forming. Each time the culprits had taken the hint, and the luminous swirl had vanished.

For the moment he was on top of things. But what was gonna happen after he'd won the planet was giving his brain a real hard time. It was going to be difficult stopping the possessed from vanishing inside the red cloud, because he was the only one among them who didn't want that to happen. Once he'd delivered the whole planet to them, they'd start looking round at what was stopping them from achieving their true goal. And some wiseass with an eye on the main chance would make his bid. Wouldn't be the first time.

'So give them something more to do,' Jezzibella said.

'Sure, right, doll. Like after the entire fucking world, what else am I gonna give them, for Christ's sake?'

'Listen, you keep telling me this whole set-up is going to end once the possessed pull New California out of the universe, right? Everyone's going to be equal and immortal.'

'Yeah, that's about it.'

'That means you'll be nothing, least nothing special.'

'That's what I'm fucking telling you.'

Jezzibella shifted again. This time she was like nothing he'd seen before: a librarian, or schoolmarm. Not the remotest bit sexy. Al sucked some breath through his teeth, the way she did that was just plain unnerving – her not having the energistic power, and all.

She leant over, and put a hand on each of his shoulders, stern eyes inches from his. 'When you're nothing, all your lieutenants and soldiers become nothing, too. Deep down they're not going to want that. You've got to find a reason – a fucking good reason – to keep the Organization intact. Once they grab that angle you can keep things humming along sweetly for quite a while yet.'

'But we've won here. There isn't a single excuse to keep going the way we have.'

'There are plenty,' she said. 'You simply don't know enough about the way the modern galaxy works to make any long-range plans, that's all. But I'm going to cure that, starting right here. Now listen closely.'

*

New California's planetary government had always taken a progressive view on flinging tax dollars at the local defence establishment. Firstly, it provided a healthy primer for industry to pursue an aggressive export policy, boosting foreign earnings. Secondly, its navy's above-average size gave it an excellent heavyweight political stature within the Confederation.

Such enthusiasm for defence hardware had resulted in a superb C3 (command, control, and communication) set-up. The core was Monterey's naval tactical operations centre, a large chamber drilled deep into the asteroid's rock, below the first biosphere cavern, and equipped with state-of-the-art AIs and communication systems, linked in to equally impressive squadrons of sensor satellites and weapons platforms. It was capable of coordinating the defence of the entire star system against anything from a full-scale invasion to a sneak attack by a rogue antimatter-powered starship. Unfortunately, no one had ever considered the consequences should it be captured and its firepower turned inwards on the planet and orbiting asteroids.

The Organization lieutenants had split into two factions to run their operations centre. There was Avram Harwood's staff, who dealt purely with the administration and management details of the Organization, essentially the new civil service. Then there were those, a smaller number, working under the auspices of Silvano Richmann and Emmet Mordden, who were operating the military hardware they'd captured. The law enforcers. Al's laws. He'd given that task to the possessed alone, just in case any non-possessed tried to be a hero.

When Al and Jezzibella walked into the centre the huge wall-mounted hologram screens were showing satellite views of Santa Volta. Grizzled spires of smoke were rising from several of the city's blocks. Graphic symbols were superimposed over the real-time layout as the Organization advanced its troops. Silvano Richmann and Leroy Octavius stood in front of the colourful screens, heads together as they discussed the best strategy to crack open the population. Filling the eight rows of consoles behind them, the communication team were waiting patiently.

Everyone turned as Al strode forward. There were grins, smiles, whoops, sharp whistles. He did the rounds, pressing the flesh, joking, laughing, thanking, offering encouragement.

Jezzibella followed a pace behind him. She and Leroy quirked an eyebrow at each other.

'So how's it going?' Al asked a scrum of his senior lieutenants when he'd finished his processional.

'We're more or less sticking to the timetable,' Mickey Pileggi said. 'Some places put up a fight. Others just roll onto their backs and stick their legs in the air for us. We got no way of knowing in advance. Word's getting out that we aren't possessing everyone. It helps. Causes a shitload of confusion.'

'Fine from my angle, too, Al,' Emmet Mordden said. 'Our

sensor satellites have been monitoring some of the deep space message traffic. It's not easy, because most of it is directional tight-beam. But it looks like the rest of the system knows we're here, and what we're doing.'

'Is that going to be a problem?' Al asked.

'No, sir. We caught nearly forty per cent of New California's navy ships in dock when we took over the orbiting asteroids. They're still there, and another twenty per cent is on permanent assignment to the Confederation Navy fleets. That just leaves a maximum of about fifty ships left in the system which could cause us any grief. But I've got every SD platform on situation-A readiness. Even if the admirals out there get their act together they know it would be suicide to attack us.'

Al lit a cigar, and blew a stream of smoke towards the screen. The near orbit tactical display, Emmet had called it yesterday. It looked pretty calm at the moment. 'Sounds like you're handling your slice of the action, Emmet. I'm impressed.'

'Thanks, Al.' The nervous man bobbed in appreciation. 'As you can see, there's no spacecraft activity within a million kilometres of the planetary surface, except for five voidhawks. They're holding themselves stable over the poles, seven hundred thousand kilometres out. My guess is they're just watching us to see what's happening.'

'Spies?' Al enquired.

'Yes.'

'We should blow them all to shit,' Bernhard Allsop said loudly. 'Ain't that right, Al? That'll give the rest of those frigging Commie Edenists the message: don't spy on us, don't fuck with us or it's your ass.'

'Shut up,' Al said mildly.

Bernhard twitched apprehensively. 'Sure, Al. I didn't mean nothing by it.'

'Can you hit the voidhawks?' Jezzibella asked.

Emmet glanced from her to Al, and licked his suddenly sweaty lips. 'It's difficult, you know? They chose those polar positions carefully. I mean, they're out of range of our energy weapons. And if we launch a combat wasp salvo at them, they'll just dive down a wormhole. But, hey ... they can't hurt us, either.'

'Not this time,' Al said. He chewed his cigar from the left side of his mouth to the right. 'But they can see what we're about, and it'll frighten them. Pretty soon the whole goddam Confederation is going to know what's happened here.'

'I told you they'd be trouble, Al baby,' Jezzibella said, on cue. Her voice had shunted down to a tart's whinny.

'Sure you did, doll,' he said, not taking his eyes off the tactical display. 'We're gonna have to do something about them,' Al announced to the room at large.

'Well, hell, Al,' Emmet said. 'I'll give it a go, but I don't think ...'

'No, Emmet,' Al said generously. 'I ain't talking about five crappy little ships. I'm talking about what's lining up behind them.'

'The Edenists?' Bernhard asked, hopefully.

'Partly, yeah. But they ain't the whole picture, are they, boy? You gotta think big, here. You're in a big universe now.' He had their complete attention. Damn, but Jez had been right. Typical.

'The Edenists are gonna broadcast what we've done here to the whole Confederation. Then what do you think is gonna happen, huh?' He turned a full circle, arms held out theatrically. 'Any takers? No? Seems pretty goddam obvious to me, guys. They're gonna come here with every fucking battleship they got, and grab the planet back off us.'

'We can fight,' Bernhard said.

'We'll lose,' Al purred. 'But that don't matter. Does it? Because I know what you're thinking. Every goddamned dumbass one of you. You're thinking: *We won't be here. We're gonna be out of this stinking joint any day now, safe on the other side of the red cloud where there ain't no sky and there ain't no space,*

**274**

*and nobody dies any more.* Ain't that right? Ain't that what's brewing inside those thick skulls of yours?'

Shuffled feet and downcast eyes was the only response he was offered. 'Mickey, ain't that right?'

Mickey Pileggi developed an urgent wish to be somewhere else. He couldn't meet his boss's interrogation stare. 'Well, you know how it is, Al. That's a last resort, sure. But shit, we can do like Bernhard says and fight some first. I ain't afraid of fighting.'

'Sure you ain't afraid. I didn't say you were afraid. I didn't insult you, Mickey, you rube goof. I'm saying you ain't thinking level. The Confederation Navy, they're gonna turn up here with a thousand, ten thousand starships, and you're gonna do the smartest thing you can do, and hide. Right? I would if they came at me with all pieces shooting.'

The left side of Mickey's face began to tic alarmingly. 'Sure, boss,' he said numbly.

'So you think that's gonna make them give up?' Al asked. 'Come on, all of you. I want to know. Who in this room believes the big government boys are just gonna give up if you make New California disappear? Huh? Tell me. They lose a planet with eight hundred million people on it, and the admiral in charge, he's just gonna shrug and say: "Well fuck it, you can't win them all." And go home.' Al stabbed a finger at the little purple stars of light representing the voidhawks on the tactical display screen. A slim bolt of white fire lashed out, striking the glass. Glowing droplets sprinkled out. A crater bowed inwards, distorting and magnifying the graphics below. 'Is he FUCK!' Al bellowed. 'Open your Goddam eyes, shitheads! These people can fly among the stars, for Christ's sake. They know everything there is to know about how energy works, they know all about quantum dimensions, hell they can even switch off time if they feel like it. And what they don't know, they can find out pretty fucking quick. They'll see what you've done, they'll follow where you take the planet. And they'll bring it back. Those cruddy longhairs will look at what happened, and they'll work on it, and they'll work on it. And they ain't never gong to stop until they've solved the problem. I know the Feds, the governments. Believe me, of all people, I fucking know. You ain't never safe from them. They don't ever fucking stop. Never! And it won't matter diddly how much you scream, and how much you cuss and rage. They'll bring you back. Oh yeah, right back here under the stars and emptiness where you started from. Staring death and beyond in the face.' He had them now, he could see the doubt blossoming, the concern. And the fear. Always the fear. The way right into a man's heart. The way a general jerked his soldiers' strings.

Al Capone grinned like the devil himself into the daunted silence. 'There's only one fucking way to stop that from ever happening. Any of you cretins figured that out yet? No? Big surprise. Well, it's simple, assholes. You stop running scared like you have been all your life. You stop, you turn round to face what's scaring you, and you bite its fucking dick off.'

\*

For five centuries after the first successful ZTT jump governments, universities, companies, and military laboratories throughout the Confederation had been researching methods of direct supralight communication. And for all the billions of fuseodollars poured into the various projects, no one had ever produced a valid theory let alone a practical system to surmount the problem. Starships remained the only method of carrying data between star systems.

Because of this, waves of information would spread out like ripples through the inhabited star systems within the Confederation. And as the stars were not arranged in a tidy geometrical lattice, such wavefronts became more and more distorted as time went on. News companies had long since refined a set of equations defining the most effective distribution procedure between their offices. On receiving a hot item (such as the appearance of Ione Saldana), an office would typically charter eight to twelve starships to relay the flek depending on when and where the story originated. Towards the end of the distribution coverage, the information could well arrive in one system from several directions over the course of a fortnight. The nature of the starships employed also had a strong influence on the timing, depending on the marque of ship used, how good the captain was, component malfunctions, a hundred diverse circumstances all contributing to the uncertainty.

Laton's appearance had naturally received an overriding precedence from all the Time Universe offices Graeme Nicholson's flek arrived at. But Srinagar was over four hundred light-years away from Tranquillity. News of the *Yaku*'s existence, and who it was carrying, arrived several days after the *Yaku* itself had departed from Valisk.

Laton!

Rubra was astonished. They might have been fellow Serpents, but that hardly made them allies. So for the first time in a hundred and thirty years he expanded his affinity and grudgingly contacted the Edenist habitats orbiting Kohistan to tell them the starship had docked briefly.

**But Laton did not come inside, he assured them. Only three crew came through immigration: Marie Skibbow, Alicia Cochrane, and Manza Balyuzi.**

**Skibbow was definitely sequestrated, and the other two are likely recipients, the Kohistan Consensus replied. Where are they?**

**I don't know.** It was a humiliating, dismaying admission, especially making it to his former peers. But Rubra had immediately made the connection between Marie Skibbow and Anders Bospoort, in whose apartment Dariat's corpse had been found. Such a chain of events worried him enormously. But his supposedly infallible memory storage facility had failed him utterly. After Marie and Anders had gone down the starscraper that first time they had simply vanished from his perception; and the subroutine in the starscraper hadn't noticed their absence. Nor could he locate them now, not even with his perception subroutines expanded and upgraded with a new batch of safeguards.

*Do you require our assistance?* the Kohistan Consensus asked. *Our neuropathologists may be able to analyse the nature of the distortion in your subroutines.*

*No! You'd love that, wouldn't you? Getting into my mind again. Poking round to see what makes me pulse.*

*Rubra—*

*You shits don't ever give up, don't ever stop.*

*Given the circumstances, do you not think it would be sensible to put old antagonisms behind us?*

*I'll deal with it. By myself. They can only fuck with my peripheral routines. They can't touch me.*

*As far as you know.*

*I know! Believe me, I know. I'm me; same as I ever was.*

*Rubra, this is only the beginning. They will try to infiltrate your higher-order thought routines.*

*They won't succeed, not now I know what to watch for.*

*Very well. But we must recommend to the Srinagar system assembly that starships are prohibited from docking with you. We cannot risk the prospect of any contamination spreading.*

*Suits me fine.*

*Will you at least cooperate with us on that?*

*Yes, yes. But only until I've tracked down the three* Yaku *crew and exterminated them.*

*Please be careful, Rubra. Laton's proteanic virus is extremely dangerous.*

*So that's what you think I've got, why my routines are failing. Bastards!*

It took several minutes for his anger to sink back into more rational, passive, thought currents. By the time he was thinking logically again, Valisk's SD sensor network alerted him to five voidhawks emerging from their wormhole termini to take up station half a million kilometres away. Spies! They didn't trust him.

He had to find the three people from the *Yaku*, and those members of his family whose monitor routines had been tampered with.

While the rest of the Srinagar system went to an agitated stage one military alert status, he tried again and again to scan his own interior for the renegades. Standard visual-pattern recognition routines were useless. He upgraded and changed the perception-interpretation routines several times. To no avail. He tried loading similar search orders into the servitors, hoping that they might succeed where the sensitive cells woven into every polyp surface had failed. He swept through entire starscrapers with his principal consciousness, certain that they still hadn't managed to infiltrate and corrupt his identity core. He found nothing.

After ten hours, the watching voidhawks were joined by three Srinagar Navy frigates.

Inside the habitat, Time Universe played Graeme Nicholson's recording continuously, agitating the population badly. Opinions were divided. Some said Laton and Rubra were obviously colleagues, comrades in antagonism. Laton wouldn't hurt Valisk. Others pointed out that the two had never met, and had chosen very different paths through life.

There was unease, but no actual problems. Not for the first few hours. Then some idiot from the spaceport's civil traffic-control centre leaked the news (actually he was paid two hundred thousand fuseodollars by Collins for the data) that the *Yaku* had docked at Valisk. Twenty starships immediately filed for departure flights, which Rubra refused.

Unease began to slip into resentment, anger, and alarm. Given the nature of the residents, they had no trouble asserting their feelings in a manner which the rentcops employed by Magellanic Itg had a hard time damping down. Riots broke out in several starscrapers. Localized 'councils' were formed, demanding the right to petition Rubra. Who plain ignored them (after memorizing the ringleaders). More thoughtful and prudent members of the population started to hike out into the remoter sections of parkland, taking camping gear with them.

Such strife was almost designed to make Rubra's frantic search for the three *Yaku* crew-members difficult verging on impossible.

Thirty-eight hours after Graeme Nicholson's flek arrived in the Srinagar system, a voidhawk came from Avon, exposing the true nature of the threat the Confederation was facing (such was the priority it even beat the First Admiral's earlier communiqué warning of a possible energy virus).

In its wake all incoming starships were isolated and told to prepare for boarding and inspection by fully armed military teams. Civil starflight effectively shut down overnight. Proclamations were issued, requiring all newly arrived travellers to report to the police. Failure to comply was roughly equivalent to thumbprinting your own death warrant. Navy reserves were called in. Industrial astroengineering stations began producing combat wasps at full capacity.

In one respect, news of the possessed assisted Rubra. It seemed to shock Valisk's population out of their confrontational attitude. Rubra judged it an appropriate time to appeal to them for help. Every communication net processor, holoscreen, and AV pillar in the habitat relayed the same image of him: a man in his prime, handsome and capable, speaking calmly and authoritatively. Given that he'd had nothing to do with the general population for a century, it was an event unusual enough to draw everyone's attention.

'There are only three possessed at large in the habitat at this moment,' he told his audience. 'Whilst they are certainly a cause for concern, they do not as yet present a threat to us. I have issued the police with the kind of heavy-calibre weapons necessary to surmount their energistic ability. And if circumstances warrant, several citizens have the kind of experience which might prove useful in a confrontation.' An ironic, knowing curl of his lip which brought an appreciative smile from many watchers. 'However, their ability to alter their appearance means they are proving hard for me to track down. I'm therefore asking all of you to look out for them and inform me immediately. Don't trust people just because they look the same as they've always been; these bastards are probably masquerading as friends of yours. Another effect to watch for is the way they interfere with electronic equipment; if any of your processors start glitching then, again, inform me straight away. There's a half-million fuseodollar reward for the information which results in their elimination. Good hunting.'

*

'Thank you, Big Brother.' Ross Nash tipped his beer glass at the holoscreen over the Tacoul Tavern's bar. He looked away from the drastically wobbly picture of Rubra, and grinned at Kiera. She was sitting in one of the wall booths, talking in low intense tones with the small cadre she'd been building up; her staff officers, people joked. Ross was mildly bugged that she hadn't been including him in the consultation process recently. OK, so he didn't have much in the way of technical knowledge, and this habitat was a far gone trip into futureworld for a guy who was born in 1940 (and died in '89 – bowel cancer), he kept expecting Yul Brynner to turn up in his black gunslinger outfit. But damn it, his opinion counted for something. She hadn't screwed with him for days either.

He glanced round the black and silver Tavern, resisting the impulse to laugh. It was busier than it had been for years. Unfortunately for the owner, nobody was paying for their drinks and meals any more. Not this particular clientele. Tatars and cyberpunks mixed happily with Roman legionaries and heavy-leather bikers, along with several rejects from the good Dr Frankenstein's assembly lab. Music was blasting out of a magnificent 1950s Wurlitzer, allowing a flock of seraphim to strut their stuff across the neon-underlit floor. It was pure sensory overload after the deprivation of the beyond, nourishment for the mind. Ross grinned engagingly at his new buddies propping up the bar. There was poor old Dariat, also cut out of Kiera's elite command group, and really pissed by that. Abraham Canaan, too, in full preacher's ensemble, scowling at the debauchery being practised all around. One thing about the possessed, Ross thought cheerfully, they knew how to party. And they could do it in perfect safety in the Tacoul Tavern; those who were affinity capable had turned the joint into a safe enclave, completely reformatting the subroutines which operated in the neural strata behind the walls.

He gulped down the rest of his glass, then held it up in front of his nose and wished it full once again. The liquid which appeared in it really did look like gnat's piss. He frowned at it; a complicated process, coordinating that many facial muscles. For the last five hours he'd been delighted that possessing a body didn't prevent you from getting utterly smashed, but now it seemed there were disadvantages. He chucked the glass over his shoulder. He was sure he'd seen shops out in the vestibule, some of them would stock a bottle or two of decent booze.

\*

Rubra knew his thought-processing efficiency was lower than optimum. The malaise was his own fault. He should be reviewing the search, reformatting subroutines yet again. Now more than ever the effort should be made, now the true nature of his predicament was known. And it was a predicament. The possessed had conquered Pernik. Bitek was not invincible. He ought to divert every mental resource towards breaking the problem; after all, the possessed were physically present, there had to be some way of detecting them. Instead he brooded. Something an Edenist habitat personality couldn't, or wouldn't, do.

Dariat. Rubra simply couldn't forget the insignificant little shit. Dariat was dead. But now death wasn't the end. And he died happy. That passive half smile seemed to flitter through the cells of the neural strata like a menacing ghost. Not such a stretched metaphor, now.

But to kill yourself just to return ... No. He wouldn't.

But someone had taught the possessed how to glitch his thought routines. Someone very competent indeed.

That smile, though. Suppose, just suppose, he was *so* desperate for vengeance ...

Rubra became aware of a disturbance in the Diocca starscraper, the seventeenth floor, a delicatessen. Some kind of attempted hold-up. A subroutine was attempting to call for the rentcops, but it kept misdirecting the information. The new safeguard protocols he'd installed were trying to compensate, and failing. They fell back on their third-level instructions, and alerted the principal personality pattern. And barely succeeded in that. Dozens of extremely potent subversive orders were operating within the Diocca starscraper's neural strata, virtually isolating it from Rubra's consciousness.

Elated and perturbed, he focused his full attention on it—

Ross Nash was leaning on the delicatessen's counter, pressing a very large pump-action shotgun into the face of the petrified manager. He clicked the fingers of his free hand, and a thousand-dollar bill flipped out of his cuff, just like the way he'd seen a magician do it in Vegas one time. The crisp note floated down to join the small pile on the counter.

'We got enough here yet, buddy?' Ross asked.

'Sure,' the manager whispered. 'That's fine.'

'Goddam bet your ass it is. Yankee dollar, best goddam currency in the whole fucking world. Everybody knows that.' He snatched up a bottle of Norfolk Tears from beside the bills.

Rubra focused on the shotgun, not entirely sure the seventeenth floor's perception-interpretation routine wasn't entirely glitched after all. The weapon seemed to be made of wood.

Ross grinned at the trembling manager. 'I'll be back,' he said, in a very heavy accent. He did an about face and started to march away. The shotgun flickered erratically, competing with a broken chair leg to occupy the same space.

The manager snatched his shockrod from its clips under the counter, and took a wild swing. It connected with the back of Ross's head.

Along with the manager, Rubra was amazed at the result of the simple blow.

As soon as the shockrod sparked across Ross's skin, his possessed body ignited with the pristine glory of a small solar flare. All colours in the shop vanished beneath the incandescent blaze, leaving only white and silver to designate rough shapes.

Nearby processors and sensors came back on-line. Thermal alerts flashed into Valisk's net, along with a security call. Ceiling-mounted fire-suppression nozzles swivelled round, and squirted retardant foam at the blaze.

The thick streams made little difference. Ross's stolen body was dimming now, sinking to its charred knees, flakes of carbonated flesh crumbling away.

Rubra activated the audio circuit on in the shop's net processor. 'Out!' he commanded.

The manager cringed at the shout.

'Move,' Rubra said. 'It's the possessed. Get out.' He opened all the net processors on the seventeenth floor to repeat the order. Analysis routines began correlating all the information from the starscraper's sensitive cells. Even with his principal personality pattern directing the procedure, he couldn't see what was happening inside the Tacoul Tavern. Then bizarre figures started to emerge from the Tavern's doorway into the vestibule.

He'd found them, the whole damnable nest.

White fireballs shot through the air, pursuing the terrorized delicatessen manager as he ran for the lifts. One of them caught him, clinging to his shoulder. He screamed as rancid black smoke churned out of the wound.

Rubra immediately cancelled the floor's autonomic routines, and shunted himself into the operating hierarchy. The vestibule's electrophorescent cells went dead, dropping the whole area into darkness, except for the confusing strobe of white fire. A muscle-membrane door leading onto the stairwell snapped open, sending out a single fan of light. The manager altered course, put his head down, and charged straight at it.

Chips of polyp rained down on the vestibule floor. All across the ceiling the atmosphere duct tubules were splitting open as Rubra contracted and flexed the flow-regulator muscles in directions they were never designed for. Thick white vapour poured out of the jagged holes. Warm, dank, and oily, it was the concentrated water vapour breathed out of a thousand lungs, which the tubules were supposed to extract from the air and pump into specialist refining organs.

The possessed wished it gone. And the muggy fog obeyed, rushing aside to let them pass. But not before it reduced their fireballs to impotent wispy swirls of fluorescing mist.

The manager reached the stairwell. Rubra closed the muscle-membrane door behind him, clenching it tight as several balls of white fire slammed into the surface, burrowing in like lava worms.

Kiera Salter ran out into the vestibule just as the last of the stinking mist vanished. Red emergency lights had come on, bringing an antagonistic moonlight glow to the broad chamber. She saw the stairwell's muscle-membrane door slap shut ahead of the vengeful mob.

'Stop!' she yelled.

Some did. Several threw white fire at the muscle membrane.

'Stop this right now,' she said, this time there was an edge in her voice.

'Fuck you, Kiera.'

'He zapped Ross, God damn it.'

'I'm gonna make him suffer.'

'Maybe.' Kiera strode into the centre of the vestibule, and stood there, hands on her hips, staring round at her precariously allied colleagues. 'But not like this.' She gestured at the smoking muscle-membrane door, which was still shut. The grey surface was visibly quivering. 'He knows now.' She tipped her head back, calling out at the ceiling. 'Don't you, Rubra?'

The ceiling's electrophorescent cells slowly came back on, illuminating her upturned face. Lines of darkness flowed across them, taking shape. YES.

'Yes. See?' She dared any of the possessed to challenge her; a couple of her more powerful new lieutenants, Bonney Lewin and Stanyon, came forward to stand beside her for emphasis. 'We're playing a different game now, no more skulking about. Now we take over the entire habitat.'

NO, printed the ceiling.

'That wasn't a deal, Rubra,' she shouted up at him. 'I'm not offering to make you a partner. Got that? If you're real, real, lucky, then you get to live on. That's all. If you don't piss me off. If you don't get in my way. Then maybe we'll have a use for your precious Valisk afterwards. But only if you behave. Because once I've taken over your population it's going to be easy to fly away. Only before we go, I'll use the starships to cut you into little pieces; I'll split your shell open, I'll bleed your atmosphere out, I'll freeze your rivers solid, I'll blast your digestive organs out of the endcap. It'll take a long time hurting for you to die completely. Decades, maybe. Who knows. You want to find out?'

YOU ARE COMPLETELY ALONE. POLICE AND COMBAT BOOSTED MERCENARIES ON THEIR WAY. SURRENDER NOW.

Kiera laughed brutally. 'No, we're not alone, Rubra. There are billions of us.' She looked round at the possessed in the vestibule, not seeing any dissenters (except ones like Dariat and

**286**

Canaan, who really didn't count). 'OK, people, as from now we're going overt. I want procedure five enacted this minute.' A casual click of her fingers, designating tasks. 'You three, override the lift supervisor processors, have them ready to take us up into the parkland. Bonney, track down that little shit who wiped Ross, I want him creatively hurt. We'll set up our command centre in Magellanic Itg's boardroom.'

The first lift arrived at the seventeenth floor. Five of the possessed hurried in, anxious to show Kiera their eagerness to obey, anxious to reap the rewards. The doors slid shut. Rubra overrode the starscraper's power circuit safeguards, and routed eighty thousand volts through the metal tracks which lined the lift shaft.

Kiera could hear the screams from inside the lift, feel the agony of forced banishment. The silicon rubber seal between the doors melted and burned, allowing the fearsome light of the bodies' internecine flame to spew out of the crack.

NOT SO EASY, IS IT?

For about twenty seconds she stood absolutely still, face a perfect cage around any emotion. Then her finger lined up on a spindly youth in a baggy white suit. 'You, open the muscle membrane; we'll use the stairs.'

'Told you so,' the youth said. 'We should have gone for him first.'

'Do it,' Kiera snapped. 'And the rest of you, Rubra's demonstrated what he can do, it's not much compared to our ability, but it's an irritant. We'll cut through the neural strata's connections with the starscrapers eventually, but until then, proceed with caution.'

The muscle-membrane door parted smoothly, allowing the now slightly subdued possessed to troop up the seventeen flights of stairs to the parkland above.

**It wasn't a pure affinity command,** Rubra told the Kohistan Consensus. **I felt what was almost like a power surge through the neural cells around the muscle membrane. It came in with the affinity**

command, just wiped all my routines completely. But it's localized, an area roughly five metres in diameter; it can't reach into the main neural strata.

Laton claimed that Lewis Sinclair had that same kind of super-charged affinity when he took over Pernik Island, the Consensus replied. It works through brute strength, and as such can be subverted. But should one of them succeed in transferring his personality into you, the energistic ability increases in proportion to the number of cells subsumed. You must not allow that to happen.

Fat chance. You know Valisk's neural cells were sequenced from my DNA, they will only process my thought routines. I guess that's similar to what Laton did to Pernik when he altered the island's neural strata with his proteanic virus. The affinity capable possessed might be able to knock out some functions like the muscle membranes, but their personalities wouldn't function as independent entities in the neural strata, not unless they operate as a subsection of my pattern. I'd have to let them in.

Excellent news. But can you protect your general population from possession?

It's going to be tricky, Rubra admitted reluctantly. And I'll never save all of them, not even a majority. I'm going to have to take a whole load of internal damage, too.

We sympathize. We will help you rebuild afterwards.

If there is an afterwards.

# 8

Culey asteroid was an almost instinctive choice for André Duchamp. Located in the Dzamin Ude star system, a healthy sixty light-years from Lalonde, it acted as a ready haven for certain types of ships in certain circumstances. As if in reaction to its Chinese-ethnic ancestry, and all the clutter of authoritarian tradition which came with that, the asteroid was notoriously lax when it came to enforcing CAB regulations and scrutinizing the legitimacy of cargo manifests. Such an attitude hadn't done its economy any harm. Starships came for the ease of trading, and the astroengineering conglomerates came to maintain and support the ships, and where the majors went there followed a plethora of smaller service and finance companies. The Confederation Assembly subcommittee on smuggling and piracy might routinely condemn Culey's government and its policies. But nothing ever altered. Certainly in the fifteen years he'd been using it, André never had any trouble selling on cargo or picking up dubious charters, the asteroid was virtually a second home.

This time, though, when the *Villeneuve's Revenge* performed its ZTT jump into the designated emergence zone Culey spaceport was unusually reticent in granting docking permission. During the last three days the system had received first the reports of Laton's re-emergence, and secondly the warning from Trafalgar about possible energy virus contamination. Both of them designated Lalonde as the focus of the trouble.

'But I have a severely injured man on board,' André protested as his third request to be allocated a docking-bay was refused.

'Sorry, Duchamp,' the port control officer replied. 'We have no bays available.'

'There's very little traffic movement round the port,' Madeleine Collum observed; she'd accessed the starship's sensor suite, and was viewing the asteroid. 'And most of that is personnel commuters and MSVs; no starships.'

'I am declaring a first degree emergency,' André datavised to the port officer. 'They have to take us now,' he muttered to Madeleine. She simply grunted.

'Emergency declaration acknowledged, *Villeneuve's Revenge*,' the port control officer datavised back. 'We would advise you set a vector for the Yaxi asteroid. Their facilities are more appropriate to your status.'

André glared at the almost featureless communication console. 'Very well. Please open a channel to Commissioner Ri Drak for me.'

Ri Drak was André's last card, the one he hadn't quite envisioned playing in a situation such as this, not the fate of a crew-member; the likes of Ri Drak were to be held in reserve until André's own neck was well and truly on the line.

'Hello, Captain,' Ri Drak datavised. 'We would seem to have a problem evolving here.'

'Not for me,' André answered. 'No problems. Not like in the past, eh?'

The two of them switched to a high-order encryption program, much to Madeleine's annoyance; she couldn't access the rest of the conversation. Whatever was said took nearly fifteen minutes to discuss. The only give-away was André's clumsy face, registering a sneaky grin, intermingled with the sporadic indignant frown.

'Very well, Captain,' Ri Drak said at last. 'The *Villeneuve's*

*Revenge* is cleared to dock, but at your own risk should you prove to be contaminated. I will alert the security forces of your arrival.'

'Monsieur,' André acknowledged gracelessly.

Madeleine didn't press. Instead she began datavising the flight computer for systems schematics, assisting the Captain with the fusion drive's ignition sequence.

Culey's counter-rotating spaceport was a seven-pointed star, its unfortunate condition mirroring the asteroid's general attitude to space-worthiness statutes. Several areas were in darkness, silver-white insulation blankets were missing from the surface, creating strange mosaic patterns, at least three pipes were leaking, throwing up weak grey gas jets.

The *Villeneuve's Revenge* was assigned an isolated bay near one of the tips. That at least was fully illuminated, internal spotlights turning the steep-walled metal crater into a shadowless receptacle. Red strobes around the rim flashed in unison as the starship descended onto the extended cradle.

An armed port police squad were first through the airlock tube when it sealed. They rounded up André and the crew, detaining them on the bridge while a customs team examined the ship's life-support capsules from top to bottom. The search took two hours before clearance was granted.

'You put up a hell of a fight in here,' the port police captain said as he slid through the open ceiling hatch into the lower deck lounge where the possessed had stormed aboard. The compartment was a shambles, fittings broken and twisted, blackened sections of composite melted into queer shapes, dark bloodstains on various surfaces starting to flake. Despite the best efforts of the straining environmental circuit there was a nasty smell of burnt meat in the air which refused to go away. Nine black body bags were secured to the hatch ladder by short lengths of silicon fibre. Stirred by the weak columns of air which were all the broken, vibrating, conditioning duct could muster, they drifted a few centimetres above the scorched decking, bumping into each other and recoiling in slow motion.

'Erick and I saw them off,' André said gruffly. It earned him a filthy glance from Desmond Lafoe, who was helping the spaceport coroner classify the bodies.

'You did pretty well, then,' the captain said. 'Lalonde sounds as if hell has materialized inside the Confederation.'

'It was,' André said. 'Pure hell. We were lucky to escape. I've never seen a space battle more ferocious than that.'

The police captain nodded thoughtfully.

'Captain?' Madeleine datavised. 'We're ready to take Erick's zero-tau pod down to the hospital now.'

'Of course, proceed.'

'We'll need you there to clear the treatment payment orders, Captain.'

André's cheerfully chubby face showed a certain tautness. 'I will be along, we're almost through with the port clearance procedures.'

'You know, I have several friends in the media who would be interested in recordings of your mission,' the police captain said. 'Perhaps you would care for me to put you in touch with them? There may even be circumstances where you wouldn't have to pay import duty; these matters are within my discretion.'

André's malaised spirit lifted. 'Perhaps we could come to some arrangement.'

Madeleine and Desmond accompanied Erick's zero-tau pod to the asteroid's hospital in the main habitation cavern. Before the field was switched off, the doctors went through the flek Madeleine had recorded as she stabilized Erick.

'Your friend is a lucky man,' the principal surgeon told them after the initial review.

'We know,' Madeleine said. 'We were there.'

'Fortunately his Kulu Corporation neural nanonics are top of the range, very high capacity. The emergency suspension program he ran during the decompression event was correspondingly comprehensive; it has prevented major internal organ tissue death, and there's very little neural damage, the blood supply to his cranium was sustained almost satisfactorily. We can certainly clone and replace the cells he has lost. Lungs will have to be completely replaced, of course, they always suffer the most from such decompression. And quite a few blood vessels will need extensive repair. The forearm and hand are naturally the simplest operation, a straightforward graft replacement.'

Madeleine grinned over at Desmond. The flight had been a terrific strain on everyone, not knowing if they'd used the correct procedures or whether the blank pod simply contained a vegetable.

André Duchamp appeared in the private waiting room they were using, his smile so bright that Madeleine gave him a suspicious frown.

'Erick's going to be all right,' she told him.

'*Très bon*. He is a beautiful *enfant*. I always said so.'

'He can certainly be restored,' the surgeon said. 'There is the question of what kind of procedure you would like me to perform. We can use artificial tissue implants to return him to full viability within a few days, these we have in store. Following that we can begin the cloning operation and start to replace the AT units as his organs mature. Or alternatively we can simply take the appropriate genetic samples, and keep him in zero-tau until the new organs are ready to be implanted.'

'Of course.' André cleared his throat, not quite looking at his other two crew. 'Exactly how much would these different procedures cost?'

The surgeon gave a modest shrug. 'The cheapest option would just be to give him the artificial tissue and not bother with cloned replacements. AT is the technology which people use in order to boost themselves; the individual units will live longer than him, and they are highly resistant to disease.'

'*Magnifique.*' André gave a wide, contented smile.

'But we're not going to use that option, are we, Captain?' Madeleine said forcibly. 'Because, as you said when Erick saved both your ship and your arse, you would buy him an entire new clone body if that's what it took. Didn't you? So how fortunate that you don't have to clone a new body, and all the expense that entails. Now all you are going to have to pay for is some artificial tissue and a few clones. Because you certainly don't want Erick walking round in anything less than a perfectly restored, and natural condition. Do you, Captain?'

André's answering grin was a simple facial ritual. '*Non*,' he said. 'How right you are, my dear Madeleine. As ever.' He gave the surgeon a nod. 'Very well, a full clone repair, if you please.'

'Certainly, sir.' The surgeon produced a Jovian Bank credit disk. 'I must ask for a deposit of two hundred thousand fuseodollars.'

'Two hundred thousand! I thought you were going to rebuild him, not rejuvenate him.'

'Sadly, there is a lot of work to be done. Surely your insurance premium will cover it?'

'I'll have to check,' André said heavily.

Madeleine laughed.

'Will Erick be able to fly after the artificial tissue has been implanted?' André asked.

'Oh, yes,' the surgeon said. 'I won't need him back here for the clone implants for several months.'

'Good.'

'Why? Where are we going?' Madeleine asked suspiciously.

André produced his own Jovian Bank disk and proffered it towards the surgeon. 'Anywhere we can get a charter for. Who knows, we might even avoid bankruptcy until we return. I'm sure that will make Erick very happy knowing what his recklessness has reduced me to.'

*

Idria asteroid was on full strategic-defence alert, and had been for three days. For the first forty-eight hours all the asteroid council knew was that *something* had taken over the New California SD network, coincidentally knocking out (or capturing) half of the planetary navy at the same time. Details were hazy. It was almost too much to believe that some kind of coup could be successful on a modern planet, but the few garbled reports which did get beamed out before the transmitters fell ominously silent confirmed that the SD platforms were firing at groundside targets.

Then a day ago the voidhawk messenger from the Confederation Assembly arrived in the system, and people understood what had happened. With understanding came terror.

Every settled asteroid in the Lyll belt was on the same maximum alert status. The Edenist habitats orbiting Yosemite had announced a two million kilometre emergence exclusion zone around the gas giant, enforced by armed voidhawks. Such New California Navy ships which had escaped the planetary catastrophe were dispersed across several settled asteroids, while the surviving admirals gathered at the Yosemite trailing Trojan asteroid cluster to debate what to do. So far all they'd done was fall back on the oldest military maxim, and sent out scouts to fill in the yawning information gap.

Commander Nicolai Penovich was duty officer in Idria's SD command centre when the Adamist starships emerged three thousand kilometres away. Five medium-sized craft, nowhere near the designated emergence zone. Sensors showed their infra-red signature leap upward within seconds of their appearance. Tactical programs confirmed a massive combat wasp launch. Targets verified as the asteroid's SD platforms, and supplementary sensor satellites.

Nicolai datavised the fire command computer to retaliate. Electron and laser beams stabbed out. The hastily assembled home defence force fleet – basically every ship capable of launching a combat wasp – was vectored on to the intruders.

By the time most of them had got under way the attackers had jumped away.

Another four starships jumped in, released their combat wasps, and jumped out.

The assault was right out of the tactics flek, and there was nothing Nicolai could do about it. His sensor coverage had already degraded by forty per cent, and still more was dropping out as combat wasp submunitions stormed local space with electronic-warfare pulses. Nuclear explosions were surrounding the asteroid with a scintillating veil of irradiated particles, almost completely wiping out the satellites' long-range scanner returns.

It was becoming increasingly difficult to direct the platforms' fire on incoming drones. He didn't even know how many surviving salvos there were any more.

Two of the defending ships were struck by kinetic missiles, disintegrating into spectacular, short-lived, streaks of stellar flame.

Nicolai and his small staff recalled the remainder of the fleet, trying to form them into an inner defensive globe. But his communications were as bad as the sensor coverage. At least three didn't respond. Two SD platforms dropped out of his command network. Victims of combat wasps, or electronic warfare, he didn't know, and the tactics program couldn't offer a prediction.

The platforms were never really intended to ward off a full-scale assault like this, he thought despairingly. Idria's real protection came from the system's naval alliance.

A couple of close-orbit detector satellites warned him of four starships emerging barely fifty kilometres from the asteroid. Frigates popped out, spraying combat wasps in all directions. Eight were aimed at Idria's spaceport, scattering shoals of submunitions as they closed at thirty-five gees. Nicolai didn't have anything left to stop them. Small explosions erupted right across the two kilometre grid of metal and composite. Precisely targeted, they struck communication relays and sensor clusters.

Every input into the SD command centre went dead.

'Oh shit almighty!' Lieutenant Fleur Mironov yelled. 'We're gonna die.'

'No,' Nicolai said. 'They're softening us up for an assault.' He called up internal structural blueprints, studying the horribly few options remaining. 'I want whatever combat personnel we have positioned in the axial spindle tubes, they're to enforce a total blockade. And close down the transit tubes linking the caverns with the spaceport. Now. Whoever's left out there will just have to take their chances.'

'Against the possessed?' Fleur exclaimed. 'Why not just fling them out of an airlock?'

'Enough, Lieutenant! Now find me some kind of external sensor that's still functioning. I must know what's happening outside.'

'Sir.'

'We have to protect the majority of the population. Yreka and Orland will respond as soon as they see what's happened. And Orland had two navy frigates assigned to it. We only have to hold out for a couple of hours. The troops can manage that, surely. The possessed aren't that good.'

'If Yreka and Orland haven't been attacked as well,' Fleur said dubiously. 'We only saw about a dozen ships. There were hundreds in the asteroids and low-orbit station docks when the possessed took over New California.'

'Jesus, will you stop with the pessimism, already? Now where's my external sensor?'

'Coming up, sir. I got us a couple of thermo-dump panel inspection mechanoids on microwave circuits. Guess the possessed didn't bother targeting those relays.'

'OK, let's have it.'

The quality of the image which came foaming into his brain

was dreadful: silver grey smears drifting entirely at random against an intense black background, crinkled blue-brown rock across the bottom quarter of the picture. Fleur manipulated the mechanoids so that their sensors swung round to focus on the battered spaceport disc at the end of its spindle. The spaceport was venting heavily in a dozen places, girders had been mashed, trailing banners of tattered debris. Eight lifeboats were flying clear of the damaged sections. Nicolai Penovich didn't like to imagine how many people were crammed inside, nor how they could be rescued. Vivid white explosions shimmered into existence against the bent constellation of Pisces. Someone was still fighting out there.

A large starship slid smoothly into view, riding a lance of violet fusion fire. Definitely a navy craft of some kind, it was still in its combat configuration; short-range sensor clusters extended, thermo-dump panels retracted. Steamy puffs of coolant gas squirted from small nozzles ringing its midsection. Hexagonal ports were open all around its front hull, too big for combat-wasp launch-tubes.

Scale was hard to judge, but Nicolai estimated it at a good ninety metres in diameter. 'I think that's a marine assault ship,' he said.

The main drive shut off and blue ion thrusters fired, locking it into position five hundred metres away from the spindle which connected the non-rotating spaceport with the asteroid.

'I've placed a couple of squads in the spindle,' Fleur said. 'They're not much, some port police, and a dozen boosted mercenaries who volunteered.'

'Horatio had it easy compared to them,' Nicolai murmured. 'But they should be able to hold. The possessed can't possibly mount a standard beachhead operation. Their bodies screw up electronics, they'd never be able to wear an SII suit, let alone combat armour. They're going to have to dock and try and fight their way along the transit tubes, that's going to cost them.' He checked the external situation again, seeking confirmation of his assessment. The big ship was holding steady, with just intermittent orange fireballs spluttering out of the equatorial vernier-thruster nozzles to maintain attitude.

'Get me access to sensor coverage of the spaceport, and check on our internal communications,' Nicolai ordered. 'We may be able to coordinate a running battle from here.'

'Aye, sir.' Fleur started to datavise instructions into the command centre's computer, interfacing their communication circuits with the civil data channels which weaved through the spaceport.

Shadows began to flicker inside the ship's open hatches. 'What the hell have they got in there?' Nicolai asked.

The inspection mechanoids turned up their camera resolution. He saw figures emerging from the ship, hornets darting out of their nest. Dark outlines, hard to see with the mushy interference and low light level. But they were definitely humanoid in shape, riding manoeuvring packs that had enlarged nozzles for higher thrust. 'Who are they?' he whispered.

'Traitors,' Fleur hissed. 'Those NC Navy bastards must have switched sides. They never did support independent asteroid settlements. Now they're helping the possessed!'

'They wouldn't. Nobody would do that.'

'Then how do you explain it?'

He shook his head helplessly. Outside the spindle, the fast, black hornets were burning their way in through the carbotanium structure. One by one, they flew into the ragged holes.

*

Louise was actually glad to return to the quiet luxury of Balfern House. It had been an extraordinary day, and a wearyingly long one, too.

In the morning she'd visited Mr Litchfield, the family's lawyer in the capital, to arrange for money from the Cricklade account to be made available to her. The transfer had taken hours, neither the lawyer nor the bank was accustomed to young girls insisting on being issued with Jovian Bank credit disks. She stuck to her guns despite all the obstacles; Joshua had told her they were acceptable everywhere in the Confederation. She doubted Norfolk's pounds were.

That part of the day had proved to be simplicity itself compared to finding a way off Norfolk. There were only three civil-registered starships left in orbit, and they were all chartered by the Confederation Navy to act as support ships for the squadron.

Louise, Fletcher, and Genevieve had taken their coach out to Bennett Field, Norwich's main aerodrome, to talk to a spaceplane pilot from the *Far Realm*, who was currently groundside. His name was Furay, and through him she had gradually persuaded the captain to sell them a berth. She suspected it was her money rather than her silver tongue which had eventually won them a cabin. Their fee was forty thousand fuseodollars apiece.

Her original hope of buying passage directly to Tranquillity had gone straight out of the window barely a minute after starting to talk to Furay. The *Far Realm* was contracted to stay with the squadron during its Norfolk assignment; when the ship did leave, it would accompany the navy frigates. No one knew when that would be any more, the captain explained. Louise didn't care, she just wanted to get off the planet, even floating around in low orbit would be safer than staying in Norwich. She would worry about reaching Tranquillity when the *Far Realm* arrived at its next port.

So the captain appeared to give in gracefully, and negotiate terms. They were due to fly up tomorrow, where they would wait in the ship until the squadron's business was complete.

More delay. More uncertainty. But she'd actually started to accomplish her goal. Fancy, arranging to fly on a starship, all by herself. Fly away to meet Joshua.

And leave everyone else in the stew.

I can't take them all with me, though. I want to, dear Jesus, but I really can't. Please understand.

She tried not to let the guilt show as she led the maids through the house back to her room. They were carrying the parcels and cases Louise had bought after they'd left Bennett Field. Clothes more suitable to travelling on a starship (Gen had a ball choosing them), and other items she thought they might need. She remembered Joshua explaining how difficult and dangerous star travel could be. Not that it bothered him, he was so brave.

Thankfully Aunt Celina hadn't returned yet, even though it was now late afternoon. Explaining the baggage away would have been impossible.

After shooing the maids out of her room Louise kicked her shoes off. She wasn't used to high heels, the snazzy black leather was beginning to feel like some kind of torture implement. Her new jacket followed them onto the floor, and she pushed the balcony doors open.

Duke was low in the sky, emitting a lovely golden tint, which in turn made the gardens seem rich with colour. A cooling breeze was just strong enough to sway the branches on the trees. Out on the largest pond, black and white swans performed a detailed waltz around clumps of fluffy tangerine water lilies, while long fountains foamed quietly behind them. It was all so deceitfully tranquil; with the wall shielding the sound of the busy road outside she would never know she was in the heart of the largest city on the planet. Even Cricklade was noisier at times.

Thinking about her home made her skin cold. It was something she'd managed to avoid all day. I wonder what Mummy and Daddy are being made to do by their possessors? Evil, vile acts if that awful Quinn Dexter has any say in the matter.

Louise shivered, and retreated back into the room. Time for a long soak in the bath, then change for dinner. By the time

Aunt Celina rose tomorrow morning, she and Gen would be gone.

She took off her new blouse and skirt. When she removed her bra she felt her breasts carefully. Were they more sensitive? Or was she just imagining it? Were they supposed to be sensitive this early in a pregnancy? She wished she'd paid more attention to the family planning lessons at school, rather than giggling with her friends at the pictures of men's privates.

'Looks like you're getting lonely, Louise, having to do that for yourself.'

Louise yelped, grabbing up the blouse and holding it in front of her like a shield.

Roberto pushed aside the curtain at the far end of the room where he'd concealed himself, and sauntered forward. His grin was arctic.

'Get out!' Louise screamed at him. The terrible first heat of embarrassment was turning to cold anger. 'Out, you filthy fat oaf!'

'What you need is a close friend,' Roberto gloated. 'Someone who can do it for you. It's a lot better that way.'

Louise took a step back, her legs shaking with revulsion. 'Get out, now,' she growled at him.

'Or what?' His hand swept wide, the gesture taking in the pile of cases which the maids had left. 'Going somewhere? What exactly have you been up to today?'

'How I spend my time is none of your business. Now go, before I ring for a maid.'

Roberto took another step towards her. 'Don't worry, Louise, I won't say anything to my mother. I don't rat on my friends. And we are going to be friends, aren't we? Real good friends.'

She took a pace back, glancing round. The bell cord to summon a maid was on the other side of the bed, near him. She'd never make it. 'Get away from me.'

'I don't think so.' He started to undo the buttons on his

shirt. 'See, if I have to leave now I might just tell the police about that so-called farmhand friend of yours.'

'What?' she barked in shock.

'Yeah. Thought that might adjust your attitude. They make me do history at school, see. I don't like it, but I do know who Fletcher Christian was. Your friend is using a false name. Now why would he do that, Louise? In a bit of trouble back on Kesteven, was he? Bit of a rebel, is he?'

'Fletcher is not in any trouble.'

'Really? Then why don't I just go make that call?'

'No.'

Roberto licked his lips. 'Now that's a whole lot nicer, Louise. We're cooperating with each other. Aren't we?'

She just clutched the blouse closer to her, mind feverish.

'Aren't we?' he demanded.

Louise nodded jerkily.

'OK, that's better.' He peeled off his shirt.

Louise couldn't help the tears stinging her eyes. No matter what, she told herself, I won't let him. I'd sooner die; it would be cleaner.

Roberto unbuckled his belt, and started to take down his trousers. Louise waited until they were round his knees, then bolted for the bed.

'Shit!' Roberto yelled. He made a grab for her. Missed. Nearly toppled over as the trouser fabric tangled round his shins.

Louise flung herself on top of the bed, and started to scurry over the blankets. She'd left it on the other side. Roberto was cursing behind her, grappling with his trousers. She reached the end of the bed, and flopped down, hands reaching underneath.

'No, you don't.' Roberto grasped an ankle and started dragging her back.

Louise squealed, kicking backwards with her free foot.

'Bitch.'

He landed on top of her, making her cry out at the pain of such a weight. She clawed desperately at the mattress, pulling both of them to the edge of the bed. Her hands could just reach the carpet. Roberto laughed victoriously at her ineffectual struggling, and shifted round until he was straddling her buttocks. 'Going somewhere?' he taunted. Her head and shoulders hung over the edge of the bed, vast waves of hair flooding the sheets. He sat up, panting slightly, and brushed the hair off her back, enjoying the flawless skin which was exposed. Louise strained below him, as if she was still trying to wriggle free. 'Stop fighting it,' he told her. His cock was hugely erect. 'It's going to happen, Louise. Come on, you'll love it when we get started. I'm going to last all night long with you.' His hands pushed below her, reaching for her breasts.

Louise's desperate fingers finally found the cool, smooth shape of carved wood she was searching for under the bed. She grabbed at it, groaning in revulsion as Roberto's hands squeezed. But the feel of Carmitha's shotgun sent resolution surging through her veins, inflaming and chilling at the same time.

'Let me up,' she begged. 'Please, Roberto.'

The obscene prowling hands were stilled. 'Why?'

'I don't want it like this. Turn me over. Please, it'll make it easier for you. This hurts.'

There was a moment's silence. 'You won't struggle?' he sounded uncertain.

'I won't. I promise. Just not like this.'

'I do like you, Louise. Really.'

'I know.'

The weight against the small of her back lifted. Louise tensed, gathering every ounce of strength. She pulled the shotgun clear from under the bed, and twisted round, swinging it in a wide arc, trying to predict where his head would be.

Roberto saw it coming. He managed to bring his arms up in an attempt to ward off the blow, ducking to one side—

The shotgun barrel caught him a glancing blow above his left ear, the end of the pump mechanism thumping his guarding hand. Nothing like as devastating as Louise wanted it. But he cried out in pain and shock, clamping his hands over the side of his head. He started to keel over.

Louise tugged her legs out from under him, and tumbled off the bed, almost losing hold of the shotgun. She could hear Roberto sob behind her. It was a sound which sent a frightening burst of glee into her head. It freed her from all that genteel refinement which Norfolk had instilled, put civilization aside.

She climbed to her feet, got a better grip on the shotgun, and brought it crashing down on the top of Roberto's skull.

\*

The anxious knocking on the door was the next thing Louise was conscious of. For some inexplicable reason she'd sunk down onto the floor and started to weep. Her whole body was cold and trembling, yet her skin was prickled with perspiration.

The knock came again, more urgent this time. 'Lady Louise?'

'Fletcher?' she gasped. Her voice was so weak.

'Yes, my lady. Are you all right?'

'I . . .' A giggle became choked in her throat. 'One minute, Fletcher.' She looked round, and gagged. Roberto was sprawled over the bed. Blood from his head wound had produced a huge stain over the sheet.

Dear Jesus, I've killed him. They'll hang me.

She stared at the body for a long, quiet moment, then got up and wrapped a towel round her nakedness.

'Is anyone with you?' she asked Fletcher.

'No, my lady. I am alone.'

Louise opened the door, and he slipped inside. For some reason the sight of the corpse didn't seem to shake him.

'My lady.' The voice was so soft with sympathy and concern. He opened his arms, and she pressed against him, trying not to cry again.

'I had to,' she blurted. 'He was going to . . .'

Fletcher's hand stroked her wild hair, smoothing and combing it with every stroke. Within a minute it was a dry, shiny cloak again. And somehow the pain inside was lessened.

'How did you know?' she murmured.

'I could sense your anguish. A mighty silent shout, it was.'

'Oh.' Now there was a strange notion, that the possessed could listen to your thoughts. There's so much badness inside my head.

Fletcher met her troubled gaze. 'Did that animal violate you, my lady?'

She shook her head. 'No.'

'He is lucky. Had he done so, I would have dispatched him to the beyond myself. Nor would such a passage be pleasant for him.'

'But, Fletcher, he is dead. I did it.'

'No, lady, he lives.'

'The blood . . .'

'A cut to the head always looks far worse than it is. Come now, I will have you shed no more tears for this beast.'

'Oh, Lord, what a dreadful mess we're in. Fletcher, he suspects something about you. I can't just go to the police and file a rape charge. He'd tell them about you. Besides,' she drew an annoyed breath, 'I'm not quite sure which of us Aunt Celina would believe.'

'Very well. We shall have to leave now.'

'But—'

'Can you think of another course to follow?'

'No,' she said sadly.

'Then you must prepare; pack what you need. I shall go and tell the little one, also.'

'What about him?' She indicated Roberto's unconscious form.

'Dress yourself, my lady. I will deal with him.'

Louise picked through the boxes, and went into the en suite bathroom. Fletcher was already leaning over Roberto.

She put on a pair of long dark blue trousers and a white T-shirt. Black plimsolls completed the outfit. A combination unlike anything she'd ever worn before – unlike anything Mother had ever allowed her to wear. But practical, she decided. Just wearing such garments made her feel different. The rest of the things she needed went into one of the suitcases she'd bought. She was halfway through packing when she heard Roberto's frightened shout from the bedroom. It tailed off into a whimper. Her initial impulse was to rush in and find out what was happening. Instead, she took a deep breath, then looked in the mirror and finished tying back her hair.

When she did finally emerge back into the bedroom, Roberto had been trussed up with strips of blanket. He stared at her with wide, terrified eyes. The gag in his mouth muffled his desperate shouts.

She walked over to the bed and looked down at him. Roberto stopped trying to speak.

'I'm going to return to this house one day,' she said. 'When I do, I'll have my father and my husband with me. If you're smart, you won't be here when we arrive.'

*

Duchess was already rising by the time they arrived at Bennett Field. Every aircraft on Norfolk had been pressed into military service (including the aeroambulance from Bytham), ready to fly the newly formed army out to the rebel-held islands. Over a third of them were parked in long ranks over the aerodrome's close-mown grass. There were a lot of khaki-uniformed troops milling around outside the hangars.

Three guards stood beside the entrance to the administration block, a sergeant and two privates. There hadn't been any at lunchtime when Louise had met Furay.

Genevieve climbed down out of the cab, and gave them a sullen look. The young girl was becoming very grizzly.

'Sorry, miss,' the sergeant said. 'No civilians permitted in here. The aerodrome is under army control now.'

'We're not civilians, we're passengers,' Genevieve said indignantly. She glared up at the big man, who couldn't help a grin.

'Sorry, love, but you still can't come in.'

'She's telling the truth,' Louise said. She fished a copy of their transport contract with the *Far Realm* out of her bag and proffered it to the sergeant.

He shrugged and flicked through the pages, not really reading it.

'The *Far Realm* is a military ship,' Louise said hopefully.

'I'm not sure . . .'

'These two young ladies are the nieces of the Earl of Luffenham,' Fletcher said. 'Now surely your superior officer should be made aware of their travel documentation? I'm sure nobody would want the Earl to have to call the general commanding this base.'

The sergeant nodded gruffly. 'Of course. If you'd like to wait inside while I get this sorted out. My lieutenant is in the mess at the moment. It might take a while.'

'You're very kind,' Louise said.

The sergeant managed a flustered smile.

They were shown into a small ground-floor office overlooking the field. The privates brought their bags in for them, both smiling generously at Louise.

'Have they gone?' she asked after the door was closed.

'No, my lady. The sergeant is most discomfited by our presence. One of the privates has been left a few yards down the corridor.'

'Damnation!' She went over to the single window. From her position she could see nearly a third of the field. If anything the planes seemed to be packed even tighter than this morning, there were hundreds of them. Squads of militia were marching along the grass roadways, shouted at by sergeant majors. A great many people were involved with loading big cargo planes. Flat-topped trucks trundled past the squads, delivering more materièl.

'I think the campaign must be starting,' Louise said. Dear Jesus, they look so young. Just boys, my age. 'They're going to lose, aren't they? They're all going to be possessed.'

'I expect so, my lady, yes.'

'I should have done something.' She wasn't sure if she was speaking out loud or not. 'Should have left Uncle Jules a letter. Warned them. I could have given them that much of my time, enough to write a few simple lines.'

'There is no defence, dear lady.'

'Joshua will protect us. He'll believe me.'

'I liked Joshua,' Genevieve said.

Louise smiled, and ruffed her sister's hair.

'If you had warned your family and the Prince's court, and they believed you, I fear you would not have been able to buy your passage on the *Far Realm*, lady.'

'Not that it's done us much good, so far,' she said in exasperation. 'We should have gone up to the *Far Realm* as soon as Furay finalized the contract.'

Genevieve gave her an anxious look. 'We'll get up there, Louise. You'll see.'

'Not very easily. I can't see the lieutenant allowing us on to the field on the strength of that contract, not when all the troops are taking off. At the very least he'll call Uncle Jules first. Then we'll really be in trouble.'

'Why?' Genevieve asked.

Louise squeezed her sister's hand. 'I had a bit of a quarrel with Roberto.'

'Yuck! Mr Fatso. I didn't like him.'

'Me neither.' She glanced out of the window again. 'Fletcher, can you tell if Furay is out there?'

'I will try, lady Louise.' He came over to stand beside her, putting both hands flat on the windowsill and bowing his head. He shut his eyes.

Louise and Genevieve swapped a glance. 'If we can't get away into orbit, we'll have to go out onto the moors and camp there,' Louise said. 'Find somewhere isolated, like Carmitha did.'

Genevieve put her arms round her big sister's waist and hugged. 'You'll get us away, Louise. I know you will. You're so clever.'

'Not really.' She hugged the girl back. 'But at least I got us into some decent clothes.'

'Yes!' Genevieve smiled down approvingly at her jeans and sweatshirt, even though there was a horrid cartoon rabbit printed on the chest.

Fletcher's eyes flicked open. 'He's here, lady Louise. Over yonder.' He pointed out of the window in the direction of the central control tower.

Louise was fascinated by the wet palmprints he'd left on the sill. 'Excellent. That's a start. Now all we have to do is work out how to get to the spaceplane.' Her hand tightened on the new Jovian Bank credit disk in her trouser pocket. 'I'm sure Mr Furay can be persuaded to take us up straight away.'

'There are also several possessed within the aerodrome perimeter.' Fletcher gave a confused frown. 'One of them is wrong.'

'Wrong?'

'Odd.'

'What do you mean?'

'I'm not quite sure, only that he is odd.'

Louise glanced down at Genevieve, whose face had paled at the mention of the possessed. 'They won't catch us, Gen. Promise.'

'As do I, little one.'

Genevieve nodded uncertainly, wanting to believe.

Louise looked from the girl to the solders marching about

outside, and came to a decision. 'Fletcher, can you fake one of the army uniforms?' she asked. 'An officer, not too high-ranking. A lieutenant or captain, perhaps?'

He smiled. 'A prudent notion, my lady.' His grey suit shimmered, darkening to khaki, its surface roughening.

'The buttons are wrong,' Genevieve declared. 'They should be bigger.'

'If you say so, little one.'

'That'll do,' Louise said after a minute, anxious that the sergeant would return before they were done. 'Half of these boys have never seen uniforms before. They don't know if it's right or not. We're wasting time.'

Genevieve and Fletcher pulled a face together at the reprimand. The girl giggled.

Louise opened the window and peered out. There was no one in the immediate vicinity. 'Push the cases through first,' she said.

They walked over to the nearest hangar as quickly as they could; Louise immediately regretting bringing their bags and cases. She and Fletcher were carrying two apiece, and they were heavy; even Genevieve had a big shoulder bag which she was wilting under. Any attempt to be inconspicuous was doomed from the start.

It was about two hundred yards to the hangar. When they got there, the central control tower didn't look any nearer. And Fletcher just said that Furay was 'near there'. The pilot could be well on the other side for all she knew.

The hangar was being used as a store depot by the army; long rows of wooden crates were lined up along the sides, arranged so that narrow alleyways branched off at right angles leading right back to the walls. Five fork-lift trucks were parked at the far end. There were no soldiers in sight. The doors at both ends were wide open, creating a gentle breeze along the main aisle.

'See if there's a farm ranger or something like it parked

here,' Louise said. 'If not, we're going to have to dump the cases.'

'Why?' Genevieve asked.

'They're too heavy, Gen, and we're in a hurry. I'll buy you some more, don't worry.'

'Can you use such a contraption, my lady?' Fletcher asked.

'I've driven one before.' Up and down Cricklade's drive. Once. With Daddy shouting instructions in my ear.

Louise let the bags fall to the floor, and told Genevieve to wait by them.

'I will search round outside,' Fletcher said. 'My appearance will cause little concern. May I suggest you stay in here?'

'Right. I'll check down there.' She started walking towards the other end of the hangar. The ancient corrugated-iron roof panels were creaking softly as they shed the heat of Duke-day.

She was about thirty yards from the open sliding doors when she heard Fletcher calling out behind her. He was running down the wide aisle formed by the crates, waving his arms urgently. Genevieve was chasing after him.

A jeep drove into the hangar. Two people were sitting in it. The one driving wore a soldier's uniform. The second, sitting in the back, was dressed all in black.

Louise turned to face them. I'll brazen it out; after all, that's what I've been doing all day.

Then she realized the man in black was a priest, she could see the dog collar. She breathed out a sigh of relief. He must be an army padre.

The jeep braked to a halt beside her.

Louise smiled winningly, the smile which always made Daddy say yes. 'I wonder if you could help us, I'm a little bit lost.'

'I doubt that, Louise,' Quinn Dexter said. 'Not someone as resourceful as you.'

Louise started to run, but something cold and oily snaked

round her ankles. She crashed down onto the timeworn concrete floor, grazing her hands and wrists.

Quinn stepped down out of the jeep. The mockery of a cassock swirled round his feet. 'Going somewhere?'

She ignored her stinging hands and numbed knee, lifting her head to see him standing above her. 'Devil! What have you done to Mummy?'

His dog collar turned a shiny scarlet, as though it was made from blood. 'Such a fucking great hurry for knowledge. Well, don't you worry, Louise, we're going to show you exactly what happened to Mummy. I'm going to give you a personal demonstration.'

'Do not touch her, sir,' Fletcher called as he came to a halt by the front of the jeep. 'The lady Louise is my ward, under my protection.'

'Traitor,' Lawrence Dillon yelled. 'You are one of the blessed ones. God's Brother allowed you back into this world to fight the legions of the false Lord. Now you defy the Messiah chosen to lead the returned.'

Quinn clicked his fingers, and Lawrence fell silent. 'I don't know who you are, friend. But don't fuck with me or you'll die to regret it.'

'I do not wish to draw swords with any man. So stand aside and we will go our separate ways.'

'Arsehole. I'm stronger than you by myself; and there's two of us.'

Fletcher smiled thinly. 'Then why do you not take what you desire by your might? Could it be I would struggle? And that would draw the attention of the soldiers. Are you stronger than an entire army?'

'Don't push it,' Quinn warned. 'I'm off this shit-tip planet today, and nobody's gonna stop that. Now I know this bitch from before, she's smart. She'll have a starship lined up to take her away, right?'

Louise glared up at him.

'Thought so,' Quinn sneered. 'Well, lover, you're gonna hand your tickets over to me. My need is one fuck of a lot greater than yours.'

'Never!' She groaned as Lawrence Dillon grabbed her by the back of her neck and hauled her upright.

Fletcher made a start forward, but stopped as Quinn pointed at Genevieve, who was cowering behind him.

'Dumb move,' Quinn said. 'I'll blow you back to the beyond if I have to. And then it'll go real bad for your little pal. You know I mean it. I won't possess her. I'll keep her for myself. Some nights I'll hand her over to Lawrence; he knows some real kinks now. I taught him myself.'

'Sure did.' Lawrence grinned wildly at Genevieve.

'You are inhuman.' Fletcher put an arm instinctively round Genevieve.

'Wrong!' Quinn barked. His sudden fury made Fletcher take a half-pace backwards.

'Banneth. Now she's inhuman. She did things to me . . .' Spittle appeared on Quinn's chin. He giggled, and wiped it away on the back of a trembling hand. 'She did things, OK. And now. Now, I'm the one who's gonna do things right back to her. Things so sick she's never thought of them. God's Brother understands that, understands the need in me. I'm gonna let my serpent beast devour her then spew out the bits. I'll turn my whole crusade on her if I have to. I'll use biowar bugs, I'll use nukes, I'll use antimatter. I don't fucking care. I'm gonna crack Earth wide open. And I'm gonna go down there, and I'm gonna take her. And nobody is going to stand in my way.'

'Right on!' Lawrence shouted.

Quinn was breathing heavily, as if there was insufficient oxygen in the hangar. The cassock had returned to his original priest's robe, tiny crackles of energy rippling along the voluminous fabric. Louise quailed before the expression on his face. There wasn't even any point in struggling.

Quinn smiled at her, enraptured; two drops of blood dripped off his vampire fangs, running down his chin.

'Sweet Jesus.' Louise made the shape of the cross with her free hand.

'But,' Quinn said, calm again, 'right now, I'm only interested in you.'

'Fletcher!' she wailed.

'I warn you, sir, do not touch her.'

Quinn waved a dismissive hand. Fletcher doubled up as if a giant had slammed a fist into his stomach. Breath *oof*ed out of his parted lips. With a look of horrified surprise, he was flung backwards, thin slivers of white fire crawling over him, slowly constricting. His uniform began to smoulder. Blood burst out of his mouth and nose, more began to stain his crotch. He screamed, bucking about helplessly, wrestling with the air.

'Nooo!' Louise implored. 'Please stop. Stop!'

Genevieve had stumbled to her knees, white face staring brokenly.

Lawrence began to fumble at the collar of Louise's T-shirt, snickering eagerly. Then his hand froze, and he drew a breath in surprise.

Quinn was frowning, squinting along the length of the hangar.

Louise gulped, not understanding anything. But Fletcher had stopped his agonized contortions. A liquid dust, sparkling with rainbow colours, was slithering over him, and his clothes were slowly mending. He rolled round groggily, and swayed up on his knees.

'What the fuck you doing here, man?' Quinn Dexter shouted.

Louise scanned the far end of the hangar. Duchess was shining directly through the wide open doors, producing a brilliant scarlet rectangle set amid the funereal metal cavern. A blank, black human figure was silhouetted in the exact centre. It raised its arm, pointing.

A bullet bolt of white fire streaked down the hangar, almost too fast for the eye to follow. Louise saw huge shadows careering round at dizzying speeds. The bolt hit the iron roofing girder directly above Quinn Dexter. He flinched, ducking blindly as flakes of hot, tortured metal rained down. The whole roof creaked as the loading was redistributed.

'God's Brother, what the shit are you playing at?' Quinn raged.

A bass laugh rumbled down the hangar, distorted by the peculiar acoustics of the stacked crates.

Louise had time to flash one imploring look at Fletcher, who could only shrug in confusion before the strange figure spread both arms wide.

'Quinn?' Lawrence appealed. 'Quinn, what the hell is happening?'

His answer was a rosette corona of white fire which burst out of the silhouette. The crates around the figure ignited in the eerily powerful topaz flame which the energistic ability always fanned. A dry wind rose from nowhere, sending Quinn's robe thrashing.

'Shit,' Quinn gasped.

The flames were racing towards them, gorging on the crates, swirling round and round the aisle, faster and faster, the eye of a cyclonic inferno. Wood screeched and snapped as it was cremated, spilling the contents of the crates for the flames to consume, intensifying their strength.

Louise squealed as the awesome heat pummelled against her. Lawrence had let go of her, his arms waving frantically. In front of him the air was visibly flexing like a warped lens, a shield against the baneful radiance.

Fletcher scooped up Genevieve. Bending low, he scuttled

towards the open door beyond the jeep. 'Move, lady,' he shouted.

Louise barely heard him above the roaring. Dull explosions sounded somewhere behind the leading edge of flame. Corrugated-iron panels were taking flight, busting their rusty rivets to shoot off the roof, soaring high into the two-tone sky.

She staggered after Fletcher. Only when she was actually outside did she look round, just for a second.

The flames formed a furious rippling tunnel the entire length of the hangar. Dense black smoke churned out of the end. But the centre was perfectly clear.

Quinn stood before the conflagration, facing it down, arms raised to discharge his power, deflecting the devastating barrage of heat. Far ahead of him, the blank figure had adopted a similar poise.

'Who are you?' Quinn screamed into the holocaust. 'Tell me!' A large wall of crates burst apart, sending a storm of sparks charging into the fray. Several roof girders buckled, sagging down, corrugated panels scything into the flames. The tunnel began to twist, losing its stability. 'Tell me. Show your face.' Sirens were sounding. The shouts of men. And more of the ruined hangar collapsed. 'Tell me!'

The rampaging flames obscured the impudent figure. Quinn let out a wordless howl of outrage. And then even he had to retreat as metal melted and concrete turned to sluggish lava. He and Lawrence together, lurching out onto the withered grass. Men and fire engines swarmed round in chaos. It was easy to blend in and slink away. Lawrence said nothing as they made their way along a lane of parked aircraft, the darkness of Quinn's mind humbling him into silence.

Louise and Fletcher saw the first vehicles bumping over the grass, farm rangers painted military green and a couple of jeeps. A squad of militia were running round the rank of planes, urged on by their officer. Sirens were starting up in the distance. Behind her, the flames were crawling ever higher into the sky.

'Fletcher, your uniform,' she hissed.

He glanced down. His trousers had become purple. A blink, and they were khaki again; his jacket lost its rumpled appearance. His bearing was impressively imperious.

Genevieve moaned in his arms, as if she were fighting a nightmare.

'Is she all right?' Louise asked.

'Yes, my lady. Simply a faint.'

'And you?'

He nodded gingerly. 'I survive.'

'I thought . . . It was awful. That devil-brute, Quinn.'

'Never worry for me, lady. Our Lord has decreed some purpose for me, it will be revealed in time. I would not be here otherwise.'

The first vehicles were nearly upon them. Louise could see more soldiers on their way. It was going to be a complete madhouse; nobody would know what was going on, what was to be done.

'This could be our chance,' she said. 'We must be bold.' She started waving at one of the farm rangers. 'That's only a corporal driving. You outrank him.'

'As always, lady, your ingenuity is matched only by your strength of spirit. What cruel fate that our true lives are separated by such a gulf of time.'

She gave him a half-embarrassed, half-delighted smile. Then the farm ranger was pulling to a halt in front of them.

'You there,' Fletcher snapped at the startled man. 'Help me get this child away. She has been overcome by the fire.'

'Yes, sir.' The corporal rushed out of the driving seat to help Fletcher ease Genevieve on to the back seat.

'Our spaceplane is over by the tower,' Louise said, fixing Fletcher with an emphatic stare. 'It will have the medicine my sister requires. Our pilot is skilled in such matters.'

'Yes, madam,' Fletcher said. 'The tower,' he instructed the corporal.

The bewildered man looked from Louise to Fletcher, and decided not to question orders from an officer, no matter how bizarre the circumstances. Louise hopped in the back and cradled Genevieve's head as they drove away from the disintegrating hangar.

The corporal took ten minutes to find the *Far Realm*'s spaceplane, guided by Fletcher. Although she'd never seen one before, Louise could see how different it was to the aircraft it was parked among. A needle fuselage with sleek wings that didn't quite match, as if they'd come off a larger craft.

Genevieve had recovered by the time they arrived, though she was very subdued, pressing into Louise's side the whole time. Fletcher helped her down out of the farm ranger, and she glanced mournfully over to where the stain of black smoke was spreading over the crimson horizon. One hand gripped the pendant which Carmitha had given her, knuckles white.

'It's over, now, all over,' Louise said. 'I promise, Gen.' She ran her thumb over the Jovian Bank credit disk in her pocket as if it were a talisman as potent as Carmitha's charm. Thank heavens she'd kept hold of that.

Genevieve nodded silently.

'Thank you for your assistance, Corporal,' Fletcher said. 'Now I think you had better return to your commanding officer and see if you can help with the fire.'

'Sir.' He was dying to ask what was going on. Discipline defeated curiosity, and he flicked the throttle, driving off down the broad strip of grass.

Louise blew out a huge sigh of relief.

Furay waited for them at the bottom of the airstair. A half-knowing smile in place; interested rather than apprehensive.

Louise looked straight at him, grinning in return – at their arrival, the state they were in. It was a relief that for once she didn't have to concoct some ludicrous story on the spot. Furay was too smart for that. Bluntness and a degree of honesty was all she needed here.

She held up her Jovian Bank disk. 'My boarding pass.'

The pilot cocked an eyebrow towards the smoke. 'Anyone you know?'

'Yes. Just pray you never get to know them, too.'

'I see.' He took in Fletcher's uniform. When they'd met at lunchtime Fletcher had been in a simple suit. 'I see you've made lieutenant in under five hours.'

'I was once more than this, sir.'

'Right.' It wasn't quite the response Furay expected.

'Please,' Louise said. 'My sister needs to sit down. She's been through a lot.'

Furay thought the little girl looked about dead on her feet. 'Of course,' he said sympathetically. 'Come on. We've got some medical nanonics inside.'

Louise followed him up the airstair. 'Do you think you could possibly lift off now?'

He eyed the ferocious blaze again. 'Somehow, I just knew you were going to ask that.'

*

Marine Private Shaukat Daha had been standing guard outside the navy spaceplane for six hours when the hangar caught fire on the other side of Bennett Field. The major in charge of his squad had dispatched half a dozen marines to assist, but the rest were told to stand firm. 'It may just be a diversion,' the major datavised.

So Shaukat could only watch the extraordinarily vigorous flames through enhanced retinas on full resolution. The fire engines which raced across the aerodrome were quite something, though, huge red vehicles with crews in silvery suits. Naturally this crazy planet didn't have extinguisher mechanoids. Actual people had to deploy the hoses. It was fascinating.

His peripheral-senses monitor program alerted him to the

two men approaching the spaceplane. Shaukat shifted his retinal focus. It was a couple of the locals, a Christian padre and an army lieutenant. Shaukat knew that technically he was supposed to take orders from Norfolk officers, but this lieutenant was ridiculously young, still a teenager. There were limits.

Shaukat datavised his armour suit communication block to activate the external speaker. 'Gentlemen,' he said courteously as they came up to him. 'I'm afraid the spaceplane is a restricted zone. I'll have to see some identification and authorization before you come any closer.'

'Of course,' Quinn Dexter said. 'But tell me, is this the frigate *Tantu*'s spaceplane?'

'It is, yes, sir.'

'Bless you, my son.'

Annoyed at the honorific, he tried to datavise a moderately sarcastic response into the communication block. His neural nanonics had shut down completely. The armour suit suddenly became oppressively constrictive, as if the integral valency generators had activated, stiffening the fabric. He reached up to tear the shell-helmet off, but his arms wouldn't respond. A tremendous pain detonated inside his chest. Heart attack! he thought in astonishment. Allah be merciful, this cannot be, I'm only twenty-five.

Despite his disbelief the convulsion strengthened, jamming every muscle rock-solid. He could neither move nor breathe. The padre was looking at him with a vaguely interested expression. Coldness bit into his flesh, fangs of ice piercing every pore. His guttural cry of anguish was stifled by the armour suit tightening like a noose round his throat.

Quinn watched the marine tremble slightly as he earthed the man's body energy, snuffing out the chemical engines of life from every cell. After a minute he walked up to the dead statue and flicked it casually with a finger. There was a faint crystalline *ting* which faded quickly.

'Neat,' Lawrence said in admiration.

'It was quiet,' Quinn said with modest pride. He started up the spaceplane's airstair.

Lawrence examined the armour suit closely. Tiny beads of pale hoarfrost were already forming over the dark leathery fabric. He whistled appreciatively, and bounded up the airstair after Quinn.

\*

William Elphinstone rose up out of the diabolical darkness into a riot of heat, light, sound, and almost intolerable sensation. His gasp of anguish at the traumatic rebirth was deafening to his sensitive ears. Air seemed to rasp over his skin, every molecule a saw tooth.

So long! So long without a single sense. Held captive inside himself.

His possessor had gone now, departed. Freeing him. William whimpered in relief and fear.

There were terrible fragments of memory. Of a seething hatred. Of a demonic fire let loose. Of satisfaction at confounding the enemy. Of Louise Kavanagh.

Louise?

William understood so very little. He was propped up against a chain-link fence, his legs folded awkwardly below him. In front of him were hundreds of planes lined up across a broad aerodrome. It wasn't a place he'd ever seen before.

The sound of sirens rose and fell noisily. When he looked round he saw a hangar which had been gutted by fire. Flames and smoke were still rising out of the blackened ruins. Silver-suited firemen were surrounding the building, spraying it with foam from their hoses. An awful lot of militia troops were milling round the area.

'Here,' William cried to his comrades. 'I'm over here.' But his voice was a feeble croak.

A Confederation Navy spaceplane flew low over the field, wobbling slightly as if it wasn't completely under control. He blinked at it in confusion. There was another memory associated with the craft. Strong yet elusive: a dead boy hanging upside-down from a tree.

'And what do you think you're doing here?' The voice came from one of the two patrolling soldiers who were standing three yards away. One of them was pointing his rifle at William. The second was holding back a pair of growling Alsatians.

'I ... I was captured,' William Elphinstone said. 'Captured by the rebels. But they're not rebels. Please, you must listen. They're devils.'

Both soldiers exchanged a glance. The one with the rifle slung it over his shoulder, and raised a compact communication block.

'You must listen,' William said desperately. 'I was taken over. Possessed. I'm a serving officer from the Stoke County militia. I order you to listen.'

'Really, sir? Lost your uniform, did you?'

William looked at what he was wearing. It was his old uniform, but you had to look close to know. The shirt's khaki colour had faded below a blue and red check pattern, from the thighs down his regulation trousers were now tough blue denim jeans. Then he caught sight of his hands. The back of both were covered in black hair – and everyone always teased him about having delicate woman's hands.

He let out a little moan of dismay. 'I'm telling you the truth. As God is my witness.' Their blank, impersonal faces told him how useless it all was.

William Elphinstone remained slumped against the fence until the MPs came and took him off to Bennett Field's tiny police station. The detectives who arrived from Norwich's Special Branch division to interrogate him didn't believe his story either. Not until it was far too late.

\*

The Nyiru asteroid orbited at ninety thousand kilometres above Narok, one of the earliest Kenya-ethnic colony worlds. After it was knocked into position two centuries ago the construction company sliced out a five hundred metre diameter ledge for visiting bitek starships. Eager for the commerce they would bring, the asteroid council equipped the ledge with a comprehensive infrastructure; there was even a small chemical plant to provide the nutrient fluid the starships digested.

*Udat* complained it didn't taste right. Meyer wasn't up to arguing. With Haltam's best ministrations, it had taken him seven hours to recover consciousness after their escape from Tranquillity. Waking to find himself in interstellar space with a worried, hurting blackhawk and an equally unsettled crew to placate did not help his frail mental state. They had flown directly to Narok, needing eleven swallows to cover the eighty light-years, where normally they would only use five.

In all that time he had seen Dr Alkad Mzu precisely twice. She kept to herself in her cabin for most of the trip. Despite analgesic blocks and the medical nanonic packages wrapped round her legs and arms, her injuries were causing some discomfort (most curious of all she refused to let Haltam program the leg packages to repair an old knee injury). Neither of them had been in the mood to give ground. A few tersely formal words were exchanged; she apologized for his injuries and the vigour of the opposition, he filled her in on the flight parameters. And that was all.

After they arrived at Nyiru she paid the agreed sum without any quibble, added a five per cent bonus, and departed. Cherri Barnes did ask where she was headed, but the slight woman replied with one of her dead-eye smiles and said it was best nobody knew.

She vanished from their lives as much a mystery as when she entered it so dramatically.

Meyer spent thirty-six hours in the asteroid's hospital undergoing cranial deep invasion procedures to repair the damage around his neuron symbionts. Another two days of recuperation and extensive checks saw him cleared to leave.

Cherri Barnes kissed him when he walked back onto the *Udat*'s bridge. 'Nice to see you.'

He winked. 'Thanks. I was worried there for a while.'

'*You* were worried?'

**I was frightened,** *Udat* **said.**

**I know. But it's all over now. And by the way, I think you behaved commendably while I was out of it. I'm proud of you.**

**Thank you. I do not want to have to do that again, though.**

**You won't have to. I think we're finally through with trying to prove ourselves.**

**Yes!**

He glanced enquiringly round at his three crew. 'Anybody got any idea what happened to our weirdo passenger?'

''Fraid not,' Aziz said. 'I asked round the port, and all I could find out was that she's hired herself a charter agent. After that – not a byte.'

Meyer eased himself down into his command couch. A small headache was still pulsing away behind his eyes. He was beginning to wonder if it was going to be permanent. The doctor had said most probably not. 'No bad thing. I think Mzu was right when she said we'd be better off not knowing about her.'

'Fine in theory,' Cherri said irritably. 'Unfortunately all those agency people saw it was us who lifted her from Tranquillity. If she's right about how dangerous she is, then we're in some sticky shit right now. They're going to want to ask us questions.'

'I know,' Meyer said. 'God, targeted by the ESA at my age.'

'We could just go straight to them,' Haltam said. 'Because, let's be real here, they're going to catch us if they want to. If we go to them, it ought to show we aren't at the heart of whatever it is she's involved in.'

Cherri snorted in disgust. 'Yeah, but running to the King's secret police ... It ain't right. I've heard the stories, we all have.'

'Too right,' Haltam said. 'They make bad enemies.'

'What do you think, Meyer?' Aziz asked.

It wasn't something he wanted to think about. His nutrient levels had been balanced perfectly by the hospital while he was in recuperation therapy, but he still felt shockingly tired. Oh, for someone else to lift the burden from him, which of course was the answer, or at least a passable fudge.

**Good idea,** *Udat* **commented. She was nice.**

'There is somebody who might be able to help us,' Meyer told them. 'If she's still alive. I haven't seen her for nearly twenty years, and she was quite old then.'

Cherri gave him a suspicious look. 'Her?'

Meyer grinned. 'Yeah. Her. A lady called Athene, she's an Edenist.'

'They're worse than the bloody ESA,' Haltam protested.

'Stop being so prejudiced. They have one quality above all else, they're honest. Which is a damn sight more than you can say for the ESA. Besides, Edenism is one culture the ESA can never subvert.'

'Are you sure she'll help?' Cherri asked.

'No promises. All I can tell you is if she can, she will.' He looked at each of them in turn. 'Does anyone have an alternative?'

They didn't.

'OK, Cherri, file a departure notice with the port, please. We've been here quite long enough.'

'Aye, sir.'

**And you, let's have a swallow sequence for the Sol system.**

**Of course,** *Udat* **said, then added rather wistfully: I wonder if** *Oenone* **will be at Saturn when we arrive?**

**Who knows? But it would be nice to see how it developed.**

**Yes. As you say, it has been a long time.**

The first swallow manoeuvre took them twelve light-years from Narok's star. The second added another fifteen light-years. Confident the blackhawk had recovered from its ordeal, Meyer told it to go ahead with the third swallow.

Empty space twisted apart under the immense distortion which the patterning cells exerted. *Udat* moved cleanly into the interstice it had opened, shifting the energy which chased through its cells in smaller, more subtle patterns to sustain the continuity of the pseudofabric that closed around the hull. Distance without physical length flowed past the polyp.

**Meyer! Something is wrong!**

The alarmed mental shout struck like a physical blow. **What do you mean?**

**The terminus is retreating, I cannot match the distortion pattern to its coordinate.**

Linked with the blackhawk's mentality he could actually feel the pseudofabric changing, twisting and flexing around the hull as if it were a tunnel of agitated smoke. *Udat* was unable to impose the stability necessary to maintain the wormhole's uniformity.

**What's happening?** he asked, equally panicked.

**I don't understand. There is another force acting on the wormhole. It is interfering with my own distortion field.**

**Override it. Come on, get us out of here.** He felt a burst of power surge through the blackhawk's cells, amplifying the distortion field. It simply made the interference worse. *Udat* could actually sense waves forming in the wormhole's pseudofabric. The blackhawk juddered as two of them rolled against its hull.

**It doesn't work. I cannot support this energy output.**

**Keep calm,** Meyer implored. **It might just be a temporary episode.** In his own mind he could feel the energy drain reach exorbitant levels. There was barely ninety seconds' reserve left at this expenditure rate.

*Udat* reduced the strength of the distortion field, desperate to conserve its energy. A huge ripple ran down the wormhole, slapping across the hull. Loose items jumped and span over the bridge. Meyer instinctively grabbed the couch arms even as the restraint webbing folded over him.

The flight computer datavised that a recorded message was coming on-line. Meyer and the crew could only stare at the offending console in amazement as Dr Mzu's image invaded their neural nanonics. There was no background, she simply stood in the middle of a grey universe.

'Hello, Captain Meyer,' she said. 'If everything has gone according to plan you should be accessing this recording a few seconds before you die. This is just a slightly melodramatic gesture on my part to explain the how and why of your situation. The how is simple enough, you are now experiencing distortion feedback resonance. It's a spin-off discovery from my work thirty years ago. I left a little gadget in the life-support section which has set up an oscillation within the *Udat*'s distortion field. Once established, it is quite impossible to damp down, the wormhole itself acts as an amplifier. The resonance will not end while the distortion field exists, and without the field the wormhole will collapse back into its quantum state. A neat logic box you cannot escape from. You can now only survive as long as *Udat*'s patterning cells have energy, and that is depleting at quite a rate, I imagine.

'As to the why; I specifically chose you to extract me from Tranquillity because I always knew *Udat* was capable of pulling off such a difficult feat. I know because I've witnessed this blackhawk in action once before. Thirty years ago, to be precise. Do you remember, Captain Meyer? Thirty years ago, almost to the month, you were part of an Omutan mercenary squadron assigned to intercept three Garissan Navy ships, the *Chengho*, the *Gombari*, and the *Beezling*. I was on the *Beezling*, Captain, and I know it was you in the Omutan squadron because after it was over I accessed the sensor recordings we made of the attack. The *Udat* is a most distinctive ship, both in shape, colouring, and agility. You are good, and because of that you won the battle. And don't we all know exactly what happened to my home planet after that.'

The datavise ended.

Cherri Barnes looked over to Meyer, strangely placid. 'Is she right? Was it you?'

All he could do was give her a broken smile. 'Yes.' **I'm sorry, my friend.**

**I love you.**

Three seconds later, the energy stored in the *Udat*'s patterning cells was exhausted. The wormhole, which was held open purely by the artificial input of the distortion field, closed up. A straight two-dimensional fissure, fifteen light-years in length, appeared in interstellar space. For an instant it spat out a quantity of hard radiation equal to the mass of the blackhawk. Then, with the universe returned to equilibrium, it vanished.

# 9

Nicolai Penovich tried not to show how outright shit-scared he was when the po-faced gangsters ushered him into the Nixon suite. Not that the macho-routine façade would do a hell of a lot of good, they'd already let slip that the possessed could pretty much tell what was going on in your mind. But not read it direct, not pull out exact memories. And that was his ace. One memory, and a prayer.

As prayers went it was a goddam feeble one to be gambling not just his life but also his life after death.

He was shown into a giant lounge with a fluffy white shag carpet and pale pink furniture which resembled fragile glass balloons. There were several doors leading off to the rest of the suite, plain gold slabs three metres high. The far wall was a window looking down on New California. The view as the terracompatible planet slowly drifted past was magnificent.

One of the gangsters used his Thompson sub-machine-gun to prod Nicolai into the middle of the room. 'Stand there. Wait,' he grunted.

About a minute later one of the tall doors opened silently. A young girl walked out. Despite his predicament, Nicolai couldn't help staring. She was ravishing, a mid-teens face with every feature highlighted by the purest avian bones. All she wore was a long gossamer robe revealing an equally sublime physique.

When he thought about it, she was obscurely familiar. He couldn't imagine meeting her and not remembering, though.

She walked straight past him to a pile of travelling cases on the other side of the lounge. 'Libby, where's my red leather playsuit? The one with the silver chain collar. Libby!' Her foot stomped on the carpet.

'Coming, poppet.' A harried woman shuffled into the lounge. 'It's in the brown case, the one with your after-party informal collection.'

'Which one's that?' the girl complained.

'This one, poppet. Honestly, you're worse now than when we were touring.' She bent over to open the case.

Nicolai gave the nymphet a more intense scrutiny. It couldn't be . . .

Al Capone hurried in, followed by a number of cronies. And there was no doubt at all of his identity. He was a handsome man in his early twenties, with jet-black hair, slightly chubby cheeks which emphasized his near-permanent soft smile. His clothes were as antique (and as ridiculous to Nicolai's eyes) as the other gangsters', but he wore them with such panache it really didn't matter.

He took one glance at Jezzibella and grimaced. 'Jez, I told you before, will you stop goddam prancing around in front of the guys like this. You ain't wearing diddly.'

She looked back over her shoulder, pouted, and twirled a lock of hair round one finger. 'Oh come on, Al baby, it gives you a kick. The boys can all see what it is you've got, and they can never have. Living proof you're top doggy.'

'Jez-us.' He raised his eyes heavenwards.

Jezzibella sauntered over to him, and pecked him lightly on the cheek. 'Don't be long, precious. I've got parts of me that need a serious seeing to.' She beckoned Libby to follow, and made for the door. The woman walked after her, a garment made up from about five slender red leather straps draped over her arm.

Jezzibella treated Nicolai to a cutely bashful smile from the middle of a cloud of gold-blonde curls. Then she was gone.

Al Capone was staring at him. 'You got something on your mind, feller?'

'Yes, sir.'

'And what's that?'

'I've got some information for you, Mr Capone. Something that could be very useful to your Organization.'

Al nodded curtly. 'OK, you got through the door, that proves you got balls enough. Believe me, not many get this far. So now you're here, make your pitch.'

'I want to join your Organization. I hear you make room for non-possessed people with special talents.'

Al pointed a thumb at Avram Harwood III who was standing among the little cluster of lieutenants. 'Sure do. If Savvy Avvy here says what you got is good news, then you're in.'

'Is antimatter good news?' Nicolai asked. He caught the shudder of horror on the broken mayor's face.

Al rubbed a finger thoughtfully over his chin. 'Could be. You got some?'

'I know where you can get it. And I can assist your starship fleet when it comes to handling the stuff. It's a tricky substance, but I've had the training.'

'How come? You're a Fed, or close to it; a G-man for sure. I thought it was illegal.'

'It is. But Idria is a small asteroid sharing a star system with some powerful institutions. A lot of groundside politicos talk about strengthening our general assembly into a system-wide administration, or union. Some of Idria's council and SD officers don't appreciate that kind of talk. It took us a long time to gain our independence from the founding company, and it wasn't easy. So we made preparations. Just in case. Several of our companies make components that can be used to build antimatter-confinement systems and drives. Strategic Defence Command also established a link with a production station.'

'So you can get it any time you want?' Al asked.

'Yes, sir. I have the coordinate of the star which the station is orbiting. I can take you there.'

'What makes you think I want this stuff?'

'Because you're in the same position Idria was. New California is big, but the Confederation is a lot bigger.'

'You telling me I'm penny ante?'

'You might wind up that way if the First Admiral comes knocking.'

Al grinned broadly, he put his arm round Nicolai and patted his shoulders. 'I like you boy, you got what it takes. So here's the deal. You go sit in a corner with my friend Emmet Mordden, here, who is a real wiz with electric machines and stuff. And you tell him what you know, and if he says it checks out, you're in.'

*

Al shut the door behind him and leant against it, taking a moment out of life, that essential chunk of time alone in his head which allowed his worn-down resolution to build itself up again. I never realized being me was so goddam difficult.

Jezzibella had shifted to the trim athlete persona again, strong and haughty. She lay on the bed, arms stretched above her head, one knee bent. The playsuit had gripped her breasts with tight silver chains, forcing hard dark nipples to point at the ceiling. Every time she breathed her whole body flexed with feline allure.

'OK,' Al said. 'So tell me, what the fuck is antimatter?'

She arched her back, glaring defiantly at him. 'Never.'

'Jez! Just tell me. I don't have time for this crap.'

Her head was tossed from side to side.

'Goddam it!' He strode over to the bed, grabbed her jaw, and forced her to face him. 'I want to know. I gotta make decisions.'

A hand came arching through the air to strike him. He

managed to catch it just before it reached his face, but his pale grey fedora was knocked off. She started to struggle, pushing him aside.

'Games, huh?' he shouted angrily. 'You wanna play fucking games, bitch?' He grabbed both her arms, pinning them against the pillows. And the sight of her chest heaving below the playsuit's revealing confinement ignited the dragon's fire in his heart. He forced her further down into the mattress, gloating at the sight of her superb muscles straining helplessly. 'Who's in charge now? Who fucking owns you?' He ripped the leather off her crotch, and prised her legs apart. Then he was kneeling between her thighs, his clothes evaporating. She groaned, making one last desperate attempt to break free. Against him, she never stood a chance.

Somewhen later, his own fulfilment made him cry out in wonder. The orgasmic discharge from his body was primitive savagery, enrapturing every cell. He held himself rigid, prolonging the flow as long as he could bear before collapsing onto the rumpled silk sheets.

'That's better, baby,' Jezzibella said as she stroked his shoulders. 'I hate it when you're all uptight.'

Al grinned languidly at her. She'd changed back into the teen-kitten again, all worshipful concern crowned by a frizz of golden curls. 'No way, lady. No way are you human.'

She kissed his nose. 'About the antimatter,' she said. 'You need it, Al. If there's any chance at all, then grab it.'

'I don't follow,' he mumbled. 'Lovegrove says it's just a different kind of bomb. And we got ourselves plenty of the atom explosives already.'

'It's not just a better kind of bomb, Al; you can use it to power combat wasps and starships, too, bump up their performance by an order of magnitude. If you like, it's the difference between a rifle and a machine-gun. They both fire bullets, but which would you prefer in a rumble?'

'Good point.'

'Thanks. Now even with the asteroid campaign going well, we haven't got anything like numerical parity with the Confederation's conventional forces. However, antimatter is a superb force multiplier. If you've got some, they're going to think twice before launching any sort of offensive.'

'Jeeze, you are a fucking marvel. I gotta get this organized with the boys.' He swung his legs over the side of the bed, and started to reconstitute his clothes out of the magic realm where they'd been banished.

'Wait.' She pressed up against his back, arms sliding round to hug. 'Don't go rushing in to this half-cocked, Al. We've got to think this through. You're going to have problems with antimatter, it's vicious stuff. And you don't help.'

'What do you mean?' he bridled.

'This way your energistic ability gronks out electronics and power circuits, you just can't afford that with antimatter. Put a possessed anywhere near a confinement system and we're all going to be watching the last half of the explosion from the beyond. So ... it will have to be the non-possessed who work with the stuff.'

'Sheesh.' Al scratched his mussed hair, desperately uncertain. His Organization was built along the principle of keeping the non-possessed in line, under his thumb. You had to have some group at the bottom who needed to be watched on a permanent basis, it kept the Organization soldiers busy, gave them a purpose. Made them take orders. But give the non-possessed antimatter ... that would screw up the balance something chronic. 'I ain't so sure, Jez.'

'It's not that big a problem. You just have to make sure you've got a secure hold over anyone you assign to handle the stuff. Harwood and Leroy can fix that; they can arrange for you to hold their families hostage.'

Al considered it. Hostages might just work. It would take a lot of effort to arrange, and the Organization soldiers would really have to be on the ball. Risky.

'OK, we'll give it a shot.'

'Al!' Jezzibella squealed girlishly, and started kissing his throat exuberantly.

Al's half-materialized clothes vanished again.

*

The Chiefs of Staff office was as extravagant as only senior government figures could get away with; its expensive, hand-crafted furniture was arranged round a long hardwood table running down the centre. One wall could be made transparent, giving the occupants a view out over the SD Tactical Operations Centre.

Al sat himself down at the head of the table, and acknowledged his senior lieutenants with a wave of his hand. There was no smile on his face, a warning that this was strictly business.

'OK,' he said. 'So what's been happening? Leroy?'

The corpulent manager glanced along the table, a confident expression in place. 'I've more or less kept to the original pacification schedule we drew up. Eighty-five per cent of the planet is now under our control. There are no industrial or military centres left outside our influence. The administrative structure Harwood has been building up seems to be effective. Nearly twenty per cent of the population is non-possessed, and they're doing what they're told.'

'Do we need them?' Silvano Richmann asked Al, not even looking at Leroy.

'Leroy?' Al asked.

'For large urban areas, almost certainly,' Leroy said. 'The smaller towns and villages can be kept going with their possessed inhabitants providing a combined energistic operation. But cities still require their utilities to function, you just can't wish that much shit and general rubbish away. Apparently the possessed cannot create viable food out of inorganic compounds, so the transport network has to be maintained to keep edible supplies flowing in. At the moment that's just stock

**336**

from the warehouses. Which means we'll have to come up with a basic economy of some sort to persuade the farms to keep supplying the cities. The problem with that is, the possessed who are living out in the rural areas aren't inclined to do too much work, and in any case I haven't got a clue what we could use for money, counterfeiting is too damn easy for you, we may just have to resort to barter. Another problem is that the possessed cannot manufacture items which have any permanence, once outside the energistic influence they simply revert to their component architecture. So a lot of factories are going to have to be restarted. As for the military arena, non-possessed are unquestionably necessary, but that's Mickey's field.'

'OK, you done good, Leroy,' Al said. 'How long before I'm in charge of everything down there?'

'You're in charge of everything that counts right now. But that last fifteen per cent is going to be a hard slog. A lot of the resistance is coming from the hinterland areas, farm country where they're pretty individual characters. Tough, too. A lot of them are holed up in the landscape with their hunting weapons. Silvano and I have been putting together hunter teams, but from what we've experienced so far it's going to be a long dirty campaign, on both sides. They know the terrain, our teams don't; it's an advantage which almost cancels out the energistic ability.'

Al grunted sardonically. 'You mean we gotta fight fair?'

'It's a level playing field,' Leroy acknowledged. 'But we'll win in the end, that's inevitable. Just don't ask me for a timetable.'

'Fine. I want you to keep plugging away at that economy idea. We gotta maintain some kind of functioning society down there.'

'Will do, Al.'

'So, Mickey, how are you holding out?'

Mickey Pileggi scrambled to his feet, sweat glinting on his forehead. 'Pretty good, Al. We broke forty-five asteroids with that first action. They're the big ones, with the most important industrial stations. So now we've got three times as many warships as when we started. The rest of the settlements are just going to be a mopping-up operation. There's nothing out there which can threaten us any more.'

'You got crews for all these new ships?'

'We're working on it, Al. It isn't as easy as the planet. There's a lot of distance involved here, our communication lines aren't so hot.'

'Any reaction from the Edenists?'

'Not really. There were some skirmishes with armed void-hawks at three asteroids, we took losses. But no big retaliation attacks.'

'Probably conserving their strength,' Silvano Richmann said. 'It's what I would do.'

Al fixed Mickey with the look (God, the hours he'd spent practising that back in Brooklyn). And he hadn't lost it, poor old Mickey's tic started up like he'd thrown a switch. 'When we've taken over all the ships docked at the asteroids, are we gonna be strong enough to bust the Edenists?'

Mickey's eyes performed a desperate search for allies. 'Maybe.'

'It's a question of how you want them, Al,' Emmet Mordden said. 'I doubt we could ever subdue them, not make them submit to possession, or hand the habitats over to the Organization's control. You'll just have to trust me on this, they're completely different to any kind of people you have ever met before. All of them, even the kids. You might be able to kill them, destroy their habitats. But conquest? I don't think so.'

Al squeezed his lips together, and studied Emmet closely. Emmet was nothing like Mickey; timid, yeah, but he knew his stuff. 'So what are you saying?'

'That you've got to make a choice.'

'What choice?'

'Whether to go for the antimatter. You see, Edenism has a

monopoly on supplying $He_3$, and that's the fuel which all the starships and industrial stations run on, as well as the SD platforms, and we all know they have to be kept powered up. Now there's an awful lot of $He_3$ stored around the New California system, but ultimately it's going to run out. That means we must go to the source if we want to keep our starships going, and maintain our hold over the planet. Either that or use the alternative.'

'Right,' Al said reasonably. 'You've been talking to this Nicolai Penovich character, Emmet, is he on the level?'

'As far as I can make out, yeah. He certainly knows a lot about antimatter. I'd say he can take us to this production station of his.'

'We got ships which can handle that?'

Emmet gave an unhappy scowl. 'Ships, yeah, no problem now. But Al, starships and antimatter, it means using a lot of non-possessed to run them. Our energistic power, it's not good for space warfare, if anything it puts our ships at a disadvantage.'

'I know,' Al said smoothly. 'But, shit, we can turn this in our favour if we handle it right. It'll prove that the non-possessed have got a part in the Organization just as much as anyone. Good publicity. Besides, those boosted guys, they helped out in the asteroids, right?'

'Yes,' Silvano admitted reluctantly. 'They're good.'

'That's it, then,' Al said. 'We'll give our ships a crack at the Edenists, for sure. See if we can snatch the helium mines they got. But in the meantime we take out a sweet little insurance policy. Emmet, start putting together the ships you'll need. Silvano, I want you and Avvy to work on who's gonna crew them. I only want you to use non-possessed who are family guys, catch? And before they leave for the station, I want those families up here in Monterey being given the holiday of a lifetime. Shift everyone out of the resort complex, and house them there.'

Silvano produced a greedy smile. 'Sure thing, Al, I'm on it.'

Al sat back and watched as they started to implement his instructions. It was all going real smooth, which threw up its own brand of trouble. One which even Jez had overlooked – but then this was one field where he had a shitload more experience than her. The lieutenants were getting used to wielding power, they were learning how to pull levers. They all had their own territories right now, but pretty soon they'd start to think. And sure as chickens shat eggs, one of them would try for it. He looked round the table, and wondered which it would be.

*

Kiera Salter sat down in the president's chair in Magellanic Itg's boardroom, and surveyed her new domain. The office was one of the few buildings inside the habitat, a circular fifteen-storey tower situated at the foot of the northern endcap. Its windows gave her a daunting view down the interior. The shaded browns of the semi-arid desert were directly outside, slowly giving way to the tranquil greens of grassland and forest around the midsection, before finally merging into the rolling grass plains, currently dominated by some vivid pink xenoc plant. Moating that, and forming an acute contrast, was the circumfluous sea: a broad band of near-luminous turquoise shot through with wriggling scintillations. High and serene above it all, the axial light-tube poured out a glaring noon-sun radiance. The only incongruity amid the peaceful scene was the dozen or so clouds which glowed a faint red as they drifted through the air.

There was little other evidence of the coup which she had led; one or two small smudges of black smoke, a crashed rentcop plane in the parkland surrounding a starscraper lobby. Most of the real damage had occurred inside the starscrapers, but the important sections, the industrial stations and space-port, had sustained only a modest amount of battering.

Her plan had been a good one. Anyone who came into

contact with a possessed was immediately taken over, regardless of status. A ripple effect spread out from the seventeenth floor of the Diocca starscraper, slow at first, but gradually gaining strength as the numbers grew. The possessed moved on to the next starscraper.

Rubra warned people of course, told them what to look out for, told them where the possessed were. He directed the rentcops and the boosted mercenary troops, ambushing the possessed. But good as they were, the troops he had at his disposal were heavily dependent on their hardware. That gave the possessed a lethal advantage. Unless it was as basic as a chemical-projectile weapon technology betrayed them, failing at critical moments, producing false data. He didn't even attempt to take Valisk's small squad of assault mechanoids out of storage.

Out on the docking-ridges, the polyp hulls of possessed starships began to swell below a shimmer of exotic light patterns, emerging from their convulsions as full-grown hellhawks. Fantastically shaped starships and huge harpies zoomed away from the habitat to challenge the voidhawks and Srinagarian frigates that were edging in cautiously. The military ships had pulled back, abandoning their effort to assist the beleaguered population.

Kiera's authority now extended the length of the habitat, and encompassed a zone a hundred thousand kilometres in diameter outside the shell. All in all, not a bad little fiefdom for a former Society wife from New Munich. She'd glimpsed it briefly once before, this position, the influence, importance, and respect which authority endowed. It could have been hers for the taking back then; she had the breeding and family money, her husband had the ambition and skill. By rights a cabinet seat awaited, and maybe even the chancellorship (so she dreamed and schemed). But he'd faltered, betrayed by his ambition and lack of patience, making the wrong deals in search of the fast track. A weak failure condemning her to sitting out her empty life in the grand old country house, working studiously for the right charities, pitied and avoided by the social vixens she'd once counted as her closest friends. Dying bitter and resentful.

Well, now Kiera Salter was back, younger and prettier than ever before. And the mistakes and weaknesses of yesteryear were not going to be repeated again. Not ever.

'We finished going through the last starscraper three hours ago,' she told the council she'd assembled (oh so carefully selecting most of the members). 'Valisk now effectively belongs to us.'

That brought applause and some whistles.

She waited for it to die down. 'Bonney, how many non-possessed are left?'

'I'd say a couple of hundred,' the hunter woman said. 'They're hiding out, with Rubra's help, of course. Tracking them down is going to take a while. But there's no way for them to get out; I'll find them eventually.'

'Do they pose any danger?'

'The worst-case scenario would be a few acts of sabotage; but considering we can all sense them if they get close enough to us, it would be very short-lived. No, I think the only one who could hurt us now would be Rubra. But I don't know enough about him and what his capabilities are.'

Everyone turned to look at Dariat. Kiera hadn't wanted him on the council, but his understanding of affinity and the habitat routines was peerless. They needed his expertise to deal with Rubra. Despite that, she still didn't consider him a proper possessed; he was crazy, a very ruthless kind of crazy. His agenda was too different from theirs. A fact which to her mind made him a liability, a dangerous one.

'Ultimately, Rubra could annihilate the entire ecosystem,' Dariat said calmly. 'He has control over the environmental maintenance and digestive organs; that gives him a great deal of power. Conceivably he could release toxins into the water and food, replace the present atmosphere with pure nitrogen and suffocate us, even vent it out into space. He can turn off the axial light-tube and freeze us, or leave it on and cook us. None of that would damage him in the long term; the biosphere can be replanted, and the human population replaced. He cares less for the lives of humans than we do, his only priority is himself. As I told you right at the start, everything else we achieve is completely pointless until he is eliminated. But you didn't listen.'

'So, shitbrain, why hasn't he done any of that already?' Stanyon asked contemptuously.

Kiera put a restraining hand on his leg under the table. He was a good deputy for her, his intimidating strength accounting for a great deal of the obedience she was shown; he also made an excellent replacement for Ross Nash in her bed. However, vast intelligence was not one of his qualities.

'Yes,' she said levelly to Dariat. 'Why not?'

'Because we have one key element left to restrain him,' Dariat said. 'We can kill him. The hellhawks are armed with enough combat wasps to destroy a hundred habitats. We're in a deterrence situation – if we fight each other openly, we both die.'

'Openly?' Bonney challenged.

'Yes. Right now, he will be conferring with the Edenist Consensus about methods of reversing possession. And as you know, I'm investigating methods of transferring my personality into the neural strata without him blocking it. That way I could assume control of the habitat and eliminate him at the same time.'

Which isn't exactly the solution I want, Kiera thought.

'So why don't you just do it?' Stanyon asked. 'Shove yourself in there and fight the bastard on his own ground. Don't you have the balls for it?'

'The neural strata cells will only accept Rubra's thought routines. If a thought routine is not derived from his own personality pattern it will not function in the neural strata.'

'But you fucked with the routines before.'

'Precisely. I made changes to what was there, I did not replace anything.' Dariat sighed elaborately, resting his head in his hands. 'Look, I've been working on this problem for nearly thirty years now. Conventional means were utterly useless against him. Then I thought I'd found the answer with affinity enhanced by this energistic ability. I could have used it to modify sections of the neural strata, force the cells to accept my personality routines. I was exploring that angle when that drunk cretin Ross Nash blew our cover. So we went overt and showed Rubra what we can do; fine, but by doing that we threw away our stealth advantage. He is on his guard like never before. I've had enough evidence of that over the last ten hours. If I try to convert a chunk of the neural strata ready to accept me, it drops out of the homogeneity architecture, and he does something to the cells' bioelectric component, too, which kills them instantly. Don't ask me what – breaks down the natural chemical regulators, or plain electrocutes them with nerve impulse surges. I don't know! But he's blocking me every step of the way.'

'All very interesting,' Kiera said coldly. 'What we need to know, however, is can you beat him?'

Dariat smiled, his gaze unfocused. 'Yes. I'll beat him, I feel the lady Chi-ri touching me. There will be a way, and I'll find it eventually.'

The rest of the council exchanged irritated or worried glances, except for Stanyon, who merely gave a disgusted groan.

'Can we take it, then, that Rubra does not pose any immediate threat?' Kiera asked. She found Dariat's devotion to the Starbridge religion with its lords and ladies of the realms another indication of just how unstable he was.

'Yes,' Dariat said. 'He'll keep up the attrition, of course.

Electrocution, servitor housechimps cracking rocks over your skull; and we'll have to abandon the tubes and starscraper lifts. It's an annoyance, but we can live through it.'

'Until when?' Hudson Proctor asked. He was an ex-general Kiera had drafted in to her initial coterie to help plan their takeover strategy. 'Rubra is in here with us, and the Edenists are outside. Both of them are doing their damnedest to push us back into the beyond. We have to stop that, we must fight back. I'm damned if I'm prepared to sit here and let them win.' He glanced round the table, buoyed by the level of silent support shown by the council.

'Our hellhawks are easily a match for any voidhawk,' Kiera said. 'The Edenists cannot get inside Valisk, all they can do is sit at a safe distance and watch. I don't consider them a problem at all, let alone a threat.'

'The hellhawks might be as good as a voidhawk in a fight, but what's to make them stay and guard us?'

'Dariat?' Kiera said, irked at having to defer to him again. But he was the one who'd worked out how to keep the hellhawks loyal to Valisk.

'The souls possessing the hellhawks will help us for as long as we want,' Dariat said. 'We have something they ultimately want: human bodies. Rubra's descendants can all use their affinity to converse with Magellanic Itg's blackhawks. That means the souls can get out of the hellhawks and into those bodies the same way as they got in. During our takeover we captured enough of Rubra's descendants to provide each hellhawk possessor with a human body. They're all stored in zero-tau, waiting.'

'Waiting for what?' Hudson Proctor asked. 'This is what gets me. I don't even know why we're bothering with this discussion in the first place.'

'What do you suggest we should be doing, then?' Kiera asked.

'The blindingly obvious. Let's just go. Now! We know we

can do it; together we have the power to lift Valisk clean out of this universe. We can create our own universe around us; one with new laws, a place where there's no empty eternity around us, and where we're safely sealed off from the beyond. We'll be safe there, from Rubra, from the Edenists, from everybody. Safe and immortal.'

'Quite right,' Kiera said. Most possessed had only been back for a few hours, but already the urge was growing. To run, to hide from the dreadful empty sky. Enclosed Valisk was better than a planet; but Kiera had hated the starscrapers with their windows showing the naked stars, always reminding her of the beyond. Yes, she thought, we will have to leave that sight eventually. But not yet. There were other, older, instincts prising at her thoughts. For when Valisk departed to a universe where anything became possible to every individual, the need for leadership would fade away, lost among the dream of eternal sybaritic life into which they would all fall. Kiera Salter would cease to be anything special. Maybe it was inevitable, but there was no need to rush into it. 'What about the threat from ourselves?' she asked them, a high note of curiosity in her voice. As if they'd already solved the obvious problem.

'What threat?' Stanyon asked.

'Think about it. How long are we intending to leave this universe for?'

'I wasn't planning on coming back,' Hudson Proctor said caustically.

'Me neither. But eternity is rather a long time, isn't it? And those are the terms we're going to have to start thinking in nowadays.'

'So?' he demanded.

'So how many people are there in Valisk right now? Stanyon?'

'Close to nine hundred thousand.'

'Not quite nine hundred thousand people. And the purpose

of life, or the nearest definition I'll ever make, is to experience. Experience whatever you can for as long as you can.' She gave the councillors a morbid smile. 'That isn't going to change whatever universe we occupy. As it stands, there aren't enough of us; not if we want to keep providing ourselves with new and different experiences for all of eternity. We have to have variety to keep on generating freshness, otherwise we'll just be playing variants on a theme for ever. Fifty thousand years of that, and we'll be so desperate for a change that we'll even come back here just for the novelty.' She'd won them; she could see and sense the doubt and insecurity fission in their minds.

Hudson Proctor sat back in his chair, and favoured her with a languid smile. 'Go on, Kiera, you've obviously thought this through. What's the solution?'

'There are two possibilities. First, we use the hellhawks to evacuate ourselves to a terracompatible world, and begin the possession campaign all over again. Personally I'd hate to risk that. Srinagar's warships might not be able to break into Valisk, but if we tried to land on the planet it would be a shooting gallery. Alternatively, we can play it smart and gather people in to us. Valisk can support at least six or seven million, and that's without our energistic ability enhancing it. Six million should be enough to keep our society alive and fresh.'

'You're joking. Bring in over five million people?'

'Yes. It'll take time, but it can be done.'

'Bringing some people in, yes, but so many ... Surely our population is going to grow anyway?'

'Not by five million it isn't. We'd have to make permanent pregnancy compulsory for every female for the next ten years. This council might be in command now, but try implementing that and see how long we last.'

'I'm not talking about right now, I'm talking about after. We'll have children after we leave.'

'Will we? These aren't our actual bodies, they'd never be *our* children. The biological imperative isn't driving us any more; these bodies are sensory receptors for our consciousness, nothing else. I certainly don't intend to have any children.'

'All right, even assuming you're right, and I'm not saying you are, how are you going to get that kind of influx, launch the hellhawks on pirate flights to capture people?'

'No,' she said confidently. 'Invite them. You've seen the Starbridge tribes. There are the disaffected just like them in every society throughout the Confederation. I know, one of the charities I used to work for helped rehabilitate youngsters who couldn't cope with modern life. Gather them all together, and you could fill twenty habitats this size.'

'But how? What's going to make them want to come here, to Valisk?'

'We just have to find the right message, that's all.'

*

Even by day, Burley Palace stood aloof from the city of Atherstone: surrounded by extensive parkland at the top of a small rise, it surveyed the sprawling lower districts with a suitably regal detachment. At night the isolation made it positively imperious. Atherstone's lights turned the motorways, boulevards, and grand squares into a gaudy mother-of-pearl blaze which shimmered as though it was alive. Right in the centre, however, the palace grounds were a lake of midnight darkness. And in the centre of that, Burley Palace shone brighter than it ever did under the noon sun, illuminated by a bracelet of five hundred spotlights. It was visible from almost anywhere in the city.

Ralph Hiltch observed it through the Royal Marine flyer's sensor suite as they approached. A neoclassical building with innumerable wings slotting together at not-quite geometrical angles, and five quadrangles enclosing verdant gardens. Even though it was nearly one o'clock in the morning there were a lot of cars using the long drive which cut through the parkland, headlights creating a near-constant stream of white light. Although highly ornamental, the palace was the genuine centre of government; so given the planet's current state of alert, the activity was only to be expected.

The pilot brought the flyer down on one of the discreetly positioned rooftop pads. Roche Skark was waiting for Ralph as he came down the airstair, two bodyguards standing unobtrusively a few metres behind.

'How are you?' the ESA director asked.

Ralph shook his hand. 'Still in one piece, sir. Unlike Mortonridge.'

'That's a nasty case of guilt you've got there, Ralph. I hope it's not clouding your judgement.'

'No, sir. In any case, it isn't guilt. Just resentment. We nearly had them, we were so close.'

Roche gave the younger operative a sympathetic look. 'I know, Ralph. But you drove them out of Pasto, and that's got to be a colossal achievement. Just think what would have happened if it had fallen to the likes of Annette Ekelund. Mortonridge multiplied by a hundred. And if they'd possessed that many people they wouldn't have been content to stay put like they are on the peninsula.'

'Yes, sir.'

They walked into the palace.

'This idea the pair of you came up with. Is it workable?' Roche asked.

'I believe so, sir,' Ralph said. 'And I appreciate you allowing me to outline it to the Princess myself.' The notion had evolved from several strategy reviews he and Colonel Palmer had held during the occasional lull in the frantic two days of the Mortonridge evacuation. Ralph knew that it contained suggestions which had to be made to the Princess personally. He feared it being diluted by navy staff analysts and tacticians if he routed it through the correct procedural channels. Smooth minds polishing away the raw substance to present a sleek concept, one that was politically acceptable. And that wouldn't work, nothing short of hundred per cent adherence to the proposal would produce success.

Sometimes when he stood back and observed this obsessional character he'd become he wondered if he wasn't simply overdosing on arrogance.

'Given the circumstances, it was the least we could do,' Roche Skark said. 'As I told you, your efforts have not gone unnoticed.'

Sylvester Geray was waiting for them in the decagonal reception room with its gleaming gold and platinum pillars. The equerry in his perfect uniform gave Ralph's borrowed marine fatigues a reluctant appraisal, then opened a set of doors.

After the opulence of the staterooms outside, Princess Kirsten's private office was almost subdued. The kind of quietly refined study a noble landowner would run an estate from. He couldn't quite make the leap to accepting that the entire Ombey star system was ruled from this room.

He stepped up to the desk, feeling he ought to salute, but knowing it would appear ridiculous – he wasn't military. The Princess didn't look much different from her images on the news, a dignified lady who seemed to be locked in perpetual middle age. No amount of discipline was able to stop him checking her face. Sure enough, there was the classic Saldana nose, slender with a downturned end; which was almost her only delicate feature, she had an all-over robustness of a kind which made it impossible ever to imagine her growing into a frail old grandmother.

Princess Kirsten acknowledged him with a generous nod. 'Mr Hiltch. In the flesh at last.'

'Yes, ma'am.'

'Thank you so much for coming. If you'd like to sit down, we can start.' Ralph took the chair next to Roche Skark, grateful for the illusion of protection his boss gave him. Jannike

Dermot was eyeing him with what was almost a sense of amusement. The only other person in the room, apart from the equerry, was Ryle Thorne, who didn't appear to care about Ralph's presence one way or the other.

'We'll bring in Admiral Farquar now,' Kirsten said. She datavised the desk's processor for a security level one sensenviron conference. The white bubble room emerged to claim them.

Ralph found he was sitting to the right of the Admiral, down at the end of the table away from the Princess.

'If you'd like to summarize the current Mortonridge situation for us, Mr Hiltch,' Kirsten said.

'Ma'am. Our principal evacuation operation is now finished. Thanks to the warnings we broadcast, we managed to lift out over eighteen thousand people with the planes and Royal Navy transport flyers. Another sixty thousand drove up the M6 and got out that way before the motorway failed. The sensor satellites show us that there are about eight hundred boats carrying refugees which are heading up to the main continent. Our priority at the moment is to try and take people off the smaller ones, which are desperately overcrowded.'

'Which leaves us with close to two million people stranded in Mortonridge,' Admiral Farquar said. 'And not a damn thing we can do about it.'

'We believe most of them are now possessed,' Ralph said. 'After all, Ekelund's people have had two days. And those that aren't possessed will be by tomorrow. We keep running into this exponential curve. It's a frightening equation when it's translated into real life.'

'You're absolutely sure they are being possessed?' Princess Kirsten asked.

'I'm afraid so, ma'am. Our satellite images are being fudged, of course, right across the peninsula. But we can still use sections of the communication net. The possessed seem to have forgotten or ignored that. The AIs have been pulling what images they can from sensors and cameras. The overall pattern is constant. Non-possessed are tracked down, then systematically hurt until they submit to possession. They're fairly ruthless about it, though they do seem to be reticent with children. Most of those reaching the evacuation points now are under sixteen.'

'Dear Heaven,' the Princess muttered.

'Any of the possessed trying to get out?' Ryle Thorne asked.

'No, sir,' Ralph said. 'They seem to be sticking to the agreement as far as we can tell. The only anomaly at the moment is the weather. There's a considerable amount of unnatural cloud building up over Mortonridge, it started this morning.'

'Unnatural cloud?' Ryle Thorne enquired.

'Yes, sir. It's an almost uniform blanket spreading up from the south, which doesn't appear to be affected by the wind. Oh, and it's starting to glow red. We believe it could be an additional form of protection from the sensor satellites. If it continues to expand at its current rate, Mortonridge will be completely veiled in another thirty-six hours. After that we'll only have the sensors hooked into the net, and I don't believe they'll overlook them for much longer.'

'A red cloud? Is it poisonous?' Princess Kirsten asked.

'No, ma'am. We flew some drones through it, taking samples. It's just water vapour. But they're controlling it somehow.'

'What about its potential as a weapon?'

'I don't see how it could be used aggressively. The amount of power necessary to generate it is quite impressive, but that's all. In any case, the border we've established at the top of Mortonridge is an effective block. The troops are calling it a firebreak. The SD lasers have cleared a two kilometre wide line of scorched earth straight across the neck. We're combining satellite observation with ground patrols to monitor it, if anything moves out there it'll be targeted immediately.'

'What happens if the cloud tries to move over?'

'Then we'll attempt to burn it back with the SD lasers. If that doesn't work, then we'll need your authority to launch punitive strikes, ma'am.'

'I see. How will you know how to target these punitive strikes if the red cloud covers all of Mortonridge?'

'Scout teams will have to go in, ma'am.'

'Then let us pray the cloud can be halted by the lasers, then.'

'I can see you're geared up to prevent any attempt at a mass breakout,' Ryle Thorne said. 'What have you done to prevent individual possessed sneaking out among the refugees? We all know it only takes one to restart the whole nightmare. And I monitored aspects of the evacuation, it was rather chaotic at times.'

'It was chaotic getting the refugees out, sir,' Ralph said. 'But the other end was more straightforward. Everyone was tested to see if they had this energistic effect. We didn't find anybody. Even if they did manage to get through, the refugees are all being held in isolation. We think the only possessed on Ombey are on Mortonridge.'

'Good,' Princess Kirsten said. 'I know Roche Skark has already congratulated you, Mr Hiltch, but I'd like to express my own gratitude for the way you've handled this crisis. Your conduct has been exemplary.'

'Thank you, ma'am.'

'It galls me to say it, but I think that Ekelund woman was right. The final outcome isn't going to be decided here.'

'Excuse me, ma'am, but I told Ekelund I thought that was incorrect, and I still believe that.'

'Go on, Mr Hiltch,' Kirsten told him cordially. 'I don't bite, and I'd dearly love to be proved wrong in this instance. You have an idea?'

'Yes, ma'am. I think just waiting passively for this problem to be resolved somewhere else would be a vast mistake. For our own peace of mind, if nothing else, we have to know that the possessed can be beaten, can be made to give up what they've taken. We know zero-tau can force them to abandon the bodies they've stolen; and it may be that Kulu or Earth, or somewhere with real top-grade scientific resources, can find a quicker, more effective method. But the point is, whatever solution we eventually come up with we still have to get out there on the ground and implement it.'

'So you want to start now?' Admiral Farquar asked.

'The preparation stage, yes, sir. There is a lot of groundwork to be laid first. Colonel Palmer and I believe the possessed have already made one critical mistake. By possessing everyone left in Mortonridge they have given up their blackmail weapon. They cannot threaten us with a massacre as they did in Exnall, not any more, because they have no hostages left. There is only us and them now.'

'Ralph, you've had first-hand experience of how hard they fight. It would cost us a couple of marines for every four or five possessed we captured. That's a bad ratio.'

Ralph switched his attention to the Princess, wishing they were out of the sensenviron. He wanted physical eye contact, delivering her the truth of what he believed. 'I don't believe we should use our own marines, sir. Not in the front line. As you say, they would be wiped out. We know the possessed have to be completely overwhelmed before they can be subdued, and those kind of battles would demoralize the troops long before we made any real inroads.'

'So what do you want to use?' Kirsten asked curiously.

'There is, ma'am, one technology which can function effectively around a possessed, and is also available in the kind of quantities necessary to liberate Mortonridge.'

'Bitek,' Kirsten said quickly, vaguely pleased at making the connection.

'Yes, ma'am.' Ralph made an effort to rein in his surprise. 'The Edenists could probably produce some kind of warrior construct which could do the job.'

'There's even an appropriate DNA sequence which they could employ,' she said, enjoying the game, her thoughts racing ahead, mapping out possibilities. 'A Tranquillity serjeant. I've accessed sense-vises of them. Nasty looking brutes. And Ione is a cousin of ours, I'm sure acquisition wouldn't be a problem.'

The rest of the Security Committee remained silent, startled by her apparent eagerness to discard taboos.

'We would still need a massive conventional army to occupy and hold the land we regained, and support the bitek constructs,' Ralph said cautiously.

'Yes.' The Princess was lost in thought. 'You've certainly offered a valid proposal, Mr Hiltch. Unfortunately, as I'm sure you are aware, I could not conceivably approach the Edenists with such a request. The political implications of such an alliance would undermine some of the Kingdom's basic tenets of foreign policy, a policy which has been maintained for centuries.'

'I see, ma'am,' Ralph said stiffly.

'I can't petition them,' Kirsten said, enjoying herself. 'Only King Alastair can do that. So you'd better go and ask my big brother for me, hadn't you, Mr Hiltch?'

*

As soon as New California fell to the Capone Organization the Consensus of the thirty habitats orbiting Yosemite started preparing for war. It was a situation which had never before occurred in the five centuries since Edenism was founded. Only Laton had ever threatened them in the past, but he was one man; the staggering pan-Confederation resources they had were adequate to deal with him (so they considered at the time). This was different.

Adamists throughout the Confederation nearly always allowed prejudice to contaminate their thinking towards the Edenist culture. They assumed that as it was both wealthy and cloistered it would be if not decadent, then at least timorous.

**355**

They were wrong. Edenists prided themselves in their rational approach to all facets of life. They might deplore violence, favouring endless diplomatic negotiations and economic sanctions to any form of conflict, but if there was no alternative, they would fight. And fight with a coldly logical precision which was frightening.

Once the decision was taken, Consensus began the job of coordinating the gas giant's resources and priorities. The extensive clusters of industrial stations which surrounded each habitat were immediately turned over in their entirety to armaments manufacture. Component production was integrated by Consensus, matching demand to capability within hours, then going on to harmonize final fabrication procedures. Barely four hours after the operation started, the first new combat wasps were emerging from their freshly allocated assembly bays.

After conquering New California itself, Capone began his campaign against the system's asteroid settlements. Consensus knew then it would only be a matter of time. Yosemite was the source of He$_3$ for the entire system, the strategic high ground.

Perhaps if Capone had ordered an all-out assault on Yosemite as his first action he might have been successful. Instead, taking over the asteroid settlements was a tactical error. It allowed the Consensus precious days to consolidate the gas giant's defences. Not even Emmet Mordden really grasped the awesome potential of an entire civilization converted to a war footing, especially one with Edenism's technological resources. How could he? It had never happened before.

Voidhawks hovering seven hundred thousand kilometres above New California's poles observed the three new squadrons being assembled among the fifty-three asteroids orbiting the planet. Their composition, numbers, and in some cases even the armament specifications were duly noted and relayed to Yosemite. Unknown to the Organization, the voidhawks were not the summation of the Edenist Intelligence-gathering operation, they simply coordinated the observation. Thousands of stealthed spy sensor globes the size of tomatoes were falling past the asteroids like a constant black snow. All the information they gathered was passed back to the voidhawks through affinity links with their bitek processors. The possessed couldn't detect affinity, nor was it susceptible to either conventional electronic warfare or the interference by the energistic ability, all of which allowed the spy globes to reveal a minute by minute account of the build-up.

Had anyone in the Organization realized just how detailed the Edenist knowledge was, they would never have dispatched the starships.

Thirty-nine hours after Capone had given the go ahead to try and capture the Yosemite cloudscoops, two of the three squadrons of ships docked in the asteroids departed. Consensus knew both the vectors of the ships and their arrival time.

Yosemite orbited seven hundred and eighty-one million kilometres from the G5-type star of the New California system. At a hundred and twenty-seven thousand kilometres in diameter it was slightly smaller than Jupiter, although its storm bands lacked the vigour normally associated with such mass; even their coloration was uninspiring, streamers of sienna and caramel meandering among the pristine white upbursts of ammonia crystals.

The thirty Edenist habitats orbited sedately three-quarters of a million kilometres above the equator, their tracks perturbed only by gentle resonances with the eight large innermost moons. It was in that radial band where the Consensus had concentrated its new defensive structure. Each of the habitats was englobed by beefed-up strategic-defence platforms; but given the demonstrated ruthlessness of the attackers, Consensus was attempting to prevent any Organization ships getting near enough to launch a combat wasp salvo.

With the vectors identified and timed, Consensus redeployed twelve thousand of the combat wasps out of the total of three hundred and seventy thousand it had already seeded across the gas giant's equatorial zone. Their fusion drives ignited for a few minutes, putting them on a loose interception trajectory with the area of space the attackers were likely to emerge in. A hundred of the patrolling voidhawks were moved closer.

The first seven attackers to emerge, as per standard tactic programs, were all front-line navy rapid-response frigates. Their mission was to assess the level of opposition, and if necessary clear the incoming squadron's designated emergence zone of any hostile hardware. Even as their event horizons vanished, leaving them falling free, twenty-five voidhawks were accelerating towards them at ten gees. Distortion fields locked on, ruining the equilibrium of space around their hulls, preventing any of them from jumping clear. Combat wasps were already shooting over the intervening distance at twenty-five gees. The frigates immediately launched defensive salvos, but with their sensors hampered by the energistic flux of their own crews, the prized response was too slow in coming, and even when it did they were hopelessly outnumbered. Each of the frigates was the target of at least a hundred and fifty combat wasps, streaking in at them from every direction. At most, they could fire forty defenders. To have stood a good chance they would have needed close to five hundred apiece.

Within a hundred seconds all seven frigates were destroyed.

Ten minutes later, the rest of the Organization's starships started to emerge from their ZTT jumps. Their predicament was even worse. They were expecting the specialist frigates to have established a defensive perimeter. It took time for an ordinary Adamist starship to deploy its sensor clusters and scan local space for possible danger; time which in this case was lengthened by bolshie, malfunctioning equipment. When the sensors finally did relay an image of the external arena, it seemed as though a small galaxy was on the move. Yosemite was almost invisible behind a sparkling nebula of fusion drives;

thousands of combat wasps and tens of thousands of submunitions were generating a fraudulent dawn across half of the colossal planet's nightside. And the nebula was contracting, twin central whorls twisting lazily into two dense spires which were rising inexorably towards the emergence zones.

One by one, the Organization starships crashed against the terrible, moon-sized mountains of light, detonating into photonic avalanches which tumbled away into the yawning darkness.

*

Two hours later, the voidhawks on observation duty above New California reported that Capone's third squadron was leaving the orbital asteroids. When they were a quarter of a million kilometres above the planet, the starships activated their energy patterning nodes and vanished. Consensus was puzzled by the vector, they weren't aligned on any known inhabited world.

*

Not even the ending of the physical threat had brought any relief to the turmoil in Louise's head. They had flown all the way into orbit to dock with the *Far Realm* without any problem. Although Furay had grumbled constantly about bits of machinery going wrong on the ascent.

The starship itself wasn't quite as impressive as she'd been expecting. The interior was like servants' quarters, except made out of metal and plastic. There were four spheres grouped together in a pyramid shape, which the crew called life-support capsules, and that was the total available living space; apparently the rest of the ship inside the hull was solid machinery. Everything was so dreadfully small – tables, chairs, bunks; and what wasn't being used had to be folded away. And to complete her misery, free fall was an utter nightmare.

It was ironic, as Genevieve had perked up during the

spaceplane flight, so Louise had felt gradually worse. As soon as the rocket engines finally cut out, leaving them floating free, Genevieve had yelled delightedly, releasing her webbing and hurtling around the cabin, giggling as she bounced and somersaulted. Even Fletcher, after his initial alarm at the sensation, had relaxed, smiling cautiously as he attempted a few simple gymnastic manoeuvres with Genevieve cheering him on.

But not her. Oh no. She'd been wretchedly sick three times during the rendezvous, what with the spaceplane juddering around the whole time. It had taken her several goes to learn how to use the sanitation tube provided for such instances. Much to the disgusted dismay of the others in the cabin.

She had then continued to be sick, or at least have the stomach spasms, after they floated through the airlock tube into the starship's tiny lounge. Endron, the ship's systems specialist who doubled as medical officer, had towed her into the sickbay cubicle. Twenty minutes later, when the horrid warm itch inside her stomach faded, and some kind of cool fluid was sprayed into her mouth to rinse away the taste of vomit, she began to take stock for the first time. Her ears felt funny, and when she touched one she could feel something hard cupped round the back of it.

'That's a medical nanonic,' Endron told her. 'I've put one package behind each ear. Don't try and take them off, they've knitted with your inner ears. It ought to solve your balance problem.'

'Thank you,' she said meekly. 'I'm sorry to be so much trouble.'

'You're not. If only your sister was as quiet as you.'

'Oh. I'm sorry. Is she being a nuisance?'

He laughed. 'Not really. We're just not used to girls her age on board, that's all.'

Louise stopped fingering the medical package. When she brought her hand away she saw a strange green bracelet on her wrist; it was made from a substance like lustreless polythene, an inch wide and about half an inch thick. There was no join, it was solid. On closer inspection she saw it had fused to her skin, yet it wasn't painful.

'Another package,' Endron said drily. 'Again, don't touch it, please.'

'Is it for my balance as well?'

'No. That one is for your other condition. It will keep your blood chemistry stable, and if it detects any metabolic problem starting from free fall exposure it'll datavise a warning to me.'

'Other condition?' she asked timidly.

'You did know you were pregnant, didn't you?'

She closed her eyes and nodded, too ashamed to look at him. A complete stranger knowing. How awful.

'You should have told Furay,' he remonstrated gently. 'Free fall exerts some strong physiological changes on a body, especially if you're unaccustomed to it. And in your state, you really should have been prepared properly before the space-plane took off.'

A warm tear squeezed out from under her eyelids. 'It's all right, isn't it? The baby? Oh, please, I didn't know.'

'Shush.' Endron's hand stroked her forehead soothingly. 'The baby is just fine. You're a very healthy young girl. I'm sorry if I frightened you; like I said, we're not used to passengers. I suppose it must be equally strange for you, too.'

'It's all right, really?'

'Yes. And the nanonic will keep it that way.'

'Thank you. You've been very kind.'

'Just doing my job. I'll have to consult some files about your diet, though, and check what food stocks we've got on board. I'll get back to you on that one.'

Louise opened her eyes, only to find the cabin blurred by liquid stretching across her irises. A lot of blinking cleared it.

'Let's get you mobile again,' Endron said, and released the seal on the straps holding her down on the couch. 'Though you're not to whizz about like your sister, mind.'

His tone was identical to Mrs Charlsworth's. 'I won't.' The rest of the sentence died on her lips as she caught sight of him. Her first thought was that he was suffering some kind of terrible affliction.

Endron's head was ordinary enough, a man in his late fifties, she guessed, with a short crop of fading curly black hair and cheeks which appeared almost bloated, eradicating wrinkles. However, his body ... He had very broad shoulders atop an inflated ribcage, she could actually see the lines of individual ribs under his glossy green ship-suit. She'd seen holograms of terrestrial sparrows at school, and the anatomical arrangement put her in mind of that puffed-out bird, his chest was huge, and very frail looking.

'Not seen a Martian before, huh?' he asked kindly.

Furious with herself for staring Louise turned her head away. 'I'm not sure. Do all Martians look like you?'

'Yep. So you'd better get used to it. This is an SII line ship after all, the rest of the crew are the same as me. Except Furay of course; that's why he's on board. We couldn't fly the spaceplane down to terracompatible planets. Can't take the gravity.'

'How ...' She wasn't sure if this was really a fit subject to discuss so casually. It was almost as though they were talking about a terminal illness. 'Why are you like that?'

'Geneering. It's very deliberate, dates back awhile. Even with terraforming we don't have a standard atmosphere on Mars. Our ancestors decided to meet the problem halfway. As we're a Communist society, naturally everyone got the modification to expand our lung capacity; and that was on top of the earlier adaptations we made to ourselves to survive in the Moon's gravity field.'

'The Moon?' Louise asked, trying to sort things out in her mind. 'You lived on the Moon first?'

'It was the Lunar nation which terraformed Mars. Didn't they teach you that at school?'

'Uh, no. At least, we haven't got to it yet.' She decided not to question him on the Communism bit. Given Daddy's opinion on that topic, it would make life a little too complicated right now.

He was smiling gently at her. 'I think that's enough history. It's nearing midnight, Norwich time. Perhaps you'd better get some sleep, yes?'

She gave him an eager nod.

Endron coached her in the elementary movements necessary to get about in free fall. Speed was not a requirement, he insisted, arriving safely and accurately at your destination was. And you had to be careful of inertia, it created huge bruises.

With his encouragement she made her way into the life-support capsule they'd been allocated. A lounge five yards to a side, made from grubby pearl-grey composite walls which were inlaid with several instrument panels with tiny orange and green lights winking below their dark glass surfaces. Plastic doors which were like a kind of solidified liquid flowed apart to reveal three 'cabins' for them to sleep in (the wardrobes she had in her Cricklade bedroom were larger). There was a bathroom on the upper deck which Louise took one look at and promptly recoiled, vowing not to go to the toilet again until they were safely back on a planet.

Genevieve shot up to embrace her as soon as she glided through the ceiling hatch. Fletcher smiled a welcome.

'Isn't this truly wondrous!' the little girl proclaimed. She was floating with her toes six inches off the decking, spinning like a ballerina. Two ponytails stood out at right angles from her head. When she spread her arms wide her speed slowed. A neat toe kick, too quick to follow, and she soared up to the ceiling, clasping a grab hoop to kill her movement. Enchanted eyes smiled at Louise. 'Bet you I can do seven somersaults before I reach the floor.'

'You probably can,' Louise said wearily.

'Oh.' Genevieve's face was instantly contrite. She levitated back to the decking until she was level with Louise. 'I'm sorry. How are you feeling?'

'Fine now. And it's time for bed.'

'Oww, Louise!'

'Now.'

'All right.'

Endron proffered the girl a squeeze bulb. 'Here, it's a chocolate drink. Try it, I'm sure you'll like it.'

Genevieve started sucking eagerly on the nozzle.

'You are recovered, lady?' Fletcher asked.

'Yes. Thank you, Fletcher.'

They looked at each other for a long moment, unaware of Endron watching them.

One of the instrument panels let out a quiet bleep.

Endron scowled and drifted over to it, anchoring himself on a stikpad. 'Shoddy components,' he muttered.

Fletcher gave Louise an apologetic grimace, mildly embarrassed. 'I can't stop it,' he said in a whisper.

'Not your fault,' she whispered back. 'Don't worry. The ship still works.'

'Yes, lady.'

'That was nice,' Genevieve announced. She held out the empty squeeze bulb, and promptly burped.

'Gen!'

'Sorry.'

With Endron showing her how the cabin fittings worked, Louise finally got Genevieve into bed, a heavily padded sleeping bag stuck to the decking. Louise tucked her sister's hair into the hood, and kissed her gently. Genevieve gave her a drowsy smile, and immediately closed her eyes.

'She'll sleep for a good eight hours now she's got that sedative in her,' Endron said, holding up the empty squeeze bulb. 'And when she wakes up she won't be anything like as hyper. Furay told me what she was like when you boarded the spaceplane. She was having a bounceback response to the hangar fire. In a way that kind of overreaction is as bad as depressive withdrawal.'

'I see.' There didn't seem anything to add. She glanced back at Genevieve before the funny door contracted. For one whole night there would be no possessed, no Roberto, and no Quinn Dexter.

I've done what I promised, Louise thought. Thank you, Jesus.

Despite how tired she was feeling, she managed a prideful smile. No longer the worthless, pampered landowner daughter Carmitha had such contempt for just scant days ago. I suppose I've grown up a bit.

'You should rest now, lady,' Fletcher said.

She yawned. 'I think you're right. Are you going to bed?'

For once Fletcher's sedate features showed a certain lightness. 'I believe I will linger a while longer.' He indicated a holoscreen which was displaying the image from an external camera. Cloud-splattered landscape was rolling past, pastel greens, browns, and blues illuminated by Duke's radiance. 'It is not often a mortal man is permitted to view a world over the shoulder of angels.'

'Good night, Fletcher.'

'Good night, lady. May the Lord guard your dreams from the darkness.'

*

Louise didn't have time to dream. A hand pressing her shoulder woke her soon enough.

She winced at the light coming through the open door. When she tried to move, she couldn't, the sleeping bag held her too tight.

'What?' she groaned.

Fletcher's face was a few inches from hers, a gloomy frown spoiling his brow. 'I apologize, lady, but the crew is in some confusion. I thought you should know.'

'Are they on board?' she cried in dismay.

'Who?'

'The possessed.'

'No, lady Louise. Be assured, we are perfectly safe.'

'What then?'

'I think they are in another ship.'

'All right, I'm coming.' Her hand fumbled round until she found the seal catch inside the bag, she twisted it ninety degrees and the spongy fabric split open along its length. After she dressed she wrapped her hair into a single artless ponytail, and swam out into the tiny lounge.

Fletcher showed her the way to the bridge, wriggling along the tubular companionways which connected the life-support capsules, and through dimly lit decks which appeared even more cramped than their lounge. Louise's first sight of the bridge reminded her of the Kavanagh family crypt beneath the manor's chapel. A gloomy room with candlelike crystals sitting on top of instrument consoles, spilling out waves of blue and green light which crawled across the walls. Machinery, ribbed tubes, and plastic cables formed an untidy glyptic over most bulkheads. But most of all it came from the four crew-members lying prone on their bulky acceleration couches, eyes closed, limbs immobile. A thin hexagonal web was stretched over them, holding them down on the cushioning.

Furay and Endron she recognized, but that was the first time she'd seen Captain Layia, and Tilia, the *Far Realm*'s node specialist. Endron had been right, the other Martians had exactly the same anatomical features as himself. In fact there was very little difference between genders; Louise wasn't entirely sure the two women even had breasts. On top of that ribcage they would have been absurd.

'Now what?' she asked Fletcher.

'I am not sure, their repose refutes any disturbance.'

'It's not sleep, they're datavising with the flight computer. Joshua told me that's what happens on a starship bridge.

Um, I'll explain later.' Louise blushed faintly; he had become such a fixture in her life it was hard to remember who he actually was. She used some grab hoops to move herself over to Furay's couch, and tapped him experimentally on the shoulder. Somehow the thought of disturbing the others didn't arise, a child-fear of how those strange figures would respond.

Furay opened his eyes in annoyance. 'Oh, it's you.'

'I'm sorry. I wanted to know what was happening.'

'Yeah, right. Hang on.' The webbing peeled back and curled up, vanishing into the edge of the couch's cushioning. Furay pushed off, and slowly twisted his body round to the vertical, using a stikpad to anchor himself in front of Louise. 'Nothing too good, I'm afraid. The navy squadron's commanding admiral has put every ship on condition amber, which is one stage short of an actual combat alert.'

'Why?'

'The *Tantu* has dropped out of our communication net. They won't respond to any signals. She's worried that they might have been hijacked. Apparently there was some kind of garbled message a few minutes after the frigate's spaceplane docked, then nothing.'

Louise flashed a guilty glance at Fletcher, who remained unperturbed. The action did not go unnoticed by Furay. 'The *Tantu*'s spaceplane left Bennett Field about ten minutes after us. Care to comment?'

'The rebels were close behind us,' Louise said quickly. 'Perhaps they stowed away on the other spaceplane.'

'And took over an entire frigate?' Furay said sceptically.

'They have energy weapons,' Louise said. 'I've seen them.'

'Try waving a laser rifle around on the bridge of a Confederation Navy starship and the marines would cut you into barbecue ribs.'

'I have no other explanation,' she said earnestly.

'Hummm.' His stare informed her he was having big second thoughts about bringing her on board.

'What remedial action does the Admiral propose?' Fletcher asked.

'She hasn't decided yet. The *Serir* has been sent to rendezvous. The situation will be reviewed when they report.'

'She?' Fletcher asked in surprise. 'Your admiral is a lady?'

Furay pulled at his chin, trying to work out just what the hell he was dealing with.

'Yes, Fletcher,' Louise hissed. 'We don't have many female estate managers on Norfolk,' she explained brightly to Furay. 'We're not used to ladies holding important positions. Do excuse our ignorance.'

'You don't strike me as unimportant, Louise,' Furay said.

His tone was so muddled, silky, and scathing at the same time, she couldn't decide if he was making what Mrs Charlsworth called an overture, or just being plain sarcastic.

Furay suddenly stiffened. 'It's moving.'

'What is?'

'The *Tantu*. It's under way, heading up out of orbit. Your rebels must have hijacked it, there's no other reason.'

'The ship is flying away?' Fletcher asked.

'That's what I just said!' Furay told him in irritation. 'They must be heading up for a jump coordinate.'

'What's the Admiral doing about it?' Louise asked.

'I'm not sure. The *Far Realm* isn't a combat craft, we don't have access to the squadron's strategic communications.'

'We must follow it,' Fletcher announced.

'Pardon me?'

Louise glared at him with silent urgency.

'This ship must follow the frigate. People must be warned of what it carries.'

'And just what does it carry?' Furay asked mildly.

'Rebels,' Louise said hurriedly. 'People who've looted and murdered, and will do so again if they aren't arrested. But I'm sure we can leave the administering of justice to the Confederation Navy, can't we, Fletcher?'

'Lady—'

'Exactly what has got you so all-fired het up?' Captain Layia asked. Her couch webbing peeled back allowing her to glide over towards the three of them.

Her face did have a few feminine qualities, Louise admitted, but not many; the shaven scalp was too unsettling – all ladies had long hair. The judgemental way Layia took in the scene betrayed her authority; that she was in command had never been in doubt from the moment she spoke, it had nothing to do with the silver star on her epaulette.

'I am concerned that we should follow the frigate, ma'am,' Fletcher said. 'The rebels on board cannot be allowed to spread their sedition any further.'

'Nor will they be allowed to,' Layia said patiently. 'I can assure you the Admiral does not regard the hijacking of a navy frigate lightly. However, it is a navy matter, and we are just a supply ship. It is not our problem.'

'But they must be stopped.'

'How? If you use combat wasps you'll kill everyone on board.'

Fletcher appealed to Louise, who could only shrug, though the motion didn't quite come off in free fall.

'The Admiral will send a ship to pursue them,' Captain Layia said. 'When it arrives in a star system it will simply broadcast the situation to the authorities. The *Tantu* will be unable to dock at any port, and eventually their consumables will run out, forcing them to negotiate.'

'Those on board will not be allowed to disembark?' Fletcher asked apprehensively.

'Absolutely not,' the Captain assured him.

'Providing the pursuit ship manages to keep up with them through their ZTT jumps,' Furay said pessimistically. 'If *Tantu* programs for a sequential jump sequence then anyone following will be in trouble, unless it's a voidhawk. Which it won't be, because the squadron doesn't have one.' He trailed off under the Captain's stare. 'Sorry, but that's the normal method to avoid tracking, and every navy ship can perform sequential jumps. You know that.'

'Ma'am, please,' Fletcher entreated, 'if there is any chance the rebels can escape, we have to fly after them.'

'One, you're a passenger. I believe Mr Furay explained how we are obliged to stay in Norfolk orbit as long as the navy requires, and no amount of money can alter that. Two, if I broke orbit to chase the *Tantu*, then the Admiral would have me brought back and relieved of my duty. Three, as you've been so helpfully informed, the *Tantu* can perform sequential jumps; if a top-line frigate can't follow them through those manoeuvres then we certainly can't. And four, mister, if you don't get off my bridge *right now*, I'll sling you into a lifeboat and give you a one-way trip back down to the land you love so dearly. Have you got all that?'

'Yes, Captain,' Louise said, feeling an inch small. 'Sorry to bother you. We won't do it again.'

'Aw, shit,' Endron called from his acceleration couch. 'I'm getting multiple processor drop-outs. Whatever this glitch is, it's multiplying.'

Layia looked at Louise, and jabbed a finger at the hatch.

Louise grabbed Fletcher's arm and pushed off with her feet, trying to propel them towards the hatchway. She didn't like the expression of anguish on his face one bit. Her trajectory wasn't terribly accurate, and Fletcher had to flip them aside from one of the consoles.

'What are you trying to do?' Louise wailed when they were back in the lounge they'd been allocated. 'Don't you understand how dangerous it is to antagonize the Captain?' She caught herself, and clamped a hand over her mouth, distraught at the gaffe. 'Oh, Fletcher, I'm sorry. I didn't mean that.'

'Yet you spoke the truth, lady. As always. It was foolish of me, I admit, aye, and reckless too. For you and the little one must remain safe up here.' He turned and looked at the holoscreen. They were over the side of Norfolk which was turned to face Duchess, a harsh vista of reds and black.

'Why, Fletcher? What was so important about following Quinn Dexter? The navy can take care of him. Are you worried what'll happen if he gets loose on another planet?'

'Not exactly, lady. Alas, there are many possessed abroad in your fine Confederation now. No, I have seen into that man's heart, and he frightens me sorely, lady Louise, a fright more profound than the hell of beyond. He is the strange one I felt earlier. He is not as other possessed. He is a monster, a bringer of evil. I have resolved this matter in my own mind, though it has taken many hours of struggle, I must become his nemesis.'

'Dexter's?' she said weakly.

'Yes, my lady. I think he may be the reason Our Lord blessed me to return. I am vouchsafed a clarity in this regard I cannot in conscience ignore. I must raise the alarm before he can advance his schemes further to the misery of other worlds.'

'But it's not possible for us to go after him.'

'Aye, lady, such a conundrum has a fierce grip upon my heart, borrowed though it be. It squeezes like a fire. To have been so close, and to lose the scent.'

'We might not have lost him,' Louise said, her thoughts aching they were spinning so fast.

'How so, lady?'

'He said he was going to Earth. To Earth so he could hurt someone . . . Banneth. He was going to hurt Banneth.'

'Then Banneth must be warned. He will commit such terrible atrocities in pursuit of his devilsome aims. I can never purge what he said of the little one from my mind. To even think such filth. Only in his head do such ideas dwell.'

'Well, we are going to Mars anyway. I expect there will be more ships flying to Earth than to Tranquillity. But I don't have a clue how you could find Banneth once you get there.'

'Every voyage is divided into stages, lady. It is best to sail them one at a time.'

She watched him for some while as the holoscreen's pallid light washed across his rapt face. 'Why did you mutiny, Fletcher? Was it truly terrible on the *Bounty*?'

He gazed at her in surprise, then slowly smiled. 'Not the conditions, lady, though I doubt you would much care for them. It was one man, my captain. He it was, the force moving my life towards the shore of destiny. William Bligh was my friend when the voyage started, strange though it is to recount such a fact now. But – oh, how the sea changed him. He was embittered by his lack of promotion, fired by his notions of how a ship should be run. Never have I witnessed such barbarism from a man who claimed to be civilized, nor endured such treatment at his hands. I will spare you the anguish of detail, my fair lady Louise, but suffice it to say that all men have a breaking point. And mine was found during that long, dreadful voyage. However, I endure no shame over my actions. Many good and honest men were freed from his tyranny.'

'Then you were in the right?'

'I believe so. If this day I were called before the captains in a court martial, I could give a just account of my actions.'

'Now you want to do something similar again. Freeing people, I mean.'

'Yes, lady. Though I would endure a thousand voyages with Bligh as my master in preference to one with Quinn Dexter. I had thought William Bligh versed in the ways of cruelty. I see now how mistaken I was. Now, to my horror, I have looked upon true evil. I will not forget the form it takes.'

# 10

The reporters had spent several days in prison, a word which their Organization captors studiously avoided, the preferred designation being house arrest, or protective confinement. They'd been singled out and spared when the possessed spread through San Angeles, then corralled with their families in the Uorestone Tower. Patricia Mangano, who was in charge of the guard detail, allowed the children to play in the opulent lounges while parents mixed freely, speculating on their circumstances and rehashing old gossip as only their profession knew how.

Five times in the last couple of days small groups had been taken out to tour the city, observing the steady falsification of buildings which was the hallmark of a land under possession. Once-familiar suburban streets had undergone timewarps overnight, it was as though some kind of dark architectural ivy was slowly creeping its way upwards, turning chromeglass to stone, crinkling flat surfaces into arches, pillars, and statues. A plethora of era enclaves had emerged, ranging from 1950s New York avenues to timeless whitewashed Mediterranean villas, Russian dachas to traditional Japanese houses. All of them were ameliorated, more wistful renderings of real life.

The reporters recorded it all as faithfully as they could with their glitch-prone neural nanonic memory cells. This morning, though, was different. All of them had been summoned from their rooms, herded onto buses, and driven the five kilometres to City Hall. They were escorted from the buses by Organization gangsters and assembled on the sidewalk, forming a line between the autoway and the skyscraper's elaborate arched entrance. On Patricia's order the gangsters took several paces back, leaving the reporters to themselves.

Gus Remar found his neural nanonics coming back on-line, and immediately started to record his full sensorium, datavising his flek recorder block to make a back-up copy. It had been a long time since he'd covered a story in the field, these days he was a senior studio editor at the city's Time Universe bureau, but the old skill was still there. He started to scan round.

There were no vehicles using the autoway, but crowds were lining the sidewalk, five or six deep at the barrier. When he switched to long-range focus he could see they stretched back for about three blocks. The possessed were a majority, easy to spot in their epoch garments: the outlandish and the tediously uninspired. They seemed to be mingling easily enough with the non-possessed.

A slight fracas two hundred metres away at the back of the crowd caught Gus's attention. His enhanced retinas zoomed in.

Two men were pushing at each other, faces red with anger. One was a dark, handsome youth, barely twenty with perfectly trimmed black hair, dressed in leather jacket and trousers. An acoustic guitar was slung over his back. The second was older, in his forties, and considerably fatter. His attire was the most bizarre Gus had yet seen on display; some kind of white suit, smothered in rhinestones, with trousers flaring over thirty centimetres around his ankles, and collars which looked like small aircraft wings. Large amber-tinted sunglasses covered a third of his puffed-out face. If it hadn't been for the circumstances, Gus would have said it was a father quarrelling with his son. He shunted his audio discrimination program into primary mode.

'Goddam fake!' the younger man shouted with a rich

Southern drawl. 'I was never *this*.' Hands flicked insultingly over the front of the white costume, ruffling the fit. 'You're what they squeezed me into. You ain't nothing but a sick disease the record companies cooked up to make money. I would never come back as you.'

The larger man pushed him away. 'Who are you calling a fake, son? I am the King, the one and only.'

The shoving began in earnest, both of them trying to floor the other. Amber sunglasses went spinning. Organization gangsters moved in quickly to separate them, but not before the younger Elvis had unslung his guitar ready to brain the Vegas-version.

Gus never saw the outcome. The crowd started cheering. A cavalcade had turned onto the autoway. Police motorcycles (Harley Davidsons, according to Gus's encyclopedia memory file) appeared first, ten of them with blue and red lights flashing. They were followed by a huge limousine which crawled along at little more than walking pace: a 1920s Cadillac sedan which looked absurdly massive, fat tyres bulging from the weight of its armour-plated bodywork. Glass that was at least five centimetres thick shaded the interior aquarium-green. There was one man sitting in the back, waving happily at the crowd.

The city was going wild for him. Al grinned around his cigar and gave them a thumbs up. Jee-zus, but it was like the good old days, riding round in this very same bulletproof Cadillac with the pedestrians staring open-mouthed as he went past. In Chicago they'd known it contained a prince of the city. And now in San Angeles they goddam well knew again.

The Cadillac drew to a halt outside City Hall. A smiling Dwight Salerno came down the steps to open the door.

'Good to see you back, Al. We missed you.'

Al kissed him on both cheeks, then turned to face the ecstatic crowd, clasping his hands together above his head like he was a prizefighter posing over a whipped opponent. They roared their approval. White fire cascaded and fizzed over the autoway as if Zeus was putting on a fourth of July display.

'I love you guys!' Al bellowed at the faceless mass of chuckleheads. 'Together ain't no miserable Confederation fucker gonna stop us doing what we wanna do.'

They couldn't hear the words, not even those in the front rank. But the content was clear enough. The laudation increased.

With one hand still waving frantically, Al turned round and bounded up the stairs into City Hall. Always leave them wanting more, Jez said.

The conference was held in the lobby, a vaulting four-storey cavern that took up over half of the ground floor. An avenue of huge palm trees, cloned from Californian originals, stretched from the doors to the vast reception desk. Today their solar-tubes were diminished to an off-white fluorescence, their bowls of loam drying out. Other signs of neglect and hurried tidying were in evidence: defunct valet mechanoids lined up along one wall, emergency exit doors missing, scraps of rubbish swept into piles behind stilled escalators.

The reception desk had been completely cleared, and a row of chairs placed behind it. Al sat in the centre, with two lieutenants on either side. His chair had been raised slightly. He watched the nervous reporters being brought in and marshalled on the floor in front of him. When they'd shushed down he rose to his feet.

'My name is Al Capone, and I suppose you're all wondering why I asked you here,' he said, and chuckled. Their answering grins were few and far between. Tight asses. 'OK, I'll lay it on the line for you; you're here because I want the whole Confederation to know what's been going down in these parts. Once they know and understand then that's gonna save everyone a shitload of grief.' He took off his grey fedora and put it down carefully on the polished desk. 'It's an easy situation. My Organization is now in charge of the whole New California system. We're keeping the planet and the asteroid settlements in order, no exceptions. Now we ain't out to harm anyone, we just use our clout to keep things flowing along as best they'll go, same as any other government.'

'Are you running the Edenist habitats, too?' a reporter asked. The rest flinched, waiting for Patricia Mangano's retribution. It never came, though she looked far from happy.

'Smart of you, buddy,' Al acknowledged with a grudging smile. 'No, I ain't running the Edenist habitats. I could. But I ain't. Know why? Because we're about evenly matched, that's why. We could do a lot of damage to each other if we ever came to fighting. Too much. I don't want that. I don't want people sent into the beyond on account of some penny-ante dispute over territory. I've been there myself, it's worse than any fucking nightmare you can imagine; it shouldn't happen to anyone.'

'Why do you think you've been returned from the beyond, Al? Has God passed judgement on you?'

'You got me there, lady. I don't know why any of this started. But I'll tell you guys this much; I never saw no angels or no demons while I was stuck in the beyond, none of us did. All I know is we're back. It ain't no one's fault, it just happened. And now we gotta make the best of what's a pretty shitty deal, that's what the Organization is for.'

'Excuse me, Mr Capone,' Gus said, encouraged by the response to earlier questions. 'What's the point of your Organization? You don't need it. The possessed can do whatever they want.'

'Sorry, buddy, you're way wrong there. Maybe we don't need quite the same government as we had before, not all that tax, and regulations, and ideology, and shit. But you've got to have order, and that's what I provide. I'm doing everyone a favour by taking charge like this. I'm protecting the possessed from attack by the Confederation Navy. I'm looking out for a whole load of non-possessed; because I'm telling you, without me you certainly wouldn't be standing here in charge of your own body. See, I'm providing for all kinds of people, even though half of them don't appreciate it right now. The possessed didn't have jack shit worked out about where they were going until I came along. Now we're all working together, making it happen. All because of me and the Organization. If I hadn't stepped in and kept things going the cities would have busted down, we would have had a whole flood of lost boys heading for the countryside. Listen, I've seen the Depression first-hand, I know what it's like for people who don't have a job or something to do. And that's what we were heading for here.'

'So what are your long-range goals, Al? What's your Organization going to do next?'

'Smooth things out. No one is trying to deny things are still a little rough around the edges down here. We need to work on what kind of society we can build.'

'Is it true you're planning to attack the Confederation?'

'That's pure bullshit, buddy. Jee-zus, I don't know where you got that rumour from. No, of course we're not going to attack anyone. But we can defend ourselves pretty good if the Confederation Navy tries any funny stuff, we sure got the ships for that. Hell, I don't want that to happen. We just want to be peaceable neighbours with everyone. I might even ask if we can join the Confederation.' At the murmur of surprise echoing through the lobby he grinned round happily. 'Yeah. Why the hell not? Sure we can ask to join. Maybe some good will come out of it, some kind of compromise that'll make everyone happy; a solution to all the souls that wanna come back. The Organization can pay Confederation longhairs to grow us all new bodies from scratch, something like that.'

'You mean you'd give up your body if a clone was available?'

Al frowned as Emmet leant over to murmur in his ear,

explaining what a clone was. 'Sure,' he said. 'Like I told you, we're all the victims of circumstance.'

'You believe peaceful coexistence is possible?'

Al's jocularity darkened. 'You'd better fucking believe it, buddy. We're back, and we're here to stay. Grab that? What I'm trying to convince you guys is that we ain't no end-of-the-world threat, it's not us who's the Riders of the Apocalypse. We've proved possessed and non-possessed can live together on this planet. OK, so people out there are alarmed right now, that's only natural. But we're frightened too, you can't expect us to go back to the beyond. We've got to work together on this. I'm personally offering the Assembly President my hand in friendship. Now that's an offer he can't refuse.'

*

The glowing red clouds had begun to grow, small ruby speckles blossoming right across Norfolk. Louise, Fletcher, and Genevieve spent their first day in orbit watching the images received by the *Far Realm*'s external cameras. Kesteven Island was by far the worst. A solid crimson aureole had gathered to mask the land, its shape a distended mockery of the coastline it was obscuring. Strands of ordinary white cloud malingered around its disciplined edges, only to be rebuffed by invisible winds if they drifted too close.

Fletcher assured the girls that in itself the red cloud was harmless. 'A simple manifestation of will,' he proclaimed. 'Nothing more.'

'You mean it's just a wish?' Genevieve asked, intrigued. She had woken almost purged of her emotional turmoil, there were none of yesterday's periods of manic exuberance or haunted silences. Although she was quieter than usual; which Louise thought was about right. She didn't feel like talking much, either. Neither she nor Fletcher had mentioned the *Tantu*.

'Quite so, little one.'

'But why are they wishing it?'

'So that they can seek refuge below it from the emptiness of the universe. Even this planet's sky, which has little night, is not a sight to cherish.'

Over thirty islands now had traces of redness in the air. Louise likened it to watching the outbreak of some terrible disease, a swelling cancer gnawing away at the flesh of her world.

Furay and Endron had come down into the lounge a few times, keeping them informed of the navy squadron's actions, and the army's progress. Neither amounted to much. The army had landed on two islands, Shropshire and Lindsey, hoping to retake their capitals. But reports from the forward units were confused.

'Same problem as we had with Kesteven,' Furay confided when he brought them lunch. 'We can't support the lads on the ground because we don't have any reliable targeting information. And that red cloud has got the Admiral badly worried. None of the technical staff can explain it.'

By midafternoon (ship's time) the army commanders had lost contact with half of their troops. The red cloud was visible over forty-eight islands, nine of which it covered completely. As Duke-day ended for Ramsey Island slender wisps were located over a couple of villages. Teams of reserve soldiers were hurriedly flown in from Norwich. In both cases contact was lost within fifteen minutes of them entering the area.

Louise watched grimly as the coiling cloud thickened over each village. 'I was right,' she said miserably. 'There's nothing anybody here can do. It's only a matter of time now.'

*

Tolton made his way up the narrow creek, water slopping over his glittery purple shoes. The top of the steep bank, a fringe of sandy grass, was several centimetres above his head. He couldn't see out onto the parkland, and nobody could see him –

thankfully. Far overhead, Valisk's light-tube gleamed. The intensity hurt Tolton's eyes; he was a night person, used to the clubs, bars, and vestibules of the starscrapers, delivering his poet sermons to the ship crew burnouts, bluesensers, stimmed-out wasters, and mercenaries who sprawled throughout the lower floors of the starscrapers. They tolerated him, those lost entities, listening to (or laughing at) his carefully crafted words, donating their own stories to his wealth of experiences. He moved among the descriptions of shattered lives as vagrants moved through the filthy refuse of a darkened cul-de-sac, forever picking, trying to understand what they said, to bestow some grace to their wizened dreams with his prose, to explain them to themselves.

One day, he told them, I will incorporate it all into an MF album. The galaxy will know of your plight, and liberate you.

They didn't believe him, but they accepted him as one of their own. It was a status which had saved him from many a bar fight. But now, in his hour of desperate need, they had failed him. However difficult it was to acknowledge, they had lost; the toughest bunch of bastards in the Confederation had been wiped out in less than thirty-six hours.

'Take the left-hand channel at the next fork,' the processor block clipped to his belt told him.

'Yes,' he mumbled obediently.

And this was the greatest, most hurtful, joke of all: him, the aspirant anarchist poet, pathetically grateful to Rubra, the super-capitalist dictator, for helping him.

Ten metres on two gurgling streams merged together. He turned left without hesitation, the foaming water splashing his knees. Fleeing from the starscraper it was as though an insane montage of all the combat stories he'd ever been told had come scampering up out of his subconscious to torment him. Horror and laughter pursued him down every corridor, even the dis-used ones he thought only he walked. Only Rubra, a calm voice reeling off directions, had offered any hope.

Water made his black trousers heavy. He was cold, partly from the fright, partly cold turkey.

There had been no sign of pursuit for three hours now, though Rubra said they were still tracking him.

The narrow creek began to widen, its banks lowering. Tolton walked out into a tarn fifteen metres across with a crescent cliff cupping the rear half. Fat xenoc fish lumbered out of his way, apparently rolling along the bottom. There was no other exit, no feed stream.

'Now what?' he asked plaintively.

'There's an inlet at the far end,' Rubra told him. 'I've shut down the flow so you'll be able to swim through. It's only about five metres long, it bends, and there's no light; but it leads to a cave where you'll be safe.'

'A cave? I thought caves were worn into natural rock over centuries.'

'Actually, it's a surge chamber. I just didn't want to get technical on you, not with your artistic background.'

Tolton thought the voice sounded tetchy. 'Thank you,' he said, and started to wade forwards towards the cliff. A couple more directions, and he dived under the surface. The inlet was easy to find, a nightmare-black hole barely a metre and a half wide. Knowing he would never be able to turn round or even back out, he forced himself to glide into the entrance, bubbles streaming behind him.

It couldn't have been five metres long, more like twenty or thirty. The curves were sharp, one taking him down, the other up. He broke surface with a frantic gasping cry. The cave was a dome shape, twenty metres across, and every surface was coated in a film of water, thin ripples were still running down the walls. He had emerged in the pool at the centre. When he looked up there was a large hole at the apex, droplets splattered on his upturned face. A high ring of electrophorescent cells cast a weak pink-white glow into every cranny.

He paddled over to the side of the pool, and pushed himself out onto the slippery floor. A bout of shivering claimed his limbs; he wasn't sure if it was from the cold water or the nagging feeling of claustrophobia. The surge chamber was horribly confined, and the fact that it was usually full of water didn't help.

'I'll have one of the housechimps bring you some dry clothes, and food,' Rubra said.

'Thank you.'

'You should be safe here for a while.'

'I . . .' He looked round apprehensively. Everyone always said Rubra could see everything. 'I don't think I can stay very long. It's a bit . . . closed in.'

'I know. Don't worry, I'll keep you moving, keep you ahead of them.'

'Can I join up with anyone else? I need to be around people.'

'There aren't that many of you left free, I'm afraid. And meeting up with them isn't a good idea, that would just make you easier to locate. I haven't quite worked out how they track the non-possessed yet; I suspect they've got some kind of ESP ability. Hell, why not? They've got every other kind of magic.'

'How many of us are there?' he asked, suddenly panicky.

Rubra considered giving him the truth, but Tolton wasn't the strongest of characters. 'A couple of thousand,' he lied. There were three hundred and seventy-one people left free within the habitat, and assisting all of them simultaneously was pure hell.

Even as he was reassuring Tolton he perceived Bonney Lewin stalking Gilbert Van-Riytell. The tough little woman had taken to dressing in nineteenth-century African safari gear, a khaki uniform with two crossed bandolier straps holding polished brass cartridges in black leather hoops. A shiny Lee Enfield .303 rifle was slung over her shoulder.

Gilbert was Magellanic Itg's old comptroller, and had never

really stood a chance. Rubra had been trying to steer him along some service tunnels below a tube station, but Bonney and her co-hunters were boxing him in.

'There's an inspection hatch three metres ahead,' Rubra datavised to Van-Riytell. 'I want you to—'

Shadows lifted themselves off the service tunnel wall and grabbed the old man. Rubra hadn't even noticed them. His perception routines had been expertly circumvented.

Once again, he purged and reformatted local subroutines. By the time he regained some observation ability Van-Riytell's legs and arms were being tied round a long pole, ready to be carried away like a prize trophy. He wasn't even struggling any more. Bonney was supervising the procedure happily.

One of her hunting team was standing back, watching aloofly; a tall young man in a simple white suit.

Rubra knew then. It had to be him.

**Dariat!**

The young man's head jerked up. For an instant the illusion flickered. Long enough for Rubra. Under the outline of the handsome youth lurked Horgan. Horgan with a shocked expression wrenching his thin face. Incontrovertible proof.

**I knew it would be you,** Rubra said. In a way the knowledge came almost as a relief.

**Much good it will do you,** Dariat answered. **Your awareness of anything is going to come to an end real soon now. And you won't even make it to the freedom of the beyond, I won't allow you that escape.**

**You're amazing, Dariat. I mean that as a compliment. You still want me, don't you? You want revenge. It's all you've ever wanted, all that kept you alive these last thirty years. You still blame me for poor old Anastasia Rigel, even after all this time.**

**You got another suspect? If you hadn't driven me away, she and I would still be alive.**

**The pair of you would be dodging good old Bonney here, you mean.**

**Maybe so. But then maybe if I'd been happy I might have made**

**384**

something of my life. Ever think of that? I might have risen through the company hierarchy just like you always wanted. I could have made Magellanic Itg supreme; I could have turned Valisk into the kind of nation that would have had Tranquillity's plutocrats flocking to us in droves. There wouldn't be any of these misfits and losers who rally round your banner. King Alastair would have come here asking me for tips on how to run his kingdom. Do you really think a shipload of fucking zombies could have walked in here past passport, customs, and immigration without anyone even noticing if that kind of regime had been in place? Don't you dare try and avoid facing up to what you've done.

Oh, really? Tell me, by misfits, and all the other trash you'd fling out of the airlocks, do you include the kind of girl you fell in love with?

'Bastard!' Dariat screamed. Everyone in the hunting party stared at him, even Van-Riytell. 'I'll find you. I'll get you. I'll crush your soul to death.' Rage distended his face. He flung both arms out horizontally from his body, a magus Samson thrusting against the temple pillars. White fire exploded from his hands to chew into the tunnel walls. Polyp flaked and cracked, black chips spinning away though the air.

Temper, temper, Rubra mocked. I see that hasn't improved much over the years.

'Pack it in, you maniac!' Bonney yelled at him.

'Help me!' Dariat shouted back. The energistic hurricane roaring through his body was turning his brain to white-hot magma, wanting to burst clean out of his skull. 'I'm going to kill him. Help me, for Chi-ri's sake.' White fire hammered at the crumbling tunnel, desperate to reach the neural strata, to reach the very substance of the mind, and burn and burn and burn—

'Stop it, right now.' Bonney aimed her Lee Enfield at him, one eyebrow cocked.

Dariat slowly allowed the white fire to sink back into the passive energistic currents stirring the cells of his possessed body. His shoulders hunched in as smoke from the scorched polyp spun round him. He reverted to Horgan, even down to the unwashed shirt and creased trousers. Hands were pressed to his face as he resisted the onrush of tears. 'I'll get him,' Horgan's quavering, high-pitched voice proclaimed. 'I'll fucking have him. I'll roast him inside his shell like he was some kind of lobster. You'll see. Thirty years I've waited. Thirty! Thole owes me my justice. He *owes* me.'

'Sure he does,' Bonney said. 'But just so you and I are clear on this: pull another stunt like that, and you'll need a new body to work out of.' She jerked her head to the team trussing up Van-Riytell. They lifted the old comptroller off the ground, and started off down the tunnel.

The hunter woman glanced back at Dariat's hunched figure, opened her mouth to say something, then thought better of it. She followed the rest of the hunters along the tunnel.

You frightened me so bad I'm trembling, Rubra sneered. Can you feel the quakes? I expect the sea is about to flood the parkland. How's about that for wetting yourself?

Laugh away, Dariat said shakily. Go right ahead. But I'm going to come for you one day. I'll crack your safeguards. They won't last for ever, you know that. And for ever is what I've got on my side now. Then when I've busted you, I'm going to come into the neural strata with you, I'm going to crawl into you mind like a maggot, Rubra. And like a maggot I'm going to gnaw away at you.

I always was right about you. You were the best. Who else could still burn so hot after thirty years? Damn, why did you ever have to meet her? Together we could have rebuilt the company into a galaxy-challenger.

Such flattery. I'm honoured.

Don't be. Help me.

*What?* You have got to be fucking joking.

No. Together we could beat Kiera, purge the habitat of her cronies. You can rule Valisk yet.

The Edenists were right, you are insane.

The Edenists are frightened by my determination. You should know, you inherited that gene, it seems.

Yeah. So you know you can't deflect me. Don't even try.

Dariat, you're not one of them, boy, not one of the possessed. Not really. What can they possibly give you afterwards, huh? Ever thought of that? What sort of culture are they going to build? This is just an aberration of nature, a nonsense, and a transient one at that. Life has to have a purpose, and they're not alive. This energistic ability, the way you can create out of nothing, how can you square that with human behaviour? It's not possible, the two are not compatible, never will be. Look at yourself. If you want Anastasia back, bring her back. Find her in the beyond, get her back here. You can have everything now, remember? Kiera said so, did she not? Are you a part of that, Dariat? You have to decide, boy. Some day. If you don't, they'll do it for you.

'I can't bring her back,' he whispered.

What's that?

I can't. You understand nothing.

Try me.

You, a father confessor? Never.

I always have been. I am the confessor for everyone inside me, you know that. I am the repository of everyone's secrets. Including those of Anastasia Rigel.

I know everything about Anastasia. We had no secrets. We were in love.

Really? She had a life before you met her, you know. Seventeen long years. And afterwards, too.

Dariat glanced around with cold anger, his appearance sliding back to the white-suited ascetic. There was no afterwards. She died! Because of you.

If you knew of her past, you would understand what I meant.

What secrets? he demanded.

Help me, and I'll show you.

You shit! I'm going to cremate you, I'll dance on your fragments—

Rubra's principal routine watched Dariat's rage run its

course. He thought at one point that the man would revert to flailing at the tunnel walls with white fire again. But Dariat managed to hang on to that last shred of control – barely.

Rubra stayed silent. He knew it was too early to play his ace, the one final secret he had kept safe for the last thirty years. The doubt he had planted deep in Dariat's mind would have to be teased further, tormented into full-blown paranoia before the revelation was exposed.

\*

*Lady Macbeth*'s event horizon vanished, allowing her mushroom-shaped star trackers to rise out of their jump recesses and scan round. Fifteen seconds later the flight computer confirmed the starship had emerged fifty thousand kilometres above Tranquillity's non-rotational spaceport. By that time her electronic-warfare sensors registered eight of the habitat's strategic-defence platforms had locked on to the hull, despite the fact their coordinate was smack in the centre of a designated emergence zone.

'Jesus,' Joshua muttered sourly. 'Welcome home, people, nice to see you again.' He looked over to Gaura, who was lying on Warlow's acceleration couch. 'Update Tranquillity on our situation, fast, please. It seems a little trigger-happy today.' Combat sensors had located four blackhawks on interception trajectories, accelerating towards them at six gees.

Gaura acknowledged him with an indolent wrist-flick. The Edenist's eyes were closed; he'd been communicating with the habitat personality more or less from the moment the starship had completed the ZTT jump. Even with affinity it was difficult to convey their situation in a single quick summary; explanations, backed up with full memory exposure, took several minutes. He detected more than one ripple of surprise within the personality's serene thoughts as the story of Lalonde unfolded in its mentality.

When he'd finished, Ione directed her identity trait at him

in the Edenist custom. **That's some yarn you've got there,** she said. **Two days ago I wouldn't have believed a word of it, but as we've had warning fleks arriving from Avon on an almost hourly basis for the last day and a half all I can say is I'll grant you docking permission.**

**Thank you, Ione.**

**However, you will all have to be checked for possession before I'll admit you into the habitat. I can hardly expose the entire population to the risk of contamination on the word of one man, even though you seem genuine.**

**Of course.**

**How's Joshua?**

**He is well. A remarkable young man.**

**Yes.**

The flight computer's display showed the strategic-defence platforms disengaging their weapons lock. Joshua received a standard acknowledgement from the spaceport's traffic-control centre followed by a datavised approach vector.

'I need a docking-bay which can handle casualties,' he datavised back. 'And put a paediatric team on alert status, as well as some biophysics specialists. These kids have had a real hard time on Lalonde, and that only finished when they got nuked.'

'I am assembling the requisite medical teams now,' Tranquillity replied. 'They will be ready by the time you dock. I am also alerting a spaceport maintenance crew. Judging by the state of your hull, and the vapour leakages I can observe, I believe it would be appropriate.'

'Thank you, Tranquillity. Considerate as ever.' He waited for Ione to come on-line and say something, but the channel switched back to traffic control's guidance updates.

If that's the way she wants it ... Fine by me. His features slumped into a grouch.

He ignited the *Lady Mac*'s two functional fusion tubes, aligning the ship on their approach vector. They headed in for Tranquillity at one and a half gees.

'They believe all that spiel about possession?' Sarha asked Gaura, a note of worried scepticism in her voice.

'Yes.' He queried the habitat about the fleks from Avon. 'The First Admiral's precautions have been endorsed by the Assembly. By now ninety per cent of the Confederation should be aware of the situation.'

'Wait a minute,' Dahybi said. 'We only just got back here from Lalonde, and we didn't exactly hang around. How the hell could that navy squadron alert Avon two or three days ago?'

'They didn't,' Gaura said. 'The possessed must have got off Lalonde some time ago. Apparently Laton had to destroy an entire Atlantean island to prevent them from spreading.'

'Shit,' Dahybi grunted. 'You mean they're loose in the Confederation already?'

'I'm afraid so. It looks like Shaun Wallace was telling Kelly the truth after all. I had hoped it was all some subtle propaganda on his part,' the Edenist added sadly.

The news acted as a mood damper right through the starship. Their expected sanctuary wasn't so secure after all; they'd escaped a battle to find a war brewing. Not even an Edenist psyche could suppress that much gloom. The children from Lalonde picked up on it (those not squeezed into the zero-tau pods), another emotional ricochet, though admittedly not as large as all the others they'd been through. The happiness Father Horst had promised them waited at the end of their journey was proving elusive. Even the fact the voyage was ending didn't help much.

The damage *Lady Macbeth* had suffered in the fight above Lalonde didn't affect her manoeuvrability, not with Joshua piloting. She closed in on her designated docking-bay, CA 5–099, at the very centre of the spaceport disc, precisely aligned along the vector assigned by traffic control. There was no hint that fifteen attitude-control thrusters had been disabled, and she was venting steadily from emergency dump valves as well as a couple of fractured cryogenic feed-pipes.

By that time almost a quarter of the habitat population was accessing the spaceport's sensors, watching her dock. The news companies had broken into their schedules to announce that a single ship had made it back from Lalonde. Reporters had been very quick off the mark in discovering the paediatric teams were assembling in the bay. (Kelly's boss was making frantic datavises to the incoming starship, to no avail.)

The space industry people, industrial station workers, and ships' crews kicking their heels in the bars because of the quarantine observed the approach with a sense of troubled awe. Yes, Joshua had come through again, but the state of old *Lady Mac* ... Charred, flaking nultherm foam exposed sections of her hull which showed innumerable heat-stress ripples (a sure sign of energy-beam strikes), melted sensor clusters, only two fusion tubes functional. It must have been one hell of a scrap. They all knew no one else would be returning. Knowledge that every friend, colleague, or vague acquaintance who had accompanied Terrance Smith was either radioactive dust or lost to possession was hard to accept. Those starships were powerful, fast, and well armed.

The disembarkation process was, as expected, pretty shambolic. People kept emerging from the airlock tube as if *Lady Mac* was the focus of some dimensional twist, her internal space far larger than that which the hull enclosed. Edenists formed a good percentage of the exiles, much to the surprise of the rover reporters. They helped a horde of wondrously sensogenic, scared-looking refugee kids in ragged clothes. Paediatric nurses floated after them in the reception compartment, while reporters dived like airborne sharks to ask the children how they felt/ what they'd seen. Tears started to flow. **How the hell did they get in there?** Ione asked the habitat. Serjeants launched themselves to intercept the reporters.

Jay Hilton hugged her legs to her chest as she drifted across the compartment, shivering unhappily. None of this was what she'd been expecting, not the starship voyage nor their arrival. She tried to catch sight of Father Horst amid the noisy swirl of bodies bouncing around the compartment, knowing that he'd got others to look out for and probably couldn't spare much time for her. In fact she wouldn't be needed for anything much now there were plentiful adults around to take care of things again. Perhaps if she hunched up really small everyone would ignore her, and she'd be able to have a look at the habitat's park. Jay had heard stories of Edenist habitats and how beautiful they were; back in the arcology she'd often day-dreamed that one day she'd visit Jupiter, despite everything Father Varhoos preached about the evils of bitek.

The opportunity to escape the mêlée never quite presented itself. A reporter soared past her, noticed she was the oldest kid in the compartment, and used a grab hoop to brake himself abruptly. His mouth split into a super-friendly smile, the kind his neural nanonics program advised was best to interface trustfully with Young Children. 'Hi, there. Isn't this atrocious? They should have organized things better.'

'Yes,' Jay said doubtfully.

'My name is Matthias Rems.' The smile broadened further.

'Jay Hilton.'

'Well, hi there, Jay. I'm glad you've reached Tranquillity, you're quite safe here. From what we've heard it was nasty for all of you on Lalonde.'

'Yes!'

'Really? What happened?'

'Well, Mummy got possessed the first night. And then—' A hand closed on her shoulder. She glanced round to see Kelly Tirrel giving Matthias Rems an aggressive stare.

'He wants to know what happened,' Jay said brightly. She liked Kelly, admiring her right from the moment she arrived at the savannah homestead to rescue them. On the voyage to

Tranquillity she'd secretly decided that she was going to be a tough, Confederation-roaming reporter like Kelly when she grew up.

'What happened is your story, Jay,' Kelly said slowly. 'It belongs to you; it's all you've got left. And if he wants to hear it he has to offer you a great deal of money for it.'

'Kelly!' Matthias flashed her a slightly exasperated you-know-the-score grin.

It made no discernible impression on Kelly. 'Pick on some-one your own size, Matthias. Ripping off traumatized children is low even for you. I'm covering for Jay.'

'Is that right, Jay?' he asked. 'Did you thumbprint a contract with Collins?'

'What?' Jay glanced from one to the other, puzzled.

'Serjeant!' Kelly shouted.

Jay squeaked in alarm as a glitter-black hand closed around Matthias Rems's upper arm. The owner of the hand was a hard-skinned monster worse than any shape a possessed had ever worn.

'It's all right, Jay,' Kelly grinned for the first time in days. 'It's on our side. This is what Tranquillity uses for its police force.'

'Oh.' Jay swallowed loudly.

'I'd like to complain about an attempted violation of confidentiality copyright,' Kelly told the serjeant. 'Also, Matthias is breaking the sense-media ethics charter concerning the approach and enticement of minors in the absence of their parents or guardians.'

'Thank you, Kelly,' the serjeant said. 'And welcome home, I offer my congratulations on your endurance through difficult times.'

She grimaced numbly at the bitek servitor.

'Come along now, sir,' the serjeant said to Matthias Rems. It pushed away from the compartment bulkhead with its stocky legs, the pair of them heading for one of the hatchways.

'Don't ever trust reporters, Jay,' Kelly said. 'We're not nice people. Worse than the possessed really; they only steal bodies, we steal your whole life and make a profit out of it.'

'You don't,' Jay said, shoving the full child-force of trusting worship behind the words. A belief which was a sheer impossibility for any adult to live up to.

Kelly kissed her forehead, emotions in a muddle. Kids today, so knowing, which only makes them even more vulnerable. She gently pushed Jay towards one of the paediatric nurses, and left them discussing what the little girl had eaten last, and when.

'Kelly, thank Christ!'

The familiar voice made her twitch, a movement which in free fall was like a ripple running from toe to crown. She held on to a grab hoop to steady herself.

Feet first, Garfield Lunde slid down into her vision field. Her direct boss, and the man who had authorized her assignment. A big gamble, as he told her at the time, this kind of fieldwork was hardly her forte. Putting her deeper in his debt; everything he did for his workforce was a favour, an against-the-rules kindness. He owed his position entirely to his mastery of office politics, sensevise talent and investigative ability never entered into it.

'Hello, Garfield,' she said in a dull tone.

'You made it back. Great hairstyle, too.'

Kelly had almost forgotten her hair, cut to a fine fuzz to fit her armour suit's shell-helmet. Style, dress sense, cosmetic membranes: concepts which seemed to have dissolved clean out of her universe. 'Well done, Garfield; I can see why your observational ability pushed you right the way up the seniority league.'

He wagged a finger, almost catching his ponytail, which was snaking around his neck. 'Tough lady, at last. Looks like you lost your cherry on this assignment; touched a few corpses, wondered if you should have helped instead of recorded. Don't feel bad, it happens to us all.'

'Sure.'

'Is anyone else coming back, any other starships?'

'If they're not here by now, they won't be coming.'

'Christ, this is getting better by the second. We've got us a total exclusive. Did you get down to the planet?'

'Yes.'

'And is it possessed?'

'Yes.'

'Magnificent!' He glanced contentedly around the reception chamber, watching children and Edenists in free fall flight, their movements reminiscent of geriatric ballerinas. 'Hey, where are the mercs you went with?'

'They didn't make it, Garfield. They sacrificed themselves so the *Lady Mac*'s spaceplane could lift the children off.'

'Oh my God. Wow! Sacrificed themselves for kids?'

'Yes. We were outgunned, but they stood their ground. All of them. I never expected . . .'

'Stunning. You got it, didn't you? For Christ's sake Kelly, tell me you recorded it. The big fight, the last noble stand.'

'I recorded it. What I could. When I wasn't so scared I couldn't think straight.'

'Yes! I knew I made the right decision sending you. This is it, babe. Just watch our audience points go galactic. We're going to put Time Universe and the others out of business. Do you realize what you've done here? Shit, Kelly, you'll probably wind up as my boss, after this. Wonderful!'

Very calmly, Kelly let Ariadne's free fall unarmed-combat program shift into primary mode. Her sense of balance was immediately magnified, making her aware of every slight movement her body made in the minute air currents churning through the chamber. Her spacial orientation underwent a similar augmentation; distances and relative positions were obvious.

'Wonderful?' she hissed.

Garfield grinned proudly. 'You bet.'

Kelly launched herself at him, rotating around her centre of gravity as she did so. Her feet came round, seeking out his head, legs kicking straight.

Two of the serjeants had to pull her off. Luckily the paediatric team had some medical nanonic packages with them. They were able to save Garfield's eye; it would take a week before his broken nose knitted back into its proper shape, though.

\*

All the passenger refugees had left *Lady Mac*. Overstressed environmental systems were calming. The docking-bay's umbilicals sent a cool wind washing through the bridge, taking with it the air of the voyage; ugly air with its smell of human bodies, humidity, and heavy carbon dioxide. To Joshua's mind even the fans behind the grilles weren't whining so much. Perhaps it was his imagination.

Now there was only the crew left to soak up the luxuriously plentiful oxygen. The crew minus one. There hadn't been much time for Joshua to dwell on Warlow during the flight. Racing between jump coordinates, worrying about the energy patterning nodes holding out, the leakages, the damaged systems, children he had suddenly become responsible for, the desperate need to succeed.

Well, now he'd won, beaten the odds the universe had thrown at him. And it made him feel good, even though there was no happiness to accompany it. Self-satisfaction was a curious state, in this case roughly equivalent to fatigue-induced nirvana, he thought.

Ashly Hanson came up through the decking hatch, and took a swift glance round the lethargic forms still encased by their acceleration couch webbing. 'Flight's over, you know,' he said.

'Yeah.' Joshua datavised an instruction into the flight computer. Harlequin schematics of the starship's principal systems vanished from his mind, and the webbing peeled back.

'I think the cleaning up can wait until tomorrow,' Dahybi said.

'Message received,' Joshua said. 'Shore leave is now granted, and compulsory.'

Sarha glided over from her couch, and gave Joshua a tiny kiss. 'You were magnificent. After all this is over, we're going back to Aethra so we can tell him we escaped, and got the children off.'

'If he's there.'

'He's there. You know he is.'

'She's right, Joshua,' Melvyn Ducharme said as he cancelled the neurographic visualization of *Lady Mac*'s power circuits. 'He's there. And even if the transfer didn't work, his soul is going to be watching us right now.'

'Jesus.' Joshua shivered. 'I don't even want to think about that.'

'We don't have a lot of choice in the subject any more.'

'But not today,' Ashly put in heavily. He held out an arm to Sarha. 'Come along, we'll leave these morbids to moan among themselves. I don't know about you, but I'm having one very stiff drink in Harkey's first, then it's bed for a week.'

'Sounds good.' She twisted her feet off the stikpad by Joshua's couch, and followed the old time-hopper pilot through the hatch.

A vaguely nonplussed expression appeared on Joshua's face as they left together. None of your business, he told himself. Besides, there was Kelly to consider, though she'd been almost unrecognizable since returning from Lalonde. And then there was Louise. Ione, too.

'I think I'll skip the drink and go straight to bed,' he announced to the other two.

They went out of the bridge hatch one at a time. It was only when they got to the airlock that they encountered the service company's systems specialist coming the other way. She wanted the captain's authority to begin assessing the ship so she could assemble a maintenance schedule. Joshua stayed behind to discuss priorities, datavising over the files on systems which had taken punishment above Lalonde.

There was nobody about when he finally left the starship. The circus in the reception chamber had ended. The reporters had packed up. There wasn't even a serjeant left to check him over for possession. Sloppy, he thought, not like Tranquillity at all.

A commuter lift took him along the spindle which connected the spaceport disc to the centre of the habitat's northern endcap. It deposited him in one of the ten tube stations which served the hub; deserted but for a single occupant.

Ione stood outside the waiting tube carriage, dressed in a sea-blue sarong and matching blouse. He smiled ruefully at the memory that evoked.

'I remember you,' she said.

'Funny, I thought you'd forgotten.'

'No. Not you, no matter what.'

He stood in front of her, looking down at a face which owned far too much wisdom for such delicate features. 'I was stupid,' he confessed.

'I think you and I can withstand one argument, don't you?'

'I was stupid more than once.'

'Tranquillity's been reviewing the memories of the Edenists you saved. I'm very proud of what you achieved on that flight, Joshua, and I don't just mean all that fancy flying. Very proud indeed.'

All he could do was nod ineffectually. For a long time he'd dreamed about a reunion like this; going off after they'd had a fight had left too many things open ended, too much unsaid. Now it was actually happening, his mind was slipping to Louise, who had also been left behind. It was all Warlow's fault, him and that damn promise to be a little less selfish with his girls.

'You look tired,' Ione said, and held out her hand. 'Let's go home.'

Joshua looked down at her open hand, small and perfect. He twined his fingers through hers, rediscovering how warm her skin was.

*

Parker Higgens thought it must have been about twenty years since he last left Tranquillity. A short trip on an Adamist starship to a university on Nanjing so he could deliver a paper and assess some candidates for the Laymil project. He hadn't enjoyed the experience, free fall nausea seemed capable of penetrating whatever defences his neural nanonics erected across his nerve pathways.

This time it was pleasantly different. The gravity in the blackhawk's life-support capsule never fluctuated, he had a comfortable cabin to himself, the crew were friendly, and his navy escort officer was a cultured lady who made an excellent travelling companion.

At the end of the flight he even accessed the blackhawk's electronic sensors to watch their approach to Trafalgar. Dozens of navy starships swarmed round its two large spaceport globes. Avon provided a sumptuous backdrop; the warm blues, whites, greens, and browns of a terracompatible planet were so much kinder than the abrasive storm bands of Mirchusko, he realized. He almost laughed at the stereotype image he presented as he gawped like some stupefied tourist: the dusty old professor finally discovers there is life outside the research centre.

Pity he didn't have time to enjoy it. The navy officer had been datavising Trafalgar constantly since their wormhole terminus closed behind them, outlining their brief and authenticating it with a series of codes. They'd been given a priority approach vector, allowing them to curve round one of the spaceports at an exhilarating speed before sliding into the huge crater which served as a docking-ledge for bitek starships (they were the only blackhawk using it).

After that he'd had a couple of meetings with the First

Admiral's staff officers; an exchange of information which chilled both sides. Parker found out about possession, they were given the data on the Laymil home planet, Unimeron. They decided there wasn't any room for doubt.

When he was shown into Samual Aleksandrovich's big circular office the first thing Parker Higgens felt was an obscure burst of jealousy. The First Admiral had a view out over Trafalgar's biosphere which was more impressive than the one in his own office back on the Laymil project campus. A true dedicated bureaucrat's reaction, he chided himself, prestige is everything.

The First Admiral came round from behind his big teak desk to greet Parker with a firm handshake. 'Thank you for coming, Mr Director; and I'd also like to convey my gratitude to the Lord of Ruin as well for acting so promptly in this matter. It would appear she is a strong supporter of the Confederation; I just wish other heads of state followed her example.'

'I'll be sure to tell her,' Parker said.

The First Admiral introduced the others sitting round his desk: Admiral Lalwani, Captain Maynard Khanna, Dr Gilmore, and Mae Ortlieb, the President's science office liaison aide.

'Well, the Kiint did warn us, I suppose,' Admiral Lalwani said. 'All races eventually face the truth about death. It would appear the Laymil lost their confrontation.'

'They never said anything before,' Parker said bitterly. 'We have six Kiint assisting the project back at Tranquillity; I've worked with them for decades, they're helpful, cooperative, I even considered them as friends ... And never once did they drop the slightest hint. Damn them! They knew all along why the Laymil killed themselves and their habitats.'

'Ambassador Roulor did say it was something which we must come to terms with on our own.'

'Very helpful,' Dr Gilmore grunted. 'I have to say it's a

typical attitude to take given their psychology inclines towards the mystic.'

'I think any race which has uncovered the secret of death and survived the impact is inevitably going to take a highly spiritual approach to life,' the First Admiral said. 'Don't begrudge them that, Doctor. Now then, Mr Director, it would appear that our possession and the Laymil reality dysfunction are one and the same thing, correct?'

'Yes, Admiral. In fact, in the light of what we know now, the Laymil shipmaster's reference to the Galheith clan's death essence makes perfect sense. Possession was spreading across Unimeron as he left orbit.'

'I think I can confirm that,' Admiral Lalwani said. She glanced at the First Admiral for permission. He inclined his head. 'A voidhawk messenger has just returned from Ombey. Several possessed got loose there; fortunately the authorities were remarkably successful in hunting them down. However, despite that success, they've had to cede some ground to them. We have a recording of the phenomenon.'

Parker accessed the flek of images compiled by Ombey's strategic-defence sensor-satellites, seeing the remarkably smooth red cloud slowly sheathing Mortonridge. Time-lapse coverage showed the planet's terminator cruise in across the ocean. At night the peninsula's covering glowed a hostile cerise, its edges flexing in agitation over the crinkled coastline.

'Oh dear,' he said after he cancelled the visualization.

'They match,' Dr Gilmore said. 'Absolutely, the same event.'

'Admittedly Laton was in a hurry and under a great deal of stress,' Lalwani said. 'But if we understand him correctly, once that red cloud envelops a world completely, the possessed can take it right out of the universe.'

'Not outside, exactly,' Dr Gilmore said. 'If you can manipulate space-time to the extent they apparently can, then you should be able to format a favourable micro-continuum around a world. The surface simply won't be accessible through ordinary space-time. A wormhole might reach them, if we knew the correct quantum signature for its terminus.'

'The Laymil homeworld wasn't destroyed,' Parker said slowly. 'Of that we are sure. We speculated that it could have been moved, but naturally we considered only physical movement through this universe.'

'Then the possessed Laymil must have worked this vanishing trick,' Lalwani said. 'It really is possible.'

'Dear God,' the First Admiral murmured. 'As if it wasn't enough trying to find a method of reversing possession, we now have to consider how to bring back entire planets from some demented version of heaven.'

'And the Laymil in the spaceholms committed suicide rather than submit,' Lalwani said bleakly. 'The parallel between the Ruin Ring and Pernik Island is one I find most disturbing. The possessed confront us with a single choice, surrender or die. And if we do die, we enhance their own numbers. Yet Laton chose death; indeed he seemed almost happy at the prospect. Right at the end he told Oxley he would begin what he named the great journey, though he never elaborated. But the intimation that he would not suffer in the beyond was a strong one.'

'Unfortunately it's hardly something you can turn into a firm policy,' Mae Ortlieb observed. 'Nor one to reassure people with even if you did.'

'I am aware of that,' Lalwani told the woman coolly. 'What this information can do is point us towards areas which should be investigated. From the result of those investigations, policies can then be formulated.'

'Enough,' the First Admiral said. 'We are here to try and decide which is the most fruitful line of scientific enquiry. Given we now have a basic understanding of the problem confronting us I'd like some suggestions. Dr Gilmore?'

'We're continuing to examine Jacqueline Couteur to try and determine the nature of the energy which the possessing soul utilizes. So far we've had very little success. Our instruments either cannot read it or suffer glitches produced by it. Either way, we cannot define its nature.' He gave the First Admiral a timorous glance. 'I'd like your permission to move on to reactive tests.'

Parker couldn't help the disapproving snort which escaped from his lips. Again reinforcing the persona of crusty old academic; but he deplored Gilmore's wholehearted right-wing militarism.

No one would think of it to look at him now, but Parker Higgens had done his stint for radicalism and its various causes during his student days. He wondered if that was on the file Lalwani must invariably keep on him, ageing bytes in an obsolete program language detailing his protests over military development work carried out on the university campus. Had she accessed that before he'd been allowed in here, the heart of the greatest military force the human race had ever assembled? Perhaps she judged him safe these days. Perhaps she was even right in doing so. But people like Gilmore reopened all the old contemptuous thoughts. Reactive tests, indeed.

'You have a problem with that, Mr Director?' Dr Gilmore asked with formal neutrality.

Parker let his gaze wander round the office's big holoscreens, watching the starships shoaling over Avon. Readying themselves for combat. For conflict. 'I agree with the First Admiral,' he said sorrowfully. 'We must attempt to locate a scientific solution.'

'Which is only going to happen if my research can proceed unhindered. I know what you're thinking, Mr Director, and I regret the fact that we're dealing with a live human here. But unless you can offer me a valid alternative we must use her to add to our knowledge base.'

'I am aware of the argument about relative levels of suffering, Doctor. I just find it depressing that after seven centuries of adhering to the scientific method we haven't come up with a more humane principle. I find the prospect of experimenting on people to be abhorrent.'

'You should review the file Lieutenant Hewlett made when his marine squad were sent on their capture mission to obtain Jacqueline Couteur. You'd see exactly who really practises abhorrent behaviour.'

'Excellent argument. They do it to us, so we're fully justified doing it to them. We are all people.'

'I'm sorry,' the First Admiral interjected. 'But we really don't have time for the pair of you to discuss ethics and morality. The Confederation is now officially in a state of emergency, Mr Director; if that turns us into what you regard as savages in order to defend ourselves, then so be it. We did not initiate this crisis, we are simply reacting to it the only way I know how. And I am going to use you as much as Dr Gilmore will use the Couteur woman.'

Parker straightened his spine, sitting up to stare at the First Admiral. Somehow arguing with him as he had with the navy scientist wasn't even an option. Lalwani was right, he acknowledged sorely. Student politics didn't stand much chance against his adult survival instinct. We are what our genes made us. 'I don't think I would be much use to your endeavour, Admiral. I've made my contribution.'

'Not so.' He gestured to Mae Ortlieb.

'The Laymil must have tried to prevent possession from engulfing their spaceholms before they committed suicide,' she said. 'I believe that is what the essencemasters were on board the ship for.'

'Yes, but it couldn't have worked.'

'No.' She gave him a heavily ironic smile. 'So I'd like to use the scientific method, Mr Director; eliminate the impossible and all you're left with is the possible. It would be a lot of help to us if we knew what won't work against the possessed. A great deal of time would be saved. And lives, too, I expect.'

'Well, yes, but our knowledge is extremely limited.'

'I believe there are still many files in the Laymil electronics stack which have not been reformatted to human sense compatibility?'

'Yes.'

'Then that would be a good start. If you could return to Tranquillity and ask Ione Saldana to initiate a priority search for us, please.'

'That was in hand when I left.'

'Excellent. My office and the Navy Science Bureau here in Trafalgar can provide fresh teams of specialists to assist in the analysis process. They'd probably be better qualified in helping to recognize any weapons.'

Parker gave her an exasperated look. 'The Laymil didn't work like that, weapons are not part of their culture. Their countermeasures would consist principally of psychological inhibitors distributed through the spaceholms' life-harmony gestalt. They would attempt to reason with their opponents.'

'And when that failed, they might just have been desperate enough to try something else. The Laymil possessed weren't above using violence, we saw that in the recording. Their reality dysfunction was incinerating large portions of land.'

Parker surrendered, even though he knew it was all wrong. These people could so easily believe in the concept of super-weapons hidden amid the fractured debris of the Ruin Ring, a deus ex machina waiting to liberate the human race. The military mind! 'Anything is possible,' he said. 'But I'd like to go on record as saying that in this case I strongly doubt it.'

'Of course,' the First Admiral said. 'However, we do need to look, I'm sure you can appreciate that. May we send our specialists back with you?'

'Certainly.' Parker didn't like to think what Ione Saldana would say about that. Her one principal limitation on the project was the right to embargo weapons technology. But these people had outmanoeuvred him with astonishing ease. An acute lesson in the difference between political manoeuvring practised on the Confederation capital and one of its most harmless outpost worldlets.

Samual Aleksandrovich watched the old Director knuckle under, even feeling a slight sympathy. He really didn't like to invade the world of such a blatantly decent man of peace. The Parker Higgenses of this universe were what the Confederation existed to defend. 'Thank you, Mr Director. I don't want to appear an ungracious host, but if you could be ready to leave within a couple of hours, please. Our people are already being assembled.' He carefully avoided Higgens's sharp glance at that comment. 'They can travel on navy voidhawks, which should provide you a suitable escort back to Tranquillity. I really can't run the risk of your mission being intercepted. You're too valuable to us.'

'Is that likely?' Parker asked in concern. 'An interception, I mean?'

'I would certainly hope not,' the First Admiral said. 'But the overall situation is certainly less favourable than I'd hoped. We didn't get our warnings out quite fast enough. Several returning voidhawks have reported that the possessed have gained an enclave on various worlds, and there are seven asteroid settlements we know of that have been taken over completely. Most worrying is a report from the Srinagar system that they have taken over the Valisk habitat, which means they have a fleet of blackhawks at their disposal. That gives them the potential to mount a substantial military operation to assist others of their kind.'

'I see. I didn't realize the possessed had advanced so far. The Mortonridge recording is a distressing one.'

'Precisely. So you can appreciate our hurry in acquiring what information we can from the Laymil recordings.'

'I . . . I do, yes.'

'Don't worry, Mr Director,' Lalwani said. 'Our advantage at the moment is that the possessed are all small individual groups, they lack coordination. It is only if they become organized on a multistellar level that we will be in real trouble. The Assembly's prohibition on commercial starflight should give us a few weeks' grace. It will be difficult for them to spread themselves by stealth. Any interstellar movements they make from now on will have to be large scale, which gives us the ability to track them.'

'That is where the navy will face its greatest challenge,' the First Admiral said. 'Also our greatest defeat. In space warfare there is no such thing as a draw, you either win or you die. We will be shooting at complete innocents.'

'I doubt it will come to that,' Mae Ortlieb said. 'As you said, they are a disorganized rabble. We control interstellar communications, it should be enough to prevent them merging to form a genuine threat.'

'Except . . .' Parker said, he caught himself, then gave an penitent sigh. 'Some of our greatest generals and military leaders must be waiting in the beyond. They will understand just as much about tactics as we do. They'll know what they have to do in order to succeed.'

'We'll be ready for them,' the First Admiral said. He tried not to show any disquiet at Parker's suggestion. *Would I really be able to compete against an alliance between Napoleon and Richard Saldana?*

*

Dariat walked up the last flight of stairs into the foyer of the Sushe starscraper. None of the possessed used the lifts any more – too dangerous, Rubra still controlled the power circuits (and as for taking a tube carriage . . . forget it). The once-stylish circular foyer echoed a war zone. Its glass walls were cracked and tarnished with soot, furniture was mashed and flung about, dripping with water and grubby grey foam from the ceiling fire sprinklers. Black soil from broken pot plants squelched messily underfoot.

He refused to say it to the others picking their way through the wreckage: *If you'd just listened to me.* They'd heard it from him so many times they didn't listen; besides, they followed Kiera slavishly now. He had to admit the council she'd put together was effective at maintaining control within the habitat. And precious little else. He found it a telling point that the possessed hadn't bothered using their energistic power to return the lobby to its original state; it wasn't as if they had to go round with a brush and dustsponge. Rubra's continuing presence and war-of-nerves campaign was taking its toll on morale.

He stepped through the twisted doors out onto the flagstones ringing the lobby building. The surrounding parkland had, at least, retained its bucolic appearance. Emerald grass, unblemished by a single weed, extended out to the rank of sagging ancient trees two hundred metres away, crisscrossed by hard-packed gravel paths leading off deeper into the habitat interior. Dense hemispherical bushes with dark violet leaves and tiny silver flowers were scattered about. Small reptilian birds that were little more than triangular wings of muscle, with scales coloured turquoise and amber, swooped playfully through the air overhead.

The corpse spoilt the idyll; lying with its legs across one of the gravel paths, one ankle twisted at an awkward angle. There was no way of telling if it was male or female. Its head looked as if it had been shoved into a starship's fusion-exhaust jet.

The remains of the perpetrators, a pair of servitor housechimps, were smouldering on the grass twenty metres away. One of them held a melted wand which Dariat recognized as a shockrod. A lot of the possessed had been caught unawares by the harmless-looking servitors. After a couple of days of unexpected, and unpredictable, attacks most people simply exterminated them on sight now.

He walked past, wrinkling his nose at the smell. When he reached the trees he saw one of the triangular birds had alighted on the topmost branch. They eyed each other warily. It was a xenoc, so he was reasonably sure it wasn't affinity bonded. But with Rubra, you could never be certain. Now Dariat thought about it, the servitors would be an excellent way of keeping everyone under observation, circumventing the disruption he'd been inflicting on the neural strata's subroutines. He scowled up at the bird, which rippled its wings but didn't take off.

Dariat moved swiftly through the wood to a large glade which Kiera was using. Impressively tall trees with grey-green leaves formed a valley on either side of a wide stream, their black trunks host to a furry moss-analogue. Long grass fringed the water, littered with wild poppies.

Two groups of people were occupying the glade. One was comprised entirely of youngsters, couples in their late teens and early twenties; boys all with bare chests, wearing shorts or swimming trunks; girls in light summer dresses or bikinis, emphasizing their femininity. Both genders had been chosen for their beauty. Four or five children milled about looking completely bored; girls in party frocks and ribbons in their hair, boys in shorts and smart shirts. Two of the under-sevens were smoking.

At the other end of the glade four people in ordinary clothes stood in a group, talking in loud, strained voices. Arms waved around as fingers jabbed for emphasis. Various electronic modules were scattered on the grass round their feet, the paraphernalia of a professional MF recording operation.

Dariat saw Kiera Salter was standing among the recording team, and went over. She was wearing a white cotton camisole with tiny pearl buttons down the front, the top half undone to display her cleavage, and a thin white skirt showing tanned legs and bare feet. With her hair unbound over her shoulders the effect was awesomely sexy. It lasted right up until she turned her gaze on him. Marie Skibbow's body might be a male fantasy made flesh, but the maleficent intelligence now residing in her skull was instantly chilling.

'I hear you're losing it, Dariat,' she said curtly. 'I've been patient with you so far, because you've been very useful to us.

But if there's another incident like the one in the service tunnel, then I shall consider that usefulness at an end.'

'If you don't have me here to counter Rubra, then it's going to be you who'll wind up losing your temper. He'll blast every possessed back into the beyond if you let your guard down for a second. He doesn't care about the people whose bodies we've stolen.'

'You are becoming a bore, Dariat. And from what I hear that wasn't a temper loss, more like a psychotic episode. You're a paranoid schizophrenic, and people find that unsettling. Now concentrate on how to flush Rubra out of the neural strata by all means, but stop trying to spread dissension or it's going to go hard on you. Clear?'

'As crystal.'

'Good. I do appreciate what you're trying to do, Dariat. You're just going to have to learn a softer approach, that's all.' She gave him a factory-issue sympathetic smile.

Dariat saw one of the xenoc triangle birds perched on a tree behind her, watching the scene in the glade. The smirk which rose on his real lips was hidden by the energistic mirage-form he cloaked himself with. 'I expect you're right. I'll try.'

'Good man. Look, I don't want to be forced out of Valisk by him any more than you do. We're both on to a good thing here, and we can both maintain our status providing we just keep calm. If this recording works we should have recruits flocking to join us. That way we can shift Valisk to a place where Rubra's neutered. Permanently. Just keep him from causing too much trouble before then, and leave the rest to me, OK?'

'Yeah, all right. I understand.'

She nodded dismissal, then took a steadying breath and turned back to the recording team. 'Are you ready yet?'

Khaled Jaros glared at the recalcitrant sensor block in his hand. 'I think so, yes. I'm sure it will work this time. Ramon has reprogrammed it so that only the primary functions are left; we won't be able to get olfactory or thermal inputs, but the AV reception appears to be holding stable. With a bit of luck we can add some emotional activant patterns later.'

'All right, we'll try again,' she said loudly.

Under Khaled's directions the group of sybarite youths took up their positions once more. One couple started necking on the grass, another pair sported in the water. The little children stubbed their cigarettes out then ran round in dizzy circles, giggling and shrieking. 'Not so loud!' Khaled bellowed at them.

Kiera took up her own position leaning against a boulder at the side of the sparkling water. She cleared her throat, and forked her hair back with her left hand.

'Undo another couple more buttons, dear, please,' Khaled instructed. 'And bend your knees further.' He was staring straight into an AV pillar on one of the blocks.

She paused irately, and thought about it. The solidity of the camisole buttons wavered, and the hoops fell off allowing the flimsy fabric to shift still further apart. 'Is this quite necessary?' she asked.

'Trust me, darling. I've directed enough commercials in my time. Sex always sells: primary rule of advertising. And that's what this is, no matter what you want to call it. So I want legs and cleavage for the boys to drool over, and confidence to inspire the girls. That way we get them both feeding from our palm.'

'OK,' she grumbled.

'Wait.'

'Now what?'

He looked up from the AV pillar. 'You're not distinctive enough.'

Kiera glanced down at the slope of her breasts on show. 'You are making a very bad joke.'

'No no, not your tits, darling; they're just fine. No, it's the overall image, it's so passé.' Fingers plucked at his lower lip. 'I know, let's be astonishingly bold. I want you lounging there, just as you are, but have a red scarf wrapped round your ankle.'

Kiera stared at him.

'Please, love? Trust, remember?'

She concentrated again. The appropriate fabric materialized round her ankle, a silk handkerchief tied in a single knot. Blood red, and see if he caught the hint.

'That's wonderful. You look wild, gypsy exotic. I'm in love with you already.'

'Can I start now?'

'Ready when you are.'

Kiera took a moment to compose herself again, aiming for an expression which was the epitome of adolescent coyness. The water tinkled melodically beside her, other youths smiled and held each other close, children raced past her boulder. She grinned indulgently at them, and waved as they played their merry game. Then her head came round slowly to look straight at the sensor block.

'You know, they're going to tell you that you shouldn't be accessing this recording,' she said. 'In fact, they're going to get quite serious about that; your mum and dad, your big brother, the authorities in charge of wherever you live. Can't think why. Except, of course, I'm one of the possessed, one of the demons threatening "the fabric of the universe", your universe. I'm your enemy, apparently. I'm pretty sure I am, anyway; the Confederation Assembly says so. So ... that must be right. Yes? I mean, President Haaker came here and looked me over, and talked to me, and found out all about me, what I want, what I hate, who is my favourite MF artist, what frightens me. I don't remember that time when I spoke to him. But it must have happened, because the ambassadors of every government in the Assembly voted that I'm officially to be denounced as a monster. They wouldn't do that, not all those bright, serious, wise people unless they had all the facts at their disposal, now would they?

'Actually, the one lonely fact they had, and voted on, was that Laton killed ten thousand Edenists because they were possessed. You remember Laton. Some sort of hero a while back, I've been told, something about a habitat called Jantrit. I wonder if he asked the individuals on Pernik Island if they wanted to be exterminated. I wonder if they all said yes.

'They've done to us what they do to kids the universe over, lumped us together and said we're bad. One thug hits somebody, and every kid is a violent hooligan. You know that's truth, it happens all the time in your neighbourhood. You're never an individual, not to them. One wrong, all wrong. That's the way we're treated.

'Well, not here, not in Valisk. Maybe some possessed want to conquer the universe. If they do, then I hope the Confederation Navy fights them. I hope the navy wins. Those sort of possessed frighten me as much as they frighten you. That's not what we're about, it's so stupid, it's so obsolete. There's no need for that kind of behaviour, that kind of thinking, not any more. Not now.

'Those of us here on Valisk have seen what the power which comes of possession can really do when it's applied properly. Not when it's turned to destruction, but when it's used to help people. That's what frightens President Haaker, because it threatens the whole order of his precious world. And if that goes, he goes, along with all his power and his wealth. Because that's what this is really all about: money. Money buys people, money lets companies invest and consolidate their markets, money pays for weapons, tax money pays for bureaucracy, money buys political power. Money is a way of rationing what the universe has to offer us. But the universe is infinite, it doesn't need to be rationed.

'Those of us who have emerged from the dead of night can

break the restrictions of this corrupt society. We can live outside it, and flourish. We can burn your Jovian Bank ration cards and liberate you from the restrictions others impose on you.' Her smile tilted towards shy impishness. She held a hand out towards the sensor block, palm open. Her fingers closed into a fist, then parted again. A pile of ice-blue diamonds glittered in her palm, laced with slim platinum chains.

She grinned back at the sensor block, then tipped them carelessly onto the grass. 'You see, it's so simple. Items, objects, goods, the capitalist stockpile, exist only to give joy; for us living in Valisk they are an expression of emotion. Economics is dead, and true equality will rise out of the ashes. We've turned our back on materialism, rejected it completely. It has no purpose any more. Now we can live as we please, develop our minds not our finances. We can love one another without the barrier of fear now that honesty has replaced greed, for greed has died along with all the other vices of old. Valisk has become a place where every wish is granted, however small, however grand. And not just for those of us who have returned. To keep it to ourselves would be a cardinal act of greed. It is for everyone. For this aspect of our existence is the part which your society will despise the most, will curse us for. We are taking Valisk out of this physical dimension of the universe, launching it to a continuum where everyone will have our energistic power. It's a place where I can take on form, and return the body I have borrowed. All of us lost souls will be real people again, without conflict, and without the pain it takes for us to manifest ourselves here.

'And now I'll make our offer. We open Valisk to all people of goodwill, to those of a gentle disposition, to everyone sick of having to struggle to survive, and sick also of the petty limits governments and cultures place on the human heart. You are welcome to join us on our voyage. We shall be leaving soon, before the navy warships come and their bombs burn us for the crime of being what we are: people who embrace peace.

**414**

'I promise you that anyone who reaches Valisk will be granted a place among us. It will not be an easy journey for you, but I urge you to try. Good luck, I'll be waiting.'

The white cotton changed, darkening into a swirling riot of colour, as if skirt and camisole were made from a thousand butterfly wings. Marie Skibbow's smile shone through, bringing a natural warmth all of its own to the watchers. Children flocked round her, giggling merrily, hurling poppy petals into the air so that when they fell they became a glorious scarlet snowstorm. She let them take her hands and hurry her forward, eager to join their game.

The recording ended.

*

Despite being nearly fifty years old, the implant-surgery care ward boasted an impressive array of contemporary equipment. Medicine, along with its various modern sidelines, was a profitable business in Culey asteroid.

The annexe to which Erick Thakrar had been assigned (Duchamp hadn't paid for a private room) was halfway along the ward's main hall, a standardized room of pearl-white composite walls and glare-free lighting panels, the template followed by hospitals right across the Confederation. Patients were monitored by a pair of nurses at a central console just inside the door. They weren't strictly necessary, the hospital's subsentient processor array was a lot faster at spotting metabolic anomalies developing, but hospitals always adopted the person-in-the-loop philosophy; invalids wanted the human touch, it was reassuring. As well as being profitable, medicine was one of the last remaining labour-intensive industries, resisting automation with an almost Luddite zeal.

The operation to implant Erick's artificial tissue units had begun fifteen minutes after his removal from zero-tau. He'd been in surgery for sixteen hours; at one point he had four different surgical teams working on various parts of him. When he came out of theatre, thirty per cent of his body weight was accounted for by artificial tissue.

On the second day after his operation he had a visitor. A woman in her mid-thirties with unobtrusive oriental features. She smiled at the ward's duty nurse, claiming she was Erick's second cousin, and could even have proved it with an ID card if she'd been pressed. The nurse simply waved her down the ward.

When she entered the annexe two of the six beds were unoccupied, one had the privacy screen down to reveal an elderly man who gave her a hopeful talk-to-me-please look, the remaining three were fully screened. She smiled blandly at the lonely man, and turned to Erick's bed, datavising a code at the screen control processor. The screen split at the foot of the bed, shrinking back towards the walls. The visitor stepped inside, and promptly datavised a closure code at it.

She tried not to flinch when she saw the figure lying on the active shapeform mattress. Erick was completely coated in a medical package, as if the translucent green substance had been tailored into a skin-tight leotard. Tubes emerged from his neck and along the side of his ribs, linking him with a tall stack of medical equipment at the head of the bed, supplying the nanonics with specialist chemicals needed to bolster the traumatized flesh, and syphoning out toxins and dead blood cells.

Two bloodshot, docile eyes looked out at her from holes in the package smothering his face. 'Who are you?' he datavised. There was no opening in the package for his mouth, only a ventlike aperture over his nose.

She datavised her identification code, then added: 'Lieutenant Li Chang, CNIS. Hello, Captain; we received your notification code at the navy bureau.'

'Where the hell have you people been? I sent that code yesterday.'

'Sorry sir, there's been a system-wide security flap for the last two days. It's kept us occupied. And your shipmates have been hanging around the ward. I judged it best that they didn't encounter me.'

'Very smart. You know which ship I came in on?'

'Yes, sir, the *Villeneuve's Revenge*. You made it back from Lalonde.'

'Just barely. I've compiled a report of our mission and what happened. It is vital you get this data package to Trafalgar. We're not dealing with Laton, this is something else, something terrible.'

Li Chang had to order a neural nanonics nerve override to retain her impassive composure. After everything he'd been through to obtain this data ... 'Yes, sir; it's possession. We received a warning flek from the Confederation Assembly three days ago.'

'You know?'

'Yes, sir, it appears the possessed left Lalonde before you got there, presumably on the *Yaku*. They're starting to infiltrate other planets. It was Laton who alerted us to the danger.'

'Laton?'

'Yes, sir. He managed to block them on Atlantis, he warned the Edenists there before he kamikazied. The news companies are broadcasting the full story if you want to access it.'

'Oh, shit.' A muffled whimper was just audible from behind the package over his face. 'Shit, shit, shit. This was all for nothing? I went through this for a story the news companies are shoving out? This?' An arm was raised a few centimetres from the mattress, shaking heavily as though the package coating was too burdensome to lift.

'I'm sorry sir,' she whispered.

His eyes were watering. The facial package sucked the salty liquid away with quiet efficiency. 'There's some information left in the report. Important information. Vacuum can defeat them. God, can it defeat them. The navy will need to know that.'

'Yes, sir, I'm sure they will.' Li Chang hated how shallow

that sounded, but what else was there to say? 'If you'd like to datavise the report to me I'll include it on our next communiqué to Trafalgar.' She assigned the burst of encrypted data to a fresh memory cell.

'You'd better check my medical record,' Erick said. 'And run a review on the team which operated on me. The surgeons are bound to realize I was hardwired for weapons implants.'

'I'll get on to it. We have some assets in the hospital staff.'

'Good. Now for Heaven's sake, tell the head of station I want taking off this bloody assignment. The next time I see André Duchamp's face I'm going to smack his teeth so far down his throat he'll be using them to eat through his arse. I want the asteroid's prosecution office to formally charge the captain and crew of the *Villeneuve's Revenge* with piracy and murder. I have the appropriate files, it's all there, our attack on the Krystal Moon.'

'Sir, Captain Duchamp has some contacts of his own here, political ones. That's how he circumvented the civil starflight quarantine to dock here. We could probably have him arrested, but whoever that contact is, they aren't going to want the embarrassment of a trial. He'd probably be allowed to post bail, that's if he doesn't simply slope off quietly. Culey asteroid is really not the kind of place to bring that kind of charge against an independent trader. It's one of the reasons so many of them use it, which is why CNIS has such a large station here.'

'You won't arrest him? You won't stop this madness? A fifteen-year-old girl was killed when we attacked that cargo ship. Fifteen!'

'I don't recommend we arrest him here, sir, because he wouldn't stay under arrest. If the service is to have any chance of nailing him, it ought to be done somewhere else.' There was no answer, no response. The only clue she had that Erick was still alive came from the slow-blinking coloured LEDs on the medical equipment. 'Sir?'

'Yes. OK, I want him so bad I can even wait to be sure. You don't understand that people like him, ships like his, they've got to be stopped, and stopped utterly. We should fling every crew-member from every independent trader down onto a penal planet, break the ships down for scrap and spare parts.'

'Yes, sir.'

'Go away, Lieutenant. Make arrangements to have me shipped back to Trafalgar. I'll do my convalescing there, thank you.'

'Sir . . . Yes, sir. I'll relay the request. It might be some time before you can actually be transferred. As I said, there is a Confederationwide quarantine order in effect. We could have you taken to a more private area, and guarded.'

Again there was a long interval. Li Chang bore it stoically.

'No,' Erick datavised. 'I will remain here. Duchamp is paying, perhaps my injuries along with the repairs his ship needs will be enough to bankrupt the bastard. I expect Culey's authorities regard bad debts as a serious crime, after all that's money which is at stake, not morality.'

'Yes, sir.'

'The first ship out of here, Lieutenant, I want to be on it.'

'I'll set it up, sir. You can count on me.'

'Good. Go now.'

Feeling as guilty as she'd ever done in her life, she turned quickly and datavised the screen to open. One quick glance over her shoulder as she left – hoping to ease her conscience, hoping to see him relaxing into a peaceful sleep – showed his eyes were still open at the bottom of their green pits; a numbed angry stare, focused on nothing. Then the screen flowed shut.

\*

Alkad Mzu exited the Nyiru traffic control sensor display as soon as the wormhole interstice closed. At fifty thousand kilometres there hadn't been much of an optical-band return, the visualization was mostly graphics superimposed over enhanced pixel representations. But for all the lack of true visibility, there was no fooling them. *Udat* had departed.

She looked out through the observation lounge's giant window, which was set in the rock wall just above the asteroid's docking-ledge. A slender slice of stars was visible below the edge of the bulky non-rotational spaceport a kilometre and a half away. Narok itself drifted into view; seemingly smothered in white cloud, its albedo was sufficient to cast a frail radiance. Faint elongated shadows sprang up across the ledge, streaming away from the blackhawks and voidhawks perched on their docking pedestals. They tracked round over the smooth rock like a clock's second hand. Alkad waited until Narok vanished below the sharp synthetic horizon. The swallow manoeuvre would be complete now. One more, and the resonance device she had secreted on board would be activated.

There wasn't really any feeling of success, let alone happiness. A lone blackhawk and its greedy captain were hardly compensation for Garissa's suffering, the genocide of an entire people. It was a start, though. If nothing else, internal proof that she still retained the ardent determination of thirty years ago when she had kissed Peter goodbye. '*Au revoir*, only,' he'd insisted. An insistence she'd willed herself to believe in.

Maybe the easy, simple heat of hatred had cooled over the decades. But the act remained, ninety-five million dead people dependent on her for some degree of justice. It wasn't rational, she knew, this dreadful desire for revenge. But it was so sadly human. Sometimes she thought it was all she had left to prove her humanity with, a single monstrously flawed compulsion. Every other genuine emotion seemed to have disappeared while she was in Tranquillity, suppressed behind the need to behave normally. As normal as anyone whose home planet has been destroyed.

The dusky shadows appeared again, odd outlines stroking across the rock ledge, matching the asteroid's rotation. *Udat* would have performed its third swallow by now.

Alkad crossed herself quickly. 'Dear Mother Mary, please welcome their souls to heaven. Grant them deliverance from the crimes they committed, for we are all children who know not what we do.'

What lies! But the Maria Legio Church was an ingrained and essential part of Garissan culture. She could never discard it. She didn't want to discard it, stupid as that paradox was for an unbeliever. There was so little of their identity left that any remnant should be preserved and cherished. Perhaps future generations could find comfort among its teachings.

Narok fell from sight again. Alkad turned her back on the starfield and walked towards the door at the back of the observation lounge; in the low gravity field her feet took twenty seconds to touch the ground between each step. The medical nanonic packages she wore round her ankles and forearms had almost finished their repair work now, making her lazy movements a lot easier.

Two of the *Samaku*'s crew were waiting patiently for her just inside the door, one of them an imposing-looking cosmonik. They fell in step on either side of her. Not that she thought she really needed bodyguards, not yet, but she wasn't willing to take the chance. She was hauling round too much responsibility to risk jeopardizing the mission over a simple accident, or even someone recognizing her (this was a Kenyan-ethnic star system, after all).

The three of them took a commuter lift along the spindle to the spaceport where the *Samaku* was docked. Chartering the Adamist starship had cost her a quarter of a million fuseodollars, a reckless sum of money, but necessary. She needed to get to the Dorados as quickly as possible. The Intelligence agencies would be searching for her with a terrifying urgency now she'd evaded them on Tranquillity, and coincidentally proved they were right to fear her all along. *Samaku* was an independent trader; its military-grade navigational systems, and the bonuses she promised, would ensure a short voyage time.

Actually transferring over the cash to the captain had been the single most decisive moment for her; since escaping Tranquillity every other action had been unavoidable. Now, though, she was fully committed. The people she was scheduled to join in the Dorados had spent thirty years preparing for her arrival. She was the final component. The flight to destroy Omuta's star, which had started in the *Beezling* three decades ago, was about to enter its terminal phase.

*

The *Intari* started to examine the local space environment as soon as it slipped out of its wormhole terminus. Satisfied there was no immediate hazard from asteroidal rubble or high-density dust clouds it accelerated in towards Norfolk at three gees.

Norfolk was the third star system it had visited since leaving Trafalgar five days earlier, and the second to last on its itinerary. Captain Nagar had ambivalent feelings about carrying the First Admiral's warning of possession; in time-honoured fashion Adamists did tend to lay a lot of the blame on the messenger. Typical of their muddled thinking and badly integrated personalities. Nonetheless he was satisfied with the time *Intari* had made, few voidhawks could do better.

**We may have a problem,** *Intari* told its crew. **The navy squadron is still in orbit, it has taken up a ground fire-support formation.**

Nagar used the voidhawk's senses to see for himself, his mind accepting the starship's unique perception. The planet registered as a steeply warped flaw in the smooth structure of space-time, its gravity field drawing in a steady sleet of the minute particles which flowed through the interplanetary medium. A clutter of small mass points were in orbit around the flaw, shining brightly in both the magnetic and electromagnetic spectrum.

**They should have departed last week,** he said rhetorically. At his silent wish *Intari* obligingly focused its sensor blisters on the planet itself, shifting its perceptive emphasis to the optical spectrum. Norfolk's bulk filled his mind, the twin sources of illumination turning the surface into two distinctly coloured hemispheres, divided by a small wedge of genuine night. The land which shone a twilit vermilion below Duchess's radiance appeared perfectly normal, complying with *Intari*'s memory of their last visit, fifteen years ago. Duke's province, however, was dappled by circles of polluted red cloud.

**They glow,** *Intari* said, concentrating on the lone slice of night.

Before Nagar could comment on the unsettling spectacle, the communication console reported a signal from the squadron's commanding admiral, querying their arrival. When Nagar had confirmed their identity the admiral gave him a situation update on the hapless agrarian planet. Eighty per cent of the inhabited islands were now covered by the red cloud, which seemed to block all attempts at communication. The planetary authorities were totally incapable of maintaining order in the affected zones, police and army alike mutinied and joined the rebels. Even the Royal Marine squads sent in to assist the army had dropped out of contact. Norwich itself had fallen to the rebel forces yesterday, and now the streamers of red cloud were consolidating above the city. That substance more than anything had prevented the admiral from attempting any kind of retaliation using the starships' ground-bombardment weapons. How, she asked, could the rebels produce such an effect?

'They can't,' Nagar told her. 'Because they're not rebels.' He began datavising the First Admiral's warning over the squadron's secure communication channels.

Captain Layia remained utterly silent as the datavise came through. Once it was finished she looked round at her equally subdued crew.

'So now we know what happened to the *Tantu*,' Furay said. 'Hellfire, I hope the chase ship the admiral dispatched kept up with it.'

Layia gave him an agitated glance, uncomfortable notions stirring in her brain. 'You brought our three passengers up from the same aerodrome as the *Tantu*'s spaceplane, and at more or less the same time. The little girl was caught up in some sort of ruckus: a weird fire. You said so yourself. And they originally came from Kesteven Island, where it all started.'

'Oh, come on!' Furay protested. The others were all staring at him, undecided but definitely suspicious. 'They fled from Kesteven. They bought passage on the *Far Realm* hours before the hangar fire.'

'We're suffering from glitches,' Tilia said.

'Really?' Furay asked scathingly. 'You mean more than usual?'

Tilia glared at the pilot.

'Slightly more,' Layia murmured seriously. 'But nothing exceptional, I admit.' The *Far Realm* might have been an SII ship, but that didn't mean the company necessarily operated an exemplary maintenance procedure. Cost-cutting was a major company priority these days, not like when she started flying.

'They're not possessed,' Endron said.

Layia was surprised by the soft authority in his voice, he sounded so certain. 'Oh?'

'I examined Louise as soon as she came on board. The body sensors worked perfectly. As did the medical nanonics I used on her. If she was possessed the energistic effect the First Admiral spoke of would have glitched them.'

Layia considered what he said, and gave her grudging agreement. 'You're probably right. And they haven't tried to hijack us.'

'They were concerned about the *Tantu*, as well. Fletcher hated those rebels.'

'Yes. All right, point made. That just leaves us with the question of who's going to break the news to them, tell them exactly what's happened to their home world.'

Furay found himself the centre of attention again. 'Oh great, thanks a lot.'

By the time he'd drifted through the various decks to the lounge the passengers were using, the squadron admiral had begun to issue orders to the ships under her command. Two frigates, the *Ladora* and the *Levêque*, were to remain in Norfolk orbit where they could enforce the quarantine; any attempt to leave the planet, even in a spaceplane, was to be met with an instant armed response. Any commercial starship that arrived was to be sent on its way, again failure to comply was to be met with force. The *Intari* was to continue on its warning mission. The rest of the squadron was to return to 6th Fleet headquarters at Tropea in anticipation of reassignment. *Far Realm* was released from its support duties, and contract.

After a brief follow-on discussion with the admiral, Layia announced: 'She's given permission for us to fly directly back to Mars. Who knows how long this emergency is going to last, and I don't want to be stranded in the Tropea system indefinitely. Technically, we're on military service, so the civil starflight proscription doesn't apply. At the worst case it'll be something for the lawyers to argue about when we get back.'

With his mood mildly improved at the news they were going home, Furay slid into the lounge. He came through the ceiling hatch, head first, which inverted his visual orientation. The three passengers watched him flip round and touch his feet to a stikpad. He gave them an awkward grin. Louise and Genevieve were looking at him so intently, knowing something was wrong, yet still trusting. It wasn't a burden he was used to.

'First the good news,' he said. 'We're leaving for Mars within the hour.'

'Fine,' Louise said. 'What's the bad news?'

He couldn't meet her questing gaze, nor that of Genevieve. 'The reason we're leaving. A voidhawk has just arrived with an official warning from the First Admiral and the Confederation

Assembly. They think ... there's the possibility that people are being ... possessed. There was a battle on Atlantis; someone called Laton warned us about it. Look, something strange is happening to people, and that's what they're calling it. I'm sorry. The admiral thinks that's what has been happening on Norfolk, too.'

'You mean it's happening on other planets as well?' Genevieve asked in alarm.

'Yes.' Furay frowned at her, goosebumps rising along his arms. There hadn't been the slightest scepticism in her voice. Children were always curious. He looked at Fletcher, then Louise. Both of them were concerned, yes, but not doubting. 'You knew. Didn't you? You knew.'

'Of course.' Louise gave him a bashful smile.

'You knew all along. Holy Christ, why didn't you say something? If we'd known, if the admiral—' He broke off, troubled.

'Quite,' Louise said.

He was surprised by just how composed she was. 'But—'

'You find it hard enough to accept an official warning from the Confederation Assembly. You would never have believed us, two girls and an estate worker. Now would you?'

Even though there was no gravity, Furay hung his head. 'No,' he confessed.

# 11

The heavily wooded valley was as wild and beautiful as only an old habitat could be. Syrinx wandered off into the forest which came right up to the edge of Eden's single strip of town. She was heartened by just how many trees had survived from the habitat's early days. Their trunks might have swollen, and tilted over, but they were still alive. Wise ancient trees which several centuries ago had discarded the usual parkland concept of discreet order, becoming completely unmanageable, so the habitat didn't even try any more.

She couldn't remember being happier – though the verdant surroundings were only one contributing factor.

'Separation generates anticipation,' Aulie had told her with a mischievous smile as he kissed her goodbye just after lunch. He was probably right, his understanding of emotions was as extensive as his sexual knowledge. That was what made him such a fabulous lover, giving him complete control over her responses.

In fact, he was right, Syrinx admitted wistfully. They had only been parted for ninety minutes, and already her body missed him dreadfully. The very notion of what they'd do that night when she had him alone to herself again was glorious.

Their holiday visit to Eden was the talk of all her friends, and her family. She relished that aspect of their affair almost as much as the physical side. Aulie was forty-four, twenty-seven years older than her. In a culture which was too egalitarian and liberal to be shocked, she'd delighted in making a pretty good job of it so far.

There was the odd time when she was aware of the age gulf. This afternoon was one of them. Aulie had wanted to visit one of the caverns in the habitat's endcap which was full of late twenty-first-century cybernetic machinery, kept working as a functional museum. Syrinx was hard put to think of anything more boring. Here they were in the first habitat ever grown, five hundred years old, the seat of their culture; and he wanted to take a look at antique robots?

So they'd parted company. Him to his steam engines, leaving her to explore the interior. Eden was much smaller than the other habitats, a cylinder eleven kilometres long, three in diameter; a prototype, really. It didn't have starscrapers, the inhabitants lived in a small town ringing the northern endcap. Again, leftovers from a bygone age; simple, quick-to-assemble bungalows of metal and composite, laboriously preserved by their present occupants. Each of them had spruce handkerchief-sized gardens boasting ancient pure-genotype plant varieties. The vegetation might not have the size or sharpness of colour owned by their modern descendants, but their context made them a visual treat. Living history.

She picked her way along what she thought were paths, dodging gnarled roots which knitted together at ankle height, ducking under loops of sticky vine. Moss and fungi had colonized every square centimetre of bark, giving each tree its own micro-ecology. It was hot among the trunks, the motion-less air cloyingly humid. Her dress with its short skirt and tight top was intended purely to emphasize her adolescent figure for Aulie's benefit, in here it was totally impractical, damp fabric fighting every movement of her limbs. Her hair died within minutes, sodden strands flopping down to grease her shoulders. Green and brown smears multiplied over her arms and legs, nature's very own tribal war paint.

Despite the inconveniences she kept going forwards. The sensation of expectancy was growing all the while, and nothing to do with Aulie any more. This was something more ambivalent, a notion of approaching divinity.

She emerged from the jumbled trees into a glade which accommodated a calm lake that was almost sealed over with pink and white water lilies. Black swans drifted slowly along the few remaining tracts of open water. A bungalow sat on the marshy shore, very different to those in the town; it was built from stone and wood, standing on stilts above the reeds. A high, steeply curved blue slate roof overhung the walls, providing an all-round veranda, and giving the building an acutely Eastern aspect.

Syrinx walked towards it, more curious than apprehensive. The building was completely incongruous, yet apposite at the same time. Copper wind chimes, completely blue from age and exposure to the elements, tinkled softly as she climbed the rickety steps to the veranda which faced out over the lake.

Someone was waiting for her there, an oriental man sitting in a wheelchair, dressed in a navy-blue silk jacket, with a tartan rug wrapped round his legs. His face had the porcelain delicacy of the very old, almost all of his hair had gone, leaving a fringe of silver strands at the back of his head, long enough to come down over his collar. Even the wheelchair was antique, carved from wood, with big thin wheels that had chrome spokes; there was no motor. It looked as though the man hadn't moved out of it for years, he blended into its contours perfectly.

An owl was perched on the balcony, big eyes fixed on Syrinx.

The old man raised a hand with a thousand liver spots on its crinkled yellowing skin. He beckoned. **Come closer.**

Horribly aware of what a mess she looked, Syrinx took a hesitant couple of steps forward. She glanced sideways, trying to see into the bungalow through its open windows. Empty blackness prowled behind the rectangles. Blackness which hid—

**What is my name?** the old man asked sharply.

Syrinx swallowed nervously. **You are Wing-Tsit Chong, sir. You invented affinity, and Edenism.**

**Sloppy thinking, my dear girl. One does not invent a culture, one nurtures it.**

**I'm sorry. I can't ... It's difficult to think.** There were shapes flickering in the darkness, consolidating into outlines which she thought she recognized. The owl hooted softly. Guilty, Syrinx jerked her gaze back to Wing-Tsit Chong.

**Why is it difficult for you to think?**

She gestured to the window. **In there. People. I remember them. I'm sure I do. What am I doing here? I don't remember.**

**There is no one inside. Do not allow your imagination to fill the darkness, Syrinx. You are here for one reason only: to see me.**

**Why?**

**Because I have some very important questions to ask you.**

**Me?**

**Yes. What is the past, Syrinx?**

**The past is a summation of events which contribute to making the present everything which it is—**

**Stop. What is the past?**

She shrugged her shoulders, mortified that here she was in front of the founder of Edenism, and couldn't answer a simple question for him. **The past is a measure of entropic decay—**

**Stop. When did I die, what year?**

**Oh. 2090.** She twitched a smile of relief.

**And what year were you born?**

**2580.**

**How old are you now?**

**Seventeen.**

**What am I when you are seventeen?**

**Part of Eden's multiplicity.**

**What components make up a multiplicity?**

**People.**

**No. Not physically, they don't. What are the actual components, name the process involved at death.**

Transfer. Oh, memories!

So what is the past?

**Memories.** She grinned broadly, straightening her shoulders to say formally: The past is a memory.

At last, we achieve progress. Where is the only place your personal past can take form?

In my mind?

Good. And what is the purpose of life?

To experience.

**This is so, though from a personal view I would add that life should also be a progression towards truth and purity. But then I remain an intransigent old Buddhist at heart, even after so long. This is why I could not refuse the request from your therapists to talk to you. Apparently I am an icon you respect.** Humour quirked his lips for a moment. **In such circumstances, for me to assist in your deliverance is an act of *dana* I could not possibly refuse.**

*Dana*?

The Buddhist act of giving, a sacrifice which will allow the *dayaka*, the giver, a glimpse of a higher state, helping in transforming one's own mind.

I see.

I would be surprised if you did, at least fully. Edenism seems to have shied away from religion, which I admit I did not anticipate. However, our current problem is more immediate. We have established that you live to experience, and that your past is only a memory.

Yes.

Can it harm you?

No, she said proudly, the logical answer.

You are incorrect. If that were so you would never learn from mistakes.

I learn from it, yes. But I can't be hurt by it.

You can, however, be influenced by it. Very strongly. I believe we are debating how many angels dance on a pinhead, but influence can be harmful.

**431**

I suppose so.

Let me put it another way. You can be troubled by memories.

Yes.

Good. What effect does that have on your life?

If you are wise, it stops you from repeating mistakes, especially if they are painful ones.

This is so. We have established, then, that the past can control you, and you cannot control the past, yes?

Yes.

What about the future?

Sir?

Can the past control the future?

It can influence it, she said cautiously.

Through what medium?

People?

Good. This is *kamma*. Or what Western civilization referred to as reaping the seeds you have sown. In simpler terms it is fate. Your actions in the present decide your future, and your actions are based on the interpretation of past experiences.

I see.

In that respect, what we have in your case is an unfortunate problem.

We do?

Yes. However, before we go any further, I would like you to answer a personal question for me. You are seventeen years old, do you now believe in God? Not so primitive a concept as a Creator trumpeted by Adamist religions, but perhaps a higher force responsible for ordering the universe? Be honest with me, Syrinx. I will not be angry whatever the answer. Remember, I am probably the most spiritually inclined of all Edenists.

I believe . . . I think . . . No, I'm afraid that there might not be.

I will accept that for now. It is a common enough doubt amongst our kind.

It is?

Indeed. Now, I am going to tell you something about yourself in small stages, and I would like you to apply the most rigorous rational analysis to each statement.

I understand.

This is a perceptual reality, you have been brought here to help you overcome a problem. He smiled kindly, a gesture of his hand inviting her to continue.

If I am undergoing some form of treatment it can't be for physical injuries, I wouldn't need a perceptual reality for that. I must have had some kind of mental breakdown, and this is my therapy session. Even as she said it she could feel her heart rate increase, but the blood quickening in her veins only seemed to make her skin colder.

Very good. But, Syrinx, you did not have a breakdown, your own thought routines are quite exemplary.

Then why am I here?

Why indeed?

Oh, an outside influence?

Yes. A most unpleasant experience.

I've been traumatized.

As I said, your thought routines are impressive. Those of us running your therapy have temporarily blocked your access to your adult memories, thus avoiding contamination of those routines by the trauma. You can, for the moment, think without interference, even though this state does not permit your intellect to function at full capacity.

Syrinx grinned. I'm actually smarter than this?

I prefer the term swifter, myself. But what we have is adequate for our purpose.

The purpose being my therapy. With my adult mind traumatized I wouldn't listen. I was catatonic?

Partly, your withdrawal was within what the psychologist called a psychotic loop. Those responsible for hurting you were trying to force you to do something quite abhorrent. You refused, for love's sake. Edenists everywhere are proud of you for your resistance, yet that obstinacy has led to your current state.

Syrinx gave a downcast smile, not entirely perturbed. **Mother always said I had a stubborn streak.**

**She was entirely correct.**

**So what must I do now?**

**You must face the root of what was done to you. The trauma can be overcome; not instantly, but once you allow yourself to remember what happened without it overwhelming you as it has done until now, then the auxiliary memories and emotions can be dealt with one at a time.**

**That's why you talked about the past, so I can learn to face my memories without the fear, because that's all they are, memories. Harmless in themselves.**

**Excellent. I will now make them available to you.**

She steeled herself, foolish that it was, clenching her stomach muscles and fisting her hands.

**Look at the owl,** Wing-Tsit Chong instructed. **Tell me its name.**

The owl blinked at her, and half extended its wings. She stared at the flecked pattern of ochre and hazel feathers. They were running like liquid, becoming midnight-blue and purple. '*Oenone!*' she shouted. Pernik Island rushed towards her at a speed which made her grasp the balcony rail in fright.

**Please don't, Syrinx,** *Oenone* asked. The deluge of misery and longing entwined with that simple request made her eyes brim with tears. **Don't leave me again.**

**Never. Never ever ever ever, beloved.** Her whole body was trembling in reaction to the years of memory yawning open in her mind. And right at the end, the last before stinking darkness had grasped at her, most vivid of all, the dungeon and its torturers.

**Syrinx?**

**I'm here,** she reassured the voidhawk unsteadily. **It's OK, I'm fine.**

**You saved me from them.**

**How could I not?**

**I love you.**

**And I you.**

**I was right,** Wing-Tsit Chong said.

When Syrinx raised her head she saw the old man's face smiling softly, the multiplying wrinkles ageing him another decade. **Sir?**

**To do what I did all those centuries ago. To allow people to see the love and the sourness which lives in all of us. Only then can we come to terms with what we are. You are living proof of that, young Syrinx. I thank you for that. Now open your eyes.**

**They are open.**

He sighed theatrically. **So pedantic. Then close them.**

Syrinx opened her eyes to look up at a sky-blue ceiling. The dark blobs around the edges of her vision field resolved into three terribly anxious faces bending over her.

'Hello, Mother,' she said. It was very difficult to talk, and her body felt as though it was wrapped in a shrunken ship-tunic.

Athene started crying.

*

There were fifteen holoscreens in the editing suite, arranged in a long line along one wall. All of them were switched on, and the variety of images they displayed was enormous, ranging from a thousand kilometre altitude view of Amarisk with the red cloud bands mirroring the Juliffe tributary network, to the terrifyingly violent starship battle in orbit above Lalonde; and from Reza Malin's mercenaries flattening the village of Pamiers, to a flock of overexcited young children charging out of a homestead cabin to greet the arrival of the hovercraft.

Out of the five people sitting at the editing suite's table, four of them stared at the screens with the kind of nervous enthusiasm invariably suffered by voyeurs of suffering on a grand scale, where the sheer spectacle of events overcame the agony of any individual casualty. In the middle of her colleagues, Kelly regarded her work with a detachment which was mainly derived from a suppressor program her neural nanonics were running.

'We can't cut anything else,' Kate Elvin, the senior news editor, protested.

'I don't like it,' said Antonio Whitelocke. He was the head of Collins's Tranquillity office, a sixty-year career staffer who had plodded his way to the top from the Politics and Economics Division. An excellent choice for Tranquillity, but hardly empathic with young rover reporters like Kelly Tirrel. Her Lalonde report scared him shitless. 'You just can't have a three-hour news item.'

'Grow some bollocks,' Kelly snapped. 'Three hours is just dip-in highlights.'

'Lowlights,' Antonio muttered, glaring at his turbulent new megastar. Her skinhead hairstyle was devastatingly intimidating, and he'd heard all about poor Garfield Lunde. Marketing always complained about the use of non-mainstream image anchors. When he thought of that pretty, feminine young woman who used to present the breakfast round-up just last month he could only worry that one of the possessed had sneaked back from Lalonde after all.

'The balance is perfect,' Kate said. 'We've incorporated the fundamentals of the doomed mission, and even managed to end on an upbeat note with the rescue. That was a stroke of sheer brilliance, Kelly.'

'Well, gee, thanks. I would never have gone with Horst and the mercs back to the homestead unless it made a better report.'

Kate sailed on serenely through the sarcasm; unlike Antonio she'd been a rover once, which had included a fair share of combat assignments. 'This edit will satisfy both our corporate objectives, Antonio. First off, the rumour circuit has been overheating ever since *Lady Macbeth* came back, marketing haven't even needed to advertise our evening news slot. Everybody in Tranquillity is going to access us tonight, I've heard the opposition are just going to run soap repeats while Kelly's on.

And once our audience access they aren't going to stop, we're not just giving them sensenviron impressions of a war, we've got a whole story to tell them here. That always hooks them. Our advertising premium for this is going to be half a million fuseodollars for a thirty-second slot.'

'For one show,' Antonio grumbled.

'More than one, that's the beauty. Sure, everyone is going to make a flek of tonight. But Kelly brought back over thirty-six hours of her own fleks, and then we've got the recordings taken from *Lady Macbeth*'s sensors from the moment they emerged in the Lalonde system. We can milk this for a month with specialist angle interviews, documentaries, and current affairs analysis panels. We've won the ratings war for the whole goddam year, and we did it on the cheap.'

'Cheap! Do you know what we paid that bloody "Lagrange" Calvert for those sensor recordings?'

'Cheap,' Kate insisted. 'Tonight alone is going to pay for those. And with universal distribution rights we'll quadruple Collins's group profits.'

'If we can ever get it distributed,' Antonio said.

'Sure we can. Have you accessed the civil starflight prohibition order? It just prevents docking, not departure. Blackhawks can simply stay inside a planet's emergence zone and datavise a copy to our local office. We'll have to pay the captains a little more, but not much, because they're losing revenue sitting on the endcap ledges. This can work. It'll be head office seats for us after this.'

'What "after this"?' Kelly said.

'Come on, Kelly.' Kate squeezed her shoulder. 'We know it was rough, we felt it for ourselves. But the quarantine is going to stop the possessed from spreading, and now we're alert to the problem the security forces can contain them if there is an outbreak. They won on Lalonde because it's so damn backward.'

'Oh, sure.' Kelly was operating on stimulant programs alone

now, fatigue toxin antidote humming melodically in her head. 'Saving the galaxy is a doddle now we know. Hell, it's only the dead we're up against after all.'

'If you're not up to this, Kelly, then say so,' Antonio said, then played his master card. 'We can use another anchor. Kirstie McShane?'

'That bitch!'

'So we can go ahead as scheduled, can we?'

'I want to put in more of Pamiers, and Shaun Wallace. Those are the kind of events which will make people more aware of the situation.'

'Wallace is depressing, he spent that entire interview telling you that the possessed couldn't be beaten.'

'Damn right. Shaun's vital, he tells us what we really need to know, to face up to the real problem.'

'Which is?'

'Death. Everyone's going to die, Antonio, even you.'

'No, Kelly, I can't sanction this sort of slant. It's as bad as that Tyrathca Sleeping God ceremony you recorded.'

'I shouldn't have let you cut that out. Nobody even knew the Tyrathca had a religion before.'

'Xenoc customs are hardly relevant at a time like this,' he said.

'Kelly, we can use that Tyrathca segment in a documentary at a later date,' Kate said. 'Right now we need to finalize the edit. Christ, you're on-line in another forty minutes.'

'You want to keep me sweet, then put in all of Shaun's interview.'

'We've got half of it,' Antonio said. 'All the salient points are covered.'

'Hardly. Look, we have got to bring home to people what possession is really all about, the meaning behind the act,' Kelly said. 'So far all the majority of Confederation citizens have had is this poxy official warning from the Assembly. It's an abstract, a problem on another planet. People have to learn it's not that simple, that there's more to this disaster than simple physical security. We have to deal with the philosophical issues as well.'

Antonio pressed the palm of his hand onto his brow, wincing.

'You don't get it, do you?' Kelly asked hotly. Her arm waved at the holoscreens with their damning images. 'Didn't you access any of this? Don't you understand? We have to get this across to people. I can do that for you. Not Kirstie blowbrain McShane. I was there, I can make it more real for anyone who accesses the report.'

Antonio looked at the holoscreen which showed Pat Halahan running through the smoky ruins of Pamiers, blasting his bizarre attackers to shreds of gore. 'Great. Just what we need.'

\*

This just wasn't the way Ione had expected it to go. Joshua hadn't even looked at her bedroom door when they arrived back at the apartment, let alone show any eagerness. There had been times with him when she hadn't made it to the bed before her skirt was up around her waist.

Yet somehow she knew this wasn't entirely due to the traumas of the mission. He was intent and troubled, not frightened. Very unfamiliar territory as far as Joshua was concerned.

He'd simply had a shower and a light supper then settled down in her big settee. When she sat beside him she was too uncertain about the reaction to even rest her hand on his arm.

I wonder if it's that girl on Norfolk? she asked dubiously.

He has endured some difficult times, Tranquillity answered. You must expect his usual behaviour to be toned down.

Not like this. I can see he's been shaken up, but this is more.

The human mind is constantly maturing. External events dictate the speed of the maturation. If he has begun to think harder for himself because of Lalonde, surely this is no bad thing?

Depends what you want from him. He was so perfect for me

before. So very uncomplicated, the roguish charmer who would never try to claim me.

I believe you also mentioned something about sex on occasion.

Yeah, all right, that too. It was great, and completely guilt free. I picked him up, remember? What more could a girl with my kind of responsibilities want? He was someone who was never going to try and interfere with my duties as the Lord of Ruin. Politics simply didn't interest him.

A husband would be preferable to a casual lover. Someone who is always there for you.

You're my husband.

You love me, and I love you; it could never be anything else since I gave birth to you. But you are still human, you need a human companion. Look at voidhawk captains, the perfect example of mental symbiosis.

I know. Maybe I'm just feeling jealous.

Of the Norfolk girl? Why? You know how many lovers Joshua has had.

Not of her. Ione looked at Joshua's profile as he stared out of the lounge's big window. Of me. Me a year ago. The old story, you never know what you have until it's gone.

He is right next to you. Reach out. I am sure he needs comfort as much as you.

He's not there, not any more. Not my original Joshua. Did you see that flying he did? Gaura's memory of the Lagrange stunt nearly gave me a heart attack. I never realized just how good a captain he is. How could I ever take that away from him? He lives for space, for flying *Lady Mac* and what that can give him. Remember that last argument we had before he left for Lalonde? I think he was right. He's achieved his *métier*. Flying is sequenced into his genes the way dictatorship is in mine. I can't take that away from him any more than he could take you away from me.

I think you may be stretching the metaphor slightly.

Maybe. We were young, and we had fun, and it was lovely. I've got the memories.

He had fun. You are pregnant. He has responsibilities to the child.

Does he? I don't think mothers require a big tough hunter-gatherer to support them nowadays. And monogamy becomes progressively more difficult the longer we live. Geneering has done more to change the old 'till death us do part' concept than any social radicalism.

Doesn't your child deserve a loving environment?

My baby will have a loving environment. How can you even question that?

I do not question your intentions. I am simply pointing out the practicalities of the situation. At the moment you are unable to provide the child with a complete family.

That's very reactionary.

I admit I am arguing on the extreme. I am not a fundamentalist, I simply wish to concentrate your thoughts. Everything else in your life has been planned and accounted for, the child has not. Conception is something you have done all for yourself. I do not wish it to become a mistake. I love you too much for that.

Father had other children.

Who were given to the Edenists so that they would be brought up in the greatest possible family environment. A whole world of family.

She almost laughed out loud. Imagine that, Saldanas became Edenists. We made the transition in the end. Does King Alastair know about that?

You are ducking the issue, Ione. One child of the Lord of Ruin is brought up with me as a parental, the heir. The others are not. As a parent you have a responsibility to their future.

Are you saying I've been irresponsible conceiving this child?

Only you can answer that. Were you depending on Joshua to be a stay-at-home father? Even then you must have known how unlikely that was.

God, all this argument just because Joshua looks moody.

I am sorry. I have upset you.

No. You've done what you wanted to do, made me think. For some of us it's painful, especially if you're like me and hadn't really considered the consequences of your actions. It gets me all resentful and defensive. But I'll do the best for my child.

*I know you will, Ione.*

She blushed at the tenderness of the mental tone. Then she leant against Joshua. 'I was worried while you were gone,' she said.

He took a sip of his Norfolk Tears. 'You were lucky. I was scared shitless most of the time.'

'Yes. "Lagrange" Calvert.'

'Jesus, don't you start.'

'If you didn't want the publicity, you shouldn't have sold *Lady Mac*'s sensor recordings to Collins.'

'It's hard to say no to Kelly.'

Ione squinted at him. 'So I gather.'

'I meant: it's hard to refuse that kind of money. Especially given my situation. The fee I got from Terrance Smith isn't going to cover *Lady Mac*'s repairs. And I can't see the Lalonde Development Company ever handing over the balance on our contract, given there isn't a Lalonde left to develop any more. But the money I got from Collins will cover everything, and leave me happily in the black.'

'Not forgetting the money you made on the Norfolk run.'

'Yeah, that too. But I didn't want to break into that, it's kind of like a reserve I'm holding back for when everything settles down again.'

'My hero optimist. Do you think the universe is going to settle down?'

Joshua didn't like the way the conversation was progressing. He knew her well enough now, she was steering. Hoping to angle obliquely into the subject she wanted to discuss. 'Who knows? Are we going to finish up talking about Dominique?'

Ione raised her head from his shoulder to give him a puzzled glance. 'No. What made you ask that?'

'Not sure. I thought you wanted to talk about us, and what

happens after. Dominique and the Vasilkovsky Line played a heavy part in my original plans from here on in.'

'There isn't going to be an after, Joshua, not in the sense of returning to the kind of existence we had before. Knowing there's an afterlife is going to tilt people's perception on life for ever.'

'Yeah. It is pretty deep, when you think about it.'

'That's your considered in-depth analysis of the situation, is it?' For a moment she thought she'd gone and wounded him. But he just gave a gaunt smile. Not angry.

'Yeah,' he said, quiet and serious. 'It's deep. I had three bloody narrow escapes inside two days on that Lalonde mission. If I'd made one mistake, Ione, just one, I'd be dead now. Only I wouldn't, as we now know, I'd be trapped in the beyond. And if Shaun Wallace was telling the truth – and I suspect he was – then I'd be screaming silently to be let back in no matter what the cost or who had to pay it.'

'That's horrible.'

'Yes. I sent Warlow to his death. I think I knew that even before he went out of the airlock. And now he's out there, or in there – somewhere, with all the other souls. He might even be watching us now, begging to be given sensation. The trouble with that is, I do owe him.' Joshua put his head back on the silk cushions, staring up at the ceiling. 'Do I owe him big enough for that, though? Jesus.'

'If he was your friend, he wouldn't ask.'

'Maybe.'

Ione sat up and reached for the bottle to pour herself another measure of Norfolk Tears.

**I'm going to ask him,** she told Tranquillity.

**Surely you are not about to ask for my blessing?**

**No. But I'd welcome your opinion.**

**Very well. I believe he has the necessary resources to complete the task; but then he always has. Whether he is the most desirable**

candidate still presents me with something of a dilemma. I acknowledge he is maturing; and he would not knowingly betray you. Impetuosity does weigh against him, however.

Yes. Yet I value that trait above all.

I am aware of this. I even accept it, when it applies to your first child and my future. But do you have the right to make that gamble when it concerns the Alchemist?

Maybe not. Although there might be a way round it. And I have simply got to do something. 'Joshua?'

'Yeah. Sorry, didn't mean to go all moody on you.'

'That's all right. I have a little problem of my own right now.'

'You know I'll help if I can.'

'That's the first part, I was going to ask you anyway. I'm not sure I can trust anyone else with this. I'm not even sure I can trust you.'

'This sounds interesting.'

She took a breath, committed now, and began: 'Do you remember, about a year ago, a woman called Dr Alkad Mzu contacted you about a possible charter?'

He ran a quick check through his neural nanonics memory cells. 'I got her. She said she was interested in going to the Garissa system. Some kind of memorial flight. It was pretty weird, and she never followed it up.'

'No, thank God. She asked over sixty captains about a similar charter.'

'Sixty?'

'Yes, Tranquillity and I believe it was an attempt to confuse the Intelligence agency teams who keep her under observation.'

'Ah.' Instinct kicked in almost immediately, riding a wave of regret. This was big-time, and major trouble. It almost made him happy they hadn't leapt straight into bed, unlike the old days (a year is old, ha!). For him it was odd, but he was simply too ambivalent about his own feelings. And he could see how she'd been thrown by his just-old-friends approach, too.

Sex would have been so easy; he just couldn't bring himself to do it with someone he genuinely liked when it didn't mean what it used to. That would have been too much like betrayal. I can't do that to her. Which was a first.

Ione was giving him a cautious, enquiring look. In itself an offer.

I can stop it now if I want.

It was sometimes easy for him to forget that this blonde twenty-year-old was technically an entire government, the repository of state, and interstellar, secrets. Secrets it didn't always pay to know about; invariably the most fascinating kind.

'Go on,' Joshua said.

She smiled faintly in acknowledgement. 'There are eight separate agencies with stations here, they have been watching Dr Mzu for nearly twenty-five years now.'

'Why?'

'They believe that just before Garissa was destroyed she designed some kind of doomsday device called the Alchemist. Nobody knows what it is, or what it does, only that the Garissan Department of Defence was pouring billions into a crash development project to get it built. The CNIS have been investigating the case for over thirty years, ever since they first heard rumours that it was being built.'

'I saw three men following her when she left Harkey's Bar that night,' Joshua said, running a search and retrieval program through his neural nanonics. 'Oh hell, of course. The Omuta sanctions have been lifted; they were the ones who committed the Garissan Genocide. You don't think she'd . . .?'

'She already has. This is not for general release, but last week Alkad Mzu escaped from Tranquillity.'

'Escaped?'

'Yes. She turned up here twenty-six years ago, and took a job at the Laymil project. My father promised the Confederation Navy she would be allowed neither to leave nor to pass on any technical information relating to the Alchemist to other governments or astroengineering conglomerates. It was an almost ideal solution, everyone knows Tranquillity has no expansionist ambitions, and at the same time she could be observed continually by the habitat personality. The only other alternative was to execute her immediately. My father and the then First Admiral both agreed the Confederation should not have access to a new kind of doomsday device; antimatter is quite bad enough. I continued that policy.'

'Until last week.'

'Yes. Unfortunately, she made total fools out of all of us.'

'I thought Tranquillity's observation of the interior was perfect. How could she possibly get out without you knowing?'

'Your friend Meyer lifted her away clean. The *Udat* actually swallowed inside the habitat and took her on board. There was nothing we could do to stop him.'

'Jesus! I thought my Lagrange point stunt was risky.'

'Quite. Like I said, her escape leaves me with one hell of a problem.'

'She's gone to fetch the Alchemist?'

'Hard to think of any other reason, especially given the timing. The only real puzzle about this is, if it exists, why hasn't it been used already?'

'The sanctions. No . . .' He started to concentrate on the problem. 'There was only ever one navy squadron on blockade duties. A sneak raid would have a good chance of getting through. That's if one ship was all it took to fire it at the planet.'

'Yes. The more we know about Dr Mzu, the less we understand the whole Alchemist situation. But I really don't think her ultimate goal can be in any doubt.'

'Right. So she's probably gone to collect it, and use it. The *Udat* has a fair payload capacity; and Meyer's seen combat duty in his time, he can take a bit of heat.' Except . . . Joshua knew Meyer, a wily old sod, for sure, but there was one hell of a difference between the occasional mercenary contract, and annihilating an entire planet of unsuspecting innocents. Meyer wouldn't do that, no matter how much money was offered. Offhand, Joshua couldn't think of many (or even any) independent trader captains who would. That kind of atrocity was purely the province of governments and lunatic fanatics.

'The use of it is what concerns me the most,' Ione said. 'Once it's been activated, governments will finally be able to see what it can actually do. From that, they'll deduce the principles. It'll be mass-produced, Joshua. We have to try to stop that. The Confederation has enough problems with antimatter, and now possession. We cannot allow another terror factor to be introduced.'

'We? Oh, Jesus.' He let his head flop back onto the cushions – if only there was a stone wall to thump his temple against instead. 'Let me guess. You want me to chase after her. Right? Go up against every Intelligence agency in the Confederation, not to mention the navy. Find her, tap her on the shoulder, and say nicely: all is forgiven, and the Lord of Ruin would really like you to come home, oh and by the way whatever your thirty-year plan – your obsession – was to screw up Omuta we'd like you to forget it as well. Jesus fucking Christ, Ione!'

She gave him an unflustered sideways glance. 'Do you want to live in a universe where a super-doomsday weapon is available to every nutcase with a grudge?'

'Try not to weight your questions so much, you might drown.'

'The only chance we have, Joshua, is to bring her back here. That or kill her. Now who are you going to trust to do that? More to the point, who can I trust? There's nobody, Joshua. Except you.'

'Walk into Harkey's Bar any night of the week, there's a hundred veterans of covert operations who'll take your money and do exactly what you ask without a single question.'

'No, it has to be you. One, because I trust you, and I mean really trust you. Especially after what you did back at Lalonde. Two, you've got what it takes to do the job, the ship and the contacts in the industry necessary to trace her. Three, you've got the motivation.'

'Oh, yeah? You haven't said how much you'll pay me yet.'

'As much as you want, I am the national treasurer after all. That is, until young Marcus takes over from me. Did you want to bequeath our son this problem, Joshua?'

'Shit, Ione, that's really—'

'Below the belt even for me? Sorry, Joshua, but it isn't. We all have responsibilities. You've managed to duck out of yours for quite a while now. All I'm doing is reminding you of that.'

'Oh, great, now this is all my problem.'

'No one else in the galaxy can make it your problem, Joshua, only you. Like I said, all I'm doing is making the data available to you.'

'Nice cop-out. It's me that's going to be in at the shit end, not you.' When Joshua looked over at her he expected to see her usual defiant expression, the one she used when she was powering up to out-stubborn him. Instead all he saw was worry and a tinge of sorrow. On a face that beautiful it was heartbreaking. 'Look, anyway, there's a Confederationwide quarantine in effect, I can't take *Lady Mac* off in pursuit even if I wanted to.'

'It only applies to civil starflight. *Lady Macbeth* would be re-registered as an official Tranquillity government starship.'

'Shit.' He smiled up at the ceiling, a very dry reflex. 'Ah well, worth a try.'

'You'll do it?'

'I'll ask questions in the appropriate places, that's all, Ione. I'm not into heroics.'

'You don't need to be, I can help.'

'Sure.'

'I can,' she insisted, piqued. 'For a start, I can issue you with some decent combat wasps.'

'Great, no heroics please, but take a thousand megatons worth of nukes with you just in case.'

'Joshua ... I don't want you to be vulnerable, that's all. There will be a lot of people looking for Mzu, and none of them are the type to ask questions first.'

'Wonderful.'

'I can send some serjeants with you as well. They'll be useful as bodyguards when you're docked.'

He tried to think up an argument against that, but couldn't. 'Fine. Unsubtle, but fine.'

Ione grinned. She knew that tone.

'Everyone will just think they're cosmoniks,' she said.

'OK, that just leaves us with one minor concern.'

'Which is?'

'Where the hell do I start looking? I mean, Jesus; Mzu's smart, she's not going to fly straight to the Garissa system to pick up the Alchemist. She could be *anywhere*, Ione; there are over eight hundred and sixty inhabited star systems out there.'

'She went to the Narok system, I think. That's where the *Udat*'s wormhole was aligned, anyway. It makes sense, Narok is Kenyan-ethnic; she may be contacting sympathizers.'

'How the hell do you know that? I thought only blackhawks and voidhawks could sense each other's wormholes.'

'Our SD satellites have some pretty good sensors.'

She was lying; he knew it right away. What was worse than the lie, he thought, was the reason behind it. Because he couldn't think of one, certainly not one that had to be kept from him, the only person she trusted to send on this job. She must be protecting something, a something more important than the Alchemist. Jesus. 'You were right, you know that? The night we met at Dominique's party, you said something to me. And you were right.'

'What was it?'

'I can't say no to you.'

*

Joshua left an hour later to supervise the *Lady Mac*'s refit, and round up his crew. It meant he missed Kelly's report, which put him in a very small minority. Kate Elvin's earlier optimism had been well founded, the other news companies didn't even try to compete. Ninety per cent of Tranquillity's population accessed the sensevises Kelly had recorded on Lalonde. The impact was as devastating as predicted. Though not at once. The editing was too good for that, binding segments together in a fast-paced assault on the sensorium. Only afterwards, when they could duck the impact on their immediate attention, did the implications of possession begin to sink in.

The effect acted like a mild depressant program, or a communal virus. Yes, there truly was life after corporeal death. But it was perpetual misery, even for the righteous and the holy. Nor was there any sighting of God, any God, even the Creator's numerous prophets went curiously unseen; no Pearly Gates, no brimstone lakes, no judgement, no Jahannam, no salvation. The reward for any life lived in any fashion was nothing, the final absolute. The best anybody now had to hope for after death was to come back and possess the living. A poor recompense indeed for a life of virtuous strife.

Having to come to terms with the concept of a universe besieged by lost souls was a wounding process. People reacted in different ways. Getting smashed, or stoned, or stimmed out was popular. Some found religion in a big way. Some became fervently agnostic. Some turned to their shrinks for reassurance. Some (the richer and smarter) quietly focused their attention (and funding) to zero-tau mausoleums.

One thing the psychiatrists did notice, this was a depression which drove nobody to suicide. The other constants were the slow decline in efficiency at work, increased lethargy, a rise in use of tranquillizer and stimulant programs. Pop-psychology commentators took to calling it the rise of the why-bother psychosis.

The rest of the Confederation was swift to follow, and almost identical in its response no matter what ethnic culture base was exposed to the news. No ideology or religion offered much in the way of resistance. Only Edenism proved resilient, though even that culture was far from immune.

Antonio Whitelocke chartered twenty-five blackhawks and Adamist independent trader starships to distribute Kelly's fleks to Collins offices across the Confederation. Saturation took three weeks, longer than optimum, but the quarantine alert made national navies highly nervous. Some of the more authoritarian governments, fearful of the effect Kelly's recording would have on public confidence, tried to ban Collins from releasing it, an action which simply pushed the fleks underground whilst simultaneously boosting their credibility. It was an unfortunate outcome, because in many cases it clashed and interacted with two other information ripples expanding across the Confederation. Firstly there was the rapidly spreading bad news about Al Capone's takeover of New California, and secondly the more clandestine distribution of Kiera Salter's seductive recording.

* * *

The *Mindori* hit eight gees as soon as it cleared the wormhole terminus. Various masses immediately impinged on Rocio Condra's perception. The core of the Trojan point was twenty million kilometres in diameter, and cluttered with hundreds of medium-sized asteroids, tens of thousands of boulders, dust shoals, and swirls of ice pebbles, all of them gently resonating to the pull of distant gravity fields. *Mindori* opened its wings wide, and began beating them in vast sweeps.

Rocio Condra had chosen an avian form as the hellhawk's image. The three stumpy rear fins had broadened out, becoming thinner to angle back. Its nose had lengthened, creases and folds multiplying across the polyp, deepening, accentuating the creature's streamlining. Meandering green and purple patterns had vanished, washed away beneath a bloom of midnight black. The texture was crinkly, delineating tight-packed leather feathers. He had become a steed worthy of a dark angel.

Loose streamers of interplanetary dust were churned into erratic storms as he powered forwards in hungry surges. Radar and laser sensors began to pulse against his hull. It had taken Rocio Condra a long time experimenting with the energistic power pumping through his neural cells to maintain a viable operational level within the hellhawk's electronic systems, although efficiency was still well down on design specs. So long as he remained calm, and focused the power sparingly and precisely, the processors remained on-line. It helped that the majority of them were bitek, and military grade at that. Even so, combat wasps had to be launched with back-up solid rockets, but once they were clear they swiftly recovered, leaving only a small window of vulnerability. Thankfully, his mass perception, a secondary effect of the distortion field, was unaffected. Providing he wasn't outnumbered by hostile void-hawks, he could give a good account of himself.

The beams of electromagnetic radiation directed at him were coming from a point ten thousand kilometres ahead. Koblat asteroid, a new and wholly unimportant provincial settlement in a Trojan cluster which after a hundred and fifteen years of development and investment had yet to prove its economic worth. There were thousands just like it scattered across the Confederation.

Koblat didn't even rate a navy ship from the Toowoomba star system's defence alliance. Its funding company certainly didn't provide it with SD platforms. The sole concession which the asteroid's governing council had made to 'the emergency' was to upgrade their civil spaceflight sensors, and equip two interplanetary cargo ships with a dozen combat wasps apiece, grudgingly donated by Toowoomba. It was, like every response to the affairs of the outside universe, a rather pathetic token.

And now a token which had just been exposed for what it was. The hellhawk's emergence, location, velocity, flight vector, and refusal to identify itself could only mean one thing: it was hostile. Both of the armed interplanetary craft were dispatched on an interception vector, lumbering outwards at one and a half gees, hopelessly outclassed even before their fusion drives ignited.

Koblat beamed a desperate request for help to Pinjarra, the cluster's capital four million kilometres away, where three armed starships were stationed. The asteroid's inadequate internal emergency procedures were activated, sealing and isolating independent sections. Its terrified citizens rushed to designated secure chambers deep in the interior and waited for the attack to begin, dreading the follow-on, the infiltration by possessed.

It never happened. All the incoming hellhawk did was open a standard channel and datavise a sensorium recording into the asteroid's net. Then it vanished, expanding a wormhole interstice and diving inside. Only a couple of optical sensors caught a glimpse of it, producing a smudgy image which nobody believed in.

When Jed Hinton finally got back from his designated safe shelter chamber, he almost wished the alert had kept going a few more hours. It was change, something new, different. A rare event in all of Jed's seventeen years of life.

When he returned to the family apartment, four rooms chewed out of the rock at level three (a two-thirds gravity field), his mum and Digger were shouting about something or other. The rows had grown almost continual since the warning from the Confederation Assembly had reached Koblat. Work shifts were being reduced as the company hedged its bets, waiting to see what would happen after the crisis was over. Shorter shifts meant Digger spending a lot more time at home, or up at the Blue Fountain bar on level five when he could afford it.

'I wish they'd stop,' Gari said as more shouting sounded through the bedroom door. 'I can't think right with so much noise.' She was sitting at a table in the living room, trying to concentrate on a processor block. Its screen was full of text with several flashing diagrams, part of a software architecture course. The level was one his didactic imprints had covered five years ago; Gari was only three years younger, she should have assimilated it long ago. But then his sister had something in her genes which made it difficult for laser imprinters to work on her brain, she had to work hard at revising everything to make it stick.

'Girl's just plain arse-backwards,' Digger shouted some nights when he stumbled home drunk.

Jed hated Digger, hated the way he shouted at Mum, and hated the way he picked on Gari. Gari tried hard to keep up with her year, she needed encouraging. Not that there was anything to achieve in Koblat, he thought miserably.

Miri and Navar came in, and promptly loaded a games flek into the AV block. The living room immediately filled up with an iridescent laserlight sparkle. A flock of spherical, coloured-chrome chessboards swooped round Jed's head every time his eyes strayed towards the tall AV pillar. Both girls started yelling instructions at the block, and small figures jumped between the various spheres in strategic migrations, accompanied by a thumping music track. The projector was too damn large for a room this size.

'Come on, guys,' Gari wailed. 'I've got to get this stuff locked down ready for my assessment.'

'So do it,' Navar grunted back.

'Cow!'

'Dumb bitch!'

'Stop it! You played this all yesterday.'

'And we haven't finished yet. If you weren't so thick you'd know that.'

Gari appealed to Jed, chubby face quivering on the threshold of tears.

Miri and Navar were Digger's daughters (by different mothers), so if Jed lifted a finger to them Digger would hit him. He'd found that out months ago. They knew it too, and used the knowledge with tactical skill.

'Come on,' he told Gari, 'we'll go down to the day club.'

Miri and Navar laughed jeeringly as Gari shut down her processor block and glared at them. Jed shoved the door open and faced his tiny worldlet.

'It's not any quieter at the club,' Gari said as the door shut behind them.

Jed nodded dispiritedly. 'I know. But you can ask Mrs Yandell if you can use her office. She'll understand.'

'Suppose,' Gari acknowledged brokenly. Not long ago her brother had been capable of putting the whole universe to rights. A time before Digger.

Jed set off down the tunnel. Only the floor had been covered in composite tiling, the walls and ceiling were naked rock lined with power cables, data ducts, and fat environmental tubes. He took the left turning at the first junction, not even thinking. His life consisted of walking the hexagonal weave of tunnels which circled the asteroid's interior; that entire topographic web existed only to connect two places: the apartment and the day club. There was nowhere else.

Tunnels with gloomy lighting, hidden machines that made every wall in Koblat thrum quietly; that was his environment now, a worldlet without a single horizon. Never fresh air and open spaces and plants, never room, not for his body or his mind. The first biosphere cavern was still being bored out (that was where Digger worked), but it was years behind schedule and ruinously over budget. At one time Jed had lived with the faith that it would provide him an outlet for all his crushed-up feelings of confinement and anger, allowing him to run wild over fresh-planted grass meadows. Not now. His mum and Digger along with all the rest of the adults were too stupid to appreciate what possession really meant. But he knew. Nothing mattered now, nothing you did, nothing you said, nothing you thought, nothing you wished for. Die now or die in a hundred years' time, you still spent eternity with a sprained mind which was unable to extinguish itself. The final, absolute horror.

No, they didn't think about that. They were as trapped in this existence as the souls were in the beyond. Both of them trekking after the low-income jobs, going where the companies assigned them. No choice, and no escape, not even for their children. Building a better future wasn't a concept which could run in their thought routines, they were frozen in the present.

For once the dreary tunnel outside the day club centre was enlivened with bustle. Kids hurried up and down, others clumped together to talk in bursts of high-velocity chatter. Jed frowned, this was wrong. Koblat's kids never had so much energy, or enthusiasm. They came here to hang out, or access the AV projections which the company provided to absorb and negate unfocused teenage aggression. Travelling the same loop of hopelessness as their parents.

Jed and Gari gave each other a puzzled look, both of them sensitive to the abnormal atmosphere. Then Jed saw Beth winding through the press towards them, a huge smile on her narrow face. Beth was his maybe-girlfriend; the same age, and always trading raucous insults. He couldn't quite work out if that was affection or not. It did seem a solid enough friendship of some kind, though.

'Have you accessed it yet?' Beth demanded.

'What?'

'The sensevise from the hellhawk, cretin.' She grinned and pointed to her foot. A red handkerchief was tied above her ankle.

'No.'

'Come on then, mate, you're in for a swish-ride treat.' She grabbed his hand and tugged him through the kids milling round the door. 'The council tried to erase it, of course, but it was coded for open access. It got into every memory core in the asteroid. Nothing they could do about it.'

There were three AV players in the day club centre, the ones Jed always used to access vistas of wild landscapes, his one taste of freedom. Even so he could only see and hear the wonderful xenoc planets; the AV projectors weren't sophisticated (i.e. expensive) enough to transmit activent patterns which stimulated corresponding tactile and olfactory sensations.

A dense sparkle-mist filled most of the room. Twenty people were standing inside it, their arms hanging limply by their side, faces entranced as they were interacted with the recording. Curious now, Jed turned to face one of the pillars square on.

Marie Skibbow's tanned, vibrant body lounged back over a boulder five metres in front of him, all flimsy clothes and pronounced curves. It was a perfectly natural poise, such a Venus could only possibly belong in this paradisaical setting with its warmth and light and rich vegetation. Jed fell in love, forgetting all about skinny, angular Beth with her hard-edge attitude. Until now girls such as Marie had existed only in adverts or AV dramas; they weren't real, *natural*, not like this. The fact that such a person actually lived and breathed somewhere in the Confederation gave him a kick higher than any of the floaters he scored.

Kiera Salter smiled at him, and him alone. 'You know, they're going to tell you that you shouldn't be accessing this recording,' she told him.

*

When it ended Jed stood perfectly still, feeling as though a piece of his own body had been stolen from him, certainly something was missing, and he was the poorer for it. Gari was at his side, her face forlorn.

'We have to go there,' Jed said. 'We have to get to Valisk and join them.'

# 12

The hotel sat on its own plateau halfway up the mountainside, looking out across the deep bay. The only buildings to share the rocky amphitheatre with it were half a dozen weekend retreat villas belonging to old-money families.

Al could appreciate why the owners had made strenuous efforts to keep the developers out, it was a hell of a sight – an unspoilt beach that went on for miles, tiny fang rocks at the front of the headlands stirring up founts of spray, long lazy breakers rolling onto the sands. The only thing wrong about it was that he couldn't get down there to enjoy it. There was a lot of time pressure building up at the top of the Organization, dangerous amounts of work and too-tight schedules. Back in Brooklyn when he was a kid he'd sit on the docks and watch gulls pecking at dead things in the muddy shallows. One thing about those gulls, their necks never stayed still, peck peck peck all day long. Now he'd surrounded himself with people that took after them. Never ever did his senior lieutenants give him a break. Peck peck peck. 'Al, we need you to settle a beef.' Peck peck. 'Al, what do we do with the navy rebels?' Peck peck. 'Al, Arcata is pulling in the red cloud again, you want we should zap the bastards?' Peck peck.

Jee-zus. In Chicago he had days off, months on holiday. Everyone knew what to do, things ran smoothly – well, kind of. Not here. Here, he didn't have a fucking minute to himself. His head was buzzing like a fucking hornets' nest he had to think so hard on the hoof.

'But you're loving it,' Jezzibella said.

'Huh?' Al turned back from the window. She was lying across the bed, wrapped in a huge fluffy white robe, her hair lost beneath a towel turban. One hand held a slim book, the other was plucking Turkish delights out of a box.

'You're Alexander the Great and Jimi Hendrix all in one, you're having a ball.'

'Dozy dame, who the hell is Jimi Hendrix?'

Jezzibella pouted crossly at the book. 'Oh, he was the sixties, sorry. A real wildcat musician, everybody loved him. The thing I'm trying to say here is, don't knock what you've got, especially when you've got so much. Sure, things are a little rough at the start, they're bound to be. It just makes winning all the sweeter. Besides, what else have you got to do? If you don't give orders, you take orders. You told me that.'

He grinned down at her. 'Yeah. You're right.' But how come she'd known what he was thinking? 'You wanna come with me this time?'

'It's your shout, Al. I'll maybe go down to the beach later.'

'Sure.' He was beginning to resent these goddam tours. San Angeles had been a beaut, but then everyone else wanted in on the act. This afternoon it was Ukiah, tomorrow morning it was Merced. Who gave a shit? Al wanted to get back up to Monterey where the action was at.

The silver and ivory telephone at the side of the bed rang. Jezzibella picked up the handset and listened for a moment. 'That's good to hear, Leroy. Come on in; Al can give you ten minutes for news like that.'

'What?' Al mouthed.

'He thinks he's cracked our money problem,' she said as she replaced the handset.

Leroy Octavius and Silvano Richmann walked in. Leroy smiling effusively, Silvano managing a glimmer of enthusiasm as he greeted Al and ignored Jezzibella entirely. Al let the faint insult pass, Silvano was always on the level about how he hated the non-possessed, and there was no hint in Jez's mind that she'd taken offence.

'So what have you come up with?' Al asked as they sat in the chairs which gave them a splendid view out across the bay.

Leroy put a slim black case down on the coffee table in front of him, resting a proud hand on it. 'I took a look at the basics of what money is all about, Al, and tried to see how it could apply to our situation.'

'Money is just something you screw out of other people, right, Silvano?' Al laughed.

Leroy gave an indulgent smile. 'That's about it, Al. Money is principally a fancy method of accounting, it shows you how much other people owe you. The beauty of it is you can use it to collect that debt in a thousand different ways, that's how come money always grows out of a barter economy. Individual currencies are just a measure of the most universal commodity. It used to be gold, or land, something which never changed. The Confederation uses energy, which is why the fuseodollar is the base currency, because it's linked to $He_3$ production, and those costs are fixed and universal.'

Al sat back, materialized a Havana, and took a deep drag. 'Thanks for the history lesson, Leroy. Get to the point.'

'The method of accounting isn't so important, whether you use old-fashioned notes and coins or a Jovian Bank disk, it doesn't matter. What you must establish is the nature of the debt itself, the measure of what you owe. In this case it's so simple I could kick myself for not thinking of it straight off.'

'Someone's gonna kick you, Leroy, for sure. And pretty quick. What debt?'

'An energistic one. An act of magic, you promise to pay someone whatever they want.'

'For Christ's sake, that's crazy,' Al said. 'What's the sense in someone owing me a chunk of magic when I can work my

**461**

own? The original New California economy went ass-backwards in the first place because we got this ability.'

Leroy's grin became annoyingly wide. Al let him get away with it because he could see how tight and excited the fat manager's thoughts were, he'd certainly convinced himself he was right.

'You can, Al,' Leroy said. 'But I can't. This is a not so rhetorical question, but how are you going to pay me for all this work I've been doing for you? Sure you've got the threat of possession to hold me with, but you need my talent, have me possessed and you don't get that. But put me on a salary and I'm yours for life. For a day's work you promise to do five minutes of magic for me: manifest a good suit or a copy of the *Mona Lisa*, whatever I ask for. But it doesn't have to be you who owes me for the day, I take the token, or promise, or whatever, and go to any possessed for my magic to be performed.'

Al chewed round his cigar. 'Let me get this straight, here, Leroy. Any schmuck with one of your chocolate dime tokens can come along and ask me to make them a set of gold-plated cutlery any time they want?'

'Not any time, no, Al. But it's the simplest principle of all: you do something for me, I do something for you. Like I said, it's exchanging and redeeming debt. Don't think of it on such a personal level. We've been wondering how to keep the non-possessed working for the possessed, this is the answer: you'll pay them, but you pay them in whatever they want.'

Al glanced over at Jezzibella, who shrugged. 'I can't see a flaw in the idea,' she said. 'How are you going to measure it, Leroy? Surely the possessed will be able to counterfeit any currency?'

'Yes. So we don't use one.' He opened his bag and took out a small processor block, it was matt-black with a gold Thompson sub-machine-gun embossed on one side. 'Like I said, money is all accounting. We use a computer memory to keep track of what's owed to whom. You want your magic doing for you, then the computer shows how much you're entitled to. Same for the reverse, if you're a possessed it shows how much work the non-possessed have been doing for you. We just set up a planetary bank, Al, keep a ledger on everyone.'

'I must be crazy even listening to this. Me? You want me to run a bank? The First National Al Capone Bank? Jesus H. Christ, Leroy!'

Leroy held up the black processor block to stress the argument. 'That's the real beauty of it, Al. It makes the Organization utterly indispensable. The soldiers are the ones who are going to enforce and regulate payment on the ground. They make it fair, they make the whole economy slide along smoothly. We don't have to force or threaten anyone any more, at least not on the scale we have been doing with the SD network. We don't put taxes on the economy, like other governments, we become the economy. And there's nothing to stop the possessed using the system themselves. There are a lot of jobs too big for one individual. It can work, Al. Really it can.'

'I scratch your back, you scratch mine,' Al said. He eyed the black processor block suspiciously. Leroy handed it over. 'Did Emmet help with this accounting machine?' Al asked curiously. Apart from the gold emblem it could have been carved from a lump of coal for all he knew.

'Yes, Al, he designed it, and the ledger program. He says that the only way a possessed guy can tamper with it is if he gets into the computer chamber, which is why he wants to base it on Monterey. We're already making it the Organization headquarters, this will cement the deal.'

Al scaled the electric gadget back on the table. 'OK, Leroy. I see you've busted your balls to do good work for me here. So I'll tell you what we'll do; I'll grab all my senior lieutenants for a meeting in Monterey in two days' time, see what they make of it. If they buy it, I'm behind you all the way. How does that sound?'

'Achievable.'

'I like you, Leroy. You setting up any more tours for me?'

Leroy flicked a fleeting glance at Jezzibella, who gave him a tiny shake of her head. 'No, Al; Merced is the last for a while. It's more important you're up at Monterey for a while now, what with the next stage just about ready.'

'Goddam, am I glad to hear that.'

Leroy smiled contentedly, and put the accountancy block back in his slim case. 'Thanks for listening, Al.' He stood.

'No problem. I'll just have a word with Silvano, here, then the pair of you can get back into space.'

'Sure, Al.'

'So?' Al asked when Leroy had left.

'It ain't my concern, Al,' Silvano said. 'If that's the way you wanna do it, then fine by me. I admit, we gotta have some kinda dough around here, else things are gonna start falling apart pretty damn fast. We can only keep people in line with the SD platforms for so long.'

'Yeah, yeah.' Al waved a discontented hand. Money for magic, Jee-zus, even the numbers racket was more honest than that. He stared at his lieutenant, if it hadn't been for the ability to sense emotions there would have been no way for him to work out what was going on behind that Latino poker-face. But Silvano was eager about something. 'So what do you want? And it better be good fucking news.'

'I think it may be. Somebody came back from beyond who had some interesting information for us. He's an African type, name of Ambar.' Silvano smiled at the memory. 'He wound up in a blond Ivy League body, man was he pissed about that; it's taking up a lot of effort to turn himself into a true brother again.'

'Now *there's* someone who could cash in a potload of Leroy's tokens,' Jezzibella said innocently. She popped another Turkish delight in her mouth, and winked at Al as Silvano scowled.

'Right,' Al chuckled. 'What did he want to trade?'

'He's only been dead thirty years,' Silvano said. 'Came from a planet called Garissa, said it got blown away, the whole damn world. Some kind of starship attack that used antimatter. Don't know whether to believe him or not.'

'You know anything about that?' Al asked Jezzibella.

'Sure, baby, I nearly did a concept album on the Garissa Genocide once. Too depressing, though. It happened, all right.'

'Sweet shit, a whole planet. And this Ambar guy was there?'

'So he says.'

'Antimatter can really do that? Waste out an entire planet?'

'Yeah. But the thing is, Al, he says the Garissan government was working on its own weapon when it got wasted, something to fire at Omuta. The biggest weapon ever built, he swears. And he oughta know, he was some hotshot rocket scientist for their navy.'

'Another weapon?'

'Yeah. They called it the Alchemist. Ambar said it got built, but never got used. Said the whole fucking Confederation would know if it had been, that mother's got some punch.'

'So it's still around,' Al said. 'Let me guess: he'll lead us right to it.'

'No. But he says he knows someone who can. His old college lecturer, a broad called Alkad Mzu.'

\*

*Lady Macbeth* was scheduled to depart in another eight hours, though no one would ever guess by looking at her. Twenty per cent of her hull was still open to space, exposing the hexagonal stress structure; engineers on waldo platforms had the gaps completely surrounded, working with methodical haste to integrate the new systems they had installed to replace battle-damaged units.

There was an equal amount of well-ordered effort going on inside the life-support capsules, as crews from five service and astroengineering companies laboured to bring the starship up to its full combat-capable status. A status whose performance figures would surprise a lot of conventional warship captains. A status she hadn't truly enjoyed for decades. Her standard internal fittings were being stripped out, replaced by their military-grade equivalents.

Joshua wanted the old girl readied at peak performance, and as Ione was paying ... The more he thought about what he'd agreed to do for her, the more he worried about it. Immersing himself in the details of the refit was an easy escape, almost as good as flying.

He had spent most of yesterday holding conferences with astroengineering company managers discussing how to compress a fortnight's work into forty-eight hours. Now he watched attentively as their technicians clustered round the consoles manipulating the cyberdrones and waldo arms enclosing *Lady Mac*.

A pair of legs slid through the control centre's hatch, wobbling about as though the owner wasn't quite accustomed to free fall manoeuvring. Joshua hurriedly grabbed at the offending trousers, pulling the man to one side before his shoes caught one of the console operators behind her ear.

'Thank you, Joshua,' a red-faced Horst Elwes said as Joshua guided him down onto a stikpad. He gave a watery blink, and peered out into the bay. 'I was told I would find you here. I heard that you had found yourself a charter flight.'

There was no detectable irony in the priest's tone, so Joshua said: 'Yes, the Lord of Ruin contracted me to pick up some essential specialist components to enhance Tranquillity's defences. The industrial stations outside don't manufacture every component which goes into the SD platforms.' Joshua didn't actually hear anyone snigger, but there were definitely some sly grins flashing round the consoles. Nobody knew for sure what the flight was for, but they all had a good idea what it didn't entail. As an excuse the components charter was pretty feeble. Ione had reported that every Intelligence agency in the habitat had taken a sudden interest in his impending departure.

'But they can manage to build combat wasps, apparently,' Horst said with gentle amusement. Brackets on the bay walls held sixty-five combat wasps ready for loading into *Lady Macbeth*'s launch-tubes.

'One of the reasons we won the contract, Father. *Lady Mac* can carry cargo and fight her way out of trouble.'

'If you say so, young Joshua. But please, don't try that one on St Peter if you ever make it to those big white gates.'

'I'll bear it in mind. Was there something you wanted?'

'Nothing important. I was gladdened to hear your starship was being repaired for you. *Lady Macbeth* sustained a lot of damage rescuing us. I understand how expensive such machinery is. I wouldn't want you to suffer a financial penalty for such a selfless act.'

'Thank you, Father.'

'The children would like to see you before you leave.'

'Er . . . Why?'

'I believe they want to say thank you.'

'Oh, yes.' He glanced at Melvyn who appeared equally discomfited. 'I'll try, Father.'

'I thought you could combine it with the memorial service. They will all be there for that.'

'What memorial service?'

'Oh dear, didn't Sarha tell you? The Bishop has agreed that I can hold a service of commemoration to those who sacrificed themselves for the children. I think Mr Malin's team and Warlow deserve our prayers. It starts in three hours' time.'

Joshua's good humour drained away. I do not want to think about death and after, not right now.

Horst studied the young man's face, seeing both anxiety and guilt expressed in the carefully composed features. 'Joshua,' he said quietly. 'There is more to death than the beyond. Believe me, I have seen how much more with my own two eyes. The recordings your friend Kelly made, while truthful, do not contain anything like the whole story. Do you think I could retain my faith in Our Lord if Shaun Wallace had been right?'

'What did you see?'

'The one thing which could convince me. For you, I expect it would be different.'

'I see. We have to come to faith in our own way?'

'As always, yes.'

*

Tranquillity's cathedral was modelled on the old European archetype. One of the few buildings inside the habitat, it grew up out of the parkland several kilometres away from the circle of starscraper lobbies halfway along the cylinder. The polyp walls were lily-white, with an arching ceiling ribbed by smooth polygonal ridges to give the appearance of a long-abandoned hive nest. Tall gashes in the wall had been sealed by traditional stained glass, with a huge circular rosette at the end of the nave overlooking the stone altar. The Virgin Mary, baby Jesus in arm, gazed down on the slab of granite which Michael Saldana had brought from Earth.

Joshua had been given a place in the front pew, sitting next to Ione. He hadn't had time to change out of his ship-suit, while she was dressed in some exquisitely elegant black dress complete with elaborate hat. At least the rest of the *Lady Mac*'s crew shared his sartorial manner.

The service was short, perhaps because of the children who fidgeted and whispered. Joshua didn't mind. He sang the hymns and listened to Horst's sermon, and joined in with the prayers of thanks.

It wasn't quite as cathartic as he wanted it to be, but there was some sense of relief. People congregating together to tell the dead of their gratitude. And just how did that ritual start, he wondered, have we always known they'd be watching?

Ione propelled him over to the knot of children after it was over. Father Horst and several paediatric nurses were trying to keep them in order. They looked different, Joshua decided. The gaggle which closed round him could have been any junior day club on an outing. Certainly none of them resembled that subdued, frightened group who had flooded on board *Lady Mac* barely a week ago.

As they giggled and recited their rehearsed thank-yous he realized he was grinning back. Some good came out of the mission after all. In the background Father Horst was nodding approvingly. Wily old sod, Joshua thought, he set me up for this.

There were others filing out of the cathedral, the usual clutter of rover reporters, (surprisingly) the Edenists from Aethra, a large number of the clientele from Harkey's Bar and other space industry haunts, a few combat boosted, Kelly Tirrel. Joshua excused himself from the children and caught up with her in the narthex.

'*Lady Mac* is departing this evening,' he said lamely.

'I know.'

'I caught some of the Collins news shows; you've done all right for yourself.'

'Yes. Finally, I'm officially more popular than Matthias Rems.' There was humour in her voice, but not her expression.

'There's a berth if you want it.'

'No thanks, Joshua.' She glanced over at Ione, who was chatting to Horst Elwes. 'I don't know what she's conned you into doing for her, but I don't want any part of it.'

'It's only a charter to pick up components which—'

'Fuck off, Joshua. If that's all there is to it, why offer me a place? And why load *Lady Mac* full of top-grade combat wasps? You're heading straight back into trouble, aren't you?'

'I sincerely hope not.'

'I don't need it, Joshua. I don't need the fame, I don't need the risk. For fuck's sake, do you know what's going to happen to you if you die? Didn't you access any of my recordings?' She almost seemed to be pleading with him.

'Yes, Kelly, I accessed some of them. I know what happens when you die. But you can't give up hope for something better. You can't stop living just because you're frightened. You kept going on Lalonde, despite everything the dead threw at you. And you triumphed.'

'Ha!' she let out a bitter, agonized laugh. 'I wouldn't call that triumph if I were you: thirty kids saved. That's the most pathetic defeat in history. Even Custer did better than that.'

Joshua gazed at her, trying to understand where his Kelly had vanished. 'I'm sorry you feel that way, really I am. I think we did OK at Lalonde, and a lot of other people share that opinion.'

'Then they're stupid, and they'll grow out of it. Because everything now is temporary. Everything. When you're damned to exist for eternity, nothing you experience lasts for long.'

'Quite. That's what makes living worthwhile.'

'No.' She gave him a fragile smile. 'Know what I'm going to do now?'

'What?'

'Join Ashly, he's got the right idea about how to spend his time. I'm going to take million-year sojourns in zero-tau. I'm going to sleep away the rest of the universe's existence, Joshua.'

'Jesus, that's dumb. What's the point?'

'The point is, you don't suffer the beyond.'

Joshua grinned the infamous Calvert grin, then ducked forward to give her a quick kiss. 'Thanks, Kelly.'

'What the hell for, bollock-brain?'

'It's a faith thing. You have to come to it by yourself ... apparently.'

'If you go on like this, Joshua, you're going to die young.'

'And leave a beautiful corpse. Yeah, I know. But I'm still flying Ione's charter.'

Her mournful eyes regarded him with hurt and the old pain of longing. But she knew the gulf was too wide now. They both did.

'I never doubted it.' She kissed him back, so platonic it was almost formal. 'Take care.'

'It was fun while it lasted, though, wasn't it?' he enquired to her retreating back.

Her hand fluttered casually, a dismissive backward wave.

'Sod it,' he grunted.

'Ah, Joshua, good, I wanted to catch you.'

He turned to face Horst. 'Nice service, Father.'

'Why, thank you. I got rather out of practice on Lalonde, nice to see the old art hasn't deserted me entirely.'

'The children look well.'

'I should hope so, the attention they're getting. Tranquillity is an extraordinary place for an old arcology dweller like me. You know, the Church really did get it wrong about bitek. It's a wonderful technology.'

'Another cause, Father?'

Horst chuckled. 'I have my hands full, thank you. Speaking of which—' He pulled a small wooden crucifix from his cassock pocket. 'I'd like you to take this with you on your voyage. I had it with me the whole time on Lalonde. I'm not sure if it'll bring you good luck, but I suspect your need is greater than mine.'

Joshua accepted the gift awkwardly, not quite sure whether to put it round his neck or stuff it in a pocket. 'Thank you, Father. It'll come with me.'

'Bon voyage, Joshua. May the Lord look after you. And do try and be good this time.'

Joshua grinned. 'Do my best.'

Horst hurried back to the children.

'Captain Calvert?'

Joshua sucked in a breath. Now what? 'You got me.' He was telling it to a gleaming brass breastplate, one with distinctly feminine contours. It belonged to a cosmonik that resembled some steam-age concept of a robot; solid metal bodywork and rubbery flexible joints. Definitely a cosmonik, Joshua determined after a quick survey, not a combat boosted, there was too much finesse in the ancillary systems braceleting each of the forearms. This was a worker not a warrior.

'My name is Beaulieu,' she said. 'I was a friend of Warlow's. If you are looking for a replacement for his post, I would like to be considered.'

'Jesus, you're as blunt as he was, I'll give you that. But I don't think he ever mentioned you.'

'How much of his past did he mention?'

'Yeah, not much.'

'So?'

'I'm sorry?'

'So, do I have the post?' She datavised over her CV file.

The information matrix rotated slowly inside the confines of Joshua's skull. It competed for space with a sense of indignation that she should do this at Warlow's own memorial, coupled with a grudging acknowledgement that anyone this forthright probably had what it took, she wouldn't last long with an attitude that wasn't solidly backed up with competence.

Running a quick overview check on the file he saw she was seventy-seven years old. 'You served with the Confederation Navy?'

'Yes, Captain. Thirty-two years ago; it qualifies me to maintain combat wasps.'

'So I see. The navy issued an arrest warrant for me and *Lady Mac* at Lalonde.'

'I'm sure they had their reasons. I only serve one captain at a time.'

'Er, right. That's good.' Joshua could see another three cosmoniks standing in the last pew, waiting to see what the outcome would be. He datavised the cathedral's net processor block. 'Tranquillity?'

'Yes, Joshua.'

'I've got three hours before we leave, and I don't have time for games. Is this Beaulieu on the level?'

'As far as I can ascertain, yes. She has been working in my spaceport for fifteen months, and has had no contact with any foreign agency operatives. Nor does she fraternize with the combat boosted or the less savoury traders. She stays with her own kind; cosmoniks do tend to stick together. Warlow's outgoing nature was an exception rather than the rule.'

'Outgoing?' Joshua's eyebrows shot up.

'Yes. Did you not find him so?'

'Thank you, Tranquillity.'

'My pleasure to assist.'

Joshua cancelled the datavise. 'We're having to fly with one patterning node out until I can find a replacement, and there may be some trouble later on in the charter,' he told Beaulieu. 'I can't give you specifics.'

'That does not concern me. I believe your ability will minimize any threat, "Lagrange" Calvert.'

'Oh, Jesus. OK, welcome aboard. You've got two hours to collect your gear and get it stowed.'

\*

The docking cradle gently elevated *Lady Macbeth* upwards out of bay CA 5–099. Several hundred people had accessed the spaceport's sensors to watch her departure; Intelligence agency operatives, curious rumour-gorged space industry crews, news offices recording files for their library in case anything eventful did happen.

Ione saw the *Lady Macbeth*'s thermo-dump panels slide out of their recesses, a parody of a bird's wings extending ready for flight. Tiny chemical verniers ignited round the starship's equator, lifting her smoothly from the cradle.

She used her affinity to receive a montage summary of the tired company engineering teams congratulating each other, traffic control officers coordinating the starship's vector, Kelly Tirrel alone in her room accessing the spaceport sensor image.

**It is fortunate that Kelly Tirrel did not wish to go with him,** Tranquillity said. **You would have had to stop her, which would have raised the flight's profile.**

**Sure.**

**He will remain safe, Ione. We are there with him to provide assistance, and even in part to die to protect him.**

**Right.**

The *Lady Macbeth*'s bright blue ion thrusters fired, washing out the bay's floodlights. Ione used the strategic-defence platforms to track the starship as it flew in towards Mirchusko. Joshua piloted her into a perfectly circular one hundred and eighty-five thousand kilometre orbit, cutting off the triple fusion drives at the precise moment of injection. The ion thrusters only fired twice more to fine-tune the trajectory before the thermo-dump panels started to fold up.

Tranquillity sensed the gravitonic pulse as the starship's patterning nodes discharged. Then the tiny mote of mass was gone.

Ione turned back to her other problems.

\*

Demaris Coligan thought he'd done OK with his suit, dreaming up a fawn-brown fabric with silvery pinstripes, and a neat cut that wasn't half as garish as some of the Organization lieutenants wore.

At the last minute he added a small scarlet rose to his buttonhole, then nodded to the oily Bernhard Allsop who led him into the Nixon suite.

Al Capone was waiting for him in the vast lounge; his suit wasn't that different to Demaris's, it was just that Al wore it with such verve. Not even the equally snappy senior lieutenants flanking him could produce the same style.

The sight of so many heavyweights didn't do much to increase Demaris's level of confidence. But there was nothing he'd done wrong, he was sure of that.

Al gave him a broad welcoming smile, and clasped his hand in a warm grip. 'Good to see you, Demaris. The boys here tell me you been doing some good work for me.'

'Do whatever I can, Al. And that's a fact. You and the Organization's been good to me.'

'Mighty glad to hear that, Demaris. Come over here, got something to show you.' Al draped his arm around Demaris's shoulder in a companionable fashion, guiding him over to the transparent wall. 'Now ain't that a sight?'

Demaris looked out. New California itself was hidden behind the bulk of the asteroid, so he looked up. Crinkled sepia-coloured rock curved away to a blunt conical peak. Three kilometres away, hundreds of thermo-dump panels the size of football fields hung down from the rock, forming a ruff collar right round the asteroid's neck. Beyond that was the non-rotating spaceport disc, which, like the stars, seemed to be revolving. An unnervingly large constellation of Adamist star-ships floated in a rigorously maintained lattice formation just past the edge of the disc. Demaris had spent the entire previous week helping to prep them for flight; and the constellation only represented thirty per cent of the Organization's total warship fleet.

'It's, er . . . pretty fine, Al,' Demaris said. He couldn't make out Al's thoughts too clearly, so he didn't know whether he was in the shit or not. But the boss seemed pleased enough.

'Pretty fine!' Al appeared to find this hilarious, roaring with laughter. He slapped Demaris's back enthusiastically. The other lieutenants smiled politely.

'It's a fucking great ritzy miracle, Demaris. One hundred per cent proof. You know just one of those ships is packing enough firepower to blow the entire old US Navy out of the water? Now that's the kinda thought makes you shit bricks, huh?'

'Right, Al.'

'What you're seeing out there is something no one else has ever tried before. It's a fucking crusade, Demaris. We're gonna save the universe for people like us, put it to rights again. And you helped make it happen. I'm mighty grateful to you for that. Yes, sir. Mighty grateful.'

'Did what I could, Al. We all do.'

'Yeah, but you helped with getting those star-rockets ready. That takes talent.'

Demaris tapped the side of his head. 'I possessed someone who knows; he don't hold nothing back.' With great daring he gave a gentle punch to Al's upper arm. 'Least, not if he knows what's good for him.'

A split-second pause, then Al was laughing again. 'Goddam right. Gotta let 'em know who's calling the shots.' A finger was raised in caution. 'But, I gotta admit; I got one hell of a problem brewing here, Demaris.'

'Well, Christ, Al, anything I can do to help, you know that.'

'Sure, Demaris, I know that. The thing is, once we start the crusade they're gonna fight back, the Confederation guys. And they're bigger than we are.'

Demaris dropped his voice an octave, glancing from side to side. 'Well, sure they are, Al; but we got the antimatter now.'

'Yeah, that's right, we got that. But that don't make them any smaller, not numbers wise.'

Demaris's smile was a little harder to maintain. 'I don't see ... What is it you want, Al?'

'This guy you're possessing – what's his name?'

'The goof calls himself Kingsley Pryor, he was a real hotshot engineer for the Confederation Navy, a lieutenant-commander.'

'That's right, Kingsley Pryor.' Al pointed a finger at Leroy Octavius.

'Lieutenant-Commander Kingsley Pryor,' Leroy recited, glancing at the screen on his processor block. 'Attended University of Columbus, and graduated 2590 with a degree in magnetic confinement physics. Joined the Confederation Navy the same year, graduated from Trafalgar's officer cadet campus with a first. Took a doctorate in fusion engineering at Montgomery Tech in 2598. Assigned to 2nd Fleet headquarters engineering division. Rapid promotion. Currently working on the navy's project to reduce fusion rocket size. Married, with one son.'

'Yeah,' Demaris said cagily. 'That's him. So?'

'So I got a job for him, Demaris,' Al said. 'A special job, see? I'm real sorry about that, but I can't see no way out of it.'

'No need to be sorry, Al. Like I said, anything I can do.'

Al scratched the side of his cheek, just above three thin white scars. 'No, Demaris, you ain't listening. I fucking hate it when people do that. I got a job for him to do. Not you.'

'Him? You mean Pryor?'

Al gave the ever-impassive Mickey a helpless grimace. 'Jee-zus, I'm dealing with fucking Einstein here. YES, shit-for-brains. Kingsley Pryor, I want him back. Now.'

'But, but, Al, I can't give you him. I am him.' Demaris thumped his chest frantically with both hands. 'I ain't got anybody else to ride around in. You can't ask me to do that.'

Al frowned. 'Are you loyal to me, Demaris, are you loyal to the Organization?'

'What kind of a fucking question is that? Course I'm fucking loyal, Al. But it still don't mean you can't ask that. You can't!' He whirled round as he heard the smooth *snick* of a Thompson being cocked. Luigi Balsmao was cradling one of the sub-machine-guns lightly, an affable smile on his thickset face.

'I am asking you, as a loyal member of my Organization, to give me back Kingsley Pryor. I'm asking you *nicely*.'

'No. No fucking way, man!'

The scars on Al's reddening face were frost white. 'Because

you acted loyal to me I give you the choice. Because we're gonna liberate every one of those ass-backwards planets out there, you're gonna have a zillion decent bodies to choose from. Because of this, I give you the opportunity to avoid zero-tau and prove your honour like a man. Now for the last goddam time, read my lips: I want Pryor.'

*

Kingsley Pryor didn't even know why he was crying like a baby. Because he was free? Because he'd been possessed? Because death wasn't final?

Whatever the reason, the emotional fallout was running through him like an electrical discharge. Control was impossible. However, he was fairly sure he was crying. Lying on cool silk sheets, a billowingly soft mattress below his spine. Knees hooked up under his chin with arms wrapped round his shins. And in darkness. Not the sensory depravation of the mental imprisonment, but a wonderful genuine dusk, where a mosaic of grey on grey shadows delineated shapes. It was enough for a start. Had he been plunged directly into countryside on a sunny day he would probably have fried from sensory overload.

A swishing sound made him tighten his grip on himself. Currents of air stirred across his face as someone sat on the bed beside him.

'It's all right,' a girl's melodic voice whispered. 'The worst part's over now.'

Fingers stroked the nape of his neck. 'You're back. You're alive again.'

'Did . . . Did we win?' he croaked.

'No. I'm afraid not, Kingsley. In fact the real battle hasn't even begun yet.'

He shivered uncontrollably. Too much. Everything was too much for him right now. He wanted, not to die (Gods no!) but just to be away. Alone.

'That's why Al let you out again. You have a part to play in the battle, you see. A very important part.'

How could a voice so mellifluous carry such an intimation of catastrophe? He used his neural nanonics to retrieve a strong tranquillizer program and shunt it into primary mode. Sensations and palpitating emotions damped down. Something was not quite right about the neural nanonics function, but he couldn't be bothered to run a diagnostic.

'Who are you?' he asked.

A head was laid down on his shoulder, arms embracing him. For a moment he was reminded of Clarissa, the softness, the warmth, the female scent.

'A friend. I didn't want you to wake up with them taunting you. That would have been too horrible. You need my touch, my sympathy. I understand people like no other. I can prepare you for what is to come: the offer you can't refuse.'

He slowly straightened himself, and turned to look at her. The sweetest girl he'd ever seen, her age lost between fifteen and twenty-five, fair hair curling buoyantly round her face as she looked down at him in concern.

'You're beautiful,' he told her.

'They've captured Clarissa,' she said. 'And dear little Webster, too. I'm sorry. We know how much you love them. Demaris Coligan told us.'

'Captured?'

'But safe. Secure. Non-possessed. A child and a woman, they could not be hurt, not here. Al welcomes the non-possessed to his Organization. They'll have an honoured place, Kingsley. You can earn that for them.'

He struggled to resolve the image which the name Al stirred in his mind. The fleshy-faced young man in a strange grey hat. 'Earn it?'

'Yes. They can be safe for ever, they need never die, never age, never endure pain. You can bring them that gift.'

'I want to see them.'

'You could.' She kissed his brow, a tiny dry lick with her lips. 'One day. If you do what we ask, you will be able to return to them. I promise that. Not as your friend. Not as your enemy. Just one human to another.'

'When? When can I see them?'

'Hush, Kingsley. You're too tired now. Sleep. Sleep away all your anguish. And when you wake, you will learn of the fabulous destiny which is yours to fulfil.'

*

Moyo watched Ralph Hiltch walk down the road out of Exnall, the girl lying in his arms. Together they made a classic image, the hero rescuing his damsel.

The other armour-suited troops closed around their leader, as one they slipped off the road, back into the cover of the trees. Not that the snarled-up trunks of the old forest could hide them, Ralph's fury acted like a magnesium flare to the strange senses which Moyo was only just accustoming himself to.

The ESA agent's anger was of a genus which perturbed Moyo deeply. The resolution behind it was awesome. After two centuries incarcerated in the beyond, Moyo had assumed he would be immune to any kind of threat ever again. That was why he had cooperated with Annette Ekelund's scheme, no matter how callous it was by the standards of the living. Possession, a return to the universe he had thought himself banished from, brought a different, darker slant on those things he had cherished and respected before – morality, honour, integrity. With such an outlook contaminating his thinking, he had considered himself invulnerable to fear, even aloof from it. Hiltch made him doubt the arrogance of his new-found convictions. He might have been granted an escape from the beyond, but remaining free was by no means guaranteed.

The boy whom Moyo held in front of him began to squirm

again, crying out in anguish as Ralph Hiltch vanished from sight. His last hope dashed. He was about ten or eleven. The misery and terror whirling inside his head was so strong it was almost contagious.

His resolution fractured by Hiltch, Moyo began to feel shame at what he was doing. The craving which the lost souls in the beyond set up at the back of his mind was worse than any cold turkey, and it was relentless. They wanted what he had, the light and sound and sensation which dwelt so richly in the universe. They promised him fealty for ever if he granted it to them. They cajoled. Then insisted. They threatened. It would never end. A hundred billion imps of obligation and conscience whispering together were a voice more powerful than he.

He had no choice. While the living remained unpossessed, they would fight to fling him back into the beyond. While souls dwelt in the beyond they would plague him to be given bodies. The equation was so horrifically simple, the two forces cancelling each other out. Providing he obeyed.

His rebirth was only a few hours old, and already independent destiny was denied him.

'Do you see what we can do?' Annette Ekelund shouted at the ranks of her followers. 'The Saldanas reduced to bargaining with us, accepting our terms. That's the power we have now. And the first thing we must do is consolidate it. Everyone who was assigned to a vehicle, I want you ready to leave as soon as the marines withdraw; that should be in quarter of an hour at the most, so be ready. If we even appear to lack the courage to go through with this, they'll unleash the SD platforms on us. You felt Hiltch's thoughts, you know it's true. Those of you holding a hostage, get them possessed right now. We need all the numbers we can muster. This isn't going to be easy, but we can capture this whole peninsula within a couple of days. After that we'll have the power to close the sky for good.'

Moyo couldn't help but glance up. Dawn was strengthening above the barbed tree line, thankfully eradicating the stars and their hideous reminder of infinity. But even with daylight colours fermenting across the blackness the vista remained so empty, a void every bit as barren as the beyond. Moyo wanted nothing more than to seal it shut, to prevent the emptiness from draining his spirit once again.

Every mind around him had the same yearning.

Moans and shouting broke his introspection. The hostages were being dragged back inside the buildings. Nothing had been said about that, there was no prior arrangement. It was as though the possessed shared a communal unease at inflicting the necessary suffering in full view of each other and the low-orbit sensor satellites. Breaking a person's spirit was as private as sex.

'Come on,' Moyo said. He picked the boy up effortlessly, and went back into the wooden frame bungalow.

'Mummy!' the boy yelled. 'Mummy, help!' He started weeping.

'Hey now, don't panic,' Moyo said. 'I'm not going to hurt you.' It didn't make any difference. Moyo went straight through into the lounge, and opened the big patio doors. There was a lawn at the rear, extending back almost to the harandrid trees which encircled the town. Two horticultural mechanoids roamed anarchically over the trim grass, their mowing blades digging into the loamy soil as if they'd been programmed to plough deep furrows.

Moyo let go of the boy. 'Go on,' he said. 'Run. Scoot.'

Limpid eyes stared up at him, not understanding at all. 'But my mummy . . .'

'She's not here any more. She's not even her any more. Now go on. The Royal Marines are out there in the forest. If you're quick, you'll find them before they leave. They'll look after you. Now run.' He made it fiercer than he had to. The boy snatched a quick glance into the lounge, then turned and shot off over the lawn.

Moyo waited to make sure he got through the hedge without

any trouble, then went back inside. If it had been an adult he held hostage, there would have been no compunction, but a child . . . He hadn't abandoned all of his humanity.

Through the lounge window he could see vehicles rumbling down the road. It was a strange convoy which Annette Ekelund had mustered; there were modern cars, old models ranging across planets and centuries, mobile museums of military vehicles, someone had even dreamed up a steam-powered traction engine which slowly clanked and snorted its way along, dripping water from leaky couplings. If he focused his thoughts he could make out the profile of the actual cars and farm vehicles underneath the fanciful solid mirages.

There had been a coupé Moyo had always wanted back on Kochi, a combat wasp on wheels, its top speed three times the legal limit; but he never could quite manage to save enough for a deposit. Now, though, it could be his for the price of a single thought. The concept depressed him, half of the coupé's attraction had been rooted in how unobtainable it was.

He spent a long time behind the window, wishing the procession of would-be conquerors well. He'd promised Annette Ekelund he would help, indeed he'd opened five of Exnall's residents for possession during the night. But now, contemplating the days which lay ahead, repeating that barbarity ten times an hour, he knew he wouldn't be able to do it. The boy had proved that to him. He would be a liability to Ekelund and her blitzkrieg. Best to stay here and keep the home fires burning. After the campaign, they would need a place to rest.

Breakfast was . . . interesting. The thermal-induction panel in the kitchen went crazy as soon as he switched it on. So he stared at it, remembering the old range cooker his grandmother had in her house, all brushed black steel and glowing burner grille. When he was young she had produced the most magnificent meals on it, food with a tang and texture he'd never tasted since. The induction panel darkened, its outline expanding; the yellow composite cupboard unit it sat on merged into it – and the stove was there, radiant heat shining out of its grille as the charcoal blocks hissed unobtrusively. Moyo grinned at his achievement, and put the copper kettle on the hotplate. While it started to boil he searched round the remaining cupboards for some food. There were dozens of sachets, modern chemically nutritious food without any hint of originality. He tossed a couple into the iron frying pan, compelling the foil to dissolve, revealing raw eggs and several slices of streaky bacon (with the rind left on as he preferred). It began to sizzle beautifully just as the kettle started to whistle.

Chilled orange juice, light muesli flakes, bacon, eggs, sausages, kidneys, buttered wholemeal toast with thickly cut marmalade, washed down with cups of English tea – it was almost worth waiting two centuries for.

After he was finished eating, he tailored Eben Pavitt's sad casual clothes into the kind of expensive bright blue suit which the richer final year students had worn when he was a university fresher. Satisfied, he opened the bungalow's front door, and stepped out into the street.

There had never been a town like Exnall on Kochi. Moyo found it pleasantly surprising. From the media company shows he had always imagined the Kulu Kingdom planets to have a society even more formal than his own Japanese-ethnic culture. Yet Exnall lacked any sort of disciplined layout. He wandered along its broad streets, sheltered by the lofty harandrids, enjoying what he found, the small shops, gleaming clean cafés, patisseries, and bars, the little parks, attractive houses, the snow-white wooden church with its bright scarlet tile roof.

Moyo wasn't alone exploring his new environment. Several hundred people had stayed behind after Annette Ekelund had left. Most of them, like himself, were ambling round, not quite meeting the eyes of their fellow citizens. Everyone was party to the same guilty secret: what we did, what was done for us to return our souls into these bodies. The atmosphere was almost one of mourning.

The strollers were dressed in the clothes of their era and culture, solid citizens all. Those who favoured grotesquerie and mytho-beast appearances had departed with Ekelund.

He was delighted that several of the cafés were actually open; taken over by possessed proprietors who were industriously imagineering away the modern interiors, replacing them with older, more traditional decors (or in two cases retro-futuristic). Espresso machines gurgled and slurped enthusiastically, the smell of freshly baked bread wafted about. And then there was the doughnut machine. Set up in the window of one café, it was a beautiful antique contraption of dull polished metal with an enamel manufacturer's badge on the front. It was a couple of metres long, with a huge funnel at one end, filled with white dough. Raw doughnuts dropped out of a nozzle onto a metal grid conveyor belt which dunked them into a long vat of hot cooking oil where they fizzled away, effervescing golden bubbles until they rose out of the other side a rich brown in colour. After that they dropped off the end onto a tray of sugar. The smell they released into the crisp morning air was delectable. Moyo stood with his nose to the glass for a full minute, entranced by the parade of doughnuts trundling past while electric motors hummed and clicked, and the turquoise gas flames played underneath the oil. He had never guessed that anything so wondrously archaic could be found within the Confederation, so simple and so elaborate. He pushed the door open and went in.

The (new) proprietor was behind the counter, a balding man with a handkerchief knotted round his neck, and wearing a blue and white striped apron. He was wiping the counter's shiny wooden top with a dishcloth. 'Good morning, sir,' he said. 'And what can I get you?'

This is ridiculous, Moyo thought, we're both dead, we've

**485**

been rescued by some weird miracle, and all he's interested in is what I want to eat. We should be getting to know each other, trying to understand what's happened, what this means to the universe. Then he sensed the alarm burbling up in the proprietor's thoughts, the man's terribly brittle nature.

'I'll have one of the doughnuts, of course, they look delicious. And have you got any hot chocolate?'

The proprietor gave a big smile of relief, sweat was prickling his forehead. 'Yes, sir.' He busied himself with the jugs and cups behind the counter.

'Do you think Ekelund will succeed?'

'I expect so, sir. She seems to know what she's doing. I did hear she came from another star. That's one resourceful lady.'

'Yes. Where do you come from?'

'Brugge, sir. Back in the twenty-first century. A fine city it was in those days.'

'I'm sure.'

The proprietor put a mug of steaming hot chocolate on the counter along with a doughnut. Now what? Moyo wondered. I haven't got a clue what kind of coin to conjure up.

The whole situation was becoming more surreal by the second.

'I'll put it on your bill, sir,' the proprietor said.

'Thank you.' He picked up the mug and plate, glancing round. There were only three other people in the café. Two of them a young couple, oblivious to anything but each other. 'Mind if I sit here?' he asked the third, a woman in her late twenties, and making no attempt to cloak herself in any kind of image. Her head came up to show tear trails smearing chubby pale cheeks.

'I was just going,' she muttered.

'Don't, please.' He sat opposite her. 'We ought to talk. I haven't talked to anyone for centuries.'

Her eyes looked down at her coffee cup. 'I know.'

'My name's Moyo.'

'Stephanie Ash.'

'Pleased to meet you, Stephanie. I don't know what I should be saying, half of me is terrified by what's happened, the other half is elated.'

'I was murdered,' she whispered. 'He ... he— He laughed when he did it, every time I screamed it just made him laugh louder. He enjoyed it.' The tears were flowing openly again.

'I'm sorry.'

'My children. I had three children, they were only little, the eldest was six. What kind of life would they have knowing what happened to me? And Mark, my husband, I thought I saw him once, later, much later. He was all broken down and old.'

'Hey there, it's over now, finished,' he said softly. 'Me, I got hit by a bus. Which is a tricky thing to do in Kochi's capital city; there are barriers along the roads, and safety systems, all kinds of protective junk. But if you're real stupid, and loaded, and part of a group that's daring you to run the road, then you can jump in front of one before its brakes engage. Yeah, real tricky, but I managed it. So what use was my life? No girl, no kids; just mum and dad who would have been heartbroken. You had something, a family that loved you, kids you can be proud of. You were taken away from them, and that's a real evil, I'm not saying it isn't. But look at you now, you still love them after all this time. And I'll bet wherever they are, they love you. Compared to me, Stephanie, you're rich. You had it all, the whole life trip.'

'Not any more.'

'No. But then this is a fresh start for all of us, isn't it? You can't allow yourself to grieve over the past. There's too much of it now. If you do that, then you'll never do anything else.'

'I know. But it's going to take time, Moyo. Thank you, anyway. What were you, some kind of social worker?'

'No. I was at university studying law.'

'You were young, then?'

'Twenty-two.'

'I was thirty-two when it happened.'

Moyo bit into his doughnut, which tasted as good as it looked. He grinned and gave the proprietor an appreciative thumbs-up. 'I can see I'll be coming back here.'

'It seems silly to me,' she confided.

'Me too. But it's the way he's chosen to anchor himself.'

'Are you sure it was law, and not philosophy?'

He smiled round the doughnut. 'That's better. Don't go for the big issues right away, you'll only get depressed, start small and work along to quantum metaphysics.'

'You've lost me already, when I did work I was just a councillor at the local junior day club. I adored children.'

'I don't think you were just anything, Stephanie.'

She sat back in the chair, toying with the tiny coffee cup. 'So what do we do now?'

'Generally speaking?'

'We have only just met.'

'OK, generally speaking, try and live the life we always wanted to. From now on, every day is going to be a summer's day you've taken off work so that you can go out and do the one thing you've always wanted to.'

'Dance in the Rubix Hotel,' she said quickly. 'It had the most beautiful ballroom, the podium was big enough for a whole orchestra, and it looked out over the grounds to a lake. We never went to a function there; Mike always promised he'd take me. I wanted to wear a scarlet gown, with him in a dinner jacket.'

'Not bad. You're a romantic, Stephanie.'

She blushed. 'What about you?'

'Oh, no. Mine are all pretty basic male daydreams. Tropical beaches and girls with perfect figures; that kind of thing.'

'No, I don't believe that. There's more to you than simplistic clichés. And besides, I told you mine.'

'Well ... I suppose there is mountain gliding. It was a rich-kid sport on Kochi. The gliders were made out of linked molecule films, only weighed about five kilos, but they had a wingspan of about twenty-five metres. Then before you could even get in to one you had to have your retinas and cortical processor implants upgraded so that you could actually see air currents, determine their flow speed; the whole X-ray vision trip. That way you'd be able to pick out the wind stream which could carry you to the top.

'The clubs would set out courses over half a mountain range. I watched a race once. The pilots looked like they were lying in a torpedo-shaped bubble; the linked molecule film is so thin you can't even see it unless the sun catches it just right. They were skiing on air, Stephanie, and they made it seem like the easiest thing in the world.'

'I don't think either of us are going to be living our fantasies for a while.'

'No. But we will, eventually, when Ekelund takes over Mortonridge. Then we'll have the power to indulge ourselves.'

'That woman. God, she frightened me. I had to hold a man hostage while she spoke to the soldier. He was pleading and crying. I had to give him to someone else afterwards. I couldn't hurt him.'

'I let mine go altogether.'

'Really?'

'Yes. It was a boy. I think he got to the marines in time to be evacuated. Hope so, anyway.'

'That was good of you.'

'Yeah. I had the luxury this time. But if the Saldana Princess sends her troops in here to find us and claw us back, I'll fight. I'll do everything I can to stop them from evicting me from this body.'

'I hear mine,' Stephanie said. 'She's inside me, lonely and afraid. She cries a lot.'

'My host's called Eben Pavitt, he rages the whole time. But underneath he's scared.'

**489**

'They're as bad as the souls in the beyond. Everyone is making demands on us.'

'Ignore them. You can do it. Compared to the beyond, this is paradise.'

'Not really. But it's a good first step.'

He finished his chocolate, and smiled. 'Do you want to come for a walk, see what our new town is like?'

'Yes. Thank you, Moyo, I think I would.'

# 13

The Confederation Navy Intelligence Service had originally been formed with the intent of infiltrating the black syndicates that produced antimatter and hunting down their production stations. Since those early days its activities had expanded along with those of the Confederation Navy as a whole. By the time Admiral Lalwani assumed command one of its principal functions was to monitor, analyse, and assess the deplorable amount of new and ingenious weapon systems manufactured by governments and astroengineering companies across the Confederation, with emphasis on the more clandestine marques. To that end, the designers of the Service's secure Weapons Technology laboratory complex were given a brief to contain just about any conceivable emergency, from biohazards, to outbreaks of nanonic viruses, to small nuclear explosions.

There was only one entrance: a long corridor cut through the rock with two right-angle turns; it was wide and high enough to accommodate an outsize service truck or even a small flyer. Three separate doors were spaced along it, each built from a two-metre thickness of carbotanium composite strengthened by molecular-binding-force generators. The first two slabs could only be opened by the security staff outside, while the third was operated from inside the facility. Since the arrival of Jacqueline Couteur, Trafalgar's population had started calling it the demon trap – appropriate enough, Samual

Aleksandrovich conceded as the final door swung upwards amid a hiss of pressure and loud mechanical whinings. Dr Gilmore was waiting on the other side to greet him and his entourage.

'I'm delighted I can actually offer you some good news for a change,' Dr Gilmore said as he led the First Admiral up to the Biological Division's isolation facility. 'We've all heard about New California. Is it really Al Capone leading them?'

'We don't have any evidence to the contrary,' Lalwani said. 'The Edenists in the system are monitoring news broadcasts. Capone appears very fond of publicity, he's been touring cities like some kind of medieval monarch. Pressing the flesh, he calls it. A number of reporters were left unpossessed purely so they could record the event.'

'And this pre-starflight primitive had the ability to take over one of our most developed worlds?' Dr Gilmore enquired. 'I find that hard to credit.'

'Don't,' Lalwani said. 'We've been researching him. He's a genuine emperor genotype. People like him have an intuitive ability to format social structures which support their premiership, whatever their local environment, from street gangs to entire nations. Thankfully they don't occur very often, nor at such a high level; but when they do the rest of us need to watch out.'

'Even so—'

'Obviously, he's getting advice on modern life. There will be an inner cabinet to help him, but he won't share the ultimate power. We don't believe he's psychologically capable of it. That could be a significant weakness given the sheer quantity of problems he must be facing in enforcing his rule.'

'So far New California is the only planetary system we know of which has succumbed completely,' the First Admiral said. 'Seventeen more planets are suffering from large-scale incursions, and are doing their best to isolate the affected areas. Fortunately the legitimate authorities retained control of their

SD networks. The worst casualties have been among the asteroid settlements; our last estimation was that we'd lost over a hundred and twenty Confederationwide. If a possessed gets inside one, their success rate in taking it over is close to a hundred per cent. It's proving difficult to fight them in such closed environments. Other planets have had trouble, but on a much smaller scale. Our warning seems to have had the required effect. It could have been a lot worse.'

'Our main concern is that nobody attempts any foolhardy liberation missions,' Lalwani said. 'There would be few national navies capable of mounting a successful operation along those lines. At the moment any troops entering such an environment are liable to be possessed themselves.'

'There will be political pressure on the military to act, though,' the First Admiral said dourly. 'So far our only notable public success has been the destruction of the *Yaku* in the Khabrat system. Trivial. What we need above all is some kind of weapon which is able to incapacitate the possessed. That or an effective method of exorcism. Preferably both.' He gave Dr Gilmore a questing gaze.

'I believe we can now help you on the first count,' the implant specialist said confidently. They stopped before the biological isolation facility, and he datavised his code at the door.

Euru's researchers had acted swiftly as soon as they'd obtained permission to advance their studies. The First Admiral flinched at the sight which greeted him within the examination room. On his side, the monitoring consoles were fully staffed; remorselessly obsessive scientists and technicians absorbed in the displays projected by AV pillars. A scene of brisk competence and scientific endeavour, as always reinforcing the concept of impersonal efficiency.

Samual Aleksandrovich doubted there was any other way the team could cope with their objective; it must act as a psychological buffer between them and the subject. *Subject –*

he chided himself silently. Although he'd witnessed inhumanity on a far more brutal scale than this during his active service days.

With Captain Khanna at his side he walked hesitantly up to the transparent wall which cut the rock chamber in two, wondering if he should show signs of dismay or approval. In the end he settled for the same bleak acceptance which everyone else in the room had put on along with their baggy white lab overalls.

A naked and shaven Jacqueline Couteur had been immobilized on a surgical bed. Although wired into it would be a more honest evaluation, the First Admiral thought. Grey composite ribs formed a cage over the length of her body, supporting clamps which pressed pairs of large circular electrodes against her forearms, abdomen, and upper legs; clear gel was leaking out from beneath the silvery metal, ensuring better contact and conductivity. Two ceiling-mounted waldo arms had been equipped with sensor arrays, like bundles of fat white gun muzzles, which they were sweeping slowly and silently up and down the prone body. The thick circular brace which held her head fast looked as if it had melded with her skin. A plastic defecation tube had been inserted in her anus, while a free fall toilet suction catheter adhered to her vagina. He couldn't decide if that was a civilized courtesy or the final humiliation.

Not that Couteur would care, not in her present condition.

Her entire musculature twitched and rippled in random spasms. The flesh quivering on her face made it seem as though she was enduring a ten-gee acceleration.

'What the hell are you doing to her?' Maynard Khanna asked in a guttural whisper.

It was the first time the First Admiral could ever remember the staff captain speaking before his superiors.

'Neutralizing her offensive potential,' Dr Gilmore said with a tone of high satisfaction. 'The report we received from

Lalonde contained a reference from Darcy and Lori that electricity affects the possessed in an adverse fashion. We checked and discovered it's true. So we're running a current through her.'

'Dear God, that's...' His face crunched up in a disgusted grimace.

Dr Gilmore ignored him, addressing himself solely to the First Admiral. 'She is having to use her entire energistic ability to ward off the current. We experimented with the voltage level until we achieved this balance. Her physiological functions continue to operate normally, but she is completely incapable of manifesting any reality dysfunction effect. She can no longer distort matter, create illusions, or conjure up white fireballs. It means we are free to study her without any interference; even our electronic systems have recovered eighty-five per cent of their efficiency in her presence.'

'So what have you learned?' the First Admiral asked.

'Please bear in mind we are on the threshold of a completely new field here.'

'Doctor,' the First Admiral cautioned.

'Of course. Firstly, we have developed a screening method which can pick out any possessed. There is a tiny but constant discharge of static electricity right across their body. We think it must be a by-product of their beyond continuum spilling into ours. Such an influx surge would also account for the energy they constantly have at their disposal.'

'Static electricity?' a bemused Lalwani said.

'Yes, ma'am. It's beautiful, the sensors that will pick it up are cheap, easy to mass-produce, simple to use; and if they malfunction it's a certainty that a possessed is nearby anyway. Now we know what to look for they will find it impossible to hide in a crowd or infiltrate new areas.'

'Excellent,' the First Admiral said. 'We'll have to see that this information is distributed as fast as our original warning.'

He moved right up to the transparent wall, seeing his breath mist the surface, and activated the intercom. 'Do you remember me?' he asked.

Jacqueline Couteur took a long time to answer, her syllables maimed by the laboured gurgling of vocal cords not fully under control. 'We know you, Admiral.'

'Is she in communication with those in the beyond?' he asked Dr Gilmore quickly.

'I cannot give you an absolute, Admiral. However, I suspect not; at least nothing more than leaking a rudimentary form of contact back into her own continuum. Our Jacqueline is very fond of dominance games, and "we" tends to sound impressive.'

'If you are in pain,' the First Admiral told her, 'I apologize.'

'Not as sorry as that shit's going to be when I catch up with him.' Bloodshot eyes juddered round to focus on Dr Gilmore.

He responded with a thin superior smile.

'Exactly how much pain do you inflict on the mind of the body you have stolen?' Samual Aleksandrovich asked mildly.

'Touché.'

'As you see, we are learning from you as I said we would.' He gestured at the sensors which the waldo arms were sliding over her head and torso. 'We know what you are, we know something of the suffering which awaits you back in the beyond, we understand why you are driven to do what you do. I would ask you to work with me in helping to solve this problem. I do not wish there to be conflict between us. We are one people, after all, albeit at different stages of existence.'

'You will give us bodies? How generous.' Somehow she managed to grin, lips wriggling apart to dribble saliva down her cheeks.

'We could grow bitek neural networks which you could inhabit. You would be able to receive the full range of human senses. After that they could be placed in artificial bodies, rather like a cosmonik.'

'How very reasonable. But you forget that we are human,

496

too; we want to live full human lives. For ever. Possession is only the beginning of our return.'

'I am aware of your goals.'

'Do you wish to help us?'

'Yes.'

'Then terminate your life. Join us. Be on the winning side, Admiral.'

Samual Aleksandrovich gave the vibrating, abused body a final, almost disgusted glance, and turned his back to the transparent wall.

'She says the same thing to us,' Dr Gilmore said as if in apology. 'Repeatedly.'

'How much of what she says is the truth? For instance, do they really need human bodies? If not, we might just be able to force them into a compromise.'

'Verification may be difficult,' Euru said. 'The electricity has contained the worst excesses of Couteur's reality dysfunction, but a personality debrief in these circumstances may prove beyond us. If the nanonics were to malfunction during axon interface they could cause a lot of damage to her brain.'

'The possessed are certainly capable of operating within bitek neuron structures,' Lalwani said. 'Lewis Sinclair captured Pernik's neural strata; and we have confirmed that Valisk's blackhawks have also been captured.'

'Physically they're capable of it, yes,' Euru said. 'But the problem is more likely to be psychological. As ex-humans, they want human bodies, they want the familiar.'

'Acquire what information as you can without risking the actual body itself,' the First Admiral instructed. 'In the meantime, have you developed any method of subduing them?'

Dr Gilmore indicated the surgical table with a muddled gesture. 'Electricity, Admiral. Equip our marines with guns that fire a dart that contains a small electron-matrix cell, and simply push a current into them. Such weapons were in widespread use from the mid-twentieth century right up until the twenty-third. We've already produced a modern chemical-powered design with a range over five hundred metres.'

Samual Aleksandrovich didn't know whether to berate the implant specialist or commiserate with him. That was the trouble with laboratory types, all theory, no thought about how their gadgets would perform in the field. It was probably just the same in Couteur's time, he reflected. 'And how far can they project their white fire?'

'It varies depending on the individual.'

'And how will you determine what voltage to discharge from the electron-matrix cell? Some will be stronger than Couteur, while others will be weaker.'

Dr Gilmore glanced to Euru for support.

'Voltage regulation is a problem area,' the suave black-skinned Edenist said. 'We are considering if a static scanner can determine the level in advance. It may be that the quantity of static exuded might indicate the individual's energistic strength.'

'In here, possibly,' the First Admiral said. 'In combat conditions I very much doubt it. And even if it did work, what do you propose we should do with the captive?'

'Put them in zero-tau,' Dr Gilmore said. 'We know that method has enjoyed a hundred per cent success rate. They employed it on Ombey.'

'Yes,' the First Admiral acknowledged, recalling the file he'd accessed, the battle to capture the possessed inside the big department store. 'And at what cost? I don't intend to be cavilling about your endeavours, Doctor, but you really need to bring in some experienced combat personnel into your consultation process. Even conceding your stun gun could work, it would take two or three marines to subdue a possessed and place them in zero-tau. During which time those possessed remaining at liberty would have converted another five people. With that ratio we could never win. We must have a single weapon, a one-shot device which can rid a body of the possessing soul without harming it. Will electricity do that? Can you increase the voltage until the incursive soul is forced out?'

'No, Admiral,' Euru said. 'We have already tried with Couteur. The voltages necessary will kill the body. In fact we had to abandon the procedure for several hours to allow her to heal herself.'

'What about other methods?'

'There will be some we can try, Admiral,' Dr Gilmore insisted. 'But we'll need to research her further. We have so little data at the moment. The ultimate solution will of course be to seal the junction between this universe and the beyond continuum. Unfortunately we still cannot locate the interface point. Those scanners we are operating in there are some of the most sensitive gravitonic-distortion detectors ever built, yet there is no sign of any space-time density fluctuation in or around her. Which means the souls are not returning through a wormhole.'

'Not wormholes as we understand them, anyway,' Euru finished. 'But then, given Couteur's existence, our whole conception of quantum cosmology is obviously seriously incomplete. Having the ability to travel faster than light isn't nearly as smart as we once thought it was.'

*

It had taken Quinn some time to modify the *Tantu*'s bridge. It wasn't the look of the compartment which bothered him so much; the frigate was configured for high-gee acceleration, its fittings and structure were correspondingly functional. He liked that inherent strength, and emphasized it by sculpting the surfaces with an angular matt-black bas-relief of the kind he imagined would adorn the walls of the Light Brother's supreme temple. Lighting panels were dimmed to a carmine spark, flickering behind rusty iron grilles.

It was the information he was presented with, or rather the

lack of it, which displeased him, and consequently required the longest time to rectify. He had no neural nanonics, not that they would have worked even if he did have a set. Which meant he didn't know what was happening outside the ship. For all of *Tantu*'s fabulous high-resolution sensor array, he was blind, unable to react, to make decisions. To have the external universe visible was his first priority.

Possessing the frigate's nineteen-strong crew had taken barely twenty minutes after he and Lawrence had docked. Initiating the returned souls into the sect, having them accept his leadership, had required another hour. Three times he had to discipline the faithless. He regretted the waste.

Those remaining had worked hard to build the displays he wanted; fitting holoscreens to the consoles, adapting the flight computer programs to portray the external environment in the simplest possible terms. Only then, with his confidence restored, had he ordered their departure from Norfolk orbit.

Quinn settled back in his regal velvet-padded acceleration couch, and gave the order to jump away. Twenty seconds after they completed the operation, the holoscreens showed him the little purple pyramid which represented the squadron's lone pursuit ship lit up at the centre of the empty cube. According to the scale, it was three thousand kilometres away.

'How do we elude them?' he asked Bajan.

Bajan was possessing the body of the *Tantu*'s erstwhile captain. The third soul to do so since the hijacking began. Quinn had been dissatisfied with the first two, they had both lived in pre-industrial times. He needed someone with a technological background, someone who could interpret the wealth of data in the captain's captive mind. Bajan had only died two centuries ago; a civil fusion engineer, starflight was a concept he understood. He also had a sleazy, furtive mind which promised instant obedience to both Quinn and the sect's doctrines. But Quinn didn't mind that, such weaknesses simply made him easier to control.

Bajan's fists squeezed, mimicking the pressure he was placing on the mind held within. 'Sequential jumps. The ship can do it. That can throw off any pursuer.'

'Do it,' Quinn ordered simply.

Three jumps later, spanning seven light-years, and they were alone in interstellar space. Four days after that, they jumped into a designated emergence zone two hundred thousand kilometres above Earth.

'Home,' Quinn said, and smiled. The frigate's visible-spectrum sensors showed him the planet's nightside, a leaden blue-grey crescent which was widening slowly as the *Tantu's* orbit inched them towards the edge of the penumbra. First-magnitude stars blazed on the continents; the arcologies, silently boasting their vast energy consumption as the light from the streets, skyscrapers, stadiums, vehicles, parks, plazas, and industrial precincts merged into a monochrome blast of photons. Far above the equator, a sparkling haze band looped round the entire world, casting the gentlest reflection off the black-glitter oceans below.

'God's Brother, but it's magnificent,' Quinn said. They hadn't shown him this view when he'd been brought up the Brazilian orbital tower on his way to exile. There were no ports in his deck of the lift capsule, nor on the sections of the mammoth docking station through which the Ivets had passed. He'd lived on Earth all his life, and never seen it, not as it should be seen. Exquisite, and tragically fragile.

In his mind he could see the dazzling lights slowly, tortuously snuffed out as thick oily shadows slid across the land, a tide which brought with it despair and fear. Then reaching out into space, crushing the O'Neill Halo, its vitality and power. No light would be left, no hope. Only the screams, and the Night. And Him.

Tears of joy formed fat distorting lenses across Quinn's eyeballs. The image, the conviction, was so strong. Total blackness, with Earth at its centre; raped, dead, frozen, entombed.

'Is this my task, Lord? Is it?' The thought of such a privilege humbled him.

The flight computer let out an alarmed whistle.

Furious that his dreams should be interrupted, Quinn demanded: 'What is it?' He had to squint and blink to clear his vision. The holoscreens were filling with tumbling red spiders' webs, graphic symbols flashed for attention. Five orange vector lines were oozing inwards from the edge of the display to intersect at the *Tantu*'s location. 'What is happening?'

'It's some kind of interception manoeuvre!' Bajan shouted. 'Those are navy ships. And the Halo's SD platforms are locking on.'

'I thought we were in a legitimate emergence zone.'

'We are.'

'Then what—'

'Priority signal for the *Tantu*'s captain from Govcentral Strategic Defence Command,' the flight computer announced.

Quinn glowered at the AV projection pillar which had relayed the message. He snapped his fingers at Bajan.

'This is Captain Mauer, commander of the CN ship *Tantu*,' Bajan said. 'Can somebody tell me what the problem is?'

'This is SD Command, Captain. Datavise your ship's ASA code, please.'

'What code?' Bajan mouthed, completely flummoxed.

'Does anybody know what it is?' Quinn growled. *Tantu* had already datavised its identification code as soon as the jump was completed, as per standard procedure.

'The code, Captain,' SD Command asked again.

Quinn watched the fluorescent orange vectors of another two ships slide into the holoscreen display. Their weapons sensors focused on the *Tantu*'s hull.

'Computer, jump one light-year. Now,' he ordered.

'No, the sensors . . .' Bajan exclaimed frantically.

His objection didn't matter. The flight computer was programmed to respond to Quinn's voice commands alone.

The *Tantu* jumped, its event horizon slicing clean through the carbon-composite stalks which elevated the various sensor clusters out of their recesses. Ten of them had deployed as soon as the starship emerged above Earth: star trackers, mid-range optical sensors, radar, communications antennas.

All seven warships racing towards the *Tantu* saw it disappear behind ten dazzling white plasma spumes as its event horizon crushed the carbon molecules of the stalks to fusion density and beyond. Ruined sensor clusters spun out of the radioactive mist.

The SD Command Centre duty officer ordered two of the destroyers to follow the *Tantu*, cursing his luck that the interception squadron hadn't been assigned any voidhawks. It took the two starships eleven minutes to match trajectories with the *Tantu*'s jump coordinate. Everybody knew that was too long.

Soprano alarms shrilled at painful volume, drowning out all other sounds on the *Tantu*'s bridge. The holoscreens which had been carrying the sensor images turned black as soon as the patterning nodes discharged, then flicked to ship schematic diagrams. Disturbing quantities of red symbols flashed for attention.

'Kill that noise,' Quinn bellowed.

Bajan hurried to obey, typing rapidly on the keyboard rigged up next to his acceleration couch.

'We took four hull breaches,' Dwyer reported as soon as the alarm cut off. He was the most ardent of Quinn's new apostles, a former black-stimulant-program pusher who was murdered at the age of twenty-three by a faster, more ambitious rival. His anger and callousness made him ideal for the cause, he'd even heard of the sects, dealing with them on occasions. 'Six more areas have been weakened.'

'What the fuck was that? Did they shoot at us?' Quinn asked.

'No,' Bajan said. 'You can't jump with sensors extended, the distortion effect collapses any mass caught in the field.

Fortunately it's only a very narrow shell which covers the hull, just a few micrometres thick. But the atoms inside it get converted directly into energy. Most of it shoots outwards, but there's also some which is deflected right back against the hull. That's what hit us.'

'How much damage did we pick up?'

'Secondary systems only,' Dwyer said. 'And we're venting something, too; nitrogen I think.'

'Shit. What about the nodes? Can we jump again?'

'Two inoperative, another three damaged. But they're fail-soft. I think we can jump.'

'Good. Computer, jump three light-years.'

Bajan clamped down on his automatic protest. Nothing he could do about the spike of anger and exasperation in his mind though, Quinn could perceive that all right.

'Computer, jump half a light-year.'

This time the bridge lights sputtered almost to the point of extinction.

'All right,' Quinn said as the gloomy red illumination grew bold again. 'I want some fucking sensor visuals on these screens now. I want to know where we are, and if anyone followed us. Dwyer, start working round those damaged systems.'

'Are we going to be OK, Quinn?' Lawrence asked. His energistic ability couldn't hide the sweat pricking his sallow face.

'Sure. Now shut the fuck up, let me think.' He slowly unbuckled the straps holding him into his acceleration couch. Using the stikpads he shuffled on tiptoe over to Bajan's couch. His black robe swirled like bedevilled smoke around him, the hood deepening until his face was almost completely hidden. 'What,' he asked in a tight whisper, 'is an ASA code?'

'I dunno, Quinn, honest,' the agitated man protested.

'I know you don't know, dickhead. But the captain does. Find out!'

'Sure, Quinn, sure.' He closed his eyes, concentrating on the captain's mind, inflicting as much anguish as he could dream of to wrest free the information. 'It's an Armed Ship Authorization designation,' he grunted eventually.

'Go on,' Quinn's voice emerged from the shadows of his hood.

'Any military starship which jumps to Earth has to have one. There's so much industry in orbit, so many settled asteroids, they're terrified of the damage just one rogue ship could cause. So the captain of every Confederation Navy ship is given an ASA code to confirm they're legally entitled to be armed and that they're under official control. It acts as a failsafe against any hijacking.'

'It certainly does,' Quinn said. 'But it shouldn't have done. Not with us. You should have known.'

Nobody else on the bridge was looking anywhere near Bajan, all of them hugely absorbed with their own tasks of stabilizing the damage. And Quinn, looming over him like some giant carrion creature.

'This Mauer is a tough mother, Quinn. He tricked me, that's all. I'll make him suffer for it, I swear. The Light Bringer will be proud of the way I let my serpent beast loose on him.'

'There's no need,' Quinn said genially.

Bajan let out a faltering whimper of relief.

'I shall supervise his suffering myself.'

'But . . . how?'

In the absolute silence of the bridge, Lawrence Dillon sniggered.

'Leave us, Bajan, you little prick,' Quinn ordered. 'You have failed me.'

'Leave? Leave what?'

'The body I provided for you. You don't deserve it.'

'No!' Bajan howled.

'Go. Or I'll shove you into zero-tau.'

With a last sob, Bajan let himself fall back into the beyond, the glories of sensation ripping out of his mind. His soul wept its torment as the crowded emptiness closed round him once again.

Gurtan Mauer coughed weakly, his body trembling. He had lurched from one nightmare to another. The *Tantu*'s bridge had become an archaic crypt where technological artefacts protruded from whittled ebony, as if they were the foreign elements. A monk in midnight-black robes stood at the side of his couch, the hint of a face inside the voluminous hood indicated by the occasional carmine flicker striking alabaster skin. An inverted crucifix hung on a long silver chain round his neck; for some reason it wasn't drifting round as it ought in free fall.

'You didn't just defy me alone,' Quinn said. 'That I could almost accept. But when you held back that fucking ASA code you defied the will of God's Brother. Right now I should have been in the docking station, by morning I would have kissed the ground at the foot of the orbital tower. I was destined to carry the gospel of the Night to the whole motherfucking world! And you fucked with me, shithead. You!'

Mauer's ship-suit caught light. In free fall the flame was a bright indigo fluid, slithering smoothly across his torso and along his limbs. Scraps of charred fabric peeled off, exposing the charcoaled skin below. Fans whirred loudly behind the bridge's duct grilles as they attempted to suck the awful stench from the compartment's air.

Quinn ignored the agonized wailing muted by the captain's clamped mouth. He let his mind lovingly undress Lawrence.

The slight lad drifted idly in the centre of the bridge, smiling dreamily down at his naked body. He allowed Quinn to shape him, the young stable boy's skinny figure developing thick sinuous muscles, the width of his shoulders increasing. Clad only in a barbarian warrior garb of shiny leather strips, he began to resemble a dwarf addicted to body building.

The blue flame cloaking Mauer dribbled away as the last of the ship-suit was consumed. With a simple wave of his hand,

Quinn healed the captain's burns, restoring skin, nails, hair to their former state. Mauer became a picture of vitality.

'Your turn,' Quinn told Lawrence with a deviant laugh.

The pain-shocked, imprisoned captain could only stare upwards in terror as the freakishly hulking boy grinned broadly, and glided in towards him.

*

Alkad Mzu accessed the *Samaku*'s sensor suite via the flight computer, allowing the picture to share her mind with a sense of benevolent dismay. This is what we fought over? This was what a planet died for? This? Dear Mary!

Like all starships jumping insystem, the *Samaku* had emerged a safe half-million kilometres above the plane of the ecliptic. The star known as Tunja was an M4-type, a red dwarf. Bright enough from the starship's forty million kilometre distance, but hardly dazzling like a G-type, the primary of most terracompatible planets. From Alkad's excellent vantage point it hung at the centre of a vast disc of grizzled particles, extending over two hundred million kilometres in diameter.

The inner amulet, surrounding Tunja out to about three million kilometres, was a sparsely populated region where the constant gale of solar wind had stripped away the smaller particles, leaving only tide-locked boulders and asteroid fragments. With their surfaces smoothed to a crystalline gloss by the incessant red heat, they twinkled scarlet and crimson as if they were a swarm of embers flung off by the dwarf's arching typhonic prominences. Further out, the disc's opacity began to build, graduating into a sheet of what looked like dense grainy fog; bright carmine at the inner fringe, shading away to a deep cardinal red ninety million kilometres later. A trillion spiky shadows speckled the uniformity, cast by the larger chunks of rock and metal bobbing among the dust and slushy gravel.

No terracompatible planet was conceivable in such an environment. The star was barren except for a single gas giant,

Duida, orbiting a hundred and twenty-eight million kilometres out. A couple of young Edenist habitats circled above it, but the main focus of human life was scattered across the disc.

A disc of such density was usually the companion of a new-born star, but Tunja was estimated to be over three billion years old. Confederation planetologists suspected the red dwarf's disc had its genesis in a spectacularly violent collision between a planet and a very large interstellar meteor. It was a theory which could certainly explain the existence of the Dorados themselves: three hundred and eighty-seven large asteroids with a near-pure metal content. Two-thirds of them were roughly spherical, permitting the strong conclusion that they were molten core magma material when the hypothetical collision took place. Whatever their origin, such abundant ore was an immensely valuable economic resource for the controlling government. Valuable enough to go to war over.

'Ayacucho's civil traffic control are refusing us docking permission,' Captain Randol said. 'They say all the Dorados are closed to civil starflight and we have to return to our port of origin.'

Alkad exited the sensor visualization, and stared across the *Samaku*'s bridge. Randol was wearing a diplomatically apologetic expression.

'Has this ever happened before?' she asked.

'No. Not that we've been to the Dorados before, but I've never heard of anything like it.'

I have not waited this long, nor come so far, to be turned away by some bloody bureaucrat, Alkad thought. 'Let me talk to them,' she said.

Randol waved a hand, signalling permission. The *Samaku*'s flight computer opened a channel to Ayacucho asteroid's traffic control office.

'This is Immigration Service Officer Mabaki, how can I help you?'

'My name is Daphine Kigano,' Alkad datavised back – she

ignored the speculative gaze from Randol at the name on one of her passports. 'I'm a Dorado resident, and I wish to dock. I don't see why that should be a problem.'

'It isn't a problem, not under normal circumstances. I take it you haven't heard of the warning from the Confederation Assembly?'

'No.'

'I see. One moment, I'll datavise the file over.'

Alkad and the rest of the crew fell silent as they accessed the report. More than surprise, more than disbelief, she felt anger. Anger that this should happen now. Anger at the threat it posed to her mission, her life's duty. Mother Mary must have deserted the Garissan people long ago, leaving the universe to place so much heartbreak and malicious catastrophe in their path.

'I would still like to come home,' she datavised when it was over.

'Impossible,' Mabaki replied. 'I'm sorry.'

'I'm the only one who will enter the asteroid. Even if I were possessed I would present no threat. And I'm quite willing to be tested for possession, the Assembly warning says electronics malfunction in their presence. It should be simple enough.'

'I'm sorry, we simply can't take the risk.'

'How old are you, Officer Mabaki?'

'Excuse me?'

'Your age?'

'Is there some relevance to this?'

'Indeed there is.'

'I'm twenty-six.'

'Indeed? Well, Officer Mabaki, I am sixty-three.'

'Yes?'

Alkad sighed quietly. Exactly what was included in the Dorados' basic history didactic courses? Did today's youth know nothing of their tragic past? 'That means I was evacuated from Garissa. I survived the Genocide, Officer Mabaki. If our

**509**

Mother Mary had wanted me harmed, she would have done it then. Now, I am just an old woman who wishes to come home. Is that really so hard?'

'I'm sorry, really. But no civil starships can dock.'

Suppose I really can't get in? The Intelligence services will be waiting back at Narok, I can't return there. Maybe the Lord of Ruin would take me back. That would circumvent any personal disaster, not to mention personality debrief, but it would all be over then: the Alchemist, our justice.

She could see Peter's face that last time, still covered in a medical nanonic, but with his eyes full of trust. And that was the crux; too many people were relying on her; those treasured few who knew, and the blissfully ignorant masses who didn't.

'Officer Mabaki.'

'Yes?'

'When this crisis is over, I will return home, will I not?'

'I shall look forward to issuing your ship docking permission personally.'

'Good, because it will be the last docking authorization you ever do issue. The first thing I intend to do on my return will be to visit my close personal friend Ikela and tell him about this ordeal you have put me through.' She held her breath, seemingly immersed in zero-tau. It was one lone name from the past flung desperately into the unknown. Mother Mary, please let it strike its target.

Captain Randol gave a bass chuckle. 'I don't know what you did, Alkad,' he said loudly. 'But they just datavised our docking authority and an approach vector.'

\*

André Duchamp had long since come to the bitter realization that the lounge compartment would never be the same again. Between them, Erick and the possessed had wrought an appalling amount of damage, not just to the fittings, but the cabin systems as well.

The small utility deck beneath the lounge was in a similar deplorable state. And the spaceplane was damaged beyond repair. The loading clamps hadn't engaged, allowing it to twist about while the *Villeneuve's Revenge* was under acceleration. Structural spars had snapped and bent all along its sleek fuselage.

He couldn't afford to rectify half of the damage, let alone replace the spaceplane. Not unless he took on another mercenary contract. That prospect did not appeal, not after Lalonde. I am too old for such antics, he thought, by rights I should have made a fortune to retire on by now. If it wasn't for those bastard *anglo* shipping cartels I would have the money.

Anger gave him the strength to snap the last clip off the circulation fan unit he was working on; the little plastic star shattered from the pressure, chips spinning off in all directions. Bombarded by heat from a possessed's fireball, then subjected to hard vacuum for a week, the plastic had turned dismayingly brittle.

'Give me a hand, Desmond,' he datavised. They had turned off the lounge's environmental circuit in order to dismantle it, which meant wearing his SII suit for the task. Without air circulating at a decent rate the smell in the compartment was unbearable. The bodies had been removed, but a certain amount of grisly diffusion had occurred during their flight from Lalonde.

Desmond left the thermal regulator power circuit he was testing and drifted over. They hauled the cylindrical fan unit out of the duct. It was clogged solid with scraps of cloth and spiral shavings of nultherm foam. André prodded at the grille with an anti-torque keydriver, loosening some of the mangled cloth. Tiny flakes of dried blood swirled out like listless moths.

'*Merde*. It'll have to be broken down and purged.'

'Oh, come on, André, you can't use this again. The motor overloaded when Erick dumped the atmosphere. There's no telling what internal damage the voltage spike caused.'

'Ship systems all have absurdly high performance margins. The motor can withstand a hundred spikes.'

'Yeah, but the CAB . . .'

'To hell with them, data-constipated bureaucrats. They know nothing of operational flying.'

'Some systems you don't take chances with.'

'You forget, Desmond, this is my ship, my livelihood. Do you think I would risk that?'

'You mean what's left of your ship, don't you?'

'What are you implying, that I am responsible for the souls of humanity returning to invade us? Perhaps also it is my fault that the Earth is ruined, and the Meridian fleet never returned.'

'You're the captain, you took us to Lalonde.'

'On a legitimate government contract. It was honest money.'

'Have you never heard of fool's gold?'

André's answer was lost as Madeleine opened the ceiling hatch and used the crumbling composite ladder to pull herself down into the lounge. 'Listen you two, I've seen. . . . Yek!' She slapped a hand over her mouth and nose, eyes smarting from the unwholesome scents layering the atmosphere. In the deck above, an air-contamination warning sounded. The ceiling hatch started to hinge down. 'Christ, haven't the pair of you got this cycled yet?'

'*Non*,' André datavised.

'It doesn't matter. Listen, I've just seen Harry Levine. He was in a bar on the second residence level. I got out fast, I'm pretty sure he didn't see me.'

'*Merde!*' André datavised the flight computer for a link into the spaceport's civil register, loading a search order. Two seconds later it confirmed the *Dechal* was docked, and had been for ten days. His SII suit's permeability expanded, allowing a sudden outbreak of sweat to expire. 'We must leave. Immediately.'

'No chance,' Madeleine said. 'The port office wouldn't even

let us disengage the umbilicals, let alone launch, not with that civil starflight proscription order still in force.'

'The Captain's right, Madeleine,' Desmond datavised. 'There are only three of us left. We can't go up against Rawand's crew like this. We have to fly outsystem.'

'Four!' she said through clenched teeth. 'There are four of us left . . . Oh, mother of God, they'll go for Erick.'

Desmond glanced round to see a pair of nurses easing him out of the gas in a medical hypnotic mask covering Erick's

*

The fluid in Erick's inner ears began to stir, sending a volley of mild nerve impulses into his sleeping brain. The movement was so slight and smooth it made no impression on his quiescent mind. It did, however, register within his neural nanonics; the ever-vigilant basic monitor program noted the movement was consistent with a constant acceleration. Erick's body was being moved. The monitor program triggered a stimulant program.

Erick's hazy dream snuffed out, replaced by the hard-edged schematics of a personal situation display. Second-level constraint blocks were erected across his nerves, preventing any give-away twitches. His eyes stayed closed as he assessed what the hell was happening.

Quiet, easy hum of a motor. *Tap tap tap* of feet on a hard floor – an audio discrimination program went primary: two sets of feet, plus the level breathing of two people. Constant pulse of light pressure on the enhanced retinas below closed eyelids indicated linear movement, backed up by inner ear fluid motion; estimated at a fast walking pace. Posture was level: he was still lying on his bed.

He datavised a general query/response code, and received an immediate reply from a communication net processor. Its location was a corridor on the third storey of the hospital, already fifteen metres from the implant surgery care ward. Erick requested a file of the local net architecture, and found a security observation camera in the corridor. He accessed it to find himself with a fish-eye vantage point along a corridor where his own bed was sliding underneath the lens. Madeleine and Desmond were at either end of the bed, straining to supplement the motor as they hauled it along. A lift door was sliding open ahead of them.

Erick cancelled the constraint blocks and opened his eyes. 'What the fuck's going on?' he datavised to Desmond.

Desmond glanced round to see a pair of furious eyes staring at him out of the green medical nanonic mask covering Erick's face. He managed a snatched, semi-embarrassed grin. 'Sorry, Erick, we didn't dare wake you up in case someone heard the commotion. We had to get you out of there.'

'Why?'

'The *Dechal* is docked here. But don't worry, we don't think Hasan Rawand knows about us. And we intend to keep it that way. André is working on his political contact to get us a departure authorization.'

'For once he might make a decent job of it,' Madeleine muttered as they steered Erick's bulky bed into the lift. 'After all, it's his own neck on the block this time, not just ours.'

Erick tried to rise, but the medical packages were too restrictive, he could only just get his head off the pillows, and that simple motion was tiring beyond endurance. 'No. Leave me. You go.'

Madeleine pushed him down gently as the lift started upwards. 'Don't be silly. They'll kill you if they catch up with you.'

'We'll see this through together,' Desmond said, his voice full of sympathy and reassurance. 'We won't desert you, Erick.'

Encased in the protective, nurturing packages, Erick couldn't even groan in frustration. He opened a secure encrypted channel to the Confederation Navy Bureau. Lieutenant Li Chang responded immediately.

'You have to intercept us,' Erick datavised. 'These imbeciles are going to take me off Culey if no one stops them.'

'OK, don't panic, I'm calling in the Covert Duty squad. We can reach the spaceport in time.'

'Do we have any assets in the flight-control centre?'

'Yes, sir.'

'Activate one; make sure whatever departure authorization Duchamp gets is invalidated. I want the *Villeneuve's Revenge* to stay locked tight in that bloody docking-bay.'

'I'm on it. And don't worry.'

Desmond and Madeleine had obviously devoted considerable attention to planning their route in order to avoid casual observation. They took Erick straight up through the rock honeycomb which was Culey's habitation section, switching between a series of public utility lifts. When they were in the upper levels, where gravity had dropped to less than ten per cent standard, they left the bed behind and tugged him along a maze of simple passages bored straight through the rock. It was some kind of ancient maintenance or inspection grid, with few functional net processors. Lieutenant Li Chang had trouble tracking their progress.

Eighteen minutes after leaving the hospital they arrived at the base of the spaceport's spindle. Several intrigued sets of eyes followed their course as they floated across the big axial chamber to a vacant transit capsule.

'We're two minutes behind you,' Li Chang datavised. 'Thank heavens they chose a devious route, it slowed you up.'

'What about the departure authorization?'

'God knows how Duchamp did it, but Commissioner Ri Drak has cleared the *Villeneuve's Revenge* for departure. The Navy Bureau has lodged a formal protest with Culey's Governing Council. It should earn us a delay if not outright cancellation; Ri Drak's political opponents will use the complaint to make as much capital as they can.'

The transit capsule took them to the bay containing the *Villeneuve's Revenge*. It was a tedious journey; like the rest of the structure the transit tubes were in need of refurbishment, if not outright replacement. The capsule juddered frequently as it ran through lengths of rail with no power, the light-panels dimming then brightening in sympathy. It paused at several junctions, as if the spaceport route-management computer was unsure of the direction.

'Can you manoeuvre a bit now?' Madeleine asked Erick, hopeful that free fall would grant them some relief from straining at his mass. She was carrying two of the ancillary medical modules which were hooked up to his dermal armour of packages, feeding in a whole pharmacopoeia of nutrients to the new implants. The tubes were forever tangling round her limbs or snagging on awkward fixtures.

'Sorry. Tricky,' he datavised back. It might earn them thirty seconds.

Madeleine and Desmond swapped a martyred glance, and bundled Erick out of the transit capsule. The hexagonal cross-section corridors that encircled the docking-bay were white-walled composite, scuffed to a rusty grey by the boots of countless generations of crews and maintenance staff. The neat rows of grab hoops running along the walls had snapped off long ago, leaving only stumps. It didn't matter, the kind of people frequenting Culey spaceport were hardly novices. Madeleine and Desmond simply kept Erick in the middle of the corridor, imparting the odd gentle nudge to prevent him touching the walls as inertia slid him along.

Once the transit capsule door closed behind him, Erick lost his communication channel to Lieutenant Li Chang. He wished the packages didn't prevent him from sighing. Did nothing in this rat's arsehole of a settlement ever work? One of his medical support units emitted a cautionary bleep.

'Soon be over,' Madeleine soothed, misinterpreting the electronic tone.

Erick blinked rapidly, the sole method of expression left to him. They were risking themselves to save him, while he would be turning them over to the authorities as soon as they docked at a civilized port. Yet he'd killed to protect them, leaving them free to commit murder and piracy in turn. Applying for a CNIS post had seemed such a prestigious step forwards at the time. How stupid his vanity appeared with hindsight.

His eye focused on a two-centimetre burn mark scoring the composite wall. Instinct or a well-written extended sensory analysis program, it was the result which mattered. That burn mark was on the cover of a net conduit inspection panel, and it was fresh. When he switched to infra-red it still glowed a faint pink. With the spectrum active, other burns became apparent, a small ruddy constellation sprayed round the corridor walls, every glimmer corresponding to an inspection panel.

'Madeleine, Desmond, stop,' he datavised. 'Someone's deliberately screwed the net here.'

Desmond halted his ponderous glide with a semi-automatic slap at the stump of a grab hoop. He reached out to brake Erick. 'I can't even establish a channel to the ship,' he complained.

'Do you think they got into the life-support capsules?' Madeleine asked. Her own enhanced retinas were scanning round the fateful inspection panels.

'They wouldn't get past Duchamp, not while his paranoia's roused. We'll be lucky if he even opens the airlock for us.'

'They're armed, though; they could have cut their way in. And they're in front of us.'

Desmond peered down the slightly curving corridor, alarmed and uncertain. There was a four-way junction ten metres in front of him, one of its branches leading directly to the docking-bay's airlock. The only sounds he could hear were the rattly fans of the environmental maintenance system.

'Go back to the transit capsule,' Erick datavised. 'That has a working net processor, we can open a channel to the ship from there, even if we have to route it through the external antenna.'

'Good idea.' Madeleine braced her feet on a grab hoop stump, and gave Erick's shoulders a steady push, starting him off back down the corridor. Desmond was already slithering round them, lithe as a fish. When she looked back she could see shadows fluctuating within the junction. 'Desmond!' She scrambled inside her jacket for the TIP pistol she was carrying. An elbow hit the corridor wall, setting her tumbling. She tried to damp her momentum with one hand clawing at the coarse composite, while still fumbling at the obstinate holster. Her feet caught Erick, sending him thudding against the wall. He bounced, trailing long confused spirals of tubing, ancillary modules flying free.

Shane Brandes, the *Dechal*'s fusion engineer, slid out of the corridor which led to the airlock; he was wearing the copper one-piece overall of the local spaceport services company. It took him a couple of seconds to recognize the frenetic woman four metres in front of him who was grappling with a gun caught up in her jacket. He gagged in astonishment.

'Don't move, ball-head!' Madeleine screeched, half in panic, half in exhilaration. She brought the TIP pistol round to point at the terrified man. Her body was still rebounding, which meant she had to keep tracking. Five separate combat programs went into primary mode; her thoughts were so churned up she'd simply designated the classification rather than individual files. Various options for combat-wasp salvo attack formations skipped through her mind. She focused through the sleet of data and looping problematical high-gee vector lines to keep the nozzle trained on Brandes, who was doing a credible imitation of raising his hands in the air even though they were visually inverted.

'What do I do?' Madeleine yelled to Desmond. He was wrestling with Erick, trying to halt the injured man's cumbersome oscillations.

'Just keep him covered,' Desmond shouted back.

'OK.' She squeezed the pistol grip in an effort to stop it shaking so much; her legs forked wide, stabilizing her against the corridor. 'How many with you?' she asked Brandes.

'None.'

Madeleine finally tamed her wayward programs. A blue neon targeting grid slid into place over her vision, and locked. She aimed at a point ten centimetres to the side of Brandes's head, and fired. Composite snapped and boiled, sending out a puff of unhealthy black smoke.

'Jesus. Nobody, I swear! I'm supposed to disable the starship's umbilical feeds, and smash this bay's net before . . .'

'Before what?'

Everybody had shunted an audio-discrimination program into primary mode, so everybody heard the transit capsule door opening.

Desmond immediately activated a tactics program, and opened an encrypted channel to Madeleine. Their respective programs interfaced, coordinating their threat response. He turned to face the bright fan of light emerging from the door, his TIP pistol sliding round in a smooth program-controlled motion.

When Hasan Rawand came out of the commuter lift the exhilaration he was burning was hotter than any black-market stimulant program. He fancied himself as a hunting bird, powerdiving on its unsuspecting prey.

The sharp reality of the corridor *hurt*. A situation so abrupt he was still smiling confidently as Desmond's TIP pistol muzzle was locked directly on his head. Stafford Charlton and Harry Levine almost cannoned into his back as they left the commuter lift; the four mercenaries hired to provide overwhelming firepower were considerably more controlled, reaching for their own weapons.

'Rawand, I've programmed in a dead man's trigger,' Desmond said loudly. 'If you shoot me, you still die.'

The *Dechal*'s captain swore murderously. Behind him the mercenaries were having a lot of trouble deploying in the cramped corridor. Fast encrypted datavises assured him three of them were targeting the crewman from the *Villeneuve's*

*Revenge.* 'Give the word, we can vaporize his pistol first. We're sure.'

They weren't exactly the kind of odds Hasan Rawand was keen on. His eyes swept over the figure encased in medical nanonic packages. 'Is that who I think it is?' he enquired.

'Not relevant,' Desmond replied. 'Now listen, nobody makes any sudden movements at all. Clear? That way no real untimely tragic accidents occur. This is what we have here: a stand-off. With me so far? Nobody's going to win today, especially not if anyone starts shooting in here. So I'm calling time out, and we can both regroup and conspire to stab each other in the back some other happy time.'

'I don't think so,' Hasan said. 'I don't have a quarrel with you, Lafoe, nor you Madeleine. It's your captain I want, and that murdering bastard Thakrar. You two can leave any time. Nobody's going to shoot you.'

'You don't know shit about what we've been through,' Desmond said, an anger which surprised him powering his voice. 'I don't know about your ship, Rawand, but this isn't a crew which deserts each other the first second it hits the fan.'

'Very noble,' Hasan sneered.

'OK, here's what's going to happen next. The three of us are going to back up into the *Villeneuve's Revenge*, and we'll take Brandes with us for insurance. One mistake on your part, and Madeleine fries him.'

Hasan grinned rakishly. 'So? He never was much use as a fusion engineer anyway.'

'Rawand!' Shane screamed.

'Don't fuck with me!' Desmond shouted.

'Stafford, burn one of those medical modules our dear Erick is so attached to,' Hasan ordered.

Stafford Charlton laughed, and shifted his maser pistol slightly. The module he chose let out a vicious crack as the lance of radiation pierced its casing. Boiling fluid shot out of blackened fissures as the internal reserve bladders were irradiated. Tubes broke free, chemicals spraying out of their melted ends, causing them to whip about with a serpent's ferocity.

Desmond didn't even have to datavise an order; acting on the evaluation of their combined programs, Madeleine fired her TIP pistol immediately. The pulse burned away half of the flesh covering Shane Brandes's left shin. He howled in agony, clutching at the mutilated limb. His voice subsided to a sob as his neural nanonics erected axon blocks against the pain.

Hasan Rawand narrowed his eyes, enhanced retinas absorbing the entire scene. He put a tactical analysis program into primary mode, which offered him two blunt options: retreat, or open fire. Estimated casualties on his side were fifty per cent, including Shane. When he added the secondary goal of successfully entering the *Villeneuve's Revenge* the only option was retreat and reorganize.

'Want to play double or quits?' Desmond asked calmly.

Hasan glared at him; being thwarted was bad enough, but being mocked was almost intolerable.

The transit capsule doors opened again. A fist-sized sphere emitting intolerable white light soared into the corridor. Hasan Rawand and his accomplices were closest to it, receiving the full impact of the photonic blitz. Two of the mercenaries who had their retinal sensitivity cranked up wide were instantly blinded as the implants burnt out. For the others it was as though the terrible light was boring right through their eye sockets and into the soft tissue of the brain. Instinct and situation analysis response programs fused into a simple protective act: eyelids slammed shut and hands jammed over eyes.

Unseen in the glare, the three members of the CNIS Covert Duty squad dived out into the corridor, following Lieutenant Li Chang. Dressed in smooth neutral-grey armour suits, their active optical sensors were filtered for the intensity of the quasar grenade.

'Break though Rawand's people, snatch Erick,' Li Chang ordered. She fired another quasar grenade from her forearm magazine, aiming along the corridor at Desmond. It never reached its intended goal, one of the blinded mercenaries struck it as he thrashed about.

The mercenaries had linked combat programs, coordinating their response. Guidance and orientation programs allowed them to fix an accurate line on the transit capsule door and bring their weapons to bear. Thermal-induction pulses discharged, maser beams slashed about.

The dissipation layers on the suits which Li Chang's squad wore deflected or absorbed most direct hits. The composite walls of the tunnel had no such protection. Flames squirted out amid fountains of smoking composite. Fire alarms screeched in warning. Turbulent jets of thick grey extinguisher gas roared into the air, turning to blobs of oily turquoise liquid as soon as the substance came into contact with any flame, smearing the combustible surface. Huge bubbling clumps congealed around the quasar grenades, smothering them.

Answering shots from Li Chang's squad eliminated three mercenaries straight away. But their bodies formed a formidable tangled obstacle blocking off the corridor, as well as contriving a shield against further energy weapon fire. Behind it, Hasan and his remaining active cohorts rallied hurriedly.

Li Chang fought her way through the swirling extinguisher gas to grapple with one of the corpses. Her armour suit gauntlets couldn't get a decent grip on anything. The gas had slicked every damn surface. Two maser beams struck her chest and shoulder as she attempted to force her way forwards. She could actually see the gas crystallizing in long straight lines marking out the beams. One of the covert squad members was beside her, clawing at the dead man's neck. The body was bucking fitfully between them, its mass impeding every move.

Another TIP shot struck her armour, diffracting. A wide splash of skin on the dead man veered to a rancid bruise-brown as the energy punched it. His clothes were smouldering, drawing the extinguisher gas like a condensing dew.

Her neural nanonics had to activate a nausea-suppressor program. 'Use the smarts,' she said, formulating search–hunt parameter patterns. A volley of centimetre-long darts slid out of the cartridges on her belt – miniature programmable missiles with a tiny ionic exhaust. They curved and rolled through the seething air, sliding round the awkward contours of the lifeless mercenaries, and accelerated down the corridor.

Li Chang heard a savage firecracker barrage as over two hundred diminutive electron explosive warheads detonated in the space of three seconds. Sharp flickering fingers of blue-white light stabbed back past the floating bodies. Ripples of purple static surfed along the composite walls towards her. There was a sudden surge of air, sucking her towards the source of the light and sound. The three battered corpses began to move. A pressure-drop warning sounded, its metallic whistle Dopplering as the pressure thinned out fast. Emergency hatches were sliding out of the corridor walls, sealing off the damaged section.

'Captain Thakrar?' she datavised. 'Sir, are you there?'

Scrambling after the corpses she could see the butchery which the smart darts had inflicted. A galaxy of blood globules spun round the ripped torsos of Hasan Rawand and the others. She assumed there were four in total. It was hard to tell.

Chunks of gore were splatting against the cracks in the wall, producing temporary seals which would shake and wobble under pressure, before being sucked through. Holding her breath – which was ridiculous as the suit provided her with a full oxygen supply – Li Chang flung herself through the centre of the bloody pulp, flinching every time the suit's tactile sensors faithfully reported an object slithering down her side.

The corridor beyond was empty. An emergency hatch had cut off the junction. Li Chang hauled her way along to it. The wind was abating now, almost all of the air had gone.

A small transparent port was set in the centre of the hatch. When Li Chang pressed her shell-helmet sensors against it, all she could see was more hatches closed across the other corridors. Captain Thakrar and the crew-members from the *Villeneuve's Revenge* were nowhere to be seen.

That was when a new sound was added to the fading clamour of the various alarms. A deep bass rumble which she could feel through the structure as much as hear. The light-panels flickered, then went out. Small blue-white back-up globes came on.

'Oh God, no,' she whispered to herself inside the helmet. 'I promised him, I said he'd be safe now.'

The *Villeneuve's Revenge* was launching from inside its docking-bay. André had released the cradle hold-down latches, but without the bay manager to assist there was nothing he could do about the umbilical couplings and airlock tube. Secondary drive tubes ignited, power from the main generators vaporizing hydrogen at barely subfusion temperatures. Clouds of searing blue ions billowed out around the spherical starship as it rose laboriously. Hoses and cables jacked into their sockets on the lower hull tore and snapped; streams of coolant fluid, water, and cryogenic fuel sluiced round the cylindrical bay. Once the starship was above the cradle the drive exhaust played directly over the girders, reducing them to garish slag in seconds. The airlock tube stretched and flexed to its limit then ripped free of the docking ring, pulling spars, data cables, and locking pins with it.

'What the fuck are you doing, Duchamp?' an enraged traffic control broadcast at the rogue starship. 'Turn your drive off now.'

The *Villeneuve's Revenge* was rising out of the bay on a pillow of radiant ions. Walls and support girders marked its progress by melting and sagging.

André was only dimly aware of the massive damage his departure was causing. Flying the starship alone required his full concentration. Culey's SD platforms had lock-on; but he knew they would never fire, not while he was still so close. Frantically, he ordered all the open access hatches to close.

A ring of cryogenic storage tanks around the rim of the bay finally detonated under the unceasing blast of the starship's exhausts. It was a chain reaction, sending out vast plumes of white vapour and spinning chunks of debris. The entire docking-bay structure began to crumple under the force of the multiple explosions. Momentum-damping mechanisms in the spaceport spindle bearings veered towards overload as the impulse jud-dered its way through the framework.

The wavefront from the tank explosions struck the *Ville-neuve's Revenge*, fragments of wreckage puncturing the dark silicon hull in a dozen places. The starship was buffeted violently. An event horizon sealed over the hull, then shrank to nothing.

\*

It was Gerald Skibbow's third trip to the lounge; a spacious semicircular room cut into Guyana's rock, with wide glass sliding doors leading out onto a veranda that gave an excellent view down the interior of the asteroid's second habitation cavern. Despite the apparent easygoing nature, the lounge was at the centre of the navy's secure medical sanatorium, although the security measures were deliberately unobtrusive. Staff and patient-inmates mingled openly, producing what the doctors hoped was a casual atmosphere. It was intended to redevelop the social interactivity skills of the inmates who had been bruised by traumas, stress, and, in several cases, stringent interrogation. Anyone was free to come and go as they pleased; sit in the big spongy chairs and contemplate the view, have a drink and a snack, or play the simple games provided.

Gerald Skibbow didn't like the lounge at all. The artificial asteroid cavern was too removed from his experience, its cyclorama landscape unsettled him; and the lounge's expensive modern setting reminded him of the arcology he'd yearned to escape from. He didn't want memories. His family dwelt in memories, the only place they did live now.

For the first few days after his personality debrief he had begged and pleaded with his captors to end those memories with their clever devices (that or death). The nanonics were still entombed within his skull, it would take so little effort on their part to cleanse him, a purge of fiery impulses and his past would be gone. But Dr Dobbs had smiled kindly and shaken his head, saying they wanted to cure him, not persecute him further.

Gerald had come to despise that mild smile, the utter intransigence it fronted. It condemned him to live amid a swirl of wondrously awful images: those of the savannah, the shared laughter, the tired happiness which had come at the end of each day, the days themselves, filled with simple achievement. In short, happiness. And in knowing it, he knew all he had lost, and was never to regain. He convinced himself the Kulu military people were deliberately submerging him in his own recollections as a punishment for his involvement in Lalonde and the outbreak of possession. There was no other reason for them to refuse him help. They blamed him, and wanted him to remember that. Memories emphasized that he had nothing, that he was worth nothing, that he had failed the only people he'd ever loved. Memories which kept him permanently looped in his failure.

His other wounds, physical ones from the encounter with Jenny Harris's team, had been treated efficiently and effectively by medical packages, although his face and head sported fresh scars from the time a few days ago when he'd tried to claw the lovely smiling faces from within his brain; fingernails tearing at the skin to let him get at the bone of the skull and prise it open so that his darling family could escape and unfetter him. But the strong medical orderlies had jumped on him, and Dr Dobbs's smile had become sad. There had been fresh batches of chemicals to make him drowsy, and extra sessions when he had to lie on the psychiatrist's comfy couch and tell everyone how he felt. It hadn't done any good. How could it?

Gerald sat on one of the tall stools at the lounge's bar and asked for a cup of tea. The steward smiled and said: 'Yes, sir. I'll get you some biscuits, too.'

His tea and biscuits arrived on a tray. He poured, concentrating hard. These days his reactions weren't too sharp and his vision seemed to lack any real depth perception. Flat and unresponsive; so perhaps it was the world at fault, not him.

He rested his elbows on the polished wood of the bar, and cradled the cup in his hands, sipping slowly. His eyes scanned the ornamental plates and cups and vases in the showcase behind the bar. Not interesting, but at least it kept him from looking out of the veranda windows and receiving the wickedly vertiginous view of the cavern. The first time they'd brought him into the lounge he'd tried to jump over the veranda. It was a hundred and fifty metres above the ground, after all. Two of the other inmates had actually cheered and laughed as he hurdled over the metal railing. But there was a net to snag him. Dr Dobbs had smiled tolerantly after it had stopped bouncing and winched him in.

At the far end of the bar, a holoscreen was switched to a news show (presumably censored – they wouldn't give inmates anything too contentious). Gerald shifted along a couple of stools so he could hear the commentary. The presenter was a handsome silver-haired man speaking in level, measured tones. And smiling – naturally. The image changed to a low-orbit shot of Ombey, focusing on the Xingu continent. A curious appendicular finger glowed crimson amid the dour browns and greens of the earth, prodding out from the bottom of the main landmass. It was, Gerald heard, the latest anomaly to engulf Mortonridge. Unfortunately it meant that no one was able to see what was happening beneath. Royal Kulu Navy sources confirmed it matched the reality dysfunction effect observed on the Laymil homeworld; but emphasized that whatever mischief the possessed were cooking up below it there was no possibility of them removing Ombey from the universe. There simply weren't enough of them; they didn't have the strength. And the red cloud had been halted at the firebreak. After two laser shots from a low-orbit SD platform the cloud's leading edge had recoiled, yielding to the negotiated boundary.

The disconcerting image of cloud was replaced by a sequence of fast pictures of big government buildings and uniformed officials with grim faces bustling through their doors and ignoring shouted questions. Gerald found the report hard to follow, although it seemed to be hinting that the Morton-ridge situation was going to be 'resolved', that 'certain' plans were being 'initiated'.

Fools. They didn't realize. Not even sucking out every piece of knowledge in his brain had brought them understanding.

He sipped some more of his tea, thoughts calming to a more contemplative mood. Perhaps if he was lucky the possessed would begin another offensive; that way his misery would be extinguished for good as he was crushed back into the numbing darkness.

Then came the report about yesterday's hellhawk incursion. Five of them had emerged into the Ombey system, two of their number skipping high above the planet, three jumping about between the system's handful of settled asteroids. Always maintaining their distance, keeping well outside the range of SD platforms, and sliding back into wormholes as soon as Royal Navy ships were dispatched to interdict. Apparently their missions were to datavise a sensorium recording coded for open access into every communication net they could establish a channel with.

Leonard DeVille appeared to say how unfortunate the recording was, and that he hoped people would be sensible enough to see it for the crude propaganda it represented. In any case, he added contemptuously, with the civil starflight proscription in force, anyone sad enough to succumb would be safe from Kiera Salter's clutches. They would simply be unable to reach Valisk.

'There now follows,' said the handsome anchorman, 'a brief extract of the recording; though we are voluntarily complying with government wishes and not playing it in full.'

The holoscreen showed a beautiful teenage girl whose flimsy clothes were virtually falling off her.

Gerald blinked. His vision was deluged by a dizzy rush of memories, the pictures more vivid than anything his eyes provided. Past and present wrestled for dominance.

'You know, they're going to tell you that you shouldn't be accessing this recording,' the girl said. 'In fact, they're going to get quite serious about that—'

Her voice; a harmony which threaded through every memory. Gerald's teacup hit the top of the bar and spun away, flinging the hot liquid over his shirt and trousers.

' – your mum and dad, your big brother, the authorities in charge of wherever you live. Can't think why. Except, of course, I'm one of the possessed—'

'Marie?' his throat was so clogged he could barely whisper. Two of the inmate supervision staff sitting at a table behind him exchanged a troubled look.

' – one of the demons—'

'Marie.' Tears brimmed up in Gerald's eyes. 'Oh my God. Darling!'

The two supervision staff rose to their feet, one of them datavising an alert code into the sanatorium's net. Other inmates in the lounge had begun to notice Gerald's behaviour. Grins zipped around: the loony's at it again.

'You're alive!' He shoved both hands palm-down on the top of the bar and tried to vault over. 'Marie!' The steward ran towards him, an arm outstretched. 'Marie! Darling, baby.' With his wobbly senses, Gerald completely misjudged his leap and went crashing onto the floor behind the bar. The steward had time for a fast yelp of shock as his flying feet tangled with Gerald's sprawled body and sent him tumbling to smack painfully into the base of the bar. A flailing arm sent a cascade of glasses smashing down on the hard tiles.

Gerald shook the glass splinters from his hair, and jerked his head back. Marie was still there above him, still smiling coyly and invitingly. At him. She wanted Daddy back.

'MARIE.' He surged up at the same time the two supervisors arrived at the bar. The first snatched hold of Gerald's shirt, tugging him away from the holoscreen. Gerald spun round to face this new impediment, roared in rage, and swung a violent punch. The supervisor's unarmed-combat program could barely cope with the suddenness of the attack. Muscles bunched under the orders of abrupt override impulses, twisting him away from the fist. The response wasn't quite good enough. Gerald caught him a glancing blow on the side of his head. Behind that strike was the force of a body hardened by months of tough physical labour. The supervisor stumbled back into his partner, the two of them swaying desperately for balance.

Cheers and raucous whoops of encouragement were hurled from all across the lounge. Someone picked up one of the big pot plants, and threw it at a distracted nurse. An alarm shrilled. The staff began to draw their nervejam sticks.

'Marie! Baby, I'm here.' Gerald had finally reached the holoscreen, thrusting his face against the cool plastic. His nose was squashed almost flat. She grinned and flirted mere centimetres away, her figure composed from a compact cellular array of small glowing spheres. 'Marie! Let me in, Marie.' He started to thump on the screen. 'Marie!'

She vanished. The handsome anchorman smiled out. Gerald shrieked in anguish, and started pummelling the holoscreen with all his strength. 'Marie. Come back. Come back to me.' Smears of blood from torn knuckles dribbled down the anchorman's tanned features.

'Oh, Christ,' the first supervisor grunted. He aimed a

nervejam stick at Gerald's back and fired. Gerald froze, then his limbs started to quake fiercely. A long wretched wail fluted out of his lips as he crumpled onto the floor. He managed to gasp one last piteous, 'Marie,' before unconsciousness claimed him.

# 14

Given the propensity for mild paranoia among Tranquillity's plutocrats, medical facilities were always one aspect of the habitat never short of investment and generous charitable donations. Consequently, and in this case fortunately, there was always a degree of overcapacity. After twenty years of what amounted to chronic underuse, the Prince Michael Memorial Hospital's paediatric ward was now chock full, a situation which produced a permanent riot along its broad central aisle during the day.

When Ione called in, half of the kids from Lalonde were chasing each other over beds and around tables, yelling ferociously. The game was possessed and mercenaries, and mercenaries always won. The two rampaging teams charged past Ione, neither knowing nor caring who she was (her usual escort of serjeants had been left outside). A harassed Dr Giddings, the head of the Paediatric Department, caught sight of his prestigious visitor and hurried over. He was in his late twenties; effusiveness and a lanky frame married to produce a set of hectic, rushed mannerisms whenever he spoke. His face inclined towards chubby, which gave him an engagingly boyish appearance. Ione wondered if he'd undergone cosmetic tailoring; that face would be so instantly trustworthy to children, a big brother you could always confide in.

'Ma'am, I'm so sorry,' he blurted. 'We had no idea you were

coming.' He tried to reseal the front of his white house tunic, glancing round fretfully at the ward. Cushions and bedclothes were scattered everywhere, colourful animatic dolls waddled around, either laughing or repeating their catchphrases. (Probably wasted, Ione thought, none of these children would recognize the idols from this season's AV shows.)

'I don't think I'd be very popular if you made them clean up just for me,' Ione said with a smile. 'Besides, I've been watching them for the last few days. I'm really only here to confirm they're adapting properly.'

Dr Giddings gave her a careful glance, using his fingers to comb back some of his floppy ginger hair. 'Oh, yes, they're adapting all right. But then children are always easy to bribe. Food, toys, clothes, trips into the parkland, every kind of outdoor game they can play. Never fails. This is heaven's holiday camp as far as they're concerned.'

'Aren't they homesick?'

'Not really. I'd describe them as parent-sick more than anything. Separation causes some psychological problems, naturally.' He gestured round. 'But as you can see, we're doing our best to keep them busy, that way they don't have time to think about Lalonde. It's easier with the younger ones. Some of the older ones are proving recalcitrant; they can be prone to moodiness. But again, I don't think it's anything serious. Not in the short term.'

'And in the long term?'

'Long term, the only real cure is to get them back to Lalonde and their parents.'

'That's going to have to wait, I'm afraid. But you've certainly done a wonderful job with them.'

'Thank you,' Dr Giddings murmured.

'Is there anything else you need?' Ione asked.

Dr Giddings pulled a face. 'Well, medically they're all fine now apart from Freya and Shona; and the nanonic packages are taking good care of those two. They should be healed within a week. So, as I said, what the rest could really do with right now is a strong, supportive family environment. If you were to appeal for foster families, I'm sure we'd have enough volunteers.'

'I'll have Tranquillity put out an announcement, and make sure the news studios mention it.'

Dr Giddings grinned in relief. 'That's very kind, thank you. We were worried people might not come forward, but I'm sure that if you back the appeal personally . . .'

'Do my best,' she said lightly. 'Do you mind if I have a wander round?'

'Please.' He half-bowed, half-stumbled.

Ione walked on down the aisle, stepping round a thrilled three-year-old girl who was dancing with, and cuddling, a fat animatic frog in a bright yellow waistcoat.

The twin rows of beds had channelled an avalanche of toys along the main aisle. Holomorph stickers were colonizing the walls and even some of the furniture; their cartoon images swelling up from the surface to run through their cycle, making it appear as if the polyp was flexing with rainbow diffraction patterns. A blue-skinned imp appeared to be the favourite; picking its nose then flicking disgusting tacky-yellow bogies at anyone passing by. No medical equipment was actually visible, it was all built unobtrusively into the walls and bedside cabinets.

The far end opened up into a lounge section, with a big table where they all sat round for meals. Its curving wall had two large oval windows which provided a panoramic view out past the curving habitat shell. Right now Tranquillity was above Mirchusko's nightside, but the rings glinted as if they were arches of frosted glass, and the smooth beryl orb of Falsia shone with a steady aquamarine hue. The stars continued their eternal orbit around the habitat.

A girl had made a broad nest of cushions in front of a window, snuggling down in them to watch the astronomical marvels roll past her. According to the neural strata's local memory, she'd been there for a couple of hours. A ritual practised every day since *Lady Mac* had arrived.

Ione hunched down beside her. She looked about twelve, with short cropped hair so blonde it was almost silver.

**What's her name?** Ione asked.

**Jay Hilton. She's the oldest of the group, and their leader. She is one of the moody ones Dr Giddings mentioned.**

'Hello, Jay.'

'I know you.' Jay managed an aslant frown. 'You're the Lord of Ruin.'

'Oh dear, you've found me out.'

'Thought so. Everyone said my hair is the same as yours.'

'Hmm, they're almost right; I'm growing mine a bit longer these days.'

'Father Horst cut mine.'

'He did a good job.'

'Of course he did.'

'Cutting hair isn't the only thing he did right, by all accounts.'

'Yes.'

'You're not joining in with the games much, are you?'

Jay wrinkled her nose up contemptuously. 'They're just kids' games.'

'Ah. You prefer the view, then?'

'Sort of. I've never seen space before. Not real space, like this. I thought it was just empty, but this is always different. It's so pretty with the rings and everything. So's the parkland, too. Tranquillity's nice all over.'

'Thank you. But wouldn't you be better off in the parkland? It's healthier than sitting here all day long.'

'Suppose so.'

'Did I say something wrong?'

'No. It's just . . . I think it's safer here, that's all.'

'Safer?'

'Yes. I talked to Kelly on the flight here, we were in the

spaceplane together. She showed me all the recordings she'd made. Did you know the possessed were frightened of space? That's why they make the red cloud cover the sky, so they don't have to see it.'

'I remember that part, yes.'

'It's sort of funny if you think about it, the dead scared of the dark.'

'Thank heavens they're scared of something, I say. Is that why you like sitting here?'

'Yes. This is like the night; so I'll be safe from them here.'

'Jay, there are no possessed in Tranquillity, I promise.'

'You can't promise that. Nobody can.'

'OK. Ninety-nine per cent, then. How's that sound?'

'I believe that.' Jay smiled sheepishly.

'Good. You must be missing your family?'

'I miss Mummy. We went to Lalonde so we could get away from the rest of our family.'

'Oh.'

'I miss Drusilla, too. She's my rabbit. And Sango; he was Mr Manani's horse. But he's dead anyway. Quinn Dexter shot him.' The tenuous smile faded, and she glanced back at the stars in a hunt for reassurance.

Ione studied the young girl for a moment. She didn't think a foster family would be much use in this case, Jay was too clued-up to accept a substitute for anything. However, Dr Giddings had mentioned bribes . . . 'There's someone I'd like you to meet, I think you'll get on very well with her.'

'Who?' Jay asked.

'She's a friend of mine, a very special friend. But she doesn't come down into the starscrapers; it's tricky for her. You'll have to come up and visit her in the park.'

'I ought to wait for Father Horst. We normally have lunch together.'

'I'm sure he won't mind just this once. We can leave a message.'

Jay was obviously torn. 'I suppose so. I don't know where he's gone.'

To see Tranquillity's bishop, but Ione didn't say it.

*

'I wonder why you saw the demon as red?' the Bishop was asking as the two of them walked the old-fashioned grounds of the cathedral with its century-old yew hedges, rose beds, and stone-lined ponds. 'It does seem somewhat classical. One can hardly credit that Dante did actually get shown round Hell.'

'I think demon might be a simplistic term in this instance,' Horst replied. 'I've no doubt that it was some kind of spiritual entity; but given the clarity of hindsight, it seemed to be more curious than malevolent.'

'Remarkable. To come face to face with a creature not of this realm. And you say it appeared before the Ivets performed their dark mass?'

'Yes. Hours before. Though it was definitely present at the mass; right there when possession started.'

'It was the instigator, then?'

'I don't know. But I hardly think its presence can be a coincidence. It was certainly involved.'

'How strange.'

Horst was disturbed by how melancholic the old man sounded. Joseph Saro was far removed from the tough realist of a bishop Horst had served with back at the arcology; this was a genteel jolly man, whose subtlety was perfectly suited to an undemanding diocese like Tranquillity. With his almost-white beard and crinkled ebony skin he had evolved a cosy dignity. More of a social figure than religious leader.

'Your grace?' Horst prompted.

'Strange to think that it is two thousand six hundred years since Our Lord walked the earth, the last time of miracles. We are, as you said earlier, so used to dealing in the concept of faith rather than fact. And now here we are again, surrounded by miracles, although of a singularly dark countenance. The Church no longer has to teach people and then pray that they come to believe in their own way; all we have to do today is point. Who can refute what the eye beholds, even though it doth offend?' He finished with a lame smile.

'Our teachings still have purpose,' Horst said. 'More so than ever now. Believe me, your grace, the Church has endured for millennia so that people alive today can know Christ's message. That is a tremendous achievement, one we can all draw comfort from. So much has been endured, schism from within, conflict and assaults from outside. All so his word can be heard in the darkest hour.'

'Which word?' Joseph Saro asked quietly. 'We have so many true histories now: old orthodoxies, revelationist scrolls, revisionist teachings; Christ the pacifist, Christ the warrior. Who knows what was really said, what was altered to appease Rome? It was so long ago.'

'You're wrong, your grace. I'm sorry, but the details of that time are irrelevant. That he existed is all we need to know. We carried the essence of Our Lord across the centuries, it is that which we've kept alive for so long, ready for this day. Christ showed us the human heart has dignity, that everyone can be redeemed. If we have faith in ourselves, we cannot fail. And that is the strength we must gather if we are to confront the possessed.'

'I'm sure you're right; it's just that such a message seems, well . . .'

'Simplistic? Fundamentals are always simple. That is why they endure for so long.'

Joseph Saro patted Horst's shoulder. 'Ah, my boy. Which of us is the teacher now? I envy your faith, I really do. My task would be so much easier if I believed with your fervour. That we have souls is of no doubt to me; though we can be assured our wonderful scientist colleagues will seek a solid rationale among the grubby shadows of quantum cosmology. Who knows, perhaps they will even find it. Then what? And how do you explain the different faiths, Horst? You are going to have to think of that now. God knows, others will. Now spirituality is real, religion, all religion will come in for scrutiny as never before. What of the others who claim theirs is the true path to God? What of the Muslims, the Hindus, the Buddhists, the Sikhs, the Confucians, the Shintoists, even the Starbridge tribes, not to mention all those troublesome cultists?'

'The origin of each is identical, that's what's important. People must have faith. If you believe in your God, you believe in yourself. There is no greater gift than that.'

'Such murky waters we are adrift in,' Joseph Saro murmured. 'And you, Horst, you have grown into a man with the clearest of visions. I'm humbled, and even a little frightened by you. I must have you deliver the sermon next Sunday; you'll bring them flocking in. You may very well be the first of the Church's new evangelists.'

'I don't think so, your grace. I've simply passed through the eye of the needle. The Lord has tested me, as He will test all of us in the months ahead. I regained my faith. For that I have the possessed to thank.' Unconsciously, his hand went to his throat, sensitive fingertips feeling the tiny scars left from when invisible fingers had clawed at him.

'I do hope Our Lord doesn't set me too hard a test,' Joseph Saro said in a forlorn tone. 'I'm far too old and comfortable in my ways to do what you did on Lalonde. That's not to say I'm not proud of you, for I certainly am. You and I are strictly New Testament priests, yet you were set a decidedly Old Testament task. Did you really perform an exorcism, my boy?'

Horst grinned. 'Yes, I really did.'

*

Captain Gurtan Mauer was still dry retching as the lid of the zero-tau pod closed over him, blackness suspending him from time. The tortures and obscenities might have wrecked his dignity, the pitiful pleas and promises were proof of that, but he was still cold sober sane. Quinn was quite determined in that respect. Only sane, rational people were able to appreciate the nuances of their own suffering. So the pain and barbarism was always pitched a degree below the level which would tip the *Tantu*'s ex-captain into the refuge of insanity. This way he could hold out for days, or even weeks. And zero-tau would hold him ready for when Quinn's wrath rose again; for him there would be no periods of relief, just one long torment.

Quinn smiled at the prospect. His robe and hood shrank to more manageable proportions, and he pushed off from the decking. He'd needed the interlude to regain his own equilibrium after the disaster in Earth orbit, the humiliation of retreat. Gurtan Mauer provided him with a valid focus for his anger. He could hardly use the starship's crew; there were only fifteen of them left now, and few were inessential.

'Where are we going, Quinn?' Lawrence asked as the two of them drifted through the companionway to the bridge.

'I'm not sure. I'll bet most of the Confederation knows about possession now, it'll make life fucking difficult.' He wriggled through the hatch to the bridge, and checked round to see what was being done.

'We're almost finished, Quinn,' Dwyer said. 'There wasn't too much damage, and this is a warship, most critical systems have back-ups. We're flight-ready again. But people are going to know we've been in some sort of scrap. No way could we go outside to repair the hull. Spacesuits won't work on us.'

'Sure, Dwyer. You've done good.'

Dwyer's grin was avaricious.

They were all waiting for Quinn to tell them where he wanted to go next. And the truth was, he wasn't entirely sure he knew. Earth was his goal, but perhaps he'd been too ambitious trying for it first. It was the old problem, to charge in with an army of disciples or to stealthily rot the structure from within. After the dreariness of Norfolk, the prospect of action had excited him. It still did, but he obviously didn't have enough forces to break through Earth's defences. Not even the Royal Kulu Navy could do that.

He needed to get there on a different ship, one which wouldn't cause such a heated response. After he'd docked at the orbital tower station he could get down to the planet. He knew that.

But where to get another ship from? He knew so little about the Confederation worlds. Only once during his twenty years on Earth had he met anyone from offworld.

'Ah.' He grinned at Lawrence. 'Of course, Banneth's colleague.'

'What?'

'I've decided where we're going.' He checked the bridge displays, their cryogenic fuel reserves could fly them another four hundred light-years. More than enough. 'Nyvan,' he announced. 'We're going to Nyvan. Dwyer, start working out a vector.'

'What's Nyvan?' Lawrence asked.

'The second planet anyone ever found which was good enough to live on. Everyone used to flock there from the arcologies. They don't now.'

*

Nova Kong had always boasted that it was the most beautiful city to be found within the Confederation. Wisely, few challenged the claim.

No other Adamist society had the kind of money which had been lavished on the city ever since the day Richard Saldana first stepped down out of his spaceplane and (according to legend) said: 'This footstep will not depart in the sands of time.'

If he did say it, he was certainly right. The capital city of the Kulu Kingdom was a memorial which no one who saw it would ever be likely to forget. Right from the start, aesthetics was a paramount factor in planning, and pretty grandiose aesthetics at that. It had no streets, only flamboyant boulevards, greenway avenues, and rivers (half of them artificial); all powered ground traffic used the labyrinth of underground motorways. Commemorative monuments and statues dominated the junctions; the Kingdom's heroic history celebrated in hundreds of artistic styles from megalithic to contemporary.

Although it had a population of nineteen million, the building density regulations meant it was spread out over five hundred square kilometres, with Touchdown plaza at its centre. Every conceivable architectural era was to be found among the public, private, and commercial buildings so carefully sprinkled across the ground, with the exception of prefab concrete, programmable silicon, and composite ezystak panels (anything built in Nova Kong was built to last). Seventeen cathedrals strove for attention against neo-Roman government offices. Gloss-black pyramid condominiums were as popular as Napoleonic apartment blocks with conservatory roofs arching over their central wells. Sir Christopher Wren proved a heavy influence on the long curving terraces of snow-white stone town houses, while oriental and Eastern designs appeared to be favoured among the smaller individual residences.

Chilly autumn air was gusting along the boulevards when Ralph Hiltch flew in over the clean spires and ornate belfries. His vantage point was a privilege not awarded to many people. Commercial overflights were strictly forbidden; only emergency craft, police, senior government officials, and the Saldanas were ever permitted this view.

He couldn't have timed his arrival better, he thought. The trees which filled the parks, squares, and ornamental waterways below were starting to turn in the morning frosts. Green leaves were fading to an infinite variety of yellows, golds, bronzes and reds; a trillion flecks of rusty colour glinting in the strong sunlight. Soggy auburn mantles were already expanding across the damp grass, while thick dunes snuggled up in the sheltered lees of buildings. Nova Kong's million-strong army of utility mechanoids were programmed to go easy on the invasive downfall, allowing the rustic image to prevail.

Today though the refined perfection of the city was marred by twisters of smoke rising from several districts. As they passed close to one, Ralph accessed the flyer's sensor suite to obtain a better view of a Gothic castle made from blocks of amber and magenta glass which seemed to be the source. The smoke was a dense billow pouring out from the stubby remains of a smashed turret. Fires were still flickering inside the main hall. Over twenty police and Royal Marine flyers had landed on the parkland outside; figures in active armour suits walked through the castle's courtyards.

Ralph knew that depressing scene well enough. Although in his heart he'd never expected to see it here, not Nova Kong, the very nucleus of the Kingdom. He'd been born on the Principality of Jerez, and this was his first visit to Kulu. One part of his mind wryly acknowledged he would always retain a hint of the provincial attitude. Nova Kong was the capital, it ought to remain impervious to anything, any form of attack, physical or subversive. That was the reason his job, his agency, existed: the first line of defence.

'How many of these incursions have there been?' he asked the Royal Navy pilot.

'A couple of dozen in the last three days. Tough bastards to beat, I can tell you. The Marines had to call down SD fire support a couple of times. We haven't seen any new ones for eleven hours now, thank Christ. That means we've probably got them all. City's under martial law, every transport route on the planet has shut down, and the AIs are sweeping the net for any sign of activity. Nowhere the possessed can hide any more, and they certainly can't run.'

'Sounds like you people were on the ball. We did much the same thing on Ombey.'

'Yeah? You beat them there?'

'Almost.'

The ion-field flyer lined up on Apollo Palace. Awe and nerves squeezed Ralph's heart, quickening its pulse. Physically the middle of the city, politically the hub of an interstellar empire, and home to the most notorious family in the Confederation.

Apollo Palace was a small town in its own right, albeit contained under a single roof. Every wing and hall interlocked, their unions marked by rotundas and pagodas. Sumptuous stately homes, which in centuries past must have been independent houses for senior courtiers, had now been incorporated in the overall structure, ensnared by the flourishing webbing of stone cloisters which had gradually crept out from the centre. The family chapel was larger than most of the city's cathedrals, and more graceful than all.

A hundred quadrangles containing immaculate gardens flashed past underneath the flyer's fuselage as it descended. Ralph shunted a mild tranquillizer program into primary mode. Turning up electronically stoned before your sovereign probably went against every written and unwritten court protocol in existence. But, damn it, he couldn't afford a slip due to nerves now – the Kingdom couldn't afford it.

Eight armed Royal Marines were waiting at the foot of the airstair when they landed in an outer quadrangle. Their captain clicked his heels together, and saluted Ralph.

'Sorry, sir, but I must ask you to stand still.'

Ralph eyed the chemical-projectile guns trained on him. 'Of course.' Cold air turned his breath to grey vapour.

The captain signalled one of the marines who came forward holding a small sensor pad. She touched it to Ralph's forehead, then went on to his hands.

'Clear, sir,' she barked.

'Very good. Mr Hiltch, would you please datavise your ESA identification code, and your martial law transport authority number.' The captain held up a processor block.

Ralph obliged the request.

'Thank you, sir.'

The marines shouldered their weapons. Ralph whistled silent relief; happy at how seriously they were taking the threat of possession, but at the same time wishing he wasn't on the receiving end.

A tall middle-aged man stepped out of a nearby doorway, and walked over. 'Mr Hiltch, welcome to Kulu.' He put his hand out.

That he was a Saldana was not in doubt; his size, poise, and that distinct nose made it obvious for anyone to see. Trouble was, there were so many of them. Ralph ran an identity check through his neural nanonics, the file was in his classified section: the Duke of Salion, Chairman of the Privy Council's Security Commission, and Alastair II's first cousin. One of the most unobtrusive, and powerful, men in the Kingdom.

'Sir. Thank you for meeting me.'

'Not at all.' He guided Ralph back through the door. 'Princess Kirsten's message made it clear she considers you important. I have to say we're all extremely relieved to hear Ombey has survived a not inconsiderable assault by the possessed. The Principality does lack the resources available to the more developed worlds of the Kingdom.'

'I saw the smoke as I flew down. It seems nowhere is immune.'

A lift was waiting for them just inside the building. The Duke datavised an order into its processor. Ralph felt it start off, moving downwards then horizontally.

'Regrettably so,' the Duke admitted. 'However we believe we have them contained here. And preliminary indications from the other principalities are that they've also been halted. Thankfully, it looks like we're over the worst.'

'If I might ask, what was the sensor that marine used on me?'

'You were being tested for static electricity. The Confederation Navy researchers have found the possessed carry a small but permanent static charge. It's very simple, but so far it's proved infallible.'

'Some good news, that makes a change.'

'Quite.' The Duke gave him a sardonic smile.

The lift opened out into a long anteroom. Ralph found it hard not to gawp. He'd thought Burley Palace was opulent; here the concept of ornamentation and embellishment had been taken to outrageous heights. Marble was drowning under arabesque patterns of platinum leaf; the church-high ceiling was adorned with frescoes of unusual xenocs which were hard to see behind the glare of galactic chandeliers. Arched alcoves were inset with circular windows of graduated glass, each fashioned after a different flower. Trophy heads were mounted on the wall, jewelled armour helmet effigies of fantasy creatures; dragons wrought in curving jade panes inlaid with rubies, unicorns in alabaster and emeralds, hobgoblins in onyx and diamonds, mermaids in aquamarine and sapphires.

Courtiers and civil servants were walking about briskly, their footfalls completely silent on the Chinese carpet. The Duke strode diagonally across the room, with everyone melting out of his way. Ralph hurried to keep up.

Double doors opened into a library of more manageable proportions. Then Ralph was through into a snug oak-panelled study with a log fire burning eagerly in the grate, and frost-rimed French windows presenting a view out into a quadrangle planted with ancient chestnuts. Five young children were scampering about on the lawn, dressed against the cold in colourful coats, woollen bobble hats, and leather gloves. They were flinging sticks and stones into the big old trees, trying to bring down the prickly burrs.

King Alastair II stood before the fire, rubbing his hands together in front of the flames. A bulky camel-hair coat was slung over a high-backed leather chair. Damp footprints on the carpet indicated he'd just come in from the quadrangle.

'Good afternoon, Mr Hiltch.'

Ralph stood to attention. 'Your Majesty.' Despite the fact he was in the presence of his King, Ralph could only stare at the oil painting on the wall. It was the *Mona Lisa*. Which was impossible. The French state of Govcentral would never let that out of the Paris arcology. Yet would the King of Kulu really have a copy on his wall?

'I reviewed the report which came with you, Mr Hiltch,' the King said. 'You've had a busy few weeks. I can see why my sister valued your counsel so highly. One can only hope all my ESA officers are so efficient and resourceful. You are a credit to your agency.'

'Thank you, Your Majesty.'

The Duke shut the study door as the King used an iron poker to stir the fire.

'Do stand easy, Mr Hiltch,' Alastair said. He put the poker back in the rack and eased himself down in one of the leather chairs which ringed the hearth rug. 'Those are my grand-children out there.' A finger flicked towards the quadrangle. 'Got them here at the palace while their father's off with the Royal Navy. Safest place for them. Nice to have them, too. That lad in the blue coat, being pushed round by his sister, that's Edward; your future king, in fact. Although I doubt you'll be around when he ascends the throne. God willing, it won't be for another century at least.'

'I hope so, Your Majesty.'

'Course you do. Sit down, Mr Hiltch. Thought we'd have an informal session to start with. Gather you've something contro-versial to propose. This way if it is too controversial, well ... it'll simply never have happened. Can't have the monarch exposed to controversy, now can we?'

'Certainly not,' the Duke said with a modest smile as he sat between the two of them.

An arbitrator, or a buffer? Ralph mused. He sat in the remaining leather chair, mildly relieved that he wasn't having to look up at the two men any more. Both of them were half a head taller than him (another Saldana trait). 'I understand, Your Majesty.'

'Good man. So what hot little mess is dear Kirsten dropping in my lap this time?'

Ralph upped the strength of his tranquillizer program, and started to explain.

When he finished, the King rose silently and dropped a couple of logs on the fire. Flames cast a shivering amber light across his face. At seventy-two he had acquired a dignity that went far beyond the superficial physical countenance provided by his genes; experience had visibly enriched his personality. The King, Ralph decided, had become what kings were supposed to be, someone you could trust. All of which made his troubled expression more worrying than it would be on any normal politician.

'Opinion?' Alastair asked the Duke, still gazing at the fire.

'It would appear to be an even-handed dilemma, sir. Mr Hiltch's proposal is tenable, certainly. Reports we have received show the Edenists are more than holding their own against the possessed; only a handful of habitats have been penetrated, and I believe all the insurgents were rounded up effectively. And using bitek constructs as front-line troops would reduce our losses to a minimum if you committed an army to liberating Mortonridge. Politically, though, Princess Kirsten is quite right; such a course of action will mean a complete reversal of a foreign policy which has stood for over four hundred years, and was actually instigated by Richard Saldana himself.'

'For good reasons at the time,' the King ruminated. 'Those damn atheists with their $He_3$ monopoly have so much power over us Adamists. Richard knew being free of their helping hand was the only road to true independence. It might have been ruinously expensive to build our own cloudscoops in those days, but by God look at what we've achieved with that freedom. And now Mr Hiltch here is asking me to become dependent on those same Edenists.'

'I'm suggesting an alliance, Your Majesty,' Ralph said. 'Nothing more. A mutually advantageous military alliance in time of war. And they will benefit from the liberation of Mortonridge just as much as we will.'

'Really?' the King asked; he sounded sceptical.

'Yes, Your Majesty. It has to be done. We have to prove to ourselves, and every other planet in the Confederation, that the possessed can be driven back into the beyond. I expect such a war might well take decades; and who would ever agree to start it if they didn't know victory was possible? Whatever the outcome, we have to try.'

'There has to be another solution,' said the King, almost inaudibly. 'Something easier, a more final way of ridding ourselves of this threat. Our navy scientists are working on it, of course. One can only pray for progress, though so far it has been depressingly elusive.' He sighed loudly. 'But one cannot act on wishes. At least not in my position. I have to respond to facts. And the fact is that two million of my subjects have been possessed. Subjects I am sworn before God to defend. So something must be done, and you, Mr Hiltch, have offered me the only valid proposal to date. Even if it is only related to the physical.'

'Your Majesty?'

'One isn't criticizing. But I have to consider what the Ekelund woman said to you. Even if we win and banish them all from living bodies, we are still going to wind up joining them eventually. Any thoughts on how to solve that little conundrum, Mr Hiltch?'

'No, Your Majesty.'

'No. Of course not. Forgive me, I'm being dreadfully unfair. But never fear; you're not alone on that one, I'm sure. We can dump it off on the Bishop for the moment, though ultimately it will have to be addressed. And addressed thoroughly. The prospect of spending eternity in purgatory is not one I naturally welcome. Yet at the moment it seems one to which we are all destined.' The King smiled wanly, glancing out of the French windows at his grandchildren. 'I can only hope Our Lord will eventually show us some of His mercy. But for now, the problem at hand: liberating Mortonridge, and the political fallout from asking the Edenists to help. Simon?'

The Duke deliberated on his answer. 'As you say, sir, the situation today is hardly the same as when Richard Saldana founded Kulu. However, four centuries of discord has entrenched attitudes, particularly that of the average middle-Kulu citizen. The Edenists aren't seen as demons, but neither are they regarded with any geniality. Of course, as Mr Hiltch has said, in times of war allies are to be found in the most unusual places. I don't believe an alliance in these circumstances would damage the monarchy. Certainly a successful conclusion to a liberation campaign would prove your decision to be justified. That is assuming the Edenists will agree to come to our aid.'

'They'll help, Simon. We might snub them for the benefit of the public; but they are not stupid. Nor are they dishonourable. Once they see I am making a genuine appeal they will respond.'

'The Edenists, yes. But the Lord of Ruin? I find it hard to believe the Princess suggested we ask her for the DNA sequence of Tranquillity's serjeants, no matter how good they would be as soldiers.'

The King gave a dry laugh. 'Oh, come now, Simon, where's your sense of charity? You of all people should know how accommodating Ione is when it comes to the really important problems faced by the Confederation. She's proved her worth in the political arena with the Mzu woman; and she is family, after all. I'd say it was far less galling for me to request her help than it is making any approach to the Edenists.'

'Yes, sir,' the Duke said heavily.

Alastair tutted in bogus dismay. 'Never mind, Simon, it's your job to be paranoid on my behalf.' He turned his gaze back to Ralph Hiltch. 'My decision, though. As always.'

Ralph tried to appear resolute. It was quite extraordinary to witness the use of power at such a level. The thoughts and words formulated in this room would affect literally hundreds of worlds, maybe even a fate greater than that. He wanted to scream at the King to say yes, that it was bloody obvious what he should decide. Yes. Yes. YES. Say it, damn you.

'I'll give my authority to initiate the project,' Alastair said. 'That's all for now. We will ask the Edenists if they can assist us. Lord Mountjoy can sound out their ambassador to the court, that's what he's good at. While you, Mr Hiltch, will go directly to the Admiralty and begin a detailed tactical analysis of the Mortonridge liberation. Find out if it really is possible. Once I've seen how these two principal factors mature, the proposal will be brought before the Privy Council for consideration.'

'Thank you, Your Majesty.'

'It's what I'm here for, Ralph.' His stately smile became artful. 'I think you can cancel your tranquillizer program now.'

\*

'Oh, Lord, now what's he up to?' Staff Nurse Jansen Kovak asked as soon as he accessed the ceiling sensors in Gerald Skibbow's room. All the medical facility's inmates were reviewed on a regular basis; with troublesome ones like Skibbow a check was scheduled every twenty minutes.

The room had modest furnishings. A single bed and a deep settee had puffed themselves up out of the floor, ready to retract if an inmate tried to injure himself against them. All the services were voice-activated. There was nothing to grab hold of, no loose items lying around which could weight a fist.

Gerald was kneeling beside the bed as if in prayer, his hands hidden from the ceiling sensors. Jansen Kovak switched cameras, using one incorporated in the floor, giving him a mouse-eye view.

The image showed Gerald was holding a spoon with both

**551**

hands. Slowly and relentlessly he was flexing it, bending the stem just below the scoop. It was made of a strong composite; but Jansen Kovak could see the tiny white stress fractures crinkling the surface. Another minute and the spoon would break, leaving Gerald with a long spike which although not exactly sharp could certainly harm anyone caught on the end of a lunge.

'Dr Dobbs,' Jansen datavised. 'I think we have a problem with Skibbow.'

'What now?' Dobbs asked. He had only just caught up on his appointments; yesterday's episode with Skibbow in the lounge had wrecked his schedule. Skibbow had been recovering well up until that point. Bad luck his daughter had turned up again – certainly the timing, anyway. Although the fact she was still alive could eventually be worked into his therapy, give him a long-term achievement goal.

'He's smuggled a spoon out of the lounge. I think he's going to use it as a weapon.'

'Oh, great, just what I need.' Riley Dobbs hurriedly finished with the patient he was counselling, and accessed the facility's AI. He retrieved the interpretation routine which could make sense of Skibbow's unique thought patterns, and opened a channel to the debrief nanonics. This kind of grubby mental spying was totally unethical; but then he had discarded the constraints of the General Medical Council all those years ago when he came to work for the Royal Navy. Besides, if he was to effect any kind of cure on Skibbow, he needed to know exactly what kind of demons were driving the man. Resorting to a weapon, however feeble, seemed extreme for Skibbow.

The images were slow to form in Dobbs's mind. Gerald's thoughts were in turmoil, fast-paced, flicking between present reality and extrapolated fantasies.

Dobbs saw the pale blue wall of the bedroom, fringed with the redness which came from squinted eyes. Feeling the spoon in his hands, the friction heat building up in its stem. Tired arm muscles as they pushed and pulled at the stubborn composite. 'And they'll regret getting in my way. God will they ever.'

Image shift to – a corridor. Kovak screaming in pain as he sinks to his knees, the spoon handle jutting out of his white tunic. Blood spreading over his chest, drops splattering on the floor. Dr Dobbs was already sprawled face down on the corridor floor, his whole body soaked in glistening blood. 'Which is less than he deserves.' Kovak emitted a last gurgle and died. Gerald pulled the Weapon of Vengeance from his chest and carried on down the corridor. Sanatorium staff peered fearfully out of doors, only to shrink back when they saw who was coming. As well they might; they knew who had Right and Justice on his side.

Shifting back – to the bedroom, where the damn spoon still hadn't snapped. His breath was becoming ragged now. But still he persevered. A soundless mutter of: 'Come on. Please!'

Shifting – to the journey through Guyana, a confused blur of rock walls. Not actually knowing the geometry of the asteroid; but he'd find a way. Asteroid spaceports were always attached up at the axis. There would be trains, lifts . . .

Back – when the spoon finally snaps, making his taut arms judder. 'Now I can begin. I'm coming for you, darling. Daddy's coming.'

To – fly through space. Stars streaking into blue-white lightning outside the ship's hull as he rushes to the strange distant habitat. And there's Marie waiting for him at the end of the voyage, adrift in space, clad in those fragile white swirls of gauze, luscious hair blown back by the breeze. Where she says to him: 'They'll tell you that you shouldn't have come, Daddy.'

'Oh, but I should,' he replies. 'You need me, darling. I know what you're going through. I can drive the demon out. You'll feel nothing as I push you into zero-tau.' And so he lays her

**553**

gently down into the plastic coffin and closes the lid. Blackness eclipses her, then ends to show her face smiling up at him, twinkling tears of gratitude slipping from her eyes.

Which is why he's standing up now, slipping the jagged spoon handle into his sleeve. Calm. Take deep calming breaths now. There's the door. Daddy's coming to rescue you, baby. He is.

Riley Dobbs cancelled the interpretation routine. 'Oh, bugger.' He ordered Gerald's debrief nanonics to induce somnolence within the fevered brain.

Nerves and courage fired up, Gerald was reaching for the bedroom door when a wave of tiredness slapped into him with an almost physical force. He sagged, swaying on his feet as muscles became too exhausted to carry him. The bed loomed before him, and he was toppling towards it as darkness and silence poured into the room.

'Jansen,' Riley Dobbs datavised. 'Get in there and take the spoon away, and any other implements you can find. Then I want him transferred to a condition three regime; twenty-four-hour observation, and a softcare environment. He's going to be a dangerous pain until we can wean him off this new obsession.'

*

Kiera Salter had dispatched fifteen hellhawks to the Oshanko sector of the Confederation to seed dissent into the communication nets of the Imperium's worlds and asteroid settlements. That was three days ago.

Now, Rubra observed eleven wormhole termini blink open to disgorge the survivors. Two bloated warplanes and a sinister featureless black aeromissile shape kept a loose formation with eight Olympian-sized harpies who flapped their way back towards Valisk's docking-ledges with lethargic, defeated wing strokes.

**I see the Emperor's navy has lived up to its top gun reputation,** Rubra remarked in a tone of high spirits. **Just how is troop morale**

coming along these days? That's the eighth of Kiera's little jaunts in which your hellhawks have taken a beating from unfriendly natives. Any grumblings of rebellion at the new regime yet? A few discreet suggestions that priorities ought to be altered?

Screw you, Dariat retorted. He was sitting on a small riverbank of crumbling earth, dark water flowing swiftly below his dangling feet. Occasionally he caught sight of a big garpike slithering past on the way to its spawning ground upriver. Five hundred metres away in the other direction the water tipped over a shallow cliff to splatter down into the circumfluous saltwater reservoir ringing the endcap. Out here among the habitat's low rolling hills the eight separate xenoc grasses waged a continual war for primacy. As they all came to seed at different times of the year none ever won an outright victory. Right now it was a salmon-pink Tallok-aboriginal variety which was flourishing, its slender corkscrew blades tangling in a dense blanket of dry candyfloss which matted the ground. Back along the cylindrical habitat, Dariat could see the broad rosy bracelet fading to emerald around the midsection where the starscraper lobbies were; and in turn that rich terrestrial vegetation eventually petered away into the ochre scrub desert which occupied the far end. The bands of colour were as striking as they were regular; it was as if someone had sprayed them on while Valisk turned on a lathe.

Of course, you wouldn't actually know much about what's happening to the subjects of Kiera's politburo dictatorship these days, Rubra continued pleasantly. You being a loner now. Did you know dear old Bonney was shouting for you yesterday? I whisked one of the non-possessed away from her clutches, put him on a tube carriage, and shot him off to one of my safe areas. I don't think she was very happy about it. Your name came up several times.

Sarcasm is a pitiful form of wit.

Absolutely, my boy. So you won't be letting it get to you, will you?

No.

Mind you, Kiera is having some success. The second hellhawk full of kids arrived this morning; looking for that bright new world she promised in her recording. Two dozen of them; the youngest was only nine. Would you like to see what was done to them so they could be possessed? I have all the memories, nobody tried to block my perception from that ceremony.

Shut up.

Oh dear, is that a twang of conscience I detect?

As you well know, I don't care what happens to the morons who get suckered here. All I'm interested in is how badly I'm going to fuck you up.

I understand. But then I know you better than Kiera does. It's a pity you don't understand me.

Wrong. I know you completely.

You don't, my boy. You don't know what I'm holding secret. Anastasia would thank me for what I'm doing, the protection I'm extending you.

Dariat growled, sinking his head into his hands. He had chosen this spot for the seclusion it offered from Kiera's merry band of maniacs. He wanted somewhere quiet to meditate. Free from distractions, he could try and formulate a mental pattern which had the ability to penetrate the neural strata. But he wasn't free of distractions, he never could be. For Rubra would never tire of playing his game; the insinuations, the doubts, the dark hints.

During the last thirty years, Dariat thought he'd perfected patience to an inhuman degree. But now he was finding that a different kind of patience was required. Despite a herculean resolution he was beginning to question if Rubra really did have any secrets. It was stupid, of course, because Rubra was bluffing, running an elaborate disinformation campaign. However, if Anastasia did have some secret, some legacy, the only entity who would know was Rubra.

Yet if it did exist, why hadn't Rubra used it already? Both of them knew this was a struggle to the bitterest of ends.

Anastasia could never have done anything which would

make him betray himself. Not sweet Anastasia, who had always warned him about Anstid. Her Lord Thoale made sure she knew the consequences of every action. Anastasia understood destiny. Why did I never listen to her?

**Anastasia left nothing for me,** he said.

**Oh yeah? In that case, I'll do a deal with you, Dariat.**

**Not interested.**

**You should be. I'm asking you to join me.**

**What?**

**Join me, here in the neural strata. Transfer yourself over like a dying Edenist. We can become a duality.**

**You have got to be fucking joking.**

**No. I have been considering this for some time. Our current situation is not going to end well, not for either of us. Both of us are at odds with Kiera; that will never change. But together we could beat her easily, purge the habitat of her cronies. You can rule Valisk yet.**

**You used to control a multistellar industrial empire, Rubra, now look what you're reduced to. You're pathetic, Rubra. Contemptible. And the best thing is, you know it.**

Rubra shifted his principal focus from the linen-suited young man, withdrawing to contemplate a general perception of the habitat. Bonney Lewin was missing again. That damn woman was getting too good at foxing his observation routines. He automatically expanded the secondary routines surrounding and protecting the remaining non-possessed. She'd show up near one of them soon enough.

**He didn't agree,** Rubra said to the Kohistan Consensus.

**That is unfortunate. Salter is expending a great deal of effort to collect her Deadnight followers.**

**Her what?**

**Deadnight is the name which her subversive recording has acquired. Unfortunately a great many young Adamists are finding it seductive.**

**Don't I know it. You should see what she does to them when they**

get here. Those hellhawks should never have been allowed to collect them.

*There is little we can do. We do not have the capability to shadow every hellhawk flight.*

Pity.

*Yes. The hellhawks are causing us some concern. So far they have not been used in an aggressor role. If they were deployed in combat with Valisk's armament resources behind them, they would pose a formidable problem.*

So you keep telling me. Don't say you've finally come to a decision?

*We have. With your permission we would like to remove their threat potential.*

Do as you would be done by, and do it first. Well, well, you've finally started thinking like me. There's hope for all of you yet. OK, go ahead.

*Thank you, Rubra. We know this must be difficult for you.*

Just make damn sure you don't miss. Some of my industrial stations are very close to my shell.

Rubra had always maintained an above-average number of strategic-defence platforms around Valisk. Given his semi-paranoid nature it was inevitable he should want to make local space as secure as possible. Forty-five weapons platforms covered a bubble of space fifty-thousand kilometres in diameter with the habitat and its comprehensive parade of industrial stations at the centre. They were complemented by two hundred sensor satellites, sweeping both inward and outward. No one had ever attempted an act of aggression within Valisk's sphere of interest – a remarkable achievement considering the kind of ships which frequented the spaceport.

Magellanic Itg had manufactured the network, developing indigenous designs and fabricating all the components itself. It was a policy which had earned the company a healthy quantity of export orders. It also enabled Rubra to install his personality as the network's executive. He certainly wasn't about to trust any of his woefully ineffectual descendants with his own defence.

That arrangement had come to an abrupt end with the emergence of the possessed. His control over the network was via affinity with bitek management processors that were integrated into every platform's command circuitry. He hadn't even realized he'd lost control of the platforms until he'd attempted to interdict the hellhawks when they first revealed themselves. Afterwards, he'd worked out that somebody – that little shit Dariat, no doubt – had subverted his SD governor thought routines long enough to load powerdown orders into every platform.

With the power off, there was no way of regaining control through the bitek processors. Every platform would have to be reactivated manually. Which was exactly what Kiera had done. Spacecraft had rendezvoused with the platforms and taken out Rubra's bitek management processors, replacing them with electronic processors and new fire-authority codes.

A new SD command centre was established in the counter-rotating spaceport, outside Rubra's influence. He couldn't strike at that like he could the starscrapers. The possessed technicians who reactivated the network were convinced they had made it independent, a system which only Kiera and her newly installed codes could control.

What neither they nor Dariat quite appreciated was the number of physical interfaces between the neural strata and Valisk's communication net. The tube trains and the starscraper lifts were the most obvious examples, but every mechanical and electronic utility system had a similar junction, a small processor nodule which converted fibre-optic pulses to nerve impulses and vice versa. And Magellanic Itg not only built Valisk's communication net, it also supplied ninety per cent of the counter-rotating spaceport's electronics. A fact which even fewer people were aware of was that every company processor had a backdoor access function hardwired in, to which Rubra alone had the key.

Within seconds of the possessed establishing their new SD command channels he was in the system. A delicious irony, he felt, a ghost in the ghosts' machinery. The devious interface circuits he'd established to gain entry couldn't support anything like the data traffic necessary to give him full control of the platforms once more, but he could certainly do unto others what they'd done to him.

On the ready signal from the Kohistan Consensus, Rubra immediately sent a squall of orders out to the SD platforms. Command codes were wiped and replaced, safety limiters were taken off-line, fusion generator management programs were reformatted.

In the commandeered spaceport management office used to run the habitat's SD network, every single alarm tripped at once. The whole room was flooded with red light from AV projectors and holoscreens. Then the power went off, plunging the crew into darkness.

'What the holy fuck is happening?' the recently appointed network captain shouted. A bright candle flame ignited at the tip of his index finger, revealing equally confounded faces all around him. He reached for his communication block to call Kiera Salter, dreading what she would say. But his hand never made it.

'Oh shit, *look*,' someone cried.

Severe white light began to flood in through the office's single port.

In forty-five fusion generators the plasma jet had become unstable, perturbed by rogue manipulations in the magnetic-confinement field. Burnthrough occurred, plasma striking the confinement-chamber walls, vaporizing the material, which increased the pressure a thousandfold. Forty-five fusion generators ruptured almost simultaneously, tearing apart the SD platforms in a burst of five million degree shrapnel and irradiated gas.

**You're clear**, Rubra told the waiting fleet.

Three hundred wormhole termini opened, englobing the habitat. Voidhawks shot out. Two hundred were designated to eradicate the industrial stations, depriving Kiera of their enormous armament manufacturing base. The bitek starships immediately swooped round onto their assault vectors. Kinetic missiles flashed out of their launch-cradles, closing on the stations at sixteen gees. Each salvo was aimed so that the impact blast would kick the debris shower away from the habitat, minimizing the possibility of collision damage to the polyp shell.

The remaining hundred voidhawks were given suppression duties. Flying in ten-strong formations they broadcast affinity warnings to the thoroughly disconcerted hellhawks sitting on the docking-ledges, ordering them to remain where they were. Sharp ribbons of ruby-red light from targeting lasers made the ledge polyp shimmer like black ice speared by an early morning sun. Refracted beams twisted around the alien shapes perched on the pedestals as the voidhawks strove to match their discordant vectors with the habitat's rotation.

Closer to the habitat, cyclones of shiny debris were churning out from the ruined industrial stations. Victorious voidhawks dived and spun above the metallic constellations, racing away ahead of the perilous wavefront of sharp high-velocity slivers. The hellhawks sat on their pedestals, observing the carnage with mute impotence.

**Exemplary shooting**, Rubra told the Kohistan Consensus. **Just remember, when this is all over, you're paying Magellanic ltg's compensation claim.**

Three hundred wormhole interstices opened. The voidhawks vanished in an extraordinary display of synchronization. Elapsed time of the attack was ninety-three seconds.

Even in the heat of passion Kiera Salter could sense nearby minds starting to flare in alarm. She tried to dislodge Stanyon from her back and rise to her feet. When he resisted, tightening his grip, she simply smacked an energistic bolt into his chest. He grunted, the impact shoving him backwards.

'What the fuck are you playing at, bitch?' he growled.

'Be silent.' She stood up, her wishes banishing the soreness and rising bruises. Sweat vanished, her hair returned to a neatly brushed mane. A simple, scarlet summer dress materialized over her skin.

On the other side of the endcap the hellhawks were seething with resentment and anger. Beyond them was a haze of life which gave off a scent of icy determination. And Rubra, the ever-present mental background whisper, was radiating satisfaction. 'Damn it!'

Her desktop processor block started shrilling. Data scrawled over its screen. A strategic-defence alert, and red systems-failure symbols were flashing all over the network schematic.

The high-pitched sound started to cut off intermittently, and the screen blanked out. The more she glared at the block, the worse the glitches became.

'What's happening?' Erdal Kilcady asked. Her other bedroom fancy. A gormless twenty-year-old who as far as she could determine had only one use.

'We're being attacked, you fool,' she snapped. 'It's those fucking Edenists.' Shit, and her schemes had been progressing beautifully up until now. The idiot kids believed her recording; they were starting to arrive. Another couple of months would have seen the habitat population rise to a decent level.

Now this. The constant hellhawk flights must have frightened the Edenists into taking action.

The burn mark on Stanyon's chest healed over. Clothes sprang up to conceal his body. 'We'd better get along to the SD control centre and kick some butt,' he said.

Kiera hesitated. The SD centre was in the counter-rotating spaceport. She was certain the habitat itself would be safe from attack. Rubra would never allow that, but the spaceport might be a legitimate target.

Just as she took a reluctant first step towards the door the black Bakelite telephone on her bedside table started to ring. The primitive communication instrument was one which worked almost infallibly in the energistic environment exuded by the possessed. She picked it up, and pressed the handset to her ear. 'Yes?'

'This is Rubra.'

Kiera stiffened. She'd thought this room was outside of his surveillance. Exactly how many of their systems were exposed to him? 'What do you want?'

'I want nothing. I'm simply delivering a warning. The voidhawks from Kohistan are currently eliminating the habitat's industrial production capability. There will be no more combat wasps to arm the hellhawks. We don't like the threat they present. Do not attempt to resupply from other sources or it will go hard on you.'

'You can do nothing to us,' she said, squeezing some swagger into her voice.

'Wrong. The Edenists respect life, which is why no hellhawks were destroyed this time. However, I can guarantee you the next voidhawk strike will not be so generous. I have eliminated the habitat's SD platforms so that in future it won't even be as difficult for them as today's strike. You and the hellhawks will sit out the rest of the conflict here. Is that understood?' The phone went dead.

Kiera stood still, her whitened fingers tightening round the handset. Little chips of Bakelite sprinkled down onto the carpet. 'Find Dariat,' she told Stanyon. 'I don't care where he is, find him and bring him to me. Now!'

\*

Chaumort asteroid in the Châlons star system. Not a settlement which attracted many starships; it had little foreign exchange to purchase their cargoes of exotica, and few opportunities for export charters. Attendant industrial stations were old, lacking investment, their products a generation out of date; their poor sales adding to the downward cycle of the asteroid's economy. Ten per cent of the adult population was unemployed, making qualified workers Chaumort's largest (and irreplaceable) export. The fault lay in its leadership of fifteen years ago, which had been far too quick to claim independence from the founding company. Decline had been a steady constant from that carnival day onwards. Even as a refuge for undesirables, it was close to the bottom of the list.

But it was French-ethnic, and it allowed certain starships to dock despite the Confederation's quarantine edict. Life could have been worse, André Duchamp told himself, though admittedly not by much. He sat out at a table in what qualified as a pavement café, watching what there was of the worldlet passing by. The sheer rock cliff of the biosphere cavern wall rose vertically behind him, riddled with windows and balconies for its first hundred metres. Out in the cavern the usual yellow-green fields and orchards of spindly trees glimmered under the motley light of the solar-tubes which studded the axis gantry.

The view was acceptable, the wine passable, his situation if not tolerable then stable – for a couple of days. André took another sip and tried to relax. It was a pity his initial thought of selling combat wasps (post-Lalonde, fifteen were still languishing in the starship's launch-tubes) to Chaumort's government had come to nothing. The Treasury didn't have the funds, and three interplanetary ships had already been placed on defence contract retainers. Not that the money would have been much use here; the two local service companies which operated the spaceport had a very limited stock of spare parts. Of course, it would have come in useful to pay his crew. Madeleine and Desmond hadn't actually said anything, but

André knew the mood well enough. And that bloody *anglo* Erick, as soon as they'd docked Madeleine had hauled him off to the local hospital. Well, those thieving doctors would have to wait.

He couldn't actually remember a time when there had been so few options available. In fact he was down to one slender possibility now. He'd found that out as soon as he'd arrived (this time checking the spaceport's register for ships he knew). An unusually large number of starships were docked. All of them arriving recently. In other words, after the quarantine had been ratified and instituted by the Châlons system congress.

The Confederation Assembly had demonstrated a laudable goal in trying to stop the spread of the possessed, no one disputed that. However, the new colony planets and smaller asteroids suffered disproportionately from the lack of scheduled flights; they needed imported high-technology products to maintain their economies. Asteroid settlements like Chaumort, whose financial situation was none too strong to start with, were going to shoulder a heavy cost for the crisis not of their making. What most of these backwater communities shared was their remoteness; so if say an essential cargo were to arrive on a starship, then it was not inconceivable that said starship would be given docking permission. The local system congress wouldn't know, and therefore wouldn't be able to prevent it. That cargo could then (for a modest charter fee) be distributed to help other small disadvantaged communities by interplanetary ships, whose movements were not subject to any Confederation proscription.

Chaumort was quietly establishing itself as an important node in a whole new market. The kind of market where starships such as the *Villeneuve's Revenge* were uniquely qualified to exploit.

André had spoken to several people in the bars frequented by space industry crews and local merchants, voicing his approval for this turn of events, expressing an interest in being able to help Chaumort and its people in these difficult times. In short, becoming known. It was a game of contacts, and André had been playing it for decades.

Which was why he was currently sitting at a table waiting for a man he'd never seen before to show up. A bunch of teenagers hurried past, one of the lads snatching a basket of bread rolls from the café's table. His comrades laughed and cheered his bravado, and then ran off before the patron discovered the theft. André no longer smiled at the reckless antics of youth. Adolescents were a carefree breed; it was a state to which he had long aspired, and which his chosen profession had singularly failed to deliver. It seemed altogether unfair that happiness should exist only at one end of life, and the wrong end at that. It should be something you came in to, not left further and further behind.

A flash of colour caught his eye. All the delinquents had tied red handkerchiefs round their ankles. What a stupid fashion.

'Captain Duchamp?'

André looked up to see a middle-aged Asian-ethnic man dressed in a smart black silk suit with flapping sleeves. The tone and the easy body posture indicated an experienced negotiator; too smooth for a lawyer, lacking the confidence of the truly wealthy. A middleman.

André tried not to smile too broadly. The bait had been swallowed. Now for the price.

\*

The medical nanonic around Erick's left leg split open from crotch to ankle, sounding as though someone was ripping strong fabric. Dr Steibel and the young female nurse slowly teased the package free.

'Looks fine,' Dr Steibel decided.

Madeleine grinned at Erick and pulled a disgusted face. The leg was coated in a thin layer of sticky fluid, residue of the package unknitting from his flesh. Below the goo his skin was swan-white, threaded with a complicated lacework of blue veins. Scars from the burns and vacuum ruptures were patches of thicker translucent skin.

Now the package covering his face and neck had been removed, Erick sucked in a startled breath as cool air gusted over the raw skin. His cheeks and forehead were still tingling from the same effect, and they'd been uncovered two hours ago.

He didn't bother looking at the exposed limb. Why bother? All it contained was memories.

'Give me nerve channel access, please,' Dr Steibel asked. He was looking into an AV pillar, disregarding Erick completely.

Erick complied, his neural nanonics opening a channel directly into his spinal cord. A series of instructions were datavised over, and his leg rose to the horizontal before flexing his foot about.

'OK.' The doctor nodded happily, still lost in the information the pillar was directing at him. 'Nerve junctions are fine, and the new tissue is thick enough. I'm not going to put the package back on, but I do want you to apply the moisturizing cream I'll prescribe. It's important the new skin doesn't dry out.'

'Yes, Doc,' Erick said meekly. 'What about . . . ?' He gestured at the packages enveloping his upper torso and right arm.

Dr Steibel flashed a quick smile, slightly concerned at his patient's listless nature. ''Fraid not. Your AT implants are integrating nicely, but the process isn't anywhere near complete yet.'

'I see.'

'I'll give you some refills for those support modules you're dragging round with you. These deep invasion packages you're using consume a lot of nutrients. Make sure the reserves don't get depleted.'

He picked up the support module which Madeleine had repaired, and glanced at the pair of them. 'I'd strongly advise

**567**

no further exposure to antagonistic environments for a while, as well. You can function at a reasonably normal level now, Erick, but only if you don't stress your metabolism. Do not ignore warnings from your metabolic monitor program. Nanonic packages are not to be regarded as some kind of infallible safety net.'

'Understood.'

'I take it you're not flying away for a while.'

'No. All starship flights are cancelled.'

'Good. I want you to keep out of free fall as much as possible, it's a dreadful medium for a body to heal in. Check in to a hotel in the high-gravity section while you're here.' He datavised a file over. 'That's the exercise regime for your legs. Stick to it, and I'll see you again in a week.'

'Thanks.'

Dr Steibel nodded benevolently at Madeleine as he left the treatment room. 'You can pay the receptionist on your way out.'

The nurse began to spray a soapy solution over Erick's legs, flushing away the mucus. He used a neural nanonic override to stop a flinch when she reached his genitals. Thank God they hadn't been badly injured, just superficial skin damage from the vacuum.

Madeleine gave him an anxious glance over the nurse's back. 'Have you got much cash in your card?' she datavised.

'About a hundred and fifty fuseodollars, that's all,' he datavised back. 'André hasn't transferred this month's salary over yet.'

'I've got a couple of hundred, and Desmond should have some left. I think we can pay.'

'Why should we? Where the hell is Duchamp? He should be paying for this. And my AT implants were only the first phase.'

'Busy with some cargo agent, so he claimed. Leave it with me, I'll find out how much we owe the hospital.'

Erick waited until she'd left, then datavised the hospital's net processor for the Confederation Navy Bureau. The net management computer informed him there was no such eddress. He swore silently, and accessed the computer's directory, loading a search order for any resident Confederation official. There wasn't one, not even a CAB inspector, too few ships used the spaceport to warrant the expense.

The net processor opened a channel to his neural nanonics. 'Report back to the ship, please, *mon enfant* Erick,' André datavised. 'I have won us a charter.'

If his neck hadn't been so stiff, Erick would have shaken his head in wonder. A charter! In the middle of a Confederation quarantine. Duchamp was utterly unbelievable. His trial would be the shortest formality on record.

Erick swung his legs off the examination table, ignoring the nurse's martyrdom as her spray hoses were dislodged. 'Sorry, duty calls,' he said. 'Now go and find me some trousers, I haven't got all day.'

*

The middleman's name was Iain Girardi. André envied him his temperament; nothing could throw him, no insult, no threat. His cool remained in place throughout the most heated of exchanges. It was just as well, André's patience had long since been exhausted by his ungrateful crew.

They were assembled in the day lounge of the *Villeneuve's Revenge*, the only place André considered secure enough to discuss Girardi's proposition. Madeleine and Desmond had their feet snagged by a stikpad on the decking, while Erick was hanging on to the central ladder, his medical support modules clipped on to the composite rungs. André floated at Iain Girardi's side, glowering at the three of them.

'You've got to be fucking joking!' Madeleine shouted. 'You've gone too far this time, Captain. Too bloody far. How can you even listen to this bastard's offer? God in heaven, after all we went through at Lalonde. After all Erick did. Look at this ship! They did that to it, to you.'

'That's not strictly accurate,' Iain Girardi said, his voice tactfully smooth and apologetic.

'Shut the fuck up!' she bawled. 'I don't need you to tell me what's been happening to us.'

'Madeleine, please,' André said. 'You are hysterical. No one is forcing you to take part. I will not hold you to your contract if that is your wish.'

'Damn right, it's my wish. And nowhere does it say in my crew contract that I fly for the possessed. You pay me my last two months in full, plus the Lalonde combat bonus you owe me, and I'm out of here.'

'If that is what you want.'

'You've got the money?'

'*Oui*. But of course. Not that it is any of your business.'

'Bastard. Why did you leave us to pay for Erick's treatment, then?'

'I am only a captain, I do not claim to perform miracles. My account has only just been credited. Naturally it is my pleasure to pay for dear Erick's treatment. It is a matter of honour for me.'

'Just been ...' Madeleine glanced from André to Iain Girardi then back again. Understanding brought outraged astonishment. 'You accepted a retainer from him?'

'*Oui*,' André snapped.

'Oh, Jesus.' The shock of his admission silenced her.

'You spoke about Lalonde,' Iain Girardi said. 'Did the Confederation Navy rush to your aid while you were there?'

'Do not speak about an event of which you know nothing,' Desmond growled.

'I know something about it. I've accessed Kelly Tirrel's report. Everybody has.'

'And we have all accessed Gus Remar's report from New

California. The possessed have conquered that world. By rights we ought to sign on with the Confederation Navy and help eradicate every one of them from this universe.'

'Eradicate them how? This is a dreadful calamity which has befallen the human race, both halves of it. Dropping nukes on millions of innocent people is not going to bring about a resolution. Sure, it was chaos at Lalonde, and I'm sorry you were hit with the worst of it. Those possessed were a disorganized terrified rabble, lashing out blindly to protect themselves from the mercenary army you carried. But the Organization is different. For a start we're proving that possessed and non-possessed can live together.'

'Yeah, while we're convenient,' Madeleine said. 'While you need us to run the technology and fly starships. After that it's going to be a different bloody story.'

'I can appreciate your bitterness, but you are wrong. Al Capone has taken the first steps to solving this terrible dilemma, he's proposing a joint research project to find a solution. All the Confederation Navy is doing is working on methods of blowing the possessed back into the beyond. I don't know about you, but I certainly don't want them to triumph.'

Desmond bunched his fist, one toe coming off the stikpad, ready to launch himself at the man. 'You traitorous little shit.'

'You're going to die,' Iain Girardi said remorselessly. 'You, me, everyone on board this ship, everyone in Chaumort. All of us die. It can't be helped, you can't reverse entropy. And when you die, you're going to spend eternity in the beyond. Unless something is done about it, unless you can find a living neuron structure which will host you. Now I ask again, do you want Al Capone's project to fail?'

'If all Capone is interested in is spreading happiness across the galaxy, why does he want to hire a combat-capable starship?' Madeleine asked.

'Protection in the form of deterrence. There are Organization representatives like me in dozens of asteroids looking to sign up combat-capable starships. The more we have in orbit above New California, the more difficult it will be for anyone to launch a strike force against it. The Confederation Navy is going to attack New California's strategic-defence network. Everyone knows that. The First Admiral has got the Assembly screaming at him for some kind of positive action. If he can crack the SD network open he's cleared the way for an invasion; have the marines round up all the bad guys and shove them into zero-tau.' Iain Girardi let out a heartfelt pained breath. 'Can you imagine the bloodshed that'll cause? You have seen first-hand how hard the possessed can fight when they're cornered. Imagine the conflict in your lower lounge multiplied by a billion. That's what it will be like.' He gave Erick a sympathetic glance. 'Is that what you want?'

'I'm not fighting for the possessed,' Madeleine muttered sullenly. She hated the way Iain Girardi could turn her words, make her doubt her convictions.

'Nobody is asking the *Villeneuve's Revenge* to fight,' Iain Girardi said earnestly. 'You are there for show, that's all. Perimeter defence patrol, where you're visible, a demonstration of numerical strength. Hardly an onerous duty. And you get paid full combat rates, with a guaranteed six-month contract; in addition to which I have a discretionary retainer fee to offer. Obviously for a prime ship like the *Villeneuve's Revenge* it will be a substantial one. You will be able to afford to have the worst of the damage repaired here at Chaumort, plus Erick can receive the best medical treatment available. I can even arrange for a brand-new spaceplane on very favourable terms; New California astroengineering companies make the best models.'

'You see?' André said. 'This is the kind of charter to be proud of. If the Organization is right we will have helped to secure the future of the entire human race. How can you object?'

'No, Captain,' Madeleine said. 'I'm not sharing the life-support capsules with the possessed. Not ever. Period.'

'Nobody is suggesting you do,' Girardi sounded shocked. 'Obviously we understand there is a lot of suspicion at the moment. The Organization is working hard at breaking down those old prejudicial barriers. But until more trust is built up, then obviously you will have your own crew and no one else. In a way, that's part of establishing trust. The Organization is prepared to accept an armed ship crewed by non-possessed orbiting the planet providing you are integrated into its SD command network.'

'Shit,' Madeleine hissed. 'Erick?'

He knew it was some kind of trap. And yet . . . it was hard to see how the possessed proposed to hijack the ship. This was one crew totally aware of the danger in letting even one of the bastards on board. Iain Girardi might have made a major mistake in approaching André.

The CNIS could undoubtedly use first-hand intelligence data on the disposition of ships around New California, which the *Villeneuve's Revenge* would be ideally placed to gather. And he could always jump the ship away when the data was collected, no matter what objections Duchamp raised. There were items stowed in his cabin which could overcome the rest of the crew.

Which just left personal factors. I don't want to go into the front line again.

'It's an important decision,' he muttered.

André gave him a puzzled look. Naturally he was pleased some of the (diabolically expensive) medical nanonic packages were off, but obviously the poor boy's brain still hadn't completely recovered from decompression. And Madeleine was asking him to decide. *Merde.* 'We know that, Erick. But I don't want you to worry. All I need to know is which of my crew is loyal enough to come with me. I have already decided to take my ship to New California.'

'What do you mean, loyal enough?' Madeleine asked hotly.

André held his hand up in a pleading gesture. 'What does Erick have to say, eh?'

'Will we be docking with anything in the New California system? Do you expect us to take on any extra crew, for example?'

'Of course not,' Girardi said. 'Fuel loading doesn't require anyone coming into the life-support capsules. And if the unlikely event does arise, then obviously you'll have a full veto authority over anyone in the airlock tube. Whatever precautions you want, you can have.'

'OK,' Erick said. 'I'll come with you, Captain.'

\*

'Yeah?'

. . .

'Fuck, I might have guessed, who else is going to call this time of night. Don't you people ever sleep?'

. . .

'Everybody wants favours. I don't do them any more. I'm not so cheap these days.'

. . .

'Yeah? So you go run and tell my comrades; what use will I be to you then?'

. . .

'Mother Mary! You've got to be ... Alkad Mzu? Shit, that's a name I didn't expect to hear ever again.'

. . .

'Here? In the Dorados? She wouldn't dare.'

. . .

'You're sure?'

. . .

'No, of course nobody's said anything. It's been months since the partisans even bothered having a meeting. We're all too busy doing charity work these days.'

'Mother Mary. You believe it, don't you? Ha! I bet you lot are all pissing yourselves. How do you like it for a change, arsehole? After all these years waiting, us poor old wanderers have gone and got us some real sharp teeth at last.'

...

'You think so? Maybe I just resigned from your agency. Don't forget what the issue is here. I was born on Garissa.'

...

'Fuck you, don't you fucking dare say that to me, you bastard. You even so much as look at my family, you little shit, and I'll fire that fucking Alchemist at your home planet myself.'

...

'Yeah, yeah. Right, it's a sorry universe.'

...

'I'll think about it. I'm not promising you anything. Like I said, there are issues here. I have to talk to some people.'

*

The party was being thrown on the eve of the fleet's departure. It had taken over the entire ballroom of the Monterey Hilton, and then spread out to occupy a few suites on the level below. The food was real food; Al had been insistent about that, drunk possessed could never keep the illusion of delicacies going. So the Organization had run search programs through their memory cores and hauled in anyone who listed their occupation as chef, possessed or non-possessed, skill was all that counted, not its century of origin. The effort was rewarded in a formal eight-course banquet, whose raw materials had been ferried up to the asteroid in seven spaceplane flights, and resulted in Leroy Octavius handing out eleven hundred hours' worth of energistic credits to farmers and wholesalers.

After the meal Al stood on the top table and said: 'We're gonna have a bigger and better ball when you guys come back safe, and you got Al Capone's word on that.'

**575**

There was a burst of tumultuous applause, which only ended when the band struck up. Leroy and Busch had auditioned over a hundred musicians, whittling the numbers down to an eight-strong jazz band. Some of them were even genuine twenties musicians, or so they claimed. They certainly sounded and looked the part when they got up on stage to play. Nearly three hundred people were out on the dance floor jiving away to the old honky-tonk tunes which Al loved best.

Al himself led the way, hurling a laughing Jezzibella about with all the energy and panache he'd picked up at the Broadway Casino back in the old days. The rest of the guests soon picked up the rhythm and the moves. Men, Al insisted, wore their tuxes, or if they were serving in the fleet a military uniform; while the women were free to wear their own choice of ball gowns, providing the styles and fabrics weren't anything too modern. With the decorations of gossamer drapes and giant swans created out of fresh-cut flowers the overall effect was of a grand Viennese ball, but a damn sight more fun.

Possessed and non-possessed rubbed shoulders harmoniously. Wine flowed, laughter shook the windows, some couples snuck off to be by themselves, a few fights broke out. By any standard it was a roaring success.

Which was why at half-past two in the morning Jezzibella was puzzled to find Al all by himself in one of the lower-level suites, leaning against its huge window, tie undone, brandy glass in one hand. Outside, star-points of light moved busily through space as the last elements of the fleet manoeuvred into their jump formation.

'What's the matter, baby?' Jezzibella asked quietly. Soft arms circled round him. Her head came to rest on his shoulder.

'We'll lose the ships.'

'Bound to lose some, Al honey. Can't make an omelette without breaking eggs.'

'No, I mean, they're gonna be in action light-years away. What's to make them do as I say?'

'Command structure, Al. The fleet is a mini-version of the Organization. The soldiers at the bottom do what the lieutenants at the top tell them. It's worked in warships for centuries. When you're in battle you automatically follow orders.'

'So what if that piece of shit Luigi takes it into his head to dump me and set up all on his own in Arnstadt?'

'He won't. Luigi is loyal.'

'Right.' He chewed at a knuckle, thankful he was facing away from her.

'This bothers you, doesn't it?'

'Yeah. It's a goddam problem, OK? That fleet is one fuck of a lot of power to hand over to one guy.'

'Send two others.'

'What?'

'Put a triumvirate in charge.'

'What?'

'Easy, lover; if there's three of them in charge of the fleet, then each of them is going to be busting his balls to prove how loyal he is in front of the others. And let's face it, the fleet's only going to be away for a week at the most. It takes a hell of a lot longer than that to get a conspiracy up and running successfully. Besides, ninety per cent of those soldiers are loyal to you. You've given them everything Al; a life, a purpose. Don't sell yourself short, what you've done with these people is a miracle, and they know it. They cheer your name. Not Luigi's, not Mickey, not Emmet. You, Al.'

'Yeah.' He nodded, drawing his confidence back together. What she said made a lot of sense. It always did.

Al looked at her in the drizzle of starlight. The personas were combined tonight, a feminine athlete. Her dress of sparkling pearl-coloured silk hinted at rather than revealed her figure. The allure she exerted was terrifying. Al had been hard put to control his temper that evening as he picked up the swell of hunger and lust from the other men on the dance floor every time she glided past.

'Goddam,' he whispered. 'I ain't never done anything to deserve a reward as big as you.'

'I think you have,' she murmured back. Their noses touched again, arms moving gently into an embrace. 'I've got a present for you, Al. We've been saving it up as a treat, and I think the time's right.'

His hold around her tightened. 'I got the only treat I need.'

'Flatterer.'

They kissed.

'It can wait till the morning,' Jezzibella decided.

*

The lift opened onto a section of Monterey Al didn't recognize. An unembellished rock corridor with an air duct and power cables clinging to the ceiling. The gravity was about half-strength. He pulled a face at that, free fall was the one thing about this century he really hated. Jez kept trying to get him to make out with her in one of the axis hotel cubicles, but he wouldn't. Just thinking about it made his stomach churn.

'Where are we?' he asked.

Jezzibella grinned. She was the knowing and carefree girl-about-town persona this morning, wearing a snow-white ship-suit which stretched around her like rubber. 'The docking-ledges. They've not been used much since you took over. Not until now.'

Al let her lead him along the corridor and into an obser-vation lounge. Emmet Mordden, Patricia Mangano, and Mickey Pileggi were waiting in front of the window wall. All of them smiled proudly, an emotion reflected in their thought currents. Al played along with the game as Jez tugged him over to the window.

'We captured this mother on one of the asteroids a couple of weeks back,' Mickey said. 'Well, its captain was possessed, actually. Then we had to persuade the soul to transfer down the affinity link. Jezzibella said you'd like it.'

'What is this shit, Mickey?'

'It's our present to you, Al baby,' Jezzibella said. 'Your flagship.' She smiled eagerly, and gestured at the window.

Al walked over and looked out. Buck Rogers' very own rocket ship was sitting on the rock shelf below him. A beautiful scarlet torpedo with yellow fins sprouting from the sides, and a cluster of copper rocket engine tubes at the rear.

'That's for me?' he asked in wonder.

\*

The rocket ship's interior was fully in keeping with its external appearance, the pinnacle of 1930s engineering and décor. Al felt more at home than any time since he had emerged from the beyond. This was his furniture, his styling. A little chunk of his home era.

'Thank you,' he said to Jezzibella.

She kissed him on the tip of his nose, and they linked arms.

'It's a blackhawk,' she explained. 'The possessing soul is called Cameron Leung; so you be nice to him, Al. I said you'd find him a human body when the universe calms down a little.'

'Sure.'

An iron spiral stair led up to the promenade deck. Al and Jezzibella settled back on a plump couch of green leather where they could see out of the long curving windows and along the rocket's nose-cone. He put his fedora down on a cane table at the side of the couch and draped an arm round her shoulders. Prince of the city again, full time.

'Can you hear me, Cameron?' Jezzibella inquired.

'Yes,' came the reply from a silver Tannoy grille set in the wall.

'We'd like to see the fleet before it leaves. Take us over, please.'

Al winced, grabbing hold of the couch's flared arms. More fucking spaceflight! But there was none of the rush of acceleration he'd braced himself for. All that happened was the view changed. One minute the spherical silver-white grid of Monterey's spaceport was rotating slowly in front of them, the next it was sliding to one side and racing past overhead.

'Hey, I can't feel nothing,' Al whooped. 'No acceleration, none of that free fall crap. Hot damn, now this is the way to travel.'

'Yes.' Jezzibella clicked her fingers smartly, and a small boy hurried forward. He was dressed in a white high-collar steward's uniform, and his hair had been parted in the centre and slicked back with cream. 'A bottle of Norfolk Tears, I think,' she told him. 'This is definitely celebration time. I think we might make a toast, too. Make sure you chill the glasses.'

'Yes, miss,' he piped.

Al frowned after him. 'Kinda young to be doing that, ain't he?'

'It's Webster Pryor,' she said sotto voce. 'Sweet boy.'

'Kingsley's son?'

'Yes. Thought it best we keep him close to hand the whole time. Just in case.'

'I see. Sure.'

'You're right about the ship, Al. Bitek is the only way to travel. My media company was always too miserly to let me have one for touring. Blackhawks make the best warships, too.'

'Yeah? So how many have we got?'

'Three, counting this one. And we only got those because their captains were cold-footed when we snatched the asteroids.'

'Pity.'

'Yes. But we're hoping to get luckier this time.'

Al grinned out of the window as the luscious crescent of New California swung into view, and settled back to enjoy the ride.

\*

Cameron Leung accelerated away from Monterey at two gees, curving down towards the planet a hundred and ten thousand kilometres below. Far ahead of the blackhawk's sharp emerald aerospike, the Organization's fleet was sliding along its five thousand kilometre orbit, a chain of starships spaced a precise two kilometres apart. Sunlight bounced and sparkled off foil-coated machinery as they emerged from the penumbra; a silver necklace slowly threading itself around the entire planet.

It had taken two days for all of them to fly down from their assembly points at the orbiting asteroids, jockeying into their jump formation under the direction of Emmet Mordden and Luigi Balsmao. The *Salvatore* was the lead vessel, an ex-New California Navy battlecruiser, and now Luigi Balsmao's command ship.

Two million kilometres away, hanging over New California's south pole, the voidhawk *Galega* had observed the fleet gathering. The swarm of stealthed spy globes it'd showered around the planet had monitored the starships manoeuvring into their designated slot in the chain, intercepting their command communications. Given the two-degree inclination of the fleet's orbital track, *Galega* and its captain, Aralia, had calculated the theoretical number of jump coordinates. Fifty-two stars were possible targets.

The Yosemite Consensus had dispatched voidhawks to warn the relevant governments, all of whom had been extremely alarmed by the scale of the potential threat. Other than that there was little the Edenists could do. Attack was not a viable option. The Organization fleet was under the shield of New California's SD network, and its own offensive potential was equally formidable. If it was to be broken up, then it would have to be intercepted by a fleet of at least equal size. But even if the Confederation Navy did assemble a task force large enough, the admirals were then faced with the problem of where to deploy it: a fifty-two to one chance of getting the right system.

*Galega* watched Capone's scarlet and lemon blackhawk race down from Monterey to hold station fifty kilometres away from the *Salvatore*. A spy globe fell between the two. The Intelligence-gathering staff in the voidhawk's crew toroid heard Capone say: 'How's it going, Luigi?'

'OK, boss. The formation's holding true. They'll all hit the jump coordinate.'

'Goddam, Luigi, you should see what you guys look like from here. It's a powerhouse of a sight. I tell you, I wouldn't want to wake up in the morning and find you in my sky. Those jerkhead Krauts are gonna crap themselves.'

'Count on it, Al.'

'OK, Luigi, take it away, it's all yours. You and Patricia and Dwight take care now, you hear? And Jez says good luck. Go get 'em.'

'Thank the little lady for us, boss. And don't worry none, we'll deliver for you. Expect some real good news a week from now.'

The *Salvatore*'s thermo-dump panels and sensor clusters began to retract down into their jump recesses, taking a long while to do so. Several times they seemed to stick or judder. The second ship in the formation began to configure itself for a jump, then the third.

For another minute nothing happened, then the *Salvatore* vanished inside its event horizon.

Aralia and *Galega* were instinctively aware of its spacial location, and with that the jump coordinate alignment could have only one solution. **It's Arnstadt**, Aralia told the Yosemite Consensus. **They're heading for Arnstadt.**

**Thank you, Aralia,** Consensus replied. **We will dispatch a voidhawk to alert the Arnstadt government. It will take the Organization fleet at least two days to reach the system. The local navy forces will have some time to prepare.**

**Enough?**

**Possibly. It depends on the Organization's actual goal.**

When Aralia reviewed the images from the spy globes, another twelve ships had already followed the *Salvatore*. A further seven hundred and forty were gliding inexorably toward the Arnstadt jump coordinate.

\*

'No, Gerald,' Jansen Kovak said. The tone was one which parents reserved for particularly troublesome children. His hand tightened around Gerald's upper arm.

He and another supervisory nurse had walked Gerald to the sanatorium's lounge, where he was supposed to eat his lunch. Once they reached the door Gerald glanced furtively down the corridor, muscles tensing beneath his baggy sweatshirt.

Kovak was familiar with the signs. Gerald could drop into a frenzy at the slightest provocation these days, anything from an innocuous phrase to the sight of a long corridor which he assumed led directly to the outside world. When it happened he'd lash out at his supervisors and anyone else who happened to be in the way, before making yet another run for it. The concept of codelocked doors seemed utterly beyond him.

The corner of Gerald's lip spasmed at the stern warning, and he allowed himself to be led into the lounge. The first thing he did was glance at the bar to see if the holoscreen was on. It had been removed altogether (much to the annoyance of other inmates). Dr Dobbs wasn't going to risk triggering another incident of that magnitude.

Privately, Jansen Kovak considered that they were wasting their time in trying to rehabilitate Skibbow. The man had obviously tipped right over the edge and was now free-falling into his own personal inferno. He should be shipped off to a long-term care institution for treatment and maybe some selective memory erasure. But Dr Dobbs insisted the psychosis could be treated here; and Gerald was technically an ESA internee, which brought its own complications. It was a bad duty.

The lounge fell silent when the three of them came in. Not that there were many people using it; four or five inmates and a dozen staff. Gerald responded to the attention with a frightened stare, checking faces. He frowned in puzzlement as one woman with oriental features and vivid copper hair gave him a sympathetic half-smile.

Jansen quickly steered him over to a settee halfway between the window and the bar and sat him down. 'What would you like to eat, Gerald?'

'Um . . . I'll have the same as you.'

'I'll get you a salad,' Kovak said, and turned to go over to the bar. Which was his first mistake.

Something smashed into the middle of his back, knocking him forwards completely off balance. He went crashing painfully onto the ground. Auto-balance and unarmed-combat programs went primary, interfacing to roll him smoothly to one side. He regained his feet in a fluid motion.

Gerald and the other nurse were locked together, each trying to throw the other to the ground. Jansen selected an option from the neural nanonics menu. His feet took a pace and a half forwards, and his weight shifted. One arm came round in a fast arc. The blow caught Gerald on his shoulder, which toppled him sideways. Before he could compensate, the back of his legs came into contact with Jansen's outstretched leg. He tripped, the weight of the other supervisory nurse quickening his fall.

Gerald yelled in pain as he landed on his elbow, only to be smothered below the bulk of the other nurse. When he raised his head the lounge door was five metres away. So close!

'Let me go,' he begged. 'She's my daughter. I have to save her.'

'Shut up, you prize pillock,' Jansen grunted.

'Now that's not nice.'

Jansen spun round to see the redheaded woman standing behind him. 'Er . . . I. Yes.' Shame was making his face became uncomfortably warm. It also seemed to be enervating his neural nanonics display. 'I'm sorry, it was unprofessional. He's just so annoying.'

'You should try being married to him for twenty years.'

Jansen's face registered polite incomprehension. The woman wasn't an inmate. She was wearing a smart blue dress, civilian clothing. But he didn't remember her on the staff.

She smiled briskly, grabbed hold of the front of his tunic, and threw him six metres clean through the air. Jansen's scream was more of shock than of pain. Until he hit the ground. That impact was pure agony, and his neural nanonics had shut down, allowing every volt of pain to flow cleanly through his nerves.

The other nurse who was still wrapped round Gerald managed to get out one dull grunt of surprise before the woman hit him. Her fist shattered his jaw, sending a spurt of blood splashing across Gerald's hair.

By that time one of the other sanatorium staff in the lounge had enough presence of mind to datavise an alarm code at the room's net processor. Sirens started wailing. A grid of metal bars started to slide up out of the floor, sealing off the open balcony doors.

Three burly nurses were closing on the red-haired woman as Gerald blinked up at her in amazement. She winked at him and raised an arm high, finger pointing to the ceiling. A bracelet of white fire ignited round her wrist.

'Shit,' the leader of the three nurses yelped. He nearly pitched over as he tried desperately to reverse his headlong rush.

'It's a fucking possessed!'

'Back! Get back!'

'Where the hell did she come from?'

'Go for it, babe,' one of the inmates roared jubilantly.

A rosette of white fire exploded from her hand, dissolving into a hundred tiny spheres almost as soon as it appeared. They smashed into the ceiling and walls and furniture. Sparks cascaded down as small plumes of black smoke squirted out. Flames began to take hold. Fire alarms added their clamour to the initial alert. Then the lights went out and the alarms were silenced.

'Come on, Gerald,' the woman said. She pulled him to his feet.

'No,' he squeaked in terror. 'You're one of them. Let me go, please. I can't be one of you again. I can't take that again. Please, my daughter.'

'Shut up, and get a move on. We're going to find Marie.'

Gerald gaped at her. 'What do you know of her?'

'That she needs you, very badly. Now come on!'

'You know?' he snivelled. 'How can you know?'

'Come on.' She tugged at him as she started towards the lounge door. It was as if the grapple arm of a heavy-load cargo mechanoid had attached itself to him.

The steward raised his head above the bar to see what was happening. Various inmates and staff had dived for cover behind the furniture. The terrifying possessed woman was striding purposefully for the door, hauling a cowering Skibbow along. He datavised a codelock order at the door, then opened an emergency channel to the net processor. It didn't respond. His hand curled round the nervejam stick, ready to—

'Hey, you!' called the woman.

A streamer of white fire smacked straight into his forehead.

'Naughty,' she said grimly.

Gerald gibbered quietly as the steward slumped forwards, smoke rising from the shallow crater in his temple. 'Oh dear God, what are you?'

'Don't blow it for me now, Gerald.' She stood in front of the door. The room's air rushed past her, ruffling her long copper tresses. Then the air flow reversed, turning to a howling hurricane with a solid core. It smashed into the door, buckling the reinforced composite.

She stepped though the gap, pulling Gerald after her. 'Now we run,' she told him happily.

As the sanatorium was operated by the Royal Navy the guards were armed. It didn't make any difference, they weren't front-line combat troops. Whenever one of them got near to Gerald and the woman she would use her white fire to devastating effect. The asteroid's internal security centre could trace her position purely because of the wave of destruction she generated around herself. All electronics and power circuits were ruptured by flares of white fire, doors were simply ripped apart, environmental ducts were battered and split, mechanoids reduced to slag. She did it automatically, a defensive manoeuvre burning clean any conceivable threat in front of her. Crude but effective.

The asteroid went to an immediate status two defence alert. Royal Marines were rushed from their barracks to the sanatorium.

But as with all asteroid settlements, everything was packed close together, and made as compact as possible. It took the woman and Gerald ninety seconds to get from the lounge to the sanatorium's nearest entrance. Sensors and cameras in the public hall caught her emerging from the splintered door. Terrified pedestrians sprinted from the vicious tendrils of white fire she unleashed; it was almost as though she was using them as whips to drive people away from her. Then the images vanished as she hammered at the net processors and sensors.

The Royal Marine commander coordinating the emergency at least had the presence of mind to shut down the lifts around the hall. If she wanted out, she'd have to walk. And when she did, she'd run smack into the marines now deploying in a pincer movement around her.

Both squads were edging cautiously down the public hall, hurrying civilians out of the way. They approached the sanatorium's wrecked entrance from opposite directions, chemical-projectile rifles held ready, electronic-warfare blocks alert for any sign of the distortion pattern given off by a possessed. When they came into view of each other they froze, covering the length of the hall with their rifles. No one was left between them.

The squad captain of one side shouldered his weapon. 'Where the fuck did she go?'

*

'I knew they'd stop the lifts,' the redhead said in satisfaction. 'Standard tactics for dealing with the possessed is to block all nearby transport systems to prevent us from spreading. Bloody good job they were on the ball today.'

Gerald agreed, but didn't say anything. He was concentrating on the rungs in front of his face, not daring to look down.

The possessed woman might have smashed open all the doors in the medical facility, but once they were out in the hall she had stood in front of the lift doors and made a parting motion with her hands. The lift doors had obeyed, sliding open silently. After that they had started to climb down the ladder set in the wall of the shaft. There wasn't much light to see where he was putting his hands and feet, just some sort of bluish radiance coming from the woman above him. Gerald didn't want to see how she was making it.

It was cold in the shaft, the air tasting both wet and metallic. And silent, too, the darkness above and below swallowing all sounds. Every minute or so he could just make out another door in the shaft wall; the buzz of conversation and tiny slivers of light oozing round the seals.

'Careful,' she said. 'You're near the bottom now. Ten more rungs.'

The light increased, and he risked a glance down. A metal grid slicked with condensation glinted dully at the foot of the ladder. Gerald stood on it, shivering slightly and rubbing his arms. Mechanical clunks started to rumble down from above.

The possessed woman jumped nimbly past the last two rungs and gave him a enthusiastic smile. 'Stand still,' she said, and put her hands on either side of his head, spreading her fingers over his ears.

Gerald quivered at her touch. Her hands were starting to glow. This was it. The start of the pain. Soon he would hear the demented whispers emerging from the beyond, and one of them would pour into his body again. All hope would die then. I might as well refuse, and let her torture kill me. Better that than . . .

She took her hands away, their internal glimmer fading away. 'I think that should do it. I've broken down the debrief nanonics. The doctors and police would only use you to see where we were and what we were doing, then they'd send you to sleep.'

'What?' He started to probe his skull with cautious fingers. It seemed intact. 'Is that all you did?'

'Yes. Not so bad, was it?' She beckoned. 'There's a hatch here that leads to the maintenance tunnels. It's only got a mechanical lock, so we won't trigger any processors.'

'Then what?' he asked bleakly.

'Why, we get you off Guyana and on your way to Valisk to find Marie, of course. What did you think, Gerald?' She grasped the handle on the metre-high hatch, and shoved it upwards. The hatch swung open, revealing only more darkness behind.

Gerald felt like crying. His head was all funny, hot and light, which made it very hard for him to think. 'Why? Why are you doing this? Are you just playing with me?'

'Of course I'm not playing, Gerald. I want Marie back to normal more than anything. She's all we have left now. You know that. You saw the homestead.'

He sank to his knees, looking up at her flat-featured face and immaculate hair, trying desperately to understand. 'But why? Who are you to want this?'

'Oh, dearest Gerald, I'm sorry. This is Pou Mok's body. It

**589**

takes up far to much concentration to maintain my own appearance, especially with what I was doing up there.'

Gerald watched numbly as the copper hair darkened and the skin of her face began to flow into new features. No, not new. Old. So very, very old. 'Loren,' he gasped.

# 15

After five centuries of astounding technological endeavour and determined economic sacrifice by the Lunar nation, Mars, the God of War, had finally been pacified. The hostile red gleam which had so dominated Earth's night skies for millennia was extinguished. Now the planet had an atmosphere, complete with vast swirls of white and grey clouds; blooms of vegetation were expanding across the deserts, patches of sepia and dark green staining the tracts of rust-red soil. To an approaching starship it seemed, at first, almost identical to any other terracompatible planet to be found within the Confederation's boundaries. Disparities only became apparent when the extent of the remaining deserts was revealed, accounting for three-fifths of the surface; and there was a definite sparsity of free water. Although there were thousands of individual crater lakes, Mars had only one major body of water, the Lowell Sea, a gently meandering ribbon which wrapped itself round the equator. Given the scale involved it appeared as though a wide river was flowing constantly around the planet. Closer inspection showed that circumnavigation would be impossible. The Lowell Sea had formed as water collected in the hundreds of large asteroid-impact craters which pocked the planet's equator in an almost straight line.

Population, too, was one of the planet's quirks; a phenomenon which was also visible from orbit, provided you knew what to look for. Anyone searching the nightside for the usual sprawling iridescent patches of light which marked the kind of vigorous human cities normally present after five centuries of colonization would be disappointed; only six major urban areas had sprung up so far. Towns and villages were also present amid the rolling steppes; but in total the number of people living on the surface didn't exceed three million. Phobos and Deimos were heavily industrialized, providing homes for a further half-million workers and their families. They at least followed a standard development pattern.

Apart from stage one colony planets in their formative years, Mars had the smallest human population of any world in the Confederation. However, that was where comparisons ended. The Martian technoeconomy was highly developed, providing its citizens with a reasonable standard of living, though nothing like the socioeconomic index enjoyed by Edenists or the Kulu Kingdom.

One other aspect of mature Confederation societies missing from Mars was a strategic-defence network. The two asteroid moons were defended, of course, both of them were important SII centres with spaceports boasting a high level of starship traffic. But the planet was left open; there was nothing of any value on its surface to threaten or hold hostage or steal. The trillions of fuseodollars poured into the terraforming project were dispersed evenly throughout the new biosphere. Oxygen and geneered plants were not the kind of targets favoured by pirates. Mars was the most expensive single project ever undertaken by the human race, yet its intrinsic value was effectively zero. Its real value was as the focus of aspirations for a whole nation of exiles, to whom it had become the modern promised land.

None of this was readily apparent to Louise, Genevieve, and Fletcher as they observed the planet growing in the lounge's holoscreen. The difference from Norfolk was apparent (Genevieve said Mars looked worn out rather than brand new) but none of them knew how to interpret what they were seeing in geotechnical terms. All they cared about was the lack of glowing red cloud.

'Can you tell if there are any possessed down there?' Louise asked.

'Alas no, lady Louise. The planet lies far outside my second sight. All I can feel is the shape of this doughty ship. We could be alone in the universe, for all the perception I have.'

'Don't say that,' Genevieve said. 'We've come here to get away from horrible things.'

'And away from them we certainly are, little one.'

Genevieve spared a moment from watching the holoscreen to grin at him. The voyage had calmed her considerably. With very little to do for any of the passengers during the flight, the novelty of bouncing around in free fall had soon worn off, and she had swiftly learned how to access the flight computer. Furay had brought some old voice-interactive tutorial programs on-line for her, and she had been engrossed ever since with AV recordings of children's stories, educational files, and games. Genevieve adored the games, spending hours in her cabin, surrounded by a holographic haze, fighting off fantasy creatures, or exploring mythological landscapes, even piloting ships to the galactic core.

Louise and Fletcher had used the same programs to devour history encyclopedia files, reviewing the major events which had shaped human history since the mid-eighteen-hundreds. Thanks to Norfolk's restrictive information policies, most of it was as new to her as it was to him. The more she reviewed, the more ignorant she felt. Several times she had been obliged to ask Furay if a particular incident was genuinely true, the information in the *Far Realm*'s memory was so different from that which she'd been taught. Invariably, the answer was yes; though he always tempered it by saying that no one viewed anything in the same context. 'Interpretation though the filters of ideology has always been one of our race's curses.'

Even that cushion didn't make her any happier. The teachers at school hadn't exactly been lying to her, censorship was hardly practical given the number of starship crews who visited at midsummer; but they'd certainly sheltered her from an awful lot of unsavoury truths.

Louise ordered the flight computer to show a display of their approach vector. The holoscreen image shifted, showing them the view from the forward sensor clusters overlaid with orange and green graphics. Phobos was falling towards the horizon, a darkened star embedded at the heart of a large scintillating wreath of industrial stations. They watched it expand as the *Far Realm* matched orbits at a tenth of a gee. Inhabited for over five centuries, it had a weighty history. No other settled asteroid/moon of such a size orbited so close to an inhabited planet. But its proximity made it ideal to provide raw material for the early stages of the terraforming project. Since those days it had reverted primarily to being an SII manufacturing centre and fleet port. The spin imparted to provide gravity within its two biosphere caverns had flung off the last of the surface dust centuries ago. Naked grey-brown rock was all that faced the stars now; large areas had a marbled finish where mining teams had removed protrusions to enhance the symmetry, and both ends had been sheered flat. With its cylindrical shape and vast encrustations of machinery capping each end its genealogy appeared to be midway between ordinary asteroid settlements and an Edenist habitat.

Captain Layia slotted the starship into the spaceport approach vector which traffic control assigned her, then spent a further twenty minutes datavising the SII fleet operations office, explaining why their scheduled return flight from Norfolk had been delayed.

'You didn't mention our passengers, then?' Tilia said when the exchange was over.

'Life is complicated enough right now,' Layia retorted. 'Explaining to the operations office why they're on board, and the financial circumstances, isn't going to make a good entry on anyone's record. Agreed?'

She received a round of apathetic acknowledgements from the other crew-members.

'None of them have passports,' Furay commented. 'That might be a problem when we dock.'

'We could get them to register as refugees,' Endron said. 'Under Confederation law the government is obliged to accept them.'

'The first thing they would have to do is explain how they got here,' Layia said. 'Come on, think. We've got to offload them somehow, and without any comebacks.'

'They're not listed on our manifest,' Tilia said. 'So no one's going to be looking for them. And if the port Inspectorate does decide to give us a customs check we can just move them round the life-support capsules to keep them out of sight of their team. Once our port clearance comes though we can sneak them into the asteroid without any difficulty.'

'Then what?'

'They don't want to stay here,' Furay said. 'They just want to find a ship which will take them to Tranquillity.'

'You heard traffic control,' Layia said. 'All civil flights have ended. The only reason our Defence Command didn't swarm all over us is because we still have a Confederation Navy flight authorization.'

'There might not be any flights to Tranquillity from Mars, but if anyone in this system is going there, it'll be from Earth. Getting them to the O'Neill Halo shouldn't be too difficult, there are still plenty of inter-orbit flights, and Louise has enough money. She was talking about chartering the entire ship, remember?'

'That could work,' Layia said. 'And if we can acquire some passports for them first, then nobody in the Halo will ask how they got to Mars. From that distance, everything at this end will appear perfectly legitimate.'

'I might know someone who can fix passports for them,' Tilia volunteered.

Layia snorted. 'Who doesn't?'

'He's not cheap.'

'Not our problem. All right, we'll try it. Endron, tell them the way it is. And make certain they cooperate.'

*

The *Far Realm* settled lightly on a docking cradle. Umbilical hoses snaked up to jack into the lower hull. Genevieve watched the operation on the lounge's holoscreen, fascinated by all the automated machinery.

'We'd best not tell Daddy we came here, had we?' she said without looking up.

'Why not?' Louise asked. She was surprised, it was the first time Gen had mentioned either of their parents since they'd left Cricklade. *But then, neither have I.*

'Mars has a Communist government. The computer said so. Daddy hates them.'

'I think you'll find the Martians are a bit different to the people Daddy's always moaning about. In any case, he'll be glad we came here.'

'Why?'

'Because he'll be glad we got away. The route we travel isn't really important, just that we get safely to our destination.'

'Oh. I suppose you're right.' Her face became solemn for a moment. 'What do you think he's doing right now? Will that nasty knight man be making him do things he doesn't want to?'

'Daddy isn't doing anything for anyone. He's just stuck inside his own head, that's all. It's the same as being in prison. He'll be thinking a lot, he's perfectly free to do that.'

'Really?' Genevieve looked at Fletcher for confirmation.

'Indeed, little one.'

'I suppose that's not so bad, then.'

'I know Daddy,' Louise said. 'He'll be spending the whole time worrying about us. I wish there was some way we could tell him we're all right.'

'We can when it's all over. And Mummy, too. It is going to be all over, isn't it, Louise?'

'Yes. It's going to end; someday, somehow. And when we get to Tranquillity, we can stop running and do whatever we can to help.'

'Good.' She smiled primly at Fletcher. 'I don't want you to go, though.'

'Thank you, little one.' He sounded ill at ease.

Endron came gliding through the ceiling hatch, head first. He twisted neatly round the ladder, and touched his feet to a stikpad beside the holoscreen.

Fletcher kept very still. Now she knew what to look for, Louise could see how hard he was concentrating. It had taken several days of intense practice for him to learn how to minimize the disruption his energistic effect exerted on nearby electronics. In the end it had paid off; it had been fifty hours since the last time any of the *Far Realm*'s crew had come flashing through the life-support capsule searching for an elusive glitch in the starship's systems.

'We made it home,' Endron started off blithely. 'But there is a small problem with your legal status. Mainly the fact you don't have a passport between you.'

Louise deliberately avoided glancing at Fletcher. 'Is there a Norfolk Embassy here? They may be able to issue us with some documentation.'

'There will be a legal office to handle Norfolk's diplomatic affairs, but no actual embassy.'

'I see.'

'But you have a solution,' Fletcher said. 'That is why you are here, is it not?'

'We have a proposal,' Endron said edgily. 'There is an

**597**

unorthodox method of acquiring a passport for the three of you; it's expensive but has the advantage of not involving the authorities.'

'Is it illegal?' Louise asked.

'What we have here is this: the rest of the crew and I have rather a lot of Norfolk Tears on board which we can sell to our friends, so we really don't want to draw too much official attention to ourselves right now.'

'Your government wouldn't send us back, would they?' Genevieve asked in alarm.

'No. Nothing like that. It's just that this way would be easier all round.'

'We'll get our passports the way you suggested,' Louise said hurriedly. She felt like hugging the genial payload officer; it was exactly what she had been nerving herself up to ask him.

*

Moyo didn't exactly sleep, there were too many pressures being applied against his mind for that, but he did rest for several hours each night. Eben Pavitt's body wasn't in the best condition, nor was he in the first flush of youth. Of course, Moyo could use his energistic power to enhance any physical attribute such as strength or agility, but as he stopped concentrating he could feel the enervation biting into his stolen organs. Tiredness became an all-over ache.

After a couple of days he had learned the limits pretty well, and took care to respect them. He was lucky to have obtained this body, it would be the direst of follies to lose it by negligence. Another might not be so easy to come by. The Confederation was larger now than when he had been alive, but the numbers of souls back in the beyond was also prodigious. There would never be enough bodies to go around.

The slim blades of light which dawn drove through the loose bamboo blind were an unusually intense crimson. They shifted the bedroom from a familiar collection of grisaille outlines to a strong two-tone portrait of red and impenetrable black. Despite the macabre perspective, Moyo was imbued by a feeling of simple contentment.

Stephanie stirred on the mattress next to him, then sat up frowning. 'Your thoughts look indecently happy to me all of a sudden. What is it?'

'I'm not sure.' He got up and padded over to the window. His fingers pressed down the slim tubes of bamboo. 'Ah. Come and look.'

The sky above Exnall was clotting with wisps of cloud, slowly condensing into a broad disc. And they glowed a muted red. Dawn's corona was rising up to blend with them. Only in the west was there a dark crescent of night, and that was slowly being squeezed to extinction.

'The stars will never rise here again,' Moyo said happily.

There was a power thrumming through the land now, one which he could feel himself responding to, contributing a little of himself towards maintaining the whole. A vast conjunction of will, something he suspected was akin to an Edenist Consensus. Annette Ekelund had won, converting the peninsula to a land where the dead walked free once more. Now two million of them were marrying their energistic power at a subconscious level, bringing about the overriding desire which also dwelt within the latent mind.

Several shadows flittered across the bottom of the garden where the overhanging boughs granted immunity against the spreading red light. The horticultural mechanoids had long since cranked to a halt, though not before wrecking most of the flower beds and small shrubs. When he opened his mind to the dark area he found several nervous bundles of thought. It was the kids left over from the possession again. He hadn't been alone in letting one go. Unfortunately the Royal Marines had executed a fast, efficient retreat.

**599**

'Damn. They're back for the food again.'

Stephanie sighed. 'They've had all of the sachets in the kitchen. What else can we give them?'

'There are some chickens in one of the houses opposite; we could always cook them and leave the meat out.'

'Poor little mites. They must be frozen sleeping out there. Could you go and fetch some chickens, please? I'll get the range cooker hot, we'll cook them in the oven.'

'Why bother? We can just turn them straight into roasts.'

'I'm not convinced about that; and I don't want them to catch anything from food that hasn't been cooked properly.'

'If you just zap the chickens they'll be cooked properly.'

'Don't argue. Just go and get them.' She turned him round, and gave him a push. 'They'll need plucking, as well.'

'All right, I'm going.' He laughed as his clothes formed around him. Argument would be pointless. It was one of the things he enjoyed about her, she didn't have many opinions, but those she did have ... 'By the way, what are we going to do for food? There's none left in the bungalow, and people have been helping themselves to the stocks in the stores on Maingreen.' After some experimenting he'd found his energistic power wasn't quite as omnipotent as he'd first thought. He could cloak anything in an illusion, and if the wish was maintained for long enough the matter underneath would eventually flow into the shape and texture which he was visualizing. But the human body needed to ingest specific proteins and vitamins. A lump of wood that looked, tasted, and smelt like salmon was still just a lump of wood when it was in his stomach. Even with real food he had to be sensible. Once he'd actually thrown up after transforming sachets of bread into chocolate gâteau – he hadn't removed the foil wrapping first.

'That's something we can start thinking about later,' she said. 'If necessary we can move out of the town and set ourselves up in one of the farms.'

He didn't like the idea, he'd lived all his life in cities, but didn't say anything out loud.

Someone knocked on the front door before he got to it. Pat Staite, their neighbour, was standing outside dressed in elaborate blue and grey striped baseball gear.

'We're looking for people to help make up the teams,' he said hopefully.

'It's a little early in the day for me.'

'Absolutely. Terribly sorry. If you're free this afternoon . . . ?'

'Then I'll come along, certainly.'

Pat was one of Exnall's growing band of sports enthusiasts who seemed intent on playing every ball game ever devised by the human race. They had already taken over two of the town's parks.

'Thanks,' Staite said, not registering the irony in Moyo's voice or thoughts. 'There's an ex-Brit living in the street now. He said he'd teach us how to play cricket.'

'Fabulous.'

'Is there anything you used to play?'

'Strip poker. Now if you'll excuse me, I have to go and catch some chickens for my breakfast.'

The chickens had broken out of their coop, but they were still pecking and scratching round the garden. They were a geneered variety, plump, with rusty yellow feathers. They were also remarkably quick.

Moyo's first couple of attempts at catching one ended with him falling flat on his stomach. When he climbed to his feet the second time, the whole flock was squawking in alarm and vanishing fast into the shrubbery. He glared at them, banishing the mud caking his trousers and shirt, and pointed a finger. The tiny bolt of white fire caught the chicken at the base of its neck, sending out a cloud of singed feathers and quite a lot of blood. It must have looked ludicrous, he knew, using his power for this. But if it got the job done . . .

When he'd finished blasting every chicken he could see, he

walked over to the nearest corpse. And it started running away from him, head flopping down its chest on the end of a flaccid strip of skin. He stared at it disbelievingly, he'd always thought that was an urban myth. Then another of the corpses sprinted for freedom. Moyo pushed his sleeves up and summoned a larger bolt of white fire.

There were voices drifting through the open kitchen door when he returned to the bungalow. He didn't even have to use his perception to know who was in there with her.

Under Stephanie's control the range cooker was radiating waves of heat. Several children were warming themselves around it, holding big mugs of tea. They all stopped talking as he walked in.

Stephanie's bashful welcoming smile was transformed to an astonished blink as she saw the smoking remnants of chicken he was carrying. A couple of the children started giggling.

'Into the lounge, everyone,' Stephanie ordered the kids. 'Go on, I'll see what I can salvage.'

Once they had left he asked: 'What the hell are you doing?'

'Looking after them, of course. Shannon says she hasn't had a meal ever since the possessed arrived.'

'But you can't. Suppose—'

'Suppose what? The *police* come?'

He dropped the burnt carcasses onto the tile worktop next to the range cooker. 'Sorry.'

'We're responsible only to ourselves now. There are no laws, no courts, no rights and wrongs. Only what feels good. That's what this new life is for, isn't it? Indulgence.'

'I don't know. It might be.'

She leant against him, arms encircling his waist. 'Look at it selfishly. What else have you got to do today?'

'And there I was thinking I was the one who'd adjusted best to this.'

'You did, at first. I just needed time to catch up.'

He peered through the door at the children. There were

eight of them bouncing around on the lounge furniture, none over twelve or thirteen. 'I'm not used to children.'

'Nor chickens, by the look of things. But you managed to bring them back in the end, didn't you?'

'Are you sure you want to do this? I mean, how long do you want to look after them for? What's going to happen when they grow up? Do they hit sixteen and get possessed? That's an awful prospect.'

'That won't happen. We'll take this world out of the reach of the beyond. We're the first and the last possessed. This kind of situation won't arise again. And in any case, I wasn't proposing to bring them up in Exnall.'

'Where then?'

'We'll take them up to the end of Mortonridge and turn them over to their own kind.'

'You're kidding me.' A pointless statement; he could sense the determination in her thoughts.

'Don't tell me you want to stay in Exnall for all of eternity?'

'No. But the first few weeks would be fine.'

'To travel is to experience. I won't force you, Moyo, if you want to stay here and learn how to play cricket that's OK by me.'

'I surrender.' He laughed, and kissed her firmly. 'They won't be able to walk, not all that way. We'll need some sort of bus or truck. I'd better scout round and see what Ekelund left us.'

*

It was the eighth time Syrinx had walked to Wing-Tsit Chong's odd house on the side of the lake. For some of these meetings it would be just the two of them sitting and talking, on other occasions they would be joined by therapists and Athene and Sinon and Ruben for what amounted to a joint session. But today it was only the pair of them.

As ever, Wing-Tsit Chong was waiting in his wheelchair on

the veranda, a tartan rug tucked round his legs. **Greetings, my dear Syrinx. How are you today?**

She bowed slightly in the oriental tradition, a mannerism she had taken up after the second session. **They took the nanonic packages off my feet this morning. I could barely walk, the skin was so tender.**

**I hope you did not chastise the medical team for this minor discomfort.**

**No.** She sighed. **They have done wonders with me. I'm grateful. And the pain will soon be gone.**

Wing-Tsit Chong smiled thinly. **Exactly the answer you should give. If I were a suspicious old man . . .**

**Sorry. But I really have accepted the physical discomfort as transitory.**

**How fortunate, the last chain unshackled.**

**Yes.**

**You will be free to roam the stars again. And if you were to fall into their clutches once more?**

She shivered, giving him a censorious glance as she leant on the veranda rail. **I don't think I'm cured enough to want to think about that.**

**Of course.**

**All right, if you really want to know, I doubt I'll venture out of *Oenone*'s crew toroid quite so readily now. Certainly not while the possessed are still loose in the universe. Is that wrong for someone of my situation? Have I failed?**

**Answer yourself.**

**I still have some nightmares.**

**I know. Though not as many; which we all know is a good sign of progress. What other symptoms persist?**

**I want to fly again. But . . . it's difficult to convince myself to do it. I suppose the uncertainty frightens me. I could meet them again.**

**The uncertainty or the unknown?**

**You're so fond of splitting hairs.**

**Indulge an old man.**

Definitely the uncertainty. The unknown used to fascinate me. I loved exploring new planets, seeing wonders.

Your pardon, Syrinx, but you have never done these things.

What? She turned from the railing to stare at him, finding only that annoying, passive expression. *Oenone* and I spent years doing exactly that.

You spent years playing tourist. You admired what others had discovered, what they had built, the way they lived. The actions of a tourist, Syrinx, not an explorer. *Oenone* has never flown to a star which has not been catalogued; your footprint has never been the first upon a planet. You have always played safe, Syrinx. And even that did not protect you.

Protect me from what?

Your fear of the unknown.

She sat on the wickerwork chair opposite him, deeply troubled. You believe that of me?

I do. I want you to feel no shame, Syrinx, all of us have weaknesses. Mine, I know, are more terrible than you would ever believe me capable of.

If you say so.

As always, you remain stubborn to the last. I have not yet decided if this is a weakness or a strength.

Depends on the circumstances, I guess. She flashed a mischievous smile.

He inclined his head in acknowledgement. As you say. In these two circumstances, it must therefore count as a weakness.

You would rather I had surrendered myself and *Oenone*?

Of course not. And we are here to deal with the present, not dwell on what was.

So you see this alleged fear of mine to be a continuing problem?

It inhibits you, and this should not be. Your mind should not be caged, by your own bars or anyone else's. I would like you and *Oenone* to face the universe with determination.

How? I mean, I thought I was just about cured. I've been through all my memories of the torture and the circumstances around it with the therapists; we broke up each and every black spectre with rigorous logic. Now you tell me I have this deep-seated flaw. If I'm not ready now, I doubt I ever will be.

Ready for what?

I don't know exactly. Do my bit, I suppose. Help protect Edenism from the possessed, that's what all the other voidhawks are doing right now. I know *Oenone* wants to be a part of that.

You would not make a good captain at this point, not if you were to take an active part in the conflict. The unknown would always cast its shadow of doubt over your actions.

I know all about the possessed, believe me.

Do you? Then what will you do when you join them?

Join them? Never!

You propose to avoid dying? I will be interested to hear the method you plan for this endeavour.

Oh. Her cheeks reddened.

Death is always the great unknown. And now we know more of it the mystery only deepens.

How? How can it deepen when we know more?

Laton called it the great journey. What did he mean? The Kiint said they have confronted the knowledge and come to terms with it. How? Their understanding of reality cannot be so much greater than ours. Edenists transfer their memories into the neural strata when their bodies die. Does their soul also transfer? Do these questions not bother you? That such philosophical abstracts should attain a supreme relevance to our existence is most disturbing to me.

Well, yes, they are disturbing if you lay them out in clinical detail like that.

And you have never considered them?

I have considered them, certainly. I just don't obsess on them.

You are the one Edenist still with us who has come closest to knowing the truth of any of these. If it affects any of us, it affects you.

Affect, or hinder?

Answer yourself.

I wish you'd stop saying that to me.

You know I never will.

Yes. Very well, I've thought about the questions; as to the answers, I don't have a clue. Which makes the questions irrelevant.

Very good, I would agree with that statement.

You would?

With one exception. They are irrelevant only for the moment. Right now, our society is doing what it always does in times of crisis, and resorting to physical force to defend itself. Again I have no quarrel with this. But if we are to make any real progress in this arena these questions must be examined with a degree of urgency so far lacking. For answer them we must. This is not a gulf of knowledge the human race can survive. We must deliver – dare I call it – divine truth.

You expect that out of a therapy session?

My dear Syrinx, of course not. What sloppy thinking. But I am disappointed the solution to our more immediate problem has eluded you.

Which problem? she asked in exasperation.

Your problem. He snapped his fingers at her with some vexation, as if she were a miscreant child. Now concentrate, please. You wish to fly, but you retain a perfectly understandable reticence.

Yes.

Everyone wishes to know the answer to those questions I asked, yet they do not know where to look.

Yes.

One race has those answers.

The Kiint? I know, but they said they wouldn't help.

Incorrect. I have accessed the sensevise recording of the Assembly's emergency session. Ambassador Roulor said the Kiint would not help us in the struggle we faced. The context of the statement was somewhat ambiguous. Did the Ambassador mean the physical struggle, or the quest for knowledge?

We all know that the Kiint would not help us to fight. Ergo, the Ambassador was referring to the afterlife.

A reasonable assumption. One hopes the future of the human race does not rest on a single misinterpreted sentence.

So why haven't you asked the Kiint Ambassador to Jupiter to clarify it?

I doubt that even a Kiint ambassador has the authority to disclose the kind of information we now search for, no matter what the circumstances.

Syrinx groaned in understanding. You want me to go to the Kiint homeworld and ask.

How kind of you to offer. You will embark on a flight with few risks involved, and you will also be confronting the unknown. Sadly your latter task will be conducted on a purely intellectual level, but it is an honourable start.

And good therapy.

A most fortunate combination, is it not? If I were not a Buddhist I would be talking about the killing of two birds.

Assuming the Jovian Consensus approves of the flight.

An amused light twinkled in the deeply recessed eyes. Being the founder of Edenism has its privileges. Not even the Consensus would refuse one of my humble requests.

Syrinx closed her eyes, and looked up at the vaguely puzzled face of the chief therapist. She realized her lips were parted in a wide smile.

Is everything all right? he asked politely.

Absolutely. Taking a cautious breath, she eased her legs off the side of the bed. The hospital room was as comfortable and pleasant as only their culture could make it. But it would be nice for a complete change.

*Oenone.*

Yes?

I hope you've enjoyed your rest, my love. We have a long flight ahead of us.

At last!

\*

It had not been an easy week for Ikela. The Dorados were starting to suffer from the civil and commercial starflight quarantine. All exports had halted, and the asteroids had only a minuscule internal economy, which could hardly support the hundreds of industrial stations that refined the plentiful ore. Pretty soon he was going to have to start laying off staff in all seventeen of the T'Opingtu company's foundry stations.

It was the first setback the Dorados had ever suffered in all of their thirty-year history. They had been tough years, but rewarding for those who had believed in their own future and worked hard to attain it. People like Ikela. He had come here after the death of Garissa, like so many others tragically disinherited from that world. There had been more than enough money to start his business in those days, and it had grown in tandem with the system's flourishing economy. In three decades he had changed from bitter refugee to a leading industrialist, with a position of responsibility in the Dorados' Governing Council.

Now this. It wasn't financial ruin, not by any means, but the social cost was starting to mount up at an alarming rate. The Dorados were used only to expansion and growth. Unemployment was not an issue in any of the seven settled asteroids. People who found themselves suddenly without a job and regular earnings were unlikely to react favourably to the council washing its hands of the problem.

Yesterday Ikela had sat in on a session to discuss the idea of making companies pay non-salaried employees a retainer fee to tide them through the troubles, which had seemed the easy solution until the chief magistrate started explaining how difficult that would be to implement legally. As always the council had dithered. Nothing had been decided.

Today Ikela had to start making his own decisions along those same lines. He knew he ought to set an example, and pay some kind of reduced wage to his workforce. It wasn't the kind of decision he was used to making.

He strode into the executive floor's anteroom with little enthusiasm for the coming day. His personal secretary, Lomie, was standing up behind her desk, a harassed expression on her face. Ikela was mildly surprised to see a small red handkerchief tied round her ankle. He would never have thought a level-headed girl like Lomie would pay any attention to that Deadnight nonsense which seemed to be sweeping through the Dorados' younger generation.

'I couldn't stonewall her,' Lomie datavised. 'I'm sorry, sir, she was so forceful, and she did say she was an old friend.'

Ikela followed her gaze across the room. A smallish woman was rising from one of the settees, putting her cup of coffee down on the side table. She clung to a small backpack which was hanging at her side from a shoulder strap. Few Dorados residents had skin as dark as hers, though it was extensively wrinkled now. Ikela guessed she was in her sixties. Her features were almost familiar, something about them agitating his subconscious. He ran a visual comparison program through his neural nanonics personnel record files.

'Hello, Captain,' she said. 'It's been a while.'

Whether the program placed her first, or the use of his old title triggered the memory, he never knew. 'Mzu,' he choked. 'Dr Mzu. Oh Mother Mary, what are you doing here?'

'You know exactly what I'm doing here, Captain.'

'Captain?' Lomie enquired. She looked from one to the other. 'I never knew . . .'

Keeping his eyes fixed on Mzu as if he expected her to leap for his throat, Ikela waved Lomie to be silent. 'I'm taking no appointments, no files, no calls, nothing. We're not to be interrupted.' He datavised a code at his office door. 'Come through, Doctor, please.'

The office had a single window, a long band of glass which looked down on Ayacucho's biosphere cavern. Alkad gave the farms and parks an appreciative glance. 'Not a bad view, considering you've only had thirty years to build it. The

Garissans seem to have done well for themselves here. I'm glad to see it.'

'This cavern's only fifteen years old, actually. Ayacucho was the second Dorado to be settled after Mapire. But you're right, I enjoy the view.'

Alkad nodded, taking in the large office; its size, furnishings, and artwork chosen to emphasize the occupant's status rather than conforming to any notion of aesthetics. 'And you have prospered, too, Captain. But then, that was part of your mission, wasn't it?'

She watched him slump down into a chair behind the big terrestrial-oak desk. Hardly the kind of dynamic magnate who could build his T'Opingtu company into a multistellar market leader in the fabrication of exotic alloy components. More like a fraud whose bluff had just been called.

'I have some of the resources we originally discussed,' he said. 'Of course, they are completely at your disposal.'

She sat on a chair in front of the desk, staring him down. 'You're straying from the script, Captain. I don't want resources, I want the combat-capable starship we agreed on. The starship you were supposed to have ready for me the day the Omutan sanctions ended. Remember?'

'Look, bloody hell, it's been decades, Mzu. Decades! I didn't know where the hell you were, even if you were still alive. Mother Mary, things change. Life is different now. Forgive me, I know you are supposed to be here at this time, I just never expected to see you. I didn't think . . .'

A chilling anger gained control of Alkad's thoughts, unlocked from that secret centre of motivation at the core of her brain. 'Have you got a starship which can deploy the Alchemist?'

He shook his head before burying it in his hands. 'No.'

'They slaughtered ninety-five million of us, Ikela, they wrecked our planet, they made us breathe radioactive soot until our lungs bled. Genocide doesn't even begin to describe what was done to us. You and I and the other survivors were a mistake, an oversight. There's no life left for us in this universe. We have only one purpose, one duty. Revenge, vengeance, and justice, our three guiding stars. Mother Mary has given us this one blessing, providing us with a second chance. We're not even attempting to kill the Omutans. I would never use the Alchemist to do that; I'm not going to become as they are, that would be their ultimate victory. All we're going to do is make them suffer, to give them a glimpse, a pitiful glimmer of the agony they've forced us to endure every waking day for thirty years.'

'Stop it!' he shouted. 'I've made a life for myself here, we all have. This mission, this vendetta, what would it achieve after so much time? Nothing! We would be the tainted ones then. Let the Omutans carry the guilt they deserve. Every person they talk to, every planet they visit, they'll be cursed to carry the weight of their name with them.'

'As we suffer pity wherever we go.'

'Oh Mother Mary! Don't do this.'

'You will help me, Ikela. I am not giving you a choice in this. Right now you've allowed yourself to forget. That will end. I will make you remember. You've grown old and fat and comfy. I never did, I never allowed myself that luxury. They didn't allow me. Ironic that, I always felt. They kept my angry spirit alive with their eternal reminder, their agents and their discreet observation. In doing so, they also kept their own nemesis alive.'

His face lifted in bewilderment. 'What are you talking about? Have the Omutans been watching you?'

'No, they're all locked up where they belong. It's the other Intelligence agencies who have discovered who I am and what I built. Don't ask me how. Somebody must have leaked the information. Somebody weak, Ikela.'

'You mean they know you're here?'

'They don't know exactly where I am. All they know is I escaped from Tranquillity. But now they'll be looking for me.

And don't try fooling yourself, they'll track me down eventually. It's what they're good at, very good. The only question now is which one will find me first.'

'Mother Mary!'

'Exactly. Of course, if you had prepared the starship for me as you were supposed to, this wouldn't even be a problem. You stupid, selfish, petty-minded bastard. Do you realize what you've done? You have jeopardized everything we ever stood for.'

'You don't understand.'

'No, I don't; and I won't dignify you by trying to. I'm not even going to listen to any more of your pitiful whingeing. Now tell me, where are the others? Do we even have a partisan group any more?'

'Yes. Yes, we're still together. We still help the cause whenever we can.'

'Are all the originals here?'

'Yes, we're all still alive. But the other four aren't in Ayacucho.'

'What about other partisans, do you have a local leadership council?'

'Yes.'

'Then call them to a meeting. Today. They will have to be told what's happening. We need nationalist recruits for a crew.'

'Yes,' he stammered. 'Yes, all right.'

'And in the meantime, start looking for a suitable starship. There ought to be one in dock. It's a shame I let the *Samaku* go. It would have suited us.'

'But there's a Confederationwide quarantine . . .'

'Not where we're going there isn't. And you're a member of the Dorados council, you can arrange for the government to authorize our departure.'

'I can't do that!'

'Ikela, look at me very closely. I am not playing games with you. You have endangered both my life and the mission you swore to undertake when you took the oath to serve your naval commission. As far as I am concerned, that amounts to treason. Now if an agency grabs me before I can retrieve the Alchemist, I am going to make damn sure they know where the money came from to help you start up T'Opingtu all those years ago. I'm sure you remember exactly what the Confederation law has to say about antimatter, don't you?'

He bowed his head. 'Yes.'

'Good. Now start datavising the partisans.'

'All right.'

Alkad regarded him with a mixture of contempt and worry. That the others would falter had never occurred to her. They were all Garissan Navy. Thirty years ago she had secretly suspected that if anyone was destined to be the weak link it would be her.

'I've been moving round a lot since I docked,' she said. 'But I'll spend the rest of the afternoon in your apartment. I need to clean up, and that's the one place I can be sure you won't tip anyone off about. There'd be too many questions.'

Ikela recouped some of his old forcefulness. 'I don't want you there. My daughter's living with me.'

'So?'

'I don't want her involved.'

'The sooner you get my starship prepared, the sooner I'll be gone.' She hoisted the backpack over her shoulder and went out into the anteroom.

Lomie glanced up from behind her desk, curiosity haunting her narrow features. Alkad ignored her, and datavised the lift processor for a ride to the lobby. The doors opened, revealing a girl inside. She was in her early twenties, a lot taller than Mzu, with a crown of short dreadlocks at the top of a shaven skull. First impression was that someone had attempted to geneer an elf into existence, her torso was so slim, her limbs so disproportionately long. Her face could have been pretty if her personality wasn't so stern.

'I'm Voi,' she said after the doors shut.

Alkad nodded in acknowledgement, facing the doors and wishing the lift could go faster.

All movement stopped, the floor indicator frozen between four and three.

'And you're Dr Alkad Mzu.'

'There's a nervejam projector in this bag, and its control processor is activated.'

'Good. I'm glad you're not walking round unprotected.'

'Who are you?'

'I'm Ikela's daughter. Check my public record file, if you like.'

Alkad did, datavising the lift's net processor for a link to Ayacucho's civil administration computer. If Voi was some kind of agency plant, they'd made a very good job of ghosting details. Besides, if she was from an agency, the last thing they'd be doing was talking. 'Restart the lift, please.'

'Will you talk to me?'

'Restart the lift.'

Voi datavised the lift's control processor, and they started to descend. 'We want to help you.'

'Who's we?' Alkad asked.

'My friends; there are quite a few of us now. The partisans you belong to have done nothing for years. They are soft and old and afraid of making waves.'

'I don't know you.'

'Was my father helpful?'

'We made progress.'

'They won't help you. Not when it comes to action. We will.'

'How did you find out who I am?'

'From my father. He shouldn't have told me, but he did. He's so weak.'

'How much do you know?'

'That the partisans were supposed to prepare for you. That

you were bringing something to finally give us our revenge against Omuta. Logically it has to be some kind of powerful weapon. Possibly even a planet-buster. He was always afraid of you, they all were. Have they made the proper preparations? I bet they haven't.'

'As I said, I don't know you.'

Voi leaned over her, furiously intent. 'We have money. We're organized. We have people who aren't afraid. We won't let you down. We'd never let you down. Tell us what you want, we'll provide it.'

'How did you know I was seeing your father?'

'Lomie, of course. She's not one of us, not a core member, but she's a friend. It's always useful for me to know what my father is doing. As I said, we're properly organized.'

'So are children's day clubs.' For a moment Alkad thought the girl was going to strike her.

'All right,' Voi said with a calm that could only have been induced by neural nanonic overrides. 'You're being sensible, not trusting a stranger with the last hope our culture owns. I can accept that. It's rational.'

'Thank you.'

'But we can help. Just give us the chance. Please.' And please was obviously not a word which came easy from that mouth.

The lift doors opened. A lobby of polished black stone and curving white metal glinted under large silver light spires. A thirty-year-old unarmed-combat program reviewed the image from Alkad's retinal implants, deciding nobody was lurking suspiciously. She looked up at the tall, anorexically-proportioned girl, trying to decide what to do. 'Your father invited me to stay at his apartment. We can talk more when we get there.'

Voi gave a shark's smile. 'It would be an honour, Doctor.'

*

It was the woman sitting up at the bar wearing a red shirt who caught Joshua's attention. The red was very red, a bright, effervescent scarlet. And the style of the shirt was odd, though he'd be hard pressed to define exactly what was wrong with the cut, it lacked ... smoothness. The clincher was the fact it had buttons down the front, not a seal.

'Don't look,' he murmured to Beaulieu and Dahybi. 'But I think she's a possessed.' He datavised his retinal image file to them.

They both turned and looked. In Beaulieu's case it was quite a performance, twisting her bulk round in the too-small chair, streamers of light slithering round the contours of her shiny body.

'Jesus! Show some professionalism.'

The woman gave the three of them a demurely inquisitive glance.

'You sure?' Dahybi asked.

'Think so. There's something wrong with her, anyway.'

Dahybi said nothing; he'd experienced Joshua's intuition at work before.

'We can soon check,' Beaulieu said. 'Go over to her and see if any of our blocks start glitching.'

'No.' Joshua was slowly scanning the rest of the teeming bar. It was a wide room cut square into the rock of Kilifi asteroid's habitation section; with a mixed clientele mostly taken from ships' crews and industrial station staff. He was anonymous here, as much as he could be (five people had so far recognized '"Lagrange" Calvert'). And Kilifi had been a good cover, it manufactured the kind of components he was supposed to be buying for Tranquillity's defences. Sarha and Ashly were handling the dummy negotiations with local companies; and so far no one had questioned why they'd flown all the way to Narok rather than a closer star system.

He saw a couple more suspicious people drinking in solitude, then another three crammed round a table with sullen sly expressions. *I'm getting too paranoid.*

'We have to concentrate on our mission,' he said. 'If Kilifi isn't enforcing its screening procedures properly, that's their problem. We can't risk any sort of confrontation. Besides, if the possessed are wandering round this freely it must mean their infiltration is quite advanced.'

Dahybi hunched his shoulders and played with his drink, trying not to look anxious. 'There are navy ships docked here, and most of the independent traders are combat capable. If the asteroid falls, the possessed will get them.'

'I know.' Joshua met the node specialist's stare, refusing to show weakness. 'We cannot cause waves.'

'Sure, you said: don't draw attention to yourself, don't talk to the natives, don't fart loudly. What the hell are we doing here, Joshua? Why are you so anxious to trace Meyer?'

'I need to talk to him.'

'Don't you trust us?'

'Of course I do. And don't try such cheap shots. You know I'll tell all of you as soon as I can. For now, it's best you don't know. You trust me, don't you?'

Dahybi put his lips together in a tired grin. 'Cheap shot.'

'Yeah.'

The waitress brought another round of drinks to their alcove. Joshua watched her legs as she wriggled away through the crowd. A bit young for him, mid-teens. Louise's age. The thought warmed him briefly. Then he saw she was wearing a red handkerchief round her ankle. Jesus, I don't know which is worse, the horrors of possession or the pathetic dreams of the Deadnights.

He'd received one hell of a shock the first time he accessed the recording from Valisk. Marie Skibbow possessed and luring naive kids to their doom. She'd been a lovely girl, beautiful and smart, with thoughts as hard as carbotanium composite. If she could be caught, anyone could. Lalonde strummed out far too many resonances.

'Captain,' Beaulieu warned.

Joshua saw Buna approaching their alcove. He sat down and

smiled. There wasn't the slightest sign of nerves. But then, as Joshua had discovered while asking round his fellow captains, Mabaki was overfamiliar with this kind of transaction.

'Good afternoon, Captain,' Buna said pleasantly. 'Have you managed to acquire your cargo yet?'

'Some of it,' Joshua said. 'I'm hoping you were successful with the rest.'

'Indeed I was. Most of the information was quite simple to obtain. However, I am nothing if not assiduous in any freelance work I undertake. I discovered that, sadly, what you actually need falls outside our original agreement.'

Dahybi gave the man a hateful glare. He always despised bent civil servants.

'And will cost . . . ?' Joshua enquired, unperturbed.

'An additional twenty thousand fuseodollars.' Buna sounded sincerely regretful. 'I apologize for the cost, but times are hard at the moment. I have little work and a large family.'

'Of course.' Joshua held up his Jovian Bank credit disk.

Mabaki was surprised by the young captain's swift concession. It took him a moment to produce his own credit disk. Joshua shunted the money over.

'You were right,' Buna said. '*Udat* did come to this star system. It docked at the Nyiru asteroid. Apparently its captain was hurt when they arrived, he spent almost four days in hospital undergoing neural trauma treatment. When it was complete, they filed a flight plan for the Sol system, and left.'

'Sol?' Joshua asked. 'Are you sure?'

'Positive. However – and this is where the twenty thousand comes in – their passenger, Dr Alkad Mzu, didn't go with them. She hired an independent trader called the *Samaku*, and departed an hour later.'

'Flight plan?'

'Filed for a Dorado asteroid, Ayacucho. I even checked traffic control's sensor data for the flight. They were definitely aligned for Tunja when they jumped.'

Joshua resisted the impulse to swear. Ione was right, Mzu was running to the last remnants of her nation. She must be going for the Alchemist. He flicked another glance at the girl in the red shirt, her head tipped back elegantly as she drank her cocktail. Jesus, as if we don't have enough problems right now. 'Thank you.'

'My pleasure. You should also know, for no extra charge, that I'm not the only one to be asking these questions. There are three access requests logged on the Civil Spaceflight Department computer for the same files. One request was made only twenty minutes before mine.'

'Oh, Jesus.'

'Bad news?'

'Interesting news,' Joshua grunted. He rose to his feet.

'If there is anything else I can obtain for you, Captain, please call.'

'Sure thing.' Joshua was already walking for the door, Dahybi and Beaulieu a couple of steps behind.

Before he reached the exit, people watching the AV pillar behind the bar were gasping in shock; agitated murmurs of conversation rippled down the length of the room. Perfect strangers asking each other, 'Did you access that?' the way they always did with momentous news.

Joshua focused on the AV pillar's projection, allowing the hazy laserlight sparkle to form its picture behind his eyes. A planet floated below him, its geography instantly familiar. No real continents or oceans, just winding seas and thousands of medium-sized islands. Patches of glowing red cloud squatted over half of the islands, concentrated mainly in the tropic zones – though on this world tropic was a relative term.

'... Confederation Navy frigate *Levêque* confirmed that all inhabited islands on Norfolk have now been covered by the reality dysfunction cloud,' the news commentator said. 'All contact with the surface has been lost, and it must be assumed that the majority, if not all, of the population has been possessed. Norfolk is a pastoral planet with few spaceplanes available to the local government; because of this no attempt was made to evacuate any inhabitants to the navy squadron before the capital, Norwich, fell. A statement from Confederation Navy Headquarters at Trafalgar said that the *Levêque* would remain in orbit to observe the situation, but no offensive action was being considered at this time. This brings to seven the number of planets known to have been taken over by the possessed.'

'Oh, Jesus, Louise is down there.' The AV image broke up as he turned his head away from the pillar, seeing Louise running over the grassy wolds in one of those ridiculous dresses, laughing over her shoulder at him. And Genevieve, too, that irritating child who was either laughing or sulking. Marjorie, Grant (it would go worse for him, he would resist as long as possible), Kenneth, and even that receptionist at Drayton's Import. 'God damn it. No!' I should have been there. I could have got her away.

'Joshua?' Dahybi asked in concern. 'You OK?'

'Yeah. Did you catch that piece about Norfolk?'

'Yes.'

'She's down there, Dahybi. I left her there.'

'Who?'

'Louise.'

'You didn't leave her there, Joshua. It's her home, it's where she belongs.'

'Right.' Joshua's neural nanonics were plotting a course from Narok to Norfolk. He didn't remember requesting it.

'Come on, Captain,' Dahybi said. 'We've got what we came for. Let's go.'

Joshua looked at the woman in the red shirt again. She was staring at the AV pillar, abstract pastel streaks from the projection glinting dully on her ebony cheeks. A delighted smile flourished on her lips.

Joshua hated her, her invincibility, the cool arrogance sitting among her enemies. Queen of the bitch demons come to taunt him. Dahybi's hand tightened round his arm.

'OK, we're gone.'

*

'Here we are, home at last,' Loren Skibbow said with a histrionic sigh. 'Not that we can stay for long. They'll tear Guyana apart to find us now.'

The apartment was on the highest level of the biosphere's habitation complex, where gravity was only eighty per cent standard. The penthouse of some Kingdom aristocrat, presumably, furnished with dark active-contour furniture and large hand-painted silk screens; every table and alcove shelf was littered with antiques.

Gerald felt it was a somewhat bizarre setting to wind up in, considering the day's events. 'Are you creating this?' When they lived in the arcology, Loren had always badgered him for what she termed a 'grander' apartment.

She looked round with a rueful smile, and shook her head. 'No. My imagination isn't up to anything so gaudy. This is Pou Mok's place.'

'The woman you're possessing? The redhead?'

'That's right.' Loren smiled and took a step towards him.

Gerald stiffened. Not that she needed any physical signs; his mind was foaming with fear and confusion. 'OK, Gerald, I won't touch you. Sit down, we have a lot to talk about. And this time I mean talk, not just you telling me what you've decided is best for us.'

He flinched. Everything she did and said triggered memories. The unedited past seemed to have become his curse in life.

'How did you get here?' he asked. 'What happened, Loren?'

'You saw the homestead, what that bastard Dexter and his Ivets did to us.' Her face paled. 'To Paula.'

'I saw.'

'I tried, Gerald. Honestly, I tried to fight back. But it all happened so fast. They were crazy brutes; Dexter killed one of his own just because the boy would slow them down. I wasn't strong enough to stop it.'

'And I wasn't there.'

'They'd have killed you, too.'

'At least . . .'

'No, Gerald. You would have died for nothing. I'm glad you escaped. This way you can help Marie.'

'How?'

'The possessed can be beaten. Individually, in any case. I'm not so sure about overall. But that's for others to fight over, planetary governments and the Confederation. You and I have to rescue our daughter, allow her to have her own life. No one else will.'

'How?' This time it was a shout.

'The same way you were freed: zero-tau. We have to put her in zero-tau. The possessed can't endure it.'

'Why not?'

'Because we're conscious the whole time. Zero-tau suspends normal energy-wave functions, but our souls are still connected to the beyond somehow, that makes us aware of time passing. But only time, nothing else. It is the ultimate sensory deprivation, actually worse than the beyond. At least in the beyond souls have the memories of other souls to feed on, and some perception of the real universe.'

'That's why,' Gerald murmured. 'I knew Kingsford Garrigan was scared.'

'Some can hold out longer than others, it depends on how strong their personality is. But in the end, everyone retreats from the body they possess.'

'There is hope, then.'

'For Marie, yes. We can save her.'

'So that she can die.'

'Everybody dies, Gerald.'

'And goes on to suffer in the beyond.'

'I'm not sure. If it hadn't been for you and Marie, I don't think I would have remained with all the other souls.'

'I don't understand.'

Loren gave him a hapless smile. 'I was worried about the two of you, Gerald, I wanted to make sure you were all right. That's why I stayed.'

'Yes, but . . . where else could you go?'

'I'm not certain that question applies. The beyond is strange, there are no separate places within it, not like this universe.'

'So how could you leave?'

'I wouldn't leave it . . .' She fluttered her hands in exasperation as she struggled with the concept. 'I just wouldn't be in the same part of it as the rest of them.'

'You said there were no different parts.'

'There aren't.'

'So how—'

'I don't pretend to understand, Gerald. But you can leave the others behind. The beyond isn't necessarily the torment everyone is making it out to be.'

Gerald studied the pale-salmon carpet, shamed at being unable to look at his own wife. 'And you came back for me.'

'No, Gerald.' Her voice hardened. 'We might be husband and wife, but my love isn't that blind. I came back principally for Marie's sake. If it had just been you, I don't think I would have had the courage. I endured the other souls devouring my memories for her sake. Did you know you can see out of the beyond? Just. I watched Marie, and that made the horror tolerable. I hadn't seen her since that day she walked out on us. I wanted to know she was alive and safe. It wasn't easy, I almost abandoned my vigil, then she was possessed. So I stayed, waiting for an opportunity to help, for someone close to you to be possessed. And here I am.'

'Yes. Here you are. Who is Pou Mok? I thought the Principality had defeated the possessed, confined them all to Mortonridge.'

'They have, according to the news reports. But the three who arrived here on the *Ekwan* with you got to Pou Mok before they left the asteroid. They were smart choosing her; she supplies illegal stimulant programs to the personnel up here, among other things. That's why she can afford this place. It also means she's not included on any file of Guyana's inhabitants, so she never got hauled in to be tested like everyone else. The idea was that even if the three from the *Ekwan* got caught on the planet, Pou Mok's possessor would be safe to begin the process all over again. In theory, she was the perfect provocateur to leave behind. Unfortunately for the three of them, I was the one who came forward from the beyond. I don't care about their goals, I'm only interested in Marie.'

'Was I wrong taking her to Lalonde?' Gerald asked remotely. 'I thought I was doing the best possible thing for her, for all of you.'

'You were. Earth's dying; the arcologies are old, worn out. There's nothing there for people like us; if we'd stayed, Marie and Paula would have had lives no different from us, or our parents, or any of our ancestors for the last ten generations. You broke the cycle for us, Gerald. We had the chance to take pride in what our grandchildren would become.'

'What grandchildren?' He knew he was going to start crying any minute. 'Paula's dead; Marie hated our home so much she ran away at the first opportunity.'

'Good thing she did, Gerald, wasn't it? She was always headstrong, and she's a teenager. Teenagers can never look and plan ahead, having a good time is the only thing they can think of. All she knew was that two months of her life weren't as comfy as the ones which went before, and she had to do some work for the first time as well. Small surprise she ran away. It was a premature taste of adulthood that scared her off, not us being bad parents.

'You know, I perceived her before she was possessed. She'd found herself a job in Durringham, a good job. She was doing all right for herself, better than she could ever do on Earth. Knowing Marie, she didn't appreciate it.'

When Gerald found the nerve to glance up, he saw Loren's expression was a twin to his own. 'I didn't tell you before. But I was so frightened for her when she ran away.'

'I know you were. Fathers always think their daughters can't take care of themselves.'

'You were worried, too.'

'Yes. Oh, yes. But only that fate would throw something at her she couldn't survive. Which it has done. She would have done all right if this curse hadn't been unleashed.'

'All right,' he said shakily. 'What do we do about it? I just wanted to go to Valisk and help her.'

'That's my idea, too, Gerald. There's no big plan, though I do have some of the details sorted out. First thing we need to do is get you on the *Quadin*, it's one of the few starships still flying. Right now the Kingdom is busy selling weapons components to its allies. The *Quadin* is departing for Pinjarra asteroid in seven hours with a cargo of five-gigawatt maser cannons for their SD network.'

'Pinjarra?'

'It's in the Toowoomba star system, Australian-ethnic; the Kingdom is anxious to keep it locked in to its diplomatic strategy. Their asteroid settlements aren't very well defended, so they're being offered upgrades on favourable financial terms.'

Gerald fidgeted with his fingers. 'But how do I get on board? We'd never make it into the spaceport, never mind a starship. Maybe if we just asked Ombey's government if we can go to Valisk? They'll know we're telling the truth about wanting to help Marie. And that information about zero-tau would be useful. They'd be grateful.'

'Bloody hell.' Loren regarded the pathetically hopeful smile on his face more with astonishment than contempt. He had always been the forceful one, the go-getter. 'Oh, Gerald, what have they done to you?'

'Remember.' He hung his head, probing at his temples in a vain attempt to alleviate some of the sparkling pain inside. 'They made me remember. I don't want that. I don't want to remember, I just want to forget it all.'

She came over and sat beside him, her arm going round his shoulder the way she used to do with her daughters when they were younger. 'Once we free Marie, all this will be over. You can think of other things again, new things.'

'Yes.' He nodded vigorously, speaking with the slow surety of the newly converted. 'Yes, you're right. That's what Dr Dobbs told me, too; I have to formulate relevant goals for my new circumstances, and concentrate on achieving them. I must eject myself from the failings of the past.'

'Good philosophy.' Her eyebrows rose in bemusement. 'Firstly we have to buy you passage on the *Quadin*. The captain has supplied Pou Mok with various fringe-legal fleks before, which can be used to lever him into taking you. If you're firm enough with him, Gerald. Are you going to manage that?'

'Yes. I can do that.' He grasped his hands together, squeezing. 'I can tell him anything if it will help Marie.'

'Just don't be too aggressive. Stay polite and calmly determined.'

'I will.'

'Fine. Now money isn't a problem, obviously, I can give you a Jovian Bank credit disk with about half a million fuseodollars loaded in. Pou Mok also has half a dozen blank passport fleks. Our real problem is going to be your appearance, every sensor in the asteroid is going to be programmed for your features now. I can change the way you look, but only while I'm near you, which is no use at all. They can detect me easily in public places, especially if I'm using my energistic ability. So we're going to have to give you a permanent alteration.'

'Permanent?' he asked uneasily.

'Pou Mok has a set of cosmetic adaptation packages. She used to keep changing her own face in case the asteroid police became too familiar with it – she's not even a natural redhead. I think I know enough to program the control processor manually. If I don't get too close, the packages should be able to give you a basic make over. It ought to be enough.'

Loren took him through into one of the bedrooms and told him to lie down. The cosmetic adaptation packages were similar to nanonic medical packages but with warty bubbles on the outside, holding reserves of collagen ready to be implanted, firming up new contours. Gerald felt the furry inner surface knitting to his skin, then his nerves went dead.

*

It took a lot of effort on Gerald's part not to shy away from the ceiling-mounted sensors in the public hall. He still wasn't convinced about the face that appeared each time he looked in the mirror. Ten years younger, but with puffy cheeks and drooping laughter lines, skin a shade darker with an underlying red flush; a face which conveyed his internal worry perfectly. His hair had been trimmed to a centimetre fuzz and coloured a light chestnut – at least there were no silver strands any more.

He walked into the Bar Vips and ordered a mineral water, asking the barman where he could find Captain McRobert.

McRobert had brought two of his crew with him, one of whom was a cosmonik with a body resembling a mannequin: jet black with no features at all, not even on the head; he was an impressive two hundred and ten centimetres tall.

Gerald tried to retain an impassive expression as he sat at their table, but it wasn't easy. Their steely presence was conjuring up memories of the squad which had captured Kingsford Garrigan in Lalonde's jungle. 'I'm Niall Lyshol; Pou Mok sent me,' he stuttered.

'If she hadn't, we wouldn't be here,' McRobert said curtly. 'As it is . . .' He gave the cosmonik a brief signal.

Gerald was offered a processor block.

'Take it,' McRobert instructed.

He tried, but the huge black hand wouldn't let go.

'No static charge,' the cosmonik said. 'No glitches.' The block was withdrawn.

'All right, Niall Lyshol,' McRobert said. 'You're not a possessed, so what the fuck are you?'

'Someone who wants a flight out of here.' Gerald exhaled softly, reminding himself of the relaxation exercises Dr Dobbs urged him to employ: cycle down the body and the brainwaves will follow. 'As someone else who deals with Pou Mok, Captain, you should appreciate the need to keep moving on before people start to take an interest in you.'

'Don't pull that bullshit pressure routine on me, boy. I'm not taking anyone who's hot, not with the way things are right now. I don't even know if we're going to leave Guyana, the code two defence alert still hasn't been lifted. Traffic control is hardly going to clear anyone for flight while one of those bastards is running loose up here.'

'I'm not hot. Check the bulletins.'

'I have done.'

'So you'll take me when the code two is lifted?'

'You're a complication, Lyshol. I can't take passengers because of the quarantine; which means you'd have to be listed as crew. You haven't got neural nanonics; which means the line company would start asking me questions. I don't like that.'

'I can pay.'

'Be assured: you will.'

'And you'll have Pou Mok's gratitude. For what it's worth.'

'Less than she likes to think. What are you running from?'

'People. Not the authorities. There's no official trouble.'

'One hundred thousand fuseodollars, and you spend the whole voyage in zero-tau. I'm not having you throwing up all over the life-support capsule.'

'Agreed.'

'Too quickly. A hundred thousand is an awful lot of money.'

Gerald wasn't sure how much longer he could keep this up;

slow thoughts echoed in his skull, telling him that the sanatorium had been a much kinder environment than this. If I went back, Dr Dobbs would understand, he'd make sure the police didn't punish me. If it wasn't for Marie ... 'You can't have it both ways. If I stay here then a lot of secrets are going to get spilt. You probably wouldn't be able to fly to any of the Kingdom systems again. I think that would bother the line company more than taking on a crewman without neural nanonics; not that they'll know I don't have neural nanonics unless you tell them.'

'I don't like being threatened, Lyshol.'

'I'm not threatening you. I'm asking for help. I need your help. Please.'

McRobert glanced at his companions. 'All right. The *Quadin* is docked at bay 901-C, we're scheduled to depart in three hours. Like I said, I can't guarantee that time with the code two, but if you're not there I'm not waiting.'

'I'm ready now.'

'No baggage? You surprise me. Very well, you can pay me when we get on board. And, Lyshol, don't expect any crew salary.'

When the four of them came out of Bar Vips, Gerald gave what he believed to be a surreptitious glance along the public hall. There weren't many people about, the code two alert had hauled in all the asteroid's off-duty military and civil service personnel.

Loren watched him go, hunched up and tragic between his three escorts. They stepped into a lift, and the door closed behind them. She walked the other way down the public hall, a smile playing over her illusory lips.

\*

After seven and a half hours with over a hundred false alerts and not one genuine sighting, Admiral Farquar was considering running a suppressor program through his neural nanonics. He hated the artificial calm the software brought, but the tension and depression were getting to him. The hunt for the possessed woman was being run from the Royal Naval Tactical Operations Centre. It wasn't quite the operation envisaged while it was being built, but its communications were easily reconfigured to probe the asteroid's net, and its AI had been loaded with the tracker programs developed by Diana Tiernan to hunt the possessed across Xingu. Given the size of Guyana, and the density of electronic systems spread throughout the interior, they should have had a result within minutes.

But the woman had eluded them. In doing so, she had forced him to admit to Princess Kirsten that if one could, so could more. There might be any number running round Guyana. For all he knew the entire navy staff could have been possessed, which was why the Operations Centre kept saying they couldn't find her. He didn't believe it himself (he'd visited the centre personally) but no doubt it was an option the Cabinet had to consider. Even he must be considered suspect, though they'd been tactful enough not to say so.

As a result, Guyana had handed over Ombey's strategic-defence network command to a Royal Navy base in Atherstone. A complete quarantine of the asteroid had been quietly enforced under the guise of the code two defence alert.

So far it had all been for nothing.

The office management computer datavised him that Captain Oldroyd, his staff security officer, and Dr Dobbs were requesting an interview. He datavised an acknowledgement, and his office dissolved into the white bubble of a sensenviron conference room.

'Have you made any progress finding her?' Dobbs asked.

'Not yet,' Farquar admitted.

'That ties in,' the doctor said. 'We've been running analysis scenarios based on the information we've collated so far; and based on that I believe I've come up with a rationale for her actions. Extracting Skibbow from our medical facility was slightly puzzling behaviour. It was an awful risk even for a possessed. If the marines had been thirty seconds faster she would never have made it. She must have had an extremely good reason.'

'Which is?'

'I think she's Loren Skibbow, Gerald's wife, if for no other reason than what she said to Jansen Kovak: "You should try being married to him for twenty years." I checked our file, they were married for twenty years.'

'His wife?'

'Exactly.'

'OK, I've heard stranger.' The Admiral faced Captain Old-royd. 'I hope you've got some evidence to back this theory up with.'

'Yes, sir. Assuming she is who we suspect, her behavioural profile certainly fits her actions to date. First of all, we believe she's been in Guyana for some time, possibly right from the beginning when the *Ekwan* docked. She has obviously had enough time to learn how to move around without activating any of our tracer programs. Secondly, if she can do that, why hasn't she launched the kind of takeover effort we saw on Xingu? She's held back for a reason.'

'Because it doesn't fit in with her plans,' Dr Dobbs said eagerly. 'If the whole asteroid became possessed, her peers would be unlikely to allow Gerald his freedom. This is all personal, Admiral, it's not part of what's happening to Morton-ridge or New California. She's completely on her own. I don't believe she's any real danger to the Kingdom's security at all.'

'Are you telling me we've shifted the Principality to a code two alert because of a *domestic* matter?' Admiral Farquar asked.

'I believe so,' Dr Dobbs said apologetically. 'The possessed are people, too. We've had ample proof that they retain a nearly complete range of human emotions. And ... er ... we did put Gerald through quite an ordeal. If what we suspect is true, it would be quite reasonable to assume Loren would do her best to take him away from us.'

'Dear God. All right, so now what? How does this theory help us deal with her?'

'We can negotiate.'

'To what end? I don't care that she's a loving wife. She's a bloody possessed. We can't have the pair of them living happily ever after up here.'

'No. But we can offer to take better care of Gerald. From her viewpoint, of course,' Dr Dobbs added quickly.

'Maybe.' The Admiral would have dearly loved to have found a flaw in the reasoning, but the facts did seem to fit together with uncomfortable precision. 'So what do you recommend?'

'I'd like to broadcast over Guyana's net, load a message into every personal communication processor, blanket the news and entertainment companies. It'll only be a matter of time before they access it.'

'If she answers she'll give away her location. She'll know that.'

'We'll find her eventually, I'll make that quite clear. What I can offer is a solution she can accept. Do I have your permission? It will need to be a genuine offer. After all, the possessed can read the emotional content of minds. She'll know if I'm telling the truth.'

'That's a pretty broad request, Doctor. What exactly do you want to offer her?'

'Gerald to be taken down to the planet and given an Ombey citizenship. We provide full financial compensation for what we put him through, complete his counselling and therapy. And finally, if this crisis is resolved we'll do whatever we can to reunite him with his daughter.'

'You mean that Kiera girl in Valisk?'

'Yes, Admiral.'

'I doubt my authority runs to that—' He broke off as the office management computer datavised a change in Guyana's status. The Operations Centre had just issued a full combat alert.

The Admiral opened a channel to the duty officer. 'What's happening?' he datavised.

'The AI has registered an anomaly, sir. We think it could be her. I've dispatched a Royal Marine squad.'

'What sort of anomaly?'

'A camera in the spaceport spindle entrance chamber registered a man getting into a transit capsule. When the capsule stopped at section G5 a woman got out. The capsule never stopped at any other section.'

'What about processor glitches?'

'The AI is analysing all the electronics around her. There are some efficiency reductions, but well below the kind of disturbance which we were getting from the possessed down in Xingu.'

The Admiral requested a schematic of the spaceport. Section G5 was the civil spaceplane and ion-field flyer dock. 'Dear God, Dr Dobbs, I think you might have been right after all.'

*

Loren floated along the brightly lit tubular corridor towards the airlock. According to the spaceport register, a Kulu Corporation SD2002 spaceplane was docked to it, a thirty-seater craft owned by the Crossen company which used it to ferry staff up to their microgee industrial stations. One of the smallest spaceplanes at Guyana, it was exactly the kind of craft a pair of fairly ignorant desperadoes would try to steal if they wanted to get down to the planet.

There was nobody about. The last person she'd seen had been a maintenance engineer who'd boarded the transit capsule she'd arrived in. She toyed with the idea of letting her energistic ability flare out and mess up some of the electronics in the corridor. But that might make them suspicious, she'd controlled herself for so long that any change now would cause questions. She'd just have to hope that their security programs and sensors would catch her. The change of image was a subtle enough betrayal, providing their monitor routines were good enough.

The airlock tube was five metres long, and narrower than the corridor, barely two metres wide. She manoeuvred herself into it, only to find the hatch at the far end was shut.

At last, an excuse to use the energistic ability.

There was a surge of electricity around the hatch. She could sense the main power cables behind the azure-blue composite walls, thick lines that burnt with an ember glow of current. There were other cables too, smaller and dimmer. It was one of those which had come alive, connected to a small communication block set into the rim of the hatch.

'It's Loren, isn't it?' a voice from the block asked. 'Loren Skibbow; I'm sure it's you. My name is Dr Riley Dobbs. I was treating Gerald before you took him away.'

She stared at the block in shock. How the bloody hell had he figured that out?

The power flowed through her body, twisting up from the beyond like a hot spring; she could feel it squirting through every cell. Her mind shaped it as it rose inside her, transforming it into the pattern she wanted, a pattern which matched her dreamy wish. It began to superimpose itself over reality. Sparks shivered over the surface of the hatch.

'Loren, I want to help, and I've been given the authority which will allow me to help. Please listen. Gerald is my patient, I don't want him harmed. I believe the two of us agree on that.'

'Go to hell, Doctor. Better still, I'll take you there personally. You damaged my husband's mind. I'm not going to forget that.'

There were noises in the corridor behind her, soft scraping, clinking sounds. When she focused, she could perceive the minds of the marines closing on her. Cold and anxious, but very determined.

'Gerald was damaged by the possession,' Dobbs said. 'I was trying to cure him. I want to continue that process.'

The sparks had begun to swirl round the composite of the airlock tube, penetrating below the surface as if they were swimming through the material.

'Under the muzzle of a gun?' she asked scathingly. 'I know they're behind me.'

'The marines won't shoot. I promise that, Loren. It would be pointless. Shooting would just cost the life of the person you've possessed. Nobody wants that. Please, come and talk to me. I've already obtained huge concessions from the authorities. Gerald can be taken down to the planet. He'll be looked after properly, I'll continue his therapy. Perhaps some day he can even see Marie again.'

'You mean Kiera. That bitch won't let my daughter go.'

'Nothing is certain. We can discuss this. Please. You can't leave on the spaceplane. Even if you get in you can hardly pilot it down through the SD network. The only way Gerald can get down to the planet is if I take him.'

'You won't touch him again. He's safe in my hiding place now, and you never found me, not in all the time I was there.'

The airlock walls gave out a small creak. All the sparks had blurred together to form a glowing ring of composite encircling her. She smiled tightly. The subterfuge was nearly complete. Dobbs's intervention had turned out to be a beautiful bonus.

Loren could sense the marines holding back just past the edge of the airlock tube. She took a deep breath, attempting to deflect the knowledge of what was about to come. White fire burst out of her feet with a terrible screeching sound. It fountained into the corridor and broke apart into a avalanche of individual fireballs which careered into the waiting marines.

'No, Loren, don't, I can help. Please—'

She exerted herself to the full. Dobbs's voice fractured into a brassy caterwaul before vanishing altogether as the energistic effect crashed every processor within twenty-five metres.

'Don't,' Pou Mok pleaded from the heart of Loren's mind. 'I won't tell them where he is. I promise. They'll never know. Let me live.'

'I can't trust the living,' Loren told her.

'Bitch!'

The wall of the airlock tube gleamed brighter than the fireballs, then the composite vaporized. Loren flew out of the widening gap, impelled by the blast of air which stampeded away into the vacuum.

'Dear God,' Admiral Farquar grunted. The spaceport's external sensors showed him the jet of air diminishing. Three marines had followed Loren Skibbow out into space. Their armour suits would provide some protection against decompression, and they had a small oxygen reserve. The duty officer had already dispatched some MSVs to chase after them.

Loren Skibbow was a different matter. For a while she had glowed from within, a fluorescent figure spinning round and round as she left the ruptured dock behind. Now the glow was fading. After a couple of minutes it winked out. The body exploded far more violently than it should have done.

'Locate as much as you can of her, and bring the pieces back,' Admiral Farquar told the duty officer. 'We can take a DNA sample; the ISA ought to be able to identify her for us.'

'But why?' Dr Dobbs asked, mortified. 'What the hell made her do that?'

'Perhaps they don't think quite like us, after all,' the Admiral said.

'They do. I know they do.'

'When we find Skibbow, you can ask him.'

It was a task which proved harder than expected. There was no response from his debrief nanonics, so the Royal Navy began a physical search of Guyana, monitored by the AI. No room, no service tunnel, no storage chamber was overlooked. Any space larger than a cubic metre was examined.

It took two and a half days. Pou Mok's room was opened and searched thirty-three hours after it began. Because it was listed as being rented (currently unoccupied) by someone on Ombey, and the diligent search turned up nothing, it was closed up and codelocked.

The cabinet meeting which followed the end of the search decided that one missing mental patient could not justify keeping the Navy's premier defence base isolated, nor could Ombey do without the products of Guyana's industrial stations. The asteroid was stood down to a code three status, and the problem of the woman's identity and Skibbow's whereabouts handed over to a joint ISA–ESA team.

Three and a half days after its original departure time, the *Quadin* left for Pinjarra. Gerald Skibbow wasn't aware of it, he had been in zero-tau an hour before Loren's final diversion.

## 16

Arnstadt fell to the Organization fleet after a ninety-minute battle above the planet. The strategic-defence network was hammered into oblivion by Capone's antimatter-powered combat wasps. There had been some advance warning from the Edenists, giving the local navy time to redeploy its ships. Three squadrons of voidhawks had arrived from the habitats orbiting one of the system's gas giants, reinforcing the Adamist vessels.

None of the preparations altered the final outcome. Forty-seven Arnstadt Navy ships were destroyed, along with fifteen voidhawks. The remaining voidhawks swallowed away, withdrawing back to the gas giant.

The Organization fleet's transport starships moved unopposed into low orbit, and spaceplanes began to ferry a small army of possessed down to the surface. Like all modern Confederation planets, Arnstadt had few soldiers. There were several marine brigades, who were mainly trained in space warfare techniques and covert mission procedures. Wars in this era were fought between starships. The days of foreign invasion forces marching across enemy territory had vanished before the end of the twenty-first century.

With its SD network reduced to radioactive meteorites flaring through bruised skies, Arnstadt was incapable of offering the slightest resistance to the possessed marching down out of their spaceplanes. Small towns were infiltrated first, increasing the numbers of possessed available to move on to larger towns. The area of captured ground began to increase exponentially.

Luigi Balsmao set up his headquarters in one of the orbiting asteroid settlements. Information on the people captured by the advancing possessed was datavised up to the asteroid where the structure coordination programs written by Emmet Mordden decided if they should be possessed or not. Organization lieutenants were appointed, their authority backed up by the firepower of fleet starships in low orbit.

With the subjugation of the planet confidently under way, Luigi split half of the fleet into squadrons, and deployed them against the system's asteroid settlements. Only the Edenist habitats were left alone; after Yosemite, Capone wasn't about to risk a second defeat on such a scale.

Starships were dispatched back to New California, and fresh cargo ships soon began to arrive, bringing with them the basic components for a new SD network along with other equipment to help consolidate the Organization's advance. Rover reporters were allowed to see carefully selected sections of the planet under its new masters: children left non-possessed to run around freely, possessed and non-possessed working side by side to restart the economy, Luigi stamping down hard on any possessed who didn't acknowledge the Organization's leadership.

News of the successful invasion swept across the Confederation, backed up by sensevise recordings from the reporters. Surprise was total. One star system's government – no matter what its nature – taking over another was a concept always considered totally impossible. Capone had proved it wasn't. In doing so he set off a chain reaction of panic. Commentators began to talk about planetary-level exponential curves, the most extreme showing the entire Confederation falling to the Organization within six months as the industrial resources of more and more systems were absorbed by Capone's empire.

On the Assembly floor, demands that the Confederation Navy should intervene and destroy the Organization fleet became almost continuous. First Admiral Aleksandrovich had to make several appearances to explain how impractical the notion was. The best the navy could do, he said, was to seek out the source of Capone's antimatter and prevent a third system from being taken over. Arnstadt was already lost. Capone had secured a victory which couldn't be reversed without a great loss of life. At this stage, such casualties were wholly unacceptable. He also pointed out that, sadly, a great many non-possessed crews were cooperating with the Organization to operate their starships. Without them, the invasion of Arnstadt could never have happened. Perhaps, he suggested, the Assembly should consider introducing an emergency act to deal with any such traitors. Such legislation might, in future, discourage captains seeking to sign up with Capone for short-term gain.

*

'Escort duties?' André Duchamp asked wearily. 'I thought we were here to help defend New California itself. What exactly does this escort duty entail?'

'Monterey hasn't given me a detailed briefing,' Iain Girardi said. 'But you will simply be protecting cargo ships from attack by the Confederation Navy. Which is exactly what your contract stipulated.'

'Hardly,' Madeleine growled. 'Nor does it say anywhere that we help a deranged dictator who wiped out an entire fucking planet. I say jump out, Captain. Power up the patterning nodes right now, and get the fuck out of here while we still can.'

'I would have thought this was a more appealing task for you,' Iain Girardi said. His acceleration couch webbing peeled back, and he drifted off the cushioning. 'The majority of the crews in the cargo ships are non-possessed, and you won't be

**641**

permanently in range of the Organization's SD platforms. If anything, we're giving you an easier job with less risk for the same money.'

'Where would we be going?' André asked.

'Arnstadt. The Organization is shipping industrial equipment there to help restart the planetary economy.'

'If they hadn't blown it all to shit in the first place they wouldn't need to restart it,' Madeleine said.

André shushed her impatiently. 'It seems fine to me,' he told Iain Girardi. 'However, the ship will require some maintenance work before we can undertake such an assignment. An escort flight is very different from supplementing planetary defences.'

Iain Girardi's humour appeared strained for the first time. 'Yes. I'll have to discuss the nature of the repairs with Monterey.' He datavised the flight computer for a communication channel.

André waited with a neutral smile.

'The Organization will bring the *Villeneuve's Revenge* up to full combat-capable status,' Iain Girardi announced. 'Your hull and sensor suite will be repaired by us, but you must meet the cost of secondary systems.'

André shrugged. 'Take it out of our fee.'

'Very well. Please dock at Monterey's spaceport, Bay VB757. I shall disembark there; you'll be assigned a liaison officer for the mission.'

'Non-possessed,' Desmond Lafoe said sharply.

'Of course. I believe they also want you to take some reporters with you, as well. They'll require access to your sensors during the flight.'

'*Merde.* Those filth. What for?'

'Mr Capone is highly focused on the need for accurate publicity. He wants the Confederation to see that he is not a real threat.'

'Unlike Arnstadt,' Madeleine said swiftly.

André piloted the starship down from its emergence zone to

the large asteroid. Spaceflight traffic above New California was heavy, starships raced between the orbital asteroids and the emergence zones, spaceplanes and ion-field flyers flew a constant shuttle service from the planet. Although the starship only had sixty-five per cent of its sensor clusters remaining, André kept them fully extended to gather what information he could.

When the flight computer told her Girardi was talking to Monterey again, Madeleine opened an encrypted channel to André: 'I don't think we should dock,' she datavised.

The captain extended the datavise to include Erick and Desmond. 'Why not?'

'Look at those ships out there, if anything there's more activity than before the planet was possessed. I didn't realize how damn professional this Capone Organization is. We're not going to get out of this, André, we're in too deep. The second we dock they'll swarm on board and possess us.'

'Then who will crew the ship for them? *Non*, they need us.'

'She has a point about the Organization's size and motivation, though,' Erick datavised. 'The possessed are dependent on us flying the warships, but what happens when there are no more worlds left to invade? Capone took Arnstadt in less than a day, and almost doubled his military resources doing so. He's not going to stop now. If he and the rest of the possessed keep on winning at that rate, there will be no place left for nonpossessed anywhere in the Confederation. That's what we'll be helping bring about.'

'I know this.' André cast a guilty glance at Girardi to make sure he wasn't aware of the conversation. 'That is why I agreed to the escort duty.'

'I don't get it,' Madeleine said.

'Simple, *ma cherie*. The Organization repairs the *Villeneuve's Revenge* for me, fills up our cryogenic fuel tanks, equips us with combat wasps, and sends us off on a flight. Then while we're on route, we vanish. What is to stop us?'

'Their liaison officer, for a start,' Desmond said.

'Ha, one man. We can overcome him. Capone has made his greatest mistake in trying to dishonour André Duchamp. It is I who is using them now, for the benefit of my fellow man, *comme il faut*. I am no quisling. And I think we should make sure the reporters know of this savage blow we will strike against Capone.'

'You really intend to leave?' Madeleine asked.

'Naturally.'

Erick grinned, as best as his new skin would allow him. For once Duchamp's devious nature could actually work for the best. He opened a new file in his neural nanonics memory cell, and started recording the sensor images. CNIS would want to know about the Organization's disposition; though he suspected the New California system would already be under full covert surveillance.

'What about Shane Brandes?' Desmond asked.

André's face darkened. 'What about him?'

'How long were you planning to leave him in zero-tau?'

'I could hardly drop him off at Chaumort, it was too small. We want a backward planet where we can dump him in the middle of a desert or a jungle.'

'Lalonde would do,' Madeleine said under her breath.

'Well, if you're looking for somewhere he won't come back from . . .' Desmond offered maliciously.

'No,' Erick datavised.

'Why not?' André asked. 'Give him to the Organization when we dock. It is an excellent idea. Shows them how loyal we are.'

'We kill him, or dump him. But not that. You didn't see what they did to Bev.'

André flinched. 'Very well. But I'm not hanging on to that bastard for ever, his zero-tau is costing me power.'

*Villeneuve's Revenge* docked in its designated bay, its crew alert for any treachery from the Organization. There was none to see. As Iain Girardi promised, maintenance teams immediately started to work on the starship's battered hull and defunct sensors. It took eleven hours to withdraw the damaged sections and install new replacements. Integration and diagnostic checks took another two hours to complete.

Once André agreed that they were ready for escort duties, the Organization started loading combat wasps into the launch-tubes. An airlock tube slid out from the docking-bay wall to connect with the *Villeneuve's Revenge*.

It was Desmond, armed with a machine-pistol bought on Chaumort, who went down to the lower deck with Girardi. He made sure the tube was completely empty before opening the hatch and letting the Organization man out. Only when Girardi had swum down the length of the tube and closed the far hatch behind him did he give André the all clear.

'Send your liaison officer through,' André datavised to the spaceport.

As arranged, the man wore nothing, towing his clothes in a small bag behind him as he came along the tube. Desmond made every test they could think of, requesting complex datavises from the liaison officer's neural nanonics, exposing him to different processor blocks.

'I think he's clean,' Desmond datavised.

Madeleine unlocked the manual latches on the hatch to the lower deck.

The liaison officer introduced himself as Kingsley Pryor. To Erick, his subdued behaviour and quiet, stumbling voice indicated someone emerging from shock.

'There will be a convoy of twelve cargo ships departing for Arnstadt in three hours,' Kingsley Pryor told them. 'The *Villeneuve's Revenge* will be one of five combat-capable ships escorting them. Your job is to defend them from any sneak attacks from Confederation Navy ships. If it does happen, they'll probably use voidhawks against us.' He gave the bridge a thoughtful look. 'I wasn't told there would only be four of you, is that enough to operate at full combat efficiency?'

'Of course it is,' André responded hotly. 'We have survived much worse than a voidhawk attack.'

'Very well. There is one other thing you should know. The Organization is held together by fear and respect, obedience must be total. You have accepted our money and signed on with the fleet, we will not tolerate any disloyalty.'

'You come on my ship, and tell me—' André blustered loudly.

Kingsley Pryor held up a hand. Weak though the gesture was, it silenced Duchamp immediately. Something in the liaison officer's manner put a great deal of weight behind his authority. 'You signed a pact with the Devil, Captain. Now I'm explaining the small print. You don't trust us, fair enough; we don't really trust you either. I'm sure that now you've seen New California first-hand you've realized just how powerful and dedicated the Organization is, and you're having second thoughts about supporting us. Perfectly natural. After all, it would be very easy for a starship to disappear in the direction of the Confederation. Let me try and dissuade you. While your ship was being repaired, a nuclear explosive was included inside one of the new components. It has a seven-hour timer which must be reset by a code. I do not have that code, so you cannot use debrief nanonics to extract it from me. A liaison officer in one of the other escort ships will transmit that code at us every three hours, resetting the timer. In turn I will transmit the code I have been given at the other ships, which have been similarly modified. If all of us stay together, there will be no problem. If one ship leaves, they will be killing themselves and the crew of another ship.'

'Remove it now!' André shouted, furiously. 'I will not fly under such a blackmail threat.'

'It is not blackmail, Captain, it is enforcement, making sure you abide by the terms of your contract. I believe the argument goes along the lines of: "If you intended to keep the agreement you made with us you have nothing to worry about."'

'I will not fly with a bomb on board. That is final!'

'Then they will come on board, and possess you. And another crew will be found. It is the ship and its capability they want, Captain, not you as an individual.'

'This is intolerable!'

For a moment a real anger shone in Kingsley Pryor's eyes. He sneered at André. 'So is a free man agreeing to help Capone, Captain.' Then the emotion was gone, leaving only the meek expression in its wake. 'Shall we get the reporters on board now? We haven't got too much time before we have to be at the jump coordinate.'

*

Jed Hinton was still a hundred metres from the pub when he knelt down and took the red handkerchief off his ankle. Koblat's adults were starting to get nettled by Deadnight; kids that followed the cause were being hassled. Nothing serious, some jostling in public places, rows at home. The usual crap.

Digger, of course, despised the recording, descending into a rage whenever it was mentioned. For once Jed enjoyed a guilty delight at the way he intimidated Miri and Navar, forbidding them to have anything to do with it. Without realizing, he'd altered the political structure of the family. Now it was Jed and Gari who were the favoured ones, the ones who could access Kiera Salter, and talk about her ideas with their friends, and know the taste of freedom.

Jed walked into the Blue Fountain, making out like it was cool for him to be there. Normally he'd be anywhere else, it was Digger's pub. But Digger was busy these days; not working the tunnelling units, but out at the spaceport doing maintenance on the machinery in the docking-bays. There were three shifts a day now, supporting the increasing number of flights. Yet although everyone knew perfectly well starships were arriving and departing several times a day, there was no official log. Three times he'd accessed the net and asked the spaceport register for a list of ships docked only to be told there were none.

Fascinated, the Deadnight kids had asked round, and together they'd pieced together the basics of the quarantine-busting operation. They had all been excited that day, starships arriving illegally was *perfect* for them. Beth had smiled at him and said: 'Bloody hell, we might just make it to Valisk, after all.' Then she'd hugged him. She'd never done that before, not in that way.

He asked the barman for a beer, slowly scanning the pub. A room where the images within the ten-year-old landscape holograms covering the walls were diminishing to blurred smears, their colours fading. The naked rock they covered would be less depressing. Most of the scuffed composite and aluminium tables were occupied. Groups of men sat hunched over their drinks and talked in low tones. Nearly a quarter of the customers were wearing ship-suits, bright and exotic compared to the clothes favoured by Koblat's residents.

Jed located the crew from the *Rameses X*, the starship's name stencilled neatly on their breast pockets. Their captain was with them, a middle-aged woman with the silver star on her epaulette. He went over.

'I wonder if I could talk to you, ma'am?'

She glanced up at him, faintly suspicious at the respectful tone.

'What is it?'

'I have a friend who would like to go to Valisk.'

The captain burst out laughing. Jed flushed as the rest of the crew groaned, trading infuriatingly superior expressions.

'Well, son, I can certainly understand how come your friend is so interested in young Kiera.' She winked broadly.

Jed's embarrassment deepened, which must have been obvious to all of them. True, he had spent hours on his processor block with a graphics program, altering the image from the recording. Now the block's small AV pillar could project her lying beside him on the bed at night, or looming over him smiling. At first he'd worried he was being disrespectful; but she would understand the need he had for her. The love. She knew all about love, in its many forms. It was all she spoke of.

'It's what she offers,' he stammered helplessly. 'That's what we're interested in.'

That just brought another round of hearty laughter from the group.

'Please,' he said. 'Can you take us there?'

The humour sank from her face. 'Listen, son, take the advice of an older woman. That recording: it's just a big bullshit con. They want you there so they can possess you, that's all. There's no paradise waiting at the end of the rainbow.'

'Have you been there?' he asked stiffly.

'No. No, I haven't. So you're right, I can't say for certain. Let's just put it down to a healthy dose of cynicism; everybody catches it when they get older.' She turned back to her drink.

'Will you take me?'

'No. Look, son, even if I was crazy enough to fly to Valisk, do you have any idea how much it would cost you to charter a starship to take you?'

He shook his head mutely.

'From here, about quarter of a million fuseodollars. Do you have that kind of money?'

'No.'

'Well, there you are, then. Now stop wasting my time.'

'Do you know anyone who would take us, someone who believes in Kiera?'

'Goddamit!' She screwed round in her chair to glare at him. 'Can't you inbred morons pick up a simple hint when it's smacked you in the face?'

'Kiera said you'd hate us for listening to her.'

The captain let out an astonished snort of breath. 'I don't believe this. Don't you see how gullible you are? I'm doing you a favour.'

'I didn't ask you to. And why are you so blind to what she says?'

'Blind? Fuck you, you teeny shit.'

'Because you are. You're scared it's true, that she's right.'

She stared at him for a long moment, the rest of the crew fixing him with hostile stares. They'd probably beat him up in a minute. Jed didn't care any more. He hated her as much as he did Digger and all the others with closed minds and dead hearts.

'All right,' the Captain whispered. 'In your case I'll make an exception.'

'No,' one of the crew said, his hand going out to hold her arm. 'You can't, he's only a kid with a hard-on for the girl.'

She shook off the restraining hand, and brought out a processor block. 'I was going to hand this over to the Confederation Navy, even though it would be difficult to explain away given our current flight schedule. But I think you can have it instead, now.' She took a flek from its slot in the block and slapped it into an astonished Jed's hand. 'Say hello to Kiera for me. If you aren't too busy screaming while they possess you.'

Chairs were pushed back noisily. The crew of the *Rameses X* left their unfinished drinks on the table and marched out.

Jed stood at the centre of a now silent pub, every eye locked on him. He didn't even notice, he was staring raptly at the little black flek resting in his palm as if it was the key to the fountain of youth. Which in a way, he supposed, it was.

\*

The *Levêque* was orbiting fifteen thousand kilometres above Norfolk, its complete sensor suite extended to sweep the planet. Despite the Confederation Navy's hunger for information, little data was returning. Slow cyclonic swirls of red cloud had mushroomed from the islands, mating then smoothing out into a placid sheet, sealing the world behind a uniform twilight nimbus. Small ivory tufts of cirrocumulus swam above the polar zones for a few hours, the last defiant speckling of alien colour; but in time even they fell to melt into the veil.

The consolidation was five hours old when the change began. *Levêque*'s officers noticed the cloud's light emission level was increasing. The frigate's captain decided to play safe, and ordered them to raise their orbit by another twenty thousand kilometres. By the time their main fusion drive ignited, the crimson canopy was blazing brighter than any firestorm. They ascended at five gees, badly worried by the glare expanding rapidly across the stars behind them. Gravitonic sensors reported discordant ripples within the planetary mass below. If the readings were truthful, then the world should be breaking apart. Heavily filtered optical-band sensors revealed the planet's geometry remained unchanged.

Seven gees, and the cloud's surface was kindling to the intensity of a nuclear furnace.

Luca Comar looked upwards in a dreamy daze. The red cloud guarding the sky above Cricklade Manor's steep roof was writhing violently, its gold and crimson underbelly caught by potent microburst vortices. Huge churning strips were being torn open, allowing a fierce white light to slam down. He flung his arms wide, howling a rapturous welcome.

Energy stormed through him at an almost painful rate; bursting from some non-point within to vanish into the raging sky. The woman beside him was performing the same act, her features straining with effort and incredulity. In his mind he could feel the possessed all across Norfolk uniting in this final supreme sacrament.

Boiling fragments of cloud plunged through the air at giddy velocities, corkscrew lightning bolts snapping between them. Their red tint was fading, sinking behind the flamboyant dawn irradiating the universe beyond the atmosphere.

A thick, heavy light poured over Luca. It penetrated straight through his body. Through the mossy grass. Through the soil. The whole world surrendered to it. Luca's thoughts were trapped by the invasion, unable to think of anything but sustaining the moment. He hung suspended from reality as the last surge of energy unwound through his cells.

Silence.

Luca slowly let out his breath. He opened his eyes cautiously. The clouds had calmed, reverting to rumpled white smears. Warm mellow light was shining over the wolds. There was no sun, no single source point, it came from the boundary of the enclosed universe itself. Shining equally, everywhere.

And they'd gone. He could no longer hear the souls in the beyond. Those piercing pleas and promises had vanished. There was no way back, no treacherous chink in the folds of this fresh continuum. He was free inside his new body.

He looked at the woman, who was glancing round in stupefaction.

'We've done it,' he whispered. 'We escaped.'

She smiled tentatively.

He held out his arms, and concentrated. Not the smoke-snorting knight again; the moment required something more dignified. Soft golden cloth settled around his skin, an imperial toga, befitting his mood.

'Oh yes. Yes!'

The energistic ability was still there, the imposition of will upon matter. But now the cloth had a stronger, firmer texture than the artefacts he'd created before.

Before ... Luca Comar laughed. In another universe. Another life.

This time it would be different. They could establish their nirvana here. And it would last for ever.

\*

**652**

The cluster of five survey satellites from the *Levêque* gradually spread apart as they glided through the section of space where Norfolk should be. Communication links beamed a huge flow of information back to the frigate. Every sensor they had was switched to maximum sensitivity. Two distinct spectrums of sunlight fell on them. Tremulous waves of solar ions dusted their receptors. Cosmic radiation bombardment was standard.

There was nothing else. No gravity field. No magnetosphere. No atmospheric gas. Space-time's quantum signature was perfectly normal.

All that remained of Norfolk was the memory.

*

When it was discovered in 2125, Nyvan was immediately incorporated into the celebration of hope which was sweeping Earth in the wake of Felicity's discovery. The second terracompatible planet to be found, a beautiful verdant virgin land, proof the first hadn't been a fluke. Everybody on Earth wanted to escape out to the stars. And they wanted to go there now. That, ultimately, proved its downfall.

By then, people had finally realized the arcologies weren't going to be a temporary shelter from the ruined climate, somewhere to stay while Govcentral cooled the atmosphere, cleaned up the pollution, and put the weather patterns back to rights. The tainted clouds and armada storms were here to stay. Anyone who wanted to live under an open sky would have to leave and find a new one.

In the interests of fairness, and maintaining its own shaky command over individual state administrations, Govcentral agreed that everyone had the right to leave, without favouritism. It was that last worthy clause, included to pacify several vocal minorities, which in practice meant that colonists would have to be a multicultural, multiracial mix fully representative of the planet's population. No limits were placed on the numbers buying starship tickets, they just had to be balanced. For those states too poor to fill up their quota, Govcentral provided assisted placement schemes so the richer states couldn't complain they were being unfairly limited. A typical political compromise.

By and large, it worked for Nyvan and the other terracompatible planets being sought out by the new ZTT drive ships. The first decades of interstellar colonization were heady times, when common achievement easily outweighed the old ethnic enmities. Nyvan and its early siblings played host to a unity of purpose rarely seen before.

It didn't last. After the frontier had been tamed and the pioneering spirit flickered into extinction the ancient rivalries lumbered to the fore once again. Earth's colonial governance gave way to local administrations on a dozen planets, and politicians began to adopt the worst jingoistic aspects of late-twentieth-century nationalism, leading the mob behind them with absurd ease. This time there were no safeguards of seas and geographical borders between the diverse populations. Religions, cultures, skins, ideologies, and languages were all squeezed up tight in the pinch chamber of urban conglomeration. Civil unrest was the inevitable result, ruining lives and crippling economies.

Overall, the problem was solved in 2156 by the Govcentral state of California, which sponsored New California, the first ethnic-streaming colony, open only to native Californians – a trend which although initially controversial was swiftly taken up by the other states. This second wave of colonies suffered none of the strife so prevalent among the first, clearing the way for the mass emigration of the Great Dispersal.

While the new ethnic-streaming worlds successfully absorbed Earth's surplus population and flourished accordingly, the earlier colonies slowly lost ground both culturally and economically. A false dawn shading to a perpetual twilight.

*

'What happened to the asteroids?' Lawrence Dillon asked.

Quinn was gazing thoughtfully at the images which the *Tantu*'s sensors were throwing onto the hemisphere of holo-screens at the foot of his acceleration couch. In total, eleven asteroids had been manoeuvred into orbit around Nyvan, their ores mined to provide raw material for the planet's industries. Ordinarily, they would develop into healthy mercantile settlements with a flotilla of industrial stations.

The frigate's sensors showed that eight of them were more or less standard knots of electromagnetic activity, giving off a strong infra-red emission. The remaining three were cold and dark. *Tantu*'s high-resolution optical sensors focused on the closest of the defunct rocks, revealing wrecked machinery clinging to the crumpled grey surface. One of them even had a counter-rotating spaceport disc, though it no longer revolved; the spindle was bent, and the gloomy structure punctured with holes.

'They had a lot of national wars here,' Quinn said.

Lawrence frowned at him, thoughts cloudy with incomprehension.

'There's a lot of different people live here,' Quinn explained. 'They don't get on too good, so they fight a lot.'

'If they hate each other, why don't they all leave?'

'I don't know. Ask them.'

'Who?'

'Shut the fuck up, Lawrence, I'm trying to think. Dwyer, has anyone seen us yet?'

'Yes, the detector satellites picked us up straight away. We've had three separate transponder interrogations so far; they were from different defence network command centres. Everyone seemed satisfied with our identification code this time.'

'Good. Graper, I want you to be our communication officer.'

'Yes, Quinn.' Graper let the eagerness show in his voice, anxious to prove his worth.

'Stick with the cover we decided. Call each of those military centres, and tell the bastards we've been assigned a monitor mission in this system by the Confederation Navy. We'll be staying in high orbit until further notice, and if any of them want fire support against possessed targets we'll be happy to provide it.'

'I'm on it, Quinn.' He began issuing orders to the flight computer.

'Dwyer,' Quinn said. 'Get me a channel into Nyvan's communication net.' He floated away from his velvet acceleration couch, and used a stikpad to steady himself in front of his big command console.

'Er, Quinn, this is weird, the sensors are showing me like fifty communications platforms in geosync,' Dwyer said nervously. He was using grab hoops to hold himself in front of his flight station, his face centimetres from a glowing holoscreen, as though the closer he could get the more understanding of its data he would have. 'The computer says they've got nineteen separate nets on this world, some of them don't even hook together.'

'Yeah, so? I told you, dickbrain, they got a shitload of different nations here.'

'Which one do you want?'

Quinn thought back, picturing the man, his mannerisms, voice, accent. 'Is there a North American ethnic nation?'

Dwyer consulted the information on the holoscreen. 'I got five. There's Tonala, New Dominica, New Georgia, Quebec, and the Islamic Texas Republic.'

'Gimme the New Georgia one.' Information began to scroll up on his own holoscreen. He studied it for a minute, then requested a directory function and loaded in a search program.

'Who is this guy, Quinn?' Lawrence asked.

'Name's Twelve-T. He's one mean fucker, a gang lord, runs a big operation down there. Any badass shit you want, you go to him for it.'

The search program finished its run. Quinn loaded the eddress it had found for him.

'Yeah?' a voice asked.

'I want to talk to Twelve-T.'

'Crazy-ass mother, ain't no fucker got that handle living here.'

'Listen, shitbrain, this is his public eddress. He's there.'

'Yeah, so you know him, datavise him.'

'Not possible.'

'Yeah? Then he don't know you. Any mother he needs to rap with knows his private code.'

'OK; the magic word is Banneth. And if you don't think that's magic, trace where this call is coming from. Now tell the man, because if I come calling, you're going out hurting.'

Dwyer gave another myopic squint at his displays. 'He's tracing the call. Back to the satellite already. Hot program.'

'I expect they use it a lot,' Quinn muttered.

'You got a problem up there, motherfucker?' a new voice asked. It was almost as Quinn remembered it, a low purr, too damaged to be smooth. Quinn had seen the throat scar which made it that way.

'No problem at all. What I got up here is a proposition.'

'Where you at, man? What is this monk shit? You ain't Banneth.'

'No.' Quinn swayed forward slowly towards the camera lens in the centre of the console, and pulled his hood right back. 'Run your visual file search program.'

'Oh, yeah. You used to be Banneth's little rat runner; her whore, too. I remember. So what you want here, ratty?'

'A deal.'

'What you got to trade?'

'You know what I'm riding in?'

'Sure. Lucky Vin ran a trace, he's pissin' liquid nitrogen right now.'

'It could be yours.'

'No shit?'

'That's right.'

'What've I gotta do for it, hump you?'

'No, I just want to trade it in. That's all.'

The whisper lost its cool. 'You want to trade in a fucking Confederation Navy frigate? What the fuck for?'

'I need to talk to you about that. But there's some good-quality hardware on board. You'll come out ahead.'

'Talk, motherfucker? If you're hardware's so shit-hot, how come you wanna dump it?'

'God's Brother doesn't always ride to war. There are other ways to bring His word to the faithless.'

'Cut that voodoo shit, man. Damn, I hate that sect shit you arcology freaks use. Ain't no God, so he sure as shit can't have no Brother.'

'Try telling that to the possessed.'

'Motherfuck! Smartass motherfucker! That's what you are, that's all you are.'

'Do you want to deal or not?' Quinn knew he would; what gang lord could resist a frigate?

'I ain't promising shit up front.'

'That's cool. Now I need to know which asteroid to dock with. And it's going to have to be one which doesn't ask too many questions. Have you got any weight in orbit?'

'You know it, man, that's why you come to me. You might talk like you the King of Kulu's brother, but here it's me who's got the juice. And stink this, I don't trust you, rat runner.'

'With this much firepower behind me, think how much I care. Start fixing things.'

'Fuck you. A strike like this is gonna take a few days to set up, man.'

'You have forty-eight hours; then I want a docking-bay number flashing in front of me. If not, I will smite you from the face of the world.'

'Will you cut that freaky crap—'

Quinn cancelled the circuit, and threw his head back laughing.

\*

It had only taken a few hours for the screen of red cloud to engulf the sky above Exnall. The tenuous beginnings of the early morning had been supplanted by billowing masses of solid vapour sweeping up from the south. Thunder arrived in accompaniment, bass grumbles which seemed to circle and swoop around the town like jittery birds. There was no telling where the sun was now, but its light still seemed to slip through the covering to illuminate the streets in natural tones.

Moyo marched down Maingreen on his mission to find some kind of transport for Stephanie's children. The more he thought about the prospect, the happier it made him. She was right, as always, it did give him something positive to do. And no, he didn't want to spend eternity in Exnall.

He passed the doughnut café and the baseball game on the park, oblivious to both. If he searched with his mind, he could perceive the buildings around him like foggy shadows; all space was dark, while matter was amended to a translucent white gauze. Individual objects were hard to distinguish, and small ones almost impossible; but he thought he stood a good chance of recognizing something like a bus.

The street sweeper was busy again. A man in a grey jacket and cloth cap, pushing his broom in front of him as he made his way slowly along the pavement. Every day he had appeared. He never did anything else but sweep the pavements, never talked to anybody, never responded to any attempts at conversation.

Moyo was slowly coming to learn that not all of Exnall's possessed were adapting readily to their new circumstances. Some, like the sports nuts and café owners, were obsessively filling every moment of their day with activity no matter how spurious, while others would amble around in a listless mockery of their earlier existence. That assessment put his own labours perilously close to the apathetic ones.

A dense collection of shadows at the rear of one of the larger stores caught his attention. When he walked round the building there was a long van parked in the loading-bay. It had suffered some damage in the riot; struck by white fire, the front two tyres had melted into puddles of sticky plastic, the navy-blue bodywork was blackened and in some places cracked open, the windscreen was smashed. But it was certainly big enough.

He stared at the first tyre, visualizing it whole and functional. Not an illusion, but how the solid matter should actually be structured. The hardened plastic puddle started to flow, amoebic buds swelling up to engulf the naked hub.

'Yo there, man. Having some fun?'

Moyo had been so involved with the tyre he hadn't noticed the man approaching – he really should have done. At first sight the man looked as if he'd grown a dark-brown mane; his beard came down to his waist, as did the corkscrew locks of his luxuriant hair. A pair of tiny amber hexagonal glasses which were almost curtained by tresses seemed perversely prominent. The flares of his purple velvet trousers were embellished with tiny silver bells which chimed with each step, not in tune, but certainly in keeping.

'Not exactly. Is this your van?'

'Hey, property is theft, man.'

'Property is what?'

'Theft. You're like stealing from what rightfully belongs to all people. That van is an inanimate object. Unless you're into a metallic version of Gaia – which personally I'm not. However, just because it's inert that doesn't mean we can abuse its intrinsic value which is the ability to carry cats where they want to go.'

'Cats? I just want it to ferry some children out of here.'

'Yeah, well, OK that's cool, too. But what I like mean is that it's like community property. It was built by people, so all people should share it equally.'

'It was built by cybersystems.'

'Oh no, that's real heavy duty corporate shit. Man, they've got into your skull big-time. Here, take a toot, Mr Suit, take yourself out of yourself.' He held out a fat reefer which was already alight and sending out a pungent sweetness.

'No, thanks.'

'Takes your mind to other realms.'

'I've just got back from one, thank you. I have no intention of returning.'

'Yeah, right, dig your point. The baddest trip of them all.'

Moyo couldn't quite make out what he was confronting. The man didn't seem like one of the apathetic ones. On the other hand, he obviously hadn't managed to adapt very well. Perhaps he came from a pre-technology age, where education was minimal and superstition ruled everyone's life.

'What era do you come from?'

'Ho! The greatest one there ever was. I dug the era of peace, when we were busy fighting the establishment for all the freedom you cats just take for granted. Heck, I was at Woodstock, man. Can you dig that?'

'Um, I'm very happy for you. So you don't mind if I rebuild the van, then?'

'Rebuild? What are you, some kind of anti-anarchist?'

'I'm someone who's got children to look after. Unless you'd rather they were tortured by Ekelund's people.'

The man's body bucked as if he'd been struck a physical blow; his arms wove in strange jerky motions in front of him. Moyo didn't think it was a dance.

'I hate your hostility groove, but I dig your motivation. That's cool. A square cat like you is probably having a lot of trouble adjusting to this situation.'

Moyo's jaw dropped open. '*I'm* having trouble?'

'Thought so. So like what kind of magical mystery tour are you planning here?'

'We're taking the children out of Exnall. Stephanie wants to drive up to the border.'

'Oh, man!' A wide smile prised apart layers of hair. 'That is so beautiful. The border again. We're gonna roll this old bus out and set the draft dodgers free in the land of Mounties and maple leaves. What a trip! Thank you, man, thank you.' He walked over to the battered van and stroked its front wing lovingly. A small wavy rainbow appeared on the bodywork where his hand had touched it.

'What do you mean, we?'

'Come on, man, lighten up. You don't think you can handle that kind of scene alone, do you? The military mind is full of low cunning; you wouldn't get a mile out of town without them throwing up roadblocks across the freeway. Maybe a few of us would fall down some stairs while we're being arrested, too. It happens, man, all of the frigging time. The Federal pigs don't give a shit about our rights. But I've been here before, I know how to go sneaky on them.'

'You think she'd try and stop us?'

'Who, man?'

'Ekelund.'

'Hell, who knows. Chicks like that have got it real hard up their asses. Between you and me, I think they're maybe like aliens. You know, UFO people from Venus. But I can see you're sceptical right now, I won't press it. So how many kids are you planning on squirrelling away in here?'

'About seven or eight, so far.'

Without quite understanding how it happened, Moyo found a friendly arm round his shoulder, guiding him to the van's cab.

'That's worthy. I can dig that. Now you just ease yourself up in the driver's seat, or whatever the hell they call it these days,

**662**

and dream up some controls we can all handle. Once you've done that and I've given us a cool disguise we can hit the road.'

Twinkles of light were shooting all over the van's bodywork, sketching glowing lines of colour in the damaged composite. It was as if a flock of acidhead fairies had been let loose with spray cans. Moyo wanted to complain at this ideological hijack, but couldn't manage to think up the correct words. He took the easy option, and sat in the driver's seat like he'd been told.

*

There was a gap between the deuterium tank's cryostat ducts and the power feed sub-module which routed superconductor cables to nearby patterning nodes, a narrow crevice amid the boxy nultherm-foam-coated machinery. In the schematics the flight computer provided it was listed as a crawlway.

For pigmy acrobats, maybe, Erick thought irascibly. He certainly couldn't wear any protective gear over the SII suit. Sharp corners and bloated tubes jabbed and squeezed against him every time he moved. It couldn't be doing the medical nanonic packages round his arm and torso any good. Thankfully the black silicon covering his skin was an effective insulator, otherwise he would have been roasted, frozen, or electrocuted long ago.

Along with Madeleine he'd been burrowing through the innards of the *Villeneuve's Revenge* for nine hours now. It was nasty, tiring, stressful work. With his body in the state it was he had to keep a constant check on his physiological status. He was also running a mild relaxant program in primary mode; claustrophobia was a problem prowling wolfishly round the fringes of conscious thought.

The crawlway ended a metre short of the hull, opening out into a hexagonal metallic cave bordered with stress structure girders, themselves spiralled by cables. Erick squirmed out into this cramped space, and drew a sharp breath of relief; more psychological than practical, given he was breathing through a respirator tube. He switched his collar sensors to scan round, seeing the fuselage plate behind his head. It appeared perfectly normal, a smooth, slightly curving silicon surface, dark grey with red code strips printed round the edges.

With his legs still jammed in the crawlway, Erick pulled the sensor block from the straps securing it to his side. It contained six separate scanner pads which he slipped out and started fixing to the hull plate and girders.

'Plate 3–25-D is clean,' he datavised to André eight minutes later. 'No electromagnetic activity; and it's solid, too, no density anomalies.'

'Very good, Erick. 5–12-D is next.'

'How is Madeleine doing?'

'She is methodical. Between you, eighteen per cent of the possible locations have now been eliminated.'

Erick cursed. The four of them had carefully gone over the starship's schematics, working out every possible section of the hull in which the device could have been hidden by Monterey's maintenance crews. With Pryor on board observing the bridge, they were limited to two crew searching at any one time, the two supposed to be asleep. It was going to take a long time to cover all the possible areas.

'I still say it's probably a combat wasp. That would be the easiest method.'

'Oui, but we won't know for sure until you have eliminated all the other options. Who can tell with such treacherous bastards?'

'Great. How long to Arnstadt?'

'We have another five jumps to go. Two of the other escort ships are manoeuvring sluggishly, which gives us additional time. They are probably searching as we are. You have perhaps another fifteen hours, twenty at the outside.'

Not enough, Erick knew, not nearly enough. They were going to have to go to Arnstadt. After that he didn't like to think what the Organization would require from them. Nothing as simple as escort duties, that was for certain.

'All right, Captain, I'm on my way to 5–12-D.'

\*

The chamber which the Saldanas used for their Privy Council meetings was called the Fountain Room, a white marble octagon with a gold and opal mosaic ceiling. Imposing three-metre statues stood around the walls, sculpted from a dark rock which had been cut out of Nova Kong, depicting a toga-clad orator in various inspirational poses. The Fountain Room wasn't as grandiose as some of the state function rooms added to the Apollo Palace in later centuries, but it had been built by Gerald Saldana soon after his coronation for use as his cabinet room. The continuity of power was unbroken since then; the Saldanas were nothing if not respectful for the traditions of their own history.

There were forty-five members of the current Privy Council, including the princes and princesses who ruled the principalities, which meant a full meeting was only held every eighteen months. Normally the King summoned twenty to twenty-five people to advise him, family nearly always over half of them. Today there were just six sitting round the Fountain Room's triangular mahogany table with its inlaid crowned phoenix. It was the war cabinet, chaired by Alastair II himself, with the Duke of Salion on his left, followed by Lord Kelman Mountjoy, the Foreign Office Minister; on the King's right-hand side was the Prime Minister, Lady Phillipa Oshin, Admiral Lavaquar, the Defence Chief, and Prince Howard, President of Kulu Corporation. No aides or equerries were present.

Alastair II picked up a small gavel and tapped the much-battered silver bell on the table in front of him. 'The fifth meeting of this cabinet committee is now in order. I trust everyone has accessed the latest reports concerning Arnstadt?'

There was a subdued round of acknowledgement from the cabinet.

'Very well. Admiral, your assessment?'

'Bloody worrying, Your Majesty. As we all know interstellar conquest has always been regarded as completely impractical. Today's navies exist to protect civil starships from piracy, and deter potential aggressors from committing random or sneak assaults. If anyone strikes at us for political or economic reasons they damn well know we will strike back harder. But actually subduing an entire system's population was not a concept any of our strategy groups even considered until today. Ethnically-streamed populations are too diverse, you simply cannot impose a different culture on a defeated indigenous people, it will never be accepted, and you lose the peace trying to enforce it. Therefore, conquests are impractical. Possession has changed that. All Confederation worlds are vulnerable to it, even Kulu. Though had the Capone Organization fleet jumped into orbit here it would have lost.'

'Even armed with antimatter?' Prince Howard enquired.

'Oh, yes. We would have taken a pounding, no doubt about it. But we would have won; in terms of firepower our SD network is second only to Earth's. The thing which concerns our strategists most is the Organization's theoretical expansion rate. They have effectively doubled their fleet size by taking Arnstadt. If another five or six star systems were to fall into Capone's hands, we would be facing parity at the very least.'

'We have distance on our side,' Lady Phillipa said. 'Kulu is nearly three hundred light-years from New California. Deploying any kind of fleet over such a distance would be inordinately difficult. And Capone is having trouble resupplying his conquests with He$_3$, he simply isn't getting any from the Edenists.'

'Your pardon, Prime Minister,' the Admiral said, 'but you are taking a too literal interpretation of these events. Yes, it would be physically difficult for Capone to subdue Kulu, but the trend he is starting would be a different matter indeed.

Others returning from the beyond are equally capable, and some have considerably more experience in empire building than he does. Unless planetary governments remain exceptionally vigilant in searching for outbreaks of possession, what happened to New California could easily be repeated. If Capone was all we had to worry about, I would frankly be very relieved. As to the Organization's $He_3$ shortage; deuterium can and will be used as a monofuel for starship drives. It's less efficient and its radiation output has a progressively detrimental effect on the drive tube equipment. But do not imagine for a moment that will prevent them from using it. The Royal Navy has contingency plans to continue high-level operations in the event that Kulu loses every single $He_3$ cloudscoop in the Kingdom. We can fly for years, conceivably decades, using deuterium alone should the need arise.'

'So lack of $He_3$ isn't going to stop him?' the King asked.

'No, sir. Our analysts believe that given the internal nature of Capone's Organization he will have to continue his expansion efforts in order to survive. The Organization has no other purpose, growth through conquest is all it is geared up for. As a strategy for maintaining control over his own people it is excellent, but sooner or later he will run into size-management problems. Even if he realizes this and tries to stop, his lieutenants will stage a coup. If they didn't they'd lose their status along with him.'

'He seems to be running New California efficiently enough,' Lord Mountjoy said.

'That's a propaganda illusion,' the Duke of Salion said. 'The agencies have come up with a similar interpretation to the navy's. Capone boasts he has established a working government, but essentially it's a dictatorship backed by the threat of ultimate force. It survives principally because the planetary economy is on a war footing which always distorts financial reality for a while. This idea of a currency based on magic tokens is badly flawed. The energistic ability of the possessed is essentially unlimited, you cannot package it up and redistribute it to the have-nots as if it were some kind of tangible commodity.

'And so far no one has challenged Capone, he's moved too swiftly for that. But the Organization's internal political situation won't last. As soon as any kind of routine is established, people can start to look at how they are being made to live and consider it objectively. We estimate that serious underground opposition groups are going to start forming within another fortnight among both communities. From what we've actually seen and what we can filter through the propaganda, it would be very tough for possessed and non-possessed to live peacefully side by side. The society Capone has built is extremely artificial. That makes it easy to destroy, especially from within.'

Lord Mountjoy smiled faintly. 'You mean we don't have to do anything but wait? The possessed will wipe themselves out for us?'

'No. I'm not saying that. Our psychologists believe that they cannot form societies as large or as complex as ours. We have system-wide industrial civilizations because that is what it takes to maintain our socioeconomic index. But when you can live in a palace grander than this one simply by wishing it to be, what is the point of having states whose populations run into hundreds of millions? That's what will eventually neuter Capone; but it doesn't get rid of the general problem which the possessed present. Not for us.'

'I never thought a military solution was the right one, anyway,' Alastair said with a contrite nod at the Admiral. 'Not in the long term. So what kind of threat are we facing from the possessed infiltrating us? Have we really caught all of them who were at liberty in the Kingdom? Simon?'

'Ninety-nine point nine per cent, Your Majesty, certainly here on Kulu itself. Unfortunately, I can't give you absolutes. Sheer probability dictates that several have eluded us. But the AIs are becoming increasingly proficient in tracking them down through the net. And of course, if they begin to build up in any numbers they become easy for us to spot and eradicate.'

'Hardly good for morale, though,' Lady Phillipa said. 'Government can't guarantee you won't get possessed, but if it does happen don't worry, we'll see it.'

'Admittedly inconvenient for individual subjects,' Prince Howard observed. 'But it doesn't affect our overall ability to respond to the threat. And the Kulu Corporation has already built a prototype personal monitor to safeguard against possession.'

'You have?'

'Yes. It's a simple bracelet stuffed with various sensors which is linked permanently into the communication net. It'll stretch our bandwidth capacity, but two AIs can keep real-time tabs on every person on the planet. If you take it off, or if you are possessed, we'll know about it straight away and where it happened.'

'The civil rights groups will love that,' she muttered.

'The possessed will not,' Prince Howard said levelly. 'And it is their opinion which matters the most.'

'Quite,' Alastair II said. 'I shall publicly put on the first bracelet. It ought help ease public attitude to the notion. This is for their own good, after all.'

'Yes, Your Majesty,' Lady Phillipa conceded with reasonable grace.

'Very well. We cannot guarantee absolute safety for the population, but as my brother says, we can still conduct broad policy. For the moment, I have to be satisfied with that. As to the principal thrust of that broad policy, we must make a decision about Mortonridge. Admiral?'

'My staff tactical officers have been running battle simulations along the lines young Hiltch suggested. His experience has been a lot of help, but for my mind there are an awful lot of variables and unknowns.'

'Do we win any of these simulations?' the Duke of Salion asked.

'Yes. Almost all of them, providing we devote sufficient resources. That seems to be the clinching factor every time.' He gave the King a worried look. 'It's going to be risky, Your Majesty. And it is also going to be extremely costly. We must maintain our current defence status throughout the Kingdom simultaneously with running this campaign. It will take every military reserve we have, not to mention stretching our industrial capacity.'

'That should keep the baronies happy,' Lady Phillipa said.

Alastair II pretended he hadn't heard. 'But it can be done?' he pressed the Admiral.

'We believe so, Your Majesty. But it will require the full support of the Edenists. Ideally, I'd also like some material cooperation from the Confederation Navy and our allies. The more we have, the greater chance of victory.'

'Very well. Kelman, this is your field. How did your audience with the Edenist Ambassador go?'

The Foreign Minister attempted not to smile at the memory; he still wasn't sure which of them had been the more surprised. 'Actually, Ambassador Astor was extremely receptive to the notion. As we know, the old boy doesn't exactly have the easiest of jobs here. However, once I asked, he immediately put the whole embassy over to working on the practical aspects. Their military and technology attachés agree that the Jovian habitats have the capacity to produce Tranquillity serjeants in the kind of quantities we envisage.'

'What about commitment?' Prince Howard asked.

'Such a request would have to be put before their Consensus, but he was sure that given the circumstances Jupiter would consider it favourably. He actually offered to accompany whatever delegation we send and help present the argument for us. It might not sound much, but I consider such an offer to be significant.'

'Why, exactly?' the King asked.

'Because of the nature of their culture. Edenists very rarely enact a Consensus, normally there is no need. They share so much in terms of ethics and motivation that their decisions on most subjects are identical. Consensus is only required when they confront something new and radical, or they are threatened and need to select a level of response. The fact that the Ambassador himself is in agreement with our request and that he is willing to argue our case for us is a very positive factor. More than anyone, he understands what it has cost us to ask for their help in the first place, the pride we have swallowed. He can convey that for us.'

'In other words, he can swing it,' Prince Howard said.

'I consider it a high probability.'

The King paused for a moment, weighing up the troubled faces confronting him. 'Very well, I think we should proceed to the next stage. Admiral, start to prepare what forces you need to support the liberation of Mortonridge.'

'Yes, Your Majesty.'

'Kelman, the immediate burden rests upon your ministry. The Admiral says he requires support from the Confederation Navy and our allies, it will be up to the diplomatic service to secure it. Whatever interests we have, I want them realized. I suggest you confer with the ESA to see what pressure can be applied to anyone displaying less than wholehearted enthusiasm.'

'What level of assets do you want activated?' the Duke of Salion asked cautiously.

'All of them, Simon. We either do this properly or not at all. I am not prepared to commit our full military potential against such a powerful enemy unless we have total superiority. It would be morally unacceptable, as well as politically unsound.'

'Yes, sir, I understand.'

'Excellent, that's settled, then.'

'Um, what about Ione?' Lady Phillipa asked.

Alastair almost laughed openly at the Prime Minister's meekness. Not like her at all. Everyone did so tiptoe around the subject of Tranquillity in his presence. 'Good point. I think it might be best if we employ family here to complement Kelman's people. We'll send Prince Noton.'

'Yes, Your Majesty,' Lord Mountjoy said guardedly.

'Any other topics?' the King asked.

'I think we've achieved all our aims, sir,' Lady Phillipa said. 'I'd like to announce that plans to liberate Mortonridge are under way. A positive step to regain the initiative will be just what people need to hear.'

'But no mention of the Edenists,' Lord Mountjoy interjected quickly. 'Not yet, that still needs to be handled with care.'

'Of course,' she said.

'Whatever you think appropriate,' Alastair told them. 'I wish all of you good luck on your respective tasks. Let us hope Our Lord smiles on us, the sunlight seems to be decidedly lacking of late.'

*

It was only the third time Parker Higgens had been invited into Ione's apartment, and the first time he'd been in alone. He found himself disturbed by the big window in the split-level entrance lounge which looked out into the circumfluous sea; the antics of the shoals of small fish flashing their harlequin colours as they sped about did not amuse him. Strange, he thought, that the threat of pressure all that water represented should be so much more intimidating than the vacuum outside the starscraper windows.

Ione welcomed him with a smile and a delicate handshake. She was wearing a yellow robe over a glittering purple bikini, her hair still damp from her swim. Once again, as he had been right from the first moment he saw her, Parker Higgens was captivated by those enchanting blue eyes. His only comfort was that he wasn't alone in the Confederation, millions suffered as he did.

'Are you all right, Parker?' she enquired lightly.

'Yes, thank you, ma'am.'

Ione gave the window a suspicious look, and it turned opaque. 'Let's sit down.'

She selected a small circular table made from a wood so darkened with age it was impossible to identify. A pair of silent housechimps began to serve tea from a bone-china set.

'You seem to have made a lot of new friends in Trafalgar, Parker. An escort of four voidhawks, no less.'

Parker winced. Did she have any idea how penetrating that irony of hers could be? 'Yes, ma'am. The navy science analysts are here to assist with our interpretation of the Laymil recordings. The First Admiral's staff suggested the procedure, and I had to agree with their reasoning. Possession is a terrible occurrence, if the Laymil had a solution we should not stint in our efforts to locate it.'

'Please relax, Parker, I wasn't criticizing. You did the right thing. I find it most gratifying that the Laymil project has suddenly acquired so much importance. Grandfather Michael was right after all; a fact he must be enjoying. Wherever he is.'

'You have no objection to the navy people scrutinizing the recordings, then?'

'None at all. It would be a rather spectacular feather in our cap if we did produce the answer. Although I have my doubts on that score.'

'So do I, ma'am. I don't believe there is a single answer to this problem. We are up against the intrinsic nature of the universe itself, only God can alter that.'

'Humm.' She sipped her tea, lost in contemplation. 'Yet the Kiint seem to have found a way. Death and possession don't bother them.' For the first time ever she saw real anger on the old Director's gentle face.

'They're not still working here, are they, ma'am?'

'Yes, Parker, they're still here. Why?'

'I fail to see the reason. They knew all along what had happened to the Laymil. Their whole presence here is some absurd charade. They never had any intention of helping us.'

'The Kiint are not hostile to the human race, Parker. Whatever their reasons are, I'm sure they are good ones. Perhaps they were gently trying to nudge us in the right direction. Who knows? Their intellects are superior to ours, their bodies too, in most respects. You know, I've just realized we don't even know how long they live. Maybe they don't die, maybe that's how they've beaten the problem.'

'In which case they can hardly help us.'

She stared at him coolly over the rim of her cup. 'Is this a problem for you, Parker?'

'No.' His jaw muscles rippled as he fought his indignation. 'No, ma'am, if you value their input to the project I will be happy to set aside my personal objection.'

'Glad to hear it. Now, there are still four thousand hours of sensorium records in the Laymil electronics stack which we haven't accessed yet. Even with the new teams you brought it's going to take a while to review them all. We'll have to accelerate the process.'

'Oski Katsura can construct additional reformatting equipment, that ought to speed things along. The only area of conflict I can see is weapons technology. You did say you wished to retain the right of embargo, ma'am.'

'So I did.' He has a point. Do I really want to hand Laymil weapons over to the Confederation, no matter how noble the cause?

It is no longer a relevant question, Tranquillity said. We know why the spaceholms committed suicide. Our earlier assumption that it was inflicted by an external force is demonstrably incorrect. Therefore your worry that the data for some type of superweapon exist is no longer applicable. No superweapon was designed or built.

674

**You hope! What if the spaceholms built one to try and stop the approach of the possessed Laymil ships?**

Given the level of their knowledge base at the time of their destruction, any weapons built in defence of the spaceholms would not be noticeably different to our own. They did not think in terms of weapons, whereas there is a case to be made for plotting human history in terms of weapons development. It may well be that anything the Laymil came up with would be inferior.

**You can't guarantee that. Their biotechnology was considerably more advanced than Edenist bitek.**

It was impressive because of its scale. However, their actual development was not much different to the Edenists. There is little risk of you worsening the situation by allowing unlimited access to the recordings.

**But not zero?**

**Of course not. You know this, Ione.**

I know it. 'I think we'd better rescind that proscription for the time being,' she told Parker Higgens.

'Yes, ma'am.'

'Is there anything else we can do to assist the Confederation Navy? Our unique position here ought to count for something.'

'Their senior investigator came up with two suggestions. Apparently Joshua Calvert said he found the original electronics stack in some kind of fortress. If he were to supply us with the coordinates of this structure we could explore it to see what other electronics remain. If one stack can survive undamaged, then there must be others, or even parts of others. The data in those crystals is priceless to us.'

**Oh dear,** Tranquillity said.

**Don't you dare go all sarcastic on me, not after Joshua agreed to find the Alchemist. We both agreed he's grown up a lot since that time.**

**Unfortunately his earlier legacy remains.**

Just in time she guarded herself against a scowl. 'Captain

Calvert isn't here at the moment. But, Parker, I'd advise against too much optimism. Scavengers are notorious braggarts, I'd be very surprised if this fortress he spoke of exists in quite the same condition he claimed.'

**Neeves and Sipika may have the coordinate,** Tranquillity said. **They might cooperate. If not, we are in an official state of emergency; debrief nanonics could be used.**

**Well done. Send a serjeant in there now to interview them. Make it clear that if they don't tell us voluntarily it'll be extracted anyway.** 'I'll see what can be done,' she said in the hope of countering his disappointed expression. 'What was the other suggestion?'

'A thorough scan of Unimeron's orbital track. If the planet was taken into another dimension by Laymil possessed there may be some kind of trace.'

'Surely not a physical one? I thought we had this argument before.'

'No, not a physical one, ma'am. We thought, instead, there may be some residual energy overspill in the same way the possessed betray their presence, it may be there is a detectable distortion zone.'

'I see. Very well, look into it. I'll authorize any reasonable expenditure for sensor probes. The astroengineering companies should welcome the work now I've stopped ordering weapons for the SD network. We might even get some competitive prices.'

Parker finished his tea, not quite certain he should ask what he wanted to. The responsibilities of the project Directorship were sharply defined, but then he was only human. 'Are we well defended, ma'am? I heard about Arnstadt.'

Ione smiled, and bent down to scoop Augustine from the floor. He'd been trying to climb the table leg. 'Yes, Parker, our defences are more than adequate.' She ignored the old Director's astonishment at the sight of the little xenoc, and stroked Augustine's head. 'Take it from me, the Capone Organization will never get into Tranquillity.'

# 17

The Bar KF-T wasn't up to much, but after a fifty-hour trip squashed into the two-deck life-support capsule of an inter-orbit cargo tug with just the captain's family to talk to Monica Foulkes wasn't about to closet herself away in a barren hotel room. *A drink and some company, that's what I need.* She sat on a stool up at the bar sipping an imported beer while Ayacucho's meagre nightlife eddied around her. The economic downturn from the quarantine was affecting every aspect of Dorados life, even here. It was 10.30 p.m. local time and only five couples were braving the dance floor – there were even some tables free. But the young men were still reassuringly on the prowl; she'd already had three offers of a drink.

The only cause for concern was how many of them were wearing red handkerchiefs round their ankle, boys and girls. She couldn't be entirely sure if they wanted to seduce her or simply convert her. Deadnight was becoming an alarming trend; the ESA's head of station in Mapire estimated twenty per cent of the Dorados' teenage population was getting sucked in. Monica would have put it nearer to fifty per cent. Given the blandness of existence among the asteroids she was surprised it wasn't even higher.

Her extended sensory analysis program plotted the tall man's approach, only alerting her to his existence when he was two metres away and his destination obvious.

'Can I get you another bottle?'

Her intended reply perished as soon as she saw the too-long greying hair flopping over his brow. 'Sure,' she grinned whimsically.

He sat on the empty stool beside her and signalled the barmaid for a couple of bottles. 'Now this is far more stylish than our last encounter.'

'True. How are you, Samuel?'

'Overworked and underpaid. Government employees get the same deal the Confederation over.'

'You forgot unappreciated.'

'No, I didn't,' he said cheerfully. 'That's the benefit of Edenism, everyone contributes to the greater good, no matter what area we excel in.'

'Oh, God.' She accepted her new beer from the barmaid. 'An evangelical Edenist. Just my luck.'

'So, what are you doing here?'

'Negotiating armament manufacturing contracts; it actually says I'm a rep for Octagon Exports on my passport.'

'Could be worse.' Samuel tried his beer, and frowned at the bottle with some dismay. 'Take me, I'm supposed to be part of the delegation from this system's Edenist habitats, discussing mutual defence enhancement arrangements. I specialize in internal security procedures.'

Monica laughed, and tipped her bottle at the middle-aged Edenist. 'Good luck.' The humour ended. 'You must have seen them?'

'Yes. I'm afraid the possessed are definitely inside the barricades.'

'Shit! I meant the Deadnight kids.'

'Ah. Monica, please take care. Our ... examination of the Dorados has shown up several cadres of possessed. They're here, and they are expanding. I do not advise you return to Mapire. Our estimation is that it will fall within another three days, probably less.'

'Did you tell the Governing Council?'

'No. We decided it would cause too much panic and disorder. The council would institute quite draconian measures, and be completely unable to enforce them, which would only worsen the situation. The Dorados do not have the usual civil government structure; for all their size and economic import-ance, they remain company towns, without adequate law-enforcement personnel. In short, the possessed will take over here anyway. We need time to search in peace before they do. I'm afraid Mzu comes before everything, including alerting the population.'

'Oh. Thanks for the warning.'

'My pleasure. Have your assets located Daphine Kigano yet?'

Monica crinkled her face up in distaste. I shouldn't be discussing this, not with him. Standard agency doctrine. But the universe wasn't exactly standard any more. And the ESA didn't have too many resources here. 'No. But we know it's her.'

'Yes. That's what we concluded.'

'A chartered starship carrying one passenger was rather unsubtle. Our station accessed the Department of Immigra-tion's file on the *Samaku*'s docking: one hundred per cent visual confirmation. God knows what she was doing in the Narok system, though.'

'Just trading ships, we hope. An interdiction order has gone out for the *Samaku*, all voidhawks and Confederation Navy ships are alert for it.'

'Good. Look, Samuel, I don't know what your orders are—'

'Originally: find Mzu, prevent her from handing over the Alchemist to the Garissan partisan movement, retrieve the Alchemist. That's the soft option. If we can't do that, then I was instructed to terminate her and destroy her neural nanon-ics. If we don't get the Alchemist, no one else must have it.'

'Yeah. Pretty much the same as mine. Personally I think the second option would be best all round.'

'Possibly. I must admit that even after seventy-five years in the job I am reluctant to kill in cold blood. A life is a life.'

'For the greater good, my friend.'

Samuel smiled sadly. 'I know both the arguments and the stakes involved. However, there is also a new factor to consider. We absolutely cannot allow her or it to fall into the hands of the possessed.'

'God, I know that.'

'Which means, we really don't want to expedite option two, do we?'

Facing him was the same as receiving a stern glance from a loving grandfather who was dispensing homely wisdom. How infuriating that she had to have the obvious pointed out to her in such a fashion. 'How can I argue against that?' she grunted miserably.

'Just as long as you appreciate all the factors.'

'Sure. Consider my wrist firmly smacked. What have your lot got planned for her, then?'

'Following acquisition, Consensus recommended placing her in zero-tau. At the very least until the possessed situation is resolved. Possibly longer.'

'How long?' Monica almost didn't want to ask, or know.

'Consensus thought it prudent that she remains there until we have a requirement for the Alchemist. It is a large galaxy, after all; there may be other, more hostile xenocs than the Kiint and Tyrathca out there.'

'I was wrong, you're not an evangelist, you're a paranoid.'

'A pragmatist, I sincerely hope; as are all Edenists.'

'OK, Samuel, so pragmatically, what do you want to do next? And please bear in mind that I am a loyal subject of my King.'

'Concentrate on finding her first, then get her away from the Dorados. The argument over custody can come later.'

'Nine-tenths of the law,' she muttered. 'Are you offering me a joint operation?'

'Yes, if you're willing. We have more resources here, I think, which gives us the greater chance of launching a successful extraction mission. But neither of us can afford to dismiss any avenue which will locate her. I am sure your Duke of Salion would approve of any action which guaranteed her removal from the scene right now. You can accompany her on our evacuation flight; and afterwards we would allow a joint custody to satisfy the Kingdom we have not acquired Alchemist technology. Is that reasonable?'

'Yeah, very. We have a deal.'

They touched bottles.

'The local partisan leadership has been called to a meeting here tonight,' she said. 'Unfortunately, I don't know exactly where that is in the asteroid. I'm waiting for our asset to get in touch as soon as it's over.'

'Thank you, Monica. We don't know where it is, either. But we're assuming she will be there.'

'Can you track any of the partisans?'

'It is not easy. But we'll certainly make every effort.'

*

For three days the rented office suite which had become the new Edenist Intelligence Service headquarters in Ayacucho had been the centre of a remarkable breeding programme. When the agents of the 'defence delegation' team arrived they brought with them seventy thousand geneered spider eggs. Every arachnid was affinity capable, and small enough to clamber through grilles and scurry through the vast mechanical plexus of lift shafts, maintenance passages, environmental ducts, cable conduits, and waste-disposal pipes which knitted the asteroid's rooms and public halls together into a functional whole.

For over seventy hours the tiny infiltrators were coaxed and manipulated along black pipes and through chinks in the rock, slipping round cracks in badly fitted composite panels. Thousands never made it to their required destination. Victims of more predatory creatures, of working insect grids, of security barriers (most common in the corporate areas), sluices of strange liquids, smears of sticky fluids, and the most common failing of all: being lost.

But for every one which didn't make it, five did. At the end of the deployment period the Edenists had visual coverage of sixty-seven per cent of Ayacucho's interior (which was how Samuel found Monica Foulkes so easily). The three voidhawks perched on Ayacucho's docking-ledges, along with the ten armed voidhawks holding station inside Tunja's particle disc and the agents reviewed the spiders on a snapshot rotor, managing a complete sweep every four hours. As a method of locating one individual it was horribly inefficient. Samuel knew that it would only be pure chance if Mzu was spotted during one of the sweeps. It was up to the agents on the ground to lower the odds by procedural work; their dull routine of researching public files, bullying assets, bribing officialdom, and on occasion outright blackmail.

\*

For thirty years the Garissan partisan movement had pursued a course of consistently lacklustre activity. It funded several anti-Omutan propaganda campaigns to keep the hatred alive among the first of a new generation born to the refugees. Mercenaries and ex-Garissan Navy marines were recruited and sent on sabotage missions against any surviving Omutan interests. There were even a couple of attempts to fly into the Omuta system and attack asteroid settlements, both of which were snuffed by CNIS before the starships ever left dock. But for the last decade the leadership had done little except talk. Membership had dropped away steadily, as had funding, along with any real enthusiasm.

With such shoddy organization and defunct motivation it was inevitable that any Intelligence agency which had ever shown an interest in the partisans had collated files on every person who had been a member, or even attended a fringe meeting. Their leadership was perfectly documented; long since consigned to the semi-crank category and downgraded to intermittent monitoring. A status which was now abruptly reversed.

There were five people making up the executive of Ayacucho's partisan group. In keeping with the movement's deterioration none of them followed the kind of security procedures they had obeyed so rigorously in the early days. That sloppiness in conjunction with an encyclopedic knowledge of their daily activity patterns allowed the Edenists to position spiders where they could provide a comprehensive coverage of the leadership's movements in the hours leading up to the meeting.

Samuel and the voidhawks were presented with eyeblink pictures of the partisan leaders making their way through the asteroid. Respectable middle-age professionals now, they all had escorts of bodyguards, keen for any sign of trouble. These entourages were unmistakable, making them easy to follow.

'It looks like either level three or four in section twelve,' Samuel told Monica.

She datavised her processor block for a schematic of the asteroid. 'It's all offices there, corporate country. That makes sense, it's more secure, and they are all rich. It wouldn't be suspicious for them to be there together.'

'Unfortunately it makes life complicated for us. We're having trouble infiltrating that area.' He was watching an inverted image of Ikela walking along a corridor at the centre of five boosted bodyguards. They were approaching a junction. A fast check with the voidhawks revealed that there were no more spiders left ahead. He ordered the one he was using to scuttle along the ceiling after Ikela.

**There are UV lights ahead**, a voidhawk warned. **The spider is approaching a grade-five clean environment.**

**I know, but I need to see which way he turns.** It was a strange viewpoint; to Samuel the corridor wasn't particularly large, to the spider it was vast. The two visual interpretations tended to clash confusingly inside his cortex unless he maintained a high level of concentration. Drab whiteness slid smoothly past galloping legs. Far above him was the sky of hazel carpet. Footsteps crashed against the spider's pressure-sensitive cells. Stalactite mountains clad in expensive black silk marched on in front of the racing arachnid, becoming difficult to resolve as they approached the fork. He just needed a hint . . .

The affinity link vanished amid a violet flash. Damnation! A further review showed Samuel no spiders had managed to penetrate the area.

'What is it?' Monica asked as he flinched in annoyance.

'We just lost them.'

'So now what?'

He looked round at the other agents in the office suite. 'Kit up, and move out. We'll cover as many approaches as we can. Monica, are you sure your asset is reliable?'

'Don't fret; we've got him hoisted by the short and curlies. He won't be able to datavise during the meeting, but as soon as it's over we'll know where it was and if she's there. Did any of your infiltration systems see her going in?'

'No,' he admitted. 'Not even a fifty per cent characteristics match.'

'I'm not surprised.'

The Edenist agents were putting on slim equipment belts and strapping up shoulder holsters. Monica checked her own maser pistol, and ran a diagnostic program through her implants.

'Monica,' Samuel said.

She caught the tone. 'I know: I'm not in your command network, I'd be in the way if I try to front-line. It's all yours, Samuel.'

'Thank you.' **Stand by,** he told the voidhawks waiting on the docking-ledge, **if we do grab her we'll need to exit fast.** He led the team out.

*

There were only five people in the Tunja system who knew the real reason for forming the Garissan partisan movement. None of them lived on the same asteroid, so that if disaster did strike the others would be there to carry on with the plan.

In Ayacucho it was Ikela, the nominal head of the original five. It suited him to be one of the partisan group's executives rather than the leader. This way he kept up to date on the movement's activities whilst staying out of the limelight. His position was due principally to his financial support rather than any active participation. Again, according to plan.

Dan Malindi, the Ayacucho group's leader, was the first to arrive at the secure conference office of Laxa and Ahmad, the legal firm they were using as cover. He gave Ikela a puzzled, vaguely annoyed glance as he entered. No one knew why Ikela had demanded the meeting at seven hours' notice. And the executive weren't people used to being kept in ignorance, not by one of their own. The sight of the normally composed industrialist sitting mutely at the table looking as if he was suffering some kind of fever with the way he was sweating did nothing to ease the tension.

Kaliua Lamu was the second to arrive; a financier who made little secret about his growing ambivalence to the movement. Partisan membership didn't sit well alongside his new-found respectability.

Feira Ile and Cabral arrived together, the most senior ranking figures in the Dorados administration. Feira Ile had been an admiral in the Garissan Navy, and was now Ayacucho's SD chief, while Cabral had built himself the largest media group in the Dorados. His company's growth and popularity were due to the tabloid nationalism of its editorial policy, which made him a natural choice for the partisans. Most of the executive suspected his support was strictly for appearance's sake.

Bodyguards and assistants left the room. Dan Malindi glared at the small woman sitting quietly behind Ikela, who obstinately refused to be intimidated into moving.

'She's with me,' Ikela said.

Dan Malindi grunted in dissatisfaction and activated the office's security screen. 'All right, Ikela, what the hell is this about?'

Ikela gave the woman a respectful gesture, and she stood up, walking to the end of the table opposite Dan Malindi. 'My name is Dr Alkad Mzu, I'm here to finish our war with Omuta.'

Dan Malindi and Kaliua Lamu both gave her a nonplussed glance. Cabral frowned, ordering a neural nanonics file search. But it was Feira Ile who produced the strongest reaction; he half rose to his feet, openly astonished. 'The Alchemist,' he murmured. 'You built the Alchemist. Holy Mary.'

'The what?' Cabral asked.

'The Alchemist,' Alkad told them. 'It was our superweapon. I was its designer.'

'Feira?' Cabral prompted.

'She's right,' the old ex-admiral said. 'I was never given any details, the project was classified way above my security rating. But the navy built this ... thing, whatever it is, just before the Genocide. We were going to use it against Omuta.' He drew a long breath and looked at the diminutive physicist. 'What happened?'

'Our flight was intercepted by blackhawks hired by Omuta,' Alkad said. 'We never got there. The Alchemist was never used.'

'No way,' Dan Malindi said. 'This is complete bullshit. You appear on the scene thirty years after the event and spin some crap about a missing legend you heard about in some bar. I bet the next stage is asking us for money to search for this Alchemist. In fact, I bet it's going to take a lot of money to find it, right?' He was sneering contemptuously at her when he finished, but somehow her cold smile managed to rob his anger.

'I don't need to search. I know exactly where it is.'

'It wasn't lost?' Kaliua Lamu asked. His enthusiasm brought him a disgusted look from Dan Malindi.

'No, it's never been lost. It's been kept safe.'

'Where?'

Alkad merely smiled.

'Maybe it does exist,' Cabral said. 'And our illustrious admiral here was right saying someone called Alkad Mzu built it. How do we know you're her? We can't make the decisions we need to make on the word of some stranger who turns up out of the blue, especially not at this precise time.'

Alkad raised an eyebrow. 'Captain?'

'I can vouch for her,' Ikela said softly. 'This is Dr Alkad Mzu.'

'Captain?' Dan Malindi asked. 'What does she mean?'

Ikela cleared his throat. 'It was my rank in the Garissan Navy. I used to be captain of the frigate *Chengho*. We were flying escort duty on the Alchemist deployment mission. That's how I know.'

'Datavise your command authority code,' Feira Ile said sternly.

Ikela nodded reluctantly, and retrieved the code from its memory cell.

'It would appear our colleague is telling the truth,' Feira Ile told the silent office.

'Mother Mary,' Cabral muttered, glancing at the man he thought he'd known for the last thirty years. 'Why didn't you tell us?'

Ikela sank his head into his hands. 'The plan operates on a need to know basis only. Up until today you didn't need to know.'

'What plan?' Feira Ile snapped.

'To deploy the Alchemist,' Alkad said. 'After the original

mission was crippled, Ikela and four other officers were detailed to sell the antimatter we were carrying. They were supposed to invest that money so there would be sufficient funds to hire a combat-capable starship and equip it to fire the Alchemist once the sanctions were lifted and the Confederation Navy squadron assigned to blockade duties returned home. The only reason you partisans exist is to provide me with a crew that will not flinch from the job that needs to be done.' She stared at Ikela. 'And now I'm here, on schedule, and I find no ship, and no crew.'

'I told you,' Ikela shouted. 'You can have your ship if that's still what we want. I have more than enough money. Anyone of us in this room has enough money to provide a starship for you. I have never failed my duty to my people. Don't you ever say that. But things have changed.'

'Looks like you've failed to me,' Cabral said briskly. 'Looks like you've failed a lot of people.'

'Think!' Ikela stormed. 'Think for the love of Mary what she is proposing. What will the Confederation do to us if we blow up Omuta's star? What revenge will they take?'

'It can do that?' a startled Kaliua Lamu asked. 'The Alchemist will destroy their star?'

'On one setting, yes,' Alkad said. 'I don't intend using that. I propose to simply extinguish the star. No one will die, but their planet and asteroid settlements will have to be evacuated and abandoned. They will become a broken homeless people, as we are. That's fitting, surely?'

'Well, yes . . .' He searched round the table for support, finding only uneasy confusion. 'But I don't understand. If you survived the blackhawk attack, why didn't you continue with the mission? Why wait thirty years?'

'There were complications,' Alkad said tonelessly. 'By the time we were in any position to function again the sanctions had been imposed, and the blockade squadron was in place. It was decided to wait until these obstructions were removed, which would give us a much greater chance of success. We did not have limitless government resources any more, and we only have one chance to get it right. This is the optimum time to strike. We won't have another chance; the Intelligence agencies are pursuing me. And they will find me.'

Dan Malindi groaned. 'Intelligence agencies? Holy Mary, they'll find out where you've been.'

'Oh, yes, they'll know you're involved. Does that bother you?'

'Bother me? You bitch! I have a family.'

'Yes. I've heard this argument already today. It is beginning to bore me. I have lived the reality of the Genocide for thirty years. You, all of you, have just been playing patriot. Each of you has profited in your own field by chanting the cry of nationalism. Well, my being here has put an end to your pathetic game.'

'Are you threatening us?' Cabral asked.

'I have always been a threat to your cosy life, even though you never knew I existed.'

'What exactly do you want?' Feira Ile asked.

'Two things. A combat-capable starship with a decent crew of committed nationalists. And a secure environment for myself while you prepare them. Do not underestimate the agencies. They now know for certain that the Alchemist is real, which means they will go to any lengths to acquire me.'

Ikela stood up, placing his hands on the table and leaning forwards. 'I say we cannot do this. Mother Mary, we're sitting here talking about wrecking an entire star system as if it was some kind of difficult business venture. Times have changed, we are not Garissans any more. I'm sorry if that is painful for you to hear, Doctor, but we're not. We have to look to the future, not the past. This is madness.'

'And that is treachery,' Cabral said.

'Treachery to what? To a planet that was killed thirty years ago? If that's what it is, then fine, I'm a traitor to it. I don't care.'

'Other people might when they get to hear.'

'Ikela, I really don't think you're in any position to back out now,' Feira Ile said. 'Given your mission, you are still a serving officer. That means you are required to discharge your obligations.'

'Then I quit, I resign my commission.'

'Very well. In that case, I must ask you to hand over the T'Opingtu company to me.'

'What?'

'I believe we just heard that it was founded on money provided by the Garissan Navy. That means it doesn't belong to you.'

'Go fuck yourself.'

'Listen, we can't make a snap judgement over this,' Kaliua Lamu said. 'Ikela's right, we're talking about wiping out an entire solar system.'

'I might have known you'd take that attitude,' Dan Malindi said.

'Excuse me?'

'You heard. I'm willing to provide as much help as Dr Mzu wants. What the hell is the Confederation going to do to us if we're armed with Alchemists?'

'There is only one,' Alkad said.

'You can build more, can't you?'

She hesitated uncomfortably. 'If there was a requirement, it could be duplicated.'

'There you are, then. You can't leave what's left of the Garissan nation and culture unprotected, can you?'

'You want to start a damn arms race as well?' Ikela yelled. 'You're as mad as she is.'

'Curb your language. Have you forgotten the possessed?'

'In Mary's name, what have they got to do with this?'

'If we were armed with Alchemists, that bastard Capone would think twice before sending his fleet here.'

'And who precisely is going to be in charge of these Alchemists?'

'The Dorados Council, of course,' Dan Malindi said scornfully.

'Exactly, and we all know how much influence you have there.'

'Enough!' Alkad slammed her fist down. 'I will not supply Alchemists to anyone. You have no conception of what it is capable of. It is not some bigger and better bomb you can use for political advantage. It was built for one purpose, to destroy the people who threatened our world. It will be used for one purpose, our revenge against them.' She looked at each of them in turn, furious and sickened that this was all that remained of the planet she was once so proud of. Where was their dignity, their resolution? Could none of them perform one single act of remembrance? 'I will give you thirty minutes to debate this. After that you will tell me which of you support me, and which do not.'

'I certainly support you,' Kaliua Lamu said loudly, but he was talking to her back as she limped away.

The shouting had already begun again before the door closed behind her. All the bodyguards and aides in the ante-room stared; Alkad barely saw them. If she had just known or anticipated the shambles which the partisans had become then she would have been mentally geared up.

'Alkad?' Voi was bending down, giving the smaller woman an anxious look.

'Don't mind me, I'll be all right.'

'Please, I have something to show you. Now.'

The girl took Alkad's arm, hustling her across the room and out into the corridor. Alkad couldn't be bothered to protest, although force of habit made her activate a threat-analysis program. Her enhanced retinas began scanning the length of the corridor.

'Here,' Voi said triumphantly. She opened her palm to reveal a tiny squashed spider.

'Mother Mary! Have you completely flipped?'

'No, listen. You know you said you thought the Intelligence agencies were following you.'

'I should never have told you that. Voi, you don't know what you're getting involved with.'

'Oh, yes, I do. We started checking the spaceport log. There's a delegation of Edenists here to discuss strengthening our defences. Three voidhawks brought thirty of them.'

'Yes?'

'Mapire only rated one voidhawk, and six Edenists to discuss our mutual defence with the Council. It should be the other way round, the capital should have got the larger delegation, not Ayacucho.'

Alkad glanced at the little brown blob in the girl's hand, a bad feeling sinking through her. 'Go on.'

'So we thought about how Edenists would search the asteroid for you. Adamists would use spylenses and hack into the communication net to get at public security monitor cameras. Edenists would use bitek systems, either simulants or affinity-bonded animals. We started looking. And here they are. Spiders. They're everywhere, Alkad. We checked. Ayacucho is totally infested.'

'That doesn't necessarily prove . . .' she said slowly.

'Yes, it does.' The hand with the crushed blob was shaken violently. 'This is a spider from the Lycosidae family. Ayacucho's ecologists never introduced any Lycosidae into the biosphere. Check the public records if you don't believe me.'

'All sorts of things can get through bio-quarantine; irradiation screening isn't perfect.'

'Then why are they all male? We haven't found a single

female, not one. It's got to be so they can't mate, they won't reproduce. They'll die off without causing any sort of ecological imbalance. Nobody will ever notice them.'

Strangely enough, Alkad was almost impressed. 'Thank you, Voi. I'd better go back in there and tell them I need more security.'

'Them?' Voi was utterly derisory. 'Did they leap to help you? No. Of course not. I said they wouldn't.'

'They have what I need, Voi.'

'They have nothing we don't. Nothing. Why don't you trust us? Trust me? What does it take to make you believe in us?'

'I do believe in your sincerity.'

'Then come with me!' It was an agonized plea. 'I can get you out of here. They don't even have any way to get you out of the office without the spiders seeing.'

'That's because they don't know about them.'

'They don't know because they're not concerned about security. Look at them, they've got enough bodyguards in there to form a small army. Everybody in the asteroid knows who they are.'

'Truthfully?'

'All right, not everybody. But certainly every reporter. The only reason they don't say anything is because of Cabral. Anyone coming to the Dorados who really wanted to make contact with the partisan movement wouldn't need more than two hours to find a name.'

'Mary be damned!' Alkad glanced back at the door to the anteroom, then at the tall girl. Voi was everything her father was not, dedicated, determined, hurting to help. 'You have some kind of safe route out of here?'

'Yes!'

'OK. You can take me out of this section. After that I'll get in touch with your father again, see what they're going to do for me.'

'And if they won't help?'

'Then it looks like you're on.'

*

'Yeah? So, I'm late. Sue me. Listen, this meeting caused me a shitload of grief. I don't need no lecture from the ESA on contact procedures right now.'

. . .

'Yeah, she's here all right, in the flesh. Mother Mary, she's really got the Alchemist stashed away somewhere. She's not kidding. I mean, shit, she really wants to take out Omuta's star.'

. . .

'Course I don't know where it is, she wouldn't say. But Mary, Ikela used to be a frigate captain in the Omutan Navy. He flew escort on the Alchemist mission. I never knew. Twenty years we've been plotting away together, and I never knew.'

. . .

'Sure you want to know where we are. Look, you're going to come in here shooting, right? I mean, how do I know you're not going to snuff me? This is serious heavy-duty shit.'

. . .

'All right, but if you're lying you'd better make sure you finish me. I'll have you if you don't, no matter what it costs. And hey, even if you do kill me, I can come back and get you that way. Yeah. So you'd better not be fucking me over.'

. . .

'Oh, absolutely. I always believe every word you people say. OK, listen, we're in Laxa and Ahmad's conference office. The bodyguards are all in the anteroom. Tell your people to be fucking careful when they come in. You let them know I'm on your side, yeah?'

. . .

'No, she's out in the anteroom. She went out there twenty

minutes ago so we could argue about what to do. The vote was three to two for wasting Omuta's star. Guess how I voted.'

\*

'Laxa and Ahmad, the conference office,' Monica said. 'Mzu's in the anteroom along with the bodyguards.'

**Go**, Samuel ordered.

The twenty Edenist agents closed on the Laxa and Ahmad offices. Floor plans were pulled from the asteroid's civil engineering memory cores. Entry routes and tactics were formulated and finalized while they jogged towards their target, the general affinity band thick with tense exchanges.

Monica kept three paces behind Samuel the whole way. It irked her, and she wasn't looking forward to her debrief, either. Teaming up with Edenists! But at least this way the Alchemist would be neutered. Providing Samuel kept his part of the agreement. Which she was sure he would do. Although high politics could still screw everything up. God!

It took them four minutes to reach Laxa and Ahmad. One featureless corridor after another. Thankfully there were few people about; only a handful of workaholics were left. They barged past an old man carrying several flek cases, a man and a woman who looked so guilty they were obviously having an affair, a pair of teenage girls, one very tall and skinny and black, the other small and white, both wearing red handkerchiefs round their ankles.

When she reached Laxa and Ahmad the Edenist team was already inside. Two agents stood guard out in the corridor. Monica stepped wearily through the crumpled door, drawing her pistol.

Samuel drew his breath sharply. 'Damnation.'

'What?' she asked. By then they had reached the conference office anteroom. The partisan bodyguards were all sprawled on the floor with limbs twitching erratically, and six Edenists stood over them, their TIP pistols pointing down. Three scorch lines slashed the walls where laser fire had burned the composite. A pair of spent nerve-shortout grenades rolled round on the carpet.

'Where's Mzu?' Monica asked.

Samuel beckoned her into the conference office. The partisan leadership had been caught by the nerve-shortout pulses, but the door and security screening had saved them from the worst effects. They were still conscious. Four of them. The fifth was dead.

Monica grimaced when she saw the broad char mark on the side of Ikela's skull. The beam had fractured the bone in several places, roasting the brain to a black pulp. Someone had made very sure his neural nanonics were ruined. 'God, what happened here?'

Two Edenist agents were standing behind Feira Ile, their pistol muzzles pressed into his neck. His wrists had been secured in a composite zipcuff behind his back. Crumbs of vomit were sticking to his lip; he was sweating profusely from the grenade assault, but otherwise defiant. A laser pistol was lying on the table in front of him.

'He shot Ikela,' Samuel said in bewildered dismay. He squatted down beside Ikela's chair. 'Why? What was the point? He was one of yours.'

Feira Ile grinned savagely. 'My last duty for the Garissan Navy.'

'What do you mean?'

'Ikela flew escort duty on the Alchemist. He probably knew where it is. Now he can't tell you.'

Monica and Samuel swapped a grim glance.

'She's gone, hasn't she?' Monica said bitterly.

'It would seem so.'

'Fuck it!' She stamped over to Kaliua Lamu, who had an agent holding him upright in his chair. 'Where did Mzu go?' Monica asked.

'Screw you.'

Monica gave an amused glance at the other partisans round the table. 'Oh, come on, Kaliua,' she said sweetly. 'You were eager enough to tell us this meeting's location.'

'Liar!'

She took out a Royal Kulu Bank credit disk. 'A hundred thousand pounds, wasn't it?'

'Bitch whore! I never,' he shouted at his comrades. 'It wasn't me. For Mary's sake, it wasn't.'

Monica grabbed his chin, and slowly exerted her boosted grip. Kaliua Lamu gagged fearfully at the force which threatened to shatter his jawbone.

'You said I'd better be certain when I finish you. Well, I intend to be extremely thorough extinguishing your life unless I know where she went.'

'I don't know.'

'Debrief nanonics would be the pleasant option, but we don't have time for that. Fortunately, old-fashioned pain can still produce some pretty impressive results during field interrogation. And they trained me very well, Kaliua.' She pushed her face centimetres from his bugging eyes. 'Would you like to try calling my bluff? Or perhaps you think you're strong enough to resist me for a couple of hours after I've fused your neural nanonics into ash? Once they're dead you can't block the pain. And the field way to fuse neural nanonics is with electrodes. Crude, but it works. Guess where they're applied.'

'No. Please! Don't.' His eyes were watering as he started shaking.

'Where, then?'

'I don't know. I promise. She was gone when we finished. I told you she was supposed to be waiting outside for us to finish. But she wasn't there.'

'Then who did she leave with?'

'It was a girl, my bodyguard said. Ikela's daughter, Voi. She's tall, young. They were talking together and never came back. Honestly, that's all I know.'

Monica let go of his chin. He slumped back in the chair, trembling in relief.

'A tall girl,' Monica whispered. She was looking at Samuel in dawning dismay as the memory blossomed. She hurriedly accessed the neural nanonics memory cell she'd kept running to record the operation.

In the corridor on the way up. Two girls, one tall and black, the other white and small. Pressed against the wall in alarm as she and Samuel ran past. The memory cell image froze. Green neon grid lines closed round the smaller girl, calculating her height. It matched Mzu's. So did the approximate weight.

A backpack fitted with a long shoulder strap hung at the girl's side.

Monica had seen that backpack once before. Never in her life would she need help from neural nanonics to remember that time. The backpack had been flapping behind a small spacesuit-clad figure who was clinging desperately to a rope ladder.

'Dear God, we walked right bloody past her,' she told an aghast Samuel. 'The bitch is wearing a chameleon suit.'

*

*Lady Macbeth* slipped slowly into place above the docking cradle, her equatorial verniers sparkling briefly as Joshua compensated for drift. Optical-band sensors gave a poor return here; Tunja's ruby glow was insipid even in clear space, and down where Ayacucho lurked among the disc particles it was an abiding roseate gloom. Laser radar guided the starship in until the cradle latches clamped home.

The bay's rim lights sprang up to full intensity, highlighting the hull, their reflected beams twisting about at irregular angles as the thermo-dump panels folded back into the fuselage. Then the cradle started to descend.

In the bridge not a word was spoken. It was the mood which

had haunted them all the way from Narok, an infection passed down from captain to crew.

Sarha looked over the bridge at Joshua for some sign of . . . humanity, she supposed. He had flown them here, making excellent time as always. And apart from the kind of instructions necessary to keep the ship humming smoothly, he hadn't put ten words together. He'd even taken his meals alone in his cabin.

Beaulieu and Dahybi had told the rest of the crew of the Norfolk possession, and how concerned Joshua had been for Louise. So at least Sarha knew the reason for his blues, even though she found it slightly hard to believe. This was the Joshua with whom she'd had an affair for over six months last year. He was so easy about the relationship that when they did finally stop sleeping together she'd stayed on as part of the crew without any awkwardness on either side.

Which was why she found it difficult that Joshua could be so affected by what had happened to Louise, by all accounts a fairly simple country girl. He never became that entangled. Commitment wasn't a concept which nested in his skull. Part of the fascination was his easygoing nature. There was never any deceit with Joshua, you knew just where you stood.

Perhaps Louise wasn't so simple after all. Perhaps I'm just jealous.

'Going to tell us now, Captain?' she asked.

'Huh?' Joshua turned his head in her general direction.

'Why we're here? We're not chasing Meyer any more. So who is this Dr Mzu?'

'Best you don't ask.'

A circuit of the bridge showed her how irritated everyone was getting with his attitude. 'Absolutely, Joshua; I mean, you can't be sure if we're trustworthy, can you? Not after all this time.'

Joshua stared at her. Fortunately, belaboured intuition finally managed to struggle through his moping thoughts to reveal the crew's bottled-up exasperation. 'Bugger,' he winced. Sarha was right, after all they'd been through together these people deserved a better style of captaincy than this. Jesus, I'm picking up Ione's paranoia. Thank God I didn't have to make any real command decisions. 'Sorry, I just got hit by Norfolk. I wasn't expecting it.'

'Nobody expected any of this, Joshua,' Sarha said sympathetically.

'Yeah, right. OK, Dr Mzu is a physicist, who once worked for the Omutan Navy . . .'

They didn't say much while he told them what the flight was about. Which was probably a good thing, he guessed. It was one hell of a deal he'd accepted on their behalf. How would I feel if they'd dragged me along without knowing why?

When he finished he could see a mild smile on Ashly's face, but then the old pilot always did claim to chase after excitement. The others took it all reasonably stoically; though Sarha was looking at him with a kind of bemused pique.

Joshua hitched his face up into one of his old come-on grins. 'Told you, you were better off not knowing.'

She hissed at him, then relented. 'Bloody hell, wasn't there anybody else the Lord of Ruin could use?'

'Who would you trust?'

Sarha tried to come up with an answer, and failed hopelessly.

'If anyone wants to bail out, let me know,' Joshua said. 'This wasn't exactly covered in my job description when you signed on.'

'Neither was Lalonde,' Melvyn said drily.

'Beaulieu?' Joshua asked.

'I have always served my captain to the best of my ability,' the shiny cosmonik said. 'I see no reason to stop now.'

'Thanks. All of you. OK, let's get *Lady Mac* powered down. Then we'll have a quick scout round for the Doctor.'

*

The Dorados Customs and Immigration Service took seventy-five minutes to process the *Lady Mac*'s crew. Given the quarantine, Joshua had been expecting some hassle, but these officers seemed intent on analysing every molecule in the starship. Their documentation was reviewed four separate times. Joshua wound up paying a five thousand fuseodollar administration fee to the chief inspector before they were confirmed to be non-possessed, had the appropriate Tranquillity government authorization to be flying, and declared suitable citizens to enter Ayacucho.

The lawyers were waiting for him at the end of the docking-bay airlock tube. Three of them, two men and a woman, their unfussy blue suits cloned from some conservative chain store design program.

'Captain Calvert?' the woman asked. She gave him a narrow frown, as if uncertain he could be the person she wanted.

Joshua rotated slightly so his silver star on his epaulette was prominent. 'You got me.'

'You are the captain of the *Lady Macbeth*?' Again, the uncertainty.

'Yep.'

'I am Mrs Nateghi from Tayari, Usoro, and Wang, we represent the Zaman Service and Equipment company which operates here in the spaceport.'

'Sorry, guys, I don't need a maintenance contract. We just got refitted.'

She held out a flek with a gold 'scales of justice' symbol embossed on one side. 'Marcus Calvert, this is a summons for fees owing to our client since August 2586. You are required to appear before the Ayacucho civil claims court at a date to be set in order to resolve this debt.'

The flek was pressed into Joshua's palm. 'Whaa—' he managed to grunt.

Sarha started giggling, which drew a cool glare from Mrs Nateghi. 'We have also filed a court impounding order on the

*Lady Macbeth*,' she said frostily. 'Please do not try and leave as you did last time.'

Joshua kissed the flek flamboyantly and beamed at the woman. 'I'm Joshua Calvert. I think you should be talking to my father. He's Marcus Calvert.'

If the statement threw her, there was no visible sign. 'Are you the *Lady Macbeth*'s current owner?'

'Sure.'

'Then you remain liable for the debt. I will have the summons revised to reflect this. The impounding order remains unaffected.'

Joshua kept his smile in place. He datavised the flight computer for a review of all 2586 log entries. There weren't any. 'Jesus, Dad, thanks a bunch,' he muttered under his breath. No way – absolutely not – would he show the three vultures how fazed he was. 'Look, this is obviously an oversight, a computer glitch, something on those lines. I have no intention of contesting the debt. And I shall be very happy to pay off any money owing on *Lady Mac*'s account. I'm sure nobody wants this regrettable misunderstanding to come to court.' He jabbed a toe at Sarha, whose giggles had turned to outright laughter.

Mrs Nateghi gave a brisk nod. 'It is within my brief to accept payment in full.'

'Fine.' Joshua took his Jovian Bank credit disk out of his ship-suit's top pocket.

'The cost in 2586 to the Zaman company for services rendered comes to seventy-two thousand fuseodollars. I have an invoice.'

'I'm sure you do.' Joshua held out the credit disk, anxious to be finished.

The lawyer consulted her processor block, a show of formality. 'The interest accrued on your debt over twenty-five years comes to two hundred and eighty-nine thousand fuseo-dollars, as approved by the court.'

Sarha's laughter ended in a choke. Joshua had to use a

neural nanonics nerve impulse override to stop himself from snarling at the lawyer. He was sure she was doing the same to stop her equally blank face from sneering. Bitch! 'Of course,' he said faintly.

'And our firm's fee for dealing with the case is twenty-three thousand fuseodollars.'

'Yes, I thought you were cheap.'

This time, she scowled.

Joshua shunted the money over. The lawyers hauled themselves away down the corridor.

'Can we afford that?' Sarha asked.

'Yes,' Joshua said. 'I have an unlimited expense account for this trip. Ione's paying.' He didn't want to dwell on what she'd say when she saw the bill.

I wonder why Dad left in such a hurry?

Ashly patted Joshua's shoulder. 'Real chip off the old block, your dad, eh?'

'I hope he hurries up and possesses someone soon,' Joshua said through gritted teeth. 'There's a few things I'd like to talk to him about.' Then he thought about what he'd just said. Maybe not as funny and cuttingly sarcastic as he'd intended. Because Dad was there in the beyond. Suffering in the beyond. That's if he wasn't already . . . 'Come on, let's make a start.'

*

The club you wanted, according to the spaceport personnel, was the Bar KF-T; that's where the action is. Along with the dealers, pushers, and pimps, and all the rest of the people in the know.

The trouble was, Joshua found after a straight two-hour stint of surfing the tables, they didn't know the one piece of information he needed. The name of Alkad Mzu had not left a heavy impression on the citizens of Ayacucho.

At the end he gave up and went to sit with Ashly and Melvyn at a raised corner table. It gave him a good view over the dance floor, where some nice girls were moving in trim movements. He rolled his beer bottle between his palms, not much interested in the contents.

'It was only a long shot, Captain,' Melvyn said. 'We ought to start sniffing round the astroengineering companies. Right now they're so desperate for business that even the legitimate ones would happily consider selling her a frigate.'

'If she wants to disappear, she has to do it at the bottom of the heap,' Joshua said. 'You'd think the dealers would have heard something.'

'Maybe not,' Ashly said. 'There's definitely some kind of underground league here. It can't be the same as the usual asteroid independence movements; the Dorados are already sovereign. I got a few hints when they thought I was offering *Lady Mac*'s services, plenty of talk about revenge against Omuta. Mzu could have turned to them, after all they're her people. Unfortunately, the likes of you and I can hardly pass ourselves off as long-lost cousins of the cause.' He held up his hand, studying it dispassionately.

Joshua looked at his own skin. 'Yeah, you've got a point. We're not exactly obvious Kenyan-ethnic stock, are we?'

'Dahybi might make the grade.'

'I doubt it.' His eyes narrowed. 'Jesus, will you look at how many of those kids are wearing red handkerchiefs round their ankles.' Six or seven times that evening while he'd been scouting round teenagers had asked him to take them to Valisk.

'We could do worse than the Deadnights,' Melvyn said broodingly. 'At least there aren't any possessed here.'

'Don't count on it.' Ashly leant over the table, lowering his voice. 'My neural nanonics suffered a couple of program-load errors this evening. Not full glitches, but the diagnostics couldn't pinpoint the cause.'

'Humm.' Joshua looked at Melvyn. 'You?'

'My communication block had a five-second drop-out.'

'Some of my memory cells went off-line earlier, too. I should have paid more attention. Shit. We've been here barely three hours, and we've each been close enough to one to be affected. What does that come to in percentages of the population?'

'Paranoia can be worse than real dangers,' Melvyn said.

'Sure. If they are here, they're obviously not strong enough to mount an all-out takeover campaign. Yet. That gives us a little time.'

'So what's our next move?' Melvyn asked.

'Other end of the spectrum, I suppose,' Joshua said. 'Contact someone in government who can run discreet checks for us. Or maybe it wouldn't be a bad idea to let slip the *Lady Mac* is for hire. If Mzu is here to get help, the only place it'll come from is the nationalist community. They might even wind up trying to charter us to deploy the damn thing.'

'Too late now,' Ashly said. 'We're officially here to buy defence components for Tranquillity. And we've been asking too many questions.'

'Yeah. Jesus, I'm not used to thinking along these lines. I wonder if any of my fellow captains have been approached for a combat charter?'

'Only if she's actually in this asteroid,' Ashly said. 'Nothing to stop the *Samaku* docking at one of the others when it arrived. That's even if she came here in the first place. We ought to be checking that.'

'I'm not an idiot,' Joshua moaned. 'Sarha's working on it.'

\*

Sarha's smile appeared a little frayed after the third time Mabaki bumped against her. The crowd in the Bar KF-T weren't that excitable. She could certainly thread her way through without jostling anyone.

Mabaki waggled his eyebrows when she glanced back. 'Sorry,' he grinned.

It wasn't so much that he bumped her, as where. And how the touch tarried. She told herself a pathetic middle-aged lech was probably going to be one of the smaller tribulations they would encounter on this crazy course Joshua had set.

Just before she gave in and tried a datavise, she located Joshua standing over by the bar. (Where else? she asked herself.) 'That's him,' she told Mabaki.

Sarha tapped Joshua on the shoulder as he was accepting a beer bottle from the barmaid. 'Joshua, I found someone I think can . . .' She trailed off in confusion. It wasn't Joshua. That she of all people could be mistaken was astonishing. But he did look remarkably similar, especially in the treacherously shimmering light thrown out by the dance floor's holographic spray. Same broad chest to accommodate a metabolism geneered for free-fall, identical prominent jaw folding back into flat cheeks. But this man's skin was darker, though nothing like the ebony of most Dorado Kenyan-ethnics, and his glossy hair was jet black rather than Joshua's nondescript brown.

'I'm sorry,' she stammered.

'I'm not.' He could certainly manage the Joshua charm-grin, too. Possibly even better than Joshua.

'I was looking for someone else.'

'I hate him already.'

'Goodbye.'

'Oh, please, I'm too young for my life to end. And it will when you leave. At least have a drink with me first. He can wait.'

'No, he can't.' She began to move away. Some erratic impulse made her look back in perplexity. Damn, the likeness was extraordinary.

His smile widened. 'That's it. You're making the right choice.'

'No. No, I'm not.'

'At least let me give you my eddress.'

'Thank you, but we're not staying.' Sarha forced her legs to work. She just knew her face would be red. How stupidly embarrassing.

'I'm Liol,' he called out after her. 'Just ask for Liol. Everybody knows me.'

I'll bet they do, she thought, especially the girls. The crowd closed around her again, Mabaki tagging along faithfully.

\*

Second time lucky. Joshua was sitting at a table in a shadowy corner, and he was with Ashly and Melvyn, so there was no mistake this time.

'Officer Mabaki works for the Dorados Immigration Service,' Sarha explained as she pulled up a chair.

'Excellent,' Joshua said. 'I'd like to purchase some of your files.'

It cost him fifteen thousand fuseodollars to learn that the *Samaku* had definitely docked at Ayacucho. One passenger had disembarked.

'That's her,' Mabaki confirmed after Joshua datavised a visual file to him. 'Daphine Kigano. You don't forget women like that.'

'Daphine Kigano, really? Bit of a viper, was she?'

'You're telling me.' Mabaki savoured another sip of the Tennessee malt Joshua had bought him. 'She was some friend or other of Ikela's. You don't mess with those sort of connections.'

Joshua datavised the club's net processor for a civil information core, and accessed a file on Ikela. It was mostly public relations spin released by T'Opingtu, but it gave him an idea of what he was dealing with. 'So I see,' he muttered. 'Can you tell us what starships have left since Daphine Kigano arrived?'

'That's simple. None. Well, not unless you count the Edenist delegation, but they're from this system's gas giant anyway. There are still some inter-orbit ships flying, but no Adamist starships. The *Lady Macbeth* is the first starship to arrive since the *Samaku* departed.'

After Mabaki left a grin spread over Joshua's face. It was the first in a long time which didn't have to be printed there by neural nanonics. 'She's still here,' he said to the others. 'We've got her.'

'We've got a lead on her,' Melvyn cautioned. 'That's all.'

'Optimist. Now we know who to ask for, we can start focusing our efforts. I think this Ikela character would be a good place to start. Hell, we can even get a legitimate appointment. T'Opingtu is the kind of company we ought to approach for Tranquillity's SD spares, anyway.' He drained his beer bottle and put it back on the table. A flash of movement caught his eye, and he slapped his hand down on the spider scuttling clear of the soggy mat.

*

'Oh, well,' Samuel said. 'At least we know why he's here. I suppose Ione Saldana must have commissioned him to track Mzu.'

'That stupid little cow,' Monica complained. 'Doesn't she have any idea what kind of issues she's fooling with? And sending some bloody mercenary on the chase!'

'"Lagrange" Calvert,' Samuel mused. 'I suppose she could have done worse. He's certainly got the balls for a mission like this.'

'But not the style. God, if he starts blundering round asking questions everyone in the Dorados is going to know Mzu is running loose. Here of all places! I ought to terminate him; it'd save us a nasty headache in the long term.'

'I do wish you wouldn't keep on about how easier life would be if we killed everyone who poses the slightest inconvenience. Calvert is an amateur, he's not going to bother us. Besides, he won't be the one who stirs up the public.' Samuel indicated the row of AV pillars set up along one side of the rented office. Edenist agents were busy monitoring the output of every Ayacucho-based media company.

News of Ikela's death was already breaking, tying it in with reports of a 'disturbance' at the offices of Laxa and Ahmad. Police were treating the death as suspicious, refusing to comment to the rovers gathered outside the doors of the legal firm. Although they'd already let slip that they would like to question Kaliua Lamu about the death.

Monica winced at that. She shouldn't have blown him, but they had been desperate for the information. The financier had demanded that Monica protect him from his erstwhile comrades, a request she could hardly refuse. He and his family were already on board one of the Edenist delegation's voidhawks, waiting to be spirited away to safety. 'Don't I know it. That Cabral is going to make our life hell,' she grumbled. 'I don't know why you let him and the other two go.'

'You know perfectly well why. What else could we do? For goodness' sake, Feira Ile is Ayacucho's SD chief, Malindi is President of the Merchant's Association, and both of them sit on the Dorados' Governing Council. I could hardly authorize their abduction.'

'I suppose not,' she sighed.

'It's not as if they can tell people what they were doing, or even that they were there.'

'Don't count on it. They're certainly above the law here; and if any word of Mzu does leak out it'll inflame the nationalist sympathy.'

'I think we had better assume it will do. Cabral will make sure of it. After all, he voted to help her retrieve the Alchemist.'

'Yes.' She let out an exasperated groan. 'God, we walked right past her!'

'Ran past,' Samuel corrected.

Monica glared at him. 'Any sightings?'

'None at all. However, we are losing an unusual number of spiders.'

'Oh?'

'Children are going round killing them. It's some kind of

organized game. Several day clubs are running competitions to see who can find the most. There are cash prizes. Clever,' he acknowledged.

'Somebody's well organized.'

'Yes and no. Children are a most peculiar method of attack, the numbers they can eliminate will inconvenience us rather than block us. If it was another agency that discovered we were infiltrating the asteroid, they would release a tailored virus to kill the spiders.' He cast an enquiring glance. 'No?'

She puckered her lips in an ironic smile. 'I would imagine that could well be standard operating procedure for some people.'

'So ... it isn't an agency, but it is someone who has connections that reach down into local day clubs. And quickly.'

'Not the partisans. They were never that well organized, and their membership is mostly ageing reticents. The group that has Mzu?'

'By process of elimination, it must be.'

'Yes, but so far we only know one member, this Voi girl. If there is an inner core of partisans I find it hard to believe the ESA didn't know about them.'

'And us.' He looked over to the agents monitoring the news, his face flickering through a range of expressions as he exchanged a barrage of questions and answers across the general affinity band. 'Interesting.'

'What?' she asked patiently.

'Given Ikela's mysterious death and his wealth, there's been no mention of his daughter by any media company. That's normally the first thing reporters focus on: who's going to inherit.'

'Cabral's shielding her.'

'Looks like it.'

'Do you think he could be involved with this new group?'

'Very unlikely. From what we know about him, his partisan involvement was minimal, he was part of it for form's sake.'

'So what the hell group is Voi mixed up with?'

*

Much later, when he had the time to sit down and think about it, Liol gave Lalonde as the reason for being so slow off the mark. He would never have been so sluggish under normal circumstances. But after accessing Kelly Tirrel's report he hit Ayacucho's clubs and bars, drinking and stimming out with methodical determination. A lot of people were doing exactly the same thing, but for a different reason. They merely feared the possessed, while Liol had watched his life's dream crumple in less than a second.

It had always been a dangerous dream. A single hope which has lasted from the earliest days of childhood is not a sound foundation on which to build a life. But Liol had done it. His mother had always told him his father would come back one day; an assurance she kept on repeating through another three husbands and countless boyfriends. He will return, and he'll take us away with him; somewhere where the sun shines dazzling white and the land is flat and endless. A universe away from the Dorados, worldlets haunted by the momentous horror and tragedy of the past.

The dream – the sure knowledge – of his destiny gave Liol attitude, setting him apart from his peers. His was among the first generation of Garissans born after the Genocide. While others suffered from their parents' nightmares, a young Liol flourished in the expanding caverns and corridors of Mapire. He was the champion of his day club; idolized as reckless by his teeny friends, the first of all of them to get drunk, the first to have sex, the first to try soft drugs, and then not so soft, the first to run a black stimulant program through newly implanted neural nanonics. A genuine been-there-done-that kid, as much

**711**

as you could go and do within the limited scope for experience permitted in orbit around Tunja.

His zest even carried over into his early twenties, when the years of his father's non-return were beginning to pile up in an alarming quantity. He still clung to his mother's promise.

A goodly number of his contemporaries emigrated from the Dorados when they reached their majority, a migration worrying to the council. Everyone assumed Liol would be among them, surely the first who would want to seek new opportunities. But he stayed, joining in the effort to build the Dorados into a prime industrial state.

Garissa's refugees had been awarded the settlement rights to the Dorados by the Confederation Assembly as part of their restitutions against Omuta for the Genocide. Every multistellar company mining the ore had to pay a licence fee to the council, part of which was used to invest in the asteroids' infrastructure, while the remainder was paid directly to the survivors, and their descendants, by now scattered across the Confederation.

By 2606 this dividend had grown to a respectable twenty-eight thousand fuseodollars per annum. With such a guaranteed income as collateral, Liol had little trouble collecting loans and grants from the bank and the Dorados Development Agency to start his own business. In keeping with his now somewhat unhealthy obsession with spaceflight, he formed a company, Quantum Serendipity, specializing in servicing starship electronics. It was a good choice; the number of starship movements in the Tunja system was growing each year. He was awarded subcontracts by the larger service and maintenance companies, working his way up the list of approved suppliers. After two years of steady growth, he leased a docking-bay in the spaceport, and made his first bid for a complete starship-maintenance service. Year three saw Quantum Serendipity buy a majority share in a small electronics station; by producing the processors in-house he could undercut his competitors and still make a profit.

He now had the majority shares in two electronics stations, owned seven docking-bays, and employed seventy people. And six months ago, Quantum Serendipity had landed a service contract for the communication network linking Ayacucho's SD platforms, a rock-solid income which was on the verge of pushing him into a whole new level of operations.

Then news of the possession arrived from the Confederation Assembly, swiftly followed by Kelly Tirrel's report. The first didn't bother Liol half as much as his competitors; with his SD contract he could keep his company afloat throughout the crisis. But the second item, with its hero of the day, super-pilot 'Lagrange' Calvert rescuing little kiddies in his starship – that came close to breaking him. It was the end of his world.

None of his friends understood the reason behind his sudden ferocious depression, the worrying benders he launched himself into. But then they had never been told of his dream, and how much it meant to him, that was private. So after a couple of abortive attempts to 'cheer him up' had failed dismally amid his tirades of calculatingly vicious abuse they had left him alone.

Which was why he'd been surprised when the girl in the Bar KF-T had spoken to him. Surprised, and not a little bit blasted. The come-on routine he gave her was automatic, he didn't have to think. It was only when she'd gone that a frown crossed his flattish, handsome face. 'Joshua,' he said in a drink-fuddled voice. 'She called me Joshua. Why did she do that?'

The barmaid, who by now had given up on the idea of lugging him home for the night, shrugged gamely and moved on.

Liol drained his whisky chaser in one swift toss, then datavised a search request into the spaceport registration computer. The answer seemed to trojan a wickedly effective sober-up program into his neural nanonics.

*

Alkad had seen worse rooms when she was on the move thirty years ago. The hotel charged by the hour, catering for starship crews on fast stopovers, and citizens who wanted somewhere quiet and private to indulge any of a variety of vices which modern technology could provide. There was no window, the hotel was cut into rock some distance behind the cliff at the end of the biosphere cavern. It was cheaper that way. The customers never even noticed.

Big holograms covered two of the walls, showing pictures of some planetary city at dusk, its jewelscape of twinkling lights retreating into a horizon of salmon-pink sky. The bed filled half of the floor space, leaving just enough room for people to shuffle round it. There was no other furniture. The bathroom was a utilitarian cubicle fitted with a shower and a toilet. Soaps and gels were available from a pay dispenser.

'This is Lodi Shalasha,' Voi said when they arrived. 'Our electronics supremo, he's made sure the room's clean. I hope. For his sake.'

The young man rolled off the bed and smiled nervously at Alkad. He was dressed in a flamboyant orange suit with eye-twisting green spirals. Not quite as tall as Voi, and several kilos overweight.

Student-type, Alkad categorized instantly; burning with the outrage that came from a head stuffed full of fresh knowledge. She'd seen it a thousand times before when she was a lecturer; kids from an easy background expanding their minds in all the wrong directions at the first taste of intellectual freedom.

His smile was strained when he looked at Voi. 'Have you heard?'

'Heard what?' the tall girl was immediately suspicious.

'I'm sorry, Voi. Really.'

'*What?*'

'Your father. There was some kind of trouble at the Laxa and Ahmad offices. He's dead. It's all over the news.'

Every muscle in the girl's body hardened, she stared right through Lodi. 'How?'

'The police say he was shot. They want to question Kaliua Lamu.'

'That's stupid, why would Kaliua shoot my father?'

Lodi shrugged hopelessly.

'It must have been those people running to the offices. Foreign agents, they did it,' Voi said. 'We must not let this distract us.' She paused for a moment, then burst into tears.

Alkad had guessed it was coming, the girl was far too rigid. She sat Voi down on the bed and put her arm round the girl's shoulder. 'It's all right,' she soothed. 'Just let it happen.'

'No.' Voi was rocking back and forth. 'I must not. Nothing must interfere with the cause. I've got a suppressor program I can use. Give me a moment.'

'Don't,' Alkad warned. 'That's the worst thing you can do. Believe me, I've had enough experience of grief to know what works.'

'I didn't like my father,' Voi wailed. 'I told him I hated him. I hated what he did. He was weak.'

'No, Ikela was never weak. Don't think that of your father. He was one of the best navy captains we had.'

Voi wiped a hand across her face, simply broadening the tear trails. 'A navy captain?'

'That's right. He commanded a frigate during the war. That's how I knew him.'

'Daddy fought in the war?'

'Yes. And after.'

'I don't understand. He never said.'

'He wasn't supposed to. He was under orders, and he obeyed them right up to his death. An officer to the last. I'm proud of him. All Garissans can be proud of him.' Alkad hoped the hypocrisy wouldn't taint her voice. She was alarmingly aware how much she needed Voi's people now, whoever they were. And Ikela had almost kept the faith, it was only a white lie.

'What did he do in the navy?' Voi was suddenly desperate for details.

'Later, I promise,' Mzu said. 'Right now I want you to activate a somnolence program. Believe me, it's the best thing. We were having a hard enough day before this.'

'I don't want to sleep.'

'I know. But you need it. And I'm not going anywhere. I'll be here when you wake up.'

Voi glanced uncertainly at Lodi, who nodded encouragingly. 'All right.' She lay back on the bed, shuffled herself comfortable, and closed her eyes. The program took hold.

Alkad stood up and deactivated the chameleon suit. It was painful peeling the hood off her face, the thin fabric stuck possessively to her skin. But the room's cool air was a tonic; she'd sweated heavily underneath it.

She split the seal on her blouse and began to wriggle her arms out of the suit.

Lodi coughed frantically.

'Never seen a naked woman before?'

'Er, yes. But . . . I. That is—'

'Are you just playing at this, Lodi?'

'Playing at what?'

'Being a good-guy radical, a revolutionary on the run?'

'No!'

'Good. Because you're going to see a lot worse than a bare-arsed woman my age before we're done.'

His skittish attitude calmed. 'I understand. I really do. Er—'

Alkad started on the trousers, they were tighter than the hood. 'Yes?'

'Who are you, exactly?'

'Voi didn't explain?'

'No. She just told me to alert the group for possible action. She said we must be careful because the asteroid was probably under covert surveillance.'

'She was right.'

'Yeah, I know,' he said proudly. 'I was the one who worked out the Edenists were spreading those spiders.'

'Clever of you.'

'Thanks. Our junior cadres are cleaning them from critical areas, corridor junctions and places. But I made sure they skimp round this hotel; I didn't want to draw attention to it.'

'A smart precaution. So do these cadres of yours know we're here?'

'No, absolutely not; nobody else knows. I swear. Voi said she wanted a safe room; I even paid cash.'

Maybe I can still salvage this after all, Alkad thought. 'Tell you what, Lodi; I'm going to have a shower first, then afterwards you can tell me all about this little group of yours.'

\*

As with most crews when they were docked, Joshua liked to book in at a hotel even if it was only for a single night. It wasn't necessarily more convenient than staying in the *Lady Mac*, it just made a change. This time, though, the crew returned to the starship, and Joshua depressurized the airlock tube once they were all back on board. It would hardly stop anyone in an SII suit, but *Lady Mac* had her fair share of internal defence systems. And besides ... at the back of his mind was the notion that a possessed would be hard pressed to wear and operate a spacesuit; if Kelly was right their rampant energistic ability would completely screw up the suit's processors. He sealed himself up in his sleep cocoon with his paranoia reduced to its lowest level in days.

It was a sombre breakfast as they began to drift into the galley cabin and collect their food five hours later. Everyone had accessed the local news companies. Ikela's murder was the premier item.

Ashly glanced at the galley's AV pillar as he plugged his cereal packet into the milk nozzle.

'Got to be a cover-up,' the pilot grunted. 'Too much smoke,

too little fire. The police should have made an arrest by now. Where's someone as prominent as this Lamu character going to hide in an asteroid?'

Joshua glanced up from his carton of grapefruit. 'You think Mzu did it?'

'No.' Ashly retrieved the now chilly packet and gulped down a mouthful of the mushy wheat paste. 'I think someone trying to get Mzu did it; Ikela just got in their way. The police must know that. They simply can't blurt it out in public.'

'So did they get her?' Melvyn asked.

'Am I psychic?'

'Such questions are irrelevant,' Beaulieu said. 'We don't have enough information to speculate in this fashion.'

'We can certainly speculate on who else is trying to nab her,' Melvyn said. 'For my money, it's got to be the bloody Intelligence agencies. If we can confirm she made it here, so can they. And that's serious trouble, Captain. If they can kill someone like Ikela with impunity, they're not going to worry much about riding over us.'

Joshua switched his empty carton of grapefruit for a can of tea and a croissant. He stared round at his crew as he chewed on the bland pastry (another reason he liked hotels, free-fall food was always soft and tacky to avoid crumbs). Melvyn's words were unsettling, none of them were really used to personal, one on one, danger; starship combat was so very different. Then there was the possibility of encountering the possessed as well. 'Beaulieu's right, we don't have enough data yet. We'll spend the morning rectifying that. Melvyn and Ashly, you team up; I want you to concentrate on industrial defence contracts, see if you can find traces of the kind of things Mzu would require for retrieving and deploying the Alchemist. Principally, that'll be a starship, but it'll still need fitting out; if we're really lucky she could have ordered some kind of customized equipment. Dahybi, Beaulieu, try and find out what happened to the Daphine Kigano alias, where she was last seen, her credit disk number, that kind of thing. I'm going to find out what I can about Ikela and his associates.'

'What about me?' Sarha asked indignantly.

'You're on duty in here, and you don't let anyone apart from us on board. From now on, there will always be one of us on the bridge. I don't know that there are any possessed in Ayacucho, but I'm not risking it. There's also the Intelligence agencies to consider, along with local security forces, and whoever Mzu is lined up with. I think now might also be an appropriate time to take the serjeants out of zero-tau just in case events turn sour. We can pass them off as cosmoniks easily enough.'

*

Ione was finding the whole sensation of independence most peculiar, both individually and in unison with the mirror fragment minds in the other serjeants. Her thoughts were fluttering across the affinity band like birds fleeing a hurricane.

**We must try and separate more**, she said.

To which her own thoughts replied: **Absolutely**.

She felt like giggling; the kind of giggle that came from being tickled by a merciless lover: unwelcome yet inevitable.

The affinity contact with the other three serjeants reduced, paring down to essential information: location, threat status, environment interpretation. She couldn't help the little frisson of eagerness at the experience; this was the first time she had ever been anywhere outside Tranquillity. Ayacucho might not be much, but she was determined to soak in as much of it as she could.

She was following Joshua out of the transit capsule which had delivered them from the spaceport. The axial chamber was just a low-gee bubble of rock, but at the same time it was a bubble of rock which she hadn't seen before. Her first foreign world.

Joshua got into a waiting tube lift and sat down. She chose

the seat opposite him, the composite creaking as it adjusted to her weight.

'This is all so strange,' she said as the lift moved off. 'Part of me wants to be next to you.'

His face became immobile. 'Jesus, Ione, why the fuck did you shove your personality into the serjeants? Tranquillity's would've been just fine.'

'Why, Joshua Calvert, I do believe you're embarrassed.'

'Who, me? Oh no, I'm quite used to sexless two-metre monstrosities making a pass at me.'

'Don't be so grumpy. It's unbecoming. Besides, you should be grateful. My instinct is very protective towards you. That might give me an edge.'

Joshua's retort was lost somewhere in his throat.

The lift's doors opened on a public hall in the asteroid's commercial district where several late office workers scurried to work, a pair of mechanoids were cleaning the walls and floor. It was less spartan than the axial chamber, with a high, arched roof, and troughs of plants spaced at regular intervals. But it was still only a tunnel through rock, nothing exuberant. Unfortunately the serjeant didn't have lips that could easily be compressed into a pout, otherwise she would have done it. She really wanted to see the biosphere cavern.

Joshua started off down the hall.

'What do you hope to accomplish here?' she asked.

'T'Opingtu is a big company; someone will have been appointed to run it straight away. And Ikela would make sure his replacement is someone he can trust, someone from his immediate circle. It's not much, but it's the best lead we've got.'

'I really don't think you'll be able to get an appointment today.'

'Don't be such a downer, Ione. Your trouble is Tranquillity is incorruptible and logical, that's all you're used to. Asteroids like Ayacucho are neither. The size of the contract I'm going to dangle in their faces will get me straight into the top office. There's an etiquette to this kind of business.'

'Very well; you get in. Then what?'

'I won't know until I get there. Remember this is strictly a data-acquisition mission, everything is helpful even if it is only negative. So keep your senses open and your memory on full record.'

'Aye, Captain.'

'OK, now we're primarily interested in anything we can learn about Ikela's life. We know he was a Garissan refugee, so who did he move with from the past, was he a strong nationalist? Names, contacts, that kind of stuff.'

'My personality didn't suffer any damage during the replication process, I can think for myself.'

'Wonderful. A bodyguard with an attitude.'

'Joshua, darling, this isn't attitude.'

He stopped and jabbed a finger at the husky construct. 'Now look—'

'That's Pauline Webb,' Ione said.

'What? Who?'

Three people were marching down the public hall towards Joshua. Two African-ethnic men flanking a white woman. He didn't like the look of the men at all; they were wearing civilian suits, but combat armour would have been more appropriate. Boosted, and no doubt containing a wide variety of extremely lethal implants.

Pauline Webb stopped a couple of metres short of Joshua, and gave the serjeant a curious glance. 'Your appointment is cancelled, Calvert. Collect your crew, get back in your starship, and go home. Today.'

Joshua produced his most nonchalant grin. 'Pauline Webb. Fancy seeing you here.'

Her narrowed eyes gave the serjeant another suspicious glance. 'This situation is not your concern any more.'

'It is everybody's concern,' Ione said. 'Especially mine.'

'I didn't know you things could operate independently.'

'Now you do,' Joshua said politely. 'So if you'll just step aside . . .'

The man directly in front of Joshua folded his arms and planted his feet slightly apart, a true immovable object. He smiled carnivorously down at Joshua.

'Er, perhaps we could come to an arrangement?'

'The arrangement is simple,' Webb said. 'If you leave, you get to live.'

'Come on, Joshua,' Ione said. The serjeant's all-too-human hand closed on his shoulder, forcing him to turn.

'But—'

'Come on.'

'That's smart advice,' Webb said. 'Listen to it.'

Ione let go of his shoulder after a few paces. A fuming Joshua allowed her to escort him back down the hall towards the lift. When he glanced over his shoulder Webb and her two troopers were standing watching him.

'This isn't her turf,' he hissed at the serjeant. 'We could have caused a scene, made trouble for her. The police would have sorted her out as well as us.'

'Any incident with the authorities here would have been resolved in her favour. She's a CNIS officer assigned to Mzu; the local Navy Bureau would have backed her, and you and I would be in deep shit, not to mention jail.'

'How the hell did Webb know where I was going?'

'I imagine *Lady Mac*'s crew is under clandestine surveillance right now.'

'Jesus!'

'Quite. We will have to withdraw and come up with a new strategy.'

They reached the lift doors, and Joshua datavised for a ride back to the axial chamber. He cast another glance over his shoulder to check on Webb, a sly smile germinating on his face. 'You know what this means, don't you?'

'What?'

'The agencies don't have her yet. We're still in with a chance.'

'That's logical.'

'Of course it's logical. We may even be able to turn this to our advantage.'

'How?'

'I'll tell you when we're back in *Lady Mac*. Everyone's going to have to undergo decontamination first. Christ knows what sort of covert nanonic they've stung us with. We'll be broadcasting our own thoughts back to them if we're not careful.'

The lift doors opened and he stepped inside. Someone had slapped half a dozen twenty-centimetre circular holomorph stickers at random over the walls, with a couple more on the ceiling. One was at head height; it started its cycle, a tight bud of lavender photons swelling out from the centre into the form of a scantily clad teenage cheerleader. She shook her silver baton enthusiastically. 'Run, Alkad, run!' she yelled. 'You're our last hope; don't let them catch you. Run, Alkad, run!'

Joshua stared at it in stupefaction. 'Jesus wept.'

The cheerleader winked saucily, and syphoned back down below the sticker's surface. Three more began their cycle.

# 18

our, Kingsley.

Hull plate 8-92-K: lustreless grey, a few scratches where tools
and careless gauntlets had caught it, red stripe codes designating
its manufacturing batch and CAB permitted usage, reactive
indicator tabs to measure radiation and vacuum ablation still a
healthy green; exactly the same as all the other hexagonal plates
protecting the delicate systems of the *Villeneuve's Revenge* from
direct exposure to space. Except it was leaking a minute level
of electromagnetic activity. That was what the first scanner pad
indicated. Erick hurriedly applied the second over the centre of
the source. The sensor block confirmed a radiation emission
point. Density analysis detailed the size of the entombed unit,
and a rough outline of its larger components.

'I got it, Captain,' Erick datavised. 'They incorporated it in
a hull plate. It's small, electron-compressed deuterium tritium
core, I think; maybe point two of a kiloton blast.'

'You're sure?'

Erick was too tired to be angry. This was his ninth search,
and they were all imposing far too much stress on his convales-
cent body. When he finished each ten-hour session spent
snaking through the starship's innards he had to go straight on
bridge duty to maintain the illusion of normal shipboard
routine for Kingsley Pryor and the eight rover reporters they
were carrying. On top of that the Organization had played
dirty. Just as he knew they would.

'I'm sure.'

'Thank the blessed saints. Finally! Now we can escape these devils. You can deactivate it, can't you, *mon enfant*?'

'I think the best idea would be to detach the plate and use the X-ray lasers to vaporize it as soon as it's clear.'

'Bravo. How long will it take?'

'As long as it does. I'm not about to rush.'

'Of course.'

'Are there any reasonable jump coordinates in this orbit?'

'Some. I will begin plotting them.'

Erick slowly swept the rest of the little cavity for any further incongruous processors. Opposite the hull plate was a spiral of ribbed piping, resembling a tightly coiled dragon's tail, which led to a heat-exchange pump. He had emerged at its rim, wedged between the curving titanium and a cluster of football-sized cryogenic nitrogen tanks which pressurized the vernier rockets. A small, cramped space, but one providing a hundred crannies and half-hidden curves. It took him half an hour to sweep it properly, forcing himself to be methodical. Not easy with an armed mini-nuke eighty centimetres from his skull, its timer counting down.

When he was satisfied there were no booby triggers or alarms secreted in the cavity, he squirmed round to face the hull, and eased himself further out of the crawlway like paste from a tube.

Normally, a starship's hull plates were detached from the outside, with the seam rivets and load pins easily accessible. This was a lot more difficult. The arcane procedure for an internal jettison ran through Erick's neural nanonics, an operation which must surely have been dreamed up by committees of civil servant lawyers on permanent lunch breaks and with no knowledge of astroengineering. It was highly tempting just to shove a fission blade into the silicon and saw round the mini-nuke in a wide circle. Instead he datavised the flight computer to switch off the sector's molecular-binding-force generator,

**725**

then applied the anti-torque screwdriver to the first feed coupling. It might have been imagination, but he thought his new AT arm was slower than the other. The nutrient reserves were almost depleted. His thoughts were too cluttered to really bother about it.

Eighty minutes later, the plate was ready. The little cavity swarmed with discarded rivets, load pins, flakes of silicon, and several tool heads he'd lost. His suit sensors were having trouble supplying him with a decent image through all the junk. He slotted the last tools back in his harness, and wriggled even further out of the crawlway, feeling round with his toes for a solid foothold to brace himself against. When he was in position he was bent almost double with his back pressing against the plate. He started to shove, his leg muscles straining hard. Physiological monitor programs began signalling caution warnings almost immediately. Erick ignored them, using a tranquillizer program to damp down the swelling worry about the further damage he was causing himself.

The plate moved. Neural nanonics recorded a minute shift in his posture. Then he was rising in millimetre increments. He waited until the neural nanonics reported the plate had shifted five centimetres, then stopped pressing. Inertia would complete the work now. Cramp persecuted his abdomen.

A wide sliver of silver-blue light shone into the cavity as he retreated back down into the crawlway. One edge of the plate was loose, rising up out of alignment. His suit collar sensors hurriedly reduced their receptivity as the beam animated the rivet fragments into a glittering storm.

The plate lumbered upwards. Erick checked the edges one last time to see if they were all clear, then datavised: 'OK, Captain, it's free. Fire the verniers. Let's separate.'

He could actually see the silent eruptions of the tiny chemical rocket nozzles ringing the starship's equator, quick luminous yellow fountains. The hull plate appeared to be moving faster now, receding from the cavity.

Kursk was visible outside. The *Villeneuve's Revenge* was in low orbit, soaking in the wellspring of lambent light shimmering off the planet's cloud-daubed oceans.

It was the Capone Organization's second conquest; a stage three world, six light-years from Arnstadt. With a population of just over fifty million, it was evolving from its purely planetary-based economic phase to develop a small space industry. Consequently, it was an easy target. There was no SD network, yet it had valuable modern astroengineering stations and a reasonable population. The squadron of twenty-five starships which Luigi Balsmao dispatched to subdue the planet had encountered almost no opposition. Five independent trader starships docked at Kursk's single orbiting asteroid settlement had been armed with combat wasps; but the weapons were third-rate, and the captains less than enthusiastic about flying out to die bravely against the Organization's superior firepower.

Along with the other escort ships, the *Villeneuve's Revenge* had been assigned to the new Organization squadron within eight hours of arriving at Arnstadt. A subdued but furious André was unable to refuse. They had even seen action, firing half a dozen combat wasps against the two defenders who had responded to their arrival.

With their depleted crew numbers, everyone had to be on the bridge during the last stage of the mission, which meant they couldn't continue their search for the bomb. Which in turn meant they couldn't duck out of the final engagement.

With the small battle won, and the planet open to Capone's landing forces, the *Villeneuve's Revenge* had been given orbital clearance duties by the squadron commander. Tens of thousands of tiny fragments thrown out by detonating combat wasps now contaminated space around the planet, each one presenting a serious potential impact hazard to approaching starships. Combat sensor clusters on the *Villeneuve's Revenge* were powerful enough to track anything larger than a snowflake that came within a hundred kilometres of the fuselage. And

André was using the X-ray laser cannons to vaporize any such fragment they located.

Erick watched hull plate 8–92-K shrink, a small perfect black hexagon against the glittery deep-turquoise ocean. It turned brilliant orange in an eyeblink, then burst apart.

'I think it is time we had a small discussion with M. Pryor,' André Duchamp datavised to his crew.

It was almost as if the Organization's liaison man was expecting them when André datavised his command code to open the cabin door. It was Kingsley Pryor's designated sleep period, but he was fully dressed, floating in the lotus position above the decking. His eyes were open, showing no surprise at the two laser pistols levelled at him.

Nor fear, Erick thought.

'We have eliminated the bomb,' André said triumphantly. 'Which means you have just become surplus to requirements.'

'So you're going to slaughter the other crews, are you?' Kingsley said quietly.

'Pardon?'

'I have to transmit a code every four hours – seven at the most, remember? If that doesn't happen one of the other starships will explode. Then they won't be in any position to transmit their code, and another will go. You'll start a chain reaction.'

André maintained his poise. 'Obviously, we will warn them we are leaving before we jump outsystem. Do you take me for a barbarian? They will have time to evacuate. And Capone will have five ships less.' There was a glint in his eye. 'I will make sure the rover reporters understand that. My ship and crew are striking right at the heart of the Organization.'

'I expect Capone will be devastated at the news. Deprived of a warrior like you.'

André glared furiously; he could never manage sarcasm,

however crude, and he hated being on the receiving end. 'You may inform him yourself. We will return you to him via the beyond.' His grip on the laser pistol tightened.

Kingsley Pryor switched his glacial eyes to Erick, and datavised: 'You have to stop them murdering me.'

The message was encrypted with a Confederation Navy code.

'Knowing the nature of the possessed, I expect that code was compromised a long time ago,' Erick datavised back.

'Very likely. But do your shipmates know you are a CNIS officer? You'd join me in the beyond if they did. And I'll tell them. I have absolutely nothing to lose, now. I haven't for some time.'

'Who the fuck are you?'

'I served a duty tour in the CNIS Weapons Division as a technical evaluation officer. That's why I know who you are, Captain Thakrar.'

'As far as I'm concerned that makes you a double traitor, to humanity and the Navy. And Duchamp won't believe a word you say.'

'You need to keep me alive, Thakrar, very badly. I know which star system the Organization is planning to invade next. Right now, there is no more important piece of information in this whole galaxy. If Aleksandrovich and Lalwani know the target, they can intercept and destroy the Organization fleet. You now have no other duty but to get that information to them. Correct?'

'Filth like you would say anything.'

'You can't risk the possibility that I'm lying. I obviously have access to the Organization's command echelons, I wouldn't be in this position if I didn't. Therefore I could quite easily know their overall strategy planning. At the very least, procedure says I should be debriefed.'

The decision seemed more enervating than all that time spent in the cavity working on the hull plate. Erick was repelled by the notion that a piece of shit like Pryor could manipulate him. 'Captain?' he said wearily.

'*Oui?*'

'How much do you think he's worth if we turn him over to the Confederation authorities?'

André gave his crewman a surprised look. 'You have changed since you came on board, *mon enfant.*'

Since Tina . . . who wouldn't? 'We're going to be in the shit with the Confederation when we return. We did sign up with Capone, remember, and we helped with this invasion. But if we bring them a prize like this, especially if we do it in full view of the rovers, we'll be heroes; it'll wipe the slate clean.'

As always, avarice won with Duchamp. His gentle face's natural smile expanded with admiration. 'Good thinking, Erick. Madeleine, help Erick stuff this pig into zero-tau.'

'Yes, Captain.' She pushed off the hatch rim and grabbed hold of Pryor's shoulder. On the way she couldn't resist giving Erick a troubled look.

He couldn't even raise a regretful grin in response. I thought it was over, that getting rid of the bomb would finish it. We would dock at some civilized spaceport, and I could turn them all over to the local navy bureau. Now all I've done is swapped one problem for another. Great God Almighty, when is this all going to end?

\*

The beyond was different, not changed, but the rents which tore open into the real universe fired in flashes of sensation. They enraged and exhilarated the souls which dwelt there; a pathetic taster, a reminder of what used to be. Proof that corporeal life could be theirs again.

There was no pattern to the rents. The beyond did not have a structured topology. They occurred. They ended. And each time, a soul would wriggle through to possess. Luck, chance, dictated their appearance.

The souls screamed for more, scrabbling at the residual traces of their more fortunate comrades who had made it through. Pleading, praying, promising, cursing. The tirade was one-way. Almost.

The possessed had the power to look back, to listen harder.

One of them said: We want somebody.

The gibbering souls shrieked their lies in return. I know where they are. I know how to help. Take me. Me! I will tell you.

The chant of a billion tormented entities is not to be ignored.

Another rent appeared, loud sunlight piercing an ebony cloud. There was a barrier at the top, preventing any soul from surging through into the glory. Its extended existence ignited an agonized desire within those who flocked around it.

See? A body awaits you, a reward for the information we need.

What? What information?

Mzu. Dr Alkad Mzu, where is she?

The question rippled through the beyond, a virus rumour, passed – ripped – from one soul to another. Until, finally, the woman came forth, rising from the degradations of perpetual mind-rape to embrace and adore the pain which saturated her new body. Feelings rushed in to inflate consciousness: warmth, wetness, cool air. Eyes blinked open, half-laughing half-weeping at the agony of her scalded, skinless limbs. 'Ayacucho,' Cherri Barnes coughed to the gangsters standing over her. 'Mzu went to Ayacucho.'

*

The top-secret file contained a report which the First Admiral found even more worrying than any naval defeat. It had been written by an economist on President Haaker's staff, detailing the strain which possession was placing on the Confederation economy. The major problem was that modern conflicts tended to be resolved by fifteen-minute engagements between oppos-ing squadrons of starships; fast, and usually pretty decisive. It was an exceptional dispute which led to more than three navy engagements.

Possession, though, was shutting down the interstellar econ-omy. Tax revenue was falling, and with it government ability to support its forces on month-long deployment missions. And the Confederation Navy placed the primary drain on everyone's finances. Enforcing the quarantine was good strategic policy, but it wasn't going to solve the problem. A new strategy, one which had to include a final solution, had to be found within six months. After that, the Confederation would start to fragment.

Samual Aleksandrovich exited the file as Maynard Khanna ushered the two visitors into his office. Admiral Lalwani and Mullein, the captain of the voidhawk *Tsuga*, both saluted.

'Good news?' Samual Aleksandrovich asked Lalwani. It had become a standing joke at the start of their daily situation meetings.

'Not entirely negative,' she said.

'You amaze me. Sit down.'

'Mullein has just arrived from Arnstadt; *Tsuga* has been on Intelligence-gathering duties in that sector.'

'Oh?' Samual cocked a thick eyebrow at the youngish Edenist.

'Capone has invaded another star system,' Mullein said.

Samual Aleksandrovich swore bitterly. 'That's not negative?'

'It's Kursk,' Lalwani said. 'Which is interesting.'

'Interesting!' he grunted. His neural nanonics supplied him with the planet's file. Not *knowing* the world he was supposed to protect kindled obscure feelings of guilt. Its image appeared on one of the office's long holoscreens, just a perfectly ordinary terracompatible world, dominated by large oceans.

'Population fifty million plus,' Samual Aleksandrovich

recited from the file. 'Hell. The Assembly will combust, Lalwani.'

'They've no right,' she said. 'Your original confinement strategy is working very effectively.'

'Apart from Kursk.'

She ducked her head in acknowledgement. 'Apart from Kursk. But then that isn't due to the quarantine order failing. The quarantine was intended to prevent stealthy infiltration, not armed invasions.'

Samual's mind went back to the classified report. 'Let's hope the noble ambassadors see it that way. Why did you say it was interesting?'

'Because Kursk is a stage three world; no naval forces, no SD network. A pushover for the Organization. However, all they earned themselves was a few orbital industrial stations and a big struggle to quash the planetary population, the majority of whom live in the countryside – they're still very agrarian. In other words, the possessed are up against small, solid communities of well-armed farmers who have had plenty of advance warning.'

'But possessed forces backed up by starships, nonetheless,' Samual observed.

'Yes, but why bother possessing fifty million people who can make no positive contribution to the Organization?'

'Possession makes no sense generally.'

'No, but Capone's Organization needs sound economic support, certainly his fleet does. It won't operate without a functioning industrial capacity behind it.'

'All right, you've convinced me. So what analysis have your staff come up with?'

'We believe it was principally a propaganda move. A stunt, if you like. Kursk wasn't a challenge to him, and it isn't an asset. Its sole benefit comes from the psychology. Capone has conquered another world. He's a force to be reckoned with, the

King of the Possessed. That kind of garbage. People aren't going to look at how strategically insignificant Kursk is, all they'll think about is that damn exponential expansion curve. It's going to place a lot of political pressure on us.'

'The President's office has requested a briefing on the new development in two hours, sir,' Maynard Khanna said. 'It will be reasonable to assume the Assembly will follow that up with a request for some kind of large-scale high-visibility military deployment. And a victory. It will be expedient for the politicians to demonstrate the Confederation can strike at the enemy, that they're not sitting back doing nothing.'

'Wonderfully precise thinking,' Samual Aleksandrovich grumbled. 'National navies have only released seventy per cent of the forces pledged to us; we are barely managing to enforce the quarantine; we can't track down where the hell Capone's antimatter is coming from. Now they expect me to ransack what forces I have to build some kind of interdiction flotilla. I wonder if they'll give me a target, too, because I certainly can't see one. When will people learn that if we kill the possessed bodies all we're doing is simply adding to the numbers of souls in the beyond; and I doubt the families of those we kill will thank us.'

'If I can offer a suggestion, sir,' Mullein said.

'By all means.'

'As Lalwani said, *Tsuga* has been collecting Intelligence from Arnstadt. It's our contention that Capone isn't having it all his own way, not down on the planet itself. The SD platforms are having to fire on an almost hourly basis to support the Organization lieutenants on the surface. There is a lot of resistance down there. The Yosemite Consensus believes that if we were to start harassing the ships and industrial stations Capone has in orbit, it would make life very difficult for him. Constant reinforcement over interstellar distances is going to place a considerable strain on his resources.'

'Maynard?' the First Admiral asked.

'Possible, sir. The General Staff already has appropriate contingency plans.'

'When don't they?'

'Primarily, it would mean the observation voidhawks seeding Arnstadt's orbital space with stealthed fusion mines; a decent percentage should manage to trickle past the SD sensors. Equip them with mass-proximity fuses and any ships down there would be in deep trouble. No one would know when an attack was coming; it would rattle the crews once they realized we were blitzing them. Fast-strike missions could also be mounted against the asteroid settlements; jump a ship in, fire off a random salvo of combat wasps, and jump out again. Something similar to the Edenist attack against Valisk. It would have the advantage that we were mainly destroying hardware rather than people.'

'I want the feasibility studies run today,' the First Admiral said. 'Include Kursk as well as Arnstadt. That'll give me something concrete when I'm called to explain this latest fiasco to the Assembly.' He gave the young voidhawk captain a speculative gaze. 'What exactly is Capone's fleet doing right now?'

'Most of it is spread through the Arnstadt system, keeping the asteroid settlements in line until their populations are fully possessed. A lot of captured ships are being flown back to New California, we assume to be armed ready for his next invasion. But it's a slow job; he's probably short of crews.'

'For once,' Lalwani said sorely. 'I can't get over how many of those independent trader bastards went to work for him.'

'Recruitment is slowing considerably now the quarantine is in place,' Maynard Khanna said. 'Even the independent traders are reluctant to take Capone's money now they've heard about Arnstadt, and the Assembly's proclamation must have had some effect.'

'That or they're too busy raking it in by breaking the quarantine, I expect.' She shrugged. 'We've been getting reports; some of the smaller asteroids are still open to flights.'

'There are times when I wonder why we bother,' Samual Aleksandrovich marvelled. 'Thank you for the briefing, Mullein, and my gratitude to *Tsuga* for a swift flight.'

'Has Gilmore made any progress?' Lalwani asked when the captain had left.

'He won't admit it, but the science teams are stumped,' Samual Aleksandrovich said. 'All they can come up with is a string of negatives. We're learning a lot about the capabilities of this energistic ability, but nothing about how it is generated. Nor have Gilmore's people acquired any hard data on the beyond. I think that worries me the most. It obviously exists, therefore it must have some physical parameters, a set of governing laws; but they simply cannot detect or define them. We know so much about the physical universe and how to manipulate its fabric, yet this has defeated our most capable theorists.'

'They'll keep at it. The research teams at Jupiter have done no better. I know that Govcentral have established a similar project; and no doubt the Kulu Kingdom will be equally industrious.'

'I think in this instance they might all even be persuaded to cooperate,' Samual Aleksandrovich mused. 'I'll mention it during my presidential briefing, it'll give Olton something to concentrate on.'

Lalwani shifted round in her chair, leaning forward slightly as if she was discomforted. 'The one piece of genuinely good news is that we believe Alkad Mzu has been sighted.'

'Praise the Lord. Where?'

'The Dorados. Which lends a considerable degree of weight to the report. That's where seventy per cent of the Garissan refugees finished up. There is a small underground movement there. She'll probably try to contact them. We infiltrated them decades ago, so there shouldn't be any problem.'

Samual Aleksandrovich gave his Intelligence chief a pensive stare. He had always been able to rely on her utterly. The height of the stakes these days, though, were breaking apart all the old allegiances. Damn Mzu's device, he thought, the alleged potency of the thing even gnaws at trust. 'Which *we* is that, Lalwani?' he asked quietly.

'Both. Most Intelligence agencies have assets in the underground.'

'That's not quite what I meant.'

'I know. It's going to be down to the agents on the ground, and who reaches her first. For me personally, Edenist acquisition would not be an unwelcome outcome. I know we won't abuse the position. If CNIS obtains her, then as Admiral of the service I will follow whatever orders the Assembly's Security Commission delivers concerning her disposal. Kulu and the others could give us a problem, though.'

'Yes. What do the Edenists propose to do if you get her?'

'Our Consensus recommends zero-tau storage. That way she will be available should the Confederation ever face an external threat which needs something as powerful as the Alchemist to defend it.'

'That seems a logical course. I wonder if the Alchemist could help us against the possessed?'

'Supposedly, it's a weapon of enormous destructive power. If that's true, then like every weapon we have in our arsenal today, it will be utterly ineffective against the possessed.'

'You're right, of course. Unfortunately. So I suppose we are going to have to depend on Dr Gilmore and his ilk for a solution.' And I wish I had the confidence I should have in him. Saviour-to-be is a terrible burden for anyone to carry round.

\*

It was the one sight Lord Kelman Mountjoy had never expected to see. His job had taken him to countless star systems; he had stood on a beach to watch a binary dawn over the sea, admired Earth's astonishing O'Neill Halo from a million kilometres above the north pole, enjoyed lavish hospitality in the most exotic locations. But as Kulu's Foreign Minister, Jupiter was always destined to be *verboten*.

Now, though, he accessed the battlecruiser's sensor suite throughout the entire approach phase. The starship was accelerating at one and a half gees, carrying them down towards the five hundred and fifty thousand kilometre orbital band occupied by the Jovian habitats. Two armed voidhawks from the Jovian defence fleet were escorting the warship in. Just a precaution, Astor had assured them. Kelman had accepted gracefully, though most of the Royal Navy officers were less charitable.

The habitat Azara was looming large ahead of them, a circular spaceport disc extending out of its northern endcap. Although Edenism didn't have a capital, Azara played host to all of the foreign diplomatic missions. Even the Kingdom maintained an embassy at Jupiter.

'I still can't get used to the scale here,' Kelman confessed as the acceleration began to fluctuate. Their approach was in its final stages, the battlecruiser flowing through the thick traffic lanes of inter-orbit ships towards the spaceport. 'Whenever we build anything large it always seems so ugly. Of course, technically the Kingdom does own one bitek habitat.'

'I thought Tranquillity was independent,' Ralph Hiltch said.

'Great-grandfather Lukas granted its title to Michael as an independent duchy,' Prince Collis said affably. 'So, strictly speaking, in Kulu law, my father is still its sovereign. But I'd hate to try and argue the case in court.'

'I didn't know,' Ralph said.

'Oh, yes. I'm quite the amateur expert on the situation,' Prince Collis said. 'I'm afraid we do all harbour a rather baroque interest in cousin Ione and her fiefdom. All of my siblings access the official file on Tranquillity at some time while we're growing up. It's fascinating.' Alastair II's youngest child smiled whimsically. 'I almost wish I'd been sent with that delegation instead of Prince Noton. No offence,' he added for Astor's benefit.

'Your Highness,' the Edenist Ambassador murmured, 'this would seem to be the time for breaking taboos.'

'Indeed. And I shall do my best to throw off my childhood prejudices. But it will be hard. I'm not accustomed to the notion of the Kingdom being dependent on anyone.'

Ralph looked across the small lounge. All of the acceleration couches had tilted down from the horizontal, transforming into oversized armchairs. Ambassador Astor lay back bonelessly in his, a politely courteous expression on his face, as always. Ralph had no idea how he maintained it without the benefit of neural nanonics.

'Attempting to remedy a situation not of your making is hardly dishonourable, Your Highness.'

'Oh, Ralph, do stop blaming yourself for Ombey,' Kelman Mountjoy protested. 'Everyone thinks you've done a superb job so far. Even the King; which makes it official. Right, Collis?'

'Father thinks very highly of you, Mr Hiltch,' the Prince confirmed. 'I dare say you'll be lumbered with a title once this is over.'

'In any case, I don't believe this proposed alliance could be said to make the Kingdom dependent on us,' Astor said. 'Liberating the possessed of Mortonridge is both necessary and advantageous to everyone. And if, afterwards, we understand each other a little better, then surely that's for the best, too.'

Kelman exchanged an amused glance with Astor as Ralph Hiltch shuffled round in discomfort. For all that they came from totally different cultures, he and the Edenist shared remarkably similar rationalities. Communication and understanding came swiftly between them. It was a cause of growing dismay to Kelman that the freedom he'd enjoyed all his life, allowing him to develop his intellect, was maintained by guardians such as Ralph and the Navy, who could never share his more liberal outlook. Small wonder, he thought, that history showed empires always rotted from the core outward.

There were checks as soon as they docked. Brief almost-formalities; the inevitable test for static, confirmation that processors worked in their presence; verifications which everybody had to comply with. Including the Prince. Ambassador Astor made sure his own examination was a very public one. And Collis was charm personified to the two Edenists running sensors over him.

Azara's administrator was waiting with a small official reception committee at the spaceport's tube station. In most Edenist habitats, the post of administrator was largely ceremonial; in Azara's case it had evolved into something approaching Edenism's Foreign Minister.

Quite a considerable crowd had assembled to see the delegation; mostly young, curious Edenists, and staff from the foreign embassies.

A smiling Collis listened to the administrator's short speech, replied with a few appropriate words, and said he was eager to see the inside of a habitat. The whole group ignored the waiting tube carriage, and walked out of the station.

Ralph had never been inside a habitat either. He stood on the lawn outside the tube station and stared along the cylindrical landscape, mesmerized by the beauty of the sight. This was a lush, dynamic nature at its most majestic.

'Makes you wonder why we ever rejected bitek, doesn't it?' Kelman said quietly.

'Yes, sir.'

The Prince was mingling among the crowd, smiling and shaking hands. Walkabouts were hardly a novelty for him, but this was unplanned, and he didn't have his usual retinue of ISA bodyguards, just a couple of dour-faced Royal Marines that everyone ignored. He was clearly enjoying himself.

Kelman watched a couple of the girls kiss him, and grinned. 'Well, he is a real live prince, after all. I don't suppose they get to meet very many of them around here.' He glanced up at the radiant axial light-tube and the verdant arch of land overhead. There was something distinctly unnerving about knowing the vast structure was alive, and looking right back at him, its huge thoughts contemplating him. 'I think I'm glad to be here, Ralph. And I think you had the right idea to ask for an alliance. This society really has a frightening potential, I never actually appreciated that before. I always thought it would be they who were the losers as a result of our foreign policy. I was wrong; no matter all the barriers and distance we throw up, they won't make the slightest difference to these people.'

'It's too late to alter that now, sir. We're free of their energy monopoly. And I'm not sorry about that.'

'No, Ralph, I don't suppose you are. But there are more aspects to life than the purely materialistic. I think both our cultures would benefit from stronger ties.'

'You could say the same about every star system in the Confederation, sir.'

'So you could, Ralph, so you could.'

\*

The second general Consensus within a month, and probably not the last within this year, it acknowledged wryly amid itself as it formed.

The most unfortunate aspect of Lord Kelman Mountjoy's request, Consensus decided, is its innate logic. Examination of the war simulations presented to us by Ralph Hiltch show a very real possibility that the liberation of Mortonridge will succeed. We acknowledge those among us who point out that this success is dependent on no further external factors being applied in the favour of the possessed. So already we see the risk rising.

Our major problem derives from the projected victory being almost totally illusory. We have already concluded that physical confrontation is not the answer to possession. Mortonridge simply confirms this. If it takes the combined strength of the two most powerful cultures in the Confederation to liberate a mere two million people on a single small peninsula, then freeing an entire planet by such a method clearly verges on the impossible.

Hopes across the Confederation would be raised to unreasonable heights by success at Mortonridge. Such hopes would be dangerous, for they would unleash demands local politicians will be unable to refuse and equally unable to satisfy. However, for us to refuse the Kingdom's request would cast us in the role of villain. Lord Kelman Mountjoy has been ingenious in placing us in this position.

'I would disagree,' Astor told the Consensus. 'The Saldanas know as well as us that military intervention is not the final answer. They too are presented with an enormously difficult dilemma by Mortonridge. As they are more susceptible to political pressures, they are responding in the only way possible.

'I would also say this: by sending the King's natural son with their delegation they are signalling the importance they attach to our decision, and an acknowledgement of what must inevitably come to be should our answer favour them. If both of us commit ourselves to the liberation there can be no return to the policies of yesterday. We will have established a strong bond of trust with one of the most powerful cultures in the Confederation currently contrary to us. That is a factor we cannot afford to ignore.'

Thank you, Astor, Consensus replied, as always you speak well. In tribute of this, we acknowledge that the future must be safeguarded in conjunction with the present. We are given an opportunity to engender a more peaceful and tolerant universe when the present crisis is terminated.

Such a *raison d'être* is not a wholly logical one to place ourselves on a war footing. Nor is the kindling of false hope which will be the inevitable outcome.

However, there are times when people do need such a hope.

And to err is human. We embrace our humanity, complete with all those flaws. We will tell the Saldana prince that until such time that we can provide a permanent solution to possession he may have our support for this foolhardy venture.

*

After a five-day voyage, *Oenone* slipped out of its wormhole terminus seventy thousand kilometres above Jobis, the Kiint homeworld. As soon as they had identified themselves to the local traffic control (a franchise run by humans) and received permission to orbit, Syrinx and the voidhawk immediately started to examine the triad moons.

The three moons orbited the planet's Lagrange One point, four million kilometres in towards the F2 star. Equally sized at just under eighteen hundred kilometres in diameter, they were also equally spaced seventy thousand kilometres apart, taking a hundred and fifty hours to rotate about their common centre.

They were the anomaly which had attracted the attention of the first scoutship in 2356. The triad was an impossible formation, too regular for nature to produce. Worse, the three moons massed exactly the same (give or take half a billion tonnes – a discrepancy probably due to asteroid impacts). In other words, someone had built them.

It was to the scoutship captain's credit she didn't flee. But then fleeing was probably a null term when dealing with a race powerful enough to construct artefacts on such a scale. Instead, she beamed a signal at the planet, asking permission to approach. The Kiint said yes.

It was about the most forthcoming thing they ever did say. The Kiint had perfected reticence to an art form. They never discussed their history, their language, or their culture.

As to the triad moons, they were an 'old experiment', whose nature was unspecified. No human ship had ever been permitted to land on them, or even launch probes.

Voidhawks, however, with their mass-perception ability, had added to the sparse data over the centuries. Using *Oenone*'s senses, Syrinx could feel the moons' uniformity; globes of a solid aluminium silicon ore right down to the core, free of any blemishes or incongruities. Their gravity fields pressed into space-time, causing a uniquely smooth three-dimensional stretch within the local fabric of reality. Again, all three fields were precisely the same, and perfectly balanced, ensuring the triad's orbital alignment would hold true for billions of years.

A pale silver-grey in colour, they each had a small scattering of craters. There were no other features, perhaps the strongest indicator of their artificial origin. Nor could centuries of discreet probing by the voidhawks find any mechanical structures or instruments left anywhere. The triad moons were totally inert. Presumably, whatever the 'experiment' was, it had finished long ago.

Syrinx couldn't help but wonder if the triad had something to do with the beyond and the Kiint's understanding of their own nature. No human astrophysicist had ever come up with any halfway convincing explanation as to what the experiment could be.

Maybe the Kiint just wanted to see what the shadows would look like from Jobis's surface, Ruben said. The penumbra cones do reach back that far.

It seems a trifle extravagant for a work of art, she countered.

Not really. If your society is advanced enough to build something like the triads in the first place, then logic dictates that such a project would only represent a fraction of your total ability. In which case it might well be nothing other than a chunk of performance art.

*Some chunk.* She felt his hand tighten around hers, offering comfort in return for the brief hint of intimidation she had leaked into the affinity band.

*Remember,* he said, *we really know very little about the Kiint. Only what they choose to tell us.*

*Yes. Well, I hope they choose to let slip a little more today.*

The question over the true extent of the Kiint's abilities nagged at her as *Oenone* swept in to a six hundred kilometre parking orbit. From space Jobis resembled an ordinary terra-compatible world, although at fifteen thousand kilometres in diameter it was appreciably larger, with a gravity of 1.2 Earth standard. It had seven continents, and four principal oceans; axial tilt was less than one per cent, which when coupled with a suspiciously circular orbit around the star produced only mild climate variations; there were no real seasons.

For a world housing a race which could build the triads there was astonishingly little in the way of a technological civilization visible. Conventional wisdom had it that as Kiint technology was so advanced it could never resemble anything like human machinery and industrial stations, so nobody knew what to look for; either that or it was all neatly folded away in hyperspace. Even so, they must have gone through a stage of conventional engineering, an industrial age with hydrocarbon combustion and factory farming, pollution and exploitation of natural planetary resources. If so, there was no sign of it ever existing. No old motorways crumbling under the grasslands, no commercial concrete cities abandoned to be swallowed by avaricious jungles. Either the Kiint had done a magnificent job of restoration, or they had achieved their technological maturity a frighteningly long time ago.

Today, Jobis supported a society comprised of villages and small towns, municipalities perched in the centre of land only marginally less wild than the rest of the countryside. Population was impossible to judge, though the best guesstimate put it at slightly less than a billion. Their domes, which were the only kind of buildings, varied in size too much for anyone to produce a reliable figure.

Syrinx and Ruben took the flyer down, landing at Jobis's only spaceport. It was situated beside a coastal town whose buildings were all human-built. White-stone apartment blocks and a web of small narrow streets branching out from a central marina made it resemble a holiday destination rather than the sole Confederation outpost on this placid, yet most eerily alien of worlds.

The residents were employed either by embassies or companies. The Kiint did not encourage casual visits. Quite why they participated in the Confederation at all was something of a mystery, though one of the lesser ones. Their only interest and commercial activity was in trading information. They bought data on almost any subject from anyone who wanted to sell, with xenobiology research papers and scoutship logs fetching the highest prices. In exchange, they sold technological data. Never anything new or revolutionary, you couldn't ask for anti-gravity machines or a supralight radio; but if a company wanted its product improving, the Kiint would deliver a design showing a better material to use in construction or a way of reconfiguring the components so they used less power. Again, a huge hint to their technological heritage. Somewhere on Alpha there must be a colossal memory bank full of templates for all the old machines they'd developed and then discarded God alone knew how long ago.

Syrinx never got a chance to explore the town. She had contacted the Edenist Embassy (the largest diplomatic mission on Jobis) while *Oenone* flew into parking orbit, explaining her mission. The embassy staff had immediately requested a meeting with a Kiint called Malva, who had agreed.

**She's our most cooperative contact**, Ambassador Pyrus

explained as they walked down the flyer's airstairs. **Which I concede isn't saying much, but if any of them will answer you, she will. Have you had much experience dealing with the Kiint?**

**I've never even met one before,** Syrinx admitted. The landing field reminded her of Norfolk, just a patch of grass designated to accommodate inconvenient visitors. Although it was warmer, sub-tropical, it had the same temporary feel. Few formalities, and fewer facilities. Barely twenty flyers and spaceplanes were parked outside the one service hangar. The difference from Norfolk came from the other craft sharing the field, lined up opposite the ground-to-orbit machines. Kiint-fabricated, they resembled smaller versions of human ion-field flyers; ovoid but less streamlined.

**Then why were you sent?** Pyrus asked, diffusing a polite puzzlement into the thought.

**Wing-Tsit Chong thought it was a good idea.**

**Did he, now? Well I can hardly contradict him, can I?**

**Is there anything I should know before I meet her?**

**Not really. They'll either deal with you, or not.**

**Did you explain the nature of the questions I have?**

Pyrus waved an empty hand round at the scenery. **You told me when you contacted the Embassy. We don't know if they can intercept singular-engagement mode, but I expect they can if they want. Next question of course is whether they would bother. You might like to ask Malva exactly how important we are to them. We've never worked that out either.**

**Thank you.** Syrinx patted the top pocket of her ship-tunic, feeling the outline of her credit disk. Eden had loaded it with five billion fuseodollars before she left, just in case. **Will I have to pay for the information, do you think?**

Pyrus gestured at the Kiint transport craft, and a hatch opened, the fuselage material flowing apart. It was close enough to the ground not to need airstairs. Syrinx couldn't quite judge if its belly was resting on the ground, or if it was actually floating.

**Malva will tell you,** Pyrus said. **I advise total openness.**

Syrinx stepped into the craft. The interior was a lounge, with four fat chairs as the only fittings. She and Ruben sat down gingerly, and the hatch flowed shut.

**Are you all right?** an anxious *Oenone* asked straight away.

**Of course I am. Why?**

**You started accelerating at roughly seventy gees and are currently travelling at Mach thirty-five.**

**You're kidding!** Even as she thought it, she was sharing *Oenone*'s mind, perceiving herself streaking across a tall mountain range eight hundred kilometres inland from the town at an awesome velocity for atmospheric travel. **They must be very tolerant of sonic booms on this planet.**

**I suspect your vehicle isn't producing one. My current orbital position doesn't allow optimum observation, but I can't locate any turbulence in your wake.**

According to *Oenone*, the craft decelerated at seventy gees as well, landing some six thousand kilometres from the space-port field. When she and Ruben stepped out a balmy breeze plucked at her silky ship-tunic. The craft had come to rest in a broad valley, just short of a long lake with a shingle beach. Cooler air was breathing down from the snow-capped peaks guarding the skyline, ruffling the surface of the water. Avocado-green grass-analogue threw thin coiling blades up to her knees. Trees with startlingly blue bark grew in the shape of melting lollipops, colonizing the valley all the way up to the top of the foothills. Birds were circling in the distance; they looked too fat to be flying in the heavy gravity.

A Kiint dome was situated at the head of the lake, just above the beach. Despite the fresh mountain air, Syrinx was perspiring inside her ship-tunic by the time they had walked over to it.

It must have been very old, made from huge blocks of a yellow-white stone that had almost blurred together. The weathering had given it a grainy surface texture, which local ivy-analogues put to good use. Broad clusters of tiny flowers dripped out of the dark leaves, raising their pink and violet petals to the sun.

The entrance was a wide arch, its border blocks carved with worn crestlike symbols. A pair of the blue-bark trees stood outside, gnarled from extreme age, half of their branches dead, but nonetheless casting a respectable shadow over the dome. Malva stood just inside, a tractamorphic arm extended, its tip formshifting to the shape of a human hand. Breathing vents issued a mildly spicy breath as Syrinx touched her palm to impossibly white fingers.

**I extend my greetings to you and your mind sibling, Syrinx,** the Kiint broadcast warmly. **Please enter my home.**

**Thank you.** Syrinx and Ruben followed the Kiint along the passage inside, down to what must have been the dome's central chamber. The floor was a sheet of wood with a grain close to red and white marble, dipping down to a pool in the middle which steamed and bubbled gently. She was sure the floor was alive, in fact the whole chamber's decor was organic based. Benches big enough to hold an adult Kiint were like topiary bushes without leaves. Smaller ones had been grown to accommodate the human form. Interlocked patches of amber and jade moss with crystalline stems matted the curving walls, threaded with naked veins of what looked to be mercury. Syrinx was sure she could see them pulsing, the silver liquid oozing slowly upwards. An aura of soft iridescent light bounced and ricocheted off the glittery surface in playfully soothing patterns.

Above her, the dome's blocks capped the chamber. Except from inside they were transparent; she could see the geometric reticulation quite plainly.

All in all, Malva's home was interesting rather than revelatory. Nothing here human technology and bitek couldn't reproduce with a bit of effort and plenty of money. Presumably it had been selected to put Confederation visitors at ease, or damp down their greed for high-technology gadgets.

Malva eased herself down on one of the benches. **Please be seated. I anticipate you will require physical comfort for this session.**

Syrinx selected a seat opposite her host. It allowed her to see some small grey patches on Malva's snowy hide, so pale they could have been a trick of the light. Did grey indicate ageing in all creatures? **You are very gracious. Did Ambassador Pyrus indicate the information I would ask for?**

**No. But given the trouble which now afflicts your race, I expect it is of some portent.**

**Yes. I was sent by the founder of our culture, Wing-Tsit Chong. We both appreciate you cannot tell me how we can rid ourselves of the possessed. However, he is curious about many aspects of the phenomenon.**

**This ancestor of yours is an entity of some vision. It is my regret I never encountered him.**

**You would be most welcome to visit Jupiter and talk to him.**

**There would be little point; to us a memory construct is not the entity, no matter how sophisticated the simulacrum.**

**Ah. That was my first question: have the souls of Edenists transferred into the neural strata of our habitats along with their memories?**

**Is this not obvious to you yet? There is a difference between life and memory. Memory is only one component which comprises a corporeal life. Life begets souls, they are the pattern which sentience and self-awareness exerts on the energy within the biological body. Very literally: you think, therefore you are.**

**Life and memory, then, are separate but still one?**

**Whilst the entity remains corporeal, yes.**

**So a habitat would have its own soul?**

**Of course.**

**So voidhawks have as well.**

**They are closer to you than your habitats.**

**How wonderful,** *Oenone* said. **Death will not part us, Syrinx. It has never parted captains and ships.**

A smile rose to her face, buoyed by the euphoria of the

voidhawk's thoughts. *I never expected it to, my love. You were always a part of me.*

*And you I,* it replied adoringly.

*Thank you,* Syrinx told Malva. *Do you require payment for this information?*

*Information is payment. Your questions are informative.*

*You are studying us, aren't you?*

*All of life is an opportunity to study.*

*I thought so. But why? You gave up star travel. That must be the ultimate way to experience, to satisfy a curious mind. Why show an interest in an alien race now?*

*Because you are here, Syrinx.*

*I don't understand.*

*Explain the human urge to gamble, to place your earned wealth on the random tumble of a die. Explain the human urge to constantly drink a chemical which degrades your thought processes.*

*I'm sorry,* she said, contrite at the gentle chiding.

*Much we share. Much we do not.*

*That's what puzzles Wing-Tsit Chong and me. You are not that different from us, ownership of knowledge doesn't alter the way the universe ultimately works. Why then should this prevent you from telling us how to combat the possessed?*

*The same facts do not bring about the same understanding. This is so even between humans. Who can speak of the gulf between races?*

*You faced this knowledge, and you survived.*

*Logic becomes you.*

*Is that why you gave up starflight? Do you just wait to die knowing it isn't the end?*

*Laton spoke only the truth when he told you that death remains difficult. No sentient entity welcomes this event. Instinct repels you, and for good reason.*

*What reason?*

*Do you embrace the prospect of waiting in the beyond for the universe to end?*

*No. Is that what happens to Kiint souls, too?*

**751**

The beyond awaits all of us.

And you've always known that. How can you stand such knowledge? It is driving humans to despair.

Fear is often the companion of truth. This too is something you must face in your own way.

Laton also called death the start of the great journey. Was he being truthful then as well?

It is a description which could well apply.

Syrinx glanced over to Ruben for help, not daring to use the singular-engagement mode. She felt she was making progress, of sorts, even if she wasn't sure where it was leading. Though some small traitor part of her mind resented learning that Laton hadn't lied.

Do you know of other races which have discovered the beyond? Ruben asked.

Most do. There was a tinge of sadness in Malva's thoughts.

How? Why does this breakthrough occur?

There can be many reasons.

Do you know what caused this one?

No. Though we do not believe it to be entirely spontaneous. It may have been an accident. If so, it would not be the first time.

You mean it wasn't supposed to happen?

The universe is not that ordered. What happens, happens.

Did these other races who found the beyond all triumph like the Kiint?

Triumph is not the object of such an encounter.

What is?

Have you learnt nothing? I cannot speak for you, Ruben.

You deal with many humans, Malva, Syrinx said. You know us well. Do you believe we can resolve this crisis?

How much faith do you have in yourself, Syrinx?

I'm not sure, not any more.

Then I am not sure of the resolution.

But it is possible for us.

Of course. Every race resolves this moment in its history.

752

**Successfully?**

Please, Syrinx. There are only differing degrees of resolution. Surely you have realized this of all subjects cannot be a realm of absolutes.

Why won't you tell us how to begin resolving the crisis? I know we are not so different. Couldn't we adapt your solution? Surely your philosophy must allow you some leeway, or would helping us negate the solution entirely?

It is not that we cannot tell you how we dealt with the knowledge, Syrinx. If it would help, then of course we would; to do otherwise would be the infliction of cruelty. No rational sentient would condone that. We cannot advise you because the answer to the nature of the universe is different for each sentient race. This answer lies within yourselves, therefore you alone can search for it.

Surely a small hint—

You persist in referring to the answer as a solution. This is incorrect. Your thoughts are confined within the arena of your psychosocial development. Your racial youth and technological dependence blinds you. As a result, you look for a quick fix in everything, even this.

Very well. What should we be looking for?

Your destiny.

\*

The hold-down latches locked the *Tantu* into the docking cradle, producing a mechanical grinding. Quinn didn't like the sound, it was too final, metal fingers grasping at the base of the starship, preventing it from leaving unless the spaceport crew granted permission.

Which, he told himself, they would. Eventually.

It had taken Twelve-T almost a week to organize his side of the deal. After several broken deadlines and threats and high-velocity abuse, the necessary details had finally been datavised to the *Tantu*, and they'd flown down to Jesup, an asteroid owned by the government of New Georgia. The flight plan they'd filed with Nyvan's traffic control was for a cryogenic resupply, endorsed and confirmed by the Iowell Service & Engineering company who had won the contract. As the fuel transfer didn't require the *Tantu*'s crew to disembark, there was no requirement for local security forces to check for signs of possession. The whole routine operation could be handled by Iowell's personnel.

When the docking cradle had lowered the frigate into the bay, an airlock tube wormed its way out of the dull metal wall to engage the starship's hatch. Quinn and Graper waited in the lower deck for the environmental circuit to be established.

The next five minutes, Quinn knew, were going to be crucial. He was going to have to use the encounter to establish his control over Twelve-T, while the gang lord would undoubtedly be seeking to assert his superiority at the same time. And although he didn't know it, Twelve-T had a numerical advantage. Quinn guessed there would be a troop of gang soldiers on the other side of the hatch; congested with weapons, and hyped on attitude. It's what *he* would have done.

What I need, he thought, is the kind of speed which boosting gives the military-types. He felt the energistic power shifting inside his body, churning through his muscles to comply with his wishes. Light-panels in the airlock chamber began to flicker uncertainly as his robe shrank around his body, eradicating any fabric which could catch against obstructions.

A cold joy of anticipation seeped up within his mind as he prepared to unleash his serpent beast on the waiting foe. For so long now he had been forced to restrain himself. It would be good to advance the work of God's Brother again, to watch pride shatter beneath cruelty.

Twelve-T waited nervously in the docking-bay's reception chamber as the airlock pressurized. His people were spread around the dilapidated chamber, wedged behind tarnished support ribs, sheltered by bulky, broken-down cubes of equipment. All of them covering the ash-grey circular carbotanium hatch with their weapons, sensors focused and fire-control programs switched to millisecond-response triggers.

That shit Quinn might have raged about the delays, but Twelve-T knew he'd put together a slick operation. This whole deal needed the master's touch. A fucking frigate, for shit's sake! He'd busted his balls arranging for the starship to dock without the cops realizing what was going down. But then the gang had interests all over New Georgia, half their money came from legitimate businesses. Companies like Iowell were easy to muscle in on, a small operation established decades ago; the spaceport crew did as the union told them, managers could be persuaded to take their cut.

Getting his soldiers up to Jesup had been a bitch, too. Like him, they all had the gang's distinctive silver skull, skin from their eyebrows back to the nape of the neck replaced by a smooth cap of chrome flexalloy. Metal and composite body parts were worn like medals, showing how much damage you'd taken for the gang.

Try slipping twenty of them into Jesup without the administration cops taking an interest.

But he'd done it. And now he was going to find out just what the fuck was really going on. Because sure as turds floated to the top, Quinn Dexter wasn't on the level.

The instrument panel beside the hatch let out a weak bleep.

'It's ready,' Lucky Vin datavised. 'Shit, Twelve-T, I can't get anything from the sensors in the tube. They've crashed.'

'Quinn do that, man?'

'I ain't too sure. This place ... it ain't the maintenance hotspot of the galaxy, you know.'

'OK. Pop the hatch.' He opened the datavise to include the rest of his soldiers. 'Sharpen up, people, this is it.'

The hatch seal disengaged, allowing the actuators to hinge it back. Absolute blackness filled the airlock tube.

Twelve-T craned his neck forwards, scar tissue stretching tightly. Even with his retinal implants switched to infra-red there was nothing to see in the tube. 'Screw this—'

The blackness at the centre of the tube bulged out, a bulbous cone devouring the chamber's photons. Five maser carbines and a TIP pistol fired, skewering the antilight chimera from every direction. It broke open, petals of night peeling apart from the centre to splash against the chamber walls.

Twelve-T's neural nanonics began to crash. Blocks clipped to his belt chased them into electronic oblivion. The last datavise he received was from his maser carbine, telling him the power cells were dropping out. He tried to grasp the ten-millimetre machine-gun velcroed to his hip, only to find his arm shuddering, the pistonlike actuators he'd replaced the forearm muscles with were seizing up.

A missile composed of tightly whorled shadow swelled up out of the centre of the flowering blackness. Too fast for the eye to follow in real-time (certainly as far as Twelve-T's faltering retinal implants were concerned), it shot across the chamber and bounced.

The first scream clogged the chamber's air. One of the soldiers was crumpling up, his body imploding in a series of rapid strikes. He seemed to be dimming, as if he were caught at the middle of a murky nebula. Then his head caved in, and it was blood not the sounds of agony that went spraying across the chamber.

A second soldier convulsed, as if she was trying to jam her head down towards her buttocks. She managed a single bewildered grunt before her spine snapped.

The third victim darkened, his clothes starting to smoulder. Both of his titanium hands turned cherry red, glowing brightly. When he opened his mouth to scream a column of pink steam puffed out.

Twelve-T had it worked out by then. There was always a translucent cloud around the soldiers as they were slaughtered, a grey shadow that flickered at subliminal speed. His disabled arm levered the machine-gun off the velcro, and he turned desperately towards the source of the latest screams. His soldiers were losing it. Flinging themselves at the exit hatch, wrestling with each other in their struggle to escape.

The light panels were turning a dark tangerine and beginning to sputter, black iron grids had materialized across them, growing thicker. Oily smoke began to pour forth. The fractured buzzing sound of the conditioning fans was dying away. Globules of blood oscillated through the air, fringes rippling like restive jellyfish. Twelve-T knew then he'd been fucked. It wasn't Quinn Dexter, rat boy from the arcologies. This was the worst it could possibly get.

He'd never liked Nyvan. But what the fuck, it was his home planet. Now the possessed were going to violate it, subdue every living body. And he was the total fucking asshole who'd let them in.

Another of his soldiers was being chopped apart; haloed in quivering dusk. Pure fury powered Twelve-T's malfunctioning body into a final act of obedience. He swung the machine-gun round on the macerated soldier, and squeezed back on the trigger. It was only a short burst. A blue flame spat out of the muzzle to the accompaniment of a thunderous roar. Without a neural nanonics operational procedure program to help him, the recoil was far more powerful than he expected. His shoes were ripped free of the stikpad, and he was somersaulting backwards through the air, hollering in surprise.

The universe paused.

'Shatter!' a furious voice bellowed.

The machine-gun obeyed: its cool silicolithium fragmented like a shrapnel grenade. Needle slivers sliced deep into Twelve-T's flesh, some ricocheting off the metal casings of his replacement parts. He was flailing wildly now, trailing fantails of blood from his shredded hand.

'Hold him,' someone instructed curtly.

**757**

Quinn slowed himself back from the speedstate, energistic currents sinking down to quiescent levels. As they did, the rest of the world began to accelerate. It had been awesome, moving through an airlock chamber populated by statues, time solidified to a single heartbeat. Their time, not his. God's Brother had granted him impunity from the actions of any non-possessed. What greater sign that he was indeed the chosen one?

'Thank you, my Lord,' he whispered, humbled. Planets would truly bow before him now; just as Lawrence had prophesied.

Most of the blood had impacted on a surface, splattering wide into big smears and sticking tenaciously. Grotesque corpses drifted peacefully in the warm air streams. The remnants of the gang were in a sorry state. With four possessed in the airlock chamber and pulsing with malevolent power, their artificial body parts had either frozen or were running out of control. And they were all combat-vets, heavily dependent on replacements, almost up to cosmonik level. Lawrence and Graper were plucking weapons from unresisting hands, claws, and wrist sockets.

Quinn kicked off towards Twelve-T. His robe resumed its usual extravagant cut as he glided across the compartment.

Twelve-T was sweating heavily. One of the soldiers whose arms were mostly the original organic was bandaging the gang lord's ruined hands with strips torn from his own T-shirt.

'I admire your strength,' Quinn said. 'It can be harnessed to serve God's Brother.'

'Ain't no God, can't have no fucking—' Pain gripped his left arm, forcing him to cry out. His skin hissed as it rose in huge blisters.

'You wanted to irritate me,' Quinn said mildly.

Twelve-T glowered helplessly. He wasn't used to so much pain, none of them were. Neural nanonics always protected them. That meant it was going to get bad, he realized, real bad. Unless . . .

'And I won't allow you to suicide,' Quinn said. 'I know that's what you were thinking. Everybody does when they grab what's gonna happen.'

The strips of cloth bandaging Twelve-T's hands hardened into shiny nylon. Their ends flexed up like blind snakes, then slowly knotted together.

'You're so close to me, Twelve-T,' Quinn said earnestly. 'Your serpent beast is almost free. You would never have become what you are without realizing what your true nature is. Don't hold back, embrace God's Brother. Live in the Night with us.'

'You'll make a mistake, asshole. And I'll be around waiting for it.'

'I don't make mistakes. I am the chosen one.'

'Holy fuck.'

'Follow me, Twelve-T. Submit to your true self and know the glory of His word. Betray your people for greed and profit. That way you will never know defeat again. My disciples fuck who they want when they want. They see their enemies burn in torment. Enjoy rewards you have never dared take before. Help me, Twelve-T. Tell me where the asteroid cops are. Shunt your gang's money into my credit disk. Show me where the space-planes are that can take my disciples down to the surface. Do it, Twelve-T.'

'You won't get down to the planet,' Twelve-T grunted. 'People are too frightened of the possessed landing. There's all kinds of weird checks going on down there. You might have beaten my troops, big deal; but you dead freaks ain't going to turn my planet into holiday hellpark.'

'You understand nothing,' Quinn said. 'I don't give a fuck about the souls in the beyond. I'm not here to save anyone, least of all them. God's Brother has chosen me to help Him bring down the Night.'

'Oh sweet shit,' Twelve-T whimpered. Quinn was a loon. A motherfucking twenty-four-carat loon.

'I want two things from this planet,' Quinn continued. 'A starship I can use to take me home to Earth; because that's where I can hurt the Confederation most. It'll have to be a cargo ship of some kind, one which Govcentral's defences will accept is harmless. I'm sure there are plenty docked here right now, right?'

A small jaw muscle twitched on Twelve-T's face.

'Good,' said Quinn. The gang lord's thoughts had betrayed him, bitter defeat mingling with the dregs of resentment and anger. 'You want to know what the other thing is, don't you? It's simple, I intend Nyvan to be the first planet the Light Brother can bring into His kingdom. I'm going to bring the Night to this planet, Twelve-T. Endless Night. Night without hope. Until He comes from the other side of the beyond to grant you salvation.'

Making sure every word was perfectly clear, Twelve-T said: 'Go fuck yourself.' He braced himself for the retribution.

Quinn laughed softly. 'Not that easy, shithead. I told you, I want your help. I need a local smartarse to straighten out crap like a ship and how to sneak my possessed disciples past the pigs guarding the planet. Someone who knows all the access codes around here. And that's you, Twelve-T. As He chose me, so I have chosen you.' He glanced round at the gang's remaining soldiers. 'We'll open the rest of this worthless trash for possession, then convert all of Jesup. After that, nobody down below will be able to resist us.'

'Oh, Jesus, help us,' Twelve-T begged. 'Please.'

'Ain't no God,' Quinn mimicked savagely. 'So he ain't got no son, has he.' Laughing, he pushed Twelve-T down towards the decking. The gang lord's knees bent, allowing the stikpad to fasten to his trousers. Quinn stood in front of the supplicant and beckoned Lawrence over. 'I know you're a tough mother, Twelve-T. If you're possessed you'll only try to fool your new owner, jazz me about as best you can. You and your dumb pride. I can't afford that kind of shit any more. That means I'm gonna have to squeeze what I want to know out of you myself, so I know you're being honest.'

Kneeling before the monster, head bowed, Twelve-T said: 'I will never help you.'

'You will. I have many ways of binding my disciples to me. For most it is love or fear. For you, I choose dependence.' He placed his hands on either side of Twelve-T's silver head. The feat was the converse of a coronation. Quinn lifted the silver cap from the gang lord's skull with an almost gentle reverence. It came loose with a soft sucking sound. The bone underneath was covered in a sticky red mucus. Ichor dribbled over Twelve-T's face, mingling with sticky tears.

Lawrence took the cap from Quinn, acting as jester to the king. A little mad giggle escaped from the boy's lips as he held it in front of the stricken gang lord, its mirror surface ensuring he witnessed his own reduction to impotent vassal.

Quinn's hands descended again. This time the noise was louder as the bone creaked and split. He lifted the top of the skull high, smiling at the bloody trophy. Twelve-T's naked brain glistened below him, wrapped in delicate membranes, small beads of fluid weeping up from the tightly packed ribbons of tissue.

'Now I can keep a real close eye on what you're thinking,' Quinn said.

# 19

'So your group has no organized structure, as such?' Alkad asked.

'We're organized, all right,' Lodi Shalasha insisted. 'But nothing formal. We're just like-minded people who keep in touch and help each other out.'

Alkad pushed her legs down into the chameleon-suit trousers. There was still a residue of cold sweat smearing the fabric from when she'd worn the suit last night. Her nose wrinkled up in distaste, but she kept on working the trousers up her shins. 'You said you had junior cadres, the ones clearing the spiders away. That sounds like a regular underground movement hierarchy to me.'

'Not really. Some of us work in day clubs, that way we help to keep the memory of the Genocide alive for the children. Nobody should be allowed to forget what was done to us.'

'I approve.'

'You do?' He sounded surprised.

'Yes. The original refugees seem to have forgotten. That's why I'm in this mess right now.'

'Don't worry, Doctor; Voi will get you off Ayacucho.'

'Perhaps.' Alkad prided herself that the somnolence program had been for the best. When the girl had woken this morning she'd been subdued, but still functional. The grief for her father was still there, as it should be, but it hadn't debilitated her.

Over breakfast, Alkad had explained what her priorities were: to get away from the Dorados as fast as possible now her location was blown to the Intelligence agencies; and the remaining principal requirement for a combat-capable starship (she still couldn't bring herself to mention the Alchemist). It would be too much to hope for the ship to be crewed by Garissan patriot-types, a mercenary crew would just have to do now. The three of them had discussed possible options, and Voi and Lodi had started arguing over names, who to contact for what.

Voi had left by herself to secure a starship. It would be inviting disaster for Alkad to be seen with her again. As a pair they were too distinctive, however adroit the chameleon suits were at hiding their peripheral features.

'Hey, you've made the news,' Lodi waved his communication block enthusiastically. He'd entered a reference search program to monitor the media output. 'Access the Cabral NewsGalactic studio.'

Alkad struggled the suit on over her shoulders, then datavised the room's net processor for a channel to the studio.

Cabral NewsGalactic were showing a recording of a holomorph sticker which had a young cheerleader shouting: 'Run, Alkad, run!'

'Mother Mary,' Alkad muttered. 'Is this the work of your people?'

'No. I swear. I've never seen one before. Besides, only Voi and I know your name. None of the others even know you exist.'

Alkad went back to the studio. A rover reporter was walking down one of Ayacucho's main public halls. The stickers were everywhere. A cleaner mechanoid was trying to spray one off the wall, but its solvent wasn't strong enough. Smears of black semi-dissolved plastic dribbled down the metallic wall panel.

'It is as if a plague has visited Ayacucho,' the rover reporter said cheerfully. 'The first of these stickers appeared about six hours ago. And if I didn't know better I'd say they've been breeding like bacteria. Police say that the stickers are being handed out to children, and detectives are currently correlating security monitor recordings to see if they can identify the main distributors. Though sources inside the Public Prosecutor's Office tell me they're not sure exactly what charges could be brought.

'The question everyone is asking is: exactly who is Alkad, and what is she running from?'

The image went back to the studio anchorman. 'Our company's investigations have uncovered one possible answer to the mystery,' he said in a sombre bass voice. 'At the time of the Genocide, the Garissan Navy employed a Dr Alkad Mzu to work on advanced defence projects. Mzu is said to have survived the Genocide, and spent the last thirty years under an assumed name teaching physics at the Dorados university. But now foreign Intelligence agencies, acting in response to Omutan propaganda, have started hunting her under the pretext of illegal technology violations. A senior member of the Dorados Governing Council, who asked not to be named, said today: "Such an action by these foreign agents is a gross violation of our sovereignty. I find it obscene that the Omutans can lay these unfounded allegations against one of our citizens who has dedicated her life to educating our brightest youngsters. If this is their behaviour after thirty years of sanctions, then we must ask why the Confederation ever lifted those sanctions in the first place. They certainly do not seem to have had the desired effect in remedying the aggressive nature of the Omutan government. Their current cabinet is just a new collar on the same dog."

'The council member went on to say that if Alkad Mzu turned up at his apartment he would certainly offer her sanctuary, and that every true Dorados citizen would do the same. He said he would not rest until all suspected foreign agents had been expelled from the asteroids.'

'Holy Mother Mary,' Alkad groaned.

She cancelled the channel and slumped down onto the bed, the suit's hood hanging flaccidly over her shoulder. 'I don't believe this is happening. Mother Mary, they're turning me into a media celebrity.'

'That's my uncle for you,' Lodi said. 'Did you check out the positive bias in those reports? Mary, you'd be elected president tomorrow if we were ever allowed to vote around here.'

'Your uncle?'

He flinched. 'Yeah, sure. Cabral's my uncle. He's made a mint out of exploiting the little-Garissan attitude. I mean, just look at the kind of people living here, they lap it up.'

'He's insane. What does he think he's doing, giving me this kind of public profile?'

'Whipping up public support in your favour. This kind of propaganda is going to make life ten times harder for the agencies chasing you. Anyone tries to take you out of Ayacucho against your will today, they'll wind up getting lynched.'

She stared at him. That eager face which permitted so much inner anger to show without ever dimming the natural innocence. Child of the failed revolutionaries. 'You're probably right. But this isn't happening the way I ever expected it to.'

'I'm sorry, Doctor.' He pulled a worn shoulder bag out of the cupboard. 'Do you want to try some of these clothes now?'

He was proffering some long sports shorts and an Ayacucho Junior Curveball Team sweatshirt. With a short-cut wig and the chameleon suit reprogrammed, they intended her to walk out of the room as an average sports-mad teenager. A male one.

'Why not?'

'Voi will call soon. We ought to be ready.'

'You really believe she can get us off this asteroid in a starship, don't you?'

'Yes.'

'Lodi, do you have any idea how difficult that is to arrange, now of all times? Underground movements need to have contacts infiltrated right through the local administrative structure; dedicated devoted people who will risk everything for the cause. What have you got? You're rich kids who've found a new way to rebel against their parents.'

'Yes, and we can use that money to help you, if you'd just let us. Voi taught us that. If we need something, we buy it. That way there's no network for the agencies to discover and penetrate. We've never been compromised. That's why you stayed in this room all night without anyone storming the door with an assault mechanoid.'

'You may have a point there. I have to admit the old partisans didn't do too well, did they.' She gave the chameleon-suit hood a reluctant grimace, then started to smooth back her hair ready to slip it on.

*

Joshua held the Petri dish up to the cabin's light-panel, squinting at the clear glass. It looked completely empty, his enhanced retinas couldn't even find dust-motes. But lurking inside the optically pure dish were thirteen nanonic monitor bugs which the medical packages had extracted from *Lady Mac*'s crew and the serjeants. They were subcutaneous implants; agents stung them by casually brushing up against an unsuspecting victim.

'How come I rated three?' Ashly complained.

'Obvious subversive type,' Sarha said. 'Bound to be up to no good.'

'Thanks.'

'You're all in the clear,' she said. 'The medical analysis program can't spot any unusual infections or viruses. Looks like they weren't playing nasty.'

'This time,' Joshua said. As soon as the scanners in the starship's surgery had located the first of the monitor bugs he'd ordered Sarha to run a full biochemical analysis on everyone.

Microbes and viruses were far easier to introduce in a target than nanonics.

Fortunately, the agencies had been curious rather than hostile. But this was the sharpest reminder to date of the stakes involved. They'd been lucky thus far. It wouldn't last, he thought. And he wasn't the only one who realized that. The cabin had a kind of after-game locker-room atmosphere, with a team that was very relieved to have scraped a draw.

'Let's start from the beginning,' he said. 'Sarha, are we secure now?'

'Yes. These bugs can't datavise through *Lady Mac*'s screening. They're only a problem outside.'

'But you don't know when we got stung?'

'There's no way of knowing, sorry.'

'Your friend Mrs Nateghi,' Melvyn suggested. 'It was rather odd.'

'You're probably right,' Joshua said reluctantly. 'OK, assume everything we've done up until now has been compromised. First off, is there any point in continuing? Jesus, it's not as if we don't know she's here. The bloody news studios have been broadcasting nothing else. Our problem is how difficult it's going to be to contact her without anyone else tagging along. They're bound to try and sting us again. Sarha, will our electronic-warfare blocks work against these monitor bugs?'

'They should be able to scramble them; we picked up top-of-the-range systems before we left Tranquillity.'

'Fine. From now on, nobody goes into Ayacucho without one. We also take a serjeant each when we venture out. Ione, I want you to carry those chemical-projectile guns we brought.'

'Certainly, Joshua,' said one of the four serjeants in the cabin.

He couldn't tell if it was the one who'd accompanied him earlier. 'Right, what kind of data have we pulled in so far? Melvyn?'

'Ashly and I got round to the five major defence contractors,

Captain. The only orders coming in are for upgrades to the asteroid's SD platforms, and there's precious few of them. We got offered some magnificent discounts when we asked about supplying *Lady Mac* with new systems. They're absolutely desperate for work. Mzu hasn't ordered any equipment from anybody. And nobody is refitting starships.'

'OK. Beaulieu?'

'Nothing, Captain. Daphine Kigano disappeared within fifteen minutes of arriving here. There's no address for her, no credit records, no hotel booking, no citizenship register, no public record file.'

'All right. That just leaves us with Ikela.'

'He's dead, Joshua,' Dahybi said. 'Hardly the best lead.'

'Pauline Webb was very keen to stop me having any contact with T'Opingtu's management. Which means that's the direction to take. I've been reviewing every byte I can find on Ikela and T'Opingtu. He came to the Dorados with a lot of money to start up that company. There's no mention of where it came from, according to his biography he used to work for a Garissan engineering company as a junior manager. Which doesn't add up.

'Now if you were Alkad Mzu, on the run and in need of a starship that can deploy the Alchemist, who are you going to go to when you get here? Ikela fits the search program perfectly: the owner of a company which manufactures specialist astro-engineering components. Remember she fooled the Intelligence agencies for close on thirty years. Whatever plan she formatted with her colleagues after the Genocide, it was well thought out.'

'Not perfect, though,' Ashly said. 'If it was, Omuta's star would be turning nova right now.'

'The possessed glitched it for them, that's all,' Sarha said. 'Who could anticipate this quarantine?'

'Whatever,' Joshua said. 'The point is, T'Opingtu was probably set up to provide Mzu with the means to deploy the

Alchemist. Ikela would have made sure that policy continued in the event he didn't live long enough to see her arrive.'

'Which he did, but only just,' Ashly said. 'It must have been the agencies who snuffed him.'

'But not Mzu,' Melvyn said. 'This media campaign backing her sprang up too quickly after the murder. Somebody knows she's out there. Somebody with a shitload of influence, but not in contact with her. It's going to be almost impossible for us to snatch her with public opinion being whipped up like this, Captain.'

'Which is exactly the intention,' Dahybi said. 'Though it's more likely aimed at the Intelligence agencies than us.'

'We'll deal with that problem if we ever get to it,' Joshua said. 'Right now our priority is to establish a trace on Mzu.'

'How?' Sarha asked.

'Ikela has a daughter; according to his public record file she's the only family he's got.'

'She'll inherit,' Beaulieu said bluntly.

'You got it. Her name's Voi, and she's twenty-one. She's our way in to whatever organization her Daddy built up in preparation for Mzu.'

'Oh, come on, Joshua,' Ashly protested. 'Her father's just been murdered, she's not going to make appointments with perfect strangers, let alone tell us anything about the Garissan underground, even if she has any data. Which is questionable. I wouldn't involve my daughter in anything like that. And the agencies will be wanting to question her, too.'

Joshua wasn't going to argue. As soon as he reviewed Ikela's public record file he'd known Voi was the link. Ione would call it his intuition. She might even have been right. The old burn of conviction was there. 'If we can just get close to her, we stand a chance,' he said firmly. 'Mzu can't afford to remain here now. She's going to have to make a break for it, and sooner rather than later. One way or another, Voi will be involved. It's our best shot.'

'I'm not disagreeing with you,' Dahybi said. 'It's as good a chance as any. But how the hell are you going to get near her?'

'Weren't you listening?' asked one of the serjeants. 'Voi is female and twenty-one.'

Joshua grinned evilly at Dahybi.

'You have got to be joking,' the stupefied node specialist insisted.

'I'll just lie back and think of the Confederation.'

'Joshua . . .'

Joshua burst out laughing. 'Your faces! Don't worry, Dahybi, I'm not that conceited. But she will have friends. There are quite a lot of rich entrepreneurs in the Dorados, their kids will cling together in their own little social clique. And I am a starship owner–captain, after all. One of them will get us in. All I have to do now is find her.' He smiled broadly at his crew, who were regarding him with a mixture of umbrage and resignation. 'Time to party.'

\*

Prince Lambert sealed the straps around the lanky girl's wrists, then activated the sensenviron program. His bedroom dissolved into a circular stone-walled chamber at the top of a castle tower, its bed at the centre of the flagstone floor. His male slaves began to file through the iron-bound door. Ten of them stood round the bed, looking down dispassionately at the spread-eagle figure.

He took the remote response collar from under the pillow and fastened it round her neck.

'What is it?' the girl asked, anxiety rising into her voice. She was very young, it was highly probable she'd never heard of the device before.

He kissed her silent, and datavised the collar's activation sequence. The technology was a bastardization of medical nanonic packages, sending filaments to merge with her spinal cord. He could use it to manipulate her body into reacting exactly how he wanted, fulfilling each of the fantasies in turn.

'Do hope I'm not interrupting,' one of the slaves said in a sharp female voice.

Prince Lambert gave a start, jumping up from the bed. The girl wailed in dismay as the collar began to knit smoothly with her skin.

He cancelled the sensenviron program, retrieving the reality of his darkened bedroom, and stared at the tall skinny figure which replaced the muscle-bound slave. 'For Mary's sake, Voi! I'm going to change this bloody apartment's door code, I should never have let you have it.' He squinted at the figure. 'Voi?'

She was pulling her chameleon suit hood off, allowing her little crown of dreadlocks to wriggle free. A wig of unkempt gingerish hair was held carelessly in her hand. Her clothes were standard-issue biosphere agronomist overalls. 'I want to talk to you.'

His jaw dropped. One hand gestured ineffectually at the girl on the bed, who was tugging at the straps. 'Voi!'

'Now.' She went back out into the living room.

He swore, then datavised a shutdown order at the collar, and started to open the strap seals.

'How old is she?' Voi asked when he emerged into the living room.

'Does it matter?'

'It might to Shea. Has she found out about your little kinks yet?'

'Why the sudden interest in my sex life? Do you miss it?'

'Like a sunbather misses bird crap.'

'That's not what you said at the time.'

'Who cares?'

'I do. We were good together, Voi.'

'History.'

**771**

'Then why have you come running back?'

'I need something of yours.'

'Mother Mary, that detox procedure was a big mistake. I preferred you as you were before.'

'I'm really interested in everything you say, PL.'

'What the hell are you doing here?'

'I want you to flight-prep the *Tekas*, and take me and some friends outsystem.'

'Oh, sure, no problem.' He collapsed into the leather settee, and favoured her with a pitying gaze. 'Any particular destination? New California? Norfolk? Hey, why don't we go for the big one, and see if we can break through Earth's SD network?'

'It's important. It's for Garissa.'

'Oh, Mary. Your poxy revolution.'

'It isn't revolution, it's called honour. Access your dictionary file.'

'Haven't got one. And for your information, there's a civil starflight quarantine in operation. I couldn't fly the *Tekas* away if I wanted to.'

'Do you?'

'Yes. All right, one–nil. If I'd known about this quarantine in advance I would have left. The Dorados might be home, but I don't think they're the best place to live while the possessed are roaming around. You've got the right idea, Voi, you're just too late.'

She held up a flek. 'The Dorados Governing Council flight authorization; it'll be an official voyage.'

'How the hell . . .'

'Daddy was on the council. I have his access codes.'

Temptation haunted him like a curse. 'Is it still valid?'

'Yes. Me and three others. Deal?'

'There's a few people I'd like to bring along.'

'No. You can operate that yacht by yourself, that's why I chose it. This isn't a bloody pleasure cruise, PL. I need you to fly some complex manoeuvres for me.'

'*Tekas* isn't combat capable, you know. Who are these others?'

'Need-to-know only. And you don't. Do we have a deal?'

'Do we get to try out free-fall sex?'

'If fucking me means you'll fly the yacht for me, fuck away.'

'Mother Mary, you are a complete bitch!'

'Deal?'

'All right. Give me a day to wind things up here.'

'We leave in three hours.'

'No way, Voi. I doubt I could even fill the cryogenic tanks by then.'

'Try.' She waved the flek. 'If you don't; no authorization.'

'Bitch.'

*

The girl was extravagantly attractive; early twenties with lustrous ebony skin and dry-chestnut hair that fell just below her bottom. Her dress was a shimmering metallic grey-blue with a skirt hem higher than the dangling ends of her hair.

Melvyn suspected she was a typical insecure rich kid. Though Joshua didn't seem to mind; the two of them were busy French-kissing on the Bar KF-T's dance floor.

'He's a devil for it,' Melvyn said peevishly. He felt he should explain to Beaulieu, who was sitting at the table with him. 'Never works for me. I mean, fusion specialist is a tough job. And I'm crew, that's glamorous enough, isn't it? But they just bloody stampede at him when we dock. I think he got his pheromones geneered along with everything else.' He started searching through the cluster of beer bottles on the table for one that had something left inside. There were rather a lot of them.

'You don't think it's anything to do with the fact he's thirty years younger than you?' the cosmonik asked.

'Twenty-five!' Melvyn corrected indignantly.

'Twenty-five.'

'Certainly not.'

The cosmonik gave the Bar KF-T another automatic scan. Joshua's direction of investigation was obviously puzzling the Intelligence agents who were on observation duty. Melvyn and Beaulieu had identified five of them in the club, making a game of it as they sat drinking beer and waiting for Joshua to score. It wasn't that the agents didn't mix; they drank, they danced, they chatted to people, the betraying factor was the way they maintained a rigid distance from the *Lady Mac*'s crew.

Joshua waved a sunny farewell to the girl, and sat down at Melvyn's table with a satisfied sigh. 'Her name's Kole, and she's invited me to a party this evening.'

'I'm surprised she can hold back that long,' Melvyn muttered.

'I'm meeting her and her friends at tonight's benefit gig, then they're going on to a private bash at someone's apartment.'

'A benefit gig?' Beaulieu questioned.

'Some local MF bands are getting together so they can raise money for Alkad Mzu's legal costs, should she ever need to fight Confederation extradition warrants.'

'She's becoming a bloody religion,' Melvyn said.

'Looks that way.' Joshua started counting the bottles on the table. 'Come on, we need to get back to *Lady Mac*.' He slipped his arm under Melvyn's shoulder, and signalled Beaulieu to help. Between them, they got the drunk fusion specialist to his feet. Ashly and Sarha walked over from the bar. All four serjeants rose from their seats.

None of the agents moved. That would have been too blatant.

A pair of possessed walked into Bar KF-T. A man and woman, dressed in clothes which almost matched current fashions.

Joshua's electronic-warfare block datavised an alarm.

'Get down!' the four serjeants shouted in unison.

The threat-response program which had gone primary as soon as the alarm came on sent Joshua diving for cover amid the tables and chairs. He hit the floor, rolling expertly to absorb the impact. A couple of empty chairs went flying as his legs struck them. His crew was following him down; even Melvyn, though his alcohol-polluted nerves made him slower.

Screams broke out across the club as the serjeants drew their stubby machine-guns. The agents were also moving, boosted muscles turning their actions into a blur.

Both the possessed gasped at the near-instantaneous reaction to their appearance. An unnerving number of weapons were lining up on them amid the chaos of a terrified and bewildered clientele.

'Freeze,' a quadraphonic voice ordered them.

They didn't have functional neural nanonics to run combat programs, but instinct was almost as fast. Both of them started to raise their arms, white fire bursting from their fingertips.

Six machine-guns, three semi-automatic pistols, and a carbine opened fire.

Joshua had never heard a chemical-projectile weapon before. Ten of them shooting at once was louder than a fusion-rocket exhaust. He slammed his hands over his ears. The fusillade couldn't have lasted more than a couple of seconds. He risked raising his head.

Only the agents (there were actually six – Melvyn had missed one) and the serjeants were standing. Everyone else was on the floor, sprawled flat or curled up in foetal balls. Tables and chairs rolled and spun. The music and dance floor holograms were still playing.

He heard several peculiar mechanical *snicking* sounds as fresh magazines were slammed into the guns.

Bullets had shredded the wall behind the possessed, chewing apart the composite panelling. Large splatters of blood covered the tattered splinters of composite. The two bodies—

Joshua squirmed at the sight. There wasn't much left to

identify as human. A nausea-suppression program switched smoothly into primary mode, though that only stopped the physical symptoms.

Moans and cries rose over the music. Several people had been hit by ricochets.

'Joshua!'

It was Sarha. She had her hand clamped round Ashly's left thigh. Blood was staining her fingers scarlet. 'He's been hit.'

The pilot was staring with a calm morbid interest at his wound. 'Damn stupid thing.' He blinked in confusion.

'Ione,' Joshua shouted. 'Medical nanonic.'

One of the serjeants took a package from its equipment belt. Beaulieu was slitting Ashly's trouser fabric with a small metal blade that had slid out of her left wrist attachments. A dribble of grey-green fluid was leaking from a bullet hole in her brass breastplate.

'I say, do be careful,' Ashly murmured.

When the wound had been fully exposed, Sarha slapped the package over it.

'Let's go,' Joshua said. 'Beaulieu, take Melvyn. Sarha and I will handle Ashly. Ione, cover us.'

'Now wait a minute,' one of the agents said. Joshua recognized him as one of the heavyweights accompanying Pauline Webb. 'You're staying right here until the police arrive.'

It was a barman who had recovered fast enough to think of the financial possibilities who started recording the scene in a memory cell. Later that day and all through the night the news companies repeated it almost constantly. Six armed men in a shouting match with a young starship captain (later everyone realized it was 'Lagrange' Calvert himself) and his crew. The captain saying that no one was going to prevent him from taking his injured friend to get proper treatment. And what authority did they have, anyway? Four identical and disturbingly menacing cosmoniks stood between Calvert and the armed men. There was a short pause, then everyone's guns seemed to disappear. The starship crew left the club, carrying their wounded with them.

Anchormen speculated long and loud on the possibility that the six armed men were in fact foreign Intelligence agents. Rover reporters tried desperately to hunt them down, with no success.

The police officially confirmed that the two people shot dead by the agents had been possessed (though no details about how they knew for sure were forthcoming). Ayacucho's Governing Council issued a statement urging everyone to remain calm. Total priority was given to search and identification procedures which were being put into operation to locate any further possessed in the asteroid. All citizens and residents were asked to cooperate fully.

There was no physical expression of panic, no angry mobs gathering in the biosphere cavern or marches on the council chamber. People were too fearful of what might be lying in wait outside their apartment doors. Those companies and offices which had remained open started to wind down or conduct their businesses purely over the communication net; anything as long as personal contact was reduced. Parents took their children out of day clubs. Emergency services were brought up to full alert status. Company security staff were seconded to the police to help with the search.

By late afternoon several starships had been given official flight authorization by the council. Most of them were taking councillors, their families, and close aides away for conferences or defence negotiations with allies.

'And we can't stop them,' Monica complained bitterly. She was sitting at the back of the office which the Edenists were using, sipping a mug of instant tea. There was little else for her to do now, which aggravated her intensely. All the ESA's assets had been activated. None of them had any idea where Mzu was, few had even heard of Voi, let alone any underground group the girl was connected with.

Locating Mzu was all down to the Edenist observation operation now, and the slender hope they would get a lucky break.

'She has not embarked on any starship,' Samuel said. 'We are sure of that. Both axial chambers have been under constant observation, and not just by us. Nobody who comes within twenty-five per cent of Mzu's height and mass has passed into the spaceports without being positively identified.'

'Yes, yes,' Monica said irritably.

'If we don't find her in another four hours we are going to withdraw from Ayacucho.'

She'd known it was coming, but that didn't make it any easier. 'That bad?'

'Yes. I'm afraid so.' He had just finished watching another possession through a spider in one of the residential sections. It was the apartment of an ordinary family of five, doing as they'd been advised, staying at home and not allowing anyone else in. Until the police arrived. All three officers were possessed; and after seven minutes so were the family. 'We estimate eight per cent of the population has been possessed now. With everyone isolated and sitting tight, it is becoming easier for them to spread. They have taken over the police force in its entirety.'

'Bastards. They've gone for officialdom every time since Capone used the police and civil service to take over New California.'

'A remarkably perceptive man, Mr Capone.'

'I don't suppose it would do any good broadcasting a general warning now?'

'We think not. There are few weapons available to the general populace, and most of those are energy weapons, which are worse than useless. We would be adding to the suffering.'

'And since that bloody media campaign, nobody would trust us.'

'Exactly.'

'What do we do if Mzu doesn't escape?'

'That depends on what happens here. If the possessed take Ayacucho out of this universe, the problem is solved, albeit not very satisfactorily. If they remain here, then the voidhawks will enforce a permanent blockade.'

She gritted her teeth, hating the mounting feeling of frustration. 'We could try broadcasting a message to her, offer to take her off.'

'I've considered it; and I might well use it as a last resort before we evacuate.'

'Great. So now we just sit and pray she walks in front of a spider.'

'You have an alternative?'

'No. I don't think any of us do.'

'Perhaps not; though I remain intrigued by what Joshua Calvert and his crew were doing in that club.'

'Trying to get laid, by the look of it.'

'No. Calvert is shrewd. If you want my guess he is attempting to approach Voi through her friends.'

'He can't know who her friends are, he doesn't have the resources. We've only got three of her friends on our list, and that took five hours to acquire.'

'Possibly. But he's already inserted himself in her social stratum with that invitation to a party. And it's a small asteroid.'

'If Voi is hiding Mzu, she's not going to reveal herself.'

'True.' His grin was childlike in its mischievousness.

'What?' Monica asked in annoyance.

'The irony. From being an amateur irritant, Calvert is now our only lead.'

\*

Ashly had said very little during the trip back to the spaceport. Joshua guessed the pilot's neural nanonic programs were busy suppressing the shock. But Sarha didn't seem unduly worried, and she was monitoring the medical package round his thigh.

Melvyn was doing his best to sober up fast. One of the

serjeants had given him a medical nanonic package which was now wrapped round his neck to form a thick collar. It was busy filtering all traces of alcohol out of the blood entering his brain.

Joshua's only concern was the fluid which was still trickling out of the bullet hole in Beaulieu's breastplate. Medical nanonics would be of no value at all in treating the cosmonik. None of them had standardized internal systems; each was unique, and proud of it. He wasn't even sure if she was mostly mechanical or biological underneath her brass carapace.

'How are you doing?' he asked her.

'The bullet damaged some of my nutrient synthesis glands. It's not critical.'

'Do you have any ... er, spares?'

'No. That function has multiple redundancy back-up. It looks worse than it is.'

'Don't tell me, just a flesh wound,' Ashly grunted.

'Correct.'

The commuter lift's doors opened. Two serjeants slid out into the corridor first, checking for any possessed between them and the docking-bay's airlock tube. 'Joshua,' one of them called.

His electronic-warfare detector block wasn't acting up. 'What?'

'Someone here for you.'

He learned nothing from the tone, so he pushed off with his feet and glided out into the corridor. 'Oh, Jesus wept.'

Mrs Nateghi and her two fellow goons from Tayari, Usoro and Wang were waiting outside the airlock tube. Another man was floating just behind them.

The crew followed Joshua out of the lift.

'Captain Calvert.' Mrs Nateghi's voice was indecently happy.

'Can't get enough of me, can you? So what is it this time? A million-fuseodollar fine for littering? Ten years' hard labour for not returning my empties to the bar? Penal colony exile for farting in public?'

'Humour is an excellent defence mechanism, Captain Calvert. But I would advise you to have something stronger in court.'

'I've just saved your asteroid from being taken over by the possessed. Will that do?'

'I've accessed the NewsGalactic recording. You were lying on the floor with your hands over your head the whole time. Captain Calvert, I have a summons for you to be present at a preliminary hearing to establish proceedings which will determine the ownership of the starship *Lady Macbeth*, pursuant to the claim my client has filed upon said ship.'

Joshua stared at her, too incredulous to speak.

'Ownership?' Sarha asked. 'But it's Joshua's ship; it always has been.'

'That is incorrect,' Mrs Nateghi said. 'It was Marcus Calvert's ship. I have a sensorium recording of Captain Calvert admitting that.'

'He was never trying to deny it. His father is dead. *Lady Mac*'s registration is filed with the CAB. You can't challenge that.'

'Yes, I can.' The man who had been keeping himself behind the other two lawyers slowly edged forward.

'You!' Sarha exclaimed.

'Me.'

Joshua stared at him, a very unpleasant chill sluicing into his thoughts. The angular, ebony face was ... Jesus, I know him. But where from? 'So who the hell are you?'

'My name is Liol. Liol Calvert, actually. I'm your big half-brother, Joshua.'

\*

The last place Joshua wanted to bring this ... this *fraud* was the captain's cabin. It was his father's cabin, for Christ's sake, even though most of the old fittings and personal mementoes had been removed during the last refit. This was the closest Joshua had ever come to knowing a home.

But Ashly needed the deep invasion packages in *Lady Mac*'s sickbay to remove the bullet in his thigh. That bitch-queen Mrs Nateghi wasn't going to be deflected, and the summons was real enough. He also had a mission. So it was back to basics.

As soon as the cabin hatch shut behind them, Joshua asked: 'OK, shithead, how much?'

Liol didn't answer immediately, he was gazing round the cabin. His face carried an expression which was close to trepidation. 'I'm finally here,' he said falteringly. 'This must be very strange for you, Joshua. It is for me.'

'Cut the crap, how much?'

Liol's face cleared. 'How much for what?'

'To drop the claim and bugger off, of course. It's a neat scam, I'll give you that. Normally I'd just let the courts break you apart, but I'm a little pushed for time right now. I don't need complications. So name your price, but you'd better make it less than fifty grand.'

'Nice one, Josh.' Liol smiled, and held out his Jovian Bank credit disk, silver side up. Green figures glowed on the surface.

Joshua blinked as he read out the amount of money stored inside: eight hundred thousand fuseodollars. 'I don't understand.'

'It's very simple, I *am* your brother. I'm entitled to joint ownership, at the very least.'

'Not a chance. You're a con artist who knows how to use a cosmetic adaptation package, that's all. Right now, my face is as famous as Jezzibella's. You saw an opportunity to make a nuisance of yourself, and remodelled your features.'

'This is my face. I've had it ever since I was born, which was before you. Access my public file if you want proof.'

'I'm sure someone as smart as you has planted all the appropriate data in Ayacucho's memory cores. You've done your research, and you've shown me you have the money to buy official access codes.'

'Really? And what about you?'

'Me?'

'Yes. How come you acquired this ship after my father died? In fact, how did he die? Is he even dead at all? Prove you're a Calvert. Prove you are Marcus's son.'

'I didn't acquire it, I inherited it. Dad always wanted me to have it. His will is on file in Tranquillity. Anybody can access it.'

'Oh, that's nice. So Tranquillity's public records are beyond reproach, while anything stored in the Dorados was put there by criminals. How convenient. I wouldn't try that one in court if I were you.'

'He's my father!' Joshua shouted angrily.

'Mine too. And you know it.'

'I know you're a fake.'

'If you were a true Calvert, you'd know.'

'What the fuck are you talking about?'

'Intuition. What does your intuition tell you about me, Josh?'

For the first time in his life, Joshua knew what vertigo must feel like. To be teetering on the edge of some monstrously deep chasm.

'Ah,' Liol's grin was triumphant. 'Our little family quirk can be a real downer at times. After all, I knew you were real the second I accessed Kelly Tirrel's report. I also know what you're going through, Joshua. I felt exactly the same way about you. All that terrible anger, refusing to believe despite all the evidence. We're more than brothers, we're almost twins.'

'Wrong. We don't even come from the same universe.'

'What exactly worries you the most, Josh? That I am your brother, or I'm not?'

'I'll scuttle *Lady Mac* before I let anyone else have her. If you've got any intuition, you'll know how true that is.'

'My mistake.' Liol stroked the acceleration couch beside the hatch, the longing obvious in his eyes. 'I can see the ship means as much to you as it does to me. No surprise there, we've both got the Calvert wanderlust. Hitting you with a big legal scene first off was bound to create some hostility. But I've been waiting for this starship to dock here for every day of my life. Dad left Ayacucho before I was even born. In my mind the *Lady Macbeth* has always been mine. She's my inheritance, too, Josh. I belong here just as much as you do.'

'A starship only has one captain. And you, asteroid boy, don't know the first thing about piloting or captaining. Not that it's relevant, you'll never be in a position to fly *Lady Mac*.'

'Don't fight this, Josh. You're my brother, I don't want to alienate you. Christ, just finding out you existed was a hell of a shock. Family feuds are the worst kind. Don't let's start one the moment we meet. Think how Dad would feel, his sons going at each other like this.'

'You are *not* family.'

'Where was *Lady Macbeth* docked in 2586, Josh? What ports?'

Joshua clenched his fists, a free-fall assault program working out possible trajectories he could leap along. He hated how smug this arrogant bastard was. Wiping that knowing superiority from his ugly flat face would be wonderful.

'The disadvantage with white skin like yours, Josh, is that I can see every blush. It's a dead give-away. Me? I always win at poker.'

Joshua seethed silently.

'So, do you want to discuss this sensibly?' Liol asked. 'Personally, I'd hate to face Mrs Nateghi across a courtroom.'

'I don't suppose, *Lie*, this sudden urge to acquire a starship has anything to do with your asteroid being overrun by possessed?'

'Lovely.' Liol clapped his hands enthusiastically. 'You're a

Calvert, all right. Never see a belt without wanting to hit below it.'

'That's right. So, I'll see you in court here in about a week's time. How does that sound?'

'Would you really abandon your own brother to the possessed?'

'If I had one, probably not.'

'I think I'm going to like you after all, Josh. I thought you'd be soft; after all, you've had it dead easy. But you're not.'

'*Easy?*'

'Compared to me. You knew Dad. You had the big inheritance waiting. I'd call that easy.'

'I'd call that bollocks.'

'If you don't believe in your own intuition, a simple DNA profile will tell you if we're related. I'm sure your sickbay could run one for you.'

And Joshua was absolutely stumped at that. There was something about this complete stranger that was deeply unsettling, yet obscurely comforting at the same time. Jesus, he does look like me, and he knows about the intuition, and Dad wiped the log for 2586. It's not utterly impossible. But *Lady Mac* is mine. I could never share her.

He stared at Liol for a moment longer, then made a command decision.

The crew were all hanging round on the bridge, along with Mrs Nateghi. Nobody would make eye contact. Joshua shot out of the captain's cabin, rotated ninety degrees, and slapped his feet on a stikpad. 'Sarha. Take our guest down to the sickbay. Get a blood sample, use a dagger if you want, and run a DNA profile.' He jabbed a finger at Mrs Nateghi. 'Not you. You're leaving. Right now.'

She ignored him whilst managing to project her complete disdain at the same time. 'Mr Calvert, what are your instructions?'

'I just told you . . . Oh.'

'Thank you so much for your help,' Liol said with flawless courtesy. 'I'll be in touch with your office if I decide any further legal action is required against my brother.'

'Very well. Tayari, Usoro and Wang will be delighted to help. Forcing recidivists to acknowledge their responsibilities is always rewarding.'

Combating her amusement, Sarha held up a warning finger as Joshua's face turned beacon red.

'Dahybi, show the lady out, please,' he said.

'Aye, Captain.' The node specialist gestured generously at the floor hatch, and followed Mrs Nateghi through.

Liol flashed Sarha an engaging grin. 'You wouldn't really use a dagger on me, would you?'

She winked. 'Depends on the circumstances.'

'Fancy that, Joshua,' one of the serjeants said as the pair of them left the bridge. 'There's two of you.'

Joshua glared at the bitek construct, then executed a perfect mid-air somersault and zoomed back into his cabin.

'Thanks very much,' Ashly said mordantly. 'But don't any of you worry. I'm fine.'

*

Alkad's tranquillizer program wasn't nearly strong enough to keep the claustrophobia at bay. Eventually she had to admit defeat and switch a somnolence program to primary. Her only thought as she fell into oblivion was: I wonder who will be there when I wake?

The rendezvous was an elaborate one, which decreased the chances of success. But even that wasn't her main worry. Getting out of Ayacucho undetected was the big problem.

The asteroid had two counter-rotating spaceports, one at each end. The main one was used by starships and larger inter-orbit craft, while the second was mainly for heavy-duty cargo and utility tankers delivering fresh water and liquid oxygen for the biosphere. It was also the operations base for the personnel commuters and MSVs and tugs which flew between the asteroid and its necklace of industrial stations.

Both were under heavy surveillance by agents. There was no chance of getting through the axial chambers and taking a commuter lift to the docking-bays, so Voi had arranged for Alkad and herself to be shipped out in cargo-pods.

Lodi and another youth called Eriba, who claimed to be a molecular structures student, worked on a couple of standard pods in one of T'Opingtu's storage facilities. They were converted into heavily padded coffins moulded to hold someone wearing an SII spacesuit. Both boys swore the insulation would prevent any thermal or electromagnetic leakage. The cargo-pods would appear perfectly inert to any sensor sweep.

Of course, the insulation meant that Alkad couldn't datavise out for help if anything went wrong and nobody opened her pod. She believed she held her composure pretty well while she allowed them to seal her in. After that there was nothing but the tranquillizer program for the twenty minutes before she sought refuge in sleep.

A tug was scheduled to take the cargo-pods out to one of T'Opingtu's foundry stations. From there they would be transferred to an inter-orbit craft that was heading for Mapire.

Alkad woke to find herself in free fall. *At least we got out of the asteroid.*

Her neural nanonics reported they were picking up a datavise.

'Stand by, Doctor, we're cracking the pod now.'

She could feel vibrations through her suit, then the collar sensors were showing her slash-lines of red light cavorting around her. The top of the cargo-pod came free, and someone in an SII suit and a manoeuvring pack was sliding into view in front of her.

'Hello, Doctor, it's me, Lodi. You made it, you're out.'

'Where's Voi?' she datavised.

'I'm here, Doctor. Mary, but that was horrible. Are you all right?'

'Yes. Fine, thank you.' As well as relief for herself, she was strangely glad the girl had come through unscathed.

She made sure she had a secure grip on her crumpled old backpack before she let Lodi draw her out of the pod. Held in front of him, with the manoeuvring pack puffing out fast streamers of gas, she sank into the déjà vu of Cherri Barnes towing her back to the *Udat*. Then space had been frighteningly empty, with so little light her collar sensors had struggled to resolve anything. Now she was deep within Tunja's disc, gliding through a red-out blizzard. No stars were visible anywhere, the particles were too thick. Their size was inordinately difficult to judge: a grain of dust a centimetre from her nose or a boulder a kilometre away, both looked exactly the same.

Ahead of her she could see the waiting starship. Its fuselage shone a dim burgundy, much darker than the particles skipping across it like twisters of interference in an empty AV projection. Two thermo-dump panels were extended, resembling slow-motion propeller blades as rills of dust swirled around them. The airlock hatch was open, emitting a welcoming beam of white light.

She sank along it, relishing the return of normal colour. They entered a cylindrical chamber with grab hoops, utility sockets, harsh light-tubes, environment grilles, and small instrument panels distributed at random. The sensation that reality was solidifying around her was inescapable.

The hatch closed, and she clung to a grab hoop as air flooded in. Her SII suit flowed back into a globe hanging off the collar, and she was inundated with sounds.

'We did it!' Voi was jubilant. 'I told you I could get you out.'

'Yes, you did.' She looked round at them, Voi, Lodi, and Eriba, so dreadfully young to be sucked in to this world of subterfuge, hatred, and death. Beaming faces desperate for her approval. 'And I'd like to thank you; you did a magnificent job, all of you.'

Their laughter and gratitude made her shake her head in wonder. Such odd times.

Five minutes later Alkad was dressed in her old ship-suit, backpack tight against her waist, following Voi into the *Tekas*'s upper-deck lounge. The yacht was only large enough for one life-support capsule, with three decks. Despite the lack of volume, the fittings were compact and elegant, everything blending seamlessly together to provide the illusion of ample space.

Prince Lambert was reclining in a deep circular chair, datavising a constant stream of instructions to the flight computer. *Tekas* was under way, accelerating at a twentieth of a gee, though the gravity plane was flicking about.

'Thank you for offering us the use of your ship,' Alkad said after they were introduced.

He gave Voi a sterling glance. 'Not at all, Doctor, the least I could do for a national heroine.'

She ignored the sarcasm, wondering what the story was with him and Voi. 'So what's our current status? Did anyone follow you?'

'No. I'm fairly sure about that. I flew outside the disc for a million kilometres before I went through it. Your inter-orbit craft did the same thing, but on the other side. In theory no one will realize we rendezvoused. Even the voidhawks can't sense what happens inside the disc, not from a million kilometres away, it's too cluttered.'

Unless they want to follow me right to the Alchemist, Alkad thought. 'What about a stealthed voidhawk just outside the disc, or even inside with us?' she asked.

'Then they've got us cold,' he said. 'Our sensors are good, but they're not military-grade.'

'We'd know by now if we were being followed,' Voi said. 'As soon as we rendezvoused they would have moved to intercept.'

'I expect so,' Alkad said. 'How long before we can clear the disc and jump outsystem?'

'Another forty minutes. You don't rush a manoeuvre like this; there are too many sharp rocks out there. I'm going to have to replace the hull foam as it is; dust abrasion is wearing it down to the bare silicon.' He smiled unconvincingly at Alkad. 'Am I going to be told what our mission is?'

'I require a combat-capable starship, that's all.'

'I see. And I suppose that is connected with the work you did for the Garissan Navy before the Genocide?'

'Yes.'

'Well, you'll excuse me if I leave the party before that.'

Alkad thought of the remaining devices in her backpack, and just how tight her security margin had become. 'Nobody will force you to do anything.'

'Nice to hear.' He gave Voi another pointed glance. 'For once.'

'What jump coordinate does this course give us?' Alkad asked.

'Nyvan,' he said. 'It's a hundred and thirty light-years away, but I can get a reasonable alignment on it without using up too much fuel. Voi told me you wanted a planet with military industrial facilities, and wouldn't ask too many questions.'

\*

The last of the starships with official flight authorization had departed ninety minutes earlier, when Joshua made his way out of the spaceport. Service and maintenance staff had gone home to be with their families. Utility umbilicals supporting the remaining starships were becoming less than reliable.

Three agents were loitering in the axial chamber, talking in quiet tones. They were the only people there. Joshua gave them a blasé wave as he and his escort of three serjeants emerged from the commuter lift.

One of the agents frowned. 'You're going back in there?' she asked incredulously.

'Try keeping me from a party.'

He could hear the argument start behind him as the lift doors closed. Holomorph sticker cheerleaders began their chant all around him.

'If she's worried enough to question you openly, then the possessed must be gaining ground,' a serjeant said.

'Look, we've been over this. I'm just going to check out the gig, and see if Kole has turned up. If she hasn't, we head straight back.'

'It would have been much safer if I'd gone alone.'

'I don't think so.' Joshua wanted to say more, but the lift was probably overloaded with nanonic bugs. He datavised the net for a channel to *Lady Mac*.

'Yes, Joshua?' Dahybi responded.

'Certain people out here are getting twitchy about the possessed. I want you to monitor the asteroid's internal systems; transportation, power, environment, the net, everything. If any of them start downgrading I want to know right away.'

'OK.'

Joshua glanced at the rigid, expressionless face of the nearest serjeant. Right now he really wanted Ione to confide in, to be able to ask her opinion, to talk things through. If anyone knew how to handle awkward family, it was her. Some deep-buried prejudice prevented him from saying anything to the serjeants. 'One other thing, Dahybi. Call Liol, tell him to get himself over to the *Lady Mac* right away. Give him a passenger cabin in C capsule. Don't let him on the bridge. Don't give him any access codes for the flight computer. And make sure you check him for possession when he arrives.'

'Yes, Captain. Take care.'

A datavise couldn't convey emotional nuances, but he knew Dahybi well enough to guess at the amused approval.

'You accept his claim, then?' Ione asked.

'The DNA profile seems similar to mine,' Joshua said grudgingly.

'Yes, I'd say ninety-seven per cent compatibility is roughly in the target area. It's not unusual for starship crews to have extended families spread over several star systems.'

'Thank you for reminding me.'

'If your father was ever anything like you, then it's possible Liol isn't your only sibling.'

'Jesus.'

'I'm just preparing you for the eventuality. Kelly Tirrel's recording has enhanced your public visibility rating by a considerable factor. Others may seek you out in the same way.'

He pulled an ironic face. 'Wouldn't that be something? The gathering of the Calverts. I wonder if there are more of us than there are Saldanas?'

'I very much doubt it; not if you include our illegitimates.'

'And black sheep.'

'Quite. What do you intend to do about Liol?'

'I haven't got a clue. He's not touching the *Lady Mac*, though. Can you imagine having board meetings every time to decide her next destination? It's the opposite of everything I am, not to mention the old girl herself.'

'He'll probably come to realize this. I'm sure you can come to some arrangement. He appears to be quite smart.'

'The word is smarmy.'

'There's very little difference between you.'

The lift dropped him off in a public hall a couple of hundred metres from the Terminal Terminus club where the benefit gig was being played. Not everyone was obeying the Governing Council's request to stay put at home. Kids filled the hall with laughter and shouts. Everyone was wearing a red handkerchief on their ankle.

For a moment Joshua felt disconnected from his own generation. He had formidable responsibilities (not to mention problems), they were just stimheads sliding round their perpetual circuit from one empty good time to the next, they didn't understand the universe at all.

Then a couple of them recognized 'Lagrange' Calvert, and wanted to know what it was like rescuing the children from Lalonde, and had there really been possessed in Bar KF-T? They were peppy, and the girls in the group were giving him the eye. He began to loosen up; the barriers weren't so solid after all.

The Terminal Terminus looked like some kind of chasmic junction between tunnels. Big old mining machines were parked in arching recesses, their conical, worn-down drill mechanisms jutting out into the main chamber. Obsolete mechanoids clung to the ceiling, spider-leg waldos dangling down inertly. Drinks were served over a long section of heavy-duty caterpillar track.

A fantasy wormhole squatted in the centre, a rippling gloss-black column five metres wide stretching between floor and ceiling. Things were trapped inside, undefined creatures who clawed at the distortion effect in desperate attempts to escape; the black surface bent and distended, but never broke.

'Very tasteful, under the circumstances,' Joshua muttered to a serjeant.

A stage had been set up between two of the mining machines. AV projectors powerful enough to cover a stadium stood on each side.

One of the serjeants went off to guard an emergency exit. The remaining two stuck by Joshua.

He found Kole standing with a group of her friends under one of the mining machines. Her hair had been woven through with silver and chrome-scarlet threads, which every now and then made it fan open like a peacock tail.

He paused for a moment. She was so phoney; rich without Dominique's cosmopolitan verve, and absolute trash compared to Louise's simple honesty.

Louise.

Kole caught sight of him, and squealed happily, kissed him, rubbed against him. 'Are you all right? I accessed what happened after I left.'

He grinned brashly, the legend in the flesh. 'I'm fine. My . . . er, cosmoniks here are a tough bunch. We've seen worse.'

'Really?' She cast a respectful eye over the two serjeants. 'Are you male?'

'No.'

Joshua couldn't tell if Ione was annoyed, amused, or plain didn't care. On second thoughts, he doubted the latter.

Kole kissed him again. 'Come and meet the gang. They didn't believe I'd hooked you. Mother, I can't believe I hooked you.'

He braced himself for the worst.

From her vantage point lounging casually on a coolant feed duct a third of the way up the side of a mining machine, Monica Foulkes watched Joshua greeting Kole's posse of friends. He knew exactly the attitude to take to be accepted within seconds. She took a gulp of iced mineral water as her enhanced retinas scanned the young faces below. It was hot wearing the chameleon suit, but it gave her the skin tone of Ayacucho's Kenyan-ethnic population; 'foreign agents' were about as popular as the possessed right now. Except Calvert, of course, she thought sorely, he was being greeted like a bloody hero. Her characterization-recognition program ran a comparison against the youngsters she was scanning, and signalled a ninety-five per cent probable match.

'Damn!'

Samuel (now black-skinned, twenty-five years old, and wearing jazzy purple sports gear) looked up from the base of the mining machine. 'What?'

'You were right. Kole has just introduced him to Adok Dala.'

'Ah. I knew it. He was Voi's boyfriend up until she dumped him eighteen months ago.'

**794**

'Yes, yes, I can access the file for myself, thank you.'

'Can you hear what's being said?'

She glanced down contemptuously. 'Not a chance. This place is really filling up now. My audio-discrimination programs can't filter over that distance.'

'Come down, please, Monica.'

Something in his tone halted any protest. She slithered down the pitted yellow-painted titanium bodywork of the mining machine.

'We have to decide what to do. Now.'

She flinched. 'Oh, God.'

'Do you believe Adok Dala will know where Voi is?'

'I don't think so, but there's no guarantee. And if we snatch Dala now, it isn't going to make a whole lot of difference as far as official repercussions are concerned. He's hardly going to complain about being taken off Ayacucho, is he?'

'You're right. And it will prevent Calvert from learning anything.'

Joshua's neural nanonics reported a call from Dahybi. 'Two voidhawks from the defence delegation have just left the docking-ledge, Captain. Our sensors can't see much from inside the bay, but we think they're keeping station five kilometres off the spaceport.'

'OK, keep monitoring them.'

'No problem. But you should know that Ayacucho is suffering localized power failures. They're completely random, and the supervisor programs can't locate any physical problem in the supply system. One of the news studios has gone off-line, as well.'

'Jesus. Start flight-prepping *Lady Mac*; I'll wind things up here and get back to you within thirty minutes.'

'Aye, Captain. Oh, and Liol has arrived. He's not possessed.'

'Wonderful.'

Kole was still clinging magnetically to his side. No one she'd introduced him to had mentioned Voi. His original idea had been to ask them about Ikela's murder and see what was said. But now time was running out. He looked round to find out where the serjeants were, hoping Ione wasn't going to make an issue of pulling out. Hell, we gave it our best.

The compère was striding out on the stage, holding her arms out for silence as the rowdy crowd cheered and started catcalling. She started into her spiel about the Fuckmasters.

'This is Shea,' Kole told him.

It was hard for Joshua to smile; Shea was tall and skinny, almost identical to Voi's size and height. He datavised his electronic-warfare block to scan her, but she was clean. What he saw was real, not a chameleon suit. It wasn't Voi.

'This is Joshua Calvert,' Kole boasted, raising her voice against the rising whistle of the giant AV projectors. 'He's my starship captain.'

Shea's melancholia became outright distress. She started crying.

Kole gave her an astonished look. 'What's the matter?'

Shea shook her head, lips sealed together.

'I'm sorry,' Joshua said, earnestly sympathetic. 'What did I do?'

Shea smiled bravely. 'It's not you. It's just ... my boyfriend left this afternoon. He's captaining a starship, too, and that reminded me. I don't know when I'm going to see him again. He wouldn't say.'

Intuition was starting a major-league riot in Joshua's skull. The first MF band was strolling on stage. He put a protective arm round Shea's shoulders, ignoring Kole's flash of ire. 'Come on, I'll buy you a drink. You can tell me about it. You never know, I might be able to help. Stranger things happen in space.'

He signalled the two serjeants frantically, and turned away from the stage just as the AV projectors burst into life. A thick haze of coherent light filled the Terminal Terminus. Even though he was looking away, sensations spirited down his nerves; fragmented signals saturated with crude activant sequences. He felt good. He felt hot. He felt randy. He felt slippery.

A glance back over his shoulder had him sitting on a saddle astride a giant penis, urging it forwards.

Honestly, kids today. When he was younger MF was about the giddy pursuit, how it felt when your partner adored you in return, or spurned you without reason. Making up and breaking up. The infinite states of the heart, not the dick.

The kids around him were laughing and giggling, joyous expressions on their incredulous faces as the AV dazzle poured down their irises. They all swayed from side to side in unison.

'Joshua, four Edenists are coming this way,' a serjeant warned.

Joshua could see them in the sparkling light cloud which pervaded the audience. Taller than everyone else, some kind of visor over their eyes, moving intently through the swinging throng.

He grabbed Shea's hand tightly. 'This way,' he hissed urgently, and veered off towards the mock wormhole in the centre of the club. One of the serjeants cleared a path, forcing people aside. Frowns and snarls lined his route.

'Dahybi,' he datavised. 'Get the rest of the serjeants out of zero-tau, fast. Secure a route through the spaceport from the axial chamber to *Lady Mac*. I might be needing it.'

'It's being done, Captain. Parts of the asteroid's net are crashing.'

'Jesus. OK, we've got the serjeants' affinity to keep communications open if it goes completely. You'd better keep one in the bridge with you.'

He reached the writhing black column and looked back. Shea was breathless and confused, but not protesting. The Edenists weren't chasing after him. 'What ... ?' Some sort of struggle had broken out over where he'd left Kole's friends. Two of the tall agents were pulling an inert body between them. It was Adok Dala, unconscious and shaking, victim of a nervejam shot. The other pair of agents and someone else were holding back some irate kids. A nervejam stick was raised and fired.

Joshua turned his head a little too far, and he was tasting nipple while he slid over dark pigmentation as if he was snowboard slaloming, leaving a huge trail of glistening saliva behind him. His neck muscles flicked back a couple of degrees, and the Edenists were retreating, completely unnoticed by the entranced euphoric audience they were shoving their way through. Behind them, Kole's friends clung together; those still standing wept uncomprehendingly over those felled by the violence which had stabbed so unexpectedly into their moment of erotic rapture.

Shea gasped at the scene, and made to rush over.

'No!' Joshua shouted. He pulled her back, and she recoiled, as frightened by him as the agents. 'Listen to me, we have to get out of here. It's only going to get worse.'

'Is it the possessed?'

'Yeah. Now come on.'

Still keeping hold of her hand he slid around the wormhole. It felt like dry rubber against his side, flexing in queasy movements.

'Nearest exit,' he told the serjeant in front of him. 'Go.' It began to plough through tightly packed bodies at an alarming speed. Blissfully unaware people were sent tumbling. Joshua followed on grimly. The Edenists must have wanted Adok Dala for the same reason he wanted Shea. Had he got the wrong friend? Oh, hell.

The cavern wall was only ten metres ahead of him now, a red circle shining above an exit. His electronic-warfare block datavised an alarm.

Jesus! 'Ione.'

'I know,' the lead serjeant shouted. It drew its machine-gun.

'No,' he cried. 'You can't, not in here.'

'I'm not inhuman, Joshua,' the burly figure retorted.

They reached the wall, and hurried along to the exit. That was when he realized Kole was still with them.

'Stay here,' he told her. 'You'll be safe with all these people.'

'You can't leave me here,' she gasped imploringly. 'Joshua! I know what's happening. You can't. I don't want that to happen to me. You can't let them. Take me with you, for Mary's sake!'

And she was just a stricken young girl whose broken hair was flapping wildly.

The first serjeant slammed the door open and went through. 'I'll stay here,' the second said. The machine-gun was held ready in one hand. It took out an automatic pistol and held it in the other. 'That's a bonus, these things are ambidextrous. Don't worry, Joshua. They'll suffer if they try and get past me.'

'Thanks, Ione.' Then he was out in the corridor, urging the two girls along. 'Dahybi,' he datavised. His neural nanonics reported they couldn't acquire a net processor. 'Bugger.'

'The other serjeants are securing the spaceport,' the serjeant told him. 'And the *Lady Mac* is flight-prepped. Everything is ready.'

'Great.' His electronic-warfare block was still datavising its alarm. He took his own nine-millimetre pistol out of its holster. Its operating procedure program went primary.

They came to a crossroads in the corridor. And Joshua wasted a second querying the net on the direction he wanted. Cursing, he requested the Ayacucho layout he'd stored in a memory cell. There would be too much risk using a lift now; power supplies were dubious, transport management processors more so. His neural nanonics devised the shortest route to the axial chamber, it seemed depressingly far.

'This way.' He pointed down the left-hand corridor.

'Excuse me,' someone said.

Joshua's electronic-warfare block gave out one final warning, then shut down. He whirled round. Standing ten metres down the other corridor were a man and a woman, dressed in heavy black leather jackets and trousers with an improbable number of shiny zips and buckles.

'Run,' the serjeant ordered. It stepped squarely into the middle of the corridor, and levelled its compact machine-gun.

Joshua didn't hesitate. Shoving at the girls, he started running. He heard a few heated words being shouted behind him. Then the machine-gun fired.

He took the first turning, desperate to escape from the line of sight. His neural nanonics immediately revised his route. The corridors were all identical, three metres high, three metres wide, and apparently endless. Joshua hated that, trapped in a maze and utterly reliant on a guidance program susceptible to the possessed. He wanted to know exactly where he was, and be able to prove it. Being unaware of his exact location was an alien experience. Human doubt was superseding technological prowess.

He was looking over his shoulder as he took the next turning, making sure the girls were keeping up and there was no sign of any pursuit. His peripheral-vision monitor program indexed the figure striding down the corridor towards him milliseconds before his neural nanonics crashed.

It was a man in white Arab robes. He smiled in simple gratitude as Joshua and the girls stumbled to a halt in front of him.

Joshua swung his pistol round, but the lack of any procedural program meant he misjudged its weight. The arc was too great. Before he could bring it back to line up on the target, a ball of white fire struck his hand.

Joshua howled at the flare of terrible pain as the pistol fell from his grip. No matter how vigorously he waved his arm the deadly white flame could not be dislodged from its grip around his fingers. Oily stinking smoke spouted out.

'Time to say goodbye to your life,' the smiling possessed said.

'Fuck you.'

He could hear the girls crying out behind him, the wails of their revulsion and horror. Shock was diminishing the pain in his hand slightly. He could feel the puke rising in his throat as more and more of his flesh charred. His whole right arm was stiffening. Somewhere behind his assailant a vast crowd of invisible people were whispering all at once. 'No.' It wasn't a coherent word, just a defiant grunt mangled by his contorted throat muscles. *I will not submit to that. Never.*

A cascade of water burst out of the corridor's ceiling to the accompanying sound of a high-pitched siren. The edge of the lighting panels turned red, and started to flash.

Shea was laughing with brittle hysteria as she withdrew her fist from the fire-alarm panel. Dots of blood oozed up from her grazed knuckles. Joshua punched his own hand upwards, straight underneath a nozzle. He roared triumphantly. The white flame vanished in a gust of steam, and he collapsed down onto his knees, his whole body shaking violently.

The Arab regarded the three of them with a degree of aristocratic annoyance, as if any hint of defiance was unprecedented. Water splattered on his dark headgear, turning his robe translucent as it clung to his body.

Joshua raised his head against the icy torrent to snarl at his enemy. His right hand was dead now, a supreme crush of coldness had devoured his wrist. A few spittles of vomit emerged from his mouth before he managed to growl: 'OK, shithead, my turn.'

The Arab frowned as Joshua reached into a pocket with his left hand and brought out Horst Elwes's small crucifix. He thrust it forward.

'Holy Father, Lord of Heaven and the mortal world, in humility and obedience, I do ask Your aid in this act of sanctification, through Jesus the Christ Who walked among us to know our failings, grant me Your blessing in this task.'

'But I am a Sunni Muslim,' the bemused Arab said.

'Eh?'

'A Muslim. I have no belief in your false Jewish prophet.' He raised his arms, palms upwards. The deluge of water from the nozzles turned to snow. Every flake stuck to Joshua's shipsuit, smearing him in a coat of slush. Most of his skin was numb now.

'But I believe,' Joshua ground out through vibrating teeth. And did. The revelation was as shocking as the cold and the pain. But he'd come to this moment of pure clarity through reason and ordeal. All he knew, all he'd seen, all he'd done; it spoke to him that there was order in the universe. Reality was too complex for chance evolution.

Medieval prophets were a convenient lie, but something had made sense out of the chaos which existed before time began. Something started time itself flowing.

'My Lord God, look upon this servant of Yours before me, fallen to a misguided and unclean spirit.'

'Misguided?' The Arab glowered, trickles of static electricity crawling up his robes. 'You brain-dead infidel! Allah is the only true— oh, shit.'

The serjeant fired, aiming for the Arab's head.

Joshua drooped limply onto the floor. 'That's always how religious arguments end, isn't it?' He was only dimly conscious of the serjeant dragging him out of the downpour. His neural nanonics came back on-line, and immediately started erecting axon blockades. It was a different kind of numbness than the snow had brought, less severe. The sergeant wrapped a medical nanonic package around his hand. A stimulant program coaxed Joshua's brain back to full alertness. He blinked up at the three faces peering down at him. Kole and Shea were clinging together, both of them in a shambolic state, drenched and stupefied. The serjeant had taken a bad pounding, deep scorch marks crisscrossed its body, all-too-human blood was bubbling out from crusted wounds.

Joshua climbed slowly to his feet. He wanted to smile

reassuringly at the girls, but the will just wasn't there. 'Are you OK?' he asked the serjeant.

'I'm mobile.'

'Good. What about you two, any damage?'

Shea shook her head timidly, Kole was still sobbing.

'Thanks for helping,' he said to Shea. 'That was fast thinking. I don't know what I would have done without the water. It was all a little bit too close for comfort. But we're through the worst now.'

'Joshua,' the serjeant said. 'Dahybi says that three of the Capone Organization's warships have just arrived.'

*

Seven Edenists in full body armour were guarding the docking-ledge departure lounge. Monica was tremendously glad to see them. Along with Samuel, she'd been covering their retreat from the Terminal Terminus, no easy duty. There had been three encounters with the possessed on the way, and the shapeshifting magicians terrified her. Nerves and neural nanonics were hyped to the maximum. Never once had she given them the opportunity to surrender or back off. Locate and shoot, that was the way to do it. And she noticed that for all his worthiness and respect for life, Samuel was wired pretty much the same.

The light-panels were flickering and dimming as the group rushed across the lounge towards the airlock door, and the waiting crew bus outside. Monica waited until the airlock hatch slid shut before taking her combat programs off-line. She flicked the machine-gun's safety catch on, and slowly pulled off her chameleon suit hood. The bus's cool air felt gloriously refreshing as it gusted over her sweat-soaked hair.

'Well, that was easy,' she said.

The bus was rolling towards *Hoya*, the last voidhawk left on the ledge. Nothing else moved on the shelf of smooth dark rock.

'Unfortunately, you might be right,' Samuel said. He was bent over the unconscious form of Adok Dala, checking the boy with a sensor from a medical block. 'Capone's ships are here.'

'What?'

'Don't worry. The Duida Consensus has dispatched a squadron of voidhawks to support us. We are in little physical danger.'

An insane impulse made Monica stare out through the bus's window in search of the Organization ships. She could barely make out the non-rotational spaceport, an eclipsed crescent with the funereal red mist of the disc swirling around its edges. 'We're a long way from New California. Is this another invasion?'

'No, there are only three ships.'

'Then why ... Oh God, you don't think he's looking for Mzu as well?'

'It is the most obvious possibility.'

They reached the voidhawk, and the bus extended its airlock tube over the upper hull. Despite their situation, Monica glanced round curiously once she was on board. The crew toroid wasn't that much different from an Adamist's starship's life-support capsule in terms of technology; it was a lot roomier, though. Samuel led her round the central corridor to the bridge, and introduced her to Captain Niveu.

'My thanks to *Hoya*,' she said, remembering her etiquette.

'Our pleasure, you have been performing a difficult job under extreme circumstances.'

'Tell me about it. What's happening with the Capone ships?'

'They are accelerating down into the disc, though they have made no threatening moves. The squadron from the Duida habitats is here, we're moving out to join them now. What happens next depends on the Capone ships.'

'We're under way?' Monica asked. The gravity field was rock steady.

'Yes.'

'Are there any electronic sensors I can access?'

'Certainly.'

Monica's neural nanonics received a datavise from the bridge's bitek processor array. *Hoya* was already sliding up through the fringes of the disc, like a bird emerging from a rain cloud. Purple and green symbols outlined the three Capone Organization ships, half a million kilometres away, and heading in towards Ayacucho at a steady third of a gravity. The squadron of voidhawks was clustered together just outside the top of the disc.

'They're not in any hurry,' Monica observed.

'They probably don't wish to appear hostile,' Niveu said. 'If it came to a battle with us they would lose.'

'Are you going to allow them to dock?'

Niveu glanced at Samuel.

'Consensus is undecided,' Samuel said. 'We don't have sufficient information yet. To attack them without reason is not an action we can undertake lightly.'

'They can't be here on an assault mission,' Niveu said. 'Ayacucho has almost fallen now, attacking it would be pointless. The asteroid's new masters would probably welcome an alliance with Capone.'

'Destroying them now might be the best course for us all in the long run,' Monica said. 'If they walk in, they'll be able to squeeze every byte of data from Voi's friends. And if Voi and Mzu didn't get off, then we really are up shit creek.'

'Good point,' Samuel said. 'We must find out what we can. Time to talk to our guest.'

\*

Only Sarha, Beaulieu, and Dahybi were on the bridge when Joshua sailed through the floor hatch. He'd told the serjeants to take both girls to C capsule, where Melvyn, Liol, and Ashly were waiting in the sickbay.

Sarha's expression was a blend of anger and worry as he drifted past her acceleration couch. 'God, Joshua!'

'I'm all right, really.' He showed her the medical nanonic which had enveloped his right hand. 'All under control.'

She scowled as he moved away trailing droplets of cold water. A neat mid-air twist, and he was lying on his acceleration couch with the webbing folding over him.

'The net has gone completely,' Dahybi said. 'We can't monitor the asteroid's systems.'

'It doesn't matter,' Joshua said. 'I know exactly what's happening in there. That's why we're leaving.'

'Did the girl help?' Beaulieu asked.

'Not yet. I just want to get us clear first. Dahybi, are any of the voidhawks screwing round with our nodes?'

'No, Captain; we can jump.'

'Good.' Joshua optimistically ordered the flight computer to release the cradle clamps. He was rather pleased to see them disengage, some processors were still working back in the spaceport.

The chemical verniers fired, lifting them straight up out of the bay. Sarha winced as the drab metal wall slid past the tips of the sensor clusters, there was only about five metres' clearance. But *Lady Mac* never wavered. As soon as they emerged from the bay Joshua cut the rockets, letting the starship fly free. The sensor clusters sank down into their jump recesses. An event horizon claimed the hull. They jumped half a light-year. A second after they emerged energy flashed through the patterning nodes again. This time the jump was three light-years.

Joshua let out a juddering sigh.

Sarha, Beaulieu, and Dahybi looked at him. He was completely motionless, staring at the ceiling.

'Why don't you join the others in the sickbay?' Sarha said compassionately. 'Your hand should be checked properly.'

'I heard them, you know.'

Sarha gave Dahybi an anxious look. The node specialist gave her a curt gesture with his hand.

'Heard who?' she asked. Her webbing peeled back, allowing her to haul herself over to Joshua. A stikpad at the side of his couch captured her feet.

He didn't acknowledge her presence. 'The souls in the beyond. Jesus, they're real all right, they're there waiting. One tiny act of weakness, that's all it takes, and they've got you.'

Her fingers stroked his waterlogged hair. 'They didn't get you.'

'No. But they lie and lie about how they can help. I was angry, and stupid enough to think Horst's damn cross would save me.' He held up the little crucifix, and snorted at it. 'Jesus, he was a Muslim.'

'You're not making a lot of sense.'

He looked up at her with bloodshot eyes. 'Sorry. They can hurt you very badly, you know. He'd only just started with my hand, that was a warm-up. I don't know if I could have held out. I told myself I would, or at least that I wouldn't give in. I think the only way to do that is to die.'

'But you didn't give in, and you're still alive, and it's only you inside your skull. You won, Joshua.'

'Luck, and the tank is about empty.'

'It wasn't luck you had three serjeants with you. It was healthy paranoia and good planning. You knew the possessed are extremely dangerous, and took it into account. And that's what we'll do again next time.'

He gave a nervous laugh. 'If I can manage a next time. It's quite something to look right down into the abyss and see what's there waiting for you, one way or the other, as possessed or possessor.'

'We were up against it at Lalonde, and we're still flying.'

'That was different, I was ignorant, then. But now I know for sure. We're going to die, and be condemned to live in the beyond. All of us. Every sentient entity in the universe.' His face screwed up in pain and anger. 'Jesus, I can't believe that's all there is: life and purgatory. After tens of thousands of years, the universe finally reveals that we have souls, and then we have the glory snatched right back and replaced with terror. There has to be something more, there has to be. He wouldn't do that to us.'

'Who?'

'God, He, She, It, whatever. This torment, it's too . . . I don't know. Personal. Why the fuck build a universe that does this to people? If you're that powerful, why not make death final, or make everyone immortal? Why this? We have to know, have to find out why it works the way it does. That way we can know what the answer to all this is. We have to find something that's permanent, something which will last until the end of time.'

'How do you propose to do that?' she asked quietly.

'I don't know,' he snapped, then just as suddenly he was thoughtful again. 'Maybe the Kiint. They say they've solved all this. They won't tell us outright, but they might at least point me in the right direction.'

Sarha looked down at his intense expression in astonishment. Joshua taking life so seriously was strange, Joshua mounting a crusade was frankly astonishing. For one second she thought that he had been possessed after all. 'You?' she blurted.

All the suffering and angst vanished from his angular face. The old Joshua swept back. He started chuckling. 'Yeah, me. I might be catching religion a little late in life, but the born-again are always the most insufferable, and devout.'

'It's more than your hand which needs checking out in the sickbay.'

'Thank you, my loyal crew.' His restraint webbing parted, allowing him up. 'But we're still going to ask the Kiint.' He ordered the flight computer to run a full star track search and correlate their exact position. Then he ran an almanac search for Jobis's file.

'Right now?' Dahybi asked tartly. 'You're going to throw away all you achieved on Ayacucho just like that?'

'Of course not,' Joshua said smoothly.

'Good. Because if we don't find Mzu and the Alchemist before the possessed do, there probably won't be any Confederation left for you to save.'

*

Adok Dala returned to consciousness with a loud cry. He looked round fearfully at the *Hoya*'s sickbay. Not reassured by his surroundings. Not at all.

Samuel removed the medical nanonic package from the base of his neck. 'Easy there. You're quite safe, Adok. Nobody is going to hurt you here. And I must apologize for the way we treated you in the club, but you are rather important to us.'

'You're not the possessed?'

'No. We're Edenists. Well, apart from Monica, here; she's from the Kulu Kingdom.'

Monica did her best to smile at the nervous boy.

'You're foreign agents, then?'

'Yes.'

'I won't tell you anything. I'm not helping you catch Mzu.'

'That's very patriotic. But we're not interested in Mzu. Frankly, we hope she got away clean. You see, the possessed are in charge of Ayacucho now.'

Adok moaned in distress, clamping his hand over his mouth.

'What we'd like to know about is Voi,' Samuel said.

'Voi?'

'Yes. Do you know where she is?'

'I haven't seen her for days. She put us all on stand-by. It was silly, we had to organize the kids in the day clubs to kill spiders. She said Lodi figured out you were using them to spy on us.'

'Clever man, Lodi. Do you know where he is?'

'No. Not for a couple of days.'

**809**

'Interesting. How many are there in this group of yours?'

'About twenty, twenty-five. There's no real list. We're just friends.'

'Who started it?'

'Voi. She'd changed when she came out of detox. The Genocide became a real cause for her. We just got sucked along by her. Everybody does when Voi gets serious about an issue.'

Monica datavised a request to her processor block, retrieving a memory image from the file she'd recorded at the Terminal Terminus. It had bothered her since the snatch. The last glimpse she had of Joshua Calvert showed him tugging a girl along. She showed the enhanced image to Adok. 'Do you know her?'

He blinked blearily at the little screen. Whatever drugs Samuel had administered to loosen his tongue were making him drowsy. 'That's Shea. I like her, but . . .'

'Is she one of your group?'

'Not really, but she's Prince Lambert's girlfriend. He's sort of a member; and she's done a few things for us occasionally.'

Monica looked at Samuel. 'What have we got on this Prince Lambert character?'

'A moment.' He consulted his bitek processor block. 'He's registered as a pilot for the *Tekas*, an executive yacht owned by his family corporation. Monica, it was one of the starships which left Ayacucho this afternoon.'

'Damn it!' She slammed her fist down on one of the cabinets beside Adok Dala's couch. 'Does Voi know Prince Lambert?'

Adok smiled blithely. 'Yes. They used to be lovers. He was the reason she wound up in detox.'

**Do you have a jump coordinate for the *Tekas*?** Samuel asked Niveu.

**No. It flew outside our mass-perception range. None of the voidhawks registered its jump. But we do have the flight vector. It was an odd course, the ship was heading back down to the disc when it passed beyond us. If it didn't perform any drastic realignment**

manoeuvres there are three possible stars it could have flown to: Shikoku, Nyvan, and Torrox.

Thank you. We'll check them.

Of course. I'll inform Duida's Defence Command. We'll leave immediately.

*

Shea had changed into a grey ship-suit when Joshua floated into the sickbay. She was talking quietly to Liol, but broke off to give him a shy grin. Ashly and Melvyn were busy packing equipment away. One of the serjeants held on to a grab hoop just inside the hatch.

'How are you feeling?' Joshua asked her.

'Fine. Ashly gave me a tranquillizer. I think it helps.'

'I wish he'd give me one.'

Her grin brightened. 'Is your hand very bad?'

He held it up. 'Most of the bone is intact, but I'm going to need some clone-vat tissue to build the fingers up. The package can't regenerate quite that much.'

'Oh. I'm sorry.'

'Tranquillity will pay for it,' he said, straight-faced. 'Where's Kole?'

'Zero-tau,' Melvyn said.

'Good idea.'

'Do you want me to go in as well?' Shea asked.

'Up to you. But I need some help before you decide.'

'From me?'

'Yes. Let me explain. Contrary to everything the news studios were saying, I'm not a foreign agent.'

'I know that, you're "Lagrange" Calvert.'

Joshua smiled. 'I knew it would come in useful one day. The thing is, we are looking for Alkad Mzu, but not because of any Omutan propaganda.'

'Why, then?'

He took her hand in his, squeezing emphatically. 'There is a reason, Shea, it's a good reason, but not a very nice one. I'll tell you if you really want to know; because if you're anything like the person I think you are, you'd help us find her if you knew what's actually going on. But if you'll trust me on this, you don't want to know. It's up to you.'

'Are you going to kill her?' she asked sheepishly.

'No.'

'Promise?'

'I promise. We just want to take her back to Tranquillity, where she's been living since the Genocide. As prisons go, it isn't bad. And if we can get to her in time, it'll save an awful lot of people. Maybe an entire planet.'

'She's going to drop a planet-buster on Omuta, isn't she?'

'Something like that.'

'I thought so,' she said in a tiny voice. 'But I don't know where she is.'

'I think you do. You see, we believe she's with Voi.'

'Oh, her.' Shea's face darkened.

'Yes, her. I'm sorry, this sounds painful for you. I didn't realize.'

'She and Prince Lambert had a thing. He still ... well, he'd go back to her if she'd have him.'

'This Prince Lambert is your boyfriend, the starship captain?'

'Yes.'

'Which ship?'

'The *Tekas*.'

'And it left Ayacucho today?'

'Yes. Do you really think Alkad Mzu was on board?'

'I'm afraid so.'

'Is he going to be in trouble with the authorities?'

'I couldn't care less about him. I just want to locate Mzu. Once I've done that, once she knows I'm on her tail and watching every move, the threat will be neutered. She'll have to come back with me then. Now, are you going to tell me where the *Tekas* went?'

'I'm sorry, I wish I could help, but he wouldn't tell me where they were going.'

'Shit!'

'PL is flying the *Tekas* to Nyvan,' Liol said. He looked round enquiringly at the startled faces. 'Did I say something wrong?'

'How the bloody hell do you know where he was going?' Joshua demanded.

'PL's a good friend of mine; we grew up together. Quantum Serendipity has the contract to service the *Tekas*. He's not the most experienced pilot, and Voi had given him a very odd manoeuvre to fly. So I helped him program the flight vector.'

# 20

André Duchamp had half expected to be shot at by the Ethenthia asteroid's SD platforms when the *Villeneuve's Revenge* jumped into its dedicated emergence zone three thousand kilometres away. He certainly had a lot of explaining to do to the local defence command, followed up by testimony from the rover reporters. When he did finally receive docking permission he assumed the famed Duchamp forcefulness and integrity had won through again.

What actually happened was that while he was busy claiming to be a defector from the Capone Organization, Erick opened a channel to the local Confederation Navy Bureau and asked them to press the local authority for clearance. Even so, the authorities were extremely cautious. Three SD platforms were locked on to the *Villeneuve's Revenge* as it approached the spaceport.

The security teams which ransacked the life-support capsules in search of treachery were exceptionally thorough. André put on a brave face as composite panels were split open and equipment modules broken down into component parts for high-definition scanning. The cabins hadn't exactly been in optimum shape before. It would take weeks to reassemble the trashed fittings to comply with even the minimum of CAB flight-worthiness requirements.

But Kingsley Pryor was hauled away by the emotionless

officers from an unnamed division of the defence forces. A big credit bonus to the intrepid crew who had outsmarted Capone.

The only possible flaw was Shane Brandes. So the *Dechal*'s fusion engineer was brought out of zero-tau while they were still on the approach phase and given a simple ultimatum: cooperate or you're going to be a dead crewman who we're in mourning over. He chose cooperation; explaining to the Ethenthia authorities why they'd abducted him in the first place would have been a little too confusing, he felt.

Thirteen hours after they docked, the last of Ethenthia's security officers departed. André gazed round lugubriously at his bridge. The consoles were little more than open grids of processor boards; walls and decking had been stripped down to the bare metal; environmental ducts were making stressed whining sounds, and dirty condensation was building up on every surface.

'We did it.' His clown face exhibited a genuine smile as he looked from Erick, to Madeleine, and finally Desmond. 'We're home free.'

Madeleine and Desmond began to chuckle, sharing the realization. They really had come through.

'I have a few bottles in my cabin,' André said. 'If that thieving scum *anglo* police haven't stolen them. We must celebrate. Ethenthia is as good a place as any to sit out this war. We can keep busy with some proper maintenance. I'm sure I can get the insurance to pay for some of this wreckage; after all, we're war heroes now. Who will argue, eh?'

'Tina might,' Erick said.

The flatness in the voice dispelled André's smile. 'Tina who?'

'The girl we killed on the *Krystal Moon*. Murdered, actually.'

'Oh, Erick. Dear *enfant*. You are tired. You have done more work than most.'

'Certainly more than you. But what's new there?'

'Erick,' Desmond said, 'come, now, it has been a terrible

time for all of us. Perhaps we should get some rest before we decide what to do next.'

'Good suggestion. I admit I haven't quite made up my mind what to do with you yet.'

'What *you* are going to do with us?' André asked indignantly. 'I think your medical modules are malfunctioning, your brain is being fed the wrong chemicals. Come, we will go to bed, and in the morning none of this will be mentioned again.'

'Shut up, you pompous geek,' Erick said. It was the contemptuous indifference of the voice which shocked André into silence.

'My problem is, that I owe Madeleine and Desmond my life,' Erick went on. 'But then, if you hadn't been such an arsehole, Duchamp, none of us would ever have been put in the crazy position we were. That's the kind of hazard I have to accept when I take on missions like this.'

'Missions?' André didn't like the cold passion which had suddenly overtaken his crewman.

'Yes, I'm an undercover officer in the CNIS.'

'Oh, fuck,' Madeleine grunted helplessly. 'Erick ... Shit, I liked you.'

'Yeah. That's my problem, too. I'm in a little bit deeper than I ever expected. We made a good team fighting the possessed.'

'So now what?' she asked numbly. 'A penal colony?'

'After everything we went through, I'm prepared to make you an offer. I owe you that, I think.'

'What sort of offer?' André asked.

'An exchange. You see, I'm your case officer, I'm the one who decides if the Service prosecutes, I'm the one who provides the evidence that we attacked the *Krystal Moon* and killed a fifteen-year-old girl because you're such an incompetent captain you can't keep up the payments on a ship that isn't worth ten fuseodollars.'

'Ah! Of course, money is no problem, my dear *enfant*. I can mortgage the ship, it will be done for you by tomorrow. What currency do you—'

'*Shut up!*' Madeleine bellowed. 'Just shut the fuck up, Duchamp. What is it, Erick? What's he got to do? Because whatever it is, he's going to do it with a big smile on his fat, stupid face.'

'I want to know something, Duchamp,' Erick said. 'And I think you can tell me. In fact, I'm sure you can. Because it's information which only the vilest, most deceitful pieces of shit in the galaxy are entrusted with.' He drifted over until he was centimetres from the captain. Duchamp had started to tremble.

'What is the coordinate of the antimatter station, André?' he asked softly. 'I know you know.'

André blanched. 'I . . . I cannot. Not that.'

'Oh, really? Do you know why the Confederation is so unsuccessful in finding antimatter production stations, Madeleine?' Erick asked. 'It's because we can't use debrief nanonics on people we suspect of knowing where they are. Nor can we use drugs, or even torture. It's their neural nanonics, you see. The price of learning a station's coordinates is a very special set of neural nanonics. The black cartel supplies them absolutely free of charge. Top-of-the-range, whatever marque you like, but always with one small modification. If they detect the owner is being subjected to any form of interrogation, such as debrief nanonics, they kamikaze. The only way the coordinate is passed on is voluntarily. So what is it, Duchamp?'

'They'll kill me,' André whimpered. He made to reach out and clasp Erick's shoulder, but his hand fisted just before contact and drew back. 'Did you not hear? They'll kill me!'

'Fucking tell him!' Madeleine shouted.

'*Non.*'

'It won't be a penal colony after the trial,' Erick said. 'We'll take you away to a quiet little laboratory deep in Trafalgar, and try and see if this time we can beat the kamikaze mechanism.'

**817**

'They'll know. They always find out. Always!'

'One of the stations is supplying Capone with antimatter. That means the cartel has already lost it to the possessed, so they're not going to care. And what about you? Do you care, do you want Capone to keep winning? And if he does beat us, what do you think he'll do with you when he finally catches up with you?'

'But suppose the station I know of isn't the one?'

'The only good antimatter station is one which has been destroyed. Now what's it going to be? The CNIS lab? The cartel? Capone? Or do I load a "no further action" code in your file? Make your mind up.'

'I despise you, *anglo*. I want your precious Confederation to die right in front of you. I want your entire family possessed and made to fuck animals. I want your soul trapped in the beyond for all time. Only then will I have justice for what you and your kind have done to me and my life.'

'The coordinate, Duchamp,' Erick said impassively.

André datavised the star's almanac file over.

\*

Lieutenant-Commander Emonn Verona, the CNIS's Head of Station on Ethenthia, sat behind his desk and stared at Erick in what was almost a state of reverence. 'You have the name of the next system Capone intends to invade, and an antimatter station coordinate?'

'Yes, sir. According to Pryor, Capone is going to send his fleet to the Toi-Hoi system.'

'Good God. If we can ambush that fleet, we've got the bastard cold. He'll be finished.'

'Yes, sir.'

'Right. This Bureau's only goal now is to get your information back to Trafalgar. There aren't any navy ships stationed here; I'm going to have to signal the Edenist habitats orbiting Golmo and request some voidhawks. That's fifteen light-hours away.' He eyed the exhausted captain, whose skin seemed to be half nanonic packages; the medical ancillary modules fastened to his belt had several orange LEDs winking on them. 'We ought to have a voidhawk here within sixteen hours. That'll give you some time to have a decent rest first.'

'Thanks. All of us got pretty strung out searching the ship for that nuke.'

'I'll bet. Are you sure you want to drop the charges against Duchamp?'

'Not really. But I gave my word, even though that means nothing to a man like him. Besides, he knows the navy has a file on him now, he knows we'll be watching him, he'll never trust another crew-member again. He'll never be able to fly another illegal flight again. And given the state of that ship, and his own abilities, he isn't going to be able to make enough from legal charters to keep going. The banks will take the *Villeneuve's Revenge* off him. For someone like him, that's worse than a penal colony or the death sentence.'

'I hope I never get you at my court martial,' Emonn Verona said.

'He deserves it.'

'I know. What do you want to do about Pryor?'

'Where is he now?'

'He's being remanded in custody. There are any number of charges we can bring. I can't believe a Confederation Navy officer turned like that.'

'It will be interesting to find out the reason. I think there's a lot more to Kingsley Pryor than we know. The best course would be for me to take him back to Trafalgar. He can be debriefed properly there.'

'OK. I'm going to step up security round the Bureau, and I don't want you to leave it until the voidhawk arrives. There's a spare office you can use to sleep in, my executive officer will show you. And I'll organize a medical team to examine you before you depart.'

'Thank you, sir.' Erick stood up, saluted, and walked out.

Emonn Verona had been fifteen years in the navy, and undercover officers like Erick Thakrar still unnerved him.

The office light-panel dimmed for a few seconds, then flickered annoyingly up to its full brightness. Emonn Verona gave it a resigned glare, the damn thing had been getting worse for a couple of days now. He made a note in his neural nanonics general file to get an engineer in once Thakrar was safely on his way.

\*

Right from the start, Gerald Skibbow had disliked asteroid settlements. They were worse than an arcology; the corridors were claustrophobic, while the biosphere caverns had a forced grandeur which lessened them considerably. Those initial impressions had come from Pinjarra, where the *Quadin* had left him. Now he was in Koblat, which made Pinjarra seem like an Edenist habitat by comparison.

It hadn't taken long, even for someone as ingenuous as himself, to find out that, despite the quarantine, non-governmental cargoes were still arriving at Pinjarra from outsystem. They didn't arrive on starships, though, *Quadin* was virtually the only one docked to the asteroid's spaceport, the rest were inter-orbit craft. Hours spent in the bars which their crews used gave him an outline of the operation, and a name: Koblat. An asteroid which was open to quarantine-busting flights, acting as a distribution hub for the Trojan cluster. A berth on an inter-orbit ship returning empty cost him five thousand fuseodollars.

It was the starships Gerald wanted; their captains might conceivably accept a charter to Valisk. He had money in his Jovian Bank credit disk, so perhaps it was his manner which caused them all to shake their heads and turn their backs on him. He knew he was too anxious, too insistent, too desperate. He'd made progress in controlling the extremes of his behaviour; there were fewer tantrums when his requests were refused, and he really tried to remember to wash and shave and find clean clothes. But still the captains rejected him. Perhaps they could see the ghosts and demons dancing inside his head. They didn't understand. It was Marie they were condemning, not him.

This time he had come very close to screaming at the captain as she made a joke of his pleas. Very close to raising his fists, to punching the truth and the need into her.

Then she had looked into his eyes and realized the danger caged in there, and her smile had emptied away. Gerald knew the barman was watching closely, one hand under the bar to grip whatever it was he used to quell trouble. There was a long moment spent looking down at the captain as silence rippled out from her table to claim the Blue Fountain. He took the time to think the way Dr Dobbs said he should, to focus on goals and the proper way to achieve them, how to make himself calm when his thoughts were febrile with rage.

The possibility of violence passed. Gerald turned and made for the door. Outside, naked rock pressed in on him, procreating a sense of suffocation. There were too few light-panels in the corridor. Hologram signs and low-wattage AV projections tried to entice him into other clubs and bars. He shuffled past, reaching the warren of smaller corridors which served the residential section. He thought his rented room was close, the signs at every intersection were confusing, numbers and letters jumbled together; he wasn't used to them yet. Voices rumbled down the corridor, male laughs and jeers, the tone was unpleasant. They were coming from the junction ahead. Dim shadows moved on the walls. He almost stopped and turned round. Then he heard the girl's cry, angry and fearful at the same time. He wanted to run away. Violence frightened him now. The possessed seemed to be at the heart of all conflicts, all evil. It would be best to leave, to call others to help. The girl cried out again, cursing. And Gerald thought of Marie, and how lonely and afraid she must have been when the possessed claimed her. He edged forward, and glanced round the corner.

At first, Beth had been furious with herself. She prided herself on how urbanwise she was. Koblat might be small, but that didn't mean it had much community spirit. There were only the company cops to keep order, and they didn't much bother unless they'd had their bung. The corridors could get tough. Men in their twenties, the failed rebels who now had nothing in front of them but eighty years' work for the company, went together in clans. They had their own turf, and Beth knew which corridors they were, where you didn't go at any time.

She hadn't been expecting any trouble when the three young men walked down the corridor towards her. She was only twenty metres from her apartment, and they were in company overalls, some kind of maintenance crew. Not a clan, nor mates coming back from a clubbing session. Mr Regulars.

The first one whistled admiringly when they were a few metres away. So she gave them the standard blank smile and moved over to one side of the corridor. Then one of them groaned and pointed at her ankle. 'Christ, she's wearing one too, a deadie.'

'Are ya gay, doll? Fancy giving that Kiera one, do ya? Me too.'

They all laughed harshly. Beth tried to walk past. A hand caught her arm. 'Where you going, doll?'

She attempted to pull herself free, but he was too strong.

'Valisk? Going to shag Kiera? We not good enough for you here? You got something against your own kind?'

'Let go!' Beth started to struggle. More hands grabbed her. She lashed out with her free arm, but it was no good. They were bigger, older, stronger.

'Little cow.'

'She's got some fight in her.'

'Hold the bitch. Take that arm.'

Her arms were forced behind her back, holding her still. The man in front of her grinned slowly as she twisted about. He grabbed her hair suddenly, and pushed her head back. Beth flinched, very near to losing it. His face was centimetres from hers, triumphant eyes gloating.

'Gonna take you home with us,' he breathed. 'We'll straighten you out good and proper, doll; you won't want girls again, not after we've finished with you.'

'Fuck off!' Beth screamed. She kicked out. But he caught her leg, and shoved it high into the air.

'Dumb slut.' He tugged at the knot which held the red handkerchief round her ankle. 'Reckon this might come in useful, guys. She's got a mouth on her.'

'You . . . you just bloody well leave her alone.'

All four of them stared at the speaker.

Gerald stood in the corridor's junction, his grey ship-suit wrinkled and dirty, hair ruffled, three days of beard shading his face. Even more alarming than the nervejam stick he was pointing at them in a two-handed grip, was the way it shook. He was blinking as if he was having great difficulty focusing.

'Whoa there, feller,' the man holding Beth's leg said. 'Let's not get excited here.'

'*Get away from her!*' The nervejam stick juddered violently.

Beth's leg was hurriedly dropped. The hands let go of her arms. Her three would-be rapists began to back off down the corridor. 'We're going, OK? You got this all wrong, feller.'

'Leave! I know what you are. You're part of it. You're part of them. You're helping *them*.'

The three men were retreating fast. Beth looked at the unstable nervejam stick and the persecuted face behind it, and almost felt like joining them. She tried to get her breathing back under control.

'Thanks, mate,' she said.

Gerald sucked on his lower lip, and gradually slid down the wall until he was squatting on his heels. The nervejam stick dropped from his fingers.

'Hey, you OK?' Beth hurried forwards.

Gerald looked up at her with a pathetically placid face, and started whimpering.

'Jeez—' She looked round to make certain her assailants had gone, then hunkered down beside him. Something made her hold back from making a grab for the nervejam. She was desperately uncertain what he'd do. 'Listen, they'll probably come back in a minute. Where do you live?'

Tears started streaming down from his eyes. 'I thought you were Marie.'

'No such luck, mate, I'm Beth. Is this your corridor?'

'I don't know.'

'Well, do you live near here?'

'Help me, please, I have to get to her, and Loren's left me here all alone. I don't know what to do next. I really don't.'

'You're not the only one,' Beth grunted.

*

'Well, who is he?' Jed asked.

Gerald was sitting at the lounge table in Beth's apartment, staring at the mug of tea he was holding. It was a pose he'd maintained for the last ten minutes.

'Says his name's Gerald Skibbow,' Beth said. 'Reckon he's telling the truth.'

'OK. How about you? You all right now?'

'Yeah. Those manky bastards got a real fright. Don't reckon we'll be seeing them again.'

'Good. You know, we might be better off if we stop wearing our handkerchiefs. People are getting real uptight about it.'

'What? No way! Not now. It says what I am; a Deadnight. If they can't stomach that, it ain't my problem.'

'It nearly was.'

'It won't happen again.' She held up the nervejam, and gave a brutish smirk.

'Jeez. Is that his?'

'Yep. Said I could borrow it.'

Jed regarded Gerald in dismayed confusion. 'Blimey. Bloke must be pretty far gone.'

'Hey.' She tapped his belly with the tip of the nervejam. 'Watch what you're saying. Maybe he's a little cranky, but he's my mate.'

'A *little* cranky? Look at him, Beth, the guy's a walking dunny.' He saw the way she tensed up. 'OK. He's your mate. What are you going to do with him?'

'He'll have a room somewhere.'

'Yeah, a nice quiet one with lots of padding on the walls.'

'Quit that, will you. How much you've changed, huh? We're supposed to be wanting a life where people don't jump down each other's throats the whole time. Least, that's what I thought. Am I wrong?'

'No,' he grumbled. Beth these days was hard to understand. Jed had thought she'd appreciate the fact he wasn't making moves on her any more. If anything that had made her even more intractable. 'Hey, look, don't worry. My head'll get straightened when we reach Valisk.'

Gerald slewed round in his chair. 'What did you say?'

'Hey, mate, thought you'd gone switch-off on us there,' Beth said. 'How you feeling?'

'What did you say about Valisk?'

'We want to go there,' Jed said. 'We're Deadnights, see. We believe in Kiera. We want to be part of the new universe.'

Gerald stared at him, then gave a twisted giggle. 'Believe her? She's not even Kiera.'

'You're just like all the others. You don't want us to have a chance just because you blew yours. That stinks, man!'

'Wait, wait.' Gerald held up his arms in placation. 'I'm sorry. I didn't know you were a Deadnight. I don't know what Deadnights are.'

'It's what she said, that Kiera. *Those of us who have emerged from the dead of night can break the restrictions of this corrupt society.*'

'Oh, right, that bit.'

'She's going to take us away from all this,' Beth said. 'Where arseholes like those three blokes don't do what they did. Not any more. There won't be any of that in Valisk.'

'I know,' Gerald said solemnly.

'What? You taking the piss?'

'No. Honestly. I've been searching for a way to Valisk ever since I saw the recording. I came here all the way from Ombey on the one hope that I'd find a way. I thought one of the starships might take me.'

'No way, mate,' Jed said. 'Not the starships. We tried. The captains have all got closed minds. I told you, they hate us.'

'Yes.'

Jed glanced at Beth, trying to judge what she thought, if he should risk it. 'You must have quite a bit of money, you come here from Ombey,' he said.

'More than enough to charter a starship,' Gerald said bitterly. 'But they just won't listen to me.'

'You don't need a starship.'

'What do you mean?'

'I'll tell you how to get to Valisk if you take us with you. It's ten times cheaper than the way you were planning, but we still can't put that much together ourselves. As you've got to charter a whole ship for the flight anyway, it won't cost you any more for us to be on board.'

'All right.'

'You'll take us?'

'Yes.'

'Promise?' Beth asked, her voice betraying a multitude of vulnerabilities.

'I promise, Beth. I know what it's like to be let down, to be abandoned. I wouldn't do that to anyone, least of all you.'

She shifted round uncomfortably, rather pleased by what he'd said, the fatherly way he'd said it. Nobody on Koblat ever spoke to her like that.

'OK,' Jed said. 'Here it is: I've got a pick-up coordinate timetable for this system.' He took a flek from his pocket, and slotted it in the desktop block. The block's holoscreen flashed up a complex graphic. 'This shows where and when a starship from Valisk will be waiting to take on anyone who wants to go there. All you have to do is charter an inter-orbit craft to get us to it.'

*

As always, Syrinx found Athene's house relaxing. No doubt Wing-Tsit Chong and the psychological team would call it a return to the womb. And if she found that amusing, she told herself, she must be virtually recovered.

She had returned from Jobis two days earlier. After relating everything she had learned from Malva to Wing-Tsit Chong, *Oenone* had flown to Romulus and a berth in an industrial station.

I suppose I ought to be glad you're flying courier duty for our Intelligence service, Athene said. The doctors must think you're recovered.

And you don't? Syrinx was walking with her mother across the garden which seemed to grow shaggier with each passing year.

If you're not sure yourself, how can I be, my dear?

Syrinx grinned, somehow cheered by the uncanny perception. Oh, Mother, don't fuss. Work is always a great anodyne, especially if you love your work. Voidhawk captains do nothing else.

*I want us flying missions together again,* Oenone insisted. *It is good for both of us.*

For a moment, mother and daughter were aware of the gridwork surrounding *Oenone*. Technicians were busy working on the lower hull, installing combat-wasp launch-cradles, maser cannons, and military-grade sensor pods.

*Ah, well,* Athene said. *Looks like I'm outvoted.*

*I'll be all right, Mother, really. Going straight into the defence force would be a little too confrontational. But courier work is important. We have to act with unity against the possessed; that's vital. Voidhawks have an important role to play in that.*

*I'm not the one you're trying to convince.*

*Jesus, Mother. Everyone I know is mutating into a psychiatrist. I'm a big girl now, and my brain's back in good enough shape to make decisions.*

*Jesus?*

Oh. Syrinx could feel the blush rising to her cheeks – only Mother could do that! *Someone I met always used it as an expletive. I just thought it was appropriate these days.*

*Ah, yes. Joshua Calvert. Or 'Lagrange' Calvert, as everyone calls him now. You had quite a thing about him, once, didn't you?*

*I did not! And why is he called 'Lagrange' Calvert?*

Syrinx listened with growing incredulity as Athene explained the events which had occurred in orbit around Murora. *Oh, no, fancy Edenism having to be grateful to him. And what a stupid stunt jumping inside a Lagrange point at that velocity. He could have killed everybody on board. How thoughtless.*

*Dear me, it must be love.*

*Mother!*

Athene laughed in delight at being able to needle her daughter so successfully. They'd come to the first of the big lily ponds which verged one side of the garden. It was heavily shaded now, the rank of golden yews behind it had swelled considerably in the last thirty years, their boughs reaching right across the water. She looked into the black water. Bronze-coloured fish streaked for the cover of the lily pads.

*You ought to get the servitor chimps to prune the yews,* Syrinx said. *They steal too much light. There are far fewer lilies than there used to be.*

*Why not see what happens naturally?*

*It's untidy. And a habitat isn't natural.*

*You never did like losing arguments, did you?*

*Not at all. I'm always willing to listen to alternative viewpoints.*

A burst of good-humoured scepticism filled the affinity band. *Is that why you're turning to religion all of a sudden? I always thought you would be the most susceptible.*

*What do you mean?*

*Remember when Wing-Tsit Chong called you a tourist?*

*Yes.*

*It was a polite way of saying that you lack the confidence in yourself to find your own answers to life. You are always searching, Syrinx, though you never know what for. Religion was inevitably going to exert a fascination on you. The whole concept of salvation through belief offers strength to those who doubt themselves.*

*There's a big difference between religion and spirituality. That is something the Edenist culture is going to have to come to terms with; us, the habitats, and the voidhawks.*

*Yes, you're uncomfortably right there. I have to admit I was rather pleased to know that* Iasius *and I will be reunited again, no matter how terrible the circumstances. It does make life more tolerable.*

*That's one aspect. I was thinking more about transferring our memories into the habitat when we die. It forms the basis of our entire society. We never feared death as much as Adamists, which always strengthened our rationality. Now we know we're destined to the beyond, it rather makes a mockery of the whole process. Except—*

*Go on.*

*Laton, damn him. What did he mean? Him and his great journey, and telling us that we don't have to worry about being trapped in the* beyond. And then Malva as good as confirmed he was telling the truth.

You think that's a bad thing?

No. If we're interpreting this properly, there is more to the beyond than eternal purgatory. That would be wondrous.

I agree.

Then why didn't he tell us exactly what awaits? And why would it only be us who escape the entrapment, and not the Adamists?

Perhaps Malva was being more helpful than you realized when she told you the answer lies within us. If you were told, you would not have found it for yourself. You wouldn't have known it, you would simply have been taught.

It had to be Laton, didn't it? The one person we can never truly trust.

Even you can't trust him?

Not even I; despite the fact I owe him my life. He's Laton, Mother.

Perhaps that's why he didn't tell us. He knew we wouldn't trust him. He did urge us to research this thoroughly.

And so far we've failed thoroughly.

We've only just started, Syrinx. And he gave us one clue, the kind of souls that have returned. You encountered them, darling, you have the most experience of them. What type are they?

Bastards. All of them.

Calm down, and tell me what they were like.

Syrinx smiled briefly at the reprimand, then gazed at the pink water lilies, trying to make herself remember Pernik. Something she still shied away from. I was being truthful. They really were bastards. I didn't see that many. But none of them cared about me, about how much they were hurting me. It didn't bother them, as if they were emotionally dead. I suppose being in the beyond for so long does that to them.

Not quite. Kelly Tirrel recorded a series of interviews with a possessed called Shaun Wallace. He wasn't callous, or indifferent. If anything he seemed a rather sad individual.

Sad bastards, then.

You're being too flippant. But consider this; how many Edenists are sad bastards?

No, Mother, I can't accept that. You're saying that there's some kind of selection process involved. That something is imprisoning sinners in the beyond and letting the righteous go on this final journey into the light. That cannot be right. You're saying there is a God. One that takes an overwhelming interest in every human being, that cares how we behave.

I suppose I am. It would certainly explain what's happened.

No, it wouldn't. Why was Laton allowed to go on the great journey?

He wasn't. Souls and memory separate at death, remember? It was Laton's personality operating within Pernik's neural strata that freed you and warned us, not his soul.

Do you really believe this?

I'm not sure. As you say, a god who takes this much interest in us as individuals would be awesome. Athene turned from the pool, and slipped her arm through her daughter's. I think I'll keep hoping for another explanation.

Good!

Let's hope you find it for me.

Me?

You're the one gallivanting round the galaxy again. It gives you a much better chance than me.

All we're going to do is pick up routine reports from embassies and agents about possible infiltrations by the possessed, and how local governments are coping with the problem. Tactics and politics, that's all, not philosophy.

How very dull-sounding. She pulled Syrinx a little closer, allowing the worry and concern in her mind to flow freely through affinity. Are you sure you're going to be all right?

Yes, Mother. *Oenone* and the crew will take good care of me. I don't want you to worry any more.

\*

When Syrinx had left to supervise the last stages of *Oenone*'s refit, Athene sat in her favourite chair on the patio and attempted to involve herself in the household routine again. There were plenty of children to supervise at the moment, the adults were all away working long hours, mainly in support of the defence force. Jupiter and Saturn were both gearing up for the Mortonridge Liberation.

You shouldn't try to hold her so tight, Sinon said. It doesn't help her confidence seeing you have so little in her.

I have every confidence, she bridled.

Then show it. Let go.

I'm too frightened.

We all are. But we should be free to face it by ourselves.

How do you feel, then, knowing your soul has gone on?

Curious.

That's all?

Yes. I already exist in tandem with the others of the multiplicity. The beyond is not too different from that.

You hope!

One day we will know.

Let's pray it's later rather than sooner.

Like daughter, like mother.

I don't think I need a priest right now. More like a stiff drink.

Sinner. He laughed.

She watched the shadows deepen under the trees as the lighttube enacted a rose-gold dusk. 'There can't be a God, can there? Not really.'

*

He doesn't look terribly happy, Tranquillity said as Prince Noton stepped into one of the ten tube stations which served the hub.

Ione pivoted her perceptual viewpoint through a complete circle, as if she was walking around the Prince. She was intrigued by his air of stubborn dignity, the kind of face and body posture that indicated he knew he was old and outdated but still insisted on interpreting the universe the way he wanted to. He wore the dress uniform of a Royal Kulu Navy admiral, with five small medal pins on his chest. When he removed his cap to climb into the tube carriage there was little hair left, and that grey; a telling sign for a Saldana.

**I wonder how old he is?** she mused.

**A hundred and seventy. He is King David's youngest exowomb sibling. He ran the Kulu Corporation for a hundred and three years until Prince Howard took over in 2608.**

**How strange.** Her attention flicked back to the Royal Kulu Navy battlecruiser docked in the spaceport (the first active duty ship from the Kingdom in a hundred and seventy-nine years). A diplomatic mission of the highest urgency, its captain had said when he requested permission to approach. And Prince Noton had an entourage of five Foreign Office personnel. **He's part of the old order. We're hardly likely to have anything in common. If Alastair wants something from me, surely someone younger would have been a better bet? Maybe even a princess.**

**Possibly. Though it would be hard not to respect Prince Noton. His seniority is part of the message the King is sending.**

For a moment she felt a twist of worry. **I wonder. If anyone knows your true capabilities, it is my royal cousins.**

**I doubt he will ask anything dishonourable.**

Ione had to jog down the last twenty metres of the corridor, fumbling with the seal on the side of her skirt. She had chosen a formal business suit of green tropical-weave cotton and a plain blouse; smart but not imperious. Trying to impress Prince Noton with power dressing, she suspected, would be a waste of time.

The tube carriage had already arrived at the station of De Beauvoir Palace, her official residence. Two serjeants were escorting the Prince and his entourage down the long central hall. Ione raced across the audience chamber in her stockinged feet, sat behind the central desk, and jammed her shoes on.

**How do I look?**

**Beautiful.**

She growled at the lack of objectivity, and combed her hair back with a hand. **I knew I should have had this cut.** She glanced round to check the arrangements. Six high-backed chairs were positioned in front of the desk. Human caterers were preparing a buffet in one of the informal reception rooms (housechimps would have been a faux pas given the Kingdom's attitude to bitek, she felt). **Change the lighting.**

Half of the floor-to-ceiling panes of glass darkened; the remainder altered their diffraction angle. Ten large planes of light converged on the desk, surrounding her in a warm astral glow. **Too much – oh, hell.**

The doors swung open. Ione rose to her feet as Prince Noton walked across the floor.

**Go around the desk to greet him. Remember you are family, and technically there has never been any rift between us and the Kingdom.**

Ione did as she was told, putting on a neutral smile; one she could turn to charm or ice. It was up to him.

When she put out her hand, there was only the slightest hesitation on Prince Noton's part. He gave her a politely formal handshake. His eyes did linger on her signet ring, though.

'Welcome to Tranquillity, Prince Noton. I'm very flattered that Alastair should honour me with an emissary of your seniority. I only wish we were meeting in happier times.'

The staff from the Foreign Office were staring ahead rigidly. If she didn't know better she would have said they were praying.

Prince Noton took an awkwardly long time to answer. 'It is a privilege to serve my King by coming here.'

Ah! 'Touché, cousin,' she drawled.

They locked gazes while the Foreign Office staff watched nervously.

'You had to be female, didn't you?'

'Naturally, though it was completely random. Daddy never

had any exowomb children. Our family tradition of primogeniture doesn't apply here.'

'You hate tradition so much?'

'No, I admire a lot of tradition. I uphold a lot of tradition. What I will not tolerate is tradition for tradition's sake.'

'Then you must be in your element. Order is falling across the Confederation.'

'That, Noton, was below the belt.'

He nodded gruffly. 'Sorry. I don't know why the King chose me for this. Never was a bloody diplomat.'

'I don't know, I think he chose rather well, actually. Sit down, please.' She went back to her own chair. Tranquillity showed her the Foreign Office personnel exchanging relieved expressions behind her back. 'So what exactly does Alastair want?'

'These fellers.' Prince Noton clicked his finger in the direction of a serjeant. 'I'm supposed to ask you if we can have their DNA sequence.'

'Whatever for?'

'Ombey.'

She listened with dawning unease as Prince Noton and the Foreign Office personnel related the details of the proposed Mortonridge liberation. Do you think this will work?

I don't have the kind of information available to the Royal Navy, so I cannot provide an absolute. But the Royal Navy would not undertake such an action unless it was confident of the outcome.

I can't believe this is the right way to go about saving people who have been possessed. They're going to destroy Mortonridge, and a lot of people will get killed in the process.

Nobody ever claimed war is clean.

Then why do it?

For the overall objective, which is usually political. Certainly it is in this case.

So I can halt it, then? If I refuse to give Alastair the sequence.

You can be the voice of sanity, certainly. Who would thank you?

The people who wouldn't get killed, for a start.

Who are the people currently possessed, and would endure any sacrifice to be freed. They do not have the luxury of your academic moral choices.

That's not fair. You can't condemn me for wanting to prevent bloodshed.

Unless you can offer an alternative, I would recommend handing over the sequence. Even if you prevaricated, you would not halt the liberation campaign. At the most you would delay it for a few weeks while the Edenists spliced together a suitable warrior servitor.

You know damn well I don't have any alternative.

This is politics, Ione; you cannot prevent the liberation from going ahead. By helping, you will form valuable alliances. Do not overlook that. You are pledged to defend all those who live within me. We may need help to do this.

No, we don't. You alone of all the habitats are the final sanctuary against the possessed.

Even that is not definite. Prince Noton is correct: old orders, old certainties, are falling everywhere.

What must I do, then?

You are the Lord of Ruin. Decide.

When she looked at the old prince, his immobile face and his impassioned thoughts, she knew there was no choice, that there never had been. The Saldanas had sworn to defend their subjects. And in return their subjects believed in them to provide that defence. Over the Kingdom's history, hundreds of thousands had died to maintain that mutual trust.

'Of course I will provide the DNA sequence for you,' Ione said. 'I only wish there was more I could do.'

*

With an irony Ione found almost painful, two days after Prince Noton departed for Kulu with the DNA sequence, Parker

Higgens and Oski Katsura told her they had located a Laymil memory of the spaceholm suicide.

Almost all other research work on the Laymil Project campus had stopped to allow staff from every division to assist in reviewing the decrypted sensorium memories. However, despite being the prime focus of activity, the Electronics Division was no busier than the last time she had visited. The decryption operation had been finalized, allowing all of the information within the Laymil electronics stack to be reformatted into a human access standard.

'It's only the review process itself which is causing a bottleneck now,' Oski Katsura said as she ushered Ione into the hall. 'We have managed to copy all of the memories in the stack, so we now have permanent access. In the end, only twelve per cent of the files were scrambled, which leaves us with eight thousand two hundred and twenty hours of recordings available. Though of course we have a team working on the lost sequences.'

The Laymil electronics stack had finally been powered down. Technicians were gathered round its transparent environment sphere, checking and disconnecting it from the conditioning units.

'What are you going to do with it?' Ione asked.

'Zero-tau,' Oski Katsura said. 'Unfortunately, it is really too venerable to be put on exhibition. That is, unless you want it displayed to the public for a little while first?'

'No. This is your field, that's why I appointed you as division chief.'

Ione saw the members of the Confederation Navy Science Bureau mingling with the ordinary project staff at the various research stations in the hall. It was a sign of the times that she drew no more than a few idly curious glances.

Parker Higgens, Kempster Getchell, and Lieria were standing together to watch the technicians prepare the stack for zero-tau.

'End of an era,' Kempster said as Ione joined them. He appeared oblivious to any connotations in the statement. 'We can't go on depending on stolen knowledge any more. Much to the distress of the navy people, of course, no giant ray guns for them to play with. Looks like we'll have to start thinking for ourselves again. Good news, eh?'

'Unless you happen to have a possessed knocking on your door,' Parker Higgens said coldly.

'My dear Parker, I do access the news studios occasionally, you know.'

'How is the search for Unimeron going?' Ione asked.

'From a technical point of view, very well,' Kempster said enthusiastically. 'We've finished the revised design for the sensor satellite we want to use. Young Renato has taken a blackhawk down to the orbital band we intend to cover to test-fly a prototype. If all goes well, the industrial stations will begin mass production next week. We can saturate the band by the end of the month. If there are any unusual energy resonances there, we ought to find them.'

It wasn't going to be as quick as Ione had hoped for. 'Excellent work,' she told the old astronomer. 'Oski tells me you have found a memory of the spaceholm suicide.'

'Yes, ma'am,' Parker Higgens said.

'Did they have a weapon to use against the possessed?'

'Not a physical one, I'm happy to say. They seemed inordinately complacent about the suicide.'

'What do the navy people think?'

'They were disappointed, but they concur the spaceholm culture made no attempt to physically defeat the possessed Laymil approaching from Unimeron.'

Ione sat at an empty research station. 'Very well.' Show me.

She never could get used to the illusive sensorium squeeze of emerging into a Laymil body. This time, her appropriated frame was one of the two male varieties, an egg producer. He was standing amid a group of Laymil, his current family and co-habitees, on the edge of their third marriage community. His clarion heads bugled softly, a keening joined by hundreds of throats around him. The melody was a slow one, rising and falling across the gentle grassy slope. Its echo sounded in his mind, gathered by the mother entity from every community in the spaceholm. Together they sang their lament, a plainsong in unison with the life spirit of the forests and meadows, the shoalminds of the animals, the mother entity. A chant taken up by every spaceholm as the cozened dead approached their constellation.

The ether was resonant with sadness, its weight impressing every organic cell within the spaceholm. Sunspires were dipping to their early and final dusk, draining away the joyful colours he had lived with all his life. Flowers relaxed into closure, their curling petals sighing for the loss of light, while their spirits wept for the greater loss which was to follow.

He linked arms with his mates and children, ready to share death as they shared life: together. The families linked arms. Drinking strength from the greater concord. They had become a single triangle on the valley floor. Component segments of three adults. Inside them, the children, protected, cherished. The whole, a symbol of strength and defiance. As with minds, so with bodies; as with thoughts, so with deeds.

'Join into rapture,' he instructed his children.

Their necks wove round, heads bobbing with enchanting immaturity. '**Sorrow. Fear failure. Death essence triumphant.**'

'**Recall essencemaster teaching,**' he instructed. '**Laymil species must end. Knowledge brings birthright fulfilment. Eternal exaltation awaits strong. Recall knowledge. Believe knowledge.**'

'**Concur.**'

Beyond the rim of the spaceholm constellation, the ships from Unimeron slid out of the darkness. Stars gleaming red with the terrible power of the death essence, riding bright prongs of fusion flame.

'Know truth,' the massed choir of spaceholms sang at them. 'Accept knowledge gift. Embrace freedom.'

They would not. The pernicious light grew as the ships advanced, silent and deadly.

The Laymil in the spaceholms raised their heads to the vertical, and bellowed a single last triumphant note. Air rippled at the sound. The sunspires went out, allowing total darkness to seize the interior.

'Recall strength,' he pleaded with his children. 'Strength achievement final amity.'

'Confirm essencemaster victory.'

The spaceholm mother entity cried into the void. A pulse of love which penetrated to the core of every mind. Deep within its shell, cells ruptured and spasmed, propagating fractures clean through the polyp.

Sensation ended, but the darkness remained for a long time. Then Ione opened her eyes.

'Oh my God. That was their only escape. They were so content about it. Every Laymil rushed into death. They never tried to outrun them, they never tried to fight them. They wilfully condemned themselves to the beyond to avoid being possessed.'

'Not quite, ma'am,' Parker Higgens said. 'There are some very interesting implications in those last moments. The Laymil didn't consider they had lost. Far from it. They showed enormous resolution. We know full well how much they worship life; they would never sacrifice themselves and their children simply to inconvenience the possessed Laymil, for that is all suicide is. There are any number of options they could have explored before resorting to such an extreme measure. Yet the one whose sensorium we accessed made constant references to knowledge and truth derived from the essencemasters. That knowledge was the key to their "eternal exaltation". I suspect the essencemasters solved the nature of the beyond. Am I right, Lieria?'

'An astute deduction, Director Higgens,' the Kiint said through her processor block. 'And one which confirms the statement Ambassador Roulor made to your Assembly. For each race, the solution is unique. Surely you do not anticipate suicide as the answer for the problems facing humankind?'

Parker Higgens faced the big xenoc, his anger visible. 'It was more than suicide. It was a victory. They won. Whatever the knowledge was they carried with them, it meant they were no longer afraid of the beyond.'

'Yes.'

'And you know what it was.'

'You have our sympathy, and whatever support we can provide.'

'Damn it! How dare you study us like this! We are not laboratory creatures. We are sentient entities, we have feelings, we have fears. Have you no ethics?'

Ione stood behind the trembling director, and laid a cautionary hand on his shoulder.

'I am well aware of what you are, Director Higgens,' Lieria said. 'And I am empathic to your distress. But I must repeat, the answer to your problem lies within you, not us.'

'Thank you, Parker,' Ione said. 'I think we're all now quite clear on where we stand.'

The director gave a furious wave of his hand and walked away.

I apologize for his temper, Ione told the Kiint. But as I'm sure you know, this terrifies us all. It is frustrating for us to know you have a solution, even though it cannot apply to us.

Justly so, Ione Saldana. And I do understand. History records our race was in turmoil when we first discovered the beyond.

You give me hope, Lieria. Your existence is proof that satisfactory solutions can be found for a sentient race, something other than genocidal suicide. That inspires me to keep searching for our own answer.

*

Erick was woken by his neural nanonics. He had routinely set up programs to monitor his immediate environment, physical and electronic, alert for anything which fell outside nominal parameters.

As he sat up in the darkened office, his neural nanonics reported an outbreak of abnormal fluctuations in Ethenthia's power supply systems. When he datavised a query at the supervisor programs, it turned out that no one in the asteroid's civil engineering service was even examining the problem. A further review showed that fifteen per cent of the habitation section's lifts appeared to be inoperative. The number of datavises into the net was also reducing.

'Oh dear God. Not here, too!' He swung his legs off the settee. A wave of nausea twisted along his spine. Medical programs sent out several caution warnings; the team Emonn Verona promised hadn't been to see him yet.

When he datavised the lieutenant-commander's eddress to the office's net processor there was no response. 'Bloody hell.' Erick pulled on his ship-suit, easing it over his medical packages. There were two ratings standing guard outside the office, both armed with TIP carbines. They came to attention as soon as the door opened.

'Where's the Lieutenant-Commander?' Erick asked.

'Sir, he said he was going to the hospital, sir.'

'Bugger. Right, you two come with me. We're getting off this asteroid, right away.'

'Sir?'

'That was an order, mister. But in case you need an incentive, the possessed are here.'

The two of them swapped a worried glance. 'Aye, sir.'

Erick started accessing schematics of the asteroid as they

went through the Navy Bureau and out into the public hall. He followed that up by requesting a list of starships currently docked at the spaceport. There were only five, one of which was the *Villeneuve's Revenge*, which cut his options down to four.

His neural nanonics designed a route to the axial chamber which didn't use any form of powered transportation. Seven hundred metres, two hundred of which were stairs. But at least the gravity would be falling off.

They went in single file, with Erick in the centre. He ordered both ratings to put their combat programs into primary mode. People turned to stare as they marched down the middle of the public hall.

Six hundred metres to go. And the first stairwell was directly ahead. The hall's light-panels started dimming.

'Run,' Erick said.

*

Kingsley Pryor's cell measured five metres by five. It had one bunk, one toilet, and one washbasin; there was a small AV lens on the wall opposite the bed, accessing one local media company. Every surface – fittings, floor, walls – was the same blue-grey lofriction composite. It was fully screened, preventing any datavises.

For the last hour the light-panel on the ceiling had been flickering. At first, Kingsley had thought the police were doing it to irritate him. They had been almost fearful as they escorted him from the *Villeneuve's Revenge* with a Confederation Navy officer. A member of the Capone Organization. It was only to be expected that they would try to re-establish their superiority with such sad psychology, demonstrating who was in control. But the shifts of illumination had been too fitful for any determined effort. The AV images were also fragmenting, but not at the same time as the light. Then he found the call button produced no response.

Kingsley realized what was happening, and sat patiently on his bunk. A quarter of an hour later the humming sound from the conditioning grille fan faded away. Nothing he could do about it. Twice in the next thirty minutes the fan started up again briefly, once to blow in air which stank of sewage. Then the light-panel went out permanently. Still Kingsley sat quietly.

When the door did finally open, it shone a fan of light directly across him, highlighting his almost prim posture. A werewolf crouched in the doorway, blood dripping from its fangs.

'Very original,' Kingsley said.

There was a confused puppy-like *yap* from the creature.

'I really must insist you don't come any closer. Both of us will wind up in the beyond if you do. And you've only just got here, haven't you?'

The werewolf outline shimmered away to reveal a man wearing a police uniform. Kingsley recognized him as one of his escorts. There was a nasty pink scar on his forehead which hadn't been there before.

'What are you talking about?' the possessed man asked.

'I am going to explain our situation to you, and I want you to observe my thoughts so that you know I'm telling the truth. And after that, you and your new friends are going to let me go. In fact, you're going to give me every assistance I require.'

\*

A hundred and fifty metres to the axial chamber. They were almost at the top of the last flight of stairs when the well's lights went out. Erick's enhanced retinas automatically switched to infra-red. 'They're close,' he shouted in warning.

A narrow flare of white fire fountained up the centre of the stairwell, arching round to burst over the rating behind him. He grunted in pain and swung round, firing his TIP carbine at the base of the streamer. Purple sparks bounced out of the impact point.

'Help me,' he cried. A smear of white fire was cloaking his entire shoulder. Terror and panic were negating all the suppression programs which his neural nanonics had doused his brain with. He stopped firing to flail at the fire with his free hand.

The other rating slithered past Erick to fire back down the stairs. A flat circle of brilliant emerald light sprang over the floor of the stairwell, then started to rise as if it were a fluid. The flare of white fire withdrew below its surface. Shadows were just visible beneath it, darting about sinuously.

The burned rating had collapsed onto the stairs. His partner was still shooting wildly down into the advancing cascade of light. The TIP pulses were turning to silver spears as they penetrated the surface, trailing bubbles of darkness.

The next door was eight metres above Erick. The ratings would never last against the possessed, he knew, a few seconds at best. That few seconds might enable him to escape. The information he had was vital, it had to get to Trafalgar. Millions of innocents depended on it, on him. Millions. Against two.

Erick turned and flung himself up the last few steps. In his ears he could hear a voice shouting: '. . . two of my crew are dead. Fried! Tina was fifteen years old!'

He barged through the door, ten per cent gravity projecting him in a long flat arc above the corridor floor, threatening to crack his head against the ceiling. The persecuting noises and fog of green light shut off as the door slid shut behind him. He touched down, and powered himself in another long leap forward along the corridor. Neural nanonics outlined his route for him as if it was a starship vector plot; a tube of orange neon triangles that flashed past. Turning right. Right again. Left.

Gravity had become negligible when he heard the scream ahead of him. Fifteen metres to the axial chamber. That was all; fifteen bloody metres! And the possessed were ahead of him. Erick snatched at a grab hoop to halt his forward flight. He didn't have any weapons. He didn't have any back-up. He didn't even have Madeleine and Desmond to call on, not any more.

More screams and pleas were trickling down the corridor from the axial chamber as the possessed chased down their victims. It wouldn't be long before one of them checked this corridor.

*I have to get past. Have to!*

He called up the schematic again, studying the area around the axial chamber. Twenty seconds later, and he was at the airlock hatch.

It was a big airlock, used to service the spaceport spindle. The prep room which led to it had dozens of lockers, all the equipment and support systems required to maintain space hardware; even five deactivated free-flying mechanoids.

Erick put his decryption program into primary mode, and set it to work cracking the first locker's code. He stripped off his ship-suit as the lockers popped open one after the other. Physiological monitor programs confirmed everything he saw as the fabric parted. Pale fluid tinged with blood was leaking out of his medical nanonic packages where the edges were peeling from his flesh; a number of red LEDs on the ancillary modules were flashing to indicate system malfunctions. His new arm was only moving because of the reinforced impulses controlling the muscles.

But he still functioned. That was all that mattered.

It was the fifth locker which contained ten SII spacesuits. As soon as his body was sealed against the vacuum he hurried into the airlock, carrying a manoeuvring pack. He didn't bother with the normal cycle, instead he tripped the emergency vent. Air rushed out. The outer hatch irised apart as he secured himself into the manoeuvring pack. Then the punchy gas jets fired, sending him wobbling past the hatch rim and out into space.

*

André hated the idea of Shane Brandes even being inside the *Villeneuve's Revenge*. And as for the man actually helping repair and reassemble the starship's systems ... *Merde*. But as with most events in André's life these days, he didn't have a lot of choice. Since the showdown with Erick, Madeleine had retreated into her cabin and refused to respond to any entreaties. Desmond, at least, performed the tasks requested of him, though not with any obvious enthusiasm. And, insultingly, he would only work alone.

That just left Shane Brandes to help André with the jobs that needed more than one pair of hands. The *Dechal*'s exfusion engineer was anxious to please. He swore he had no allegiance to his previous captain, and harboured no grudges or ill will towards the crew of the *Villeneuve's Revenge*. He was also prepared to work for little more than beer money, and he was a grade two technician. One could not afford to overlook gift horses.

André was re-installing the main power duct in the wall of the lower-deck lounge, which required Shane to feed the cable to him when instructed. Someone glided silently through the ceiling hatch, blocking the beam from the bank of temporary lights André had rigged up. André couldn't see what he was doing. 'Desmond! Why must ...' He gasped in shock. 'You!'

'Hello again, Captain,' Kingsley Pryor said.

'What are you doing here? How did you get out of prison?'

'They set me free.'

'Who?'

'The possessed.'

'*Non*,' André whispered.

'Unfortunately so. Ethenthia has fallen.'

The anti-torque tool André was holding seemed such a pitiful weapon. 'Are you one of them now? You will never have my ship. I will overload the fusion generators.'

'I'd really rather you didn't,' Pryor datavised. 'As you can see, I haven't been possessed.'

'How? They take everybody, women, children.'

'I am one of Capone's liaison officers. Even here, that carries enormous weight.'

'And they let you go?'

'Yes.'

A heavy dread settled in André's brain. 'Where are they? Are they coming?' He datavised the flight computer to review the internal sensors (those remaining – curse it). As yet no systems were glitching.

'No,' Pryor said. 'They won't come into the *Villeneuve's Revenge*. Not unless I tell them to.'

'Why are you doing this?' *As if I didn't know.*

'Because I want you to fly me away from here.'

'And they'll let us all go, just like that?'

'As I said, Capone has a lot of influence.'

'What makes you think I will take you? You blackmailed me before. It will be simple to throw you out of the airlock once we are free of Ethenthia.'

Pryor smiled a dead man's smile. 'You've always done exactly as I wanted, Duchamp. You were always supposed to break away from Kursk.'

'Liar.'

'I have been given other, more important, objectives than ensuring a third-rate ship with its fifth-rate crew stay loyal to the Organization. You have never had any free will since you arrived in the New California system. You still don't. After all, you don't really think there was only one bomb planted on board, do you?'

\*

Erick watched the *Villeneuve's Revenge* lift from its cradle. The starship's thermo-dump panels extended, ion thrusters took over from the verniers. It rose unhurriedly from the spaceport. When he switched his collar sensors to high resolution he could see the black hexagon on the fuselage where plate 8–92-K was missing.

He didn't understand it, Duchamp was making no attempt to flee. It was almost as if he was obeying traffic control, departing calmly along an assigned vector. Had the crew been possessed? Small loss to the Confederation.

His collar sensors refocused on the docking-bay he was approaching; a dark circular recess in the spaceport's gridiron exterior. It was a maintenance bay, twice as wide as an ordinary bay. The *Clipper*-class starship *Tigara* which sat on the docking cradle seemed unusually small in such surroundings.

Erick fired his manoeuvring-pack jets to take him down towards the *Tigara*. There were no lights on in the bay; all the gantries and multi-segment arms were folded back against the walls. Utility umbilicals were jacked in, and an airlock tube had mated with the starship's fuselage; but apart from that there was no sign of any activity.

The silicon hull showed signs of long-term vacuum exposure – faded lettering, micrometeorite impact scuffs, surface-layer ablation stains – all indicating hull plates long overdue for replacement. He drifted over the blurred hexagons until he was above the EVA airlock, and datavised the hatch-control processor to cycle and open. If anyone was on board, they would know about him now. But there were no datavised questions, no active sensor sweeps.

The hatch slid open, and Erick glided inside.

*Clipper*-class starships were designed to provide a speedy service between star systems, carrying small high-value cargoes. Consequently, as much of their internal volume as possible was given over to cargo space. There was only one life-support capsule, which accommodated an optimum crew of three. That was the principal reason Erick had chosen the *Tigara*. In theory, he would be able to fly it solo.

Most of the starship systems were powered down. He kept

his SII suit on as he moved through the two darkened lower decks to the bridge. As soon as he was secured in the captain's acceleration couch he accessed the flight computer and ordered a full status review.

It could have been a lot better. *Tigara* was in the maintenance bay for a complete refit. One of the fusion generators was inoperative, two energy patterning nodes were dead, heat exchangers were operating dangerously short of required levels, innumerable failsoft components had been allowed to decay below their safety margins.

None of the maintenance work had even been started. The owners hadn't been prepared to commit that much money while the quarantine was in force.

Dear Lord, Erick thought, the *Villeneuve's Revenge* was in better condition than this.

He datavised the flight computer to disengage the bay's airlock tube, then initiated a flight-prep procedure. The *Tigara* took a long time to come on-line. At every stage he had to order back-up sequences to take over, or override safety programs, or re-route power supplies. He didn't even bother with the life-support functions, all he wanted was power in the energy patterning nodes and secondary drive tubes.

With a fusion generator active, he ordered some sensor clusters to deploy. An image of the bay filled his mind, overlaid with fragile status graphics. He scanned the electromagnetic spectrum for any traffic, but there was only the background hash of cosmic radiation. Nobody was saying anything to anybody. What he wanted was someone asking Ethenthia what was happening, why they'd gone off the air. A ship close by that could help.

Nothing.

Erick fired the emergency release pins which the docking cradle's load clamps were gripping. Verniers sent out a hot deluge of gas which shimmered across the bay's walls, shaking loose blankets of thermal insulation from the gantries. *Tigara* rose a metre off its cradle, straining at the nest of umbilical hoses jacked into its rear fuselage. The snapfree couplings began to break, sending the hoses writhing.

The starship was low on cryogenic fuel; he couldn't afford to waste delta-V reserve aligning himself on an ideal vector. The astrogration program produced a series of options for him.

None of them were what he'd been hoping for. So what else was new?

The last of the umbilicals broke, and the *Tigara* lurched up out of the bay. Erick ordered the flight computer to extend the communication array and align it on Golmo and the Edenist habitats orbiting there. Sensor clusters began to sink down into their recesses as energy poured into the patterning nodes.

The flight computer alerted him that an SD platform was sweeping the ship with its radar. Then it relayed a signal from traffic control into his neural nanonics.

'Is that you, Erick? We think it's you. Who else is this stupidly ballsy? This is Emonn Verona, Erick, and I'm asking you: don't do it. That ship is completely fucked; I've got the CAB logs in front of me. It can't fly. You're only going to hurt yourself, or worse.'

Erick transmitted a single message to Golmo, then retracted the communication array down into its jump configuration. The SD platform had locked on. Some of the patterning nodes were producing very strange readings in the pre-jump diagnostic run-through. CAB monitor programs flashed up jump-proscription warnings. He switched them off.

'Game over, Erick. Either return to the docking-bay, or you join our comrades in the beyond. You don't want that. Where there's life, there's hope. Right? Of all people, you must believe that.'

Erick ordered the flight computer to activate the jump sequence.

# 21

The hellhawk *Socratous* was a flat V-shaped mechanical space-craft with a grey-white fuselage made up from hundreds of different component casings, a veritable jigsaw of mismatched equipment, not all of it astronautic. Two long engine nacelles were affixed to the stern, transparent tubes filled with a heavy opaque gas which fluoresced its way through the spectrum in a three-minute cycle.

It was an impressive sight as it slid down out of the starfield for a landing on Valisk's docking-ledge. Had it been real, it would be capable of taking on an entire squadron of Confederation Navy ships with its exotic weapons.

The illusion popped as a crew bus rolled across the ledge towards it. *Socratous* reverted to a muddy-brown egg-shape with a crew toroid wrapped around its midsection. Rubra could just see two small ridges on the rear quarter which hadn't been there before. They corresponded roughly with the nacelles of the fantasy starship. He wondered if the tumours would be benign. Did the energistic ability prevent metastasis from exploding inside possessed bodies as the wished-for changes became less illusion and cells multiplied to obey the will of the dominant soul? It seemed an awfully complex requirement for such a crude power, modifying the molecular structure of DNA and taming the mitosis process. The apparent milieux of their energistic ability was blasting holes through solid walls and contorting matter into new shapes; he'd never seen any demonstrations of subtlety.

Perhaps the whole possession problem would burn itself out in an orgy of irreversible cancer. Few of the returned souls were ever content with the physical appearance of the bodies they had claimed.

How superbly ironic, Rubra thought, that vanity could be the undoing of entities who had acquired near-godlike powers. It was also a dangerous prospect, once they realized what was happening. Those people remaining free would become even more valuable, the attempts to possess them ever more desperate. And Edenism would be the last castle to besiege.

He decided not to mention the prospect to the Kohistan Consensus. It was another small private advantage; no one else in the Confederation had such an individual and extensive vantage point of the possessed and their behaviour as him. He wasn't sure if he could exploit the knowledge, but he wasn't going to give it away until he was certain.

A subroutine of his principal personality was designated to observe the aberrant melanomata and carcinomas developing on the possessed inside the habitat. If the growths turned malignant the current situation would change drastically right across the Confederation.

The crew bus had left the *Socratous* to trundle back across the ledge. Kiera and about forty of her cronies were flocking into a reception lounge. When the bus docked, it disgorged about thirty-five Deadnight kids, eager besotted youngsters with red handkerchiefs worn proudly round their ankles and wonder in their eyes that they'd reached the promised land after so much difficulty.

**Damn it, you have to stop these flights,** Rubra complained to the Kohistan Consensus. **That's nearly two thousand victims this week. There must be something you can do.**

**We really cannot interdict every hellhawk flight. Their objective**

does not affect the overall balance of strategic events, and is relatively harmless.

Not to these kids, it isn't!

Agreed. But we cannot be everyone's keeper. The effort and risk involved in arranging clandestine rendezvous to pick up the Deadnights is disproportionate to the reward.

In other words, as long as the hellhawks are busy with this, they can't cause much trouble elsewhere.

Correct. Unfortunately.

And you used to call me a heartless bastard.

Everybody is suffering from the effects of possession. Until we discover a solution to the entire problem, all we can hope for is to reduce it to an absolute minimum wherever possible.

Right. I'd like to point out that when Kiera reaches the magic number, it's me who is going to be the one suffering.

That is some time off yet. Asteroid settlements have been alerted to these clandestine rendezvous flights. There should be less of them in future.

I bloody well knew I could never trust you lot.

We did not inflict any of this on you, Rubra. And you are quite welcome to transfer into the neural strata of one of our habitats should it look like Kiera Salter is preparing to shift Valisk out of this universe.

I'll keep it in mind. But I don't think you'll need to welcome this particular prodigal. Dariat is almost ready. Once he comes over, it'll be Kiera who is going to have to worry about where I shift Valisk.

Your attempt at subversion is a risky strategy.

That's how I built Magellanic Itg, through sheer balls. It's also why I rejected you. You don't have any.

This is not getting us anywhere.

If it works, I'll be able to start fighting back on a level you can't conceive of. Risk makes you alive, that's what you never understood. That's the difference between us. And don't try coming over all smarmy superior with me. It's me who's got an idea, me who stands a chance. Have you got any suggestions to make, an alternative?

**No.**

**Exactly. So don't lecture me.**

**We would urge caution, though. Please.**

**Urge away.**

Rubra dismissed the affinity link with his usual contempt. Circumstances might have forced him into an alliance with his old culture, but all the renewed contact had done was convince him how right he had been to reject them all those centuries ago.

He switched his primary routine's attention inward. The group of newly arrived Deadnights had been split up and taken away to be opened for possession. A temporary village had sprung up at the base of the northern endcap, extravagant tents and small cosy cottages for the possessed to dwell in. A smaller version of the camps which ringed the starscraper foyers halfway down the interior. The teams Kiera had working to make the starscrapers safe were finding progress difficult. And in any case, the possessed didn't entirely trust the areas they claimed to have secured. Rubra had never stopped his continual harassment. Nearly ten per cent of the servitor population had been killed as he deployed them on sneak attacks, but he still managed to eliminate a couple of possessed every day.

Separated from their companions, the Deadnights were easily overwhelmed. Piteous screams and pleas hung over the village like smog.

One of Rubra's newest monitor routines alerted him to a minuscule electrical discrepancy within the starscraper where Tolton was hiding. He had discovered electricity was the key to locating Bonney Lewin when she was using her energistic ability to fox his visual observation. A series of extremely sensitive routines which now monitored his own bioelectric patterns could sometimes detect a possessed from the backwash of their energistic power. In effect, the entire polyp structure had become an electronic-warfare detector. It was hardly reliable, but he was constantly refining the routines.

He tracked down the wraithish presence to the twenty-seventh floor vestibule where it was moving towards the stairwell muscle-membrane door. Visually, the vestibule was empty. At least, according to his local autonomic subroutines it was. The current in one of the organic conductor cables buried behind the wall fluctuated subtly.

Rubra reduced the power to the electrophorescent cells covering the polyp ceiling. The visual image remained the same for a couple of seconds, then the ceiling darkened. It should have been instantaneous. Whatever was causing the electrical disturbance stopped moving.

He opened a channel to Tolton's processor block. 'Get going, boy. They're coming for you.'

Tolton rolled off the bed where he'd been dozing. He'd been staying in the apartment for five days. The original occupant's wardrobes had been ransacked for a new ensemble. He'd accessed a good number of the MF and bluesense fleks in the lounge. And he'd sampled all of the imported delicacies in the kitchen, washing them down with fine wines and a lot of Norfolk Tears. For a suffering social poet, he'd adapted to hedonism with the greatest of ease. Small wonder there was a graceless scowl on his face as he snatched up his leather trousers and wriggled his bulk into them.

'Where are they?'

'Ten floors above you,' Rubra assured him. 'Don't worry, you've got plenty of time. I've got your exit route ready for you.'

'I've been thinking, maybe you ought to steer me toward some weapons hardware. I could start evening up the score a little.'

'Let's just concentrate on the essentials, shall we? Besides, if you get close enough to a possessed to use a weapon, they're close enough to turn it against you.'

Tolton addressed the ceiling. 'You think I can't handle it?'

'I thank you for the offer, son, but there are just too many of them. You staying free is my victory against all of them, don't blow it for me.'

Tolton clipped the processor block to his belt, and fastened his straggly hair back in a ponytail. 'Thanks, Rubra. We all got it way wrong about you. I know it don't mean shit to you probably, but when this is over, I'm going to tell the whole wide Confederation what you done.'

'That's one MF album I'll buy. First in a long time.'

Tolton stood in front of the apartment's door, breathed in like a yoga-master, flexed his shoulders like a sport-pro warming up, nodded briskly, and said: 'OK, let's hustle.'

Rubra felt an obdurate burst of sympathy, and, strangely enough, pride as the poet stepped out into the vestibule. When Kiera started her takeover he assumed Tolton would last a couple of days. Now he was one of only eighty non-possessed left. One of the reasons he'd survived was because he followed instructions to the letter; in short, he trusted Rubra. And Rubra was damned if Bonney would get him now.

The invisible energistic swirl was on the move again, descending the stairwell. Rubra started to modify the output of the electrophorescent cells in the ceiling. HELLO, BONNEY, he printed. I HAVE A PROPOSITION FOR YOU.

The swirl stopped again.

COME ON, TALK TO ME. WHAT HAVE YOU GOT TO LOSE?

He waited. A column of air shimmered silver, as if a giant cocoon had sprung up out of the polyp. Rubra experienced it most as a slackening of pressure in the local subroutines; a pressure he hadn't even been aware of until then. Then the silver air lost its lustre, darkening to khaki. Bonney Lewin stood on the stairs, her Lee Enfield searching for hazards.

'What proposition?'

ABANDON YOUR CURRENT VICTIM, I WILL GIVE YOU A BETTER ONE.

'I doubt it.'

DOESN'T KIERA WANT DARIAT ANY MORE?

Bonney gave the glowing letters a thoughtful stare. 'You're trying to sucker me.'

NO. THIS IS GENUINE.

'You're lying. Dariat hates you; he's totally bonkers about beating seven bells out of you. If we help him, he'll succeed.'

SO WHY HASN'T HE COME TO YOU FOR HELP?

'Because he's . . . weird.'

NO. IT IS BECAUSE USING YOU TO DEFEAT ME WOULD MEAN HAVING TO SHARE THE POWER WHICH WOULD RESULT FROM HIS DOMINATION OF THE NEURAL STRATA. HE WANTS IT ALL. HE HAS SPENT THIRTY YEARS WAITING FOR AN OPPORTUNITY LIKE THIS. DO YOU THINK HE WILL GIVE THAT AWAY? AND AFTER ME, KIERA IS GOING TO BE NEXT. THEN PROBABLY YOU.

'So you hand him over to us. That still doesn't make any sense; either way, we get to nail you.'

DARIAT AND I ARE PLAYING OUR OWN GAME. I DO NOT EXPECT YOU TO UNDERSTAND. BUT I DO NOT INTEND TO LOSE TO HIM.

She worried at a fingernail. 'I don't know.'

EVEN WITH MY HELP, HE WILL BE DIFFICULT TO CATCH. DO YOU FEAR FAILURE?

'Don't try working that angle on me, it's pathetic.'

VERY WELL. SO DO YOU ACCEPT?

'Difficult one. I really don't trust you. But it would be a superb hunt, you've got me there. I haven't had a single sniff of that tricky little boyo yet, and I've been trying for long enough.' She shouldered her rifle. 'All right, we've got a deal. But just remember, if you are trying to get me to walk into some ten thousand volt power cable, I can still come back. Kiera's recording is hauling in thousands of morons. I'll return in one of them, and then you'll wish all you had to worry about was Dariat.'

UNDERSTOOD. FIND A PROCESSOR BLOCK, AND SWITCH IT TO ITS BASIC ROUTINES, THAT SHOULD KEEP IT FUNCTIONING. I WILL UPDATE YOU ON HIS LOCATION.

*

Dariat walked along the shoreline of the circumfluous salt-water reservoir as the light-tube languished to a spectacular golden orange. The cove was backed by a decaying earth bluff which tipped an avalanche of the pink Tallok-aboriginal grass onto the sand. Curving outgrowths of the xenoc plant resembled a meandering tideline, which gave him the impression of walking along a spit between two different coloured seas. The only sounds were of the water lapping against the sand, and the birds crying out as they flew back to land for the night.

He had walked here many times as a child. An era when being alone meant happiness. Now he welcomed the solitude again; it gave him the mindspace to think, to formulate new subversion routines to insert into the neural strata; and he was free of Kiera and her greed and shallow ambitions. That second factor was becoming a dominant one. They had been looking for him ever since the Edenists destroyed the industrial stations. With both his knowledge of the habitat and energistically enhanced affinity it was absurdly easy to elude them. Few ever ventured down to the vast reservoir, preferring to cling to the camps around starscraper foyers. Without the tubes, it was a long journey across the grassland where malevolent servitor creatures lay in wait for the negligent.

**Trouble**, Rubra announced.

Dariat ignored him. He could hide himself from the possessed easily enough. None of them knew enough about affinity to access the neural strata properly. As a consequence he no longer bothered hiding himself from Rubra any more, nor did he bother with the linen-suited persona. It was all too stressful.

The price of release came in the form of taunts and nerve games emanating from Rubra with unimaginative regularity.

She's found you, Dariat, she's coming for you. And boy is she pissed.

Certain he'd regret it, Dariat asked: Who?

Bonney. There's nine of them heading right at you in a couple of trucks. I think Kiera was saying something about returning with your head. Apparently, attachment to your body was considered optional.

Dariat opened his affinity link with the neural strata just wide enough to hitch onto the observational subroutines. Sure enough, two of the rugged trucks which the rentcops used were arrowing across the rosy grassland. 'Shit.' They were heading straight for the cove, with about five kilometres left to go. How the hell did she find me?

Beats me.

Dariat stared straight up, following the line of the coast which looped behind the light-tube. Is there someone above me with a high-res sensor?

If there is, I can't spot them. In any case, I doubt a sensor would work for a possessed.

Binoculars? Hell, it hardly matters.

He couldn't see the trucks with his eyes yet, the tall grass hid them. And his mind couldn't perceive their thoughts, they were too far away. So just how had they found him?

There is a tube station at the end of the cove, Rubra said. They'll never be able to catch you in that. I can take you to anywhere in the habitat.

Thanks. And you'll be able to run a thousand volts through me as soon as I step inside a carriage. Or had you forgotten?

I don't want you blown into the beyond. You know that. I've made my offer, and it stands. Come into the neural strata. Join your mind with me. Together we will annihilate them. Valisk can be purged. We will take them to dimensions where simply existing is an agony for them. Both of us will have revenge.

You're crazy.

**Make your mind up. I can hide you for a time while you decide. Is it to be me? Or is it to be Kiera?**

Dariat was still receiving the image of the trucks from the sensitive cells. They were rocking madly over the uneven ground as the drivers held them at their top speed.

**I think I'll take a while longer to make up my mind.** Dariat started jogging for the tube station. After a minute, the trucks swung round to intercept him. *Bloody hell.* Horgan's body was reasonably fit, but he was only fifteen years old. Dariat's imagination bestowed him with athlete's legs, bulky slabs of muscle packed tight under oil-glossed skin. His speed picked up.

**I wonder what that kind of overdrive does to your blood-sugar levels? I mean, the power has to come from somewhere. Surely you're not converting the energistic overspill from the beyond directly into protein?**

**Save the science class till later.** He could see the station ahead of him, a squat circular polyp structure bordering the bluff, like some kind of storage tank half buried in the sand. The trucks were only a kilometre away. Bonney was standing up in the passenger seat of the lead vehicle, aiming her Lee Enfield at him over the windscreen. Motes of white fire punched into the sand around him. He ducked down for the last fifty metres, using the bluff as cover as he scuttled for the station entrance.

Inside, two broad escalators spiralled round each other, their steps moving sedately. A garishly coloured tubular hologram punctured the air up the centre of the shaft, adverts sliding along it. Dariat leapt on to the down escalator, and sprinted recklessly, hands barely touching the rail.

He made it to the bottom just as the trucks braked outside; Bonney charged towards the entrance. There was a carriage waiting on the station, a shiny white aluminium bullet. Dariat stopped, panting heavily, staring at the open door.

**Get in!**

Rubra's mental voice contained a strong intimation of alarm, which Dariat could hardly credit. **If you're fucking me, I'll come back. I'll promise myself to Anstid for that one wish to be granted.**

**Imagine my terror. I've told you, I need you intact and cooperative. Now get in.**

Dariat closed his eyes and took a step forward, directly into the carriage. The door slid shut behind him, and there was a faint vibration as it started accelerating along the track. He opened his eyes.

**See?** Rubra taunted. **Not such a bogey man, after all.**

Dariat sat down and took some deep breaths to calm his racing heart. He used the sensitive cells to watch an apoplectic Bonney Lewin jump down from the empty platform to fire her Lee Enfield along the dark tunnel. She was screaming obscenities. The accompanying hunters were standing well back. One of her boots was treading on the magnetic guide rail.

**Fry her,** Dariat said. **Now!**

**Oh, no. This is much more fun. This way I get to find out if the dead can have heart attacks.**

**You are a complete bastard.**

**That's right. And to prove it, I'm going to show you Anastasia's secret now. The one thing she never showed you.**

Dariat was instantly wary. **More lies.**

**Not this time. Don't tell me you don't want to find out. I know you, Dariat. Fully. I've always known. I know what she means to you, I know how much she means to you. Your memory of her was strong enough to power a grudge over thirty years. That's almost inhuman, Dariat. I respect it enormously. But it leaves you wide open to me. Because you want to know, don't you? There's something I've got, or heard, or saw, that you didn't. A little segment of Anastasia Rigel you don't have. You won't be able to live with that knowledge.**

**I'll be able to ask her soon. Her soul is waiting for me in the beyond. When I've dealt with you, I'll go to her, and we'll be together again.**

**Soon will be too late.**

**You're unbelievable, you know that?**

**Good. I'll take you there.**

**Whatever you like.** Dariat pushed his weariness behind the thought, showing just how unconcerned he was. Behind that, clutched away from the bravado and outward confidence, his teenage self huddled in worry. That same self which so idolized her. Now there was the chance, the remotest possibility that the image was flawed, less than honest. The doubt cut into him, weakening the core of resolution which had supported him for so terribly long.

Anastasia would never keep anything from him. Would she? She loved him, she said so. The last thing she ever said, ever wrote.

Rubra guided the tube carriage to a starscraper lobby station and opened the door. **It's waiting on the thirty-second floor.**

Dariat glanced cautiously out onto the little station and the wide passage which led to the lobby itself. His mind could sense the thoughts of the possessed camped outside the lobby. No one showed any interest in him. He hurried across the floor to the bank of lifts in the centre, reaching them unnoticed.

The lift deposited him at the thirty-second floor vestibule. A completely normal residential section; twenty-four mechanical doors leading to apartments, and three muscle membranes for the stairwells. One of the mechanical doors slid open to show a darkened lounge.

Dariat could sense someone inside, a dozing mind, its thought currents placid. When he tried to use the observation subroutines for the bedroom he found he couldn't, Rubra had wiped them.

**Oh, no, my boy, you go right in there and face your fate like a man.**

Dariat flinched. But ... one unaware non-possessed. How bad could it be? He walked into the apartment, ordering the electrophorescent cells to full intensity. Thankfully, they responded.

It was a woman who lay on the big bed, a duvet had worked

**863**

downwards to reveal her shoulders. Her skin was very black, with the minute crinkles which spelt out the onset of middle age and the start of weight problems for anyone without much geneering in their ancestry. A tangle of finely braided jet-black hair was fanned out over the pillows, every strand tipped with a moondust-white bead.

She groaned sleepily as the light came on, and turned over. Despite a face which cellulite was busy inflating, she had a petite nose.

NO! For one moment horror claimed his senses. She was similar to Anastasia. Features, colour, even the age was almost right. If a medical team had gone out to the tepee, they might have reanimated the body, a hospital might conceivably have used extensive gene-therapy to regenerate the dead brain cells. It could be done, for the President of Govcentral or Kulu's heir apparent, the effort would be made. But not a Starbridge girl regarded as vermin by the personality of the habitat in which she dwelt. The cold shock subsided.

Whoever she was, as soon as she saw him, she screamed.

'It's all right,' Dariat said. He couldn't even hear his own voice above her distraught wails.

'Rubra! One of them's here. Rubra, help me.'

'No,' Dariat said. 'I'm not. Well . . .'

'Rubra! RUBRA.'

'Please,' Dariat implored.

That silenced her.

'I'm not going to hurt you,' he said. 'I'm running from them myself.'

'Uh huh?' Her gaze darted to the door.

'Really. Rubra brought me here, too.'

The duvet was readjusted. Slim bronze and silver bracelets tinkled as she moved.

Dariat's chill returned. They were exactly the same kind of bracelets Anastasia wore. 'Are you a Starbridge?'

She nodded, wide-eyed.

**Wrong question**, Rubra said. **Ask her what her name is.**

He hated himself. For giving in, for playing to Rubra's rules.

'Who are you?'

'Tatiana,' she gulped. 'Tatiana Rigel.'

Rubra's mocking, triumphant laughter shook his skull from the inside. **Got it now, boy? Meet Anastasia's little sister.**

\*

Another day, another press conference. At least this new technology had progressed beyond flashbulbs; Al had always hated them back in Chicago. More than once he had been photographed raising a hand to ward off the brilliant bursts of light; photos which the papers always ran, because it looked as if he was trying to hide, confirming his guilt.

He had held the press conference in the Monterey Hilton's big ballroom, sitting at a long table with his back to the window. The idea was that the reporters would see the formation of victorious fleet ships which had just returned from Arnstadt, and were holding station five kilometres off the asteroid. Leroy Octavius said it should make an impressive backdrop for the dramatic news announcement.

Except the starships weren't quite in the right coordinate, so they were only just visible when rotation did bring them into view; the reporters had to look round the side of the table to see them. And everybody knew the Organization had conquered Arnstadt and Kursk, it wasn't new even though this made it sort of official.

Drama and impact, that was the sole purpose. So Al sat at the long table with its inappropriate vases of flowers; Luigi Balsmao on one side, and a couple of other ship captains on the other. He told the reporters how easy it had been to break open Arnstadt's SD network, the eagerness of the population to accept the Organization as a government after a 'minimum number' of key administrative people had been possessed. How the star system's economy was turning round.

'Did you use antimatter, Al?' Gus Remar asked. A weary veteran of these affairs now, he reckoned he knew what liberties he could take. Capone did have a weird sense of honour operating; nobody got blasted for trying to work an angle, only outright opposition earned his disapprobation.

'That's a dumb kinda question, pal,' Al replied, keeping the scowl from his face. 'What do you want to ask that for? We got plenty of interesting dope on how the Organization is curing all sorts of medical problems which the non-possessed bring to our lieutenants. You people, you always look for the bad side. It's like a goddam obsession with you.'

'Antimatter is the biggest horror the Confederation knows, Al. People are bound to be interested in the rumours. Some of the ships' crews say they fired antimatter-powered combat wasps. And the industrial stations here are producing anti-matter-confinement systems. Have you got a production station, Al?'

Leroy Octavius, who was standing behind Al, leant forward and whispered something in his ear. Some of the humour returned to Al's stony face. 'I can neither confirm or deny the Organization has access to invincible weapons.'

It didn't stop them from asking again and again. He lost the press conference then. There wasn't any chance to read out the dope Leroy had prepared on the medical bonus, and how they'd prevented the kind of food shortages on Arnstadt which were being reported as affecting other possessed worlds.

Asked at the end if he was planning another invasion, Al just growled: 'Wait and see,' then walked out.

'Don't worry about it, we'll embargo the whole conference,' Leroy said as they took a lift down to the bottom of the hotel.

'They ought to show some goddam respect,' Al grunted. 'If it wasn't for me they'd be possessed and screaming inside their own heads. Those bastards never fucking change.'

'You want us to lean on them a little?' Bernhard Allsop asked.

'No. That would be stupid. The only reason the Confederation news companies take our reports is because they're from non-possessed.' Al hated it when Bernhard tried to be tough and demonstrate his loyalty. *I should have him wasted, he's becoming a complete pain in the ass.*

But wasting people wasn't so easy these days. They'd come back in another body, and carry a grudge the size of Mount Washington.

God *damn*, the problems kept hitting on him.

*

The lift doors opened on the hotel basement, a windowless level given over to environmental machinery, large pumps, and condensation-smeared tanks. A boxing ring had been set up at the centre, surrounded by the usual training paraphernalia of exercise bikes, histeps, weights, and punchbags; Malone's gym.

Whenever he wanted to loosen up, Al came down here. He'd always enjoyed sports back in Chicago; going to the game was an event in those days. One he missed. If he could bring back the Organization, and the music, and the dancing from that time, he reasoned, then why not the sports, too?

Avram Harwood had run a check on professions listed in the Organization's files, and found Malone, who claimed to have worked as a boxing trainer in New York during the 1970s.

Al marched into the gym area trailed by five of his senior lieutenants, Avram Harwood, and a few other hangers on like Bernhard. It was noisy in the basement anyway, with the pumps thrumming away, and in the gym with music playing and men pounding away at leather punchbags you had to shout to be heard. This was the way it should be: the smell of leather and sweat, grunts as sparring blows hit home, Malone yelling out at his star pupils.

'How's it going?' Al asked the trainer.

Malone shrugged, his heavy face showing complete misery. 'Today's people, they gone soft, Al. They don't want to hit each other, they think it's immoral or something. We ain't gonna find no Ali or Cooper on this world. But I got a few contenders, kids who've had it hard. They're working out OK.' A fat finger indicated the two young men in the ring. 'Joey and Gulo, here, they could have what it takes.'

Al cast an eye over the two boxers dancing round in the ring. Both of them were big, fit-looking kids, wearing colourful protective gear. He knew enough about the basics to see they were holding themselves right, though they were concentrating too much on defence.

'I'll just watch a while,' Al told Malone.

'Sure thing, Al. Help yourself. Hey! Gulo, close the left, the left, ass-wipe.'

Joey saw his opening and landed a good right on Gulo's face. Gulo went for a body lock, and both of them bounced on the ropes.

'Break, break,' the ref cried.

Al pulled up a stool and gazed contentedly at the two combatants. 'All right, what's the order of play for today? Speak to me, Avvy.' The ex-mayor's body twitches were getting worse, Al noticed. And some of the weals still hadn't healed over despite a couple of attempts by Al's possessed lieutenants to heal them. Al didn't like having so much resentment and hostility festering close by. But the guy sure knew how to administrate; replacing him now would be a bitch.

'We now have fifteen delegations from outsystem who have arrived,' Avram Harwood said. 'They all want to see you.'

'Outsystem, huh?' Al's flagging interest started to perk up. 'What do they want?'

'Your assistance, basically,' Avram said. He didn't hide his displeasure.

Al ignored it. 'For what?'

'All of them are from asteroid settlements,' Patricia Mangano said. 'The first bunch that came here are from Toma, that's in the Kolomna system. Their problem is that the asteroid only has a population of ninety thousand. That gives them enough energistic power to shift it out of this universe easily enough. But then they realized that spending the rest of eternity inside a couple of modestly sized biosphere caverns which are totally dependent on technology wasn't exactly going to be a whole load of fun. Especially when nearly a third of the possessed come from pre-industrial eras.'

'Goddam, this is what I've been telling people all along,' Al said expansively. 'There ain't no point in vanishing whole planets away, not until we got the Confederation licked.'

Several of the trainee boxers had drifted over to stand close by. As if aware of the growing interest, Joey and Gulo were increasing their efforts to knock each other senseless. Malone's rapid-fire monotone picked up momentum.

'So what has this got to do with me?' Al asked.

'The Toma people want to move everyone to Kolomna.'

'Jee-zus!'

'They want our fleet to help them. If we choose Kolomna as our next invasion target we will receive their total cooperation for as long as you want it. Every industrial station in the system will be given over to supporting the fleet, every starship captured will be converted to carry weapons or troops, they'll bring the planetary population into order along Organization lines. They say they want to sign up as your lieutenants.'

Al was flattered, it turned his whole day around.

Out in the ring, both boxers were perspiring heavily. Blood was tricking out of Gulo's mouth. Joey's left eye was bruising. Cheers and whistles were swelling from the spectators.

'Risky,' Luigi said. 'Kolomna is First Admiral Aleksandrovich's homeworld. He probably wouldn't take too kindly to it. I wouldn't if I was him. Besides, we're still getting things in order for Toi-Hoi.'

Al rocked back on the stool and materialized one of his Havanas, its end already alight. 'I'm not too worried about that admiral getting pissed with me, not with what I've got in store for him. Any chance we can split the fleet, send some ships to Kolomna?'

'Sorry, boss, that's some of the bad news I've got for you,' Luigi said. 'The Confederation is really hassling us bad at Arnstadt. They've got voidhawks flying above both poles dropping invisible bombs on the SD platforms in orbit. Stealth, the bastards call it. We're losing a shitload of hardware every day. And the non-possessed population are putting up some resistance – quite a lot, actually. The new lieutenants we've appointed are having to use a whole load of force to establish our authority. It gives them a sense of independence, so we have to use the SD platforms to make them see reason, too. Except the Confederation is knocking the platforms out one at a time, so instead we gotta use starships to substitute, and they're just as vulnerable.'

'Well, fuck it, Luigi,' Al stormed. 'Are you telling me we're gonna lose?'

'No way!' an indignant Luigi protested. 'We're launching our own patrols up above the poles. We're hassling them right back, Al. But it takes five or six of our ships to block one of their goddam voidhawks.'

'They're bogging us down out there,' Silvano Richmann said. 'It's quite deliberate. We're also losing ships out among Arnstadt's settled asteroids. The voidhawks make lightning raids, fling off a dozen combat wasps, and duck away before we can do anything about it. It's a shitty way of fighting, Al, nothing is head on any more.'

'Modern navies are built around the concept of rapid tactical assault,' Leroy said. 'Their purpose is to inflict damage over a wide front so that you have to overstretch your defences. They've adopted a guerrilla policy to try and wear down our fleet.'

'Fucking coward's way of fighting,' Silvano grumbled.

'It'll get worse,' Leroy warned. 'Now they've seen how effective it is against Arnstadt, they'll start doing it here. New

California's SD network is just as vulnerable to stealth mines. Our advantage is that the Organization is now up and running on the planet. We don't need to enforce it the way we do on Arnstadt. I think we only used a groundstrike ten times last week.'

'Twelve,' Emmet corrected. 'But we do have a lot of industrial capacity in orbit. I'd hate to lose much of it to a stealth strike campaign. Our outer system asteroid settlements really aren't supplying us with anything like the material they should be, production simply doesn't match capacity at all.'

'That's because we essentially have the same problem as the outsystem delegations,' Leroy said.

'Go on,' Al said glumly; he was rolling the cigar absently between his fingers, its darkened tip pointing down. But he still hadn't taken his eyes off the fight. Joey was sagging now, swaying dazedly, while the blood from Gulo's face was flowing freely down his chest to splatter the floor of the ring. No bell was going to be rung; it wouldn't finish now until one of them fell.

'Every possessed wants to live on a planet,' Leroy said. 'Asteroids don't have an adequate population base to sustain a civilization for eternity. We've started to see a lot of inter-orbit craft heading towards New California from the settlements. And for every possessed on their way, there are another ten waiting for the next ship.'

'Goddam it,' Al shouted. 'When those skid-row assholes get here, you send them right back where they came from. We need those asteroid factories working at full steam ahead. You got that?'

'I'll notify SD Command,' Leroy said.

'Make sure they know I ain't fucking joking.'

'Will do.'

Al relit his cigar by glaring at it. 'OK, so, Luigi, when can we start to take out the Toi-Hoi system?'

Luigi shrugged. 'I'll be honest with you, Al, our original timetable ain't looking too good here.'

'Why not?'

'We thought we'd almost double the fleet size with Arnstadt's ships. Which we have done. But then we need a lot of them to keep order in that system, and reliable crews are getting hard to find. Then there's Kursk. We made a mistake with that one, Al, the place ain't worth a bucket of warm spit. It's those hillbilly redneck farmers. They just won't roll over.'

'That's where Mickey is right now,' Silvano said. 'He's trying to run an offensive which will bring them to heel. It's not easy. The tricky bastards have taken to the countryside. They're hiding in trees and caves, a whole load of places the satellite sensors can't find them. And the Confederation is hitting us big-time with those stealth weapons, like Arnstadt was just a warm-up. We're losing three or four ships a day.'

'I think Luigi is right when he said we made a mistake invading Kursk,' Emmet said. 'It's costing us a bundle, and returning zippo. I say pull the fleet out; let the possessed on the ground take care of the planet in their own time.'

'That'll mean the Organization won't have any clout there,' Patricia said. 'Once everyone's possessed, they'll snatch it clean out of the universe.'

'The only thing it ever gave to us was propaganda,' Leroy said. 'We can't work that angle any more. Emmet's right. I don't think we should be aiming at any planet lower than stage four, one that can replace our losses, as a minimum requirement.'

'That sounds solid to me,' Al agreed. 'I don't like losing Kursk, but spelt out like that I don't see that we've got one whole hell of a choice. Luigi, get Mickey back here, tell him to bring all the ships and as many of our soldiers as he can. I want to go for Toi-Hoi as soon as you can load up with supplies. People will think we've stalled otherwise, and it's important to keep the momentum going.'

'You got it, boss. I'd like to send Cameron Leung as the messenger, if you ain't using him. It'll be the quickest way, cut down on any more of our losses.'

'Sure, no problem. Send him pronto.' Al blew a smoke ring at the distant ceiling. 'Anything else?'

Leroy and Emmet gave each other a resigned look.

'There's a lot of currency cheating going on,' Emmet said. 'I suppose you could call it forgery.'

'Jee-zus, I thought you rocket scientists had that all figured out.'

'Foolproof, you said,' Silvano said with a demon's grin.

'It should have been,' Emmet insisted. 'Part of it is due to the way it's being implemented. Our soldiers aren't being entirely honest about the amount of time the possessed are devoting to redeeming their energistic debts. People are starting to complain. There's a lot of restlessness building up down there, Al. You're going to have to make it clear to the lieutenants how important it is to stick with the rules. The economy we've rigged up is shaky enough already without suffering this confidence crisis. If it fails then we lose control and the planet goes wild, just like Kursk. You can't use the SD platforms to waste everyone who disagrees with us; we need to be subtle about how we keep the majority in line.'

'All right, all right,' Al waved a hand, nettled at the schoolmaster tone Emmet was using.

'Based on what we've seen so far, I'm not sure a wild possessed population could even feed themselves. Certainly the cities would have to be abandoned as soon as the supply infrastructure collapses. You do need a large area of land under cultivation to support a city like San Angeles.'

'Will you cut this crap. I fucking understand, OK? What I want to know is, what are you going to do about it?'

'It's about time you met with the groundside lieutenants again, Al,' Leroy said. 'We can build on the fleet's return, show

how together we are up here, how they'd be nothing without us. Make them toe the line.'

'Oh, Jesus H. Christ, not another fucking tour. I just got back!'

'You're in charge of two star systems, Al,' Leroy said matter of factly. 'There are some things which have to be done.'

Al winced. The fatboy manager was right, as goddam always. This wasn't a game to be picked up when he felt like it, this was different to before. In Chicago he'd climbed on the back of the power structure to advance himself; now he was the structure. That was when he finally realized the responsibility, and enormity, of what he'd created.

If the Organization crashed, millions – living and resurrected – would fall beside him, their hopes smashed on the rocks of his selfish intransigence. Alcatraz was the result of his last brush with hubris. Alcatraz would be bliss compared to the suffering focused on him should he fail again.

The fight which was limping to its conclusion was no longer the centre of attention; most of the possessed in the gym were staring at him strangely. They could see the muddle and horror in his mind. Leroy and Avram were waiting, puzzled by the sudden, uneasy silence.

'Sure thing, Leroy,' Al said meekly. 'I know what I'm in charge of. And I ain't never been scared of doing what has to be done. Remember that. So set up that tour. You got that?'

'Yes, sir.'

'Makes a fucking change. Right, you guys all know what you gotta do. Do it.'

Gulo landed one final blow in Joey's stomach which sent him staggering backwards to collapse in a corner. Malone hopped over the ropes to examine the fallen man. Gulo stood over them, uncertain what to do next. Blood was dripping swiftly from his chin.

'OK, kid,' Malone said. 'That's it for the day.'

Al flicked his cigar away and stood by the ropes. He beckoned Gulo over. 'You did pretty damn good out there, boy. How long you been training?'

Gulo slipped a blood-soaked gumshield from his mouth. 'Nine days, Mr Capone, sir,' he mumbled. Little flecks of blood splattered Al's suit jacket as he wheezed painfully.

Al took hold of the kid's head with one hand, and turned it from side to side, examining the bruises and cuts inside the sparring helmet. He concentrated hard, feeling a cold tingle sweeping along his arm to infect the kid's face through his fingertips. The bleeding stopped, and the grazed bruising deflated slightly. 'You'll do OK,' Al decided.

\*

Jezzibella was lounging on the circular bed. A wall-mounted holoscreen showing her an image of the gym relayed by a sensor high in the ceiling. Emmet, Luigi, and Leroy clustered together, discussing something in sober tones, their amplified murmurs filling the bedroom.

'Hard day at the office, lover?' Jezzibella asked. It was a persona of toughness wrapping a tender heart. Her face was very serious, fine features slightly flushed. A longish bob hairstyle cupped her cheeks.

'You saw it,' he said.

'Yeah.' She uncurled her legs and stood up, wrestling with the fabric of her long silky white robe. There was no belt, and it was open to the waist, allowing a very shapely navel to peek out. 'Come here, baby. Lie down.'

'Best goddam offer I've had all day.' He was bothered by his own lack of enthusiasm.

'Not that; you need to relax.'

Al grunted disparagingly, but did as he was told. When he was lying on his back he stuck his hands behind his head, frowning at the ceiling. 'Crazy. Me of all people; I should've known what was going to happen with the money. Everyone skims and everyone scams. What made me think my soldiers were going to be square shooters?'

Jezzibella planted a foot on either side of his hips, then sat down. Her robe's fabric must have carried one hell of a static charge, he guessed, there was no other reason why it should cling to her skin at all the strategic zones. Her fingers dug into the base of his neck, thumbs probing deep.

'Hey, what is this?'

'I'm trying to get you to relax, remember? You're so tense.' Her fingers were moving in circles now, almost strumming his hot muscle cords.

'That's good,' he admitted.

'I should really have some scented oils to do this properly.'

'You want I should try and dream some up?' He wasn't too certain he could imagine smells the way he could shapes.

'No. Improvising can be fun, you never know what you might discover. Turn over, and get rid of your shirt.'

Al rolled over, yawning heavily. He rested his chin on his hands as Jezzibella began to move her fingertips along his spine.

'I dunno what I hate most,' Al said. 'Retreating from Kursk, or admitting how right that shitty slob Leroy was.'

'Kursk was a strategic withdrawal.'

'Running away is running away, doll. Don't matter how you dress it up.'

'I think I've found something that might help you with Arnstadt.'

'What's that?'

She leant over to the bedside cabinet and picked up a small processor block, tapping the keyboard. 'I only saw this recording today. Leroy should have brought it to me earlier. Apparently it's all over the Confederation. We got it from one of the outsystem delegations that arrived to plead with you.'

The holoscreen switched from the gym to showing Kiera Salter lounging on her boulder.

'Yep, that certainly perks me up,' Al said cheerfully.

Jezzibella slapped his rump. 'Just you behave, Al Capone. Forget her tits, listen to what she's saying.'

He listened to the enticing words.

'She's actually rather good,' Jezzibella said. 'Especially considering it's AV only, no naughty sensory activants to hammer home the message. I could have done it better, of course, but then I'm a professional. But that recording is pulling in dissatisfied kids from every asteroid settlement that ever received a copy. They call it Deadnight.'

'So? Valisk is one of those frigging freaky habitat places. She's hardly gonna be a threat to us no matter how many people go there.'

'It's how they get there which interests me. Kiera has managed to take over Valisk's blackhawks, they call them hellhawks.'

'Yeah?'

'Yes. And all they're doing is ferrying idiot kids to the habitat. She is facing the same problem as all the possessed asteroid settlements. They're not the kind of places you want to spend eternity in. My guess is that she's trying to beef up Valisk's population so the ones already there don't push to land on a planet. It makes sense. If they did move, Kiera won't be top dog any more.'

'So? I never said she was dumb.'

'Exactly. She's organized. Not on the scale you are, but she's smart, she understands politics. She'd make an excellent ally. We can supply her with people a lot faster than she can acquire them through clandestine flights. And in return, she loans us a couple of squadrons of these hellhawks, which the fleet desperately needs. They'd soon put a stop to the Confederation's stealth attacks.'

'Damn!' He shuffled round inside the cage of her legs to see her poised above him, hands on her hips, content smile on her lips. 'That's good, Jez. No, it ain't, it's fucking brilliant. Hell, you don't need me, you could run this Organization by yourself.'

'Don't be silly. I can't do what you do to me, not solitaire.'

He growled hungrily, and reached for the robe. Marie Skibbow's golden face smiled down on them as more and more of their clothing vanished, some into thin air, some into torn strips.

*

The First Admiral waited until Captain Khanna and Admiral Lalwani seated themselves in front of his desk, then datavised the desktop processor for a security level one sensenviron conference. Six people were waiting round the oval table in the featureless white bubble room which formed around him. Directly opposite Samual Aleksandrovich was the Confederation Assembly President, Olton Haaker, with his chief aide Jeeta Anwar next to him; the Kulu Ambassador, Sir Maurice Hall, was on her left, accompanied by Lord Elliot, a junior minister from the Kulu Foreign Office; the Edenist Ambassador, Cayeaux, and Dr Gilmore took the remaining two chairs.

'This isn't quite our usual situation briefing today, Admiral,' President Haaker said. 'The Kulu Kingdom has made a formal request for military aid.'

Samual Aleksandrovich knew his face was showing a grimace of surprise, his sensenviron image, however, retained a more dignified composure. 'I had no idea any of the Kingdom worlds were under threat.'

'We are not facing any new developments, Admiral,' Sir Maurice said. 'The Royal Navy is proving most effective in protecting our worlds from any strikes by possessed starships. Even Valisk's hellhawks have stopped swallowing into our systems to peddle their damnable Deadnight subversion. And our planetary forces have contained all the incursions quite successfully. With the sorry exception of Mortonridge, of course. Which is why we are requesting your cooperation and assistance. We intend to mount a liberation operation, and free the citizens who have been possessed.'

'Impossible,' Samual said. 'We have no viable method of purging a body of its possessor, Dr Gilmore.'

'Unfortunately, the First Admiral is correct,' the navy scientist said. 'As we have found, forcing a returned soul to relinquish a body it has captured is extremely difficult.'

'Not if they are placed in zero-tau,' Lord Elliot said.

'But there are over two million people on Mortonridge,' Samual said. 'You can't put that many into zero-tau.'

'Why not? It's only a question of scale.'

'You'd need . . .' Samual trailed off as various tactical programs went primary in his neural nanonics.

'The help of the Confederation Navy,' Lord Elliot concluded. 'Exactly. We need to move a large number of ground troops and matériel to Ombey. You have transport and assault starships which aren't really involved with enforcing the civil starflight quarantine. We'd like them to be reassigned to the campaign. The combined resources of our own military forces, our allies, and the Confederation Navy ought to be sufficient to liberate Mortonridge.'

'Ground troops?'

'We will initially be providing the Kingdom with half a million bitek constructs,' Ambassador Cayeaux said. 'They should be able to restrain individual possessed, and force them into a zero-tau pod. Their deployment will ensure the loss of human life is kept to a minimum.'

'You are going to help the Kingdom?' Samual couldn't be bothered to filter his surprise out of the question. But . . . the Edenists and the Kingdom allied! At one level he was pleased, prejudice can be abandoned if the incentive is great enough. What a pity it had to be this, though.

'Yes.'

'I see.'

'The Edenist constructs will have to be backed up by a

considerable number of regular soldiers to hold the ground they take,' Sir Maurice said. 'We would also like you to assign two brigades of Confederation Marines to the campaign.'

'I've no doubt your tactical evaluations have convinced you about the plausibility of this liberation,' Samual said. 'But I must go on record as opposing it, and certainly I do not wish to devote my forces to what will ultimately prove a futile venture. If this kind of combined effort is to be made, it should at least be directed at a worthwhile target.'

'His Majesty has said he will go to any lengths to free his subjects from the suffering being inflicted on them,' Lord Elliot said.

'Does his obligation only extend to the living?'

'Admiral!' Haaker warned.

'I apologize. However, you must appreciate, I have a responsibility to the Confederation worlds as a whole.'

'Which so far you have demonstrated perfectly.'

'So far?'

'Admiral, you know the status quo within the Confederation cannot be maintained indefinitely,' Jeeta Anwar said. 'We cannot afford it.'

'We have to consider the political objectives of this conflict,' Haaker said. 'I'm sorry, Samual, but logic and sound tactics aren't the only factors at play here. The Confederation must be seen to be doing something. I'm sure you appreciate that.'

'And you have chosen Mortonridge as that something?'

'It is a goal which the Kingdom and the Edenists think they can achieve.'

'Yes, but what would happen afterwards? Do you propose to take on every possessed planet and asteroid in a similar fashion? How long would that take? How much would it cost?'

'I sincerely hope such a process would not have to be repeated,' Cayeaux said. 'We must use the time it takes to liberate Mortonridge to search for another approach to the problem. However, if there is no answer, then similar campaigns may indeed have to be mounted.'

'Which is why this first one must succeed,' Haaker said.

'Are you ordering me to redeploy my forces?' Samual asked.

'I'm informing you of the request the Kulu Kingdom and the Edenists have made. It is a legitimate request made by two of our strongest supporters. If you have an alternative proposal, then I'll be happy to receive it.'

'Of course I don't have an alternative.'

'Then I don't think you have any reason to refuse them.'

'I see. If I might ask, Ambassador Cayeaux, why does your Consensus agree to this?'

'We agreed to it for the sake of the hope it will provide to all the living in the Confederation. We do not necessarily approve.'

'Samual, you've done a magnificent job so far,' Lalwani said. 'We know this liberation is only a sideshow, but it will gain us a great deal of political support. And we are going to need every scrap of support we can find in the coming weeks.'

'Very well.' Samual Aleksandrovich paused in distaste. What upset him most was how well he understood their argument, almost sympathizing with it. Image had become the paramount motivation, the way every war was fought for politicians. But in this I am no different to military commanders down the centuries, we always have to play within the political arena in order to fight the real battle. I wonder if my illustrious predecessors felt so soiled? 'Captain Khanna, please ask the General Staff to draw up fleet redeployment orders based on the request from the Kulu Kingdom Ambassador.'

'Yes, sir.'

'I wish your King every success, Ambassador.'

'Thank you, Admiral. We do not wish to disrupt your current naval operations. Alastair does understand the importance of the role you are playing.'

'I'm glad of that. There are going to be some difficult decisions for all of us ahead, his patronage will be essential. As I have said from the beginning, this requires an ultimate solution that can never be purely military.'

'Have you considered the proposal Capone made?' Sir Maurice asked. 'I know if any of the possessed can be seen in terms of a conventional enemy, it's him. But could bitek construct bodies be made to work?'

'We examined it,' Maynard Khanna said. 'In practical terms it is completely unviable. The numbers are impossible. A conservative estimate for the Confederation's current population is nine hundred billion, which averages out at just over one billion per star system. Even if you assume only ten dead people for everyone living, there must be approximately ten trillion souls in the beyond. If they were each given a construct body, where would they live? We would have to find between three to five thousand new terracompatible planets for them. Clearly an impossible task.'

'I would contend that number,' Cayeaux said. 'Laton quite clearly said that not every soul remains imprisoned in the beyond.'

'Even if it was only a single trillion, that would still mean locating several hundred planets for them.'

'Laton's information interests me,' Dr Gilmore said. 'We have been assuming all along that it is incumbent on us to provide a final solution. Yet if souls can progress from the beyond to some other state of existence, then clearly it is up to them to do so.'

'How would we make them?' Haaker asked.

'I'm not sure. If we could just find one of them who would cooperate we could make so much more progress; someone like that Shaun Wallace character who was interviewed by Kelly Tirrel. Those we have here in Trafalgar are all so actively hostile to our investigation.'

Samual thought about making a comment concerning relevant treatment and behaviour, but Gilmore didn't deserve public rebukes. 'I suppose we could try a diplomatic initiative. There are several isolated asteroid settlements which have been possessed and yet haven't yet moved themselves out of the universe. We could make a start with them; send a message asking them if they will talk to us.'

'An excellent proposal,' Haaker said. 'It would cost very little, and if we obtain a favourable response I would be prepared to give a joint research project my full support.'

\*

The senseviron ended, leaving Dr Gilmore alone in his office. He did nothing for several minutes while the last part of the meeting ran through his mind. A man who prided himself on his methodical nature, the embodiment of the scientific method, he wasn't angry with himself, at the most he felt a slight irritation that he hadn't reasoned this out earlier. If Laton was correct about souls moving on, then the beyond was not the static environment he had assumed until now. That opened up a whole range of new options.

Dr Gilmore entered the examination room containing Jacqueline Couteur to find the staff on an extended break. Both quantum signature sensor arrays were missing from the overhead waldo arms. The electronics lab was rebuilding them once again, a near-continual process of refinement as they sought out the elusive transdimensional interface.

Jacqueline Couteur was being fed. A trolley had been wheeled in beside the surgical bed, sprouting a thick hose which hung just over her mouth. Her black head restraint had been loosened slightly, allowing her to switch between the two nipples; one for water, the other a meat paste.

Dr Gilmore walked through to stand next to the surgical bed. Her eyes followed his movement.

'Good morning, Jacqueline; how are you today?'

Her eyes narrowed contemptuously. Little wisps of steam

licked up from the electrodes pressing against her skin. She opened her mouth, and circled the plastic nipple with her tongue. 'Fine, thank you, Dr Mengele. I'd like to speak to my lawyer, please.'

'That's interesting. Why?'

'Because I'm going to sue you for every fuseodollar you own, and then have you shot down to a penal world in a one-way capsule. Torture is illegal in the Confederation. Read the Declaration of Rights.'

'If you are in discomfort, you should leave. We both know you can do that.'

'We're not discussing my options at the moment. It is your actions which are in question. Now may I have my one phone call?'

'I had no idea an immortal soul had civil rights. You certainly don't show your victims much in the way of autonomy.'

'My rights are for the courts to decide. By denying me access to legal representation for such a test case you are compounding your crime. However, if it bothers you, then I can assure you that Kate Morley would like to see a lawyer.'

'Kate Morley?'

'This body's co-host.'

Dr Gilmore gave an uncertain smile. This wasn't going to plan at all. 'I don't believe you.'

'Again, you take the role of the court upon yourself. Do you really think Kate enjoys being strapped down and electrocuted? You are violating her basic human rights.'

'I'd like to hear her ask for a lawyer.'

'She just has done. If you don't believe me, try running a voiceprint analysis. She said it.'

'This is absurd.'

'I want my lawyer!' Her voice rose in volume. 'You, marine, you are sworn to uphold the rights of Confederation citizens. I want a lawyer. Get me one.'

The captain of the marine guard looked at Dr Gilmore for guidance. Everyone on the other side of the glass partition was staring in.

Dr Gilmore relaxed, and smiled. 'All right, Jacqueline. You cooperate with us, we'll cooperate with you. I will raise the topic with the First Admiral's legal staff to see if they consider you are entitled to legal representation. But first I want you to answer a question for me.'

'The accused have a right of silence.'

'I'm not accusing you of anything.'

'Clever, Doctor. Ask, then. But don't insult me by asking me to incriminate myself.'

'When did your body die?'

'In 2036. Do I get my lawyer now?'

'And you were conscious the whole time you were in the beyond?'

'Yes, you moron.'

'Thank you.'

Jacqueline Couteur gave him a highly suspicious glance. 'That's it?'

'Yes. For now.'

'How did that help you?'

'Time passes in the beyond. That means it is subject to entropy.'

'So?'

'If your continuum decays, then the entities within it can die. More pertinently, they can be killed.'

* * *

'She wants a *what*? Maynard Khanna asked.

Dr Gilmore flinched. 'A lawyer.'

'This is a joke, right?'

'I'm afraid not.' He sighed reluctantly. 'The problem is, whilst ordinarily I would dismiss such a request as sheer nonsense, it has opened something of a debate amongst the investigating staff. I know the Intelligence Service has extremely wide-ranging powers that supersede the Declaration of Rights, but personality debrief is normally conducted by another division. I'm not saying that what we're doing to Couteur and the others isn't necessary, I would just like to establish that our orders were drafted correctly, that is: legally. Naturally, I don't wish to bother the First Admiral with such trivia at this time. So if you could raise the matter with the Provost General's office I'd be grateful. Just for clarification, you understand.'

\*

In appearance, Golomo was no different to any of the other gas giants found amongst the star systems of the Confederation. A hundred and thirty-two thousand kilometres in diameter, its ring band slightly denser than usual, its storm bands a raucous mix of twirled vermilion, pale-azure, splashed with coffee-cup swirls of white strands. The abnormality for which it was renowned lurked several hundred kilometres below the furrowed surface of the outer cloud layer, down where the density and temperature had risen considerably. That was where the Edenists whose habitats colonized the orbital space above located life; a narrow zone where pressure reduced the speed of the turbulence, and the strange hydrocarbon gases developed an easy viscosity. Single cells like airborne amoebas, but the size of a human fist, could survive there. They always clustered together in great colonies, resembling blankets of beluga. Why they did it, nobody could work out, none of them were specialized, all of them were independent. Yet to find singletons was unusual, at least in the areas so far observed by the probes, which admittedly was a minute percentage of the planet.

At any other time, Syrinx would dearly have loved to pay the research sites a visit. The old curiosity was still itching when *Oenone* slid out of its wormhole above the gas giant.

**Other days, other priorities,** the voidhawk chided.

Syrinx felt a hand patting hers; affinity was filled with, if not quite sympathy, then certainly tolerance. She gave Ruben a droll glance, and shrugged. **OK, another time.** She borrowed the voidhawk's powerful affinity voice to identify them to the Golomo Consensus; SD sensors were already locking on.

The routine for each system they visited was identical: impart a summary of the Confederation's strategic disposition, then there were accounts of new developments in neighbouring systems, which asteroids and planets faced the possibility of takeovers. In exchange, the Consensus provided an Intelligence update on the local system. *Oenone* could cover two, sometimes three star systems a day. So far the picture of conditions they were building up was depressing. The Edenist habitats were managing to stay on top of the situation, remaining loyal to the designated 'isolation and confinement' policy. Adamist populations were less observant. Everywhere she went there were complaints about the hardships resulting from the quarantine, Edenist worries of local navies falling short of their designated duties, stories of illegal starship flights, a steady trickle of asteroids falling to the possessed, of political manoeuvring and advantage-trading.

**We are generally more law abiding than Adamists,** Oxley said. **And there are more of them than us. That's bound to produce a weighted picture.**

**Don't make excuses for them,** Caucus said.

**Lack of education, and fear,** Syrinx said. **That's what's doing it. We have to make allowances, I suppose. But at the same time, their attitude is going to be a real problem in the long term. In fact, it might mean there won't even be a long term as far as they're concerned.**

**Apart from the Kulu Kingdom, and one or two other of the more disciplined societies.** Ruben's suggestion was infected with irony.

She delayed her answer as she grew aware of a growing unease in Golomo's Consensus. Voidhawks from the local defence force were popping in and out of wormholes, filling the affinity band with an excited buzz. **What is the problem?** she enquired.

**We are confirming that the Ethenthia asteroid settlement has fallen to possession,** Consensus informed *Oenone* and its crew. **We have just received a message from its Confederation Navy Bureau concerning the arrival of a CNIS captain, Erick Thakrar, from Kursk. According to the Bureau chief, Thakrar had obtained information of an extremely important nature. A voidhawk was requested to carry the captain and his prisoner to Trafalgar. Unfortunately there is a fifteen-hour delay to Ethenthia, in the intervening time the possessed appear to have ...**

Along with everyone else attuned to Consensus, Syrinx and her crew were immediately aware of the incoming message. Habitat senses perceived it as a violet star-point of microwaves, shining directly at Golomo from Ethenthia.

'This is Erick Thakrar, CNIS Captain; I'm the one Emonn Verona told you about. Or at least I hope he did. God. Anyway, the possessed have taken over Ethenthia now. You probably know that by now. I managed to make it to a starship, the *Tigara*, but they're on to me. Listen, the information I've got is vital. I can't trust it to an open com link; if they find out what I know, it'll become useless. But right now my problem is that this ship is totally fucked, and I'm not much better. I've got a partial alignment on the Ngeuni system, but there's sod all about it in this almanac. I think it's a stage-one colony. If I can't transfer to a flightworthy starship there, I'll try and slingshot back here. God, the SD platform is locking on. OK, I'm jumping now—'

**Ngeuni is a stage-one colony,** *Oenone* responded immediately.

Syrinx was automatically aware of its spacial location eleven light-years away. When correlated with Ethenthia's current position the alignment must have been very tenuous indeed. If Thakrar's ship was as bad as he implied ...

**The colony is still in its start-up stage,** *Oenone* continued. **However, there may be some starships available.**

**This is something I should follow up,** Syrinx told Consensus.

**We concur. It will be another day before Thakrar returns here, assuming his ship remains flightworthy.**

**We'll check Ngeuni to see if he got there.** Even as she spoke, energy was flowing through the voidhawk's patterning cells.

\*

Stephanie heard a loud mechanical screeching sound followed by a raucous siren blast. She grinned round at the children sitting at the kitchen table. 'Looks like your uncle Moyo has found us some transport.'

Her humour faded when she reached the bungalow's front porch. The bus which was parked on the road outside was spitting light in every spectrum, its bodywork a tight-packed mass of cartoon flowers growing out of Paisley fields. LOVE, PEACE, and KARMA flashed in nightclub neon on the sides. The darkest areas were its gleaming chrome hubcaps.

Moyo climbed down out of the cab, busily radiating embarrassment. The doors at the back of the bus hissed open, and another man climbed down. She'd never seen anyone with so much hair before.

The children were crowding round her, gazing out eagerly at the radiant carnival apparition.

'Is that really going to take us to the border?'

'How do you make it light up?'

'Please, Stephanie, can I get inside?'

Stephanie couldn't say no to them, so she waved them on with a casual gesture. They swarmed over the small front lawn to examine the wonderment.

'I can see how this should help us avoid any undue attention,' she said to Moyo. 'Have you lost your mind?'

A guilty finger indicated his new companion. 'This is Cochrane, he helped me with the bus.'

'So it was your idea?'

'Surely was.' Cochrane bowed low. 'Man, I always wanted a set of wheels like this.'

'Good. Well now you've had it, you can say goodbye. I have to take these children out of here, and they're not going in that thing. We'll change it into something more suitable.'

'Won't do you no good.'

'Oh?'

'He's right,' Moyo said. 'We can't sneak about, not here. You know that. Everybody can sense everything in Mortonridge now.'

'That's still no reason to use this . . . this—' She thrust an exasperated arm out towards the bus.

'It's like gonna be a mobile Zen moment for those with unpure thoughts,' Cochrane said.

'Oh, spare me!'

'No, really. Any cat catches sight of that bus and they're gonna have to confront like their inner being, you know. It's totally neat, a soul looking into its own soul. With this, you're broadcasting goodness at them on Radio Godhead twenty-four hours a day; it's a mercy mission that makes mothers weep for their lost children. My Karmic Crusader bus is going to shame them into letting you through. But like if you hit on people with a whole heavy military scene, like some kind of covert behind-the-lines hostility raid, you'll waste all those good vibes your karma has built up. It'll make it easy for all the cosmically uncool redneck dudes running loose out there to make it hard for us.'

'Humm.' He did make an odd kind of sense, she admitted grudgingly. Moyo gave her a hopeful shrug, a loyalty which leant her a cosy feeling. 'Well, we could try it for a few miles, I suppose.' Then she gave Cochrane a suspicious look. 'What do you mean, us?'

He smiled and held his arms out wide. A miniature rainbow sprang up out of his palms, arching over his head. The children laughed and clapped.

'Hey, I was at Woodstock, you know. I helped rule the world for three days. You need the kind of peaceful influence I exert over the land. I'm a friend to all living things, the unliving, too, now.'

'Oh, hell.'

*

Erick still hadn't activated the life-support capsule's internal environmental systems. He was too worried what the power drain would do to the starship's one remaining functional fusion generator. There certainly wasn't enough energy stored in the reserve electron-matrix cells to power up the jump nodes.

Ngeuni's star was a severe blue-white point a quarter of a light-year away. Not quite bright enough to cast a shadow on the hull, but well above first magnitude, dominating the starfield. His sensor image was overlaid with navigation graphics, a tunnel of orange circles which seemed to be guiding the *Tigara* several degrees south of the star. After five jumps he was still matching delta-v.

Thankfully, the clipper's fusion drive was capable of a seven-gee acceleration, and they weren't carrying any cargo. It meant he had enough fuel to align the ship properly. Getting back to Golomo was going to be a problem, though.

The flight computer warned him that the alignment manoeuvre was almost complete. *Tigara* was flashing towards the jump coordinate at nineteen kilometres per second. He started to reduce thrust, and ordered the fusion generator to power up the nodes. As soon as the plasma flow increased he started receiving datavised caution warnings. The confinement field which held the ten million degree stream of ions away from the casing was fluctuating alarmingly.

Erick quickly loaded an emergency dump order into the flight computer, linking it to a monitor. If the confinement field fell below five per cent the generator would shut down and vent.

For some reason he was devoid of all tension. Then he realized his medical program was flashing for attention. When he accessed it, he saw the packages were filtering out a deluge of toxins and neurochemicals from his bloodstream at the same time as they were issuing chemical suppressors.

He grinned savagely around the SII suit's oxygen tube. Neutering his own reflexes at precisely the time he needed them the most. Too many factors were building up against him. And still it didn't really bother him, not snug in the heart of his semi-narcotic hibernation.

The flight computer signalled that the jump coordinate was approaching. Sensors and heat-dump panels began to sink down into their recesses. The main drive reduced thrust to zero. Erick fired the ion thrusters, keeping the *Tigara* on track.

Then the energy patterning nodes were fully charged. Finally he felt a distant sense of relief, and reduced the fusion generator output. The straining confinement field surged as the plasma stream shrank by ninety per cent inside half a second. Decaying failsoft components didn't respond in time. An oscillation rippled along the tokamak chamber, tearing the plasma stream apart.

The *Tigara* jumped.

It emerged deep inside the Ngeuni system; at that instant a perfect inert sphere. The poise was shattered within an instant as the raging plasma tore through the tokamak's casing, and ripped out through the hull, loosing incandescent swords of ions in all directions. A chain reaction of secondary explosions began as cryogenic tanks and electron matrices detonated.

The ship disintegrated amid a blaze of radioactive gases and ragged molten debris. Its life-support capsule came spinning out of the core of the explosion, a silvered sphere whose surface was gashed by veins of black carbon where energy bursts and tiny fragments had peppered the polished nultherm foam.

As soon as it was clear of the boiling gases, emergency rockets fired to halt the capsule's wild tumbling motion; a solid kick into stability. The beacon began to broadcast its shrill distress call.

# 22

Like most enterprises mounted by governments and institutions on Nyvan, the Jesup asteroid was chronically short of finance, engineering resources, and qualified personnel. The rock's major ore reserves had been mined out a long time ago. Ordinarily, the revenue would have been invested in the development of the asteroid's astroengineering industry. But the New Georgia government had diverted the initial windfall income to pay for more immediate and voter-friendly projects on the ground.

After the ore was exhausted, Jesup spent the next decades limping along both economically and industrially. Fledgling manufacturing companies shrank back to service subsidiaries and small indigenous armament corporations. Its ageing infrastructure was maintained one degree from breakdown. Of the three planned biosphere caverns only one had ever been completed, leaving a vast number of huge empty cavities spaced strategically throughout the rock which would have been the kernels of fresh mining activity.

It was when Quinn was striding along one of the interminable bare-rock tunnels linking the discarded cavities that he sensed the first elusive presence. He stopped so abruptly that Lawrence almost bumped into him.

'What was that?'

'What?' Lawrence asked.

Quinn turned full circle, slowly scanning the dust-encrusted rock of the wide tunnel. Dribbles of condensation ran along the curving walls and roof, cutting small forked channels through the ebony dust as they generated fragile miniature stalactites. It was as if the tunnel was growing a fur of cactus spikes. But there was no place for anyone to hide, only the waves of shadow between the widely spaced lighting panels.

His entourage of disciples waited with nervous patience. After two days of slickly brutal initiation ceremonies the asteroid now belonged to him. However, Quinn remained disappointed with the number of true converts among the possessed. He had assumed that they of all people would despise Jesus and Allah and Buddha and the other false gods for condemning them to an agonizing limbo. Showing them the path to the Light Bringer ought to have been easy. But they continued to demonstrate a bewildering resistance to his teachings. Some even interpreted their return to be a form of redemption.

Quinn could find nothing in the tunnel. He was sure he had caught a wisp of thought which didn't belong to any of the entourage. It had been accompanied by a tiny flicker of motion: grey on black. His first reaction was that someone was sneaking along behind them.

Irritated by the distraction, he strode off again, his robe rising to glide above the filthy rock floor. It was cold in the tunnel, his breath turning to snowy vapour before his eyes. His feet began to crunch on particles of ice.

A frigid gust of air swept against him, making an audible swoosh. His robe flapped about.

He stopped again, angry this time. 'What the fuck is going on here? There's no environment ducts in this tunnel.' He held up a hand to feel the air, which was now perfectly still.

Someone laughed.

He whirled round. But the disciples were looking at each other in confusion. None of them had dared mock his bewilderment. For a moment he thought of the unknown figure at the spaceport on Norfolk, the powerful swirl of flames he had unleashed. But that was lightyears away, and no one else had escaped the planet except the Kavanagh girl.

'These tunnels are always acting erratically, Quinn,' Bonham said. Bonham was one of the new converts, possessing Lucky Vin's body, which he was twisting into a ghoul-form, bleaching the skin, sharpening the teeth, and swelling the eyes. Thick animal hair was sprouting out of his silver skull. He said he had been born into a family of Venetian aristocrats in the late nineteenth century, killed before his twenty-seventh birthday in the First World War, but only after having tasted both the decadence and blind cruelty of the era. A taste which had become a voracious appetite. He had needed no persuading to embrace Quinn's doctrines.

'I asked one of the maintenance chappies, and he said it's because there aren't any ducts in the tunnels to regulate them properly. There are all sorts of weird surges.'

Quinn wasn't satisfied. He was sure he'd sensed someone sneaking about. A dissatisfied grunt, and he was on his way once more.

No further oddities waylaid him before he reached the cavity where one of the teams was working. It was an almost spherical chamber, with a small flat floor, acting as a junction to seven of the large tunnels. A single fat metal tube hung downwards from the apex, rattling loudly as it blew out a wind of warm dry air. Quinn scowled up at it, then went over to the knot of five men working to secure the fusion bomb to the floor.

The device's casing was a blunt cone seventy centimetres high. Several processor blocks had been plugged into its base with optical cables. The men stopped working and stood up respectfully as Quinn approached.

'Did anyone come through here earlier?'

They assured him no one had. One of them was non-possessed, a technician from the New Georgia Defence Force. He was sweating profusely, his thoughts a mixture of dread and outrage.

Quinn addressed him directly. 'Is everything going OK?'

'Yes,' the technician murmured meekly. He kept glancing at Twelve-T.

The gang lord was in a sorry state. Tiny jets of steam spluttered out of his mechanical body parts. Rheumy crusts were building up around the rim of bone in which his brain was resting, as though candle wax was leaking out. The membrane that clothed his brain had thickened (as Quinn wished) but was now acquiring an unhealthy green tint. He was blinking and squinting constantly as he fought the pain.

Quinn followed the man's gaze with pointed slowness. 'Oh yeah. The most feared gangster on the planet. Real hard-arsed mother who isn't gonna believe in God's Brother no matter what I do to him. Pretty dumb, really. But the thing is, he's useful to me. So I let him live. As long as he doesn't stray too far from me, he keeps on living. It's sort of like a metaphor, see? Now, you going to be a hard-arse?'

'No, sir, Mr Quinn.'

'That's fucking smart.' Quinn's head came forward slightly from the umbra of the hood to allow a faint light to strike his ashen skin. The technician closed his eyes to hide from the sight, lips mumbling a prayer.

'Now is this bomb going to work?'

'Yes, sir. It's a hundred-megaton warhead, they all are. Once they're linked into the asteroid's net we can detonate them in sequence. As long as there are no possessed near them, they'll function properly.'

'Don't worry about that. My disciples won't be here when Night dawns in the sky.' He turned back to the tunnel, giving it a suspicious look. Again he had the intimation of motion, a flicker no larger than the flap of a bird's wing, and twice as fast.

He was sure that someone had been watching the incident. A spoor of trepidation hung in the air like the scent of a summer flower.

When he stood at the entrance he could see the line of light-panels shrink into distance before a curve took them from sight. The gentle sound of pattering water was all that emerged. He was half expecting to see that same blank human silhouette which had appeared at the hangar on Norfolk.

'If you are hiding, then you are weaker than me,' he told the apparently empty shaft. 'That means you will be found and brought before me for judgement. Best you come out now.'

There was no response.

'Have it your way, shithead. You've seen what happens to people I don't like.'

*

The rest of Quinn's day was spent issuing the instructions that would cause Night to fall on the innocent planet below. He commanded New Georgia's SD network now. It would be a simple matter for the platforms to interfere with Nyvan's two other functional networks, and various national sensor satellites. Under cover of this electronic-warfare barrage, space-planes would slide down undetected to the surface. Every nation would be seeded by a group of possessed from Jesup. And Nyvan's curse of national antagonism would prevent a unified planetary response to the problem, which was the only response that could ever stand a chance of working.

The possessed would conquer here, probably with greater ease than anywhere in the Confederation. They were a single force, knowing nothing of borders and limits.

As for those who would actually be sent down, Quinn chose carefully. A couple of the devout for every spaceplane to make sure they followed their flight vectors and landed at the designated zone; but the rest were ones only fear and his own proximity kept in line: unbelievers. It was quite deliberate. Free of his thrall, they would do what they always did, and seek to possess as many people as they could.

He didn't care that he would not be there to move among them and bring the word of God's Brother. Norfolk had shown him that mistake. Conversion on an individual basis was totally impractical when dealing with planetary populations.

Quinn's duty, and that of the disciples, was the same as all priests'; they were simply to prepare the ground for God's Brother to walk upon, to build the temples and prepare the sacrament. It was He who would bring the final message, showing all the light.

The spaceplanes were only half of the scheme. Quinn was preparing to dispatch inter-orbit ships to the three derelict asteroids under the command of his most trusted followers. Those worthless rocks had now become a cornerstone in his plans to advance the Night.

\*

It was after midnight when Quinn returned to the tunnel. This time he was by himself. He stood motionless under the arching entrance for a full minute, allowing whoever was there to notice him. Then he raised a hand, and fired a single bolt of white fire at the electrical cable which ran along the crest of the tunnel. All the light-panels went out.

'Now we will know which of us is the master of darkness,' he shouted into the black air. He searched with his mind alone as he walked forwards, aware of the rock as an insubstantial pale grey tube around him. It was all that existed in a blank universe.

Feeble zephyrs of cold air rustled his robe. While out on the very cusp of perception, a tiny buzz increased; similar to the Babel of the beyond, but so much weaker.

He experienced no fright, nor even curiosity at confirming such an alien phenomenon existed. The Lords who battled for the heart of the universe and its denizens worked in ways he could never understand. All he had was his strength, and the knowledge that he knew himself. He would never quail, no matter what.

'I got you now, fuckers,' Quinn whispered back at the tremulous voices.

As if in response, the air grew colder, its churning stronger. He concentrated hard, trying to focus his eldritch sight on the air currents themselves. Elusive, twisting strands; they were hard for his mind to grasp. But he persisted, seeking out the points where heat was draining out of the gas molecules.

As he delved further and further into the convoluted waves of energy a tide of light began to thicken in the air around him, sending faint streaks of colour dancing across the tunnel. It was as if the atmosphere's atoms had expanded into vast vacuous blobs, rushing around each other in frantic motion. When he slashed at one of the gliding luminescent baubles, his hand was a matt-black shape that passed clean through the hazy apparition. His fingers closed, snatching at nothing.

The misty glowing ball changed direction, ploughing through the others of its kind, rushing away from Quinn.

'Come back!' Quinn bellowed in fury, and let loose a blast of white fire in the direction it had gone. The aerial swell of colour shrank back from the bolt of energy.

Quinn saw them then, people huddled together in the darkness of the tunnel. Illuminated by the energistic discharge, they had dour frightened faces. All of them were staring at him.

The energy bolt vanished, and with it the vision. Quinn gaped at the nebulous shoal which bobbled in agitation. They were flowing away from him steadily, picking up speed.

He thought he knew what they were then. A whole group of possessed who had discovered how to make themselves invisible. His own energistic power began to boil through his body, mimicking the patterns inside the effervescent air. It was inordinately difficult, requiring almost his entire strength. As the energy crackled round him in the novel formation he realized what was happening. This was an effect similar to the one sought by the wild possessed on their quest to escape this universe, forcing open one of the innumerable chinks in quantum reality.

Quinn persevered, exerting himself fully, clawing at the elusive opening. After all, if they could do it, he, the chosen one, could achieve the same state. He hurried after the fleeing spectres, down the tunnel to the cavity where the bomb had been placed. The very last thing he could allow was a whole group of souls out of his control or sight.

His emergence into the new realm was gradual. The shadowy outlines of matter which his mind perceived began to take on more substance, becoming less translucent. His skin tingled, as if he was passing through a membrane of static. Then he was there. Weight was different, his body felt as if it was lighter than a drop of rain. He realized he wasn't breathing. His heart had stopped, too. Though somehow his body still functioned. Sheer will-power, he supposed.

He walked into the cavity to find them all, maybe a couple of hundred people; men, women, and children. A large knot were gathered round the fusion bomb; if it wasn't for their blatant dismay they could have been praying to it. They were turning to face him; a collective fearful gasp went up. Children were clutched to their parents. Several held up shaking hands to ward him off.

'Peekaboo,' Quinn said. 'I see you, arseholes.'

There was something wrong, something different between him and them. His own body glowed from the energistic power he was exerting, an image of vigour. They, by contrast, were uniformly pallid, almost monochrome. Wasted.

'Nice try,' he told them. 'But there's nowhere you can hide from God's Brother. Now I want you to all come back to reality with me. I won't be too hard; I've learned a useful trick tonight.' He fixed his eyes on a teenage lad with flowing hair, and smiled.

**901**

The lad shook his head. 'We can't return,' he stammered.

Quinn took five fast steps forward, and made a grab for the lad's arm. His fingers didn't exactly connect, but they did slow down as they passed through the sleeve. The lad's arm suddenly flared with brilliant colour, and he screeched in shock, stumbling backwards. 'Don't,' he pleaded. 'Please, Quinn. It hurts.'

Quinn studied his pain-furrowed face, rather enjoying the sight. 'So you know my name, then.'

'Yes. We saw you arrive. Please leave us alone. We can't harm you.'

Quinn prowled along the front rank of the cowed group, looking at each of them as they pressed together. All of them shared the same dejection, few could meet his gaze. 'You mean you were like this when I came here?'

'Yes,' the lad replied.

'How? I was the first to bring the possessed here. What the fuck are you?'

'We're . . .' He glanced round at his peers for permission. 'We're ghosts.'

\*

The hotel suite was two storeys from the ground, which gave it a gravity field roughly a fifth of that which Louise was used to on Norfolk. She found it even more awkward than free fall. Every movement had to be well thought out in advance. Genevieve and Fletcher didn't much care for it either.

And then there was the air, or rather the lack of it. Both of Phobos's biosphere caverns were maintained at a low pressure. It was an intermediate stage, double that of Mars to help people en route to the planet to acclimatize themselves. Louise was glad she wasn't going down to the surface, each breath was a real effort to suck enough oxygen down into her lungs.

But the asteroid was a visual thrill – once she got used to the ground curving up over her head. The balcony gave them an excellent view across the parkland and fields. She would have loved to walk through the forests, many of the trees were centuries old. Their dignity reassured her, making the worldlet seem less artificial. From where she stood on the balcony she could see several cedars, their distinctive layered grey-green boughs standing out against the more verdant foliage. There had been no time for such leisurely activities, though. As soon as they'd left the *Far Realm*, Endron had booked them in here (though it was her money which paid for the suite). Then they'd been out shopping. She thought she would enjoy that, but unfortunately Phobos was nothing like Norwich. There were none of the city's department stores and exclusive boutiques. Their clothes had all come from the SII general merchandise depository which was half shop, half warehouse, but of course none of them fitted her or Gen. Their bodies were a completely different shape to the asteroid's Martian and Lunar residents. Everything they chose had to be made up. After that had come processor blocks (everyone in the Confederation used them, Endron explained, certainly travellers). Genevieve had plumped for one with a high-wattage AV projector and went on to load it with over fifty games from the depository's central memory core. Louise bought herself a block which could control the medical nanonic package round her wrist, allowing her to monitor her own physiological state.

Equipped and appearing like any normal visiting Confederation citizen, Louise had then accompanied Endron to the hostelries frequented by spaceship crews. It was a rerun of her attempts to buy passage off Norfolk; but this time she had some experience in the matter, and Endron knew his way around Phobos. Between them they took a mere two hours to find the *Jamrana*, an inter-orbit cargo ship bound for Earth, and agree a price for Louise and the others.

That just left the passports.

Louise dressed herself in a tartan skirt (with stiffened fabric to stop it dancing up in the low gravity), black leggings, and a green polo-neck top. Clothes were the same as computers, she thought; after using the *Far Realm*'s flight computer she could never go back to the stupid keyboard-operated terminals on Norfolk, and now she had a million styles of dress available, none of them shaped by absurd concepts of what was *appropriate*...

She went out into the lounge. Genevieve was in her bedroom, the thin sounds of music and muffled dialogue leaking through the closed door as yet another game was run through her processor block. Louise didn't strictly approve, but objecting now would seem churlish, and it did keep her out of mischief.

Fletcher was sitting on one of the three powder-blue leather settees which made up the lounge's conversation area. He was sitting with his back to the glass window. Louise glanced at him, then the view which he was ignoring.

'I know, my lady,' he said quietly. 'You believe me foolish. After all, I have undertaken a voyage between the stars themselves, in a ship where I swam through the air with the grace of a fish in the ocean.'

'There are stranger things in the universe than asteroid settlements,' she said sympathetically.

'As ever, you are right. I wish I could understand why the ground above us doesn't fall down to bury us. It is ungodly, a defiance of the natural order.'

'It's only centrifugal force. Do you want to access the educational text again?'

He gave her an ironic smile. 'The one which the teachers of this age have prepared for ten-year-old children? I think I will spare myself repeated humiliation, my lady Louise.'

She glanced at her gold watch, which was almost the last surviving personal item from Norfolk. 'Endron should be here in a minute. We'll be able to leave Phobos in a few hours.'

'I do not relish our parting, lady.'

It was the one topic which she had never mentioned since

the day when they had flown up to the *Far Realm*. 'You are still intent on going to go down to Earth, then?'

'Aye, I am. Though in my heart I fear what awaits me there, I will not shirk from the task I have found for my new body. Quinn must be thwarted.'

'He's probably there already. Goodness, by the time we reach the O'Neill Halo all of Earth could be possessed.'

'Even if I knew that beyond all doubt, I would still not allow myself to turn back. I am truly sorry, lady Louise, but my course is set. But do not worry yourself unduly, I will stay with you until you have found passage to Tranquillity. And I will make sure that there are no possessed on your vessel before it casts off.'

'I wasn't trying to stop you, Fletcher. I think I'm a little fearful of your integrity. People in this age always seem to put themselves first. I do.'

'You put your baby first, dearest Louise. Of that resolution, I am in awe. It is my one regret that by embarking on my own reckless venture I will in all likelihood never now meet your beau, this Joshua of whom you speak. I would dearly like to see the man worthy of your love, he must be a prince among men.'

'Joshua isn't a prince. I know now he is nowhere near perfect. But ... he does have a few good points.' Her hands touched her belly. 'He'll be a good father.'

Their eyes met. Louise didn't think she had ever seen so much loneliness before. In all the history texts they'd reviewed, he had always taken care to avoid any which might have told him what became of the family he'd left behind on Pitcairn Island.

It would have been so very easy for her to sit beside him and put her arms round him. Surely a person so alone deserved some comfort? What made her emotions worse was that she knew he could see her uncertainty.

The door processor announced that Endron was waiting.

**905**

Louise made light of the moment with a chirpy smile, and went to fetch Genevieve from her room.

'Do we all have to go?' a reticent Genevieve asked Endron. 'I'd reached the third strata in Skycastles. The winged horses were coming to rescue the princess.'

'She'll still be there when we get back,' Louise said. 'You can play it on the ship.'

'He needs you there for a full image scan,' Endron said. 'No way out of it, I'm afraid.'

Genevieve looked thoroughly disgusted. 'All right.'

Endron led them along one of the public halls. Louise was slowly mastering the art of walking in the asteroid's effete gravity field. Nothing you could do to stop yourself leaving the ground at each step; so push strongly with your toes, angling them to project you along a flat trajectory. She knew she'd never be as fluid as the Martians, no matter how much practice she had.

'I wanted to ask you,' Louise said as they slid into a lift. 'If you're all Communists, how can the *Far Realm*'s crew sell Norfolk Tears here?'

'Why shouldn't we? It's one of the perks of being a crew-member. The only thing we don't like about bringing it in is paying import duty. And so far we haven't actually done that.'

'But doesn't everybody own everything anyway? Why should they pay for it?'

'You're thinking of super-orthodox Communism. People here retain their own property and money. No society could survive without that concept; you have to have something to show for your work at the end of the day. That's human nature.'

'So you have landowners on Mars as well?'

Endron chuckled. 'I don't mean that sort of property. We only retain personal items. Things like apartments are the property of the state; after all, the state pays for them. Farming collectives are allocated their land.'

'And you accept that?'

'Yes. Because it works. The state has enormous power and wealth, but we vote on how it's used. We're dependent on it, and control it at the same time. We're also very proud of it. No other culture or ideology would ever have been able to terraform a planet. Mars has absorbed our nation's total wealth for five centuries. Offworlders have no idea of the level of commitment that requires.'

'That's because I don't understand why you did it.'

'We were trapped by history. Our ancestors modified their bodies to live in a Lunar gravity field before the ZTT drive was built. They could have sent their children to settle countless terracompatible worlds, but then those children would have needed geneering to adapt them back to the human "norm". Parent and child would have been parted at birth; they wouldn't have been descendants, just fosterlings in an alien environment. So we decided to make ourselves a world of our own.'

'If I have followed this discourse correctly,' Fletcher said, 'you have spent five centuries turning Mars from a desert to a garden?'

'That's right.'

'Are you really so powerful that you can rival Our Lord's handiwork?'

'I believe He only took six days. We've got a long way to go yet before we equal that. Not that we'll ever do it again.'

'Is the whole Lunar nation emigrating here now?' Louise asked, anxious to halt Fletcher's queries. She had caught Endron giving him puzzled glances at odd times during the voyage. It was something to watch out for; she was used to his naivety, thinking little of it. Others were not so generous.

'That was the idea. But now it's happened, the majority of those living in the Lunar cities are reluctant to leave. Those who do come here to settle are mostly the younger generation. So the shift is very gradual.'

'Will you live on Mars once you've finished flying starships?'

'I was born in Phobos; I find skies unnatural. Two of my children live in Thoth City. I visit when I can, but I don't think I would fit in down there anyway. After all this time, our nation is finally beginning to change. Not very swiftly, but it's there, it's happening.'

'How? How can Communism change?'

'Money, of course. Now the terraforming project no longer absorbs every single fuseodollar earned by our state industries, there is more cash starting to seep into the economy. The younger generation adore their imported AV blocks and MF albums and clothes, they are placing so much value on these status symbols, ignoring our own nation's products purely for the sake of difference, which they see as originality. And they have a whole planet to range over; some of us actually worry that they might walk off into the countryside and reject us totally. Who knows? Not that I'd mind if they do discard our tenets. After all, it is their world. We built it so they could know its freedom. Trying to impose the old restrictions on them would be the purest folly. Social evolution is vital if any ethnic-nationhood is to survive; and five centuries is a long time to remain static.'

'So if people did claim land for themselves, you wouldn't try to confiscate it back?'

'Confiscate? You say that with some malice. Is that what the Communists on your world say they're going to do?'

'Yes, they want to redistribute Norfolk's wealth fairly.'

'Well, tell them from me, it won't work. All they'll ever do is cause more strife if they try and change things now. You cannot impose ideologies on people who do not embrace them wholeheartedly. The Lunar nation functions because it was planned that way from the moment the cities gained independence from the companies. It's the same concept as Norfolk, the difference being your founders chose to write a pastoral constitution. Communism works here because everybody supports it, and the net allowed us to eliminate most forms of corruption within the civil service and local governing councils that plagued most earlier attempts. If people don't like it, they leave rather than try and wreck it for everyone else. Isn't that what happens on Norfolk?'

Louise thought back to what Carmitha had said. 'It's difficult for the Land Union people. Starflight is expensive.'

'I suppose so. We're lucky here, the O'Neill Halo takes all our malcontents, some asteroids have entire low-gee levels populated by Lunar émigrés. Our government will even buy your ticket for you. Perhaps you should try that on Norfolk. The whole point of the Confederation's diversity is that it provides every kind of ethnic culture possible. There's no real need for internal conflict.'

'That's a nice idea. I ought to mention it to Daddy when I get back. I'm sure a one-way starship ticket would be cheaper than keeping someone at the Arctic work camps.'

'Why tell your father? Why not campaign for it yourself?'

'Nobody would listen to me.'

'You won't be your age for ever.'

'I meant because I'm a girl.'

Endron gave her a mystified frown. 'I see. Perhaps that would be a better issue to campaign about. You'd have half of the population on your side from day one.'

Louise managed an uncomfortable smile. She didn't like having to defend her home world from sarcasm, people should show more courtesy. The trouble was, she found it hard to defend some of Norfolk's customs.

Endron took them to one of the lowest habitation levels, a broad service corridor which led away from the biosphere cavern deep into the asteroid's interior. It was bare rock, with one wall made up from stacked layers of cable and piping. The floor was slightly concave, and very smooth. Louise wondered how old it must be for people's feet to have worn it down.

They reached a wide olive-green metal door, and Endron datavised a code at its processor. Nothing happened. He had to datavise the code another two times before it opened. Louise didn't dare risk a glance at Fletcher.

Inside was a cathedral-sized hall filled with three rows of high-voltage electrical transformers. Great loops of thick black cabling emerged from holes high up in the walls, stretching over the aisles in a complicated weave that linked them to the fat grey-ribbed cylinders. There was a strong tang of ozone in the air.

A flight of metal stairs pinned against the rear wall led up to a small maintenance manager's office cut into the rock. Two narrow windows looked down on the central aisle as they walked towards it, the outline of a man just visible inside. Fletcher's alarm at the power humming savagely all around them was clear in the sweat on his forehead and hands, his small, precisely controlled steps.

The office had a large desk with a computer terminal nearly as primitive as the models Louise used on Norfolk. A screen took up most of the back wall, its lucidly coloured symbols displaying the settlement's power grid.

There was a Martian waiting for them inside; a man with very long snow-white hair brushed back neatly, and a bright orange silk suit worn in conjunction with a midnight-black shirt. He carried a slim, featureless grey case in his left hand.

Faurax didn't know what to make of his three new clients at all; if they hadn't been with Endron he wouldn't even have let them into the office. These were not the times to dabble in his usual sidelines. Thanks to the current Confederation crisis, the Phobos police were becoming quite unreasonable about security procedures.

'If you don't mind me asking,' he said after Endron had introduced everybody, 'why haven't you got your own passports?'

'We had to leave Norfolk very quickly,' Louise said. 'The possessed were sweeping through the city. There was no time to apply to the Foreign Office for passports. Although there's no reason why we shouldn't have been issued with them, we don't have criminal records or anything like that.'

It even sounded reasonable. And Faurax could guess the kind of financial package which the *Far Realm*'s crew would engineer concerning their passage. Nobody wanted questions at this stage.

'You must understand,' he said, 'I had to undertake a considerable amount of research to obtain the Norfolk government's authentication codes.'

'How much?' Louise asked.

'Five thousand fuseodollars. Each.'

'Very well.'

She didn't even sound surprised, let alone shocked. Which tweaked Faurax's curiosity; he would have dearly liked to ask Endron who she was. The call he'd got from Tilia setting up the meeting had been very sparse on detail.

'Good,' he said, and put his case on the desk, datavising a code at it. The upper surface flowed apart, revealing a couple of processor blocks and several fleks. He picked up one of the fleks, which was embossed with a gold lion: Norfolk's national symbol. 'Here we are. I loaded in all the information Tilia gave me; name, where you live, age, that kind of thing. All we need now is an image and a full body biolectric scan.'

'What do we have to do?' Louise asked.

'First, I'm afraid, is the money.'

She gave a hollow laugh, and took a Jovian Bank credit disk from her small shoulder bag. Once the money had been shunted over to Faurax's disk, he said: 'Remember not to wear these clothes when you go through the Halo's immigration. These images were supposedly taken on Norfolk before you left, and the clothes are new. In fact, I'd advise dumping them altogether.'

'We'll do that,' Louise said.

'OK.' He slotted the first flek into his processor block, and read the screen. 'Genevieve Kavanagh?'

The little girl smiled brightly.

'Stand over there, dear, away from the door.'

She did as he asked, giving the sensor lens a solemn stare. After he'd got the visual image filed, he used the second processor block to sweep her so he could record her biolectric pattern. Both files were loaded into her passport, encrypted with Norfolk's authentication code. 'Don't lose it,' he said, and dropped the flek into her hand.

Louise was next. Faurax found himself wishing she was a Martian girl. She had a beautiful face, it was just her body which was so alien.

Fletcher's image went straight into his passport flek. Then Faurax ran the biolectric sensor over him. Frowned at the display. Ran a second scan. It took a long time for his chilly disquiet to give way into full-blown consternation. He gagged, head jerking up from the block to stare at Fletcher. 'You're a—' His neural nanonics crashed, preventing him from data-vising any alarm. The air solidified in front of his eyes; he actually saw it flowing like a dense heat shiver, contracting into a ten-centimetre sphere. It hit him full in the face. He heard the bone in his nose break before he lost consciousness.

Genevieve squealed in shock as Faurax went crashing to the floor, blood flowing swiftly from his nose .

Endron looked at Fletcher in total shock, too numb to move. His neural nanonics had shut down, and the office light-panel was flickering in an epileptic rhythm. 'Oh my God. No! Not you.' He glanced at the door, gauging his chances.

'Do not try to run, sir,' Fletcher said sternly. 'I will do whatever I must to protect these ladies.'

'Oh, Fletcher,' Louise groaned in dismay. 'We were almost there.'

'His device exposed my nature, my lady. I could do naught else.'

Genevieve ran over to Fletcher and hugged him tightly round his waist. He patted her head lightly.

'Now what are we going to do?' Louise asked.

'Not you as well?' Endron bewailed.

'I'm not possessed,' she said with indignant heat.

'Then what . . . ?'

'Fletcher has been protecting us from the possessed. You don't think I could stand against them by myself, do you?'

'But he's one of them.'

'One of whom, sir? Many men are murderers and brigands, does that make all of us so?'

'You can't apply that argument. You're a possessed. You're the enemy.'

'Yet, sir, I do not consider myself to be your enemy. My only crime, so it sounds, is that I have died.'

'And come back! You have stolen that man's body. Your kind want to do the same to mine and everyone else's.'

'What would you have us do? I am not so valiant that I can resist this release from the torture of the beyond. Perhaps, sir, you see such weakness as my true crime. If so, I plead guilty to that ignominy. Yet know you this, I would grasp at such an escape every time it is offered, though I know it to be the most immoral of thefts.'

'He saved us,' Genevieve protested hotly. 'Quinn Dexter was going to do truly beastly things to me and Louise. Fletcher stopped him. No one else could. He's not a bad man; you shouldn't say he is. And I won't let you do anything horrid to him. I don't want him to have to go back there into beyond.' She hugged Fletcher tighter.

'All right,' Endron said. 'Maybe you're not like the Capone Organization, or the ones on Lalonde. But I can't let you walk round here. This is my home, damn it. Maybe it is unfair, and unkind that you suffered in the beyond. You're still a possessor, nothing changes that. We are opposed, it's fundamental to what we are.'

'Then you, sir, have a very pressing problem. For I am sworn to see these ladies to their destination in safety.'

'Wait,' Louise said. She turned to Endron. 'Nothing has changed. We still wish to leave Phobos, and you know Fletcher is not a danger to you or your people. You said so.'

Endron gestured at the crumpled form of Faurax. 'I can't,' he said desperately.

'If Fletcher opens your bodies to the souls in the beyond, who knows what the people who come through will be like,' Louise said. 'I don't think they will be as restrained as Fletcher, not if the ones I've encountered are anything to judge by. You would be the cause of Phobos falling to the possessed. Is that what you want?'

'What the hell do you think? You've backed me into a corner.'

'No, we haven't, there's an easy way out of this, for all of us.'

'What?'

'Help us, of course. You can finish recording Fletcher's passport for us, you can find a zero-tau pod for Faurax and keep him in it until this is all over. And you'll know for certain that we've gone and that your asteroid is safe.'

'This is insane. I don't trust you, and you'd be bloody stupid to trust me.'

'Not really,' she said. 'If you tell us you'll do it, Fletcher will know if you're telling us the truth. And once we're gone you still won't change your mind, because you could never explain away what you've done to the police.'

'You can read minds?' Endron's consternation had deepened.

'I will indeed know of any treachery which blackens your heart.'

'What do you intend to do once you reach Tranquillity?'

'Find my fiancé. Apart from that, we have no plans.'

Endron gave Faurax another fast appraisal. 'I don't think I have a lot of choice, do I? If you stop this electronic-warfare effect, I'll get a freight mechanoid to take Faurax to the *Far*

*Realm.* I can use one of the on-board zero-tau pods without anyone asking questions. Lord knows what I'll say when this is over. They'll just fling me out of an airlock, I expect.'

'You're saving your world,' Louise said. 'You'll be a hero.'

'Somehow, I doubt that.'

\*

The cave went a long way back into the polyp cliff, which allowed Dariat to light a fire without having to worry about it being spotted. He'd chosen the beach at the foot of the endcap as today's refuge. Surely here at least he and Tatiana would be safe? There were no bridges over the circumfluous reservoir. If Bonney came for them she'd have to use either a boat or one of the tube carriages (however unlikely that was). Which meant that for once they'd have a decent warning.

The hunter's ability to get close before either he or Rubra located her was unnerving. Even Rubra seemed genuinely concerned by it. Dariat never could understand how she ever located them in the first place. But locate them she did. There hadn't been a day since he met Tatiana when Bonney hadn't come after them.

His one guess was that her perception ability was far greater than anyone else's, allowing her to see the minds of everybody in the habitat. If so, the distance was extraordinary; he couldn't feel anything beyond a kilometre at the most, and ten metres of solid polyp blocked him completely.

Tatiana finished gutting the pair of trout she'd caught, and wrapped them in foil. Both were slipped into the shallow hole below the fire. 'They ought to be done in about half an hour,' she said.

He smiled blankly, remembering the fires he and Anastasia had made, the meals she had prepared for him. Campfire cooking was an outlandish concept to him then. Used to regulated heat-inducted sachets, he was always impressed by the cuisine she produced from such primitive arrangements.

'Did she ever say anything about me?' he asked.

'Not much. I didn't see much of her after she set herself up as a mistress of Thoale. Besides which, I was discovering boys myself about then.' She gave a raucous laugh.

Apart from the physical resemblance, it was difficult to accept any other connection between Tatiana and Anastasia. It was inconceivable that his beautiful love would have ever grown into anything resembling this cheery, easygoing woman, with an overloud voice. Anastasia would have kept her quiet dignity, her sly humour, her generous spirit.

It was hard for him to feel much sympathy for Tatiana, and harder still to tolerate her behaviour, especially given their circumstances. He persisted, though, knowing that to desert her now would make him unworthy, a betrayal of his own one love.

Damn Rubra for knowing that.

'Whatever she did say, I'd appreciate you telling me.'

'OK. I suppose I owe you that at least.' She settled herself more comfortably into the thin sand, her bracelets tinkling softly. 'She said her new boy – that's you – was very different. She said you'd been hurt by Anstid since the day you were born, but that she could see the real person buried underneath all the pain and loneliness. She thought she could free you from his thrall. Strange, she really believed it; as if you were some sort of injured bird she'd rescued. I don't think she realized what a mistake she'd made. Not until the end. That was why she did it.'

'I am true to her. I always have been.'

'So I see. Thirty years' planning.' She whistled a single long note.

'I'm going to kill Anstid. I have the power now.'

Tatiana began to laugh, a big belly rumble that shook her loose cotton dress about. 'Ho, yes, I can see why she'd fall for you. All that sincerity and retention. Cupid tipped his arrows with a strong potion that day you two met.'

'Don't mock.'

Her laughter vanished in an instant. Then he could see the resemblance to Anastasia, the passion in her eyes. 'I would never mock my sister, Dariat. I pity her for the trick Tarrug played on her. She was too young to meet you, too damn young. If she'd had a few more years to gather wisdom, she would have seen you are beyond any possible salvation. But she was young, and stupid the way we all are at that age. She couldn't refuse the challenge to do good, to bring a little light into your prison. When you get to my age, you give lost causes a wide passage.'

'I am not lost, not to Chi-ri, not to Thoale. I will slay Anstid. And that is thanks to Anastasia, she broke that lord's spell over me.'

'Oh dear, oh dear, listen to him. Stop reading the words, Dariat, learn with your heart. Just because she told you the names of our Lords and Ladies doesn't mean you know them. You won't kill Anstid. Rubra is not a realm Lord, he's a screwed-up old memory pattern. Sure, his bananas mind makes him bitter and vindictive, which is an aspect of Anstid, but he's not the real thing. Hatred isn't going to vanish from the universe just because you nuke a habitat. You can see that, can't you?'

**Yes, go on, boy, answer the question. I'm interested.**

**Fuck off!**

**Pity you never went to university; the old school of hard knocks is never quite enough when you need to stand up for yourself in the intellectual debating arena.**

Dariat made an effort to calm himself, aware of the little worms of light scurrying over his clothing. A sheepish grin unfurled on his lips. 'Yes, I can see that. Besides, without hatred you could never know how sweet love is. We need hatred.'

'That's more like it.' She started applauding. 'We'll make a Starbridge of you yet.'

'Too late for that. And I'm still going to nuke Rubra.'

'Not before I'm out of here, I hope.'

'I'll get you out.'

**Yeah, and whose help are you going to need for that?**

'How?' Tatiana asked.

'I'll be honest. I don't know. But I'll find a way. I owe you and Anastasia that much.'

**Bravo, Sir Galahad. In the meantime, three ships have arrived.**

**So?**

**So they're from New California, a frigate and two combat-capable traders. I think our current status quo might be changing.**

\*

The voidhawks on observation duty perceived the three Adamist starships emerge from their ZTT jump twelve thousand kilometres out from Valisk. As their thermo-dump panels, sensor clusters, and communication arrays deployed, the voidhawks started to pick up high-bandwidth microwave transmissions. The ships were beaming out news reports all over the Srinagar system, telling everyone who was interested how well the Organization was doing, and how New California was prospering. There were several long items on the possessed curing injuries and broken bones in the non-possessed.

The one thing the voidhawks couldn't intercept was the signal between the ships and Valisk. Whatever was said, it resulted in eight hellhawks arriving to escort the New California starships to the habitat's spaceport.

Alarmed by the implication of Capone extending his influence into the Srinagar system, Consensus requested Rubra monitor developments closely. For once, he wasn't inclined to argue.

\*

Kiera waited for Patricia Mangano at the end of the passageway which led up to the axial chamber three kilometres above her.

Without the tube carriages, every ascent and descent had to be on foot. Starting at the axial chamber, the passageway contained a ladder for the first kilometre, then gave way to a staircase for the final two as the curvature became more pronounced. It ended two kilometres above the base of the endcap, emerging from the polyp shell onto a shelf-like plateau which was reached by a switchback road.

Thankfully, similar plateaux around the endcap gave them admission to the docking ledge lounges. Which meant they'd all but stopped using the counter-rotating spaceport.

If Patricia was annoyed by the time and physical effort it took her to descend, it was hidden deeper than Kiera's perception was able to discern. Instead, when Capone's envoy emerged into the light, she smiled with a simple delight as she looked round. Kiera had to admit, the little plateau was an excellent vantage point. The distinct bands of colour which comprised Valisk's interior shone lucidly in the light-tube's relentless emission.

Patricia shielded her eyes with one hand as she gazed about the worldlet. 'Nothing anybody says can prepare you for this.'

'Didn't you have habitats in your time?' Kiera asked.

'Absolutely not. I'm strictly a twentieth-century gal. Al prefers us as his lieutenants, that way we understand each other better. Some modern types, I can only comprehend about one word in ten.'

'I'm from the twenty-fourth century myself. Never set foot on Earth.'

'Lucky you.'

Kiera gestured at the open-top truck parked at the end of the road. Bonney was sitting in the back seat, ever vigilant.

Kiera switched on the motor and began the drive down the road. 'I'll warn you from the start, anything you say in the open is overheard by Rubra. We think he tells the Edenists just about everything that goes on in here.'

'What I have to say is private,' Patricia said.

'I thought so. Don't worry, we have some clean rooms.'

*

It wasn't too difficult for Rubra to infiltrate the circular tower at the base of the northern endcap. He just needed to be careful. The possessed could always detect small animals like mice and bats, which were simply blasted by a bolt of white fire. So he had to resort to more unusual servitors.

Deep in the birthing caverns of the southern endcap, incubators were used to nurture insects whose DNA templates had been stored unused since the time when Valisk was germinated. Centipedes and bees began to emerge, each one affinity controlled by a subroutine.

The bees flew straight out into the main cavern, where they hovered and loitered among all the temporary camps set up round the starscraper lobbies. Coverage wasn't perfect, but they provided him with a great deal of information about what went on inside the tents and cottages, where his usual perception was blocked.

The centipedes were carried aloft by birds, to be deposited on the roof of the tower and other substantial buildings. Like the spiders which the Edenist Intelligence agency used to infiltrate their observation targets, they scuttled along conditioning ducts and cable conduits, hiding just behind grilles and sockets where they could scrutinize the interior.

Their deployment allowed Rubra and the Kohistan Consensus to watch as Kiera led Patricia Mangano into Magellanic Itg's boardroom. Patricia had one assistant with her, while Kiera was accompanied by Bonney and Stanyon. No one else from Valisk's new ruling council had been invited.

'What happened?' Patricia asked after she had claimed a chair at the big table.

'In what respect?' Kiera replied, cautiously.

'Come on. You've got your hellhawks flitting about the

Confederation with impunity to bring back warm bodies. And when they get here, the habitat looks like it's a Third World refugee camp left over from my own century. You're living in the Iron Age here. It doesn't make any sense. Bitek is the one technology that keeps working around us. You should be lording it up in the starscraper apartments.'

'Rubra happened,' Kiera said bitterly. 'He's still in the neural strata. The one expert we had on affinity who could possibly remove him has ... failed. It means we've got to go through the starscrapers a centimetre at a time to make them safe. We're getting there. It'll take time, but we've got eternity, after all.'

'You could leave.'

'I don't think so.'

Patricia lounged back, grinning. 'Ah, right. That would mean evacuating to a planet. How would you keep your position and authority there?'

'The same way Capone does. People need governments, they need organizing. We're a very socially oriented race.'

'So why didn't you?'

'We're doing all right here. Have you really come all this way just to take cheap shots?'

'Not at all. I'm here to offer you a deal.'

'Yes?'

'Antimatter in return for your hellhawks.'

Kiera glanced at Bonney and Stanyon; the latter's face was alive with interest. 'What exactly do you think we can do with antimatter?'

'The same as us,' Patricia said. 'Blow Srinagar's SD network clean to hell. Then you'll be able to get off this dump. The planet will be wide open to you. And as you'll be running the invasion, you'll be able to shape whatever society springs up among the possessed down there. That's the way it works for the Organization. We begin it, we rule it. Whether it works here depends on how good you are. Capone is the best.'

'But not perfect.'

'You have your problems, we have ours. The Edenist voidhawks are causing a lot of disruption to our fleet activities. We need the hellhawks to deal with them. Their distortion fields can locate the stealth bombs being flung at us.'

'Interesting proposition.'

'Don't try and bargain, please. That would be insulting. We have an irritant; you have a potential disaster looming.'

'If you don't take too much offence at the question, I'd like to know how much antimatter you'll deliver.'

'As much as it takes, and the ships to deploy them, providing you can keep your end. How many hellhawks can you offer?'

'We have several out collecting Deadnight kids. But I can probably let you have seventy.'

'And you can keep them under control, make them follow orders?'

'Oh, yes.'

'How?'

Kiera gloated. 'It's not something you'll ever be able to duplicate. We can give the possessing souls human bodies without having to return them to the beyond first.'

'Smart. So do we have a deal?'

'Not with you. I'll travel to New California myself and talk to Capone. That way we'll both know how much we can trust the other.'

*

Kiera hung back after Patricia left the boardroom. 'This changes everything,' she said to Bonney. 'Even if we don't get enough antimatter to knock over Srinagar, it'll give us the deterrence to prevent another voidhawk attack.'

'It looks like it. Do you think Capone is on the level?'

'I'm not sure. He must need the hellhawks pretty badly, or he wouldn't have offered us the antimatter. Even if he's got a production station, it won't exactly be plentiful.'

'You want me to come with you?'

'No.' The tip of her tongue licked over her lips, a fast movement by a lash of forked flesh. 'We're either going to be leaving here for Srinagar, or I'll deal with Capone to provide us with enough bodies to fill the habitat. Either way, we won't be needing that shit Dariat any more. See to it.'

'You bet.'

**Can you stop the hellhawks from leaving?** Rubra asked.

**No,** the Kohistan Consensus said. **Not seventy of them. They are still armed with a considerable number of conventional combat wasps.**

**Bugger.**

**If Kiera does acquire antimatter combat wasps from Capone, we don't think we will be able to provide an adequate level of reinforcement to Srinagar's Strategic Defence network. The planet may fall to her.**

**Then call in the Confederation Navy. Srinagar's been paying its taxes, hasn't it?**

**Yes. But there is no guarantee the Navy will respond. Its resources are being deployed over a wide area.**

**Then call Jupiter. They're bound to have spare squadrons.**

**We will see what can be done.**

**Do that. In the meantime, there are some important decisions to be taken. By me and Dariat both. And I don't think Bonney Lewin is going to give us much more time.**

\*

Erick was sure that the explosion, followed by the capsule's equally violent stabilization manoeuvre, had torn loose some of his medical nanonic packages. He could feel peculiar lines of pressure building up under the SII suit, and convinced himself it was fluid leakage. Blood or artificial tissue nutrient from the packages and their supplements, he wasn't sure which. Over half of them no longer responded to his datavises.

At least it meant they couldn't contribute to the medical

program's dire pronouncements on his current physiological state. His right arm wouldn't respond to any nerve impulses at all, nor was he receiving any sensation from it. The only positive factor was a confirmation that blood was still circulating inside the new muscles and artificial tissue.

There wasn't much he could do to rectify the situation. The capsule's reserve electron matrices didn't have enough power to activate the internal life-support system. The thin atmosphere was already ten degrees below zero, and falling rapidly. Which meant he was unable to take the suit off and replace the nanonic packages. And just to twist the knife, an emergency survival gear locker containing fresh medical nanonic packages had popped open in the ceiling above him.

Back-up lighting had come on, casting a weak pale-blue glow across the compartment. Frost was forming on most of the surfaces, gradually obscuring the few remaining active holoscreen displays. Various pieces of refuse had been jolted loose from their nesting places to twirl whimsically through the air, throwing avian-style shadows across the acceleration couches.

Potentially the most troubling problem was the intermittent drop-outs which the flight computer's datavises were suffering from. Erick wasn't entirely sure he could trust its status display. It still responded to simple commands, though.

With his personal situation stable for a moment, he instructed the capsule's sensors to deploy. Three of the five responded, pistonlike tubes sliding up out of the nultherm foam coating. They began to scan round.

Astrogration programs slowly correlated the surrounding starfield. If they were working correctly, then the *Tigara* had emerged approximately fifty million kilometres from the coordinate he was aiming for. Ngeuni was only an unremarkable blue-green star to one side of the glaring A2 primary.

He wasn't sure if they would pick up the capsule's distress beacon. Stage-one colonies did not have the most sophisticated communication satellites. When he instructed the capsule's phased-array antenna to focus on the distant planet, it didn't acknowledge. He repeated the instruction, and there was still no activity.

The flight computer ran a diagnostic, which gave him a System Unviable code. Without actually going outside to examine it, there was no way of telling what was wrong.

Alone.

Cut off.

Fifty million kilometres from possible rescue.

Light-years from where he desperately needed to be.

All that was left for him now was to wait. He began switching off every piece of equipment apart from the attitude rockets, the guidance system which drove them, and the computer itself. Judging by the frequency of the thruster firings, the capsule was venting something. The last diagnostic sweep before he shut down the internal sensors couldn't pinpoint what it was.

After he'd reduced the power drain to a minimum, he pressed the deactivation switch for his restraint webbing. Even that seemed reluctant to work, taking a long time to fold back below the side of the cushioning. At this movement, levering himself up from the couch, fluid stirred across his abdomen. He found that by moving very slowly, the effect (and perhaps the harm) was moderated.

Training took over, and he began to index the emergency gear which had deployed from the ceiling. That was when the emotional shock hammered him. He suddenly found himself shaking badly as he clung to a four-person programmable silicon dinghy.

Indexing his position! Like a good little first-year cadet.

A broken laugh bubbled round the SII suit's respirator tube. The glossy black silicon covering his eyes turned permeable to vent the salty fluid burning his squeezed-up eyelids.

Never in his life had he felt so utterly helpless. Even when the possessed were boarding the *Villeneuve's Revenge* he'd been able to do something. Fight back, hit them. Orbiting above New California with the Organization poised to obliterate them at the first false move, he'd been able to store most of the sensor images. There had always been something, some way of being positive.

Now he was humiliatingly aware of his mind crumbling away in mimicry of his tattered old body. Fear had risen to consume him, flowing swiftly out of the dark corners of the bridge. It produced a pain in his head far worse than any physical injury ever could.

Those muscles which still functioned disobeyed any lingering wishes he might have, leaving him ignominiously barnacled to the dinghy. Every last reserve of determination and resolve had been exhausted. Not even the ubiquitous programs could shore up his mentality any more.

Too weak to continue living, too frightened to die: Erick Thakrar had come to the end of the line.

\*

Eight kilometres west of Stonygate, Cochrane tooted the horn on the Karmic Crusader bus, and turned off the road. The other three vehicles in the convoy jounced over the grass verge and came to a halt behind it.

'Yo, dudettes,' Cochrane yelled back to the juvenile rioters clambering over the seats. 'Time out for like the big darkness.' He pressed the red button on the dash, and the doors hissed open. Kids poured out like a dam burst.

Cochrane put his purple glasses back on and climbed down out of the cab. Stephanie and Moyo walked over to him, arm in arm. 'Good place,' she said. The convoy had halted at the head of a gentle valley which was completely roofed over by the rumbling blanket of crimson cloud, rendering the mountain peaks invisible.

'This whole righteous road trip is one major groove.'

'Right.'

He materialized a fat reefer. 'Hit?'

'No, thanks. I'd better see about cooking them some supper.'

'That's cool. I can't psych out any hostile vibes in this locale. I'll like keep watch, make sure the nazgul aren't circling overhead.'

'You do that.' Stephanie smiled fondly at him and went to the back of the bus, where the big luggage hold was. Moyo started pulling out the cooking gear.

'We should manage to reach Chainbridge by tomorrow evening,' he said.

'Yes. This isn't quite what I expected when we started out, you know.'

'Predictability is boring.' He put a big electric camping grill on the ground, adjusting the aluminium legs to make it level. 'Besides, I think it's worked out for the best.'

Stephanie glanced round the improvised campsite, nodding approval; nearly sixty children were scampering around the parked vehicles. What had started off as a private mission to help a handful of lost children had rapidly snowballed.

Four times during the first day they had been stopped by residents who had told them where non-possessed children were lurking. On the second day there were over twenty children packed on board; that was when Tina Sudol had volunteered to come with them. Rana and McPhee joined up on the third day, adding another bus.

Now there were four vehicles, and eight possessed adults. They were no longer making a straight dash for the border at the top of Mortonridge. It was more of a zigzag route, visiting as many towns as they could to pick up children. Ekelund's people, who had evolved into the closest thing to a government on Mortonridge, maintained the communication net between the larger towns, albeit with a considerably reduced bit capacity than previously. News of Stephanie's progress had spread widely. Children were already waiting for the buses when they reached some towns, on a couple of occasions dressed smartly and given packed lunches by the possessed who had taken care of them. They had borne witness to some very tearful partings.

After the children had eaten and washed and been settled in their tents, Cochrane and Franklin Quigley sliced branches off a tree and piled them up to form a proper campfire. The adults came to sit round it, enjoying the yellow light flaring out to repel the clouds' incessant claret illumination.

'I think we should forget going back to a town when we're done with the kids,' McPhee said. 'All of us get along OK, we should try a farm. The towns are starting to run out of food now. We could grow some and sell it to them. That would give us something to do.'

'He's been back a whole week, and he's already bored,' Franklin Quigley grunted.

'Bor-ing,' Cochrane said. He blew twin streams of smoke out of his nostrils. They spiralled through the air to jab at McPhee's nose like a cobra.

The giant Scot made a pass of his hand, and the smoke wilted, turning to tar and splattering on the ground. 'I'm not bored, but we have to do something. It makes sense to think ahead.'

'You might be right,' Stephanie said. 'I don't think I'd like to live in any of the towns we've passed through so far.'

'The way I see it,' said Moyo, 'is that the possessed are developing into two groups.'

'Please don't use that word,' Rana said. Sitting cross-legged next to the flamboyantly feminine Tina Sudol, Rana appeared fastidiously androgynous with her short hair and baggy blue sweater.

'What word?' Moyo asked.

'Possession. I find it offensive and prejudicial.'

'That's right, babe,' Cochrane chortled. 'We're not possessors, we're just like dimensionally disadvantaged.'

'Call our cross-continuum placement situation whatever

you wish,' she snapped back. 'You cannot alter the fact that the term is wholly derogatory. The Confederation's military industrial complex is using it to demonize us so they can justify increased spending on their armaments programmes.'

Stephanie pressed her face into Moyo's arm to smother her giggles.

'Come on, we're not exactly on the side of the saints,' Franklin observed.

'The perception of common morality is enforced entirely by the circumstances of male-dominated society. Our new and unique circumstances require us to re-evaluate that original morality. As there are clearly not enough living bodies to go around the human race, sensory ownership should be distributed on an equitable basis. It's no good the living protesting about us. We have as much right to sensory input as they do.'

Cochrane took the reefer from his mouth, and gave it a sad stare. 'Man, I wish I could manifest your trips.'

'You ignore him, darling,' Tina Sudol said to Rana. 'He's a perfect example of male brutality.'

'I suppose a fuck is out of the question tonight, then?'

Tina sucked in her cheeks theatrically as she glowered at the unrepentant hippy. 'I'm only interested in men.'

'And always have been,' McPhee said, in an unsubtle whisper.

Tina flounced her glossy, highlighted hair back with a manicured hand. 'You men are animals, all of you, simply rancid with hormones. No wonder I wanted to escape that prison of flesh I was in.'

'*The two groups*,' Moyo said, 'seem to be divided into those that stay put, like the café proprietors, and the restless ones – like us, I suppose, though we're an exception. They complement each other perfectly. The wanderers go around playing tourist, drinking down the sights and experiences. And wherever they go, they meet the stayers and tell them about their journeys. That way both types get what they want. Both of us exist to relish experience; some like to go out and find it, others like it brought to them.'

'You think that's what it's going to be like from now on?' McPhee asked.

'Yes. That's what we'll settle down into.'

'But for how long? Wanting to see and feel is just a reaction from the beyond. Once we've had our fill, human nature will come back. People want to settle down, have a family. Procreation is our biological imperative. And that's one thing we never can do. We will always be frustrated.'

'I'll like give it a try,' Cochrane said. 'Me and Tina can make babies in my tepee any time.'

Tina gave him a single disgusted look, and shuddered.

'But they wouldn't be yours,' McPhee said. 'That isn't your body, and it certainly isn't your DNA. You will never have a child again, not one of your own. That phase of our lives is over, it cannot be regained no matter how much of our energistic ability we expend.'

'You're also forgetting the third type walking amongst us,' Franklin said. 'The Ekelund type. And I do know her. I signed up with her for the first couple of days. She seemed to know what she was doing. We had "objectives" and "target assignments", and "command structures" – and God help anyone who disobeyed those Fascists. She's a straight power nut with a Napoleon complex. She's got her little army of wannabe toughs running round in combat fatigues thinking they're reborn Special Forces brigades. And they're going to keep sniping away at the Royal Marines over the border until the Princess gets so pissed with us she nukes Mortonridge down to the bedrock.'

'That situation won't last,' McPhee said. 'Give it a month, or a year, and the Confederation will fall. Don't you listen to the whispers in the beyond? Capone is getting his act together out there. It won't be long before the Organization fleet jumps to Ombey. Then there will be nobody left for Ekelund to fight, and her command structure will simply fade away. Nobody is going to do what she tells them for the rest of time.'

'I don't want to live for the rest of time,' Stephanie said. 'I really don't. That's almost as frightening as being trapped in the beyond. We're not made to live for ever, we can't handle it.'

'Lighten up, babe,' Cochrane said. 'I don't mind giving eternity a try; it's the flipside which is the real bummer.'

'We've been back a week, and Mortonridge is already falling apart. There's hardly any food left, nothing works properly—'

'Give it a chance,' Moyo said. 'We're all badly shocked, we don't know how to control this new power we've got, and the non-possessed want to hunt us down and fling us back. You can hardly expect instant civilization under those circumstances. We'll find a way to adjust. As soon as the rest of Ombey is possessed we'll take it out of this universe altogether. Once that happens, things will be different. You'll see; this is just an interim stage.' He put his arm round her as she leant into him. She kissed him lightly, mind shining with appreciation.

'Yo, love machines,' Cochrane said. 'So while you two screw like hot bunnies for the rest of the night, who's going into town to track down some food?'

\*

**Got a beacon**, Edwin announced. His mind was hot with triumph.

Around *Oenone*'s bridge the communal tension level reduced with a strong mental sigh. They had arrived above Ngeuni twenty minutes ago. Every sensor extended. The crew in alert status one. Weapons powered up. Ready for anything. To retrieve Thakrar. To fight possessed starships that had captured Thakrar.

And there had been nothing. No ships in orbit. No response

from the small development company advance camp on the planet.

*Oenone* accelerated into a high-polar orbit, and Edwin activated every sensor they had.

**It's very weak, some kind of capsule emergency signal. Definitely the *Tigara*'s identification code, though. The ship must have broken up.**

**Lock on to it, please,** Syrinx said. She was aware of the astrogration data from the sensors flooding into the bitek processor array. From that, she and *Oenone* understood exactly where the signal was in relation to themselves.

**Go.**

The voidhawk swallowed through a wormhole that barely had any internal length at all. Starlight blue-shifted slightly as it twisted into a tight rosette, kissing the hull then expanding. A life-support capsule was spinning idly ten kilometres in front of the terminus as *Oenone* shot out. Local space was smeared with scraps of debris from the *Tigara*'s violent end. Syrinx could feel the capsule's mass in her mind as it hung in *Oenone*'s distortion field. Sensors and communication dishes in the lower hull pods swung round to point at the dingy sphere.

**There's no response from the capsule,** Edwin said. **I'm registering some power circuits active in there, but they're very weak. And it's been venting its atmosphere.**

**Oxley, Serina, take the MSV over there,** Syrinx ordered. **Bring him back.**

*

*Oenone*'s crew watched through Serina's armour-suit sensors as she crept through the decks of the life-support capsule, searching for Captain Thakrar. It was a shambles inside, with equipment torn off bulkheads, hatches jammed, lockers broken open to send junk and old clothes floating free. The air had gone, allowing several pipes to burst and release globules of fluid, which had subsequently frozen solid. She had to use a high-powered fission cutter on the latches around the final hatch before she could worm her way into the bridge. At first she didn't even recognize the SII-suited figure clutching at one of the emergency supply cases on the ceiling. Granules of frost had solidified on him, as they had on every surface, glinting a dusty grey in the beams thrown out by her helmet lights. In his foetal position he looked like some kind of giant mummified larva.

At least he got into a suit, Oxley said. Is there any infra-red emission?

Check the electronic-warfare block first, Syrinx said.

Negative electronic-warfare emission. He's not possessed. But he is alive. The suit's a couple of degrees above ambient.

Are you sure it's not just natural body heat residue? Those suits are a good insulator. If he's alive then he hasn't moved since the frost formed on him. That must have been hours ago.

Serina's bitek processor block converted her affinity voice into a straight datavise. 'Captain Thakrar? Are you receiving this, sir? We're Edenists from Golomo; we received your message.' The ice-encrusted figure didn't move. She waited a moment, then made her way towards him. I've just datavised his suit processor for a status update. He's still breathing. Oh, damn.

They all saw it at the same time: ancillary medical modules anchored to Thakrar by small plastic tubes which burrowed through the SII suit material. Two of the modules had red LEDs shining under their coating of frost, the others were completely dark. The tubes had all frozen solid.

Get him back here, Syrinx instructed. Fast as you can, Serina.

*

Caucus was waiting with a stretcher right outside the MSV's airlock. *Oenone* had stopped generating a gravity field in the crew torus so that Serina and Oxley could tow Thakrar's inert form through the cramped little tube without too much difficulty. He was shedding droplets as they went, the layer of frost melting in the warm air. They got him onto the stretcher, and *Oenone* immediately reinstated gravity in the torus, tugging the crew down to the decking again. Oxley held on to the dead medical modules as they raced round the central corridor to the sickbay.

**Deactivate the suit, please,** Caucus told Serina as the stretcher was wheeled under the diagnostic scanner. She issued the order to the suit's control processor, which examined the external environment before obeying. The black silicon retreated from Thakrar's skin, sliding from his extremities to glide smoothly toward his throat. Dark fluids began to stain the stretcher. Syrinx wrinkled her nose up at the smell, putting a hand over her nose.

**Is he all right?** *Oenone* asked.

**I don't know yet.**

**Please, Syrinx, it is him who is hurt, not you. Please don't remember like this.**

**I'm sorry. I didn't know I was being so obvious.**

**To the others, perhaps not.**

**It does make me remember, I won't deny that. But his injuries are very different.**

**Pain is pain.**

**My pain is only a memory.** She recited; in her mind it was Wing-Tsit Chong's voice which spoke the phrase. **Memories do not hurt, they only influence.**

Caucus winced at the sight that was unveiled. Thakrar's lower right arm was new, that much was obvious. The medical packages wrapped round it had shifted, opening large gashes in the translucent immature skin. AT muscles lay exposed, their drying membranes acquiring a nasty septic tint. Scars and skin grafts on the legs and torso were a livid red against the snowy skin. The remainder of his packages appeared to have withered, green surfaces crinkling up like ageing rubber, pulling the edges back from the flesh they were supposed to heal. Sour nutrient fluids dripped out of torn inlet plugs.

For a moment, all Caucus could do was stare in a kind of revolted dismay. He simply didn't know where to start.

Erick Thakrar's bruised eyelids slowly opened. What alarmed Syrinx the most was the lack of confusion they showed.

'Can you hear me, Erick?' Caucus said in an overloud voice. 'You're perfectly safe now. We're Edenists, we rescued you. Now please don't try and move.'

Erick opened his mouth, lips quivering.

'We're going to treat you in just a moment. Are your axon blocks functional?'

'No!' It was very clear, very determined.

Caucus picked an anaesthetic spray from the bench. 'Is the program faulty, or have your neural nanonics been damaged?'

Erick brought his good arm round, and pressed his knuckles into Caucus's back. 'No, you will not touch me,' he datavised. 'I have a nerve-burst implant. I will kill him.'

The spray fell from Caucus's hand to clatter on the deck.

Syrinx could barely credit what was happening. Her mind instinctively opened to Caucus, offering support to his own frightened thoughts. All the crew were doing the same.

'Captain Thakrar, I am Captain Syrinx, this is my voidhawk *Oenone*. Please deactivate your implant. Caucus was not going to harm you.'

Erick laughed, an unsteady gulp which shook his whole body. 'I know that. I don't want to be treated. I'm not going back, not out there. Not again.'

'Nobody is going to send you anywhere.'

'They will. They always do. You do, you navy people. Always one final mission, one little bit of vital information to collect then it will all be over. It never is, though. Never.'

'I understand.'

'Liar.'

She gestured to the outlines of the medical packages visible through her ship-tunic. 'I do have some knowledge of what you have been through. The possessed had me for a brief time.'

Erick gave her a scared glance. 'They'll win. If you saw what they can do, you'll know that. There's nothing we can do.'

'I think there is. I think there must be a solution.'

'We'll die. We'll become them. They're us, all of us.'

**Captain? I've got a clean shot at him.**

Syrinx was aware of Edwin, out in the central corridor, a maser carbine raised. The blank muzzle was pointing at Erick Thakrar's back. A feed from the weapon's targeting processor showed it was aimed precisely on Thakrar's spinal column. The coherent microwaves would sever his nerves before he could use the implant.

**No**, she said. **Not yet. He deserves our efforts to talk him out of this.** For the first time in a long time, she was angry at an Adamist for being just that, an Adamist. Closed mind, locked up tight in its skull. No way of knowing what others were thinking, never really knowing love, kindness, or sympathy. She couldn't take the simple truth to him directly. Not the easy way.

'What do you want us to do?' she asked.

'I have information,' Erick datavised. 'Strategic information.'

'We know. Your message to Golomo said it was important.'

'I will sell it to you.'

There was a collective burst of surprise from the crew.

'OK,' Syrinx said. 'If I have the price on board, you will have it.'

'Zero-tau.' Erick's face became pleading. 'Tell me you have a pod on board. For God's sake.'

'We have several.'

'Good. I want to be put inside. They can't get to you in there.'

'All right, Erick. We'll put you in zero-tau.'

'For ever.'

'What?'

'For ever. I want to stay in zero-tau for ever.'

'Erick . . .'

'I thought about this; I thought about it a lot, it can work. Really it can. Your habitats can resist the possessed. Adamist starships don't work for them, not properly. Capone is the only one who has any military ships, and he won't be able to keep them going for long. They'll need maintenance, spares. He'll run out eventually. Then there won't be any more invasions, only infiltrations. And you won't let your guard down. We will, Adamists will. But not you. In a hundred years from now there will be nothing left of our race, except for you. Your culture will live for ever. You can keep me in zero-tau for ever.'

'There's no need for this, Erick. We can beat them.'

'No,' he brayed. 'Can't can't can't.' The effort of speaking made him cough painfully. His breathing was very heavy now. 'I'm not going to die,' he datavised. 'I'm not going to be one of them; not like little Tina. Dear little Tina. God, she was only fifteen. Now she's dead. But you don't die in zero-tau. You're safe. It's the only way. No life, but no beyond, either. That's the answer.' Very slowly, he took his hand away from Caucus. 'I'm sorry. I wouldn't have hurt you. Please, you have to do this for me. I can tell you where Capone is going to invade next. I can give you the coordinate of an antimatter station. Just give me your word, as an Edenist, as a voidhawk captain; your word that you will take my pod to a habitat, and that your culture will always keep me in zero-tau. Your word, please it's so little to ask.'

**What do I do?** she asked her crew.

Their minds merged, awash with compassion and distress. The answer, she felt, was inevitable.

Syrinx walked over and took Erick's cold, damp hand in hers. 'All right, Erick,' she said softly. Wishing once more for a single second of genuine communication. 'We'll put you in zero-tau. But I want you to promise me something in return.'

Erick's eyes had closed. His breathing was very shallow now. Caucus was exuding concern at the read-out from the diagnostic scanner. **Hurry,** he urged.

'What?' Erick asked.

'I want your permission to take you out of zero-tau if we find a proper solution to all this.'

'You won't.'

'But if we do!'

'This is stupid.'

'No, it isn't. Edenism was founded on hope, hope for the future, the belief that life can get better. If you have faith in our culture to preserve you for eternity, you must believe in that. Jesus, Erick, you have to believe in something.'

'You are a very strange Edenist.'

'I am a very typical Edenist. The rest just don't know it yet.'

'Very well, deal.'

'I'll talk to you soon, Erick. I'll be the one who wakes you up and tells you.'

'At the end of the universe, perhaps. Until then . . .'

# 23

Alkad hadn't seen snow since she left Garissa. Back in those days she'd never bothered indexing a memory of winter in her neural nanonics. Why waste capacity? The season came every year, much to Peter's delight and her grudging acceptance.

The oldest human story of all: I never knew what I had until I lost it.

Now, from her penthouse in the Mercedes Hotel, she watched it falling over Harrisburg, a silent cascade as inexorable as it was gentle. The sight made her want to go outside and join the children she could see capering about in the park opposite.

The snow had begun during the night, just after they landed at the spaceport, and hadn't let up in the seven hours since. Down on the streets tempers were getting shorter as the traffic slowed and the pavements turned slippery with the slush. Ancient municipal mechanoids, backed up by teams of men with shovels, struggled to clear the deep drifts which blockaded the main avenues.

The sight didn't exactly bode well. If the Tonala nation's economy was so desperate that they used human labour to clean the streets of their capital . . .

So far Alkad had managed to keep her objective in focus. She was proud of that, after every obstacle thrown in her way she had proved herself resourceful enough to keep the hope alive. Even back on the *Tekas* she'd thought she would soon be retrieving the Alchemist.

Nyvan had done much to wreck her mood and her confidence. There were starships docked at the orbiting asteroids, and the local astroengineering companies could probably provide her with the equipment she wanted; yet the decay and suspicion native to this world made her doubt. The task was slipping from her grasp once more. Difficulties were piling up against her, and now she had no more fall-back positions. They were on their own now; her, Voi, Lodi, and Eriba, with money as their only resource. True to his word, Prince Lambert had taken the *Tekas* out of orbit as soon as they'd disembarked. He said he was flying to Mondul, it had a strong navy, and he knew people there.

Alkad resisted accessing her time function. Prince Lambert must have made his third ZTT jump by now, and another potential security hazard was no more.

'That's a new one,' Eriba announced. He was stretched out along the settee, bare feet dangling over the armrest. It meant he could just see the holoscreen on the far wall. A local news show was playing.

'What is?' Alkad asked him. He had been consuming news ever since they arrived, switching between the holoscreen and the communication net's information cores.

'Tonala has just ordered every border to be closed and sealed. The cabinet claims that New Georgia's actions are overtly hostile, and other nations can't be trusted. Apparently, the SD networks are still blasting each other with electronic-warfare pulses.'

Alkad grimaced. That clash had been going on when the *Tekas* arrived. 'I wonder how that affects us? Are those the land borders, or are they going to prohibit spaceflight as well?'

'They haven't said.'

The door chimed as it admitted Voi. She strode into the big lounge shrugging out of her thick navy-blue coat and shaking grubby droplets of melted snow on the white carpet. 'We've got an appointment for two o'clock this afternoon. I told the Industry Ministry we were here to buy defence equipment for the Dorados, and they recommended the Opia company. Lodi ran a check through the local data cores, and they own two asteroid industrial stations along with a starship service subsidiary.'

'That sounds promising,' Alkad said guardedly. She had left all the organization to Voi. The agencies would be looking for her; zipping around town would be asking for trouble. As it was, using the Daphine Kigano passport when they arrived was a risk, but she didn't have any others prepared.

'Promising? Mary, it's spot on. What do you want, the Kulu Corporation?'

'I wasn't criticizing.'

'Well, it sounded like it.'

Voi had slowly reverted to her original temper during the voyage. Alkad wasn't sure if the waspy girl was recovering from her father's death, or reacting to it.

'Has Lodi found out if there are any suitable starships for hire?'

'He's still checking,' Voi said. 'So far he's located over fifty commercial vehicles stranded insystem due to the quarantine. Most of them are docked in low-orbit stations and the asteroid ports. He's running performance comparisons against the requirements you gave us. I just hope he can find us one at a Tonala facility. Did you hear about the border restrictions? They're even closing down net-interface points with the other nations.'

'That's a minor problem compared to the one we'll have crewing the ship.'

'What do you mean?'

'Our flight is not the kind of job you normally give mercenaries. I'm not sure money will guarantee loyalty for this mission.'

'Why didn't you say so, then? Mary, Alkad, how can I help if you keep complaining after the fact? Be more cooperative.'

'I'll bear it in mind,' Alkad said mildly.

'Is there anything else we should know?'

'I can't think of anything; but you'll be the first to be told if I do.'

'All right. Now, I've arranged for a car to take us to Opia's offices. The security company which supplied it is also providing bodyguards. They will be here in an hour.'

'Good thinking,' Eriba said.

'Elementary thinking,' Voi shot back. 'We're foreigners who have arrived in the middle of an Assembly-imposed quarantine. That's hardly an optimum low-visibility scenario. I want to downgrade our risk to a minimum.'

'Bodyguards ought to help, then,' Alkad said, prosaically. 'You should go and take a rest before we visit Opia. You haven't slept since we landed. I'll need you to be fresh for the negotiations.'

Voi gave a distrustful nod, and went into her bedroom.

Alkad and Eriba exchanged a glance, and smiled simultaneously.

'Did she really say low-visibility scenario?' he asked.

'Sounded like it to me.'

'Mary, that detox therapy was a bad idea.'

'What was she like before?'

'About the same,' he admitted.

Alkad turned back to the window and the snow softening the city skyline.

The door chimed again.

'Did you order something from room service?' she asked Eriba.

'No.' He gave the door a worried look. 'Do you think it's the bodyguards Voi hired?'

'They're very early, then; and if they're professional they would datavise us first.' She picked up her shoulder bag and selected one of the devices inside. When she datavised the penthouse's net processor to access the camera in the corridor outside there was no response. The cut crystal wall lights began to flicker. 'Stop!' she told Eriba, who had drawn his laser pistol. 'That won't work against the possessed.'

'Do you think . . .'

He trailed off just as Voi burst back into the lounge. She was gripping a maser carbine tight in her hand.

The penthouse's entrance door swung open. Three people were standing behind it, their features lost in the darkened corridor.

'Do not come in,' Alkad said loudly. 'My weapons will work, even against you.'

'Are you quite sure, Doctor?'

Sections of Alkad's neural nanonics were dropping out. She datavised a primer code at the small sphere she held in her hand before she lost even that ability. 'Fairly sure. Do you want to be the first experimental subject?'

'You haven't changed; you were always so confident you were right.'

Alkad frowned. It was a female voice, but she couldn't place it. She didn't have the processing power left in her neural nanonics to run an audio-comparison program. 'Do I know you?'

'You used to. May we come in, please? We really aren't here to harm you.'

Since when did the possessed start saying please? Alkad thought the circumstances out, and said: 'It only needs one of you to speak. And if you're not a threat, stop glitching our electronics.'

'That last request is difficult, but we will try.'

Alkad's neural nanonics started to come back on-line. She quickly re-established full control over the device.

'I'll call the police,' Voi datavised. 'They can send a Tac Squad. The possessed won't know until it's too late.'

'No. If they wanted to hurt us, they would have done it by now. I think we'll hear what she has to say.'

'You shouldn't expose yourself to a negative personal safety context. You are the only link we have to the Alchemist.'

'Oh, shut up,' Alkad said aloud. 'All right, come in.'

The young woman who walked into the penthouse was in her early twenties. Her skin was several shades lighter than Alkad's, though her hair was jet black, and her face was rounded by a little too much cellulite for her to be pretty; it fixed her expression to one of continual shy resentment. She wore a long tartan-print summer dress, with a kilt-style skirt that had been the fashion on Garissa the year of the Genocide.

Alkad ran a visual-comparison program search through her memory cells. 'Gelai? Gelai, is that really you?'

'My soul, yes,' she said. 'Not my body. This is just an illusion, of course.' For a moment the solid mirage vanished, revealing a teenaged Oriental girl with fresh jagged scars on her legs.

'Mother Mary!' Alkad croaked. She'd hoped the tales of torture and atrocity were just Confederation propaganda.

Gelai's usual profile returned. The flicker of exposure was so fast, it made Alkad's mind want to believe Gelai's was the true shape; the abused girl was something decency rejected.

'What happened?' Alkad asked.

'You know her?' Voi demanded indignantly.

'Oh, yes. Gelai was one of my students.'

'Not one of your best, I'm sorry to say.'

'You were doing all right, as I recall.'

'This enhances stress relief nicely,' Voi said. 'But you haven't told us why you're here.'

'I was killed in the planet-buster attack,' Gelai said. 'The university campus was only five hundred kilometres from one of the strikes. The earthquake levelled it. I was in my residence hall when it hit. The thermal flash set half of the building alight. Then the quake arrived; Mary alone knows how powerful it was. I was lucky, I suppose. I died in the first hour. That was reasonably quick. Compared to a lot of them, anyway.'

'I'm so sorry,' Alkad said. She had rarely felt so worthless; confronted by the pitiful evidence of the greatest failure it was possible to have. 'I failed you. I failed everybody.'

'At least you were trying,' Gelai said. 'I didn't approve at the time. I took part in all the peace demonstrations. We held vigils outside the continental parliament, sang hymns. But the media said we were cowards and traitors. People actually spat on us in the streets. I kept going, though, kept protesting. I thought if we could just get our government to talk to the Omutans then the military would stop attacking each other. Mary, how naive.'

'No, Gelai, you weren't naive, you were brave. If enough of us had stood for that principle then maybe the government would have tried harder to find a peaceful solution.'

'But they didn't, did they?'

Alkad traced Gelai's cheeks with her finger, touching the past she'd thought was so far behind her, the cause of the present. Feeling the ersatz skin was all she needed to know she had been right to do what she'd done thirty years ago. 'I was going to protect you. I thought I'd sold my very soul so that you would all be safe. I didn't care about that. I thought you were worth the sacrifice; all you bright young minds so full of the silliest hopes and proudest ideals. I would have done it, too, for you. Slain Omuta's star, the biggest crime in the galaxy. And now all that's left of us are the ones like these.' She waved a hand limply at Voi and Eriba. 'Just a few thousand kids living in rocks that mess with their heads. I don't know which of you suffered the worst fate. At least you had a taste of what our people might have achieved if we'd lived. This new generation are just poor remnants of what they could've been.'

Gelai puffed up her lips, and stared firmly at the floor. 'I wasn't sure what I was going to do when I came here. Warn you or kill you.'

'And now?'

'I didn't realize why you were doing it, why you went off to help the military. You were this aloof professor we were all a bit in awe of, you were so smart. We respected you so much, I never gave you human motives, I thought you were a lump of chilled bitek on legs. I see I was wrong, though I still think you are wrong to have built anything as evil as the Alchemist.'

Alkad stiffened. 'How do you know about the Alchemist?'

'We can see this universe from the beyond, you know. It's very faint, but it's there. I watched the Confederation Navy trying to get people off Garissa before the radiation killed them. I've seen the Dorados, too. I even saw you a few times in Tranquillity. Then there are the memories that we tear from each other. Some soul I encountered knew about you. Perhaps it was more than one, I don't know. I never kept count; you don't, not when you do that hundreds of times a day. So that's how I know what you built, although no one knows what it is. And I'm not the only one, Doctor; Capone knows about it too, and quite a few other possessed.'

'Oh, Mother Mary,' Alkad groaned.

'They've shouted into the beyond, you see. Promised every soul bodies if they cooperated in finding you.'

'You mean the souls are watching us now?' Voi asked.

Gelai smiled dreamily. 'Yes.'

'Fuck!'

Mzu glanced at the penthouse's door, which was closed on Gelai's two companions. 'How many possessed are on Nyvan?'

'Several thousand. It will belong to us within a week.'

'That doesn't leave us much time,' Alkad said.

Voi and Eriba were starting to look panic-stricken.

'Forget the Alchemist,' Voi said heatedly. 'We must get ourselves outsystem.'

'Yes. But we have a few days' grace. That gives us time to be certain about our escape, we can't afford a mistake now. We'll

**946**

charter a ship as we always intended; Opia's service subsidiary can do that for us. But I don't think there will be enough time to have the carrier built. Ah, well, if it comes to it, we can always load the Alchemist onto a combat wasp.'

'You can fit it on a combat wasp?' Voi was suddenly intrigued. 'Just how big is it?'

'You don't need to know.'

The tall girl scowled.

'Gelai, will you warn us if any of the possessed come close?'

'Yes, Doctor, we'll do that much. For a couple of days anyway, just while you find a ship. Are you really going to use the Alchemist after all this time?'

'Yes, I am. I've never been as sure about it as I am now.'

'I don't know if I want you to, or not. I can never accept that revenge wrought on such a scale is right. What can it ever achieve except make a few bitter old refugees feel better? But if you don't use it against Omuta, then someone else will take it from you and fire it at another star. So if it must be fired, then I suppose I'd rather it was Omuta.' Naked distress swarmed over her face. 'Funny how we all lose our principles at the end, isn't it?'

'You haven't,' Alkad told her. 'Killed by the Omutans, thirty years in the beyond, and you would still spare them. The society that can produce you is a miracle. Its destruction was a sin beyond anything our race had committed before.'

'Except perhaps possession.'

Alkad slipped her arms round the distraught girl, and hugged her. 'It will be all right. Somehow, this dreadful conflict will finish up without us destroying ourselves. Mother Mary wouldn't condemn us to the beyond for ever, you'll see.'

Gelai broke away to study Mzu's face. 'You think so?'

'Strange as it seems for a semi-atheist, yes. But I know the structure of the universe better than most, I've glimpsed order in there, Gelai. There has always been a solution to the problems we've posed. Always. This won't be any different.'

'I'll help you,' Gelai said. 'I really will. We'll make sure all four of you get off the planet unharmed.'

Mzu kissed her forehead. 'Thank you. Now what about the two who came with you, are they Garissans as well?'

'Ngong and Omain? Yes. But not from the same time as me.'

'I'd like to meet them. Ask them to come in, then we can all decide what to do next.'

*

'What bloody high life?' Joshua challenged. 'Listen, I risked everything – balls included – to earn the money to refit *Lady Mac*. You wouldn't catch me crawling to the banks and finance companies like you did. True Calverts are independent. I'm independent.'

'How we established ourselves was due entirely to circumstances,' Liol retorted. 'My only prospect came from the Dorados Development Agency grants. And by God, did I take it. Quantum Serendipity was built up from nothing. I'm self-made and proud of it, I wasn't born with your kind of privileges.'

'Privileges? All Dad left me was a broken-down starship and eighteen years' unpaid docking fees. Hardly a plus factor.'

'Crap. Just living in Tranquillity is a privilege which half of the Confederation aspires to. A plutocrat's paradise floating in the middle of a xenoc gold mine. You were never not going to make money. All you had to do was stick your hand out to grab a nugget or two.'

'They tried to kill me in that fucking Ruin Ring.'

'Then you shouldn't have been so sloppy, should you? Earning your wealth is always only half of the problem. Hanging on to it, now that's tough. You should have taken precautions.'

'Absolutely,' Joshua purred. 'Well, I've certainly learnt that lesson. I'm hanging on to what I've got now.'

'I'm not going to stop you from captaining *Lady Mac*. But—'

'*If it's of any interest*,' Sarha announced loudly, 'we've emerged in the middle of a hostile electronic environment. I've got two of Nyvan's SD networks asking for our flight authorization at the same time they're saturating our sensors with overload impulses.'

Joshua grunted disparagingly, and returned his attention to the datavised displays from the flight computer. He chided himself for the lapse, it wasn't like him not to pay attention to the jump emergence sequence. But when you've got a so-called brother with a lofriction conscience . . .

Sarha was right. Space between Nyvan and its orbiting asteroids was being subjected to a variety of powerful electronic disruption effects. *Lady Mac*'s sensors and discrimination programs were sophisticated enough to pierce most of the clutter; Nyvan's SD networks were using archaic techniques, it was the sheer wattage behind them that was causing the trouble.

With Sarha's help Joshua managed to locate the network command centres, and transmit *Lady Mac*'s standard identification code, followed by their official Tranquillity flight authorization. Only Tonala and Nangkok responded, giving him permission to approach the planet. New Georgia's SD network, based at Jesup, remained silent.

'Keep trying them,' Joshua told Sarha. 'We'll head in anyway. Beaulieu, how are you doing tracing the *Tekas*?'

'Give me a minute more, Captain, please. This planet has a very strange communications architecture, and their usual interfaces seem to be down today. I expect that is a result of the network barrage. I am having to access several different national nets to find out if the ship arrived.'

On the other side of the bridge from the cosmonik, Ashly snorted bitterly. 'Boneheads, nothing on this damned world ever changes. They always brag about how different they are from each other; I never noticed myself.'

'When were you here last?' Dahybi asked.

'About 2400, I think.'

Joshua watched Liol slowly turn his head to look at the pilot; his eyebrow was raised in quizzical dissension.

'When?' Liol asked.

'2400. I remember it quite well. King Aaron was still on Kulu's throne. There was some kind of dispute between Nyvan's countries because the Kingdom had sold one of them some old warships.'

'Right,' Liol said. He was waiting for the punchline.

*Lady Mac*'s crew propagated dispassionate expressions right across the bridge.

'I've found a reference,' Beaulieu said. 'The *Tekas* arrived yesterday. According to Tonala's public information core it had an official flight authorization issued by the Dorados Council. It docked at one of their national low-orbit stations, the Spirit of Freedom, then departed an hour later, with a flight plan filed for Mondul. Four people disembarked, Lodi, Voi, Eriba, and Daphine Kigano.'

'Jackpot,' Joshua said. He datavised traffic control for an approach vector to the Spirit of Freedom. After the eighth attempt, traffic control confirmed contact through the jamming and gave him a vector.

\*

Spirit of Freedom was Tonala's main low-orbit civil spaceport, orbiting seven hundred and fifty kilometres above the equator, a free-floating hexagonal grid two kilometres in diameter and a hundred metres thick. Tanks, lounges, corridor tubes, thermo-dump panels, and docking-bays were sandwiched between the framework of grey-white alloy struts; tapering spires extended out from each corner, tipped with a cluster of fusion-drive tubes to hold the structure's attitude stable.

As well as a port for commercial starships and cargo spaceplanes, it was also the flight hub for the huge tugs which brought down the metal mined from Floreso asteroid. Several of the heavy-duty craft were keeping station alongside the Spirit of Freedom as *Lady Mac* approached; open-lattice pyramids with a clump of ten big fusion-drive tubes at the tip, and load-attachment points at each corner.

They were designed to ferry down four ironbergs apiece. Seventy-five thousand tonnes of spongesteel: incredibly pure metal foamed with nitrogen while it was still in its molten state. Floreso's industrial teams solidified it into a squat pear-shape, with a base that was scalloped by twenty-five gently rounded ridges. After that, the ironbergs were attached to the tugs for a three-week flight, spiralling down into a slightly elliptical two hundred kilometre orbit. For the last two days of the voyage, electric motors in the load-attachment points would spin them up to one rotation per minute. In effect, they became the biggest gyroscopes in the galaxy, their precession keeping them perfectly aligned as they flew free along the final stretch of their trajectory.

Injecting the ironbergs into the atmosphere was an inordinately difficult operation for the tugs, requiring extreme precision. Each ironberg had to be at the correct attitude, and following its designated flight path exactly, so that its blunt base could strike the upper atmosphere at an angle which would create the maximum aerobrake force. Once its velocity started to drop off, gravity would pull it down in a steepening curve, which created yet more drag, accelerating the whole process. Hypersonic airflow around the scalloped base would also perpetuate the spin, maintaining stability, keeping it on track.

If everything went well – if the asteroid crews had got the internal mass distribution balanced right, if the injection point was correct – the ironberg would be aerobraked to subsonic velocity about five kilometres above the ocean. After that, nothing else mattered, no force in the universe could affect that much mass hanging in the sky in a standard gravity field. It fell straight down at terminal velocity to splash into the water amid an explosion of steam that resembled the mushroom cloud of a small nuclear bomb. And there it bobbed among the waves, its foamed interior making it buoyant enough to float without any aids.

When all four ironbergs from one tug had splashed down, the recovery fleet would sail in. The ironbergs would be towed into a foundry port ready to be broken up and fed to Tonala's eager mills. An abundant supply of cheap metal, obtained without any ecological disturbance, was a healthy asset to the nation's economy.

So not even the chaotic electronic war being fought between the SD networks was allowed to interrupt the operation. The tugs around the Spirit of Freedom continued to receive their regular maintenance schedule. SII-suited engineering crews crawled over the long struts, while MSVs and tankers drifted in close attendance. The service craft were the only other vehicles flying apart from *Lady Mac*. Joshua had a trouble-free approach, making excellent time. As they flew over the station, sensors showed him eleven other starships nestled snugly in the docking-bays.

The inspection from port officers was one he was expecting: checking everyone on board for possession, then going through the life-support capsules and the two ancillary craft with electronic-warfare blocks to make sure there were no unexplained glitches. Once they'd been cleared, Joshua received an official datavised welcome from Tonala's Industry Ministry, with an invitation to discuss his requirements and how local firms could help. They were also authorized to fly *Lady Mac*'s spaceplane down to Harrisburg.

'I'll take a pair of serjeants, Dahybi, and Melvyn,' Joshua announced. 'You too, Ashly, but you stay in the spaceplane in case we need evacuating. Sarha, Beaulieu, I want *Lady Mac* maintained at flight-ready status. Same procedure as before, we may have to leave in a hurry, so keep monitoring groundside, I want to be told if and when the crap hits the fan.'

'I can come with you,' Liol said. 'I know how to handle myself if it gets noisy down there.'

'Do you trust my command judgement?'

'Of course I do, Josh.'

'Good. Then you stay up here. Because my judgement is that you won't follow my orders.'

*

It was dark in Jesup's biosphere cavern now, a permanent joyless twilight. And cold with it. Quinn had ordered it so. The solar-tubes strung out along the axial gantry were producing an enfeebled opalescent glow, whose sole purpose was to show people where they were going.

As a result, an impossible autumn had visited the lush tropical vegetation. After a futile search twisting round on their stems in search of light, the leaves were yellowing. In many places they had begun to fall, their edges crisping black from the bitter air. Already the neat filigree of pretty streams was clogging with soggy mush, overspill channels were blocked, pools were flooding the surrounding ground.

The experience of accelerated decay was one which Quinn savoured. It demonstrated his power over his surroundings. No reality dysfunction this, making things different as long as you didn't blink. This was solid change, irreversible. Potent.

He stood before the stone altar which had been built in the park, studying the figure bound to the inverted cross on top. It was an old man, which in some ways was good. This way Quinn confirmed his zero-rated compassion; only children held equal status.

His loyal disciples stood in a circle round him, seven of them clad in blood-red robes. Faces shining as bright as their minds, fuelled by greed and ominous desire.

Twelve-T was also in attendance, sagging with the formidable burden of merely staying alive. His maltreated head was permanently bowed now. No possessed was imposing change upon him, but he was becoming almost Neanderthal in his posture.

Outside the elite coterie the acolytes formed a broad semicircle. All of them were wearing grey robes with the hoods thrown back. Their faces illuminated by the unnaturally hot bonfires flanking the altar, a flickering topaz light caressing their skin with fake expressions.

Quinn could sense several ghosts standing amongst them. Frightened and demoralized as always; and as he had discovered, utterly harmless. They were completely unable to affect any aspect of the physical world. Trivial creatures with less substance than the shadows they craved.

In a way he was glad they were attending. Spying. This ceremony would show them what they were dealing with. They could be tyrannized, he was sure; in that they were no different to any other human. He wanted them to realize that he would never hesitate to inflict what pain he could upon them if they chose not to obey.

Satisfied, Quinn sang: 'We are the princes of the Night.'

'We are the princes of the Night,' the acolytes chorused. It was a sound similar to the threat of thunder beyond the horizon.

'When the false lord leads his legions away into oblivion, we will be here.'

'We will be here.'

The old man was shaking now, moving his lips in prayer. He was a Christian priest, which was why Quinn had selected him. A double victory. Victory over the false lord. And victory for the serpent beast. Taking a life for no reason other than you wished it, for the pain it would cause others.

Such sacrifices had always focused on authority and its

enforcement. A spectacle to coerce the weak. In pre-industrial times, this rite might have been about the summoning of dark witchcraft; but in an age of nanonic technology man had long surpassed magic, black or white. The sect had known and encouraged the value of image, the psychology of precise brutality. And it worked.

Who now amongst this gathering would stand to challenge him? It was more ordination than anything else, confirming his right to reign.

He held out a hand, and Lawrence placed the dagger in his palm. Its handle was an elaborate ebony carving, but the blade was plain carbotanium, and very sharp.

The priest cried out as Quinn slid the tip into his paunchy abdomen. It deepened to a whimper as Quinn recited: 'Accept this life as a token of our love and devotion.'

'We love you, and devote ourselves to you, Lord,' growled the acolytes.

'God grant you deliverance, son,' the priest choked.

Blood was running down Quinn's arm, splattering the altar. 'Go fuck yourself.'

Lawrence laughed delightedly at the priest's anguish. Quinn was immensely proud of the boy; he'd never know anyone to offer himself up to God's Brother so unreservedly.

The priest was dying to the harsh cheers of the acolytes. Quinn could sense the old man's soul rising from the body, twining like smoke in a listless sky to vanish through a chink in reality. He pressed himself forward to lick ravenously at the ephemeral stream with a narrow black tongue, enraptured.

Then another soul was pushing back down the trickle of energy, surging into the body.

'Shithead!' Quinn spat. 'This body is not for you. It is our sacrament. Get the fuck out of it.'

The skin on the priest's upside-down face began to flow like treacle. The features twisted themselves through a hundred and eighty degrees so that the mouth was superimposed on the forehead. Then the skin hardened again and the eyes snapped open.

Quinn took a pace back in surprise. It was his own face staring at him.

'Welcome to the beyond, you little prick,' it told him. Then it smiled wickedly. 'Remember this part?'

A streamer of white fire lashed out of the knife which was plunged deep into the priest's chest. It struck Twelve-T's right arm, puncturing his chrome and steel wrist. The smoking mechanical hand dropped to the floor, fingers waggling as if they were playing piano keys. His wrist joint was reduced to a jagged bracelet of metal with green hydraulic fluid spraying out, and the frayed end of a power cable fluttering about.

'Do it!' the forged face yelled.

Twelve-T lunged towards Quinn, shoving his broken arm forward. A mad smile cracked his face.

Lawrence wailed, 'No,' and flung himself into Twelve-T's path.

The broken wrist joint rammed into Lawrence's throat. A bright spark of electricity twinkled at the end of the ragged power cable as it touched the boy's skin.

Lawrence shrieked as his whole body silently detonated into sunlit brilliance. He froze with his arms still outstretched, a frantic expression etched on his face. The light was so fierce he became translucent. A naked angel bathing in the heart of a star. Then his extremities began to shrivel, turning black. He had time to shriek once more before the internecine fire ate him away.

The dreadful light shrank, revealing a patch of baked earth and droppings of fine white ash. Twelve-T lay next to it where he had stumbled, the fall jolting his brain out of his half-skull like wine from a goblet. It was rolling over the grass.

'Ah, well,' said the forged face. 'I guess we both lost this time around. Be seeing you, Quinn.' It began to untwist, reverting to the priest's startled death rictus. The incursive soul flowed away, retreating into the beyond.

'COME BACK!' Quinn roared.

There was a last ironic laugh, and his tormentor was gone.

For all his power and strength, there was nothing Quinn could do. Absolutely nothing. His impotence was an agonizing humiliation. He screamed, and the altar shattered, sending the priest's battered body tumbling. The acolytes began to run. Quinn kicked Twelve-T's brain, and the grisly organ burst apart, sending a splat of gore across his terrified disciples. He turned back and discharged a bolt of searing white fire into the priest's remnants. The body ignited instantly, but the flames were only a effete mockery of the incendiary heat which had consumed Lawrence.

The disciples shrank away as Quinn sent blast after blast of white fire into the pyre, reducing the body and the crumbling stones to radiant magma. When they reached the boundary of light given off from the bonfires, they too turned and fled after the acolytes.

Only the ghosts remained, safe from the fury of the black-robed figure in their secluded lifeless realm. After a while they saw him sink to his knees, and make the sign of the inverted cross on his chest.

'I will not fail you, my Lord,' he said quietly. 'I will quicken the Night as I promised. All I ask as the price of my soul, is that when it has fallen you bring me the fucker who did this.'

He rose and made his way out of the park. This time he was truly alone. Even ghosts quailed before the terrifying thoughts alight inside his head.

\*

*Hoya* was the first of the four voidhawks to emerge above Nyvan. Niveu and his crew immediately began scanning the local environment for threats.

'No ships within twenty thousand kilometres,' he said, 'but

the SD networks are shooting off electronic-warfare blitzes at each other. Looks like the nations are in their usual confrontational state.'

Monica accessed the sensor suite in the voidhawk's lower hull, and the starfield projected into her mind came alive with vivid coloured icons. Two more voidhawks were holding formation a hundred kilometres away. As she watched, another wormhole terminus opened to disgorge the fourth. 'Are we being targeted by the platforms?' she asked. She appreciated the way the Edenists unfailingly spoke out loud in her presence, keeping her informed. But their display symbology was very different to that used by the Royal Navy, she hadn't quite mastered the program yet.

'There are very few specific targets,' Samuel said. 'The networks appear intent on jamming and disrupting every processor out to geosync orbit.'

'Is it safe for us to approach?'

Niveu shrugged. 'Yes. For now. We'll monitor the local news to find out what's going on. If there's any indication of them advancing the hostilities to an active stage, I'll review the situation again.'

'Does your service have any stations down there?' she asked Samuel.

'There are some assets, but we don't have any active operatives. We don't even have an embassy. There's no gas-giant in this system, it was colonized long before their presence was deemed necessary to develop an industrialized economy. Frankly, the price of having to import all their He$_3$ is partly responsible for Nyvan's current state.'

'It also means we have no back-up,' Niveu said.

'OK, let me have a communication circuit. We have a couple of embassies and several consuls. They should be monitoring starship traffic.'

It took a long time to establish contact. After hours subjected to the output from the SD platforms, the national civil communication satellites were now almost completely inoperative. She eventually got round the problem by aligning one of *Hoya*'s antennas directly on the cities she wanted, which limited her to those on the half of the planet ahead of the voidhawks.

'Mzu's here,' she said at last. 'I got through to Adrian Redway, our station chief in the Harrisburg embassy. The *Tekas* arrived yesterday. It docked at Tonala's principal low-orbit station, and four people took a spaceplane down to Harrisburg. Voi was one of them, and so was Daphine Kigano.'

'Excellent,' Samuel said. 'Is the *Tekas* still here?'

'No. It departed an hour later. And no other starship has left since. She's still down there. We've got her.'

'We have to go in,' Samuel told Niveu.

'I understand. But you should know that several governments are claiming New Georgia has fallen to the possessed. New Georgia is denying it of course, though it does seem as though they have lost their asteroid, Jesup. Apparently Jesup dispatched some inter-orbit ships to the three abandoned asteroids. It is being heralded as a breach of sovereignty, which of course is taken extremely seriously here.'

'Could the ships be carrying escapees?' Monica asked.

'It is possible, I suppose. Although I can't think of any reason why anyone should consider those asteroids to be a refuge; they were badly damaged in the '32 conflict. No one even bothered to salvage them. But we ought to know what the Jesup ships are doing before too long; the governments which own the abandoned asteroids have dispatched their own ships to investigate.'

'If it turns out those ships from Jesup are crewed by possessed, then the situation will deteriorate rapidly,' Samuel said. 'The other governments are unlikely to come to New Georgia's aid.'

'True enough,' Monica said pensively. 'They're more likely to nuke the whole country.'

'I don't imagine we will be staying long,' Samuel said. 'And we will have the flyers with us, we can evacuate within minutes.'

'Yeah, sure. There's one other thing.'

'Oh?'

'Redway said one other starship has arrived since the *Tekas* left. The *Lady Macbeth*; she's docked at Tonala's main low-orbit station.'

'How intriguing. The Lord of Ruin obviously knew what she was doing when she chose this "Lagrange" Calvert.'

Monica was sure there was a note of admiration in his voice.

The four voidhawks accelerated in towards Nyvan. After receiving permission from traffic control, they slotted into a six hundred kilometre orbit, adopting a diamond formation. Four ion-field flyers left their hangars and curved down towards the planet, heading into the huge swirl of angry cloud that covered most of Tonala.

*

Jesup's Strategic Defence Control Centre had been hollowed out of the rock deep behind the habitation section. It was New Georgia's ultimate citadel; safe from any external attack which didn't actually crack Jesup open, equipped with enough security systems to fend off an open mutiny by the asteroid's population, and fitted with a completely independent environmental circuit. No matter what happened to Jesup and New Georgia's government, the SD officers could continue to fight on for weeks.

Quinn waited for the monolithic innermost door to slide open, displaying a serenity that was harrowing in its depth. Only Bonham accompanied him now as he strode around the asteroid, the other disciples were too afraid.

There had been a few modifications to the control centre. Console technology had devolved considerably; in most cases processors and AV projectors had abated to a simple telephone. A whole rank of the black and silver machines were lined up along a wall, where they were jangling incessantly. A group of officers in stiff grey uniforms were snatching up the handsets as fast as they could. In front of them was a big square table with a picture of Nyvan and its orbiting asteroids covering its surface. Five young women were busy moving wooden markers across it with long poles.

The adrenalin-powered clamour faltered as Quinn walked in. There was no sign of any face inside his robe's hood, light fell into the oval opening never to return. Only the pearl-white hands emerging from his sleeves suggested a human was in residence.

'Keep going,' he told them.

The voices sprang back, far louder than before so as to demonstrate their loyalty and commitment.

Quinn went over to the commander's post, a pulpit-like podium which overlooked the table. 'What is the problem?'

Shemilt, who was running the control centre, saluted sharply. He was wearing a heavily decorated Luftwaffe uniform from the Second World War, every inch the Teutonic warrior aristocrat. 'I regret to inform you, sir, that ships have been sent to intercept our teams working in the other asteroids. The first will make contact in forty minutes.'

Quinn studied the table; it was becoming cluttered. Four vultures were grouped together just above the planet. New Georgia's SD platforms were diamond-studded pyramids. Ruby pentagons showed opposing platforms. Three red-flagged markers were being shoved slowly over the star map. 'Are they warships?'

'Our observation stations are having a lot of trouble in this foul weather, but we don't think so. Not frigates, anyway. I expect they will be carrying troops, though; they're definitely big enough for that.'

'Don't get too carried away, Shemilt.'

Shemilt stood to attention. 'Yes, sir.'

Quinn pointed at one of the red flags. 'Can our SD platforms hit these ships?'

'Yes, sir.' Shemilt pulled a clipboard off a hook inside his command post, and flicked through the typewritten sheets. 'Two of them are in range of our X-ray lasers, and the third can be destroyed with combat wasps.'

'Good. Kill the little shits.'

'Yes, sir.' Shemilt hesitated. 'If we do that, the other networks will probably shoot at us.'

'Then shoot back, engage every target you can reach. I want an all-out confrontation.'

Activity round the table slowed as operators glanced at Quinn. Resentment was building in their thoughts, capped, as always, by fear.

'How do we get out, Quinn?' Shemilt asked.

'We wait. Space warfare is very fast, and very destructive. By the end of today, there won't be a working laser cannon or a combat wasp left orbiting Nyvan. We'll get hit a few times, but fuck, these walls are two kilometres thick. This is the mother of all fallout shelters.' He gestured at the table, and every marker ignited, yellow candlelike flames squirting out black smoke. 'Then when it's over, we can fly away in perfect safety.'

Shemilt nodded hurriedly, using speed to prove he'd never doubted. 'I'm sorry, Quinn, it's obvious really.'

'Thank you. Now kill those ships.'

'Yes, sir.'

Quinn left the control centre with Bonham scurrying after him, always trailing by a few paces. The giant door slid shut behind them, its bass grumbles echoing along the broad corridor.

'Are there really enough ships here to take everyone off?' Bonham asked.

'I doubt it. And even if there were, the spaceport will be a prime target.'

'So . . . some of us should leave early, then?'

'Fast, Bonham, very fast. That's probably why you got where you did.'

'Thank you, Quinn.' He quickened his steps; Quinn's voice was slightly fainter.

'Of course, if they see me leaving now, they'd know I'd abandoned them. Discipline would go straight to shit.'

'Quinn?' He could hardly hear the dark figure at all now.

'After all, it's not as if you could bind them . . .'

Bonham squinted at the figure he was now almost running to catch up with. Quinn seemed to be gliding smoothly over the rock floor without moving his legs. His black robe had faded to grey. In fact it was almost translucent. 'Quinn?' This latest performance was frightening him more than anything to date. The anger and wrath which Quinn radiated so easily were simple to understand, almost reassuring in comparison. This though, Bonham didn't know if it was something being done to Quinn, or something he was doing to himself. 'What is this? Quinn?'

Quinn had become completely transparent now, only the slightest rippling outline of rock betrayed his position; even his thoughts were evaporating from Bonham's perception. He stumbled to a halt. Panic set in. Quinn was no longer present anywhere in the corridor.

'Holy Christ, now what?'

He felt a breath of cold air stroke his face. He frowned.

A bolt of white fire smashed into the back of his skull. Two souls were cast out of the corpse as it collapsed onto the floor, both of them keening in dread at the fate which awaited.

'Wrong god.' A chuckle drifted down the empty corridor.

*

When Joshua landed just after midday local time, rumour was blanketing Harrisburg as thickly as the snow. It seemed to be the one weapon in the armoury of the possessed that was the same the Confederation over. The more people heard, the less they knew, the more fearful they became. One freak outbreak of urban mythology and entire populations would become paralysed, either that or regress straight into survivalist siege mode.

On most worlds, government assurances and rover reporters on the scene managed to restart the engines of ordinary existence. People would creep sheepishly back to work and wait for the next canard of Genghis Khan riding a Panzer tank into the suburbs.

Not on Nyvan. Here governments were the ones gleefully shooting out savage accusations at their old antagonists. A coordinated global response to the prospect of the possessed landing was never even considered, an impossibility in realpolitik.

As soon as they landed Joshua loaded a search request into the city's commercial data core. The number of armed guards and lack of flights at the spaceport made his intuition rebel. He knew they didn't have much time; the quiet approach – questions, contacts, money – would never work here.

They hired a car and set off down 'hotel row', a potholed six-lane motorway which linked the spaceport to the city ten kilometres away. Only two lanes were cleared of snow, and there was hardly any other traffic.

Dahybi used his electronic-warfare detector block to sweep the eight-seater cabin for bugs. 'Seems clean,' he told the others.

'OK,' Joshua said. 'Our processor technology is probably more advanced than the locals, but don't count on it for a permanent advantage. I need to find her as fast as we can, which is going to mean sacrificing subtlety.'

As they approached the hotel they'd booked, Joshua datavised an update into the car's control processor. The car swept past the hotel's entrance, heading for the city.

'There goes our deposit,' Melvyn complained.

'It bothers me,' Joshua said. 'Ione, are we being followed?'

One of the serjeants was sitting at the back of the cab, pointing a small circular sensor pad through the rear window.

'One car, possibly two. I think there are three people in the first one.'

'Probably some kind of local security police,' Joshua decided. 'I'd be surprised if they weren't keeping tabs on foreigners right now.'

'So what do we do about them?' Dahybi asked.

'Not a damn thing. I don't want to give them an excuse to interfere.' He accessed the car's net processor, and established an encrypted link to the spaceplane. 'What's your situation, Ashly?'

'So far so good. I'll have the electron matrices completely recharged in another three minutes. That'll expand your options.'

'Good. We'll keep a channel open to you from now on. If the city's net starts to crash, come get us. That's our cut-off point.'

'Aye, Captain. *Lady Macbeth* just fell below the horizon, so I've lost contact. Every civil communication satellite is out now.'

'If their situation alters, they'll change orbit and re-establish a link. Sarha knows what to do.'

'I certainly hope so. Before I lost contact, Beaulieu told me four voidhawks have arrived. They're heading for low orbit.'

'They must have come from the Dorados,' Joshua decided. 'Ashly, when *Lady Mac* comes back on-line, tell Sarha to monitor them as best she can. And let me know if any of their spaceplanes land.'

*

The snowfall had thickened considerably by the time Joshua's car reached the address his search program had identified for him. It reduced Harrisburg to a sequence of shabby granite streets that were hard to tell apart. Nothing was alive apart from people, wrapped in their insulated coats as they kicked their way through the pavement slush. Hologram hoardings and neon signs were all that remained unaffected by the weather, flashing and morphing as always.

'I should have brought Liol down,' Joshua muttered, half to himself. 'He said he wanted a taste of exotic worlds.'

'You're going to have to come to terms with him eventually, Joshua,' Melvyn said.

'Maybe. Jesus, if he just wasn't such a pushy bastard. Can't you tell him to lighten up, Ione? You spend a lot of time talking to him.'

'It didn't work before,' one of the serjeants said.

'You've already told him?'

'Let's say I've been through the procedure earlier. He's not the only one who needs to relax, Joshua. Neither of you are going to make any progress the way you both carry on.'

He wanted to explain. How it was. How he didn't feel quite so alone any more, and how that left him troubled. How he wanted to welcome his brother, but at the same time knew him so well he didn't trust him. To be honest with him would be seen as a weakness. Liol was the interloper. Let him make the first gesture. *I saved his arse from the Dorados, I was the honourable one, and what thanks do I get?*

When he glanced round the car, he knew that anything he said which verged on truth would make him sound petulant. A year ago I would've told the lot of them to bugger off. Jesus, life was simpler then, when there was just me. 'I'll do what I can,' he conceded.

Their car turned off the street and dipped down into an underground garage. The building it served was a ten-storey block with small shops at street level (half of them empty), and the upper floors given over to offices and design bureaux.

'Going to tell us why we're here now?' Dahybi asked as they climbed out of the car.

'Simple,' Joshua said. 'When you need a job doing fast and effectively, go to a professional.'

The office of Kilmartin and Elgant, Data Security Specialists, was on the seventh floor. There was nobody behind the desk in the reception room. Joshua paused for a second, expecting a secretarial program to query them; but the desktop processor wasn't switched on. The inner door slid open when he approached it.

In a rash of optimistic bravado accompanying their firm's launch, Kilmartin and Elgant had taken a fifty-year lease on sufficient floor space to house fifteen operatives. There were still enough desks for fifteen in the open-plan office; seven of them had dust covers thrown over processors which were fairly dubious even by Nyvan's technological standards; four desks had niches where processors used to be; one patch of carpet showed imprints where a desk used to stand.

Only one desk had a decent cluster of modern blocks, which shared the surface with a thoroughly dead pot plant. Two men were sitting behind it, staring intently into the hazy aura of an AV pillar. The first was tall, young, and broad-shouldered, sporting a long blond pony-tail tied with a colourful leather lace. He wore an expensive black suit, tailored to provide maximum freedom of movement. Not openly belligerent, but with a presence that would make people think twice before tackling him. The second was well into middle age, dressed in a faded grey-brown jacket, tufty chestnut hair askew. He looked as if he belonged behind the complaints desk in a tax office.

They regarded Joshua and his odd delegation with mild surprise.

Joshua looked from one to the other, slightly uncertain as intuition tickled his skull. Then he clicked his fingers decisively, and pointed at the younger of the two. 'I bet you're the data expert and your friend handles the combat routines. Good disguise, right?'

The aura from the AV pillar faded as the younger man tilted his chair back and put his hands behind his head. 'Clever. Are we expecting you, Mr—?'

Joshua gave a faint smile. 'You tell me.'

'All right, Captain Calvert, what do you want?'

'I need to access some information, and fast. Can you manage that for me?'

'Sure. Nationwide net access, no problem, whatever file you want. Hey, listen, I know what this place looks like. Forget that. Talent isn't something you can eyeball. And I'm so far on top of things I'm getting oxygen starvation. Someone's search program locates my public file, I know about it before they do. You came down from the *Lady Macbeth* an hour ago. One of your crew is still with your spaceplane. Want to know how much the service company is ripping you off for your electron matrix recharge? You're in the right place.'

'I don't care. Money doesn't concern me.'

'OK, I think we've reached interface here.' He turned to his colleague, and muttered something. The older man gave him a disgruntled look, then shrugged. He walked out of the office, giving the two sergeants a curious glance as he passed.

'Richard Keaton.' The athletic young man leant over the desk, holding his hand out and smiling broadly. 'Call me Dick.'

'I certainly will.' They shook hands.

'Sorry about Matty there. He's got enough implants to chop up a squad of marines. But he gets overprotective, and I don't need him hovering right now. Smart of you to see which of us was which. I don't think anyone's ever done that before.'

'Your secret's safe with me.'

'So what can I do for you, Captain Calvert?'

'I need to find someone.'

Keaton raised a forefinger. 'If I could just interrupt. First, there is my fee.'

'I'm not going to quibble. I might even pay a bonus.'

One of the serjeants tapped a foot pointedly on the worn carpet.

'Nice to hear, Captain. OK, then; my fee is one flight off this planet on the *Lady Macbeth*, just as soon as you leave. Destination: who cares.'

'That's an ... unusual fee. Any particular reason?'

'Like I said, Captain, you came to the right place. This might not be the biggest firm in town, but I fish the data streams. There are possessed on Nyvan. They've already taken over Jesup, that wasn't just propaganda by our upstanding government. The electronic-warfare barrage in orbit? That was cover to help them get down here. There aren't too many in Tonala yet – not according to the Special Investigation Bureau, anyway. But they're spreading through the other countries.'

'So you want to be gone?'

'I sure do. And I figure you won't be here when they reach Harrisburg, either. Look, I won't be any trouble on board. Hell, shove me into zero-tau, I don't mind.'

Joshua didn't have the time to argue. Besides, taking Keaton with them actually reduced the risk of exposure. A flight off Nyvan wasn't such a high price. 'You bring only what you've got with you; I'm not waiting while you go home to pack. We don't have any slack built into our mission profile.'

'We have a deal, Captain.'

'Very well, welcome aboard, Dick. Now, the person I want is called Dr Alkad Mzu, alias Daphine Kigano. She arrived on the starship *Tekas* last night with three companions. I don't know where she is or who she might attempt to contact; however, she will be trying to stay hidden.' He datavised over a visual file. 'Find her.'

\*

Twenty thousand kilometres above Nyvan, the Organization frigate *Urschel* emerged from its ZTT jump. It was swiftly followed by the *Raimo* and the *Pinzola*. They were nowhere near a designated emergence zone, but only the four void-hawks were aware of their arrival. None of Nyvan's gravitonic distortion detector satellites were functioning, the waves of electronic-warfare assaults had crashed them beyond repair.

After five minutes assessing the local situation their fusion drives came on, pushing them towards a low-orbit injection point. Once they were on their way, Oscar Kearn, the small flotilla's commander, concentrated on the eternal, beseeching voices crying into his head.

Where is Mzu? he asked them.

The possessed among the crew, including Cherri Barnes, joined his silky cajoling, adding to the tricksy promises he made. Theirs was a multiple chant which hummed through the beyond, a harmonic passed between every desperate soul. It agitated them, its very existence a taunt; plots and scheming were an exquisitely tortuous reminder of what lay on the other side of their dreadful continuum, what they could partake of once again if they just helped.

Where is Mzu?

What is she doing?

Who is with her?

There are bodies waiting for worthy hosts. Millions of bodies, out here among the light and air and experience, held ready for Capone's friends. One could be yours. If—

Where is Mzu? Exactly?

Ah.

When they reached a five hundred kilometre orbit, each of the frigates dispatched a spaceplane. The three black delta shapes sliced down through Nyvan's atmosphere, their tapering noses lining up on Tonala, hidden behind the planet's curvature seven thousand kilometres ahead.

Oscar Kearn ordered the frigates to manoeuvre again, and they began to raise their orbit.

*

'This really doesn't look good,' Sarha said. 'The sensors are showing three of them. I don't think their transponders are responding to the station.'

'You don't think?' Beaulieu queried.

'Who knows? Those bloody SD platforms are still at it. I doubt we could pick up an EM pulse through all this jamming.'

'What are their drive exhausts like?' Liol asked.

Sarha ignored the datavised displays inside her skull long enough to fire a disgusted glance at him. The three of them were alone on *Lady Mac*'s bridge. All the remaining serjeants were down in B capsule, guarding the airlock tube. 'What?' There were times when he was a little bit too much like Joshua, that is: quite infuriating.

'If there are possessed on board, they'll be affecting the ship's systems,' Liol recited. 'Their drives will fluctuate. The recordings from Lalonde taught us that. Remember?'

Sarha didn't trust herself to answer directly. Yes, he was like Joshua, gallingly right the whole time. 'I'm not sure our discrimination programs will be much use at this distance. I can't get a radar lock to determine their velocity.'

'Want me to try?'

'No, thank you.'

'When Josh said don't give me access to the flight computer, I don't think he meant I wasn't supposed to help you survive an assault by the possessed,' Liol said peevishly.

'You will be able to ask him directly soon,' Beaulieu said. 'We should be over Ashly's horizon in another ninety seconds.'

'Those ships are definitely heading for a rendezvous with the Spirit of Freedom,' Sarha said. 'The optical image is good enough for a rough vector analysis.'

'I'd like to point out that the three highly similar ships which appeared at the Dorados before we left were all from New California,' Liol said.

'I am aware of that,' Sarha snarled back.

'Jolly good. I'd hate to be possessed by anyone I didn't know.'

'What are the voidhawks doing?" Beaulieu asked.

'I don't know. They're on the other side of the planet.' Sarha was uncomfortably aware of the perspiration permeating her ship-suit. She datavised the conditioning grille above her for some cool, dry air – cooler, dryer air. And to think I'd always been slightly envious about Joshua having command of a starship. 'I'm disengaging the airlock,' she told the other two. 'Station staff might try to come on board once they realize those starships are heading here.' It was a logical action. And actually doing something made her feel a whole lot better.

'I've got the spaceplane beacon,' Beaulieu announced.

'You're still intact, then?' Ashly datavised.

'Yeah, still here,' Sarha replied gamely. 'What's your situation?'

'Stable. Nothing much is moving at the spaceport. The four Edenist flyers arrived half an hour ago. They're parked about two hundred metres away from me right now. I tried datavising them, but they're not answering. A whole group of people set off into town as soon as they landed. There were cars here waiting for them.'

The flight computer signalled that Joshua was coming on-line. 'Any signs of possession on the planet yet?' he asked.

'I'd have to say yes, Captain,' Beaulieu told him. 'The national nets are suffering considerable degrees of drop-out. But there's no real pattern to it. Several countries don't have a single glitch.'

'They will,' Joshua datavised.

'Joshua, three Adamist starships appeared an hour ago,' Sarha datavised. 'We believe they sent some spaceplanes or flyers down to the planet; they were in the right orbit for it. Liol thinks they're the same Organization ships that were at the Dorados.'

'Oh, well, if the starflight expert says so . . .'

'Josh, those frigates are heading for this station,' Liol datavised.

'Oh, Jesus. OK, get clear of the station. And Sarha, try to get a positive ident.'

'Will do. How are things your end?'

'Promising, I think. Expect us . . . today, what . . . outcome.'

'I'm losing the link,' Beaulieu warned. 'Heavy interference, and it's focused directly at us.'

'Josh, let me have access authority for the flight computer. Sarha and Beaulieu are being overloaded up here, for Christ's sake. I can help.'

'. . . think . . . Mummy's boy . . . on my ship . . . fucking . . . because I'll . . . first . . . trust . . .'

'Lost them,' Beaulieu said.

'The frigates have started jamming us directly,' Sarha said. 'They know we're here.'

'They're softening up the station for an assault,' Liol said. 'Give me the access codes, I can fly *Lady Mac* away.'

'No, you heard Joshua.'

'He said he trusted me.'

'I don't think so.'

'Look, you two have to operate the on-board systems, monitor the electronic-warfare battle, and now you've got to watch the frigates as well. If we launch now they might think we're going to defend the station. Can you fly *Lady Mac* and fight at the same time as everything else?'

'Beaulieu?' Sarha asked.

'Not my decision, but he does have a point. We need to leave, now.'

'Sarha, Josh is all emotionally tangled up when it comes to me. Fair enough, I didn't handle him well. But you can't endanger his life and ours on a single bad decision made from ignorance. I'll do my best here. Trust me. Please.'

'All right! Damn it. But fusion drive authority only. You're not jumping us anywhere.'

'Fine.' And the dream finally happened, just as he'd always known it would. *Lady Mac*'s flight computer opened to him, and all the systems were on-line, filling his mind with glorious wing-sweeps of colour. They fitted just perfectly.

He designated the procedure menus he needed, bringing the thrusters and drive tubes up to active flight status. Beaulieu and Sarha were working smoothly together, activating the remaining on-board systems. Umbilicals retracted from the fuselage, and the cradle started to elevate them out of the shallow docking-bay. The viewfield which the flight computer was datavising at him expanded as more of *Lady Mac*'s sensor clusters lifted above the rim. Three bright, expanding stars were ringed in antagonistic red as they crept up over the curvature of the brilliant blue horizon.

Liol fired the verniers to take them off the cradle, not caring if the other two could see the stupid smile on his face. For a moment, all the envy and bitterness returned, the irrational pique he'd felt when he first learned that Joshua existed, a usurper brother who was captaining the ship which was rightfully his. This was the rush that belonged to him. The power to traverse the galaxy.

One day, he and Joshua were going to have to settle this.

But not today. Today was when he proved himself to his brother and the crew. Today was when he started living the life he knew belonged to him.

When they were a hundred metres above the docking bay, Liol fired the secondary drive, selecting a third of a gee acceleration. *Lady Mac* immediately veered off the vector he'd plotted. He pumped a fast correction order into the flight computer, deflecting the exhaust angle. Overcompensating. 'Wowshit!' The acceleration couch webbing gripped him tighter.

'The spaceplane hangar is empty,' Sarha said witheringly. 'That means our mass distribution is off centre. Perhaps you'd care to bring the level seven balance-calibration programs on-line?'

'Sorry.' He searched desperately round the flight control menus, and found the right program. *Lady Mac* juddered back onto her original vector.

'Joshua is going to throw me out of the airlock,' Sarha decided.

*

It had taken some time for Lodi to get used to having Omain sitting in the hotel suite with him. A possessed, for Mary's sake! But Omain turned out to be quiet and polite (a little sad, to be honest), keeping out of the way. Lodi slowly managed to relax, though this must surely be the strangest episode in his life. Nothing was ever going to out-weird this.

At first he had jumped every time Omain even spoke. Now, he was relatively cool about the whole scene. His processor blocks were spread out over one of the tables, enabling him to cast trawl programs into the net streams, fishing out relevant information. It was what he did best, so Voi had left him to it while she, Mzu and Eriba went to the Opia company. His main concern at the moment was monitoring the civil situation now the government had closed the borders. Voi wanted to make sure they would be allowed to get back into orbit. So far, it looked as if they could. There had even been one piece of good luck; the first since they arrived at Nyvan. A starship called *Lady Macbeth* had docked at the Spirit of Freedom, and it was exactly the type of ship Mzu wanted.

'They are asking for her,' Omain said.

'Huh?' Lodi cancelled the datavised displays, blinking away the after-image the graphics left in his mind.

'Capone's people are in orbit,' Omain said. 'They know Mzu is here. They are asking for her.'

'You mean you can tell what's going on in orbit? Mary! I can't, not with all the interference from the SD platforms.'

'Not tell, exactly. This is whispered gossip, distorted by the many souls it has passed through. I have only the vaguest notion of the facts.'

Lodi was fascinated. Once he began talking, Omain knew some seriously interesting facts. He'd lived on Garissa, and was quite willing to share his impressions. (Lodi had never summoned the courage to ask Mzu what their old world was like.) From Omain's melancholic descriptions it sounded like a good place to live. The Garissans, Lodi was sure, had lost more than their world by the sound of it; their whole culture was different now, too tight-arsed and Western-ethnic orientated.

One of the processor blocks datavised a warning into Lodi's neural nanonics. 'Oh, bollocks!'

'What is it?'

They had to speak in raised voices, almost shouting at each other. Omain was sitting in the corner of the lounge furthest from Lodi; it was the only way the blocks would remain functional.

'Someone has accessed the hotel's central processor. They've loaded a search program for the three of us, and it's got a visual reference for Mzu, too.'

'It cannot be the possessed, surely?' Omain said. 'Neural nanonics don't function for us.'

'Might be the Organization ships. No. They'd never be able to access Tonala's net from orbit, not with the platforms still going at it. Hang on, I'll see what I can find out.' He felt almost happy as he started retrieving tracker programs from the memory fleks he'd brought. The net dons in this city probably had ten times the experience he'd got from snooping round Ayacucho's communication circuits, but his programs were still able to flash back through the junctions, tracing the origin of the searchers.

The answer sprang into his mind just as the hotel's central processor crashed. 'Wow, that was some guardian program. But I got them. You know anything about a local firm called Kilmartin and Elgant?'

'No. But I haven't been here long, not in this incarnation.'

'Right.' Lodi twitched a smile. 'I'll see what . . . that's odd.'

Omain had risen from his chair. He was frowning at the suite's double door. 'What is?'

'The suite's net processor is down.'

The door chimed.

'Did you . . .' Lodi began.

Something very heavy smashed into the door. Its panels bulged inwards. Splintering sounds were spitting out of the frame.

'Run!' Omain shouted. He stood before the door, both arms held towards it, palms outwards. His face was clenched with effort. The air twisted frantically in front of him, whipping up a small gale.

Another blow hammered the door, and Omain was sent staggering backwards. Lodi turned to run for the bedroom. He was just in time to see a fat three-metre-long serpent slither vertically up the outside of the window. Its huge head reared back, levelling out to stare straight at him. The jaws parted to display fangs as big as fingers. Then it lunged forward, shattering the glass.

\*

From his elevated position in the command post, Shemilt studied the ops table below him. One of the girls leant over and pushed a red-flagged marker closer to the deserted asteroid.

'In range, sir,' she reported.

Shemilt nodded, trying not to show too much dismay. All three of the inter-orbit ships were in range of New Georgia's SD network now. And Quinn had not returned to change his orders. His very specific orders.

If only we weren't so bloody terrified of him, Shemilt thought. He still felt sick every time he remembered the zero-tau pod containing Captain Gurtan Mauer. Quinn had opened it up during two of the black mass ceremonies.

If we all grouped together— But of course, death was no longer the end. Throwing the dark messiah into the beyond would solve nothing.

There was a single red telephone in his command post. He picked up the handset. 'Fire,' he ordered.

*

Two of the three inter-orbit ships on their way to find out what the teams from Jesup were doing in the deserted asteroids were struck by X-ray lasers. The beams shone clean through the life-support capsules and the fusion-drive casings. Both crews died instantly. Electronics flash evaporated. Drive systems ruptured. Two wrecks tumbled through space, their hulls glowing a dull orange, vapour squirting from split tanks.

The third was targeted by a pair of combat wasps.

The officers of the other two national SD networks saw them streaking away from New Georgia's platform, heading towards the helpless inter-orbit ship. They requested and received fire authority codes. By then the attacking combat wasps had begun dispensing their submunition drones. Infra-red decoys shone like micronovas amid the shoal of drive exhausts; electronic-warfare pulses screamed at the sensors of any SD platform within five thousand kilometres. The offensive was a valid tactic; combat wasps launched to try and protect the remaining ship were confused for several seconds. A time period which in space warfare was critical.

A flock of one-shot pulsers finally got close enough to discharge into the remaining inter-orbit ship, killing it immediately. That didn't prevent the kinetic missiles from arrowing in on it at thirty-five gees. Nor submunitions with nuclear war-heads from detonating when they were within range.

*Lady Mac*'s sensors picked up most of the brief battle, though the overspill from the electronic-warfare submunitions overlapping the general assault waged by the SD platforms caused several overload drop-outs.

'This is becoming a seriously hazardous location,' Sarha mumbled. The external sensor image was quivering badly as if something was shaking the starship about. Artificial circles of green, blue, and yellow were splashing open against the starfield like raindrop graffiti. Intense blue-white flares started to appear among them.

'It just went nuclear,' Beaulieu said. 'I don't think I've seen overkill on that scale before.'

'What the hell is going on up there?' Sarha asked.

'Nothing good,' Liol said. 'A possessed would have to be very determined to make a trip to one of those abandoned asteroids; there are no biospheres left, that'll leave them heavily dependent on technology.'

'How are the Organization ships reacting?' Sarha asked. Twenty minutes after *Lady Mac* had left the Spirit of Freedom, the three frigates had docked. A quarter of an hour after that all communication with the station had ceased. They were now holding orbit eight hundred kilometres ahead of Spirit of Freedom, which gave their sensors a reasonable resolution.

'I'm way ahead of you,' Liol said. 'Two of them are launching – wait, they all are. They're going down into a lower orbit. Damn, I wish we could see what the voidhawks are doing.'

'I'm registering activity within the station's defence sensor suite,' Beaulieu said. 'They're sweeping us.'

'Liol, take us another five hundred kilometres away.'

'No problem.'

Sarha consulted the orbital display. 'We'll be over Tonala in another thirty minutes. I'm going to recommend Joshua pulls out.'

'There's a lot of ship movements beginning down here,' Beaulieu said. 'Two more low-orbit stations are launching ships; and those are the ones we can see.'

'Bugger it,' Sarha grunted. 'OK, go to defence-ready status.'

*Lady Mac*'s standard sensor clusters retreated down into their recesses; the smaller, bulbous combat sensors slid smoothly upwards to replace them, gold-chrome lenses reflecting the last twinkling explosions in high orbit. Her combat-wasp launch-tubes opened.

All around her, Nyvan's national navies and SD platforms were switching to the same status.

\*

Since arriving at Jesup, Dwyer had spent almost every hour helping to modify the bridge systems of the cargo clipper *Mount's Delta*. Given his minimal technical background, his time was spent supervising the non-possessed technicians who did most of the installation.

The bridge compartment was badly cramped, which meant only a couple of people could work in it at any one time. Dwyer had become highly proficient at dodging flying circuit boards and loose console covers. But he was satisfied with the result, which was far less crude than the changes they'd made to the *Tantu*. With the huge stock of component spares available in the spaceport, the consoles looked as if they'd slipped off the factory production line mere hours earlier. Their processors were now all military grade, capable of functioning while they were subjected to the energistic effect of the possessed. And the flight computer had been augmented until it was capable of flying the ship following the simplest of verbal orders.

This time there was none of the black sculpture effect, every surface was standard. Quinn had insisted the clipper's life-support capsule must stand up to inspection when they arrived at Earth. Dwyer was confident he had reached that objective.

Now he was hovering just outside the small galley alcove on the mid-deck watching a female technician replacing the old hydration nozzles with the latest marque. A portable sanitation sucker hovered over her shoulder, its fan humming eagerly as it ingested the occasional stale globule which burped out of the tubes she'd unscrewed.

The unit's hum rose sharply, becoming strident. A draught of cold air brushed Dwyer's face.

'How's it going?' Quinn asked.

Dwyer and the technician both yelped in surprise. The

clipper's airlock was in the lower deck, and the floor hatch was closed.

Dwyer spun round, grabbing at support struts to wrestle his inertia back under control. Sure enough, Quinn was sliding down through the ceiling hatch from the bridge. His robe's hood was folded back, sticking to his shoulders as if he was in his own private gravity field. For the first time in days his flesh tone was almost normal. He grinned cheerfully at Dwyer.

'God's Brother, Quinn. How did you do that?' Dwyer glanced over his shoulder to check the floor hatch again.

'It's like style,' Quinn said. 'Some of us have it . . .' He winked at the female technician, and flung a bolt of white fire straight into her temple.

'Fuck!' Dwyer gasped.

The corpse banged back into the galley alcove. Tools fluttered out of her hands like iron butterflies.

'We'll dump her out of the airlock when we're under way,' Quinn said.

'We're leaving?'

'Yes. Right now. And I don't want anyone to know.'

'But . . . what about the engineering crew in the bay's control centre? They have to direct the umbilical retraction.'

'There is no more crew. We can relay the launch instructions to the management computer through the bay's datanet.'

'Whatever you say, Quinn.'

'Come on, you'll enjoy Earth. I know I will.' He performed a somersault in mid-air, and slow-dived back up through the hatch.

Dwyer took a moment to compose himself, clenching his hands so the way his fingers trembled didn't show; then he followed Quinn up into the bridge.

*

Anger and worry isolated Alkad from the mundanities of the drive back to the hotel. She hadn't thought this fast and hard since the days she was working on the Alchemist theory. Options were closing all around her, like the sound of prison doors slamming shut.

The meeting with two of Opia's vice-presidents had been a typical sounding-you-out session. All very cordial, and achieving very little. They had agreed on the principle of the company finding her a starship and crew, which at some yet-to-be-specified time would be equipped with specialist defence systems for duties in the Dorados' defence force.

The one hold she had over them was the prospect that this would be the first order by the Dorados Council; and if all went smoothly, more would follow. Possibly a great deal more.

Greed had taken root. She had seen it so many times before in the industrialists who had been supplying Garissa's navy.

They would have followed her requests, ignoring the oddities of the situation. She was convinced of it. Then just as the meeting was winding down the Tonalan government announced a state of emergency. New Georgia's SD platforms had opened fire on three ships, one of which belonged to Tonala. Such an action, the Defence Ministry insisted, proved beyond any doubt that the possessed had captured Jesup, that the New Georgia government was lying, and possibly even possessed itself.

Once again Nyvan's national factions were at war with each other.

The Opia executives loaded a program for a crestfallen expression into their neural nanonics. Sorry, but the contract would have to go into suspension. Temporarily. Just until Tonalan might has reigned triumphant.

The car drew up underneath the sweeping portico of the Mercedes Hotel. Ngong was first out, scouring the broad street for threats. Now they had him and Gelai protecting them, Alkad had dispensed with the security firm Voi had hired, although they'd kept the company's car with its armoured bodywork and secure circuitry.

There wasn't much traffic on the street. The team of men shovelling snow had vanished, leaving the dilapidated mechanoids to struggle on by themselves. Ngong nodded and beckoned. Alkad eased herself off the seat and scurried over to the lobby's rotating door, Gelai a pace behind her the whole time. They had told her of the Organization's ships during the trip back. It baffled Alkad how Capone had ever heard of her. But there was no disguising Gelai's rising concern.

The five of them bundled into the penthouse lift, which rose smoothly. Only the annoying flicker of the light-panel betrayed Gelai and Ngong for what they were.

Alkad ignored the lighting. The state of emergency was dangerous. It wouldn't be long before Tonala retaliated against New Georgia's SD network. Those starships docked above Nyvan would be pressed into service, if the captains didn't simply ignore the quarantine and leave. She would soon be trapped here without any transport and the Capone Organization closing in. Unless she did something fast, she would belong to the possessed one way or the other, and with her came the Alchemist.

The spectre of what the device could do to the Confederation if it was used on a target other than Omuta's star was now preying on her mind. What if it was used against Jupiter? The Edenist habitats would die, Earth would be deprived of the He$_3$ without which it could never survive. Or what if it was used against Sol itself? What if it was switched to the nova function?

There had never been any conceivable prospect of this before. I was always in control. Mother Mary, forgive my arrogance.

She cast a sideways glance at Voi, who was looking as irritable as always with the lift's progress. Voi would never entertain any change in their mission priorities. The concept of failure was not allowed for.

Like me at that age.

I have to get off this planet, she realized abruptly. I have to reopen the options again. I can't let it end like this.

The lift's floor indicator said they were three floors below the penthouse when Gelai and Ngong exchanged a questioning glance.

'What's the matter?' Voi asked.

'We can't sense Omain, or Lodi,' Gelai said.

Alkad immediately tried to datavise Lodi. There was no response. She ordered the lift to stop. 'Is there anyone up there?'

'No,' Gelai said.

'Are you sure?'

'Yes.'

Of all the facets of possession, the perception ability fascinated Alkad the most. She'd only just started considering the mechanism of possession. The whole concept would ultimately mean quantum cosmology having to be completely restructured again. So far, she'd made very little theoretical progress.

'I told him to stay put,' Voi said indignantly.

'If his neural nanonics aren't responding then this is rather more serious than him simply wandering off,' Alkad told her.

Voi pulled a face, unconvinced.

Alkad ordered the lift to restart.

Gelai and Ngong were standing in front of the doors when they opened on the penthouse vestibule. Trickles of static skipped over their clothes as they readied themselves for trouble.

'Oh Mary,' Eriba said. The double doors to the penthouse had been smashed apart.

Gelai waved the others back as she edged cautiously into the lounge. Alkad heard an intake of breath.

The body Omain had been possessing was lying across one of the big settees, covered with deep scorch marks. Snow was blowing in through a gaping hole in the window.

Ngong hurriedly checked the other rooms. 'No body. He's not here,' he told them.

'Oh, Mother Mary, now what?' Alkad exclaimed. 'Gelai, have you got any idea who did this?'

'None. Aside from the obvious that it was some possessed.'

'They know about us,' Voi said. 'And now Lodi's been possessed, they know too much about us. We must leave immediately.'

'Yes,' Alkad said reluctantly. 'I suppose so. We'd better go directly to the spaceport, see if we can hook up with a starship there.'

'Won't they know we're going to do that?' Eriba said.

'What else can we do? This planet can't help us any more.'

One of the processor blocks on the table let out a bleep. Its AV projector sparkled.

Alkad looked straight into it. And she was looking out through a set of eyes at a man dressed in a traditional Cossack costume.

'Can you hear me, Dr Mzu?' he asked.

'Yes. Who are you?'

'My name is Baranovich, not that it particularly matters. The important fact here is that I have agreed to work for Mr Capone's Organization.'

'Oh, shit,' Eriba groaned.

Baranovich smiled and held a small circular mirror up. Alkad could see Lodi's frightened face reflected in the surface.

'So,' Baranovich said. 'As you can see, we have not harmed your comrade. This is his datavise you are receiving. If he was possessed, he would be unable to do this. No? Say something, Lodi.'

'Voi? Dr Mzu? I'm sorry. I couldn't— Look there are only seven of them. Omain tried . . .' Something hissed loudly behind him. The image blurred. Then he blinked.

'A brave boy,' Baranovich clapped Lodi on the shoulder. 'The Organization has a place for those with such integrity. I would hate to see another come to use this body.'

'You might have to,' Alkad said. 'I cannot consider swapping a lone man for the device, no matter how well I know him. There have been far bigger sacrifices made to get me to this point. I would be betraying those who made them, and that I can never do. I'm sorry, Lodi, really I am.'

'My dear Doctor,' Baranovich said. 'I was not offering you Lodi in exchange for the Alchemist. I am simply using him as a convenient instrument through which I can deal with you, and perhaps demonstrate our intent.'

'I don't need to deal with you.'

'Your pardon, Doctor, I believe you do. You will not get off this planet unless the Organizations takes you off. I think you know that now. After all, you weren't going to try and run to the spaceport, now were you?'

'I'm not about to discuss my departure arrangements with you.'

'Bravo, Doctor. Resistance to the very end. I respect that. But please understand, the circumstances in which you find yourself have changed radically since you began your quest for vengeance. There will be no revenge against Omuta any more. What would be the point? In a few short months Omuta as it is today will not exist. Whatever you can do to it will not exceed the coming of possession. Will it, Doctor?'

'No.'

'So you see, you have only yourself to consider now, and what will happen in your personal future. The Organization can offer you a decent future. You know that with us millions of valuable people remain unpossessed, and secure in their jobs. You can be one of them, Doctor. I have the authority to offer you a place with us.'

'In return for the Alchemist.'

Baranovich shrugged magnanimously. 'That is the deal. We

will take you – and your friends too if you want them – off this planet today, before the orbital battle becomes any worse. Nobody else will do that. You either stay here and become possessed, eternity spent in the humiliation of physical and mental bondage; or you come with us and live out the rest of your life as fruitfully as possible.'

'As destructively as possible, you mean.'

'I doubt the Alchemist would have to be used many times, not if it's as good as rumour says. Yes?'

'It wouldn't need many demonstrations,' Alkad agreed slowly.

'Alkad!' Voi protested.

Baranovich beamed happily. 'Excellent, Doctor, I see you are acknowledging the truth. Your future is with us.'

'There's something you should know,' Alkad said. 'The activation code is stored in my neural nanonics. If I am killed and moved into another body in a bid to make me more compliant, I will not be able to access them. If I am possessed, the possessor will not be able to access them. And, Baranovich, there are no copies of the code.'

'You are a prudent woman.'

'If I come with you, then my companions are to be given passage to a world of their choice.'

'No!' Voi shouted.

Alkad turned from the projection, and told Gelai: 'Keep her quiet.'

Voi squirmed helplessly as the possessed woman pinned her arms behind her back. A membrane of thick skin sprouted up over her lips.

'Those are my terms,' Alkad told Baranovich. 'I have spent most of my life in pursuit of my goal. If you do not agree to my terms, then I will not hesitate to defy you in the only way I have left. I have that determination, it is the one real weapon I have always had. You have pushed me into this position, do not doubt that I will use it.'

'Please, Doctor, there is no need for such vehemence. We will be happy to carry your young friends to a safe place.'

'All right. We have a deal.'

'Excellent. Our spaceplanes will pick you and your friends up at the ironberg foundry yard outside the city. We'll be waiting at Disassembly Shed Four with Lodi. Be there in ninety minutes.'

# 24

Admiral Motela Kolhammer and Syrinx arrived at the First Admiral's office just as the Provost General was coming out. He almost bumped into them, head down and scowling. Kolhammer was given a brief grunt of apology before he strode off, chased by three aides in an equally flustered mood. The Admiral gave them a curious look before stepping into the office.

Captain Maynard Khanna and Admiral Lalwani were sitting in front of the First Admiral's desk. Two more blue-steel chairs were distending up out of the circular pools of silver on the floor.

'What was all that about?' Kolhammer asked.

'We have a small legal problem with one of our guests,' Lalwani said drily. 'It's just a question of procedures, that's all.'

'Bloody lawyers,' Samual Aleksandrovich muttered. He gestured Kolhammer and the voidhawk captain to sit.

'Is it relevant to Thakrar's information?' Kolhammer asked.

'No, fortunately.' Samual smiled a fast welcome at Syrinx. 'My thanks to *Oenone* for such a swift flight.'

'I'm happy to be contributing, sir,' Syrinx said. 'Our journey time from Ngeuni was eighteen hours.'

'That's very good.'

'Good enough?' Kolhammer asked.

'We believe so,' Lalwani said. 'According to our New California surveillance operation, Capone is only just starting to refuel and rearm his fleet again.'

'How up to date is that information?' Kolhammer asked.

'There's a voidhawk flight each day from the Yosemite Consensus, so at the most we're only thirty hours behind. According to the Consensus, it will be another week at the most before they're ready to launch.'

'At Toi-Hoi, allegedly,' Kolhammer mused. 'Sorry to play the heretic, but how reliable is this Captain Thakrar?'

Syrinx could only give an empty gesture. *If only I had some way of imparting Erick's intensity, his devotion, to them.* 'I have no doubt Captain Thakrar's data is genuine, Admiral. Apart from his unfortunate collapse at the finish of his mission he's proved an absolute credit to the CNIS. Capone does intend to invade Toi-Hoi next.'

'I accept the information as essentially accurate,' Lalwani affirmed. 'We really are going to be able to intercept the Organization fleet.'

'Which is going to eliminate the Capone problem completely,' Maynard Khanna said. 'With him gone, all we have to concern ourselves with is the quarantine.'

'And that damn-fool Mortonridge liberation which the Kingdom's foisted on to us,' Kolhammer complained.

'Psychologically, the elimination of Capone's fleet will be considerably more important,' Lalwani said. 'Capone is interpreted as a far more active threat by Confederation citizens—'

'Yeah, thanks to the damn media,' Kolhammer said.

'—so when they see there is no further chance of his fleet appearing in their skies, and the Navy has achieved that for them, we will have a great deal more leverage with the Assembly when it comes to implementing our policy.'

'Which is?' Samual Aleksandrovich asked sardonically. 'Yes, yes, Lalwani. I know. I simply don't welcome the notion of holding things together while we pray that Gilmore and all the others like him can find a solution for us; it smacks of inactivity.'

'The more we thwart them, the more we can expect them to cooperate in finding a solution,' she said.

'Very optimistic,' Kolhammer said.

Samual datavised a request into his desktop processor and the fat AV cylinder hanging from the middle of the ceiling began to sparkle. 'This is our current strategic disposition,' he said as the chairs swivelled their occupants round to face the projection. They were looking down on the Confederation stars from galactic south, where tactical situation icons orbited round the suns of inhabited worlds like technicolour moons. At the centre, Earth's forces were portrayed by enough symbols to form a ring of gas giant proportions. 'You're going to get your chance, Motela,' the First Admiral said quietly. 'That 1st Fleet squadron you assembled to deal with Laton is the only possible force we can engage Capone with. We don't have time to put anything else together.'

Kolhammer studied the projection. 'What does the Yosemite Consensus estimate Capone's fleet size to be this time?'

'Approximately seven hundred,' Lalwani said. 'Numerically, that's slightly down on last time. Arnstadt is tying up a lot of his mid-capacity ships. However, he has acquired a disturbing number of Arnstadt's naval ships. Consensus believes the fleet will contain at least three hundred and twenty front-line warships. The rest are made up from combat-capable traders and civil craft modified to carry combat wasps.'

'And they're armed with antimatter,' Kolhammer said. 'My squadron has a maximum of two hundred ships. We both went to the same academy, Lalwani, you need a two to one advantage to guarantee success. And that's just theoretically.'

'The Organization crews are not highly motivated or efficient,' she replied. 'Nor do their ships function at a hundred per cent capacity with possessed on board screwing up the systems.'

'Neither of which will matter a damn to their damn forty-gee combat wasps once they're launched. They function just fine.'

'I will assign you half of the 1st Fleet vessels here at Avon,' the First Admiral said. 'That will bring your strength up to four hundred and thirty, including eighty voidhawks. In addition, Lalwani has suggested that we request support from every Edenist Consensus within a seventy light-year radius of Toi-Hoi.'

'Even if they only release ten per cent of their voidhawks, that should give you nearly three hundred and fifty voidhawks,' she said.

'Seven hundred and eighty front-line warships,' Kolhammer said. 'A force that big is very cumbersome.'

Lalwani turned from the projection to give him a reproachful stare. She found him grinning straight at her.

'But I think I can cope.'

'Our tactical staff want to use Tranquillity as the rendezvous point,' Khanna said. 'It's only eighteen light-years from Toi-Hoi; which means you can be there in five hours once you know the Organization fleet is on its way.'

'One ship takes five hours, yes, but we're dealing with nearly eight hundred. I wasn't joking about such a force being cumbersome. Why don't the tactical staff want us to use Toi-Hoi itself?'

'Capone must have it under observation. If he sees that kind of task force arrive he'll simply abort and choose another target. We'd be back at square one. Tranquillity is close, and it's not an obvious military base. Once our observation operation confirms the Organization fleet is leaving for Toi-Hoi a void-hawk will fly directly to Tranquillity and alert you. You can be at Toi-Hoi before Capone's ships arrive. You can destroy them as they jump in.'

'Perfect tactics,' Kolhammer said, almost to himself. 'How long before the rest of the 1st Fleet ships can join the squadron?'

'I've already issued recall orders,' the First Admiral said. 'The bulk will be at Trafalgar within fifteen hours. The remainder can fly directly to Tranquillity.'

Kolhammer consulted the AV projection again, then datavised a series of requests into the desktop processor. The scale changed, expanding while the viewpoint slipped round to put Toi-Hoi at the centre. 'The critical factor here is that Tranquillity is secure. We need to prevent any ship from leaving, and also make sure it's not under any kind of stealth observation before we arrive.'

'Suggestion?' Samual asked.

'It'll be four and a half days before the task force gets to Tranquillity. But Meredith Saldana's squadron is still at Cadiz, correct?'

'Yes, sir,' Khanna said. 'The ships were docked at a 7th Fleet supply base. The Cadiz government requested they remain and support local forces.'

'So, a voidhawk could reach Cadiz within . . .' He gave Syrinx an enquiring glance.

'From Trafalgar? Seven to eight hours.'

'And Meredith could get to Tranquillity in a further twenty hours. Which would give him almost three days to check local space for any kind of clandestine surveillance activity, as well as preventing any locals from leaving.'

'Get the orders drafted,' the First Admiral told Khanna. 'Captain Syrinx, my compliments to the *Oenone*, I'd be obliged if you can convey them to Cadiz for me.'

**Now this is real flying**, *Oenone* said excitedly.

Syrinx concealed her own delight at the voidhawk's enthusiasm. 'Of course, Admiral.'

Samual Aleksandrovich cancelled the AV projection. He felt the same kind of anxiety that had beset him the day he turned his back on his family and his world for a life in the navy. It came from standing up and taking responsibility. Big decisions were always made solo; and this was the biggest in his career.

He couldn't remember anyone sending close on eight hundred starships on a single combat assignment before. It was a frightening number, the firepower to wreck several worlds. And by the look of him, Motela was beginning to acknowledge the same reality. They swapped a nervous grin.

Samual stood up and put out his hand. 'We need this. Very badly.'

'I know,' Kolhammer said. 'We won't let you down.'

*

Nobody in Koblat's spaceport noticed the steady procession of kids slipping quietly down the airlock tube in bay WJR-99, where the *Leonora Cephei* was docked. Not the port officials, not the other crews (who would have taken a dim view of Captain Knox's charter), and certainly not the company cops. For the first time in Jed's life, the company's policy meant that things were swinging his way.

The spaceport's internal security surveillance systems were turned off, the CAB docking-bay logs had been disabled, customs staff were on extended leave. No inconvenient memory file would ever exist of the starships that had come and gone since the start of the quarantine; nor would there be a tax record of the bonuses everyone was earning.

Even so, Jed was taking no chances. His small chosen tribe convened in the day club where he and Beth checked them over, making them take off their red handkerchiefs before dispatching them up to the spaceport at irregular intervals.

There were eighteen Deadnights he and Beth reckoned they could trust to keep quiet; and that was stretching the *Leonora Cephei*'s life-support capacity to its legal limit. Counting himself and Beth, there were four left when Gari finally arrived. That part was pre-arranged; if both of them had been gone from the apartment for the whole day, Mother might have wondered what they were up to. What had definitely not been arranged was Gari having Navar in tow.

'I'm coming, too,' Navar said defiantly as she saw Jed's face darken. 'You can't stop me.'

Her voice was that same priggish bark he had come to loathe over the last months, not just the tone but the way it always got what it wanted. 'Gari!' he protested. 'What are you doing, doll?'

His sister's lips squeezed up as a prelude to crying. 'She saw me packing. She said she'd tell Digger.'

'I will, I swear,' Navar said. 'I'm not staying here, not when I can go and live in Valisk. I'm going, all right.'

'OK.' Jed put his arm round Gari's quivering shoulders. 'Don't worry about it. You did the right thing.'

'No, she bloody didn't,' Beth exclaimed. 'There's no room on board for anyone else.'

Gari started crying. Navar folded her arms, putting on her most stubborn expression.

'Thanks,' Jed said over his sister's head.

'Don't leave me here with Digger,' Gari wailed. 'Please, Jed, don't.'

'No one's leaving you behind,' Jed promised.

'What then?' Beth asked.

'I don't know. Knox is just going to have to find room for one more, I suppose.' He glared at Gari's erstwhile antagonizer. How bloody typical that even now she was messing things up, right when he thought he was going to escape the curse of Digger for ever. By rights he should deck her one and lock her in a dunny until they'd gone. But in the world Kiera promised them all animosities would be forgiven and forgotten. Even a mobile pain-in-the-arse like Navar. It was an ideal he was desperate to achieve. Would dumping her here make him unworthy of Kiera?

Seeing his indecision, Beth stormed: 'Christ, you're so useless.' She rounded on Navar, the nervejam suddenly in her hand. Navar's smirk faded as she found herself confronting someone who for once wasn't going to be wheedled or threatened. 'One word out of you, one complaint, one show of your usual malice, and I use this on your bum before I shove you out of the airlock. Got that?' The nervejam was pressed against the end of Navar's nose for emphasis.

'Yes,' the girl squeaked. She looked as miserable and frightened as Gari. Jed couldn't remember seeing her so disconcerted before.

'Good,' Ruth said. The nervejam vanished into a pocket. She flashed Jed a puzzled frown. 'I don't know why you let her give you so much grief the whole time. She's only a girly sprog.'

Jed realized he must be blushing as red as Gari. Explanations now would be pointless, not to mention difficult.

He pulled his shoulder bag out from under the table. It was disappointingly light to be carrying everything he considered essential to his life.

*

Captain Knox was waiting for them in the lounge at the end of the airlock tube. A short man with the flat features of his Pacific island ancestry, but the pale skin and ash-blond hair which one of those same ancestors had bought as he geneered his family for free fall endurance. His light complexion made his anger highly conspicuous.

'I only agreed to fifteen,' he said as Beth and Jed drifted through the hatch. 'You'll have to send some back; three at least.'

Jed tried to push his shoes onto a stikpad. He didn't like free fall, which made his stomach wobble, his face swell, and clogged his sinuses. Nor was he much good at manoeuvring himself by hanging on to a grab hoop and using his wrists to angle his body. Inertia fought every move, making his tendons burn. When he did manage to touch his sole to the pad there was little adhesion. Like everything else in the inter-orbit ship, it was worn down and out of date.

'Nobody is going back,' he said. Gari was clinging to his

side, the mass of her floating body trying hard to twist him away from the stikpad. He didn't let go of the grab hoop.

'Then we don't leave,' Knox said simply.

Jed saw Gerald Skibbow at the back of the lounge; as usual he was in switch-off, staring at the bulkhead with glazed eyes. Jed was beginning to wonder if he had a serious habit. 'Gerald.' He waved urgently. 'Gerald!'

Knox muttered under his breath as Gerald came awake in slow stages, his body twitching.

'How many passengers are you licensed for?' Beth asked.

Knox ignored her.

'What is it?' Gerald asked. He was blinking as if the light was too bright.

'Too many people,' Knox said. 'You've gotta chuck some off.'

'I have to go,' Gerald said quietly.

'No one is saying you don't, Gerald,' Beth said. 'It's your money.'

'But my ship,' Knox said. 'And I'm not carrying this many.'

'Fine,' Beth said. 'We'll just ask the CAB office how many people you're licensed to carry.'

'Don't be stupid.'

'If you won't carry us, then return the fee and we'll find another ship.'

Knox gave Gerald a desperate glance, but he looked equally bewildered.

'Just three, did you say?' Beth asked.

Sensing things were finally flowing in his favour, Knox smiled. 'Yes, just three. I'll be happy to fly a second charter for your friends later.'

Which was rubbish, Beth knew. He was only worried about his own precious skin. A ship operating this close to the margin really would be hard put to sustain nineteen Deadnights plus the crew. It was the first time Knox had shown the slightest concern about the flight. The only interest he'd shown in them

**997**

before was their ability to pay. Which Gerald had done, and well over the odds, too. They didn't deserve to be pushed around like this.

But Gerald was totally out of the argument. Back in one of his semi-comatose depressions again. And Jed ... Jed these days was focused on one thing only. Beth still hadn't made up her mind if she was annoyed about that or not.

'Put three of us in the lifeboat, then,' she said.

'What?' Knox asked.

'You do have a lifeboat?'

'Of course.'

Which is where he and his precious family would shelter if anything did go wrong, she knew. 'We'll put the three youngest in there. They'd be the first in anyway, wouldn't they?'

Knox glared at her. Ultimately, though, money won the argument. Skibbow had paid double the price of an ordinary charter, even at the inflated rates flights to and from Koblat were currently worth.

'Very well,' Knox said gracelessly. He datavised the flight computer to close the airlock hatch. Koblat's flight control was already signalling him to leave the docking-bay. His filed flight plan gave a departure time of five minutes ago, and another ship was waiting.

'Give him the coordinate,' Beth told Jed. She took Gerald by the arm, and gently began to tug him to his couch.

Jed handed the flek over to Knox, wondering how come Beth was suddenly in charge.

The *Leonora Cephei* rose quickly out of the docking-bay; a standard drum-shaped life-support capsule separated from her fusion drive by a thirty-metre spine. Four thermo-dump panels unfolded from her rear equipment bay, looking like the cruciform fins of some atmospheric plane. Ion thrusters flared around her base and nose. Without any cargo to carry, manoeuvring was a lot faster and easier than normal. She rotated through ninety degrees, then the secondary drive came on, pushing her out past the rim of the spaceport.

Before *Leonora Cephei* had travelled five kilometres, the *Villeneuve's Revenge* settled onto the waiting cradle of bay WJR-99. Captain Duchamp datavised a request to the spaceport service company for a full load of deuterium and He₃. His fuel levels were down to twenty per cent, he said, and he had a long voyage ahead.

*

The clouds over Chainbridge formed a tight stationary knot of dark carmine amid the ruby streamers which ebbed and swirled across the rest of the sky. Standing behind Moyo as he drove the bus towards the town, Stephanie could sense the equally darkened minds clustered among the buildings. There were far more than there should have been; Chainbridge was barely more than an ambitious village.

Moyo's concern matched hers. His foot eased off the accelerator. 'What do you want to do?'

'We don't have a lot of choice. That's where the bridge is. And the vehicles need recharging.'

'Go through?'

'Go through. I can't believe anyone will hurt the children now.'

Chainbridge's streets were clogged with parked vehicles. They were either military jeeps and scout rangers or lightly armoured infantry carriers. Possessed lounged indolently amongst them. They reminded Moyo of ancient revolutionary guerrillas, with their bold-print camouflage fatigues, heavy lace-up boots, and shoulder-slung rifles.

'Uh oh,' Moyo said. They had reached the town square, a pleasant cobbled district bounded by tall aboriginal leghorn trees. Two light tracked tanks were drawn up across the road. The machines were impossibly archaic with their iron-slab bodywork and chuntering engines coughing up diesel smoke. But that same primitive solidity gave them a unique and unarguable menace.

The Karmic Crusader had already stopped, its cheap effervescent colours quite absurd against the tank's solid armour. Moyo braked behind it.

'You stay in here,' Stephanie said, squeezing his shoulder. 'The children need someone. This is frightening for them.'

'This is frightening for me,' he groused.

Stephanie stepped down onto the cobbles. Sunglasses spread out from her nose in the same fashion as a butterfly opening its wings.

Cochrane was already arguing with a couple of soldiers who were standing in front of the tanks. Stephanie came up behind him, and smiled pleasantly at them. 'I'd like to talk to Annette Ekelund, please. Would you tell her we're here.'

One of them glanced at the Karmic Crusader and the inquisitive children pressed against its windscreen. He nodded, and slipped away past the tanks.

Annette Ekelund emerged from the town hall a couple of minutes later. She was wearing a smart grey uniform, its leather jacket lined in scarlet silk.

'Oh, wow,' Cochrane said as she approached. 'It's Mrs Hitler herself.'

Stephanie growled at him.

'We heard you were coming,' Annette Ekelund said in a tired voice.

'So why have you blocked the road?' Stephanie asked.

'Because I can, of course. Don't you understand anything?'

'All right, you've demonstrated you're in charge. I accept that. None of us has the slightest intention of challenging you. Can we go past now, please?'

Annette Ekelund shook her head in bemused wonder. 'I just had to see you for myself. What do you think you're doing with these kids? Do you think you're saving them?'

'Frankly, yes. I'm sorry if that's too simple for you, but they're really all I'm interested in.'

'If you genuinely cared, you would have left them alone. It would have been kinder in the long run.'

'They're children. They're alone now, and they're frightened now. Abstract issues don't mean very much compared to that. And you're scaring them.'

'Not intentionally.'

'So what is all this martial jingoism for? Keeping us under control?'

'You don't show a lot of gratitude, do you? I risked everything to bring lost souls back to this world, including yours.'

'And so you think that gives you a shot at being our empress. You didn't risk anything, you were compelled, just like all of us. You were simply the first, nothing more.'

'I was the first to see what needed to be done. The first to organize. The first to fight. The first to claim victory. The first to stake out our land.' She swept an arm out towards a squad of troops who had taken over a pavement café on the other side of the square. 'That's why they follow me. Because I'm right, because I know what needs to be done.'

'What these people need is some kind of purpose. Mortonridge is falling apart. There's no food left, no electricity, nobody knows what to do. With authority comes responsibility. Unless you're just a bandit queen, of course. If you're a real leader, you should apply your leadership skills where they'll do the most good. You made a start, you kept the communication net working, you gave most towns a council of sorts. You should have built on that.'

Annette Ekelund grinned. 'What exactly were you before? They told me you were just a housewife.'

'It doesn't matter,' Stephanie said, impatient with the whole charade. 'Will you let us through?'

'If I didn't, you'd only find another way. Of course you can go through. We even have a few children scooting round the town that you can take with you. See? I'm not a complete monster.'

'The buses need recharging first.'

'Naturally.' Ekelund sighed. She beckoned one of the tank guards. 'Dane will show you where a working power point is. Please don't ask us for any food, I haven't got enough to spare. I'm having trouble supplying my own troops as it is.'

Stephanie looked at the tanks; if she concentrated hard she could make out the phantasm shapes of the farm tractor mechanoids behind the armour. 'What are you and your army doing here?'

'I would have thought that was obvious. I've taken that responsibility you prize so highly. I'm protecting Mortonridge for you. We're only thirty kilometres from the firebreak they slashed across the top of the ridge; and on the other side, the Saldana Princess is preparing. They're not going to leave us alone, Stephanie Ash. They hate us and they fear us. It's a nasty combination. So while you go gallivanting around doing your good deeds, just remember who's holding back the barbarians.' She started back for the tanks, then paused. 'You know, one day you're really going to have to decide where your loyalties lie. You said you'd fight to stop them throwing you back; well, if you do, it'll be at my side.'

'Hoh, wow, one iron-assed lady,' Cochrane muttered.

'Definitely,' Stephanie agreed.

Dane climbed into the Karmic Crusader with Cochrane and showed them the way to a line of warehouses which served the wharf. Their long roofs were all made from solar-collector panels. When the buses were plugged in, Stephanie called her people together and told them what Ekelund had said.

'If any of you want to wait here while the buses go to the firebreak, I'll understand,' she said. 'The Kingdom military might get nervous about four large vehicles heading towards them.'

'They won't shoot us out of hand,' McPhee said. 'Not as long as we don't cross the line. They'll be curious.'

'Do you think so?' Tina said anxiously. A large lace hanky was pressed to her lips.

'I've been there,' Dane said. 'It was a scout mission. I watched them watching me. They won't start any trouble. Like your friend said, they'll be curious.'

'We're almost there,' Stephanie's fixed smile betrayed her nerves. 'Just a few more hours, that's all.' She glanced back at the buses, putting on a cheerful expression as she waved at the children pressed up against the windows. They had all picked up on the gloomy aura of the darkened clouds overhead. 'McPhee, Franklin; give me a hand with them, will you. We'll let them stretch their legs here and use a toilet.'

'Sure.'

Stephanie let Moyo hold her for a moment. He planted a kiss on her forehead. 'Don't give up now.'

She smiled shyly. 'I won't. Can you take a look in the warehouses for me, see if you can find some working toilets. If not, we'll have to make do with tissues and the river.'

'I'll go check.'

The big sliding doors of the closest warehouse were open. It was used to store tubing, row after row of floor-to-ceiling stacks. All its lights were off, but there was enough pink-tinged sunlight coming through the doors for him to see by. He started checking round for an office.

Silent fork-lift mechanoids were standing in the aisles, holding up bundles of tubing that had been destined for urgent delivery. It wouldn't take much effort to start them up again, he thought. But what would be the point? Did a society of possessed need factories and farms? Some infrastructure was necessary, yes, but how much and of what kind? Something simple and efficient, and extremely long lasting. He was quietly glad that kind of decision wasn't his.

A pyramid of tubing shielded the man from Moyo's perception. So he convinced himself later. Whatever the reason, he didn't notice him until he had rounded a corner and was barely five metres away. And he wasn't a possessed. Moyo knew his own kind, the internal glimmer of cells excited by the energistic overspill. This man's bioelectric currents were almost black, while his thoughts were fast and quiet. He was excessively ordinary in appearance; wearing pale green trousers, a check shirt, and a sleeveless jacket with DataAxis printed on its left breast pocket.

Moyo was chilled by a rush of panic. Any non-possessed creeping round here had to be a spy; which meant he'd be armed, most likely with something potent enough to terminate a possessed with minimum fuss.

White fire punched out of Moyo's palm; an instinctive response.

The seething streamer splashed against the man's face and flowed round him to strike the tubing behind him. Moyo grunted in disbelief. The man simply stood there as if it was water pouring over him.

The white fire dimmed, its remnants retreating into Moyo's hand. He whimpered, expecting the worst. I'm going to be blown back into the beyond. They've found a way of neutralizing our energistic power. We've lost. There's only the beyond now. For always.

He closed his eyes. Thinking: Stephanie. Tinged with fond longing.

Nothing happened. He opened his eyes again. The man was looking at him with a mildly embarrassed expression. Behind him, molten metal was dribbling down the side of the stacked tubing.

'Who are you?' Moyo asked hoarsely.

'My name's Hugh Rosler. I used to live in Exnall.'

'Did you follow us here?'

'No. Although I did watch your bus leave Exnall. It's just coincidence I'm here now.'

'Right,' Moyo said carefully. 'You're not a spy, then?'

The question was one which Rosler apparently found quite amusing. 'Not for the Kulu Kingdom, no.'

'So how come the white fire didn't affect you?'

'I have a built-in resistance. It was thought we should have some protection when this time came around. And the reality dysfunction ability has proved inordinately useful over the years. I've been in a few tight corners in my time; completely inadvertently, I might add. I'm not supposed to be obtrusive.'

'Then you are an agent. Who do you work for?'

'*Agent* implies an active role. I only observe, I'm not part of any faction.'

'Faction?'

'The Kingdom. The Confederation. Adamists. Edenists. The possessed. Factions.'

'Uh huh. Are you going to shoot me, then, or something?'

'Good heavens, no. I told you, I'm here purely on observation duty.'

What was being said, apparently in all sincerity, wasn't helping to calm Moyo at all. 'For which faction?'

'Ah. That's classified, I'm afraid. Technically, I shouldn't even be telling you this much. But circumstances have changed since my mission began. These things aren't quite so important today. I'm just trying to put you at ease.'

'It's not working.'

'You really do have nothing to fear from me.'

'You're not human, are you?'

'I'm ninety-nine per cent human. That's good enough to qualify, surely?'

Moyo thought he would have preferred it if Hugh Rosler had launched into an indignant denial. 'What's the one per cent?'

'Sorry. Classified.'

'Xenoc? Is that it? Some unknown race? We always had

**1005**

rumours of pre-technology contact, men being taken away to breed.'

Hugh Rosler chuckled. 'Oh, yes, good old Roswell. You know I'd almost forgotten about that; the papers were full of it for decades afterwards. But I don't think it ever really happened. At least, I never detected any UFOs when I was on Earth, and I was there quite a while.'

'You were ... ? But ...'

'I'd better be going. Your friends are starting to wonder where you've got to. There's a toilet in the next warehouse which the children can use. The tank is gravity fed, so it's still working.'

'Wait! What are you observing us for?'

'To see what happens, of course.'

'Happens? You mean when the Kingdom attacks?'

'No, that's not really important. I want to see what the outcome is for your entire race now the beyond has been revealed to you. I must say, I'm becoming quite excited by the prospect. After all, I have been waiting for this for a very long time. It's my designated goal function.'

Moyo simply stared at him, astonishment and indignation taking the place of fear. 'How long?' was all he managed to whisper.

'Eighteen centuries.' Rosler raised an arm in a cheery wave, and walked away into the shadows at the back of the warehouse. They seemed to lap him up.

'What's the matter with you?' Stephanie asked when Moyo shambled slowly out into the gloomy light of the rumbling clouds.

'Don't laugh, but I think I've just met Methuselah's younger brother.'

*

Louise heard the lounge hatch slide open, and guessed who it was. His duty watch had finished fifteen minutes ago.

Just long enough to show he wasn't in any sort of rush to see her.

The trouble with the *Jamrana*, Louise thought, was its layout. Its cabin fittings were just as good as those in the *Far Realm*, but instead of the pyramid of four life-support capsules, the inter-orbit cargo craft had a single cylindrical life-support section riding above the cargo truss. The decks were stacked one on top of the other like the layers of a wedding cake. To find someone, all you had to do was start at the top, and climb down the central ladder. There was no escape.

'Hello, Louise.'

She reached for a polite smile. 'Hello, Pieri.'

Pieri Bushay had just reached twenty, the second oldest of three brothers. Like most inter-orbit ships, *Jamrana* was run as a family concern; all seven crew-members were Bushays. The strangeness of the extended family, the looseness of its internal relationships, was one which Louise found troubling; it was more a company than any family she understood. Pieri's elder brother was away serving a commission in the Govcentral Navy; which left his father, twin mothers, brother, and two cousins to run the ship.

Small wonder that a young female passenger would be such an attraction to him. He was shy, and uncertain, which was endearing; nothing like the misplaced assurance of William Elphinstone.

'How are you feeling?'

His usual opening line.

'Fine.' Louise tapped the little nanonic package behind her ear. 'The wonders of Confederation technology.'

'We'll be flipping over in another twenty hours. Halfway there. Then we'll be flying ass- ... er, I mean, bottom-backwards to Earth.'

She was impatient with the fact it was going to take longer to fly seventy million kilometres between planets than it had to fly between stars. But at least the fusion drive was scheduled to be on for a third of the trip. The medical packages didn't have to work quite so hard to negate her sickness. 'That's good.'

'Are you sure you don't want me to datavise the O'Neill Halo to see if there's a ship heading for Tranquillity?'

'No.' That had been too sharp. 'Thank you, Pieri, but if a ship is going, then it's going, if not, there's nothing I can do. Fate, you see.'

'Oh, sure. I understand.' He smiled tentatively. 'Louise, if you have to stay in the Halo till you find a starship, I'd like to show you round. I've visited hundreds of the rocks. I know what's hot out there, what to see, what to miss. It would be fun.'

'Hundreds?'

'Fifty, at least. And all the major ones; including Nova Kong.'

'I'm sorry, Pieri, that doesn't mean much to me. I've never heard of Nova Kong.'

'Really? Not even on Norfolk?'

'No. The only one I know is High York, and that's only because we're heading to it.'

'But Nova Kong is famous; one of the first to be flown into Earth orbit and be made habitable. Nova Kong physicists invented the ZTT drive. And Richard Saldana was the asteroid's chairman once; he used it as his headquarters to plan the Kulu colonization.'

'How fabulous. I can't really imagine a time when the Kingdom didn't exist, it seems so ... substantial. In fact all of Earth's pre-starflight history reads like a fable to me. So, have you ever visited High York before?'

'Yes, it's where the *Jamrana* is registered.'

'That's your home, then?'

'We mostly dock there, but the ship's my real home. I wouldn't swap it for anything.'

'Just like Joshua. You space-types are all the same. You've got wild blood.'

'I suppose so.' His face tightened at the mention of Joshua; the guardian angel fiancé Louise managed to mention in every conversation.

'Is High York very well organized?'

He seemed puzzled by the question. 'Yes. Of course. It has to be. Asteroids are nothing like planets, Louise. If the environment isn't maintained properly you'd have a catastrophe on your hands. They can't afford not to be well organized.'

'I know that. What I meant was, the government. Does it have very strong law-enforcement policies? Phobos seemed fairly easy going.'

'That's the devout Communists for you; they're very trusting, Dad says they always give people the benefit of the doubt.'

It confirmed her worries. When the four of them had arrived at the *Jamrana* a couple of hours before its departure, Endron had handed over their passport fleks to the single Immigration Officer on duty. He had known the woman, and they'd spoken cheerfully. She'd been laughing when she slotted the fleks into her processor block, barely glancing at the images they stored. Three transient offworlders with official documentation, who were friends of Endron ... She even allowed Endron to accompany them on board.

That was when he'd taken Louise aside. 'You won't make it, you know that, don't you?' he asked.

'We've got this far,' she said shakily. Though she'd had her doubts. There had been so many people as they made their tortuous way to the spaceport with the cargo mechanoid concealing Faurax's unconscious body. But they'd got the forger on board the *Far Realm*, and into a zero-tau pod without incident.

'So far you've had a lot of luck, and no genuine obstacle. That's going to end as soon as the *Jamrana* enters Govcentral-controlled space. You don't understand what it's going to be like, Louise. There's no way you'll ever get inside High York. Look, the only reason you ever got inside Phobos was because we smuggled you in, and no one bothered to inspect the *Far Realm*. You got out because no one is bothered about departing ships. And now you're heading straight at Earth, which has the largest single population in the Confederation, and runs the greatest military force ever assembled. A military force which along with the leadership is very paranoid right now. Three forged passports are not going to get you in. They are going to run every test they can think of, Louise, believe me, Fletcher is not going to get through High York's spaceport.' He was almost pleading with her. 'Come with me, tell our government what's happened. They won't hurt him, I'll testify that he's not a danger. Then after that we can find you a ship to Tranquillity, all above board.'

'No. You don't understand, they'll send him back to the beyond. I saw it on the news; if you put a possessed in zero-tau it compels them out of the body they're using. I can't turn Fletcher in, not if they're going to force him back there. He's suffered for seven centuries. Isn't that enough?'

'And what about the person whose body he's possessing?'

'I don't know!' she cried. 'I didn't want any of this. My whole planet's been possessed.'

'All right. I'm sorry. But I had to say it. You're doing a damn sight worse than playing with fire, Louise.'

'Yes.' She held on to his shoulder with one hand to steady herself, and brushed her lips to his cheek. 'Thank you. I'm sure you could have blown the whistle on us if you really wanted to.'

His reddening cheeks were confirmation enough. 'Yeah, well. Maybe I learned from you that nothing is quite black and white. Besides, that Fletcher, he's so . . .'

'Decent.'

Louise gave Pieri the kind of look that told him she was

immensely interested in every word he spoke. 'So what will happen when we arrive at High York, then? I want to know everything.'

Pieri started to access all his neural nanonic filed memories of High York spaceport. With luck, and a surfeit of details, he could make this last for a good hour.

*

The Magistrature Council was the Confederation's ultimate court. Twenty-five judges sat on the Council, appointed by the Assembly to deal with the most serious violations of Confederation law. The majority of cases were the ones brought against starship crews captured by navy ships, those accused of piracy or owning antimatter. Less common were the war crimes trials, inevitably resulting from asteroid independence struggles. There were only two possible sentences for anyone found guilty by the Magistrature: death, or deportation to a penal colony.

The full Magistrature Council also had the power to sit in judgement of sovereign governments. The last such sitting had determined, in absentia, Omuta to be guilty of genocide, and ordered the execution of its cabinet and military high command.

The Council's final mandate was the authority to declare a person, government, or entire people to be an Enemy of Humanity. Laton had been awarded such a condemnation, as had members of the black syndicates producing antimatter, and various terrorists and defeated warlords. Such a proclamation was essentially a death warrant which empowered a Confederation official to pursue the renegade across all national boundaries, and required all local governments to cooperate.

That was the pronouncement the Provost General was now aiming to have applied against the possessed. With that in the bag, the CNIS would be free to do whatever they wanted to Jacqueline Couteur and the other prisoners in the demon trap. But first her current status had to be legally established, whether she was a hostile prisoner under the terms of the state of emergency or a hapless victim. In either case, she was still entitled to a legal representative.

The courtroom in Trafalgar chosen for the preliminary hearing was maximum security court three. It had none of the trimmings of the public courts, retaining only the very basic layout of docks, desks for the prosecution and defence counsels, the judge's bench, and a small observer gallery. There was no permitted or designated place for the media or the public.

Maynard Khanna arrived five minutes before the hearing was scheduled to begin, and sat at the front of the small gallery. As someone used to the order of military life, he had an intense distrust and dislike of the legal profession. Lawyers had abolished the simple concept of right and wrong, turning it into degrees of guilt. And in doing so they cut themselves in for fees which came only in large multiples of a navy captain's salary.

The accused were entitled to a defence, Maynard conceded, but he still never understood how their lawyers avoided feeling equally guilty when they got them off.

Lieutenant Murphy Hewlett sat down behind Maynard, pulling unhappily at the jacket of his dress uniform. He leant forward and murmured: 'I can't believe this is happening.'

'Me neither,' Maynard grumbled back. 'But the Provost General says it should be a formality. No court in the galaxy is going to let Jacqueline Couteur walk out of the door.'

'For God's sake, Maynard, she shouldn't even be let out of the demon trap. You know that.'

'This is a secure court; and we can't give her defence lawyer an opportunity to mount an appeal on procedural grounds.'

'Bloody lawyers!'

'Too right. What are you doing here, anyway?'

'Provost General's witness. I'm supposed to tell the judge how we were in a war situation on Lalonde, which makes Couteur's capture legitimate under the Assembly's rules of engagement. It's in case her lawyer goes for a wrongful jurisdiction plea.'

'You know, this is the first time I've ever disagreed with the First Admiral. I said we should just keep her in the demon trap, and screw all this legal crap. Gilmore is losing days of research time over this.'

Murphy hissed in disgust and sat back. For the eighth time that morning, his hand ran over his holster. It contained a nine-millimetre semi-automatic pistol, loaded with dumdum bullets. He loosened the cover, allowing his fingers to rest on the grip. Yesterday evening he had spent two hours at the range in the officers' mess, shooting the weapon without any aid from neural nanonics programs. Just in case.

An eight-strong marine squad and their sergeant, each of them armed with a machine-gun, marched the four prisoners into the court. Jacqueline Couteur was the first in line, dressed in a neat grey suit. If it hadn't been for the carbotanium manacles she would have been a picture of middle-class respectability. A slim sensor bracelet had been placed round her right wrist, monitoring the flow of energy through her body. She looked round, noting the marine guards at each of the three doors. Then she saw Murphy Hewlett scowling, and grinned generously at him.

'Bitch,' he grunted under his breath.

The marine squad sat Jacqueline in the dock, and fastened her manacles to a loop of chain. The other three possessed, Randall, Lennart, and Nena were made to sit on the bench beside her. Once their manacles were secured, the marines took up position behind them. The sergeant datavised his processor block to check that the sensor bracelets were working, then gave the clerk of the court a brief nod.

The four defence lawyers were ushered in. Jacqueline manoeuvred a polite welcoming smile into place, this was the third time she'd seen Udo DiMarco. The lawyer wasn't entirely happy to be appointed her counsel, he'd admitted that much to her, but then went on to say he'd do his best.

'Good morning, Jacqueline,' he said, doing his nervous best to ignore the marines behind her.

'Hello, Udo. Did you manage to obtain the recordings?'

'I filed a release request with the court, yes. It may take some time; the navy claims their Intelligence Service research is classified and exempt from the Access Act of 2503. I'll challenge that, of course, but as I said this is all going to take some time.'

'They tortured me, Udo. The judge has to see those recordings. I'll walk free in seconds if the truth is ever known.'

'Jacqueline, this is only a preliminary hearing to establish that all the required arrest procedures were followed, and clarify your legal custody status.'

'I wasn't arrested, I was abducted.'

Udo DiMarco sighed, and plunged on. 'The Provost General's team is going to argue that as a possessor you have committed a kidnap, and are therefore a felon. That will give them a basis for holding you in custody. They're also arguing that your energistic power constitutes a new and dangerous weapons technology, which will validate the Intelligence Service's investigation. Please don't expect to walk out of court this morning.'

'Well, I'm sure you'll do your best.' She gave him an encouraging smile.

Udo DiMarco flexed his shoulders uncomfortably and withdrew to the defence counsel's bench. His sole comfort was the fact that the media weren't allowed in; no one would know he was defending a possessed. He datavised his processor block, reviewing the files he'd assembled. Ironically, he could put up quite a good case for Couteur's release, but he'd made the decision five minutes after having the case dumped on him that he was only going to make a show of defending her. Jacqueline could never know, but Udo DiMarco had a lot of family on New California.

The clerk of the court rose to his feet and announced: 'Please stand for Judge Roxanne Taynor. This Magistrature Council court is now in session.'

Judge Taynor appeared at the door behind the bench. Everyone stood, including the four possessed. Their movement meant the marine guards had to alter the angle they were pointing their machine-guns. For a moment their concentration was less than absolute. Everybody's neural nanonics crashed. The light-panels became incandescent. Four balls of white fire exploded around the machine-guns, smashing them into a shower of molten fragments.

Murphy Hewlett bellowed a wordless curse, yanking his pistol up, thumb flicking at the safety catch. Like most people he was caught halfway to his feet, an awkward position. A brutally white light was making him squeeze his eyelids closed; retinal implants were taking a long time to filter out the excess photons. The sound of the detonating machine-guns was audible above the startled cries. He swung the pistol round to line up on Couteur. Marines were screaming as their hands and lower arms were shredded along with their weapons. The lights went out.

From dazzling brilliance to total blackness was too much for his eyes. He couldn't see a thing. A machine-gun fired. Muzzle blasts sent out a flickering orange light.

The possessed were all moving. Fast. The gunfire turned their motions into speedy flickers. They'd run straight through the dock, smashing the tough composite apart. Fragments tumbled through the air.

Two lightning streaks of white fire lashed out, striking a couple of marines. The lawyers were scrambling for the closest door. Roxanne Taynor was already through the door to her chambers. One of the marines was standing in front of it, sweeping her machine-gun in a fast arc as she tried to line it up on a possessed.

'Close the doors!' Murphy yelled. 'Seal this place.'

A machine-gun was firing again as the light from the white fire shrank away. People screamed as they dived and stumbled for cover. Ricochets hummed lethally through the blackness.

Murphy caught sight of Couteur in the segments of illumination thrown out by another burst of gunfire. He twisted his pistol round and fired five shots, anticipating her direction for the last two. Dumdum bullets impacted with penetrating booms. Murphy dropped to his knees, and rolled quickly. A pulse of white fire ripped through the air where he'd been standing. 'Shit!' Missed her.

He could hear a siren wailing outside. Sensor modules on the walls were starting to burn, jetting out long tongues of turquoise flame which dissolved into a fountain of sparks. Three more bolts of white fire zipped over the gallery seats. There were heavy thuds of bodies hitting the floor.

When he risked a quick glance above the seat backs he could see Nena and Randall crouched low and zigzagging towards the door behind him. Eyeblink image of the door to one side of the smashed dock: three marines standing in defensive formation round it, almost flinging a lawyer out into the corridor beyond. But the door behind him was still open. It was trying to slide shut, but the body of a dead marine was preventing it from closing.

Murphy didn't have an option. They couldn't be allowed out into Trafalgar, it was inconceivable. He vaulted over the seats just as an odd rosette of white fire spun upwards from behind the judge's bench. It hit the ceiling and bounced, expanding rapidly into a crown made up from writhing flames which coiled around and around each other. The three marines guarding the door fired at it as it swooped down at them, bullets tearing out violet bubbles which erupted into twinkling starbursts. Murphy started firing his pistol at Randall as he sprinted for the door, trigger finger pumping frantically. Seeing the dumdum rounds rip ragged chunks out of the possessed's chest. Shifting his aim slightly. Half of Randall's neck blew away in a twister of blood and bone chippings. A screaming Nena cartwheeled backwards in panic, limbs thrashing out of control.

The crown of agitated white fire dropped around one of the marines like an incendiary lasso. It contracted with a vicious snapping sound, slicing clean through his pelvis. His machine-gun was still firing as his torso tumbled down, spraying the whole courtroom with bullets. He tried to say something as he fell, but shock had jammed his entire nervous system. All that came out was a coughed grunt as his head hit the ground. Dulled eyes stared at his legs which were still standing above him, twitching spastically as they slowly buckled.

The other two marines froze in terror. Then one vomited.

'Close it!' Murphy gagged. 'For Christ's sake, get out and close it.' His eyes were hot and sticky with fluid, some of it red. His foot hit something, and he half-tripped flinging himself at the gap. He landed flat on the dead marine and rolled forward. Figures were running around at the far end of the corridor, confused movements blurring together. White fire enveloped his ankle.

'Does it hurt? We can help.'

'No, fuck you!' He flopped onto an elbow and aimed the pistol back through the door, firing wildly. Pain from his ankle was making his hand shake violently. Noxious smoke sizzled up in front of him.

Then hands were gripping his shoulders, pulling him back along the floor. Bullish shouts all around him. The distinctive thud of a Bradfield slammed against his ears, louder than thunder in the close confines of the corridor. A marine in full combat armour was standing above him, firing the heavy-calibre weapon into the courtroom. Another suited marine was pulling the corpse clear of the door.

Murphy's neural nanonics started to come back on-line. Medical programs established axon blocks. The courtroom door slid shut, locks engaging with a clunk. A fire extinguisher squirted thick white gas against Murphy's smouldering dress uniform trousers. He sank down onto the corridor floor, too stunned to say anything for a while. When he looked round he could see three people he recognized from the court, all of them ashen-faced and stupefied, slumped against the walls. The marines were tending to two of them. That was when Murphy realized the corridor floor was smeared with blood. Spent cartridge cases from his pistol rolled around.

He was dragged further away from the courtroom door, allowing the marine squad to set up two tripod-mounted Bradfields, pointing right at the grey reinforced silicon.

'Hold still,' a woman in a doctor's field uniform told him. She began to cut his trousers away; a male nurse was holding a medical nanonic package ready.

'Did any of them get out?' Murphy asked weakly. People were tramping up and down the corridor, paying no attention to him.

'I don't know,' the doctor said.

'Fuck it, find out!'

She gave him a calculating look.

'Please?'

One of the marines was called over. 'The other doors are all closed,' he told Murphy. 'We got a few people out, but the possessed are safely locked up in there. Every exit is sealed tight. The captain is waiting for a CNIS team to advise him what to do next.'

'A few people?' Murphy asked. 'A few people got out?'

'Yeah. Some of the lawyers, the judge, court staff, five marines. We're proud of the fight you put up, sir, you and the others. It could have been a lot worse.'

'And the rest?'

The marine turned his blank shell-helmet towards the door. 'Sorry, sir.'

The roar of the machine-gun ended, leaving only the screams and whimpers to fester through the darkened courtroom. Maynard Khanna could hear his own feeble groans contributing to the morass of distress. There was little he could do to prevent it, the tiniest movement sent sickening spires of pain leaping into his skull. A gout of white fire had struck him seconds into the conflict, wrapping round his leg like a blazing serpent, felling him immediately. His temple had struck one of the seats, dazing him badly. After that, all the noise and flaring light swarmed around him, somehow managing to leave him isolated from the affray.

Now the white fire had gone, leaving him alone with its terrible legacy. The flesh from his leg had melted off. But his bones had remained intact, perfectly white. He could see his skeletal foot twitching next to his real one, its tiny bones fitting together like a medical text.

The splintered remnants of the dock were burning with unnatural brightness, throwing capering shadows on the wall. Maynard turned his head, crying out as red stars gave way to an ominous darkness. When he flushed the involuntary tears from his eyes he could see the heavy door at the back of the court was shut.

They hadn't got out!

He took a few breaths, momentarily puzzled by what he was doing in the dark, the waves of pain seemed to prevent his thoughts from flowing. The screams had died, along with every other sound except for the sharp crackling of the flames. Footsteps crunched through the debris. Three dark figures loomed above him; humanoid perhaps, but any lingering facet of humanity had been bred out generations ago.

The whispers began, slithering up from a bottomless pit to comfort him with the sincerity of a two-timing lover. Then came the real pain.

*

Dr Gilmore studied the datavised image he was receiving direct from Marine Captain Rhodri Peyton's eyes. He was standing in the middle of a marine squad which was strung out along one of the corridors leading to maximum security court three. Their machine-guns and Bradfields were deployed to cover the engineering officers, who were gingerly applying sensor pads to the door.

When Dr Gilmore attempted to access the officers' processor blocks there was no response. The units were too close to the possessed inside the courtroom. 'Have they made any attempt to break out?' he asked.

'No, sir,' Rhodri Peyton datavised. His eyes flicked to brown scorch lines on the walls just outside the door. 'Those marks were caused when Lieutenant Hewlett was engaging them. There's been nothing since then. We've got them trapped, all right.'

Gilmore accessed Trafalgar's central computer and requested a blueprint of the courtroom. There were no service tunnels nearby, and the air-conditioning ducts weren't large enough for anyone to crawl down. It was a maximum security court, after all. Unfortunately it wasn't the kind of security designed with the possessed in mind. He knew it would only be a matter of time before they got out. Then there really would be hell to pay.

'Have you confirmed the number of people in the courtroom?'

'We're missing twelve people, sir. But we know at least four of those are dead, and the others sustained some injuries. And Hewlett claims he terminated one of the possessed, Randall.'

'I see. That means we now have a minimum of eleven possessed to contend with. That much energistic potential is extremely dangerous.'

'This whole area is sealed sir, and I've got a squad covering each door.'

'I'm sure you have, Captain. One moment.' He datavised

the First Admiral, and gave him a brief summary. 'I have to advise we don't send the marines in. Given the size of the courtroom and the number of possessed, I'd estimate marine casualties of at least fifty per cent.'

'Agreed,' the First Admiral datavised back. 'The marines don't go in. But are you certain everyone in there is now possessed?'

'I think it's an inevitable conclusion, sir. This whole legal business was quite obviously just a ploy by Couteur to gain a foothold here. That many possessed represent a significant threat. My guess is that they may simply try to tunnel their way out, I expect they'll be able to dissolve the rock around them. They must be neutralized as swiftly as possible. We can always acquire further individuals to continue my team's research.'

'Dr Gilmore, I'd remind you that my staff captain is in there, along with a number of civilians. We must make at least one attempt to subdue them. You've had weeks to research this energistic ability, you must be able to suggest something.'

'There is one possibility, sir. I accessed Thakrar's report; he used decompression against the possessed when they tried to storm the *Villeneuve's Revenge*.'

'To kill them.'

'Yes. But it does indicate a weakness. I was going to recommend that we vent the courtroom's atmosphere. That way we wouldn't have to risk opening one of the doors to fire any sort of weapon in there. However, we could try gas against them first. They can force matter into new shapes, but I think altering a molecular structure would probably be beyond them. It needn't even be a chemical weapon, we could simply increase the nitrogen ratio until they black out. Once they've been immobilized, they could be placed into zero-tau.'

'How would you know if a gas assault worked? They destroyed the sensors, we can't see in.'

'There are a number of electronic systems remaining in the courtroom; if the possessed do succumb to the gas those systems should come back on-line. But whatever we do, Admiral, we will have to open the door at some stage to confirm their condition.'

'Very well, try the gas first. We owe Maynard and the others that much.'

*

'We're not going to have much time to get out,' Jacqueline Couteur said.

Perez, who had come into Maynard Khanna's body a few minutes earlier, was struggling to keep his thoughts flowing lucidly under a torrent of pain firing in from every part of his new frame. He managed to focus on some of the most badly damaged zones, seeing the blood dry up and torn discoloured flesh return to a healthier aspect. 'Mama, what did you to this guy?'

'Taught him not to be so stubborn,' Jacqueline said emotionlessly.

He winced as he raised himself up onto his elbows. Despite his most ardent wishes, his damaged leg felt as if fireworms were burrowing through it. He could imagine it whole and perfect, and even see the image forming around reality, but that wasn't quite enough to make it so. 'OK, so now what?' He glanced round. It was not the most auspicious of environments to welcome him back. Bodies were straddling the court's wrecked fittings, small orange fires gnawed hungrily at various jagged chunks of composite, and hatred was beaming through each of the doors like an emotive X-ray.

'Not much,' she admitted. 'But we have to look for some kind of advantage. We're at the very centre of the Confederation's resistance to us. There must be something we can do to help Capone and the others. I had hoped we could locate their nuclear weapons. The destruction of this base would be a significant blow to the Confederation.'

'Forget that; those marines were good,' Lennart said grudgingly. He was standing in front of the judge's bench, one hand pulling on his chin as he gazed intently at the floor. 'You know, there's some kind of room or corridor about twenty metres straight down.' The tiling started to flow away from his feet in fast ripples, exposing the naked rock below. 'It won't take long if we break this rock together.'

'Maybe,' Jacqueline said. 'But they'll know we're doing it. Gilmore will have surrounded us with sensors by now.'

'What, then?' asked one of the others they'd brought back. 'For Christ's sake, we can't stay in here and wait for the Confederation Marines to bust down the door. I've only just returned. I'm not giving this body up after only ten minutes. I couldn't stand that.'

'Christ?' Jacqueline queried bitingly.

'You might have to anyway,' Perez said. 'We all might wind up back there in the beyond.'

'Oh, why?' Jacqueline asked.

'This Khanna knows of an ambush the Confederation Navy is planning against Capone. He is confident they will destroy the Organization fleet. Without Capone to crack new star systems open, we're going to be stalled. Khanna is convinced the quarantine will prevent possession from spreading to any new worlds.'

'Then we must tell Capone,' Jacqueline said. 'All of us together must shout this news into the beyond.'

'Fine,' Nena said. 'Do that. But what about us? How are we going to get out of here?'

'That is a secondary concern for us now.'

'Not for me it bloody well isn't.'

When Jacqueline scowled at her, she saw beads of sweat pricking the woman's brow. Nena was swaying slightly, too. Some of the others looked as if they were exhausted, their eyes glazing over. Even Jacqueline was aware her body had grown heavier than before. She sniffed the air suspiciously, finding it contaminated with the slightly clammy ozone taint of air-conditioning.

'What exactly is the navy planning to do to Capone?' she asked.

'They know he's going to attack Toi-Hoi. They're going to hide a fleet at Tranquillity, and intercept him when they know he's on the way.'

'We must remember that,' Jacqueline said firmly, fixing each of them in turn with a compelling stare. 'Capone must be told. Get through to him.' She ignored everything else but the wish that the air in the courtroom was pure and fresh, blown down straight from some virgin mountain range. She could smell a weak scent of pine.

One of the possessed sat down heavily. The others were all panting.

'What's happening?' someone asked.

'Radiation, I expect,' Jacqueline said. 'They're probably bombarding us with gamma rays so they don't have to come in to deal with us.'

'Blast a door open,' Lennart said. 'Charge them. A few of us might get through.'

'Good idea,' Jacqueline said.

He pointed a finger at the door behind the judge's bench, its tip wavering about drunkenly. A weak crackle of white fire licked out. It managed to stain the door with a splatter of soot, but nothing more. 'Help me. Come on, together!'

Jacqueline closed her eyes, imagining all the clean air in the courtroom gathering around her and her alone. A light breeze ruffled her suit.

'I don't want to go back,' Perez wailed. 'Not there!'

'You must,' Jacqueline said. Her breathing was easier now. 'Capone will find you a body. He'll welcome you. I envy you for that.'

Two more of the possessed toppled over. Lennart sagged to his knees, hands clutching at his throat.

'The navy must never know what we discovered,' Jacqueline said thickly.

Perez looked up at her, too weak to plead. It wouldn't have been any use, he realized, not against that mind tone.

*

The shaped-electron explosive charge sliced clean through the courtroom door with a lightning-bolt flash. There was very little blowback against the marine squad crouched fifteen metres away down the corridor. Captain Peyton yelled 'Go!' at the same time as the charge was triggered. His armour suit's communication block was switched to audio, just in case the possessed were still active.

Ten sense-overload ordnance rounds were fired through the opening as the wrecked door spun round like a dropped coin. A ferocious blast of light and sound surged back along the corridor. The squad rushed forward into the deluge.

It was a synchronized assault. All three doors into the courtroom were blown at the same time. Three sets of sense-overload ordnance punched in. Three marine squads.

Dr Gilmore was still hooked in to Peyton's neural nanonics, receiving the image direct from the captain's shell-helmet sensors. The scene which greeted him took a while to interpret. Dimming flares were sinking slowly through the air as tight-beams of light from each suit formed a crazy jumping crisscross pattern above the wrecked fittings. Bodies lay everywhere. Some were victims of the earlier fight. Ten of them had been executed. There was no other explanation. Each of the ten had been killed by a bolt of white fire through the brain.

Peyton was pushing his way through a ring of nearly twenty marines that had formed in the middle of the courtroom. Jacqueline Couteur stood at the centre, her shape blurred by a grey twister that had formed around her. It looked as if she'd been cocooned by solid strands of air. The twister was making a high-pitched whining sound as it undulated gently from side to side.

Jacqueline Couteur's hands were in the air. She gazed at the guns levelled against her with an almost sublime composure. 'OK,' she said. 'You win. And I think I may need my lawyer again.'

# 25

There were nearly three thousand people in the crowd which assembled outside the starscraper lobby. Most of them looked fairly pissed off at being summoned, but nobody actually argued with Bonney's deputies when they came calling. They wanted a quiet life. On a planet they could have just walked away into the wilderness, here that option did not exist.

Part of the lobby's gently arching roof had crumpled, a remnant of an early battle during their takeover of the habitat. Bonney started to walk up the pile of rubble. She held a processor block in one hand, turning it so she could see the screen.

'Last chance, Rubra,' she said. 'Tell me where the boyo is, or I start getting serious.' The block's screen remained blank. 'You overheard what Patricia said. I know you did, because you're a sneaky little shit. You've been manipulating me for a while now. I'm always told where he is, and he's always gone when I get there. You're helping him as much as you're helping me, aren't you? Probably trying to frighten him into cooperating with you. Was that it? Well, not any more, Rubra, because Patricia has changed everything; we're playing big boys' rules now. I don't have to be careful, I don't have to respect your precious, delicate structure. It was fun going one-on-one against all those little bastards you stashed around the place. I enjoyed myself. But you were cheating the whole time. Funny, that's what Dariat warned us about right from the start.' She reached the roof, and walked to the edge above the crowd. 'You going to tell me?'

The screen printed: THOSE LITTLE DEADNIGHT GIRLS THAT COME HERE, YOU REALLY ENJOY WHAT YOU DO WITH THEM, DON'T YOU, DYKE?

Bonney dropped the processor block as if it was a piece of used toilet paper. 'Game over, Rubra. You lose; I'm going to use nukes to crack you in half.'

**Dariat, I think you'd better listen to this.**

**What now?**

**Bonney, as usual. But things have just acquired an unpleasant edge. I don't think Kiera should have left her unsupervised.**

Dariat hooked into the observation routines in time to see Bonney raise her hands for silence. The crowd gazed up at her expectantly.

'We've got the power of genii,' she said. 'You can grant yourself every wish you want. And we still have to live like dogs out in these shanty towns, grabbing what food we can, whipped into line, told where we can and can't go. Rubra's done that to us. We have starships, for fuck's sake. We can travel to another star system in less time than it takes your heart to beat once. But if you want to go from here to the endcap, you have to walk. Why? Because that shit Rubra won't let us use the tubes. And up until now, we've let him get away with it. Well, not any more.'

**Passionate lady,** Dariat said uncomfortably.

**Psycho lady, more like. They're not going to disobey her, they wouldn't dare. She's going to marshal them together and send them after you. I can't keep you ahead of an entire habitat of possessed hunting you. For once, boy, I'm not lying.**

**Yeah. I can see that.** Dariat went over to the fire at the back of the cave. It had almost burnt out, leaving a pyramid of coals cloaked in a powder of fine grey ash. He stood looking at it, feeling the slumbering heat contained within the pink fragments.

I have to decide. I can't beat Rubra. And Rubra will be destroyed by Kiera when she returns. For thirty years I would have welcomed that. Thirty fucking years. My entire life.

But he's willing to sacrifice his mental integrity, to join my thoughts to his. He's going to abandon two centuries of his belief that he can go it alone.

Tatiana stirred on the blanket, and sat up, bracelets chinking noisily. Sleepy confusion drained from her face. 'That was a strange dream.' She gave him a shrewd glance. 'But then this is a strange time, isn't it?'

'What was your dream?'

'I was in a universe which was half light, half darkness. And I was falling out of the light. Then Anastasia caught me, and we started to fly back up again.'

'Sounds like your salvation.'

'What's the matter?'

'Things are changing. That means I have to decide what to do. And I don't want to, Tatiana. I've spent thirty years not deciding. Thirty years telling myself this was the time I was waiting for. I've been a kid for thirty years.'

Tatiana rose and stood beside him. He refused to meet her gaze, so she put an arm lightly on his shoulder. 'What do you have to decide?'

'If I should help Rubra; if I should join him in the neural strata and turn this into a possessed habitat.'

'He wants that?'

'I don't think so. But he's like me, there's not much else either of us can do. The game's over, and we're running out of extra time.'

She stroked him absently. 'Whatever you decide, I don't want you to take me into account. There are too many issues at stake, big issues. Individuals don't matter so much; and I had a good run against that Bonney. We annoyed her a lot, eh? That felt nice.'

'But individuals do matter. Especially you. It's odd, I feel like I've come full circle. Anastasia always told me how precious a single life was. Now I have to decide your fate. And I can't let you suffer, which is what's going to happen if Rubra and I take on the possessed together. I'm responsible for her death, I can't have yours on my hands as well. How could I ever face her with that weighing in my heart? I have to be true to her. You know I do.' He tilted his head back, his voice raised in anger. 'Do you think you've won?'

I never even knew we were fighting until this possession happened, Rubra said sadly. You know what hopes I had for you in the old days, even though you never shared them. You know I never wanted anything to spoil my dreams for you. You were the golden prince, the chosen one. Fate stopped you from achieving your inheritance. That's what Anastasia was, for you and for me. Fate. You would call it an act of Thoale.

You believe all this was destined to be?

I don't know. All I know is that our union is the last chance either of us has to salvage something from all this shit. So now you have to ask yourself, do the living have a right to live, or do the dead rule the universe?

That's so like you, a loaded question.

I am what I am.

Not for very much longer.

You'll do it?

Yes.

Come in, then, I'll accept you into the neural strata.

Not yet. I want to get Tatiana out first.

Why?

We may be virtually omnipotent after I come into the neural strata, but Bonney and the hellhawks still have the potential to damage the habitat shell very badly. I doubt we can quell them instantaneously, yet they will know the second I come into the neural strata. We are going to have a fight on our hands, I don't want Tatiana hurt.

Very well, I will ask the Kohistan Consensus for a voidhawk to take her off.

You have a method?

I have a possible method. I make no promises. You'd better get yourselves along to the counter-rotating spaceport before Bonney starts her hunt.

*

It wasn't merely a hunting party Bonney was organizing. She was keenly aware that Dariat could always flee her in the tube carriages, while she was reduced to chasing after him in one of the rentcop force's open-top trucks. If Dariat was to be caught, then she would first have to cripple his mobility.

The crowd she had assembled was split into teams, given specific instructions, and dispatched to carry them out. Each major team had one of her deputies to ensure it didn't waver.

Every powered vehicle in the habitat set out from the starscraper lobby, driving along the tracks through the overgrown grass. Most of them travelled directly to the other camps ringing starscraper lobbies, coercing their occupants into Bonney's scheme. It was a domino effect, spreading rapidly round Valisk's midsection.

Kiera had wanted the tubes left alone so that when they moved Valisk out of the universe the transport system could be brought back on-line to serve them. Bonney had no such inhibitions. The possessed made their reluctant way into the starscraper lobbies, and down into the first-floor stations. There they combined their energistic power, and started to systematically smash the tube tunnels. Huge chunks of polyp were torn out of the walls and roof to crash down on the magnetic guide rail. Power cables were ripped up and shorted out. Carriages were fired, adding to the blockages, and sending thick plumes of black smoke billowing deep into the tunnels. Management-processor blocks were blasted to cinders, exposing their interface with Valisk's nerve fibres. Wave after wave of static discharges were pumped at the raw ends, sending what they hoped were pulses of pure pain down into the neural strata.

Bolstered by their successful vandalism, and Rubra's apparent inability to retaliate, the possessed began to move en masse down into the starscrapers. They sent waves of energistic power surging ahead of them, annihilating any mechanical or electrical system, wrecking artefacts and fittings. Every room, every corridor, every stairwell, was searched for non-possessed. Floor by floor they descended, recapturing the heady excitement and spirit of the original takeover. Unity infected them with strength. Individuals began to shapeshift into fantastic monsters and Earthly heroes. They weren't just going to flush out the traitor enemy, they were going to do it with malevolent finesse.

Hellhawks fluttered up from the docking-ledges, and began to spiral round the tubular starscrapers. An infernal flock peering into the bright oval windows with their potent senses, assisting their comrades inside.

Together they would flush him out. It was only a matter of time now.

*

Dariat sat opposite Tatiana in the tube carriage they took from the southern endcap. 'We're going to put you in one of the spaceport's emergency escape pods,' he told her. 'It's going to be tough to start with, they launch at about twelve gees to get away fast. But it only lasts for eight seconds. You can take that. There's a voidhawk squadron from Kohistan standing by to pick you up as soon as you're clear.'

'What about the possessed?' she asked. 'Won't they try and stop me, shoot at me or something?'

'They won't know what the hell's going on. Rubra is going to fire all two hundred pods at once. The voidhawks will swallow in and snatch your pod before the hellhawks even know you're out there.'

A smirk of good-humoured doubt stroked Tatiana's face. 'If you say so. I'm proud of you, Dariat. You've come through when it really counts, shown your true self. And it's a good self. Anastasia would be proud of you, too.'

'Why, thank you.'

'You should enjoy your victory, take heart from it. Lady Chi-ri will be smiling on you tonight. Bask in that warmth.'

'We haven't won yet.'

'You have. Don't you see? After all those years of struggle you've finally beaten Anstid. He hasn't dictated what you're doing now. This act is not motivated by hatred and revenge.'

Dariat grinned. 'Not hatred. But I'm certainly enjoying putting one over on that witch-queen Bonney.'

Tatiana laughed. 'Me too!'

Dariat had to grab at his seat as the carriage braked sharply. Tatiana gasped as she clung to one of the vertical poles, hanging on frantically as the lights began to dim.

'What's happening?' she asked.

The carriage juddered to a halt. The lights went out, then slowly returned as the vehicle's back-up electron matrix came on-line.

**Rubra?**

**Little bastards are smashing up the station you were heading for. They've cut the power to the magnetic rail, I haven't even got the reserve circuits.**

Dariat hooked into the neural strata's observation routines to survey the damage. The starscraper station was a scene of violent devastation. Smouldering lumps of polyp were chiselled out of the tunnel by invisible surges of energy; the guidance rail writhed and flexed, screaming shrilly as its movements yanked its own fixing pins out of the floor; severed electrical cables swung from broken conduits overhead, spitting sparks. Laughter and catcalls rang out over the noise of the violence.

A rapid flick through other stations showed him how widespread the destruction was.

**Bloody hell.**

**Damn right,** Rubra said. **She's overdosing on the fury routine, but she's playing smart with it.**

A schematic of the tube network appeared in Dariat's mind. **Look, there are plenty of alternative routes left up to the spindle.**

**Yes, right now there are. But you'll have to go back two stations before I can switch you to another tunnel. I can't restore power to the rail in your tunnel, they've fucked the relays. The carriage will have to make it there on its own power reserve. You'd almost be quicker walking. And by the time you get there, the possessed will have wrecked a whole lot more stations. Bonney's thought this out well; the way she's isolating each stretch of tunnel will break up the entire network in another forty minutes.**

**So how the hell do we get to the spindle now?**

**Forward. Go up to the station, and walk through it. I can bring another carriage to the tunnel on the other side; that'll get you directly up to the endcap.**

**Walk through? You're kidding.**

**There's only a couple of possessed left to guard each station after they've had their rampage. Two won't be a problem.**

**All right, do it.**

The lights dipped again as the carriage slid forwards slowly.

'Well?' Tatiana asked.

Dariat began to explain.

Starscrapers formed the major nodes in the habitat's tube network; each of them had seven stations ringing the lobby, enabling the carriages to reach any part of the interior. Individual stations were identical; chambers with a double-arch ceiling and a central platform twenty metres long which served two tubes. The polyp walls were a light powder-blue, with strips of electrophorescent cells running the entire length above the rails. There were stairs at each end of the platform, one set leading up to the starscraper lobby, the other an emergency exit to the parkland.

In the station ahead of Dariat, the possessed finished their wrecking spree and went off up the stairs to start searching the starscraper. As Rubra predicted, they left two of their number behind to watch over the four tunnel entrances. Smoke from the attack was layering the air. Flames were still licking round the big piles of ragged polyp slabs blocking the end of each tunnel. Several hologram adverts flashed on and off overhead; an already damaged projector suffering from the proximity of the possessed turned the images to a nonsense splash of colours.

Given that the fire was dying away naturally, the two possessed were somewhat bemused when, seven minutes after everyone else left, the station's sprinklers suddenly came on.

Dariat was three hundred metres down the tube tunnel, helping Tatiana out of the carriage's front emergency hatch. The tunnel had only the faintest illumination, a weak blue glow coming from a couple of narrow electrophorescent strips on the walls. It curved away gently ahead of him, putting enough solid polyp between him and the station to prevent the two possessed from perceiving him.

Tatiana jumped down the last half-metre and steadied herself.

'Ready?' Dariat asked. He was already using the habitat's sensitive cells to study the pile of polyp they would have to climb over to get into the station. It didn't look too difficult, there was an easy metre and a half gap at the top.

'Ready.'

**Let's go**, Dariat said.

The two possessed guards had given up any attempt to shield themselves from the torrent of water falling from the sprinklers. They were retreating back to the shelter of the stairs. Their clothes had turned to sturdy anoraks, streaked with glistening runnels. Every surface was slick with water now: walls, platform, floor, the piles of polyp.

Rubra overrode the circuit breakers governing the cables which powered the tube, then shunted thirteen thousand volts back into the induction rail. It was the absolute limit for the habitat's integral organic conductors, and three times the amount the carriages used. The broken guide rail jumped about as it had while it was being tormented by the possessed. Blinding white light leapt out of the magnetic couplings as it split open. It was as though someone had fired a fusion drive into the station. Water droplets spraying out of the overhead nozzles fluoresced violet, and vaporized. Metal surfaces erupted into wailing jets of sparks.

At the heart of the glaring bedlam, two bodies ignited, flaring even brighter than the seething air.

It wasn't just the one station, that would have drawn Bonney's attention like a combat wasp's targeting sensor. Rubra launched dozens of attacks simultaneously. Most of them were electrical, but there were also mass charges of servitor animals, as well as mechanoids switched back on, slashing round indiscriminately with laser welders and fission blades as energistic interference crashed their processors.

Reports of the tumult poured into the starscraper lobby where Bonney had set up her field headquarters. Her deputies shouted warnings into the powerful walkie-talkies they used to keep in contact with each other.

As soon as the blaze of white light shone down the tunnel, Dariat started to run towards it. He kept hold of Tatiana's hand, pulling her onward. A loud caterwaul reverberated along the tunnel.

'What's Rubra doing to them?' she shouted above the din.

'What he had to.'

The abusive light died and the sound faded away. Dariat could see the pile of polyp now, eighty metres ahead. A crescent-shaped sliver of light straddled it, seeping in from the station beyond.

Their feet began to splash through rivulets of water flowing down the tunnel. Tatiana grimaced as they reached the foot of the blockage, and hitched her skirt up.

Bonney listened to the frantic shouting all around her, counting up the incidents, the number of casualties. They'd got off lightly. And she knew that was wrong.

'Quiet,' she bellowed. 'How many stations attacked? Total?'

'Thirty-two,' one of the deputies said.

'And over fifty attacks altogether. But we've only lost about seventy to eighty people in the stations. Rubra's just getting rid of the sentries we posted. If he wanted to seriously harm us he'd do it when the wrecking crews were down there.'

'A diversion? Dariat's somewhere else?'

'No,' she said. 'Not quite. We know he uses the tubes to get around. I'll bet the little shit's in one right now. He must be. Only we've already blocked him. Rubra is clearing the sentries out of the way so Dariat can sneak through. That's why he spread the attacks round, so we'd think it was a blanket assault.' She whirled round to face a naked polyp pillar, and grinned with malicious triumph. 'That's it, isn't it, boyo? That's what you're doing. But which way is he going, huh? The starscrapers are dead centre.' She shook her head in annoyance. 'All right you people, get sharp. I want someone down in each and every station Rubra attacked. And I want them down there now. Tell them to make sure they don't step in the water, and be on the look out for servitors. But get them down there.'

The image of her yelling orders at her deputies boiled into Dariat's mind like a particularly vigorous hangover. He had just reached the top of the polyp pile, and squeezed under the ceiling. The station was filled with thick white mist, reducing visibility to less than five metres. Condensation had penetrated everywhere, making this side of the polyp mound dangerously unstable.

**Smart bitch,** Rubra said. **I didn't expect that.**

**Can you delay them?**

**Not in this station, I can't. I haven't got any servitors nearby, and the cables have all burnt out. You'll have to run.**

Image relay of a deputy with a walkie-talkie pressed to his ear hurrying across the lobby above. 'I'm on it, I'm on it,' he was yelling into the mike.

'Tatiana, move it!' Dariat shouted.

Tatiana was still wriggling along on her belly as she slithered over the top of the pile. 'What's the matter?'

'Someone's coming.'

She gave one final squirm, and freed her legs. Together they scooted down the side of the pile, bringing a minor avalanche of slushy gravel with them.

'This way.' Dariat pointed into the mist. His perception filled in glass-grey outlines of the station walls through the swirls of cold vapour, enabling him to see the tunnel entrance. Valisk's sensitive cells showed him the carriage waiting a hundred and fifty metres further on. They also showed him the deputy reaching the top of the stairs.

'Wait here,' he told Tatiana, and vaulted up onto the platform. His appearance changed drastically, the simple one piece thickening to an elaborate purple uniform, complete with gold braid. The most imposing figure to dominate his youth: Colonel Chaucer. A weekly AV show of a renegade Confederation officer, a super vigilante.

Rubra was laughing softly in his head.

The deputy was halfway down the stairs when he started to slow up. He raised the walkie-talkie. 'Somebody's down here.'

Dariat reached the bottom of the stairs. 'Only me,' he called up cheerfully.

'Who the hell are you?'

'You first. This is my station.'

The deputy's mind revealed his confusion as Dariat started up towards him with powerful, confident strides. This was not the action of someone trying to hide.

Dariat opened his mouth wide, and spat a ball of white fire directly at the deputy's head. Two souls bawled in terror as they vanished into the beyond. The body tumbled past Dariat.

'What's happening?' The walkie-talkie was reverting back to a standard communication block as it clattered down the stairs. 'What's happening? Report. Report.'

There's four more on their way up from the first floor, Rubra said. Bonney ordered them to the station as soon as the deputy said he sensed someone.

Shit! We'll never make it to the carriage. They can outrun Tatiana, no problem.

Call her up. I'll hide you in the starscraper.

What?

Just move!

'Tatiana! Up here, now!' He was aware of all the lift doors in the lobby sliding open. The four possessed had reached the bottom of the first-floor stairs. Tatiana jogged along the platform. She gave the corpse a quick, appalled, glance.

'Come on.' Dariat caught her hand, and tugged hard. Her expression was resentful, but the rising anxiety in his voice spurred her. They raced up the stairs together.

Daylight shone through the circular lobby's glass walls. It had suffered very little damage; scorch marks on the polyp pillars and cracked glass were the only evidence that the possessed had arrived to search the tower.

Dariat could hear multiple footsteps pounding up one of the stairwells on the other side of the lobby, hidden by the central bank of lifts. His perception was just starting to register their minds emerging from behind the shield of polyp. Which meant they'd also be able to sense him.

He scooped Tatiana up, ignoring her startled holler, and sprinted for the lifts. Huge muscles pumped his legs in an effortless rhythm. She weighed nothing at all.

The phenomenal speed he was travelling at meant there was no chance at all of slowing once he passed the lift doors; he would have needed ten metres to come to a halt. They slammed straight into the rear wall. Tatiana shrieked as her shoulder, ribs, and leg hit flat on, with Dariat's prodigious inertia driving into her. Then his face smacked into silvery metal, and there was no energistic solution to the blast of pain jabbing into his brain. Blood squirted out of his nose, smearing the wall. As he fell he was dimly aware of the lift doors sliding shut. The light outside was growing inordinately bright.

Dariat reeled round feebly, clutching at his head as if the pressure from his fingers alone could squeeze the bruises back down out of existence. Slowly the pain subsided, which allowed him to concentrate on vanquishing the remainder. 'Ho, fuck.' He slumped back against a wall, and let his breathing calm. Tatiana was lying on the lift floor in front of him, hands pressed against her side, cold sweat on her brow.

'Anything broken?' he asked.

'I don't think so. It just hurts.'

He went onto his hands and knees and crawled over to her. 'Show me where.'

She pointed, and he laid his hand on it. With his mind he could see the smooth glowing pattern of living flesh distorted and broken below his fingers, the fissures extending deep inside her. He willed the pattern to return to its unblemished state.

Tatiana hissed in relief. 'I don't know what you did, but it's better than a medical nanonic.'

The lift stopped at the fiftieth floor.

**Now what?** Dariat asked.

Rubra showed him.

**You are one evil bastard.**

**Why, thank you, boy.**

\*

Stanyon was leading the possessed down through the star-scraper in pursuit of Dariat. He'd started off with thirty-five under his command, and that number was rapidly swelling as

Bonney directed more and more from neighbouring starscrapers to assist him. She'd announced she was on her way herself. Stanyon was going balls-out to find Dariat before she arrived. He got hot just thinking about the praise (and other things) Kiera would direct at the champion who erased her *bête noire* from the habitat.

Eight different teams of possessed were searching, assigned a floor each. They were working their way steadily downwards, demolishing every mechanical and electrical device as they went.

He strode out of the stairwell onto the thirty-eighth-floor vestibule. For whatever reason, Rubra was no longer putting up any resistance. Muscle-membrane doors opened obediently, the lighting remained on, there wasn't a servitor in sight. He looked round, happy with what he found. The floor's mechanical utilities office had been broken open, and the machinery inside reduced to slag, preventing the sprinklers from being used. Doors into the apartments and bars and commercial offices were smashed apart, furniture and fittings inside were blazing with unnatural ferocity. Big circles of polyp flooring were cracking under the intense heat, grainy white marble surface blackening. Wisps of dirty steam fizzed up from the crannies.

'Die,' Stanyon snarled. 'Die a little bit at a time. Die hurting big.'

He was walking towards the stairwell door when his walkie-talkie squawked: 'We got him! He's down here.'

Stanyon snatched the unit from his belt. 'Where? Who is this? Which floor are you on?'

'This is Talthorn the Greenfoot; I'm on floor forty-nine. He's just below us. We can all sense him.'

'Everybody hear that?' Stanyon yelled gleefully. 'Fiftieth floor. Get your arses down there.' He sprinted for the stairwell.

*

'They're coming,' Dariat said.

Tatiana flashed him a worried-but-brave grin, and finished tying the last cord around her pillow. They were in a long-disused residential apartment; its polyp furniture of horseshoe tables and oversized scoop armchairs dominated the lounge. The chairs had been turned into cushion nests to add a dash of comfort. The foam used to fill the cushions was a lightweight plastic that was ninety-five per cent nitrogen bubbles.

They were, Rubra swore, perfect buoyancy aids.

Dariat tried on his harness one last time. The cords which he'd torn from the gaudy cushion fabric held a pillow to his chest and another against his back. Seldom had he felt so ridiculous.

His doubt must have leaked onto his face.

**If it works, don't try to fix it,** Rubra said.

**Ripe, from someone who's devoted his existence to meddling.**

**Game, set, and match, I won't even appeal. Would you like to get ready?**

Dariat used the starscraper's observation routines to check on the possessed. There were twelve of them on the floor above. A rock-skinned troll was leading the pack, followed by a pair of cyber-ninjas in black flak jackets, a xenoc humanoid that was all shiny amber exoskeleton and looked like it could rip metal apart with its talons, a faerie prince wearing his forest hunting tunic and carrying a longbow in one hand, a walkie-talkie in the other, three or four excessively hairy Neanderthals, and regular soldiers in the uniforms of assorted eras.

'The loonies are on the warpath tonight,' Dariat muttered under his breath. 'Finished?' he asked Tatiana.

She shifted her front pillow around, and tightened the last strap to hold it in place. 'I'm ready.'

The bathroom's muscle-membrane door parted silently. Inside was an emerald-green suite. A circular spar bath, vaguely Egyptian in design, matched by the basin, bidet, and toilet. They were still all in perfect condition. It was the plumbing which had degraded. Water was dripping from the brass shower head above the bath; over the years it had produced a big orange stain on the bottom. Slimy blue-green algae was growing out of the plug. The sink was piled high with bars of soap, so old and dry now that they'd started to crumble, snowing flecks over the rim.

Dariat stood in the doorway, with Tatiana pressed against him, looking eagerly over his shoulder. 'What's supposed to be happening?' she asked.

'Watch.'

A bass crunching sound was coming from the toilet. Cracks appeared round its base, expanding rapidly outwards. Then the whole bowl lurched upwards, spinning round precariously before toppling over. A two-metre circle of floor around it was rising up like a miniature volcanic eruption. Polyp splintered with a continual brassy crackling. A fine jet of water sprayed out of the fractured flush pipe.

'Lord Tarrug, what are you doing?' Tatiana asked.

'That's not Tarrug, that's Rubra,' Dariat told her. 'No dark arts involved.'

Affinity with the local subroutines allowed him to feel the toilet's sphincter muscle straining as it contorted in directions it was never intended, rupturing the thin shell of polyp floor. It halted, fully expended. The cone which it had produced quivered slightly, then stilled. Dariat hurried over. There was a crater at the centre, leading down to an impenetrable darkness. The muscle tissue which made up the sides was a tough dark-red flesh, now badly lacerated. Pale yellow fluid was oozing out of the splits, running down to disappear in the unseen space below.

'Our escape route,' Dariat said, echoing Rubra's pride.

'A toilet?' she asked incredulously.

'Sure. Don't go squeamish on me now, please.' He sat on the edge of the sphincter, and swung his legs over the crater. It was a three-metre slither down into the sewer tubule below.

When his feet touched the bottom he knelt down, and held a hand out. His skin began to glow with a strong pink light. It revealed the tubule stretching on ahead of him, a circular shaft just over a metre in diameter, and angled slightly downwards.

'Throw the pillows down,' he said.

Tatiana dropped them, peering over the edge of the crater with a highly dubious expression. Dariat shoved the two harnesses into the tubule, and started to worm his way in after them. 'When I'm in, you follow me, OK?' He didn't give her the chance to answer. It was awkward going, pushing the pillows ahead of him as he crawled along. The grey polyp was slippery with water and faecal sludge. Dariat could hear Tatiana grunting and muttering behind him as she discovered the residue smearing the sides.

There were ridges encircling the tubule every four metres, peristaltic muscle bands that assisted the usual water flow. Despite Rubra expanding them wide, they formed awkward constrictions which Dariat had to pull himself through. He had just squeezed past the third when Rubra said: **They've reached the fiftieth floor. Can you sense them?**

**Not a chance. So in theory they won't be able to find me.**

**They know the general direction, and they're heading towards the apartment.**

Dariat was too intent on inching himself along to review the images. **What about the rest?**

**On their way down. The stairwells are absolutely packed. It's like a freak-show stampede out there.**

He elbowed his way through another muscle band. The light from his hand showed the tubule walls ending two metres ahead. A thick ring of muscle membrane surrounded the rim. Beyond that was a clear empty space. He could hear a steady patter of rain in the darkness.

'We made it!' he shouted.

His only answer was another outbreak of grunted curses.

Dariat pushed the filthy pillows and their tangled cords over the edge, hearing them splash into the water. Then he was sliding himself over.

The main ingestion tract into which the sewer tubule emptied ran vertically up the entire height of the starscraper. It collected the human waste, discarded organic matter, and dirty water from every floor and carried it down to the large purification organs at the base of the starscraper. They filtered out organic compounds which were pumped back to the principal nutrient organs inside the southern endcap via their own web of specialist tubules. Poisons and toxins were disposed of directly into space. Fresh water was recirculated up to the habitat's storage reservoirs and parkland rivers.

Normally the main ingestion tract was a continual waterfall. Now, though, Rubra had closed the inlet channels, and reversed the flow from the purification organs, allowing the water level to rise up the tract until it was level with the fiftieth floor.

The cold surface closed over Dariat's head, and he felt his feet clear the tubule. A couple of swift kicks and he surfaced, puffing a spray of droplets from his mouth. Thankfully this water was clean – relatively.

He held an arm up in the air, a sharp blue flame flickering up from his fingertips. Its light showed the true extent of the tract; twenty metres in diameter, with walls of neutral-grey polyp that had the same crinkly surface texture as granite. Sewer tubule outlets formed black portals all around, their muscle membrane rims flexing like fish mouths. The pillows were bobbing about a few metres away.

Tatiana had pushed her shoulders past the tubule's muscle membrane, and was craning her head back to look round. The tract's height defeated the illumination thrown out by Dariat's small flame, revealing barely fifteen metres of the walls above the water level. A heavy shower was falling out of the darkness which roofed them, chopping up the water's surface with small ripples.

'Come on, out you come,' Dariat said. He swam back to her,

and helped ease her though the opening. She gasped at the water's chilly grip, arms thrashing about for a moment.

Dariat retrieved the two sets of pillows, and strapped himself into the harness. He had to tie Tatiana's cords for her, the cold had numbed her fingers. When he was finished, the sewer tubules all started to close silently.

'Where are we going now?' Tatiana asked nervously.

'Straight up,' he grinned. 'Rubra will pump fresh water back into the base of the tract. It should take about twenty minutes to reach the top. But expect an interruption.'

'Yeah?'

'Oh, yeah.'

*

Stanyon arrived at the fiftieth floor to find it in turmoil. The vestibule was packed with excitable possessed. None of them seemed to know what was going on.

'Anybody seen him?' Stanyon shouted. Nobody had.

'Search round, there must be some trace. I want the teams that were searching floors thirty-eight and thirty-nine to go down to fifty-one and check it out.'

'What's happening?' Bonney's voice asked from the walkie-talkie; there was a lot of crackling interference.

Stanyon held the unit to his face, pulling out more aerial. 'He's dodged us again. But we know he's here. We'll have him any minute now.'

'Make sure you stick with procedure. Remember it's not just Dariat we're up against.'

'You're not the only council member left. I know what I'm doing.'

'I'm a minute away from the lobby. I'll join you as fast as I can.'

He gave the walkie-talkie a disgusted look and switched it off. 'Terrific.'

'Stanyon,' someone called from the other end of the vestibule. 'Stanyon, we've found something.'

It was the troll, the faerie prince, and both of the cyber-ninjas who had broken into the apartment. They were hanging round the bathroom door when Stanyon arrived. He pushed his way past them impatiently.

The sides of the ruptured toilet sphincter had sagged, squeezing more of the yellow fluid out. It was running down the outside of the cone to smear the surrounding dune of polyp chippings. Water from the fractured pipe was sloshing over the floor.

Stanyon edged forwards, and peered cautiously over the crater's lip. There was nothing to see, nothing to sense. He pointed at the smaller of the two cyber-ninjas. 'You, go see where it leads to.'

The cyber-ninja looked at him. Red LEDs on his visor flashed slowly, an indolent blinking to mirror the thoughts they fronted.

'Go on,' Stanyon said, impatiently.

After a brief rebellious moment, the cyber-ninja dematerialized his flak jacket, and lowered himself down into the sewer tubule.

*

Dariat had been worried about the undercurrents. Needlessly, as it turned out. They were rising fast up the giant tract with only the occasional swirl of bubbles twisting round them. It was still raining heavily; but the whole process was eerily silent.

He maintained the small flame burning coldly from his fingers, mainly for Tatiana's benefit. There was nothing to see above them, only the empty blackness. They slid smoothly past the intermittent circlets of closed tubules with monotonous regularity, which was their only real measure of progress.

Dariat was warm enough, circulating heat through his skin

to hold the water's numbing encroachment at bay. But he did worry about Tatiana. She'd stopped talking, and her chattering teeth were clearly audible. That left him alone with his own thoughts of what was to come. And the whispers of the dammed, they were always there.

*Rubra, have you ever heard of someone called Alkad Mzu?* he asked.

*No. Why?*

*Capone is very interested in finding her. I think she's some kind of weapons expert.*

*How the hell do you know what Capone wants?*

*I can hear it. The souls in the beyond are calling for her. They're quite desperate to find her for the Organization.*

Affinity suddenly gave him a sense of space opening around him. Then an astonishingly resolute presence emerged from the new distance. Dariat was at once fearful and amazed by its belief in itself, a contentment which was almost the opposite of hubris; it knew and accepted itself too well for arrogance. There was a nobility about it which he had never experienced, certainly not during the life he had led. Yet he knew exactly what it was.

*Hello, Dariat,* it said.

*The Kohistan Consensus. I'm flattered.*

*It is intriguing for us to communicate with you. It is a rare opportunity to talk to any non-Edenist, and you are a possessor as well.*

*Make the most of it, I won't be around for much longer.*

*The action you and Rubra are undertaking is an honourable one, we applaud your courage. It can not have been easy for either of you.*

*It was realistic.*

His answer was accompanied by Rubra's emission of irony.

*We would like to ask a question,* Consensus said. *Several, in fact.*

*On the nature of possession, I assume. Fair enough.*

*Your current viewpoint is unique, and extremely valuable to us.*

**It's going to have to wait a minute**, Rubra said. **They've found the toilet.**

*

The cyber-ninja had squeezed down into the sewer tubule, and was squirming along on his belly. His mind tone was one of complete disgust. Pale violet light illuminated the lenses on his low-light enhancement goggles, casting a faint glow across the polyp directly in front of him. 'They were in here,' he yelled back over his shoulder. 'This shit's all been smeared round.'

'Yes!' Stanyon banged a fist against the muscle-membrane door. 'Get down there,' he told the second cyber-ninja. 'Help him.'

The cyber-ninja did as he was told, sitting on the edge of the crater and slinging his legs over.

'Anyone know where these pipes lead?' Stanyon asked.

'I've never been in one myself,' the faerie prince said, airily. 'But it'll empty into the lower floor eventually. You could try searching down there. Unless, of course, he's simply popped up inside someone else's john and walked out.'

Stanyon gave the slack cone an irritated look. The prospect of Dariat simply walking through the habitat's pipes to escape in the throng was intolerable. But with everyone wearing their illusionary form it would be appallingly easy. *Why can we never* organize *ourselves properly?*

With extreme reluctance he switched the walkie-talkie back on. 'Bonney, come in, please.'

Rubra opened the sphincter muscle below every single toilet on the forty-ninth, fiftieth, and fifty-first floor. It was an action nobody noticed. There were over a hundred and eighty possessed milling round on those three levels, with more still arriving. Some were obediently searching through the rooms; most were now there simply for a piece of the action. As there was no organized plan none of them were suspicious when all the remaining apartment doors slid open. At the same time, emergency fire-control doors quietly closed off the lift shafts.

Dariat pulled Tatiana to his chest, and held her tight, locking his fingers together behind her back. 'Stay with it,' he said. The surface of the water was just rising over the sewer tubules of the twenty-first floor.

Bonney reached the twelfth floor well ahead of the five deputies accompanying her. She could hear them clumping down the stairwell above her. They competed against her heart hammering away inside her ribs. So far she didn't feel any fatigue, but she knew she'd have to slow down soon. It was going to take a good twenty minutes to reach the fiftieth floor.

'Bonney,' her walkie-talkie said. 'Come in, please.'

She started down the stairs to the thirteenth floor, and raised the walkie-talkie to her face. 'Yes, Stanyon.'

'He's vanished into the pipes. I've sent some of my people after him, but I don't know where they all lead to. It's possible he might have doubled back on us. It might be an idea to leave some guards in the lobby.'

'Fuckhead.' Bonney slowed to a halt as mystification overshadowed her initial anger. 'What pipes?'

'The waste pipes. There's kilometres of them under the floors. We found one of the toilets all smashed up. That's how he got in there.'

'You mean sewer pipes?'

'Yeah.'

Bonney stared at the wall. She could sense the thought routines gliding through the neural strata a metre or so behind the naked polyp. In his own fashion, Rubra was staring right back at her. He was content.

She didn't know anything about the sewer pipes, except how obvious they were in hindsight. And Rubra had absolute control over every single environmental aspect of the habitat. And Dariat had been spotted for a few brief seconds, which had sent everyone chasing after him. Then he'd vanished. If the sewers could hide him so thoroughly, he should never have been found in the first place.

'Out!' she yelled at the walkie-talkie. 'Get out of there! Stanyon, for fuck's sake, move!'

Rubra opened the muscle-membrane rims of the sewer tubules which served the forty-ninth, fiftieth, and fifty-first floors. The pressure exerted by a thirty-storey-high column of water filling the ingestion tract was a genuinely irresistible force.

Stanyon saw the cyber-ninja bullet out of the cone of ruined muscle to smash against the ceiling. The gust of air which blew him there gave way to a massive fist of water which howled upwards to strike the spread-eagled man full on. Its roar was pitched at roughly the level of a sense-overload sonic. Stanyon's skin blistered scarlet as his capillaries ruptured. Before he could even scream the bathroom was filled with high-velocity rain which knocked him to his feet as if he was being hammered by a fusillade of rubber bullets. He crashed back into the bath where a slim laser-straight pillar of water had burst out of the plughole. It might just as well have been a chainsaw.

Throughout the three condemned floors, every bathroom, every kitchen, every public toilet was host to the same lethal eruption of water. The lights had gone out, and into this tormented night came the water itself, icy foaming waves that rushed through rooms and vestibules like a horizontal guillotine.

Tatiana cried out fearfully as the water began to drop. The two of them began to circulate round the edge of the ingestion tract; slowly to start with, then picking up speed. Small waves rippled back and forth, slapping against each other to produce wobbling spires. A loud gurgling sound rose as the water fell faster.

Dariat watched in dismay as the surface tilted. At the centre of the tract it was discernibly lower than it was at the walls. They began to spiral in towards it. The gurgling grew louder still.

**Rubra!**

**Don't worry. Another thirty seconds, that's all.**

Bonney was helpless against the torrent of anguish rushing around her – the flock of souls arising from those trapped below to depart the universe, their sobs of bitterness and fright striking her harder than any physical blow. They were too near, too strong, to avoid; raw emotion amplified to insufferable levels.

She fell to her knees, muscles knotted. Tears dripped steadily from her eyes. Her own soul was in danger of being pulled along with them, a migration which commanded attendance. She fisted her hands, and punched the polyp step. The pain was no more than a gentle tweak against the compulsion to join the damned once more. So she punched again, harder. Again.

Finally the carnage was over, the three floors filled to capacity with water. Narrow fan-sprays squirted out from the rim seals on several of the lift fire-control doors, filling the empty shafts with a fine drizzle, but the doors themselves held against the pressure. As did the stairwell muscle-membrane doors on the fifty-second floor, preventing the lower half of the starscraper from flooding. Pulverized bodies that had pressed against the ceiling were sinking slowly as pockets of air leaked out of their wounds, trailing ribbons of blood as they went.

*

The starscraper's ingestion tract did strange things to the gurgling sound produced by the frothing water, channelling it into an organlike harmonic that rattled Tatiana's bones. She was inordinately glad when it began to subside. Dariat was moaning feebly in her embrace as if he was in great pain. The flame he'd produced had snuffed out, leaving them in absolute blackness. Although she couldn't see anything, she knew the water was slowing, its surface levelling out. The cold was giving her a pounding headache.

Dariat started coughing. 'Bloody hell.'

'Are you OK?' she asked.

'I'll survive.'

'What happened?'

'We're not being chased any more,' he said, flatly.

'So what's next?'

'Rubra is going to start pumping water back into the tract. We should reach the top in about fifteen minutes.' He held up his hand, and rekindled the little blue flame. 'Think you can last that long?'

'I can last.'

* * *

Bonney walked slowly out of the starscraper lobby, still shivering despite the balmy parkland air ruffling her khaki jacket. Nearly a dozen possessed were loitering outside on the grass. They were gathered together in small clusters, talking quietly in worried tones. When she appeared, all conversation ended. They stared at her, thoughts dominated by resentment, their expressions hard, unforgiving. It was the germ of the revolution.

She gazed back at them, coldly defiant. But she knew they would never take orders from her again. The authority of Kiera's council had drowned back there in the starscraper. If she wanted to go up against Dariat and Rubra now, it would be on her own. One on one, the best kind of hunt there was. She brought a hand up to her face, licking the bloody grazes which scarred each knuckle. Her smile made the possessed closest to her back away.

There were several trucks parked beside the lobby. She chose the nearest and twisted the accelerator hard. Spinning tyres tore up long scars of grass as she tugged the steering wheel round. Then the truck was speeding away from the lobby, heading for the northern endcap.

Her walkie-talkie gave a bleep. 'Now what?' Rubra asked. 'Come on, it was a grand hunt, but you lost. Drive over to a decent bar, have a drink. My shout.'

'I haven't lost yet,' she said. 'He's still out there. That means I can win.'

'You've lost everything. Your so-called colleagues are evacuating the starscrapers. Your council is busted. There's going to be nothing left of Kiera's little empire with this lot running round out of control.'

'That's right, there's nothing left. Nothing except me and the boyo. I'm going to catch him before he can escape. I worked that one out already. You're helping him reach the spaceport. Lord knows why, but I can still spoil your game, just as you did mine. That's justice. It's also fun.'

\*

**One wacko lady,** Dariat commented.

**She's genuine trouble, though. Always has been,** Rubra said.

**And continues to be so by the look of it. Especially if she gets to the spindle before me. Which is a good possibility.** The water was now up to the second floor. Dariat could see the top of the ingestion tract now, the black tube puncturing a bubble of hazy pink light.

Another ninety seconds brought him level with the floor of the cistern chamber. He had emerged into the centre of a big hemispherical cavern whose walls were pierced by six huge water pipe outlets. Ribbons of water were still trickling across the sloping floor to the lip of the tract.

He struck out for the edge with a strong sidestroke, towing Tatiana along. She was almost unconscious; the cold had penetrated her body to the core. Even with his energistic strength, hauling her out of the water was tough going. Once she was clear he flopped down beside her, wishing himself warm and dry. Steam began to pour out of their clothes.

Tatiana tossed her head about, moaning as if she were caught in a nightmare. She sat up with a spasm of muscle, her few remaining bangles chiming loudly. Vapour was still effervescing out of her dress and dreadlocks. She blinked at it in amazement. 'I'm warm,' she said in astonishment. 'I didn't think I would ever be warm again.'

'The least I could do.'

'Is it over now?'

The wishful childlike tone made him press his lips together in regret. 'Not quite. We still have to get up to the spaceport; there's a route through these water pipes which will eventually take us to a tube tunnel, we don't have to go up to the surface. But Bonney survived. She'll try to stop us.'

Tatiana rested her chin in her hands. 'Lord Thoale is testing us more than most. I'm sure he has his reasons.'

'I'm not.' Dariat lumbered to his feet, and untied the pillow harness. 'I'm sorry, but we have to get going.'

She nodded miserably. 'I'm coming.'

\*

The search teams which Bonney and her deputies had organized were wending their way out of Valisk's starscrapers. Shock from the flooding was evident in their shuffling footsteps and tragic eyes. They emerged from the lobbies, consoling each other as best they could.

*It shouldn't have happened* was the thought which rang amongst them like an Edenist Consensus. They'd made it back to the salvation of reality. They were the chosen ones, the lucky ones, the blessed. Eternal life, and the precious congruent gift of sensation, had been within their grasp. Now Rubra had shown them how tenuous that claim was.

He was able to do that because they remained in a universe where his power was a match to theirs. It shouldn't be like that.

Whole planets had escaped from open skies and Confederation retribution, while they stayed to entrap new bodies. Kiera's idea – and it had been a good one, bold and vigorous. Eternity spent within the confines of a single habitat would be a difficult prospect, and she had seen a way forward.

That was why they'd acquiesced to her rule and that of the council, because she'd been right. At the start. Now though, they had increased their numbers, Kiera had flown off to negotiate their admission to a dangerous war, and Bonney committed them against Rubra to satisfy her personal vendettas.

No more. No more risks. No more foolhardy adventures. No more sick savagery of hunting. The time had come to leave it all behind.

*

The truck raced along the hardened track which countless wheels had compacted across the semi-arid plain surrounding Valisk's northern endcap. Bonney had the throttle at maximum, the axial motors complemented by her energistic power. Small flattened stones and cracked ridges which lay along the track sent the vehicle flying through the air in long shallow hops.

Bonney didn't even notice the jouncing, which would have caused whiplash injuries to any non-possessed riding beside her. Her mind was focused entirely on the endcap whose base was five kilometres in front of her. She imagined her beefy old vehicle beating the sleek tube capsule slicing along its magnetic rail in the tunnel below her. The one she knew he would be riding.

Up ahead she could just make out the dark line of the switchback road which wound up to the small plateau two kilometres above the plain. If she could only reach the passage-way entrance before Dariat got out of the sewer tunnels and into a tube carriage she might conceivably reach the axis chamber before him.

A feeling of contentment began to seep into her mind. An insidious infiltration which called on her to respond, to generate her own dreamy satisfaction, to pledge it to the whole.

'Bastards!' She slapped furiously at the steering wheel, anger insulating her from the loving embrace which was rising up all around her. They had begun it, the gathering of power, the sharing, linking their wills. They'd submitted, *capitulated*, to their craven fear. Valisk would soon sail calmly out of this universe, sheltering them from any conceivable threat, committing them to a life of eternal boredom.

Well, not for her. One of the hellhawks could take her off, away where there was struggle and excitement. Only after she'd dealt with Dariat, though. There would be time. There had to be.

The truck's speed began to pick up. Her stubborn insistence was diverting a fraction of the prodigious reality dysfunction which was coalescing around the habitat. The utterly implausible was becoming hard fact.

Bonney laughed gleefully as the truck shot along the track, ripping up a churning cloud of thick ochre dust behind it, while all around her, the tiny clumps of scrub grass, cacti, and lichen sprawls were sprouting big adventitious flower buds. The bland desert was quietly and miraculously transforming itself into a rich colour-riot garden as Valisk's new masters prepared to enact their vision of paradise.

\*

The Kohistan Consensus had a thousand and one questions on the nature of possession and the beyond. Dariat sat quietly in the tube carriage taking him to the axis chamber and tried to supply answers for as many as he could. He even let them hear the terrible cries of the lost souls that infested his every thought. So that they'd know, so they'd understand the dreadful compulsion driving each possessor.

*I feel strange,* Rubra announced. *It's like being drunk, or light headed. I think they're starting to penetrate my thought routines.*

*No,* Dariat said. He was aware of it himself now, the reality dysfunction starting to pervade the polyp of the shell. In the distance, a chorus of minds was singing a joyous hymn of ascension. *They're getting ready to leave the universe. We don't have much time.*

*We can confirm that,* the Consensus said. *Our voidhawks on observation duty are reporting large squalls of red light appearing on your shell, Rubra. The hellhawks appear most agitated. They are leaving their docking pedestals.*

*Don't let it happen, boy,* Rubra said. *Come into me, please, transfer over now. We can win, we can stop them taking Valisk to their bloody haven. We can screw them yet.*

*Not with Tatiana here. I won't condemn her to that. We've still got time.*

*Bonney's almost at the plateau.*

*And we're almost at the base of the endcap. This carriage can go straight up to the axis chamber. She's got to climb three kilometres of stairs. We'll make it easily.*

\*

Blue smoke spouted out of the truck's tyres as Bonney skid-braked the vehicle outside the passageway's dark entrance. When she jumped down from the driver's seat her sharp upper teeth were protruding over her lower lip, producing a permanent feral grin. Her painfully red-rimmed eyes narrowed to lethargic slits as she gazed up at the steepening cliff of grey polyp in front of her, as if puzzled by its appearance. Every movement took on a dullard's slowness. Breath wheezed heavily out of her nostrils.

She ignored the passageway and stood perfectly still, bringing her arms to rest in front of her so her hands crossed above her crotch. Her head drooped, bowing deeply, the eyes closing completely.

*

**What the hell is she doing now?** Dariat asked. **She was frantic to get up there.**

**It looks like she's praying.**

**Somehow, I really doubt that.**

The tube carriage reached the base of the endcap, and started to sweep up the slope towards the hub. An urgent whining sound permeated the inside. Dariat could feel it slowing, then it accelerated again.

**Damn it, I'm getting power drop-outs right across the habitat. That's in the sections of myself I can still perceive. I'm shrinking, boy, there are places where my thoughts have ceased. Help me!**

**The reality dysfunction is strengthening. Five minutes. Hang on for five more minutes.**

*

Bonney's khaki suit was darkening, at the same time its texture changed to a glossier aspect. She was starting to hunch up, her legs bowing out and becoming spindly. Pointed ears emerged from a shortening crop of hair. There was no suit any more, only a black pelt.

She suddenly raised her rodent head, and emitted an ear-piercing screech through a circular mouth caged by fangs. Eyes glittered a devilish red. She opened what had been her arms to spread her new wings wide. The leathery membrane was thin enough to be translucent, revealing a lacework of minute black veins beneath the dark-amber surface.

**Oh fuck!** Rubra exclaimed. **No bloody way! I don't care what she looks like, she weighs too much to fly.**

**That won't matter any more,** Dariat said. **The reality dysfunction**

is powerful enough to sustain her; we're in the universe of fables now. If she wants to fly, she will.

Bonney ran a couple of paces across the plateau, then her wings gave a fast downward sweep, and she was airborne. She beat her wings steadily, rising quickly, her triumphant screeching echoing over the blank polyp. Her flight curved round sharply as she gained altitude, evolving into a spiral as the beats became smoother, more insistent.

She'll catch me, a stricken Dariat said. She's going to reach the axis chamber before me. I'll never get Tatiana out. 'Anastasia!' he cried. 'My love, it can't end like this. Not again. I can't fail you again.'

Tatiana stared at him in fright, not understanding.

Do something, he begged.

Like what? Rubra's mental voice was faint, lacking interest.

Remember your classics, the Kohistan Consensus said. Before today, Icarus and Daedalus were the only people ever to fly with their own wings. Only one survived. Think what happened to Icarus.

Bonney was already three hundred metres above the plateau, swooping upwards on a tempestuous thermal, when she noticed the change. The light was altering, which it could never do in a habitat. She shifted her balance, twisting on a wing-tip, howling at the sheer exhilaration of the wind buffeting her face. The cylindrical landscape stretched out in front of her, dabbed with curving smears of flushed red cloud. For the first time, the lively sparkle coming off the circumfluous reservoir was absent. The entire band of water seemed to be darkened; she could barely see a single feature on the southern endcap. Yet around her the light was growing. That should never be. Both endcaps were always maintained in a dappled shade. The effect was due entirely to the nature of the light-tube, a slender cylindrical mesh of organic conductors which mimicked the shape of the habitat itself. At each end the mesh narrowed to a near-solid bundle of cable which suspended the main segment between the two hubs. The plasma it contained dwindled to a mild violet haze eight hundred metres from the hub itself.

She could now see that horn of ions retreating from the southern hub as Rubra increased the power flowing through the cables at that end. The magnetic field was expanding to squeeze the plasma along the tube. At the northern end, he cut the power completely to one specific section of the mesh. Plasma rushed out of the gap, inflating flamboyantly as it liberated itself from the constricting flux lines.

From Bonney's position it was as if a small fusion bomb had detonated above her, sending its billowing mushroom cloud hurtling downwards.

'All this,' she cried disbelievingly, 'for me?'

The air caught in the cup of the endcap was torn asunder by the racing plasma, sending her spinning madly, broken wings wrapping her body like a velvet cloak. Then the wavefront of inflamed atoms swept across her like the breath of an enraged sun god. It had none of the fury and strength of a genuine fusion explosion; by the time it reached her the plasma was nothing more than a tenuous electrically charged fog that was rapidly losing cohesion. But nevertheless, it was moving five times faster than any natural tornado, and with a temperature of tens of thousands of degrees. Her body disintegrated into splinters of vivid copper light which trailed contrails of black smoke all the way down to the resplendent desert far below.

\*

A siren started to whistle as soon as Dariat broke the hatch seal; half of the corridor lighting panels turned red, flashing urgently. He ignored the clamour and floated through the small metallic airlock chamber.

The escape pod was a simple one-deck sphere, four metres in diameter, with twelve thickly padded acceleration couches laid out petal fashion. Dariat emerged from a hatch set at their centre. There was only one instrument panel, barely more than a series of power-up switches. He flicked them all on, watching the status schematics turn green.

Tatiana hauled herself gingerly through the airlock, looking dangerously queasy. Her dreadlocks swarmed round her head, their beads making tiny clacking sounds as they knocked against each other.

'Take any couch,' Dariat instructed. 'We're coming on-line.'

She rotated herself carefully into one of the couches. Webbing unfurled from its sides to creep over her.

Dariat took the couch opposite to her, so that they were feet to feet. **Are the other pods armed?**

**Yes. Most of them. Dariat, I don't exist on the other side of the starscrapers any more; I see nothing, I feel nothing, I don't even think down there.**

**A minute more, that's all.** He reached up and pressed the launch sequencer. The airlock hatch hinged down. 'I'm going to leave soon, Tatiana. Horgan will be back in charge of his own body again. Take care of him, he's only fifteen. He's going to be suffering.'

'Of course I will.'

'I . . . I know Rubra only forced us together to put pressure on me. But I'm still glad I met you.'

'Me too. It laid a lot of old demons to rest. You showed me I was wrong.'

'How?'

'I thought she'd made a mistake with you. She hadn't. The cure just took a very long time. She's going to be proud of you when you finally catch up with her.'

Two-thirds of Valisk's shell was now fluorescing a lambent crimson; dazzling dawn-red light shone out of the starscraper windows. Inside, the possessed were united, they could perceive the entire habitat now. The flow of its fluids and gases through the plexus of tubules and pipes and ducts was as intimate to them as the blood pumping round their own veins and arteries. Rubra's flashing thought routines, too, were apparent, snapping through the neural strata like volleys of sheet lightning. Under their auspices his thoughts were slowing and dimming, retreating down the length of the cylinder as their will to banish the curse of him from their lives grew dominant.

They knew now of all the remaining non-possessed Rubra had hidden throughout the interior. Twenty-eight had survived Bonney's pursuit; cowering in obscure niches and alcoves dotted about the shell structure; frightened and uncertain at the ruby glimmer that was emerging within the polyp. The possessed didn't care about them, not any more. That struggle was over. They even perceived Dariat and Tatiana lying prone on the escape pod's acceleration couches as the computer counted down the seconds. Nobody objected if they wanted to leave.

Profound changes were propagating outside the habitat. Nanonic-sized interstices flicked open, only to decay within milliseconds. The incessant foam of fluctuations was creating distortion waves similar to those generated by voidhawks. But these lacked any sort of order or focus. Chaos had visited local space-time, weakening the fabric around the shell.

Furious hellhawks swarmed above the northern endcap. Harpies and hyperspace starships spun and swooped around each other at hazardous velocities. Their flights were dangerously unstable as the massive distortion effects buffeted them as a tempest treated leaves.

**The bodies!** they clamoured to these possessed snug inside who were capable of affinity. **Kiera promised us the bodies in zero-tau. If you leave now we will never have them. You are condemning us to a life in these constructs.**

**Sorry,** was the only, sheepishly embarrassed reply.

Combat sensors deployed as the hunger for retribution reverberated across the affinity band. Activation codes were loaded into combat wasps.

**If we are denied eternity in human form, then you will join us in the same abyss.**

The only functional thought routines Rubra had left were those in the northern endcap. Everything else was blank to him, his senses amputated. A few mysterious images were still reaching him from those bitek processors which interfaced him with the electronic architecture of the counter-rotating spaceport. Wavering sepia pictures of empty corridors, stationary transit capsules, and barren external grid sections. With them came the data streams from the spaceport's communication network.

And he'd almost lost interest in it. Dariat, he thought, had left the transfer too late; the boy was too caught up in his obsession and guilt. The end is here, night is finally eclipsing me after all these centuries. A shame. A crying shame. But at least they'll remember my name with a curse as they vegetate their way through eternity.

He jettisoned every escape pod in the spaceport.

**Now**, Dariat sighed.

Twelve gees rammed him down into the acceleration couch. His vision disappeared into a purple sparkle. And after thirty years the neural strata no longer resisted him.

Two entities – two egos – collided. Memories and personality patterns merged at a fundamental level. Hostility, antipathy, anger, regret, shame, an abundance of it all pouring out from both sides, and there could be no hiding from it any more. The neural strata thrummed from collective moments of outraged pique as secrets long hidden were exposed to searing scrutiny. But the indignation cooled as the two differing strands of thought began the process of twining and integrating into a functional whole.

One half brought size to the mating, the huge neural strata, alive yet quiescent under the spell of the reality dysfunction; from the other half came the energistic effect, small in a single human, but with unlimited potential. For the first five seconds of the transfer, Dariat's essence was operating within a section of the neural strata only a few cubic metres in volume. At that level it was sufficient to halt the reality dysfunction of the possessed from paralysing any more of the neural strata. As the integration progressed and the thought routines amalgamated and multiplied it began to expand. More and more of the neural strata awoke to accommodate it.

The horrified possessed, quite literally, watched their dreams shatter around them.

**OK, you fuckers**, bespoke Valisk's new personality. *PARTY'S OVER.*

As soon as the escape pods launched, a hundred voidhawks from the Kohistan Consensus swallowed in. Their appearance ten kilometres from Valisk's counter-rotating spaceport startled the already frantic hellhawks. The gulf between the two antagonistic swarms of bitek starships was slashed by targeting lasers and radar pulses.

**Do not engage any targets**, the voidhawks ordered. **The habitat is to be left intact, the escape pods must not be harmed.**

Two hellhawks immediately launched a salvo of combat wasps. Solid rockets had barely propelled them clear of their launch-cradles before they were struck by X-ray lasers from the voidhawks. It was a perfect demonstration of the disadvantage the hellhawks suffered in any short-range combat situation. The energistic effect downgraded their electronic systems to a woefully inferior state.

Wormhole interstices sprang open, and the hellhawks dived down them, eluding any further conflict; abandoning their erstwhile abode with nothing more dangerous than a backwash of obscenities and threats.

Over two hundred escape pods were plunging away from Valisk's spaceport. Solid-fuel rockets burned a glaring topaz, gifting the drab, grey gridiron of the spaceport with an unrivalled dawn. As the distended skirts of flame and smoke died away, a cluster of five voidhawks surged forward to intercept a single pod.

Tatiana knew Dariat had gone; his body had shrunk some-how, not in size, but certainly in presence. It was as if the terrible crush of acceleration had left him behind, diminishing the teenage boy lying on the couch. Horgan began to wail. She released her webbing, and floated over to him, her own free-fall nausea forgotten in the face of someone whose suffering was far worse.

'It's all right,' Tatiana whispered as she hugged him. 'It's all over now. He's left you for good.' She even managed to surprise herself at the note of regret which had crept into her voice.

The voidhawks rendezvoused with Tatiana's pod, claimed its occupants, then swooped away from the habitat at seven gees. Valisk was now host to a war of light. The original red fluorescence was besieged by a vigorous purple shimmer sweep-ing down the shell from the northern endcap. As the purple area grew in size, so it grew in intensity.

Ten minutes after the escape pods were launched, the last glimmer of red was extinguished. The voidhawks were seven hundred kilometres away when it happened, and still retreating at two gees. Nobody quite knew what constituted a safe separation distance. Then their distortion fields detected Val-isk's mass starting to reduce. The last image of the habitat which their sensor blisters received was of a purple-white micro-star blazing coldly. At the core of the photonic rupture, space itself broke down as bizarre energy patterns exerted a catastrophic stress.

When the glare faded and space regained its equipoise there was no evidence of the habitat's existence. However hard the voidhawks probed, they could find no residue of energy, no particles larger than a mote of dust. Valisk had neither vaporized nor shattered, it had simply and cleanly departed the universe.

*

Dariat did the one thing which he had never expected to do again. He opened his eyes and looked around. His own eyes in his own body; fat unpleasant thing that it was, clad in his usual grubby toga.

The sight which greeted him was familiar: one of Valisk's innumerable shallow valleys out among the pink grass plains. If he wasn't completely mistaken, it was the same patch of ground Anastasia's tribe had occupied the day she died.

'This is the final afterlife?' he asked aloud.

It couldn't be. There was an elusive memory, the same befuddlement as a dream leaves upon waking. Of a sundering, of being torn out of...

He had fused with Rubra, the two of them becoming one, vanquishing the foe by shunting Valisk to a realm, or dimension, or state, that the two of them grasped was intrinsically adverse to the possessing souls. Perhaps they had even created the new location by simply willing it to be. And then time went awry.

He gave his surroundings a more considered examination. It was Valisk, all right. The circumfluous sea was about four kilometres away, its clusters of atolls easily recognizable. When he turned the other way, he could see a fat black scar running down two-thirds of the northern endcap.

The light-tube was dimmer than it should be, even accounting for the loss of some plasma. It proffered a kind of twilight, but grey rather than the magnificent golden sunset Dariat had experienced every day of his life. The grass plain echoed that malaised atmosphere, it was uneasily torpid. Its resident insects had curled up into dormancy; birds and rodents slunk back reticently to their nests, even the flowers had shrugged off their natural gloss.

Dariat bent down to pick an enervated poppy. And his chubby hand passed clean through the stem. He stared at it in astonishment, for the first time seeing that he was faintly translucent.

Shock finally liberated comprehension. A location hostile to possessors, one which would exorcise them from their enslaved hosts, denying them their energistic power. That was the destination he and Rubra had committed the habitat to.

'Oh, Thoale, you utter bastard. I'm a ghost.'

# 26

The Kulu Embassy was situated just outside Harrisburg's central governmental district, a five-storey building in the civic tradition, granite-block walls and elaborately carved windows. Slender turrets and retro-modernist sculptures lined the roof in an attempt to grant the stark façade some degree of interest. To no avail; Harrisburg's ubiquitous granite reduced the most ornate architecture to the level of a neo-Gothic fortress. Even the setting, in one of the wealthier districts laid out with parks, wide streets, and century-old trees, didn't help. An office cube was an office cube, no matter what cosmetics it dabbed on.

Its neighbours comprised rich legal practices, capital city headquarters of large companies, and expensive maisonette blocks. Directly opposite, in an office which claimed to be an aircraft charter broker, Tonala's security police kept a twenty-four-hour watch on everyone who went in or out. Forty minutes ago they had gone up to alert condition amber three (foreign covert action imminent) when five large screened cars from the diplomatic fleet slid down into the embassy's underground car park. None of the officers on duty were sure if that particular alert status applied in this case; according to their colleagues at the city spaceport, the cars were full of Edenists.

The arrival of Samuel and his team had also drawn considerable interest from staff inside the embassy, too. Curious, slightly apprehensive, faces peered out of almost every doorway as

Adrian Redway led Monica Foulkes and her new allies through the building. They took a lift eight storeys below ground, to a floor which didn't exist on any blueprints logged on the city council's civil engineering computer.

Adrian Redway stopped at the door to the ESA station's operational centre, and gave Samuel an awkward look. His eyes slid over the tall Edenist's shoulders to the other six Edenists waiting patiently in the corridor.

'Listen,' he said heavily. 'I don't mean to be an oaf about this. But we do run and correlate our entire Tonala asset network from here. Surely, you don't all need to come in?' His eyebrows quivered hopefully.

'Of course not,' Samuel said graciously.

Monica gave a disgruntled sigh. She knew Samuel well enough now not to need affinity to hear the thought in his head: strange concept. If one Edenist went inside, then technically all of them did. Her hand fluttered towards him in a modestly embarrassed gesture. He winked back.

The operations centre could have been the office of any medium-sized commercial enterprise. Air-conditioned yet strangely airless, it had the standard desks with (more sophisticated than usual) processor blocks, big wall-screens, ceiling-mounted AV pillars, and side offices with heavily tinted glass walls. Eleven ESA staffers were sitting in big leather chairs, monitoring what they could of the planet's current military and politico-strategic situation. Information was becoming a precious resource as Tonala's communication net started to suffer glitches; the only certainty gained from the overall picture was how close the orbital situation was getting to all-out confrontation.

Tonala's state of emergency had been matched by the other nations. Then in the last twenty minutes Tonala's high command had confirmed it had lost the Spirit of Freedom station to unknown foreign elements. In response, five warships had been dispatched to intercept the *Urschel*, *Raimo*, and *Pinzola* to try and find out what had happened. Every other government was complaining that their deployment at this time constituted a deliberately provocative act.

Adrian led Monica and Samuel though into a conference room on the far side of the operations centre. 'My chief analyst gives us two hours tops before the shooting starts for real,' he said glumly as he sat at the head of the table.

'I hate to say this, but that really is secondary to our mission,' Monica said. 'We must secure Mzu. She cannot be killed or captured. It would be a disaster for the Confederation.'

'Yeah, I accessed the report,' Adrian said glumly. 'The Alchemist by itself is bad enough, in the hands of the possessed . . .'

'A fact you may not have yet,' Samuel said. 'The frigates *Urschel*, *Raimo*, and *Pinzola* are all Organization starships. Capone must know Dr Mzu is here; his representatives will not demonstrate any restraint or subtlety at all. Their actions could well trigger the war.'

'Jeeze; they sent some spaceplanes down after they arrived. Nobody knows where the hell to, the planetary sensor coverage is wiped.'

'What about local air defence coverage for the city?' Monica asked.

'Reasonably intact. Kulu supplied the hardware about eleven years ago; hardly top grade but it's still functioning. The embassy has an over-the-shoulder feed from the Tonala Defence Force Headquarters.'

'So if the Organization spaceplanes approach Harrisburg you'll be able to warn us.'

'No problem.'

'Good, that ought to give us a couple of minutes' breathing space. Next question, did you find her?'

Adrian pretended offence. 'Of course we found her,' he grinned. 'We're the ESA, remember?'

'Right; truth is always worse than rumour. Where is she?'

Adrian datavised the officer running the surveillance mission on Mzu. 'She booked in at the Mercedes Hotel, or rather Voi did, as soon as they arrived. They made very little effort to cover their tracks; Voi used a credit disk registered under an alias, but it's still got her biolectric pattern. I mean, how amateur can you get?'

'They're not even amateurs, they're just kids,' Samuel said. 'They eluded us on their home ground because we were rushed. Out here they're completely defenceless against any professional agency.'

'Voi did approach a local security firm,' Adrian said. 'But she hasn't followed it up. Her request for bodyguards was cancelled. They seem to have linked up with some locals instead. We're not sure who they are. There certainly aren't any Garissa partisan cadres on Nyvan.'

'How many locals?' Monica asked.

'Three or four, we think. As we don't know who they are, it's hard to be sure.'

'Any interest from other agencies?'

'There have been three probes launched into the hotel's computer system. We couldn't get an origin on any of them. Whoever it was, their blocker programs are first-rate.'

'Is Mzu still at the Mercedes?' Monica asked.

'Not at this exact moment, but she is on her way back there from a meeting with the Opia company. Her group are passing themselves off as representatives from the Dorados' Defence Force, which gives them a valid reason to buy armaments. I should be receiving a report on the meeting from our asset in the company any minute.'

'Fine,' Monica said. 'We'll intercept her at the hotel.'

'Very well.' Adrian gave her an edgy glance. 'The local police won't appreciate that.'

'Sad, but irrelevant. Can you load a priority flight clearance authorization into the city's air-defence network?'

'Sure, we supplied it, we have the ultimate authority codes.'

'Fine, stand by to do it for the Edenist flyers. We'll use them to evac as soon as we've acquired her.'

'The Kingdom will probably get expelled from this entire system if you pull a stunt like that,' Adrian said. 'If there's one thing Nyvan's nations hate more than each other, it's outsystem foreigners.'

'Mzu wanted somewhere that was dishonest and greedy enough to supply her with weapons on a no questions asked basis. If this planet had built itself a decent civilization in the first place, she wouldn't even be here. They've only themselves to blame. I mean, they've had five centuries, for God's sake.'

Samuel groaned chidingly.

Adrian paused, not meeting Monica's stare. 'Um, my second surveillance team leader is reporting in. I've had them following that Calvert character, as you asked.'

'Yes?' There was a sense of grudging inevitability in this moment, Monica thought.

'The Captain contacted a data security expert as soon as he landed, a Richard Keaton. It would seem Keaton has done a good job for him. In fact, he probably origined one of the probes into the hotel computer. They're currently in a car which is heading in the general direction of the Mercedes Hotel. He'll get there before you can.'

'Shit! That bloody Calvert.'

'Do you want him eliminated?'

'No,' Samuel said. He stopped Monica's outburst with a firm stare. 'Any action at the hotel now will draw the police to it before we can get there. Our interception will be difficult enough as it is.'

'All right,' she grumbled.

'My team could intercept Mzu for you,' Adrian said.

Monica was tempted – anything to get this resolved. 'How many have you got on her?'

'Three cars, seven personnel.'

'Mzu has at least four people with her,' Samuel said.

'Agreed,' Monica said regretfully. 'That's too many, and God knows what they're carrying, especially these unknown locals. We have to guarantee first-attempt success. Tell your team to continue their observation, Adrian, we'll join them as soon as we can.'

'Do you think she'll resist?' Adrian asked.

'I would hope not,' Samuel said. 'After all, she is not stupid; she must know Nyvan's situation is decaying by the minute. That may well make this easier for us. We should start with an open approach to fly her outsystem. Once she realizes she has to leave with us, either willingly or by force, it would be logical for her to capitulate.'

'Easier?' Monica gave him a pitying look. 'This mission?'

\*

'Mother Mary, *why*?' Voi demanded as soon as the five of them crowded back into the penthouse lift. 'You can't sell out now. Think of what you've been through – Mary, what we've done for you. You can't hand it over to Capone!'

Her impassioned outburst stopped dead as Alkad turned to stare at her. 'Do not argue with one of my decisions ever again.'

Even Gelai and Ngong were daunted by the tone, but then they could sense the thoughts powering her.

'As Baranovich made quite clear, the Omutan option is now closed to me,' Alkad said. 'Worthless piece of trash though he is, he happens to be right. You cannot begin to imagine how much I resent that, because it means the one thing I never allowed myself to think in thirty years has become real. Our vengeance has become irrelevant.'

'Nonsense,' Voi said. 'You can still hit the Omutans before the possessed.'

'Please don't display your ignorance in public, it's offensive.'

'Ignorance, you bitch. Mary, you're giving the Alchemist to Capone. Giving it! You think I'm going to keep quiet about that?'

Alkad squared her shoulders; with an immense effort she spoke in a level voice to the ireful girl. 'You are a simple immature child, with an equally childish fixation. You have never once thought through the consequences should your wish be granted, the suffering it will cause. For thirty years I have thought of nothing else. I created the Alchemist, Mary have mercy on me. I understand the full reality of what it can do. The responsibility for that machine is mine alone. I have never, nor will ever, shirk that. To do so would be to divorce myself from what remains of my humanity. And the consequences of the possessed obtaining it are very bad indeed. Therefore I will accept Baranovich's offer to leave this doomed planet. I will lead Capone's forces to the Alchemist. And I will then activate it. It will never be available for anyone to study and duplicate.'

'But—' Voi looked round the others for support. 'If you activate it, surely...'

'I will die. Oh, yes. And with me will die the one man I ever loved. We've been separated for thirty years, and I still love him. That purely human entanglement doesn't matter. I will even sacrifice him for this. Now do you understand my commitment and responsibility? Maybe I will come back as a possessor, or maybe I will stay in the beyond. Whatever my fate, it will be no different to any other human being. I am afraid of that, but I don't reject it. I'm not arrogant enough to think I can cheat our ultimate destination.

'Gelai and Ngong have shown me that we do retain our basic personality. That's good, because if I do come back in someone else's body, my resolve will remain intact. I *will not* build another Alchemist. Its reason for being is gone, it must go too.'

Voi bent her knees slightly so her eyes were closer to Alkad's face, as if that would give her a deeper insight into the physicist's mind. 'You really will, won't you? You'll kill yourself.'

'I think kamikaze is a more appropriate term. But don't worry, I'm not going to dragoon you two along. I don't even consider this to be your fight, I never did. You're not Garissans, not really; you have no reason to dip your hands into blood this deep. Now be quiet and pray to Mother Mary that we can save something from this pile of shit, and get the pair of you as well as Lodi out of here. But be assured, I still consider you expendable to my goal.' She turned to Gelai. 'If either of you have any objection to this, then speak now, please.'

'No, Doctor,' Gelai said, with the faintest smile on her lips. 'I don't object. In fact, I'm rather glad it won't be used against a planet by you or Capone. But believe me, you don't want to kill yourself; once you've known the beyond, the pressure Capone can exert by promising you a body is going to be extraordinary.'

'I know,' Alkad said. 'But choice has never played a large part in my life.'

*

Tonala's state of emergency had drastically reduced the volume of road traffic in the capital. Normally, the churning wheels of the afternoon gridlock would turn the snow to mush and spray it over the pedestrians. Now, however, the big flakes were beginning to accumulate on the roads. Harrisburg's civic mechanoids were losing their battle to clear it away.

The Transport Department considered the effects such an icy blanket would have on brake-response time, and ordered a general speed reduction to avoid accidents. The proscription was datavised into the control processor of individual vehicles.

'You want me to neutralize the order for this car?' Dick Keaton asked as Joshua fretted impatiently.

The answer was yes, but he said no anyway, because speeding when you're a suspect foreigner in a nation on the brink of war and being followed by two local police cars is an essentially dumb thing to do.

Thanks to the general lack of cars, their tail was a prominent one, keeping a precise fifty metres behind. Their presence didn't have much effect on Joshua and his companions. The two serjeants were as vigilant as mechanoids, while Melvyn stared out at the city covered in its crisp grey mantle, the opposite of Dahybi, who sat hunched up in his seat, hands clasped and paying no attention to their surroundings, almost as if he was at prayer. Dick Keaton was enjoying the ride – a pre-teen excitement which Joshua found annoying. He was trying to balance mission priorities at the same time as he reviewed what he was going to say to Mzu. A sincere but insistent invitation to return to Tranquillity, point out the shit she was in, how he had a starship waiting. It wasn't that he was bad with words, but these were just so damn important. Exactly how do you tell the semi-psychotic owner of a doomsday device to come along quietly and not make any fuss?

His communication block accepted Ashly's secure datavise and relayed it straight into his neural nanonics.

'New development,' Ashly reported. 'The Edenist flyers just activated their ion fields.'

'Are they leaving?'

'No sign of that yet. They're still on the ground, but they're in a rapid-response condition. Their agents must be close to Mzu.'

'Bugger. Any news from orbit?'

'Not a thing. *Lady Macbeth* isn't due above the horizon for another eight minutes, but the spaceplane sensors haven't detected any low-orbit weapons activity yet.'

'OK. Stand by, we're approaching the hotel now. I might need you in a hurry.'

'Do my best. But if these flyers don't want me to lift off, it could get tricky.'

'*Lady Mac* is your last resort. She can take them out. Use her if you have to.'

'Understood.'

Dahybi was leaning forward in his seat to catch a glimpse of the Mercedes Hotel as the car swept along the last two hundred metres of road.

'That park would make a handy landing spot for Ashly,' Melvyn commented.

'Acknowledged,' Joshua said. He squinted through the windscreen as the car turned on to the loop of road which led to the hotel's broad portico. There was a car already parked in front of the doors.

Joshua datavised a halt order into their car's control processor, then directed it to one of the parking slots outside the portico. Tyres crunched on the virgin snow as they pulled in.

The two police cars stopped on the road outside.

'What is it?' Dick Keaton asked, he was almost whispering.

Joshua pointed a forefinger at the car under the portico. Several people were climbing in.

'That's Mzu,' one of the serjeants said.

After so long on the trail, so much endured, Joshua felt something akin to awe now he could finally see her. Mzu hadn't changed much from the visual file stored in his neural nanonics during their one brief encounter. Features and hair the same, and she was wrapped up well in a thick navy-blue coat, but the flaky professor act had been dumped. This woman carried a deadly confidence.

If he'd ever doubted the Alchemist and Mzu's connection to it, that ended now.

'What do you want to do?' Dahybi asked. 'We can stop her car. Make our pitch now.'

Joshua held up a hand for silence. He'd just noticed the last two people getting into the car with Mzu. It wasn't a premonition he got from them, more like fear hot-wired direct into his brain. 'Oh, Jesus.'

Melvyn's electronic-warfare blocks datavised a warning. He accessed the display. 'What the hell?'

'I don't want to alarm you guys,' Dick Keaton said. 'But the people in the next car are giving us a real unfriendly look.'

'Huh?' Joshua glanced over.

'And they're aiming a multiband sensor at us, too,' Melvyn said.

Joshua returned the hostile stare from the two ESA agents in the car parked beside them. 'Oh, fucking wonderful.'

'She's leaving,' one of the serjeants called.

'Jesus,' Joshua grumbled. 'Melvyn, are you blocking that sensor?'

'Absolutely.' He gave the agents a broad toothy smile.

'OK, we follow her. Let's just hope she's going somewhere I can have a civilized chat.'

*

The five embassy cars carrying Monica, Samuel, and a mixed crew of ESA and Edenist operatives disregarded the city's new speed limit altogether as they raced for the hotel. All the security police did was follow and observe; they were anxious to see where this was all leading.

They were still a kilometre from the Mercedes Hotel when Adrian Redway datavised Monica to advise her that Mzu was on the move again. 'There's definitely only four people with her this time. The observation team launched a skyspy outside the hotel. It looks like there's been some sort of fight in the penthouse. Do you want access?'

'Please.'

The image from the small synthetic bird hovering above the park filled her brain. Its artificial-tissue wings were flapping constantly to hold it steady in the middle of the snowstorm, producing an awkward juddering. A visual-wavelength optical sensor was scanning across the penthouse's broad windows. One of them had a large jagged hole in the middle.

'I can see a lot of glass on the carpet,' Monica datavised. 'Something came in through that window, not out.'

'But what?' Adrian asked. 'That's the twenty-fifth floor.'

Monica continued her review. The lounge doors had been smashed open. Long black scorch marks were chiselled deep into the one lying on the floor.

Then she switched focus to a settee. There was a foot dangling over the armrest.

'No wonder Mzu was in a hurry to leave again,' she said out loud. 'The possessed have tracked her down.'

'Her car isn't heading for the spaceport,' Samuel said. 'Could the two locals with her be possessed?'

'Possible,' Monica agreed hesitantly. 'But the observation team said she seemed to be leading the others. They didn't think she was being coerced.'

'Calvert has started following her,' Adrian datavised.

'OK. Let's see where they're all so eager to get to.' She datavised the car's control processor to catch up with the observation team's vehicles.

\*

'Someone else has now joined us,' Ngong said. His voice was split between amusement and surprise. 'That makes over a dozen cars now.'

'And poor old Baranovich said to come alone,' Alkad said. 'Is he in one of them?'

'I don't know. One car certainly has some possessed in it.'

'Doesn't that bother you?' Voi asked.

Alkad sank down deeper into her seat, getting herself comfortable. 'Not really. This is like old times for me.'

'What if they stop us?'

'Gelai, what are the police thinking?'

'They're curious, Doctor. Make that very curious.'

'That's OK, then; as long as they aren't going to stop us we're all right. I know the agencies, they will want to know where we're going first before they make their move.'

'But Baranovich—'

'They're his problem, not ours. If he doesn't want me followed then it's up to him to do something about it.'

*

Alkad's car navigated itself along Harrisburg's abandoned streets at a doggedly legal speed. Despite that, they made good progress, leaving the closely packed buildings of the city centre behind to venture out into the more industrial suburbs. Thirty minutes into the journey, the last of the urban clutter was discarded behind them. The slightly elevated carriageway cut straight across a flat alluvial plain that was open all the way to the sea eighty kilometres away. It was a vast expanse of huge fallow fields from which tractor mechanoids and tailored bugs had eradicated any unauthorized vegetation. Trees were stunted and bent by the wind that blew in from the shore, standing hunched along the line of the drainage canals which had been dug to tame the rich black soil.

Nothing moved off the road, no animals or vehicles. They were driving across a snow desert. Large, stiff flakes were hurled horizontally against the car by the wind, taxing the guarantee of the lofriction windscreen to stay clear. Even so, that didn't prevent them from seeing the fifteen cars which were now following them: a convoy that made no attempt to hide itself.

*

Adrian Redway had settled himself into one of the chairs in the ESA's operation centre and datavised his desktop processor for a filter program to access the station's incoming information streams. Even with the filter he was almost overwhelmed by the quantity of data available. Neural nanonics assigned priority gradings. Subroutines took over from his mind's natural cross-indexing ability, leaving his consciousness free to absorb relevant details.

He focused on Mzu, principally through the observation team, then defined a peripheral-activity key to alert him of any incoming factors which would affect her situation. The rate at which external events were developing on Nyvan made it unlikely he would be able to secure Monica much advance warning, but as a veteran of twenty-eight years' ESA service he knew even seconds could change the entire outcome of a field operation.

'It has to be the ironberg foundry yard,' he datavised to Monica after they had been driving over the farmland for twenty uneventful minutes.

'We think so, too,' Monica replied. 'Are the foundry's landing pads equipped with beacon guidance? If she's looking for a spaceplane pick-up, they'll need a controlled approach in this weather.'

'Unless they have military-grade sensors. But yes, the foundry's pads have beacons. I wouldn't like to vouch for their reliability, mind. I doubt they've been serviced since the day they were installed.'

'OK, can you run a data sweep of the foundry? And if you can access it, a security sensor review would be helpful. I'd like to know if there's anyone there waiting for her.'

'I don't think you quite understand what you're asking for, that foundry is big. But I'll put a couple of my analysts on it. Just don't expect too much.'

'Thanks.' She gave Samuel a forlorn look. 'Something wrong?'

The Edenist had been accessing their exchange via his bitek processor block. 'I am reminded of the time she left Tranquillity. We were all following after her rather like this, and look what happened that time. Possibly we should be the ones taking the initiative. If the foundry is her intended destination, she may well have a method of eluding us already in place.'

'Could be. But the only way of stopping her now is to shoot the car. That would bring the police storming in.'

Samuel accessed the ESA operations centre computer, and reviewed the security police deployment status. 'We are a long way from their designated reinforcements; and we can have the flyers here in minutes. Hurting the feelings of the Tonalan government is an irrelevance compared to securing the Alchemist. Mzu has done us a favour by coming to such a remote place.'

'Yeah. Well, if you're willing to bring your flyers in to evac us, I'm certainly prepared to commit our people. We've got enough firepower to stomp on the police if—' She broke off as Adrian datavised again.

'The city air-defence network has just located those missing Organization spaceplanes,' he told her. 'They're heading right at you, Monica; three of them coming in over the sea at Mach five. Looks like you were right about the foundry being a pick-up zone.'

'My God, she was selling out to Capone. What a bitch.'

'Looks that way.'

'Can you direct the city network to shoot the spaceplanes?'

'Yes, if they get closer, but at the moment they're out of range.'

'Will they be in range at the foundry?' Samuel asked.

'No. The network doesn't have any missiles, it's all beam weapons. Tonala relies on its SD platforms to kill any threat approaching from outside its boundaries.'

'The flyers,' Monica asked Samuel. 'Can they intercept?'

'Yes.' **Launch, please,** he instructed the pilots.

Monica datavised her armour suit management processor to run a readiness diagnostic, then pulled her shell-helmet on and sealed it. The other agents began checking their own weapons.

\*

'Joshua, the flyers are all leaving,' Ashly datavised.

'I was wondering about that,' Joshua replied. 'We're only about ten kilometres from the ironberg foundry now. Mzu must have arranged some kind of rendezvous there. Dick's been running some checks for us; he says that sections of the foundry electronics are glitched. There could be some possessed up ahead.'

'Do you need an evac?'

Joshua glanced round the car. Melvyn and Dahybi weren't giving anything away, while Dick Keaton was merely curious. 'We're not in any danger yet,' one of the serjeants said.

'No. But if it happens, it's going to happen fast; and we're not in the strongest position.'

'You can't pull out now. We're too close.'

'You're telling me,' he muttered. 'All right, we'll keep on her for now. If we can get close enough to make our offer, well and good. But if the agencies start getting aggressive, then we back off. Understood, Ione?'

'Understood.'

'I may be able to offer some assistance,' Dick Keaton said.

'Oh?'

'The cars in this convoy are all local models. I have some program commands which could cause trouble in their control processors. It might help us get closer to your target.'

'If we start doing that to the agencies, they'll use their own electronic-warfare capability on us,' Melvyn said. 'That's if they don't just use a TIP carbine. Everybody knows what's at stake.'

'They won't know it's us,' Dick Keaton said.

'You hope,' Melvyn said. 'They're good, Joshua. No offence to Dick, but the agencies have entire departments of computer science professors writing black software for them.'

Joshua enjoyed the idea of bollixing up the other cars; but the way they were driving further and further into isolation was a big mitigating factor. Normal agency rules of minimum visibility wouldn't apply out here. If he upset the status quo, Melvyn was probably right about the reaction he'd get. What he really wanted was *Lady Mac* above the horizon to give them some fire support, although even her sensors would struggle to resolve anything through this snowstorm, and she wasn't due up for another forty minutes. 'Dick, see what you can do to strengthen our car processors against agency software. I'll use your idea if it looks like she's getting away from us.'

'Sure thing.'

'Ashly, can you launch without causing undue attention?'

'I think so. There has to be someone observing me, but I'm not picking up any active sensor activity.'

'OK, launch and fly a low-visibility holding pattern ten kilometres from the yard. We'll shout for you.'

*

The four Edenist flyers picked up velocity as they curved round the outskirts of Harrisburg, hitting Mach 2 thirty kilometres from the coast. Their smoothly rounded noses lined up on the ironberg foundry. Snowflakes flowing through their coherent magnetic field sparkled a vivid blue around the forward fuselage then vaporized to fluorescent purple streamers. To anyone under their path, it appeared as though four sunburst comets were rumbling through the atmosphere.

It was the one failing of Kulu's ion-field technology that it could never be successfully hidden from sensors. The three Organization spaceplanes streaking in from the sea spotted them as soon as they lifted from the spaceport. Electronic-warfare arrays were activated, seeking to blind the flyers with a full-spectrum barrage. Air-to-air missiles dropped out of their wing recesses, and shot ahead at Mach 10.

The Edenist flyers saw them coming through the electronic hash. They peeled away from each other, arcing through the sky in complex evasion manoeuvres. Chaff and signature decoys spewed out of the flyers. Masers locked on and fired continuous pulses at the incoming drones.

Explosions thundered unseen above the farmland. Some of the missiles succumbed to the masers, while others followed their programs to detonate in preloaded patterns. Clouds of kinetic shrapnel threw up lethal blockades along the trajectories they predicted the flyers would use. But there were too few missiles left to create an effective kill zone.

The flyers stormed through.

It should have ended then, a duel between energy-beam weapons and fuselage shielding, the two opponents so far away that in all probability they would never even see each other. But the snow forbade that: absorbing maser and thermal induction energy, it cut the effective strike range of both sides to less than five hundred metres. Flyers and spaceplanes had to get close to each other, spiralling round and round, looping, twisting, diving, climbing. Aggressors desperate to keep their beams on one point of their target's fuselage; targets frantic to keep moving, spinning to disperse the energy input. A genuine dogfight developed, with pilots blinded by the snow and clouds, dependent on sensors harassed by unremitting electronic-warfare impulses. Given that both the flyers and the spaceplanes were multi-role craft, the manoeuvres lacked any real acrobatic innovation. Predication programs were the true knights of the sky, allowing pilots to keep a steady lock-on on their opponent. The flyers' superior agility began to pay dividends. The spaceplanes were limited by the ancient laws of aerodynamic lift and stability, restricting their tactics to classical aerial manoeuvres, while the flyers could move in any direction they wanted to providing their fusion generators had enough power.

The Organization was always going to lose.

One by one, the crippled spaceplanes tumbled out of the sky. Two of them smashed into the frozen soil outside the foundry yard, the third into the sea.

Overhead, the flyers closed formation, and began to circle the vast foundry yard in anticipation of claiming their prize.

*Urschel* and *Pinzola* slid up over the horizon. Warned by the screams of souls torn back into the beyond, they knew what to look for. X-ray lasers stabbed down four times, their power unchecked by gravid clouds or swirling ice crystals.

*

The docking cradle rose out of the spaceport bay, exposing the fuselage of the *Mount's Delta* to a blaze of sunlight. At this juncture of a normal departure, a starship would spread its thermo-dump panels before it disengaged. Quinn told Dwyer to switch their heat-exchange circuits to an internal store. Umbilical feeds withdrew from their couplings in the lower hull, then the hold-down latches retracted.

'Fly us fifty kilometres along Jesup's spin axis,' Quinn said. 'Then hold us there.'

Dwyer flicked a throat mike down from his headset and muttered instructions to the flight computer. Ion thrusters lifted the *Clipper*-class ship clear of the bay, then the secondary drive came on. *Mount's Delta* accelerated away at a fifteenth of a gee, following a clean arc above the surface of the counter-rotating spaceport.

Quinn used the holoscreens surrounding his acceleration couch to display images from the external sensor suite. Nothing else moved around the gigantic asteroid. The surrounding industrial stations had been shut down for days, and were now drifting out of alignment. An inert fleet of personnel commuters, MSVs, inter-orbit cargo craft, and tankers were all docked to Jesup's counter-rotating spaceport, filling nearly every bay.

As soon as the starship rose away from the apex of the spaceport, Quinn switched the optical sensors to track the other asteroids. Dwyer watched the screens in silence as the three deserted asteroids appeared. This time there was movement visible, tiny stars were closing on the dark rocks at high velocity.

'Looks like we're just in time,' Quinn said. 'The nations are getting upset about losing their ships.' He spoke briefly into his mike, instructing the flight computer.

Four secure military-grade laser communicators deployed from the starship's fuselage. One pointed back at Jesup, while the other three acquired a lock-on on the abandoned asteroids. Each one fired an ultraviolet beam at its target, the encrypted code requesting a response. In answer, four similar ultraviolet beams transfixed the *Mount's Delta*. Impossible to intercept or interfere with, they linked Quinn into the equipment his teams had been setting up.

Diagrams flashed up on the bridge screens as modulated information flooded back along the beams. Quinn entered a series of codes, and watched in satisfaction as the equipment acknowledged his command authority.

'Ninety-seven nukes on-line,' he said. 'By the look of it, they're rigging another five as we speak. Dumb arseholes.'

'Is that enough?' Dwyer asked anxiously. Loyalty would probably not be any defence if things weren't going precisely to plan. He just wished he knew what that plan was.

Quinn's grin was playful. 'Let's find out, shall we?'

*

'No survivors,' Samuel said. 'None.' His dignified face betrayed a profound sorrow, one hardened by the grey light of the snow-veiled landscape.

For Monica the loss was heightened by the terrible remoteness of the event. A few swift diffuse flashes of light lost among the occluded sky above the convoy, as if sheet lightning was flaring amid the snowstorm. They had seen and heard nothing of the decimated flyers crashing on the eastern edge of the foundry yard.

**We have the pilots safe,** the *Hoya* told Samuel and the other Edenists. **Fortunately the flyers' shielding held out long enough for the transfer to complete.**

**Thank you, that's excellent news,** Samuel said. 'But not their souls,' he whispered under his breath.

Monica heard him, and met his gaze. Their minds were a

unison of grief, less than affinity but certainly sharing awareness.

'Practicalities,' he said forlornly.

'Yes.'

The car gave a fast unexpected lurch as the brakes suddenly engaged then cut out. Everyone inside was flung forwards against their seat straps.

'Electronic warfare!' shouted the ESA electronics expert who was riding with them. 'They're glitching our processor.'

'Is it the possessed?' Monica asked.

'No. Definitely coming through the net.'

The car braked again. This time the wheels locked for several seconds, starting to skid across the slushy road before an emergency program released them.

'Go to manual,' Monica instructed. She could see other cars in the convoy twisting and slithering across the dual carriage-way. One of the police vehicles hit the safety barrier and shot down the embankment into a frozen ditch, spraying snow as it went. Another of the big embassy cars thumped into the rear of Monica's car, crunching some of the bodywork. The impact spun them around. Monica's armour suit stiffened as she was shaken from side to side.

'It's not affecting Mzu,' Samuel said. 'She's pulling away from us.'

'Disable the police cars,' Monica told the electronics expert. 'And that bloody Calvert, too.' She felt a sincerely unprofessional glee as she ordered that, but it was perfectly legitimate. By separating herself and Mzu from the police and Calvert she was reducing the opportunity for interference in the mission goal.

Their driver finally seemed to master the intricacies of the car's manual controls, and they shot forward, weaving round the other disorientated cars. 'Adrian?' Monica datavised.

'With you. Nobody here can origin that electronic-warfare outbreak.'

'Doesn't matter, we're on top of it.'

'Calvert's in front of us,' the driver said. 'He's right on Mzu's tail, this hasn't affected him at all.'

'Shit!' Monica directed her shell-helmet sensors to switch to infra-red, and just caught the pink blob of Calvert's car hidden by snow a hundred and twenty metres ahead of them. Behind her, two embassy cars were already pulling away from the stalled police vehicles, while another one was creeping along the verge, trying to get round.

'Adrian, we're going to need an evac. Fast.'

'Not easy.'

'What do you fucking mean? Where are the embassy's Royal Marine utility planes? They should be on back-up, for God's sake!'

'They're both liaising with the local defence force. It would have been suspicious if I'd called them back.'

'Do it *now!*'

'I'm on it. You should have one there in about twenty minutes.'

Monica thumped an armoured fist into the seat, splitting some of the fabric. The car was racing on through the snow, surprisingly stable for one under manual control. Four sets of headlights were visible behind them, and a fast datavised review informed Monica they were all embassy cars, which gave her some satisfaction.

She put her machine-gun down and picked up a maser carbine, then undid her seat belt.

'Now what?' Samuel asked as she leant forward to get a better view through the windscreen.

'Joshua Calvert, your time is up.'

'Uh oh,' said the electronics expert. He looked up in reflex.

*

Ashly approached the ironberg foundry yard from the west, following five minutes behind the Edenist flyers. The space-plane's forward passive-sensor suite revealed the basics of the missile launch and dogfight. Then the X-ray lasers had fired from orbit. He held his breath as the sensors reported a microwave radar beam sweep across the fuselage. It came from the starships seven hundred kilometres above.

*Now is not a good time to die. Especially as I know what's in store if I do. Kelly was right, screw fate and destiny, just spend the rest of time in zero-tau. I think I might try that if I get out of this.*

Nothing happened.

Ashly let out a shudder of breath, finding his palms sweating. 'Thank you, God,' he said out loud. With its top-grade stealth systems active, and following a subsonic nap of the earth flight path twenty metres above the ground, the spaceplane was probably invisible to any sensor on, or orbiting, Nyvan. His only worry had been an infra-red signature, but the thick snow eradicated that.

He ordered the spaceplane's computer to open a secure channel to Tonala's net, hoping no one with heavy weaponry would detect the tiny signal. 'Joshua?' he datavised.

'Jesus, Ashly, we thought you'd been hit.'

'Not in this machine.'

'Where are you?'

'Thirty kilometres from the foundry yard. I'm about to go into a holding pattern. What's happening down there?'

'Some idiot used electronic warfare on the cars. We're OK; Dick hardened our programs. But the police are out of it for the moment. We're still on Mzu's tail. I think a couple of embassy cars are behind us, maybe more.'

'Is Mzu still heading for the foundry yard?'

'Looks like it.'

'Well, unless the cavalry comes up over the hill, we're the only pick-up she's got left. There's nothing flying within my sensor range.'

'Unless they're stealthed, too.'

'You've always got to look on the bleak side, haven't you?'

'Just being cautious.'

'Well, if they're stealthed, I—' Ashly broke off as the flight computer warned him of another radar sweep emanating from the starships. The beam was configured differently this time, a ground-scan profile. 'Joshua, they're hunting you. Get out! Get out of the car!'

\*

Every electronic-warfare block in the embassy car was datavising frantic alerts.

**We are being targeted by the Organization frigates**, Samuel told *Hoya* and Niveu. There was little he could do to conceal his rising panic. Once, the knowledge that his memories would be held safely in the *Hoya* would have been enough for him. Now he wasn't so sure that was all that mattered. **You must stop them. If they kill Mzu, it's all over.**

The snow-lashed sky behind the car flashed purple.

After tens of kilometres of entirely passive pursuit across the tundra-like farmland, the Tonala security police had been caught out badly by the sudden electronic-warfare attack. Of all the cars, theirs came off worse, leaving them scattered across both carriageways as their surveillance suspects, quite infuriatingly, dodged round them as if they were nothing more than inconvenient bollards. It took time for them to rally; processors had to be disengaged to allow the manual controls to be activated, officers from cars that had gone over the embankment or smashed into the barrier sprinted for cars that were still functional, swiping huge gobs of crash-cushion foam from their suits. Once they had reorganized they began to drive fast after their quarry.

It meant that their cars were still bunched together, supplying the Organization starships with the biggest target. Oscar Kearn, uncertain which one contained Mzu, decided to start there and eliminate the other cars one at a time until her soul was claimed by the beyond. With that, they would have won.

Bringing her back, one way or another, was all that mattered. Now the spaceplanes had been destroyed, she would have to die. Fortunately, as an ex-military man himself, he had prepared his fall-back options. So far Mzu had proved amazingly elusive, or just plain lucky. He was determined to put an end to that.

The ironberg foundry yard pick-up had been planned in some detail with Baranovich, its location and timing quite critical – although Oscar Kearn hadn't actually mentioned how critical to the newly allied Cossack, nor why. But he was satisfied that if things went bad for the Organization on the ground, Mzu would never survive.

Firstly, the frigates would be overhead, able to initiate a groundstrike. And if she somehow escaped that . . .

While the Organization starships were docked with the Spirit of Freedom they had gained command access to the tugs delivering Tonala's ironbergs for splashdown. A small alteration had been made to the trajectory of one tug.

Far above Nyvan's ocean, to the west of Tonala, an ironberg was already slipping through the ionosphere. This time, no recovery fleet would be needed. No ships would be employed to tow it on a week-long voyage to the foundry yard.

It was taking the direct route.

\*

The first X-ray laser blast struck the police car which was lying down the embankment, bonnet embedded in the ditch. It vaporized in a violent shock wave, sending droplets of molten metal, roasted earth, and superheated steam churning into the air. All the snow within a two hundred metre radius was ripped from the ground before the heat turned it back into water. The other car abandoned on the road was somersaulted over and over, smashing its windows and sending wheels spinning through the air.

\*

The first explosion made Alkad wince. She glanced out of the rear window, seeing an orange corona slowly shrinking back down into the road.

'What the hell did that?' Voi asked.

'Not us,' Gelai said. 'Not one of the possessed, not even a dozen. We don't have that much power.'

A second explosion sounded, rattling the car badly.

'It's me,' Alkad said. 'They want me.'

Another explosion lit up the sky. This time the pressure wave pushed at their car, sending it skidding sideways before the control processor could compensate.

'They're getting closer,' Eriba cried. 'Mother Mary, help us.'

'There's not much She can do for us now,' Alkad said. 'It's up to the agencies.'

*

The four voidhawks were in a standard five hundred kilometre equatorial parking orbit above Nyvan when *Hoya* received Samuel's frantic call. Their position allowed them to shadow the Organization frigates which were strung out along a high-inclination orbit. At the time, only *Urschel* and *Pinzola* were above the ironberg foundry yard's horizon, *Raimo* was trailing them by two thousand kilometres.

Although it was four thousand kilometres from *Urschel* and *Pinzola*, *Hoya*'s sensors could just detect the brilliant purple discharge in the clouds below the Organization frigates as they fired on a fourth car. The voidhawk began to accelerate at seven gees, followed by its three cousins. All four went to full combat alert status. A salvo of fifteen combat wasps slid out of *Hoya*'s lower hull cradles, each one charging away in a different direction at thirty gees, leaving the voidhawk at the centre of an expanding and dimming nimbus of exhaust plasma. After five seconds, the drones curved round to align themselves on the Organization frigates.

*Urschel* and *Pinzola* had no choice but to defend themselves.

Their reaction time was hardly optimum, but twenty-five combat wasps flew out of each frigate to counter the attackers, antimatter propulsion quickly pushing them up to forty gees. The frigates broke off their attack on the cars, realigning their X-ray lasers ready for the inevitable swarm of submunitions.

*Raimo* launched its own salvo of combat wasps in support of its confederates, opening up a new angle of attack against the voidhawks. Two of them responded with defensive salvos.

Over a hundred combat wasps launched in less than twenty seconds. The glare from their drives shimmered off the night-time clouds below, a radiance far exceeding any natural moonlight.

Despite the continuing electronic-warfare emission from the SD platforms, none of the orbiting network sensors could miss such a deadly spectacle. Threat-analysis programs controlling each network initiated what they estimated was an appropriate level of response.

*

Officially, Tonala's ironberg foundry yard sprawled for over eighteen kilometres along the coast, extending back inland between eight and ten kilometres according to the lie of the land. That, anyway, was the area which the government had originally set aside for the project in 2407, with an optimism which matched the one prevalent during Floreso's arrival into Nyvan orbit three years earlier. Apart from the asteroid's biosphere cavern, the foundry became Tonala's largest ever civil engineering development.

It started off in a promising enough fashion. First came a small coastal port to berth the tugs which recovered the ironbergs from their mid-ocean splashdown. With that construction under way, the engineers started excavating a huge sea water canal running parallel to the coastline. A hundred and twenty metres wide and thirty deep, it was designed to accommodate the ironbergs, allowing them to be towed into the Disassembly Sheds which were to be the centrepiece of the yard. The main canal branched twenty times, sprouting kilometre-long channels which would each end at a Shed.

After the first seven Disassembly Sheds were completed, an audit by the Tonalan Treasury revealed the nation didn't require the metal-production capacity already built. Funds for the remaining Disassembly Sheds were suspended until the economy expanded to warrant them. That was in 2458. Since then, the thirteen unused branch canals gradually choked up with weeds and silt until they eventually became nothing more than large, perfectly rectangular, salt-water marshes. In 2580, Harrisburg University's biology department successfully had them declared part of the national nature park reserve.

Those Disassembly Sheds which did get built were massive cuboid structures, three hundred metres a side, and very basic. An immense skeletal framework was thrown up, bridging the end of the branch canal, then cloaked in flat composite panels. A vertical petal door above the canal allowed the ironberg egress. Inside, powerful fission blades on the end of gantry arms performed a preprogrammed dissection, slicing the ironberg into thousand-tonne segments like some gigantic metal fruit.

A second network of smaller canals connected the Disassembly Sheds with the actual foundry buildings, allowing the bulky, awkwardly shaped segments of spongesteel to be floated directly to the smelter intakes. The desolate land between the Disassembly Sheds, foundry buildings, and canals was crisscrossed by a maze of roads, some no more than dirt tracks, while others were broad decaying carriageways built to carry heavy plant during the heady early days of construction. None of them had modern guidance-tracking cables; foundry crews didn't care, they knew the layout and drove manually. It meant that any visitors venturing deep into the yard invariably took wrong turnings. Not that they could ever get lost, the gargantuan Disassembly Sheds were visible for tens of kilometres, rising up out of the featureless alluvial plain like the blocks some local god had forgotten to sculpt mountains out of during Nyvan's creation. They made perfect navigational reference aides. Under normal conditions.

*

The road was over eighty years old; coastal winters had washed soil away from under it and frozen the surface, flexing it up and down until it snapped. There wasn't a single flat stretch anywhere, a fact disguised by fancifully wind-sculpted drifts of snow. Alkad's car lumbered along at barely more than walking pace as the suspension rocked the body from side to side.

They'd driven into the yard at a dangerously high speed along the carriageway. A fifth car had been wiped out behind them, then the blasts of energy from space seemed to stop. Alkad datavised the car's control processor to turn off at the first junction. According to the map she had loaded into her neural nanonics memory cell, the Disassembly Sheds were strung out across the yard's northern quadrant.

But as she was rapidly discovering: the map is not the territory.

'I can't see a bloody thing,' Voi said. 'I don't even know if we're on a road any more.'

Eriba peered forward, his nose almost touching the windscreen. 'The Sheds have to be out there somewhere. They're huge.'

'The guidance processor says we're heading north,' Alkad said. 'Keep looking.' She glanced out of the back window to see the car following her bouncing about heavily, its headlight beams slashing about through the snow. 'Can you sense Baranovich?' she asked Gelai.

'Faintly, yes.' Her hand waved ahead and slightly to the left. 'He's out there; and he's got a lot of friends with him.'

'How many?'

'About twenty, maybe more. It's difficult at this distance, and they're moving about.'

Voi sucked her breath in fiercely. 'Too many.'

'Is Lodi with them?'

'Possibly.'

A massive chunk of machinery lay along the side of the road. Some metallic fossil from the age of greater ambitions. Once they'd passed it, a strong red-gold radiance flooded over the car. A faint roar made the windows tremble.

'One of the smelters,' Ngong said.

'Which means the Disassembly Sheds are on this side.' Voi pointed confidently.

The road became smoother, and the car picked up speed. Its tyres began to squelch through slush that had melted in the radiance of the smelter. They could see the silhouette of the furnace building now, a long black rectangle with hangarlike doors fully open to show eight streams of radiant molten metal pouring out of the hulking smelter into narrow channels which wound away deeper into the building. Thick jets of steam were shooting out of vents in the roof. Snowflakes reverted to sour rain as they fell through them.

Alkad yelled in fright, and datavised an emergency stop order to the car's control processor. They juddered to a halt two metres short of the canal. A segment of ironberg was sliding along sedately just in front of them, a tarnished silver banana-shape with its skin pocked by millions of tiny black craters.

The sky above turned a brilliant silver, stamping a black and white image of the canal and the ironberg segment on the back of Alkad's retina. 'Holy Mother Mary,' she breathed.

The awesome light faded.

'My processor block's crashed,' Eriba said. He was twisting his head round, trying to find the source of the light. 'What was that?'

'They're shooting at the cars again,' Voi said.

Alkad datavised the car's control processor, not surprised when she couldn't get a response. It confirmed the cause: EMP.

'I wish it was only that,' she told them, marvelling sadly at their innocence. Even now they didn't grasp the enormity of what was involved, the length to which others would go. She reached under the dashboard and twisted the release for the manual steering column. Thankfully, it swung up in front of a startled Eriba. 'Drive,' she instructed. 'There'll be a bridge or something in a minute. But just drive.'

\*

'Oh, bloody hell,' Sarha grumbled. 'Here we go again.'

*Lady Mac*'s combat sensor clusters were relaying an all-too-clear image of space above Nyvan into her neural nanonics. Ten seconds ago all had been clear and calm. The various SD platforms were still conducting their pointless electronic war unabated. Ships were moving towards the three abandoned asteroids, two squadrons of frigates from different nations were closing on Jesup, while Tonala's low-orbit squadron was moving to intercept the Organization ships. This orbital chess game between the nations could have gone on for hours yet, allowing Joshua and the others plenty of time to get back up to the ship, and for all of them to jump the hell away from this deranged planet.

Then the Organization frigates had started shooting. The voidhawks accelerated out of parking orbit. And space was full of combat wasps.

'Velocity confirmed,' Beaulieu barked. 'Forty gees, plus. Antimatter propulsion.'

'Christ,' Liol said. 'Now what do we do?'

'Nothing,' Sarha snapped. So far, the conflict was ahead of them and at a slightly higher altitude. 'Stand by for EMP.' She datavised a procedural stand-by order into the flight computer. 'Damn, I wish Joshua was here, he could fly us out of this in his sleep.'

Liol gave her a hurt look.

Four swarms of combat wasps were in flight, etching

dazzling strands of light across the darkened continents and oceans. They began to jettison their submunitions, and everything became far too complicated for the human mind to follow. Symbols erupted across the display Sarha's neural nanonics provided as she asked the tactical-analysis program for simplified interpretations.

Nyvan's nightside had ceased to become dark, enlivened by hundreds of incandescent exhausts blurring together as they engaged each other. It was the fusion bombs which went off first, then an antimatter charge detonated.

Space ahead of *Lady Mac* went into blazeout. No sensor was capable of penetrating that stupendous energy release.

Tactically, it wasn't the best action. The blast destroyed every combat wasp submunition, friend or foe, within a hundred kilometres, while its EMP disabled an even larger number.

'Damage report?' Sarha asked.

'Some sensor damage,' Beaulieu said. 'Back-ups coming on-line. No fuselage energy penetration.'

'Liol!'

'Uh? Oh. Yeah. Flight systems intact, generators on-line. Attitude stable.'

'The SD platforms are launching,' Beaulieu warned. 'They're really letting loose. Saturation assault!'

'I can get us out of here,' Liol said. 'Two minutes to jump altitude.'

'No,' Sarha said. 'If we move, they'll target us. Right now we stay low and inert. We don't launch, we don't emit. If anything does lock on, we kill it with the masers and countermeasure its launch origin. Then you shift our inclination three degrees either way, not our altitude. Got that?'

'Got it.' His voice was hot and high.

'Relax, Liol, everyone's forgotten about us. We just stay intact to pick Joshua up, that's our mission, that's all we do. I want you cool for a smooth response when it comes. And it will. Use a stim program if you have to.'

'No. I'm all right now.'

Another antimatter explosion obliterated a vast section of the universe. Broken submunitions came spinning out of the epicentre.

'Lock on,' Beaulieu reported. 'Three submunitions. One kinetic, two nukes. I think; catalogue match is sixty per cent. Twenty gees only, real geriatrics.'

'OK,' Sarha said, proud to find how calm she was. 'Kick-ass time.'

\*

A deluge of light from the second antimatter explosion revealed the Disassembly Sheds to all the cars speeding across the foundry yard. A row of blank two-dimensional squares receding to the horizon.

'Go for it!' Alkad urged.

Eriba thumbed the throttle forward. The snow was abating now, revealing more of the ground ahead, giving him confidence. Furnaces glowed in the distance, coronae of slumbering dragons smeared by flurries of grey flakes. The battered road took them past long-forsaken fields of carbon concrete where ranks of sun-bleached gantries stood as memorials to machinery and buildings aborted by financial reality. Pipes wide enough to swallow the car angled up out of the stony soil like metallized worms, their ends capped by rusting grilles which issued strange heavy vapours. Lonely wolf-analogues prowled among the destitute technological carcasses, skulking in the shadows whenever the car's headlights ventured close.

Seeing the other cars falling behind, Eriba aimed for a swing-bridge over the next small canal. The car wheels left the floor as it charged over the apex of the two segments. Alkad was flung forward as it banged down on the other side.

'That's Shed Six,' Voi said eagerly looking out of a side window. 'One more canal to go.'

**1101**

'We're going to make it,' Eriba shouted back. He was completely absorbed by the race, adrenalin rush giving his world a provocative edge.

'That's good,' Alkad said. Anything else would have sounded churlish.

The snow clouds above the yard were slowly tearing open, showing ragged tracts of evening sky. It was alight with plasma fire, drive exhausts and explosions merging and expanding into a single blanket of iridescence that was alive with choppy internal tides.

Joshua kinked his neck back at a difficult angle to watch it. The car jounced about, determined to deny him an uninter-rupted view. Since the first antimatter bomb's EMP had wrecked their car's electronics Dahybi had been driving them manually. It was a bumpy ride.

Another antimatter explosion turned the remaining clouds transparent. Joshua's retinal implants prevented any lasting damage to his eyes, but he still had to blink furiously to clear the brilliant purple after-image away.

'Jesus, I hope they're all right up there.'

'Sarha knows what she's doing,' Melvyn said. 'Besides, we've got another twenty minutes before they're above the horizon, and that blast was almost directly overhead.'

'Sure, right.'

'Hang on,' Dahybi called.

The car shot over a swing-bridge, taking flight at the top. They thumped down, skittling sideways until the rear bumper smacked into the road's side barrier. A wicked grinding sound told them they'd lost more bodywork until Dahybi managed to straighten out again.

'She's pulling ahead,' Melvyn pointed out calmly.

'Can you do any fucking better?' Dahybi yelled back.

Joshua couldn't remember the composed node specialist ever getting so aggrieved before. He heard another *crunch* behind them as the first embassy car cleared the bridge.

'Just keep on her,' Joshua said. 'You're doing fine.'

'Where the hell is she going?' Melvyn wondered out loud.

'More to the point, why doesn't she care that this circus procession is following her?' Joshua replied. 'She has to be pretty confident about whoever she's meeting.'

'Who or what.' Melvyn sucked in a breath. 'You don't think the Alchemist is hidden around here, do you? I mean, look at this place, you could lose a squadron of starships out here.'

'Don't let's imagine things worse than they are,' Joshua said. 'My main concern is those two possessed with her.'

'I should be able to deal with them,' a serjeant said. It touched one of the weapons clipped to its belt.

Joshua managed a twitched smile. It was becoming harder for him to associate these increasingly combat-adept serjeants with the old sweet, sexy Ione.

'What's the Alchemist?' Dick Keaton asked.

When Joshua turned back to their passenger, he was startled by the flood of curiosity emanating from the man. It was what he imagined Edenist affinity must be like. The emotion dominated. 'Need to know only, sorry.'

Dick Keaton seemed to have some trouble returning to his usual blasé cockiness.

It bothered Joshua quite badly for some reason. The first glimpse of something hidden behind the mask. Something very wrong, and very deeply hidden.

'They're changing direction,' Dahybi warned.

Mzu's car had left the narrow road which ran between the swing-bridges, turning onto a more substantial road which led towards Disassembly Shed Four. Dahybi tugged the steering column over as far as it would go, almost missing the junction as they careered round after her.

After standing up against two centuries of salt-water corrosion, cheap slipshod maintenance, bird excrement, algae, and in one memorable instance a small aircraft crash, the walls and roof of Disassembly Shed Four were in a sorry state. Despite that, the structure's scale was still impressive to the point of intimidating. Joshua had seen far bigger buildings, but not in isolation like this.

'Joshua, look at the last car,' a serjeant said.

Five other cars were still part of the chase. Four of them were big saloons from the Kulu Embassy; smooth dark bodies with opaque windows and powerful fanbeam headlights. The fifth had started out an ordinary car with dark green bodywork: now it was some primitive monstrosity with bright scarlet paint that was covered in brash stickers. Six round headlights were affixed to a lattice of metal struts which covered the front grille. Primitive it might have been, but it was closing up fast on the last embassy car; its broad tyres gave it excellent traction on the slush.

'Jesus, they're in front and behind.'

'This might be a good time for us to retire gracefully,' Melvyn said.

Joshua glanced ahead. They were already in the shadow thrown by Disassembly Shed Four. Mzu's car was almost at the base of the colossal wall, and braking to a halt.

It was very tempting. And he was in an agony of denial not knowing what had happened to *Lady Mac*.

'Trouble,' Dick Keaton said. He was holding up a processor block, swinging it round to try and locate something. 'Some kind of electronic distortion is focusing on us. Don't know what kind, it's more powerful than the EMP, though.'

Joshua ordered his neural nanonics to run a diagnostic. The program never completed. 'Possessed!' Intuition was screaming at him. 'Out, everybody out. Go for cover.'

Dahybi slammed the brakes on. The doors were opening before they stopped. Mzu's car was fifteen metres in front of them. Stationary and empty.

Joshua threw himself out of the car, taking a couple of fast steps before flinging himself flat onto the slush. One of the serjeants hit the road beside him.

A tremendous jet of white fire squirted down from the Shed. It swamped the top of the car, sending ravenous tentacles curling down through the open doors. Glass blew out, and the interior combusted instantly, burning with eerie fury.

Ione knew exactly what she had to do, one consciousness puppeting two bodies. As soon as the first wave of heat swelled overhead she was rising, adopting a crouch position. Four hands were bringing four different guns to bear. As there was one serjeant on either side of the car, she could triangulate the source of the energistic attack perfectly. A line of dirt-greyed windows thirty metres up the Shed wall; two of them had swung open.

She opened fire. First priority was to suppress the possessed, give them so much to worry about they'd be unable to continue their own assault. Two of the guns she held were rapid-fire machine-pistols, capable of firing over a hundred rounds a second. She used them in half-second bursts, swinging them in fast arcs. The windows, surrounding panels, stress rods, and secondary structural girders disintegrated into an avalanche of scything chips as the bullets savaged them. The heavy-calibre rifles followed, explosive-tipped shells chewing ferociously at the edges of the initial devastation. Then she began slamming rounds into the panelling where she estimated the walkway the possessed were using was situated.

'Go!' she bellowed from both throats. 'Get inside, there's cover there.'

Joshua rolled over fast, and started sprinting. Melvyn was right behind him. There was nothing to hear above the bone-jarring vibration of the rifles, no pounding footsteps or shouts of alarm. He just kept running.

A streamer of white fire churned through the air above him. It was hard to distinguish in the light fluxing down from the orbital battle. The foundry yard was soaking in a brightness twice as great as the noonday sun, a glare made all the worse by the snow.

Ione saw the fire coming right at her down one half of her vision, and pointed the rifle and machine-gun along the angle of approach. She held the triggers down on both of them, bullets flaring indigo as if they were tracer rounds. The white fire struck, and she cancelled the serjeant's tactile nerves, banishing pain. Her machine-gun magazine was exhausted, but she kept on firing the rifle, holding it steady even though the fire burned away her eyes along with her leathery skin.

Then her consciousness was only in one of the bitek constructs; she could see the flaming outline of the other fall to the ground. And shadows were flittering in the dusk behind the yawning hole she'd blasted in the wall. She slapped a new magazine in the machine-gun, and raised both barrels.

Joshua had just passed Mzu's car when the explosive round went *crack* mere centimetres from his skull. He flinched, throwing his arms up defensively. A small door in the Shed wall just in front of him disintegrated. It took a tremendous act of trust, but he kept on going. Ione had opened the way. There had to be some kind of sanctuary in there.

Alkad Mzu didn't regard the interior of Disassembly Shed Four as sanctuary, exactly, but she was grateful to reach it nonetheless. The cars were still pursuing her, berserk high-speed skids and swerves across the road showing just how intent their occupants were. At least inside the Shed she could choose her opponents.

Just as Ngong closed the small door she caught a glimpse of the surviving police cars leaping the swing-bridge, their blue and red strobes flashing. The snow was hot with irradiated light from the battle above, and growing ever brighter. Ngong clanged the door to, and slammed the bolts across.

Alkad stood waiting for her retinal implants to adjust to the sombre darkness. It took them longer than it should; and her neural nanonics were totally off-line. Baranovich was close.

They made their way forwards through a forest of metal pillars. The Shed's framework structure extended some distance from the panel wall it was supporting, uncountable trusses and struts melding together in asymmetric junctions. Looking straight up, it was impossible to see the roof, only the labyrinthine intertexture of black metal forming an impenetrable barrier. Each tube and I-beam was slick with water, beads of condensation tickled by gravity until they dropped. With the Shed's conditioning turned off, the inside was a permanent drizzle.

Alkad led the others forward, out from under the artless pillars. There was no ironberg in the huge basin at the middle of the Shed, so the water was slopping quietly against the rim. The cranes, the gantry arms with their huge fission blades, the mobile inspection platforms, all hung still and silent around the sides of the central high bay. Sounds didn't echo here, they were absorbed by the prickly fur of metal inside the walls. Scraps of light escaped through lacunas in the roof buttresses, producing a crisscross of white beams that always seemed to fade away before they reached the ground. Big sea birds scurried about through the air, endlessly swapping perches as if they were searching for the perfect vantage point.

'Up here, Dr Mzu,' a voice called out.

She turned round, head tilted back, hand held in a salute to shield her face from the gentle rain. Baranovich was standing on a walkway forty metres above the ground, leaning casually against the safety railing. His colourful Cossack costume shone splendidly amid the gloom. Several people stood in the shadows behind him.

'All right,' she said. 'I'm here. Where's my transport off-planet? From what I can see, there's some difficulty in orbit right now.'

'Don't get smart with me, Doctor. The Organization isn't going to be wiped out by one small war between SD platforms.'

'Lodi is up there,' Gelai said quietly. 'The other possessed are becoming agitated by the approaching cars.'

'I don't suppose it will,' Alkad shouted back. 'So our

arrangement still stands. You let Lodi go, and I'll come with you.'

'The arrangement, Doctor, was that you come alone. But I'm a reasonable man. I'll see to it that you reach the Organization. Oh, and here's Lodi.'

He was flung over the safety barrier just as Ione's guns started to demolish the windows and panelling. His screams were lost amid the roar of the explosive rounds. Arms windmilled in pathetic desperation, their motion caught by the strobe effect of the explosions. He hit the carbon concrete with a dreadful wet thud.

'See, Doctor? I let him go.'

Alkad stared at the lad's body, desperate to reject what she'd seen. It was, she realized in some shock, the first time she'd actually witnessed somebody being killed. Murdered.

'Mother Mary, he was just a boy.'

Voi whimpered behind her.

Baranovich was laughing. Those on the walkway with him joined hands. A plume of white fire speared down towards Alkad.

Both Gelai and Ngong grabbed hold of her arms. When the white fire hit, it was like a sluice of dazzling warm water. She swayed backwards under the impact, crying out from surprise rather than pain. The strike abated, leaving her itching all over.

'Step aside,' Baranovich shouted angrily. 'She belongs to us.'

Gelai grinned evilly, and raised a hand as if to wave. The walkway under Baranovich's feet split with a loud brassy creak. He gave a dismayed yell, and made a grab for the safety rail.

'Run!' Gelai urged.

Alkad hesitated for an instant, looking back at Lodi's body for any conceivable sign of life. There was too much blood for that. Together with the others, she pelted back to the relative safety of the metal support pillars.

'I can't die yet,' she said frantically. 'I have to get to the Alchemist first. I have to, it's the only way.'

A figure stepped out in front of her. 'Dr Mzu, I presume,' said Joshua. 'Remember me?'

She gaped at him, too incredulous to speak. Three other men were standing behind him; two of them were nervously pointing machine-guns at Gelai and Ngong.

'Who is *this*?' a very confused Voi asked.

Alkad gave a little laugh that was close to hysteria. 'Captain Calvert, from Tranquillity.'

Joshua clicked his heels and did a little bow. 'On the button, Doc. I'm flattered. And *Lady Mac*'s in orbit here ready to take you back home. The Lord of Ruin is pretty pissed off at you for disappearing, but she says she'll forgive you providing your nasty little secret stays secret for ever.'

'You work for Ione Saldana?'

'Yeah. She'll be here in the sort-of flesh in a minute to confirm the offer. But right now, my priority is to get you and your friends out of here.' He gave Gelai and Ngong the eye. 'Some of your friends. I don't know what the story with these two is, but I'm not having—' The cold, unmistakable shape of a pistol muzzle was pressed firmly into the back of his neck.

'Thank you, Captain Calvert.' Monica's voice purred with triumph. 'But we professionals will take it from here.'

\*

The air on board the *Urschel* was clotted by rank gases and far too much humidity. Those conditioning filters still functioning emitted an alarmingly loud buzzing as fan motors spun towards overload. Innumerable light-panels had failed, hatch actuators were unreliable at best, discarded food wrappers fluttered about everywhere.

Cherri Barnes hated the sloppiness and disorder. Efficiency on a starship was more than just habit, it was an essential survival requirement. A crew was utterly dependent on its equipment.

But two of the possessed (her fellow possessed, she tried to tell herself) were from the late nineteenth and early twentieth century. Arrogant oafs who didn't, or wouldn't, understand the basic preconditions of shipboard routine. And their so-called commander, Oscar Kearn, didn't seem too bothered, either. He just assumed that the non-possessed crew would go around scooping up the shit. They didn't.

Cherri had given up advising and demanding. She was actually quite surprised that they'd survived the orbital battle for so long, although antimatter-powered combat wasps did load the odds in their favour. And for once the non-possessed were understandably performing their duties with a high level of proficiency. There was little for the possessed to do except wait. Oscar Kearn occupied himself by studying the hologram screen displays, and muttering the odd comment to his non-possessed subordinate. In reality he was contributing little, other than continually urging their combat wasps be directed at the voidhawks. The concept of keeping a reserve for their own defence seemed elusive.

When the explosions and energy cascades outside the hull were reaching an appalling crescendo, Cherri slipped quietly out of the bridge. Under ordinary combat conditions the companionways linking the frigate's four life-support capsules should have been sealed tight. Now she glided past open hatches as she made her way along to B capsule's maintenance engineering deck. As soon as she was inside she closed the ceiling hatch and engaged the manual lock.

She pulled herself over to one of the three processor consoles, and tapped the power stud. Not being able to datavise the frigate's flight computer was a big hindrance, she wasn't used to voice-response programs. Eventually, though, she established an auxiliary command circuit, cutting the bridge officers out of the loop. The systems and displays she wanted slowly came on-line.

Combat wasps and their submunitions still flocked through space above Nyvan, though not quite as many as before. And the blanket electronic-warfare interference had ended; quite simply, there were no SD platforms left intact to wage that aspect of the conflict.

One of the ten phased-array antennas positioned round the *Urschel*'s hull focused on the *Lady Macbeth*. Cherri pulled herself closer to the console's mike.

'Is anyone receiving this? Sarha, Warlow, can you hear me? If you can, use a five millimetre aperture signal maser for a direct com return. Do not, repeat *not*, lock on to *Urschel*'s main antenna.'

'Signal acknowledged,' a synthesized voice replied. 'Who the hell is this?'

'Warlow, is that you?'

'No, Warlow isn't with us any more. This is Sarha Mitcham, Acting First Officer. Who am I speaking with?'

'Sarha, I'm sorry, I didn't know about Warlow. It's Cherri Barnes, Sarha.'

'God, Cherri, what the hell are you doing on an Organization frigate?'

Cherri stared at the console, trying to get a grip on her raging emotions. 'I ... I belong here, Sarha. I think. I don't know any more. You just don't know what it's like in the beyond.'

'Oh, fuck, you're a possessor.'

'Guess so. Not by choice.'

'Yeah. I know. What happened to *Udat*, Cherri? What happened to you?'

'It was Mzu. She killed us. We were a complication to her. And Meyer ... she had a grudge. Be careful of her, Sarha, be very careful.'

'Christ, Cherri, is this on the level?'

'Oh, yes, I'm on the level.'

'Acknowledged. And ... thanks.'

'I haven't finished. Joshua's down on Nyvan chasing after Mzu, we know that much.'

'OK, he's down there. Cherri, please don't ask me why. I can't discuss it.'

'That's OK. I understand. It doesn't matter; we know about the Alchemist, and you know we know. But you have to tell Joshua to back off, he must get away from Mzu. Right away. We know we can't get her offplanet now our spaceplanes are gone. That means the Organization has only one option. If she's dead, she'll have to join us.'

'Is that why *Urschel* and *Pinzola* were shooting at the ground?'

'Yes. But that's not all—'

*

The timid, halting voice echoed round *Lady Macbeth*'s bridge. It sent something like cold electricity racing down Liol's nerves. He turned his head to look at Sarha, who seemed equally stupefied.

'Is she for real?' he asked, praying the answer would be no.

'I knew her,' was all Sarha would say, and that reluctantly. 'Beaulieu, can you confirm that ironberg's trajectory?'

'I will have to use active-sensor analysis to obtain its precise flight path.'

'Do it.'

'We're thirty minutes from Joshua's horizon,' Liol said. Alternative orbital trajectories were flashing through his mind as he datavised the flight computer for possible vectors.

'Nothing I can do about that,' Sarha said. 'We can try calling him through the Tonala communication net.'

'The net – bollocks. You know there isn't a working processor left on that planet after all this EMP activity. I can drop us down; if we skim the atmosphere we can be above his horizon in eight minutes.'

'No! If we start changing our orbit we'll be targeted.'

'There's nothing left out there to target us. Access the sensors, damn you. The combat wasps are all spent.'

'They've deployed all their submunitions, you mean.'

'He's my brother!'

'He's my captain, and we can't risk it.'

'*Lady Mac* can beat any poxy submunition. Take fire control, I can pilot this manoeuvre.'

'Ironberg trajectory confirmed,' Beaulieu said. 'Barnes was telling the truth. It's heading straight at them.'

'Altitude?' Sarha asked. 'Can we nuke it?'

'Ninety kilometres. That's too deep into the ionosphere for the combat wasps. They can't operate in that kind of pressure.'

'Shit!' Sarha groaned.

'Get positive, Sarha,' Liol demanded. 'We have to get over Joshua's horizon.'

'I've got lock-on,' Beaulieu said calmly. 'Two nukes, active-seeker heads. They acquired our radar emission.'

Sarha initiated the maser cannon targeting program without conscious thought. Her brain was churning with too much worry and indecision to actually think. Bright violet triangles zeroed the approaching submunitions.

'Would Josh leave one of us down there?' Liol asked.

'You piece of shit!' The masers fired, triggered by the heatlash in her mind. Both submunitions broke apart, their fusion drives dying.

'We can beat them,' Beaulieu said.

The imperturbability of the cosmonik's synthetic voice chided Sarha. 'OK. I'll handle fire control. Beaulieu, switch to active sensors, full suite; I want long-range warning of any incoming hostiles. Liol, take us down.'

*

They were hammering on the maintenance engineering deck's hatch. Its edges had started to shine cherry red, paint was blistering.

Cherri gave the circle of metal a jaded look. 'All right, all right,' she mumbled. 'I'll make it easy all round. Besides, what would you lot ever know about fraternity?'

After the hatch's locking mechanism melted away, an equally hot Oscar Kearn dived through the smouldering rim. Any hope of retribution died instantly as he saw the figure curled up and sobbing dejectedly in front of the console. The soul of Cherri Barnes had already vacated the flesh, retreating to the one place where he was never going to chase after her.

\*

Monica finally felt as though she was regaining control of the mission. There were twelve operatives with her in the Disassembly Shed providing overwhelming firepower, and their evac craft were on the way. None of their processor blocks were working, nor their neural nanonics. Everyone had taken off their shell-helmets so they could see; the sensors were glitched, too. The lack of protection made her nervous, but she could live with that. *I've got Mzu!*

She applied some pressure to the pistol barrel at the side of Calvert's neck, and he moved aside obediently. One of the Edenists claimed his machine-gun. He didn't protest when he was made to stand with his three compatriots, all of them with their hands in the air, and covered by a couple of operatives.

'Doctor, please take your hand away from that backpack,' Monica said. 'And don't try to datavise any activation codes.'

Alkad shrugged and held her hands up. 'I can't datavise anything anyway,' she said. 'There are too many possessed in here.'

Monica signalled one of the operatives to retrieve Mzu's backpack.

'You were in Tranquillity,' Alkad said. 'And the Dorados too, if I'm not mistaken. Which agency?'

'ESA.'

'Ah. Yet some of your friends are obviously Edenists. How odd.'

'We both consider your removal from this planet to be of

paramount importance, Doctor,' Samuel said. 'However, you have my assurance you will not be harmed.'

'Of course,' Alkad told them equitably. 'If I am, we all know who I'll end up with.'

'Exactly.'

Gelai looked up. 'They're coming, Doctor.'

Monica frowned. 'Who?'

'The possessed from the Organization,' Alkad told her. 'They're up in the Shed's framework somewhere.'

The operatives responded smoothly, scanning the metal lattice above them for any sign of movement. Monica stepped smartly over to Alkad's side, and grabbed her arm. 'OK, Doctor, we'll take care of them, now let's move.'

'Damn,' Samuel said. 'The police are here.'

Monica glanced back to the hole blown into the wall where they'd entered. Two Edenists had been left to cover their retreat back to the cars. 'We can deal with them.'

Samuel gave a resigned grimace. The operatives formed a protective cordon around Monica and Mzu, and started to walk back towards the wall.

Monica realized that Joshua and the others were hurrying after them. 'Not you,' she said.

'I'm not staying in here,' Joshua said indignantly.

'We can't—' Samuel began.

A portcullis slammed down out of the tangle of girders above. It struck two of the operatives, punching them to the ground. The valency generators in their armour suits were glitched, preventing the fabric from stiffening into a protective exoskeleton as it should have done. Long iron spikes along the bottom of the portcullis punctured the suit fabric, skewering their bodies to the wet carbon concrete.

Four of the operatives opened fire with their machine-guns, shooting straight up. Bullets ricocheted madly, grazing sprays of sparks off the metal.

Training compelled Monica to look round and locate the

follow-up. It was coming at her from the left, a huge pendulum blade swinging straight at Mzu. If her neural nanonics had been on-line and running threat-response programs she might have made it. As it was, boosted muscles slewed her weight around to pirouette Mzu out of the blade's arc. They went tumbling onto the floor together. The blade caught Monica's left leg a glancing blow. Her armoured boot saved her foot from being severed, but her ankle and lower shin bone were shattered by the impact. Shock dulled the initial pain. She sat up, groaning in dismay, and clutched at the ruined bones. Bile was rising in her throat, and it was very difficult to breathe.

Something extraordinarily heavy hit her shoulder, sending her sprawling. Joshua landed on the ground right beside her, rolling neatly to absorb the impact. A burst of hatred banished Monica's pain. Then the blade sliced through the air where she had been a second before, a tiny whisper the only sound of its passing. Pendulum, she thought dazedly, it comes back.

One of the embassy operatives raced over to Monica. He was holding a square medical nanonic package and cursing heavily. 'It's glitched, too, I can't get a response.'

Joshua glanced at the package glove covering his hand. Ever since he'd come into the Shed, it had been stinging like crazy. 'Tell me about it,' he grumbled.

Gelai joined them, squatting down, her face full of concern. She put her hand over Monica's ankle.

The original intensity of the pain had frightened Monica, but this was plain horrifying. She could feel the fragments of bone shifting round inside her skin, she could even see the suit's trouser fabric ripple around Gelai's hand – her glowing hand. Yet it didn't hurt.

'I think that's it,' the bashful girl said. 'Try standing.'

'Oh, my God. You're a . . .'

'Didn't you professionals know?' Joshua said evilly.

Samuel dodged round the pendulum, and crouched beside them, alert, his machine-gun pointing high. 'I thought you'd been hit,' he said as Monica gingerly applied some weight to her left foot.

'I was. She cured me.'

He gave Gelai a fast appraisal. 'Oh.'

'We'd better get going,' Monica said.

'They'll hit us again if we move.'

'They'll hit us if we stay.'

'I wish I could see them,' he moaned, blinking away the drizzle. 'There's no target for us. Shooting wild is pointless, there's too much metal.'

'They're up there,' Gelai said. 'Three of them are just above the pendulum hinge. They're the ones giving it substance.'

Samuel jerked his head about. 'Where?'

'Above it.'

'Damn it.' If he could have just switched his retinal implants to infra-red there might have been something other than mangled bleakness. He fired his machine-gun anyway, sluicing the bullets over the area he imagined Gelai was talking about. The magazine was spent in less than a second. He ejected it, and slapped in a fresh one – mindful of how many were left clipped to his belt. When he looked up again, the pendulum had vanished. Instead, a length of thick black cabling was swaying to and fro. 'That's it? Did I get them?'

'You hurt two,' Gelai told him. 'They're backing off.'

'Hurt? Great.'

'Come on,' Monica said. 'We can get to the cars.' She raised her voice. 'Random suppression fire, vertical. I want those bastards fleeing us. OK, move.'

Eight machine-guns opened fire into the overhead lattice as everyone rushed towards the hole in the wall.

High above them, and safe in his web of metal cables, Baranovich looked out of a filthy window at the three Tonalan police cars drawn up outside. There were long skid marks in the snow behind each of them, evidence of their hard braking. One other surviving police car was chasing after the twenty-first-century rally car, siren blaring and lights flashing as they both tore along the bottom of the Shed wall. Dark-clad officers were advancing towards the embassy cars.

'Let's liven things up a little,' he said above the fractious roar of the machine-guns and whining ricochets. He joined hands with the three possessed beside him. Together they launched a huge fireball, and sent it curving down on one of the stationary police cars.

The response was immediate and overwhelming. After having their car processors glitched, then crashing, being shot at by starship X-ray lasers, losing their suspects, and now having to verify whether the embassy cars were occupied by armed ESA operatives, the Tonalan security police were by now understandably a little tense. Every weapon they had was abruptly trained on Disassembly Shed Four.

Monica was twenty metres from the smashed door when the ancient, brittle panels were bombarded by hollow-case bullets, TI pulses, maser beams, and small EE rounds. Blinding light ruptured the gloom ahead of her. She hit the floor hard as white-hot fragments slashed through the air. Smoking particles rained down around her, sizzling on the moist concrete. Several landed on her head, singeing through her hair to sting her scalp.

'THIS IS THE POLICE. ABANDON YOUR WEAPONS. COME OUT ONE AT A TIME WITH YOUR BLOCKS AND IMPLANTS DEACTIVATED. YOU WILL NOT BE TOLD AGAIN.'

'Holy fuck,' Monica grunted. She raised her head. A huge strip of the wall had vanished; maleficent shifting light from the orbital battle shone in. It illuminated a multitude of broken girders whose fractured ends dripped glowing droplets. The framework structure emitted a distressed groan; weakened junctions were snapping under the stress of the new loading, starting a chain reaction. She could see whole levels of metal bending then dropping in juddery motions.

'Move!' she shouted. 'It's going to land on us.'

A flare of white fire billowed down out of the darkness, pummelling an operative to her knees. Her screams vanished beneath the plangent crackling of her armour suit and skin igniting.

Four machine-guns opened up in response.

'No!' Monica said. That was exactly what they wanted. It was a near-perfect snare manoeuvre, she admitted angrily as she flung her arms over her head again. *And we blundered right into it.*

The security police heard the machine-guns, and opened fire once more.

Baranovich hadn't been expecting quite such a emphatic rejoinder from the forces of law and order – these modern weapons were so fearsomely powerful. Twice now the weakened framework had shifted around him, forcing him to snatch at the girders and reinforce their solidity with his energistic power. That was dangerous. The metal was grounding out the EE rounds, and while he was some distance away from their impact zone those kind of voltages were lethal to a possessed and it only took one wild shot.

When the second round of shooting started he jumped down onto the nearest walkway and sprinted away. His impressive costume's shiny leather boots changed to Yankee-style trainers with inch-thick soles – a fervent hope in his mind that imagined rubber would be as effective an insulator as the real stuff. He could sense others of his group on the move, shaken by the ferocity of the attack.

Joshua looked up to see the last frayed streamers of electrons writhing down the metal pillars. The whole of the smashed-up framework above and around him was grinding loudly. It was going to collapse any second. Self-preservation kicked in strong – *Fuck Mzu, I'm going to die if I stay here.* He scrambled to his feet and slapped Melvyn, who still had his hands over his head, face jammed against the floor.

'Shift it, both of you, now!' He started running, out from

under the framework, and angling away from the gigantic hole the police had blown in the wall. There were a lot of footsteps splashing through the puddles behind him. He scanned round quickly. It wasn't just Melvyn, Dahybi, and Keaton who were following him; all the agency operatives and Mzu's wacko entourage were coming too. Everybody racing across the Disassembly Shed's high bay floor in pursuit as if he was showing them the way to salvation. 'Jesus wept!' He didn't want this! Just having Melvyn and Dahybi coming with him across an open space would have proved tempting for the possessed, but Mzu too...

Unlike the Baranovich group which had set up the meeting, the ESA and the Edenists who had unlimited access to the Kulu Embassy's memory files, and the security police who knew their home territory, Joshua didn't quite appreciate the layout of the Disassembly Sheds. Even their madcap drive through the foundry yard hadn't conclusively demonstrated to him that the canals ran straight through the centre of every Shed. So he certainly didn't know that the only way over the water was a bridge which ran along the door above the smaller canal.

What he did know was that there was a perilously dark and wide gulf in the floor ahead of him, and getting closer very fast. Only now did he hear the gentle slopping of the water, and realize what it was. He nearly went sprawling headlong as he came to a confounded halt a metre from the edge, arms flapping eccentrically for balance. He turned to see everyone rushing en masse towards him, because they'd thought he knew what he was doing, and there hadn't been time to ask questions. Behind them, Baranovich's possessed were mustering on the walkway, garish costumes agleam in the rainy dusk.

Alkad was running with her head ducked down, forcing her game leg along. Gelai and Ngong were on either side of her, holding her tight. A bubble of air around the three of them swirled with tiny glimmers of silver light.

Baranovich's laughter poured out into the vast enclosed space of the central high bay. He pointed, and Joshua could do nothing but stare dumbly as the bolt of white fire streaked across the intervening space straight at him.

Dick Keaton was leading the pack of desperadoes on the floor of the high bay, running hard. He was less than four metres from an aghast Joshua when Baranovich's fire bolt hit the data security expert clean between his shoulder blades. It burst open in a spectacular cloud of dancing twisters that drained away into the drizzle. And Dick Keaton was completely unharmed.

'Close one,' he jeered happily. His arms wrapped round Joshua, momentum carrying the pair of them over the edge of the central basin just as the mutilated framework collapsed. Fractured girders were tossed out of the crumpling wreckage in all directions, clanging loudly as they hit the floor. A huge split tore up the wall like a lightning bolt in reverse. It was a hundred and seventy metres high when it finally stopped. The framework structure settled into an uneasy silence.

The black water in the ironberg basin was freezing. Joshua yelled out as it closed round him, seeing bubbles bumble past his face. The coldshock was intense enough to make his heart jump – frightening him badly. Salt water rushed into his open mouth. And – Jesus, *thank you* – his neural nanonics came back on-line.

Nerve impulse overrides squeezed his throat muscles tight, preventing any water flooding his lungs. Analysis of his spinning inner ears revealed his exact orientation. His thrashing became purposeful, shunting him straight up.

He broke surface to draw down a huge desperate gulp of air. People in flexible armour suits were flying through the air above him; human lemmings landing in the basin with a tremendous splash. He saw Mzu, her small figure unmistakable in its prim business suit.

Keaton shook his head dog-fashion, blowing his cheeks out. 'Hell, it's *cold*.'

'Who the fuck are you?' Joshua demanded. 'They hit you dead on, and it never even blistered you.'

'Right question, sir, but unfortunately the wrong pronoun. As I once said to Oscar Wilde. Stumped him completely; he wasn't quite as hot on the riposte as legend says.'

All Joshua could do was cough. The cold was crippling. His neural nanonics were battling hard to prevent his muscles from cramping. And they were going to lose.

White fire smashed against the basin rim five metres above him. Radiant dribbles of magma ran down the basin wall.

'What in God's name did you bring us here for?' Monica shouted.

'I didn't fucking bring you!'

Her hand grabbed the front of his ship-suit. 'How do we get out?'

'Jesus, I don't know.'

She let go, her arm shaking badly. Another strike of white fire lashed above them. The rim was outlined like a dawn horizon from orbit.

'They can't hit us here,' Samuel said, his long face was dreadfully strained.

'God, so what,' Monica answered. 'They've only got to walk over here and we'll be dead.'

'We won't last that long. Hypothermia will get us before then.'

Monica glared at Joshua. 'Can anyone see some steps?'

'Dick,' Joshua said. 'Are your neural nanonics working?'

'Yes.'

'Access the Shed's management computer. Find us a way out. Now!'

This is a last-ditch madness, I know, Samuel called to the *Hoya*. But is there anything you can do?

Nothing. I am so sorry. You're too far away, we cannot provide fire support.

We're retreating, Niveu told him, his tone full of savage

regret. It's this diabolical antimatter. We've fired every combat wasp in defence, and they're still coming through. The nations have gone insane, every SD platform went offensive. *Ferrea* was damaged by a gamma-ray pulser, and *Sinensis* had to swallow out to avoid a direct impact. There's only the two of us left now. We can't last much longer. Do you wish to transfer? We can delay a few seconds more.

No. Go, warn the Consensus.

But your situation—

Doesn't matter. Go!

'Half the Shed's processors are glitched,' Dick Keaton said. 'The rest are in stand-by mode. It's been mothballed.'

'What?' Joshua had to shout to make his mouth work. His kicks to tread water were difficult now.

'Mothballed. That's why there's no ironberg in here. The small canal leaks. They drained it for repairs.'

'Drained it? Let me have the file.'

Keaton datavised it over, and Joshua assigned it to a memory cell. Analysis programs went primary, tearing into the information. What he wanted was a way to drain the basin, or at the very least a ladder. Which wasn't quite what he found when the schematics display rose into his mind. 'Ione!' he shouted. 'Ione.' His voice was pathetically weak. He worked his elbows, swivelling round to face Samuel. 'Call her.'

'Who?' the bewildered Edenist asked.

'Ione Saldana, the Lord of Ruin. Call her with affinity.'

'But—'

'Do it or we're going to die in here.'

\*

The gee force on *Lady Macbeth*'s bridge began to abate, sliding down from a tyrannical eight to an unpleasant three.

He certainly flies the same way as Joshua, Sarha thought. The few seconds she'd spared from fire control to monitor their vector had shown her a starship which was keeping pretty close to the course which the navigation program had produced. Not bad for a daydreamer novice.

'The *Urschel* is accelerating,' Beaulieu said. 'Seven gees, they're going for altitude. Must be a jump.'

'Good,' Sarha said firmly. 'That means no more of those bloody antimatter combat wasps.'

All three of them had cheered when the *Pinzola* was struck by a fusion blast. The resulting explosion as all the frigate's antimatter-confinement chambers were destroyed had blown half of *Lady Mac*'s sensors, and *Pinzola* had been eleven thousand kilometres away, almost below the horizon.

The orbital conflict had been played out hard and fast over the last eleven minutes. Several starships had been hit, but over fifteen had risen to a jump altitude and escaped. There were no more SD platforms left in low orbit, although plenty of combat wasps were still prowling. But they were all a long way from *Lady Mac*. That was Sarha's prime concern. As Beaulieu had said, the old girl could cope with Nyvan's geriatric weapons. They had a couple of new scars on the hull from kinetic debris, and three radioactive hotspots from pulser shots. But the worst of it was over now.

'Gravitonic distortion,' Beaulieu said. 'Another voidhawk has left.'

'Sensible ship,' Sarha muttered. 'Liol, how long until we're over Joshua's horizon?'

'Ninety seconds – mark.'

She datavised an order into the starship's communication system. The main dish slid out of its recess, and swung around, pointing at the horizon ahead.

\*

Ione eased herself round the metal pillar to take another look out into the Shed's high bay. The possessed up on the walkway were squirting a continual stream of white fire at the rim of the basin. That must mean Joshua and the others were still alive.

Now appeared to be the optimum time to enter the fray. She had hung back ever since she'd sprinted into the Shed ahead of the agency operatives. This whole situation was so fluid, the outcome could well be decided by who had the greatest tactical reserve. She wasn't quite sure where that decision had come from; some tactics file her 'original' self and Tranquillity had loaded into the serjeant, or internal logic. How much inventiveness she owned in this aspect she wasn't sure of. But wherever it had come from, it had been proved right.

She had watched the events play out from the cover of the framework, hovering on the brink of intervention. Then the police had arrived and fouled up everything. And Joshua had fled across the high bay to the basin.

She couldn't work that one out. It was sea water in the basin, which must be close to freezing point. Now he was pinned down.

If she could get a clear shot at the walkway the possessed were using she might be able to bring them all crashing down. But she wasn't sure how effective even the heavy-calibre rifle would be against such a concentration of energistic power.

**Ione. Ione Saldana?**

Cold accompanied the affinity call, she knew exactly what it was like to be immersed in the basin. **Agent Samuel**, she acknowledged.

**I have a message.**

He widened his mind still further. She looked out at anguished heads bobbing in the water. Joshua was right in front of her, hair plastered down over his forehead. His throat laboured hard to force the words out. 'Ione – shoot – out – the – small – canal – lock – gate – blow – that – fucker – away – good – and – be – quick – we – can't – last – long.'

She was already running towards the end of the Shed. There was a rectangular gap in the framework structure over the small canal. It framed the door which slid up to allow the ironberg segments through. The bottom of the door closed to within a

**1125**

metre of the water itself. Below that, she could see the two lock gates which held back the water while the canal outside was being repaired. They were solid metal, tarnished by age, and thick with fronds of sapphire-coloured seaweed.

She squatted down beside the edge of the canal, and fired the heavy-calibre rifle. Trying to puncture the gates themselves would be hopeless: they weren't made from any modern laced-molecule alloy, but their thickness made them completely impenetrable. Instead, the explosive-tipped shells pounded into the canal's old carbon concrete walls, demolishing the hinges and their mountings.

The gates moved slightly as water squirted round the crumbling concrete. Their top hinges were almost wrecked, making them gradually pivot downwards, a motion which prised them further apart. A V-shaped gap appeared between them, with water gushing out horizontally. Ione fired again and again, concentrating on one wall now, mauling it to smithereens. One of the hinges gave way.

**Look out**, Samuel warned. **They have stopped attacking us. That must mean—**

Ione saw the shadows shifting behind her, knowing what it meant. Then the shadows were fading away as the light grew brighter. She switched her aim to the stubborn gate itself, using the explosions to punch it down, adding their weight to that of the water.

White fire engulfed her.

The gates were wrenched apart, and the water plummeted into the empty canal beyond.

'Go with it,' Joshua datavised as the first stirrings of a current stroked his faltering legs. 'Stay afloat.'

A waterfall roar reverberated round the Shed's high bay, and he was pulled along the basin wall. The others were twirling round him. Quiet, unseen currents sucked them towards the end of the basin where it narrowed like a funnel into the small canal. They started to pick up speed as they drew closer to the mouth. Then the basin was behind them. Water was surging along the canal.

'Joshua, please acknowledge. This is Sarha, acknowledge please, Joshua.' His neural nanonics told him the signal was being routed to his communication block via the spaceplane. Everyone, it seemed, had survived the orbital battle.

'I'm here, Sarha,' he datavised. The canal water was boiling tempestuously as it flowed under the door, dipping down sharply; and he was racing towards it at a hazardous rate. It was becoming very hard to keep afloat, even here the level was sinking. He tried a few feeble sidestrokes to get away from the wall where the churning was at its worst.

'Joshua, you're entering into an emergency situation.'

Two curling vortex waves recoiled off the canal walls to converge above him as he passed under the Shed door. 'No shit!' The waves closed over his head. Neural nanonics triggered a massive adrenalin secretion, enabling him to fight his way back to the surface with recalcitrant limbs. Distorted daylight and iron-hard foam crashed around him as he floundered back into the air.

'I'm serious, Joshua. The Organization has tampered with one of the ironbergs. They altered its aerobrake trajectory so that it will land on the foundry yard. If they can't get Mzu offplanet with them, they want her dead so she'll have to join the Organization that way. It's timed to crash after the space-plane pick-up was scheduled, so that if anything went wrong they'd still win.'

The canal opened up ahead of Joshua, a rigid gully stretching away to the foundry building three kilometres distant. Water rampaged along it, a thundering white-water torrent which propelled him along helplessly. He wasn't alone. Voi came close enough for him to touch if the pounding water hadn't been so strong, snatching her away again immediately.

'Jesus, Sarha, this *is* after the spaceplanes were scheduled.'

'I know. We're tracking the ironberg, it's going to hit you in seven minutes.'

'What? Nuke the bastard, now, Sarha.'

The leading edge of the water reached the first of the scaffolding gantries erected against the rotting canal walls. It swept the lower members away, toppling the rest of the structure. The gantry rolled for a few revolutions in the spume, then began to break apart, metal poles sinking to the bottom.

'We can't, Joshua. It's already in the lower atmosphere. The combat wasps can't reach it.'

The water reached the second stretch of scaffolding. This was larger than the first, supporting big construction mechanoids and concrete hoppers. Their weight lent a degree of stability to the edifice as the water seethed around it; several members broke free, but it managed to remain relatively intact against the initial onrush.

'Don't worry, Joshua,' Ashly datavised. 'I'm on my way. Fifty seconds and I'll be there. We'll be airborne long before the ironberg crashes. I can see the Sheds already.'

'No, Ashly, stay back, there are possessed here; a lot of them. They'll hit the spaceplane if they see you.'

'Target them for me; I've got the masers.'

'Impossible.' He saw the scaffolding up ahead, and knew this was his one chance. The physiological monitor program had been issuing cautions for some time, the cold was killing him. His muscles were already badly debilitated, slow to respond. He had to get out of the water while he had some strength left. 'Everybody,' he datavised, 'grab the scaffolding, or just crash into it if that's all you can manage. But make sure you don't go past. We have to get out.'

The first rusty poles were coming up very fast. He reached out a hand. None of his fingers worked inside the medical package glove, not even when his neural nanonics commanded them. 'Mzu?' he datavised. 'Get to the scaffolding.'

'Acknowledged.'

It wasn't much practical use to him, but the relief that she was still alive kept that small core-flame of hope flickering. The mission wasn't an utter disaster, he still had purpose. Surprisingly important right now.

Dahybi had already reached the scaffolding, hugging a post as the water stormed past. Then Joshua was there, trying to hook his arm around a V-junction and shift his head out of the way at the same time to avoid a crack on the temple. The metal banged against his chest, and he never even felt it.

'You OK?' Dahybi datavised.

'Fucking wonderful.'

Voi was flashing past, just succeeding in jamming an arm on a pole.

Joshua inched himself further into the shaking structure. There was a ladder two metres away, and he flopped against it. The water wasn't quite so strong now, but it was rising fast.

Mzu came thumping into the end of the scaffolding. 'Mother Mary, my ribs,' she datavised. Samuel landed beside her, and wrapped a protective arm around her.

Joshua clambered up the ladder, thankful it was at a low angle. Dahybi followed him. Two more operatives caught the scaffolding, then Monica snagged herself. Gelai and Ngong swam quite normally across the canal, the cold having no effect on them at all. They grabbed the scaffolding and started shoving the numb survivors up out of the water.

'Melvyn?' Joshua datavised. 'Where are you, Melvyn?' He'd been one of the first to reach the canal after Ione blew the lock gate. 'Melvyn?' There wasn't even a carrier band from the fusion specialist's neural nanonics.

'What's happening?' Ashly datavised. 'I can't acquire any of you on the sensors.'

'Stay back, that's an order,' Joshua replied. 'Melvyn?'

One of the ESA operatives floated past, face down.

'Melvyn?'

'I'm sorry, Captain Calvert,' Dick Keaton datavised. 'He went under.'

'Where are you?'

'End of the scaffolding.'

Joshua looked over his shoulder, seeing the limp figure suspended in the crisscross of poles thirty metres away. He was alone.

Jesus, no. Another friend condemned to the beyond. Looking back at reality and begging to return.

'That's all of us now,' Monica datavised.

Altogether six of the operatives from the combined Edenist–ESA team had survived along with her and Samuel. Eriba's corpse was swirling past amid a scum of brown foam. Fifteen people, out of the twenty-three who had entered Disassembly Shed Four; more if you counted the two serjeants.

'What now?' Dahybi asked.

'Climb,' Joshua told him. 'We've got to get up to the top of the scaffolding. Our spaceplane is on its way.'

'So is a bloody ironberg.'

'Gelai, where are the possessed?' Joshua croaked.

'Coming,' she said. 'Baranovich is already out of the Shed. He won't let the spaceplane land.'

'I don't have a weapon,' Monica said. 'There's only two machine-guns left between all of us. We can't hold them back.' Her body was trembling violently as she crawled along a narrow conveyor belt connected to one of the concrete hoppers.

Joshua went up another three rungs on the ladder, then sagged from the effort.

'Captain Calvert,' Mzu datavised. 'I won't give anybody the Alchemist no matter what. I want you to know that. And thank you for your efforts.'

She'd given up, sitting huddled limply in a junction. Ngong was holding her, concentrating hard. Steam began to spout out of her suit. Joshua looked round at the rest of them, defeated and tortured by the cold. If he was going to do anything to salvage this, it would have to be extreme.

'Sarha, give me fire support,' he datavised.

'Our sensor returns are being corrupted,' she replied. 'I can't resolve the foundry yard properly. It's the same effect we encountered on Lalonde.'

'Jesus. OK, target me.'

'Joshua!'

'Don't argue. Activate the designator laser, and target my communication block. Do it. Ashly, stand by. The rest of you: come on, move, we have to be ready.' He took another couple of steps up the ladder.

*Lady Macbeth*'s designator laser pierced the wispy residue of snow clouds. A slim shaft of emerald light congested with hazy sparkles as gusting snowflakes evaporated inside it. It was aligned on a road three hundred metres away.

'Is that on you?' Sarha asked.

'No, track north-east, two-fifty metres.'

The beam shifted fast enough to produce a blurred sheet of green light across the sky.

'East eighty metres,' Joshua instructed. 'North twenty-five.'

His retinal implants had to bring their strongest filters on-line as the scaffolding was swamped by brilliant green light.

'Lock coordinate – mark. Preclude one-five-zero metres. Switch to ground-strike cannon. Spiral one kilometre. Scorch it, Sarha.'

The beam moved away, its colour blooming through the spectrum until it was a deep ruby red. Then its intensity grew; snowflakes drifting into it no longer evaporated, they burst apart. Thick brown fumes and smoking pumice gravel jetted up from the disintegrating carbon concrete at its base. It changed direction, curving round to gouge a half-metre groove in the ground. A perfect circle three hundred metres in diameter was etched out in polluted flame, with the canal scaffolding at the centre. Then the beam began to speed up, creating a hollow cylinder of vivid red light which expanded inexorably. The ground underneath it ignited; vaporizing the cloak of snow into a rolling cloud which broiled the land ahead of the beam.

It slashed across the corner of Disassembly Shed Four. Cherry-red embers flew out of the panels up the entire height of the wall. A thin sliver of composite and metal began to peel away from the bulk of the Shed. Then the laser struck it again. It cut a deeper chunk this time, which started to pitch over in pursuit of the first. Both of them were surrounded by a cascade of embers. The beam continued round on its spiral.

Disassembly Shed Four died badly: chopped into thin curving slices by the relentless laser. The individual wedges collapsed and crumpled against each other, softened and sagging from the immense thermal input to descend in slippery serpentine riots. When almost a fifth of it had gone, the remaining framework could no longer sustain itself. The walls and roof buckled groggily, twisting and imploding. Its final convulsions were illuminated by the laser, which continued to chop the falling wreckage into ribbons of slag. Steam geysers roared upwards as pyrexic debris slithered into the basin, flattening out to obscure the bubbling ruin in a virgin white funeral shroud.

Nothing could survive the groundstrike. The security police raced for their cars as soon as it began, only to be overtaken by the outward spiral. Baranovich and his fellow possessed took refuge back in the Disassembly Shed under the assumption that anything that massive was bound to be safe. When that folly was revealed, some of them dived into the canal, only to be parboiled. A couple of hapless foundry yard staff on their way to investigate the noises and light coming from the mothballed Shed were caught and reduced to a fog of granular ash.

The laser beam vanished.

Secure at the vestal centre of the remorseless sterilization he had unleashed, Joshua datavised the all-clear to Ashly. The spaceplane streaked out of the roiling sky to land beside the canal. Joshua and the others waited at the top of the scaffolding, hunched up as the warm wind created by the laser's passage blew against them.

'Hanson evac service,' Ashly datavised as the airstair slid out from the airlock. 'Close shaves a speciality. Shift your arses, we've only got two minutes till it hits.'

Alkad Mzu was first up the airstair, followed by Voi.

'I won't take you as you are,' Joshua told Gelai and Ngong. 'I can't, you know that.' Monica and Samuel were standing behind the two ex-Garissans, machine-guns cradled ready.

'We know,' Gelai said. 'But do you know you will be in our position one day?'

'Please,' Joshua said. 'We don't have time for this. None of us are going to jeopardize Mzu now, not after what we've been though to get her. Not even me. They'll shoot you, and I won't try to stop them.'

Gelai nodded morosely. Her black skin faded to a pasty white, ruffled ginger hair tumbled down over her shoulders. The girl sank to her knees, jaw open to wail silently.

Joshua put his arms under her shoulders to carry her into the spaceplane. Samuel was doing the same for the old man who had been possessed by Ngong.

'Dick, give me a hand,' Joshua grunted as he reached the bottom of the airstair.

'Sorry, Captain,' Dick Keaton said. 'But this is where necessity dictates we part company. I have to say, though, it's been quite an experience. Wouldn't have missed it for anything.'

'Jesus, there's an ironberg falling on us!'

'Don't worry. I'll be perfectly safe. And I can hardly come with you now my cover's been blown, now can I?'

'What the fuck are you?'

'Closer, Captain,' he grinned. 'Much closer, this time. Goodbye, and good luck.'

Joshua glared at the man – if that's what he really was – and hauled the semiconscious girl up the airstair.

Keaton stood back as the spaceplane took off, its compressor efflux whipping his ice-speckled hair about. He waved solemnly as it pitched up and accelerated away over the ruined smoking land.

High in the western sky, a red dot glimmered malevolently, growing larger by the second.

The spaceplane cabin canted up sharply, slinging Joshua back into a chair. Acceleration was two gees and rising fast. 'What's our status, Ashly?'

'Good. We've got an easy twenty seconds left. Not even a real race against the clock. Did I tell you about the time when I was flying covert landings for the Marseille Militia?'

'You told me. Pump the cabin temperature up, please, we're freezing back here.' He accessed the spaceplane's sensor suite. They were already two kilometres high, well out over the lacklustre grey sea. The ironberg was level with them, and sinking rapidly.

Joshua, who had grown up in a bitek habitat and captained a faster-than-light starship for a living, regarded it in dismayed awe. Something that big simply did not belong in the air. It was falling at barely subsonic velocity, spinning with slow elegance to maintain its trajectory. A thick braided vapour trail streaked away from its rounded tip, creating a perfectly straight line through the sky before rupturing two hundred metres higher up when the massive horizontal shock waves created by its turbulence crashed back together. Aerobrake friction made its scalloped base shine a baleful topaz at the centre, grading down to bright coral pink at the rim.

For the doomed staff left in the yard the strangest aspect of its drop was the silence. It was unreal, looking up at the Devil's fist as it descended upon you, and hearing nothing but the lazy squawking of sea birds.

The energy burst from seventy-five thousand tonnes of steel striking the ground at three hundred metres per second was cataclysmic. The blast wave razed the remaining Disassembly Sheds, sending hundreds of thousands of shattered composite panels ripping through the air. They were instantly ignited by the accompanying thermal release, crowning the maelstrom with a raging halo of flame. Last came the groundshock, a mini-quake which rippled out for several kilometres through the boggy soil, plucking the huge smelters from the skeletal remains of their furnace buildings and flinging them across the marshy wasteland at the rear of the yard. The sea retreated hastily from the catastrophe, deserting the shoreline in a series of huge breakers which fought against the incoming tide for several minutes. But in the end, the tremors ceased, and the water came rushing back to obliterate any last sign that the yard had ever existed.

*

'Ho, man, that is just orgasmic,' Quinn said. The bridge's holoscreens were pumping out a blaze of white light as the first of the antimatter explosions blossomed above Nyvan. So much destruction excited him; he could see hundreds of combat wasps in flight above the nightside continents. 'God's Brother is helping us, Dwyer. This is His signal to start. Just look at those mothers go at it. There won't be a single nuke left on the planet to fight off the fall of Night.'

'Quinn, the other nations are firing combat wasps at Jesup. We're naked out here, we've got to jump.'

'How long till they arrive?'

'Three, four minutes.'

'Plenty of time,' Quinn said smoothly. He checked the communication displays to ensure the starship's secure lasers were still linked with Jesup and the three abandoned asteroids. 'An occasion like this, I ought to say something, but fuck it, I'm not in the dignity business.' He typed in the arming code, and watched as the display symbology turned a beautiful dangerous red. His finger went straight to the execute command key, and tapped it eagerly.

Ninety-seven fusion bombs detonated, the majority of them one hundred megaton blasts.

The sensors which were protruding above the fuselage of *Mount's Delta* observed Jesup wobble. Quinn had ordered his trusted disciples to place the bombs in a line below the biosphere cavern where the rock was thinnest. Huge flakes of rock fell away from the asteroid's crinkled outer surface, allowing jets of raw plasma to stab out. It was a precision application of force, splitting the rock clean open. The biosphere cavern was ruined instantly as nuclear volcanoes erupted out of the floor to exterminate all the life it sustained. Shock waves hurtled through the rock, opening up immense fracture patterns and shattering vast sections already weakened from centuries of mining.

Centrifugal force took over from the bombs to complete the destruction, applying intolerable torque stresses on the remaining sections of rock. Hill-sized chunks of regolith crumbled away, rotation flinging them clear. Tornadoes of hot, radioactive air poured into space, forming a thin cyclone around the fragmenting asteroid.

Quinn slammed a fist into his console. 'Fucked!' he yelled victoriously. 'Totally fucking fucked. I did it. Now they'll know His might is for real. The Night is going to fall, Dwyer, sure as shit floats to the top.'

Sensors aligned on the three abandoned asteroids revealed similar scenes of devastation.

'But— Why? Why, Quinn?'

Quinn laughed joyfully. 'Back on Earth we learned everything there was to know about climate, all those doomsdays waiting to bite our arses if we aren't good obedient little Govcentral mechanoids. Don't violate the environment laws else you'll wind up drowning in your own crap. Bollocks like that. Everybody knows the entire flekload, the whole arcology from the tower nerds to the Downtown kids. I heard about nuclear winters and dinosaur killers before I could walk.' He banged a finger on the holoscreen's surface. 'And this is it. Earth's nightmare out of the box. Those rocks are going to pulverize Nyvan. Doesn't matter if they smash down on land or water; they're going to blast gigatonnes of shit up into the atmosphere. I'm not talking some crappy little smog layer up in the sky, it's going to be the fucking sky. Wet black soot stretching from the ground to the stratosphere, so thick it'll give you cancer just breathing it for five minutes. They'll never see sunlight again, never. And when the possessed take over the whole fucking ball game down there, it still ain't going to help them. They can shunt Nyvan out of the universe, but they haven't got the power to clean the air. Only He can do that. God's Brother will bring them light.' Quinn hugged Dwyer energetically. 'They'll pray to Him to come and liberate them. They can't do anything else. He is their only salvation now. And I did it for Him. Me! I've brought Him a whole fucking planet to join His legions. Now I know it works, I'm going to do it to every planet in the Confederation. Every single one, that's my crusade now. Starting with Earth.'

Secure communication lasers slid back down inside the fuselage, along with the sensors, and the *Mount's Delta* vanished inside an event horizon. Behind it, the low-orbit battle ran its course, the protagonists unaware of the true holocaust growing above them. The four tremendous clouds of rocky detritus were expanding at a constant rate, watched by the horrified surviving asteroids. Seventy per cent of the mass would miss the planet. But that still left thousands of fragments which would rain down through the atmosphere over the next two days. Each one would have a destructive potential hundreds of times greater than the ironberg. And with their planet's electronics reduced to trash, its spaceships smashed, its SD platforms vaporized, and its astroengineering stations in ruins, there was absolutely nothing Nyvan's population could do to prevent the onrush. Only pray.

Just as Quinn prophesied.

# 27

The *Leonora Cephei*'s radar was switched to long-range scanning mode, searching for any sign of another ship. After five hours gliding inertly along its orbital path, there hadn't been a single contact.

'How much longer do you expect me to muck in with this charade of yours?' Captain Knox asked scathingly. He indicated the holoscreen which was displaying the ship's radar return. 'I've seen Pommie cricket teams with more life in them than this bugger.'

Jed looked at the console; its symbology meant nothing to him, for all he knew the flight computer could be displaying schematics for *Leonora Cephei*'s waste-cycling equipment. He felt shamed by his own technological ignorance. He only ever came into the compartment when he was summoned by Knox; and the only summonses he got was when the captain found something new to complain about. He now made damn sure he brought Beth and Skibbow with him each time; it made the whole experience a little less like being humiliated by Digger.

'If this is the coordinate, they'll be here,' Jed insisted. This was the right time for the rendezvous. So where was the starship? He didn't want to look at Beth again. She didn't appear entirely sympathetic to his plight.

'Another hour,' Knox said. 'That's what I'll give you, then

we head for Tanami. There are some cargoes for me there. Real ones.'

'We'll wait a damn sight more than one hour, matey,' Beth said.

'You get what you paid for.'

'In that case we'll be here for six months; that's how much cash we bloody well shelled out.'

'One hour.' Knox's pale skin was reddening again; he wasn't used to his command decisions being questioned on his own bridge.

'Balls. We're here for as long as it takes, pal. Right, Jed?'

'Er. Yes. We should wait a bit longer.' Beth's silent contempt made him want to cringe.

Knox gestured broadly in mock-reasonableness. 'Long enough for the oxygen to run out, or can we head for port before that?'

'You regenerate the atmosphere,' Beth said. 'Stop being such a pain. We wait until our transport turns up. That's final.'

'You flaming kids, you're all crazy. You don't see my children become Deadnights. Deadheads, more like. What do you think is going to happen to you if you ever reach Valisk? That Kiera is bullshitting you.'

'No, she's not!' Jed said heatedly.

Knox was surprised at his resentment. 'OK, kid. I understand, I used to let my balls think for me when I was your age.' He winked at Beth.

She glowered back at him.

'We wait as long at it takes,' Gerald said quietly. 'We are going to Valisk. All of us. That's what I paid you for, Captain.' It was hard for him to be silent when people talked about Marie, especially the way they talked about her, as if she was some kind of communal girlfriend. Since the voyage started he had managed to hold his tongue. He found life a lot easier on board the small ship; the simple daily routine in which everything was laid out for him in advance was quite a comfort.

So what they said about Marie, their idolization of the demon who controlled her, didn't snarl him up with anguish. They spoke from ignorance. He was wise to that. Loren would be proud of him for exercising such control.

'All right, we'll wait a while,' Knox said. 'It's your charter.' It always embarrassed him when Skibbow spoke. The man had *episodes*, you never knew how he was going to behave. So far there had been no anger or violence. So far.

Fifteen minutes later, Captain Knox's little quandaries and problems were banished as the radar detected a small object three kilometres away which hadn't been there a millisecond before. There was the usual weird peripheral fuzz indicating a wormhole terminus, and the object was expanding rapidly. He accessed the *Leonora Cephei*'s sensors to watch the bitek starship emerging.

'Oh, sweet Christ Almighty,' he groaned. 'You crazy bastards. We're dead meat now. Bloody dead!'

*Mindori* slipped out of the wormhole terminus and stretched its wings wide. Its head swung round so that one eye could fix the *Leonora Cephei* with a daunting stare.

Jed looked into one of the bridge's AV pillars, seeing the huge hellhawk flap its wings in slow sweeps, closing the distance with deceptive speed. Disquiet gave way to a kind of reverence. He whooped enthusiastically, and hugged Beth. She grinned indulgently back at him.

'That's something, huh?'

'Sure is.'

'We did it, we bloody did it.'

A terrified Captain Knox ignored the babbling, insane kids, and ordered the main communication dish to point at Pinjarra so he could call the Trojan cluster capital for help. Not, he guessed, that it would do the slightest good.

Rocio Condra was ready for it. After several dozen clandestine pick-ups he knew exactly how the captains reacted to his appearance. Out of the eight short-range defence lasers secured to his hull, only three were still functioning, and that was only because they utilized bitek processor-control circuitry. The rest had succumbed to the vagaries of his energistic power, which he could never quite contain. He targeted the dish as it started to track round, and sent a half-second pulse into its central transmission module.

'Do not attempt to contact anyone,' he broadcast.

'I understand,' a shaken Knox datavised.

'Good. Are you carrying Deadnights for transfer?'

'Yes.'

'Stand by for rendezvous and docking. Tell them to be ready.'

The monster bird folded its wings as it manoeuvred closer to the spindly inter-orbit craft. Its outline began to waver as it rolled around its long axis, feathers giving way to dull-green polyp, avian shape reverting to the earlier compressed-cone hull. There were changes, though, the scattered purple rings were now long ovals, mimicking its feather pattern. Of the three rear fins, the central one had shrunk, while the two outer ones had elongated and flattened back.

With the roll manoeuvre complete, *Mindori*'s life-support module lay parallel to the *Leonora Cephei*. Rocio Condra extended the airlock tube. Now he could sense the minds inside the inter-orbit ship's life-support capsule. It contained the usual split between trepidatious crew and ridiculously exuberant Deadnights. This time there was an addition, a strange mind, dulled yet happy, with thoughts moving in erratic rhythms.

He watched with idle curiosity through the internal optical sensors as the Deadnights came aboard. The interior of the life-support module had come to resemble a nineteenth-century steamship, with a profusion of polished rosewood surfaces and brass fittings. According to the pair of possessed, Choi-Ho and Maxim Payne, who served as maintenance crew, there was also a fairly realistic smell of salt water. Rocio was pleased with the realism, which was far more detailed and solid than the possessed usually achieved. That was due to the nature of the hellhawk's neuron cell-structure which contained hundreds of subnodes arranged in processorlike lattices. They were intended to act as semi-autonomic regulators for his technological modules. Once he had conjured up the image he wanted and loaded it into a subnode it was maintained without conscious thought, and with an energistic strength unavailable to an ordinary human brain.

The last few weeks had been a revelation to Rocio Condra. After the initial bitter resentment, he had discovered that life as a hellhawk was about as rich as it was possible to have, although he did miss sex. And he'd been talking to some of the others about that; theoretically they could simply grow the appropriate genitalia (those that didn't insist on imagining themselves as techno starships). If they accomplished that, there was no real reason to go back into human bodies. Which of course would make them independent of Kiera. For an entity that lived for ever, the variety which would come from trying out a new creature's body and life cycle every few millennia might just be the final answer to terminal ennui.

Accompanying the revelation was a growing resentment at the way Kiera was using them – to which the prospect of fighting for Capone was a worrying development. Even if he was offered a human body now, Rocio was doubtful he wanted to go with the habitat. He wasn't frightened of space like the rest of the returned souls, not any more, not possessing this magnificent creature. Space and all its emptiness was to be loved for its freedom.

Gravity returned slowly as Gerald drifted through the airlock tube, his shoulder bag in tow. The airlock compartment he landed in was almost identical to the one he had left behind. Larger, its technology more discreet, and outside the hatch Choi-Ho and Maxim Payne greeted him with smiles and comforting words where behind Knox and his eldest son had stood guard over their hatch with TIP carbines and scowls.

'There are several cabins available,' Choi-Ho said. 'Not enough for everyone, so you'll probably have to double up.'

Gerald smiled blankly, which came over more as a frightened grimace.

'Pick any one,' she told him kindly.

'When will we get there?' Gerald asked.

'We have a rendezvous in the Kabwe system in eight hours, after that we'll be going back to Valisk. It should be about twenty hours.'

'Twenty? Is that all?'

'Yes.'

'Twenty.' It was said with deference. 'Are you sure?'

'Yes, quite sure.' People were starting to bunch up in the airlock behind him; all of them curiously reluctant to push past. 'A cabin,' she suggested hopefully.

'Come on, Gerald, mate,' Beth said breezily. She took his arm and pulled gently. He walked obediently down the corridor with her. He only stopped once, and that was to look over his shoulder and say an earnest thank-you to an oddly intrigued Choi-Ho.

Beth kept going right to the end of the U-shaped corridor. She thought it would be best to get Gerald a cabin away from the rest of the Deadnights. 'Can you believe this place?' she said. She was walking on a deep red carpet past portholes that shone brilliant beams of sunlight into the corridor (although she couldn't see out through them); the doors were all golden wood. In her usual sweatshirt, two jackets, and baggy jeans she felt uncomfortably out of place.

She peered round a door and found an empty cabin. There were two bunk beds clipped to a wall, and a small sliding door to the bathroom. The plumbing was similar to the toilet in the *Leonora Cephei*, except this was all heavy brass with small white glazed ceramic buttons.

'This ought to do you,' she said confidently. A quiet pule made her turn round. Gerald was standing just inside the door, his knuckles pressed into his mouth.

'What's the matter, Gerald?'

'Twenty hours.'

'I know. But that's good, isn't it?'

'I'm not sure. I want to be there, to see her again. But she's not her any more, not my Marie.'

He was quaking. Beth put an arm round his shoulder and eased him down onto the bottom bunk. 'Easy there, Gerald. Once we're at Valisk, all this is going to seem like a bad dream; honestly, mate.'

'It doesn't end there, it starts there. And I don't know what to do, I don't know how to save her. I can't put her in zero-tau by myself. They're so strong, and evil.'

'Who, Gerald? Who are you talking about? Who's Marie?'

'My baby.'

He was crying now, his head pressed into her shoulder. She patted the back of his neck instinctively.

'I don't know what to do,' he gasped out. 'She's left me again.'

'Marie's left you?'

'No. Loren. She's the only one that can help me. She's the only one who can help any of us.'

'It's all right, Gerald, really, you'll see.'

The reaction wasn't what she expected at all. Gerald started a hysterical laugh which was half screams. Beth wanted to let go and get out of the cabin fast. He'd flipped, totally flipped now. The only reason she kept hold of him was because she didn't know what would happen if she did. He might get worse.

'Please, Gerald,' she begged. 'You're frightening me.'

He grabbed both of her shoulders, squeezing hard enough to make her flinch. 'Good!' His face had reddened with anger. 'You should be frightened, you stupid, stupid little girl. Don't you understand where we're going?'

'We're going to Valisk,' Beth whispered.

'Yes, Valisk. That doesn't frighten me, I'm bloody terrified. They're going to torture us, hurt you so bad you'll beg a soul to possess you and stop them. I know they will. That's all they ever do. They did it to me before, and then Dr Dobbs made me go through it again, and again and again just so he could know what it was like.' The anger drained out of him, and he sagged forward into her awkward embrace. 'I'll kill myself. Yes. Maybe that's it. I can help Marie that way. I'm sure I can. Anything's better than possession again.'

Beth started rocking him as best she could, soothing him as she would any five-year-old who'd woken from a nightmare. The things he was saying plagued her badly. After all, they only had Kiera's word that she was building a fresh society for them. One recording that promised she was different to the rest. 'Gerald?' she asked after a while. 'Who's this Marie you want to help?'

'My daughter.'

'Oh. I see. Well how do you know she's at Valisk?'

'Because she's the one Kiera's possessing.'

Rocio Condra parted his beak in what passed for a smile. The sensor in Skibbow's cabin wasn't the best, and his affinity link with its bitek processor suffered annoying drop-outs. But what had been said was plain enough.

He wasn't entirely sure how he could use the knowledge, but it was the first sign of any possible chink in Kiera's armour. That was a start.

*

Stephanie could finally see the end of the red cloud cover. The heavy ceiling had been dropping closer to the ground for some time now as the convoy drove unimpeded along the M6. Individual clumps and streamers churned against each other in a motion reminiscent of waves crashing on rocks, bright slivers of pink and gold rippled amongst the distorted underbelly.

They acted like a conductor for a current of pure agitation. The will of the possessed was being thwarted, their shield against the sky arrested by the Kingdom's firebreak.

The cliff of white light sleeting down along the boisterous edge appeared almost solid. Certainly it took her eyes a while to acclimatize, slowly resolving the grainy shadows which crouched at the end of the road.

'I think it might be a good idea to slow down now,' Moyo said in her ear.

She applied the brakes, reducing their speed to a crawl. The other three buses behind matched her caution. Two hundred metres from the flexing curtain of sunlight she stopped altogether. The cloud base was only four or five hundred metres high here, hammering on the invisible boundary in perpetual ferment.

Two sets of bright orange barriers had been erected across the road. The first was under the edge of the cloud, sometimes bathed in red light, sometimes in white; the second was three hundred metres north, guarded by a squad of Royal Marines. Behind them, several dozen military vehicles were drawn up on the hard shoulder, armoured troop transports, ground tanks, general communication vehicles, lorries, a canteen, and several field headquarters caravans.

Stephanie opened the bus doors, and stepped down onto the road. The thunder was an aggressive growl here, warning outsiders to keep back.

'What did they do to the grass?' Moyo shouted. Just inside the line of sunlight, the grass was dead, its blades blackened and desiccated. Already it was crumbling into dust. The dead zone lay parallel to the border of the red cloud as far as the eye could see, forming a rigid stripe that cut cleanly across every contour.

Stephanie looked along the broad swath of destruction: trees and bushes had been burned to charcoal stumps. 'Some kind of no-man's-land, I suppose.'

'That's a bit extreme, isn't it?'

She laughed, and pointed up at the glowing cloud.

'OK, you got a point. What do you want to do next?'

'I'm not sure.' She resented her indecision immediately. This was the culmination of enormous emotional investment. For all that, the practicalities of the moment had been ignored. I almost wish we were still travelling, it gave me such a sense of satisfaction. What have we got after this?

Cochrane, McPhee, and Rana joined them.

'Some terminally unfriendly looking dudes we have here,' Cochrane yelled above the thunder. The Marines lining the barrier were motionless, while more were hurrying from the cluster of vehicles to reinforce them.

'I'd better go and talk to them,' Stephanie said.

'Not alone?' Moyo protested.

'I'll look a lot less threatening than a delegation.' A white handkerchief sprouted from Stephanie's hand; she held it up high and clambered over the first set of barriers.

Lieutenant Anver watched her coming and gave his squad their deployment assignments, sending half of them out to flank the road and watch for any other possessed trying to sneak over, not that they'd ever get past the satellites. His helmet sensors zoomed in for a close-up on the woman's face. She was squinting uncomfortably at the light as she emerged from under the dappled shadow of the red cloud. A pair of sunglasses materialized on her face.

'Definitely possessed, sir,' he datavised to Colonel Palmer.

'We see that, thank you, Anver,' the Colonel replied. 'Be advised, the Security Committee is accessing your datavise now.'

'Sir.'

'There's no other activity along the firebreak,' Admiral Farquar datavised. 'We don't think she's a diversion.'

'Go see what she wants, Anver,' Colonel Palmer ordered. 'And be very careful.'

'Yes, sir.'

Two of his squad slid a section of the barrier aside, and he stepped forward. For all that it was only a hundred metre walk, it lasted half of his life. He spent the time trying to think what to say to her; but when they stopped a few paces from each other, all he said was: 'What do you want?'

She lowered her hand with the handkerchief, and gave him a cautious smile. 'We brought some children out. They're in the buses back there. I, um ... wanted to tell you so you wouldn't ... you know.' The smile became one of embarrassment. 'We weren't sure how you'd react.'

'Children?'

'Yes. About seventy. I don't know the exact number, I never actually counted.'

'Does she mean non-possessed?' Admiral Farquar datavised.

'Are these children possessed?'

'Of course not,' Stephanie said indignantly. 'What do you think we are?'

'Lieutenant Anver, this is Princess Kirsten.'

Anver stiffened noticeably. 'Yes, ma'am.'

'Ask her what she wants, what the deal is.'

'What do you want for them?'

Stephanie's lips tightened in anger. 'I don't want anything. Not in return, they're just children. What I'd like is an assurance that you military types aren't going to shoot them when we send them over.'

'Oh, dear,' Princess Kirsten datavised. 'Apologize to her, Lieutenant, on my behalf, please. And tell her that we're very grateful to her and those with her for bringing the children back to us.'

Anver cleared his throat, this wasn't quite what he expected when he started his lonely walk out here. 'I'm very sorry ma'am. The Princess sends her apologies for assuming the worst. We're very grateful to you for what you've done.'

'I understand. This isn't easy for me, either. Now, how do you want to handle this?'

Twelve Royal Marines came back to the buses with her; volunteers, without their armour suits and weapons. The bus doors were opened, and the children came down. There were a lot of tears, and running round in confusion. Most of them wanted a last kiss and a hug from the adults who had rescued them (Cochrane was especially popular), much to the amazement of the marines.

Stephanie found herself almost in tears as the last batch started off down the broad road, clustering round the big marine, one of them was even being given a piggyback. Moyo's arm was round her shoulder to hold her tight.

Lieutenant Anver came over to stand in front of her, and saluted perfectly (to which Cochrane managed a quite obscene parody). He looked badly troubled. 'Thank you again, all of you,' he said. 'That's me saying it, I can't datavise under the cloud.'

'Oh, do take care of the little darlings,' Tina said, sniffing hard. 'Poor Analeese has the most dreadful cold, none of us could cure her. And Ryder hates nuts; I think he's got an allergy, and . . .' She fell silent as Rana squeezed her forearm.

'We'll take care of them,' Lieutenant Anver said gravely. 'And you, you take care of yourselves.' He glanced pointedly out to the firebreak where a procession of vehicles was massing round the barrier to greet the children. 'You might want to do that away from here.' A crisp nod at Stephanie, and he was walking back towards the barrier.

'What did he mean?' Tina asked querulously.

'Wowee,' Cochrane let out a long breath. 'We like did it, man, we showed the forces of bad vibes not to mess with us.'

Moyo kissed Stephanie. 'I'm very proud of you.'

'Ugh,' Cochrane exclaimed. 'Don't you two cats ever stop?'

A smiling Stephanie leant forwards and kissed him on his forehead, getting hair caught on her lips. 'Thank you, too.'

'Will somebody tell me what he meant,' Tina said. 'Please.'

'Nothing good,' McPhee said. 'That's a fact.'

'So now what do we do?' Rana asked. 'Go round up another group of kids? Or split up? Or settle that farm we talked about? What?'

'Oh, stay together, definitely,' Tina said. 'After everything we've done I couldn't bear losing any of you, you're my family now.'

'Family. That's cosmic, sister. So like what's your position on incest?'

'I don't know what we'll decide,' Stephanie said. 'But I think we should take the Lieutenant's advice, and do it a long way away from here.'

*

The spaceplane rose out of Nyvan's stratosphere on twin plumes of plasma flame, arching up towards its orbital injection coordinate a thousand kilometres ahead. Submunitions were still peppering space with explosions and decoy flares, while electronic-warfare drones blasted gigawatt pulses at any emission they could detect. Now its reaction-drive rockets were on, the spaceplane was no longer invisible to the residuals of the combat wasp battle.

*Lady Macbeth* flew cover a hundred kilometres above it, sensors and maser cannon deployed to strike any missile which acquired lock-on. The starship had to make continual adjustments to its flight vector to keep the spaceplane within its protective radius. Joshua watched its drive flaring, reducing velocity, accelerating, switching altitude. Five times its masers fired to destroy incoming submunitions.

By the time the spaceplane had reached orbit and was manoeuvring to dock the sky above Nyvan had calmed considerably. Only three other starships were visible to *Lady Mac*'s sensors, all of them frigates belonging to local defence forces. None of them seemed interested in *Lady Mac*, or even each other. Beaulieu began a thorough sensor sweep, alert for the inevitable chaotic showers of post-explosion debris which would make low orbit hazardous for some time to come. Some of the returns were odd, making her redefine the sweep's parameters. *Lady Mac*'s sensors shifted their focus away from the planet itself.

Joshua slid cleanly through the hatchway into the bridge. His clothes had dried out in the hot air of the spaceplane's cabin, but the dirt and stains remained. Dahybi's ship-suit was in a similar state.

Sarha gave him an apprehensive glance. 'Melvyn?' she asked quietly.

'Not a chance. Sorry.'

'Bugger.'

'You two did a good job up here,' Joshua said. 'Well done, that was some fine piloting to stay above the spaceplane.'

'Thanks, Josh.'

Joshua looked from Liol who was anchored to a stikpad by the captain's acceleration couch to Sarha whose expression was utterly unrepentant.

'Oh, Jesus, you gave him the access codes.'

'Yes, I did. My command decision. There was a war up here, Joshua.'

It wasn't, he decided, worth making an issue out of, not in view of everything else that was happening. 'That's why I left you in charge,' he said. 'I had confidence in you, Sarha.'

She frowned suspiciously, he sounded sincere. 'So you got Mzu, then. I hope it was worth it.'

'For the Confederation I suppose it is. For individuals ... you'd have to ask them. But then individuals have been dying because of her for some time now.'

'Captain, please access our sensor suite,' Beaulieu said.

'Right.' He rolled in mid-air, and landed on his acceleration couch. The images from the external sensor clusters expanded into his mind. Wrong. They had to be wrong. 'Jesus wept!' His brain was already acting in conjunction with the flight computer's astrogration program to plot a vector before he'd fully admitted the reality of the tide of rock descending on the planet. 'Prepare for acceleration, thirty seconds – mark. We have to leave.' A fast internal sensor check showed him his new passengers hurrying towards couches; images superimposed with purple and yellow trajectory plots that wriggled frantically as he refined their projected trajectory.

'Who did that?' he asked.

'No idea,' Sarha said. 'It happened during the battle, we didn't even know until afterwards. But it sure as hell wasn't random combat wasp strikes.'

'I'll monitor the drive tubes,' Joshua said. 'Sarha, take systems coverage, please. Liol you've got fire control.'

'Aye, Captain,' Liol said.

It was a strictly neutral tone. Joshua was satisfied with that. He triggered *Lady Mac*'s fusion drives, bringing them up to a three-gee acceleration.

'Where are we going?' Liol asked.

'Bloody good question,' Joshua said. 'For now I just want us out of here. After that, it rather depends on what Ione and the agents decide, I expect.'

*

There must be someone who knows. One of you.

We know it is real. We know it is hidden.

Two bodies await. A male and a female. Youthful, splendid. Do you hear them? Do you taste them? Pleading for one of you to enter them. You can. All the riches and pleasures of reality can be yours again. If you have the admission price, one tiny piece of information. That's all.

She didn't hide it by herself. She had help from somebody. Probably many. Were you one?

Ah. Yes. You. You are being truthful. You know.

**1152**

Come then. Come forward, come through. We reward you with—

He cried out in wonder and misery as he struggled his way into the victim's agonized nervous system. There was pain, and shame, and humiliation to cope with; tragic, terrible pleas from the body's true soul. One by one, he faced them down, mending the broken flesh, suppressing and ignoring the protest, until there was only his own shame left. Not so easily abandoned.

'Welcome to the Organization,' said Oscar Kearn. 'So, you were part of Mzu's mission?'

'Yes. I was with her.'

'Good. She's a clever woman, that Mzu. I'm afraid she's eluded us once again, thanks to that traitor bitch Barnes. Even so, only the amazingly resourceful can duck an ironberg when it's falling on their heads. I didn't realize what I was dealing with before. I don't suppose she would have helped us even if we had caught her. She's like that, tough and determined. But now her luck's run out. You can tell me, can't you? You know where the Alchemist is.'

'Yes,' Ikela said. 'I know where it is.'

*

Alkad Mzu floated into the bridge, accompanied by Monica and Samuel. She acknowledged Joshua with a small twitch of her lips, then blinked when she saw Liol. 'I didn't know there were two of you.'

Liol grinned broadly.

'Before we all start arguing over what to do with you, Doctor,' a serjeant said, 'I'd like you to confirm the Alchemist does or did exist.'

Alkad tapped her toe on a stikpad beside the captain's couch, preventing herself from drifting about. 'Yes, it exists. And I built it. I wish to Mary I hadn't, now, but the past is the past. My only concern now is that it doesn't fall into anybody's hands, not yours, and certainly not the possessed.'

'Very noble,' Sarha said, 'from someone who was going to use it to kill an entire planet.'

'They wouldn't have been killed,' Alkad said wearily. 'It was intended to extinguish Omuta's star, not turn it nova. I'm not an Omutan barbarian; they're the ones who kill entire worlds.'

'Extinguish a star?' Samuel mused in puzzlement.

'Please don't ask for details.'

'I propose Dr Mzu is taken back to Tranquillity,' the serjeant said. 'We can formalize the observation to ensure she doesn't pass the information on. I don't think you will anyway, Doctor, but Intelligence agencies are highly suspicious entities.'

Monica consulted Samuel. 'I can live with that,' she said. 'Tranquillity is neutral territory. It isn't all that different from our original agreement.'

'It isn't,' Samuel agreed. 'But, Doctor, you do realize you cannot be allowed to die. Certainly not until the problem of possession has been resolved.'

'Fine by me,' Alkad said.

'What I mean, Doctor, is that when you are very old, you must be placed in zero-tau to prevent your soul from entering the beyond.'

'I will not give anyone the Alchemist technology, no matter what the circumstances.'

'I'm sure that is your intention at the moment. But how will you feel after a hundred years trapped in the beyond? A thousand? And to be indelicate, the choice is not yours to make. It is ours. You lost the right to self-determination when you built the Alchemist. If you give yourself enough power to make a galaxy fear you and what you can achieve, you abrogate that right to those whom your actions affect.'

'I agree,' the serjeant said. 'You will be placed in zero-tau before you die.'

'Why not just put me in now?' Alkad said crustily.

'Don't tempt me,' Monica said. 'I know the kind of contempt you moron intellectuals hold the government services in. Well, listen good, Doctor, we exist to protect the majority so they can run around living their lives as decently and as best they can. We protect them from shits like you, who never fucking stop to think what you're doing.'

'You didn't protect my bloody planet, did you!' Alkad yelled back. 'And don't you dare lecture me on responsibility. I'm prepared to die to stop the Alchemist being used by anybody else, especially your imperialist Kingdom. I know my responsibilities.'

'You do now. Now you realize what a mistake you made, now people are dying just to keep your precious arse safe.'

'OK, that's it,' Joshua said loudly. 'We're all agreed where the Doc is going, end of discussion. Nobody is going to start shouting about moral philosophy on my bridge. We're all tired, we're all emotional. Pack it in, the pair of you. I'm going to plot a course to Tranquillity, you go to your cabins and cool off. We'll be home inside of two days.'

'Understood,' Monica said through clenched teeth. 'And ... thank you for getting us off. It was—'

'Professional?'

She almost snapped back at him, but that grin ... 'Professional.'

Alkad cleared her throat. 'I'm sorry,' she said apologetically. 'But there is a problem. We can't go straight back to Tranquillity.'

Joshua massaged his temple and asked, 'Why not?' if only to stop Monica from flying at Mzu's throat.

'The Alchemist itself.'

'What about it?' Samuel asked.

'We have to collect it.'

'All right,' Joshua said in a far-from-reasonable tone. 'Why?'

'Because it isn't secure where it is.'

'It's managed to stay secure for thirty years. Jesus, just take the secret of its location to zero-tau with you. If the agencies haven't found it by now, they never will.'

'They won't have to look any more, nor will the possessed; especially if our current situation continues for more than a few years.'

'Go on, we may as well hear it all.'

'There were three ships on our strike mission against Omuta,' Alkad said, 'the *Beezling*, the *Chengho*, and the *Gombari*. The *Beezling* was the Alchemist's deployment vessel, I was on board; the other two were our escort frigates. We were intercepted by blackhawks before we could deploy the Alchemist. They destroyed the *Gombari*, and hit us and the *Chengho* pretty badly. We were left for dead in interstellar space, neither of us could jump, and the nearest inhabited star was seven light-years away.

'After the attack, we spent a couple of days repairing our internal systems, then we rendezvoused. It was Ikela and Captain Prager who came up with the eventual solution. *Chengho* was smaller than *Beezling*, it didn't need as many energy patterning nodes to perform a ZTT jump. So the crew removed some of the *Beezling*'s intact nodes and installed them in the *Chengho*. We didn't have the proper tools for that kind of job; and then the nodes had different power ratings and performance factors, they had to be completely reprogrammed. It took us three and a half weeks, but we did it. We rebuilt ourselves a ship that could make a ZTT jump – not very well, and not very far, but it was functional. That was when things started to get difficult. The *Chengho* was too small to take both crews, even for just a small jump. There was only one life-support capsule, and it could hold eight of us at a push. We knew we couldn't risk a flight back to Garissa, the nodes would never last that long; and we guessed that Ombey would have launched some kind of big attack by then. After all, that's why we'd been dispatched in the first place, to stop them. So we jumped to the nearest inhabited star system, Crotone. The idea was that we'd charter a ship and get back to Garissa that way. Of course, when we arrived at Crotone, we heard about the Genocide.

'Ikela and Prager had even formulated a worst-case option. Just in case, they said. We'd brought some antimatter with us on the *Chengho*; if we sold that together with the frigate it would fetch millions. Assuming the Garissan government no longer existed, we would have all the money we needed to operate independently for decades.'

'The Stromboli Separatist Council,' Samuel said suddenly.

'Right,' Alkad acknowledged. 'That's who we sold it to.'

'Ah, we never did find out how they got their antimatter. They blew up two of Crotone's low-orbit port stations with the stuff.'

'After we left, yes,' Alkad said.

'So Ikela took the money, and founded T'Opingtu.'

'Correct; once we found out that the Confederation Assembly granted the Dorados to the survivors of the Genocide, all seven navy officers were given an equal share. The plan was for them to invest the money in various companies, the profits from which would be used to help fund the partisans. We needed committed nationalists to crew the ship that they were supposed to prepare for me. After that, they would buy or charter a combat-capable starship to complete the Alchemist mission. As you know, Ikela didn't fulfil the last part of the plan. I don't know about the others.'

'Why wait thirty years?' Joshua asked. 'Why didn't you just hire a combat-capable starship as soon as you had the money from the sale of the frigate, and go straight back to the *Beezling*?'

'Because we couldn't be sure exactly where it was. You see, we didn't just repair the *Chengho*. There were thirty people and the Alchemist left behind on the *Beezling*. Suppose the *Chengho* didn't make it, or suppose we were caught and interrogated by the CNIS or some other agency? There was even the possibility the blackhawks might return. We had to plan for all those factors as well, the remaining crew had to be given their chance, too.'

'They went into zero-tau,' Joshua said. 'How does that prevent you from knowing the exact coordinate?'

'Yes, obviously they went into zero-tau, but that's not all. We also repaired their reaction drive. They flew a vector to an un-inhabited star which was only two and a half light-years away.'

'Jesus, a sub-lightspeed journey through interstellar space? You've got to be kidding. That's impossible, it would take—'

'Twenty-eight years, we estimated.'

'Ah!' Realization came to Joshua like the silent detonation of Norfolk Tears after it hit the stomach. He felt a surge of admiration for those lost desperate crews of thirty years ago. Not caring what the odds were, just going for it. 'They used antimatter propulsion.'

'Yes. We transferred every gram from our remaining combat wasps into the *Beezling*'s confinement chambers. It was enough to accelerate them up to about nine per cent lightspeed. So now tell me, Captain, how difficult would it be to locate a ship that is moving away from its last known coordinate at eight or nine per cent lightspeed? And if you did find it, how would you rendezvous?'

'Not possible. OK, you'd have to wait until the *Beezling* decelerated and arrived at that uninhabited star. How come you didn't make a dash for them two years ago?'

'Because we weren't sure just how efficient the drive would be over such a long period of use. Two years gave us an adequate safety margin; and of course, as it turned out, the sanctions would be over. There was always a remote chance the Confederation Navy blockade squadron would detect us, after all it's their job to be looking for sanction-buster starships emerging in odd places around Omuta. So after we sold the *Chengho* we decided on thirty years.'

'You mean the *Beezling* is just orbiting that star waiting for you to make contact?' Liol asked.

'Yes. Providing everything worked as it was supposed to. They are supposed to wait for another five years; the time is irrelevant in zero-tau, but the support systems cannot last indefinitely. If they hadn't been contacted by then, either by me and the *Chengho* crew or by the Garissan government, they were to destroy the Alchemist and start signalling for help. Uninhabited star systems within the Confederation boundaries are inspected on a regular basis by navy patrol ships to make sure they aren't being used by antimatter production stations. They would have been rescued eventually.'

Joshua glanced round to the serjeant, wishing the construct had some way of displaying emotion; he'd like to know what Ione made of the story. 'Makes sense,' he said. 'What do you want to do?'

'We have to see if the *Beezling* completed its journey,' the serjeant said.

'And if it has?' Samuel asked.

'Then the Alchemist must be destroyed. After that, any surviving crew will be taken back to Tranquillity.'

'Question, Doc,' Joshua said. 'If anybody sees the Alchemist, will that give them a clue to its nature?'

'No. You have no worries on that score, Captain. There is, however, someone among the crew who could tell you how to build another. His name is Peter Adul, he will have to remain in Tranquillity with me. After that, you will be safe again.'

'OK, what's the star's coordinate?'

It was a long time before Alkad said: 'Mother Mary, this is not what was meant to be.'

'Nothing ever is, Doc. I learned that long ago.'

'Ha! You're too young.'

'Depends how you fill the years, doesn't it?'

Alkad Mzu datavised the coordinate over.

*

**A wormhole terminus is opening,** Tranquillity announced.

At the time, Ione was standing knee deep in the warm water of the cove, rubbing Haile's flank with a big yellow bath sponge. She straightened her back, and began wringing out the sponge. Her real attention was focused on a point in space a hundred and twenty thousand kilometres away from the habitat, where the vacuum's gravity density was building rapidly. Three SD platforms orbiting the emergence zone locked their X-ray lasers on to the terminus as it expanded. Five patrol blackhawks accelerated in at four gees.

A large voidhawk slipped out of the two-dimensional rent. *Oenone*, **Confederation Navy ship SLV-66150, requesting approach and docking permission,** it said. **Our official flight authentication code follows.**

**Granted,** Tranquillity replied after it verified the code. The SD platforms were switched back to alert status. Three of the blackhawks resumed their patrol, while the remaining two curved round to form an escort as *Oenone* accelerated in towards the habitat.

'I'm going to have to leave you,' Ione said.

Jay Hilton's vexed face peeped over the top of Haile's gleaming white back. 'What is it this time?' she asked petulantly.

'Affairs of state.' Ione started wading towards the shore. She scooped some water up and tried to flush the sand out of her bikini top.

'You always say that.'

Ione gave the disgruntled girl a forlorn smile. 'Because it always is, these days.' **Sorry,** she added.

Haile formshifted the tip of an arm into a human hand and waved. **Goodbye, Ione Saldana. I have much sorrow you are leaving, my endlegs itch like bollocks.**

**Haile!**

**I form a communication wrongness? I have shame.**

**Not wrong, exactly.**

**Gladness. That was a Joshua Calvert expression. Much favoured.**

Ione snapped her teeth together. That bloody Calvert! Anger gave way to something more confusing, a sort of resentment ... possibly. Hundreds of light-years away, and he still intrudes.

**It would be. Please don't use it around Jay.**

**Understanding is me. I have a great many human emphasis phrases conveyed by Joshua Calvert.**

**I'll bet you have.**

**I want properness in my communication. I ask your assistance in reviewing my word collection. You may edit me.**

**Yes, all right.**

**Much gladness!**

Ione took another pace, then laughed. Reviewing everything Joshua had said to the young Kiint would take hours. Hours she hadn't been spending on the beach of late. Haile was becoming very crafty.

Jay leaned against her friend, watching Ione put her sandals on and start back up the path to the tube station. There was a slightly distracted expression on the woman's face, that Jay knew meant she was busy talking to the habitat personality. She didn't like to dwell on the topic. More than likely, it would be the possessed again. That was all the adults talked about these days, and it was never reassuring talk.

Haile's arm twined round Jay's, the tip stroking her gently.

**You taste of sadness.**

'I don't think these horrible possessed will ever go away.'

**They will. Humans are clever. You will find a way.**

'I hope so. I do want Mummy back.'

**Shall we build the castles of sand now?**

'Yes!' Jay grinned enthusiastically, and started splashing her way back up to the beach. They'd made the discovery together that Haile with her tractamorphic arms was the universe's best ever builder of sand castles. With Jay directing, they had made some astonishing towers along the shoreline.

Haile emerged from the water in a small explosion of spray.

**Betterness. You have happiness again.**

'So do you. Ione promised to come back for the words.'

**It is the best niceness when the three of us play together. She knows this really.**

Jay giggled. 'She turned purple when you said that. Good job you didn't say fuck to her.'

*

**The *Oenone*, Ione reflected. Why do I know that name?**

**Atlantis.**

**Oh, yes.**

**And a certain interception in the Puerto de Santa Maria star system. We received an intelligence update from the Confederation Navy last year.**

**Oh, bloody hell, yes.**

**Captain Syrinx wishes to talk to you.**

Ione sat down in the tube carriage, and began towelling her hair. **Of course.** The affinity contact broadened, allowing Syrinx to proffer her identity trait.

**Captain,** Ione acknowledged.

**I apologize for the haste, but please be advised a Confederation Navy squadron will start arriving in another nine minutes and thirty seconds – mark.**

**I see. Is Tranquillity in danger?**

**No.**

**What, then?**

**I am carrying the squadron's commander, Admiral Meredith Saldana. He requests an interview at which he can explain our full strategic situation to you.**

**Granted. Welcome to Tranquillity.** The Captain faded from the affinity band.

**She was curious about you,** Tranquillity said. **It was quite plain from her emotional content.**

**Everybody's always curious about me.** She borrowed the habitat's external senses to observe local space. They were in Mirchusko's umbra, with Choisya and Falsia hovering just above the gas giant's crescent horizon. Apart from the flotilla of blackhawks on patrol around the habitat's shell, there was little spaceship activity. The *Oenone* was the first starship to arrive in seventy-six hours. Some MSVs and personnel commuters continued to glide between the counter-rotating spaceport and Tranquillity's bracelet of industrial stations, but they were running a much reduced flight schedule. A lone dazzlepoint of fusion flame was rising up past the drab grey loop of the Ruin Ring, an He$_3$ tanker en route from the habitat's cloudscoop to the spaceport. **Program the squadron's arrival into the SD platforms,** she said. **And warn the blackhawks, we don't want any mistakes.**

**Naturally.**

**Meredith Saldana. That's two family visits in less than a month.**

**I don't think this is a family visit.**

**You're probably right.**

&ast;

It was a suspicion which was proved unpleasantly correct soon after Syrinx and the Admiral were shown in to the audience chamber of De Beauvoir Palace. As she listened to Meredith Saldana explain the proposed ambush of Capone's fleet at Toi-Hoi a swarm of ambiguous feelings laid siege to her mind.

**I don't want to involve us in front-line campaigns,** she confided to Tranquillity.

**To be pedantic, we're in the campaign, not the front line itself. And the eradication of the Organization fleet is not a strategic opportunity which can be overlooked.**

**No choice?**

**No choice.**

**I still think we're too important for this.**

**But safe. The safest place in the Confederation, remember that.**

**We hope. I'd hate to put that to the test, right now.**

**I don't see how it will. Not from this action. We will essentially be a supply and rendezvous base.**

'Very well,' she told the Admiral. 'You have my permission to use Tranquillity for your task force's port station. I'll see that you get all the He₃ you need.'

'Thank you, ma'am,' Meredith said.

'I'm slightly concerned by this flight restriction you wish to place on starships until the ambush, although I do appreciate the logic behind it. I currently have over twenty blackhawks deploying sensor satellites around the orbit where the Laymil home planet used to be. It's extremely important research work. I'd hate to see it jeopardized.'

'They would only have to be recalled for three or four days at the most,' Syrinx said. 'Our scheduling is very tight here. Surely a small delay wouldn't affect the research too much?'

'I'll recall them for now. But if you're still here after a week, I'll have to review the policy. As I said, this is part of the effort to find an overall solution. That is not to be regarded lightly.'

'Believe me, we don't, ma'am,' Meredith said.

She stared at him, trying to work out what was going on behind his blue eyes. But his answering stare offered no clue. 'I have to say, I find it ironic that Tranquillity has become so important to the Confederation and the Kingdom after all this time,' she said.

'Ironic or pleasing? Chance has finally brought you the chance to vindicate your grandfather's actions.'

There was no humour in his tone, which surprised her. She'd assumed he would be more sympathetic than Prince Noton. 'You think grandfather Michael was wrong?'

'I think he was wrong to pursue such an unorthodox course.'

'Unorthodox to the family, perhaps. But I assure you it's not chance which has brought us together. This whole situation will prove how right he was to act on his foresight.'

'I wish you every success.'

'Thank you. And who knows, one day I might earn your approval, too.'

For the first time, he produced a grudging smile. 'You don't like losing arguments, do you, cousin Ione?'

'I am a Saldana.'

'That much is painfully obvious.'

'As are you. I don't think every Confederation admiral would have coped as well as you at Lalonde.'

'I did not cope well. I ensured my squadron survived; most of it, anyway.'

'A Confederation officer's first duty is to follow orders. Second duty is to the crew. So I believe,' she said. 'As your original orders didn't cover what you encountered, I'd say you did all right.'

'Lalonde was . . . difficult,' he said heavily.

'Yes. I know all about Lalonde from Joshua Calvert.'

Syrinx, who had been looking considerably ill-at-ease while the two Saldanas conducted their verbal fencing, glanced sharply at Ione, her eyebrows raised in interest.

'Oh yes,' Meredith reflected. '"Lagrange" Calvert. Who could forget him?'

'Is he here?' Syrinx asked. 'This is his registered port.'

'He's away at the moment, I'm afraid,' Ione told her. 'But I'm expecting him back any day now.'

'Good.'

Ione couldn't quite fathom the Edenist's attitude. **Why do you think she's interested in Joshua?**

**I have no idea. Unless she wants to punch him on the nose for Puerto de Santa Maria.**

**I doubt it. She's an Edenist, they don't do things like that. You don't suppose she and Joshua . . .?**

**I doubt it. She's an Edenist, they have more taste.**

\*

Athene didn't want him to come to the house. It would be too upsetting for the children, she explained. Though they both knew it was she who was discomforted by the whole idea; keeping him away was a way of establishing a psychological barrier.

Instead, she chose one of the spaceport reception lounges in the habitat's endcap. There was nobody else in the spacious room when she arrived, not that there could be any mistake. The hulking figure was sitting on a deep settee in front of the long window, watching service crews bustling round the void-hawks on their pedestals outside.

I missed this, he said, not turning round, I watched the voidhawks through the sensitive cells, of course, but I still miss this. The habitat perception doesn't provide any sense of urgency. And my emotions were, not suppressed exactly, but less colourful, not so keenly felt. Do you know, I think I'm actually becoming excited.

She walked over to the settee, an extraordinary sense of trepidation simmering in her mind. The figure stood, revealing its true height, several centimetres taller than her. As with all Tranquillity serjeants, its exoskeleton was a faint ruddy colour, although a good forty per cent of its body was covered in bright green medical nanonic packages. It held up both hands, and turned them round, studying them intently, its eyes just visible at the back of their protective slits.

I must be quite a sight. They force-cloned all the organs separately, then stitched them together. Serjeants take fifteen months to grow to full size usually; that would be far too long. So here we are, Frankenstein's army, patched together and rushed off the assembly line. The packages should have done their work before we reach Ombey.

Athene's shoulders drooped, mirroring the dismay in her mind. Oh, Sinon, what have you done?

What I had to. The serjeants must have some controlling consciousness. And seeing as how there were all us individual personalities already available...

Yes, but not you!

Somebody has to volunteer.

I didn't want you to be one.

I'm just a copy, my darling, and an edited down one at that. My real personality is still in the neural strata, suspended for now. When I get back, or if this serjeant is destroyed, I'll return to the multiplicity.

This is so wrong. You've had your life. It was a wonderful life, rich and exciting, and full of love. Transferring into the multiplicity is our reward for living true to our culture, it should be like being a grandparent for ever, a grandparent with the largest family of relatives in the universe. You carry on loving, and you become part of something precious to all of us. She looked up at the hard mask that was its face, her own frail cheeks trembling. You don't come back. You just don't. It's not right, Sinon, it isn't. Not for us, not for Edenists.

If we don't do this, there may not be any Edenists for very much longer.

No! I won't accept that. I never have. I believe Laton if no one else does. I refuse to fear the beyond like some inadequate Adamist.

It's not the beyond we have to worry about, it's those that have returned from it.

I was one of those who opposed this Mortonridge Liberation absurdity.

I know.

By committing ourselves to it, we're no better than animals. Beasts lashing out; it's filthy. Humans can be so much more.

But rarely are.

That's what Edenism was supposed to be about, to lift us above this primitivism. All of us.

The serjeant put its arm out towards her, then withdrew it hurriedly. Shame leaked out into the affinity band. I'm sorry. I shouldn't have asked you to come. I see how much this hurts you. I just wanted to see you with my own eyes one last time.

They're not your own eyes; and you're not even Sinon, not really. I think that's what I hate most about this. It's not just Adamist religions the beyond undermines, it's ruined the whole concept of transference. What's the point? You are your soul, if you are anything. The Kiint are right, simulacrum personalities are nothing more than a sophisticated library of memories.

In our case, the Kiint are wrong. The habitat personality has a soul. Our individual memories are the seeds of its consciousness. The more there are of us in the multiplicity, the richer its existence and heritage becomes. Knowledge of the beyond hasn't ruined our culture; Edenism can adapt, it can learn and grow. Surmounting this time intact will be our triumph. And that's what I'm fighting for, to give us that physical chance. I know the Mortonridge Liberation is a fraud, we all do. But that doesn't stop it from being valid.

You're going to kill people. However careful you are, however well intentioned you are, they will die.

Yes. I didn't start this, and I won't be the one who stops it. But I must play my part. To do nothing would be to sin by omission. What I and the others do on Mortonridge might buy you enough time.

Me?

You, Consensus, the Adamist researchers, maybe even priests. All of you have to keep looking. The Kiint found a way to face the beyond and survive. It's here somewhere.

I'll do what I can, which at my age is very limited.

Don't underestimate yourself.

Thank you. You haven't been edited down that much, you know.

Some parts of me can't be edited, not if I want to keep being me. Bearing that in mind, I have one last favour to ask of you.

Go on.

I'd like you to explain this to Syrinx for me. I know my little Slyminx, she'll go nova when she hears I volunteered for this.

I'll tell her. I don't know if I can explain, but . . .

The serjeant bowed as best the medical packages would allow. Thank you, Athene.

I can't give you my blessing. But do please take care.

\*

There was no lavish farewell party this time. Monterey had a more serious, less triumphant, air these days. But Al chose the

Hilton's ballroom anyway to watch the fleet coming together, and to hell with any bad feelings and resentment it stirred up in his head. He stood in front of the window, gazing out at the starships clustered round Monterey. There were over a hundred and fifty of them, dwindling away until the more distant ones were nothing more than big stars. Ion thrusters fired microsecond jets of gauzy blue neon to keep their attitude locked. MSVs and personnel commuters swam among them, delivering new crew and combat wasps.

The stealthed mines which the voidhawks from Yosemite had scattered were no more, returning space around New California to a more peaceful state. Even the voidhawks sent to observe the Organization were finding it increasingly difficult to maintain their inspection high above New California's poles.

As if to emphasize the change in local strategic fortunes, a hellhawk hurtled past the Hilton tower, twisting about in complex curves to dodge the stationary Adamist starships. It was one of the harpies, a red-eyed beast with a hundred and eighty metre wingspan and a vicious-looking beak.

Al pressed himself up against the window to watch as it skirred around the asteroid. 'Go, you beaut,' he yelled after it. 'Go get 'em. Go!'

A small puff of pink dust erupted from nowhere as a stealthed spyglobe was masered. The hellhawk performed a victory roll, wing-tip feathers standing proud to twist the solar wind.

'Wow!' Al pulled back from the window, smiling magnanimously. 'Ain't that something else?'

'Glad I can live up to my part of the bargain,' Kiera said with cool objectivity.

'Lady, after this, you got as many fresh bodies as you want for Valisk. Al Capone knows how to reward his friends. And believe me, this is what I call friendly.'

A serene smile ghosted her beautiful young face. 'Thank you, Al.'

The cluster of Organization lieutenants at the rear of the ballroom kept their expressions stoic, while their minds palpitated with jealousy. Al liked that; introduce a new favourite in court, and see how the old-timers bid to prove themselves. He sneaked a look at Kiera's profile; she was wearing a loose-fitting purple blouse and second-skin-tightness trousers, hair tied back with fussy decorum. Her face was beguiling, with its prim features kept firmly under control. But smouldering deep behind it was the old familiar illness of powerlust. She had more class than most, but she wasn't so different.

'How we doing, Luigi?' Al bellowed.

'Pretty good, Al. The hellhawk crews say they should have cleared away every mine and spyglobe in another thirty-two hours. We're pushing those asshole voidhawks back further and further, which means they can't launch any more crap at us. They don't know what we're doing any more, and they can't hurt us so bad. It makes one hell of a difference. The fleet's shaping up a treat now. The guys, they're getting their morale back, you know.'

'Glad to hear it.' Which was an understatement. It had been looking bad for a while, what with the voidhawks launching their unseen weapons and the lieutenants down on the planet abusing their authority to carve themselves out some territory. Funny how all problems locked together. Now the hellhawks had arrived the situation in space was improving by the hour. The crews were no longer living in constant fear of a strike by a stealthed mine, which improved their efficiency and confidence by orders of magnitude. People on the ground sensed the fresh tide above them and wanted to play ball again. The number of beefs was dropping; and the guys Leroy had working the Treasury electric adding machines said fraud was levelling out – not falling yet, but shit you couldn't expect miracles.

'How do you keep the hellhawks in line?' Al asked.

'I can guarantee them human bodies when their work's finished,' Kiera said. 'Bodies which they can go straight into without having to return to the beyond first. They're very special bodies, and you don't have any.'

'Hey.' Al spread his arms wide, puffing out a huge cloud of cigar smoke. 'I wasn't trying to muscle in on you, sister. No way. You got a neat operation. I respect that.'

'Good.'

'We need to talk terms about another squadron. I mean, between you and me, I'm in deep shit over Arnstadt – pardon my French. The goddam voidhawks there are wasting a couple of my ships each day. Something's gotta be done.'

Kiera gave a noncommittal moue. 'And what about this fleet? Won't you need a squadron to protect it from voidhawks at Toi-Hoi?'

Al didn't need to consult Luigi over that one, he could sense the hunger in the fleet commander's mind. 'Now you come to mention it, it might not be a bad idea.'

'I'll see to it,' Kiera said. 'There should be another group of hellhawks returning to Valisk today. If I dispatch a messenger now, they should be back here within twenty-four hours.'

'Sounds pretty damn good to me, lady.'

Kiera raised her walkie-talkie, and pulled a long length of chrome aerial out of it. 'Magahi, would you return to Monterey's docking-ledge, please.'

'Roger,' a crackling voice said from the walkie-talkie. 'Give me twenty minutes.'

Al was aware of an uncomfortable amount of satisfaction in Kiera's mind. She was pretty sure she'd just won something. 'Couldn't you just tell Magahi to go straight back to the habitat?' he enquired lightly.

Kiera's smile widened gracefully. It was the same welcoming promise which had ended the Deadnight recording. 'I don't think so. There's a big security factor if we radio the order; after all there are still some spyglobes out there. I don't want the Edenists to know Magahi is flying escort on a frigate convoy.'

'Escort? What frigates?'

'The frigates carrying the first batch of my antimatter combat wasps to Valisk. That was your part of the bargain, Al, wasn't it?'

Damn the bitch! Al's cigar had gone out. Emmet said their stocks of antimatter were nearly exhausted, and the fleet needed every gram to ensure success at Toi-Hoi. He looked at Leroy, then Luigi. Neither of them could offer him a way out. 'Sure thing, Kiera. We'll get it organized.'

'Thank you, Al.'

Tough little ironass. Al couldn't decide if he respected that or not. He didn't need any more complications right now. But he was awful glad that she was lining up on his side.

He took another sidelong look at her figure. Who knows? We could get to be real close allies. Except Jez would kill me for real . . .

The ballroom's huge double doors swung open to admit Patricia and someone Al had never seen before. A possessed man, who managed to cringe away from Patricia at the same time as he scampered along beside her. Judging by the perilously fragile state of his thoughts he had only just come into his new body.

He saw Al, and made an effort to compose himself. Then his eyes darted to the huge window. His discipline crumpled. 'Holy cow,' he whispered. 'It is true. You are going to invade Toi-Hoi.'

'Who the fuck is this goofball?' Al shouted at Patricia.

'His name's Perez,' she said calmly. 'And you need to listen to him.'

If it had been anyone else who spoke to him like that, they would've been kiboshed. But Patricia was one he really trusted. 'You're shitting me, right?'

'Think what he just said, Al.'

Al did. 'How did you know about Toi-Hoi?' he asked.

'Khanna! I got it from Khanna. She told me to tell you. She

said one of us must get through. Then she killed me. She killed all of us. No, not killed, executed, that's what she did, executed us. Smash smash smash with the white fire. Straight through my brain. That bitch! I'd only been back for five minutes. Five sodding minutes!'

'Who told you, feller? Who's this she you got the beef with?'

'Jacqueline Couteur. Back in Trafalgar. The Confederation Navy got her banged up in the demon trap. I hope she rots there. Bitch.'

Patricia smiled a superior I-told-you-so, which Al acknowledged frugally. He put his arm round Perez's shaking shoulders, and proffered the man a Havana. 'OK, Perez. You got my word, the word of Al Capone, which is the toughest currency of all, that nobody here is gonna send you back into the beyond again. Now, you wanna start at the beginning for me?'

# 28

Earth.

A planet whose ecology was ruined beyond repair; the price it paid for elevating itself to be the Confederation's supreme industrial and economic superpower. Overpopulated, ancient, decadent, and utterly formidable. This was the undeniable imperial heart of the human dominion.

It was also home.

Quinn Dexter admired the images building up on the bridge's holoscreens. This time he could savour them with unhurried joy. Their official Nyvan flight authority code had been accepted by Govcentral Strategic Defence Command. As far as anyone was concerned, they were a harmless ship sent by a tiny government to buy defence components.

'Traffic control has given us a vector,' Dwyer said. 'We have permission to dock at the Supra-Brazil tower station.'

'That's good. Can you fly it?'

'I think so. It's tough, we have to go around the Halo, and they've given us a narrow flight path, but I can handle that.'

Quinn nodded his permission without saying anything. Dwyer had been a perfect pain in the arse for the whole voyage, making out how difficult everything was before the flight computer performed whatever was required with faultless efficiency. An extraordinarily transparent attempt to show how indispensable he was. But then Quinn knew the effect he had on people, it was part of the fun.

Dwyer was immediately busy talking to the flight computer. Icons flurried over the console displays. Eight minutes later they were under power, accelerating at a third of a gee to curve southwards around the O'Neill Halo.

'Are we going down to the planet first?' Dwyer asked. He was growing progressively twitchier in contrast to Quinn's deadly calm. 'I didn't know if you wanted to take over an asteroid.'

'Take over?' Quinn asked faintly.

'Yeah. You know, bring them the gospel of God's Brother. Like we did for Jesup and the other three.'

'No, I don't think so. Earth isn't so arse-backwards as Nyvan, it would never be that simple to convene the Night here. It must be corrupted from within. The sects will help me do that. Once I show them what I've become they'll welcome me back. And of course, my friend Banneth is down there. God's Brother understands.'

'Sure, Quinn, that's good. Whatever you say.' The communication console bleeped for attention, which Dwyer happily gave it. Script flowed down one of the screens, which only amplified his distress as he read it. 'Hell, Quinn, have you seen this?'

'God's Brother gave me a great many gifts, but being psychic wasn't one of them.'

'It's the clearance procedures we have to comply with after we dock. Govcentral security wants to ensure no possessed are on board.'

'Fuck that.'

'Quinn!'

'I do hope, I really fucking do hope that you're not questioning me, Dwyer.'

'Shit, no way, Quinn. You're the man, you know that.' His voice was verging on hysteria.'

'Glad to hear it.'

The Brazilian orbital tower sprouted from the very heart of the South American continent, extending fifty-five thousand kilometres out into space. When it was in Earth's penumbra, as it was when the *Mount's Delta* approached, it was invisible to every visual sensor. However, in other electromagnetic wavelengths, and particularly the magnetic spectrum, it gleamed. A slim golden strand of impossible length, with minute scarlet particles skimming along it at tremendous speed.

There were two asteroids attached to the tower. Supra-Brazil, the anchor, was in geostationary orbit thirty-six thousand kilometres above the ground, where it had been mined to extract the carbon and silicon used in the tower's construction. The second asteroid sat right at the tip, acting as a mass counterbalance to ensure the anchor remained stable, and damp down any dangerous harmonic oscillations in the tower which built up from running the lift capsules.

Because Supra-Brazil was the only section of the tower that was actually in orbit, it was the one place where ships could dock. Unlike every settled asteroid it didn't rotate, nor were there any internal biosphere caverns. The three hundred metre diameter tower ran clean through the rock's centre, its principal structure perfectly black, and perfectly circular. Positioned around the lower segment that stretched down to Earth were twenty-five magnetic rails along which the lift capsules rode, delivering tens of thousands of passengers and up to a hundred thousand tonnes of cargo a day. The other segment, reaching up to the counterbalance, supported a single rail, which was used barely once a month to ferry inspection and maintenance mechanoids to the individual section platforms.

The surface of the asteroid was covered with docking-bays and all the usual spaceport support equipment. After three hundred and eighty-six years of continual operation, and the tower's steady capacity expansion, there wasn't a square metre of rock left visible.

Even with the Confederation quarantine operating, over six thousand ships a day were still using it, the majority of them from the Halo. They approached by positioning themselves ahead of the port, a long ribbon of diverse craft dropping down from a higher orbit. Navigation strobes and secondary drives produced twinkling cataracts of light as they split into a complex braid of traffic lanes a kilometre above the surface to reach their allocated bays. Departing ships formed an equally intricate helical pattern as they rose away into a higher orbit.

*Mount's Delta* slotted into its designated traffic lane, gliding round the vast stem of the tower to dock in the floor of a valley formed by pyramids of heat exchangers, tanks, and thermo-dump panels, three times the size of the Egyptian originals. When the docking cradle had drawn it down into the bottom of the bay, a necklace of lights around the rim came on, illuminating every centimetre of the hull. Figures in black space armour were secured around the bay walls, ready to deal with anyone trying to leave the ship by irregular means.

'Now what?' Quinn asked.

'We have to give the security service total access to our flight computer. They're going to run a complete diagnostic to make sure there aren't any unexplained glitches anywhere in the ship. They'll also monitor us through the internal sensors at the same time. Once they're satisfied there's no glitch we're allowed out into the bay. We have to undergo a whole series of tests, including datavises from our neural nanonics. Quinn, we haven't got any bloody neural nanonics, and a starship's crew always have them fitted. Always!'

'I told you,' Quinn's hollow voice said from deep within his hood, 'I will deal with it. What else?'

Dwyer gave the display a wretched stare. 'Once we've been cleared we're put in a secure holding area while the ship is searched by an armed security team. After it's cleared, we will be allowed out.'

'I'm impressed.'

Dwyer's communication console was showing a demand from the port's security service to access the flight computer. 'What do we do?' he shrieked. 'We can't fly away, we can't comply. We're trapped. They'll storm us. They'll have projectile weapons we can't beat. Or they'll rip the capsule bulkhead open and decompress us. Or electrocute us with—'

'You're trapped.' It was only a tiny whisper, but it stopped Dwyer's rant dead.

'You can't! Quinn, I did everything you asked. Everything! I'm loyal. I've always been fucking loyal to you.'

Quinn extended an arm, a single white finger emerging from the end of his black sleeve.

Dwyer threw out both hands. White fire screamed out of his palms to lash at the black-robed incarnation of Death. Bridge consoles flickered madly as corkscrews of pale flame bounced off Quinn, flashing through the air to bury themselves in bulkheads and equipment.

'Finished?' Quinn asked.

Dwyer was sobbing.

'You're weak. I like that. It means you'll serve me well. I will find you again, and use you.'

Dwyer evacuated his stolen body just before the first burn of pain smashed along his spinal cord.

*

The security team assigned to the *Mount's Delta* knew something was wrong as soon as the starship docked. Its routine datavises began to drop out for seconds at a time. When the bay's management officer tried to contact the captain there was no reply. A level one alert was declared.

The docking-bay and its immediate surroundings were sealed up and isolated from the rest of Supra-Brazil. One squad of combat officers and another of technical experts were rushed to the docking-bay to complement the original team. Communication lines were opened to an advisory panel made up from senior commanders in the Govcentral Internal Security Directorate and the Strategic-Defence Force.

Four minutes after it docked, the *Clipper*-class starship's datavises had returned to normal, but there was still no response from the captain nor any other member of crew. The security advisory panel authorized the team to go to the next stage.

A datalink umbilical jacked into a socket on the starship's hull. The GISD's most powerful decryption computers were brought on-line to crack the flight computer's access codes; it took less than thirty seconds. The nature of the bridge's modified processors and programs was obvious: customized to be run by possessed. Almost simultaneously, the sensors began relaying their images from the interior of the small life-support capsule. There was nobody inside. However, there was one anomaly whose cause wasn't immediately apparent. A thick red paste was splashed across almost every surface in the bridge. Then an eyeball drifted past one of the sensors, and that mystery was solved – leaving a bigger paradox. The blood hadn't yet congealed, some one or thing on board had slaughtered the crew-member only minutes ago. GISD could not permit an unknown threat to remain at large; if the possessed had developed a fresh method of attack it had to be investigated.

An airlock tube extended out from the side of the bay. After arming themselves with chemical explosive fragmentation grenades and sub-machine-guns, five GISD combat officers advanced through it to the life-support capsule. Each of them encountered a small squall of cold air in the tube as they pulled themselves along, it was barely noticeable through their armour.

Once inside, they opened every storage locker and cabinet to try to locate the missing crew-members. There was nobody to be found. Even the flight computer confirmed no atmosphere was being consumed.

An engineering crew from the port was sent in, and started to strip down the life-support capsule. It took them six hours to remove every single fitting, including the decking. The advisory council was left with an empty sphere seven metres in diameter with severed cables and hoses poking through sealed inlets. A meticulous examination of the flight computer records, evaluating power consumption, command interfaces, fuel expenditure, and utilities usage showed that there must have been two people on board when the *Mount's Delta* docked. But DNA analysis on the blood and tissue smearing the bridge showed it had all come from one body.

The *Mount's Delta* was powered down, and its cryogenic tanks emptied. Then the entire ship was slowly and methodically cut up into sections, from the support framework to the fusion generators, even the energy patterning nodes. No unit or module bigger than a cubic metre was left intact.

The media, of course, soon discovered the 'ghost flight' from Nyvan; and rover reporters swarmed around the bay, demanding and bribing information from anyone they could find connected to the security operation. It wasn't long before they managed to gain legal access to a sensor in the bay itself thanks to two judges whose motives were somewhat financially inclined. Several tens of millions of people in Earth's arcologies started accessing the investigation directly, watching the starship being cut up by mechanoids, and waiting eagerly for a possessed to be captured.

*

Quinn saw no reason to stay inside the dry deprivation of the ghost realm once he had passed unseen through all the security checks; so he rematerialized and sat in a luxurious active contour leather seat in the lift capsule's Royale Class lounge. He was near one of the panoramic windows, which would allow him to watch the dawn rise over South America as he descended vertically towards it at three thousand kilometres an hour. With his hawkish, stressed face, and expensively conservative blue silk suit, he slotted perfectly into the character of an aristocratic businessman.

For the last quarter of the journey down the tower he sipped his complimentary Norfolk Tears, which was continually topped up by a stewardess, and gave the AV projector above the cocktail bar an occasional glance. Earth's media companies competed enthusiastically to update him on the progress of the search through the dissected components of the *Mount's Delta*. If the rest of the lounge wondered at his intermittent guffaws of contempt, Earth's obsessive cult of personal privacy forbade them from enquiring as to the reason.

\*

Jed spent most of the voyage sitting on the pine floorboards in the *Mindori*'s lounge, gazing out at the starfield. There had never been a time in his life when he felt more content. The stars themselves were beautiful seen like this, and every now and then the hellhawk would swallow through a wormhole. That was exciting, even though there wasn't much to see then, just a kind of dark-grey fog swirling round outside that was never quite in focus. Coupled with the sense of invulnerability generated by riding in the hellhawk was the anticipation of Valisk. Never stronger than now.

I did it. For the first time in my life I set myself a solid goal and saw it through. Against some pretty nasty odds, too. Me and all the other kids from nowhere, we made it to Valisk. And Kiera.

He had brought his modified recording of her, although he no longer needed it. Every time he closed his eyes he could see that smile, thick soft hair falling over her bare shoulders, perfectly rounded cheeks. She would congratulate him personally when they arrived. She must do, because he was the leader. So they would probably get to talk, because she'd want to know how difficult it was for them, how they had struggled. She would be sympathetic, because that was her nature. Then perhaps—

Gari and Navar bounded into the lounge, laughing happily together. Some kind of truce had been declared since they came on board. A minor omen, Jed thought, things were steadily getting better.

'What are you doing?' Gari asked.

He grinned up at her, and gestured to the window with its thick rim of brass. 'Just looking. So what are you two doing?'

'We came to tell you. We just talked to Choi-Ho. She says this is the last swallow before we get to Valisk. Another hour, Jed!' Her face rose with elation.

'Yeah, another hour.' He snatched another glance at the alien greyness outside. Any minute now they'd be back in real space. Then he realized Beth wasn't here to witness their triumph. 'Back in a minute,' he told the two girls.

The *Mindori* was quite crowded now. The rendezvous in the Kabwe system had brought another twenty-five Deadnights on board. Everyone was doubling up in the cabins. He walked right to the end of the main corridor, where the light was slightly darker. 'Beth?' He gave her cabin door a fast knock and turned the handle. 'Come on, girl, we're almost there. You'll miss the—'

Both of Beth's jackets and her lace-up boots were lying on the floor, looking like they'd just been flung there. Beth herself was stirring on the bed, a skinny hand clawing lank strands of hair away from her face as she peered round blearily. Gerald Skibbow was next to her, sound asleep.

Indignation and pure anger made it impossible for Jed to move.

'What is it?' Beth grunted.

Jed couldn't believe it; she didn't display the slightest hint of shame. Skibbow was old enough to be her bloody great-grandfather! He glared at her, then stomped out, slamming the door loudly behind him.

Beth stared after him, her puzzled thoughts slowly slotting together. 'Oh, Jeeze, you've got to be bloody joking,' she groaned. Not even Jed was that stupid. Surely? She swung her legs out from under the duvet, taking care not to pull it off Gerald. It had taken her hours to get him to sleep. Holding him, reassuring him.

Despite her best efforts, she did dislodge the cover. The fabric seemed to stick to her jeans, and her sweatshirt was all twisted round, making every movement difficult.

Gerald Skibbow woke with a cry, looking round fearfully. 'Where are we?'

'I don't know, Gerald,' she said as calmly as she could. 'I'll go find out, then I'll bring you back some breakfast. OK, mate?'

'Yes. Um, I think so.'

'You go slip into the shower. Leave everything else to me.' Beth laced her boots up then retrieved one of her jackets from the floor. She gave the inside pocket a determined pat to make sure the nervejam was there before she left the cabin.

\*

Rocio Condra sensed the voidhawks waiting before he even started to emerge from the wormhole terminus. Seven of them, spiralling slowly around the point where he expected Valisk to be.

The terminus closed behind him, and he spread his wings wide, letting the thin streamers of solar ions gust against the feathers. All he did was glide along his orbital path while he tried to understand. Confusion was almost total. At first he thought he might even have emerged above the wrong gas giant, however unlikely that was. But no, this was Opuntia, its system of moons easily distinguishable. He could even feel the mass of Valisk's wrecked industrial stations in their proper coordinate. The only thing missing was the habitat itself.

**What has happened to Valisk?** he asked his erstwhile enemies. **Did you destroy it?**

**Obviously not,** one of the voidhawks replied. **There is no debris. Surely you can sense that?**

**I can sense that. But I don't understand.**

**Rubra and Dariat finally settled their differences, and merged. The entire neural strata became possessed, creating an enormously powerful reality dysfunction. Valisk left the universe, taking everyone inside with it.**

**No!**

**I am not lying to you.**

**My body is inside.** Even as he protested, he knew he wasn't really bothered. The decision he had been nerving himself up to make had been taken for him. He allowed energy to flow through his patterning cells, exerting pressure on a particular point in space.

**Wait,** the voidhawk called. **You have nowhere to go to. We can help, we want to help.**

**Me, join your culture? I don't think so.**

**You have to ingest nutrients to sustain yourself. You know that, even the possessed have to eat. Only habitats can provide you with the correct fluids.**

**So can most asteroid settlements.**

**But how long will the production machinery function when the settlement becomes possessed? You know they have no interest in such matters.**

**One of them does.**

**Capone? He will send you to fight to earn your food. How long will you last? Two battles? Three? With us you will be safe.**

**There are other tasks I can perform.**

**For what purpose? Now Valisk has gone, you have no human body into which you can return. They cannot reward you, only threaten.**

**How do you know that was promised to us?**

**From Dariat; he told us everything. Join us. Your assistance would be invaluable.**

**Assistance for what?**

**Finding a solution to this whole crisis.**

**I have solved it for myself.** Energy flashed through the cells, forcing an interstice open. The wormhole's non-length deepened to accept his bulk.

**The offer remains,** the voidhawk proclaimed. **Consider it. Come back to us at any time.**

Rocio Condra closed the interstice behind his tail. His mind instinctively retrieved the coordinate for New California from the *Mindori*'s infallible memory. He would see what Capone had to offer before making any hasty decisions. And the other hellhawks would be there; whatever final choice they made, they would make it together.

After he explained what had happened to Choi-Ho and Maxim Payne, they agreed not to burden the Deadnights with the knowledge that their false dream had ceased to be.

*

Jay peeled the gold insulating wrapper off her chocolate and almond lolly; it was her fifth that morning. She lay back happily on her towel and started licking the nuts off the lolly's surface. The beach was such a lovely place, and her new friend made it just about perfect.

'Sure you don't want one?' she asked. There were several more lollies scattered over the warm sand; she had stuffed her bag full of them when she left the paediatric ward that morning.

**No, with many thanks,** Haile said. **Coldness makes me sneeze. The chocolate tastes like raw sugar with much additional acid.**

Jay giggled. 'That's mad. Everyone likes chocolate.'

**Not I.**

She bit off a huge chunk and let it slither round her tongue. 'What do you like?'

**Lemon is acceptable. But I am still milking from my parent.**

'Oh, right. I keep forgetting how young you are. Do you eat solid stuff when you're older?'

**Yes. In many months away.**

Jay smiled at the wistfulness carried by the mental voice.

She had often felt the same at her mother's rules; restrictions designed purely to stop her enjoying herself. 'Do your parents all go out for fancy meals and things in the evening like we do? Are there Kiint restaurants?'

**Not here in the all around. I know not exactly about our home.**

'I'd love to see your home planet. It must be super, like the arcologies but clean and silver, with huge towers built right up into the sky. You're so advanced.'

**Some of our worlds have that form,** Haile said with cautious uncertainty. **I believe. Racial history cosmology educationals have not fully begun yet.**

'That's OK.' Jay finished the lolly. 'Gosh, that's lovely,' she mumbled round the freezing mouthful. 'I didn't have any ice cream the whole time I was on Lalonde. Can you imagine that!'

**You should ingest properly balanced dietary substances. Ione Saldana says too much niceness is bad for you. Query correctness?**

'Completely wrong.' Jay sat up and tossed the lolly stick into her bag. 'Oh, Haile, that's wonderful!' She scrambled to her feet and ran over to the baby Kiint. Haile's tractamorphic arms were withdrawing from the sandcastle like a nest of snakes that had been routed. She'd built a central tapering tower two and a half metres tall, surrounded by five smaller matching pinnacles; elaborate arching fairy bridges linked them all together. There were turrets leaning out of the sides at cockeyed angles, rings of pink shell windows, and a solid fortress wall with a deep moat round the outside.

'Best yet.' Jay stroked the Kiint's facial ridge just above the breathing vents. Haile shivered in gratitude, big violet eyes looked directly into Jay.

**I like, muchness.**

'We should build something from your history,' Jay said generously.

**I have no intricacy to contribute, only home domes,** the Kiint said sadly. **Our full past has not been made available. I must do much growth before I am ready for acceptance.**

Jay put her arms round the Kiint's neck, pressing up against her supple white hide. 'That's all right. There are lots of things Mummy and Father Horst wouldn't tell me, either.'

**Much regret. Little patience.**

'That's a shame. But the castle looks great now it's finished. I wish we had some flags to stick on top. I'll see what I can find to use for tomorrow.'

**Tomorrow the sand will be dry. The top will crumble in air, and we must start again.**

Jay looked along the row of shapeless mounds that now ran along the shoreline. Each one carried its own particular memory of joy and satisfaction. 'Honestly, Haile, that's the whole point. It's even better when there's a tide, then you can see how strong you've built.'

**So much human activity is intentionally wasteful. I doubt my ever knowing you.**

'We're simple, really. We always learn more from our mistakes, that's what Mummy says. It's because they're more painful.'

**Much oddness.**

'I've got an idea; we'll try and build a Tyrathca tower tomorrow. That's nice and different. I know what they look like, Kelly showed me.' She put her hands on her hips, and considered the castle warmly. 'Pity we can't build their Sleeping God altar or whatever it was, but I don't think it would balance, not if you make it out of sand.'

**Query Sleeping God altar or whatever?**

'It was sort of like a temple that you couldn't get inside. The Tyrathca on Lalonde all sat round it and worshipped with chanting and stuff. It was this shape, really elaborate.' Her hands swept through the air in front of the Kiint, tracing broad curves. 'See?'

**Lacking perception, I. This is worship like your ritual to support Jesus the Christ?**

'Um, sort of, I suppose. Except their god isn't our god.

Theirs is sleeping somewhere far away in space; ours is everywhere. That's what Father Horst says.'

**There are two gods, query?**

'I don't know,' Jay said, desperately wishing she hadn't got on to this topic. 'Humans have more than two gods, anyway. Religion is funny, especially if you start thinking about it. You're just sort of supposed to believe. Until you get old, that is, then it all becomes theology.'

**Query theology?**

'Grown-up religion. Look here, don't you have a god?'

**I will query my parents.**

'Good; they'll explain everything much better than me. Come on, let's go and wash this horrid sand off, then we can go riding together.'

**Much welcome.**

\*

The Royal Kulu Navy ion-field flyer swept in over Mortonridge's western seaboard, its glowing nose pointed directly at the early morning sun. Ten kilometres to the south the red cloud formed a solid massif right across the horizon. It was thicker than Ralph Hiltch remembered. None of the peninsula's central ridge of mountains had managed to rise above it, they'd been swallowed whole.

The upper surface was as calm as a lake during a breathless dawn. Only when it started to dip earthwards along the firebreak border were the first uneasy stirrings visible, while right on the edge there appeared to be a full-scale storm whipping up individual streamers. Ralph had the uncomfortable impression than the cloud was aching to be let free. Perhaps he was picking up the emotional timbre of the possessed who created it? In this situation he could never be quite sure that any feeling was the genuine article.

He thought he could see a loose knot swirling along the side of the cloud, a twist of vermilion shadow amid the scarlet, keeping pace with his flyer. But when he ordered the sensor suite to focus on it, all he could see were random patterns. A trick of the eye, then, but a strong one.

The pilot began to expand the ion field, reducing the flyer's velocity and altitude. Up ahead, the grey line of the M6 was visible, slicing clean across the virgin countryside. Colonel Palmer's advance camp was situated a couple of kilometres outside the black firebreak line. Several dozen military vehicles were drawn up along the side of the motorway, while a couple were speeding along the carbon concrete towards the unnervingly precise band of incinerated vegetation.

Any possessed marching up to the end of the red cloud would see a predictably standard garrison operation being mounted with the Kingdom's usual healthy efficiency. What they couldn't see was the new camp coming together twenty-five kilometres further to the north; a city of programmable silicon laid out in strict formation which was erupting across the endless green undulations of the peninsula's landscape. With typical military literalism it had been named Fort Forward. Over five hundred programmable silicon buildings had already been activated, two-storey barracks, warehouses, mess halls, maintenance shops, and various ancillary structures; though as yet its only residents were the three battalions of Royal Kulu Marine Engineers whose job it was to assemble the camp. Their mechanoids had ploughed the ground up around each building, installing water and sewage pipes, power lines, and datalinks. Huge drums of micro-mesh composite were being unrolled over the fresh soil to provide roads that wouldn't turn to instant quagmires. Five large filter pump houses had been established on the banks of a river eight kilometres away to feed the expanding districts.

Mechanoids were already busy digging out vast new utility grids ready for more buildings, giving an indication of just how big Fort Forward would be when it was completed. Long convoys of lorries were using the M6 to deliver matériel from the nearest city spaceport, fifty kilometres away, though that arrangement would soon be cancelled as Fort Forward's own spaceport became operational. Marine Engineers were levelling long strips of land in preparation for three prefabricated runways. The spaceport's hangars and control tower had been activated two days before so that technical crews could fit and integrate their systems.

When Ralph's battleship emerged above Ombey he had seen nine Royal Navy *Aquilae*-class bulk-transport starships in parking formation around a low-orbit port station along with their escort of fifteen front-line frigates. There were only twenty-five of the huge transporters left on active service: capable of carrying seventeen thousand tonnes of cargo they were the largest starships ever built, and hugely expensive to fly and maintain. Kulu was gradually phasing them out in favour of smaller models based on commercial designs.

They were being supported by big old delta-wing CK500-090 *Thunderbird* spaceplanes, the only atmospheric craft capable of handling the four hundred tonne cargo-pods carried by the *Aquilae* transporters. Again, a fleet on the verge of retirement; they had been the first consignment ferried to Ombey by the transports. Most of the *Thunderbird*s had spent the last fifteen years in mothball status at the Royal Navy's desert storage facility on Kulu. Now they were being reactivated as fast as the maintenance crews could fit new components from badly depleted war stocks.

Even more portentous than the build-up of navy ships were the voidhawks. Nearly eighty had arrived so far, with new ones swallowing in every hour, their lower hull cargo cradles full of pods (which could be handled by conventional civil flyers). Never before had so many of the bitek starships been seen orbiting a Kingdom world.

Ralph had experienced the same kind of uncomfortable awe he'd known at Azara as he observed them flitting around the docking stations. He was the one who had started this, creating a momentum which had engulfed entire star systems. It was unstoppable now. All he could do was ride it to a conclusion.

The ion-field flyer landed at Colonel Palmer's camp. The Colonel herself was waiting for him at the base of the airstair; Dean Folan and Will Danza were prominent in the small reception committee behind her, both grinning broadly.

Colonel Palmer shook his hand, giving his new uniform a more than casual inspection. 'Welcome back, Ralph, or should I say sir?'

He wasn't completely used to the uniform himself yet, a smart dark-blue tunic with three ruby pips glinting on his shoulder. 'I don't know, exactly. I'm a general in the official Liberation campaign army now, its very first officer. Apart from the King, of course. The formation was made official three days ago, announced in the court of the Apollo Palace. I've been appointed Chief Strategic Coordination Officer.'

'You mean you're the Liberation's numero uno?'

'Yeah,' he said with quiet surprise. 'I guess I am at this end.'

'Rather you than me.' She gestured northwards. 'Talk about coming back with reinforcements.'

'It's going to get wonderfully worse. Half a million bitek serjeants are on their way, and God alone knows how many human troops to back them up. We've even had mercenaries volunteering.'

'You accepted them?'

'I've no idea. But I'll use whatever I'm given.'

'All right, so what are your orders, sir?'

He laughed. 'Just keep up the good work. Have any of them tried to break out?'

She turned her head to face the wall of angry cloud, her expression stern. 'No. They stick to their side of the firebreak. There have been plenty of sightings. We think they're keeping an eye on us. But it's only my patrols who are visible to them.' A thumb jabbed back over her shoulder. 'They don't know anything about all this.'

'Good. We can't keep it secret for ever, of course; but the longer the better.'

'Some kids came out last week. It was the first interesting thing to happen since you left.'

'Kids?'

'A woman called Stephanie Ash bussed seventy-three non-possessed children right up to the firebreak. Gave the roadblock guard a hell of a fright, I can tell you. Apparently she'd collected them from all over the peninsula. We evacuated them to a holding camp. I think your friend Jannike Dermot has got her experts debriefing them on conditions over there.'

'Now that's a report I'd like to access.' He squinted at the red cloud. That elusive knot of shadow seemed to have returned, it was elliptical this time, hanging over the M6. It didn't take much imagination to suspect it of staring at him. 'I think I'll take a closer look before I set up my command at Fort Forward,' he announced.

Will and Dean rode shotgun on the Marine Corps runabout which took him up to the orange roadblock. It was good to talk with them again, they'd been attached to Palmer's brigade as combat liaison for the agency, supporting the various technical teams Roche Skark had dispatched to the firebreak. Both of them wanted to know every detail of his meetings with the King. They were annoyed he wouldn't datavise his visual files of Prince Edward playing at the Apollo Palace, but they were confidential. And so grows the mystique, Ralph thought, amused that he should be contributing to it.

The Marines at the roadblock saluted smartly as Ralph and the Colonel arrived. Ralph chatted to them as cordially as he could manage. They didn't seem to mind the red cloud; he found it intimidating in the extreme. It loomed barely three hundred metres above him, vigorous thrashing streamers packed so close together there was no gap between them, layer upon layer stacked up to what seemed like the edge of space.

The sonorous reverberations from its internal brawling were diabolically attuned to the harmonic of human bones. Millions of tonnes of contaminated water hanging suspended in the air by witchcraft, ready to crash down like the waterfall at the end of the world. He wondered how little effort on behalf of the possessed it would take to do just that. Could it be he really had underestimated their power? It wasn't the scale of the cloud which perturbed him so much as the intent.

'Sir!' one of the barrier guards shouted in alarm. 'Visible hostile, on foot, three hundred metres.'

Dean and Will were abruptly standing in front of Ralph, their gaussguns pointing across the firebreak.

'I think this is enough front-line inspection for today,' Colonel Palmer said. 'Let's get you back to the runabout, please, Ralph.'

'Wait.' Ralph looked between the two G66 troopers to see a single figure walking up the M6. A woman dressed in a neatly cut leather uniform, her face stained warrior-scarlet by the nimbus of the seething clouds. He knew exactly who it was, in fact he would almost have been disappointed if she hadn't appeared. 'She's not a threat. Not yet, anyway.'

He slipped between Will and Dean to stand full square in the middle of the road, facing her down.

Annette Ekelund stopped at the forward barrier on her side of the firebreak. She took a slim mobile phone from her pocket, extended its ten centimetre aerial, then tapped in a number.

Ralph's communication block announced a channel opening. He switched it to audio function.

'Hello, Ralph. I thought you would come back, you're the kind that does. And I see you've brought some friends with you.'

'That's right.'

'Why don't you bring them on over and join the party?'

'We'll pick our own time.'

'I have to say I'm disappointed; that's not quite what we agreed back in Exnall, now is it. And with a Saldana princess, too. Dear me, you can't trust anyone these days.'

'A promise made under duress is not legally binding. I'm sure you'll have enough lawyers on your side to confirm that.'

'I thought I explained all this to you, Ralph. We can't lose, not against the living.'

'I don't believe you. No matter what the cost, we must defeat you. The human race will end if you are allowed to win. I believe we deserve to keep on going.'

'You and your ideals; the original Mr Focused. No wonder you found a profession which allowed you to give loyal service. It suits you perfectly. Congratulations, Ralph, you have found yourself, not everyone can say that. In another universe, one that isn't so warped as this, I'd envy you.'

'Thank you.'

'There was a nasty little phrase coined in my era, Ralph; but it's still appropriate today, because it too came from a dogmatic soldier in a pointless war. *We had to destroy the village in order to save it.* What do you think you're going to do to Mortonridge and its people with this crusade of yours?'

'Whatever I have to.'

'But we'll still be here afterwards, Ralph, we'll always be here. The finest minds in the galaxy have been working on this problem. Scientists and priests scurrying for hard answers and bland philosophies. Millions – billions – of man-hours have already been spent on the quandary of what to do with us poor returned souls. And they've come up with nothing. Nothing! All you can do is mount this pathetic, vindictive campaign of violence in the hope that some of us will be caught and thrown into zero-tau.'

'There isn't an overall solution yet. But there will be.'

'There can't be. We outnumber you. It's simple arithmetic, Ralph.'

'Laton said it can be done.'

She chuckled. 'And you believe him?'

'The Edenists think he was telling the truth.'

'Oh, yes, the newest and most interesting of all your friends. You realize, don't you, that they could well survive this while you Adamists fall? It's in their interest for this monstrous diversion to work. Adamist planets will topple one by one while your Confederation is engrossed here.'

'And what about the Kiint?'

There was a slight pause. 'What about them?'

'They survived their encounter with the beyond. They say there is a solution.'

'Which is?'

He gripped the communication block tighter. 'It doesn't apply to us. Each race must find its own way. Ours exists, somewhere. It will be found. I have a lot of faith in human ingenuity.'

'I don't, Ralph. I have faith in our sick nature to hate and envy, to be greedy and selfish, to lie. You forget, for six centuries I couldn't hide from the naked emotions which drive all of us. I was condemned to them, Ralph. I know exactly what we are in our true hearts, and it's not nice, not nice at all.'

'Tell that to Stephanie Ash. You don't speak for all the possessed, not even a majority.'

Her stance changed. She no longer leaned casually on the barrier but stood up straight, her head thrust forward challengingly. 'You'll lose, Ralph, one way or the other. You, personally, will lose. You cannot fight entropy.'

'I wish your faith wasn't so misdirected. Think what you could achieve if you tried to help us instead.'

'Stay away from us, Ralph. That's what I really came here to tell you. One simple message: *Stay away.*'

'You know I can't.'

Annette Ekelund nodded sharply. She pushed the phone's aerial back in, and closed the little unit up.

Ralph watched her walk back down the M6 with a degree of

sorrow he hadn't expected. Shadows cavorted around her, hoaxing with her silhouette before swallowing her altogether.

'Ye gods,' Colonel Palmer muttered.

'That's what we're up against,' Ralph said.

'Are you sure half a million serjeants is going to be enough?'

Ralph didn't get to answer. The discordant bellows of thunder merged together into a continuous roar.

Everyone looked up to see the edge of the red cloud descending. It was as if the strength of the possessed had finally waned, allowing the colossal weight of water to crash down. Torrents of gaudy vapour plunged out of the main bank, hurtling earthwards faster than mere gravity could account for.

Along with the others, Ralph sprinted away from the roadblock, neural nanonics compelled a huge energy release from his muscle tissue, increasing his speed. Animal fear was pounding on his consciousness to turn and fire his TIP pistol at the virulent cascade.

His neural nanonics received a plethora of datavises from SD Command on Guyana. Low-orbit observation satellites were tracking them. Reports from patrols and sensors positioned along the firebreak: the whole front of cloud was moving.

'SD platforms are now at ready one status,' Admiral Farquar datavised.

'Do you want us to counterstrike? We can slice that bastard apart.'

'It's stopping,' Will yelled.

Ralph risked a glance over his shoulder. 'Wait,' he datavised to the Admiral. A hundred and fifty metres behind him, the base of the cloud had reached the ground, waves rebounding in all directions to furrow the surface. But the bulk of it was holding steady, not advancing. Even the thunder was muffled.

'They are not aggressing, repeat *not*, aggressing,' Ralph datavised. 'It looks like ... hell, it looks as though they've slammed the door shut. Can you confirm the situation along the rest of the firebreak?'

When he looked from side to side, the cloud was clinging to the scorched soil as far as his enhanced retinas could see. A single, simple barrier that curved back gently until it reached an apex at about three kilometres high. In a way it was worse than before; without the gap this was so uncompromisingly final.

'Confirm that,' Admiral Farquar datavised. 'It's closed up right the way along the firebreak. The coastline edges are lowering, too.'

'Great,' Colonel Palmer swore. 'Now what?'

'It's a psychological barrier, that's all,' Ralph said quietly. 'After all, it's only water. This changes nothing.'

Colonel Palmer slowly tilted her head back, scanning the height of the quivering fluorescent precipice. She shivered. 'Some psychology.'

\*

Ione.

A chaotic moan fluttered out between her lips. She was sprawled on her bed, sliding quietly into sleep. In her drowsy state, the pillow she was cuddling could so easily have been Joshua. **Oh, now what, for Heaven's sake? Can't I even dream my fantasies any more?**

**I am sorry to disturb you, but there is an interesting situation developing concerning the Kiint.**

She sat up slowly, feeling stubbornly grumpy despite Tranquillity's best efforts to emphasize its tender concern. It had been a long day, with Meredith's squadron to deal with on top of all her normal duties. And the loneliness was starting to get to her, too. **It's all right.** She scratched irritably at her hair. **Being pregnant is making me feel dreadfully randy. You're just going to have to put up with me being like this for another eight months. Then you'll have post-natal depression to cope with.**

**You have many lovers to choose from. Go to one. I want you to feel better. I do not like it when you are so troubled.**

That's a very cold solution. If getting physical was all it took, I'd just swallow an antidote pill instead.

From what I observe, most human sex is a cold activity. There is an awful lot of selfishness involved.

Ninety per cent of it is. But we put up with that because we're always looking for the other ten per cent.

And you believe Joshua is your ten per cent?

Joshua is floating somewhere between the ninety and the ten. I just want him right now because my hormones are completely out of control.

Hormonal production does not usually peak until the later months of a pregnancy.

I always was an early developer. A swift thought directed at the opaqued window allowed a dappled aquamarine light into the bedroom. She reached lethargically for her robe. All right, self-pity hour over. Let's see what our mysterious Kiint are up to. And God help you if it isn't important.

Lieria has taken a tube carriage to the StClément starscraper.

So bloody what?

It is not an action which any Kiint has performed before. I have to consider it significant, especially at this time.

*

Kelly Tirrel hated being interrupted while she was running her Present Time Reality programs. It was an activity she was indulging more often these days.

Some of the black programs she had bought were selective memory blockers, modified from medical trauma erasure programs, slithering deep into her natural brain tissue to cauterize her subconscious. They should have been used under supervision, and it certainly wasn't healthy to suppress the amount of memory she was targeting, nor for as long. Others amplified her emotional response to perceptual stimuli, making the real world slow and mundane in comparison.

One of the pushers she'd met while she was making a

documentary last year had shown her how to interface black programs with standard commercial sensenvirons to produce PTRs. Such integrations were supposedly the most addictive stim you could run. Compulsive because they were the zenith of denial. Escape to an alternative personality living in an alternative reality, where your past with all its inhibitions had been completely divorced, allowing only the present to prevail. Living for the now, yet stretching that now out for hours.

In the realms through which Kelly moved, possession and the beyond were concepts which did not, nor could ever, exist. When she did emerge, to eat, or pee, or sleep, the real world was the one which seemed unreal; terribly harsh by comparison to the hedonistic existence she had on the other side of the electronic divide.

This time when she exited the PTR she couldn't even recognize the signal her neural nanonics were receiving. Memories of such things were submerged deep in her brain, rising to conscious levels with the greatest of reluctance (and taking longer each time). It was a few moments before she even understood where she was, that this wasn't hell but simply her apartment. The lights off, the window opaqued, the sheet on which she was lying disgustingly damp, and stinking of urine, the floor littered with disposable bowls.

Kelly wanted to plunge straight back into her electronic refuge. She was losing her grip on her old personality, and didn't give a fuck. The only thing she did monitor was her own decay; overriding fear saw to that.

I will *not* allow myself to die.

No matter how badly the black stimulant programs screwed up her neurons, she wouldn't permit herself to go completely over the edge, not physically. Before that would be zero-tau. The wonderful simplicity of eternal oblivion.

And until then, her brain would live a charmed life, providing pleasure and excitement, and not even knowing it was artificial. Life was to be enjoyed, was it not? Now she knew the truth about death, how did it matter how that enjoyment was achieved?

Her brain finally identified the signal from the apartment's net processor. Someone was at the door, requesting admission. Confusion replaced her dazed resentful stupor. Collins hadn't called on her to present a show for a week (or possibly longer); not since her interview with Tranquillity's bishop when she shouted at him, angry about how cruel his God was to inflict the beyond upon unsuspecting souls.

The signal repeated. Kelly sat up, and promptly vomited down the side of the bed. Nausea swirled inside her brain, shaking her thoughts and memories into a collage which was the exact opposite of the PTR: Lalonde in all its infernal glory. She coughed as her pale limbs trembled and the scar along her ribs flamed. There was a glass on the bedside table, half full of a clear liquid which she fervently hoped was water. Her shaking hand grabbed at it, spilling a quantity before she managed to jam it to her lips and swallow. At least she didn't throw it all back up.

Almost suffocating in misery she struggled off the bed and pulled a blanket around her shoulders. Her neural nanonics medical program cautioned her that her blood sugar level was badly depleted and she was on the verge of dehydration. She cancelled it. The admission request was repeated again.

'Piss off,' she mumbled. Light seemed to be shining straight through her eye sockets to scorch her fragile brain. Sucking down air, she tried to work out why her neural nanonics had stopped running the PTR program. It shouldn't happen just because someone datavised her apartment's net processor. Perhaps the slender filaments meshed with her synaptic clefts were getting screwed by her disturbed body chemistry?

'Who is it?' she datavised as she tottered unsteadily through into the main lounge.

'Lieria.'

Kelly didn't know any Lieria; at least not without running a memory cell check. She slumped down into one of her deep recliners, pulled the blanket over her legs, and datavised the door processor to unlock.

An adult Kiint was standing in the vestibule. Kelly blinked against the light which poured in around its snow-white body, gawped, then started laughing. She'd done it, she'd totally fucked her brain with the PTR.

Lieria lowered herself slightly, and moved into the lounge, taking care not to knock any of the furniture. She had to wriggle to fit the major section of her body through the door, but she managed it. An intensely curious group of residents peered in behind her.

The door slid shut. Kelly hadn't ordered it to do that. Her laughter had stopped, and her shakes were threatening to return. This was actually happening. She wanted to go back into the PTR real bad now.

Lieria took up nearly a fifth of the lounge, both tracta-morphic arms were withdrawn into large bulbs of flesh, her triangular head was swinging slightly from side to side as her huge eyes examined the room. No housechimp had been in for weeks to clean up; dust was accumulating; the door to the kitchen was open, showing worktops overflowing with empty food sachets; a loose pile of underwear decorated one corner; her desk was scattered with fleks and processor blocks. The Kiint returned her gaze to Kelly, who curled her limbs up tighter in the recliner.

'H . . . how did you get down here?' was all Kelly could ask.

'I took the service lift,' Lieria datavised back. 'It was very cramped.'

Kelly started. 'I didn't know you could do that.'

'Use a lift?'

'Datavise.'

'We have some command of technology.'

'Oh. Yes. It's just ... skip it.' Her reporter's training began to assert itself. A private visit from a Kiint was unheard of. 'Is this confidential?'

Lieria's breathing vents whistled heavily. 'You decide, Kelly Tirrel. Do you wish your public to know what has become of you?'

Kelly stiffened her facial muscles, whether to combat tears or shame she wasn't sure. 'No.'

'I understand. Knowledge of the beyond can be disturbing.'

'How did you beat it? Tell me, please. For pity's sake. I can't be trapped there. I couldn't stand it!'

'I am sorry. I cannot discuss this with you.'

Kelly's cough had come back. She used the back of her hand to wipe her eyes dry. 'What do you want, then?'

'I wish to purchase information. Your sensevises of Lalonde.'

'My ... why?'

'They are of interest to us.'

'Sure. I'll sell them. The price is knowing how to avoid the beyond.'

'Kelly Tirrel, you cannot buy that, the answer is inside you.'

'Stop being so fucking obtuse!' she shouted, fury surmounting her consternation of the big xenoc.

'It is the profound wish of my race that one day you will understand. I had intended that by purchasing the data directly from you the money would bring or buy you some peace of mind. If I go directly to the Collins corporation, it will become lost in their accounts. You see, we do not mean you harm. It is not our way.'

Kelly stared at the xenoc, depressed by her own incomprehension. OK, girl, she thought, let's try and work this one out logically. She put her medical monitor program into primary mode, and used the results to bring appropriate suppressor and stimulant programs on-line to try and stabilize body and brain. There wasn't a great deal they could do, but at least she felt calmer and her breathing steadied. 'Why do you want to buy them?'

'We have little data on humans who are possessed by returned souls. We are interested. Your visit to Lalonde is an excellent first-hand account.'

Kelly felt the first stirrings of excitement; reporter's instinct inciting her interest. 'Bullshit. That's not what I meant. If all you wanted was information on possessed humans, you could have recorded my reports directly from Collins as soon as they were released. God knows, they've been repeated often enough.'

'They are not complete. Collins has edited them to provide a series of highlights. We understand their commercial reasons for doing so, but this is of no use to us. I require access to the entire recording.'

'Right,' she said with apparent gravity, as if she was giving the proposition appropriately weighty thought. An analysis program had gone primary, refining possible questions in an attempt to narrow the focus. 'I can give you full access to the times I came up against the possessed, and my observations of Shaun Wallace. That's no problem at all.'

'We require a full record from the time you arrived in the Lalonde star system until you departed. All details are of interest to us.'

'All details? I mean, this is a human sensevise, I kept the flek recording the whole time. Standard company procedure. Unfortunately, that includes time when I was visiting the little girls' room, if you catch on.'

'Human excretion functions do not embarrass us.'

'Shall I cut the time in *Lady Macbeth* for you?'

'Observations and crew impressions of the reality dysfunction from orbit are an integral part of the record.'

'So, how much were you thinking of offering me for this?'

'Please name your price, Kelly Tirrel.'

'One million fuseodollars.'

'That is expensive.'

'It's a lot of hours you're asking for. But the offer to edit it down still stands.'

'I will pay you the required amount for a complete recording only.'

Kelly pressed her teeth together in annoyance; it wasn't going to work, the Kiint was far too smart for verbal traps. Don't push, she told herself, get what you can and work out the why later on. 'Fair enough. Agreed.'

Lieria's tractamorphic flesh extended out into an arm, a Jovian Bank credit disk held between white pincers.

Kelly gave it an interested glance, and rose stiffly from the recliner. Her own credit disk was somewhere on her desk. She walked over to it, all three paces, then plonked herself down in the grey office chair a little too quickly.

'I would suggest you eat something and rest properly before you return to your sensenviron,' Lieria datavised.

'Good idea. I was going to.' She froze in the act of shoving the fleks and their empty storage cases around. How the hell had the Kiint known what she'd been running? *We have some command of technology.* She gripped the blanket harder with one hand as the other fished her disk from under a recorder block. 'Found it,' she said with forced lightness.

Lieria shunted the full amount across. The soft flesh of the pincers engulfed the Jovian Bank disk, then parted again to reveal a small dark blue processor block. It was like a conjuring trick which Kelly was in no state to unravel.

'Please insert your fleks in the block,' Lieria datavised. 'It will copy the recordings.'

Kelly did as she was told.

'I thank you, Kelly Tirrel. You have contributed valuable information to our race's store of knowledge.'

'Make the most of it,' she said grumpily. 'The way you're treating us we probably won't be around to contribute for much longer.'

The lounge door slid open, scattering a startled crowd of StClément residents. Lieria backed out with surprising ease. When the door closed again Kelly was left by herself with the disconcerting impression that it could all very easily have been a dream. She picked up her credit disk, looking at it in wonder. One million fuseodollars.

It was the key to permanent zero-tau. Her lawyer had been negotiating with Collins to transfer her pension fund into an Edenist trust account, just like Ashly Hanson. Except she wouldn't be coming out to take a look around every few centuries. Collins's accountants had been reluctant.

Another problem which had sent her into the sham escape of PTR. Now all she needed to do was get to an Edenist habitat. Only their culture had a chance of holding her safe through eternity.

Although ... that stubborn old part of her mind was asking a thousand questions. What the hell did the Kiint really want?

'Think,' she ordered herself fiercely. 'Come on, damn it. Think!' Something happened on Lalonde. Something so important that a Kiint walks into my apartment and pays me a million fuseodollars for a record of it. Something we didn't think was important or interesting, because it wasn't released by Collins. So if it wasn't released, how the hell did the Kiint know about it?

Logically, someone must have told them – presumably today or very recently. Someone who has reviewed the whole recording themselves, or at least more of it than Collins released.

Kelly smiled happily; an unfamiliar expression of late. And someone who must have a lot of contact with the Kiint.

*

Review every single conversation which the Kiint were involved in over the last week, Ione said. Anything that anyone mentioned about Lalonde, anything at all, however trivial. And if you can't find it, start going through your earlier memories.

**1205**

I am already reviewing the relevant scenes. There may be a problem with going back further than four days, my short-term memory capacity is only a hundred hours, after that the details are discarded so I may retain salient information. Without this procedure even my memory would be unable to cope with events inside me.

I know that! But it has to be recent for Lieria to go visiting in the middle of the night. I don't suppose the Kiint said anything among themselves? Grandfather's non-intrusion agreement can hardly apply in this case.

I concur that it cannot be considered. However, I have never been able to intercept detailed affinity conversations between the adult Kiint. At best I can sometimes distinguish what I would define as a murmur.

Bugger! If you can't remember, we'll have to haul all the Laymil project staff in and question them individually.

Not necessary. I have found it.

'Brilliant!' Show me.

The memory burst open around her. Bright light was shining down on the beach while glassy ripples lapped quietly against the shoreline. A huge sandcastle stood directly in front of her. *Oh bloody hell.*

*

Jay was woken by a hand shaking her shoulder with gentle insistence. 'Mummy,' she cried fearfully. Wherever she was, it was dark, and even darker shadows loomed over her.

'Sorry, poppet,' Kelly stage-whispered. 'It's not your mum, it's only me.'

Horror fled from the little girl's face, and she hitched herself up in the bed, wrapping her arms round her legs. 'Kelly?'

'Yep. And I am really sorry, I didn't mean to frighten you like that.'

Jay sniffed the air, highly curious now. 'What's that smell? And what time is it?'

'It's very late. Nurse Andrews is going to kill me if I stay for more than a couple of minutes. She only let me in because she knows you and I spent all that time together on *Lady Mac*.'

'You haven't visited for ages.'

'I know.' Kelly was almost crushed by the surge of emotion the girl triggered, the accusation in her tone. 'I haven't been terribly well lately. I didn't want you to see me the way I was.'

'Are you all right now?'

'Sure. I'm on the way back.'

'Good. You promised you'd show me round the studios you work in.'

'And I'll keep it, too. Listen, Jay, I've got some really important questions. They're about you and Haile.'

'What?' she asked suspiciously.

'I need to know if you told Haile anything about Lalonde, especially in the last couple of days. It's vital, Jay, honest. I wouldn't ask if it wasn't.'

'I know.' She screwed up her lips, thinking hard. 'There was some stuff about religion this morning. Haile doesn't understand it very well, and I'm not very good at explaining it.'

'What about religion, exactly?'

'It was how many gods there are. I'd told her about the Tyrathca's Sleeping God temple, you know, the one you showed me, and she wanted to know if that was the same thing as Jesus.'

'Of course,' Kelly hissed. 'It wasn't human possession, it was the Tyrathca section, we never released any of that.' She leant over and kissed Jay. 'Thank you, poppet. You've just performed a miracle.'

'Was that all?'

'Yeah. That was all.'

'Oh.'

'You snuggle down and get some sleep now. I'll come visit tomorrow.' She helped pull Jay's duvet back up and gave the girl another kiss. Jay sniffed inquisitively again, but didn't comment.

**1207**

'So?' Kelly asked softly as she walked away from the bed. 'You've been watching, you know this must be serious. I want to talk to the Lord of Ruin.'

The paediatric ward's net processor opened a channel to Kelly's neural nanonics. 'Ione Saldana will see you now,' Tranquillity datavised. 'Please bring the relevant recordings.'

*

Despite being on what he considered excellent terms with the Lord of Ruin, Parker Higgens could still be chilled to the marrow when she gave him one of her expectant looks.

'But I don't know anything about the Tyrathca, ma'am,' he complained. Being dragged out of bed straight into a highly irregular crisis conference was playing havoc with his thought processes. Accessing the sensevise recording of Coastuc-RT and seeing the strange silvery structure which the builder-caste Tyrathca had constructed in the middle of the village didn't contribute much to his composure, either.

When he glanced at Kempster Getchell for support he saw the astronomer's eyes were closed as he accessed the recording a second time.

'You're the only xenoc specialists I've got, Parker.'

'Laymil specialists.'

'Don't quibble. I need advice, and I need it fast. How important is this?'

'Well ... I don't think we knew the Tyrathca had a religion before this,' he ventured.

'We didn't,' Kelly said. 'I ran a full search program through the Collins office encyclopedia. It's as good as any university library. There's no reference to this Sleeping God at all.'

'And neither did the Kiint, so it would seem,' Parker said. 'They actually came and woke you to ask for the recording?'

'That's right.'

Parker was somewhat put out by the reporter's dishevelled appearance. She sat wedged into one corner of the sofa in

Ione's private study, a thick cardigan tugged round her shoulders as if it was midwinter. For the last five minutes she had been snatching up salmon sandwiches from a large plate balanced on the sofa's arm, pushing them forcefully into her mouth.

'Well, I have to say, ma'am, that it's a relief to find out they don't know everything.' A housechimp silently handed him a cup of coffee.

'But is it relevant?' Ione asked. 'Were they just so surprised they didn't know about the Sleeping God myth that Lieria simply rushed over to Kelly to confirm it? Or does it have some bearing on our current situation?'

'It's not a myth,' Kelly said around another sandwich. 'That's exactly what I said to Waboto-YAU, and it bloody nearly set the soldiers on me for that remark. The Tyrathca believe absolutely in their Sleeping God. Crazy race.'

Parker stirred his coffee mechanically. 'I've never known the Kiint to be excited about anything. But then I've never known them to be in a rush either, which they obviously were tonight. I think we should examine this Sleeping God in context. You are aware, ma'am, that the Tyrathca do not have fiction? They simply do not lie, and they have a great deal of trouble understanding human falsehoods. The nearest they ever come to lying is withholding information.'

'You mean there really is a Sleeping God?' Kelly asked.

'There has to be a core of truth behind the story,' Parker said. 'They are a highly formalized clan species. Individual families maintain professions and responsibilities for generations. Sireth-AFL's family was obviously entrusted with the knowledge of the Sleeping God. At a guess, I'd say that Sireth-AFL is a descendant of the family which used to deal with electronics while they were on their arkship.'

'Then why not just store the memory electronically?' Kelly asked.

'It probably is stored, somewhere. But Coastuc-RT is a very

primitive settlement, and the Tyrathca only ever use appropriate technology. There will be Tyrathca families in that village who know exactly how to build fusion generators and computers, but they don't actually need them yet, therefore the information isn't used. They employ water wheels and mental arithmetic instead.'

'Weird,' Kelly said.

'No,' Parker corrected. 'Merely logical. The product of a mind that is intelligent without being particularly imaginative.'

'Yet they were praying,' Ione said. 'They believe in a god. That requires a leap of imagination, or at least faith.'

'I don't think so,' Kempster Getchell said. He grinned round, clearly enjoying himself. 'We're messing about with semantics here, and an electronic translator, which is never terribly helpful, it's too literal. Consider when this God appeared in their history. Human gods are derived from our pre-science era. There are no new religions, there haven't been for thousands of years. Modern society is far too sceptical to allow for prophets who have personal conversations with God. We have the answer for everything these days, and if it isn't recorded on a flek it's a lie.

'Yet here we have the Tyrathca, who not only don't lie, but encounter a god while they're in a starship. They have the same intellectual analytical tools as we do, and they still call it a god. And they found it. That's what excites me, that's what is so important to this story. It isn't indigenous to their planet, it isn't ancient. One of their arkships encountered something so fearfully powerful that a race with the technology to travel between the stars calls it a god.'

'That would also mean it isn't exclusive to them,' Parker said.

'Yes. Although, whatever it is, it was benign, or even helpful to the arkship in question. They wouldn't consider it to be their Sleeping God otherwise.'

'Powerful enough to defend the Tyrathca from possessed humans,' Ione said. 'That's what they claimed.'

'Yes, indeed. A defence mounted from several hundred light-years distant, at least.'

'What the fuck could do that?' Kelly asked.

'Kempster?' Ione prompted as the old astronomer stared away at the ceiling.

'I have absolutely no idea. Although "sleeping" does imply an inert status, which can be reversed.'

'By prayer?' Parker said sceptically.

'They thought it would be able to hear them,' Kempster said. 'Stronger than all living things, was what that breeder said. Interesting. And that mirror-spire shape was supposed to be what it looked like. I'd like to say some kind of celestial event or object, that would fit in finding it in deep space. Unfortunately, there is no natural astronomical object which resembles that.'

'Take a guess,' Ione said icily.

'Powerful, and in space.' The astronomer's face wrinkled up with effort. 'Humm. Trouble is, we have no idea of the scale. Some kind of small nebula around a binary neutron star; or a white hole emission jet – which might account for the shape. But none of those are exactly inert.'

'Nor would they be much use against the possessed,' Parker said.

'But its existence is enough to fluster the Kiint,' Ione said. 'And they can manufacture moons, plural.'

'Do you think it could help us?' Kelly asked the astronomer.

'Good point,' Kempster said. 'A highly literal race thinks it can help them against the possessed. Ergo, it would be able to do the same thing for us. Although the actual encounter must have taken place thousands of years ago. Who knows how much the account had been distorted in that time, even by the Tyrathca? And if it was an event rather than an object, it would presumably be finished by now. After all, Confederation astronomers have catalogued our galaxy pretty thoroughly; and certainly anything odd within ten thousand light-years would be listed. Which is why I'm inclined to go for the inert object hypothesis. I must say, this is a delightful puzzle you've brought to us, young lady; I'd love to know what they did actually find.'

Kelly made an impatiently dismissive gesture, and leant forward. 'See?' she said to Ione. 'This is critical, just like I said. I've provided you with enough to go on. Haven't I?'

'Yes,' Ione said with considerable asperity.

'Do I get my flight authorization?'

'What is this? What flight?' Parker asked.

'Kelly wishes to visit Jupiter,' Ione said. 'To do that she needs my official authorization.'

'Do I get it?' Kelly was almost shouting.

Ione's nose crinkled with distaste. 'Yes. Now please be silent unless you have a cogent point to make.'

Kelly flung herself back into the sofa, a fearsome grin on her face.

Parker studied her for a moment, not at all liking what he found, but forwent any comment. 'The evidence we have so far is depressingly small, but to my mind it does seem to indicate that the Sleeping God is something other than a natural object. Perhaps it is a functional Von Neumann machine, that would certainly have godlike abilities ascribed to it by any culture with inferior technology. Or, I regret to say, some kind of ancient weapon.'

'A manufactured artefact which can attack the possessed over interstellar space. Now that really is an unpleasant thought,' Kempster said. 'Although the "sleeping" qualifier would admittedly be more pertinent in such a case.'

'As you say,' Ione said, 'we don't have nearly enough information to make anything other than wild guesses at this time. That must be rectified. Our real problem is that the

Tyrathca have severed all contact with us. And I really don't think we have any alternative but to ask them.'

'I would certainly advise we pursue that avenue, ma'am. The very possibility that the Sleeping God is real, and may even be able to defeat the possessed on some level, warrants further investigation. If we could...' His voice died away as Ione gripped the arms of her chair, blue eyes widening to express something Parker had never thought he would see there: horror.

*

Meredith Saldana drifted into the *Arikara*'s bridge; every one of the acceleration couches in the C&C section of the bridge was occupied as his staff officers dedicated themselves to scanning and securing space around Mirchusko.

He slid onto his own acceleration couch and accessed the tactical situation computer. The flagship was hanging a thousand kilometres off Tranquillity's counter-rotating spaceport, with every sensor cluster and communication system extended. Some spacecraft moved around the habitat's spaceport and outlying industrial stations, a couple of blackhawks were curving round the spindle to land on the outermost docking-ledge, and three He$_3$ cryogenic tankers were rising over the gas giant's natural rings en route for the habitat. Apart from that, the only ships flying were squadron members. The frigates were moving smoothly into their englobing positions, forming a protective eight thousand kilometre sphere around Tranquillity, complementing the habitat's own formidable SD platforms. His squadron's nine voidhawks were currently deployed right around the gas giant in an attempt to probe the rings for any observation system or hidden ship. An unlikely event, but Meredith was aware of just how much was riding on the Toi-Hoi ambush. When it came to this duty, he was a firm believer in the motto: I'm paranoid, but am I paranoid enough?

'Lieutenant Grese, our current situation, please?' he asked.

'One hundred per cent on-line, sir,' the Squadron Intelligence Officer reported. 'All starship traffic is shut down. Those blackhawks you can see docking are the last of the flight deploying sensor satellites looking for an energy-displacement signature from the Laymil home planet. All of them have obeyed the recall order. We're allowing personnel commuters and tugs to fly out to the industrial stations providing we're informed of their movements in advance. Tranquillity is supplying us with a direct feed from its SD sensor network, which is extremely comprehensive out to one million kilometres. Our only problem with that is that it doesn't appear to have any gravitonic-distortion detectors.'

Meredith frowned. 'That's ridiculous, how does it detect emerging starships?'

'I'm not sure, sir. We did ask, but it just said we're receiving the full datavise from each sensor satellite. My only explanation is that the Lord of Ruin doesn't want us to know the habitat's full detection capability.'

Which wasn't something Meredith believed. Somewhat to his surprise, he'd been quite impressed by his young cousin; especially as he'd gone in to meet her with a lot of firmly held preconceptions. He'd been forced to revise most of them under her unyielding dignity and astute political grasp. One thing he was sure of, if she was deliberately imposing limits on her cooperation she wouldn't be duplicitous about it.

'Can our own sensors compensate?' he asked.

'Yes, sir. At the moment, the voidhawks will provide us with an immediate warning of any emergence. But we've launched a full complement of gravitonic-distortion detector satellites. They'll provide coverage out to quarter of a million kilometres when they're in position; that's in about another twenty minutes, which will free the voidhawks for their next duty.'

'Good, in that case we won't make an issue of this.'

'Sir.'

'Lieutenant Rhoecus, voidhawk status, please.'

'Yes, Admiral,' the Edenist replied. 'There are definitely no ships inside any of Mirchusko's rings. However, we cannot give any guarantees about smaller stealthed spy satellites. Two hundred and fifty ELINT satellites have been deployed so far, which gives us a high probability of detecting any transmission should there be a spy system observing the habitat. The *Myoho* and the *Oenone* are launching further ELINTs into orbit around each of Mirchusko's moons in case there's anything hiding on or under the surface.'

'Excellent. What about covering the rest of the system?'

'We've already worked out a swallow flight plan for each voidhawk which will allow them to conduct a preliminary survey in fifteen hours. It will be somewhat cursory, but if there is another ship within two AUs of Mirchusko they should find it. Clear space provides much fewer problems than a gas giant environment.'

'Several blackhawk captains offered to assist us, Admiral,' Commander Kroeber said. 'I declined for now, but told them that Admiral Kolhammer may want them for the next stage.'

Meredith resisted a glance in the Flag-captain's direction. 'I see. Have you ever served with Admiral Kolhammer, Mircea?'

'No, sir, I haven't had that pleasure.'

'Well, for your information, I consider it unlikely he'd want the blackhawks along.'

'Yes, sir.'

Meredith raised his voice to address the bridge officers in general. 'Well done, ladies and gentlemen. You seem to have organized this securement most efficiently. My compliments. Captain, please take the *Arikara* out to our englobement coordinate, in your own time.'

'Aye, aye, sir.'

Acceleration returned to the bridge, building to a third of a gee. Meredith studied the tactical situation display, familiarizing himself with the squadron's formation. He was quietly content with the way his ships and crews were performing, especially after the trauma of Lalonde. Unlike some navy officers, Meredith didn't regard the blackhawks as universally villainous, he liked to consider himself a more sophisticated realist than that. If they were going to be betrayed, it was likely to be by an outside agency such as a stealthed spy satellite. But even then, a starship would have to collect the information.

'Lieutenant Lowie, would it be possible to eliminate any spy system hiding in the rings by EMPing them?'

'Sir, it would require complete saturation,' the Weapons Officer said. 'If the Organization has hidden a satellite out there its circuitry will be hardened. The fusion explosion would have to be inside twenty kilometres to guarantee elimination. We don't have that many bombs.'

'I see. Just an idea. Rhoecus, I'd like to keep a couple of voidhawks in orbit around Mirchusko so they can monitor starships emerging outside our own sensor range. What effect will that have on the survey?'

'Approximate increase of six hours, Admiral.'

'Damn, that's pushing our time envelope.' He consulted the tactical situation display again, running analysis programs to calculate the most effective option.

A red dot flared into existence barely ten thousand kilometres away, surrounded by symbols: a wormhole terminus disgorging a ship. And it was nowhere near any of Tranquillity's designated emergence zones. Another red dot appeared less than a second later. A third. A fourth. Three more.

'What the hell?'

'Not voidhawks, sir,' Lieutenant Rhoecus said. 'No affinity broadcasts at all. They're not responding to Tranquillity or squadron voidhawks, either.'

'Commander Kroeber, squadron to combat status. Rhoecus, recall the voidhawks. Can someone get me a visual identification?'

'Coming, sir,' Lieutenant Grese datavised. 'Two of the intruders are close to an SD sensor satellite.'

More wormhole termini were opening. *Arikara*'s thermo-dump panels and long-range sensor clusters sank back into their fuselage recesses. The warship's acceleration increased as it sped out to its englobement coordinate.

'Got it, Admiral. Oh, Lord, definitely hostile.'

The image relayed into Meredith's neural nanonics showed him a charcoal-grey eagle with a wingspan of nearly two hundred metres; its eyes gleamed yellow above a long chrome-silver beak. His body tensed in reflex, pushing him deeper into the acceleration couch. That was one massively evil-looking creature.

'Hellhawk, sir. Must be from Valisk.'

'Thank you, Grese. Confirm the other intruder identities, please.'

The tactical situation display showed him twenty-seven bitek starships had now emerged from their wormholes. Another fifteen termini were opening. It was only seven seconds since the first had appeared.

'All of them are hellhawks, sir; eight bird types, four bogus starships, the rest conform to standard blackhawk profile.'

'Admiral, the voidhawks have all swallowed back to Tranquillity,' Rhoecus said. 'Moving out to reinforce the englobement formation.'

Meredith watched their purple vector lines slice across the tactical situation display, twisting round to reach the other squadron ships. No use, Meredith thought, no use at all. Fifty-eight hellhawks were ranged against them now, forming a loose ring around the habitat. Tactical analysis programs were giving him an extremely small probability of a successful defensive engagement, even with the squadron backed up by Tranquillity's SD platforms. And that was reducing still further as more hellhawks continued to swallow in.

'Commander Kroeber, get those blackhawks Tranquillity was using as patrol ships out here as fast as possible.'

'Aye, sir.'

'Sir!' Grese shouted. 'We're registering more gravitonic distortions. Adamist ships, this time. Multiple emergence patterns.'

The tactical situation display showed Meredith two small constellations of red dots lighting up. The first was fifteen thousand kilometres ahead of Tranquillity, while the second trailed it by roughly the same amount. *Dear God, and I thought Lalonde was bad.* 'Lieutenant Rhoecus.'

'Yes, Admiral?'

'The *Ilex* and the *Myoho* are to disengage. They are ordered to fly to Avon immediately and warn Trafalgar what has happened here. Under no circumstances is Admiral Kolhammer to bring his task force to Mirchusko.'

'But, sir . . .'

'That was an order, Lieutenant.'

'Aye, sir.'

'Grese, can you identify the new intruders?'

'I think so, sir. I think it's the Organization fleet. Visual sensors show front-line warships; I've got frigates, some battle-cruisers, several destroyers, and plenty of combat-capable commercial vehicles.'

Large sections of the tactical situation display dissolved into yellow and purple hash as electronic-warfare pods spun away from the hellhawks, coming on-line as soon as they were clear of the energistic effect. The voidhawks continued to supply information on emerging starships. There were now seventy hellhawks ringing Tranquillity, with a hundred and thirty Adamist ships holding station on either side of it.

*Arikara*'s bridge had fallen completely silent.

'Sir,' Rhoecus said. '*Ilex* and *Myoho* have swallowed out.'

Meredith nodded. 'Good.' There wasn't a hell of a lot more

he could say. 'Commander Kroeber, please signal the enemy fleet. Ask them . . . Ask them what they want.'

'Aye, sir.'

The tactical situation computer datavised an alarm.

'Combat wasp launch!' Lowie shouted. 'The hellhawks have fired.'

At such close range, there was nothing the electronic-warfare barrage could do to hide the burst of yellow solid-rocket exhausts from Meredith's squadron. Each of the hellhawks had launched fifteen combat wasps. Spent solid-rocket casings separated as the dazzling plumes of fusion fire sprang out, and they began to accelerate in towards the habitat at twenty-five gees. Over a thousand drones forming an immense noose of light which was swiftly contracting.

Tactical programs went primary in Meredith's neural nanonics. In theory, they had the capacity to fight off this assault, which would leave them with practically zero reserves. And he had to decide now.

It was a hopeless situation, one where instinct fought against duty. But Confederation citizens were being attacked; and to a Saldana duty was instinct.

'Full defensive salvo,' Meredith ordered. 'Fire.'

Combat wasps leapt out of their launch-tubes in every squadron ship. Tranquillity's SD platforms launched simultaneously. For a short while, space around the habitat's shell ceased to be an absolute vacuum. Hot streams of energized vapour from the exhausts of four thousand combat wasps sprayed in towards Tranquillity, creating a faint iridescent nebula beset with giddy squalls of turquoise and amber ions. Jagged petals of lightning flared out from the tip of every starscraper, ripping away into the chaotically unstable vortex.

Blackhawks were rising from Tranquillity's docking-ledges, over fifty of them sliding out under heavy acceleration to join the fight. Meredith's tactical analysis program began revising the odds. Then he saw several swallow away. In his heart he didn't blame them.

'Message coming in, Admiral,' the communications officer reported. 'Someone called Luigi Balsmao, he claims he's the Organization fleet's commander. He says: "Surrender and join us, or die and join us."'

'What a melodramatic arsehole,' Meredith grunted. 'Please advise the Lord of Ruin, it's as much her decision as it is mine. After all, it's her people who will suffer.'

'Oh fuck! *Sir!* Another combat wasp launch. It's the Adamist ships this time.'

Under Luigi's command, all one hundred and eighty Organization starships fired a salvo of twenty-five combat wasps apiece. Their antimatter drives accelerated them in towards Tranquillity at forty gees.

# 29

The star wasn't important enough to have a name. The Confederation Navy's almanac office simply listed it as DRL0755–09-BG. It was an average K-type, with a gloomy emission in the lower end of the orange spectrum. The first scoutship to explore its planets, back in 2396, took less than a fortnight to complete a survey. There were only three unremarkable inner, solid, planets for it to investigate; none of them were terracompatible. Of the two outer gas giants, the one further from the star had an equatorial diameter of forty-three thousand kilometres, its outer cloud layer a pale green with none of the usual blustery atmospheric conditions. As worthless as the solid planets. The innermost gas giant did raise the interest of the scoutship's crew for a short while. Its equatorial diameter was a hundred and fifty-three thousand kilometres, making it larger than Jupiter, and coloured by a multitude of ferocious storm bands. Eighteen moons orbited round it, two of which had high-pressure atmospheres of nitrogen and methane. The complex interaction of their gravity fields prohibited any major ring system from forming, but all of the larger moons shepherded substantial quantities of asteroidal rubble.

The scoutship crew thought that such abundant resources of easily accessible minerals and ores would make it an ideal location for Edenist habitats. Their line company even managed to sell the survey's preliminary results to Jupiter. But once lagain,

DRL0755-09-BG's mediocrity acted against it. The gas giant was a good location for habitats, but not exceptional; without a terracompatible planet the Edenists weren't interested. DRL0755-09-BG was ignored for the next two hundred and fifteen years, apart from intermittent visits from Confederation Navy patrol ships to check that it wasn't being used by an antimatter production station.

As the *Lady Mac*'s sensor clusters gave him a visual sweep of the penurious star system, Joshua wondered why the navy wasted its time.

He cancelled the image and looked round the bridge. Alkad Mzu was lying prone on one of the spare acceleration couches, her eyes tight shut as she absorbed the external panorama. Monica and Samuel were hovering in the background, as always. Joshua really didn't want them on the bridge, but the agencies weren't prepared to allow Mzu out of their sight now.

'OK, Doc, now what?' he asked. He'd followed Mzu's directions so that *Lady Mac* emerged half a million kilometres above the inner gas giant's southern pole, near the undulating boundaries of the planet's enormous magnetosphere. It gave them an excellent viewpoint across the entire moon system.

Alkad stirred on her couch, not opening her eyes. 'Please configure the ship's antenna to broadcast the strongest signal it can at the one hundred and twenty-five thousand kilometre equatorial orbital band. I will give you the code to transmit when you're ready.'

'That was the *Beezling*'s parking orbit?'

'Yes.'

'OK. Sarha, get the dish ready for that, please. I think you'd better allow for a twenty thousand kilometre error when you designate the beam. No telling what state they were in when they got here. If they don't respond, we'll have to widen the sweep pattern out to the furthest moon.'

'Aye, Captain.'

'How many people left on this old warship of yours, Doc?' Joshua asked.

Alkad broke away from the image feeding into her neural nanonics. She didn't want to. This was it, the star represented by that stupid little alphanumeric she had carried with her like a talisman for thirty years. Always expecting him to be waiting here for her; there had been a million first lines rehearsed in those decades, a million loving looks. But now she'd arrived, seen that pale-amber star with her own eyes, doubt was gripping her like frostbite. Every other aspect of their desperate plan had fallen to dust thanks to fate and human fallibility. Would this part of it really be any different? A sublight voyage of two and a half light-years. What had the young captain called it? Impossible. 'Nine,' she said faintly. 'There should be nine of them. Is that a problem?'

'No. *Lady Mac* can take that many.'

'Good.'

'Have you thought what you're going to tell them?'

'I'm sorry?'

'Jesus, Doc; their home planet has been wiped out, you can't use the Alchemist for revenge, the dead are busy conquering the universe, and they are going to have to spend the rest of their lives locked up in Tranquillity. You've had thirty years to get used to the Genocide, and a couple of weeks to square up to the possessed. To them it's still good old 2581, and they're on a navy combat mission. You think they're going to take all this calmly?'

'Oh, Mother Mary.' Another problem, before she even knew if they'd survived.

'The dish is ready,' Sarha said.

'Thanks,' Joshua said. 'Right, Doc, datavise the code into the flight computer. Then start thinking what you're going to say. And think good, because I'm not taking *Lady Mac* anywhere near a ship armed with antimatter that isn't extremely pleased to see me.'

Mzu's code was beamed out by the *Lady Macbeth* in a slim fan of microwave radiation. Sarha monitored the operation as it tracked slowly round the designated orbital path. There was no immediate response – she hadn't been expecting one. She allowed the beam another two sweeps, then shifted the focus to cover a new circle just outside the first.

It took five hours to get a response. The tension and expectation which had so dominated the bridge for the first thirty minutes had expired long ago. Ashly, Monica, and Voi were all in the galley preparing food sachets when a small artificial green star appeared in the display which the flight computer was feeding Sarha's neural nanonics. Analysis and discrimination programs came on-line, filtering out the gas giant's constant radio screech to concentrate on the signal. Two ancillary booms slid up out of *Lady Macbeth*'s hull, unfolding wide broad-spectrum multi-element receiver meshes to complement the main communication dish.

'Somebody's there, all right,' Sarha said. 'Weak signal, but steady. Standard CAB transponder response code, but no ship registration number. They're in an elliptical orbit, ninety-one thousand kilometres by one hundred and seventy, four degree inclination. Right now they're ninety-five kilometres out from the upper atmosphere.' A strangely muffled gulp make her abandon the flight computer's display to check the bridge.

Alkad Mzu was lying flat on her acceleration couch, with every muscle unnaturally stiff. Neural nanonics were busy censoring her body-language with nerve overrides. But Sarha could see a film of liquid over her red-rimmed eyes which was growing progressively thicker. When she blinked, tiny droplets spun away across the compartment.

Joshua whistled. 'Impressive, Doc. Your old crewmates have got balls, I'll say that for them.'

'They're alive,' Alkad cried. 'Oh, Mother Mary, they're really alive.'

'The *Beezling* made it here, Doc,' Joshua said, deliberately curt. 'Let's not jump to conclusions without facts. All we've got so far is a transponder beacon. What is supposed to happen next, does the captain come out of zero-tau?'

'Yes.'

'OK. Sarha, keep monitoring the *Beezling*. Beaulieu, Liol, let's get back to flight status, please. Dahybi, charge up the nodes, I want to be ready to jump clear if things turn out bad.' He started plotting a vector which would take them over to the *Beezling*.

*Lady Mac*'s triple fusion drive came on, quickly building up to three gees. She followed a shallow arc above the gas giant, sinking towards the penumbra.

'Signal change,' Sarha announced. 'Much stronger now, but it's still an omnidirectional broadcast, they're not focusing on us. Message coming in, AV only.'

'OK, Doc,' Joshua said. 'You're on. Be convincing.'

They were still four hundred and fifty thousand kilometres away from the *Beezling*, which produced an awkward time delay. Pressed back into her couch, Alkad could only move her eyes to one side, glancing up at a holoscreen which angled out of the ceiling above her. A magenta haze slowly cleared to show her the *Beezling*'s bridge compartment. It looked as though some kind of salvage team had ransacked the place: consoles had been broken open to show electronic stacks with their circuit cards missing, wall panels had been removed exposing chunks of machinery which were half-dismantled. To add to the disorder, every surface was dusted with grubby frost. Over the years, chunks of packaging, latch pins, small tools, items of clothing, and other shipboard debris had all stuck where they'd drifted to rest, giving the impression of inorganic chrysalides frozen in the act of metamorphosis. Awkward, angular shadows overlapped right around the compartment, completing the image of Gothic anarchy. There was only one source of illumination, a slender emergency light-tube carried by some-one in an SII spacesuit.

'This is Captain Kyle Prager here. The flight computer reports we've picked up our activation trigger code. Alkad, I want this to be you. Are you receiving this? I've got very little left in the way of working sensors. Hell, I've got little in the way of anything that works any more.'

'I'm receiving you, Kyle,' Alkad said. 'And it is me, it's Alkad. I came back for you. I promised I would.'

'Mother Mary, is that really you, Alkad? I'm getting a poor image here, you look . . . different.'

'I'm old, Kyle. Very, very old now.'

'Only thirty years, unless relativity is weirder than we thought.'

'Kyle, please, is Peter there? Did he make it?'

'He's here, he's fine.'

'Almighty Mary. You're sure?'

'Yes. I just checked his zero-tau pod. Six of us made it.'

'Only six? What happened?'

'We lost Tane Ogilie a couple of years ago, after he went outside to work on the drive tube. It had to be repaired before we could decelerate into this orbit; there was a lot of systems decay over twenty-eight years. Trouble is, the whole antimatter unit is badly radioactive now. Not even armour could save him from receiving a lethal dose.'

'Oh, Mother Mary, I'm sorry. What about the other two?'

'Like I said, we've had a lot of systems decay. Zero-tau can keep you in perfect stasis, but its own components wear out. They went sometime during the voyage, we only found out when we came out to start the deceleration. Both of them suicided.'

'I see,' she said shakily.

'What happened, Alkad? You're not in any Garissan Navy uniform I remember.'

'The Omutans did it, Kyle. Just like we thought they would. The bastards went ahead and did it.'

'How bad?'

'The worst. Six planet-busters.'

Joshua cancelled his link to the communication circuit, turning to the more mundane details of the flight. Some things he just didn't want to hear: the reaction of a man being told his home planet has died.

*Lady Mac*'s sensors were slowly gathering more information on the *Beezling*, allowing the flight computer to refine the warship's location beyond Sarha's initial rough estimate. The gas giant's violent magnetic and electromagnetic emissions were making it difficult. Even this far above the outer atmosphere space was a thick ionic soup, congested with severe energy currents which degraded sensor efficiency.

Joshua altered their flight vector several times as the new figures came in. *Lady Mac* was well over the nightside now, the swirl of particles around her forward fuselage glowing a faint pink as they were buffeted through the planetary magnetosphere. It played havoc with the support circuitry.

Beaulieu and Liol would datavise flurries of instructions to contain the drop-outs, returning the systems to operational status. Joshua monitored Liol's performance, unable to find fault. He'd make a good crewman. *Maybe I could offer him Melvyn's slot, except his ego would never allow him to accept. There has to be a way we can settle this.*

He turned his attention back to the communication link. After the shocks he'd received, Kyle Prager was reacting badly to Mzu's news of her deal with the agencies and Ione.

'You know I cannot hand it over to anybody else,' Prager said. 'You should never have brought them here, no matter what you agreed with them.'

'What, and leave you to rot?' Alkad replied. 'I couldn't do that. Not with Peter here.'

'Why not? We planned for it. We would have destroyed the Alchemist and signalled the Confederation Navy for help. You know that. And as for this fable about the dead being alive . . .'

'Mother Mary. We can barely pick up your signal now, and

I knew where to look. What sort of condition would you be in five years from now? Besides, there might not be any Confederation left in another five months, let alone five years.'

'Better that than risk others learning how to build an Alchemist.'

'Nobody is going to learn from me.'

'Of course not, but there are so many temptations for governments now the knowledge of its existence has leaked.'

'It leaked thirty years ago, and the technology is still safe. This rescue mission is designed to clear up the last loose end.'

'Alkad, you're asking too much. I'm sorry my answer has to be no. If you try to rendezvous I will switch off the confinement chambers. We still have a quantity of antimatter left.'

'No!' Alkad yelled. 'Peter's on board.'

'Then stay away.'

'Captain Prager, this is Captain Calvert. I'd like to offer a simple solution.'

'Please do,' Prager answered.

'Shoot the Alchemist down into the gas giant. We'll pick you up after it's gone. Because I can assure you, I'm not going to come anywhere near the *Beezling* with that kind of threat hanging over me.'

'I'd like to, Captain, but it will take some time to check over the Alchemist's carrier vehicle. Then the antimatter would have to be reloaded. And even if it still works, you might be able to intercept it.'

'That's a very unhealthy case of paranoia you've got there, Captain.'

'One that has kept me alive for thirty years.'

'All right, try this. If we were possessed or simply wanted to acquire Alchemist technology we wouldn't even have come here. We already have the Doc. You're military, you know there are a great many ways information can be extracted from unwilling donors. And we certainly wouldn't have thrown in a crazy story like the possessed to confuse the issue. But we're

**1228**

not possessed, or even hostile to you, so we told you the truth. So I'll tell you what. If you're still not convinced that we want to end the Alchemist threat, then go right ahead and kamikaze.'

'No!' Alkad yelled.

'Quiet, Doc. First though, Captain, you put this Peter Adul character in a spacesuit, boot him out the airlock, and let us pick him up. He cannot be allowed to die, not if he knows how to build an Alchemist. The possessed would have him then. Guarding against that technology leakage is part of your duty, too, now. Once we have him, I'll blow you to shit myself if that's what it takes.'

'You would, too, wouldn't you?' Prager asked.

'Jesus, yes. After what I've been through chasing the Doc, it'll be a pleasure to finish this properly.'

'It may be just the lousy reception I'm getting, but you look very young, Captain Calvert.'

'Compared to most starship captains, I probably am. But I'm also the only option you have. You either die, or you come with me.'

'Kyle,' Alkad pleaded. 'For Mary's sake!'

'Very well. Captain Calvert, you can rendezvous with the *Beezling* and take my crew off. After that the *Beezling* will be scuttled with the Alchemist on board.'

Joshua heard someone on the bridge let out a heavy breath. 'Thank you, Captain.'

'Christ, what an ungrateful sod,' Liol complained. 'Just make sure you invoice him a huge rescue bill, Josh.'

'Well, that finally settles that question,' Ashly chuckled. 'You're definitely a Calvert, Liol.'

The *Beezling* was in a sorry state. That became increasingly apparent on *Lady Mac*'s final approach phase, when they were rising up behind it from a slightly lower orbit. Both ships were deep inside the penumbra now, although the gigantic orange and white crescent they were fleeing from still cast a glorious coronal glow across them. It was enough for *Lady Mac*'s visual sensors to provide a detailed image while they were still ten kilometres away.

Almost the entire lower quarter of the warship's fuselage plates were missing, with only a simple silver petal pattern left surrounding the drive tubes. The hexagonal stress structure was clearly visible, fencing in black and tarnished-chrome segments of machinery. Some units were obviously foreign, jutting up through the centre of the hexagons where they'd been hurriedly inserted to complement or enhance original components. From the midsection forward, the fuselage was relatively intact. There was very little protective foam remaining, just a few dabs of blackened cinderlike flakes. Long silvery scars etched across the dark monobonded silicon told the story of multiple particle impacts. There were hundreds of small craters where the fuselage's molecular-binding generators had suffered localized overloads, punctures whose vapour and shrapnel had been absorbed by whatever module or tank was directly underneath. None of the delicate sensor clusters had survived. Only two thermo-dump panels were extended, and they were badly battered; one had a large chunk missing, as if something had taken a bite out of it.

'I'm registering a strong magnetic emission,' Beaulieu said as they closed the last kilometre. 'But the ship's thermal and electrical activity is minimal. Apart from an auxiliary fusion generator and three confinement chambers the *Beezling* is basically inert.'

'No thruster activity, either,' said Liol. 'They've picked up a tumble. One rotation every eight minutes nineteen seconds.'

Joshua checked the radar return, computing a vector around the crippled old ship so he could reach its airlock. 'I can dock and stabilize you,' he datavised to Captain Prager.

'Not much point,' Prager replied. 'Our airlock chamber was breached by particle impact; and I doubt the latches will work anyway. If you just hold station we'll transfer across in suits.'

'Acknowledged.'

'Captain,' Beaulieu said. 'Two fusion drives. They're on an approach vector.'

'Jesus!' He accessed the sensors. Half of the image was a ghostly apricot-coloured ocean illuminated by the planetary-sized aurora borealis storms which floated serenely above it. The night-time sky which vaulted it was a perfect orrery, a dome of stars where the only movement came from tiny moons racing along their ordained pathways. Red icons were bracketing two of the brighter stars just outside the ecliptic. When Joshua keyed in the infra-red they became brilliant. Purple vector lines sprouted out of them, projecting their trajectory in towards him.

'Approximately two hundred thousand kilometres away,' Beaulieu said, her synthesized voice sounding completely uncaring. 'I think I can confirm the drive signatures; it appears to be our old friends the *Urschel* and the *Raimo*. Both plasma exhausts have very similar instabilities. If not them, then there are certainly possessed on board.'

'Who else?' Ashly grunted morosely.

Alkad looked round frantically, trying to make eye contact with the crew. They were all looking at Joshua as he lay on his couch, eyes closed, his flat brow producing neat parallel furrows as he frowned in concentration. 'What are you waiting for?' she asked. 'Take the survivors on board and run. Those ships are too far away to threaten us.'

Sarha waved her hand in annoyance. 'They are now,' she said in a low voice. 'They won't be for long. And we're too close to the gas giant to jump out. We need to be another hundred and thirty thousand kilometres away. In other words, up where they are. That means we can't boost straight up; we'd fly straight into them.'

'So . . . what then?'

Sarha pointed a finger at Joshua. 'He'll tell us. If there's a vector out of here, Joshua will find it.'

Alkad was surprised by the amount of respect in the

normally volatile crew-woman. But then all of the crew were regarding their captain with the kind of hushed expectancy that was usually the province of holy gurus. It made Alkad very uneasy.

Joshua's eyes flipped open. 'We have a problem,' he announced grimly. 'Their altitude gives them too much tactical advantage. I can't find us a vector.' A small regretful dip at the corner of his mouth. 'There isn't even a convenient Lagrange point this time. And I wouldn't like to risk it anyway, not while we're so close to a gas giant as big as this one.'

'Fly a slingshot,' Liol said. 'Dive straight at the gas giant and go for a jump on the other side.'

'That's over three hundred thousand kilometres away. *Lady Mac* can probably accelerate harder than the Organization ships, but they've got antimatter combat wasps, remember. Forty-five gee acceleration; we'd never make it.'

'Christ.'

'Beaulieu, put a com beam on them,' Joshua said. 'If they respond, ask them what they want. I'm sure we know, but if nothing else I'd like confirmation.'

'Yes, Captain.'

'Doc, how do we go about firing the Alchemist at them?'

'You can't,' she said simply.

'Jesus, Doc, this is no time for principles. Don't you understand? We have no other way out. None. That weapon is the only advantage we've got left. If we don't kill them, they'll get you, and Peter.'

'This is not a question of principle, Captain. It's not physically possible to deploy the Alchemist against starships.'

'Jesus.' He couldn't believe it. But the Doc looked frightened enough. Intuition convinced him she was telling the truth. The navigation program was still producing flight vectors. Dumb forced-calculation, trying out every conceivable probability to find one which would let them escape. The plots flickered in and out of existence at a subliminal speed, miniature purple lightning bolts crackling round the inside of his head. Throw in wild-card manoeuvres, lunar slingshots, Lagrange points. Pray! It didn't make the slightest difference. The Organization frigates had thoroughly outmanoeuvred him. His one hope had been the Alchemist, a super-doomsday machine, a nuke to kill a couple of ants.

I have come so far I can actually see the ship it's stored in. I can't lose now, not with these stakes.

'OK, Doc, I want to know exactly what your Alchemist does, and how it does it.' He clicked his fingers at Monica and Samuel. 'You two, I'll stay in Tranquillity if we survive this, but I have to know.'

'God, Calvert, I'll stay there with you if that's what it takes,' Monica told him. 'Just get us out of this.'

'Joshua,' Sarha said. 'You can't.'

'Give me an alternative. It gets Liol's vote. He'll be captain then.'

'I'm crew, Josh. This is your ship.'

'Now he tells me. Datavise the file, Doc. Now, please.' Information leapt into his mind as the files came over. Theory, application, construction, deployment, operational parameters. All neatly indexed with helpful cross-referencing. The blue-prints of how to slay a star; in fact, build enough and you could slay an entire galaxy; or even just ... Joshua flicked instanta-neously back to the operational aspects. Pumped a few figures of his own into Mzu's coldly simple equations.

'Jesus, Doc, it wasn't a rumour. You really are dangerous, aren't you.'

'Can you do it?' Monica asked. She wanted to shout the question at him, jolt him out of that infuriating complacency.

Joshua winked at her. 'Absolutely. Look, we came off badly down in that ironberg yard because that's not my territory. This is. In space, we win.'

'Is he serious?' Monica appealed to the rest of the bridge.

'Oh, yes,' Sarha said. 'If anyone gets hostile with *Lady Mac*, they just crash straight into his ego.'

\*

High York posed a difficult problem of interpretation for Louise. The AV pillar in the *Jamrana*'s lounge shone its image down her optic nerve throughout the entire approach phase. There was no colour, space was so black she couldn't even see the stars. The asteroid was different from Phobos's chiselled cylinder, a grizzled irregular lump which the ship's sensors seemed incapable of bringing into proper focus. Mechanical artefacts were shunting out of its puckered surface at all angles, though she wasn't quite sure if she had the scale right. If she had, then they were bigger than the largest ship ever to ply Norfolk's seas.

Fletcher was in the lounge with her. From the few comments he made he understood even less of the image than she did.

Genevieve, of course, was in her tiny cabin playing games on her processor block. She'd found a soulmate in one of Pieri's younger cousins; the pair of them had taken to locking themselves away for hours at a time to tackle battalions of Trafalgar Greenjackets or skate through puzzles of five-dimensional topology. Louise wasn't entirely happy with her sister's new hobby, but on the other hand she was grateful she didn't have the duty of keeping her amused during the flight.

High York's disc-shaped spaceport traversed the AV image, eclipsing the asteroid itself. A high-pitched whine vibrated out of the lounge walls, and the *Jamrana* drifted forwards. And still there was no glimpse of Earth. Louise had really been looking forward to that. Pieri would align a sensor on the planet for her if she asked, she was sure; but right now the whole Bushay family was involved in the docking procedure.

Louise asked her processor block for an update on their

approach, and studied the display which appeared on its screen while it accessed the ship's flight computer. 'Four minutes until we dock,' she said. Assuming she was reading the tables of figures and coloured lines correctly.

She'd spent a large portion of the flight working through the block's tutorial programs until she could manage the unit's more basic display and operation modes. She didn't need to ask anyone's help to manage her medical nanonic packages, and she could monitor the baby's health continually. It gave her a good feeling. So much of Confederation life was centred round the casual use of electronics.

'Why so nervous, my lady?' Fletcher asked. 'Our voyage ends. With our Lord's mercy we have prevailed once more against the most inopportune circumstances. We have returned to the good Earth, the cradle of humanity. Though I fear that which has befallen me, I can do naught but rejoice at our homecoming.'

'I'm not nervous,' she protested unconvincingly.

'Come now, lady.'

'All right. Look, it's not getting here; I'm really delighted we've made it. I suppose it's silly of me, but something about being on Earth is very reassuring. It's old and it's very strong, and if people are going to be safe anywhere, then it'll be here. That's the problem. Something Endron said about it keeps bothering me.'

'You know that if I can assist you, I will.'

'No. It's nothing you can help with. That's the point. Endron told me we wouldn't get through High York's spaceport; that there would be inspections and examinations, awfully strict ones. It'll be nothing like arriving at Phobos. And everything I've heard from Pieri just confirms that. I'm sorry, Fletcher, I don't think we're going to make it, I really don't.'

'And yet we must,' he said softly. 'That fiend Dexter cannot prevail. Should the necessity become apparent, I will surrender myself and warn Earth's rulers.'

'Oh, no, Fletcher, you can't do that. I don't want you to be hurt.'

'Yet still you doubt me, lady Louise. I see your heart crying in pain. That is a source of grief for me.'

'I don't doubt you, Fletcher. It's just that . . . If we can't get through, then Quinn Dexter won't manage it either. That would mean your whole journey is for nothing. I hate that.'

'Dexter is stronger than I, lady. I hold that bitter memory quite plainly. He is also more cunning and ruthless. If there is but a single chink in the armour of Earth's valiant harbourmasters he will find it.'

'Heavens, I hope not. Quinn Dexter loose on Earth is too horrible to think about.'

'Aye, my lady.' His fingers clasped hers to emphasize his determination – something he rarely did, shying away from physical contact with people. It was almost as if he feared contamination.

'That is why you must swear faithfully to me that should I stumble in my task you must pick up the torch and carry on. The world must be warned of Quinn Dexter's devilish intent. And if possible you must also seek out this Banneth of whom he spoke with such animosity. Alert her to his presence, emphasize the danger she will face.'

'I'll try, Fletcher, really I will. I promise.' Fletcher was prepared to sacrifice his new life and eternal sanity to save others. Her own goal of reaching Joshua seemed so petty and selfish in comparison. 'Be careful when we disembark,' she urged.

'I place my trust in God, my lady. And if they catch me—'

'They won't!'

'Ah, now who has adopted a frail bravado? As I recall, 'twas you who warned me of what lies crouched beside the road ahead.'

'I know.'

'Forgive me, lady. I see that once again my tact is left wanting.'

'Don't worry about me, Fletcher. I'm not the one they'll put into zero-tau.'

'Aye, lady, I confess that prospect is one I shrink from. I know in my heart I will not last long in such black confinement.'

'I'll get you out,' she vowed. 'If they put you in zero-tau I'll get it switched off, or something. There will be lawyers I can hire.' She patted her ship-suit's breast pocket, feeling the outline of the Jovian bank credit disk. 'I have money.'

'Let us hope it proves sufficient, my lady.'

She gave him what she hoped was a bright smile, making out that everything was settled. So that's that.

The *Jamrana* trembled, shaking loose small flocks of jumble. Clangs rumbled down the central ladder shaft as the spaceport docking latches engaged.

'That's funny,' Louise said. The display on the block's screen was undergoing a drastic change.

'Is something the matter, lady?'

'I don't think so. It's just odd, that's all. If I'm reading this right, the captain has given the spaceport total access to the flight computer. They're running some really comprehensive diagnostic programs, checking everything on board.'

'Is that bad?'

'I'm not sure.' Louise stiffened, glancing round self-consciously. She cleared her throat. 'They're also accessing the internal cameras. Watching us.'

'Ah.'

'Come along, Fletcher. We must get ready to leave.'

'Yes, ma'am, of course.'

He had dropped right back into the estate servant role without a blink. Louise hoped the cameras wouldn't pick up her furtive smile as she pushed off from the deck.

Genevieve's cabin was full of four-inch light cubes, each of them a different colour. Little creatures were imprisoned inside them, as if they were cages made of tinted glass. The projection froze as Louise activated the door, an orchestral rock track faded away.

'Gen! You're supposed to be packed. We're here, you know, we've arrived.'

Her little sister peered at her through the transparent lattice, red-eyed and frazzled. 'I'd just disarmed eight of the counter-program's Trogolois warriors, you know. I've never got that far before.'

'Bully for you. Now get packed, you can play it again later. We're leaving.'

Genevieve's face darkened in petulant rebellion. 'It's not fair! We're always having to leave places the moment we arrive.'

'Because we're travelling, silly. We'll get to Tranquillity in another couple of weeks, then you can put down roots and sprout leaves out of your ears for all I care.'

'Why can't we just stay in the ship? The possessed can't get inside if we're flying about.'

'Because we can't fly about for ever.'

'I don't see—'

'*Gen*, do as you're told. Turn this off and get packed. Now!'

'You're not Mother.'

Louise glared at her. Genevieve's stubborn mask collapsed, and she started to blub.

'Oh, Gen.' Louise skimmed across the narrow space and caught hold of the small girl. She ordered the processor block off, and the glowing bricks flickered into dewy sparkles before vanishing altogether.

'I want to go home,' Genevieve blurted. 'Home to Cricklade, not Tranquillity.'

'I'm sorry,' Louise cooed. 'I haven't being paying you much attention on this flight, have I?'

'You've got things to worry about.'

'When did you go to sleep last?'

'Last night.'

'Humm.' Louise put a finger under her sister's chin and lifted her face, studying the dark lines under her eyes.

'I can't sleep much in zero-gee,' Genevieve confessed. 'I keep thinking I'm falling, and my throat all clogs up. It's awful.'

'We'll book into a High York hotel, one that's on the biosphere's ground level. Both of us can have a real sleep in a proper bed then. How does that sound?'

'All right, I suppose.'

'That's the way. Just imagine. If Mrs Charlsworth could see us now. Two unmarried landowner girls, travelling without chaperones, and about to visit Earth with all its decadent arcologies.'

Genevieve attempted a grin. 'She'd go loopy.'

'Certainly would.'

'Louise, how am I going to take this block back home? I really don't want to give it up now.'

Louise turned the slim innocuous unit round in front of her. 'We escaped the possessed, and we've flown halfway across the galaxy. You don't really think smuggling this back to Cricklade is going to be a problem for the likes of us, do you?'

'No.' Genevieve perked up. 'Everyone's going to be dead jealous when we get back. I can't wait to see Jane Walker's face when I tell here we've been to Earth. She's always going on about how exotic her family holidays on Melton Island are.'

Louise kissed her sister's forehead and gave her a warm hug. 'Get packed. I'll see you up at the airlock in five minutes.'

There was only one awkward moment left. All of the Bushay family had gathered by the airlock at the top of the life-support section to say goodbye. Pieri was torn between desperation and having to contain himself in front of his parents and his cluster of extended siblings. He managed a platonic peck on Louise's cheek, pressing against her for longer than required. 'Can I still show you round?' he mumbled.

'I hope so,' she smiled back. 'Let's see how long I'm there for, shall we.'

He nodded, blushing heavily.

Louise led the way along the airlock tube, her flight bag riding on her back like a haversack. A man was floating just beyond the hatch at the far end, dressed in a pale-emerald tunic with white lettering on the top of the sleeve. He smiled politely.

'You must be the Kavanagh party?'

'Yes,' Louise said.

'Excellent. I'm Brent Roi, High York customs. There are a few formalities we have to go through, I'm afraid. We haven't had any outsystem visitors since the quarantine started. That means my staff are all sitting round kicking their heels with nothing to do. A month ago you could have shot straight though here and we wouldn't even have noticed you.' He grinned at Genevieve. 'That's a huge bag you've got there. You're not smuggling anything in, are you?'

'No!'

He winked at her. 'Good show. This way, please.' He started off down the corridor, flipping at the grab hoops to propel himself along.

Louise followed with Genevieve at her heels. She heard a whirring sound behind. The hatch back to the *Jamrana* was closing.

No way back now, she thought. Not that there ever had been.

At least the customs man appeared friendly. Perhaps she had been fretting too much about this.

The compartment Brent Roi led her into was just like a broader section of the corridor, cylindrical, ten metres long and eight wide. There were no fittings apart from five lines of grab hoops radiating out from the entrance.

Brent Roi bent his legs and kicked off hard as soon as he was through the hatch. When Louise went in he had already joined the others lining the walls. She looked round, her heart fluttering apprehensively. A dozen people were anchored to stikpads all around her, she couldn't see their faces, they all wore helmets with silver visors. Each of them was holding some sort of boxy gun. The stubby muzzles were pointed at Fletcher the instant he popped out of the hatchway.

'Is this customs?' she asked in a failing voice.

Genevieve's small hand curled round her ankle. 'Louise!' She clambered up her big sister's body like mobile ivy. The two girls clung to each other fearfully.

'The ladies are not possessed,' Fletcher said calmly. 'I ask you not to endanger them. I shall not resist.'

'Too fucking right you won't, you son of a bitch,' Brent Roi snarled.

*

Ashly fired the MSV's thrusters: too hard, too long. He cursed. The drift had been reversed, not halted. Pressure was wiring him close to overload. Mistakes like this could cost them a lot more than their lives. He datavised another set of directives into the craft's computer, and the thrusters fired again, a shorter, milder burst this time.

The MSV came to rest three metres above the launch-tube's hatch. Like the rest of the *Beezling*'s fuselage it was badly scarred and mauled. But intact.

'No particle penetration,' he datavised. 'It seems to be undamaged.'

'Good. Get it open,' Joshua answered.

Ashly was already extending three of the MSV's waldo arms. He shoved a clamp hand straight into the mounting hole left by a broken sensor cluster, and expanded the segments, securing the MSV in place. A fission blade came on, burning a lambent saffron at the tip of the second arm. Ashly used it to slice into the fuselage at the rim of the hatch, then began to saw round.

Both the *Beezling* and the MSV trembled energetically. The computer datavised a series of clamp stress cautions, their grip on the mounting had shifted slightly. 'Joshua, another one of those and you're going to shake me loose.'

'Sorry. Won't happen again, we're docked now.'

Ashly accessed the MSV's small sensor suite. The *Lady Mac* had attached herself to the rear of the *Beezling*, her aft hold-down latches engaging with the warship's corresponding locks. A slim silver piston slid out of her ring of umbilical couplings, weaving round slowly as it sought out a socket on the *Beezling* to mate with.

Spacesuited figures wearing manoeuvring packs were flitting towards the bright circle of light which was *Lady Macbeth's* open airlock. A third of the way round her fuselage one of her combat-wasp launch-tubes had opened. The front section of a combat wasp had risen up out of it, a dark tapering cylinder bristling with sensors and antennas. Beaulieu was working on it, her glossy body alive with reflected streaks of salmon-pink light that rippled fluidly with every movement. She had anchored her feet in the midsection grid which contained the drone's tanks and generators. One of the submunition chamber covers had already been removed; now she was busy extracting the cluster of electronic-warfare pods from inside.

The MSV's waldo arm finished cutting round the *Beezling's* hatch. Ashly grabbed it with the heavy-load arm and pulled it free. A strew of dust-motes and composite shavings popped out, quickly dwindling away. The MSV's external lights swung round, and he was looking straight down into a smooth white cylinder which nested a sleek conical missile whose silver surface was polished brighter than any mirror.

'Is this the right one?' he asked, including his retinal image into the datavise.

'That is the Alchemist carrier, yes,' Mzu replied.

'There's no response from any processors in there. Temperature is a hundred and twenty absolute.'

'It won't have affected the Alchemist.'

Ashly said nothing, hoping her self-confidence was as justified as Joshua's. He extended one of the MSV's manipulator waldos into the launch-tube, and fastened it around the apex of the carrier vehicle's nose-cone. Triangular keys found the locking pins, and turned them. He retracted the arm carefully, bringing the nose-cone with it. The base was studded with junctions for the thermal-shunt circuits, which were reluctant to separate; after thirty years the vacuum and the cold had melded them together. Ashly increased the tension on the waldo, and they tore free with a judder which the arm's inertia absorber could barely cope with.

'That's it?' Ashly datavised when the nose-cone was lifted clear.

'That's it,' Mzu confirmed.

The Alchemist was a single globe one and a half metres in diameter, its seamless surface a neutral grey colour. It was held in place by five carbotanium spider-leg struts which encased it neatly, their inner surfaces lined with adjustable pads to maintain a perfect grip.

'You should be able to detach the entire restraint mechanism,' Mzu datavised. 'Sever the data and power cables if necessary; they're not necessary any more.'

'OK.' He moved the manipulator waldo down the side of the Alchemist and used its small sensors to inspect the machinery he found below it. 'This shouldn't take long, the rivets are standard. I can cut them.'

'Fast, please, Ashly,' Joshua datavised. 'The Organization ships are only twenty-four minutes away.'

'Gotcha. I'll have this with Beaulieu in three minutes.' He moved the first of the manipulator's tools forward. 'Doctor?'

'Yes.'

'Why bother with a specialist carrier vehicle if it can be deployed in an ordinary combat wasp?'

'That carrier vehicle is designed to shoot the Alchemist into

**1243**

a star. Admittedly that's a large target, but we can't take starships very close to one. The carrier has to be fully insulated from the star's heat and radiation, and it also has to be fast enough to avoid interception from combat wasps in the event we were detected. We built it to accelerate up to sixty-five gees.'

Ashly would have liked to have called her bluff. But given their current situation, ignorance and blind faith made life altogether less stressful.

*

Monica didn't leave Alkad alone in the EVA preparation compartment, but she did permit her a discreet distance. Two other operatives were with her, ready to inspect the *Beezling*'s crew to make sure they brought nothing threatening with them into the *Lady Macbeth*.

Alkad didn't really notice the agent's presence, every aspect of her life had been under continual observation for so long now that intrusion meant nothing. Not even for this most precious occasion.

She anchored herself to a stikpad in front of the airlock hatch, waiting with outward patience. When she sorted through her feelings she found the rightful edgy anticipation, but perhaps not so much of it as there should have been. Thirty years. Can you really stay in love with someone for that long? Or did I just keep the ideal of love alive? One small illusion of humanity in a personality which deliberately and methodically set about excluding any other form of emotional weakness.

Well enough, there were memories of the good times. Memories of shared ideals. And of course memories of affection, adoration, and intimacy. But shouldn't real love require the continuing presence of the loved one in order to sustain itself and constantly renew? Has Peter really become nothing more than a concept suborned, just another excuse to retain my commitment?

The doubts tempted her to turn and flee from the moment.

In any case, I'm over sixty and he's still thirty-five. A hand started up towards her face, wanting to fork her hair back, or tidy it. Silly. If she was so concerned about her appearance she should have done something about it long ago. Cosmetic packages, hormone gland implants, gene therapy. Except Peter would have hated her resorting to such untruthful indignities.

Alkad forced the delinquent hand down. The LEDs on the airlock's control processor changed from red to green, and the circular hatch swung back.

Peter Adul was first out, the others had allowed him that civility. His SII suit's silicon film had withdrawn from his head so she could see all the features she remembered so well. He stared back at her, a frightened smile on his lips. 'White hair,' he said gently. 'I never imagined that. Lots of things, but never that.'

'It's not so bad. I imagined much worse happening to you.'

'But it didn't. And we're here. And you came to rescue us. After thirty years, you really came back here for us.'

'Of course I did,' she said, abruptly indignant.

Peter grinned wickedly. She laughed back, and launched herself into his arms.

\*

Joshua was accessing the MSV's external sensors to monitor Ashly and Beaulieu's efforts to integrate the Alchemist with their combat wasp. Ashly was using a waldo arm to edge the device down into the submunition chamber which the cosmonik had cleared. The Alchemist would fit, but the restraint arms folded round it were causing problems. Beaulieu had already sliced a couple of chunks off the carbotanium struts when they scraped against the chamber walls. This was one incredibly crude kludge-up from start to finish. But it didn't need excessive sophistication to work, just a secure mounting.

Superimposed across the sensor image were the *Lady Mac*'s

systems schematics, enabling him to keep a slightly more than cursory eye on their performance. Liol and Sarha were prepping the ship for high acceleration, shutting down all redundant ancillary equipment, cycling fluids back out of weight-vulnerable pipes and into their tanks, bringing the tokamaks up to full capacity so their power would be available for the molecular-binding-force generators. Dahybi was running diagnostics through all the zero-tau facilities on board.

By rights the expectancy should have reduced his brain to a small knot of psychoses by now. Instead he had the oldest excuse of being too busy to worry. That and a wonderful burn of pure arrogance. It can work. After all, it was only marginally more crazy than the Lagrange point stunt.

Too bad I'll never be able to brag about this one in Harkey's Bar.

Which was actually more of a concern than the manoeuvre itself. I can't stay in Tranquillity for the rest of my life. I should never have mentioned it to the agents.

He saw Ashly extract the waldo from the combat wasp, leaving the Alchemist behind. Beaulieu reached forward to hold a hose over the top of the submunitions chamber. A frayed jet of treacly topaz-coloured foam shot out of the nozzle, surging all around the Alchemist. It was a duopoxy sealant, used by the astronautics industry for quick, temporary repairs. The cosmonik moved the nozzle in smooth, assured motions, making sure the foam completely encapsulated the Alchemist, cementing it into the combat wasp.

'Ashly, take the MSV round to the main airlock and transfer over in your suit,' Joshua datavised.

'What about the MSV?'

'I'm dumping it here. It was never designed to withstand the kind of acceleration we'll be undergoing. That makes it a hazard, especially with all the reaction thruster volatiles it has in its tanks.'

'You're the captain. But what about the spaceplane?'

'I know. You just get back in; we've only got sixteen minutes left before the Organization ships get here.'

'Acknowledged, Captain.'

'Liol.'

'Yes, Captain?'

'Jettison the spaceplane, please. Beaulieu, how's it going?'

'Fine, Captain. I've got it covered. The sealant is bonding, should be set in another fifty seconds.'

'Excellent work. Get back inside.' Joshua datavised the flight computer for a secure channel to the combat wasp. The drone came on-line, and he started its launch-sequence program. Once its internal processors were operative he loaded in the flight vector he'd formatted. 'Doc, it's time to find out how good you are.'

'I understand, Captain.'

She accessed the processor governing the combat wasp's chamber which the Alchemist was riding in and used it to datavise a long activation code at the device. It datavised an acknowledgement back to her. The display in Joshua's mind opened out rapidly to accommodate the new iconic representation: parallel sheets of dark information stacked as high as heaven. They came alive with interlocking grids of purple and yellow that shone like channelled starfire. Perspective switch, and the sheets were concentric spherical shells, coming alight from the core outwards. Information and energy arranging themselves in a precise, and very specific, pattern.

'It's working,' Alkad datavised.

'Jesus Christ.' The neurovirtual jewel glimmered at the centre of his brain, complex beyond human comprehension. It was an outrageous irony that something so deliciously intricate and beautiful should be the harbinger of so much destruction. 'OK, Doc, set it for neutronium. I'm launching in twenty seconds – mark.'

\*

*Lady Mac*'s spaceplane had risen up out of her hangar as thermo-dump panels and sensor cluster booms shrank back the other way. Ashly caught one last glimpse of it as he swept down into the airlock. The circular docking ring clamped around its nose-cone had just disengaged, allowing it to drift free, then Beaulieu's shiny brass silhouette occluded the airlock hatch behind him, and that was the end of it.

Pity, he thought, it was a lovely little machine.

As soon as the airlock's outer hatch closed, the cylindrical chamber was fast-flooded with air. The flight computer's datavised display revealed their status. Joshua was already firing the thrusters to align them on their new flight vector. Combat-wasp launch-tubes were opening.

Ashly and Beaulieu dived out of the airlock, racing for the bridge. There was nobody in any of the decks they passed through. Several open cabin doors showed them active zero-tau pods.

The combat wasp carrying the Alchemist completed its fusion-drive ignition sequence, and launched. A quick cheer from the bridge echoed through *Lady Mac*'s empty compartments. Then ten more combat wasps were firing out of their tubes and chasing after the first. The whole salvo headed down towards the gas giant at twenty-five gees.

Ashly flew through the bridge's floor hatch just behind Beaulieu.

'Stations, please,' Joshua said. He triggered *Lady Mac*'s three fusion tubes, giving Ashly barely enough time to roll onto his acceleration couch before gravity pushed down. Restraint webbing closed over him.

'Signal from the Organization ships,' Sarha said. 'They know who we are, they're asking for you by name, Joshua.'

Joshua accessed the communication circuit. The image which his neural nanonics provided was shaky and stormed with static. It showed him a frigate's bridge, with figures lying flat on acceleration couches. One of them was dressed in a double-breasted suit of chocolate-brown worsted with slim silver-grey pinstripes, a wide-brimmed black fedora resting on the console beside him. Joshua puzzled at that one for a moment, the frigate was decelerating at seven gees. The fedora should have been squashed flat.

'Captain Calvert?'

'You got me.'

'I'm Oscar Kearn, and Al put me in charge around here.'

'Joshua,' Liol datavised. 'The frigates are flipping over again. They're starting to chase us.'

'Acknowledged.' He increased the *Lady Mac*'s acceleration, taking her up to seven gees.

Ashly groaned in chagrin before activating his acceleration couch's zero-tau field. Black stasis closed around him, ending the punishing force. Alkad Mzu and Peter Adul joined him.

'Glad to meet you, Oscar.' Joshua had to datavise, his jaw was far too heavy to move.

'My people, they tell me you just fired something down at the big planet. I hope you ain't been stupid, pal, I really do. Was it what I think it was?'

'Absolutely. No more Alchemist for anybody.'

'You dumb asshole. That's a third of your options gone. Now you listen good, sonny boy, you switch off your ship's engines and you hand over Mzu to me and there ain't nobody gonna get hurt. That's your second option.'

'No shit? Let me guess what the third is.'

'Don't be a pumpkinhead, sonny. Remember, after we waste you and your rinky-dink ship, we're only interested in giving the Mzu dame a new body. It's the beyond for you, pal, for the rest of time. And take a tip from someone who's been there, it ain't worth it. Nothing is. So you just hand her over nice and smooth, and I don't say nothing to the boss about you deep-sixing the Alchemist.'

'Mr Kearn, go screw yourself.'

'You call that Alchemist back, sonny. I know you got a radio control on the combat wasp. You call it back or I tell my crews to open fire.'

'If you blow up the *Lady Mac* you'll definitely never get it, will you? Think about it, I'll give you as much time as you need.' Joshua closed the communication link.

'How much more of this bloody acceleration?' Monica datavised.

'Seven gees?' Joshua replied. 'None at all.' He increased the thrust up to a full ten gees.

Monica couldn't even groan; her throat was sagging under its own weight. It was ridiculous, her lungs couldn't inhale properly, her artificial-tissue muscle implants were all in her limbs, not her chest. If she tried to hang on she'd end up asphyxiating. Keeping Mzu under observation was no longer an option. She would simply have to trust Calvert and the other crew-members. 'Good luck,' she datavised. 'See you on the other side.'

The flight computer informed Joshua she'd activated her acceleration couch's zero-tau field. That left him with only three people who hadn't sought refuge in stasis: Beaulieu, Dahybi, and, of course, Liol.

'Status report, please,' he datavised to them.

*Lady Mac*'s systems and structure were both holding up well. But then Joshua knew she was capable of withstanding this acceleration, her real test was going to come later.

Seventy thousand kilometres behind her, the two Organization frigates were accelerating at eight gees, which was the limit of their afflicted drives. Their crews were hurriedly assembling situation outlines and summaries for Oscar Kearn, detailing how long it would be before the *Lady Macbeth* was outside the interception range of their combat wasps.

Ahead of all three ships, the salvo of eleven combat wasps was rushing towards the gas giant. There was no way any sensor could determine which was carrying the Alchemist, making any interdiction virtually impossible.

The status quo was held for over fifteen minutes before Oscar Kearn reluctantly admitted to himself that Calvert and Mzu weren't going to hand over the device, nor surrender themselves. He ordered the *Urschel* and the *Raimo* to launch their combat wasps at *Lady Macbeth*.

'No good,' Joshua grunted savagely as *Lady Mac*'s sensors showed him the sudden upsurge in the frigates' infra-red emission signature. 'You can't dysfunction this chunk of reality, pal.'

The Alchemist was ninety seconds away from the gas giant's upper atmosphere. Its management programs began to orchestrate the complex energy patterns racing through its nodes into the sequence Mzu had selected. Once it was primed, activation occurred within two pico-seconds. Visually it could hardly be less spectacular; the Alchemist's surface turned infinitely black. The physics behind the change was somewhat more involved.

\*

'What I did,' Alkad had datavised to Joshua when he asked her how it functioned, 'was to work out how to combine a zero-tau field and the energy-compression technique which a starship jump node utilizes. In this case, just as the energy density approaches infinite the effect is frozen. Instead of expelling the patterning node out of the universe, you get a massive and permanent space-time curvature forming around it.'

'Space-time curvature?'

'Gravity.'

\*

Gravity at its strongest is capable of bending light itself, pulling at individual photons with the same tenacity as it once did Newton's apple. In nature, the only mass dense enough to produce this kind of gravity is formed at the heart of a stellar implosion. A singularity whose gravity permits nothing to escape: no matter, no energy.

At its highest setting the Alchemist would become such a cosmological entity; its surface concealed by an event horizon into which everything can fall and nothing return. Once inside the event horizon, electromagnetic energy and atoms alike would be drawn to the core's surface and compress to phenomenal densities. The effect is cumulative and exponential. The more mass which the black hole swallows, the heavier and stronger it becomes, increasing its surface area and allowing its consumption rate to rise accordingly.

If the Alchemist was fired into a star, every gram of matter would eventually plunge below the invincible barrier which gravity erected. That was Alkad Mzu's humane solution. Omuta's sun would not flare and rupture, would never endanger life on the planet with waves of heat and radiation. Instead the sun would shrink and collapse into a small black sphere, with every erg of its fusing nuclei lost to the universe for ever. Omuta would be left circling a non-radiative husk, its warmth slowly leaking away into the now permanent night. Ultimately, the air itself would become cold enough to condense and fall as snow.

But there was the second setting, the aggressive one. Paradoxically, it actually produced a weaker gravity field.

\*

The Alchemist turned black as zero-tau claimed it. However, the gravity it generated wasn't strong enough to produce a singularity with an event horizon, though it was easily capable of overcoming the internal forces which designate an atom's structure. The combat wasp immediately flashed into plasma and enfolded it. All electrons and protons within the envelope were crushed together, producing a massive pulse of gamma radiation. The emission faded rapidly, leaving the Alchemist cloaked in a uniform angstrom-deep ocean of superfluid neutrons.

When it struck the outer fringes of the atmosphere a searing white light flooded out to soak hundreds of square kilometres of the upper cloud bands. Seconds later the deeper cloud layers were fluorescing rosy pink while internal shadows surged through torn cyclones like mountain-sized fish. Then the light vanished altogether.

The Alchemist had reached the semisolid layers of the gas giant's interior, and was punching through with almost no resistance. Matter under tremendous pressure was crushed against the device, which absorbed it greedily. Every impacting atom was squeezed directly into a cluster of neutrons that plated themselves around the core. The Alchemist was swiftly buried under a mantle of pure neutronium, which boasted a density that exceeded that of atomic nuclei.

As the particles were compressed by the device's extraordinary gravity field they liberated colossal quantities of energy, a reaction far more potent than mere fusion. The surrounding semisolid material was heated to temperatures which destroyed every atomic bond. A vast cavity of nuclear instability inflated around the Alchemist as it soared ever deeper into the gas giant. Ordinary convection currents were wholly inadequate to syphon off the heat at the same rate it was being produced, so the energy abscess simply had to keep on expanding. Something had to give.

*Lady Mac's* sensors detected the first upwelling while the ship was still seven minutes from perigee. A smooth-domed tumour of cloud, three thousand kilometres in diameter, glowing like gaseous magma as it swelled up through the storm bands. Unlike the ordinary great spots infesting gas giants it didn't spiral, its sole purpose was to elevate planetary masses of tortuously heated hydrogen up from the interior. Hurricanes and cyclones which had blasted their way through the upper atmosphere for centuries were thrust aside to allow the thermal monster its bid for freedom. Its apex distended over a thousand kilometres above the tropopause, casting a pernicious copper light over a third of the nightside.

Right at the centre, the glow had become unbearably bright.

A spire of solid white light punctured the top of the cloud dome, streaking out into space.

'Holy Christ,' Liol datavised. 'Was that it? Did it just detonate?'

'Nothing like,' Joshua replied. 'This is only the start. Things are going to get a little nasty from now on.'

*Lady Mac* was already far ahead of the fountaining plasma stream, racing round the gas giant's curvature for the dawn terminator. Even so, thermal circuits issued a grade three alarm as the plasma's radiance washed over the hull. Emergency cryogenic exchangers vented hundreds of litres of inflamed fluid to shunt the heat out. Processors were failing at a worrying rate in the immense EMP backlash of the wavering plasma stream, even the military-grade electronics were suffering. On top of that, electric currents started to eddy through the fuselage stress structure as the planetary flux lines trembled.

Dahybi had withdrawn into zero-tau, leaving Joshua and Liol to datavise instructions into the flight computer, bringing back-ups on-line, isolating leakages, stabilizing power surges. They worked perfectly together, keeping the flight systems on-line, each intuitively knowing what was required to support the other.

'Something very odd is happening to the planetary magneto-sphere,' Beaulieu reported. 'Sensors are registering extraordinary oscillations within the flux lines.'

'Irrelevant,' Joshua replied. 'Concentrate on keeping our primary systems stable. Four minutes more, that's all, we'll be on the other side of the planet then.'

On board the *Urschel*, Ikela watched the lightstorm eruption on one of the bridge screens. 'Holy Mary, it works,' he whispered. 'It actually bloody works.' A perverse sense of pride mingled with fatalistic dismay. If only ... But then, fruitless wishes were ever the province of the damned.

He ignored Oscar Kearn's semi-hysterical (and totally impossible) orders to turn the ship round and get them the hell away from this badass planet. Twentieth-century man simply didn't understand orbital mechanics. They had been accelerating along their present course for twenty-two minutes now, and their trajectory effectively committed them to a slingshot flyby. Their best hope was to stay on track, and pray they got past perigee before another upwell exploded out of the atmosphere. That was what the *Lady Macbeth* was attempting. Good tactic, Ikela acknowledged grudgingly.

Somehow, he didn't think the *Urschel* would make it. He didn't know exactly how the Alchemist worked, but he doubted one eruption was the end of it.

With a sense of inevitability that curiously neutralized any regret or gloom, he settled back passively in his acceleration couch and watched the screens. The original spout of plasma was dying away, the cloud dome flattening out to dissipate into a thousand new hypervelocity storms. But underneath the frothing upper atmosphere a fresh stain of light was spreading, and it was an order of magnitude larger than the first.

He smiled contentedly at his god's-eye view of what promised to be a truly dazzling Armageddon.

The Alchemist was slowing: it had passed through the semisolid layers into the true core of the planet. Now the density of surrounding matter was intense enough to affect its flight. That meant matter was being pressed against it in ever greater quantities, and with it the rate of neutronium conversion was accelerating fast. The energy abscess which it generated stretched out back along its course through the planet's interior like a comet's tail. Sections of it were breaking apart; ten thousand kilometre lengths pinching into elongated bubbles which rose up through the disrupted tiers of the planet's internal structure. Each one greater than the last.

The second upwelling rampaged out of the upper atmosphere, its tremendous scale making it appear absurdly ponderous. Vast founts of ions cascaded from its edges as the centre broke open, twisting into scarlet arches which fell gracefully back towards the boiling cloudscape. A coronal fireball spat out of the central funnel, bigger than a moon, its surface slippery with webs of magnetic energy which condensed the plasma into deeper purple curlicues. Ghost gases flowered around it, translucent gold petal wings unfurling to beat with the harmonic of the planetary flux lines.

Lost somewhere amongst the rising glory of light were two tiny sparkles produced by antimatter detonating inside both Organization frigates.

*Lady Mac* swept triumphantly across the terminator and into daylight, surfing at a hundred and fifty kilometres per second over the hurricane rivers of phosphorescence which flowed through the troposphere. An arrogant saffron dawn waxed behind her, far outshining the natural one ahead.

'Time to leave,' Joshua datavised. 'You ready?'

'All yours, Josh.'

Joshua datavised his order into the flight computer. Zerotau claimed the last three acceleration couches on the bridge. *Lady Mac*'s antimatter drive ignited.

The starship accelerated away from the gas giant at forty-two gees.

*

Finally, the Alchemist had come to rest at the centre of the gas giant. Here was a universe of pressure unglimpsed except through speculative mathematical models. The heart of the gas giant was only slightly less dense than the neutronium itself. Yet the difference was there, permitting the inflow of matter to continue. The conversion reaction burned unabated. Pure alchemy.

Energy blazed outwards from the Alchemist, unable to escape. The abscess was spherical now, nature's preferred geometry. A sphere at the heart of a sphere; dangerously tormented matter confined by the perfectly symmetrical pressure exerted by the mass of seventy-five thousand kilometres of hydrogen piled on top of it. This time there was no escape valve up through the weak, nonsymmetrical, semisolid layers. This time, all it could do was grow.

\*

For six hundred seconds *Lady Macbeth* accelerated away from the mortally wounded gas giant. Behind her, the Alchemist's trail of fragmented energy abscesses pumped up out of the darkside clouds, transient volcanoes of feculent gas rising higher than worlds. The planet began to develop its own billowing photosphere, a dark burgundy orb enclosed by a glowing azure halo. Its ebony moons sailed on indomitably through their new sea of lightning.

The starship's multiple drive tubes cut out. Joshua's zero-tau switched off, depositing him abruptly into free fall. Sensor images and flight data flashed straight into his brain. The planet's death convulsions were as fascinating as they were deadly. It didn't matter, they were over a hundred and eighty thousand kilometres from the disintegrating storm bands. Far enough to jump.

Deep beneath the benighted clouds, the central energy abscess had swollen to an intolerable size. The pressure it was exerting against the confining mass of the planet had almost reached equilibrium. Titanic fissures began to tear open.

An event horizon engulfed *Lady Macbeth*'s fuselage.

With a timing that was the ultimate tribute to the precision of Mzu's decades-old equations, the gas giant went nova.

\*

The singularity surged into existence five hundred and eighty thousand kilometres above Mirchusko's pale jade blizzards of ammonia-sulphur cirrus. Its event horizon blinked off to reveal the *Lady Macbeth*'s dull silicon fuselage. Omnidirectional antennas were already broadcasting her CAB identification code. Given the reception they got on returning from Lalonde, Joshua wasn't going to take any chances this time.

Sensor clusters telescoped outwards, passive elements scanning round, radars pulsing. The flight computer datavised a class three proximity alert.

'Charge the nodes,' Joshua ordered automatically. His mistake, he never expected to jump into trouble here. Now that might cost them badly.

The bridge lights dimmed fractionally as Dahybi initiated an emergency power-up sequence. 'Eight seconds,' he said.

The external sensor image flashed up in Joshua's mind. At first he thought they were being targeted by electronic-warfare pods. Space was flecked with small white motes. But the electronic sensors were the only ones not being taxed, the whole electromagnetic environment was eerily silent. The flight computer reported its radar track-while-scan function was approaching capacity overload as it designated multiple targets. Each of the white motes was being tagged by purple icons to indicate position and trajectory. Three were flashing red, approaching fast.

It wasn't interference. *Lady Mac* had emerged in the middle of a massive debris storm.

The first chunk thumped into the fuselage, tolling like a church bell.

'Beaulieu, damage report?'

'Negative, Captain. It was too small to penetrate, the binding generators maintained our integrity.'

'Jesus, what is this stuff?' He datavised a set of instructions into the flight computer. The standard sensor booms began to retreat, replaced by the smaller, tougher combat sensors. Discrimination and analysis programs went primary.

The debris was mostly metallic, melted and fused scraps no bigger than snowflakes. They were all radioactive.

'There's been one brute of a fight here,' Sarha said. 'This is all combat wasp wreckage. And there's a lot of it. I think the swarm is about forty thousand kilometres in diameter. It's dissipating, clearing from the centre.'

'No response to our identification signal,' Beaulieu said. 'Tranquillity's beacons are off-air, I cannot locate a single artificial electromagnetic transmission. There isn't even a ship's beacon active.'

The centre of the debris storm had a coordinate Joshua didn't even have to run a memory check on. Tranquillity's orbital vector. *Lady Mac*'s sensor suite revealed it to be a large empty zone. 'It's gone,' he said numbly. 'They blew it up. Oh, Jesus, no. Ione. My kid. My kid was in there!'

'No, Joshua,' Sarha said firmly. 'It hasn't been destroyed. There isn't nearly enough mass in the swarm to account for that.'

'Then where is it? Where the hell did it go?'

'I don't know. There's no trace of it, none at all.'

# Timeline

**2020**  Clavius base established. Mining of Lunar sub-crustal resources starts.

**2037**  Beginning of large-scale geneering on humans; improvement to immunology system, eradication of appendix, organ efficiency increased.

**2041**  First deuterium-fuelled fusion stations built, inefficient and expensive.

**2044**  Christian reunification.

**2047**  First asteroid capture mission. Beginning of Earth's O'Neill Halo.

**2049**  Quasi-sentient bitek animals employed as servitors.

**2055**  Jupiter mission.

**2055**  Lunar cities granted independence from founding companies.

**2057**  Ceres asteroid settlement founded.

**2058**  Affinity symbiont neurons developed by Wing-Tsit Chong, providing control over animals and bitek constructs.

**2064**  Multinational industrial consortium JSKP (Jovian Sky

Power Corporation) begins mining Jupiter's atmosphere for $He_3$ using aerostat factories.

**2064** Islamic secular unification.

**2067** Fusion stations begin to use $He_3$ as fuel.

**2069** Affinity bond gene spliced into human DNA.

**2075** JSKP germinates Eden, a bitek habitat in orbit around Jupiter, with UN Protectorate status.

**2077** New Kong asteroid begins FTL stardrive research project.

**2085** Eden opened for habitation.

**2086** Habitat Pallas germinated in Jupiter orbit.

**2090** Wing-Tsit Chong dies, and transfers memories to Eden's neural strata. Start of Edenist culture. Eden and Pallas declare independence from UN. Launch buyout of JSKP shares. Pope Eleanor excommunicates all Christians with affinity gene. Exodus of affinity capable humans to Eden. Effective end of bitek industry on Earth.

**2091** Lunar referendum to terraform Mars.

**2094** Edenists begin exowomb breeding programme coupled with extensive geneering improvement to embryos, tripling their population over a decade.

**2103** Earth's national governments consolidate into Govcentral.

**2103** Thoth base established on Mars.

**2107** Govcentral jurisdiction extended to cover O'Neill Halo.

**2115**  First instantaneous translation by New Kong spaceship, Earth to Mars.

**2118**  Mission to Proxima Centauri.

**2123**  Terracompatible planet found at Ross 154.

**2125**  Ross 154 planet named Felicity, first multiethnic colonists arrive.

**2125–2130**  Four new terracompatible planets discovered. Multiethnic colonies founded.

**2131**  Edenists germinate Perseus in orbit around Ross 154 gas giant, begin He$_3$ mining.

**2131–2205**  One hundred and thirty terracompatible planets discovered. Massive starship building programme initiated in O'Neill Halo. Govcentral begins large-scale enforced outshipment of surplus population, rising to two million a week in 2160: Great Dispersal. Civil conflict on some early multiethnic colonies. Individual Govcentral states sponsor ethnic-streaming colonies. Edenists expand their He$_3$ mining enterprise to every inhabited star system with a gas giant.

**2139**  Asteroid Braun impacts on Mars.

**2180**  First orbital tower built on Earth.

**2205**  Antimatter production station built in orbit around sun by Govcentral in an attempt to break the Edenist energy monopoly.

**2208**  First antimatter drive starships operational.

**2210**  Richard Saldana transports all of New Kong's industrial facilities from the O'Neill Halo to an asteroid orbiting Kulu. He claims independence for the

Kulu star system, founds Christian-only colony, and begins to mine He$_3$ from the system's gas giant.

**2218** First voidhawk gestated, a bitek starship designed by Edenists.

**2225** Establishment of a hundred voidhawk families. Habitats Romulus and Remus germinated in Saturn orbit to serve as voidhawk bases.

**2232** Conflict at Jupiter's trailing Trojan asteroid cluster between belt alliance ships and an O'Neill Halo company hydrocarbon refinery. Antimatter used as a weapon; twenty-seven thousand people killed.

**2238** Treaty of Deimos outlaws production and use of antimatter in the Sol system: signed by Govcentral, Lunar nation, asteroid alliance, and Edenists. Antimatter stations abandoned and dismantled.

**2240** Coronation of Gerrald Saldana as King of Kulu. Foundation of Saldana dynasty.

**2267–2270** Eight separate skirmishes involving use of antimatter among colony worlds. Thirteen million killed.

**2271** Avon summit between all planetary leaders. Treaty of Avon, banning the manufacture and use of antimatter throughout inhabited space. Formation of Human Confederation to police agreement. Construction of Confederation Navy begins.

**2300** Confederation expanded to include Edenists.

**2301** First Contact. Jiciro race discovered, a pre-technology civilization. System quarantined by Confederation to avoid cultural contamination.

**2310** First ice asteroid impact on Mars.

| 2330 | First blackhawks gestated at Valisk, independent habitat. |
|---|---|
| 2350 | War between Novska and Hilversum. Novska bombed with antimatter. Confederation Navy prevents retaliatory strike against Hilversum. |
| 2356 | Kiint homeworld discovered. |
| 2357 | Kiint join Confederation as 'observers'. |
| 2360 | A voidhawk scout discovers Atlantis. |
| 2371 | Edenists colonize Atlantis. |
| 2395 | Tyrathca colony world discovered. |
| 2402 | Tyrathca join Confederation. |
| 2420 | Kulu scoutship discovers Ruin Ring. |
| 2428 | Bitek habitat Tranquillity germinated by Crown Prince Michael Saldana, orbiting above Ruin Ring. |
| 2432 | Prince Michael's son, Maurice, geneered with affinity. Kulu abdication crisis. Coronation of Lukas Saldana. Prince Michael exiled. |
| 2550 | Mars declared habitable by Terraforming office. |
| 2580 | Dorado asteroids discovered around Tunja, claimed by both Garissa and Omuta. |
| 2581 | Omutan mercenary fleet drops twelve antimatter planet-busters on Garissa, planet rendered uninhabitable. Confederation imposes thirty-year sanction against Omuta, prohibiting any interstellar trade or transport. Blockade enforced by Confederation Navy. |
| 2582 | Colony established on Lalonde. |

# Cast of Characters

## SHIPS

### Lady Macbeth

Joshua Calvert *Captain*

Melvyn Ducharme *Fusion specialist*

Ashly Hanson *Pilot*

Sarha Mitcham *Systems specialist*

Dahybi Yadev *Node specialist*

Beaulieu *Cosmonik*

### Oenone

Syrinx *Captain*

Ruben *Fusion systems*

Oxley *Pilot*

Cacus *Life support*

Edwin *Toroid systems*

Serina *Toroid systems*

Tyla *Cargo officer*

## Villeneuve's Revenge

André Duchamp *Captain*

Desmond Lafoe *Fusion specialist*

Madeleine Collum *Node specialist*

Erick Thakrar *Systems specialist/CNIS undercover agent*

## Udat

Meyer *Captain*

Cherri Barnes *Cargo officer*

## Far Realm

Layia *Captain*

Furay *Pilot*

Endron *Systems specialist*

Tilia *Node specialist*

## Arikara

Rear-Admiral Meredith Saldana *Squadron commander*

Lieutenant Grese *Squadron Intelligence Officer*

Lieutenant Rhoecus *Voidhawk Liaison Officer*

Kroeber *Commander*

## Beezling

Kyle Prager *Captain*

Peter Adul *Alchemist team physicist*

## HABITATS

### Tranquillity

Ione Saldana  *Lord of Ruin*

Dr Alkad Mzu  *Inventor of the Alchemist*

Parker Higgens  *Director, Laymil project*

Oski Katsura  *Laymil project, Electronics Division chief*

Kempster Getchell  *Laymil project, Astronomer*

Monica Foulkes  *ESA agent*

Lady Tessa  *ESA Head of Station*

Samuel  *Edenist Intelligence agent*

Pauline Webb  *CNIS agent*

Father Horst Elwes  *Priest and refugee*

Jay Hilton  *Refugee*

Kelly Tirrel  *Rover reporter*

Lieria  *Kiint*

Haile  *Juvenile Kiint*

### Valisk

Rubra  *Habitat personality*

Dariat  *Horgan's possessor*

Kiera Salter  *Marie Skibbow's possessor*

Stanyon  *Council member*

Rocio Condra  *Possessor of the blackhawk* Mindori

Bonney Lewin  *Hunter*

Tolton  *Fugitive*

Tatiana  *Fugitive*

## ASTEROIDS

### Trafalgar

Samual Aleksandrovich *First Admiral, Confederation Navy*
Admiral Lalwani *CNIS Chief*
Captain Maynard Khanna *First Admiral's staff officer*
Admiral Motela Kolhammer *1st Fleet commander*
Dr Gilmore *CNIS Research Division Director*
Jacqueline Couteur *Possessor*
Lieutenant Murphy Hewlett *Confederation Marine*

### Koblat

Jed Hinton *Deadnight*
Beth *Deadnight*
Gari Hinton *Jed's sister*
Navar *Jed's half-sister*

### Ayacucho

Ikela *Owner of T'Opingtu company and partisan leader*
Liol *Owner of Quantum Serendipity*
Voi *Ikela's daughter*
Prince Lambert *Captain of the starship* Tekas
Dan Malindi *Partisan leader*
Kaliua Lamu *Partisan leader*
Feira Ile *Ayacucho SD commander and partisan leader*
Cabral *Media magnate and partisan leader*

Mrs Nateghi *Lawyer*

Lodi Shalasha *Garissan radical*

Eriba *Garissan radical*

Kole *Socialite*

Shea *Prince Lambert's girlfriend*

## Jesup

Quinn Dexter *Messiah of the Light Bringer sect*

Lawrence Dillon *Disciple*

Twelve-T *Gang lord*

Bonham *Disciple*

Shemilt *Disciple and SD commander*

Dwyer *Disciple and systems specialist*

# PLANETS

## Norfolk

Louise Kavanagh *Refugee*

Genevieve Kavanagh *Refugee*

Luca Comar *Grant Kavanagh's possessor*

Marjorie Kavanagh *Louise's mother*

Mrs Charlsworth *Kavanagh sisters' nanny*

Carmitha *Romany*

Titreano *Possessor*

Celina Hewson *Louise's aunt*

Roberto Hewson *Louise's cousin*

## Ombey

Ralph Hiltch *ESA Head of Station, Lalonde*

Cathal Fitzgerald *Ralph's deputy*

Dean Folan *ESA G66 division*

Will Danza *ESA G66 division*

Kirsten Saldana *Princess of Ombey*

Roche Skark *ESA Director*

Jannike Dermot *ISA Director*

Landon McCullock *Police commissioner*

Diana Tiernan *Police Technology Division chief*

Admiral Farquar *Commander, Royal Navy, Ombey*

Captain Nelson Akroid *Armed Tactical Squad*

Finnuala O'Meara *Rover reporter*

Hugh Rosler *DataAxis technician*

Neville Latham *Exnall's chief inspector*

Colonel Janne Palmer *Royal Marine*

Annette Ekelund *Possessor*

Gerald Skibbow *Refugee*

Dr Riley Dobbs *Royal Navy personality debrief psychology expert*

Jansen Kovak *Royal Naval Medical Institute nurse*

Moyo *Possessor*

Stephanie Ash *Possessor*

Cochrane *Possessor*

Rana *Possessor*

Tina Sudol *Possessor*

## New California

Jezzibella *Mood Fantasy artist*

Leroy Octavius *Jezzibella's manager*

Libby *Jezzibella's dermal technology expert*

Al *Brad Lovegrove's possessor*

Avram Harwood III *Mayor of San Angeles*

Emmet Mordden *Organization lieutenant*

Silvano Richmann *Organization lieutenant*

Mickey Pileggi *Organization lieutenant*

Patricia Mangano *Organization lieutenant*

Gus Remar *Rover reporter*

Lieutenant-commander Kingsley Pryor
   *Confederation Navy*

Luigi Balsmao *Commander of the Organization fleet*

Cameron Leung *Possessor of the blackhawk* Zahan

Oscar Kearn *Captain of the Organization frigate*
   Urschel

## Kulu

Alastair II *The King*

Simon Blake, Duke of Salion *Chairman security
   commission*

Lord Kelman Mountjoy *Foreign Office minister*

Lady Phillipa Oshin *Prime Minister*

Admiral Lavaquar *Defence Chief*

Prince Howard *President of the Kulu Corporation*

Prince Noton *Ex-president of the Kulu Corporation*

## Nyvan

Gelai *Possessor and Garissan Genocide victim*
Ngong *Possessor and Garissan Genocide victim*
Omain *Possessor and Garissan Genocide victim*
Richard Keaton *Data security expert*
Baranovich *Organization lieutenant*
Adrian Redway *ESA Head of Station*

## OTHERS

### Confederation

Olton Haaker *Assembly President*
Jeeta Anwar *Chief Presidential Aide*
Mae Ortlieb *Presidential Science Aide*
Cayeaux *Edenist ambassador*
Sir Maurice Hall *Kulu Kingdom Ambassador*

### Edenists

Wing-Tsit Chong *Edenism's Founder*
Athene *Syrinx's mother*
Astor *Ambassador to the Kulu Kingdom*
Sinon *Syrinx's father*

extracts reading groups
competitions books new
discounts extracts
competitions
books
new events
events books
extracts
new reading groups
interviews
events extracts
discounts
new books events
events new
reading groups
reading groups
books
events
books

**www.panmacmillan.com**

extracts events reading groups
competitions books extracts new
books